Tor Books by David G. Hartwell

Editor
The Ascent of Wonder (with Kathryn Cramer)
The Dark Descent
Foundations of Fear
Christmas Magic
Christmas Stars
Christmas Forever
Northern Stars (with Glenn Grant)
Spirits of Christmas (with Kathryn Cramer)

Nonfiction
Age of Wonders

Edited by
DAVID G. HARTWELL

TOR

Dedication

To Tom Doherty and Harriet P. McDougal and Tor Books, and especially Melissa Ann Singer, editor, for support and patience.

To Kathryn Cramer and Peter D. Pautz for their hard work and enthusiasm, as well as provocative discussion.

To Patricia W. Hartwell for letting the books pile up and the piles of paper fall over throughout the house.

THE DARK DESCENT

A Tor Book
Published by Tom Doherty Associates, Inc.
175 Fifth Avenue
New York, NY 10010

Tor Books on the World Wide Web:
http://www.tor.com

Tor® is a registered trademark of Tom Doherty Associates, Inc.

ISBN 0-312-86217-2

Printed in the United States of America

0 9 8 7 6 5 4

Copyright Acknowledgments

Acknowledgments

This anthology grew out of three years of weekly discussions with Peter D. Pautz and Kathryn Cramer on the nature and virtues of horror literature, and its evolution. Peter's knowledge of the contemporary field and Kathryn's theoretical bent were seminal in the genesis of my own thoughts on what horror literature is and has become. Jack Sullivan, Kirby McCauley and Peter Straub were particularly helpful in discussing aspects of horror, and Samuel R. Delany contributed valuable insights, as well as the title for Part III. And I owe an incalculable debt to the great anthologists—from M. R. James and Dashiell Hammett, Elizabeth Bowen, Dorothy Sayers through Wise and Fraser, Boris Karloff and August Derleth to Kirby McCauley, Ramsey Campbell and Jack Sullivan —whose research and scholarship and taste guided my reading over the decades. Robert Hadji and Jessica Salmonson gave valuable support in late-night convention discussions, and the World Fantasy Convention provided an annual environment for advancing ideas in the context of the fine working writers and experts who make horror literature a vigorous and growing form in our time. Finally, my sincere thanks to Stephen King for *Danse Macabre*.

Table of Contents

Introduction

To taste the full flavor of these stories you must bring an orderly mind to them, you must have a reasonable amount of confidence, if not in what used to be called the laws of nature, at least in the currently suspected habits of nature. . . . To the truly superstitious the "weird" has only its Scotch meaning: "Something which actually takes place."
—Dashiell Hammett, *Creeps by Night*

The appeal of the spectrally macabre is generally narrow because it demands from the reader a certain degree of imagination and a capacity for detachment from everyday life. Relatively few are free enough from the spell of daily routine to respond. . . .
—H. P. Lovecraft, *Supernatural Horror in Literature*

I

On a July Sunday morning, I was moderating a panel discussion at Necon, a small New England convention devoted to dark fantasy. The panelists included Alan Ryan, Whitley Strieber, Peter Straub, Charles L. Grant and, I believe, Les Daniels, all of them horror novelists. The theme of the discussion was literary influences, with each participant naming the horror writers he felt significant in the genesis of his career. As the minutes rolled by and the litany of names, Poe and Bradbury and Leiber and Lovecraft and Kafka and others, was uttered, I realized that except for a ritual bow to Stephen King, every single influential writer named had been a short story writer. So I interrupted the panel and asked them all to spend the last few minutes commenting on my observation. What they said amounted to this: the good stuff is pretty much all short fiction.

After a few months of thought, I spent a late Halloween night with Peter Straub at the World Fantasy Convention, getting his response to my developing ideas on the recent evolution of horror from a short story to a novel genre. My belief that the long-form horror story is avant-garde and experimental, an unsolved aesthetic problem being attacked with energy and determination by Straub and King and others in our time, solidified as a result of that conversation.

But it seemed to me too early to generalize as to the nature of the new horror novel form. What, then, I asked myself, has happened to the short story? The horror story has certainly not up and vanished after 160 years of development and popularity; far from it. As an administrator of the annual World Fantasy Awards since 1975, I was aware of significant growth in short fiction in the past decade. And so the idea of this book was conceived, to conclude the era of the dominance of short-form horror with a definitive anthology that attempts to represent the entire evolution of the form to date and to describe and point out the boundaries of horror as it has been redefined in our contemporary field. For it seemed apparent to me that the conventional approach to horror codified by the great anthologies of the 1940s is obsolete, was indeed becoming obsolete as those books were published, and has persisted to the detriment of a clearer understanding of the literature to the present. It has persisted to the point where fans of horror fiction most often restrict their reading to books and stories given the imprimateur of a horror category label, thus missing some of the finest pleasures of this century in that fictional mode. I have gathered as many as could be confined within one huge volume here in *The Dark Descent*, with the intent of clearing the air and broadening future considerations of horror.

> Fear has its own aesthetic—as Le Fanu, Henry James, Montagu James and Walter de la Mare have repeatedly shown—and also its own propriety. A story dealing in fear ought, ideally, to be kept at a certain pitch. And that austere other world, the world of the ghost, should inspire, when it impacts on our own, not so much revulsion or shock as a sort of awe.
>
> —Elizabeth Bowen, *The Second Ghost Book*

> The one test of the really weird is simply this—whether or not there be excited in the reader a profound sense of dread, and of contact with unknown spheres and powers.
>
> —H. P. Lovecraft, *Supernatural Horror in Literature*

II   The Evolution of Horror Fiction

For more than 150 years horror fiction has been a vital component of English and American literature, invented with the short story form itself and contributing intimately to the evolution of the short story. Until the last decade, the dominant literary form of horror fiction was the short story and novella. This is simply no longer the case. Shortly after the beginning of the 1970s, within a very few years, the novel form assumed the position of leadership. First came a scattering of exceptionally popular novels—*Rosemary's Baby*, *The Other*, *The Exorcist*, *The Mephisto Waltz*, with attendant film successes—then, in 1973, the deluge, with Stephen King on the crest of the wave, altering the nature of horror fiction for the foreseeable future and sweeping along with it all the living generations of short fiction writers. Very few writers of horror fiction, young or old, resisted the commercial or aesthetic temptation to expand into the novel form, leading to the creation of some of the best horror novels of all time as well as a large amount of popular trash rushed into print. The models for these works were the previous bestsellers, popular films and the short fiction masterpieces of previous decades.

When the tide ebbed in the 1980s, much of the trash was left dead in the backlists of paperback publishers, but the horror novel had become firmly established. This is significant from a number of perspectives. Rapid evolution and experimentation was encouraged. All kinds of horror literature benefited from the incorporation of every conceivable element of horrific effect and technique from other literature and film and video and comics.

The most useful and provocative view we can take on the horror novel in recent years is that it constitutes an avant-garde and experimental literary form which attempts to translate the horrific effects previously thought to be the nearly exclusive domain of the short forms into newly conceived long forms that maintain the proper atmosphere and effects. Certainly isolated examples of more or less successful novel-length horror fiction exist, from *Frankenstein* and *Dracula* to *The Haunting of Hill House*, but they are comparatively infrequent next to the constant, rich proliferation and development of horror in shorter forms in every decade from Poe to the present. The horror novels of the past do not in aggregate form a body of traditional literature and technique from which the present novels spring and upon which they depend.

It is evident both from the recent novels themselves and from the public statements of many of the writers that Stephen King, Peter Straub and Ramsey Campbell, and a number of other leading novelists, have been discussing among themselves—and trying to solve in their works—the perceived problems of developing the horror novel into a sophisticated and effective form. In so doing, they have highlighted the desirability of a volume such as *The Dark Descent*, which represents the context from which the literature springs and attempts to elucidate the whole surround of horror today.

Horror novels grow to a very large extent out of the varied and highly evolved novellas and short stories exemplified in this book. Our perceptions of the nature of horror literature have been changing and evolving rapidly in recent decades, to the point where a compilation of the horror story, organized according to new principles, is needed to manifest the broadened nature of the literature.

Before proceeding in the next section to begin an anatomy of horror, it is interesting to note that there has been a renewed fashion for horror in every decade since the First World War, but this is the first such "revival" that has produced numerous novels.

There was a general increase in horror, particularly the ghost story, in the 1920s under the influence of M. R. James, both a prominent writer and anthologist, and such masters as Algernon Blackwood, Walter de la Mare, Edith Wharton and others. At that time the great horror magazine, *Weird*

Tales, was founded in the U.S. In the 1930s, the dark fantasy story or weird tale became prominent, influenced by the magazine mentioned above, the growth of the H. P. Lovecraft circle of writers, and a proliferation of anthologies, either in series or as huge compendiums celebrating the first century of horror fiction. After the films and books of the 1930s, the early 1940s produced the finest "great works" collections, epitomized by *And the Darkness Falls,* edited by Boris Karloff, and *Great Tales of Terror and the Supernatural,* edited by Herbert Wise and Phyllis Fraser; and Arkham House, the great specialty publisher devoted to this day to bringing into print collections by great horror authors, was founded by writer Donald Wandrei to print the collected works of H. P. Lovecraft. After the war came the science fiction horrors of the 1950s, in all those monster films and in the works of Richard Matheson, Jack Finney, Theodore Sturgeon and Ray Bradbury. In the early sixties we had the craze for "junk food" paperback horror anthologies and collections, under the advent of the midnight horror movie boom on TV. But as we remarked above, short fiction always remained at the forefront. Even the novelists were famous for their short stories.

A lot has changed.

> Atmosphere is the all-important thing, for the final criterion of authenticity is not the dovetailing of a plot but the creation of a given sensation.
>
> —H. P. Lovecraft, *Supernatural Horror in Literature*

> Much as we ask for it, the *frisson* of horror, among the many oddities of our emotional life, is one of the oddest. For one thing, it is usually a response to something that is not there. Under normal circumstances, that is, it attends only such things as nightmares, phobias and literature. In that respect it is unlike terror, which is extreme and sudden fear in the face of a material threat. . . . The terror can be dissipated by a round of buckshot. Horror, on the other hand, is fascinated dread in the presence of an immaterial cause. The frights of nightmares cannot be dissipated by a round of buckshot; to flee them is to run into them at every turn.
>
> —Sigmund Freud, *The Uncanny*

III   What It Is

Sigmund Freud remarked that we immediately recognize scenes that are supposed to provoke horror, "even if they actually provoke titters." It seems to me, however, that horror fiction has usually been linked to or categorized by manifest signs in texts, and this has caused more than a little confusion among commentators over the years. Names such as weird tales, gothic tales, terror tales, ghost stories, supernatural tales, macabre stories—all clustered around the principle of a real or implied or fake intrusion of the supernatural into the natural world, an intrusion which arouses fear—have been used as appellations for the whole body of literature, sometimes interchangeably by the same writer. So often, and in so many of the best works, has the intrusion been a ghost, that nearly half the time you will find "horror story" and "ghost story" used interchangeably. And this is so in spite of the acknowledged fact that supernatural horror in literature embodies many manifestations (from demons to vampires to werewolves to pagan gods and more) and, further, that ghosts are recognizably not supposed to horrify in a fair number of ghost stories.

J. A. Cuddon, a thorough scholar, has traced the early connections between ghost and horror stories from the 1820s to the 1870s, viewing them as originally separable: "The growth of the ghost story and the horror story in this mid-century period tended to coalesce; indeed, it is difficult to establish objective criteria by which to distinguish between the two. A taxonomical approach invariably begins to break down at an early stage. . . . On balance, it is probable that a ghost story will contain an element of horror." Jack Sullivan, another distinguished scholar and anthologist, sums up the problems of definition and terminology thusly: "We find ourselves in a tangled morass of definitions and permutations that grows as relentlessly as the fungus in the House of Usher." Sullivan chooses "ghost story" as generic, presumably to have one leg to stand on facing in each direction.

We choose "horror" as our term, both in accordance with the usage of the marketplace (Tor Books has a Tor Horror line; horror is a label for the marketing category under which novels and collections appear), and because it points toward a transaction between the reader and the text that is the essence of the experience of reading horror fiction, and not any thing contained within that text (such as a ghost, literal or implied). And moreover, H. P. Lovecraft, the theoretician and critic who most carefully described the literature in his *Supernatural Horror in Literature*, who was certainly the most important American writer of horror fiction in the first half of this century, has to the best of my memory not a single conventional ghost story in the corpus of his works.

It is Lovecraft's essay that provides the keystone upon which any architecture of horror must be built: atmosphere. And it seems to me that Freud is in accord. What this means is that you can experience true horror in, potentially, any work of fiction, be it a western, a contemporary gothic, science fiction, mystery, whatever category of content the writer may choose. A work may be a horror story (and indeed included in this anthology) no matter what, as long as the atmosphere allows. This means that horror is set free from the supernatural, that it is unnecessary for the story to contain any overt or implied device or manifestation whatsoever. The emotional transaction is paramount and definitive, and we recognize its presence even when it doesn't work as it is supposed to.

> To them [people who don't read horror] it is a kind of pornography, inducing horripilation instead of erection. And the reader who appears to relish such sensations—why he's an emotional

masochist, the slave of an unholy drug, a decadent psychotic beast.
—David Aylward, *Revenge of the Past*

First, the longing for mystic experience which seems always to manifest itself in periods of social confusion, when political progress is blocked: as soon as we feel that our own world has failed us, we try to find evidence for another world; second, the instinct to inoculate ourselves against panic at the real horrors loose on the earth . . . by injections of imagery horror, which soothe us with the momentary illusion that the forces of madness and murder may be tamed and compelled to provide us with a mere dramatic entertainment.
—Edmund Wilson, *A Literary Chronicle*

I used to read horror when I was depressed to jump-start my emotions—but it only gave me temporary relief.
—Kathryn Cramer (personal correspondence)

It proves that the tale of horror and/or the supernatural *is* serious, *is* important, *is* necessary . . . not only to those human beings who read to think, but to those who read to feel; the volume may even go a certain distance toward proving the idea that, as this mad century races toward its conclusion—a conclusion which seems ever more ominous and ever more absurd—it may be the most important and useful form of fiction which the moral writer may command.
—Stephen King, Introduction to *The Arbor House Treasury of Horror and the Supernatural*

IV   The Death of Horror

The death of the novel and the death of the short story are literary topics we joke about, so it should come as no particular surprise that a recent, and otherwise excellent, collection of essays on supernatural fiction in America from 1820–1920 states that supernatural fiction died around 1920 ("dematerialized"), to be replaced by psychoanalysis, which took over its function. Now it seems to me surprising to maintain that fiction that embodies psychological truth in metaphor is replaceable by science—it sounds rather too much like replacing painting with photography. Yet this is only a recent example of the obituary approach, an effective gambit when dealing with material you wish to exterminate, and often used by self-appointed arbiters of taste.

Let's resurrect the great Modernist critic, Edmund Wilson, for a few minutes. Wilson wrote an essay on horror in the early 1940s that challenged the whole canon of significant works established by the anthologists of the 1930s and '40s, from Dorothy Sayers and M. R. James and Hugh Walpole and Marjorie Bowen to Wise and Fraser, and Karloff. Wilson proposed his own list of masterpieces, from Poe and Gogol ("the greatest master") and Melville and Turgenev through Hardy, Stevenson, Kipling, Conrad's *The Heart of Darkness* and Henry James' *The Turn of the Screw* to Walter de la Mare and, ultimately, Kafka ("he went straight for the morbidities of the psyche"). He, Wilson, seems to be reaching toward a redefinition of horror literature, but unfortunately his essay vibrates with the discomfort of the humanist and rationalist confronting the supernatural. He rejects nearly every classic story in the horror canon and every single writer principally known for work in the field, reserving particular antipathy for H. P. Lovecraft, the anti-Modernist (to whom he devoted a whole separate essay of demolition).

Wilson's comments on Kafka are instructive. Kafka's "visions of moral horror" are "narratives that compel our attention, and fantasies that generate more shudders than the whole of Algernon Blackwood or M. R. James combined." Kafka's characters "have turned into the enchanted denizens of a world in which, prosaic though it is, we can find no firm foothold in reality and in which we can never even be certain whether souls are being saved or damned . . . he went straight for the morbidities of the psyche with none of the puppetry of specters and devils that earlier writers still carried with them." Wilson's view of the evolution of horror is implicit in these comments. He sees the literature as evolving in a linear fashion into fantasies of the psyche removed entirely from supernatural trappings. Any audience interested in these trappings is regressive. He sees no value to a modern reader in obsolete fiction.

Since Wilson's presupposition is that the evolution of horror ended with Kafka, his theory of horror reading among his contemporaries—that they are indulging in a "revived" taste for an obsolete form—allows him to start from the premise that the ghost story is dead, that it died with the advent of the electric light, and to conclude immediately that contemporary versions are doomed attempts to revive the corpse of the form. Sound familiar? It's the familiar "death of literature" obituary approach. Well, back to the grave, Edmund. You're dead, and horror literature is alive and well, happily evolving and diversifying.

But Wilson's approach to the horror canon was and remains generally stimulating. For it appears that as horror has evolved in this century it has grown significantly in the areas of "the morbidities of the psyche" and fantasies of "a world in which, prosaic though it is, we can find no firm foothold in reality."

> In order to achieve the fantastic, it is neither necessary nor sufficient to portray extraordinary things. The strangest event will enter into the order of the universe if it is alone in a world governed by laws. . . . You cannot impose limits on the fantastic; either it does not exist at all, or else it extends throughout the universe. It is an entire world in which things manifest a captive, tormented

thought, a thought both whimsical and enchained, that gnaws away from below at the mechanism's links without ever managing to express itself. In this world, matter is never entirely matter, since it offers only a constantly frustrated attempt at determinism, and mind is never completely mind, because it has fallen into slavery and has been impregnated and dulled by matter. All is woe. Things suffer and tend towards inertia, without ever attaining it; the debased, enslaved mind unsuccessfully strives toward consciousness and freedom.

—Jean-Paul Sartre, *AMINADAB or The Fantastic Considered as a Language*

V   The Three Streams

We return to the life and state of horror fiction in the present. Contemporary horror fiction occurs in three streams, in three principal modes or clusters of emphasis: 1. moral allegorical 2. psychological metaphor 3. fantastic. The stories in this anthology are separated according to these categories. These modes are not mutually exclusive, but usually a matter of emphasis along a spectrum from the overtly moral at one extreme to the nearly totally ambiguous at the other, with human psychology always a significant factor but only sometimes the principal focus. Perhaps we might usefully imagine them as three currents in the same ocean.

Stories that cluster at the first pole are characteristically supernatural fiction, most usually about the intrusion of supernatural evil into consensus reality, most often about the horrid and colorful special effects of evil. These are the stories of children possessed by demons, of hauntings by evil ghosts from the past (most ghost stories), stories of bad places (where evil persists from past times), of witchcraft and satanism. In our day they are often written and read by lapsed Christians, who have lost their firm belief in good but still have a discomforting belief in evil. Stories in this stream imply or state the Manichean universe that is so difficult to perceive in everyday life, wherein evil is so evident, horror so common that we are left with our sensitivities partly or fully deadened to it in our post-Holocaust, post-Vietnam, six-o'clock news era. A strong extra-literary appeal of such fiction, it seems to me, is to jump-start the readers' deadened emotional sensitivities.

And the moral allegory has its significant extra-literary appeal in itself to that large audience that desires the attribution of a moral calculus (usually teleological) deriving from ultimate and metaphysical forms of good and evil behind events in an everyday reality. Ginjer Buchanan says that "all the best horror is written by lapsed Catholics."

In speaking of stories and novels in this first stream, we are speaking of the most popular form of horror fiction today, the commercial bestseller lineage of *Rosemary's Baby* and *The Exorcist*, and a majority of the works of Stephen King. These stories are taken to the heart of the commercial-category audience that is characteristically style-deaf (regardless of the excellence of some of the works), the audience that requires repeated doses of such fiction for its emotional effect to persist. This stream is the center of category horror publishing.

The second group of horror stories, stories of aberrant human psychology embodied metaphorically, may be either purely supernatural, such as *Dracula*, or purely psychological, such as Robert Bloch's *Psycho*. What characterizes them as a group is the monster at the center, from the monster of Frankenstein, to Carmilla, to the chain-saw murderer—an overtly abnormal human or creature, from whose acts and on account of whose being the horror arises. D. H. Lawrence's little boy, Faulkner's Emily, and, more subtly, the New Yorker of Henry James' "The Jolly Corner" show the extent to which this stream interpenetrates and blends with the mainstream of psychological fiction in this century. Both Lovecraft and Edmund Wilson, from differing perspectives, see Joseph Conrad's *The Heart of Darkness* as essentially horror fiction. There has been strong resistance on the part of critics, from Wilson to the present, to admitting nonsupernatural psychological horror into consideration of the field, allowing many to declare the field a dead issue for contemporary literature, of antiquarian interest only since the 1930s. This trend was probably aided by the superficial examination of the antiquarianism of both M. R. James and H. P. Lovecraft.

But by 1939 an extremely significant transition is apparent, particularly in the U.S. *Weird Tales* and the Lovecraft circle of writers, as well as the popular films, had made horror a vigorous part of popular culture, had built a large audience among the generally nonliterary readership for pulp fiction, a "lower-class" audience. And in 1939 John W. Campbell, the famous science fiction editor, founded the revolutionary pulp fantasy magazine, *Unknown*. From 1923 to 1939, the leading source of horror and supernatural fiction in the English language was *Weird Tales*, publishing all traditional styles but tending toward the florid and antiquarian. *Unknown* was an aesthetic break with traditional horror fiction. Campbell demanded stories with contemporary, particularly urban, settings, told in clear, unornamented prose style. *Unknown* featured stories by all the young science fiction writers whose work was changing that genre in Campbell's *Astounding*: Alfred Bester, Eric Frank Russell, Robert A. Heinlein, A. E. Van Vogt, L. Ron Hubbard and others, particularly such fantasists as Theodore Sturgeon, Jane Rice, Anthony Boucher, Fredric Brown and Fritz Leiber.

The stories tended to focus equally on the supernatural and the psychological. Psychology was often quite overtly the underpinning for horror, as in, for example, Hubbard's "He Didn't Like Cats," in which there is an extended discussion between the two supporting characters as to whether the central character's problem is supernatural or psychological . . . and we never know, for either way he's doomed. *Unknown* broke the dominance of *Weird Tales* and influenced such significant young talents as Ray Bradbury and Shirley Jackson. The magazine encouraged the genrification of certain types of psychological fiction and, at the same time, crossbred a good bit of horror into the growing science fiction field. This reinforced a cultural trend apparent in the monster and mad scientist films of the 1930s, giving us the enormous spawn of SF/horror films of the 1950s and beyond.

It is interesting to note that as our perceptions of horror fiction and what the term includes change over the decades, differing works seem to fall naturally into or out of the category. The possibilities of psychological horror seem in the end to blur distinctions, and there is no question that horror is becoming ever more inclusive.

Stories of the third stream have at their center ambiguity as to the nature of reality, and it is this very ambiguity that generates the horrific effects. Often there is an overtly supernatural (or certainly abnormal) occurrence, but we know of it only by allusion. Often, essential elements are left undescribed so that, for instance, we do not know whether there was really a ghost or not. But the difference is not merely supernatural versus psychological explanation: third stream stories lack any explanation that makes sense in everyday reality—we don't know, and that doubt disturbs us, horrifies us. This is the fiction to which Sartre's analysis alludes, the fantastic. At its extreme, from Kafka to the present, it blends indistinguishably with magic realism, the surreal, the absurd, all the fictions that confront reality through paradoxical distance. It is the fiction of radical doubt. Thomas M. Disch once remarked that Poe can profitably be considered as a contemporary of Kierkegaard, and it is evident that this stream develops from the beginnings of horror fiction in the short story. In the contemporary field it is a major current.

Third stream stories tend to cross all category lines but usually they do not use the conventional supernatural as a distancing device. While most horror fiction declares itself at some point as violating the laws of nature, the fantastic worlds of third stream fiction use as a principal device what Sartre has called the language of the fantastic.

At the end of a horror story, the reader is left with a new perception of the nature of reality. In the moral allegory strain, the point seems to be that this is what reality was and has been all along (i.e., literally a world in which supernatural forces are at work) only you couldn't or wouldn't recognize it. Psychological metaphor stories basically use the intrusion of abnormality to release repressed or unarticulated psychological states. In her book, *Powers of Horror*, critic Julia Kristeva says that horror deals with material just on the edge of repression but not entirely repressed and inaccessible. Stories from our second stream use the heightening effect of the monstrously abnormal to achieve this release. Third stream stories maintain the pretense of everyday reality only to annihilate it, leaving us with another world entirely, one in which we are disturbingly imprisoned. It is in perceiving the changed reality and its nature that the pleasure and illumination of third stream stories lies, that raises this part of horror fiction above the literary level of most of its generic relations. So the transaction between the reader and the text that identifies all horror fiction is to an extent modified in third stream stories (there is rarely, if ever, any terror), making them more difficult to classify and identify than even the borderline cases in the psychological category. Gene Wolfe's "Seven American Nights" is, in my opinion, a story on the borderline of third stream, deeply disturbing but not conventionally horrifying. The mass horror audience is not much taken with third stream stories, regardless of craft or literary merit, because they modify the emotional jolt.

> Although the manifest images of horror fiction are legion, their latent meanings are few. Readers and writers of horror fiction, like those of all the popular genres, seem under a compulsion to repeat. Certainly the needs satisfied by horror fiction are recurrent and ineradicable.
> —George Stade, *The New York Times*, Oct. 27, 1985

> I recognize terror as the finest emotion and so I will try to terrorize the reader. But if I find that I cannot terrify, I will try to horrify, and if I find that I cannot horrify, I'll go for the gross-out.
> —Stephen King, *Danse Macabre*

VI   The Dark Descent

The descent of horror fiction from its origins in the nineteenth century to the many and sophisticated forms of the contemporary field has taken place in shorter stories. Now that the novel has taken over, the major writers are unlikely to devote their principal efforts to short fiction. So we have reached a point in the evolution of this literary mode at which we can take stock of its achievements in short fiction and assess its qualities and contributions to all of literature. The stories assembled in this book are divided according to the three streams we have identified, both to provide extended examples and to provoke further discussion. The short story is vigorously alive in horror today, in magazines, anthologies, and collections. Let it, for a moment, occupy the center of your attention. The best short fiction in modern horror is the equal of the best of all times and places.

PART I

The Color of Evil

Stephen King

The Reach

Stephen King is the single most popular writer of horror fiction since Charles Dickens; one of the most popular writers of fiction in the English language today. He is a pop culture phenomenon, the king of horror just as Elvis Presley was the king of rock and roll. He has millions of fans. He has written the best book on contemporary horror, *Danse Macabre*, full of enthusiasm for the horrific effects of radio, film, television, comics, and stories, and best of all sympathetic and illuminating comments on the works of living writers, with extensive comments from the writers themselves often provided. King's eclectic taste and willingness to respond to a variety of styles and approaches points out rich pathways for broadening our conceptions of the nature of horror stories and their virtues. And then there are the stories and novels: *Salem's Lot* and *Carrie*, *The Shining* and *The Stand*, *Night Shift* and *Skeleton Crew* and more each year. King by precept and example is the greatest force for change in horror literature in our time, unfettered by category boundaries. Whatever he writes is mainstream fiction. His example has drawn nearly every short fiction writer of the past decade into attempting the novel form, creating a publishing boom and a fertile chaos of creativity that has outlasted the boom. "The Reach," originally published as "Do the Dead Sing," is often considered his best short story. It is a work of unusual subtlety and sentiment, a ghost story of love and death, a virtuoso performance in which the horror is distanced but underpins the whole. It represents the theme of the first section of this book, embodying King's feeling that horror fiction "may be the most important and useful form of fiction which the moral writer may command."

"The Reach was wider in those days," Stella Flanders told her great-grandchildren in the last summer of her life, the summer before she began to see ghosts. The children looked at her with wide, silent eyes, and her son, Alden, turned from his seat on the porch where he was whittling. It was Sunday, and Alden wouldn't take his boat out on Sundays no matter how high the price of lobster was.

"What do you mean, Gram?" Tommy asked, but the old woman did not answer. She only sat in her rocker by the cold stove, her slippers bumping placidly on the floor.

Tommy asked his mother: "What does she mean?"

Lois only shook her head, smiled, and sent them out with pots to pick berries.

15

Stella thought: She's forgot. Or did she ever know?

The Reach had been wider in those days. If anyone knew it was so, that person was Stella Flanders. She had been born in 1884, she was the oldest resident of Goat Island, and she had never once in her life been to the mainland.

Do you love? This question had begun to plague her, and she did not even know what it meant.

Fall set in, a cold fall without the necessary rain to bring a really fine color to the trees, either on Goat or on Raccoon Head across the Reach. The wind blew long, cold notes that fall, and Stella felt each note resonate in her heart.

On November 19, when the first flurries came swirling down out of a sky the color of white chrome, Stella celebrated her birthday. Most of the village turned out. Hattie Stoddard came, whose mother had died of pleurisy in 1954 and whose father had been lost with the *Dancer* in 1941. Richard and Mary Dodge came, Richard moving slowly up the path on his cane, his arthritis riding him like an invisible passenger. Sarah Havelock came, of course; Sarah's mother Annabelle had been Stella's best friend. They had gone to the island school together, grades one to eight, and Annabelle had married Tommy Frane, who had pulled her hair in the fifth grade and made her cry, just as Stella had married Bill Flanders, who had once knocked all of her schoolbooks out of her arms and into the mud (but she had managed not to cry). Now both Annabelle and Tommy were gone and Sarah was the only one of their seven children still on the island. *Her* husband, George Havelock, who had been known to everyone as Big George, had died a nasty death over on the mainland in 1967, the year there was no fishing. An ax had slipped in Big George's hand, there had been blood—too much of it!—and an island funeral three days later. And when Sarah came in to Stella's party and cried, "Happy birthday, Gram!" Stella hugged her tight and closed her eyes

(do you do you love?)

but she did not cry.

There was a tremendous birthday cake. Hattie had made it with her best friend, Vera Spruce. The assembled company bellowed out "Happy Birthday to You" in a combined voice that was loud enough to drown out the wind . . . for a little while, anyway. Even Alden sang, who in the normal course of events would sing only "Onward, Christian Soldiers" and the doxology in church and would mouth the words of all the rest with his head hunched and his big old jug ears just as red as tomatoes. There were ninety-five candles on Stella's cake, and even over the singing she heard the wind, although her hearing was not what it once had been.

She thought the wind was calling her name.

"I was not the only one," she would have told Lois's children if she could. "In my day there were many that lived and died on the island. There was no mail boat in those days; Bull Symes used to bring the mail when there was mail. There was no ferry, either. If you had business on the Head, your man

took you in the lobster boat. So far as I know, there wasn't a flushing toilet on the island until 1946. 'Twas Bull's boy Harold that put in the first one the year after the heart attack carried Bull off while he was out dragging traps. I remember seeing them bring Bull home. I remember that they brought him up wrapped in a tarpaulin, and how one of his green boots poked out. I remember . . ."

And they would say: "What, Gram? What do you remember?"

How would she answer them? Was there more?

On the first day of winter, a month or so after the birthday party, Stella opened the back door to get stovewood and discovered a dead sparrow on the back stoop. She bent down carefully, picked it up by one foot, and looked at it.

"Frozen," she announced, and something inside her spoke another word. It had been forty years since she had seen a frozen bird—1938. The year the Reach had frozen.

Shuddering, pulling her coat closer, she threw the dead sparrow in the old rusty incinerator as she went by it. The day was cold. The sky was a clear, deep blue. On the night of her birthday four inches of snow had fallen, had melted, and no more had come since then. "Got to come soon," Larry McKeen down at the Goat Island Store said sagely, as if daring winter to stay away.

Stella got to the woodpile, picked herself an armload and carried it back to the house. Her shadow, crisp and clean, followed her.

As she reached the back door, where the sparrow had fallen, Bill spoke to her—but the cancer had taken Bill twelve years before. "Stella," Bill said, and she saw his shadow fall beside her, longer but just as clear-cut, the shadow-bill of his shadow-cap twisted jauntily off to one side just as he had always worn it. Stella felt a scream lodged in her throat. It was too large to touch her lips.

"Stella," he said again, "when you comin across to the mainland? We'll get Norm Jolley's old Ford and go down to Bean's in Freeport just for a lark. What do you say?"

She wheeled, almost dropping her wood, and there was no one there. Just the dooryard sloping down to the hill, then the wild white grass, and beyond all, at the edge of everything, clear-cut and somehow magnified, the Reach . . . and the mainland beyond it.

"Gram, what's the Reach?" Lona might have asked . . . although she never had. And she would have given them the answer any fisherman knew by rote: a Reach is a body of water between two bodies of land, a body of water which is open at either end. The old lobsterman's joke went like this: know how to read y'compass when the fog comes, boys; between Jonesport and London there's a mighty long Reach.

"Reach is the water between the island and the mainland," she might have amplified, giving them molasses cookies and hot tea laced with sugar. "I know that much. I know it as well as my husband's name . . . and how he used to wear his hat."

"Gram?" Lona would say. "How come you never been across the Reach?"
"Honey," she would say, "I never saw any reason to go."

In January, two months after the birthday party, the Reach froze for the first time since 1938. The radio warned islanders and mainlanders alike not to trust the ice, but Stewie McClelland and Russell Bowie took Stewie's Bombardier Skiddoo out anyway after a long afternoon spent drinking Apple Zapple wine, and sure enough, the skiddoo went into the Reach. Stewie managed to crawl out (although he lost one foot to frostbite). The Reach took Russell Bowie and carried him away.

That January 25 there was a memorial service for Russell. Stella went on her son Alden's arm, and he mouthed the words to the hymns and boomed out the doxology in his great tuneless voice before the benediction. Stella sat afterward with Sarah Havelock and Hattie Stoddard and Vera Spruce in the glow of the wood fire in the town-hall basement. A going-away party for Russell was being held, complete with Za-Rex punch and nice little cream-cheese sandwiches cut into triangles. The men, of course, kept wandering out back for a nip of something a bit stronger than Za-Rex. Russell Bowie's new widow sat red-eyed and stunned beside Ewell McCracken, the minister. She was seven months big with child—it would be her fifth—and Stella, half-dozing in the heat of the woodstove, thought: *She'll be crossing the Reach soon enough, I guess. She'll move to Freeport or Lewiston and go for a waitress, I guess.*

She looked around at Vera and Hattie, to see what the discussion was.

"No, I didn't hear," Hattie said. "What *did* Freddy say?"

They were talking about Freddy Dinsmore, the oldest man on the island (two years younger'n me, though, Stella thought with some satisfaction), who had sold out his store to Larry McKeen in 1960 and now lived on his retirement.

"Said he'd never seen such a winter," Vera said, taking out her knitting. "He says it is going to make people sick."

Sarah Havelock looked at Stella, and asked if Stella had ever seen such a winter. There had been no snow since that first little bit; the ground lay crisp and bare and brown. The day before, Stella had walked thirty paces into the back field, holding her right hand level at the height of her thigh, and the grass there had snapped in a neat row with a sound like breaking glass.

"No," Stella said. "The Reach froze in '38, but there was snow that year. Do you remember Bull Symes, Hattie?"

Hattie laughed. "I think I still have the black-and-blue he gave me on my sit-upon at the New Year's party in '53. He pinched me *that* hard. What about him?"

"Bull and my own man walked across to the mainland that year," Stella said. "That February of 1938. Strapped on snowshoes, walked across to Dorrit's Tavern on the Head, had them each a shot of whiskey, and walked back. They asked me to come along. They were like two little boys off to the sliding with a toboggan between them."

They were looking at her, touched by the wonder of it. Even Vera was looking at her wide-eyed, and Vera had surely heard the tale before. If you believed the stories, Bull and Vera had once played some house together, although it was hard, looking at Vera now, to believe she had ever been so young.

"And you didn't go?" Sarah asked, perhaps seeing the reach of the Reach in her mind's eye, so white it was almost blue in the heatless winter sunshine, the sparkle of the snow crystals, the mainland drawing closer, walking across, yes, walking across the ocean just like Jesus-out-of-the-boat, leaving the island for the one and only time in your life on *foot*—

"No," Stella said. Suddenly she wished she had brought her own knitting. "I didn't go with them."

"Why *not?*" Hattie asked, almost indignantly.

"It was washday," Stella almost snapped, and then Missy Bowie, Russell's widow, broke into loud, braying sobs. Stella looked over and there sat Bill Flanders in his red-and-black-checked jacket, hat cocked to one side, smoking a Herbert Tareyton with another tucked behind his ear for later. She felt her heart leap into her chest and choke between beats.

She made a noise, but just then a knot popped like a rifle shot in the stove, and neither of the other ladies heard.

"Poor *thing*," Sarah nearly cooed.

"Well shut of that good-for-nothing," Hattie grunted. She searched for the grim depth of the truth concerning the departed Russell Bowie and found it: "Little more than a tramp for pay, that man. She's well out of *that* two-hoss trace."

Stella barely heard these things. There sat Bill, close enough to the Reverend McCracken to have tweaked his nose if he so had a mind; he looked no more than forty, his eyes barely marked by the crow's-feet that had later sunk so deep, wearing his flannel pants and his gum-rubber boots with the gray wool socks folded neatly down over the tops.

"We're waitin on you, Stel," he said. "You come on across and see the mainland. You won't need no snowshoes this year."

There he sat in the town-hall basement, big as Billy-be-damned, and then another knot exploded in the stove and he was gone. And the Reverend McCracken went on comforting Missy Bowie as if nothing had happened.

That night Vera called up Annie Phillips on the phone, and in the course of the conversation mentioned to Annie that Stella Flanders didn't look well, not at all well.

"Alden would have a scratch of a job getting her off-island if she took sick," Annie said. Annie liked Alden because her own son Toby had told her Alden would take nothing stronger than beer. Annie was strictly temperance, herself.

"Wouldn't get her off 'tall unless she was in a coma," Vera said, pronouncing the word in the downeast fashion: *comer*. "When Stella says 'Frog,' Alden jumps. Alden ain't but half-bright, you know. Stella pretty much runs him."

"Oh, ayuh?" Annie said.

Just then there was a metallic crackling sound on the line. Vera could hear Annie Phillips for a moment longer—not the words, just the sound of her voice going on behind the crackling—and then there was nothing. The wind had gusted up high and the phone lines had gone down, maybe into Godlin's Pond or maybe down by Borrow's Cove, where they went into the Reach sheathed in rubber. It was possible that they had gone down on the other side, on the Head . . . and some might even have said (only half-joking) that Russell Bowie had reached up a cold hand to snap the cable, just for the hell of it.

Not 700 feet away Stella Flanders lay under her puzzle-quilt and listened to the dubious music of Alden's snores in the other room. She listened to Alden so she wouldn't have to listen to the wind . . . but she heard the wind anyway, oh yes, coming across the frozen expanse of the Reach, a mile and a half of water that was now overplated with ice, ice with lobsters down below, and groupers, and perhaps the twisting, dancing body of Russell Bowie, who used to come each April with his old Rogers rototiller and turn her garden.

Who'll turn the earth this April? she wondered as she lay cold and curled under her puzzle-quilt. And as a dream in a dream, her voice answered her voice: *Do you love?* The wind gusted, rattling the storm window. It seemed that the storm window was talking to her, but she turned her face away from its words. And did not cry.

"But Gram," Lona would press (she never gave up, not that one, she was like her mom, and her grandmother before her), "you still haven't told why you never went across."

"Why, child, I have always had everything I wanted right here on Goat."

"But it's so small. We live in Portland. There's buses, Gram!"

"I see enough of what goes on in cities on the TV. I guess I'll stay where I am."

Hal was younger, but somehow more intuitive; he would not press her as his sister might, but his question would go closer to the heart of things: "You never wanted to go across, Gram? Never?"

And she would lean toward him, and take his small hands, and tell him how her mother and father had come to the island shortly after they were married, and how Bull Symes's grandfather had taken Stella's father as a 'prentice on his boat. She would tell him how her mother had conceived four times but one of her babies had miscarried and another had died a week after birth—she would have left the island if they could have saved it at the mainland hospital, but of course it was over before that was even thought of.

She would tell them that Bill had delivered Jane, their grandmother, but not that when it was over he had gone into the bathroom and first puked and then wept like a hysterical woman who had her monthlies p'ticularly bad. Jane, of course, had left the island at fourteen to go to high school; girls didn't get married at fourteen anymore, and when Stella saw her go off in the boat with Bradley Maxwell, whose job it had been to ferry the kids back and forth that month, she knew in her heart that Jane was gone for good, although she would come back for a while. She would tell them that Alden had come along ten years later, after they had given up, and as if to make up for his tardiness, here was Alden still, a lifelong bachelor, and in some ways Stella was grateful for that because Alden was not terribly bright and there are plenty of women willing to take advantage of a man with a slow brain and a good heart (although she would not tell the children that last, either).

She would say: "Louis and Margaret Godlin begat Stella Godlin, who became Stella Flanders; Bill and Stella Flanders begat Jane and Alden Flanders and Jane Flanders became Jane Wakefield; Richard and Jane Wakefield begat Lois Wakefield, who became Lois Perrault; David and Lois Perrault begat Lona and Hal. Those are your names, children: you are Godlin-Flanders-Wakefield-Perrault. Your blood is in the stones of this island, and I stay here because the mainland is too far to reach. Yes, I love; I have loved, anyway, or at least tried to love, but memory is so wide and so deep, and I cannot cross. Godlin-Flanders-Wakefield-Perrault . . ."

That was the coldest February since the National Weather Service began keeping records, and by the middle of the month the ice covering the Reach was safe. Snowmobiles buzzed and whined and sometimes turned over when they climbed the ice-heaves wrong. Children tried to skate, found the ice too bumpy to be any fun, and went back to Godlin's Pond on the far side of the hill, but not before little Justin McCracken, the minister's son, caught his skate in a fissure and broke his ankle. They took him over to the hospital on the mainland where a doctor who owned a Corvette told him, "Son, it's going to be as good as new."

Freddy Dinsmore died very suddenly just three days after Justin Mc-Cracken broke his ankle. He caught the flu late in January, would not have the doctor, told everyone it was "Just a cold from goin out to get the mail without m'scarf," took to his bed, and died before anyone could take him across to the mainland and hook him up to all those machines they have waiting for guys like Freddy. His son George, a tosspot of the first water even at the advanced age (for tosspots, anyway) of sixty-eight, found Freddy with a copy of the *Bangor Daily News* in one hand and his Remington, unloaded, near the other. Apparently he had been thinking of cleaning it just before he died. George Dinsmore went on a three-week toot, said toot financed by someone who knew that George would have his old dad's insurance money coming. Hattie Stoddard went around telling anyone who would listen that old George Dinsmore was a sin and a disgrace, no better than a tramp for pay.

There was a lot of flu around. The school closed for two weeks that February instead of the usual one because so many pupils were out sick. "No snow breeds germs," Sarah Havelock said.

Near the end of the month, just as people were beginning to look forward to the false comfort of March, Alden Flanders caught the flu himself. He walked around with it for nearly a week and then took to his bed with a fever of a hundred and one. Like Freddy, he refused to have the doctor, and Stella stewed and fretted and worried. Alden was not as old as Freddy, but that May he would turn sixty.

The snow came at last. Six inches on Valentine's Day, another six on the twentieth, and a foot in a good old norther on the leap, February 29. The snow lay white and strange between the cove and the mainland, like a sheep's meadow where there had been only gray and surging water at this time of year since time out of mind. Several people walked across to the mainland and back. No snowshoes were necessary this year because the snow had frozen to a firm, glittery crust. They might take a knock of whiskey, too, Stella thought, but they would not take it at Dorrit's. Dorrit's had burned down in 1958.

And she saw Bill all four times. Once he told her: "Y'ought to come soon, Stella. We'll go steppin. What do you say?"

She could say nothing. Her fist was crammed deep into her mouth.

"Everything I ever wanted or needed was here," she would tell them. "We had the radio and now we have the television, and that's all I want of the world beyond the Reach. I had my garden year in and year out. And lobster? Why, we always used to have a pot of lobster stew on the back of the stove and we used to take it off and put it behind the door in the pantry when the minister came calling so he wouldn't see we were eating 'poor man's soup.'

"I have seen good weather and bad, and if there were times when I wondered what it might be like to actually be in the Sears store instead of ordering from the catalogue, or to go into one of those Shaw's markets I see on TV instead of buying at the store here or sending Alden across for something special like a Christmas capon or an Easter ham . . . or if I ever wanted, just once, to stand on Congress Street in Portland and watch all the people in their cars and on the sidewalks, more people in a single look than there are on the whole island these days . . . if I ever wanted those things, then I wanted this more. I am not strange. I am not peculiar, or even very eccentric for a woman of my years. My mother sometimes used to say, 'All the difference in the world is between work and want,' and I believe that to my very soul. I believe it is better to plow deep than wide.

"This is my place, and I love it."

One day in middle March, with the sky as white and lowering as a loss of memory, Stella Flanders sat in her kitchen for the last time, laced up her boots over her skinny calves for the last time, and wrapped her bright red woolen scarf (a Christmas present from Hattie three Christmases past) around her neck for the last time. She wore a suit of Alden's long underwear under her dress. The waist of the drawers came up to just below the limp vestiges of her breasts, the shirt almost down to her knees.

Outside, the wind was picking up again, and the radio said there would be snow by afternoon. She put on her coat and her gloves. After a moment of debate, she put a pair of Alden's gloves on over her own. Alden had recovered from the flu, and this morning he and Harley Blood were over rehanging a storm door for Missy Bowie, who had had a girl. Stella had seen it, and the unfortunate little mite looked just like her father.

She stood at the window for a moment, looking out at the Reach, and Bill was there as she had suspected he might be, standing about halfway between the island and the Head, standing on the Reach just like Jesus-out-of-the-boat, beckoning to her, seeming to tell her by gesture that the time was late if she ever intended to step a foot on the mainland in this life.

"If it's what you want, Bill," she fretted in the silence. "God knows I don't."

But the wind spoke other words. She did want to. She wanted to have this adventure. It had been a painful winter for her—the arthritis which came and went irregularly was back with a vengeance, flaring the joints of her fingers and knees with red fire and blue ice. One of her eyes had gotten dim and blurry (and just the other day Sarah had mentioned—with some unease—that the fire-spot that had been there since Stella was sixty or so now seemed to be growing by leaps and bounds). Worst of all, the deep, griping pain in her stomach had returned, and two mornings before she had gotten up at five o'clock, worked her way along the exquisitely cold floor into the bathroom, and had spat a great wad of bright red blood into the toilet bowl. This morning there had been some more of it, foul-tasting stuff, coppery and shuddersome.

The stomach pain had come and gone over the last five years, sometimes better, sometimes worse, and she had known almost from the beginning that it must be cancer. It had taken her mother and father and her mother's father as well. None of them had lived past seventy, and so she supposed she had beat the tables those insurance fellows kept by a carpenter's yard.

"You eat like a horse," Alden told her, grinning, not long after the pains had begun and she had first observed the blood in her morning stool. "Don't you know that old fogies like you are supposed to be peckish?"

"Get on or I'll swat ye!" Stella had answered, raising a hand to her gray-haired son, who ducked, mock-cringed, and cried: "Don't, Ma! I take it back!"

Yes, she had eaten hearty, not because she wanted to, but because she believed (as many of her generation did), that if you fed the cancer it would leave you alone. And perhaps it worked, at least for a while; the blood in her stools came and went, and there were long periods when it wasn't there at all. Alden got used to her taking second helpings (and thirds, when the pain was particularly bad), but she never gained a pound.

Now it seemed the cancer had finally gotten around to what the froggies called the *pièce de résistance*.

She started out the door and saw Alden's hat, the one with the fur-lined ear flaps, hanging on one of the pegs in the entry. She put it on—the bill came all the way down to her shaggy salt-and-pepper eyebrows—and then looked around one last time to see if she had forgotten anything. The stove was low, and Alden had left the draw open too much again—she told him and told him, but that was one thing he was just never going to get straight.

"Alden, you'll burn an extra quarter-cord a winter when I'm gone," she muttered, and opened the stove. She looked in and a tight, dismayed gasp escaped her. She slammed the door shut and adjusted the draw with trembling fingers. For a moment—just a moment—she had seen her old friend Annabelle Frane in the coals. It was her face to the life, even down to the mole on her cheek.

And had Annabelle winked at her?

She thought of leaving Alden a note to explain where she had gone, but she thought perhaps Alden would understand, in his own slow way.

Still writing notes in her head—*Since the first day of winter I have been seeing your father and he says dying isn't so bad; at least I think that's it*—Stella stepped out into the white day.

The wind shook her and she had to reset Alden's cap on her head before the wind could steal it for a joke and cartwheel it away. The cold seemed to find every chink in her clothing and twist into her; damp March cold with wet snow on its mind.

She set off down the hill toward the cove, being careful to walk on the cinders and clinkers that George Dinsmore had spread. Once George had gotten a job driving plow for the town of Raccoon Head, but during the big blow of '77 he had gotten smashed on rye whiskey and had driven the plow smack through not one, not two, but three power poles. There had been no lights over the Head for five days. Stella remembered now how strange it had been, looking across the Reach and seeing only blackness. A body got used to seeing that brave little nestle of lights. Now George worked on the island, and since there was no plow, he didn't get into much hurt.

As she passed Russell Bowie's house, she saw Missy, pale as milk, looking out at her. Stella waved. Missy waved back.

She would tell them this:
"On the island we always watched out for our own. When Gerd Henreid broke the blood vessel in his chest that time, we had covered-dish suppers one whole summer to pay for his operation in Boston—and Gerd came back alive, thank God. When George Dinsmore ran down those power poles and the Hydro slapped a lien on his home, it was seen to that the Hydro had their money and George had enough of a job to keep him in cigarettes and booze . . . why not? He was good for nothing else when his workday was done, although when he was on the clock he would work like a dray-horse. That one time he got into trouble was because it was at night, and night was always George's drinking time. His father kept him fed, at least. Now Missy Bowie's alone with another baby. Maybe she'll stay here and take her welfare and ADC money here, and most likely it won't be enough, but she'll get the help she needs. Probably she'll go, but if she stays she'll not starve . . . and listen, Lona and Hal: if she stays, she may be able to keep something of this small world with the little Reach on one side and the big Reach on the other, something it would be too easy to lose hustling hash in Lewiston or donuts in Portland or drinks at the Nashville North in Bangor. And I am old enough not to beat around the bush about what that something might be: a way of being and a way of living—a feeling."

They had watched out for their own in other ways as well, but she would not tell them that. The children would not understand, nor would Lois and David, although Jane had known the truth. There was Norman and Ettie Wilson's baby that was born a mongoloid, its poor dear little feet turned in, its bald skull lumpy and cratered, its fingers webbed together as if it had dreamed too long and too deep while swimming that interior Reach; Reverend McCracken had come and baptized the baby, and a day later Mary Dodge came, who even at that time had midwived over a hundred babies, and Norman took Ettie down the hill to see Frank Child's new boat and although she could barely walk, Ettie went with no complaint, although she had stopped in the door to look back at Mary Dodge, who was sitting calmly by the idiot baby's crib and knitting. Mary had looked up at her and when their eyes met, Ettie burst into tears. "Come on," Norman had said, upset. "Come on, Ettie, come on." And when they came back an hour later the baby was dead, one of those crib-deaths, wasn't it merciful he didn't suffer. And many years before that, before the war, during the Depression, three little girls had been molested coming home from school, not badly molested, at least not where you could see the scar of the hurt, and they all told about a man who offered to show them a deck of cards he had with a different kind of dog on each one. He would show them this wonderful deck of cards, the man said, if the little girls would come into the bushes with him, and once in the bushes this man said, "But you have to touch this first." One of the little girls was Gert Symes, who would go on to be voted Maine's Teacher of the Year in 1978, for her work at Brunswick High. And Gert, then only five years old, told her father that the man had some fingers gone on one hand. One of the other little girls agreed that this was so. The third remembered nothing. Stella remembered Alden going out one thundery day that summer without telling her where he was going, although she asked. Watching from the window, she had seen Alden meet Bull Symes at the bottom of the path, and then Freddy Dinsmore had joined them and down at the cove she saw her own husband, whom she had sent out that morning just as usual, with his dinner pail under his arm. More men joined them, and when they finally moved off she counted just one under a dozen. The Reverend McCracken's predecessor had been among them. And that evening a fellow named Daniels was found at the foot of Slyder's Point, where the rocks poke out of the surf like the fangs of a dragon that drowned with its mouth open. This Daniels was a fellow Big George Havelock had hired to help him put new sills under his house and a new engine in his Model A truck. From New Hampshire he was, and he was a sweet-talker who had found other odd jobs to do when the work at the Havelocks' was done . . . and in church, he could carry a tune! Apparently, they said, Daniels had been walking up on top of Slyder's Point and had slipped, tumbling all the way to the bottom. His neck was broken and his head was bashed in. As he had no people that anyone knew of, he was buried on the island, and the Reverend McCracken's predecessor gave the graveyard eulogy, saying as how this Daniels had been a hard worker and a good help even though he was two fingers shy on his right hand. Then he read the benediction and the graveside group had gone back to the town-hall basement where they drank Za-Rex punch and ate cream-cheese sandwiches, and Stella never asked her men where they had gone on the day Daniels fell from the top of Slyder's Point.

"Children," she would tell them, "we always watched out for our own. We had to, for the Reach was wider in those days and when the wind roared and the surf pounded and the dark came early, why, we felt very small—no more than dust motes in the mind of God. So it was natural for us to join hands, one with the other.

"We joined hands, children, and if there were times when we wondered what *it was all for, or if there was ary such a thing as love at all, it was only because we had heard the wind and the waters on long winter nights, and we were afraid.*

"No, I've never felt I needed to leave the island. My life was here. The Reach was wider in those days."

Stella reached the cove. She looked right and left, the wind blowing her dress out behind her like a flag. If anyone had been there she would have walked further down and taken her chance on the tumbled rocks, although they were glazed with ice. But no one was there and she walked out along the pier, past the old Symes boathouse. She reached the end and stood there for a moment, head held up, the wind blowing past the padded flaps of Alden's hat in a muffled flood.

Bill was out there, beckoning. Beyond him, beyond the Reach, she could see the Congo Church over there on the Head, its spire almost invisible against the white sky.

Grunting, she sat down on the end of the pier and then stepped onto the snow crust below. Her boots sank a little; not much. She set Alden's cap again—how the wind wanted to tear it off!—and began to walk toward Bill. She thought once that she would look back, but she did not. She didn't believe her heart could stand that.

She walked, her boots crunching into the crust, and listened to the faint thud and give of the ice. There was Bill, further back now but still beckoning. She coughed, spat blood onto the white snow that covered the ice. Now the Reach spread wide on either side and she could, for the first time in her life, read the "Stanton's Bait and Boat" sign over there without Alden's binoculars. She could see the cars passing to and fro on the Head's main street and thought with real wonder: *They can go as far as they want . . . Portland . . . Boston . . . New York City. Imagine!* And she could almost do it, could almost imagine a road that simply rolled on and on, the boundaries of the world knocked wide.

A snowflake skirled past her eyes. Another. A third. Soon it was snowing lightly and she walked through a pleasant world of shifting bright white; she saw Raccoon Head through a gauzy curtain that sometimes almost cleared. She reached up to set Alden's cap again and snow puffed off the bill into her eyes. The wind twisted fresh snow up in filmy shapes, and in one of them she saw Carl Abersham, who had gone down with Hattie Stoddard's husband on the *Dancer*.

Soon, however, the brightness began to dull as the snow came harder. The Head's main street dimmed, dimmed, and at last was gone. For a time longer she could make out the cross atop the church, and then that faded out too, like a false dream. Last to go was that bright yellow-and-black sign reading "Stanton's Bait and Boat," where you could also get engine oil, flypaper, Italian sandwiches, and Budweiser to go.

Then Stella walked in a world that was totally without color, a gray-white dream of snow. *Just like Jesus-out-of-the-boat,* she thought, and at last she looked back but now the island was gone, too. She could see her tracks going back, losing definition until only the faint half-circles of her heels could be seen . . . and then nothing. Nothing at all.

She thought: *It's a whiteout. You got to be careful, Stella, or you'll never get to the mainland. You'll just walk around in a big circle until you're worn out and then you'll freeze to death out here.*

She remembered Bill telling her once that when you were lost in the woods, you had to pretend that the leg which was on the same side of your body as your smart hand was lame. Otherwise that smart leg would begin to lead you and you'd walk in a circle and not even realize it until you came around to your backtrail again. Stella didn't believe she could afford to have that happen to her. Snow today, tonight, and tomorrow, the radio had said, and in a whiteout such as this, she would not even know if she came around to her backtrail, for the wind and the fresh snow would erase it long before she could return to it.

Her hands were leaving her in spite of the two pairs of gloves she wore, and her feet had been gone for some time. In a way, this was almost a relief. The numbness at least shut the mouth of her clamoring arthritis.

Stella began to limp now, making her left leg work harder. The arthritis in her knees had not gone to sleep, and soon they were screaming at her. Her white hair flew out behind her. Her lips had drawn back from her teeth (she still had her own, all save four) and she looked straight ahead, waiting for that yellow-and-black sign to materialize out of the flying whiteness.

It did not happen.

Sometime later, she noticed that the day's bright whiteness had begun to dull to a more uniform gray. The snow fell heavier and thicker than ever. Her feet were still planted on the crust but now she was walking through five inches of fresh snow. She looked at her watch, but it had stopped. Stella realized she must have forgotten to wind it that morning for the first time in twenty or thirty years. Or had it just stopped for good? It had been her mother's and she had sent it with Alden twice to the Head, where Mr. Dostie had first marveled over it and then cleaned it. Her watch, at least, had been to the mainland.

She fell down for the first time some fifteen minutes after she began to notice the day's growing grayness. For a moment she remained on her hands and knees, thinking it would be so easy just to stay here, to curl up and listen to the wind, and then the determination that had brought her through so much reasserted itself and she got up, grimacing. She stood in the wind, looking straight ahead, willing her eyes to see . . . but they saw nothing.

Be dark soon.

Well, she had gone wrong. She had slipped off to one side or the other. Otherwise she would have reached the mainland by now. Yet she didn't believe she had gone so far wrong that she was walking parallel to the mainland or even back in the direction of Goat. An interior navigator in her head whispered that she had overcompensated and slipped off to the left. She believed she was still approaching the mainland but was now on a costly diagonal.

That navigator wanted her to turn right, but she would not do that. Instead, she moved straight on again, but stopped the artificial limp. A spasm of coughing shook her, and she spat bright red into the snow.

Ten minutes later (the gray was now deep indeed, and she found herself in the weird twilight of a heavy snowstorm) she fell again, tried to get up, failed at first, and finally managed to gain her feet. She stood swaying in the snow, barely able to remain upright in the wind, waves of faintness rushing through her head, making her feel alternately heavy and light.

Perhaps not all the roaring she heard in her ears was the wind, but it surely was the wind that finally succeeded in prying Alden's hat from her head. She made a grab for it, but the wind danced it easily out of her reach and she saw it only for a moment, flipping gaily over and over into the darkening gray, a bright spot of orange. It struck the snow, rolled, rose again, was gone. Now her hair flew around her head freely.

"It's all right, Stella," Bill said. "You can wear mine."

She gasped and looked around in the white. Her gloved hands had gone instinctively to her bosom, and she felt sharp fingernails scratch at her heart.

She saw nothing but shifting membranes of snow—and then, moving out of that evening's gray throat, the wind screaming through it like the voice of a devil in a snowy tunnel, came her husband. He was at first only moving colors in the snow: red, black, dark green, lighter green; then these colors resolved themselves into a flannel jacket with a flapping collar, flannel pants, and green boots. He was holding his hat out to her in a gesture that appeared almost absurdly courtly, and his face was Bill's face, unmarked by the cancer that had taken him (had that been all she was afraid of? that a wasted shadow of her husband would come to her, a scrawny concentration-camp figure with the skin pulled taut and shiny over the cheekbones and the eyes sunken deep in the sockets?) and she felt a surge of relief.

"Bill? Is that really you?"

"Course."

"Bill," she said again, and took a glad step toward him. Her legs betrayed her and she thought she would fall, fall right through him—he was, after all, a ghost—but he caught her in arms as strong and as competent as those that had carried her over the threshold of the house that she had shared only with Alden in these latter years. He supported her, and a moment later she felt the cap pulled firmly onto her head.

"Is it really you?" she asked again, looking up into his face, at the crow's-feet around his eyes which hadn't sunk deep yet, at the spill of snow on the shoulders of his checked hunting jacket, at his lively brown hair.

"It's me," he said. "It's all of us."

He half-turned with her and she saw the others coming out of the snow that the wind drove across the Reach in the gathering darkness. A cry, half joy, half fear, came from her mouth as she saw Madeline Stoddard, Hattie's mother, in a blue dress that swung in the wind like a bell, and holding her hand was Hattie's dad, not a mouldering skeleton somewhere on the bottom with the *Dancer*, but whole and young. And there, behind those two—

"Annabelle!" she cried. "Annabelle Frane, is it you?"

It *was* Annabelle; even in this snowy gloom Stella recognized the yellow dress Annabelle had worn to Stella's own wedding, and as she struggled toward her dead friend, holding Bill's arm, she thought that she could smell roses.

"Annabelle!"

"We're almost there now, dear," Annabelle said, taking her other arm. The yellow dress, which had been considered Daring in its day (but, to Annabelle's credit and to everyone else's relief, not quite a Scandal), left her shoulders bare, but Annabelle did not seem to feel the cold. Her hair, a soft, dark auburn, blew long in the wind. "Only a little further."

She took Stella's other arm and they moved forward again. Other figures came out of the snowy night (for it *was* night now). Stella recognized many of them, but not all. Tommy Frane had joined Annabelle; Big George Havelock, who had died a dog's death in the woods, walked behind Bill; there was the fellow who had kept the lighthouse on the Head for most of twenty years and who used to come over to the island during the cribbage tournament Freddy Dinsmore held every February—Stella could almost but not quite remember his name. And there was Freddy himself! Walking off to one side of Freddy, by himself and looking bewildered, was Russell Bowie.

"Look, Stella," Bill said, and she saw black rising out of the gloom like the splintered prows of many ships. It was not ships, it was split and fissured rock. They had reached the Head. They had crossed the Reach.

She heard voices, but was not sure they actually spoke:

Take my hand, Stella—

(do you)

Take my hand, Bill—

(oh do you do you)

Annabelle . . . Freddy . . . Russell . . . John . . . Ettie . . . Frank . . . take my hand, take my hand . . . my hand . . .

(do you love)

"Will you take my hand, Stella?" a new voice asked.

She looked around and there was Bull Symes. He was smiling kindly at her and yet she felt a kind of terror in her at what was in his eyes and for a moment she drew away, clutching Bill's hand on her other side the tighter.

"Is it—"

"Time?" Bull asked. "Oh, ayuh, Stella, I guess so. But it don't hurt. At least, I never heard so. All that's before."

She burst into tears suddenly—all the tears she had never wept—and put her hand in Bull's hand. "Yes," she said, "yes I will, yes I did, yes I do."

They stood in a circle in the storm, the dead of Goat Island, and the wind screamed around them, driving its packet of snow, and some kind of song burst from her. It went up into the wind and the wind carried it away. They all sang then, as children will sing in their high, sweet voices as a summer evening draws down to summer night. They sang, and Stella felt herself going to them and with them, finally across the Reach. There was a bit of pain, but not much; losing her maidenhead had been worse. They stood in a circle in the night. The snow blew around them and they sang. They sang, and—

—and Alden could not tell David and Lois, but in the summer after Stella died, when the children came out for their annual two weeks, he told Lona and Hal. He told them that during the great storms of winter the wind seems to

sing with almost human voices, and that sometimes it seemed to him he could almost make out the words: "Praise God from whom all blessings flow/Praise Him, ye creatures here below . . ."

But he did not tell them (imagine slow, unimaginative Alden Flanders saying such things aloud, even to the children!) that sometimes he would hear that sound and feel cold even by the stove; that he would put his whittling aside, or the trap he had meant to mend, thinking that the wind sang in all the voices of those who were dead and gone . . . that they stood somewhere out on the Reach and sang as children do. He seemed to hear their voices and on these nights he sometimes slept and dreamed that he was singing the doxology, unseen and unheard, at his own funeral.

There are things that can never be told, and there are things, not exactly secret, that are not discussed. They had found Stella frozen to death on the mainland a day after the storm had blown itself out. She was sitting on a natural chair of rock about one hundred yards south of the Raccoon Head town limits, frozen just as neat as you please. The doctor who owned the Corvette said that he was frankly amazed. It would have been a walk of over four miles, and the autopsy required by law in the case of an unattended, unusual death had shown an advanced cancerous condition—in truth, the old woman had been riddled with it. Was Alden to tell David and Lois that the cap on her head had not been his? Larry McKeen had recognized that cap. So had John Bensohn. He had seen it in their eyes, and he supposed they had seen it in his. He had not lived long enough to forget his dead father's cap, the look of its bill or the places where the visor had been broken.

"These are things made for thinking on slowly," he would have told the children if he had known how. "Things to be thought on at length, while the hands do their work and the coffee sits in a solid china mug nearby. They are questions of Reach, maybe: do the dead sing? And do they love the living?

On the nights after Lona and Hal had gone back with their parents to the mainland in Al Curry's boat, the children standing astern and waving good-bye, Alden considered that question, and others, and the matter of his father's cap.

Do the dead sing? Do they love?

On those long nights alone, with his mother Stella Flanders at long last in her grave, it often seemed to Alden that they did both.

John Collier

Evening Primrose

John Collier's characteristic stories of satirical horror (a small but distinguished tradition including certain works of Saki and Avram Davidson)
have fallen out of print in recent years. "Evening Primrose" is a particularly vivid example of the subversive little moral tale, so psychologically
acute that it leaves us more than a bit uncomfortable about what goes
on at night in the most ordinary and seductive of middle-class environ-
ments: the department store, the abode of grotesques, human and otherwise.

*In a pad of Highlife Bond, bought by
Miss Sadie Brodribb at Bracey's for 25¢*

MARCH 21

Today I made my decision. I would turn my back for good and all upon
the *bourgeois* world that hates a poet. I would leave, get out, break
away——

And I have done it. I am free! Free as the mote that dances in the
sunbeam! Free as a house-fly crossing first-class in the largest of luxury liners!
Free as my verse! Free as the food I shall eat, the paper I write upon, the
lamb's-wool-lined softly slithering slippers I shall wear.

This morning I had not so much as a car-fare. Now I am here, on velvet.
You are itching to learn of this haven; you would like to organize trips
here, spoil it, send your relations-in-law, perhaps even come yourself.
After all, this journal will hardly fall into your hands till I am dead. I'll
tell you.

I am at Bracey's Giant Emporium, as happy as a mouse in the middle of
an immense cheese, and the world shall know me no more.

Merrily, merrily shall I live now, secure behind a towering pile of carpets,
in a corner-nook which I propose to line with eiderdowns, angora vestments,
and the Cleopatræan tops in pillows. I shall be cosy.

I nipped into this sanctuary late this afternoon, and soon heard the dying
footfalls of closing time. From now on, my only effort will be to dodge the
night-watchman. Poets can dodge.

I have already made my first mouse-like exploration. I tiptoed as far as the
stationery department, and, timid, darted back with only these writing
materials, the poet's first need. Now I shall lay them aside, and seek other

31

necessities: food, wine, the soft furniture of my couch, and a natty smoking-jacket. This place stimulates me. I shall write here.

DAWN, NEXT DAY

I suppose no one in the world was ever more astonished and overwhelmed than I have been tonight. It is unbelievable. Yet I believe it. How interesting life is when things get like that!

I crept out, as I said I would, and found the great shop in mingled light and gloom. The central well was half illuminated; the circling galleries towered in a pansy Piranesi of toppling light and shade. The spidery stairways and flying bridges had passed from purpose into fantasy. Silks and velvets glimmered like ghosts, a hundred pantie-clad models offered simpers and embraces to the desert air. Rings, clips, and bracelets glittered frostily in a desolate absence of Honey and Daddy.

Creeping along the transverse aisles, which were in deeper darkness, I felt like a wandering thought in the dreaming brain of a chorus girl down on her luck. Only, of course, their brains are not as big as Bracey's Giant Emporium. And there was no man there.

None, that is, except the night-watchman. I had forgotten him. As I crossed an open space on the mezzanine floor, hugging the lee of a display of sultry shawls, I became aware of a regular thudding, which might almost have been that of my own heart. Suddenly it burst upon me that it came from outside. It was footsteps, and they were only a few paces away. Quick as a flash I seized a flamboyant mantilla, whirled it about me and stood with one arm outflung, like a Carmen petrified in a gesture of disdain.

I was successful. He passed me, jingling his little machine on its chain, humming his little tune, his eyes scaled with refractions of the blaring day. "Go, worldling!" I whispered, and permitted myself a soundless laugh.

It froze on my lips. My heart faltered. A new fear seized me.

I was afraid to move. I was afraid to look around. I felt I was being watched by something that could see right through me. This was a very different feeling from the ordinary emergency caused by the very ordinary night-watchman. My conscious impulse was the obvious one: to glance behind me. But my eyes knew better. I remained absolutely petrified, staring straight ahead.

My eyes were trying to tell me something that my brain refused to believe. They made their point. I was looking straight into another pair of eyes, human eyes, but large, flat, luminous. I have seen such eyes among the nocturnal creatures, which creep out under the artificial blue moonlight in the zoo.

The owner was only a dozen feet away from me. The watchman had passed between us, nearer him than me. Yet he had not seen him. I must have been looking straight at him for several minutes at a stretch. I had not seen him either.

He was half reclining against a low dais where, on a floor of russet leaves, and flanked by billows of glowing home-spun, the fresh-faced waxen girls modeled spectator sports suits in herringbones, checks, and plaids. He leaned against the skirt of one of these Dianas; its folds concealed perhaps his ear, his shoulder, and a little of his right side. He, himself, was clad in dim but large patterned Shetland tweeds of the latest cut, suède shoes, a shirt of a rather broad *motif* in olive, pink, and grey. He was as pale as a creature found under a stone. His long thin arms ended in hands that hung floatingly, more like trailing, transparent fins, or wisps of chiffon, than ordinary hands.

He spoke. His voice was not a voice; it was a mere whistling under the tongue. "Not bad, for a beginner!"

I grasped that he was complimenting me, rather satirically, on my own, more amateurish, feat of camouflage. I stuttered. I said, "I'm sorry. I didn't know anyone else lived here." I noticed, even as I spoke, that I was imitating his own whistling sibilant utterance.

"Oh, yes," he said. "*We* live here. It's delightful."

"We?"

"Yes, all of us. Look!"

We were near the edge of the first gallery. He swept his long hand round, indicating the whole well of the shop. I looked. I saw nothing. I could hear nothing, except the watchman's thudding step receding infinitely far along some basement aisle.

"Don't you see?"

You know the sensation one has, peering into the half-light of a vivarium? One sees bark, pebbles, a few leaves, nothing more. And then, suddenly, a stone breathes—it is a toad; there is a chameleon, another, a coiled adder, a mantis among the leaves. The whole case seems crepitant with life. Perhaps the whole world is. One glances at one's sleeve, one's feet.

So it was with the shop. I looked, and it was empty. I looked, and there was an old lady, clambering out from behind the monstrous clock. There were three girls, elderly *ingénues*, incredibly emaciated, simpering at the entrance of the perfumery. Their hair was a fine floss, pale as gossamer. Equally brittle and colourless was a man with the appearance of a colonel of southern extraction, who stood regarding me while he caressed mustachios that would have done credit to a crystal shrimp. A chintzy woman, possibly of literary tastes, swam forward from the curtains and drapes.

They came thick about me, fluttering, whistling, like a waving of gauze in the wind. Their eyes were wide and flatly bright. I saw there was no colour to the iris.

"How raw he looks!"

"A detective! Send for the Dark Men!"

"I'm not a detective. I am a poet. I have renounced the world."

"He is a poet. He has come over to us. Mr. Roscoe found him."

"He admires us."

"He must meet Mrs. Vanderpant."

I was taken to meet Mrs. Vanderpant. She proved to be the Grand Old Lady of the store, almost entirely transparent.

"So you are a poet, Mr. Snell? You will find inspiration here. I am quite the oldest inhabitant. Three mergers and a complete rebuilding, but they didn't get rid of me!"

"Tell how you went out by daylight, dear Mrs. Vanderpant, and nearly got bought for Whistler's *Mother*."

"That was in pre-war days. I was more robust then. But at the cash desk they suddenly remembered there was no frame. And when they came back to look at me——"

"——She was gone."

Their laughter was like the stridulation of the ghosts of grasshoppers.

"Where is Ella? Where is my broth?"

"She is bringing it, Mrs. Vanderpant. It will come."

"Tiresome little creature! She is our foundling, Mr. Snell. She is not quite our sort."

"Is that so, Mrs. Vanderpant? Dear, dear!"

"I lived alone here, Mr. Snell, for many years. I took refuge here in the terrible times in the eighties. I was a young girl then, a beauty, people were kind enough to say, but poor Papa lost his money. Bracey's meant a lot to a young girl, in the New York of those days, Mr. Snell. It seemed to me terrible that I should not be able to come here in the ordinary way. So I came here for good. I was quite alarmed when others began to come in, after the crash of 1907. But it was the dear Judge, the Colonel, Mrs. Bilbee——"

I bowed. I was being introduced.

"Mrs. Bilbee writes plays. *And* of a very old Philadelphia family. You will find us quite *nice* here, Mr. Snell."

"I feel it a great privilege, Mrs. Vanderpant."

"And of course, all our dear *young* people came in '29. *Their* poor papas jumped from skyscrapers."

I did a great deal of bowing and whistling. The introductions took a long time. Who would have thought so many people lived in Bracey's?

"And here at last is Ella with my broth."

It was then I noticed that the young people were not so young after all, in spite of their smiles, their little ways, their *ingénue* dress. Ella was in her teens. Clad only in something from the shop-soiled counter, she nevertheless had the appearance of a living flower in a French cemetery, or a mermaid among polyps.

"Come, you stupid thing!"

"Mrs. Vanderpant is waiting."

Her pallor was not like theirs; not like the pallor of something that glistens or scuttles when you turn over a stone. Hers was that of a pearl.

Ella! Pearl of this remotest, most fantastic cave! Little mermaid, brushed over, pressed down by objects of a deadlier white—tentacles—! I can write no more.

MARCH 28

Well, I am rapidly becoming used to my new and half-lit world, to my strange company. I am learning the intricate laws of silence and camouflage which dominate the apparently casual strollings and gatherings of the midnight clan. How they detest the night-watchman, whose existence imposes these laws on their idle festivals!

"Odious, vulgar creature! He reeks of the coarse sun!"

Actually, he is quite a personable young man, very young for a night-watchman, so young that I think he must have been wounded in the war. But they would like to tear him to pieces.

They are very pleasant to me, though. They are pleased that a poet should have come among them. Yet I cannot like them entirely. My blood is a little chilled by the uncanny ease with which even the old ladies can clamber spider-like from balcony to balcony. Or is it because they are unkind to Ella?

Yesterday we had a bridge party. Tonight, Mrs. Bilbee's little play, *Love in Shadowland*, is going to be presented. Would you believe it?—another colony, from Wanamaker's, is coming over *en masse* to attend. Apparently people live in all the great stores. This visit is considered a great honour, for there is an intense snobbery in these creatures. They speak with horror of a social outcast who left a high-class Madison Avenue establishment, and now leads a wallowing, beachcomberish life in a delicatessen. And they relate with tragic emotion the story of the man in Altman's, who conceived such a passion for a model plaid dressing jacket that he emerged and wrested it from the hands of a purchaser. It seems that all the Altman colony, dreading an investigation, were forced to remove beyond the social pale, into a five-and-dime. Well, I must get ready to attend the play.

APRIL 14

I have found an opportunity to speak to Ella. I dared not before; here one has a sense always of pale eyes secretly watching. But last night, at the play, I developed a fit of hiccups. I was somewhat sternly told to go and secrete myself in the basement, among the garbage cans, where the watchman never comes.

There, in the rat-haunted darkness, I heard a stifled sob. "What's that? Is it you? Is it Ella? What ails you, child? Why do you cry?"

"They wouldn't even let me see the play."

"Is that all? Let me console you."

"I am so unhappy."

She told me her tragic little story. What do you think? When she was a child, a little tiny child of only six, she strayed away and fell asleep behind a counter, while her mother tried on a new hat. When she woke, the store was in darkness.

"And I cried, and they all came around, and took hold of me. 'She will tell, if we let her go,' they said. Some said, 'Call in the Dark Men.' 'Let her stay here,' said Mrs. Vanderpant. 'She will make me a nice little maid.'"

"Who are these Dark Men, Ella? They spoke of them when I came here."

"Don't you know? Oh, it's horrible! It's horrible!"

"Tell me, Ella. Let us share it."

She trembled. "You know the morticians, 'Journey's End,' who go to houses when people die?"

"Yes, Ella."

"Well, in that shop, just like here, and at Gimbel's, and at Bloomingdale's, there are people living, people like these."

"How disgusting! But what can they live upon, Ella, in a funeral home?"

"Don't ask me! Dead people are sent there, to be embalmed. Oh, they are terrible creatures! Even the people here are terrified of them. But if anyone dies, or if some poor burglar breaks in, and sees these people, and might tell——"

"Yes? Go on."

"Then they send for the others, the Dark Men."

"Good heavens!"

"Yes, and they put the body in Surgical Supplies—or the burglar, all tied up, if it's a burglar—and they send for these others, and then they all hide, and in they come, the others——Oh! they're like pieces of blackness. I saw them once. It was terrible."

"And then?"

"They go in, to where the dead person is, or the poor burglar. And they have wax there—and all sorts of things. And when they're gone there's just one of these wax models left, on the table. And then our people put a dress on it, or a bathing suit, and they mix it up with all the others, and nobody ever knows."

"But aren't they heavier than the others, these wax models? You would think they'd be heavier."

"No. They're not heavier. I think there's a lot of them—gone."

"Oh, dear! So they were going to do that to you, when you were a little child?"

"Yes, only Mrs. Vanderpant said I was to be her maid."

"I don't like these people, Ella."

"Nor do I. I wish I could see a bird."

"Why don't you go into the pet-shop?"

"It wouldn't be the same. I want to see it on a twig, with leaves."

"Ella, let us meet often. Let us creep away down here and meet. I will tell you about birds, and twigs and leaves."

MAY 1

For the last few nights the store has been feverish with the shivering whisper of a huge crush at Bloomingdale's. Tonight was the night.

"Not changed yet? We leave on the stroke of two." Roscoe has appointed himself, or been appointed, my guide or my guard.

"Roscoe, I am still a greenhorn. I dread the streets."

"Nonsense! There's nothing to it. We slip out by two's and three's, stand on the sidewalk, pick up a taxi. Were you never out late in the old days? If so, you must have seen us, many a time."

"Good heavens, I believe I have! And often wondered where you came from. And it was from here! But, Roscoe, my brow is burning. I find it hard to breathe. I fear a cold."

"In that case you must certainly remain behind. Our whole party would be disgraced in the unfortunate event of a sneeze."

I had relied on their rigid etiquette, so largely based on fear of discovery, and I was right. Soon they were gone, drifting out like leaves aslant on the wind. At once I dressed in flannel slacks, canvas shoes, and a tasteful sport shirt, all new in stock today. I found a quiet spot, safely off the track beaten by the night-watchman. There, in a model's lifted hand, I set a wide fern frond culled from the florist's shop, and at once had a young, spring tree. The carpet was sandy, sandy as a lake-side beach. A snowy napkin; two cakes, each with a cherry on it; I had only to imagine the lake and to find Ella.

"Why, Charles, what's this?"

"I'm a poet, Ella, and when a poet meets a girl like you he thinks of a day in the country. Do you see this tree? Let's call it *our* tree. There's the lake—the prettiest lake imaginable. Here is grass, and there are flowers. There are birds, too, Ella. You told me you like birds."

"Oh, Charles, you're so sweet. I feel I hear them singing."

"And here's our lunch. But before we eat, go behind the rock there, and see what you find."

I heard her cry out in delight when she saw the summer dress I had put there for her. When she came back the spring day smiled to see her, and the lake shone brighter than before. "Ella, let us have lunch. Let us have fun. Let us have a swim. I can just imagine you in one of those new bathing suits."

"Let's just sit there, Charles, and talk."

So we sat and talked, and the time was gone like a dream. We might have stayed there, forgetful of everything, had it not been for the spider.

"Charles, what are you doing?"

"Nothing, my dear. Just a naughty little spider, crawling over your knee. Purely imaginary, of course, but that sort are sometimes the worst. I had to try to catch him."

"Don't, Charles! It's late. It's terribly late. They'll be back any minute. I'd better go home."

I took her home to the kitchenware on the sub-ground floor, and kissed her good-day. She offered me her cheek. This troubles me.

MAY 10

"Ella, I love you."

I said it to her just like that. We have met many times. I have dreamt of her by day. I have not even kept up my journal. Verse has been out of the question.

"Ella, I love you. Let us move into the trousseau department. Don't look so dismayed, darling. If you like, we will go right away from here. We will live in that little restaurant in Central Park. There are thousand of birds there."

"Please—please don't talk like that!"

"But I love you with all my heart."

"You mustn't."

"But I find I must. I can't help it. Ella, you don't love another?"

She wept a little. "Oh, Charles, I do."

"Love another, Ella? One of these? I thought you dreaded them all. It must be Roscoe. He is the only one that's any way human. We talk of art, life, and such things. And he has stolen your heart!"

"No, Charles, no. He's just like the rest, really. I hate them all. They make me shudder."

"Who is it, then?"

"It's him."

"Who?"

"The night-watchman."

"Impossible!"

"No. He smells of the sun."

"Oh, Ella, you have broken my heart."

"Be my friend, though."

"I will. I'll be your brother. How did you fall in love with him?"

"Oh, Charles, it was so wonderful. I was thinking of birds, and I was careless. Don't tell on me, Charles. They'll punish me."

"No. No. Go on."

"I was careless, and there he was, coming round the corner. And there was no place for me; I had this blue dress on. There were only some wax models in their underthings."

"Please go on."

"I couldn't help it. I slipped off my dress, and stood still."

"I see."

"And he stopped just by me, Charles. And he looked at me. And he touched my cheek."

"Did he notice nothing?"

"No. It was cold. But Charles, he said—he said—'Say, honey, I wish they made 'em like you on Eighth Avenue.' Charles, wasn't that a lovely thing to say?"

"Personally, I should have said Park Avenue."

"Oh, Charles, don't get like these people here. Sometimes I think you're getting like them. It doesn't matter what street, Charles; it was a lovely thing to say."

"Yes, but my heart's broken. And what can you do about him? Ella, he belongs to another world."

"Yes, Charles, Eighth Avenue. I want to go there. Charles, are you truly my friend?"

"I'm your brother, only my heart's broken."

"I'll tell you. I will. I'm going to stand there again. So he'll see me."

"And then?"

"Perhaps he'll speak to me again."

"My dearest Ella, you are torturing yourself. You are making it worse."

"No, Charles. Because I shall answer him. He will take me away."

"Ella, I can't bear it."

"Ssh! There is someone coming. I shall see birds—real birds, Charles— and flowers growing. They're coming. You must go."

MAY 13

The last three days have been torture. This evening I broke. Roscoe had joined me. He sat eying me for a long time. He put his hand on my shoulder.

He said, "You're looking seedy, old fellow. Why don't you go over to Wanamaker's for some skiing?"

His kindness compelled a frank response. "It's deeper than that, Roscoe. I'm done for. I can't eat, I can't sleep. I can't write, man, I can't even write."

"What is it? Day starvation?"

"Roscoe—it's love."

"Not one of the staff, Charles, or the customers? That's absolutely forbidden."

"No, it's not that, Roscoe. But just as hopeless."

"My dear old fellow, I can't bear to see you like this. Let me help you. Let me share your trouble."

Then it came out. It burst out. I trusted him. I think I trusted him. I really think I had no intention of betraying Ella, of spoiling her escape, of keeping her here till her heart turned towards me. If I had, it was subconscious, I swear it.

But I told him all. All! He was sympathetic, but I detected a sly reserve in his sympathy. "You will respect my confidence. Roscoe? This is to be a secret between us."

"As secret as the grave, old chap."

And he must have gone straight to Mrs. Vanderpant. This evening the atmosphere has changed. People flicker to and fro, smiling nervously, horribly, with a sort of frightened sadistic exaltation. When I speak to them they answer evasively, fidget, and disappear. An informal dance has been called off. I cannot find Ella. I will creep out. I will look for her again.

LATER

Heaven! It has happened. I went in desperation to the manager's office, whose glass front overlooks the whole shop. I watched till midnight. Then I saw a little group of them, like ants bearing a victim. They were carrying Ella. They took her to the surgical department. They took other things.

And, coming back here, I was passed by a flittering, whispering horde of them, glancing over their shoulders in a thrilled ecstasy of panic, making for their hiding places. I, too, hid myself. How can I describe the dark inhuman creatures that passed me, silent as shadows? They went there—where Ella is.

What can I do? There is only one thing. I will find the watchman. I will tell him. He and I will save her. And if we are overpowered——Well, I will leave this on a counter. Tomorrow, if we live, I can recover it.

If not, look in the windows. Look for the three new figures: two men, one rather sensitive-looking, and a girl. She has blue eyes, like periwinkle flowers, and her upper lip is lifted a little.

Look for us.

Smoke them out! Obliterate them! Avenge us!

M. R. James

The Ash-Tree

M. R. James was the master of the ghost story in which an evil from the distant past persists into the present and is visited upon us as a legacy. His antiquarian ghost stories are a body of work that codified a main tradition of horror for the twentieth century. The weight of the past haunts us in Jamesian fiction, a bleak, stern moral landscape rich in detail. "The Ash-Tree" is thematically interesting in contrast to Hawthorne and Wellman as a witchcraft story. James looks back to J. S. Le Fanu as his paradigm (he is responsible for the modern revival of interest in Le Fanu, through his famous edition of Le Fanu stories, *Madame Crowl's Ghost*, 1923), but the onstage horror at the climax of "The Ash-Tree" is James' own contribution, striking and monstrous, to the genre.

Everyone who has travelled over Eastern England knows the smaller country-houses with which it is studded—the rather dark little buildings, usually in the Italian style, surrounded with parks of some eighty to a hundred acres. For me they have always had a very strong attraction, with the grey paling of split oak, the noble trees, the meres with their reed-beds, and the line of distant woods. Then, I like the pillared portico—perhaps stuck on to a red-brick Queen Anne house which has been faced with stucco to bring it into line with the "Grecian" taste of the end of the eighteenth century; the hall inside, going up to the roof, which hall ought always to be provided with a gallery and a small organ. I like the library, too, where you may find anything from a Psalter of the thirteenth century to a Shakespeare quarto. I like the pictures, of course; and perhaps most of all I like fancying what life in such a house was when it was first built, and in the piping times of landlords' prosperity, and not least now, when, if money is not so plentiful, taste is more varied and life quite as interesting. I wish to have one of these houses and enough money to keep it together and entertain my friends in it modestly.

But this is a digression. I have to tell you of a curious series of events which happened in such a house as I have tried to describe. It is Castringham Hall in Suffolk. I think a good deal has been done to the building since the period of my story, but the essential features I have sketched are still there—Italian portico, square block of white house, older inside than out, park with fringe of woods, and mere. The one feature that marked out the house from a score of others is gone. As you looked at it from the park, you saw on the right a great old ash-tree growing within half a dozen yards of the wall, and almost or quite touching the building with its branches. I suppose it had stood there ever since Castringham ceased to be a fortified place, and since the moat was filled in and the Elizabethan dwelling-house built. At any rate, it had well-nigh attained its full dimensions in the year 1690.

In that year the district in which the Hall is situated was the scene of a number of witch-trials. It will be long, I think, before we arrive at a just estimate of the amount of solid reason—if there was any—which lay at the root of the universal fear of witches in old times. Whether the persons accused of this offence really did imagine that they were possessed of unusual power of any kind; or whether they had the will at least, if not the power, of doing mischief to their neighbours; or whether all the confessions, of which there are so many, were extorted by the mere cruelty of the witch-finders—these are questions which are not, I fancy, yet solved. And the present narrative gives me pause. I cannot altogether sweep it away as mere invention. The reader must judge for himself.

Castringham contributed a victim to the *auto-da-fe*. Mrs. Mothersole was her name, and she differed from the ordinary run of village witches only in being rather better off and in a more influential position. Efforts were made to save her by several reputable farmers of the parish. They did their best to testify to her character, and showed considerable anxiety as to the verdict of the jury.

But what seems to have been fatal to the woman was the evidence of the then proprietor of Castringham Hall—Sir Matthew Fell. He deposed to having watched her on three different occasions from his window, at the full of the moon, gathering sprigs "from the ash-tree near my house." She had climbed into the branches, clad only in her shift, and was cutting off small twigs with a peculiarly curved knife, and as she did so she seemed to be talking to herself. On each occasion Sir Matthew had done his best to capture the woman, but she had always taken alarm at some accidental noise he had made, and all he could see when he got down to the garden was a hare running across the path in the direction of the village.

On the third night he had been at the pains to follow at his best speed, and had gone straight to Mrs. Mothersole's house; but he had had to wait a quarter of an hour battering at her door, and then she had come out very cross, and apparently very sleepy, as if just out of bed; and he had no good explanation to offer of his visit.

Mainly on this evidence, though there was much more of a less striking and unusual kind from other parishioners, Mrs. Mothersole was found guilty and condemned to die. She was hanged a week after the trial, with five or six more unhappy creatures, at Bury St. Edmunds.

Sir Matthew Fell, then Deputy-Sheriff, was present at the execution. It was a damp, drizzly March morning when the cart made its way up the rough grass hill outside Northgate, where the gallows stood. The other victims were apathetic or broken down with misery; but Mrs. Mothersole was, as in life so in death, of a very different temper. Her "poysonous Rage," as a reporter of the time puts it, "did so work upon the Bystanders—yea, even upon the Hangman—that it was constantly affirmed of all that saw her that she presented the living Aspect of a mad Divell. Yet she offer'd no Resistance to the Officers of the Law; onely she looked upon those that laid Hands upon her with so direfull and venomous an Aspect that—as one of them afterwards assured me—the meer Thought of it preyed inwardly upon his Mind for six Months after."

However, all that she is reported to have said were the seemingly meaningless words: "There will be guests at the Hall." Which she repeated more than once in an undertone.

Sir Matthew Fell was not unimpressed by the bearing of the woman. He had some talk upon the matter with the Vicar of his parish, with whom he travelled home after the assize business was over. His evidence at the trial had not been very willingly given; he was not specially infected with the witch-finding mania, but he declared, then and afterwards, that he could not give any other account of the matter than that he had given, and that he could not possibly have been mistaken as to what he saw. The whole transaction had been repugnant to him, for he was a man who liked to be on pleasant terms with those about him; but he saw a duty to be done in this business, and he had done it. That seems to have been the gist of his sentiments, and the Vicar applauded it, as any reasonable man must have done.

A few weeks after, when the moon of May was at the full, Vicar and Squire met again in the park, and walked to the Hall together. Lady Fell was with her mother, who was dangerously ill, and Sir Matthew was alone at home; so the Vicar, Mr. Crome, was easily persuaded to take a late supper at the Hall.

Sir Matthew was not very good company this evening. The talk ran chiefly on family and parish matters, and, as luck would have it, Sir Matthew made a memorandum in writing of certain wishes or intentions of his regarding his estates, which afterwards proved exceedingly useful.

When Mr. Crome thought of starting for home, about half past nine o'clock, Sir Matthew and he took a preliminary turn on the gravelled walk at the back of the house. The only incident that struck Mr. Crome was this: they were in sight of the ash-tree which I described as growing near the windows of the building, when Sir Matthew stopped and said:

"What is that that runs up and down the stem of the ash? It is never a squirrel? They will all be in their nests by now."

The Vicar looked and saw the moving creature, but he could make nothing of its colour in the moonlight. The sharp outline, however, seen for an instant, was imprinted on his brain, and he could have sworn, he said, though it sounded foolish, that, squirrel or not, it had more than four legs.

Still, not much was to be made of the momentary vision, and the two men parted. They may have met since then, but it was not for a score of years.

Next day Sir Matthew Fell was not downstairs at six in the morning, as was his custom, nor at seven, nor yet at eight. Hereupon the servants went and knocked at his chamber door. I need not prolong the description of their anxious listenings and renewed batterings on the panels. The door was opened at last from the outside, and they found their master dead and black. So much you have guessed. That there were any marks of violence did not at the moment appear; but the window was open.

One of the men went to fetch the parson, and then by his directions rode on to give notice to the coroner. Mr. Crome himself went as quick as he might to the Hall, and was shown to the room where the dead man lay. He has left some notes among his papers which show how genuine a respect and sorrow was felt for Sir Matthew, and there is also this passage, which I transcribe for the sake of the light it throws upon the course of events, and also upon the common beliefs of the time:

"There was not any the least Trace of an Entrance having been forc'd to the Chamber: but the Casement stood open, as my poor Friend would always have it in this Season. He had his Evening Drink of small Ale in a silver vessel of about a pint measure, and tonight had not drunk it out. This Drink was examined by the Physician from Bury, a Mr. Hodgkins, who could not, however, as he afterwards declar'd upon his Oath, before the Coroner's quest, discover that any matter of a venomous kind was present in it. For, as was natural, in the great Swelling and Blackness of the Corpse, there was talk made among the Neighbours of Poyson. The Body was very much Disorder'd as it laid in the Bed, being twisted after so extream a sort as gave too probable Conjecture that my worthy Friend and Patron had expir'd in great Pain and Agony. And what is as yet unexplain'd, and to myself the Argument of some Horrid and Artfull Designe in the Perpetrators of this Barbarous Murther, was this, that the Women which were entrusted with the laying-out of the Corpse and washing it, being both sad Pearsons and very well Respected in their Mournfull Profession, came to me in a great Pain and Distress both of Mind and Body, saying, what was indeed confirmed upon the first View, that they had no sooner touch'd the Breast of the Corpse with their naked Hands than they were sensible of a more than ordinary violent Smart and Acheing in their Palms, which, with their whole Forearms, in no long time swell'd so immoderately, the Pain still continuing, that, as afterwards proved, during many weeks they were forc'd to lay by the exercise of their Calling; and yet no mark seen on the Skin.

"Upon hearing this, I sent for the Physician, who was still in the House, and we made as carefull a Proof as we were able by the Help of a small Magnifying Lens of Crystal of the condition of the Skinn on this Part of the Body: but could not detect with the Instrument we had any Matter of Importance beyond a couple of small Punctures or Pricks, which we then concluded were the Spotts by which the Poyson might be introduced, remembering that Ring of *Pope Borgia*, with other known Specimens of the Horrid Art of the Italian Poysoners of the last age.

"So much is to be said of the Symptoms seen on the Corpse. As to what I am to add, it is meerly my own Experiment, and to be left to Posterity to judge whether there be anything of Value therein. There was on the Table by the Beddside a Bible of the small size, in which my Friend—punctuall as in Matters of less Moment, so in this more weighty one—used nightly, and upon his First Rising, to read a sett Portion. And I taking it up—not without a Tear duly paid to him wich from the Study of this poorer Adumbration was now pass'd to the contemplation of its great Originall—it came into my Thoughts, as at such moments of Helplessness we are prone to catch at any the least Glimmer that makes promise of Light, to make trial of that old and by many accounted Superstitious Practice of drawing the *Sortes*; of which a Principall Instance, in the case of his late Sacred Majesty the Blessed Martyr King *Charles* and my Lord *Falkland*, was now much talked of. I must needs admit that by my Trial not much Assistance was afforded me: yet, as the Cause and Origin of these Dreadfull Events may hereafter be search'd out, I set down the Results, in the case it may be found that they pointed the true Quarter of the Mischief to a quicker Intelligence than my own.

"I made, then, three trials, opening the Book and placing my Finger upon certain Words: which gave in the first these words, from Luke xiii. 7, *Cut it down*; in the second. Isaiah xiii. 20, *It shall never be inhabited*; and upon the third Experiment, Job xxxix. 30, *Her young ones also suck up blood.*"

This is all that need be quoted from Mr. Crome's papers. Sir Matthew Fell was duly coffined and laid into the earth, and his funeral sermon, preached by Mr. Crome on the following Sunday, has been printed under the title of "The Unsearchable Way; or, England's Danger and the Malicious Dealings of Antichrist," it being the Vicar's view, as well as that most commonly held in the neighbourhood, that the Squire was the victim of a recrudescence of the Popish Plot.

His son, Sir Matthew the second, succeeded to the title and estates. And so ends the first act of the Castringham tragedy. It is to be mentioned, though the fact is not surprising, that the new Baronet did not occupy the room in which his father had died. Nor, indeed, was it slept in by anyone but an occasional visitor during the whole of his occupation. He died in 1735, and I do not find that anything particular marked his reign, save a curiously constant mortality among his cattle and live-stock in general, which showed a tendency to increase slightly as time went on.

Those who are interested in the details will find a statistical account in a letter to the *Gentlemen's Magazine* of 1772, which draws the facts from the Baronet's own papers. He put an end to it at last by a very simple expedient, that of shutting up all his beasts in sheds at night, and keeping no sheep in his park. For he had noticed that nothing was ever attacked that spent the night indoors. After that the disorder confined itself to wild birds, and beasts of chase. But as we have no good account of the symptoms, and as all-night watching was quite unproductive of any clue, I do not dwell on what the Suffolk farmers called the "Castringham sickness."

The second Sir Matthew died in 1735, as I said, and was duly succeeded by his son, Sir Richard. It was in his time that the great family pew was built out on the north side of the parish church. So large were the Squire's ideas that several of the graves on that unhallowed side of the building had to be disturbed to satisfy his requirements. Among them was that of Mrs. Mothersole, the position of which was accurately known, thanks to a note of a plan of the church and yard, both made by Mr. Crome.

A certain amount of interest was excited in the village when it was known that the famous witch, who was still remembered by a few, was to be exhumed. And the feeling of surprise, and indeed disquiet, was very strong when it was found that, though her coffin was fairly sound and unbroken, there was no trace whatever inside it of body, bones, or dust. Indeed, it is a curious phenomenon, for at the time of her burying no such things were dreamt of as resurrection-men, and it is difficult to conceive any rational motive for stealing a body otherwise than for the uses of the dissecting-room.

The incident revived for a time all the stories of witch-trials and of the exploits of the witches, dormant for forty years, and Sir Richard's orders that the coffin should be burnt were thought by a good many to be rather foolhardy, though they were duly carried out.

Sir Richard was a pestilent innovator, it is certain. Before his time the Hall had been a fine block of the mellowest red brick; but Sir Richard had travelled in Italy and become infected with the Italian taste, and, having more money than his predecessors, he determined to leave an Italian palace where he had found an English house. So stucco and ashlar masked the brick; some indifferent Roman marbles were planted about in the entrance-hall and gardens; a reproduction of the Sibyl's temple at Tivoli was erected on the opposite bank of the mere; and Castringham took an entirely new, and, I must say, a less engaging, aspect. But it was much admired, and served as a model to a good many of the neighbouring gentry in after-years.

One morning (it was in 1754) Sir Richard woke after a night of discomfort. It had been windy, and his chimney had smoked persistently, and yet it was so cold that he must keep up a fire. Also something had so rattled about the window that no man could get a moment's peace. Further, there was the prospect of several guests of position arriving in the course of the day, who would expect sport of some kind, and the inroads of the distemper (which continued among his game) had been lately so serious that he was afraid for his reputation as a game-preserver. But what really touched him most nearly was the other matter of his sleepless night. He could certainly not sleep in that room again.

That was the chief subject of his meditations at breakfast, and after it he began a systematic examination of the rooms to see which would suit his notions best. It was long before he found one. This had a window with an eastern aspect and that with a northern; this door the servants would be always passing, and he did not like the bedstead in that. No, he must have a room with a western look-out, so that the sun could not wake him early, and it must be out of the way of the business of the house. The housekeeper was at the end of her resources.

"Well, Sir Richard," she said, "you know that there is but the one room like that in the house."

"Which may that be?" said Sir Richard.

"And that is Sir Matthew's—the West Chamber."

"Well, put me in there, for there I'll lie tonight," said her master. "Which way is it? Here, to be sure"; and he hurried off.

"Oh, Sir Richard, but no one has slept there these forty years. The air has hardly been changed since Sir Matthew died there."

Thus she spoke, and rustled after him.

"Come, open the door, Mrs. Chiddock. I'll see the chamber, at least."

So it was opened, and, indeed, the smell was very close and earthy. Sir Richard crossed to the window, and, impatiently, as was his wont, threw the shutters back, and flung open the casement. For this end of the house was one which the alterations had barely touched, grown up as it was with the great ash-tree, and being otherwise concealed from view.

"Air it, Mrs. Chiddock, all today, and move my bed-furniture in in the afternoon. Put the Bishop of Kilmore in my old room."

"Pray, Sir Richard," said a new voice, breaking in on this speech, "might I have the favour of a moment's interview?"

Sir Richard turned around and saw a man in black in the doorway, who bowed.

"I must ask your indulgence for this intrusion, Sir Richard. You will, perhaps, hardly remember me. My name is William Crome, and my grandfather was Vicar in your grandfather's time."

"Well, sir," said Sir Richard, "the name of Crome is always a passport to Castringham. I am glad to renew a friendship of two generations' standing. In what can I serve you? for your hour of calling—and, if I do not mistake you, your bearing—shows you to be in some haste."

"That is no more than the truth, sir. I am riding from Norwich to Bury St. Edmunds with what haste I can make, and I have called in on my way to leave with you some papers which we have but just come upon in looking over what my grandfather left at his death. It is thought you may find some matters of family interest in them."

"You are mighty obliging, Mr. Crome, and, if you will be so good as to follow me to the parlour, and drink a glass of wine, we will take a first look at these same papers together. And you, Mrs. Chiddock, as I said, be about airing this chamber . . . Yes, it is here my grandfather died . . . Yes, the tree, perhaps, does make the place a little dampish . . . No; I do not wish to listen to any more. Make no difficulties, I beg. You have your orders—go. Will you follow me, sir?"

They went to the study. The packet which young Mr. Crome had brought—he was then just become a Fellow of Clare Hall in Cambridge, I may say, and subsequently brought out a respectable edition of Polyaenus—contained among other things the notes which the old Vicar had made upon the occasion of Sir Matthew Fell's death. And for the first time Sir Richard was confronted with the enigmatical *Sortes Biblicae* which you have heard. They amused him a good deal.

"Well," he said, "my grandfather's Bible gave one prudent piece of advice—*Cut it down.* If that stands for the ash-tree, he may rest assured I shall not neglect it. Such a nest of catarrhs and agues was never seen."

The parlour contained the family books, which, pending the arrival of a collection which Sir Richard had made in Italy, and the building of a proper room to receive them, were not many in number.

Sir Richard looked up from the paper to the bookcase.

"I wonder," says he, "whether the old prophet is there yet? I fancy I see him."

Crossing the room, he took out a dumpy Bible, which, sure enough, bore on the flyleaf the inscription: "To Matthew Fell, from his Loving Godmother, Anne Aldous, 2 September 1659."

"It would be no bad plan to test him again, Mr. Crome. I will wager we get a couple of names in the Chronicles. H'm! what have we here? 'Thou shalt

seek me in the morning, and I shall not be.' Well, well! Your grandfather
would have made a fine omen of that, hey? No more prophets for me! They
are all in a tale. And now, Mr. Crome, I am infinitely obliged to you for your
packet. You will, I fear, be impatient to get on. Pray allow me—another
glass."

So with offers of hospitality, which were genuinely meant (for Sir Richard
thought well of the young man's address and manner), they parted.

In the afternoon came the guests—the Bishop of Kilmore, Lady Mary
Hervey, Sir William Kentfield, etc. Dinner at five, wine, cards, supper, and
dispersal to bed.

Next morning Sir Richard is disinclined to take his gun with the rest. He
talks with the Bishop of Kilmore. This prelate, unlike a good many of the
Irish Bishops of his day, had visited his see, and, indeed, resided there, for
some considerable time. This morning, as the two were walking along the
terrace and talking over the alterations and improvements in the house, the
Bishop said, pointing to the window of the West Room:

"You could never get one of my Irish flock to occupy that room, Sir
Richard."

"Why is that, my lord? It is, in fact, my own."

"Well, our Irish peasantry will always have it that it brings the worst of
luck to sleep near an ash-tree, and you have a fine growth of ash not two
yards from your chamber window. Perhaps," the Bishop went on, with a
smile, "it has given you a touch of its quality already, for you do not seem, if
I may say it, so much the fresher for your night's rest as your friends would
like to see you."

"That, or something else, it is true, cost me my sleep from twelve to four,
my lord. But the tree is to come down tomorrow, so I shall not hear much
more from it."

"I applaud your determination. It can hardly be wholesome to have the air
you breathe strained, as it were, through all that leafage."

"Your lordship is right there, I think. But I had not my window open last
night. It was rather the noise that went on—no doubt from the twigs
sweeping the glass—that kept me open-eyed."

"I think that can hardly be, Sir Richard. Here—you see it from this point.
None of these nearest branches even can touch your casement unless there
were a gale, and there was none of that last night. They miss the panes by a
foot."

"No, sir, true. What, then, will it be, I wonder, that scratched and rustled
so—ay, and covered the dust on my sill with lines and marks?"

At last they agreed that the rats must have come up through the ivy. That
was the Bishop's idea, and Sir Richard jumped at it.

So the day passed quietly, and night came, and the party dispersed to their
rooms, and wished Sir Richard a better night.

And now we are in his bedroom, with the light out and the Squire in bed.
The room is over the kitchen, and the night outside still and warm, so the
window stands open.

There is very little light about the bedstead, but there is a strange
movement there; it seems as if Sir Richard were moving his head rapidly to

and fro with only the slightest possible sound. And now you would guess, so deceptive is the half-darkness, that he had several heads, round and brownish which move back and forward, even as low as his chest. It is a horrible illusion. Is it nothing more? There! something drops off the bed with a soft plump, like a kitten, and is out of the window in a flash; another—four —and after that there is quiet again.

Thou shalt seek me in the morning, and I shall not be.

As with Sir Matthew, so with Sir Richard—dead and black in his bed!

A pale and silent party of guests and servants gathered under the window when the news was known. Italian poisoners, Popish emissaries, infected air—all these and more guesses were hazarded, and the Bishop of Kilmore looked at the tree, in the fork of whose lower boughs a white tom-cat was crouching, looking down the hollow which years had gnawed in the trunk. It was watching something inside the tree with great interest.

Suddenly it got up and craned over the hole. Then a bit of the edge on which it stood gave way, and it went slithering in. Everyone looked up at the noise of the fall.

It is known to most of us that a cat can cry; but few of us have heard, I hope, such a yell as came out of the trunk of the great ash. Two or three screams there were—the witnesses are not sure which—and then a slight and muffled noise of some commotion or struggling was all that came. But Lady Mary Hervey fainted outright, and the housekeeper stopped her ears and fled till she fell on the terrace.

The Bishop of Kilmore and Sir William Kentfield stayed. Yet even they were daunted, though it was only at the cry of a cat; and Sir William swallowed once or twice before he could say:

"There is something more than we know of in that tree, my lord. I am for an instant search."

And this was agreed upon. A ladder was brought, and one of the gardeners went up, and, looking down the hollow, could detect nothing but a few dim indications of something moving. They got a lantern, and let it down by a rope.

"We must get at the bottom of this. My life upon it, my lord, but the secret of these terrible deaths is there."

Up went the gardener again with the lantern, and let it down the hole cautiously. They saw the yellow light upon his face as he bent over, and saw his face struck with an incredulous terror and loathing before he cried out in a dreadful voice and fell back from the ladder—where, happily, he was caught by two of the men—letting the lantern fall inside the tree.

He was in a dead faint, and it was some time before any word could be got from him.

By then they had something else to look at. The lantern must have broken at the bottom, and the light in it caught upon dry leaves and rubbish that lay there, for in a few minutes a dense smoke began to come up, and then flame; and, to be short, the tree was in a blaze.

The bystanders made a ring at some yards' distance, and Sir William and the Bishop sent men to get what weapons and tools they could; for, clearly, whatever might be using the tree as its lair would be forced out by the fire.

So it was. First, at the fork, they saw a round body covered with fire—the size of a man's head—appear very suddenly, then seem to collapse and fall back. This, five or six times; then a similar ball leapt into the air and fell on the grass, where after a moment it lay still. The Bishop went as near as he dared to it, and saw—what but the remains of an enormous spider, veinous and seared! And, as the fire burned lower down, more terrible bodies like this began to break out from the trunk, and it was seen that these were covered with greyish hair.

All that day the ash burned, and until it fell to pieces the men stood about it, and from time to time killed the brutes as they darted out. At last there was a long interval when none appeared, and they cautiously closed in and examined the roots of the tree.

"They found," says the Bishop of Kilmore, "below it a rounded hollow place in the earth, wherein were two or three bodies of these creatures that had plainly been smothered by the smoke; and, what is to me more curious, at the side of this den, against the wall, was crouching the anatomy or skeleton of a human being, with the skin dried upon the bones, having some remains of black hair, which was pronounced by those that examined it to be undoubtedly the body of a woman, and clearly dead for a period of fifty years."

Lucy Clifford

The New Mother

Lucy Clifford was a Victorian writer of children's fantasies. "The New Mother" is from *Anyhow Stories, Moral and Otherwise* (London, 1882). It is a curious example of the often-noted tendency of Victorian morality to be at odds in an unsettling way with human psychology. "Step on a crack, break your mother's back," or step out of line and you will be punished horribly, out of all proportion to the sin, seems to be the moral, familiar from horrid children's rhymes. It represents herein the whole tradition of tales calculated to terrify and horrify children into good behavior through moral allegory. The allegory may be awry, but the horror is real.

I

The children were always called Blue-Eyes and the Turkey. The elder one was like her dear father who was far away at sea; for the father had the bluest of blue eyes, and so gradually his little girl came to be called after them. The younger one had once, while she was still almost a baby, cried bitterly because a turkey that lived near the cottage suddenly vanished in the middle of the winter; and to console her she had been called by its name.

Now the mother and Blue-Eyes and the Turkey and the baby all lived in a lonely cottage on the edge of the forest. It was a long way to the village, nearly a mile and a half, and the mother had to work hard and had not time to go often herself to see if there was a letter at the post-office from the dear father, and so very often in the afternoon she used to send the two children. They were very proud of being able to go alone. When they came back tired with the long walk, there would be the mother waiting and watching for them, and the tea would be ready, and the baby crowing with delight; and if by any chance there was a letter from the sea, then they were happy indeed. The cottage room was so cosy: the walls were as white as snow inside as well as out. The baby's high chair stood in one corner, and in another there was a cupboard, in which the mother kept all manner of surprises.

"Dear children," the mother said one afternoon late in the autumn, "it is very chilly for you to go to the village, but you must walk quickly, and who knows but what you may bring back a letter saying that dear father is already on his way to England. Don't be long," the mother said, as she always did before they started. "Go the nearest way and don't look at any strangers you meet, and be sure you do not talk with them."

"No, mother," they answered; and then she kissed them and called them dear good children, and they joyfully started on their way.

The village was gayer than usual, for there had been a fair the day before. "Oh, I *do* wish we had been here yesterday," Blue-Eyes said as they went on to the grocer's, which was also the post-office. The post-mistress was very busy and just said "No letter for you to-day." Then Blue-Eyes and the Turkey turned away to go home. They had left the village and walked some way, and then they noticed, resting against a pile of stones by the wayside, a strange wild-looking girl, who seemed very unhappy. So they thought they would ask her if they could do anything to help her, for they were kind children and sorry indeed for any one in distress.

The girl seemed to be about fifteen years old. She was dressed in very ragged clothes. Round her shoulders there was an old brown shawl. She wore no bonnet. Her hair was coal-black and hung down uncombed and unfastened. She had something hidden under her shawl; on seeing them coming towards her, she carefully put it under her and sat upon it. She sat watching the children approach, and did not move or stir till they were within a yard of her; then she wiped her eyes just as if she had been crying bitterly, and looked up.

The children stood still in front of her for a moment, staring at her. "Are you crying?" they asked shyly.

To their surprise she said in a most cheerful voice, "Oh dear, no! quite the contrary. Are you?"

"Perhaps you have lost yourself?" they said gently.

But the girl answered promptly, "Certainly not. Why, you have just found me. Besides," she added, "I live in the village."

The children were surprised at this, for they had never seen her before, and yet they thought they knew all the village folk by sight.

Then the Turkey, who had an inquiring mind, put a question. "What are you sitting on?" she asked.

"On a peardrum," the girl answered.

"What is a peardrum?" they asked.

"I am surprised at your not knowing," the girl answered. "Most people in good society have one." And then she pulled it out and showed it to them. It was a curious instrument, a good deal like a guitar in shape; it had three strings, but only two pegs by which to tune them. But the strange thing about the peardrum was not the music it made, but a little square box attached to one side.

"Where did you get it?" the children asked.

"I bought it," the girl answered.

"Didn't it cost a great deal of money?" they asked.

"Yes," answered the girl slowly, nodding her head, "it cost a great deal of money. I am very rich," she added.

"You don't look rich," they said, in as polite a voice as possible.

"Perhaps not," the girl answered cheerfully.

At this, the children gathered courage, and ventured to remark, "You look rather shabby."

"Indeed?" said the girl in a voice of one who had heard a pleasant but surprising statement. "A little shabbiness is very respectable," she added in a satisfied voice. "I must really tell them this," she continued. And the children wondered what she meant. She opened the little box by the side of the peardrum, and said, just as if she were speaking to some one who could hear her, "They say I look rather shabby; it is quite lucky isn't it?"

"Why, you are not speaking to any one!" they said, more surprised than ever.

"Oh dear, yes! I am speaking to them both."

"Both?" they said, wondering.

"Yes. I have here a little man dressed as a peasant, and a little woman to match. I put them on the lid of the box, and when I play they dance most beautifully."

"Oh! let us see; do let us see!" the children cried.

Then the village girl looked at them doubtfully. "Let you see!" she said slowly. "Well, I am not sure that I can. Tell me, are you good?"

"Yes, yes," they answered eagerly, "we are very good!"

"Then it's quite impossible," she answered, and resolutely closed the lid of the box.

They stared at her in astonishment. "But we are good," they cried, thinking she must have misunderstood them. "We are very good. Then can't you let us see the little man and woman?"

"Oh dear, no!" the girl answered. "I only show them to naughty children. And the worse the children the better do the man and woman dance."

She put the peardrum carefully under her ragged cloak, and prepared to go on her way. "I really could not have believed that you were good," she said reproachfully, as if they had accused themselves of some great crime. "Well, good day."

"Oh, but we will be naughty," they said in despair.

"I am afraid you couldn't," she answered, shaking her head. "It requires a great deal of skill to be naughty well."

And swiftly she walked away, while the children felt their eyes fill with tears, and their hearts ache with disappointment.

"If we had only been naughty," they said, "we should have seen them dance."

"Suppose," said the Turkey, "we try to be naughty today; perhaps she would let us see them to-morrow."

"But, oh!" said Blue-Eyes, "I don't know how to be naughty; no one ever taught me."

The Turkey thought for a few minutes in silence. "I think I can be naughty if I try," she said. "I'll try to-night."

"Oh, don't be naughty without me!" she cried. "It would be so unkind of you. You know I want to see the little man and woman just as much as you do. You are very, very unkind."

And so, quarrelling and crying, they reached their home.

Now, when their mother saw them, she was greatly astonished, and, fearing they were hurt, ran to meet them.

"Oh, my children, oh, my dear, dear children," she said; "what is the matter?"

But they did not dare tell their mother about the village girl and the little man and woman, so they answered, "Nothing is the matter," and cried all the more.

"Poor children!" the mother said to herself, "They are tired, and perhaps they are hungry; after tea they will be better." And she went back to the cottage, and made the fire blaze; and she put the kettle on to boil, and set the tea-things on the table. Then she went to the little cupboard and took out some bread and cut it on the table, and said in a loving voice, "Dear little children, come and have your tea. And see, there is the baby waking from her sleep; she will crow at us while we eat."

But the children made no answer to the dear mother; they only stood still by the window and said nothing.

"Come, children," the mother said again. "Come, Blue-Eyes, and come, my Turkey; here is nice sweet bread for tea." Then suddenly she looked up and saw that the Turkey's eyes were full of tears.

"Turkey!" she exclaimed, "my dear little Turkey! what is the matter? Come to mother, my sweet." And putting the baby down, she held out her arms, and the Turkey ran swiftly into them.

"Oh, mother," she sobbed, "Oh, dear mother! I do so want to be naughty. I do so want to be very, very naughty."

And then Blue-Eyes left her chair also, and rubbing her face against her mother's shoulder, cried sadly. "And so do I, mother. Oh, I'd give anything to be very, very naughty."

"But, my dear children," said the mother, in astonishment, "Why do you want to be naughty?"

"Because we do; oh, what shall we do?" they cried together.

"I should be very angry if you were naughty. But you could not be, for you love me," the mother answered.

"Why couldn't we?" they asked.

Then the mother thought a while before she answered; and she seemed to be speaking rather to herself than to them.

"Because if one loves well," she said gently, "one's love is stronger than all bad feelings in one, and conquers them."

"We don't know what you mean," they cried; "and we do love you; but we want to be naughty."

"Then I should know you did not love me," the mother said.

"If we were very, very, very naughty, and wouldn't be good, what then?"

"Then," said the mother sadly—and while she spoke her eyes filled with tears, and a sob almost choked her—"then," she said, "I should have to go away and leave you, and to send home a new mother, with glass eyes and wooden tail."

"Good-day," said the village girl, when she saw Blue-Eyes and the Turkey approach. She was again sitting by the heap of stones, and under her shawl the peardrum was hidden.

"Are the little man and woman there?" the children asked.

"Yes, thank you for inquiring after them," the girl answered; "they are both here and quite well. The little woman has heard a secret—she tells it while she dances."

"Oh do let us see," they entreated.

"Quite impossible, I assure you," the girl answered promptly. "You see, you are good."

"Oh!" said Blue-Eyes, sadly; "but mother says if we are naughty she will go away and send home a new mother, with glass eyes and a wooden tail."

"Indeed," said the girl, still speaking in the same unconcerned voice, "that is what they all say. They all threaten that kind of thing. Of course really there are no mothers with glass eyes and wooden tails; they would be much too expensive to make." And the common sense of this remark the children saw at once.

"We think you might let us see the little man and woman dance."

"The kind of thing you would think," remarked the village girl.

"But will you if we are naughty?" they asked in despair.

"I fear you could not be naughty—that is, really—even if you tried," she said scornfully.

"But if we are very naughty tonight, will you let us see them to-morrow?"

"Questions asked to-day are always best answered to-morrow," the girl said, and turned round as if to walk on. "Good-day," she said blithely; "I must really go and play a little to myself."

For a few minutes the children stood looking after her, then they broke down and cried. The Turkey was the first to wipe away her tears. "Let us go home and be very naughty," she said; "then perhaps she will let us see them to-morrow."

And that afternoon the dear mother was sorely distressed, for, instead of sitting at their tea as usual with smiling happy faces, they broke their mugs and threw their bread and butter on the floor, and when the mother told them to do one thing they carefully did another, and only stamped their feet with rage when she told them to go upstairs until they were good.

"Do you remember what I told you I should do if you were very, very naughty?" she asked sadly.

"Yes, we know, but it isn't true," they cried. "There is no mother with a wooden tail and glass eyes, and if there were we should just stick pins into her and send her away; but there is none."

Then the mother became really angry, and sent them off to bed, but instead of crying and being sorry at her anger, they laughed for joy, and sat up and sang merry songs at the top of their voices.

The next morning quite early, without asking leave from the mother, the children got up and ran off as fast as they could to look for the village girl. She was sitting as usual by the heap of stones with the peardrum under her shawl.

"Now please show us the little man and woman," they cried, "and let us hear the peardrum. We were very naughty last night." But the girl kept the peardrum carefully hidden.

"So you say," she answered. "You were not half naughty enough. As I remarked before, it requires a great deal of skill to be naughty well."

"But we broke our mugs, we threw our bread and butter on the floor, we did everything we could to be tiresome."

"Mere trifles," answered the village girl scornfully. "Did you throw cold water on the fire, did you break the clock, did you pull all the tins down from the walls, and throw them on the floor?"

"No," exclaimed the children, aghast, "we did not do that."

"I thought not," the girl answered. "So many people mistake a little noise and foolishness for real naughtiness." And before they could say another word she had vanished.

"We'll be much worse," the children cried, in despair. "We'll go and do all the things she says"; and then they went home and did all these things. And when the mother saw all that they had done she did not scold them as she had the day before, but she just broke down and cried, and said sadly—

"Unless you are good to-morrow, my poor Blue-Eyes and Turkey, I shall indeed have to go away and come back no more, and the new mother I told you of will come to you."

They did not believe her; yet their hearts ached when they saw how unhappy she looked, and they thought within themselves that when they once had seen the little man and woman dance, they would be good to the dear mother for ever afterwards.

The next morning, before the birds were stirring, the children crept out of the cottage and ran across the fields. They found the village girl sitting by the heap of stones, just as if it were her natural home.

"We have been very naughty," they cried. "We have done all the things you told us; now will you show us the little man and woman?" The girl looked at them curiously. "You really seem quite excited," she said in her usual voice. "You should be calm."

"We have done all the things you told us," the children cried again, "and we do so long to hear the secret. We have been so very naughty, and mother says she will go away to-day and send home a new mother if we are not good."

"Indeed," said the girl. "Well, let me see. When did your mother say she would go?"

"But if she goes, what shall we do?" they cried in despair. "We don't want her to go; we love her very much."

"You had better go back and be good, you are really not clever enough to be anything else; and the little woman's secret is very important; she never tells it for make-believe naughtiness."

"But we did all the things you told us," the children cried.

"You didn't throw the looking-glass out of the window, or stand the baby on its head."

"No, we didn't do that," the children gasped.

"I thought not," the girl said triumphantly. "Well, good-day. I shall not be here to-morrow."

"Oh, but don't go away," they cried. "Do let us see them just once."

"Well, I shall go past your cottage at eleven o'clock this morning," the girl said. "Perhaps I shall play the peardrum as I go by."

"And will you show us the man and woman?" they asked.

"Quite impossible, unless you have really deserved it; make-believe naughtiness is only spoilt goodness. Now if you break the looking-glass and do the things that are desired . . ."

"Oh, we will," they cried. "We will be very naughty till we hear you coming."

Then again the children went home, and were naughty, oh, so very very naughty that the dear mother's heart ached and her eyes filled with tears, and at last she went upstairs and slowly put on her best gown and her new sun-bonnet, and she dressed the baby all in its Sunday clothes, and then she came down and stood before Blue-Eyes and the Turkey, and just as she did so the Turkey threw the looking-glass out of the window, and it fell with a loud crash upon the ground.

"Good-bye, my children," the mother said sadly, kissing them. "The new mother will be home presently. Oh, my poor children!" and then weeping bitterly, the mother took the baby in her arms and turned to leave the house.

"But mother, we will be good at half-past eleven, come back at half-past eleven," they cried, "and we'll both be good; we must be naughty till eleven o'clock." But the mother only picked up the little bundle in which she had tied up her cotton apron, and went slowly out at the door. Just by the corner of the fields she stopped and turned, and waved her handkerchief, all wet with tears, to the children at the window; she made the baby kiss its hand; and in a moment mother and baby had vanished from their sight.

Then the children felt their hearts ache with sorrow, and they cried bitterly, and yet they could not believe that she had gone. And the broken clock struck eleven, and suddenly there was a sound, a quick, clanging, jangling sound, with a strange discordant note at intervals. They rushed to the open window, and there they saw the village girl dancing along and playing as she did so.

"We have done all you told us," the children called. "Come and see; and now show us the little man and woman."

The girl did not cease her playing or her dancing, but she called out in a voice that was half speaking half singing. "You did it all badly. You threw the water on the wrong side of the fire, the tin things were not quite in the middle of the room, the clock was not broken enough, you did not stand the baby on its head."

She was already passing the cottage. She did not stop singing, and all she said sounded like part of a terrible song. "I am going to my own land," the girl sang, "to the land where I was born."

"But our mother is gone," the children cried; "our dear mother will she ever come back?"

"No," sang the girl, "she'll never come back. She took a boat upon the river; she is sailing to the sea; she will meet your father once again, and they will go sailing on."

Then the girl, her voice getting fainter and fainter in the distance, called out once more to them. "Your new mother is coming. She is already on her way; but she only walks slowly, for her tail is rather long, and her spectacles are left behind; but she is coming, she is coming—coming—coming."

The last word died away; it was the last one they ever heard the village girl utter. On she went, dancing on.

Then the children turned, and looked at each other and at the little cottage home, that only a week before had been so bright and happy, so cosy and spotless. The fire was out, the clock all broken and spoilt. And there was the baby's high chair, with no baby to sit in it; there was the cupboard on the wall, and never a sweet loaf on its shelf; and there were the broken mugs, and the bits of bread tossed about, and the greasy boards which the mother had knelt down to scrub until they were as white as snow. In the midst of all stood the children, looking at the wreck they had made, their eyes blinded with tears, and their poor little hands clasped in misery.

"I don't know what we shall do if the new mother comes," cried Blue-Eyes. "I shall never, never like any other mother."

The Turkey stopped crying for a minute, to think what should be done. "We will bolt the door and shut the window; and we won't take any notice when she knocks."

All through the afternoon they sat watching and listening for fear of the new mother; but they saw and heard nothing of her, and gradually they became less and less afraid lest she should come. They fetched a pail of water and washed the floor; they found some rag, and rubbed the tins; they picked up the broken mugs and made the room as neat as they could. There was no sweet loaf to put on the table, but perhaps the mother would bring something from the village, they thought. At last all was ready, and Blue-Eyes and the Turkey washed their faces and their hands, and then sat and waited, for of course they did not believe what the village girl had said about their mother sailing away.

Suddenly, while they were sitting by the fire, they heard a sound as of something heavy being dragged along the ground outside, and then there was a loud and terrible knocking at the door. The children felt their hearts stand still. They knew it could not be their own mother, for she would have turned the handle and tried to come in without any knocking at all.

Again there came a loud and terrible knocking.

"She'll break the door down if she knocks so hard," cried Blue-Eyes.

"Go and put your back to it," whispered the Turkey, "and I'll peep out of the window and try to see if it is really the new mother."

So in fear and trembling Blue-Eyes put her back against the door, and the Turkey went to the window. She could just see a black satin poke bonnet with a frill round the edge, and a long bony arm carrying a black leather bag.

From beneath the bonnet there flashed a strange bright light, and Turkey's heart sank and her cheeks turned pale, for she knew it was the flashing of two glass eyes. She crept up to Blue-Eyes. "It is—it is—it is!" she whispered, her voice shaking with fear, "it is the new mother!"

Together they stood with the two little backs against the door. There was a long pause. They thought perhaps the new mother had made up her mind that there was no one at home to let her in, and would go away, but presently the two children heard through the thin wooden door the new mother move a little, and then say to herself—"I must break the door open with my tail."

For one terrible moment all was still, but in it the children could almost hear her lift up her tail, and then, with a fearful blow, the little painted door was cracked and splintered. With a shriek the children darted from the spot and fled through the cottage, and out at the back door into the forest beyond. All night long they stayed in the darkness and the cold, and all the next day and the next, and all through the cold, dreary days and the long dark nights that followed.

They are there still, my children. All through the long weeks and months have they been there, with only green rushes for their pillows and only the brown dead leaves to cover them, feeding on the wild strawberries in the summer, or on the nuts when they hang green; on the blackberries when they are no longer sour in the autumn, and in the winter on the little red berries that ripen in the snow. They wander about among the tall dark firs or beneath the great trees beyond. Sometimes they stay to rest beside the little pool near the copse, and they long and long, with a longing that is greater than words can say, to see their own dear mother again, just once again, to tell her that they'll be good for evermore—just once again.

And still the new mother stays in the little cottage, but the windows are closed and the doors are shut, and no one knows what the inside looks like. Now and then, when the darkness has fallen and the night is still, hand in hand Blue-Eyes and the Turkey creep up near the home in which they once were so happy, and with beating hearts they watch and listen; sometimes a blinding flash comes through the window, and they know it is the light from the new mother's glass eyes, or they hear a strange muffled noise, and they know it is the sound of her wooden tail as she drags it along the floor.

Russell Kirk

There's a Long, Long Trail A-Winding

Russell Kirk is one of the most articulate Conservatives in the U.S. and also one of the contemporary masters of the Gothic, the supernatural and the uncanny in fiction. He is the great living exponent of the Christian moral allegory in the horror mode. His approach is set forth in an essay appendix to his first collection, *The Surly Sullen Bell* (1962), "A Cautionary Note on the Ghostly Tale." Kirk and T. S. Eliot were close friends and they shared an intellectual and emotional commitment to the Christian supernatural that informs all of Kirk's fiction. "There's a Long, Long Trail A-Winding" is one of Kirk's later works and the winner of the World Fantasy Award for best short fiction of the year in 1977. It epitomizes the overtly allegorical mode in contemporary horror (stories written as allegory as opposed to stories, such as much of the works of Stephen King, that may be interpreted using the moral coordinates of the allegorical method). Kirk's body of work in this mode makes him the C. S. Lewis of the supernatural genre in our day.

> *Then he said unto the disciples, It is impossible but that offenses will come; but woe unto him, through whom they come!*
> *It were better for him that a millstone were hanged about his neck, and he cast into the sea, than that he should offend one of these little ones.*
>
> LUKE 17:1–2

Along the vast empty six-lane highway, the blizzard swept as if it meant to swallow all the sensual world. Frank Sarsfield, massive though he was, scudded like a heavy kite before that overwhelming wind. On his thick white hair the snow clotted and tried to form a Phrygian cap; the big flakes so swirled about his Viking face that he scarcely could make out the barren country on either side of the road.

Somehow he must get indoors. Racing for sanctuary, the last automobile had swept unheeding past his thumb two hours ago, doubtless bound for the county town some twenty miles eastward. Westward among the hills, the highway must be blocked by snowdrifts now. This was an unkind twelfth of January. "Blow, blow, thou winter wind!" Twilight being almost upon him, soon he must find lodging or else freeze stiff by the roadside.

He had walked more than thirty miles that day. Having in his pocket the sum of twenty-nine dollars and thirty cents, he could have put up at either of the two motels he had passed, had they not been closed for the winter. Well, as always, he was decently dressed—a good wash-and-wear suit and a neat black overcoat. As always, he was shaven and clean and civil-spoken. Surely some farmer or villager would take him in, if he knocked with a ten-dollar bill in his fist. People sometimes mistook him for a stranded well-to-do motorist, and sometimes he took the trouble to undeceive them.

But where to apply? This was depopulated country, its forests gone to the sawmills long before, its mines worked out. The freeway ran through the abomination of desolation. He did not prefer to walk the freeways, but on such a day as this there were no cars on the lesser roads.

He had run away from a hardscrabble New Hampshire farm when he was fourteen, and ever since then, except for brief working intervals, he had been either on the roads or in the jails. Now his sixtieth birthday was imminent. There were few men bigger than Frank Sarsfield, and none more solitary. Where was a friendly house?

For a few moments, the rage of the snow slackened; he stared about. Away to the left, almost a mile distant, he made out a grim high clump of buildings on rising ground, a wall enclosing them; the roof of the central building was gone. Sarsfield grinned, knowing what that complex must be: a derelict prison. He had lodged in prisons altogether too many nights.

His hand sheltering his eyes from the north wind, he looked to his right. Down in a snug valley, beside a narrow river and broad marshes, he could perceive a village or hamlet: a white church-tower, three or four commercial buildings, some little houses, beyond them a park of bare maple trees. The old highway must have run through or near this forgotten place, but the new freeway had sealed it off. There was no sign of a freeway exit to the settlement; probably it could be reached by car only along some detouring country lane. In such a little decayed town there would be folk willing to accept him for the sake of his proffered ten dollars—or, better, simply for charity's sake and talk with an amusing stranger who could recite every kind of poetry.

He scrambled heavily down the embankment. At this point, praise be, no tremendous wire fence kept the haughty new highway inviolable. His powerful thighs took him through the swelling drifts, though his heart pounded as the storm burst upon him afresh.

The village was more distant than he had thought. He passed panting through old fields half-grown up to poplar and birch. A little to the west he noticed what seemed to be old mine-workings, with fragments of brick buildings. He clambered upon an old railroad bed, its rails and ties taken up; perhaps the new freeway had dealt the final blow to the rails. Here the going was somewhat easier.

Mingled with the wind's shriek, did he hear a church-bell now? Could they be holding services at the village in this weather? Presently he came to a burnt-out little railway depot, on its platform signboard still the name "Anthonyville." Now he walked on a street of sorts, but no car-tracks or footprints sullied the snow.

Anthonyville Free Methodist Church hulked before him. Indeed the bell was swinging, and now and again faintly ringing in the steeple; but it was the wind's mockery, a knell for the derelict town of Anthonyville. The church door was slamming in the high wind, flying open again, and slamming once more, like a perpetual-motion machine, the glass being gone from the church windows. Sarsfield trudged past the skeletal church.

The front of Emmons's General Store was boarded up, and so was the front of what may have been a drugstore. The village hall was a wreck. The school may have stood upon those scanty foundations which protruded from the snow. And from no chimney of the decrepit cottages and cabins along Main Street—the only street—did any smoke rise.

Sarsfield never had seen a deader village. In an upper window of what looked like a livery-stable converted into a garage, a faded cardboard sign could be read—

> REMEMBER YOUR FUTURE
> BACK THE TOWNSEND PLAN

Was no one at all left here—not even some gaunt old couple managing on Social Security? He might force his way into one of the stores or cottages—though on principle and prudence he generally steered clear of possible charges of breaking and entering—but that would be cold comfort. In poor Anthonyville there must remain some living soul.

His mittened hands clutching his red ears, Sarsfield had plodded nearly to the end of Main Street. Anthonyville was Endsville, he saw now: river and swamp and new highway cut it off altogether from the rest of the frozen world, except for the drift-obliterated country road that twisted southward, Lord knew whither. He might count himself lucky to find a stove, left behind in some shack, that he could feed with boards ripped from walls.

Main Street ended at that grove or park of old maples. Just a sugarbush, like those he had tapped in his boyhood under his father's rough command? No: had the trees not been leafless, he might not have discerned the big stone house among the trees, the only substantial building remaining to Anthonyville. But see it he did for one moment, before the blizzard veiled it from him. There were stone gateposts, too, and a bronze tablet set into one of them. Sarsfield brushed the snowflakes from the inscription: "Tamarack House."

Stumbling among the maples toward this promise, he almost collided with a tall glacial boulder. A similar boulder rose a few feet to his right, the pair of them halfway between gateposts and house. There was a bronze tablet on this boulder, too, and he paused to read it:

> SACRED TO THE MEMORY OF
> JEROME ANTHONY
> JULY 4, 1836–JANUARY 14, 1915
> BRIGADIER-GENERAL IN THE CORPS OF ENGINEERS,
> ARMY OF THE REPUBLIC, FOUNDER OF THIS TOWN
> ARCHITECT OF ANTHONYVILLE STATE PRISON
> WHO DIED AS HE HAD LIVED, WITH HONOR

"And there will I keep you forever,
Yes, forever and a day,
Till the walls shall crumble in ruin,
And moulder in dust away."

There's an epitaph for a prison architect, Sarsfield thought. It was too bitter an evening for inspecting the other boulder, and he hurried toward the portico of Tamarack House. This was a very big house indeed, a bracketed house, built all of squared fieldstone with beautiful glints to the masonry. A cupola topped it.

Once, come out of the cold into a public library, Sarsfield had pored through a picture-book about American architectural styles. There was a word for this sort of house. Was it "Italianate"? Yes, it rose in his memory—he took pride in no quality except his power of recollection. Yes, that was the word. Had he visited this house before? He could not account for a vague familiarity. Perhaps there had been a photograph of this particular house in that library book.

Every window was heavily shuttered, and no smoke rose from any of the several chimneys. Sarsfield went up to the stone steps to confront the oaken front door.

It was a formidable door, but it seemed as if at some time it had been broken open, for long ago a square of oak with a different grain had been mortised into the area round lock and keyhole. There was a gigantic knocker with a strange face worked upon it. Sarsfield knocked repeatedly.

No one answered. Conceivably the storm might have made his pounding inaudible to any occupants, but who could spend the winter in a shuttered house without fires? Another bronze plaque was screwed to the door:

TAMARACK HOUSE
PROPERTY OF THE ANTHONY FAMILY TRUST
GUARDED BY PROTECTIVE SERVICE

Sarsfield doubted the veracity of the last line. He made his way round to the back. No one answered those back doors, either, and they too were locked.

But presently he found what he had hoped for: an oldfangled slanting cellar door, set into the foundations. It was not wise to enter without permission, but at least he might accomplish it without breaking. His fingers, though clumsy, were strong as the rest of him. After much trouble and with help from the Boy Scout knife that he carried, he pulled the pins out of the cellar door's three hinges and scrambled down into the darkness. With the passing of the years, he had become something of a jailhouse lawyer— though those young inmates bored him with their endless chatter about Miranda and Escobedo. And now he thought of the doctrine called "defense of necessity." If caught, he could say that self-preservation from freezing is the first necessity; besides, they might not take him for a bum.

Faint light down the cellar steps—he would replace the hinge-pins later—showed him an inner door at the foot. That door was hooked, though hooked only. With a sigh, Sarsfield put his shoulder to the door; the hook clattered to the stone floor inside; and he was master of all he surveyed.

In that black cellar he found no light-switch. Though he never smoked, he carried matches for such emergencies. Having lit one, he discovered a providential kerosene lamp on a table, with enough kerosene still in it. Sarsfield went lamp-lit through the cellars and up more stone stairs into a pantry. "Anybody home?" he called. It was an eerie echo.

He would make sure before exploring, for he dreaded shotguns. How about a cheerful song? In that chill pantry, Sarsfield bellowed a tune formerly beloved at Rotary Clubs. Once a waggish Rotarian, after half an hour's talk with the hobo extraordinary, had taken him to Rotary for lunch and commanded him to tell tales of the road and to sing the members a song. Frank Sarsfield's untutored voice was loud enough when he wanted it to be, and he sang the song he had sung to Rotary:

"There's a long, long trail a-winding into the land of my dreams,
Where the nightingale is singing and the white moon beams;
There's a long, long night of waiting until my dreams all come true,
Till the day when I'll be walking down that long, long trail to you!"

No response: no cry, no footstep, not a rustle. Even in so big a house, they couldn't have failed to hear his song, sung in a voice fit to wake the dead. Father O'Malley had called Frank's voice "stentorian"—a good word, though he was not just sure what it meant. He liked that last line, though he'd no one to walk to; he'd repeat it:

"Till the day when I'll be walking down that long, long trail to you!"

It was all right. Sarsfield went into the dining room, where he found a splendid long walnut table, chairs with embroidered seats, a fine sideboard and china cabinet, and a high Venetian chandelier. The china was in that cabinet, and the silverware was in that sideboard. But in no room of Tamarack House was any living soul.

Sprawled in a big chair before the fireplace in the Sunday parlor, Sarsfield took the chill out of his bones. The woodshed, connected with the main house by a passage from the kitchen, was half filled with logs—not first-rate fuel, true, for they had been stacked there three or four years ago, to judge by the fungi upon them, but burnable after he had collected old newspapers and chopped kindling. He had crisscrossed elm and birch to make a noble fire.

It was not very risky to let white woodsmoke eddy from the chimneys, for it would blend with the driving snow and the blast would dissipate it at once. Besides, Anthonyville's population was zero. From the cupola atop the house, in another lull of the blizzard, he had looked over the icy countryside and had seen no inhabited farmhouse up the forgotten dirt road—which, anyway, was hopelessly blocked by drifts today. There was no approach for vehicles from the freeway, while river and marsh protected the rear. He speculated that Tamarack House might be inhabited summers, though not in any very recent summer. The "Protective Service" probably consisted of a farmer who made a fortnightly inspection in fair weather.

It was good to hole up in a remote county where burglars seemed unknown as yet. Frank Sarsfield restricted his own depredations to church poor-boxes (Catholic, preferably, he being no Protestant) and then under defense of necessity, after a run of unsuccessful mendicancy. He feared and detested strong thieves, so numerous nowadays; to avoid them and worse than thieves, he steered clear of the cities, roving to little places which still kept crime in the family, where it belonged.

He had dined, and then washed the dishes dutifully. The kitchen wood-range still functioned, and so did the hard-water and soft-water hand pumps in the scullery. As for food, there was enough to feed a good-sized prison: the shelves of the deep cellar cold-room threatened to collapse under the weight of glass jars full of jams, jellies, preserved peaches, apricots, applesauce, pickled pork, pickled trout, and many more good things, all redolent of his New England youth. Most of the jars had neat paper labels, all giving the year of canning, some the name of the canner; on the front shelves, the most recent date he had found was 1968, on a little pot of strawberry jam, and below it was the name "Allegra" in a feminine hand.

Everything in this house lay in apple-pie order—though Sarsfield wondered how long the plaster would keep from cracking, with Tamarack House unheated in winter. He felt positively virtuous for lighting fires, one here in the Sunday parlor, another in the little antique iron stove in the bedroom he had chosen for himself at the top of the house.

He had poked into every handsome room of Tamarack House, with the intense pleasure of a small boy who had found his way into an enchanted castle. Every room was satisfying, well-furnished (he was warming by the fire two sheets from the linen closet, for his bed), and wondrously old-fashioned. There was no electric light, no central heating, no bathroom; there was an indoor privy, at the back of the woodshed, but no running water unless one counted the hand pumps. There was an oldfangled wall telephone: Frank tried, greatly daring, for the operator, but it was dead. He had found a crystal-set radio that didn't work. This was an old lady's house, surely, and the old lady hadn't visited it for some years, but perhaps her relatives kept it in order as a "holiday home" or in hope of selling it—at ruined Anthonyville, a forlorn hope. He had discovered two canisters of tea, a jar full of coffee beans, and ten gallons of kerosene. How thoughtful!

Perhaps the old lady was dead, buried under the other boulder among the maples in front of the house. Perhaps she had been the General's daughter—but no, not if the General had been born in 1836. Why those graves in the lawn? Sarsfield had heard of farm families, near medical schools in the old days, who had buried their dead by the house for fear of body-snatchers; but that couldn't apply at Anthonyville. Well, there were family graveyards, but this must be one of the smallest.

The old General who built this house had died on January fourteenth. Day after tomorrow, January fourteenth would come round again, and it would be Frank Sarsfield's sixtieth birthday. "I drink your health in water, General," Sarsfield said aloud, raising his cut-glass goblet taken from the china cabinet. There was no strong drink in the house, but that didn't distress Sarsfield, for he never touched it. His mother had warned him against it—and sure enough, the one time he had drunk a good deal of wine, when he was new to the road, he had got sick. "Thanks, General, for your hospitality." Nobody responded to his toast.

His mother had been a saint, the neighbors had said, and his father a drunken devil. He had seen neither of them after he ran away. He had missed his mother's funeral because he hadn't known of her death until months after; he had missed his father's, long later, because he chose to miss it, though that omission cost him sleepless nights now. Sarsfield slept poorly at best. Almost always there were nightmares.

Yet perhaps he would sleep well enough tonight in that little garret room near the cupola. He had found that several of the bedrooms in Tamarack House had little metal plates over their doorways. There were "The General's Room" and "Father's Room" and "Mama's Room" and "Alice's Room" and "Allegra's Room" and "Edith's Room." By a happy coincidence, the little room at the top of the back stair, on the garret floor of the house, was labelled "Frank's Room." But he'd not chosen it for that only. At the top of the house, one was safer from sheriffs or burglars. And through the skylight—there was only a frieze window—a man could get to the roof of the main block. From that roof, one could descend to the woodshed roof by a fire-escape of iron rungs fixed in the stone outer wall; and from the woodshed, it was an easy drop to the ground. After that, the chief difficulty would be to run down Main Street and then get across the freeway without being detected, while people searched the house for you. Talk of Goldilocks and the Three Bears! Much experience had taught Sarsfield such forethought.

Had that other Frank, so commemorated over the bedroom door, been a son or a servant? Presumably a son—though Sarsfield had found no pictures of boys in the old velvet-covered album in the Sunday parlor, nor any of manservants. There were many pictures of the General, a little roosterlike man with a beard; and of Father, portly and pleasant-faced; and of Mama, elegant; and of three small girls, who must be Alice and Allegra and Edith. He had liked especially the photographs of Allegra, since he had tasted her strawberry jam. All the girls were pretty, but Allegra—who must be about seven in most of the pictures—was really charming, with long ringlets and kind eyes and a delicate mouth that curved upward at its corners.

Sarsfield adored little girls and distrusted big girls. His mother had cautioned him against bad women, so he had kept away from such. Because he liked peace, he never had married—not that he could have married anyway, because that would have tied him to one place, and he was too clumsy to earn money at practically anything except dish-washing for summer hotels. Not marrying had meant that he could have no little daughters like Allegra.

Sometimes he had puzzled the prison psychiatrists. In prison it was well to play stupid. He had refrained cunningly from reciting poetry to the psychiatrists. So after testing him they wrote him down as "dull normal" and he was assigned to labor as "gardener"—which meant going round the prison yards picking up trash by a stick with a nail in the end of it. That was easy work, and he detested hard work. Yet when there was truly heavy work to be done in prison, sometimes he would come forward to shovel tons of coal or carry hods of brick or lift big blocks into place. That, too, was his cunning: it impressed the other jailbirds with his enormous strength, so that the gangs left him alone.

"Yes, you're a loner, Frank Sarsfield," he said to himself, aloud. He looked at himself in that splendid Sunday-parlor mirror, which stretched from floor to ceiling. He saw a man overweight but lean enough of face, standing six feet six, built like a bear, a strong nose, some teeth missing, a strong chin, and rather wild light-blue eyes. He was an uncommon sort of bum. Deliberately he looked at his image out of the corners of his eyes—as was his way, because he was nonviolent, and eye-contact might mean trouble.

"You look like a Viking, Frank," old Father O'Malley had told him once, "but you ought to have been a monk."

"Oh, Father," he had answered, "I'm too much of a fool for a monk."

"Well," said Father O'Malley, "you're no more fool than many a brother, and you're celibate, and continent, I take it. Yet it's late for that now. Look out you don't turn berserker, Frank. Go to confession, sometime, to a priest that doesn't know you, if you'll not go to me. If you'd confess, you'd not be haunted."

But he seldom went to mass, and never to confession. All those church boxes pilfered, his mother and father abandoned, his sister neglected, all the ghastly humbling of himself before policemen, all the horror and shame of the prisons! There could be no grace for him now. *There's a long, long trail a-winding into the land of my dreams. . . ."* What dreams! He had looked up "berserker" in Webster. But he wouldn't ever do that sort of thing: a man had to keep a control upon himself, and besides he was a coward, and he loved peace.

Nearly all the other prisoners had been brutes, guilty as sin, guilty as Miranda or Escobedo. Once, sentenced for rifling a church safe, he had been put into the same cell with a man who had murdered his wife by taking off her head. The head never had been found. Sarsfield had dreamed of that head in such short intervals of sleep as he had enjoyed while the wife-killer was his cellmate. Nearly all night, every night, he had lain awake surreptitiously watching the murderer in the opposite bunk, and feeling his own neck now and again. He had been surprised and pleased when eventually the wife-killer had gone hysterical and obtained assignment to another cell. The murderer had told the guards that he just couldn't stand being watched all night by that terrible giant who never talked.

Only one of the prison psychiatrists had been pleasant or bright, and that had been the old doctor born in Vienna who went round from penitentiary to penitentiary checking on the psychiatric staffs. The old doctor had taken a liking to him, and had written a report to accompany Frank's petition for parole. Three months later, in a parole office, the parole officer had gone out hurriedly for a quarter of an hour, and Sarsfield had taken the chance to read his own file that the parole man had left in a folder on his desk.

"Francis Sarsfield has a memory that almost can be described as photographic"—so had run one line in the Vienna doctor's report. When he read that, Sarsfield had known that the doctor was a clever doctor. "He suffers chiefly from an arrest of emotional development, and may be regarded as a rather bright small boy in some respects. His three temporarily successful escapes from prison suggest that his intelligence has been much underrated. On at least one of those three occasions, he could have eluded the arresting officer had he been willing to resort to violence. Sarsfield repeatedly describes himself as nonviolent and has no record of aggression while confined, nor in connection with any of the offenses for which he was arrested. On the contrary, he seems timid and withdrawn, and might become a victim of assaults in prison, were it not for his size, strength, and power of voice."

Sarsfield had been pleased enough by that paragraph, but a little puzzled by what followed:

"In general, Sarsfield is one of those recidivists who ought not to be confined, were any alternative method now available for restraining them from petty offenses against property. Not only does he lack belligerence against men, but apparently he is quite clean of any record against women and children. It seems that he does not indulge in autoeroticism, either— perhaps because of strict instruction by his R.C. mother during his formative years.

"I add, however, that conceivably Sarsfield is not fundamentally so gentle as his record indicates. He can be energetic in self-defense when pushed to the wall. In his youth occasionally he was induced, for the promise of five dollars or ten dollars, to stand up as an amateur against some travelling professional boxer. He admits that he did not fight hard, and cried when he was badly beaten. Nevertheless, I am inclined to suspect a potentiality for violence, long repressed but not totally extinguished by years of 'humbling himself,' in his phrase. This possibility is not so certain as to warrant additional detention, even though three years of Sarsfield's sentence remain unexpired."

Yes, he had memorized nearly the whole of that old doctor's analysis, which had got his parole for him. There had been the concluding paragraphs:

"Francis Sarsfield is oppressed by a haunting sense of personal guilt. He is religious to the point of superstition, an R.C., and appears to believe himself damned. Although worldly-wise in a number of respects, he retains an almost unique innocence in others. His frequent humor and candor account for his success, much of the time, at begging. He has read much during his wanderings and terms of confinement. He has a strong taste for good poetry of the popular sort, and has accumulated a mass of miscellaneous information, much of it irrelevant to the life he leads.

"Although occasionally moody and even surly, most of the time he subjects himself to authority, and will work fairly well if closely supervised. He possesses no skills of any sort, unless some knack for woodchopping, acquired while he was enrolled in the Civilian Conservation Corps, can be considered a marketable skill. He appears to be incorrigibly footloose, and therefore confinement is more unpleasant to him than to most prisoners. It is truly remarkable that he continues to be rational enough, his isolation and heavy guilt-complex considered.

"Sometimes evasive when he does not desire to answer questions, nevertheless he rarely utters a direct lie. His personal modesty may be described as excessive. His habits of cleanliness are commendable, if perhaps of origins like Lady Macbeth's.

"Despite his strength, he is a diabetic and suffers from a heart murmur, sometimes painful.

"Only in circumstances so favorable as to be virtually unobtainable could Sarsfield succeed in abstaining from the behavior-pattern that has led to his repeated prosecution and imprisonment. The excessive crowding of this penitentiary considered, however, I strongly recommend that he be released upon parole. Previous psychiatric reports concerning this inmate have been shallow and erroneous, I regret to note. Perhaps Sarsfield's chief psychological difficulty is that, from obscure causes, he lacks emotional communication with other adults, although able to maintain cordial and healthy relations with small children. He is very nearly a solipsist, which in large part may account for his inability to make firm decisions or pursue any regular occupation. In contradiction of previous analyses of Sarsfield, he should not be described as 'dull normal' intellectually. Francis Xavier Sarsfield distinctly is neither dull nor normal."

Sarsfield had looked up "solipsist," but hadn't found himself much the wiser. He didn't think himself the only existent thing—not most of the time, anyway. He wasn't sure that the old doctor had been real, but he knew that his mother had been real before she went straight to Heaven. He knew that his nightmares probably weren't real; but sometimes, while awake, he could see things that other men couldn't. In a house like this, he could glimpse little unaccountable movements out of the corners of his eyes, but it wouldn't do to worry about those. He was afraid of those things which other people couldn't see, yet not so frightened of them as most people were. Some of the other inmates had called him Crazy Frank, and it had been hard to keep down his temper. If you could perceive *more* existent things, though not flesh-and-blood things, than psychiatrists or convicts could—why, were you a solipsist?

There was no point in puzzling over it. Dad had taken him out of school to work on the farm when he hadn't yet finished the fourth grade, so words like "solipsist" didn't mean much to him. Poets' words, though, he mostly understood. He had picked up a rhyme that made children laugh when he told it to them:

> *"Though you don't know it,*
> *You're a poet.*
> *Your feet show it:*
> *They're Longfellows."*

That wasn't very good poetry, but Henry Wadsworth Longfellow was a good poet. They must have loved Henry Wadsworth Longfellow in this house, and especially "The Children's Hour," because of those three little girls named Alice, Allegra, and Edith, and those lines on the General's boulder. Allegra: that's the prettiest of all names ever, and it means "merry," someone had told him.

He looked at the cheap wristwatch he had bought, besides the wash-and-wear suit, with his last dishwashing money from that Lake Superior summer hotel. Well, midnight! It's up the wooden hill for you, Frank Sarsfield, to your snug little room under the rafters. If anybody comes to Tamarack House tonight, it's out the skylight and through the snow for you, Frank, my boy—and no tiny reindeer. If you want to survive, in prison or out of it, you stick to your own business and let other folks stew in their own juice.

Before he closed his eyes, he would pray for Mother's soul—not that she really needed it—and then say the little Scottish prayer he had found in a children's book:

"From ghosties and ghoulies, long-leggitie beasties, and things that go bump in the night, good Lord deliver us!"

The next morning, the morning before his birthday, Frank Sarsfield went up the circular stair to the cupola, even before making his breakfast of pickled trout and peaches and strong coffee. The wind had gone down, and it was snowing only lightly now, but the drifts were immense. Nobody would make his way to Anthonyville and Tamarack House this day; the snowplows would be busy elsewhere.

From this height he could see the freeway, and nothing seemed to be moving along it. The dead village lay to the north of him. To the east were river and swamp, the shores lined with those handsome tamaracks, the green gone out of them, which had given this house its name. Everything in sight belonged to Frank.

He had dreamed during the night, the wind howling and whining round the top of the house, and he had known he was dreaming, but it had been even stranger than usual, if less horrible.

In his dream, he had found himself in the dining room of Tamarack House. He had not been alone. The General and Father and Mama and the three little girls had been dining happily at the long table, and he had waited on them. In the kitchen an old woman who was the cook, and a girl who cleaned, had eaten by themselves. But when he had finished filling the family's plates, he had sat down at the end of the table, as if he had been expected to do that.

The family had talked among themselves and even to him as he ate, but somehow he had not been able to hear what they said to him. Suddenly he had pricked up his ears, though, because Allegra had spoken to him.

"Frank," she had said, all mischief, "why do they call you Punkinhead?"

The old General had frowned at the head of the table, and Mama had said, "Allegra, don't speak that way to Frank!"

But he had grinned at Allegra, if slightly hurt, and had told the little girl, "Because some men think I've got a head like a jack-o'-lantern's and not even seeds inside it."

"Nonsense, Frank," Mama had put in, "you have a very handsome head."

"You've got a pretty head, Frank," the three little girls had told him then, almost in chorus, placatingly. Allegra had come round the table to make her peace. "There's going to be a big surprise for you tomorrow, Frank," she had whispered to him. And then she had kissed him on the cheek.

That had waked him. Most of the rest of that howling night he had lain awake trying to make sense of his dream, but he couldn't. The people in it had been more real than the people he met on the long, long trail.

Now he strolled through the house again, admiring everything. It was almost as if he had seen the furniture and the pictures and the carpets long, long ago. The house must be over a century old, and many of the good things in it must go back to the beginning. He would have two or three more days here until the roads were cleared. There were no newspapers to tell him about the great storm, of course, and no radio that worked; but that didn't matter.

He found a great big handsome *Complete Works of Henry Wadsworth Longfellow,* in red morocco, and an illustrated copy of the *Rubaiyat.* He didn't need to read it, because he had memorized all the quatrains once. There was a black silk ribbon as marker between the pages, and he opened it there—at Quatrain 44, it turned out:

> *"Why, if the Soul can fling the Dust aside,*
> *And naked on the Air of Heaven ride,*
> *Were't not a Shame—were't not a Shame for him*
> *In this clay carcass crippled to abide?"*

That old Vienna doctor, Frank suspected, hadn't believed in immortal souls. Frank Sarsfield knew better. But also Frank suspected that his soul never would ride, naked or clothed, on the Air of Heaven. Souls! That put him in mind of his sister, a living soul that he had forsaken. He ought to write her a letter on this the eve of his sixtieth birthday.

Frank travelled light, his luggage being mostly a safety razor, a hairbrush, and a comb; he washed his shirt and socks and underclothes every night, and often his wash-and-wear suit, too. But he did carry with him a few sheets of paper and a ballpoint pen. Sitting down at the library table—he had built a fire in the library stove also, there being no lack of logs—he began to write to Mary Sarsfield, alone in the rotting farmhouse in New Hampshire. His spelling wasn't good, he knew, but today he was careful at his birthday letter, using the big old dictionary with the General's bookplate in it.

To write that letter took most of the day. Two versions were discarded. At last Frank had done the best he could.

"Dearest Mary my sister,
"Its been nearly 9 years since I came to visit you and borrowed the $78 from you and went away again and never paid it back. I guess you dont want to see your brother Frank again after what I did that time and other times but the Ethiopian can not change his skin nor the leopard his spots and when some man like a Jehovahs

Witness or that rancher with all the cash gives me quite a lot of money I mean to send you what I owe but the post office isnt handy at the time and so I spend it on presents for little kids I meet and buying new clothes and such so I never get around to sending you that $78 Mary. Right now I have $29 and more but the post office at this place is folded up and by the time I get to the next town the money will be mostly gone and so it goes. I guess probably you need the money and Im sorry Mary but maybe some day I will win in the lottery and then Ill give you all the thousands of dollars I win.

"Well Mary its been 41 years and 183 days since Mother passed away and here I am 60 years old tomorrow and you getting on toward 56. I pray that your cough is better and that your son and my nephew Jack is doing better than he was in Tallahassee Florida. Some time Mary if you would write to me c/o Father Justin O'Malley in Albatross Michigan where he is pastor now I would stop by his rectory and get your letter and read it with joy. But I know Ive been a very bad brother and I dont blame you Mary if you never get around to writing your brother Frank.

"Mary Ive been staying out of jails and working a little here and there along the road. Now Mary do you know what I hate most about those prisons? Why not being on the road you will say. No Mary the worst thing is the foul language the convicts use from morning till night. Taking the name of their Lord in vain is the least they do. There is a foul curse word in every sentence. I wasnt brought up that way any more than you Mary and I will not revile woman or child. It is like being in H—— to hear it.

"Im not in bad shape except the diabetes is no better but I take my pills for it when I can buy them and dont have to take needles for it and my heart hurts me dreadfully bad sometimes when I lift heavy things hours on end and sometimes it hurts me worse at night when Ive been just lying there thinking of the life Ive led and how I ought to pay you the $78 and pay back other folks that helped me too. I owe Father O'Malley $497.11 now altogether and I keep track of it in my head and when the lottery ticket wins he will not be forgot.

"Some people have been quite good to me and I still can make them laugh and I recite to them and generally I start my reciting with what No Person of Quality wrote hundreds of years ago

'Seven wealthy towns contend for Homer dead
Through which the living Homer begged his bread.'

"They like that and also usually they like Thomas Grays Elegy in a Country Churchyard leaving the world to darkness and to me and I recite all of that and sometimes some of the Quatrains of Omar. At farms when they ask me I chop wood for these folks and I help with the dishes but I still break a good many as you learned Mary 9

years ago but I didnt mean to do it Mary because I am just clumsy
in all ways. Oh yes I am good at reciting Frosts Stopping by Woods
and his poem about the Hired Man. I have been reading the
poetical works of Thomas Stearns Eliot so I can recite his The
Hollow Men or much of it and also his Book of Practical Cats
which is comical when I come to college towns and some professor
or his wife gives me a sandwich and maybe $2 and maybe a ride to
the next town.

"Where I am now Mary I ought to study the poems of John
Greenleaf Whittier because theres been a real blizzard maybe the
biggest in the state for many years and Im Snowbound. Years ago I
tried to memorize all that poem but I got only part way for it is a
whopper of a poem.

"I dont hear much good Music Mary because of course at the
motels there isnt any phonograph or tape recorder. Id like to hear
some good string quartet or maybe old folk songs well sung for
music hath charms to soothe the savage breast. Theres an old
Edison at the house where Im staying now and what do you know
they have a record of a song you and I used to sing together Theres
a Long Long Trail A Winding. Its about the newest record in this
house. Ill play it again soon thinking of you Mary my sister. O
there is a long long night of waiting.

"Mary right now Im at a big fine house where the people have
gone away for awhile and I watch the house for them and keep
some of the rooms warm. Let me assure you Mary I wont take
anything from this good old house when I go. These are nice people
I know and I just came in out of the storm and Im very fond of
their 3 sweet little girls. I remember what you looked like when I
ran way first and you looked like one of them called Alice. The one
I like best though is Allegra because she makes mischief and laughs
a lot but is innocent.

"I came here just yesterday but it seems as if Id lived in this
house before but of course I couldnt have and I feel at home here.
Nothing in this house could scare me much. You might not like it
Mary because of little noises and glimpses you get but its a lovely
house and as you know I like old places that have been lived in lots.

"By the way Mary once upon a time Father O'Malley told me
that to the Lord all time is eternally present. I think this means
everything that happens in the world in any day goes on all at once.
So God sees what went on in this house long ago and whats going
on in this house today all at the same time. Its just as well we dont
see through Gods eyes because then wed know everything thats
going to happen to us and because Im such a sinner I dont want to
know. Father O'Malley says that God may forgive me everything
and have something special in store for me but I dont think so
because why should He?

"And Father O'Malley says that maybe some people work out
their Purgatory here on earth and I might be one of these. He says

we are spirits in the prisonhouse of the body which is like we were serving Time in the world here below and maybe God forgave me long ago and Im just waiting my time and paying for what I did and it will be alright in the end. Or maybe Im being given some second chance to set things right but as Father O'Malley put it to do that Id have to fortify my Will and do some Signal Act of contrition. Father O'Malley even says I might not have to do the Act actually if only I just made up my mind to do it really and truly because what God counts is the intention. But I think people who are in Purgatory must know they are climbing up and have hope and Mary I think Im going down down down even though Ive stayed out of prisons some time now.

"Father O'Malley tells me that for everybody the battle is won or lost already in Gods sight and that though Satan thinks he has a good chance to conquer actually Satan has lost forever but doesnt know it. Mary I never did anybody any good but only harm to ones that loved me. If just once before I die I could do one Signal Act that was truly good then God might love me and let me have the Beatific Vision. Yet Mary I know Im weak of will and a coward and lazy and Ive missed my chance forever.

"Well Mary my only sister Ive bored you long enough and I just wanted to say hello and tell you to be of good cheer. Im sorry I whined and complained like a little boy about my health because Im still strong and deserve all the pain I get. Mary if you can forgive your big brother who never grew up please pray for me some time because nobody else does except possibly Father O'Malley when he isnt busy with other prayers. I pray for Mother every night and every other night for you and once a month for Dad. You were a good little girl and sweet. Now I will say good bye and ask your pardon for bothering you with my foolishness. Also Im sorry your friends found out I was just a hobo when I was with you 9 years ago and I dont blame you for being angry with me then for talking too much and I know I wasnt fit to lodge in your house. There arent many of us old real hobos left only beatniks and such that cant walk or chop wood and I guess that is just as well. It is a degrading life Mary but I cant stop walking down that long long trail not knowing where it ends.

> "Your Loving Brother
> "Francis (Frank)

"P.S.: I dont wish to mislead so I will add Mary that the people who own this house didnt exactly ask me in but its alright because I wont do any harm here but a little good if I can. Good night again Mary."

Now he needed an envelope, but he had forgotten to take one from the last motel, where the Presbyterian minister had put him up. There must be some in Tamarack House, and one would not be missed, and that would not be very wrong because he would take nothing else. He found no envelopes in the drawer of the library table: so he went up the stairs and almost knocked at the closed door of Allegra's Room. Foolish! He opened the door gently.

He had admired Allegra's small rosewood desk. In its drawer was a leather letter-folder, the kind with a blotter, he found, and in the folder were several yellowed envelopes. Also lying face up in the folder was a letter of several small pages, in a woman's hand, a trifle shaky. He started to sit down to read Allegra's letter that was never sent to anybody, but it passed through his mind that his great body might break the delicate rosewood chair that belonged to Allegra, so he read the letter standing. It was dated January 14, 1969. On that birthday of his, he had been in Joliet prison.

How beautifully Allegra wrote!

"Darling Celia,

"This is a lonely day at Tamarack House, just fifty-four years after your great-great-grandfather the General died, so I am writing to my grand-niece to tell you how much I hope you will be able to come up to Anthonyville and stay with me next summer—if I still am here. The doctor says that only God knows whether I will be. Your grandmother wants me to come down your way to stay with her for the rest of this winter, but I can't bear to leave Tamarack House at my age, for they might have to put me in a rest-home down there and then I wouldn't see this old house again.

"I am all right, really, because kind Mr. Connor looks in every day, and Mrs. Williams comes every other day to clean. I am not sick, my little girl, but simply older than my years, and running down. When you come up next summer, God willing, I will make you that soft toast you like, and perhaps Mr. Connor will turn the crank for the ice-cream, and I may try to make some preserves with you to help me.

"You weren't lonely, were you, when you stayed with me last summer for a whole month? Of course there are fewer than a hundred people left in Anthonyville now, and most of those are old. They say that there will be practically nobody living in the town a few years from now, when the new highway is completed and the old one is abandoned. There were more than two thousand people here in town and roundabout, a few years after the General built Tamarack House! But first the lumber industry gave out, and then the mines were exhausted, and the prison-break in 1915 scared many away forever. There are no passenger trains now, and they say the railway line will be pulled out altogether when the new freeway—they have just begun building it to the east—is ready for traffic. But we still have the maples and the tamaracks, and there are ever so many raccoons and opossums and squirrels for you to watch—and a lynx, I think, and an otter or two, and many deer.

"Celia, last summer you asked me about the General's death and all the things that happened then, because you had heard something of them from your Grandmother Edith. But I didn't wish to frighten you, so I didn't tell you everything. You are older now, and you have a right to know, because when you grow up you will be one of the trustees of the Anthony Family Trust, and then this old house will be in your charge when I am gone. Tamarack House is not at all frightening, except a little in the morning on every January 14. I do hope that you and the other trustees will keep the house always, with the money that Father left to me—he was good at making money, even though the forests vanished and the mines failed, by his investments in Chicago—and which I am leaving to the Family Trust. I've kept the house just as it was, for the sake of the General's memory and because I love it that way.

"You asked just what happened on January 14, 1915. There were seven people who slept in the house that month—not counting Cook and Cynthia (who was a kind of nannie to us girls and also cleaned), because they slept at their houses in the village. In the house, of course, was the General, my grandfather, your great-great-grandfather, who was nearly eighty years old. Then there were Father and Mama, and the three of us little sisters, and dear Frank.

"Alice and sometimes even that baby Edith used to tease me in those days by screaming, 'Frank's Allegra's sweetheart! Frank's Allegra's sweetheart!' I used to chase them, but I suppose it was true: he liked me best. Of course he was about sixty years old, though not so old as I am now, and I was a little thing. He used to take me through the swamps and show me the muskrats' houses. The first time he took me on such a trip, Mama raised her eyebrows when he was out of the room, but the General said, 'I'll warrant Frank; I have his papers.' Alice and Edith might just as well have shouted, 'Frank's Allegra's slave!' He read to me—oh, Robert Louis Stevenson's poems and all sorts of books. I never had another sweetheart, partly because almost all the young men left Anthonyville as I grew up when there was no work for them here, and the ones that remained didn't please Mama.

"We three sisters used to play Creepmouse with Frank, I remember well. We would be the Creepmice, and would sneak up and scare him when he wasn't watching, and he would pretend to be terrified. He made up a little song for us—or, rather, he put words to some tune he had borrowed:

'Down, down, down in Creepmouse Town
All the lamps are low,
And the little rodent feet
Softly come and go

'There's a rat in Creepmouse Town
And a bat or two:

Everything in Creepmouse Town
Would swiftly frighten you!'

"Do you remember, Celia, that the General was State Supervisor of Prisons and Reformatories for time out of mind? He was a good architect, too, and designed Anthonyville State Prison, without taking any fee for himself, as a model prison. Some people in the capital said that he did it to give employment to his county, but really it was because the site was so isolated that it would be difficult for convicts to escape.

"The General knew Frank's last name, but he never told the rest of us. Frank had been in Anthonyville State Prison at one time, and later other prisons, and the General had taken him out of one of those other prisons on parole, having known Frank when he was locked up at Anthonyville. I never learned what Frank had done to be sentenced to prison, but he was gentle with me and everybody else, until that early morning of January 14.

"The General was amused by Frank, and said that Frank would be better off with us than anywhere else. So Frank became our hired man, and chopped the firewood for us, and kept the fires going in the stoves and fireplaces, and sometimes served at dinner. In summer he was supposed to scythe the lawns, but of course summer didn't come. Frank arrived by train at Anthonyville Station in October, and we gave him the little room at the top of the house.

"Well, on January 12 Father went off to Chicago on business. We still had the General. Every night he barred the shutters on the ground floor, going round to all the rooms by himself. Mama knew he did it because there was a rumor that some life convicts at the Prison 'had it in' for the Supervisor of Prisons, although the General had retired five years earlier. Also they may have thought he kept a lot of money in the house—when actually, what with the timber gone and the mines going, in those times we were rather hard pressed and certainly kept our money in the bank at Duluth. But we girls didn't know why the General closed the shutters, except that it was one of the General's rituals. Besides, Anthonyville State Prison was supposed to be escape-proof. It was just that the General always took precautions, though ever so brave.

"Just before dawn, Celia, on the cold morning of January 14, 1915, we all were waked by the siren of the Prison, and we all rushed downstairs in our nightclothes, and we could see that part of the Prison was afire. Oh, the sky was red! The General tried to telephone the Prison, but he couldn't get through, and later it turned out that the lines had been cut.

"Next—it all happened so swiftly—we heard shouting somewhere down Main Street, and then guns went off. The General knew what that meant. He had got his trousers and his boots on, and now he struggled with his old military overcoat, and he took his old army revolver. 'Lock the door behind me, girl,' he told Mama. She cried and tried to pull him back inside, but he went down into the snow, nearly eighty though he was.

"Only three or four minutes later, we heard the shots. The General had met the convicts at the gate. It was still dark, and the General had cataracts on his eyes. They say he fired first, and missed. Those bad men had broken into Mr. Emmons's store and taken guns and axes and whiskey. They shot the General—shot him again and again and again.

"The next thing we knew, they were chopping at our front door with axes. Mama hugged us.

"Celia dear, writing all this has made me so silly! I feel a little odd, so I must go lie down for an hour or two before telling you the rest. Celia, I do hope you will love this old house as much as I have. If I'm not here when you come up, remember that where I have gone I will know the General and Father and Mama and Alice and poor dear Frank, and will be ever so happy with them. Be a good little girl, my Celia."

The letter ended there, unsigned.

Frank clumped downstairs to the Sunday parlor. He was crying, for the first time since he had fought that professional heavyweight on October 19, 1943. Allegra's letter—if only she'd finished it! What had happened to those little girls, and Mama, and that other Frank? He thought of something from the Holy Bible: "It were better for him that a millstone were hanged about his neck, and he cast into the sea, than that he should offend one of these little ones."

Already it was almost evening. He lit the wick in the cranberry-glass lamp that hung from the middle of the parlor ceiling, standing on a chair to reach it. Why not enjoy more light? On a whim, he arranged upon the round table four silver candlesticks that had rested above the fireplace. He needed three more, and those he fetched from the dining room. He lit every candle in the circle: one for the General, one for Father, one for Mama, one for Alice, one for Allegra, one for Edith—one for Frank.

The dear names of those little girls! He might as well recite aloud, it being good practice for the approaching days on the long, long trail:

> *"I hear in the chamber above me*
> *The patter of little feet,*
> *The sound of a door that is opened,*
> *And voices soft and sweet. . . ."*

Here he ceased. Had he heard something in the passage—or "descending the broad hall stair"? Because of the wind outside, he could not be certain. It cost him a gritting of his teeth to rise and open the parlor door. Of course no one could be seen in the hall or on the stair. "Crazy Frank," men had called him at Joliet and other prisons: he had clenched his fists, but had kept a check upon himself. Didn't Saint Paul say that the violent take Heaven by storm? Perhaps he had barked up the wrong tree; perhaps he would be spewed out of His mouth for being too peaceful.

Shutting the door, he went back to the fireside. Those lines of Longfellow had been no evocation. He put "The Long, Long Trail" on the old phonograph again, strolling about the room until the record ran out. There was an old print of a Great Lakes schooner on one wall that he liked. Beside it, he noticed, there seemed to be some pellets embedded in a closet door-jamb, but painted over, as if someone had fired a shotgun in the parlor in the old days. "The violent take it by storm . . ." He admired the grand piano; perhaps Allegra had learned to play it. There was one or two big notches or gashes along one edge of the piano, varnished over, hard though that wood was. Then Frank sank into the big chair again and stared at the burning logs.

Just how long he had dozed, he did not know. He woke abruptly. Had he heard a whisper, the faintest whisper? He tensed to spring up. But before he could move, he saw reflections in the tall mirror.

Something had moved in the corner by the bookcase. No doubt about it; that small something had stirred again. Also something crept behind one of the satin sofas, and something else lurked near the piano. All these were at his back: he saw the reflections in the glass, as in a glass darkly, more alarming than physical forms. In this high shadowy room, the light of the kerosene lamp and of the seven candles did not suffice.

From near the bookcase, the first of them emerged into candlelight; then came the second, and the third. They were giggling, but he could not hear them—only see their faces, and those not clearly. He was unable to stir, and the gooseflesh prickled all over him, and his hair rose at the back of his big head.

They were three little girls, barefoot, in their long muslin nightgowns, ready for bed. One may have been as much as twelve years old, and the smallest was little more than a baby. The middle one was Allegra, tiny even for her tender years, and a little imp: he knew, he knew! They were playing Creepmouse.

The three of them stole forward, Allegra in the lead, her eyes alight. He could see them plain now, and the dread was ebbing out of him. He might have risen and turned to greet them across the great gulf of time, but any action—why, what might it do to these little ones? Frank sat frozen in his chair, looking at the nimble reflections in the mirror, and nearer they came, perfectly silent. Allegra vanished from the glass, which meant that she must be standing just behind him.

He must please them. Could he speak? He tried, and the lines came out hoarsely:

> "Down, down, down in Creepmouse Town
> All the lamps are low,
> And the little rodent feet . . ."

He was not permitted to finish. Wow! There came a light tug at the curly white hair on the back of his head. Oh, to talk with Allegra, the imp! Reckless, he heaved his bulk out of the chair, and swung round—too late.

The parlor door was closing. But from the hall came another whisper, ever so faint, ever so unmistakable: "Good night, Frank!" There followed subdued giggles, scampering, and then the silence once more.

He strode to the parlor door. The hall was empty again, and the broad stair. Should he follow them up? No, all three would be abed now. Should he knock at Mama's Room, muttering, "Mrs. Anthony, are the children all right?" No, he hadn't the nerve for that, and it would be presumptuous. He had been given one moment of perception, and no more.

Somehow he knew that they would not go so far as the garret floor. Ah, he needed fresh air! He snuffed out lamp and candles, except for one candlestick—Allegra's—that he took with him. Out into the hall he went. He unfastened the front door with that oaken patch about the middle of it, and stepped upon the porch, leaving the burning candle just within the hall. The wind had risen again, bringing still more snow. It was black as sin outside, and the temperature must be thirty below.

To him the wind bore one erratic peal of the desolate church-bell of Anthonyville, and then another. How strong the blast must be through that belfry! Frank retreated inside from that unfathomable darkness and that sepulchral bell which seemed to toll for him. He locked the thick door behind him and screwed up his courage for the expedition to his room at the top of the old house.

But why shudder? He loved them now, Allegra most of all. Up the broad stairs to the second floor he went, hearing only his own clumsy footfalls, and past the clay-sealed doors of the General and Father and Mama and Alice and Allegra and Edith. No one whispered, no one scampered.

In Frank's Room, he rolled himself in his blankets and quilt (had Allegra helped stitch the patchwork?), and almost at once the consciousness went out of him, and he must have slept dreamless for the first night since he was a farm boy.

So profound had been his sleep, deep almost as death, that the siren may have been wailing for some minutes before at last it roused him. Frank knew that horrid sound: it had called for him thrice before, as he fled from prisons. Who wanted him now? He heaved his ponderous body out of the warm bed. The candle that he had brought up from the Sunday parlor and left burning all night was flickering in its socket, but by that flame he could see the hour on his watch: seven o'clock, too soon for dawn.

Through the narrow skylight, as he flung on his clothes, the sky glowed an unnatural red, though it was long before sunup. The prison siren ceased to wail, as if choked off. Frank lumbered to the little frieze-window, and saw to the north, perhaps two miles distant, a monstrous mass of flame shooting high into the air. The prison was afire.

Then came shots outside: first the bark of a heavy revolver, followed irregularly by blasts of shotguns or rifles. Frank was lacing his boots with a swiftness uncongenial to him. He got into his overcoat as there came a crashing and battering down below. That sound, too, he recognized, wood-chopper that he had been: axes shattering the front door.

Amid this pandemonium, Frank was too bewildered to grasp altogether where he was or even how this catastrophe might be fitted into the pattern of time. All that mattered was flight; the scheme of his escape remained clear in his mind. Pull up the chair below the skylight, heave yourself out to the upper roof, descend those iron rungs to the woodshed roof, make for the other side of the freeway, then—why, then you must trust to circumstance, Frank. It's that long, long trail a-winding for you.

Now he heard a woman screaming within the house, and slipped and fumbled in his alarm. He had got upon the chair, opened the skylight, and was trying to obtain a good grip on the icy outer edge of the skylight-frame, when someone knocked and kicked at the door of Frank's Room.

Yet those were puny knocks and kicks. He was about to heave himself upward when, in a relative quiet—the screaming had ceased for a moment —he heard a little shrill voice outside his door, urgently pleading: "Frank, Frank, let me in!"

He was arrested in flight as though great weights had been clamped to his ankles. That little voice he knew, as if it were part of him: Allegra's voice.

For a brief moment he still meant to scramble out the skylight. But the sweet little voice was begging. He stumbled off the chair, upset it, and was at the door in one stride.

"Is that you, Allegra?"

"Open it, Frank, *please* open it!"

He turned the key and pulled the bolt. On the threshold the little girl stood, indistinct by the dying candlelight, terribly pale, all tears, frantic.

Frank snatched her up. Ah, this was the dear real Allegra Anthony, all warm and soft and sobbing, flesh and blood! He kissed her cheek gently.

She clung to him in terror, and then squirmed loose, tugging at his heavy hand: "Oh, Frank, come on! Come downstairs! They're hurting Mama!"

"Who is, little girl?" He held her tiny hand, his body quivering with dread and indecision. "Who's down there, Allegra?"

"The bad men! *Come on,* Frank!" Braver than he, the little thing plunged back down the garret stair into the blackness below.

"Allegra! Come back here—come back now!" He bellowed it, but she was gone.

Up two flights of stairs, there poured to him a tumult of shrieks, curses, laughter, breaking noises. Several men were below, their speech slurred and raucous. He did not need Allegra to tell him what kind of men they were, for he heard prison slang and prison foulness, and he shook all over. There still was the skylight.

He would have turned back to that hole in the roof, had not Allegra squealed in pain somewhere on the second floor. Dazed, trembling, unarmed, Frank went three steps down the garret staircase. "Allegra! Little girl! What is it, Allegra?"

Someone was charging up the stair toward him. It was a burly man in the prison uniform, a lighted lantern in one hand and a glittering axe in the other. Frank had no time to turn. The man screeched obscenely at him, and swung that axe.

In those close quarters, wielded by a drunken man, it was a chancy weapon. The edge shattered the plaster wall; the flat of the blade thumped upon Frank's shoulder. Frank, lurching forward, took the man by the throat with a mighty grip. They all tumbled pellmell down the steep stairs—the two men, the axe, the lantern.

Frank's ursine bulk landed atop the stranger's body, and Frank heard his adversary's bones crunch. The lantern had broken and gone out. The convict's head hung loose on his shoulders, Frank found as he groped for the axe. Then he trampled over the fallen man and flung himself along the corridor, gripping the axe-helve. "Allegra! Allegra girl!"

From the head of the main stair, he could see that the lamps and candles were burning in the hall and in the rooms of the ground floor. All three children were down there, wailing, and above their noise rose Mama's shrieks again. A mob of men were stamping, breaking things, roaring with amusement and desire, shouting filth. A bottle shattered.

His heart pounding as if it would burst out of his chest, Frank hurried rashly down that stair and went, all crimson with fury, into the Sunday parlor, the double-bitted axe swinging in his hand. They all were there: the little girls, Mama, and five wild men. "Stop that!" Frank roared with all the power of his lungs. "You let them go!"

Everyone in the parlor stood transfixed at that summons like the Last Trump. Allegra had been tugging pathetically at the leg of a dark man who gripped her mother's waist, and the other girls sputtered and sobbed, cornered, as a tall man poured a bottle of whiskey over them. Mrs. Anthony's gown was ripped nearly its whole length, and a third man was bending her backward by her long hair, as if he would snap her spine. Near the hall door stood a man like a long lean rat, the Rat of Creepmouse Town, a shotgun on his arm, gape-jawed at Frank's intervention. Guns and axes lay scattered about the Turkey carpet. By the fireplace, a fifth man had been heating the poker in the flames.

For that tableau-moment, they all stared astonished at the raving giant who had burst upon them; and the giant, puffing, stared back with his strange blue eyes. "Oh, Frank!" Allegra sobbed: it was more command than entreaty—as if, Frank thought in a flash of insane mirth, he were like the boy in the fairy tale who could cry confidently, "All heads off but mine!"

He knew what these men were, the rats and bats of Creepmouse Town: the worst men in any prison, lifers who had made their hell upon earth, killers all of them and worse than killers. The rotten damnation showed in all those flushed and drunken faces. Then the dark man let go of Mama and said in relief, with a coughing laugh, "Hell, it's only old Punkinhead Frank, clowning again! Have some fun for yourself, Frank boy!"

"Hey, Frank," Ratface asked, his shotgun crooked under his arm, "where'd the old man keep his money?"

Frank towered there perplexed, the berserker-lust draining out of him, almost bashful—and frightened worse than ever before in all his years on the trail. What should he shout now? What should he do? Who was he to resist such perfect evil? They were five to one, and those five were fiends from down under, and that one a coward. Long ago he had been weighed in the balance and found wanting.

Mama was the first to break the tableau. Her second captor had relaxed his clutch upon her hair, and she prodded the little girls before her, and she leaped for the door.

The hair-puller was after her at once, but she bounded past Ratface's shotgun, which had wavered toward Frank, and Alice and Edith were ahead of her. Allegra, her eyes wide and desperate, tripped over the rung of a broken chair. Everything happened in half a second. The hair-puller caught Allegra by her little ankle.

Then Frank bellowed again, loudest in all his life, and he swung his axe high above his head and downward, a skillful dreadful stroke, catching the hair-puller's arm just below the shoulder. At once the man began to scream and spout, while Allegra fled after her mother.

Falling, the hair-puller collided with Ratface, spoiling his aim, but one barrel of the shotgun fired, and Frank felt pain in his side. His bloody axe on high, he hulked between the five men and the door.

All the men's faces were glaring at Frank, incredulously, as if demanding how he dared stir against them. Three convicts were scrabbling tipsily for weapons on the floor. As Frank strode among them, he saw the expression on those faces change from gloating to desperation. Just as his second blow descended, there passed through his mind a kind of fleshly collage of death he had seen once at a farmyard gate: the corpses of five weasels nailed to a gatepost by the farmer, their frozen open jaws agape like damned souls in Hell.

"All heads off but mine!" Frank heard himself braying. "All heads off but mine!" He hacked and hewed, his own screams of lunatic fury drowning their screams of terror.

For less than three minutes, shots, thuds, shrieks, crashes, terrible wailing. They could not get past him to the doorway.

"Come on!" Frank was raging as he stood in the middle of the parlor. "Come on, who's next? All heads off but mine! Who's next?"

There came no answer but a ghastly rattle from one of the five heaps that littered the carpet. Blood-soaked from hair to boots, the berserker towered alone, swaying where he stood.

His mind began to clear. He had been shot twice, Frank guessed, and the pain at his heart was frightful. Into his frantic consciousness burst all the glory of what he had done, and all the horror.

He became almost rational; he must count the dead. One upstairs, five here. One, two, three, four, five heaps. That was correct: all present and accounted for, Frank boy, Punkinhead Frank, Crazy Frank: all dead and accounted for. Had he thought that thought before? Had he taken that mock roll before? Had he wrought this slaughter twice over, twice in this same old room?

But where were Mama and the little girls? They mustn't see this blood-splashed inferno of a parlor. He was looking at himself in the tall mirror, and he saw a bear-man loathsome with his own blood and others' blood. He looked like the Wild Man of Borneo. In abhorrence he flung his axe aside. Behind him sprawled the reflections of the hacked dead.

Fighting down his heart pain, he reeled into the hall. "Little girls! Mrs. Anthony! Allegra, oh, Allegra!" His voice was less strong. "Where are you? It's safe now!"

They did not call back. He labored up the main stair, clutching his side. "Allegra, speak to your Frank!" They were in none of the bedrooms.

He went up the garret stair, then, whatever the agony, and beyond Frank's Room to the cupola stair, and ascended that slowly, gasping hard. They were not in the cupola. Might they have run out among the trees? In that cold dawn, he stared on every side; he thought his sight was beginning to fail.

He could see no one outside the house. The drifts still choked the street beyond the gateposts, and those two boulders protruded impassive from untrodden snow. Back down the flights of stairs he made his way, clutching at the rail, at the wall. Surely the little girls hadn't strayed into that parlor butcher-shop? He bit his lip and peered into the Sunday parlor.

The bodies all were gone. The splashes and ropy strands of blood all were gone. Everything stood in perfect order, as if violence never had touched Tamarack House. The sun was rising, and sunlight filtered through the shutters. Within fifteen minutes, the trophies of his savage victory had disappeared.

It was like the recurrent dream which had tormented Frank when he was little: he separated from Mother in the dark, wandering solitary in empty lanes, no soul alive in all the universe but little Frank. Yet those tremendous ax blows had severed living flesh and blood, and for one moment, there on the stairs, he had held in his arms a tiny quick Allegra; of that reality he did not doubt at all.

Wonder subduing pain, he staggered to the front door. It stood un-shattered. He drew the bar and turned the key, and went down the stone steps into the snow. He was weak now, and did not know where he was going. Had he done a Signal Act? Might the Lord give him one parting glimpse of little Allegra, somewhere among these trees? He slipped in a drift, half rose, sank again, crawled. He found himself at the foot of one of those boulders—the farther one, the stone he had not inspected.

The snow had fallen away from the face of the bronze tablet. Clutching the boulder, Frank drew himself up. By bringing his eyes very close to the tablet, he could read the words, a dying man panting against deathless bronze:

IN LOVING MEMORY OF
FRANK
A SPIRIT IN PRISON, MADE FOR ETERNITY
WHO SAVED US AND DIED FOR US
JANUARY 14, 1915

"Why, if the Soul can fling the Dust aside,
And naked on the Air of Heaven ride,
    Were't not a Shame—were't not a Shame for him
In this clay carcass crippled to abide?"

H. P. Lovecraft

The Call of Cthulhu

Between Poe and King, the great American master of horror is H. P. Lovecraft. As a critic, his *Supernatural Horror in Literature* is the most important essay on horror literature. His influence as mentor and correspondent on his generation was overwhelming and is still felt. His emphasis on cosmic scale, his New England antiquarianism and his elevated and florid style, his consistent juxtaposition of the supernatural to the rational, combined to make him a literary outcast in his day. But his reputation has grown steadily in France (as did Poe's) and, in spite of Edmund Wilson's attempt to dispose of him once and for all in the 1940s, persists in the U.S. Lovecraft rejected conventional morality and the supernatural and yearned to have been born in the eighteenth century a rationalist. But "The Call of Cthulhu" is about a cosmic evil that waits to overcome us with "such terrifying vistas of reality, and of our frightful position therein, that we shall either go mad from the revelation or flee from the deadly light into the peace and safety of a new dark age." Psychologically interesting, but not about the psychological life of characters, concerned with the nature of reality, but with no doubt as to its nature, "The Call of Cthulhu" is about "some things man was not meant to know." Lovecraft was the giant of the pulp horror story and *Weird Tales* was the magazine where much of his work found a home, along with the stories of his friends and correspondents such as Clark Ashton Smith, Frank Belknap Long, Robert E. Howard, throughout the 1920s and 1930s. The influence of the "Lovecraft circle" was dominant until the 1940s and remained strong in *Weird Tales* until its demise in the 1950s.

(Found Among the Papers of the Late Francis Wayland Thurston, of Boston)

"Of such great powers or beings there may be conceivably a survival . . . a survival of a hugely remote period when . . . consciousness was manifested, perhaps, in shapes and forms long since withdrawn before the tide of advancing humanity . . . forms of which poetry and legend alone have caught a flying memory and called them gods, monsters, mythical beings of all sorts and kinds. . . ."

—Algernon Blackwood

I   The Horror in Clay

The most merciful thing in the world, I think, is the inability of the human mind to correlate all its contents. We live on a placid island of ignorance in the midst of black seas of infinity, and it was not meant that we should voyage far. The sciences, each straining in its own direction, have hitherto harmed us little; but some day the piecing together of dissociated knowledge will open up such terrifying vistas of reality, and of our frightful position therein, that we shall either go mad from the revelation or flee from the deadly light into the peace and safety of a new dark age.

Theosophists have guessed at the awesome grandeur of the cosmic cycle wherein our world and human race form transient incidents. They have hinted at strange survivals in terms which would freeze the blood if not masked by a bland optimism. But it is not from them that there came the single glimpse of forbidden aeons which chills me when I think of it and maddens me when I dream of it. That glimpse, like all dread glimpses of truth, flashed out from an accidental piecing together of separated things—in this case an old newspaper item and the notes of a dead professor. I hope that no one else will accomplish this piecing out; certainly, if I live, I shall never knowingly supply a link in so hideous a chain. I think that the professor, too, intended to keep silent regarding the part he knew, and that he would have destroyed his notes had not sudden death seized him.

My knowledge of the thing began in the winter of 1926–27 with the death of my grand-uncle George Gammell Angell, Professor Emeritus of Semitic Languages in Brown University, Providence, Rhode Island. Professor Angell was widely known as an authority on ancient inscriptions, and had frequently been resorted to by the heads of prominent museums; so that his passing at the age of ninety-two may be recalled by many. Locally, interest was intensified by the obscurity of the cause of death. The professor had been stricken whilst returning from the Newport boat; falling suddenly, as witnesses said, after having been jostled by a nautical-looking negro who had come from one of the queer dark courts on the precipitous hillside which formed a short cut from the waterfront to the deceased's home in Williams Street. Physicians were unable to find any visible disorder, but concluded after perplexed debate that some obscure lesion of the heart, induced by the brisk ascent of so steep a hill by so elderly a man, was responsible for the end. At the time I saw no reason to dissent from this dictum, but latterly I am inclined to wonder—and more than wonder.

As my grand-uncle's heir and executor, for he died a childless widower, I was expected to go over his papers with some thoroughness; and for that purpose moved his entire set of files and boxes to my quarters in Boston. Much of the material which I correlated will be later published by the American Archaeological Society, but there was one box which I found exceedingly puzzling, and which I felt much adverse from shewing to other eyes. It had been locked, and I did not find the key till it occurred to me to examine the personal ring which the professor carried always in his pocket. Then indeed I succeeded in opening it, but when I did so seemed only to be confronted by a greater and more closely locked barrier. For what could be the meaning of the queer clay bas-relief and the disjointed jottings, ramblings, and cuttings which I found? Had my uncle, in his latter years, become credulous of the most superficial impostures? I resolved to search out the eccentric sculptor responsible for this apparent disturbance of an old man's peace of mind.

The bas-relief was a rough rectangle less than an inch thick and about five by six inches in area; obviously of modern origin. Its designs, however, were far from modern in atmosphere and suggestion; for although the vagaries of cubism and futurism are many and wild, they do not often reproduce that cryptic regularity which lurks in prehistoric writing. And writing of some kind the bulk of these designs seemed certainly to be; though my memory, despite much familiarity with the papers and collections of my uncle, failed in any way to identify this particular species, or even to hint at its remotest affiliations.

Above these apparent hieroglyphics was a figure of evidently pictorial intent, though its impressionistic execution forbade a very clear idea of its nature. It seemed to be a sort of monster, or symbol representing a monster, of a form which only a diseased fancy could conceive. If I say that my somewhat extravagant imagination yielded simultaneous pictures of an octopus, a dragon, and a human caricature, I shall not be unfaithful to the spirit of the thing. A pulpy, tentacled head surmounted a grotesque and scaly body with rudimentary wings; but it was the *general outline* of the whole which made it most shockingly frightful. Behind the figure was a vague suggestion of a Cyclopean architectural background.

The writing accompanying this oddity was, aside from a stack of press cuttings, in Professor Angell's most recent hand; and made no pretence to literary style. What seemed to be the main document was headed "CTHULHU CULT" in characters painstakingly printed to avoid the erroneous reading of a word so unheard-of. This manuscript was divided into two sections, the first of which was headed "1925—Dream and Dream Work of H. A. Wilcox, 7 Thomas St., Providence, R.I.," and the second, "Narrative of Inspector John R. Legrasse, 121 Bienville St., New Orleans, La., at 1908 A. A. S. Mtg.—Notes on Same, & Prof. Webb's Acct." The other manuscript papers were all brief notes, some of them accounts of the queer dreams of different persons, some of them citations from theosophical books and magazines (notably W. Scott-Elliot's *Atlantis and the Lost Lemuria*), and the rest comments on long-surviving secret societies and hidden cults, with references to passages in such mythological and anthropological source-books as Frazer's *Golden Bough* and Miss Murray's *Witch-Cult in Western Europe*. The cuttings largely alluded to outré mental illnesses and outbreaks of group folly or mania in the spring of 1925.

The first half of the principal manuscript told a very peculiar tale. It appears that on March 1st, 1925, a thin, dark young man of neurotic and excited aspect had called upon Professor Angell bearing the singular clay bas-relief, which was then exceedingly damp and fresh. His card bore the name of Henry Anthony Wilcox, and my uncle had recognised him as the youngest son of an excellent family slightly known to him, who had latterly been studying sculpture at the Rhode Island School of Design and living alone at the Fleur-de-Lys Building near that institution. Wilcox was a precocious youth of known genius but great eccentricity, and had from childhood excited attention through the strange stories and odd dreams he was in the habit of relating. He called himself "psychically hypersensitive," but the staid folk of the ancient commercial city dismissed him as merely "queer." Never mingling much with his kind, he had dropped gradually from social visibility, and was now known only to a small group of aesthetes from other towns. Even the Providence Art Club, anxious to preserve its conservatism, had found him quite hopeless.

On the occasion of the visit, ran the professor's manuscript, the sculptor abruptly asked for the benefit of his host's archaeological knowledge in identifying the hieroglyphics on the bas-relief. He spoke in a dreamy, stilted manner which suggested pose and alienated sympathy; and my uncle shewed some sharpness in replying, for the conspicuous freshness of the tablet implied kinship with anything but archaeology. Young Wilcox's rejoinder, which impressed my uncle enough to make him recall and record it verbatim, was of a fantastically poetic cast which must have typified his whole conversation, and which I have since found highly characteristic of him. He said, "It is new, indeed, for I made it last night in a dream of strange cities; and dreams are older than brooding Tyre, or the contemplative Sphinx, or garden-girdled Babylon."

It was then that he began that rambling tale which suddenly played upon a sleeping memory and won the fevered interest of my uncle. There had been a slight earthquake tremor the night before, the most considerable felt in New England for some years; and Wilcox's imagination had been keenly affected. Upon retiring, he had had an unprecedented dream of great Cyclopean cities of titan blocks and sky-flung monoliths, all dripping with green ooze and sinister with latent horror. Hieroglyphics had covered the walls and pillars, and from some undetermined point below had come a voice that was not a voice; a chaotic sensation which only fancy could transmute into sound, but which he attempted to render by the almost unpronounceable jumble of letters, "*Cthulhu fhtagn.*"

This verbal jumble was the key to the recollection which excited and disturbed Professor Angell. He questioned the sculptor with scientific minuteness; and studied with almost frantic intensity the bas-relief on which the youth had found himself working, chilled and clad only in his night-clothes, when waking had stolen bewilderingly over him. My uncle blamed his old age, Wilcox afterward said, for his slowness in recognising both hieroglyphics and pictorial design. Many of his questions seemed highly out-of-place to his visitor, especially those which tried to connect the latter with strange cults or societies; and Wilcox could not understand the repeated promises of silence which he was offered in exchange for an admission of membership in some widespread mystical or paganly religious body. When Professor Angell became convinced that the sculptor was indeed ignorant of any cult or system of cryptic lore, he besieged his visitor with demands for future reports of dreams. This bore regular fruit, for after the first interview the manuscript records daily calls of the young man, during which he related startling fragments of nocturnal imagery whose burden was always some terrible Cyclopean vista of dark and dripping stone, with a subterrene voice or intelligence shouting monotonously in enigmatical sense-impacts uninscribable save as gibberish. The two sounds most frequently repeated are those rendered by the letters "*Cthulhu*" and "*R'lyeh.*"

On March 23d, the manuscript continued, Wilcox failed to appear; and inquiries at his quarters revealed that he had been stricken with an obscure sort of fever and taken to the home of his family in Waterman Street. He had cried out in the night, arousing several other artists in the building, and had manifested since then only alternations of unconsciousness and delirium. My uncle at once telephoned the family, and from that time forward kept close watch of the case; calling often at the Thayer Street office of Dr. Tobey, whom he learned to be in charge. The youth's febrile mind, apparently, was dwelling on strange things; and the doctor shuddered now and then as he spoke of them. They included not only a repetition of what he had formerly dreamed, but touched wildly on a gigantic thing "miles high" which walked or lumbered about. He at no time fully described this object, but occasional frantic words, as repeated by Dr. Tobey, convinced the professor that it must be identical with the nameless monstrosity he had sought to depict in his dream-sculpture. Reference to this object, the doctor added, was invariably a prelude to the young man's subsidence into lethargy. His temperature, oddly enough, was not greatly above normal; but his whole condition was otherwise such as to suggest true fever rather than mental disorder.

On April 2nd at about 3 p.m. every trace of Wilcox's malady suddenly ceased. He sat upright in bed, astonished to find himself at home and completely ignorant of what had happened in dream or reality since the night of March 22nd. Pronounced well by his physician, he returned to his quarters in three days; but to Professor Angell he was of no further assistance. All traces of strange dreaming had vanished with his recovery, and my uncle kept no record of his night-thoughts after a week of pointless and irrelevant accounts of thoroughly usual visions.

Here the first part of the manuscript ended, but references to certain of the scattered notes gave me much material for thought—so much, in fact, that only the ingrained scepticism then forming my philosophy can account for my continued distrust of the artist. The notes in question were those descriptive of the dreams of various persons covering the same period as that in which young Wilcox had had his strange visitations. My uncle, it seems, had quickly instituted a prodigiously far-flung body of inquiries amongst nearly all the friends whom he could question without impertinence, asking for nightly reports of their dreams, and the dates of any notable visions for some time past. The reception of his request seems to have been varied; but he must, at the very least, have received more responses than any ordinary man could have handled without a secretary. This original correspondence was not preserved, but his notes formed a thorough and really significant digest. Average people in society and business—New England's traditional "salt of the earth"—gave an almost completely negative result, though scattered cases of uneasy but formless nocturnal impressions appear here and there, always between March 23d and April 2nd—the period of young Wilcox's delirium. Scientific men were little more affected, though four cases of vague description suggest fugitive glimpses of strange landscapes, and in one case there is mentioned a dread of something abnormal.

It was from the artists and poets that the pertinent answers came, and I know that panic would have broken loose had they been able to compare notes. As it was, lacking their original letters, I half suspected the compiler of having asked leading questions, or of having edited the correspondence in corroboration of what he had latently resolved to see. That is why I continued to feel that Wilcox, somehow cognisant of the old data which my uncle had possessed, had been imposing on the veteran scientist. These responses from aesthetes told a disturbing tale. From February 28th to April 2nd a large proportion of them had dreamed very bizarre things, the intensity of the dreams being immeasurably the stronger during the period of the sculptor's delirium. Over a fourth of those who reported anything, reported scenes and half-sounds not unlike those which Wilcox had described; and some of the dreamers confessed acute fear of the gigantic nameless thing visible toward the last. One case, which the note describes with emphasis, was very sad. The subject, a widely known architect with leanings toward theosophy and occultism, went violently insane on the date of young Wilcox's seizure, and expired several months later after incessant screamings to be saved from some escaped denizen of hell. Had my uncle referred to these cases by name instead of merely by number, I should have attempted some corroboration and personal investigation; but as it was, I succeeded in tracing down only a few. All of these, however, bore out the notes in full. I have often wondered if all the objects of the professor's questioning felt as puzzled as did this fraction. It is well that no explanation shall ever reach them.

The press cuttings, as I have intimated, touched on cases of panic, mania, and eccentricity during the given period. Professor Angell must have employed a cutting bureau, for the number of extracts was tremendous and the sources scattered throughout the globe. Here was a nocturnal suicide in London, where a lone sleeper had leaped from a window after a shocking cry. Here likewise a rambling letter to the editor of a paper in South America, where a fanatic deduces a dire future from visions he has seen. A despatch from California describes a theosophist colony as donning white robes en masse for some "glorious fulfilment" which never arrives, whilst items from India speak guardedly of serious native unrest toward the end of March. Voodoo orgies multiply in Hayti, and African outposts report ominous mutterings. American officers in the Philippines find certain tribes bothersome about this time, and New York policemen are mobbed by hysterical Levantines on the night of March 22–23. The west of Ireland, too, is full of wild rumour and legendry, and a fantastic painter named Ardois-Bonnot hangs a blasphemous "Dream Landscape" in the Paris spring salon of 1926. And so numerous are the recorded troubles in insane asylums, that only a miracle can have stopped the medical fraternity from noting strange parallelisms and drawing mystified conclusions. A weird bunch of cuttings, all told; and I can at this date scarcely envisage the callous rationalism with which I set them aside. But I was then convinced that young Wilcox had known of the older matters mentioned by the professor.

II   The Tale of Inspector Legrasse

The older matters which had made the sculptor's dream and bas-relief so significant to my uncle formed the subject of the second half of his long manuscript. Once before, it appears, Professor Angell had seen the hellish outlines of the nameless monstrosity, puzzled over the unknown hieroglyphics, and heard the ominous syllables which can be rendered only as "*Cthulhu*"; and all this in so stirring and horrible a connexion that it is small wonder he pursued young Wilcox with queries and demands for data.

This earlier experience had come in 1908, seventeen years before, when the American Archaeological Society held its annual meeting in St. Louis. Professor Angell, as befitted one of his authority and attainments, had had a prominent part in all the deliberations; and was one of the first to be approached by the several outsiders who took advantage of the convocation to offer questions for correct answering and problems for expert solution.

The chief of these outsiders, and in a short time the focus of interest for the entire meeting, was a commonplace-looking middle-aged man who had travelled all the way from New Orleans for certain special information unobtainable from any local source. His name was John Raymond Legrasse, and he was by profession an Inspector of Police. With him he bore the subject of his visit, a grotesque, repulsive, and apparently very ancient stone statuette whose origin he was at a loss to determine. It must not be fancied that Inspector Legrasse had the least interest in archaeology. On the contrary, his wish for enlightenment was prompted by purely professional considerations. The statuette, idol, fetish, or whatever it was, had been captured some months before in the wooded swamps south of New Orleans during a raid on a supposed voodoo meeting; and so singular and hideous were the rites connected with it, that the police could not but realise that they had stumbled on a dark cult totally unknown to them, and infinitely more diabolic than even the blackest of the African voodoo circles. Of its origin, apart from the erratic and unbelievable tales extorted from the captured members, absolutely nothing was to be discovered; hence the anxiety of the police for any antiquarian lore which might help them to place the frightful symbol, and through it track down the cult to its fountain-head.

Inspector Legrasse was scarcely prepared for the sensation which his offering created. One sight of the thing had been enough to throw the assembled men of science into a state of tense excitement, and they lost no time in crowding around him to gaze at the diminutive figure whose utter strangeness and air of genuinely abysmal antiquity hinted so potently at unopened and archaic vistas. No recognised school of sculpture had animated this terrible object, yet centuries and even thousands of years seemed recorded in its dim and greenish surface of unplaceable stone.

The figure, which was finally passed slowly from man to man for close and careful study, was between seven and eight inches in height, and of exquisitely artistic workmanship. It represented a monster of vaguely anthropoid outline, but with an octopus-like head whose face was a mass of feelers, a scaly, rubbery-looking body, prodigious claws on hind and fore feet, and long, narrow wings behind. This thing, which seemed instinct with a fearsome and unnatural malignancy, was of a somewhat bloated corpulence, and squatted evilly on a rectangular block or pedestal covered with undecipherable characters. The tips of the wings touched the back edge of the block, the seat occupied the centre, whilst the long, curved claws of the doubled-up, crouching hind legs gripped the front edge and extended a quarter of the way down toward the bottom of the pedestal. The cephalopod head was bent forward, so that the ends of the facial feelers brushed the backs of huge fore paws which clasped the croucher's elevated knees. The aspect of the whole was abnormally life-like, and the more subtly fearful because its source was so totally unknown. Its vast, awesome, and incalculable age was unmistakable; yet not one link did it shew with any known type of art belonging to civilisation's youth—or indeed to any other time. Totally separate and apart, its very material was a mystery; for the soapy, greenish-black stone with its golden or iridescent flecks and striations resembled nothing familiar to geology or mineralogy. The characters along the base were equally baffling; and no member present, despite a representation of half the world's expert learning in this field, could form the least notion of even their remotest linguistic kinship. They, like the subject and material, belonged to something horribly remote and distinct from mankind as we know it; something frightfully suggestive of old and unhallowed cycles of life in which our world and our conceptions have no part.

And yet, as the members severally shook their heads and confessed defeat at the Inspector's problem, there was one man in that gathering who suspected a touch of bizarre familiarity in the monstrous shape and writing, and who presently told with some diffidence of the odd trifle he knew. This person was the late William Channing Webb, Professor of Anthropology in Princeton University, and an explorer of no slight note. Professor Webb had been engaged, forty-eight years before, in a tour of Greenland and Iceland in search of some Runic inscriptions which he failed to unearth; and whilst high up on the West Greenland coast had encountered a singular tribe or cult of degenerate Esquimaux whose religion, a curious form of devil-worship, chilled him with its deliberate bloodthirstiness and repulsiveness. It was a faith of which other Esquimaux knew little, and which they mentioned only with shudders, saying that it had come down from horribly ancient aeons before ever the world was made. Besides nameless rites and human sacrifices there were certain queer hereditary rituals addressed to a supreme elder devil or *tornasuk*; and of this Professor Webb had taken a careful phonetic copy from an aged *angekok* or wizard-priest, expressing the sounds in Roman letters as best he knew how. But just now of prime significance was the fetish which this cult had cherished, and around which they danced when the aurora leaped high over the ice cliffs. It was, the professor stated, a very crude bas-relief of stone, comprising a hideous picture and some cryptic writing. And so far as he could tell, it was a rough parallel in all essential features of the bestial thing now lying before the meeting.

This data, received with suspense and astonishment by the assembled members, proved doubly exciting to Inspector Legrasse; and he began at once to ply his informant with questions. Having noted and copied an oral ritual among the swamp cult-worshippers his men had arrested, he besought the professor to remember as best he might the syllables taken down amongst the diabolist Esquimaux. There then followed an exhaustive comparison of details, and a moment of really awed silence when both detective and scientist agreed on the virtual identity of the phrase common to two hellish rituals so many worlds of distance apart. What, in substance, both the Esquimau wizards and the Louisiana swamp-priests had chanted to their kindred idols was something very like this—the word-divisions being guessed at from traditional breaks in the phrase as chanted aloud:

"Ph'nglui mglw'nafh Cthulhu R'lyeh wgah'nagl fhtagn."
Legrasse had one point in advance of Professor Webb, for several among his mongrel prisoners had repeated to him what older celebrants had told them the words meant. This text, as given, ran something like this:

"In his house at R'lyeh dead Cthulhu waits dreaming."
And now, in response to a general and urgent demand, Inspector Legrasse related as fully as possible his experience with the swamp worshippers; telling a story to which I could see my uncle attached profound significance. It savoured of the wildest dreams of mythmaker and theosophist, and disclosed an astonishing degree of cosmic imagination among such half-castes and pariahs as might be least expected to possess it.

On November 1st, 1907, there had come to the New Orleans police a frantic summons from the swamp and lagoon country to the south. The squatters there, mostly primitive but good-natured descendants of Lafitte's men, were in the grip of stark terror from an unknown thing which had stolen upon them in the night. It was voodoo, apparently, but voodoo of a more terrible sort than they had ever known; and some of their women and children had disappeared since the malevolent tom-tom had begun its incessant beating far within the black haunted woods where no dweller ventured. There were insane shouts and harrowing screams, soul-chilling chants and dancing devil-flames; and, the frightened messenger added, the people could stand it no more.

So a body of twenty police, filling two carriages and an automobile, had set out in the late afternoon with the shivering squatter as a guide. At the end of the passable road they alighted, and for miles splashed on in silence through the terrible cypress woods where day never came. Ugly roots and malignant hanging nooses of Spanish moss beset them, and now and then a pile of dank stones or fragment of a rotting wall intensified by its hint of morbid habitation a depression which every malformed tree and every fungous islet combined to create. At length the squatter settlement, a miserable huddle of huts, hove in sight; and hysterical dwellers ran out to cluster around the group of bobbing lanterns. The muffled beat of tom-toms was now faintly audible far, far ahead; and a curdling shriek came at infrequent intervals when the wind shifted. A reddish glare, too, seemed to filter through the pale undergrowth beyond endless avenues of forest night. Reluctant even to be left alone again, each one of the cowed squatters refused point-blank to advance another inch toward the scene of unholy worship, so Inspector Legrasse and his nineteen colleagues plunged on unguided into black arcades of horror that none of them had ever trod before.

The region now entered by the police was one of traditionally evil repute, substantially unknown and untraversed by white men. There were legends of a hidden lake unglimpsed by mortal sight, in which dwelt a huge, formless white polypous thing with luminous eyes; and squatters whispered that bat-winged devils flew up out of caverns in inner earth to worship it at midnight. They said it had been there before D'Iberville, before La Salle, before the Indians, and before even the wholesome beasts and birds of the woods. It was nightmare itself, and to see it was to die. But it made men dream, and so they knew enough to keep away. The present voodoo orgy was, indeed, on the merest fringe of this abhorred area, but that location was bad enough; hence perhaps the very place of the worship had terrified the squatters more than the shocking sounds and incidents.

Only poetry or madness could do justice to the noises heard by Legrasse's men as they ploughed on through the black morass toward the red glare and the muffled tom-toms. There are vocal qualities peculiar to men, and vocal qualities peculiar to beasts; and it is terrible to hear the one when the source should yield the other. Animal fury and orgiastic licence here whipped themselves to daemoniac heights by howls and squawking ecstasies that tore and reverberated through those nighted woods like pestilential tempests from the gulfs of hell. Now and then the less organised ululation would cease, and from what seemed a well-drilled chorus of hoarse voices would rise in sing-song chant that hideous phrase or ritual:

"Ph'nglui mglw'nafh Cthulhu R'lyeh wgah'nagl fhtagn."

Then the men, having reached a spot where the trees were thinner, came suddenly in sight of the spectacle itself. Four of them reeled, one fainted, and two were shaken into a frantic cry which the mad cacophony of the orgy fortunately deadened. Legrasse dashed swamp water on the face of the fainting man, and all stood trembling and nearly hypnotised with horror.

In a natural glade of the swamp stood a grassy island of perhaps an acre's extent, clear of trees and tolerably dry. On this now leaped and twisted a more indescribable horde of human abnormality than any but a Sime or an Angarola could paint. Void of clothing, this hybrid spawn were braying, bellowing, and writhing about a monstrous ring-shaped bonfire; in the centre of which, revealed by occasional rifts in the curtain of flame, stood a great granite monolith some eight feet in height; on top of which, incongruous in its diminutiveness, rested the noxious carven statuette. From a wide circle of ten scaffolds set up at regular intervals with the flame-girt monolith as a centre hung, head downward, the oddly marred bodies of the helpless squatters who had disappeared. It was inside this circle that the ring of worshippers jumped and roared, the general direction of the mass motion being from left to right in endless Bacchanal between the ring of bodies and the ring of fire.

It may have been only imagination and it may have been only echoes which induced one of the men, an excitable Spaniard, to fancy he heard antiphonal responses to the ritual from some far and unillumined spot deeper within the wood of ancient legendry and horror. This man, Joseph D. Galvez, I later met and questioned; and he proved distractingly imaginative. He indeed went so far as to hint of the faint beating of great wings, and of a glimpse of shining eyes and a mountainous white bulk beyond the remotest trees—but I suppose he had been hearing too much native superstition.

Actually, the horrified pause of the men was of comparatively brief duration. Duty came first; and although there must have been nearly a hundred mongrel celebrants in the throng, the police relied on their firearms and plunged determinedly into the nauseous rout. For five minutes the resultant din and chaos were beyond description. Wild blows were struck, shots were fired, and escapes were made; but in the end Legrasse was able to count some forty-seven sullen prisoners, whom he forced to dress in haste and fall into line between two rows of policemen. Five of the worshippers lay dead, and two severely wounded ones were carried away on improvised stretchers by their fellow-prisoners. The image on the monolith, of course, was carefully removed and carried back by Legrasse.

Examined at headquarters after a trip of intense strain and weariness, the prisoners all proved to be men of a very low, mixed-blooded, and mentally aberrant type. Most were seamen, and a sprinkling of negroes and mulattoes, largely West Indians or Brava Portuguese from the Cape Verde Islands, gave a colouring of voodooism to the heterogeneous cult. But before many questions were asked, it became manifest that something far deeper and older than negro fetichism was involved. Degraded and ignorant as they were, the creatures held with surprising consistency to the central idea of their loathsome faith.

They worshipped, so they said, the Great Old Ones who lived ages before there were any men, and who came to the young world out of the sky. Those Old Ones were gone now, inside the earth and under the sea; but their dead bodies had told their secrets in dreams to the first men, who formed a cult which had never died. This was that cult, and the prisoners said it had always existed and always would exist, hidden in distant wastes and dark places all over the world until the time when the great priest Cthulhu, from his dark house in the mighty city of R'lyeh under the waters, should rise and bring the earth again beneath his sway. Some day he would call, when the stars were ready, and the secret cult would always be waiting to liberate him.

Meanwhile no more must be told. There was a secret which even torture could not extract. Mankind was not absolutely alone among the conscious things of earth, for shapes came out of the dark to visit the faithful few. But these were not the Great Old Ones. No man had ever seen the Old Ones. The carven idol was great Cthulhu, but none might say whether or not the others were precisely like him. No one could read the old writing now, but things were told by word of mouth. The chanted ritual was not the secret—that was never spoken aloud, only whispered. The chant meant only this: "In his house at R'lyeh dead Cthulhu waits dreaming."

Only two of the prisoners were found sane enough to be hanged, and the rest were committed to various institutions. All denied a part in the ritual murders, and averred that the killing had been done by Black Winged Ones which had come to them from their immemorial meeting-place in the haunted wood. But of those mysterious allies no coherent account could ever be gained. What the police did extract, came mainly from an immensely aged mestizo named Castro, who claimed to have sailed to strange ports and talked with undying leaders of the cult in the mountains of China.

Old Castro remembered bits of hideous legend that paled the speculations of theosophists and made man and the world seem recent and transient indeed. There had been aeons when other Things ruled on the earth, and They had had great cities. Remains of Them, he said the deathless Chinamen had told him, were still to be found as Cyclopean stones on islands in the Pacific. They all died vast epochs of time before men came, but there were arts which could revive Them when the stars had come round again to the right positions in the cycle of eternity. They had, indeed, come themselves from the stars, and brought Their images with Them.

These Great Old Ones, Castro continued, were not composed altogether of flesh and blood. They had shape—for did not this star-fashioned image prove it?—but that shape was not made of matter. When the stars were right, They could plunge from world to world through the sky; but when the stars were wrong, They could not live. But although They no longer lived, They would never really die. They all lay in stone houses in Their great city of R'lyeh, preserved by the spells of mighty Cthulhu for a glorious resurrection when the stars and the earth might once more be ready for Them. But at that time some force from outside must serve to liberate Their bodies. The spells that preserved Them intact likewise prevented Them from making an initial move, and They could only lie awake in the dark and think whilst uncounted millions of years rolled by. They knew all that was occurring in the universe, for Their mode of speech was transmitted thought. Even now They talked in Their tombs. When, after infinities of chaos, the first men came, the Great Old Ones spoke to the sensitive among them by moulding their dreams; for only thus could Their language reach the fleshly minds of mammals.

Then, whispered Castro, those first men formed the cult around small idols which the Great Ones shewed them; idols brought in dim aeras from dark stars. That cult would never die till the stars came right again, and the secret priests would take great Cthulhu from His tomb to revive His subjects and resume His rule of earth. The time would be easy to know, for then mankind would have become as the Great Old Ones; free and wild and beyond good and evil, with laws and morals thrown aside and all men shouting and killing and revelling in joy. Then the liberated Old Ones would teach them new ways to shout and kill and revel and enjoy themselves, and all the earth would flame with a holocaust of ecstasy and freedom. Meanwhile the cult, by appropriate rites, must keep alive the memory of those ancient ways and shadow forth the prophecy of their return.

In the elder time chosen men had talked with the entombed Old Ones in dreams, but then something had happened. The great stone city R'lyeh, with its monoliths and sepulchres, had sunk beneath the waves; and the deep waters, full of the one primal mystery through which not even thought can pass, had cut off the spectral intercourse. But memory never died, and high-priests said that the city would rise again when the stars were right. Then came out of the earth the black spirits of earth, mouldy and shadowy, and full of dim rumours picked up in caverns beneath forgotten sea-bottoms. But of them old Castro dared not speak much. He cut himself off hurriedly, and no amount of persuasion or subtlety could elicit more in this direction. The *size* of the Old Ones, too, he curiously declined to mention. Of the cult, he said that he thought the centre lay amid the pathless deserts of Arabia, where Irem, the City of Pillars, dreams hidden and untouched. It was not allied to the European witch-cult, and was virtually unknown beyond its members. No book had ever really hinted of it, though the deathless Chinamen said that there were double meanings in the *Necronomicon* of the mad Arab Abdul Alhazred which the initiated might read as they chose, especially the much-discussed couplet:

"That is not dead which can eternal lie,
And with strange aeons even death may die."

Legrasse, deeply impressed and not a little bewildered, had inquired in vain concerning the historic affiliations of the cult. Castro, apparently, had told the truth when he said that it was wholly secret. The authorities at Tulane University could shed no light upon either cult or image, and now the detective had come to the highest authorities in the country and met with no more than the Greenland tale of Professor Webb.

The feverish interest aroused at the meeting by Legrasse's tale, corroborated as it was by the statuette, is echoed in the subsequent correspondence of those who attended; although scant mention occurs in the formal publications of the society. Caution is the first care of those accustomed to face occasional charlatanry and imposture. Legrasse for some time lent the image to Professor Webb, but at the latter's death it was returned to him and remains in his possession, where I viewed it not long ago. It is truly a terrible thing, and unmistakably akin to the dream-sculpture of young Wilcox.

That my uncle was excited by the tale of the sculptor I did not wonder, for what thoughts must arise upon hearing, after a knowledge of what Legrasse had learned of the cult, of a sensitive young man who had *dreamed* not only the figure and exact hieroglyphics of the swamp-found image and the Greenland devil tablet, but had come *in his dreams* upon at least three of the precise words of the formula uttered alike by Esquimau diabolists and mongrel Louisianans? Professor Angell's instant start on an investigation of the utmost thoroughness was eminently natural; though privately I suspected young Wilcox of having heard of the cult in some indirect way, and of having invented a series of dreams to heighten and continue the mystery at my uncle's expense. The dream-narratives and cuttings collected by the professor were, of course, strong corroboration; but the rationalism of my mind and the extravagance of the whole subject led me to adopt what I thought the most sensible conclusions. So, after thoroughly studying the manuscript again and correlating the theosophical and anthropological notes with the cult narrative of Legrasse, I made a trip to Providence to see the sculptor and give him the rebuke I thought proper for so boldly imposing upon a learned and aged man.

Wilcox still lived alone in the Fleur-de-Lys Building in Thomas Street, a hideous Victorian imitation of seventeenth-century Breton architecture which flaunts its stuccoed front amidst the lovely colonial houses on the ancient hill, and under the very shadow of the finest Georgian steeple in America. I found him at work in his rooms, and at once conceded from the specimens scattered about that his genius is indeed profound and authentic. He will, I believe, some time be heard from as one of the great decadents; for he has crystallised in clay and will one day mirror in marble those nightmares and phantasies which Arthur Machen evokes in prose, and Clark Ashton Smith makes visible in verse and in painting.

Dark, frail, and somewhat unkempt in aspect, he turned languidly at my knock and asked me my business without rising. When I told him who I was, he displayed some interest; for my uncle had excited his curiosity in probing his strange dreams, yet had never explained the reason for the study. I did not enlarge his knowledge in this regard, but sought with some subtlety to draw him out. In a short time I became convinced of his absolute sincerity, for he spoke of the dreams in a manner none could mistake. They and their subconscious residuum had influenced his art profoundly, and he shewed me a morbid statue whose contours almost made me shake with the potency of its black suggestion. He could not recall having seen the original of this thing except in his own dream bas-relief, but the outlines had formed themselves insensibly under his hands. It was, no doubt, the giant shape he had raved of in delirium. That he really knew nothing of the hidden cult, save from what my uncle's relentless catechism had let fall, he soon made clear; and again I strove to think of some way in which he could possibly have received the weird impressions.

He talked of his dreams in a strangely poetic fashion; making me see with terrible vividness the damp Cyclopean city of slimy green stone—whose *geometry*, he oddly said, was *all wrong*—and hear with frightened expectancy the ceaseless, half-mental calling from underground: *"Cthulhu fhtagn,"* *"Cthulhu fhtagn."* These words had formed part of that dread ritual which told of dead Cthulhu's dream-vigil in his stone vault at R'lyeh, and I felt deeply moved despite my rational beliefs. Wilcox, I was sure, had heard of the cult in some casual way, and had soon forgotten it amidst the mass of his equally weird reading and imagining. Later, by virtue of its sheer impressiveness, it had found subconscious expression in dreams, in the bas-relief, and in the terrible statue I now beheld; so that his imposture upon my uncle had been a very innocent one. The youth was of a type, at once slightly affected and slightly ill-mannered, which I could never like; but I was willing enough now to admit both his genius and his honesty. I took leave of him amicably, and wish him all the success his talent promises.

The matter of the cult still remained to fascinate me, and at times I had visions of personal fame from researches into its origin and connexions. I visited New Orleans, talked with Legrasse and others of that old-time raiding-party, saw the frightful image, and even questioned such of the mongrel prisoners as still survived. Old Castro, unfortunately, had been dead for some years. What I now heard so graphically at first-hand, though it was really no more than a detailed confirmation of what my uncle had written, excited me afresh; for I felt sure that I was on the track of a very real, very secret, and very ancient religion whose discovery would make me an anthropologist of note. My attitude was still one of absolute materialism, *as I wish it still were,* and I discounted with almost inexplicable perversity the coincidence of the dream notes and odd cuttings collected by Professor Angell.

One thing I began to suspect, and which I now fear I *know,* is that my uncle's death was far from natural. He fell on a narrow hill street leading up from an ancient waterfront swarming with foreign mongrels, after a careless push from a negro sailor. I did not forget the mixed blood and marine pursuits of the cult-members in Louisiana, and would not be surprised to learn of secret methods and poison needles as ruthless and as anciently known as the cryptic rites and beliefs. Legrasse and his men, it is true, have been let alone; but in Norway a certain seaman who saw things is dead. Might not the deeper inquiries of my uncle after encountering the sculptor's data have come to sinister ears? I think Professor Angell died because he knew too much, or because he was likely to learn too much. Whether I shall go as he did remains to be seen, for I have learned much now.

III   The Madness from the Sea

If heaven ever wishes to grant me a boon, it will be a total effacing of the results of a mere chance which fixed my eye on a certain stray piece of shelf-paper. It was nothing on which I would naturally have stumbled in the course of my daily round, for it was an old number of an Australian journal, the *Sydney Bulletin* for April 18, 1925. It had escaped even the cutting bureau which had at the time of its issuance been avidly collecting material for my uncle's research.

I had largely given over my inquiries into what Professor Angell called the "Cthulhu Cult," and was visiting a learned friend in Paterson, New Jersey; the curator of a local museum and a mineralogist of note. Examining one day the reserve specimens roughly set on the storage shelves in a rear room of the museum, my eye was caught by an odd picture in one of the old papers spread beneath the stones. It was the *Sydney Bulletin* I have mentioned, for my friend has wide affiliations in all conceivable foreign parts; and the picture was a half-tone cut of a hideous stone image almost identical with that which Legrasse had found in the swamp.

Eagerly clearing the sheet of its precious contents, I scanned the item in detail; and was disappointed to find it of only moderate length. What it suggested, however, was of portentous significance to my flagging quest; and I carefully tore it out for immediate action. It read as follows:

MYSTERY DERELICT FOUND AT SEA

Vigilant Arrives With Helpless Armed New Zealand Yacht in Tow.
One Survivor and Dead Man Found Aboard. Tale of
Desperate Battle and Deaths at Sea.
Rescued Seaman Refuses
Particulars of Strange Experience.
Odd Idol Found in His Possession. Inquiry
to Follow.

The Morrison Co.'s freighter *Vigilant,* bound from Valparaiso, arrived this morning at its wharf in Darling Harbour, having in tow the battled and disabled but heavily armed steam yacht *Alert* of Dunedin, N. Z., which was sighted April 12th in S. Latitude 34° 21', W. Longitude 152° 17' with one living and one dead man aboard.

The *Vigilant* left Valparaiso March 25th, and on April 2nd was driven considerably south of her course by exceptionally heavy storms and monster waves. On April 12th the derelict was sighted; and though apparently deserted, was found upon boarding to contain one survivor in a half-delirious condition and one man who had evidently been dead for more than a week. The living man was clutching a horrible stone idol of unknown origin, about a foot in height, regarding whose nature authorities at Sydney University, the Royal Society, and the Museum in College Street all profess complete bafflement, and which the survivor says he found in the cabin of the yacht, in a small carved shrine of common pattern.

This man, after recovering his senses, told an exceedingly strange story of piracy and slaughter. He is Gustaf Johansen, a Norwegian of some intelligence, and had been second mate of the two-masted schooner *Emma* of Auckland, which sailed for Callao February 20th with a complement of eleven men. The *Emma,* he says, was delayed and thrown widely south of her course by the great storm of March 1st, and on March 22nd, in S. Latitude 49° 51', W. Longitude 128° 34', encountered the *Alert,* manned by a queer and evil-looking crew of Kanakas and half-castes. Being ordered peremptorily to turn back, Capt. Collins refused; whereupon the strange crew began to fire savagely and without warning upon the schooner with a peculiarly heavy battery of brass cannon forming part of the yacht's equipment. The *Emma's* men shewed fight, says the survivor, and though the schooner began to sink from shots beneath the waterline they managed to heave alongside their enemy and board her, grappling with the savage crew on the yacht's deck, and being forced to kill them all, the number being slightly superior, because of their particularly abhorrent and desperate though rather clumsy mode of fighting.

Three of the *Emma*'s men, including Capt. Collins and First Mate Green, were killed; and the remaining eight under Second Mate Johansen proceeded to navigate the captured yacht, going ahead in their original direction to see if any reason for their ordering back had existed. The next day, it appears, they raised and landed on a small island, although none is known to exist in that part of the ocean; and six of the men somehow died ashore, though Johansen is queerly reticent about this part of his story, and speaks only of their falling into a rock chasm. Later, it seems, he and one companion boarded the yacht and tried to manage her, but were beaten about by the storm of April 2nd. From that time till his rescue on the 12th the man remembers little, and he does not even recall when William Briden, his companion, died. Briden's death reveals no apparent cause, and was probably due to excitement or exposure. Cable advices from Dunedin report that the *Alert* was well known there as an island trader, and bore an evil reputation along the waterfront. It was owned by a curious group of half-castes whose frequent meetings and night trips to the woods attracted no little curiosity; and it had set sail in great haste just after the storm and earth tremors of March 1st. Our Auckland correspondent gives the *Emma* and her crew an excellent reputation, and Johansen is described as a sober and worthy man. The admiralty will institute an inquiry on the whole matter beginning tomorrow, at which every effort will be made to induce Johansen to speak more freely than he has done hitherto.

This was all, together with the picture of the hellish image; but what a train of ideas it started in my mind! Here were new treasuries of data on the Cthulhu Cult, and evidence that it had strange interests at sea as well as on land. What motive prompted the hybrid crew to order back the *Emma* as they sailed about with their hideous idol? What was the unknown island on which six of the *Emma*'s crew had died, and about which the mate Johansen was so secretive? What had the vice-admiralty's investigation brought out, and what was known of the noxious cult in Dunedin? And most marvellous of all, what deep and more than natural linkage of dates was this which gave a malign and now undeniable significance to the various turns of events so carefully noted by my uncle?

March 1st—our February 28th according to the International Date Line—the earthquake and storm had come. From Dunedin the *Alert* and her noisome crew had darted eagerly forth as if imperiously summoned, and on the other side of the earth poets and artists had begun to dream of a strange, dank Cyclopean city whilst a young sculptor had moulded in his sleep the form of the dreaded Cthulhu. March 23d the crew of the *Emma* landed on an unknown island and left six men dead; and on that date the dreams of sensitive men assumed a heightened vividness and darkened with dread of a giant monster's malign pursuit, whilst an architect had gone mad and a sculptor had lapsed suddenly into delirium! And what of this storm of April 2nd—the date on which all dreams of the dank city ceased, and Wilcox emerged unharmed from the bondage of strange fever? What of all this— and of those hints of old Castro about the sunken, star-born Old Ones and their coming reign; their faithful cult *and their mastery of dreams?* Was I tottering on the brink of cosmic horrors beyond man's power to bear? If so, they must be horrors of the mind alone, for in some way the second of April had put a stop to whatever monstrous menace had begun its siege of mankind's soul.

That evening, after a day of hurried cabling and arranging, I bade my host adieu and took a train for San Francisco. In less than a month I was in Dunedin; where, however, I found that little was known of the strange cult-members who had lingered in the old sea-taverns. Waterfront scum was far too common for special mention; though there was vague talk about one inland trip these mongrels had made, during which faint drumming and red flame were noted on the distant hills. In Auckland I learned that Johansen had returned *with yellow hair turned white* after a perfunctory and inconclu-sive questioning at Sydney, and had thereafter sold his cottage in West Street and sailed with his wife to his old home in Oslo. Of his stirring experience he would tell his friends no more than he had told the admiralty officials, and all they could do was to give me his Oslo address.

After that I went to Sydney and talked profitlessly with seamen and members of the vice-admiralty court. I saw the *Alert,* now sold and in commercial use, at Circular Quay in Sydney Cove, but gained nothing from its non-committal bulk. The crouching image with its cuttlefish head, dragon body, scaly wings, and hieroglyphed pedestal, was preserved in the Museum at Hyde Park; and I studied it long and well, finding it a thing of balefully exquisite workmanship, and with the same utter mystery, terrible antiquity, and unearthly strangeness of material which I had noted in Legrasse's smaller specimen. Geologists, the curator told me, had found it a monstrous puzzle; for they vowed that the world held no rock like it. Then I thought with a shudder of what old Castro had told Legrasse about the primal Great Ones: "They had come from the stars, and had brought Their images with Them."

Shaken with such a mental revolution as I had never before known, I now resolved to visit Mate Johansen in Oslo. Sailing for London, I reëmbarked at once for the Norwegian capital; and one autumn day landed at the trim wharves in the shadow of the Egeberg. Johansen's address, I discovered, lay in the Old Town of King Harold Haardrada, which kept alive the name of Oslo during all the centuries that the greater city masqueraded as "Christiana." I made the brief trip by taxicab, and knocked with palpitant heart at the door of a neat and ancient building with plastered front. A sad-faced woman in black answered my summons, and I was stung with disappointment when she told me in halting English that Gustaf Johansen was no more.

He had not long survived his return, said his wife, for the doings at sea in 1925 had broken him. He had told her no more than he had told the public, but had left a long manuscript—of "technical matters" as he said—written in English, evidently in order to safeguard her from the peril of casual perusal. During a walk through a narrow lane near the Gothenburg dock, a bundle of papers falling from an attic window had knocked him down. Two Lascar sailors at once helped him to his feet, but before the ambulance could reach him he was dead. Physicians found no adequate cause for the end, and laid it to heart trouble and a weakened constitution.

I now felt gnawing at my vitals that dark terror which will never leave me till I, too, am at rest; "accidentally" or otherwise. Persuading the widow that my connexion with her husband's "technical matters" was sufficient to entitle me to his manuscript, I bore the document away and began to read it on the London boat. It was a simple, rambling thing—a naive sailor's effort at a post-facto diary—and strove to recall day by day that last awful voyage. I cannot attempt to transcribe it verbatim in all its cloudiness and redundance, but I will tell its gist enough to shew why the sound of the water against the vessel's sides became so unendurable to me that I stopped my ears with cotton.

Johansen, thank God, did not know quite all, even though he saw the city and the Thing, but I shall never sleep calmly again when I think of the horrors that lurk ceaselessly behind life in time and in space, and of those unhallowed blasphemies from elder stars which dream beneath the sea, known and favoured by a nightmare cult ready and eager to loose them on the world whenever another earthquake shall heave their monstrous stone city again to the sun and air.

Johansen's voyage had begun just as he told it to the vice-admiralty. The *Emma,* in ballast, had cleared Auckland on February 20th, and had felt the full force of that earthquake-born tempest which must have heaved up from the sea-bottom the horrors that filled men's dreams. Once more under control, the ship was making good progress when held up by the *Alert* on March 22nd, and I could feel the mate's regret as he wrote of her bombardment and sinking. Of the swarthy cult-fiends on the *Alert* he speaks with significant horror. There was some peculiarly abominable quality about them which made their destruction seem almost a duty, and Johansen shews ingenuous wonder at the charge of ruthlessness brought against his party during the proceedings of the court of inquiry. Then, driven ahead by curiosity in their captured yacht under Johansen's command, the men sight a great stone pillar sticking out of the sea, and in S. Latitude 47° 9', W. Longitude 126° 43' come upon a coast-line of mingled mud, ooze, and weedy Cyclopean masonry which can be nothing less than the tangible substance of earth's supreme terror—the nightmare corpse-city of R'lyeh, that was built in measureless aeons behind history by the vast, loathsome shapes that seeped down from the dark stars. There lay great Cthulhu and his hordes, hidden in green slimy vaults and sending out at last, after cycles incalculable, the thoughts that spread fear to the dreams of the sensitive and called imperiously to the faithful to come on a pilgrimage of liberation and restoration. All this Johansen did not suspect, but God knows he soon saw enough!

I suppose that only a single mountain-top, the hideous monolith-crowned citadel whereon great Cthulhu was buried, actually emerged from the waters. When I think of the *extent* of all that may be brooding down there I almost wish to kill myself forthwith. Johansen and his men were awed by the cosmic majesty of this dripping Babylon of elder daemons, and must have guessed without guidance that it was nothing of this or of any sane planet. Awe at the unbelievable size of the greenish stone blocks, at the dizzying height of the great carven monolith, and at the stupefying identity of the colossal statues and bas-reliefs with the queer image found in the shrine on the *Alert,* is poignantly visible in every line of the mate's frightened description.

Without knowing what futurism is like, Johansen achieved something very close to it when he spoke of the city; for instead of describing any definite structure or building, he dwells only on broad impressions of vast angles and stone surfaces—surfaces too great to belong to any thing right or proper for this earth, and impious with horrible images and hieroglyphs. I mention his talk about *angles* because it suggests something Wilcox had told me of his awful dreams. He had said that the *geometry* of the dream-place he saw was abnormal, non-Euclidean, and loathsomely redolent of spheres and dimensions apart from ours. Now an unlettered seaman felt the same thing whilst gazing at the terrible reality.

Johansen and his men landed at a sloping mud-bank on this monstrous Acropolis, and clambered slipperily up over titan oozy blocks which could have been no mortal staircase. The very sun of heaven seemed distorted when viewed through the polarising miasma welling out from this sea-soaked perversion, and twisted menace and suspense lurked leeringly in those crazily elusive angles of carven rock where a second glance shewed concavity after the first shewed convexity.

Something very like fright had come over all the explorers before anything more definite than rock and ooze and weed was seen. Each would have fled had he not feared the scorn of the others, and it was only half-heartedly that they searched—vainly, as it proved—for some portable souvenir to bear away.

It was Rodriguez the Portuguese who climbed up the foot of the monolith and shouted of what he had found. The rest followed him, and looked curiously at the immense carved door with the now familiar squid-dragon bas-relief. It was, Johansen said, like a great barn-door; and they all felt that it was a door because of the ornate lintel, threshold, and jambs around it, though they could not decide whether it lay flat like a trap-door or slantwise like an outside cellar-door. As Wilcox would have said, the geometry of the place was all wrong. One could not be sure that the sea and the ground were horizontal, hence the relative position of everything else seemed phantasmally variable.

Briden pushed at the stone in several places without result. Then Donovan felt over it delicately around the edge, pressing each point separately as he went. He climbed interminably along the grotesque stone moulding—that is, one would call it climbing if the thing was not after all horizontal—and the men wondered how any door in the universe could be so vast. Then, very softly and slowly, the acre-great panel began to give inward at the top; and they saw that it was balanced. Donovan slid or somehow propelled himself down or along the jamb and rejoined his fellows, and everyone watched the queer recession of the monstrously carven portal. In this phantasy of prismatic distortion it moved anomalously in a diagonal way, so that all the rules of matter and perspective seemed upset.

The aperture was black with a darkness almost material. That tenebrousness was indeed a *positive quality;* for it obscured such parts of the inner walls as ought to have been revealed, and actually burst forth like smoke from its aeon-long imprisonment, visibly darkening the sun as it slunk away into the shrunken and gibbous sky on flapping membraneous wings. The odour arising from the newly opened depths was intolerable, and at length the quick-eared Hawkins thought he heard a nasty, slopping sound down there. Everyone listened, and everyone was listening still when It lumbered slobberingly into sight and gropingly squeezed Its gelatinous green immensity through the black doorway into the tainted outside air of that poison city of madness.

Poor Johansen's handwriting almost gave out when he wrote of this. Of the six men who never reached the ship, he thinks two perished of pure fright in that accursed instant. The Thing cannot be described—there is no language for such abysms of shrieking and immemorial lunacy, such eldritch contradictions of all matter, force, and cosmic order. A mountain walked or stumbled. God! What wonder that across the earth a great architect went mad, and poor Wilcox raved with fever in that telepathic instant? The Thing of the idols, the green, sticky spawn of the stars, had awaked to claim his own. The stars were right again, and what an age-old cult had failed to do by design, a band of innocent sailors had done by accident. After vigintillions of years great Cthulhu was loose again, and ravening for delight.

Three men were swept up by the flabby claws before anybody turned. God rest them, if there be any rest in the universe. They were Donovan, Guerrera, and Ångstrom. Parker slipped as the other three were plunging frenziedly over endless vistas of green-crusted rock to the boat, and Johansen swears he was swallowed up by an angle of masonry which shouldn't have been there; an angle which was acute, but behaved as if it were obtuse. So only Briden and Johansen reached the boat, and pulled desperately for the *Alert* as the mountainous monstrosity flopped down the slimy stones and hesitated floundering at the edge of the water.

Steam had not been suffered to go down entirely, despite the departure of all hands for the shore; and it was the work of only a few moments of feverish rushing up and down between wheel and engines to get the *Alert* under way. Slowly, amidst the distorted horrors of that indescribable scene, she began to churn the lethal waters; whilst on the masonry of that charnel shore that was not of earth the titan Thing from the stars slavered and gibbered like Polypheme cursing the fleeing ship of Odysseus. Then, bolder than the storied Cyclops, great Cthulhu slid greasily into the water and began to pursue with vast wave-raising strokes of cosmic potency. Briden looked back and went mad, laughing shrilly as he kept on laughing at intervals till death found him one night in the cabin whilst Johansen was wandering deliriously.

But Johansen had not given out yet. Knowing that the Thing could surely overtake the *Alert* until steam was fully up, he resolved on a desperate chance; and, setting the engine for full speed, ran lightning-like on deck and reversed the wheel. There was a mighty eddying and foaming in the noisome brine, and as the steam mounted higher and higher the brave Norwegian drove his vessel head on against the pursuing jelly which rose above the unclean froth like the stern of a daemon galleon. The awful squid-head with writhing feelers came nearly up to the bowsprit of the sturdy yacht, but Johansen drove on relentlessly. There was a bursting as of an exploding bladder, a slushy nastiness as of a cloven sunfish, a stench as of a thousand opened graves, and a sound that the chronicler would not put on paper. For an instant the ship was befouled by an acrid and blinding green cloud, and then there was only a venomous seething astern; where—God in heaven!— the scattered plasticity of that nameless sky-spawn was nebulously *recombining* in its hateful original form, whilst its distance widened every second as the *Alert* gained impetus from its mounting steam.

That was all. After that Johansen only brooded over the idol in the cabin and attended to a few matters of food for himself and the laughing maniac by his side. He did not try to navigate after the first bold flight, for the reaction had taken something out of his soul. Then came the storm of April 2nd, and a gathering of the clouds about his consciousness. There is a sense of spectral whirling through liquid gulfs of infinity, of dizzying rides through reeling universes on a comet's tail, and of hysterical plunges from the pit to the moon and from the moon back again to the pit, all livened by a cachinnating chorus of the distorted, hilarious elder gods and the green, bat-winged mocking imps of Tartarus.

Out of that dream came rescue—the *Vigilant,* the vice-admiralty court, the streets of Dunedin, and the long voyage back home to the old house by the Egeberg. He could not tell—they would think him mad. He would write of what he knew before death came, but his wife must not guess. Death would be a boon if only it could blot out the memories.

That was the document I read, and now I have placed it in the tin box beside the bas-relief and the papers of Professor Angell. With it shall go this record of mine—this test of my own sanity, wherein is pieced together that which I hope may never be pieced together again. I have looked upon all that the universe has to hold of horror, and even the skies of spring and the flowers of summer must ever afterward be poison to me. But I do not think my life will be long. As my uncle went, as poor Johansen went, so I shall go. I know too much, and the cult still lives.

Cthulhu still lives, too, I suppose, again in that chasm of stone which has shielded him since the sun was young. His accursed city is sunken once more, for the *Vigilant* sailed over the spot after the April storm; but his ministers on earth still bellow and prance and slay around idol-capped monoliths in lonely places. He must have been trapped by the sinking whilst within his black abyss, or else the world would by now be screaming with fright and frenzy. Who knows the end? What has risen may sink, and what has sunk may rise. Loathsomeness waits and dreams in the deep, and decay spreads over the tottering cities of men. A time will come—but I must not and cannot think! Let me pray that, if I do not survive this manuscript, my executors may put caution before audacity and see that it meets no other eye.

Shirley Jackson

The Summer People

A significant portion of the major work of Shirley Jackson is horror fiction. Aside from her novels, *The Sundial, The Haunting of Hill House* and the National Book Award winner, *We Have Always Lived in the Castle*, much of her short fiction is particularly fine horror. She chose to work often in the specialized area of the house story, of which *The Haunting of Hill House* is perhaps the most perfect example yet written. She told me in conversation in 1962 that she had a complete run of *Unknown* magazine. "It's the best," she said. Her influence on horror in the novel form continues to grow in the two decades since her death. Stephen King, in *Danse Macabre*, featured *The Haunting of Hill House* as one of his ten best since World War II. "The Summer People" is another of Jackson's house stories. Mr. and Mrs. Allison have broken a rule and will be punished. This tale is an interesting comparison to Lucy Clifford's "The New Mother." Here, however, the irony is overt, since we have the form of the moral tale without the morality at all.

The Allisons' country cottage, seven miles from the nearest town, was set prettily on a hill; from three sides it looked down on soft trees and grass that seldom, even at midsummer, lay still and dry. On the fourth side was the lake, which touched against the wooden pier the Allisons had to keep repairing, and which looked equally well from the Allisons' front porch, their side porch or any spot on the wooden staircase leading from the porch down to the water. Although the Allisons loved their summer cottage, looked forward to arriving in the early summer and hated to leave in the fall, they had not troubled themselves to put in any improvements, regarding the cottage itself and the lake as improvement enough for the life left to them. The cottage had no heat, no running water except the precarious supply from the backyard pump and no electricity. For seventeen summers, Janet Allison had cooked on a kerosene stove, heating all their water; Robert Allison had brought buckets full of water daily from the pump and read his paper by kerosene light in the evenings and they had both, sanitary city people, become stolid and matter-of-fact about their back house. In the first two years they had gone through all the standard vaudeville and magazine jokes about backhouses and by now, when they no longer had frequent guests to impress, they had subsided to a comfortable security which made the backhouse, as well as the pump and the kerosene, an indefinable asset to their summer life.

In themselves, the Allisons were ordinary people. Mrs. Allison was fifty-eight years old and Mr. Allison sixty; they had seen their children outgrow the summer cottage and go on to families of their own and seashore resorts; their friends were either dead or settled in comfortable year-round houses, their nieces and nephews vague. In the winter they told one another they could stand their New York apartment while waiting for the summer; in the summer they told one another that the winter was well worth while, waiting to get to the country.

Since they were old enough not to be ashamed of regular habits, the Allisons invariably left their summer cottage the Tuesday after Labor Day, and were as invariably sorry when the months of September and early October turned out to be pleasant and almost insufferably barren in the city; each year they recognized that there was nothing to bring them back to New York, but it was not until this year that they overcame their traditional inertia enough to decide to stay at the cottage after Labor Day.

"There isn't really anything to take us back to the city," Mrs. Allison told her husband seriously, as though it were a new idea, and he told her, as though neither of them had ever considered it, "We might as well enjoy the country as long as possible."

Consequently, with much pleasure and a slight feeling of adventure, Mrs. Allison went into their village the day after Labor Day and told those natives with whom she had dealings, with a pretty air of breaking away from tradition, that she and her husband had decided to stay at least a month longer at their cottage.

"It isn't as though we had anything to take us back to the city," she said to Mr. Babcock, her grocer. "We might as well enjoy the country while we can."

"Nobody ever stayed at the lake past Labor Day before," Mr. Babcock said. He was putting Mrs. Allison's groceries into a large cardboard carton, and he stopped for a minute to look reflectively into a bag of cookies. "Nobody," he added.

"But the city!" Mrs. Allison always spoke of the city to Mr. Babcock as though it were Mr. Babcock's dream to go there. "It's so hot—you've really no idea. We're always sorry when we leave."

"Hate to leave," Mr. Babcock said. One of the most irritating native tricks Mrs. Allison had noticed was that of taking a trivial statement and rephrasing it downwards, into an even more trite statement. "I'd hate to leave myself," Mr. Babcock said, after deliberation, and both he and Mrs. Allison smiled. "But I never heard of anyone ever staying out at the lake after Labor Day before."

"Well, we're going to give it a try," Mrs. Allison said, and Mr. Babcock replied gravely, "Never know till you try."

Physically, Mrs. Allison decided, as she always did when leaving the grocery after one of her inconclusive conversations with Mr. Babcock, physically, Mr. Babcock could model for a statue of Daniel Webster, but mentally . . . it was horrible to think into what old New England Yankee stock had degenerated. She said as much to Mr. Allison when she got into the car, and he said, "It's generations of inbreeding. That and the bad land."

Since this was their big trip into town, which they made only once every two weeks to buy things they could not have delivered, they spent all day at it, stopping to have a sandwich in the newspaper and soda shop, and leaving packages heaped in the back of the car. Although Mrs. Allison was able to order groceries delivered regularly, she was never able to form any accurate idea of Mr. Babcock's current stock by telephone, and her lists of odds and ends that might be procured was always supplemented, almost beyond their need, by the new and fresh local vegetables Mr. Babcock was selling temporarily, or the packaged candy which had just come in. This trip Mrs. Allison was tempted, too, by the set of glass baking dishes that had found themselves completely by chance in the hardware and clothing and general store, and which had seemingly been waiting there for no one but Mrs. Allison, since the country people, with their instinctive distrust of anything that did not look as permanent as trees and rocks and sky, had only recently begun to experiment in aluminum baking dishes instead of ironware, and had, apparently within the memory of local inhabitants, discarded stoneware in favor of iron.

Mrs. Allison had the glass baking dishes carefully wrapped, to endure the uncomfortable ride home over the rocky road that led up to the Allisons' cottage, and while Mr. Charley Walpole, who, with his younger brother Albert, ran the hardware-clothing-general store (the store itself was called Johnson's, because it stood on the site of the old Johnson cabin, burned fifty years before Charley Walpole was born), laboriously unfolded newspapers to wrap around the dishes, Mrs. Allison said, informally, "Course, I *could* have waited and gotten those dishes in New York, but we're not going back so soon this year."

"Heard you was staying on," Mr. Charley Walpole said. His old fingers fumbled maddeningly with the thin sheets of newspaper, carefully trying to isolate only one sheet at a time, and he did not look up at Mrs. Allison as he went on, "Don't know about staying on up there to the lake. Not after Labor Day."

"Well, you know," Mrs. Allison said, quite as though he deserved an explanation, "it just seemed to us that we've been hurrying back to New York every year, and there just wasn't any need for it. You know what the city's like in the fall." And she smiled confidingly up at Mr. Charley Walpole.

Rhythmically he wound string around the package. He's giving me a piece long enough to save, Mrs. Allison thought, and she looked away quickly to avoid giving any sign of impatience. "I feel sort of like we belong here, more," she said. "Staying on after everyone else has left." To prove this, she smiled brightly across the store at a woman with a familiar face, who might have been the woman who sold berries to the Allisons one year, or the woman who occasionally helped in the grocery and was probably Mr. Babcock's aunt.

"Well," Mr. Charley Walpole said. He shoved the package a little across the counter, to show that it was finished and that for a sale well made, a package well wrapped, he was willing to accept pay. "Well," he said again. "Never been summer people before, at the lake after Labor Day."

Mrs. Allison gave him a five-dollar bill, and he made change methodically, giving great weight even to the pennies. "Never after Labor Day," he said, and nodded at Mrs. Allison, and went soberly along the store to deal with two women who were looking at cotton house dresses.

As Mrs. Allison passed on her way out she heard one of the women say acutely, "Why is one of them dresses one dollar and thirty-nine cents and this one here is only ninety-eight?"

"They're great people," Mrs. Allison told her husband as they went together down the sidewalk after meeting at the door of the hardware store. "They're so solid, and so reasonable, and so *honest*."

"Makes you feel good, knowing there are still towns like this," Mr. Allison said.

"You know, in New York," Mrs. Allison said, "I might have paid a few cents less for these dishes, but there wouldn't have been anything sort of *personal* in the transaction."

"Staying on to the lake?" Mrs. Martin, in the newspaper and sandwich shop, asked the Allisons. "Heard you was staying on."

"Thought we'd take advantage of the lovely weather this year," Mr. Allison said.

Mrs. Martin was a comparative newcomer to the town; she had married into the newspaper and sandwich shop from a neighboring farm, and had stayed on after her husband's death. She served bottled soft drinks, and fried egg and onion sandwiches on thick bread, which she made on her own stove at the back of the store. Occasionally when Mrs. Martin served a sandwich it would carry with it the rich fragrance of the stew or the pork chops cooking alongside for Mrs. Martin's dinner.

"I don't guess anyone's ever stayed out there so long before," Mrs. Martin said. "Not after Labor Day, anyway."

"I guess Labor Day is when they usually leave," Mr. Hall, the Allisons' nearest neighbor, told them later, in front of Mr. Babcock's store, where the Allisons were getting into their car to go home. "Surprised you're staying on."

"It seemed a shame to go so soon," Mrs. Allison said. Mr. Hall lived three miles away; he supplied the Allisons with butter and eggs, and occasionally, from the top of their hill, the Allisons could see the lights in his house in the early evening before the Halls went to bed.

"They usually leave Labor Day," Mr. Hall said.

The ride home was long and rough; it was beginning to get dark, and Mr. Allison had to drive very carefully over the dirt road by the lake. Mrs. Allison lay back against the seat, pleasantly relaxed after a day of what seemed whirlwind shopping compared with their day-to-day existence; the new glass baking dishes lurked agreeably in her mind, and the half bushel of red eating apples, and the package of colored thumbtacks with which she was going to put up new shelf edging in the kitchen. "Good to get home," she said softly as they came in sight of their cottage, silhouetted above them against the sky.

"Glad we decided to stay on," Mr. Allison agreed.

Mrs. Allison spent the next morning lovingly washing her baking dishes, although in his innocence Charley Walpole had neglected to notice the chip in the edge of one; she decided, wastefully, to use some of the red eating apples in a pie for dinner, and, while the pie was in the oven and Mr. Allison was down getting the mail, she sat out on the little lawn the Allisons had made at the top of the hill, and watched the changing lights on the lake, alternating gray and blue as clouds moved quickly across the sun.

Mr. Allison came back a little out of sorts; it always irritated him to walk the mile to the mail box on the state road and come back with nothing, even though he assumed that the walk was good for his health. This morning there was nothing but a circular from a New York department store, and their New York paper, which arrived erratically by mail from one to four days later than it should, so that some days the Allisons might have three papers and frequently none. Mrs. Allison, although she shared with her husband the annoyance of not having mail when they so anticipated it, pored affectionately over the department store circular, and made a mental note to drop in at the store when she finally went back to New York, and check on the sale of wool blankets; it was hard to find good ones in pretty colors nowadays. She debated saving the circular to remind herself, but after thinking about getting up and getting into the cottage to put it away safely somewhere, she dropped it into the grass beside her chair and lay back, her eyes half closed.

"Looks like we might have some rain," Mr. Allison said, squinting at the sky.

"Good for the crops," Mrs. Allison said laconically, and they both laughed.

The kerosene man came the next morning while Mr. Allison was down getting the mail; they were getting low on kerosene and Mrs. Allison greeted the man warmly; he sold kerosene and ice, and, during the summer, hauled garbage away for the summer people. A garbage man was only necessary for improvident city folk; country people had no garbage.

"I'm glad to see you," Mrs. Allison told him. "We were getting pretty low."

The kerosene man, whose name Mrs. Allison had never learned, used a hose attachment to fill the twenty-gallon tank which supplied light and heat and cooking facilities for the Allisons; but today, instead of swinging down from his truck and unhooking the hose from where it coiled affectionately around the cab of the truck, the man stared uncomfortably at Mrs. Allison, his truck motor still going.

"Thought you folks'd be leaving," he said.

"We're staying on another month," Mrs. Allison said brightly. "The weather was so nice, and it seemed like—"

"That's what they told me," the man said. "Can't give you no oil, though."

"What do you mean?" Mrs. Allison raised her eyebrows. "We're just going to keep on with our regular—"

"After Labor Day," the man said. "I don't get so much oil myself after Labor Day."

Mrs. Allison reminded herself, as she had frequently to do when in disagreement with her neighbors, that city manners were no good with country people; you could not expect to overrule a country employee as you could a city worker, and Mrs. Allison smiled engagingly as she said, "But can't you get extra oil, at least while we stay?"

"You see," the man said. He tapped his finger exasperatingly against the car wheel as he spoke. "You see," he said slowly, "I order this oil. I order it down from maybe fifty, fifty-five miles away. I order back in June, how much I'll need for the summer. Then I order again . . . oh, about November. Round about now it's starting to get pretty short." As though the subject were closed, he stopped tapping his finger and tightened his hands on the wheel in preparation for departure.

"But can't you give us *some*?" Mrs. Allison said. "Isn't there anyone else?"

"Don't know as you could get oil anywheres else right now," the man said consideringly. "*I* can't give you none." Before Mrs. Allison could speak, the truck began to move; then it stopped for a minute and he looked at her through the back window of the cab. "Ice?" he called. "I could let you have some ice."

Mrs. Allison shook her head; they were not terribly low on ice, and she was angry. She ran a few steps to catch up with the truck, calling, "Will you try to get us some? Next week?"

"Don't see's I can," the man said. "After Labor Day, it's harder." The truck drove away, and Mrs. Allison, only comforted by the thought that she could probably get kerosene from Mr. Babcock or, at worst, the Halls, watched it go with anger. "Next summer," she told herself, "just let *him* trying coming around next summer!"

There was no mail again, only the paper, which seemed to be coming doggedly on time, and Mr. Allison was openly cross when he returned. When Mrs. Allison told him about the kerosene man he was not particularly impressed.

"Probably keeping it all for a high price during the winter," he commented. "What's happened to Anne and Jerry, do you think?"

Anne and Jerry were their son and daughter, both married, one living in Chicago, one in the far west; their dutiful weekly letters were late; so late, in fact, that Mr. Allison's annoyance at the lack of mail was able to settle on a legitimate grievance. "Ought to realize how we wait for their letters," he said. "Thoughtless, selfish children. Ought to know better."

"Well, dear," Mrs. Allison said placatingly. Anger at Anne and Jerry would not relieve her emotions toward the kerosene man. After a few minutes she said, "Wishing won't bring the mail, dear. I'm going to go call Mr. Babcock and tell him to send up some kerosene with my order."

"At least a postcard," Mr. Allison said as she left.

As with most of the cottage's inconveniences, the Allisons no longer noticed the phone particularly, but yielded to its eccentricities without conscious complaint. It was a wall phone, of a type still seen in only few communities; in order to get the operator, Mrs. Allison had first to turn the side-crank and ring once. Usually it took two or three tries to force the operator to answer, and Mrs. Allison, making any kind of telephone call, approached the phone with resignation and a sort of desperate patience. She had to crank the phone three times this morning before the operator answered, and then it was still longer before Mr. Babcock picked up the receiver at his phone in the corner of the grocery behind the meat table. He said "Store?" with the rising inflection that seemed to indicate suspicion of anyone who tried to communicate with him by means of this unreliable instrument.

"This is Mrs. Allison, Mr. Babcock. I thought I'd give you my order a day early because I wanted to be sure and get some—"

"What say, Mrs. Allison?"

Mrs. Allison raised her voice a little; she saw Mr. Allison, out on the lawn, turn in his chair and regard her sympathetically. "I said, Mr. Babcock, I thought I'd call in my order early so you could send me—"

"Mrs. Allison?" Mr. Babcock said. "You'll come and pick it up?"

"Pick it up?" In her surprise Mrs. Allison let her voice drop back to its normal tone and Mr. Babcock said loudly, "What's that, Mrs. Allison?"

"I thought I'd have you send it out as usual," Mrs. Allison said.

"Well, Mrs. Allison," Mr. Babcock said, and there was a pause while Mrs. Allison waited, staring past the phone over her husband's head out into the sky. "Mrs. Allison," Mr. Babcock went on finally, "I'll tell you, my boy's been working for me went back to school yesterday, and now I got no one to deliver. I only got a boy delivering summers, you see."

"I thought you *always* delivered," Mrs. Allison said.

"Not after Labor Day, Mrs. Allison," Mr. Babcock said firmly, "you never been here after Labor Day before, so's you wouldn't know, of course."

"Well," Mrs. Allison said helplessly. Far inside her mind she was saying, over and over, can't use city manners on country folk, no use getting mad.

"Are you *sure*?" she asked finally. "Couldn't you just send out an order today, Mr. Babcock?"

"Matter of fact," Mr. Babcock said, "I guess I couldn't, Mrs. Allison. It wouldn't hardly pay, delivering, with no one else out at the lake."

"What about Mr. Hall?" Mrs. Allison asked suddenly, "the people who live about three miles away from us out here? Mr. Hall could bring it out when he comes."

"Hall?" Mr. Babcock said. "John Hall? They've gone to visit her folks upstate, Mrs. Allison."

"But they bring all our butter and eggs," Mrs. Allison said, appalled.

"Left yesterday," Mr. Babcock said. "Probably didn't think you folks would stay on up there."

"But I told Mr. Hall . . ." Mrs. Allison started to say, and then stopped. "I'll send Mr. Allison in after some groceries tomorrow," she said.

"You got all you need till then," Mr. Babcock said, satisfied; it was not a question, but a confirmation.

After she hung up, Mrs. Allison went slowly out to sit again in her chair next to her husband. "He won't deliver," she said. "You'll have to go in tomorrow. We've got just enough kerosene to last till you get back."

"He should have told us sooner," Mr. Allison said.

It was not possible to remain troubled long in the face of the day; the country had never seemed more inviting, and the lake moved quietly below them, among the trees, with the almost incredible softness of a summer picture. Mrs. Allison sighed deeply, in the pleasure of possessing for themselves that sight of the lake, with the distant green hills beyond, the gentleness of the small wind through the trees.

The weather continued fair; the next morning Mr. Allison, duly armed with a list of groceries, with "kerosene" in large letters at the top, went down the path to the garage, and Mrs. Allison began another pie in her new baking dishes. She had mixed the crust and was starting to pare the apples when Mr. Allison came rapidly up the path and flung open the screen door into the kitchen.

"Damn car won't start," he announced, with the end-of-the-tether voice of a man who depends on a car as he depends on his right arm.

"What's wrong with it?" Mrs. Allison demanded, stopping with the paring knife in one hand and an apple in the other. "It was all right on Tuesday."

"Well," Mr. Allison said between his teeth, "it's not all right on Friday."

"Can you fix it?" Mrs. Allison asked.

"No," Mr. Allison said, "I can not. Got to call someone, I guess."

"Who?" Mrs. Allison asked.

"Man runs the filling station, I guess." Mr. Allison moved purposefully toward the phone. "He fixed it last summer one time."

A little apprehensive, Mrs. Allison went on paring apples absentmindedly, while she listened to Mr. Allison with the phone, ringing, waiting, ringing, waiting, finally giving the number to the operator, then waiting again and giving the number again, giving the number a third time, and then slamming down the receiver.

"No one there," he announced as he came into the kitchen.

"He's probably gone out for a minute," Mrs. Allison said nervously; she was not quite sure what made her so nervous, unless it was the probability of her husband's losing his temper completely. "He's there alone, I imagine, so if he goes out there's no one to answer the phone."

"That must be it," Mr. Allison said with heavy irony. He slumped into one of the kitchen chairs and watched Mrs. Allison paring apples. After a minute, Mrs. Allison said soothingly, "Why don't you go down and get the mail and then call him again?"

Mr. Allison debated and then said, "Guess I might as well." He rose heavily and when he got to the kitchen door he turned and said, "But if there's no mail—" and leaving an awful silence behind him, he went off down the path.

Mrs. Allison hurried with her pie. Twice she went to the window to glance at the sky to see if there were clouds coming up. The room seemed unexpectedly dark, and she herself felt in the state of tension that precedes a thunderstorm, but both times when she looked the sky was clear and serene, smiling indifferently down on the Allisons' summer cottage as well as on the rest of the world. When Mrs. Allison, her pie ready for the oven, went a third time to look outside, she saw her husband coming up the path; he seemed more cheerful, and when he saw her, he waved eagerly and held a letter in the air.

"From Jerry," he called as soon as he was close enough for her to hear him, "at last—a letter!" Mrs. Allison noticed with concern that he was no longer able to get up the gentle slope of the path without breathing heavily; but then he was in the doorway, holding out the letter. "I saved it till I got here," he said.

Mrs. Allison looked with an eagerness that surprised her on the familiar handwriting of her son; she could not imagine why the letter excited her so, except that it was the first they had received in so long; it would be a pleasant, dutiful letter, full of the doings of Alice and the children, reporting progress with his job, commenting on the recent weather in Chicago, closing with love from all; both Mr. and Mrs. Allison could, if they wished, recite a pattern letter from either of their children.

Mr. Allison slit the letter open with great deliberation, and then he spread it out on the kitchen table and they leaned down and read it together.

"*Dear Mother and Dad*," it began, in Jerry's familiar, rather childish, handwriting, "*Am glad this goes to the lake as usual, we always thought you came back too soon and ought to stay up there as long as you could. Alice says that now that you're not as young as you used to be and have no demands on your time, fewer friends, etc., in the city, you ought to get what fun you can while you can. Since you two are both happy up there, it's a good idea for you to stay.*"

Uneasily Mrs. Allison glanced sideways at her husband; he was reading intently, and she reached out and picked up the empty envelope, not knowing exactly what she wanted from it. It was addressed quite as usual, in Jerry's handwriting, and was postmarked Chicago. Of course it's postmarked Chicago, she thought quickly, why would they want to postmark it anywhere else? When she looked back down at the letter, her husband had turned the page, and she read on with him: "*—and of course if they get measles, etc., now, they will be better off later. Alice is well, of course, me too. Been playing a lot of bridge lately with some people you don't know, named Carruthers. Nice young couple, about our age. Well, will close now as I guess it bores you to hear about things so far away. Tell Dad old Dickson, in our Chicago office, died. He used to ask about Dad a lot. Have a good time up at the lake, and don't bother about hurrying back. Love from all of us, Jerry.*"

"Funny," Mr. Allison commented.

"It doesn't sound like Jerry," Mrs. Allison said in a small voice. "He never wrote anything like . . ." she stopped.

"Like what?" Mr. Allison demanded. "Never wrote anything like what?"

Mrs. Allison turned the letter over, frowning. It was impossible to find any sentence, any word, even, that did not sound like Jerry's regular letters. Perhaps it was only that the letter was so late, or the unusual number of dirty fingerprints on the envelope.

"I don't *know*," she said impatiently.

"Going to try that phone call again," Mr. Allison said.

Mrs. Allison read the letter twice more, trying to find a phrase that sounded wrong. Then Mr. Allison came back and said, very quietly, "Phone's dead."

"What?" Mrs. Allison said, dropping the letter.

"Phone's dead," Mr. Allison said.

The rest of the day went quickly; after a lunch of crackers and milk, the Allisons went to sit outside on the lawn, but their afternoon was cut short by the gradually increasing storm clouds that came up over the lake to the cottage, so that it was as dark as evening by four o'clock. The storm delayed, however, as though in loving anticipation of the moment it would break over the summer cottage, and there was an occasional flash of lightning, but no rain. In the evening Mr. and Mrs. Allison, sitting close together inside their cottage, turned on the battery radio they had brought with them from New York. There were no lamps lighted in the cottage, and the only light came from the lightning outside and the small square glow from the dial of the radio.

The slight framework of the cottage was not strong enough to withstand the city noises, the music and the voices, from the radio, and the Allisons could hear them far off echoing across the lake, the saxophones in the New York dance band wailing over the water, the flat voice of the girl vocalist going inexorably out into the clean country air. Even the announcer, speaking glowingly of the virtues of razor blades, was no more than an inhuman voice sounding out from the Allisons' cottage and echoing back, as though the lake and the hills and the trees were returning it unwanted.

During one pause between commercials, Mrs. Allison turned and smiled weakly at her husband. "I wonder if we're supposed to . . . *do* anything," she said.

"No," Mr. Allison said consideringly. "I don't think so. Just wait."

Mrs. Allison caught her breath quickly, and Mr. Allison said, under the trivial melody of the dance band beginning again, "The car had been tampered with, you know. Even I could see that."

Mrs. Allison hesitated a minute and then said very softly, "I suppose the phone wires were cut."

"I imagine so," Mr. Allison said.

After a while, the dance music stopped and they listened attentively to a news broadcast, the announcer's rich voice telling them breathlessly of a marriage in Hollywood, the latest baseball scores, the estimated rise in food prices during the coming week. He spoke to them, in the summer cottage, quite as though they still deserved to hear news of a world that no longer reached them except through the fallible batteries on the radio, which were already beginning to fade, almost as though they still belonged, however tenuously, to the rest of the world.

Mrs. Allison glanced out the window at the smooth surface of the lake, the black masses of the trees, and the waiting storm, and said conversationally, "I feel better about that letter of Jerry's."

"I knew when I saw the light down at the Hall place last night," Mr. Allison said.

The wind, coming up suddenly over the lake, swept around the summer cottage and slapped hard at the windows. Mr. and Mrs. Allison involuntarily moved closer together, and with the first sudden crash of thunder, Mr. Allison reached out and took his wife's hand. And then, while the lightning flashed outside, and the radio faded and sputtered, the two old people huddled together in their summer cottage and waited.

Harlan Ellison

The Whimper of Whipped Dogs

Harlan Ellison, the popular fantasist, when he writes in the horror mode, is a conduit through whom the horrors of everyday life are transformed into fictions that reawaken us, reconnect us to those daily horrors to which we have become desensitized by conventional wisdom and by habit. Ellison strives for extreme effects. Stephen King has called him the greatest contemporary horror writer: "He sums up, for me, the finest elements of the term . . . in his short stories of fantasy and horror, he strikes closest to all those things which horrify and amuse us (sometimes both at the same time) in our present lives." (*Danse Macabre,* p. 369) "The Whimper of Whipped Dogs" is a violent fantasia on everyday life in the big city with a dystopian moral and is one of the landmarks of contemporary horror fiction. It won for Ellison an Edgar Award in 1974 from the Mystery Writers of America and remains his quintessential work of horror.

On the night after the day she had stained the louvered window shutters of her new apartment on East 52nd Street, Beth saw a woman slowly and hideously knifed to death in the courtyard of her building. She was one of twenty-six witnesses to the ghoulish scene, and, like them, she did nothing to stop it.

She saw it all, every moment of it, without break and with no impediment to her view. Quite madly, the thought crossed her mind as she watched in horrified fascination, that she had the sort of marvelous line of observation Napoleon had sought when he caused to have constructed at the *Comédie-Française* theaters, a curtained box at the rear, so he could watch the audience as well as the stage. The night was clear, the moon was full, she had just turned off the 11:30 movie on channel 2 after the second commercial break, realizing she had already seen Robert Taylor in *Westward the Women,* and had disliked it the first time; and the apartment was quite dark.

She went to the window, to raise it six inches for the night's sleep, and she saw the woman stumble into the courtyard. She was sliding along the wall, clutching her left arm with her right hand. Con Ed had installed mercury-vapor lamps on the poles; there had been sixteen assaults in seven months; the courtyard was illuminated with a chill purple glow that made the blood streaming down the woman's left arm look black and shiny. Beth saw every detail with utter clarity, as though magnified a thousand power under a microscope, solarized as if it had been a television commercial.

The woman threw back her head, as if she were trying to scream, but there was no sound. Only the traffic on First Avenue, late cabs foraging for singles paired for the night at Maxwell's Plum and Friday's and Adam's Apple. But that was over there, beyond. Where *she* was, down there seven floors below, in the courtyard, everything seemed silently suspended in an invisible force-field.

Beth stood in the darkness of her apartment, and realized she had raised the window completely. A tiny balcony lay just over the low sill; now not even glass separated her from the sight; just the wrought-iron balcony railing and seven floors to the courtyard below.

The woman staggered away from the wall, her head still thrown back, and Beth could see she was in her mid-thirties, with dark hair cut in a shag; it was impossible to tell if she was pretty: terror had contorted her features and her mouth was a twisted black slash, opened but emitting no sound. Cords stood out in her neck. She had lost one shoe, and her steps were uneven, threatening to dump her to the pavement.

The man came around the corner of the building, into the courtyard. The knife he held was enormous—or perhaps it only seemed so: Beth remembered a bone-handled fish knife her father had used one summer at the lake in Maine: it folded back on itself and locked, revealing eight inches of serrated blade. The knife in the hand of the dark man in the courtyard seemed to be similar.

The woman saw him and tried to run, but he leaped across the distance between them and grabbed her by the hair and pulled her head back as though he would slash her throat in the next reaper-motion.

Then the woman screamed.

The sound skirled up into the courtyard like bats trapped in an echo chamber, unable to find a way out, driven mad. It went on and on . . .

The man struggled with her and she drove her elbows into his sides and he tried to protect himself, spinning her around by her hair, the terrible scream going up and up and never stopping. She came loose and he was left with a fistful of hair torn out by the roots. As she spun out, he slashed straight across and opened her up just below the breasts. Blood sprayed through her clothing and the man was soaked; it seemed to drive him even more berserk. He went at her again, as she tried to hold herself together, the blood pouring down over her arms.

She tried to run, teetered against the wall, slid sidewise, and the man struck the brick surface. She was away, stumbling over a flower bed, falling, getting to her knees as he threw himself on her again. The knife came up in a flashing arc that illuminated the blade strangely with purple light. And still she screamed.

Lights came on in dozens of apartments and people appeared at windows.

He drove the knife to the hilt into her back, high on the right shoulder. He used both hands.

Beth caught it all in jagged flashes—the man, the woman, the knife, the blood, the expressions on the faces of those watching from the windows. Then lights clicked off in the windows, but they still stood there, watching.

She wanted to yell, to scream, "What are you doing to that woman?" But her throat was frozen, two iron hands that had been immersed in dry ice for ten thousand years clamped around her neck. She could feel the blade sliding into her own body.

Somehow—it seemed impossible but there it was down there, happening somehow—the woman struggled erect and *pulled* herself off the knife. Three steps, she took three steps and fell into the flower bed again. The man was howling now, like a great beast, the sounds inarticulate, bubbling up from his stomach. He fell on her and the knife went up and came down, then again, and again, and finally it was all a blur of motion, and her scream of lunatic bats went on till it faded off and was gone.

Beth stood in the darkness, trembling and crying, the sight filling her eyes with horror. And when she could no longer bear to look at what he was doing down there to the unmoving piece of meat over which he worked, she looked up and around at the windows of darkness where the others still stood— even as she had stood—and somehow she could see their faces, bruise- purple with the dim light from the mercury lamps, and there was a universal sameness to their expressions. The women stood with their nails biting into the upper arms of their men, their tongues edging from the corners of their mouths; the men were wild-eyed and smiling. They all looked as though they were at cock fights. Breathing deeply. Drawing some sustenance from the grisly scene below. An exhalation of sound, deep, deep, as though from caverns beneath the earth. Flesh pale and moist.

And it was then that she realized the courtyard had grown foggy, as though mist off the East River had rolled up 52nd Street in a veil that would obscure the details of what the knife and the man were still doing . . . endlessly doing it . . . long after there was any joy in it . . . still doing it . . . again and again . . .

But the fog was unnatural, thick and gray and filled with tiny scintillas of light. She stared at it, rising up in the empty space of the courtyard. Bach in the cathedral, stardust in a vacuum chamber.

Beth saw eyes.

There, up there, at the ninth floor and higher, two great eyes, as surely as night and the moon, there were *eyes.* And—a face? Was that a face, could she be sure, was she imagining it . . . a face? In the roiling vapors of chill fog something lived, something brooding and patient and utterly malevolent had been summoned up to witness what was happening down there in the flower bed. Beth tried to look away, but could not. The eyes, those primal burning eyes, filled with an abysmal antiquity yet frighteningly bright and anxious like the eyes of a child; eyes filled with tomb depths, ancient and new, chasm-filled, burning, gigantic and deep as an abyss, holding her, compelling her. The shadow play was being staged not only for the tenants in their windows, watching and drinking of the scene, but for some *other.* Not on frigid tundra or waste moors, not in subterranean caverns or on some faraway world circling a dying sun, but here, in the city, here the eyes of that *other* watched.

Shaking with the effort, Beth wrenched her eyes from those burning depths up there beyond the ninth floor, only to see again the horror that had brought that *other.* And she was struck for the first time by the awfulness of what she was witnessing, she was released from the immobility that had held her like a coelacanth in shale, she was filled with the blood thunder pounding against the membranes of her mind: she had *stood* there! She had done nothing, nothing! A woman had been butchered and she had said nothing, done nothing. Tears had been useless, tremblings had been pointless, she *had done nothing!*

Then she heard hysterical sounds midway between laughter and giggling, and as she stared up into that great face rising in the fog and chimneysmoke of the night, she heard *herself* making those deranged gibbon noises and from the man below a pathetic, trapped sound, like the whimper of whipped dogs.

She was staring up into that face again. She hadn't wanted to see it again—ever. But she was locked with those smoldering eyes, overcome with the feeling that they were childlike, though she *knew* they were incalculably ancient.

Then the butcher below did an unspeakable thing and Beth reeled with dizziness and caught the edge of the window before she could tumble out onto the balcony; she steadied herself and fought for breath.

She felt herself being looked at, and for a long moment of frozen terror she feared she might have caught the attention of that face up there in the fog. She clung to the window, feeling everything growing faraway and dim, and stared straight across the court. She *was* being watched. Intently. By the young man in the seventh-floor window across from her own apartment. Steadily, he was looking at her. Through the strange fog with its burning eyes feasting on the sight below, he was staring at her.

As she felt herself blacking out, in the moment before unconsciousness, the thought flickered and fled that there was something terribly familiar about his face.

It rained the next day. East 52nd Street was slick and shining with the oil rainbows. The rain washed the dog turds into the gutters and nudged them down and down to the catch-basin openings. People bent against the slanting rain, hidden beneath umbrellas, looking like enormous, scurrying black mushrooms. Beth went out to get the newspapers after the police had come and gone.

The news reports dwelled with loving emphasis on the twenty-six tenants of the building who had watched in cold interest as Leona Ciarelli, 37, of 455 Fort Washington Avenue, Manhattan, had been systematically stabbed to death by Burton H. Wells, 41, an unemployed electrician, who had been subsequently shot to death by two off-duty police officers when he burst into Michael's Pub on 55th Street, covered with blood and brandishing a knife that authorities later identified as the murder weapon.

She had thrown up twice that day. Her stomach seemed incapable of retaining anything solid, and the taste of bile lay along the back of her tongue. She could not blot the scenes of the night before from her mind; she re-ran them again and again, every movement of that reaper arm playing over and over as though on a short loop of memory. The woman's head thrown back for silent screams. The blood. Those eyes in the fog.

She was drawn again and again to the window, to stare down into the courtyard and the street. She tried to superimpose over the bleak Manhattan concrete the view from her window in Swann House at Bennington: the little yard and another white, frame dormitory; the fantastic apple trees; and from the other window the rolling hills and gorgeous Vermont countryside; her memory skittered through the change of seasons. But there was always concrete and the rain-slick streets; the rain on the pavement was black and shiny as blood.

She tried to work, rolling up the tambour closure of the old rolltop desk she had bought on Lexington Avenue and hunching over the graph sheets of choreographer's charts. But Labanotation was merely a Jackson Pollock jumble of arcane hieroglyphics to her today, instead of the careful representation of eurhythmics she had studied four years to perfect. And before that, Farmington.

The phone rang. It was the secretary from the Taylor Dance Company, asking when she would be free. She had to beg off. She looked at her hand, lying on the graph sheets of figures Laban had devised, and she saw her fingers trembling. She had to beg off. Then she called Guzman at the Downtown Ballet Company, to tell him she would be late with the charts.

"My God, lady, I have ten dancers sitting around in a rehearsal hall getting their leotards sweaty! What do you expect me to do?"

She explained what had happened the night before. And as she told him, she realized the newspapers had been justified in holding that tone against the twenty-six witnesses to the death of Leona Ciarelli. Paschal Guzman listened, and when he spoke again, his voice was several octaves lower, and he spoke more slowly. He said he understood and she could take a little longer to prepare the charts. But there was a distance in his voice, and he hung up while she was thanking him.

She dressed in an argyle sweater vest in shades of dark purple, and a pair of fitted khaki gabardine trousers. She had to go out, to walk around. To do what? To think about other things. As she pulled on the Fred Braun chunky heels, she idly wondered if that heavy silver bracelet was still in the window of Georg Jensen's. In the elevator, the young man from the window across the courtyard stared at her. Beth felt her body begin to tremble again. She went deep into the corner of the box when he entered behind her.

Between the fifth and fourth floors, he hit the *off* switch and the elevator jerked to a halt.

Beth stared at him and he smiled innocently.

"Hi. My name's Gleeson, Ray Gleeson, I'm in 714."

She wanted to demand he turn the elevator back on, by what right did he pre*sume* to do such a thing, what did he mean by this, turn it on at once or suffer the consequences. That was what she *wanted* to do. Instead, from the same place she had heard the glibbering laughter the night before, she heard her voice, much smaller and much less possessed than she had trained it to be, saying, "Beth O'Neill, I live in 701."

The thing about it, was that *the elevator was stopped.* And she was frightened. But he leaned against the paneled wall, very well dressed, shoes polished, hair combed and probably blown dry with a hand dryer, and he *talked* to her as if they were across a table at L'Argenteuil. "You just moved in, huh?"

"About two months ago."

"Where did you go to school? Bennington or Sarah Lawrence?"

"Bennington. How did you know?"

He laughed, and it was a nice laugh. "I'm an editor at a religious book publisher; every year we get half a dozen Bennington, Sarah Lawrence, Smith girls. They come hopping in like grasshoppers, ready to revolutionize the publishing industry."

"What's wrong with that? You sound like you don't care for them."

"Oh, I *love* them, they're marvelous. They think they know how to write better than the authors we publish. Had one darlin' little item who was given galleys of three books to proof, and she rewrote all three. I think she's working as a table-swabber in a Horn & Hardart's now."

She didn't reply to that. She would have pegged him as an anti-feminist, ordinarily, if it had been anyone else speaking. But the eyes. There was something terribly familiar about his face. She was enjoying the conversation; she rather liked him.

"What's the nearest big city to Bennington?"

"Albany, New York. About sixty miles."

"How long does it take to drive there?"

"From Bennington? About an hour and a half."

"Must be a nice drive, that Vermont country, really pretty. They went coed, I understand. How's that working out?"

"I don't know, really."

"You don't know?"

"It happened around the time I was graduating."

"What did you major in?"

"I was a dance major, specializing in Labanotation. That's the way you write choreography."

"It's all electives, I gather. You don't have to take anything required, like sciences, for example." He didn't change tone as he said, "That was a terrible thing last night. I saw you watching. I guess a lot of us were watching. It was a really terrible thing."

She nodded dumbly. Fear came back.

"I understand the cops got him. Some nut, they don't even know why he killed her, or why he went charging into that bar. It was really an awful thing. I'd very much like to have dinner with you one night soon, if you're not attached."

"That would be all right."

"Maybe Wednesday. There's an Argentinian place I know. You might like it."

"That would be all right."

"Why don't you turn on the elevator, and we can go," he said, and smiled again. She did it, wondering why she had stopped the elevator in the first place.

* * *

On her third date with him, they had their first fight. It was at a party thrown by a director of television commercials. He lived on the ninth floor of their building. He had just done a series of spots for *Sesame Street* (the letters "U" for Underpass, "T" for Tunnel, lowercase "b" for boats, "c" for cars; the numbers 1 to 6 and the numbers 1 to 20; the words *light* and *dark*) and was celebrating his move from the arena of commercial tawdriness (and its attendant $75,000 a year) to the sweet fields of educational programming (and its accompanying descent into low-pay respectability). There was a logic in his joy Beth could not quite understand, and when she talked with him about it, in a far corner of the kitchen, his arguments didn't seem to parse. But he seemed happy, and his girlfriend, a long-legged ex-model from Philadelphia, continued to drift to him and away from him, like some exquisite undersea plant, touching his hair and kissing his neck, murmuring words of pride and barely submerged sexuality. Beth found it bewildering, though the celebrants were all bright and lively.

In the living room, Ray was sitting on the arm of the sofa, hustling a stewardess named Luanne. Beth could tell he was hustling; he was trying to look casual. When he *wasn't* hustling, he was always intense, about everything. She decided to ignore it, and wandered around the apartment, sipping at a Tanqueray and tonic.

There were framed prints of abstract shapes clipped from a calendar printed in Germany. They were in metal Bonniers frames.

In the dining room a huge door from a demolished building somewhere in the city had been handsomely stripped, teaked and refinished. It was now the dinner table.

A Lightolier fixture attached to the wall over the bed swung out, levered up and down, tipped, and its burnished globe-head revolved a full three hundred and sixty degrees.

She was standing in the bedroom, looking out the window, when she realized *this* had been one of the rooms in which light had gone on, gone off; one of the rooms that had contained a silent watcher at the death of Leona Ciarelli.

When she returned to the living room, she looked around more carefully. With only three or four exceptions—the stewardess, a young married couple from the second floor, a stockbroker from Hemphill, Noyes—*everyone* at the party had been a witness to the slaying.

"I'd like to go," she told him.

"Why, aren't you having a good time?" asked the stewardess, a mocking smile crossing her perfect little face.

"Like all Bennington ladies," Ray said, answering for Beth, "she is enjoying herself most by not enjoying herself at all. It's a trait of the anal retentive. Being here in someone else's apartment, she can't empty ashtrays or rewind the toilet paper roll so it doesn't hang a tongue, and being tightassed, her nature demands we go.

"All right, Beth, let's say our goodbyes and take off. The Phantom Rectum strikes again."

She slapped him and the stewardess's eyes widened. But the smile remained frozen where it had appeared.

He grabbed her wrist before she could do it again. "Garbanzo beans, baby," he said, holding her wrist tighter than necessary.

They went back to her apartment, and after sparring silently with kitchen cabinet doors slammed and the television being tuned too loud, they got to her bed, and he tried to perpetuate the metaphor by fucking her in the ass. He had her on elbows and kness before she realized what he was doing; she struggled to turn over and he rode her bucking and tossing without a sound. And when it was clear to him that she would never permit it, he grabbed her breast from underneath and squeezed so hard she howled in pain. He dumped her on her back, rubbed himself between her legs a dozen times, and came on her stomach.

Beth lay with her eyes closed and an arm thrown across her face. She wanted to cry, but found she could not. Ray lay on her and said nothng. She wanted to rush to the bathroom and shower, but he did not move, till long after his semen had dried on their bodies.

"Who did you date at college?" he asked.

"I didn't date anyone very much." Sullen.

"No heavy makeouts with wealthy lads from Williams and Dartmouth . . . no Amherst intellectuals begging you to save them from creeping faggotry by permitting them to stick their carrots in your sticky little slit?"

"Stop it!"

"Come on, baby, it couldn't all have been knee socks and little round circle-pins. You don't expect me to believe you didn't get a little mouthful of cock from time to time. It's only, what? about fifteen miles to Williamstown? I'm sure the Williams werewolves were down burning the highway to your cunt on weekends; you can level with old Uncle Ray. . . ."

"Why are you like this?!" She started to move, to get away from him, and he grabbed her by the shoulder, forced her to lie down again. Then he rose up over her and said, "I'm like this because I'm a New Yorker, baby. Because I live in this fucking city every day. Because I have to play patty-cake with the ministers and other sanctified holy-joe assholes who want their goodness and lightness tracts published by the Blessed Sacrament Publishing and Storm Window Company of 277 Park Avenue, when what I *really* want to do is toss the stupid psalm-suckers out the thirty-seventh-floor window and listen to them quote chapter-and-worse all the way down. Because I've lived in this great big snapping dog of a city all my life and I'm mad as a mudfly, for chrissakes!"

She lay unable to move, breathing shallowly, filled with a sudden pity and affection for him. His face was white and strained, and she knew he was saying things to her that only a bit too much Almadén and exact timing would have let him say.

"What do you expect from me," he said, his voice softer now, but no less intense, "do you expect kindness and gentility and understanding and a hand on *your* hand when the smog burns your eyes? I can't do it, I haven't got it. No one has it in this cesspool of a city. Look around you; what do you think is happening here? They take rats and they put them in boxes and when there are too many of them, some of the little fuckers go out of their minds and start gnawing the rest to death. *It ain't no different here, baby!* It's rat time for everybody in this madhouse. You can't expect to jam as many people into this stone thing as we do, with buses and taxis and dogs shitting themselves scrawny and noise night and day and no money and not enough places to live and no place to go to have a decent think . . . you can't do it without making the time right for some godforsaken other kind of thing to be born! You can't hate everyone around you, and kick every beggar and nigger and *mestizo* shithead, you can't have cabbies stealing from you and taking tips they don't deserve, and then cursing you, you can't walk in the soot till your collar turns black, and your body stinks with the smell of flaking brick and decaying brains, you can't do it without calling up some kind of awful—"

He stopped.

His face bore the expression of a man who has just received brutal word of the death of a loved one. He suddenly lay down, rolled over, and turned off.

She lay beside him, trembling, trying desperately to remember where she had seen his face before.

He didn't call her again, after the night of the party. And when they met in the hall, he pointedly turned away, as though he had given her some obscure chance and she had refused to take it. Beth thought she understood: though Ray Gleeson had not been her first affair, he had been the first to reject her so completely. The first to put her not only out of his bed and his life, but even out of his world. It was as though she were invisible, not even beneath contempt, simply not there.

She busied herself with other things.

She took on three new charting jobs for Guzman and a new group that had formed on Staten Island, of all places. She worked furiously and they gave her new assignments; they even paid her.

She tried to decorate the apartment with a less precise touch. Huge poster blowups of Merce Cunningham and Martha Graham replaced the Brueghel prints that had reminded her of the view looking down the hill toward Williams. The tiny balcony outside her window, the balcony she had steadfastly refused to stand upon since the night of the slaughter, the night of the fog with eyes, that balcony she swept and set about with little flower boxes in which she planted geraniums, petunias, dwarf zinnias, and other hardy perennials. Then, closing the window, she went to give herself, to involve herself in this city to which she had brought her ordered life.

And the city responded to her overtures:

Seeing off an old friend from Bennington, at Kennedy International, she stopped at the terminal coffee shop to have a sandwich. The counter—like a moat—surrounded a center service island that had huge advertising cubes rising above it on burnished poles. The cubes proclaimed the delights of Fun City. *New York Is a Summer Festival,* they said, and *Joseph Papp Presents Shakespeare in Central Park* and *Visit the Bronx Zoo* and *You'll Adore Our Contentious but Lovable Cabbies.* The food emerged from a window far down the service area and moved slowly on a conveyor belt through the hordes of screaming waitresses who slathered the counter with redolent washcloths. The lunchroom had all the charm and dignity of a steel-rolling mill, and approximately the same noise level. Beth ordered a cheeseburger that cost a dollar and a quarter, and a glass of milk.

When it came, it was cold, the cheese unmelted, and the patty of meat resembling nothing so much as a dirty scouring pad. The bun was cold and untoasted. There was no lettuce under the patty.

Beth managed to catch the waitress's eye. The girl approached with an annoyed look. "Please toast the bun and may I have a piece of lettuce?" Beth said.

"We dun' do that," the waitress said, turning half away as though she would walk in a moment.

"You don't do what?"

"We dun' toass the bun here."

"Yes, but I *want* the bun toasted," Beth said firmly.

"An' you got to pay for extra lettuce."

"If I was asking for *extra* lettuce," Beth said, getting annoyed, "I would pay for it, but since there's *no* lettuce here, I don't think I should be charged extra for the first piece."

"We dun' do that."

The waitress started to walk away. "Hold it," Beth said, raising her voice just enough so the assembly-line eaters on either side stared at her. "You mean to tell me I have to pay a dollar and a quarter and I can't get a piece of lettuce or even get the bun toasted?"

"Ef you dun' like it . . ."

"Take it back."

"You gotta pay for it, you order it."

"I said take it back, I don't want the fucking thing!"

The waitress scratched it off the check. The milk cost 27¢ and tasted going-sour. It was the first time in her life that Beth had said *that* word aloud.

At the cashier's stand, Beth said to the sweating man with the felt-tip pens in his shirt pocket, "Just out of curiosity, are you interested in complaints?"

"No!" he said, snarling, quite literally snarling. He did not look up as he punched out 73¢ and it came rolling down the chute.

The city responded to her overtures:

It was raining again. She was trying to cross Second Avenue, with the light. She stepped off the curb and a car came sliding through the red and splashed her. "Hey!" she yelled.

"Eat shit, sister!" the driver yelled back, turning the corner.

Her boots, her legs and her overcoat were splattered with mud. She stood trembling on the curb.

The city responded to her overtures:

She emerged from the building at One Astor Place with her big briefcase full of Laban charts; she was adjusting her rain scarf about her head. A well-dressed man with an attaché case thrust the handle of his umbrella up between her legs from the rear. She gasped and dropped her case.

The city responded and responded and responded.

Her overtures altered quickly.

The old drunk with the stippled cheeks extended his hand and mumbled words. She cursed him and walked on up Broadway past the beaver film houses.

She crossed against the lights on Park Avenue, making hackies slam their brakes to avoid hitting her; she used *that* word frequently now.

When she found herself having a drink with a man who had elbowed up beside her in the singles' bar, she felt faint and knew she should go home.

But Vermont was so far away.

Nights later. She had come home from the Lincoln Center ballet, and gone straight to bed. Lying half-asleep in her bedroom, she heard an alien sound. One room away, in the living room, in the dark, there was a sound. She slipped out of bed and went to the door between the rooms. She fumbled silently for the switch on the lamp just inside the living room, and found it, and clicked it on. A black man in a leather car coat was trying to get *out* of the apartment. In that first flash of light filling the room she noticed the television set beside him on the floor as he struggled with the door, she noticed the police lock and bar had been broken in a new and clever manner *New York* magazine had not yet reported in a feature article on apartment ripoffs, she noticed that he had gotten his foot tangled in the telephone cord that she had requested be extra-long so she could carry the instrument into the bathroom, I don't want to miss any business calls when the shower is running; she noticed all things in perspective and one thing with sharpest clarity: the expression on the burglar's face.

There was something familiar in that expression.

He almost had the door open, but now he closed it, and slipped the police lock. He took a step toward her.

Beth went back, into the darkened bedroom.

The city responded to her overtures.

She backed against the wall at the head of the bed. Her hand fumbled in the shadows for the telephone. His shape filled the doorway, light, all light behind him.

In silhouette it should not have been possible to tell, but somehow she knew he was wearing gloves and the only marks he would leave would be deep bruises, very blue, almost black, with the tinge under them of blood that had been stopped in its course.

He came for her, arms hanging casually at his sides. She tried to climb over the bed, and he grabbed her from behind, ripping her nightgown. Then he had a hand around her neck and he pulled her backward. She fell off the bed, landed at his feet and his hold was broken. She scuttled across the floor and for a moment she had the respite to feel terror. She was going to die, and she was frightened.

He trapped her in the corner between the closet and the bureau and kicked her. His foot caught her in the thigh as she folded tighter, smaller, drawing her legs up. She was cold.

Then he reached down with both hands and pulled her erect by her hair. He slammed her head against the wall. Everything slid up in her sight as though running off the edge of the world. He slammed her head against the wall again, and she felt something go soft over her right ear.

When he tried to slam her a third time she reached out blindly for his face and ripped down with her nails. He howled in pain and she hurled herself forward, arms wrapping themselves around his waist. He stumbled backward and in a tangle of thrashing arms and legs they fell out onto the little balcony.

Beth landed on the bottom, feeling the window boxes jammed up against her spine and legs. She fought to get to her feet, and her nails hooked into his shirt under the open jacket, ripping. Then she was on her feet again and they struggled silently.

He whirled her around, bent her backward across the wrought-iron railing. Her face was turned outward.

They were standing in their windows, watching.

Through the fog she could see them watching. Through the fog she recognized their expressions. Through the fog she heard them breathing in unison, bellows breathing of expectation and wonder. Through the fog.

And the black man punched her in the throat. She gagged and started to black out and could not draw air into her lungs. Back, back, he bent her further back and she was looking up, straight up, toward the ninth floor and higher . . .

Up there: eyes.

The words Ray Gleeson had said in a moment filled with what he had become, with the utter hopelessness and finality of the choice the city had forced on him, the words came back. *You can't live in this city and survive unless you have protection . . . you can't live this way, like rats driven mad, without making the time right for some godforsaken other kind of thing to be born . . . you can't do it without calling up some kind of awful . . .*

God! A new God, an ancient God come again with the eyes and hunger of a child, a deranged blood God of fog and street violence. A God who needed worshippers and offered the choices of death as a victim or life as an eternal witness to the deaths of *other* chosen victims. A God to fit the times, a God of streets and people.

She tried to shriek, to appeal to Ray, to the director in the bedroom window of his ninth-floor apartment with his long-legged Philadelphia model beside him and his fingers inside her as they worshipped in their holiest of ways, to the others who had been at the party that had been Ray's offer of a chance to join their congregation. She wanted to be saved from having to make that choice.

But the black man had punched her in the throat, and now his hands were on her, one on her chest, the other in her face, the smell of leather filling her where the nausea could not. And she understood Ray had *cared,* had wanted her to take the chance offered; but she had come from a world of little white dormitories and Vermont countryside; it was not a real world. *This* was the real world and up there was the God who ruled this world, and she had rejected him, had said no to one of his priests and servitors. *Save me! Don't make me do it!*

She knew she had to call out, to make appeal, to try and win the approbation of that God. *I can't . . . save me!*

She struggled and made terrible little mewling sounds trying to summon the words to cry out, and suddenly she crossed a line, and screamed up into the echoing courtyard with a voice Leona Ciarelli had never known enough to use.

"Him! Take him! Not me! I'm yours, I love you, I'm yours! Take him, not me, please not me, take him, take him, I'm yours!"

And the black man was suddenly lifted away, wrenched off her, and off the balcony, whirled straight up into the fog-thick air in the courtyard, as Beth sank to her knees on the ruined flower boxes.

She was half-conscious, and could not be sure she saw it just that way, but up he went, end over end, whirling and spinning like a charred leaf.

And the form took firmer shape. Enormous paws with claws and shapes that no animal she had ever seen had ever possessed, and the burglar, black, poor, terrified, whimpering like a whipped dog, was stripped of his flesh. His body was opened with a thin incision, and there was a rush as all the blood poured from him like a sudden cloudburst, and yet he was still alive, twitching with the involuntary horror of a frog's leg shocked with an electric current. Twitched, and twitched again as he was torn piece by piece to shreds. Pieces of flesh and bone and half a face with an eye blinking furiously, cascaded down past Beth, and hit the cement below with sodden thuds. And still he was alive, as his organs were squeezed and musculature and bile and shit and skin were rubbed, sandpapered together and let fall. It went on and on, as the death of Leona Ciarelli had gone on and on, and she understood with the blood-knowledge of survivors *at any cost* that the reason the witnesses to the death of Leona Ciarelli had done nothing was not that they had been frozen with horror, that they didn't want to get involved, or that they were inured to death by years of television slaughter.

They were worshippers at a black mass the city had demanded be staged; not once, but a thousand times a day in this insame asylum of steel and stone.

Now she was on her feet, standing half-naked in her ripped nightgown, her hands tightening on the wrought-iron railing, begging to see more, to drink deeper.

Now she was one of them, as the pieces of the night's sacrifice fell past her, bleeding and screaming.

Tomorrow the police would come again, and they would question her, and she would say how terrible it had been, that burglar, and how she had fought, afraid he would rape her and kill her, and how he had fallen, and she had no idea how he had been so hideously mangled and ripped apart, but a seven-storey fall, after all . . .

Tomorrow she would not have to worry about walking in the streets, because no harm could come to her. Tomorrow she could even remove the police lock. Nothing in the city could do her any further evil, because she had made the only choice. She was now a dweller in the city, now wholly and richly a part of it. Now she was taken to the bosom of her God.

She felt Ray beside her, standing beside her, holding her, protecting her, his hand on her naked backside, and she watched the fog swirl up and fill the courtyard, fill the city, fill her eyes and her soul and her heart with its power. As Ray's naked body pressed tightly inside her, she drank deeply of the night, knowing whatever voices she heard from this moment forward would be the voices not of whipped dogs, but those of strong, meat-eating beasts. At last she was unafraid, and it was so good, so very good *not* to be afraid.

"When inward life dries up, when feeling decreases and apathy increases, when one cannot affect or even genuinely touch another person, violence flares up as a daimonic necessity for contact, a mad drive forcing touch in the most direct way possible."
—Rolly May, *Love and Will*

Nathaniel Hawthorne

Young Goodman Brown

Perhaps the original horror in American myth grows out of the witchcraft trials in Puritan New England, our own regional version of the Spanish Inquisition. Nathaniel Hawthorne was the greatest American writer drawn to the matter of the Puritans and their moral horrors. It has been pointed out that the Puritan sermon, with its hair-raising images of hell and damnation, was the characteristic mode of horror literature in the U.S. before the invention of the short story. Hawthorne's awareness of horror and its effects underpins one of the great allegories of good and evil, "Young Goodman Brown." The irony that the new world of God's chosen few nurtured in its bosom its opposite, devil worship, literally or metaphorically, endures. There is more than a hint of the world of Hawthorne in Stephen King's "The Reach."

Young Goodman Brown came forth at sunset into the street at Salem village; but put his head back, after crossing the threshold, to exchange a parting kiss with his young wife. And Faith, as the wife was aptly named, thrust her own pretty head into the street, letting the wind play with the pink ribbons of her cap while she called to Goodman Brown.

"Dearest heart," whispered she, softly and rather sadly, when her lips were close to his ear, "prithee put off your journey until sunrise and sleep in your own bed tonight. A lone woman is troubled with such dreams and such thoughts that she's afeard of herself sometimes. Pray tarry with me this night, dear husband, of all nights in the year."

"My love and my Faith," replied young Goodman Brown, "of all nights in the year, this one night must I tarry away from thee. My journey, as thou callest it, forth and back again, must needs be done 'twixt now and sunrise. What, my sweet, pretty wife, dost thou doubt me already, and we but three months married?"

"Then God bless you!" said Faith, with the pink ribbons, "and may you find all well when you come back."

"Amen!" cried Goodman Brown. "Say thy prayers, dear Faith, and go to bed at dusk, and no harm will come to thee."

So they parted; and the young man pursued his way until, being about to turn the corner by the meetinghouse, he looked back and saw the head of Faith still peeping after him with a melancholy air, in spite of her pink ribbons.

"Poor little Faith!" thought he, for his heart smote him. "What a wretch am I to leave her on such an errand! She talks of dreams, too. Methought as she spoke there was trouble in her face, as if a dream had warned her what work is to be done tonight. But no, no; 'twould kill her to think it. Well, she's a blessed angel on earth; and after this one night I'll cling to her skirts and follow her to heaven."

With this excellent resolve for the future, Goodman Brown felt himself justified in making more haste on his present evil purpose. He had taken a dreary road, darkened by all the gloomiest trees of the forest, which barely stood aside to let the narrow path creep through, and closed immediately behind. It was all as lonely as could be; and there is this peculiarity in such a solitude, that the traveler knows not who may be concealed by the innumerable trunks and the thick boughs overhead; so that with lonely footsteps he may yet be passing through an unseen multitude.

"There may be a devilish Indian behind every tree," said Goodman Brown to himself; and he glanced fearfully behind him as he added, "What if the devil himself should be at my very elbow!"

His head being turned back, he passed a crook of the road, and, looking forward again, beheld the figure of a man, in grave and decent attire, seated at the foot of an old tree. He arose at Goodman Brown's approach and walked onward side by side with him.

"You are late, Goodman Brown," said he. "The clock of the Old South was striking as I came through Boston, and that is full fifteen minutes agone."

"Faith kept me back awhile," replied the young man, with a tremor in his voice, caused by the sudden appearance of his companion, though not wholly unexpected.

It was now deep dusk in the forest, and deepest in that part of it where these two were journeying. As nearly as could be discerned, the second traveler was about fifty years old, apparently in the same rank of life as Goodman Brown, and bearing a considerable resemblance to him, though perhaps more in expression than features. Still they might have been taken for father and son. And yet, though the elder person was as simply clad as the younger, and as simple in manner, too, he had an indescribable air of one who knew the world, and who would not have felt abashed at the Governor's dinner table or in King William's court, were it possible that his affairs should call him thither. But the only thing about him that could be fixed upon as remarkable was his staff, which bore the likeness of a great black snake, so curiously wrought that it might almost be seen to twist and wriggle itself like a living serpent. This, of course, must have been an ocular deception, assisted by the uncertain light.

"Come, Goodman Brown," cried his fellow traveler, "this is a dull pace for the beginning of a journey. Take my staff, if you are so soon weary."

"Friend," said the other, exchanging his slow pace for a full stop, "having kept covenant by meeting thee here, it is my purpose now to return whence I came. I have scruples touching the matter thou wot'st of."

"Sayest thou so?" replied he of the serpent, smiling apart. "Let us walk on, nevertheless, reasoning as we go; and if I convince thee not, thou shalt turn back. We are but a little way in the forest yet."

"Too far! too far!" exclaimed the goodman, unconsciously resuming his walk. "My father never went into the woods on such an errand, nor his father before him. We have been a race of honest men and good Christians since the days of the martyrs; and shall I be the first of the name of Brown that ever took this path and kept—"

"Such company, thou wouldst say," observed the elder person, interpreting his pause. "Well said, Goodman Brown! I have been as well acquainted with your family as with ever a one among the Puritans; and that's no trifle to say. I helped your grandfather, the constable, when he lashed the Quaker woman so smartly through the streets of Salem; and it was I that brought your father a pitch-pine knot, kindled at my own hearth, to set fire to an Indian village, in King Philip's war. They were my good friends, both; and many a pleasant walk have we had along this path, and returned merrily after midnight. I would fain be friends with you for their sake."

"If it be as thou sayest," replied Goodman Brown, "I marvel they never spoke of these matters; or, verily, I marvel not, seeing that the least rumor of the sort would have driven them from New England. We are a people of prayer, and good works to boot, and abide no such wickedness."

"Wickedness or not," said the traveler with the twisted staff, "I have a very general acquaintance here in New England. The deacons of many a church have drunk the communion wine with me; the selectmen of divers towns make me their chairman; and a majority of the Great and General Court are firm supporters of my interest. The Governor and I, too— But these are state secrets."

"Can this be so?" cried Goodman Brown, with a stare of amazement at his undisturbed companion. "Howbeit, I have nothing to do with the Governor and council; they have their own ways, and are no rule for a simple husbandman like me. But, were I to go on with thee, how should I meet the eye of that good old man, our minister, at Salem village? Oh, his voice would make me tremble both Sabbath day and lecture day."

Thus far the elder traveler had listened with due gravity; but now burst into a fit of irrepressible mirth, shaking himself so violently that his snakelike staff actually seemed to wriggle in sympathy.

"Ha! ha! ha!" shouted he again and again; then composing himself, "Well, go on, Goodman Brown, go on; but, prithee, don't kill me with laughing."

"Well, then, to end the matter at once," said Goodman Brown, considerably nettled, "there is my wife, Faith. It would break her dear little heart; and I'd rather break my own."

"Nay, if that be the case," answered the other, "e'en go thy ways, Goodman Brown. I would not for twenty old women like the one hobbling before us that Faith should come to any harm."

As he spoke, he pointed his staff at a female figure on the path, in whom Goodman Brown recognized a very pious and exemplary dame, who had taught him his catechism in youth, and was still his moral and spiritual adviser, jointly with the minister and Deacon Gookin.

"A marvel, truly, that Goody Cloyse should be so far in the wilderness at nightfall," said he. "But with your leave, friend, I shall take a cut through the woods until we have left this Christian woman behind. Being a stranger to you, she might ask whom I was consorting with and whither I was going."

"Be it so," said his fellow traveler. "Betake you to the woods, and let me keep the path."

Accordingly the young man turned aside, but took care to watch his companion, who advanced softly along the road until he had come within a staff's length of the old dame. She, meanwhile, was making the best of her way, with singular speed for so aged a woman, and mumbling some indistinct words—a prayer, doubtless—as she went. The traveler put forth his staff and touched her withered neck with what seemed the serpent's tail.

"The devil!" screamed the pious old lady.

"Then Goody Cloyse knows her old friend?" observed the traveler, confronting her and leaning on his writhing stick.

"Ah, forsooth, and is it your worship indeed?" cried the good dame. "Yea, truly is it, and in the very image of my old gossip Goodman Brown, the grandfather of the silly fellow that now is. But—would your worship believe it?—my broomstick hath strangely disappeared, stolen, as I suspect, by that unhanged witch, Goody Cory, and that, too, when I was all anointed with the juice of smallage, and cinquefoil, and wolfsbane—"

"Mingled with fine wheat and the fat of a newborn babe," said the shape of old Goodman Brown.

"Ah, your worship knows the recipe," cried the old lady, cackling aloud. "So, as I was saying, being all ready for the meeting, and no horse to ride on, I made up my mind to foot it; for they tell me there is a nice young man to be taken into communion tonight. But now your good worship will lend me your arm, and we shall be there in a twinkling."

"That can hardly be," answered her friend. "I may not spare you my arm, Goody Cloyse; but here is my staff, if you will."

So saying, he threw it down at her feet, where, perhaps, it assumed life, being one of the rods which its owner had formerly lent to the Egyptian magi. Of this fact, however, Goodman Brown could not take cognizance. He had cast up his eyes in astonishment, and, looking down again, beheld neither Goody Cloyse nor the serpentine staff, but his fellow traveler alone, who waited for him as calmly as if nothing had happened.

"That old woman taught me my catechism," said the young man; and there was a world of meaning in this simple comment.

They continued to walk onward, while the elder traveler exhorted his companion to make good speed and persevere in the path, discoursing so aptly that his arguments seemed rather to spring up in the bosom of his auditor than to be suggested by himself. As they went, he plucked a branch of maple to serve for a walking stick, and began to strip it of the twigs and little boughs, which were wet with evening dew. The moment his fingers touched them, they became strangely withered and dried up as with a week's sunshine. Thus the pair proceeded, at a good free pace, until suddenly, in a gloomy hollow of the road, Goodman Brown sat himself down on the stump of a tree and refused to go any farther.

"Friend," said he, stubbornly, "my mind is made up. Not another step will I budge on this errand. What if a wretched old woman do choose to go to the devil when I thought she was going to heaven: is that any reason why I should quit my dear Faith and go after her?"

"You will think better of this by and by," said his acquaintance, composedly. "Sit here and rest yourself awhile; and when you feel like moving again, there is my staff to help you along."

Without more words, he threw his companion the maple stick, and was as speedily out of sight as if he had vanished into the deepening gloom. The young man sat a few moments by the roadside, applauding himself greatly, and thinking with how clear a conscience he should meet the minister in his morning walk, nor shrink from the eye of good old Deacon Gookin. And what calm sleep would be his that very night, which was to have been spent so wickedly, but so purely and sweetly now, in the arms of Faith! Amidst these pleasant and praiseworthy meditations, Goodman Brown heard the tramp of horses along the road, and deemed it advisable to conceal himself within the verge of the forest, conscious of the guilty purpose that had brought him thither, though now so happily turned from it.

On came the hoof tramps and the voices of the riders, two grave old voices, conversing soberly as they drew near. These mingled sounds appeared to pass along the road, within a few yards of the young man's hiding place; but, owing doubtless to the depth of the gloom at that particular spot, neither the travelers not their steeds were visible. Though their figures brushed the small boughs by the wayside, it could not be seen that they intercepted, even for a moment, the faint gleam from the strip of bright sky athwart which they must have passed. Goodman Brown alternately crouched and stood on tiptoe, pulling aside the branches and thrusting forth his head as far as he durst without discerning so much as a shadow. It vexed him the more, because he could have sworn, were such a thing possible, that he recognized the voices of the minister and Deacon Gookin, jogging along quietly, as they were wont to do, when bound to some ordination or ecclesiastical council. While yet within hearing, one of the riders stopped to pluck a switch.

"Of the two, reverend sir," said the voice like the deacon's, "I had rather miss an ordination dinner than tonight's meeting. They tell me that some of our community are to be here from Falmouth and beyond, and others from Connecticut and Rhode Island, besides several of the Indian powwows, who, after their fashion, know almost as much deviltry as the best of us. Moreover, there is a goodly young woman to be taken into communion."

"Mighty well, Deacon Gookin!" replied the solemn old tones of the minister. "Spur up, or we shall be late. Nothing can be done, you know, until I get on the ground."

The hoofs clattered again; and the voices, talking so strangely in the empty air, passed on through the forest, where no church had ever been gathered or solitary Christian prayed. Whither, then, could these holy men be journeying so deep into the heathen wilderness? Young Goodman Brown caught hold of a tree for support, being ready to sink down on the ground, faint and overburdened with the heavy sickness of his heart. He looked up to the sky, doubting whether there really was a heaven above him. Yet there was the blue arch, and the stars brightening in it.

"With heaven above and Faith below, I will yet stand firm against the devil!" cried Goodman Brown.

While he still gazed upward into the deep arch of the firmament and had lifted his hands to pray, a cloud, though no wind was stirring, hurried across the zenith and hid the brightening stars. The blue sky was still visible, except directly overhead, where this black mass of cloud was sweeping swiftly northward. Aloft in the air, as if from the depths of the cloud, came a confused and doubtful sound of voices. Once the listener fancied that he could distinguish the accents of townspeople of his own, men and women, both pious and ungodly, many of whom he had met at the communion table, and had seen others rioting at the tavern. The next moment, so indistinct were the sounds, he doubted whether he had heard aught but the murmur of the old forest, whispering without a wind. Then came a stronger swell of those familiar tones, heard daily in the sunshine at Salem village, but never until now from a cloud of night. There was one voice, of a young woman, uttering lamentations, yet with an uncertain sorrow, and entreating for some favor, which, perhaps, it would grieve her to obtain; and all the unseen multitude, both saints and sinners, seemed to encourage her onward.

"Faith!" shouted Goodman Brown, in a voice of agony and desperation; and the echoes of the forest mocked him, crying, "Faith! Faith!" as if bewildered wretches were seeking her all through the wilderness.

The cry of grief, rage, and terror was yet piercing the night, when the unhappy husband held his breath for a response. There was a scream, drowned immediately in a louder murmur of voices, fading into far-off laughter, as the dark cloud swept away, leaving the clear and silent sky above Goodman Brown. But something fluttered lightly down through the air and caught on the branch of a tree. The young man seized it, and beheld a pink ribbon.

"My Faith is gone!" cried he, after one stupefied moment. "There is no good on earth; and sin is but a name. Come, devil; for to thee is this world given."

And, maddened with despair, so that he laughed loud and long, did Goodman Brown grasp his staff and set forth again, at such a rate that he seemed to fly along the forest path rather than to walk or run. The road grew wilder and drearier and more faintly traced, and vanished at length, leaving him in the heart of the dark wilderness, still rushing onward with the instinct that guides mortal man to evil. The whole forest was peopled with frightful sounds—the creaking of the trees, the howling of wild beasts, and the yell of Indians; while sometimes the wind tolled like a distant church bell, and sometimes gave a broad roar around the traveler, as if all Nature were laughing him to scorn. But he was himself the chief horror of the scene, and shrank not from its other horrors.

"Ha! ha! ha!" roared Goodman Brown when the wind laughed at him. "Let us hear which will laugh loudest. Think not to frighten me with your deviltry. Come witch, come wizard, come Indian powwow, come devil himself, and here comes Goodman Brown. You may as well fear him as he fear you."

In truth, all through the haunted forest there could be nothing more frightful than the figure of Goodman Brown. On he flew among the black pines, brandishing his staff with frenzied gestures, now giving vent to an inspiration of horrid blasphemy, and now shouting forth such laughter as set all the echoes of the forest laughing like demons around him. The fiend in his own shape is less hideous than when he rages in the breast of man. Thus sped the demoniac on his course, until, quivering among the trees, he saw a red light before him, as when the felled trunks and branches of a clearing have been set on fire, and throw up their lurid blaze against the sky, at the hour of midnight. He paused, in a lull of the tempest that had driven him onward, and heard the swell of what seemed a hymn, rolling solemnly from a distance with the weight of many voices. He knew the tune; it was a familiar one in the choir of the village meetinghouse. The verse died heavily away, and was lengthened by a chorus, not of human voices, but of all the sounds of the benighted wilderness pealing in awful harmony together. Goodman Brown cried out, and his cry was lost to his own ear by its unison with the cry of the desert.

In the interval of silence, he stole forward until the light glared full upon his eyes. At one extremity of an open space, hemmed in by the dark wall of the forest, arose a rock, bearing some rude, natural resemblance either to an altar or a pulpit, and surrounded by four blazing pines, their tops aflame, their stems untouched, like candles at an evening meeting. The mass of foliage that had overgrown the summit of the rock was all on fire, blazing high into the night and fitfully illuminating the whole field. Each pendent twig and leafy festoon was in a blaze. As the red light arose and fell, a numerous congregation alternately shone forth, then disappeared in shadow, and again grew, as it were, out of the darkness, peopling the heart of the solitary woods at once.

"A grave and dark-clad company," quoth Goodman Brown.

In truth they were such. Among them, quivering to and fro between gloom and splendor, appeared faces that would be seen next day at the council board of the province, and others which, Sabbath after Sabbath, looked devoutly heavenward, and benignantly over the crowded pews, from the holiest pulpits in the land. Some affirm that the lady of the Governor was there. At least, there were high dames well known to her, and wives of honored husbands, and widows, a great multitude, and ancient maidens, all of excellent repute, and fair young girls, who trembled lest their mothers should espy them. Either the sudden gleams of light flashing over the obscure field bedazzled Goodman Brown, or he recognized a score of the church members of Salem village famous for their especial sanctity. Good old Deacon Gookin had arrived, and waited at the skirts of that venerable saint, his revered pastor. But, irreverently consorting with these grave, reputable, and pious people, these elders of the church, these chaste dames and dewy virgins, there were men of dissolute lives and women of spotted fame, wretches given over to all mean and filthy vice, and suspected even of horrid crimes. It was strange to see that the good shrank not from the wicked, nor were the sinners abashed by the saints. Scattered also among their pale-faced enemies were the Indian priests, or powwows, who had often scared their native forest with more hideous incantations than any known to English witchcraft.

"But where is Faith?" thought Goodman Brown; and, as hope came into his heart, he trembled.

Another verse of the hymn arose, a slow and mournful strain, such as the pious love, but joined to words which expressed all that our nature can conceive of sin, and darkly hinted at far more. Unfathomable to mere mortals is the lore of fiends. Verse after verse was sung; and still the chorus of the desert swelled between like the deepest tone of a mighty organ; and with the final peal of that dreadful anthem there came a sound, as if the roaring wind, the rushing streams, the howling beasts, and every other voice of the unconcerted wilderness were mingling and according with the voice of guilty man in homage to the prince of all. The four blazing pines threw up a loftier flame, and obscurely discovered shapes and visages of horror on the smoke wreaths above the impious assembly. At the same moment, the fire on the rock shot redly forth and formed a glowing arch above its base, where now appeared a figure. With reverence be it spoken, the figure bore no slight similitude, both in garb and manner, to some grave divine of the New England churches.

"Bring forth the converts!" cried a voice that echoed through the field and rolled into the forest.

At the word, Goodman Brown stepped forth from the shadow of the trees and approached the congregation, with whom he felt a loathful brotherhood by the sympathy of all that was wicked in his heart. He could have well-nigh sworn that the shape of his own dead father beckoned him to advance, looking downward from a smoke wreath, while a woman, with dim features of despair, threw out her hand to warn him back. Was it his mother? But he had no power to retreat one step, nor to resist, even in thought, when the minister and good old Deacon Gookin seized his arms and led him to the blazing rock. Thither came also the slender form of a veiled female, led between Goody Cloyse, that pious teacher of the catechism, and Martha Carrier, who had received the devil's promise to be queen of hell. A rampant hag was she. And there stood the proselytes beneath the canopy of fire.

"Welcome, my children," said the dark figure, "to the communion of your race. Ye have found thus young your nature and your destiny. My children, look behind you!"

They turned; and flashing forth, as it were, in a sheet of flame, the fiend-worshipers were seen; the smile of welcome gleamed darkly on every visage.

"There," resumed the sable form, "are all whom ye have reverenced from youth. Ye deemed them holier than yourselves, and shrank from your own sin, contrasting it with their lives of righteousness and prayerful aspirations heavenward. Yet here are they all in my worshiping assembly. This night it shall be granted you to know their secret deeds: how hoary-bearded elders of the church have whispered wanton words to the young maids of their households; how many a woman, eager for widows' weeds, has given her husband a drink at bedtime and let him sleep his last sleep in her bosom; how beardless youths have made haste to inherit their fathers' wealth; and how fair damsels—blush not, sweet ones—have dug little graves in the garden, and bidden me, the sole guest, to an infant's funeral. By the sympathy of your human hearts for sin ye shall scent out all the places—whether in church, bedchamber, street, field, or forest—where crime has been committed, and shall exult to behold the whole earth one stain of guilt, one mighty blood spot. Far more than this. It shall be yours to penetrate, in every bosom, the deep mystery of sin, the fountain of all wicked arts, and which inexhaustibly supplies more evil impulses than human power—than my power at its utmost—can make manifest in deeds. And now, my children, look upon each other."

They did so; and, by the blaze of the hell-kindled torches, the wretched man beheld his Faith, and the wife her husband, trembling before that unhallowed altar.

"Lo, there ye stand, my children," said the figure, in a deep and solemn tone, almost sad with its despairing awfulness, as if his once angelic nature could yet mourn for our miserable race. "Depending upon one another's hearts, ye had still hoped that virtue were not all a dream. Now are ye undeceived. Evil is the nature of mankind. Evil must be your only happiness. Welcome again, my children, to the communion of your race."

"Welcome," repeated the fiend-worshipers, in one cry of despair and triumph.

And there they stood, the only pair, as it seemed, who were yet hesitating on the verge of wickedness in this dark world. A basin was hollowed, naturally, in the rock. Did it contain water, reddened by the lurid light? or was it blood? or, perchance, a liquid flame? Herein did the shape of evil dip his hand and prepare to lay the mark of baptism upon their foreheads, that they might be partakers of the mystery of sin, more conscious of the secret guilt of others, both in deed and thought, than they could now be of their own. The husband cast one look at his pale wife, and Faith at him. What polluted wretches would the next glance show them to each other, shuddering alike at what they disclosed and what they saw!

"Faith! Faith!" cried the husband, "look up to heaven, and resist the wicked one."

Whether Faith obeyed he knew not. Hardly had he spoken when he found himself amid calm night and solitude, listening to a roar of the wind which died heavily away through the forest. He staggered against the rock, and felt it chill and damp; while a hanging twig, that had been all on fire, besprinkled his cheek with the coldest dew.

The next morning, young Goodman Brown came slowly into the street of Salem village, staring around him like a bewildered man. The good old minister was taking a walk along the graveyard to get an appetite for breakfast and meditate his sermon, and bestowed a blessing, as he passed, on Goodman Brown. He shrank from the venerable saint as if to avoid an anathema. Old Deacon Gookin was at domestic worship, and the holy words of his prayer were heard through the open window. "What God doth the wizard pray to?" quoth Goodman Brown. Goody Cloyse, that excellent old Christian, stood in the early sunshine at her own lattice, catechizing a little girl who had brought her a pint of morning's milk. Goodman Brown snatched away the child as from the grasp of the fiend himself. Turning the corner by the meetinghouse, he spied the head of Faith, with the pink ribbons, gazing anxiously forth, and bursting into such joy at sight of him that she skipped along the street and almost kissed her husband before the whole village. But Goodman Brown looked sternly and sadly into her face, and passed on without a greeting.

Had Goodman Brown fallen asleep in the forest and only dreamed a wild dream of a witch meeting?

Be it so if you will; but, alas! it was a dream of evil omen for young Goodman Brown. A stern, a sad, a darkly meditative, a distrustful, if not a desperate man did he become from the night of that fearful dream. On the Sabbath day, when the congregation were singing a holy psalm, he could not listen because an anthem of sin rushed loudly upon his ear and drowned all the blessed strain. When the minister spoke from the pulpit with power and fervid eloquence, and, with his hand on the open Bible, of the sacred truths of our religion, and of saintlike lives and triumphant deaths, and of future bliss or misery unutterable, then did Goodman Brown turn pale, dreading lest the roof should thunder down upon the gray blasphemer and his hearers. Often, awaking suddenly at midnight, he shrank from the bosom of Faith; and at morning or eventide, when the family knelt down at prayer, he scowled and muttered to himself, and gazed sternly at his wife, and turned away. And when he had lived long, and was borne to his grave a hoary corpse, followed by Faith, an aged woman, and children and grandchildren, a goodly procession, besides neighbors not a few, they carved no hopeful verse upon his tombstone, for his dying hour was gloom.

J. Sheridan Le Fanu

Mr. Justice Harbottle

Le Fanu and Poe are, according to Jack Sullivan, "the first short story writers in English to work out carefully planned aesthetic strategies of horror. They were also among the first to write modern short stories. Their habitual strict attention to unity of mood and economy of means is a quality we take for granted in short fiction today, but it was virtually unknown to their more didactically inclined contemporaries." (*Horror Literature,* pp. 221–22) Sullivan goes on to maintain that "Le Fanu was more revolutionary than Poe, for he began the process of dismantling the Gothic props and placing the supernatural tale in everyday settings." M. R. James and his progeny derive from Le Fanu, and James considered him the very greatest of ghost story writers. But he was not a notable popular success in his day; his books are among the very rarest in all nineteenth-century literature. His masterpieces include "Carmilla," "Green Tea," "The Room in the Dragon Volant," and a number of others, including "Mr. Justice Harbottle" offered here. Both Poe and Le Fanu offered examinations of the human psyche in abnormal circumstances characteristically in their stories, but in Le Fanu there is unquestionably supernatural evil at work, against an evil man, Judge Harbottle. This story is offered as perhaps more characteristic of the M. R. Jamesian tradition than "Schalken the Painter," later in this book.

PROLOGUE

On this case Doctor Hesselius has inscribed nothing more than the words, "Harman's Report," and a simple reference to his own extraordinary Essay on "The Interior Sense, and the Conditions of the Opening thereof."

The reference is to Vol. I., Section 317, Note Z^a. The note to which reference is thus made, simply says: "There are two accounts of the remarkable case of the Honourable Mr. Justice Harbottle, one furnished to me by Mrs. Trimmer, of Tunbridge Wells (June, 1805); the other at a much later date, by Anthony Harman, Esq. I much prefer the former; in the first place, because it is minute and detailed, and written, it seems to me, with more caution and knowledge; and in the next, because the letters from Dr. Hedstone, which are embodied in it, furnish matter of the highest value to a right apprehension of the nature of the case. It was one of the best declared cases of an opening of the interior sense, which I have met with. It was affected too, by the phenomenon, which occurs so frequently as to indicate a law of these eccentric conditions; that is to say, it exhibited what I may term, the contagious character of this sort of intrusion of the spirit-world upon the proper domain of matter. So soon as the spirit-action has established itself in the case of one patient, its developed energy begins to radiate, more or less effectually, upon others. The interior vision of the child was opened; as was, also, that of its mother, Mrs. Pyneweck; and both the interior vision and hearing of the scullery-maid, were opened on the same occasion. After-appearances are the result of the law explained in Vol. II., Section 17 to 49. The common centre of association, simultaneously recalled, unites, or *re*unites, as the case may be, for a period measured, as we see, in Section 37. The *maximum* will extend to days, the *minimum* is little more than a second. We see the operation of this principle perfectly displayed, in certain cases of lunacy, of epilepsy, of catalepsy, and of mania, of a peculiar and painful character, though unattended by incapacity of business."

The memorandum of the case of Judge Harbottle, which was written by Mrs. Trimmer, of Tunbridge Wells, which Doctor Hesselius thought the better of the two, I have been unable to discover among his papers. I found in his escritoire a note to the effect that he had lent the Report of Judge Harbottle's case, written by Mrs. Trimmer, to Dr. F. Heyne. To that learned and able gentleman accordingly I wrote, and received from him, in his reply, which was full of alarms and regrets, on account of the uncertain safety of that "valuable MS.," a line written long since by Dr. Hesselius, which completely exonerated him, inasmuch as it acknowledged the safe return of the papers. The narrative of Mr. Harman, is therefore, the only one available for this collection. The late Dr. Hesselius, in another passage of the note that I have cited, says, "As to the facts (non-medical) of the case, the narrative of Mr. Harman exactly tallies with that furnished by Mrs. Trimmer." The strictly scientific view of the case would scarcely interest the popular reader; and, possibly, for the purposes of this selection, I should, even had I both papers to choose between, have preferred that of Mr. Harman, which is given, in full, in the following pages.

I   The Judge's House

Thirty years ago, an elderly man, to whom I paid quarterly a small annuity charged on some property of mine, came on the quarter-day to receive it. He was a dry, sad, quiet man, who had known better days, and had always maintained an unexceptionable character. No better authority could be imagined for a ghost story.

He told me one, though with a manifest reluctance; he was drawn into the narration by his choosing to explain what I should not have remarked, that he had called two days earlier than that week after the strict day of payment, which he had usually allowed to elapse. His reason was a sudden determination to change his lodgings, and the consequent necessity of paying his rent a little before it was due.

He lodged in a dark street in Westminster, in a spacious old house, very warm, being wainscoted from top to bottom, and furnished with no undue abundance of windows, and those fitted with thick sashes and small panes.

This house was, as the bills upon the windows testified, offered to be sold or let. But no one seemed to care to look at it.

A thin matron, in rusty black silk, very taciturn, with large, steady, alarmed eyes, that seemed to look in your face, to read what you might have seen in the dark rooms and passages through which you had passed, was in charge of it, with a solitary "maid-of-all-work" under her command. My poor friend had taken lodgings in this house, on account of their extraordinary cheapness. He had occupied them for nearly a year without the slightest disturbance, and was the only tenant, under rent, in the house. He had two rooms; a sitting-room and a bed-room with a closet opening from it, in which he kept his books and papers locked up. He had gone to his bed, having also locked the outer door. Unable to sleep, he had lighted a candle, and after having read for a time, had laid the book beside him. He heard the old clock at the stair-head strike one; and very shortly after, to his alarm, he saw the closet-door, which he thought he had locked, open stealthily, and a slight dark man, particularly sinister, and somewhere about fifty, dressed in mourning of a very antique fashion, such a suit as we see in Hogarth, entered the room on tip-toe. He was followed by an elder man, stout, and blotched with scurvy, and whose features, fixed as a corpse's, were stamped with dreadful force with a character of sensuality and villainy.

This old man wore a flowered silk dressing-gown and ruffles, and he remarked a gold ring on his finger, and on his head a cap of velvet, such as, in the days of perukes, gentlemen wore in undress.

This direful old man carried in his ringed and ruffled hand a coil of rope; and these two figures crossed the floor diagonally, passing the foot of his bed, from the closet door at the farther end of the room, at the left, near the window, to the door opening upon the lobby, close to the bed's head, at his right.

He did not attempt to describe his sensations as these figures passed so near him. He merely said, that so far from sleeping in that room again, no consideration the world could offer would induce him so much as to enter it again alone, even in the daylight. He found both doors, that of the closet, and that of the room opening upon the lobby, in the morning fast locked as he had left them before going to bed.

In answer to a question of mine, he said that neither appeared the least conscious of his presence. They did not seem to glide, but walked as living men do, but without any sound, and he felt a vibration on the floor as they crossed it. He so obviously suffered from speaking about the apparitions, that I asked him no more questions.

There were in his description, however, certain coincidences so very singular, as to induce me, by that very post, to write to a friend much my senior, then living in a remote part of England, for the information which I knew he could give me. He had himself more than once pointed out that old house to my attention, and told me, though very briefly, the strange story which I now asked him to give me in greater detail.

His answer satisfied me; and the following pages convey its substance.

Your letter (he wrote) tells me you desire some particulars about the closing years of the life of Mr. Justice Harbottle, one of the judges of the Court of Common Pleas. You refer, of course, to the extraordinary occurrences that made that period of his life long after a theme for "winter tales" and metaphysical speculation. I happen to know perhaps more than any other man living of those mysterious particulars.

The old family mansion, when I revisited London, more than thirty years ago, I examined for the last time. During the years that have passed since then, I hear that improvement, with its preliminary demolitions, has been doing wonders for the quarter of Westminster in which it stood. If I were quite certain that the house had been taken down, I should have no difficulty about naming the street in which it stood. As what I have to tell, however, is not likely to improve its letting value, and as I should not care to get into trouble, I prefer being silent on that particular point.

How old the house was, I can't tell. People said it was built by Roger Harbottle, a Turkey merchant, in the reign of King James I. I am not a good opinion upon such questions; but having been in it, though in its forlorn and deserted state, I can tell you in a general way what it was like. It was built of dark-red brick, and the door and windows were faced with stone that had turned yellow by time. It receded some feet from the line of the other houses in the street; and it had a florid and fanciful rail of iron about the broad steps that invited your ascent to the hall-door, in which were fixed, under a file of lamps among scrolls and twisted leaves, two immense "extinguishers," like the conical caps of fairies, into which, in old times, the footmen used to thrust their flambeaux when their chairs or coaches had set down their great people, in the hall or at the steps, as the case might be. That hall is panelled up to the ceiling, and has a large fire-place. Two or three stately old rooms open from it at each side. The windows of these are tall, with many small panes. Passing through the arch at the back of the hall, you come upon the wide and heavy well-staircase. There is a back staircase also. The mansion is large, and has not as much light, by any means, in proportion to its extent, as modern houses enjoy. When I saw it, it had long been untenanted, and had the gloomy reputation beside of a haunted house. Cobwebs floated from the ceilings or spanned the corners of the cornices, and dust lay thick over everything. The windows were stained with the dust and rain of fifty years, and darkness had thus grown darker.

When I made it my first visit, it was in company with my father, when I was still a boy, in the year 1808. I was about twelve years old, and my imagination impressible, as it always is at that age. I looked about me with great awe. I was here in the very centre and scene of those occurrences which I had heard recounted at the fireside at home, with so delightful a horror.

My father was an old bachelor of nearly sixty when he married. He had, when a child, seen Judge Harbottle on the bench in his robes and wig a dozen times at least before his death, which took place in 1748, and his appearance made a powerful and unpleasant impression, not only on his imagination, but upon his nerves.

The Judge was at that time a man of some sixty-seven years. He had a great mulberry-coloured face, a big, carbuncled nose, fierce eyes, and a grim and brutal mouth. My father, who was young at the time, thought it the most formidable face he had ever seen; for there were evidences of intellectual power in the formation and lines of the forehead. His voice was loud and harsh, and gave effect to the sarcasm which was his habitual weapon on the bench.

This old gentleman had the reputation of being about the wickedest man in England. Even on the bench he now and then showed his scorn of opinion. He had carried cases his own way, it was said, in spite of counsel, authorities, and even of juries, by a sort of cajolery, violence, and bamboozling, that somehow confused and overpowered resistance. He had never actually committed himself; he was too cunning to do that. He had the character of being, however, a dangerous and unscrupulous judge; but his character did not trouble him. The associates he chose for his hours of relaxation cared as little as he did about it.

II   Mr. Peters

One night during the session of 1746 this old Judge went down in his chair to wait in one of the rooms of the House of Lords for the result of a division in which he and his order were interested.

This over, he was about to return to his house close by, in his chair; but the night had become so soft and fine that he changed his mind, sent it home empty, and with two footmen, each with a flambeau, set out on foot in preference. Gout had made him rather a slow pedestrian. It took him some time to get through the two or three streets he had to pass before reaching his house.

In one of those narrow streets of tall houses, perfectly silent at that hour, he overtook, slowly as he was walking, a very singular-looking old gentleman.

He had a bottle-green coat on, with a cape to it, and large stone buttons, a broad-leafed low-crowned hat, from under which a big powdered wig escaped; he stooped very much, and supported his bending knees with the aid of a crutch-handled cane, and so shuffled and tottered along painfully.

"I ask your pardon, sir," said this old man, in a very quavering voice, as the burly Judge came up with him, and he extended his hand feebly towards his arm.

Mr. Justice Harbottle saw that the man was by no means poorly dressed, and his manner that of a gentleman.

The Judge stopped short, and said, in his harsh peremptory tones, "Well, sir, how can I serve you?"

"Can you direct me to Judge Harbottle's house? I have some intelligence of the very last importance to communicate to him."

"Can you tell it before witnesses?" asked the Judge.

"By no means; it must reach *his* ear only," quavered the old man earnestly.

"If that be so, sir, you have only to accompany me a few steps farther to reach my house, and obtain a private audience; for I am Judge Harbottle."

With this invitation the infirm gentleman in the white wig complied very readily; and in another minute the stranger stood in what was then termed the front parlour of the Judge's house, *tête-à-tête* with that shrewd and dangerous functionary.

He had to sit down, being very much exhausted, and unable for a little time to speak; and then he had a fit of coughing, and after that a fit of gasping; and thus two or three minutes passed, during which the Judge dropped his roquelaure on an arm-chair, and threw his cocked-hat over that.

The venerable pedestrian in the white wig quickly recovered his voice. With closed doors they remained together for some time.

There were guests waiting in the drawing-rooms, and the sound of men's voices laughing, and then of a female voice singing to a harpsichord, were heard distinctly in the hall over the stairs; for old Judge Harbottle had arranged one of his dubious jollifications, such as might well make the hair of godly men's heads stand upright for that night.

This old gentleman in the powdered white wig, that rested on his stooped shoulders, must have had something to say that interested the Judge very much; for he would not have parted on easy terms with the ten minutes and upwards which that conference filched from the sort of revelry in which he most delighted, and in which he was the roaring king, and in some sort the tyrant also, of his company.

The footman who showed the aged gentleman out observed that the Judge's mulberry-coloured face, pimples and all, were bleached to a dingy yellow, and there was the abstraction of agitated thought in his manner, as he bid the stranger good-night. The servant saw that the conversation had been of serious import, and that the Judge was frightened.

Instead of stumping upstairs forthwith to his scandalous hilarities, his profane company, and his great china bowl of punch—the identical bowl from which a bygone Bishop of London, good easy man, had baptised this Judge's grandfather, now clinking round the rim with silver ladles, and hung with scrolls of lemon-peel—instead, I say, of stumping and clambering up the great staircase to the cavern of his Circean enchantment, he stood with his big nose flattened against the window-pane, watching the progress of the feeble old man, who clung stiffly to the iron rail as he got down, step by step, to the pavement.

The hall-door had hardly closed, when the old Judge was in the hall bawling hasty orders, with such stimulating expletives as old colonels under excitement sometimes indulge in now-a-days, with a stamp or two of his big foot, and a waving of his clenched fist in the air. He commanded the footman to overtake the old gentleman in the white wig, to offer him his protection on his way home, and in no case to show his face again without having ascertained where he lodged, and who he was, and all about him.

"By ——, sirrah! if you fail me in this, you doff my livery to-night!"

Forth bounced the stalwart footman, with his heavy cane under his arm, and skipped down the steps, and looked up and down the street after the singular figure, so easy to recognize.

What were his adventures I shall not tell you just now.

The old man, in the conference to which he had been admitted in that stately panelled room, had just told the Judge a very strange story. He might be himself a conspirator; he might possibly be crazed; or possibly his whole story was straight and true.

The aged gentleman in the bottle-green coat, on finding himself alone with Mr. Justice Harbottle, had become agitated. He said,

"There is, perhaps you are not aware, my lord, a prisoner in Shrewsbury jail, charged with having forged a bill of exchange for a hundred and twenty pounds, and his name is Lewis Pyneweck, a grocer of that town."

"Is there?" says the Judge, who knew well that there was.

"Yes, my lord," says the old man.

"Then you had better say nothing to affect this case. If you do, by —— I'll commit you! for I'm to try it," says the Judge, with his terrible look and tone.

"I am not going to do anything of the kind, my lord; of him or his case I know nothing, and care nothing. But a fact has come to my knowledge which it behoves you to well consider."

"And what may that fact be?" inquired the Judge; "I'm in haste, sir, and beg you will use dispatch."

"It has come to my knowledge, my lord, that a secret tribunal is in process of formation, the object of which is to take cognisance of the conduct of the judges; and first, of *your* conduct, my lord: it is a wicked conspiracy."

"Who are of it?" demands the Judge.

"I know not a single name as yet. I know but the fact, my lord; it is most certainly true."

"I'll have you before the Privy Council, sir," says the Judge.

"That is what I most desire; but not for a day or two, my lord."

"And why so?"

"I have not as yet a single name, as I told your lordship; but I expect to have a list of the most forward men in it, and some other papers connected with the plot, in two or three days."

"You said one or two just now."

"About that time, my lord."

"Is this a Jacobite plot?"

"In the main I think it is, my lord."

"Why, then, it is political. I have tried no State prisoners, nor am like to try any such. How, then, doth it concern me?"

"From what I can gather, my lord, there are those in it who desire private revenges upon certain judges."

"What do they call their cabal?"

"The High Court of Appeal, my lord."

"Who are you, sir? What is your name?"

"Hugh Peters, my Lord."

"That should be a Whig name?"

"It is, my lord."

"Where do you lodge, Mr. Peters?"

"In Thames Street, my lord, over against the sign of the 'Three Kings.'"

"'Three Kings'? Take care one be not too many for you, Mr. Peters! How come you, an honest Whig, as you say, to be privy to a Jacobite plot? Answer me that."

"My lord, a person in whom I take an interest has been seduced to take a part in it; and being frightened at the unexpected wickedness of their plans, he is resolved to become an informer for the Crown."

"He resolves like a wise man, sir. What does he say of the persons? Who are in the plot? Doth he know them?"

"Only two, my lord; but he will be introduced to the club in a few days, and he will then have a list, and more exact information of their plans, and above all of their oaths, and their hours and places of meeting, with which he wishes to be acquainted before they can have any suspicions of his intentions. And being so informed, to whom, think you, my lord, had he best go then?"

"To the king's attorney-general straight. But you say this concerns me, sir, in particular? How about this prisoner, Lewis Pyneweck? Is he one of them?"

"I can't tell, my lord; but for some reason, it is thought your lordship will be well advised if you try him not. For if you do, it is feared 'twill shorten your days."

"So far as I can learn, Mr. Peters, this business smells pretty strong of blood and treason. The king's attorney-general will know how to deal with it. When shall I see you again, sir?"

"If you give me leave, my lord, either before your lordship's court sits, or after it rises, to-morrow. I should like to come and tell your lordship what has passed."

"Do so, Mr. Peters, at nine o'clock to-morrow morning. And see you play me no trick, sir, in this matter; if you do, by ——, sir, I'll lay you by the heels!"

"You need fear no trick from me, my lord; had I not wished to serve you, and acquit my own conscience, I never would have come all this way to talk with your lordship."

"I'm willing to believe you, Mr. Peters; I'm willing to believe you, sir."

And upon this they parted.

"He has either painted his face, or he is consumedly sick," thought the old Judge.

The light had shone more effectually upon his features as he turned to leave the room with a low bow, and they looked, he fancied, unnaturally chalky.

"D— him!" said the Judge ungraciously, as he began to scale the stairs: "he has half-spoiled my supper."

But if he had, no one but the Judge himself perceived it, and the evidence was all, as any one might perceive, the other way.

III   Lewis Pyneweck

In the meantime the footman dispatched in pursuit of Mr. Peters speedily overtook that feeble gentleman. The old man stopped when he heard the sound of pursuing steps, but any alarms that may have crossed his mind seemed to disappear on his recognizing the livery. He very gratefully accepted the proffered assistance, and placed his tremulous arm within the servant's for support. They had not gone far, however, when the old man stopped suddenly, saying,

"Dear me! as I live, I have dropped it. You heard it fall. My eyes, I fear, won't serve me, and I'm unable to stoop low enough; but if *you* will look, you shall have half the find. It is a guinea; I carried it in my glove."

The street was silent and deserted. The footman had hardly descended to what he termed his "hunkers," and begun to search the pavement about the spot which the old man indicated, when Mr. Peters, who seemed very much exhausted, and breathed with difficulty, struck him a violent blow, from above, over the back of the head with a heavy instrument, and then another; and leaving him bleeding and senseless in the gutter, ran like a lamplighter down a lane to the right, and was gone.

When, an hour later, the watchman brought the man in livery home, still stupid and covered with blood, Judge Harbottle cursed his servant roundly, swore he was drunk, threatened him with an indictment for taking bribes to betray his master, and cheered him with a perspective of the broad street leading from the Old Bailey to Tyburn, the cart's tail, and the hangman's lash.

Notwithstanding this demonstration, the Judge was pleased. It was a disguised "affidavit man," or footpad, no doubt, who had been employed to frighten him. The trick had fallen through.

A "court of appeal," such as the false Hugh Peters had indicated, with assassination for its sanction, would be an uncomfortable institution for a "hanging judge" like the Honourable Justice Harbottle. That sarcastic and ferocious administrator of the criminal code of England, at that time a rather pharisaical, bloody and heinous system of justice, had reasons of his own for choosing to try that very Lewis Pyneweck, on whose behalf this audacious trick was devised. Try him he would. No man living should take that morsel out of his mouth.

Of Lewis Pyneweck, of course, so far as the outer world could see, he knew nothing. He would try him after his fashion, without fear, favour, or affection.

But did he not remember a certain thin man, dressed in mourning, in whose house, in Shrewsbury, the Judge's lodgings used to be, until a scandal of his ill-treating his wife came suddenly to light? A grocer with a demure look, a soft step, and a lean face as dark as mahogany, with a nose sharp and long, standing ever so little awry, and a pair of dark steady brown eyes under

150

thinly-traced black brows—a man whose thin lips wore always a faint unpleasant smile.

Had not that scoundrel an account to settle with the Judge? had he not been troublesome lately? and was not his name Lewis Pyneweck, some time grocer in Shrewsbury, and now prisoner in the jail of that town?

The reader may take it, if he pleases, as a sign that Judge Harbottle was a good Christian, that he suffered nothing ever from remorse. That was undoubtedly true. He had, nevertheless, done this grocer, forger, what you will, some five or six years before, a grievous wrong; but it was not that, but a possible scandal, and possible complications, that troubled the learned Judge now.

Did he not, as a lawyer, know, that to bring a man from his shop to the dock, the chances must be at least ninety-nine out of a hundred that he is guilty.

A weak man like his learned brother Withershins was not a judge to keep the high-roads safe, and make crime tremble. Old Judge Harbottle was the man to make the evil-disposed quiver, and to refresh the world with showers of wicked blood, and thus save the innocent, to the refrain of the ancient saw he loved to quote:

> Foolish pity
> Ruins a city.

In hanging that fellow he could not be wrong. The eye of a man accustomed to look upon the dock could not fail to read "villain" written sharp and clear in his plotting face. Of course he would try him, and no one else should.

A saucy-looking woman, still handsome, in a mob-cap gay with blue ribbons, in a saque of flowered silk, with lace and rings on, much too fine for the Judge's housekeeper, which nevertheless she was, peeped into his study next morning, and, seeing the Judge alone, stepped in.

"Here's another letter from him, come by the post this morning. Can't you do nothing for him?" she said wheedlingly, with her arm over his neck, and her delicate finger and thumb fiddling with the lobe of his purple ear.

"I'll try," said Judge Harbottle, not raising his eyes from the paper he was reading.

"I knew you'd do what I asked you," she said.

The Judge clapt his gouty claw over his heart, and made her an ironical bow.

"What," she asked, "will you do?"

"Hang him," said the Judge with a chuckle.

"You don't mean to; no, you don't, my little man," said she, surveying herself in a mirror on the wall.

"I'm d—d but I think you're falling in love with your husband at last!" said Judge Harbottle.

"I'm blest but I think you're growing jealous of him," replied the lady with a laugh. "But no; he was always a bad one to me; I've done with him long ago."

"And he with you, by George! When he took your fortune, and your spoons, and your ear-rings, he had all he wanted of you. He drove you from his house; and when he discovered you had made yourself comfortable, and found a good situation, he'd have taken your guineas, and your silver, and your ear-rings over again, and then allowed you half-a-dozen years more to make a new harvest for his mill. You don't wish him good; if you say you do, you lie."

She laughed a wicked, saucy laugh, and gave the terrible Rhadamanthus a playful tap on the chops.

"He wants me to send him money to fee a counsellor," she said, while her eyes wandered over the pictures on the wall, and back again to the looking-glass; and certainly she did not look as if his jeopardy troubled her very much.

"Confound his impudence, the *scoundrel*!" thundered the old Judge, throwing himself back in his chair, as he used to do *in furore* on the bench, and the lines of his mouth looked brutal, and his eyes ready to leap from their sockets. "If you answer his letter from my house to please yourself, you'll write your next from somebody else's to please me. You understand, my pretty witch, I'll not be pestered. Come, no pouting; whimpering won't do. You don't care a brass farthing for the villain, body or soul. You came here but to make a row. You are one of Mother Carey's chickens; and where you come, the storm is up. Get you gone, baggage! get you *gone*!" he repeated, with a stamp; for a knock at the hall-door made her instantaneous disappearance indispensable.

I need hardly say that the venerable Hugh Peters did not appear again. The Judge never mentioned him. But oddly enough, considering how he laughed to scorn the weak invention which he had blown into dust at the very first puff, his white-wigged visitor and the conference in the dark front parlour was often in his memory.

His shrewd eye told him that allowing for change of tints and such disguises as the playhouse affords every night, the features of this false old man, who had turned out too hard for his tall footman, were identical with those of Lewis Pyneweck.

Judge Harbottle made his registrar call upon the crown solicitor, and tell him that there was a man in town who bore a wonderful resemblance to a prisoner in Shrewsbury jail named Lewis Pyneweck, and to make inquiry through the post forthwith whether any one was personating Pyneweck in prison, and whether he had thus or otherwise made his escape.

The prisoner was safe, however, and no question as to his identity.

IV   Interruption in Court

In due time Judge Harbottle went circuit; and in due time the judges were in Shrewsbury. News travelled slowly in those days, and newspapers, like the wagons and stage-coaches, took matters easily. Mrs. Pyneweck, in the Judge's house, with a diminished household—the greater part of the Judge's servants having gone with him, for he had given up riding circuit, and travelled in his coach in state—kept house rather solitarily at home.

In spite of quarrels, in spite of mutual injuries—some of them, inflicted by herself, enormous—in spite of a married life of spited bickerings—a life in which there seemed no love or liking or forbearance, for years—now that Pyneweck stood in near danger of death, something like remorse came suddenly upon her. She knew that in Shrewsbury were transacting the scenes which were to determine his fate. She knew she did not love him; but she could not have supposed, even a fortnight before, that the hour of suspense could have affected her so powerfully.

She knew the day on which the trial was expected to take place. She could not get it out of her head for a minute; she felt faint as it drew towards evening.

Two or three days passed; and then she knew that the trial must be over by this time. There were floods between London and Shrewsbury, and news was long delayed. She wished the floods would last for ever. It was dreadful waiting to hear; dreadful to know that the event was over, and that she could not hear till self-willed rivers subsided; dreadful to know that they must subside and the news come at last.

She had some vague trust in the Judge's good-nature, and much in the resources of chance and accident. She had contrived to send the money he wanted. He would not be without legal advice and energetic and skilled support.

At last the news did come—a long arrear all in a gush: a letter from a female friend in Shrewsbury; a return of the sentences, sent up for the Judge; and most important, because most easily got at, being told with great aplomb and brevity, the long-deferred intelligence of the Shrewsbury Assizes in the *Morning Advertiser*. Like an impatient reader of a novel, who reads the last page first, she read with dizzy eyes the list of the executions.

Two were respited, seven were hanged; and in that capital catalogue was this line:

"Lewis Pyneweck—forgery."

She had to read it half-a-dozen times over before she was sure she understood it. Here was the paragraph:

Sentence, Death—7

Executed accordingly, on Friday the 13th instant, to wit:
    Thomas Primer, *alias* Duck—highway robbery.
    Flora Guy—stealing to the value of IIs. 6d.
    Arthur Pounden—burglary.
    Matilda Mummery—riot.
    Lewis Pyneweck—forgery, bill of exchange.

And when she reached this, she read it over and over, feeling very cold and sick.

This buxom housekeeper was known in the house as Mrs. Carwell—

Carwell being her maiden name, which she had resumed.

No one in the house except its master knew her history. Her introduction had been managed craftily. No one suspected that it had been concerted between her and the old reprobate in scarlet and ermine.

Flora Carwell ran up the stairs now, and snatched her little girl, hardly seven years of age, whom she met on the lobby, hurriedly up in her arms, and carried her into her bedroom, without well knowing what she was doing, and sat down, placing the child before her. She was not able to speak. She held the child before her, and looked in the little girl's wondering face, and burst into tears of horror.

She thought the Judge could have saved him. I daresay he could. For a time she was furious with him, and hugged and kissed her bewildered little girl, who returned her gaze with large round eyes.

That little girl had lost her father, and knew nothing of the matter. She had been always told that her father was dead long ago.

A woman, coarse, uneducated, vain, and violent, does not reason, or even feel, very distinctly; but in these tears of consternation were mingling a self-upbraiding. She felt afraid of that little child.

But Mrs. Carwell was a person who lived not upon sentiment, but upon beef and pudding; she consoled herself with punch; she did not trouble herself long even with resentments; she was a gross and material person, and could not mourn over the irrevocable for more than a limited number of hours, even if she would.

Judge Harbottle was soon in London again. Except the gout, this savage old epicurean never knew a day's sickness. He laughed, and coaxed, and bullied away the young woman's faint upbraidings, and in a little time Lewis Pyneweck troubled her no more; and the Judge secretly chuckled over the perfectly fair removal of a bore, who might have grown little by little into something very like a tyrant.

It was the lot of the Judge whose adventures I am now recounting to try criminal cases at the Old Bailey shortly after his return. He had commenced his charge to the jury in a case of forgery, and was, after his wont, thundering dead against the prisoner, with many a hard aggravation and cynical gibe, when suddenly all died away in silence, and, instead of looking at the jury, the eloquent Judge was gaping at some person in the body of the court.

Among the persons of small importance who stand and listen at the sides was one tall enough to show with a little prominence; a slight mean figure, dressed in seedy black, lean and dark of visage. He had just handed a letter to the crier, before he caught the Judge's eye.

That Judge descried, to his amazement, the features of Lewis Pyneweck. He has the usual faint thin-lipped smile; and with his blue chin raised in air, and as it seemed quite unconscious of the distinguished notice he has attracted, he was stretching his low cravat with his crooked fingers, while he slowly turned his head from side to side—a process which enabled the Judge to see distinctly a stripe of swollen blue round his neck, which indicated, he thought, the grip of the rope.

This man, with a few others, had got a footing on a step, from which he could better see the court. He now stepped down, and the Judge lost sight of him.

His lordship signed energetically with his hand in the direction in which this man had vanished. He turned to the tipstaff. His first effort to speak ended in a gasp. He cleared his throat, and told the astounded official to arrest that man who had interrupted the court.

"He's but this moment gone down *there*. Bring him in custody before me, within ten minutes' time, or I'll strip your gown from your shoulders and fine the sheriff!" he thundered, while his eyes flashed round the court in search of the functionary.

Attorneys, counsellors, idle spectators, gazed in the direction in which Mr. Justice Harbottle had shaken his gnarled old hand. They compared notes. Not one had seen any one making a disturbance. They asked one another if the Judge was losing his head.

Nothing came of the search. His lordship concluded his charge a great deal more tamely; and when the jury retired, he stared round the court with a wandering mind, and looked as if he would not have given sixpence to see the prisoner hanged.

V   Caleb Searcher

The Judge had received the letter; had he known from whom it came, he would no doubt have read it instantaneously. As it was he simply read the direction:

> To the Honourable
> > The Lord Justice
> > > Elijah Harbottle,
> > One of his Majesty's Justices of
> > > the Honourable Court of Common Pleas.

It remained forgotten in his pocket till he reached home.

When he pulled out that and others from the capacious pocket of his coat, it had its turn, as he sat in his library in his thick silk dressing-gown; and then he found its contents to be a closely-written letter, in a clerk's hand, and an enclosure in "secretary hand," as I believe the angular scrivinary of law-writings in those days was termed, engrossed on a bit of parchment about the size of this page. The letter said:

> MR. JUSTICE HARBOTTLE,—MY LORD,
> I am ordered by the High Court of Appeal to acquaint your lordship, in order to your better preparing yourself for your trial, that a true bill hath been sent down, and the indictment lieth against your lordship for the murder of one Lewis Pyneweck of Shrewsbury, citizen, wrongfully executed for the forgery of a bill of

exchange, on the —th day of —— last, by reason of the wilful perversion of the evidence, and the undue pressure put upon the jury, together with the illegal admission of evidence by your lordship, well knowing the same to be illegal, by all which the promoter of the prosecution of the said indictment, before the High Court of Appeal, hath lost his life.

And the trial of the said indictment, I am farther ordered to acquaint your lordship, is fixed for the 10th day of —— next ensuing, by the right honourable the Lord Chief Justice Twofold, of the court aforesaid, to wit, the High Court of Appeal, on which day it will most certainly take place. And I am farther to acquaint your lordship, to prevent any surprise or miscarriage, that your case stands first for the said day, and that the said High Court of Appeal sits day and night, and never rises; and herewith, by order of the said court, I furnish your lordship with a copy (extract) of the record in this case, except of the indictment, whereof, notwithstanding, the substance and effect is supplied to your lordship in this Notice. And farther I am to inform you, that in case the jury then to try your lordship should find you guilty, the right honourable the Lord Chief Justice will, in passing sentence of death upon you, fix the day of execution for the 10th day of ——, being one calendar month from the day of your trial.

It was signed by   CALEB SEARCHER,
                              Officer of the Crown Solicitor in the
                              Kingdom of Life and Death.

The Judge glanced through the parchment.

" 'Sblood! Do they think a man like me is to be bamboozled by their buffoonery?"

The Judge's coarse features were wrung into one of his sneers; but he was pale. Possibly, after all, there was a conspiracy on foot. It was queer. Did they mean to pistol him in his carriage? or did they only aim at frightening him?

Judge Harbottle had more than enough of animal courage. He was not afraid of highwaymen, and he had fought more than his share of duels, being a foul-mouthed advocate while he held briefs at the bar. No one questioned his fighting qualities. But with respect to this particular case of Pyneweck, he lived in a house of glass. Was there not his pretty, dark-eyed, over-dressed housekeeper, Mrs. Flora Carwell? Very easy for people who knew Shrewsbury to identify Mrs. Pyneweck, if once put upon the scent; and had he not stormed and worked hard in that case? Had he not made it hard sailing for the prisoner? Did he not know very well what the bar thought of it? It would be the worst scandal that ever blasted Judge.

So much there was intimidating in the matter but nothing more. The Judge was a little bit gloomy for a day or two after, and more testy with every one than usual.

He locked up the papers; and about a week after he asked his housekeeper, one day, in the library:

"Had your husband never a brother?"

Mrs. Carwell squalled on this sudden introduction of the funereal topic, and cried exemplary "piggins full," as the Judge used pleasantly to say. But he was in no mood for trifling now, and he said sternly:

"Come, madam! this wearies me. Do it another time; and give me an answer to my question." So she did.

Pyneweck had no brother living. He once had one; but he died in Jamaica.

"How do you know he is dead?" asked the Judge.

"Because he told me so."

"Not the dead man."

"Pyneweck told me so."

"Is that all?" sneered the Judge.

He pondered this matter; and time went on. The Judge was growing a little morose, and less enjoying. The subject struck nearer to his thoughts than he fancied it could have done. But so it is with most undivulged vexations, and there was no one to whom he could tell this one.

It was now the ninth; and Mr. Justice Harbottle was glad. He knew nothing would come of it. Still it bothered him; and to-morrow would see it well over.

[What of the paper I have cited? No one saw it during his life; no one, after his death. He spoke of it to Dr. Hedstone; and what purported to be "a copy," in the old Judge's handwriting, was found. The original was nowhere. Was it a copy of an illusion, incident to brain disease? Such is my belief.]

VI   Arrested

Judge Harbottle went this night to the play at Drury Lane. He was one of those old fellows who care nothing for late hours, and occasional knocking about in pursuit of pleasure. He had appointed with two cronies of Lincoln's Inn to come home in his coach with him to sup after the play.

They were not in his box, but were to meet him near the entrance, and get into his carriage there; and Mr. Justice Harbottle, who hated waiting, was looking a little impatiently from the window.

The Judge yawned.

He told the footman to watch for Counsellor Thavies and Counsellor Beller, who were coming; and, with another yawn, he laid his cocked hat on his knees, closed his eyes, leaned back in his corner, wrapped his mantle closer about him, and began to think of pretty Mrs. Abington.

And being a man who could sleep like a sailor, at a moment's notice, he was thinking of taking a nap. Those fellows had no business to keep a judge waiting.

He heard their voices now. Those rake-hell counsellors were laughing, and bantering, and sparring after their wont. The carriage swayed and jerked, as one got in, and then again as the other followed. The door clapped, and the coach was now jogging and rumbling over the pavement. The Judge was a little bit sulky. He did not care to sit up and open his eyes. Let them suppose he was asleep. He heard them laugh with more malice than good-humour, he thought, as they observed it. He would give them a d—d hard knock or two when they got to his door, and till then he would counterfeit his nap.

The clocks were chiming twelve. Beller and Thavies were silent as tombstones. They were generally loquacious and merry rascals.

The Judge suddenly felt himself roughly seized and thrust from his corner into the middle of the seat, and opening his eyes, instantly he found himself between his two companions.

Before he could blurt out the oath that was at his lips, he saw that they were two strangers—evil-looking fellows, each with a pistol in his hand, and dressed like Bow Street officers.

The Judge clutched at the check-string. The coach pulled up. He stared about him. They were not among houses; but through the windows, under a broad moonlight, he saw a black moor stretching lifelessly from right to left, with rotting trees, pointing fantastic branches in the air, standing here and there in groups, as if they held up their arms and twigs like fingers, in horrible glee at the Judge's coming.

A footman came to the window. He knew his long face and sunken eyes. He knew it was Dingly Chuff, fifteen years ago a footman in his service, whom he had turned off at a moment's notice, in a burst of jealousy, and indicted for a missing spoon. The man had died in prison of the jail-fever.

The Judge drew back in utter amazement. His armed companions signed mutely; and they were again gliding over this unknown moor.

The bloated and gouty old man, in his horror considered the question of resistance. But his athletic days were long over. This moor was a desert. There was no help to be had. He was in the hands of strange servants, even if his recognition turned out to be a delusion, and they were under the command of his captors. There was nothing for it but submission, for the present.

Suddenly the coach was brought nearly to a standstill, so that the prisoner saw an omnious sight from the window.

It was a gigantic gallows beside the road; it stood three-sided, and from each of its three broad beams at top depended in chains some eight or ten bodies, from several of which the cere-clothes had dropped away, leaving the skeletons swinging lightly by their chains. A tall ladder reached to the summit of the structure, and on the peat beneath lay bones.

On top of the dark transverse beam facing the road, from which, as from the other two completing the triangle of death, dangled a row of these unfortunates in chains, a hangman, with a pipe in his mouth, much as we see him in the famous print of the "Idle Apprentice," though here his perch was ever so much higher, was reclining at his ease and listlessly shying bones, from a little heap at his elbow, at the skeletons that hung round, bringing down now a rib or two, now a hand, now half a leg. A long-sighted man could have discerned that he was a dark fellow, lean; and from continually looking down on the earth from the elevation over which, in another sense, he always hung, his nose, his lips, his chin were pendulous and loose, and drawn down into a monstrous grotesque.

This fellow took his pipe from his mouth on seeing the coach, stood up, and cut some solemn capers high on his beam, and shook a new rope in the air, crying with a voice high and distant as the caw of a raven hovering over a gibbet, "A rope for Judge Harbottle!"

The coach was now driving on at its old swift pace.

So high a gallows as that, the Judge had never, even in his most hilarious moments, dreamed of. He thought he must be raving. And the dead footman! He shook his ears and strained his eyelids; but if he was dreaming, he was unable to awake himself.

There was no good in threatening these scoundrels. A *brutum fulmen* might bring a real one on his head.

Any submission to get out of their hands; and then heaven and earth he would move to unearth and hunt them down.

Suddenly they drove round a corner of a vast white building, and under a *porte-cochère*.

VII   Chief Justice Twofold

The Judge found himself in a corridor lighted with dingy oil lamps, the walls of bare stone; it looked like a passage in a prison. His guards placed him in the hands of other people. Here and there he saw bony and gigantic soldiers passing to and fro, with muskets over their shoulders. They looked straight before them, grinding their teeth, in bleak fury, with no noise but the clank of their shoes. He saw these by glimpses, round corners, and at the ends of passages, but he did not actually pass them by.

And now, passing under a narrow doorway, he found himself in the dock, confronting a judge in his scarlet robes, in a large court-house. There was nothing to elevate this Temple of Themis above its vulgar kind elsewhere. Dingy enough it looked, in spite of candles lighted in decent abundance. A case had just closed, and the last juror's back was seen escaping through the door in the wall of the jury-box. There were some dozen barristers, some fiddling with pen and ink, others buried in briefs, some beckoning, with the plumes of their pens, to their attorneys, of whom there were no lack; there were clerks to-ing and fro-ing, and the officers of the court, and the registrar, who was handing up a paper to the judge; and the tipstaff, who was presenting a note at the end of his wand to a king's counsel over the heads of the crowd between. If this was the High Court of Appeal, which never rose day or night, it might account for the pale and jaded aspect of everybody in it. An air of indescribable gloom hung upon the pallid features of all the people here; no one ever smiled; all looked more or less secretly suffering.

"The King against Elijah Harbottle!" shouted the officer.

"Is the appellant Lewis Pyneweck in court?" asked Chief-Justice Twofold, in a voice of thunder, that shook the woodwork of the court, and boomed down the corridors.

Up stood Pyneweck from his place at the table.

"Arraign the prisoner!" roared the Chief: and Judge Harbottle felt the panels of the dock round him, and the floor, and the rails quiver in the vibrations of that tremendous voice.

The prisoner, *in limine*, objected to this pretended court, as being a sham, and non-existent in point of law; and then, that, even if it were a court constituted by law (the Judge was growing dazed), it had not and could not have any jurisdiction to try him for his conduct on the bench.

Whereupon the chief-justice laughed suddenly, and every one in court, turning round upon the prisoner, laughed also, till the laugh grew and roared all round like a deafening acclamation; he saw nothing but glittering eyes and teeth, a universal stare and grin; but though all the voices laughed, not a single face of all those that concentrated their gaze upon him looked like a laughing face. The mirth subsided as suddenly as it began.

The indictment was read. Judge Harbottle actually pleaded! He pleaded "Not Guilty." A jury were sworn. The trial proceeded. Judge Harbottle was bewildered. This could not be real. He must be either mad, or *going* mad, he thought.

One thing could not fail to strike even him. This Chief-Justice Twofold, who was knocking him about at every turn with sneer and gibe, and roaring him down with his tremendous voice, was a dilated effigy of himself; an image of Mr. Justice Harbottle, at least double his size, and with all his fierce colouring, and his ferocity of eye and visage, enhanced awfully.

Nothing the prisoner could argue, cite, or state, was permitted to retard for a moment the march of the case towards its catastrophe.

The chief-justice seemed to feel his power over the jury, and to exult and riot in the display of it. He glared at them, he nodded to them; he seemed to have established an understanding with them. The lights were faint in that part of the court. The jurors were mere shadows, sitting in rows; the prisoner could see a dozen pair of white eyes shining, coldly, out of the darkness; and whenever the judge in his charge, which was contemptuously brief, nodded and grinned and gibed, the prisoner could see, in the obscurity, by the dip of all these rows of eyes together, that the jury nodded in acquiescence.

And now the charge was over, the huge chief-justice leaned back panting and gloating on the prisoner. Every one in the court turned about, and gazed with steadfast hatred on the man in the dock. From the jury-box where the twelve sworn brethren were whispering together, a sound in the general stillness like a prolonged "hiss-s-s!" was heard; and then, in answer to the challenge of the officer, "How say you, gentlemen of the jury, guilty or not guilty?" came in a melancholy voice the finding, "Guilty."

The place seemed to the eyes of the prisoner to grow gradually darker and darker, till he could discern nothing distinctly but the lumen of the eyes that were turned upon him from every bench and side and corner and gallery of the building. The prisoner doubtless thought that he had quite enough to say, and conclusive, why sentence of death should not be pronounced upon him; but the lord chief-justice puffed it contemptuously away, like so much smoke, and proceeded to pass sentence of death upon the prisoner, having named the tenth of the ensuing month for his execution.

Before he had recovered the stun of this ominous farce, in obedience to the mandate, "Remove the prisoner," he was led from the dock. The lamps seemed all to have gone out, and there were stoves and charcoal-fires here and there, that threw a faint crimson light on the walls of the corridors through which he passed. The stones that composed them looked now enormous, cracked and unhewn.

He came into a vaulted smithy, where two men, naked to the waist, with heads like bulls, round shoulders, and the arms of giants, were welding red-hot chains together with hammers that pelted like thunderbolts.

They looked on the prisoner with fierce red eyes, and rested on their hammers for a minute; and said the elder to his companion, "Take out Elijah Harbottle's gyves"; and with a pincers he plucked the end which lay dazzling in the fire from the furnace.

"One end locks," said he, taking the cool end of the iron in one hand, while with the grip of a vice he seized the leg of the Judge, and locked the ring round his ankle. "The other," he said with a grin, "is welded."

The iron band that was to form the ring for the other leg lay still red hot upon the stone floor, with brilliant sparks sporting up and down its surface.

His companion, in his gigantic hands, seized the old Judge's other leg, and pressed his foot immovably to the stone floor; while his senior, in a twinkling, with a masterly application of pincers and hammer, sped the glowing bar round his ankle so tight that the skin and sinews smoked and bubbled again, and old Judge Harbottle uttered a yell that seemed to chill the very stones, and make the iron chains quiver on the wall.

Chains, vaults, smiths, and smithy all vanished in a moment; but the pain continued. Mr. Justice Harbottle was suffering torture all round the ankle on which the infernal smiths had just been operating.

His friends, Thavies and Beller were startled by the Judge's roar in the midst of their elegant trifling about a marriage *à-la-mode* case which was going on. The Judge was in panic as well as pain. The street lamps and the light of his own hall door restored him.

"I'm very bad," growled he between his set teeth; "my foot's blazing. Who was he that hurt my foot? 'Tis the gout—'tis the gout!" he said, awaking completely. "How many hours have we been coming from the playhouse? 'Sblood, what has happened on the way? I've slept half the night!"

There had been no hitch or delay, and they had driven home at a good pace.

The Judge, however, was in gout; he was feverish too; and the attack, though very short, was sharp; and when, in about a fortnight, it subsided, his ferocious joviality did not return. He could not get this dream, as he chose to call it, out of his head.

VIII   Somebody Has Got Into the House

People remarked that the Judge was in the vapours. His doctor said he should go for a fortnight to Buxton.

Whenever the Judge fell into a brown study, he was always conning over the terms of the sentence pronounced upon him in his vision—"in one calendar month from the date of this day"; and then the usual form, "and you shall be hanged by the neck till you are dead," etc. "That will be the 10th—I'm not much in the way of being hanged. I know what stuff dreams are, and I laugh at them; but this is continually in my thoughts, as if it forecast misfortune of some sort. I wish the day my dream gave me were passed and over. I wish I were well purged of my gout. I wish I were as I used to be. 'Tis nothing but vapours, nothing but a maggot." The copy of the parchment and letter which had announced his trial with many a snort and sneer he would read over and over again, and the scenery and people of his dream would rise about him in places the most unlikely, and steal him in a moment from all that surrounded him into a world of shadows.

The Judge had lost his iron energy and banter. He was growing taciturn and morose. The Bar remarked the change, as well they might. His friends thought him ill. The doctor said he was troubled with hypochondria, and that his gout was still lurking in his system, and ordered him to that ancient haunt of crutches and chalk-stones, Buxton.

The Judge's spirits were very low; he was frightened about himself; and he described to his housekeeper, having sent for her to his study to drink a dish of tea, his strange dream in his drive home from Drury Lane Playhouse. He was sinking into the state of nervous dejection in which men lose their faith in orthodox advice, and in despair consult quacks, astrologers, and nursery story-tellers. Could such a dream mean that he was to have a fit, and so die on the 10th? She did not think so. On the contrary, it was certain some good luck must happen on that day.

The Judge kindled; and for the first time for many days, he looked for a minute or two like himself, and he tapped her on the cheek with the hand that was not in flannel.

"Odsbud! odsheart! you dear rogue! I had forgot. There is young Tom—yellow Tom, my nephew, you know, lies sick at Harrogate; why shouldn't he go that day as well as another, and if he does, I get an estate by it? Why, lookee, I asked Doctor Hedstone yesterday if I was like to take a fit any time, and he laughed, and swore I was the last man in town to go off that way."

The Judge sent most of his servants down to Buxton to make his lodgings and all things comfortable for him. He was to follow in a day or two.

It was now the 9th; and the next day well over, he might laugh at his visions and auguries.

On the evening of the 9th, Dr. Hedstone's footman knocked at the Judge's door. The Doctor ran up the dusky stairs to the drawing-room. It was a March evening, near the hour of sunset, with an east wind whistling sharply through the chimney-stacks. A wood fire blazed cheerily on the hearth. And Judge Harbottle, in what was then called a brigadier-wig, with his red roquelaure on, helped the glowing effect of the darkened chamber, which looked red all over like a room on fire.

The Judge had his feet on a stool, and his huge grim purple face confronted the fire, and seemed to pant and swell, as the blaze alternately spread upward and collapsed. He had fallen again among his blue devils, and was thinking of retiring from the Bench, and of fifty other gloomy things.

But the Doctor, who was an energetic son of Æsculapius, would listen to no croaking, told the Judge he was full of gout, and in his present condition no judge even of his own case, but promised him leave to pronounce on all those melancholy questions, a fortnight later.

In the meantime the Judge must be very careful. He was over-charged with gout, and he must not provoke an attack, till the waters of Buxton should do that office for him, in their own salutary way.

The Doctor did not think him perhaps quite so well as he pretended, for he told him he wanted rest, and would be better if he went forthwith to his bed.

Mr. Gerningham, his valet, assisted him, and gave him his drops; and the Judge told him to wait in his bedroom till he should go to sleep.

Three persons that night had specially odd stories to tell.

The housekeeper had got rid of the trouble of amusing her little girl at this anxious time, by giving her leave to run about the sitting-rooms and look at the pictures and china, on the usual condition of touching nothing. It was not until the last gleam of sunset had for some time faded, and the twilight had so deepened that she could no longer discern the colours on the china figures on the chimneypiece or in the cabinets, that the child returned to the housekeeper's room to find her mother.

To her she related, after some prattle about the china, and the pictures, and the Judge's two grand wigs in the dressing-room off the library, an adventure of an extraordinary kind.

In the hall was placed, as was customary in those times, the sedan-chair which the master of the house occasionally used, covered with stamped leather, and studded with gilt nails, and with its red silk blinds down. In this case, the doors of this old-fashioned conveyance were locked, the windows up, and, as I said, the blinds down, but not so closely that the curious child could not peep underneath one of them, and see into the interior.

A parting beam from the setting sun, admitted through the window of a back room, shot obliquely through the open door, and lighting on the chair, shone with a dull transparency through the crimson blind.

To her surprise, the child saw in the shadow a thin man, dressed in black, seated in it; he had sharp dark features; his nose, she fancied, a little awry, and his brown eyes were looking straight before him; his hand was on his thigh, and he stirred no more than the waxen figure she had seen at Southwark fair.

A child is so often lectured for asking questions, and on the propriety of silence, and the superior wisdom of its elders, that it accepts most things at last in good faith; and the little girl acquiesced respectfully in the occupation of the chair by this mahogany-faced person as being all right and proper.

It was not until she asked her mother who this man was, and observed her scared face as she questioned her more minutely upon the appearance of the stranger, that she began to understand that she had seen something unaccountable.

Mrs. Carwell took the key of the chair from its nail over the footman's shelf, and led the child by the hand up to the hall, having a lighted candle in her other hand. She stopped at a distance from the chair, and placed the candlestick in the child's hand.

"Peep in, Margery, again, and try if there's anything there," she whispered; "hold the candle near the blind so as to throw its light through the curtain."

The child peeped, this time with a very solemn face, and intimated at once that he was gone.

"Look again, and be sure," urged her mother.

The little girl was quite certain; and Mrs. Carwell, with her mob-cap of lace and cherry-coloured ribbons, and her dark brown hair, not yet powdered, over a very pale face, unlocked the door, looked in, and beheld emptiness.

"All a mistake, child, you see."

"*There!* ma'am! see there! He's gone round the corner," said the child.

"Where?" said Mrs. Carwell, stepping backward a step.

"Into that room."

"Tut, child! 'twas the shadow," cried Mrs. Carwell, angrily, because she was frightened. "I moved the candle." But she clutched one of the poles of the chair, which leant against the wall in the corner, and pounded the floor furiously with one end of it, being afraid to pass the open door the child had pointed to.

The cook and two kitchen-maids came running upstairs, not knowing what to make of this unwonted alarm.

They all searched the room; but it was still and empty, and no sign of any one's having been there.

Some people may suppose that the direction given to her thoughts by this odd little incident will account for a very strange illusion which Mrs. Carwell herself experienced about two hours later.

IX   The Judge Leaves His House

Mrs. Flora Carwell was going up the great staircase with a posset for the Judge in a china bowl, on a little silver tray.

Across the top of the well-staircase there runs a massive oak rail; and, raising her eyes accidentally, she saw an extremely odd-looking stranger, slim and long, leaning carelessly over with a pipe between his finger and thumb. Nose, lips, and chin seemed all to droop downward into extraordinary length, as he leant his odd peering face over the banister. In his other hand he held a coil of rope, one end of which escaped from under his elbow and hung over the rail.

Mrs. Carwell, who had no suspicion at the moment, that he was not a real person, and fancied that he was some one employed in cording the Judge's luggage, called to know what he was doing there.

Instead of answering, he turned about, and walked across the lobby, at about the same leisurely pace at which she was ascending, and entered a room, into which she followed him. It was an uncarpeted and unfurnished chamber. An open trunk lay upon the floor empty, and beside it the coil of rope; but except herself there was no one in the room.

Mrs. Carwell was very much frightened, and now concluded that the child must have seen the same ghost that had just appeared to her. Perhaps, when she was able to think it over, it was a relief to believe so; for the face, figure, and dress described by the child were awfully like Pyneweck; and this certainly was not he.

Very much scared and very hysterical, Mrs. Carwell ran down to her room, afraid to look over her shoulder, and got some companions about her, and wept, and talked, and drank more than one cordial, and talked and wept again, and so on, until, in those early days, it was ten o'clock, and time to go to bed.

A scullery-maid remained up finishing some of her scouring and "scalding" for some time after the other servants—who, as I said, were few in number—that night had got to their beds. This was a low-browed, broad-faced, intrepid wench with black hair, who did not "vally a ghost not a button," and treated the housekeeper's hysterics with measureless scorn.

The old house was quiet now. It was near twelve o'clock, no sounds were audible except the muffled wailing of the wintry winds, piping high among the roofs and chimneys, or rumbling at intervals, in under gusts, through the narrow channels of the street.

The spacious solitudes of the kitchen level were awfully dark, and this sceptical kitchen-wench was the only person now up and about in the house. She hummed tunes to herself, for a time; and then stopped and listened; and then resumed her work again. At last, she was destined to be more terrified than even was the housekeeper.

There was a back kitchen in this house, and from this she heard, as if coming from below its foundations, a sound like heavy strokes, that seemed to shake the earth beneath her feet. Sometimes a dozen in sequence, at regular intervals; sometimes fewer. She walked out softly into the passage, and was surprised to see a dusky glow issuing from this room, as if from a charcoal fire.

The room seemed thick with smoke.

Looking in she very dimly beheld a monstrous figure, over a furnace, beating with a mighty hammer the rings and rivets of a chain.

The strokes, swift and heavy as they looked, sounded hollow and distant. The man stopped, and pointed to something on the floor, that, through the smoky haze, looked, she thought, like a dead body. She remarked no more; but the servants in the room close by, startled from their sleep by a hideous scream, found her in a swoon on the flags, close to the door, where she had just witnessed this ghastly vision.

Startled by the girl's incoherent asseverations that she had seen the Judge's corpse on the floor, two servants having first searched the lower part of the house, went rather frightened up-stairs to inquire whether their master was well. They found him, not in his bed, but in his room. He had a table with candles burning at his bedside, and was getting on his clothes again; and he swore and cursed at them roundly in his old style, telling them that he had business, and that he would discharge on the spot any scoundrel who should dare to disturb him again.

So the invalid was left to his quietude.

In the morning it was rumoured here and there in the street that the Judge was dead. A servant was sent from the house three doors away, by Counsellor Traverse, to inquire at Judge Harbottle's hall door.

The servant who opened it was pale and reserved, and would only say that the Judge was ill. He had had a dangerous accident; Doctor Hedstone had been with him at seven o'clock in the morning.

There were averted looks, short answers, pale and frowning faces, and all the usual signs that there was a secret that sat heavily upon their minds, and the time for disclosing which had not yet come. That time would arrive when the coroner had arrived, and the mortal scandal that had befallen the house could be no longer hidden. For that morning Mr. Justice Harbottle had been found hanging by the neck from the banister at the top of the great staircase, and quite dead.

There was not the smallest sign of any struggle or resistance. There had not been heard a cry or any other noise in the slightest degree indicative of violence. There was medical evidence to show that, in his atrabilious state, it was quite on the cards that he might have made away with himself. The jury found accordingly that it was a case of suicide. But to those who were acquainted with the strange story which Judge Harbottle had related to at least two persons, the fact that the catastrophe occurred on the morning of March 10th seemed a startling coincidence.

A few days after, the pomp of a great funeral attended him to the grave; and so, in the language of Scripture, "the rich man died, and was buried."

Ray Bradbury

The Crowd

For just over a decade, from the early 1940s to the late 1950s, Ray Bradbury produced an extraordinary body of work in the short story form, stories of science fiction, fantasy and horror, work that was quickly recognized as a significant contribution to American literature. The thread of dark fantasy is woven throughout his works. His first book, the collection *Dark Carnival* (Arkham House, 1947), was primarily supernatural horror fiction and his later masterpieces, *The Martian Chronicles* (1950), *The Illustrated Man* (1951), *The Golden Apples of the Sun* (1953), *The October Country* (1955) and *Something Wicked This Way Comes* (1959), all contain horror stories in his characteristic mode: overt moral consciousness in the face of evil. The ordinary man is faced with an evil just too big and organized to overcome. It is interesting to compare "The Crowd" to Harlan Ellison's "The Whimper of Whipped Dogs."

Mr. Spallner put his hands over his face.

There was the feeling of movement in space, the beautifully tortured scream, the impact and tumbling of the car with wall, through wall, over and down like a toy, and him hurled out of it. Then—silence.

The crowd came running. Faintly, where he lay, he heard them running. He could tell their ages and their sizes by the sound of their numerous feet over the summer grass and on the lined pavement, and over the asphalt street, and picking through the cluttered bricks to where his car hung half into the night sky, still spinning its wheels with a senseless centrifuge.

Where the crowd came from he didn't know. He struggled to remain aware and then the crowd faces hemmed in upon him, hung over him like the large glowing leaves of down-bent trees. They were a ring of shifting, compressing, changing faces over him, looking down, looking down, reading the time of his life or death by his face, making his face into a moon-dial, where the moon cast a shadow from his nose out upon his cheek to tell the time of breathing or not breathing any more ever.

How swiftly a crowd comes, he thought, like the iris of an eye compressing in out of nowhere.

A siren. A police voice. Movement. Blood trickled from his lips and he was being moved into an ambulance. Someone said, "Is he dead?" And someone else said, "No, he's not dead." And a third person said, "He won't die, he's not going to die." And he saw the faces of the crowd beyond him in the night, and he knew by their expressions that he wouldn't die. And that was strange. He saw a man's face, thin, bright, pale; the man swallowed and bit his lips, very sick. There was a small woman, too, with red hair and too much red on her cheeks and lips. And a little boy with a freckled face. Others' faces. An old man with a wrinkled upper lip, an old woman, with a mole upon her chin. They had all come from—where? Houses, cars, alleys, from the immediate and the accident-shocked world. Out of alleys and out of hotels and out of streetcars and seemingly out of nothing they came.

The crowd looked at him and he looked back at them and did not like them at all. There was a vast wrongness to them. He couldn't put his finger on it. They were far worse than this machine-made thing that happened to him now.

The ambulance doors slammed. Through the windows he saw the crowd looking in, looking in. That crowd that always came so fast, so strangely fast, to form a circle, to peer down, to probe, to gawk, to question, to point, to disturb, to spoil the privacy of a man's agony by their frank curiosity.

The ambulance drove off. He sank back and their faces still stared into his face, even with his eyes shut.

The car wheels spun in his mind for days. One wheel, four wheels, spinning, spinning, and whirring, around and around.

He knew it was wrong. Something wrong with the wheels and the whole accident and the running of feet and the curiosity. The crowd faces mixed and spun into the wild rotation of the wheels.

He awoke.

Sunlight, a hospital room, a hand taking his pulse.

"How do you feel?" asked the doctor.

The wheels faded away. Mr. Spallner looked around.

"Fine—I guess."

He tried to find words. About the accident. "Doctor?"

"Yes?"

"That crowd—was it last night?"

"Two days ago. You've been here since Thursday. You're all right, though. You're doing fine. Don't try and get up."

"That crowd. Something about wheels, too. Do accidents make people, well, a—little off?"

"Temporarily, sometimes."

He lay staring up at the doctor. "Does it hurt your time sense?"

"Panic sometimes does."

"Makes a minute seem like an hour, or maybe an hour seem like a minute?"

"Yes."

"Let me tell you then." He felt the bed under him, the sunlight on his face. "You'll think I'm crazy. I was driving too fast, I know. I'm sorry now. I jumped the curb and hit that wall. I was hurt and numb, I know, but I still remember things. Mostly—the crowd." He waited a moment and then decided to go on, for he suddenly knew what it was that bothered him. "The crowd got there too quickly. Thirty seconds after the smash they were all standing over me and staring at me . . . it's not right they should run that fast, so late at night. . . ."

"You only think it was thirty seconds," said the doctor. "It was probably three or four minutes. Your senses——"

"Yeah, I know—my senses, the accident. But I was conscious! I remember one thing that puts it all together and makes it funny, God, so damned funny. The wheels of my car, upside down. The wheels were still spinning when the crowd got there!"

The doctor smiled.

The man in bed went on. "I'm positive! The wheels were spinning and spinning fast—the front wheels! Wheels don't spin very long, friction cuts them down. And these were really spinning!"

"You're confused," said the doctor.

"I'm not confused. That street was empty. Not a soul in sight. And then the accident and the wheels still spinning and all those faces over me, quick, in no time. And the way they looked down at me, I *knew* I wouldn't die. . . ."

"Simple shock," said the doctor, walking away into the sunlight.

They released him from the hospital two weeks later. He rode home in a taxi. People had come to visit him during his two weeks on his back, and to all of them he had told his story, the accident, the spinning wheels, the crowd. They had all laughed with him concerning it, and passed it off.

He leaned forward and tapped on the taxi window.

"What's wrong?"

The cabbie looked back. "Sorry, boss. This is one helluva town to drive in. Got an accident up ahead. Want me to detour?"

"Yes. No. No! Wait. Go ahead. Let's—let's take a look."

The cab moved forward, honking.

"Funny damn thing," said the cabbie. "Hey, *you*! Get that fleatrap out the way!" Quieter, "Funny thing—more damn people. Nosy people."

Mr. Spallner looked down and watched his fingers tremble on his knee. "You noticed that, too?"

"Sure," said the cabbie. "All the time. There's always a crowd. You'd think it was their own mother got killed."

"They come running awfully fast," said the man in the back of the cab.

"Same way with a fire or an explosion. Nobody around. Boom. Lotsa people around. I dunno."

"Ever seen an accident—at night?"

The cabbie nodded. "Sure. Don't make no difference. There's always a crowd."

The wreck came in view. A body lay on the pavement. You knew there was a body even if you couldn't see it. Because of the crowd. The crowd with its back toward him as he sat in the rear of the cab. With its back toward him. He opened the window and almost started to yell. But he didn't have the nerve. If he yelled they might turn around.

And he was afraid to see their faces.

* * *

"I seem to have a penchant for accidents," he said, in his office. It was late afternoon. His friend sat across the desk from him, listening. "I got out of the hospital this morning and first thing on the way home, we detoured around a wreck."

"Things run in cycles," said Morgan.

"Let me tell you about my accident."

"I've heard it. Heard it all."

"But it was funny, you must admit."

"I must admit. Now how about a drink?"

They talked on for half an hour or more. All the while they talked, at the back of Spallner's brain a small watch ticked, a watch that never needed winding. It was the memory of a few little things. Wheels and faces.

At about five-thirty there was a hard metal noise in the street. Morgan nodded and looked out and down. "What'd I tell you? Cycles. A truck and a cream-colored Cadillac. Yes, yes."

Spallner walked to the window. He was very cold and as he stood there, he looked at his watch, at the small minute hand. One two three four five seconds—people running—eight nine ten eleven twelve—from all over, people came running—fifteen sixteen seventeen eighteen seconds—more people, more cars, more horns blowing. Curiously distant, Spallner looked upon the scene as an explosion in reverse, the fragments of the detonation sucked back to the point of impulsion. Nineteen, twenty, twenty-one seconds and the crowd was there. Spallner made a gesture down at them, wordless.

The crowd had gathered so fast.

He saw a woman's body a moment before the crowd swallowed it up.

Morgan said, "You look lousy. Here. Finish your drink."

"I'm all right, I'm all right. Let me alone. I'm all right. Can you see those people? Can you see any of them? I wish we could see them closer."

Morgan cried out, "Where in hell are you going?"

Spallner was out the door, Morgan after him, and down the stairs, as rapidly as possible. "Come along, and hurry."

"Take it easy, you're not a well man!"

They walked out on to the street. Spallner pushed his way forward. He thought he saw a red-haired woman with too much red color on her cheeks and lips.

"There!" He turned wildly to Morgan. "Did you see her?"

"See *who*?"

"Damn it; she's gone. The crowd closed in!"

The crowd was all around, breathing and looking and shuffling and mixing and mumbling and getting in the way when he tried to shove through. Evidently the red-haired woman had seen him coming and run off.

He saw another familiar face! A little freckled boy. But there are many freckled boys in the world. And, anyway, it was no use, before Spallner reached him, this little boy ran away and vanished among the people.

"Is she dead?" a voice asked. "Is she dead?"

"She's dying," someone else replied. "She'll be dead before the ambulance arrives. They shouldn't have moved her. They shouldn't have moved her."

All the crowd faces—familiar, yet unfamiliar, bending over, looking down, looking down.

"Hey, mister, stop pushing."

"Who you shovin', buddy?"

Spallner came back out, and Morgan caught hold of him before he fell. "You damned fool. You're still sick. Why in hell'd you have to come down here?" Morgan demanded.

"I don't know, I really don't. They moved her, Morgan, someone moved her. You should never move a traffic victim. It kills them. It kills them."

"Yeah. That's the way with people. The idiots."

Spallner arranged the newspaper clippings carefully.

Morgan looked at them. "What's the idea? Ever since your accident you think every traffic scramble is part of you. What are these?"

"Clippings of motor-car crackups, and photos. Look at them. Not at the cars," said Spallner, "but at the crowds around the cars." He pointed. "Here. Compare this photo of a wreck in the Wilshire District with one in Westwood. No resemblance. But now take this Westwood picture and align it with one taken in the Westwood District ten years ago." Again he motioned. "This woman is in both pictures."

"Coincidence. The woman happened to be there once in 1936, again in 1946."

"A coincidence once, maybe. But twelve times over a period of ten years, when the accidents occurred as much as three miles from one another, no. Here." He dealt out a dozen photographs. "She's in *all* of these!"

"Maybe she's perverted."

"She's more than that. How does she *happen* to be there so quickly after each accident? And why does she wear the same clothes in pictures taken over a period of a decade?"

"I'll be damned, so she does."

"And, last of all, why was she standing over *me* the night of my accident, two weeks ago!"

They had a drink. Morgan went over the files. "What'd you do, hire a clipping service while you were in the hospital to go back through the newspapers for you?" Spallner nodded. Morgan sipped his drink. It was getting late. The street lights were coming on in the streets below the office. "What does all this add up to?"

"I don't know," said Spallner, "except that there's a universal law about accidents. *Crowds gather.* They always gather. And like you and me, people have wondered year after year, why they gathered so quickly, and how? I know the answer. Here it is!"

He flung the clippings down. "It frightens me."

"These people—mightn't they be thrill-hunters, perverted sensationalists with a carnal lust for blood and morbidity?"

Spallner shrugged. "Does that explain their being at all the accidents? Notice, they stick to certain territories. A Brentwood accident will bring out one group. A Huntington Park another. But there's a norm for faces, a certain percentage appear at each wreck."

Morgan said, "They're not *all* the same faces, are they?"

"Naturally not. Accidents draw normal people, too, in the course of time. But these, I find, are always the *first* ones there."

"Who are they? What do they want? You keep hinting and never telling. Good Lord, you must have some idea. You've scared yourself and now you've got me jumping."

"I've tried getting to them, but someone always trips me up, I'm always too late. They slip into the crowd and vanish. The crowd seems to offer protection to some of its members. They see me coming."

"Sounds like some sort of clique."

"They have one thing in common, they always show up together. At a fire or an explosion or on the sidelines of a war, at any public demonstration of this thing called death. Vultures, hyenas or saints, I don't know which they are, I just don't know. But I'm going to the police with it, this evening. It's gone on long enough. One of them shifted that woman's body today. They shouldn't have touched her. It killed her."

He placed the clippings in a briefcase. Morgan got up and slipped into his coat. Spallner clicked the briefcase shut. "Or, I just happened to think . . ."

"What?"

"Maybe they *wanted* her dead."

"Why?"

"Who knows. Come along?"

"Sorry. It's late. See you tomorrow. Luck." They went out together. "Give my regards to the cops. Think they'll believe you?"

"Oh, they'll believe me all right. Good night."

Spallner took it slow driving downtown.

"I want to get there," he told himself, "alive."

He was rather shocked, but not surprised, somehow, when the truck came rolling out of an alley straight at him. He was just congratulating himself on his keen sense of observation and talking out what he would say to the police in his mind, when the truck smashed into his car. It wasn't really his car, that was the disheartening thing about it. In a preoccupied mood he was tossed first this way and then that way, while he thought, what a shame, Morgan has gone and lent me his extra car for a few days until my other car is fixed, and now here I go again. The windshield hammered back into his face. He was forced back and forth in several lightning jerks. Then all motion stopped and all noise stopped and only pain filled him up.

He heard their feet running and running and running. He fumbled with the car door. It clicked. He fell out upon the pavement drunkenly and lay, ear to the asphalt, listening to them coming. It was like a great rainstorm, with many drops, heavy and light and medium, touching the earth. He waited a few seconds and listened to their coming and their arrival. Then, weakly, expectantly, he rolled his head up and looked.

The crowd was there.

He could smell their breaths, the mingled odors of many people sucking and sucking on the air a man needs to live by. They crowded and jostled and sucked and sucked all the air up from around his gasping face until he tried to tell them to move back, they were making him live in a vacuum. His head was bleeding very badly. He tried to move and he realized something was wrong with his spine. He hadn't felt much at the impact, but his spine was hurt. He didn't dare move.

He couldn't speak. Opening his mouth, nothing came out but a gagging.

Someone said, "Give me a hand. We'll roll him over and lift him into a more comfortable position."

Spallner's brain burst apart.

No! Don't move me!

"We'll move him," said the voice, casually.

You idiots, you'll kill me, don't!

But he could not say any of this out loud. He could only think it.

Hands took hold of him. They started to lift him. He cried out and nausea choked him up. They straightened him out into a ramrod of agony. Two men did it. One of them was thin, bright, pale, alert, a young man. The other man was very old and had a wrinkled upper lip.

He had seen their faces before.

A familiar voice said, "Is—is he dead?"

Another voice, a memorable voice, responded, "No. Not yet. But he will be dead before the ambulance arrives."

It was all a very silly, mad plot. Like every accident. He squealed hysterically at the solid wall of faces. They were all around him, these judges and jurors with the faces he had seen before. Through his pain he counted their faces.

The freckled boy. The old man with the wrinkled upper lip.

The red-haired, red-cheeked woman. An old woman with a mole on her chin.

I know what you're here for, he thought. You're here just as you're at all accidents. To make certain the right ones live and the right ones die. That's why you lifted me. You knew it would kill. You knew I'd live if you left me alone.

And that's the way it's been since time began, when crowds gather. You murder much easier, this way. Your alibi is very simple; you didn't know it was dangerous to move a hurt man. You didn't mean to hurt him.

He looked at them, above him, and he was curious as a man under deep water looking up at people on a bridge. Who are you? Where do you come from and how do you get here so soon? You're the crowd that's always in the way, using up good air that a dying man's lungs are in need of, using up space he should be using to lie in, alone. Tramping on people to make sure they die, that's you. I know *all* of you.

It was like a polite monologue. They said nothing. Faces. The old man. The red-haired woman.

Someone picked up his briefcase. "Whose is this?" they asked.

It's mine! It's evidence against all of you!

Eyes, inverted over him. Shiny eyes under tousled hair or under hats.

Faces.

Somewhere—a siren. The ambulance was coming.

But, looking at the faces, the construction, the cast, the form of the faces, Spallner saw it was too late. He read it in their faces. They *knew*.

He tried to speak. A little bit got out:

"It—looks like I'll—be joining up with you. I—guess I'll be a member of your—group—now."

He closed his eyes then, and waited for the coroner.

Michael Shea

The Autopsy

Michael Shea's science fiction has twice been nominated for the Nebula Award (once for the story herein) and he has won the World Fantasy Award for his book, *Nifft the Lean*. His strength as a writer is, however, in the horror mode regardless of genre or category and he is perhaps the most under-appreciated of the major contemporary talents working in horror—although perhaps this will be remedied by his forthcoming collection from Arkham House, at least in part. "The Autopsy" is horror in the science fiction category, a transformation of the myth of demonic possession into the realm of objective science. Shea's cinematic effects compare favorably with such newer talents as Clive Barker, colorful and unflinchingly clinical. And this story uses some of Lovecraft's conventions more effectively than any other contemporary horror writer. Shea has been growing in strength for more than a decade and belongs already to the company of the best writers of horror today.

Dr. Winters stepped out of the tiny Greyhound station and into the midnight street that smelt of pines and the river, though the street was in the heart of the town. But then it was a town of only five main streets in breadth, and these extended scarcely a mile and a half along the rim of the gorge. Deep in that gorge though the river ran, its blurred roar flowed, perfectly distinct, between the banks of dark shop windows. The station's window showed the only light, save for a luminous clock face several doors down and a little neon beer logo two blocks farther on. When he had walked a short distance, Dr. Winters set his suitcase down, pocketed his hands, and looked at the stars—thick as cobblestones in the black gulf.

"A mountain hamlet—a mining town," he said. "Stars. No moon. We are in Bailey."

He was talking to his cancer. It was in his stomach. Since learning of it, he had developed this habit of wry communion with it. He meant to show courtesy to this uninvited guest, Death. It would not find him churlish, for that would make its victory absolute. Except, of course, that its victory would *be* absolute, with or without his ironies.

He picked up his suitcase and walked on. The starlight made faint mirrors of the windows' blackness and showed him the man who passed: lizard-lean, white-haired (at fifty-seven), a man traveling on death's business, carrying his own death in him, and even bearing death's wardrobe in his suitcase. For this was filled—aside from his medical kit and some scant necessities—with

175

mortuary bags. The sheriff had told him on the phone of the improvisations that presently enveloped the corpses, and so the doctor had packed these, laying them in his case with bitter amusement, checking the last one's breadth against his chest before the mirror, as a woman will gauge a dress before donning it, and telling his cancer:

"Oh, yes, that's plenty roomy enough for both of us!"

The case was heavy and he stopped frequently to rest and scan the sky. What a night's work to do, probing soulless filth, eyes earthward, beneath such a ceiling of stars! It had taken five days to dig them out. The autumnal equinox had passed, but the weather here had been uniformly hot. And warmer still, no doubt, so deep in the earth.

He entered the courthouse by a side door. His heels knocked on the linoleum corridor. A door at the end of it, on which was lettered NATE CRAVEN, COUNTY SHERIFF, opened well before he reached it, and his friend stepped out to meet him.

"Damnit, Carl, you're *still* so thin they could use you for a whip. Gimme that. You're in too good a shape already. You don't need the exercise."

The case hung weightless from his hand, imparting no tilt at all to his bull shoulders. Despite his implied self-derogation, he was only moderately paunched for a man his age and size. He had a rough-hewn face and the bulk of brow, nose, and jaw made his greenish eyes look small until one engaged them and felt the snap and penetration of their intelligence. He half-filled two cups from a coffee urn and topped both off with bourbon from a bottle in his desk. When they had finished these, they had finished trading news of mutual friends. The sheriff mixed another round, and sipped from his, in a silence clearly prefatory to the work at hand.

"They talk about rough justice," he said. "I've sure seen it now. One of those . . . patients of yours that you'll be working on? He was a killer. 'Killer' don't even half say it, really. You could say that *he* got justly executed in that blast. That much was justice for damn sure. But rough as hell on those other nine. And the rough don't just stop with their being dead either. That kiss-ass boss of yours! He's breaking his god-damned back touching his toes for Fordham Mutual. How much of the picture did he give you?"

"You refer, I take it, to the estimable Coroner Waddleton of Fordham County." Dr. Winters paused to sip his drink. With a delicate flaring of his nostrils he communicated all the disgust, contempt and amusement he had felt in his four years as Pathologist in Waddleton's office. The sheriff laughed.

"Clear pictures seldom emerge from anything the coroner says," the doctor continued. "He took your name in vain. Vigorously and repeatedly. These expressions formed his opening remarks. He then developed the theme of our office's strict responsibility to the letter of the law, and of the workmen's compensation law in particular. Death benefits accrue only to the dependents of decedents whose deaths arise *out of the course* of their employment, not merely *in* the course of it. Victims of a maniacal assault, though they die on the job, are by no means necessarily compensable under the law. We then contemplated the tragic injustice of an insurance company —*any* insurance company—having to pay benefits to unentitled persons, solely through the laxity and incompetence of investigating officers. Your name came up again."

Craven uttered a bark of mirth and fury. "The impartial public servant! Ha! The impartial brown-nose, flim-flam and bullshit man is what he *is*. Ten to one, Fordham Mutual will slip out of it *without* his help, and those men's families won't see a goddamn nickel." Words were an insufficient vent; the sheriff turned and spat into his wastebasket. He drained his cup, and sighed. "I beg your pardon, Carl. We've been five days digging those men out and the last two days sifting half that mountain for explosive traces, with those insurance investigators hanging on our elbows, and the most they could say was that there was 'strong presumptive evidence' of a bomb. Well, I don't budge for that because I don't have to. Waddleton can shove his 'extraordinary circumstances.' If you don't find anything in those bodies, then that's all the autopsy there is to it, and they get buried right here where their families want 'em."

The doctor was smiling at his friend. He finished his cup and spoke with his previous wry detachment, as if the sheriff had not interrupted.

"The honorable coroner then spoke with remarkable volubility on the subject of Autopsy Consent forms and the malicious subversion of private citizens by vested officers of the law. He had, as it happened, a sheaf of such forms on his desk, all signed, all with a rider clause typed in above the signatures. A cogent paragraph. It had, among its other qualities, the property of turning the coroner's face purple when he read it aloud. He read it aloud to me three times. It appeared that the survivors' consent was contingent on two conditions: that the autopsy be performed *in locem mortis*, that is to say in Bailey, and that only if the coroner's pathologist found concrete evidence of homicide should the decedents be subject either to removal from Bailey or to further necropsy. It was well written. I remember wondering who wrote it."

The sheriff nodded musingly. He took Dr. Winters' empty cup, set it by his own, filled both two-thirds with bourbon, and added a splash of coffee to the doctor's. The two friends exchanged a level stare, rather like poker players in the clinch. The sheriff regarded his cup, sipped from it.

"*In locem mortis*. What-all does that mean exactly?"

"'In the place of death.'"

"Oh. Freshen that up for you?"

"I've just started it, thank you."

Both men laughed, paused, and laughed again, some might have said immoderately.

"He all but told me that I *had* to find something to compel a second autopsy," the doctor said at length. "He would have sold his soul—or taken out a second mortgage on it—for a mobile x-ray unit. He's right of course. If those bodies have trapped any bomb fragments, that would be the surest and quickest way of finding them. It still amazes me your Dr. Parsons could let his x-ray go unfixed for so long."

"He sets bones, stitches wounds, writes prescriptions, and sends anything tricky down the mountain. Just barely manages that. Drunks don't get much done."

"He's gotten that bad?"

"He hangs on and no more. Waddleton was right there, not deputizing him pathologist. I doubt he could find a cannonball in a dead rat. I wouldn't say it where it could hurt him, as long as he's still managing, but everyone here knows it. His patients sort of look after *him* half the time. But Waddleton would have sent you, no matter who was here. Nothing but his best for party contributors like Fordham Mutual."

The doctor looked at his hands and shrugged. "So. There's a killer in the batch. *Was* there a bomb?"

Slowly, the sheriff planted his elbows on the desk and pressed his hands against his temples, as if the question had raised a turbulence of memories. For the first time the doctor—half harkening throughout to the never-quite-muted stirrings of the death within him—saw his friend's exhaustion: the tremor of hand, the bruised look under the eyes.

"I'm going to give you what I have, Carl. I told you I don't think you'll find a damn thing in those bodies. You're probably going to end up assuming what I do about it, but assuming is as far as anyone's going to get with this one. It is truly one of those Nightmare Specials that the good Lord tortures lawmen with and then hides the answers to forever.

"All right then. About two months ago, we had a man disappear—Ronald Hanley. Mine worker, rock-steady, family man. He didn't come home one night, and we never found a trace of him. OK, that happens sometimes. About a week later, the lady that ran the laundromat, Sharon Starker, *she* disappeared, no trace. We got edgy then. I made an announcement on the local radio about a possible weirdo at large, spelled out special precautions everybody should take. We put both our squadcars on the night beat, and by day we set to work knocking on every door in town collecting alibis for the two times of disappearance.

"No good. Maybe you're fooled by this uniform and think I'm a law officer, protector of the people, and all that? A natural mistake. A lot of people were fooled. In less than seven weeks, six people vanished, just like that. Me and my deputies might as well have stayed in bed round the clock, for all the good we did." The sheriff drained his cup.

"Anyway, at last we got lucky. Don't get me wrong now. We didn't go all hog-wild and actually prevent a crime or anything. But we *did* find a body—except it wasn't the body of any of the seven people that had disappeared. We'd took to combing the woods nearest town, with temporary deputies from the miners to help. Well, one of those boys was out there with us last week. It was hot—like it's been for a while now—and it was real quiet. He heard this buzzing noise and looked around for it, and he saw a bee-swarm up in the crotch of a tree. Except he was smart enough to know that that's not usual around here—bee hives. So it wasn't bees. It was bluebottle flies, a god-damned big cloud of them, all over a bundle that was wrapped in a tarp."

The sheriff studied his knuckles. He had, in his eventful life, occasionally met men literate enough to understand his last name and rash enough to be openly amused by it, and the knuckles—scarred knobs—were eloquent of his reactions. He looked back into his old friend's eyes.

"We got that thing down and unwrapped it. Billy Lee Davis, one of my deputies, he was in Viet Nam, been near some bad, bad things and held on. Billy Lee blew his lunch all over the ground when we unwrapped that thing. It was a man. Some of a man. We knew he'd stood six-two because all the bones were there, and he'd probably weighed between two fifteen and two twenty-five, but he folded up no bigger than a big-size laundry package. Still had his face, both shoulders, and the left arm, but all the rest was clean. It wasn't animal work. It was knife work, all the edges neat as butcher cuts. Except butchered meat, even when you drain it all you can, will bleed a good deal afterwards, and there wasn't one god-damned drop of blood on the tarp, nor in that meat. It was just as pale as fish meat."

Deep in his body's center, the doctor's cancer touched him. Not a ravening attack—it sank one fang of pain, questioningly, into new, untasted flesh, probing the scope for its appetite there. He disguised his tremor with a shake of the head.

"A cache, then."

The sheriff nodded. "Like you might keep a potroast in the icebox for making lunches. I took some pictures of his face, then we put him back and erased our traces. Two of the miners I'd deputized did a lot of hunting, were woods-smart. So I left them on the first watch. We worked out positions and cover for them, and drove back.

"We got right on tracing him, sent out descriptions to every town within a hundred miles. He was no one I'd ever seen in Bailey, nor anyone else either, it began to look like, after we'd combed the town all day with the photos. Then, out of the blue, Billy Lee Davis smacks himself on the forehead and says, 'Sheriff, *I* seen this man somewhere in town, and not long ago!'

"He'd been shook all day since throwing up, and then all of a sudden he just snapped to. Was dead sure. Except he couldn't remember where or when. We went over and over it and he tried and tried. It got to where I wanted to grab him by the ankles and hang him upside down and shake him till it dropped out of him. But it was no damn use. Just after dark we went back to that tree—we'd worked out a place to hide the cars and a route to it through the woods. When we were close we walkie-talkied the men we'd left for an all-clear to come up. No answer at all. And when we got there, all that was left of our trap was the tree. No body, no tarp, no Special Assistant Deputies. Nothing."

This time Dr. Winters poured the coffee and bourbon. "Too much coffee," the sheriff muttered, but drank anyway. "Part of me wanted to chew nails and break necks. And part of me was scared shitless. When we got back I got on the radio station again and made an emergency broadcast and then had the man at the station rebroadcast it every hour. Told everyone to do everything in groups of three, to stay together at night in threes at least, to go out little as possible, keep armed and keep checking up on each other. It had such a damn-fool sound to it, but just pairing-up was no protection if half of one of those pairs was the killer. I deputized more men and put them on the streets to beef up the night patrol.

"It was next morning that things broke. The sheriff of Rakehell called— he's over in the next county. He said our corpse sounded a lot like a man named Abel Dougherty, a millhand with Con Wood over there. I left Billy Lee in charge and drove right out.

"This Dougherty had a cripple older sister he always checked back to by phone whenever he left town for long, a habit no one knew about, probably embarrassed him. Sheriff Peck there only found out about it when the woman called him, said her brother'd been four days gone for vacation and not rung her once. Without that Peck might not've thought of Dougherty just from our description, though the photo I showed him clinched it, and one would've reached him by mail soon enough. Well, he'd hardly set it down again when a call came through for me. It was Billy Lee. He'd remembered.

"When he'd seen Dougherty was the Sunday night three days before we found him. Where he'd seen him was the Trucker's Tavern outside the north end of town. The man had made a stir by being jolly drunk and latching onto a miner who was drinking there, man named Joe Allen, who'd started at the mine about two months back. Dougherty kept telling him that he wasn't Joe Allen, but Dougherty's old buddy named Sykes that had worked with him at Con Wood for a coon's age, and what the hell kind of joke was this, come have a beer old buddy and tell me why you took off so sudden and what the hell you been doing with yourself.

"Allen took it laughing. Dougherty'd clap him on the shoulder, Allen'd clap him right back and make every kind of joke about it, say 'Give this man another beer, I'm standing in for a long-lost friend of his.' Dougherty was so big and loud and stubborn, Billy Lee was worried about a fight starting, and he wasn't the only one worried. But this Joe Allen was a natural good ol' boy, handled it perfect. We'd checked him out weeks back along with everyone else, and he was real popular with the other miners. Finally Dougherty swore he was going to take him on to another bar to help celebrate the vacation Dougherty was starting out on. Joe Allen got up grinning, said god damn it, he couldn't accommodate Dougherty by being this fellow Sykes, but he could sure as hell have a glass with any serious drinking man that was treating. He went out with him, and gave everyone a wink as he left, to the general satisfaction of the audience."

Craven paused. Dr. Winters met his eyes and knew his thought, two images: the jolly wink that roused the room to laughter, and the thing in the tarp aboil with bright blue flies.

"It was plain enough for me," the sheriff said. "I told Billy Lee to search Allen's room at the Skettles' boarding house and then go straight to the mine and take him. We could fine-polish things once we had him. Since I was already in Rakehell, I saw to some of the loose ends before I started back. I went with Sheriff Peck down to Con Wood and we found a picture of Eddie Sykes in the personnel files. I'd seen Joe Allen often enough, and it was his picture in that file.

"We found out Sykes lived alone, was an on-again, off-again worker, private in his comings and goings, and hadn't been around for a while. But one of the sawyers there could be pretty sure of when Sykes left Rakehell because he'd gone to Sykes' cabin the morning after a big meteor shower they had out there about nine weeks back, since some thought the shower might have reached the ground, and not far from Sykes' side of the mountain. He wasn't in that morning, and the sawyer hadn't seen him since.

"It looked sewed up. It *was* sewed up. After all those weeks. I was less than a mile out of Bailey, had the pedal floored. Full of rage and revenge. I felt . . . like a *bullet*, like I was one big thirty-caliber slug that was going to go right through that blood-sucking cannibal, tear the whole truth right out of his heart, enough to hang him a hundred times. That was the closest I got. So close that I *heard* it when it all blew to shit.

"I sound squirrelly. I know I do. Maybe all this gave me something I'll never shake off. We had to put together what happened. Billy Lee didn't have my other deputy with him. Travis was out with some men on the mountain dragnetting around that tree for clues. By luck, he was back at the car when Billy Lee was trying to raise him. He said he'd just been through Allen's room and had got something we could maybe hold him on. It was a sphere, half again big as a basketball, heavy, made of something that wasn't metal or glass but was a little like both. He could half-see into it and it looked to be full of some kind of circuitry and components. If someone tried to spring Allen, we could make a theft rap out of this thing, or say we suspected it was a bomb. Jesus! Anyway, he said it was the only strange thing he found, but it was plenty strange. He told Travis to get up to the mine for back-up. He'd be there first and should already have Allen by the time Travis arrived.

"Tierney, the shift boss up there, had an assistant that told us the rest. Billy Lee parked behind the offices where the men in the yard wouldn't see the car. He went upstairs to arrange the arrest with Tierney. They got half a dozen men together. Just as they came out of the building, they saw Allen take off running from the squadcar with the sphere under his arm.

"The whole compound's fenced in and Tierney'd already phoned to have all the gates shut. Allen zigged and zagged some but caught on quick to the trap. The sphere slowed him, but he still had a good lead. He hesitated a minute and then ran straight for the main shaft. A cage was just going down with a crew, and he risked every bone in him jumping down after it, but he got safe on top. By the time they got to the switches, the cage was down to the second level, and Allen and the crew had got out. Tierney got it back up. Billy Lee ordered the rest back to get weapons and follow, and him and Tierney rode the cage right back down. And about two minutes later half the god-damned mine blew up."

The sheriff stopped as if cut off, his lips parted to say more, his eyes registering for perhaps the hundredth time his amazement that there was no more, that the weeks of death and mystification ended here, with this split-second recapitulation: more death, more answerless dark, sealing all.

"Nate."

"What."

"Wrap it up and go to bed. I don't need your help. You're dead on your feet."

"I'm not on my feet. And I'm coming along."

"Give me a picture of the victims' position relative to the blast. I'm going to work and you're going to bed."

The sheriff shook his head absently. "They're mining in shrinkage stopes. The adits—levels—branch off lateral from the vertical shaft. From one level they hollow out overhand up to the one above. Scoop out big chambers and let most of the broken rock stay inside so they can stand on the heaps to cut the ceilings higher. They leave sections of support wall between stopes, and those men were buried several stopes in from the shaft. The cave-in killed *them*. The mountain just folded them up in their own hill of tailings. No kind of fragments reached them. I'm dead sure. The only ones they *found* were of some standard charges that the main blast set off, and those didn't even get close. The big one blew out where the adit joined the shaft, right where, and right when Billy Lee and Tierney got out of the cage. And there is *nothing* left there, Carl. No sphere, no cage, no Tierney, no Billy Lee Davis. Just rock blown fine as flour."

Dr. Winters nodded and, after a moment, stood up.

"Come on, Nate. I've got to get started. I'll be lucky to have even a few of them done before morning. Drop me off and go to sleep, till then at least. You'll still be there to witness most of the work."

The sheriff rose, took up the doctor's suitcase, and led him out of the office without a word, concession in his silence.

The patrol car was behind the building. The doctor saw a crueller beauty in the stars than he had an hour before. They got in, and Craven swung them out onto the empty street. The doctor opened the window and harkened, but the motor's surge drowned out the river sound. Before the thrust of their headlights, ranks of old-fashioned parking meters sprouted shadows tall across the sidewalks, shadows which shrank and were cut down by the lights' passage. The sheriff said:

"All those extra dead. For nothing! Not even to . . . *feed* him! If it *was* a bomb, and he made it, he'd know how powerful it was. He wouldn't try some stupid escape stunt with it. And how did he even know the thing was there? We worked it out that Allen was just ending a shift, but he wasn't even up out of the ground before Billy Lee'd parked out of sight."

"Let it rest, Nate. I want to hear more, but after you've slept. I know you. All the photos will be there, and the report complete, all the evidence neatly boxed and carefully described. When I've looked things over I'll know exactly how to proceed by myself."

Bailey had neither hospital nor morgue, and the bodies were in a defunct ice-plant on the edge of town. A generator had been brought down from the mine, lighting improvised, and the refrigeration system reactivated. Dr. Parsons' office, and the tiny examining room that served the sheriff's station in place of a morgue, had furnished this makeshift with all the equipment that Dr. Winters would need beyond what he carried with him. A quarter-mile outside the main body of the town, they drew up to it. Tree-flanked, unneighbored by any other structure, it was a double building; the smaller half—the office—was illuminated. The bodies would be in the big, windowless refrigerator segment. Craven pulled up beside a second squadcar parked near the office door. A short, rake-thin man wearing a large white stetson got out of the car and came over. Craven rolled down his window.

"Trav. This here's Dr. Winters."

"Lo, Nate. Dr. Winters. Everything's shipshape inside. Felt more comfortable out here. Last of those newshounds left two hours ago."

"They sure do hang on. You take off now, Trav. Get some sleep and be back at sunup. What temperature we getting?"

The pale stetson, far clearer in the starlight than the shadow-face beneath it, wagged dubiously. "Thirty-six. She won't get lower—some kind of leak."

"That should be cold enough," the doctor said.

Travis drove off and the sheriff unlocked the padlock on the office door. Waiting behind him, Dr. Winters heard the river again—a cold balm, a whisper of freedom—and overlying this, the stutter and soft snarl of the generator behind the building, a gnawing, remorseless sound that somehow fed the obscure anguish which the other soothed. They went in.

The preparations had been thoughtful and complete. "You can wheel 'em out of the fridge on this and do the examining in here," the sheriff said, indicating a table and a gurney. "You should find all the gear you need on this big table here, and you can write up your reports on that desk. The phone's not hooked up—there's a pay phone at that last gas station if you have to call me."

The doctor nodded, checking over the material on the larger table: scalpels, post-mortem and cartilage knives, intestine scissors, rib shears, forceps, probes, mallet and chisels, a blade saw and electric bone saw, scale, jars for specimens, needles and suture, sterilizer, gloves. . . . Beside this array were a few boxes and envelopes with descriptive sheets attached, containing the photographs and such evidentiary objects as had been found associated with the bodies.

"Excellent," he muttered.

"The overhead light's fluorescent, full spectrum or whatever they call it. Better for colors. There's a pint of decent bourbon in that top desk drawer. Ready to look at 'em?"

"Yes."

The sheriff unbarred and slid back the big metal door to the refrigeration chamber. Icy, tainted air boiled out of the doorway. The light within was dimmer than that provided in the office—a yellow gloom wherein ten oblong heaps lay on trestles.

The two stood silent for a time, their stillness a kind of unpremeditated homage paid the eternal mystery at its threshold. As if the cold room were in fact a shrine, the doctor found a peculiar awe in the row of veiled forms. The awful unison of their dying, the titan's grave that had been made for them, conferred on them a stern authority, Death's chosen Ones. His stomach hurt, and he found he had his hand pressed to his abdomen. He glanced at Craven and was relieved to see that his friend, staring wearily at the bodies, had missed the gesture.

"Nate. Help me uncover them."

Starting at opposite ends of the row, they stripped the tarps off and piled them in a corner. Both were brusque now, not pausing over the revelation of the swelled, pulpy faces—most three-lipped with the gaseous burgeoning of their tongues—and the fat, livid hands sprouting from the filthy sleeves. But at one of the bodies Craven stopped. The doctor saw him look, and his mouth twist. Then he flung the tarp on the heap and moved to the next trestle.

When they came out Dr. Winters took out the bottle and glasses Craven had put in the desk, and they had a drink together. The sheriff made as if he would speak, but shook his head and sighed.

"I *will* get some sleep, Carl. I'm getting crazy thoughts with this thing." The doctor wanted to ask those thoughts. Instead he laid a hand on his friend's shoulder.

"Go home, Sheriff Craven. Take off the badge and lie down. The dead won't run off on you. We'll all still be here in the morning."

When the sound of the patrol car faded, the doctor stood listening to the generator's growl and the silence of the dead, resurgent now. Both the sound and the silence seemed to mock him. The after-echo of his last words made him uneasy. He said to his cancer:

"What about it, dear colleague? We *will* still be here tomorrow? All of us?"

He smiled, but felt an odd discomfort, as if he had ventured a jest in company and roused a hostile silence. He went to the refrigerator door, rolled it back, and viewed the corpses in their ordered rank, with their strange tribunal air. "What, sirs?" he murmured. "Do you judge me? Just who is to examine whom tonight, if I may ask?"

He went back into the office, where his first step was to examine the photographs made by the sheriff, in order to see how the dead had lain at their uncovering. The earth had seized them with terrible suddenness. Some crouched, some partly stood, others sprawled in crazy, free-fall postures. Each successive photo showed more of the jumble as the shovels continued their work between shots. The doctor studied them closely, noting the identifications inked on the bodies as they came completely into view.

One man, Robert Willet, had died some yards from the main cluster. It appeared he had just straggled into the stope from the adit at the moment of the explosion. He should thus have received, more directly than any of the others, the shockwaves of the blast. If bomb fragments were to be found in any of the corpses, Mr. Willet's seemed likeliest to contain them. Dr. Winters pulled on a pair of surgical gloves.

He lay at one end of the line of trestles. He wore a thermal shirt and overalls that were strikingly new beneath the filth of burial. Their tough fabrics jarred with that of his flesh—blue, swollen, seeming easily torn or burst, like ripe fruit. In life Willet had grease-combed his hair. Now it was a sculpture of dust, spikes and whorls shaped by the head's last grindings against the mountain that clenched it.

Rigor had come and gone—Willet rolled laxly onto the gurney. As the doctor wheeled him past the others, he felt a slight self-consciousness. The sense of some judgment flowing from the dead assembly—unlike most such vagrant emotional embellishments of experience—had an odd tenacity in him. This stubborn unease began to irritate him with himself, and he moved more briskly.

He put Willet on the examining table and cut the clothes off him with shears, storing the pieces in an evidence box. The overalls were soiled with agonal waste expulsions. The doctor stared a moment with unwilling pity at his naked subject.

"You won't ride down to Fordham in any case," he said to the corpse. "Not unless I find something pretty damned obvious." He pulled his gloves tighter and arranged his implements.

Waddleton had said more to him than he had reported to the sheriff. The doctor was to find, and forcefully to record that he had found, strong "indications" absolutely requiring the decedents' removal to Fordham for x-ray and an exhaustive second post-mortem. The doctor's continued employment with the Coroner's Office depended entirely on his compliance in this. He had received this stipulation with a silence Waddleton had not thought it necessary to break. His present resolution was all but made at that moment. Let the obvious be taken as such. If the others showed as plainly as Willet did the external signs of death by asphyxiation, they would receive no more than a thorough external exam. Willet he would examine internally as well, merely to establish in depth for this one what should appear obvious in all. Otherwise, only when the external exam revealed a clearly anomalous feature—and clear and suggestive it must be—would he look deeper.

He rinsed the caked hair in a basin, poured the sediment into a flask and labeled it. Starting with the scalp, he began a minute scrutiny of the body's surfaces, recording his observations as he went.

The characteristic signs of asphyxial death were evident, despite the complicating effects of autolysis and putrefaction. The eyeballs' bulge and the tongue's protrusion were by now at least partly due to gas pressure as well as the mode of death, but the latter organ was clamped between locked teeth, leaving little doubt as to that mode. The coloration of degenerative change—a greenish-yellow tint, a darkening and mapping-out of superficial veins—was marked, but not sufficient to obscure the blue of cyanosis on the face and neck, nor the pinpoint hemorrhages freckling neck, chest, and shoulders. From the mouth and nose the doctor scraped matter he was confident was the blood-tinged mucus typically ejected in the airless agony.

He began to find a kind of comedy in his work. What a buffoon death made of a man! A blue, pop-eyed, three-lipped thing. And there was himself, his curious, solicitous intimacy with this clownish carrion. Excuse me, Mr. Willet, while I probe this laceration. How does it feel when I do this? Nothing? Nothing at all? Fine, now what about these nails. Split them clawing at the earth, did you? Yes. A nice bloodblister under this thumbnail I see—got it on the job a few days before your accident no doubt? Remarkable calluses here, still quite tough. . . .

The doctor looked for an unanalytic moment at the hands—puffed, dark paws, gestureless, having renounced all touch and grasp. He felt the wastage of the man concentrated in the hands. The painful futility of the body's fine articulation when it is seen in death—this poignancy he had long learned not to acknowledge when he worked. But now he let it move him a little. This Roger Willet, plodding to his work one afternoon, had suddenly been scrapped, crushed to a nonfunctional heap of perishable materials. It simply happened that his life had chanced to move too close to the passage of a more powerful life, one of those inexorable and hungry lives that leave human wreckage—known or undiscovered—in their wakes. Bad luck, Mr. Willet. Naturally, we feel very sorry about this. But this Joe Allen, your co-worker. Apparently he was some sort of . . . cannibal. It's complicated. We don't understand it all. But the fact is we have to dismantle you now to a certain extent. There's really no hope of your using these parts of yourself again, I'm afraid. Ready now?

The doctor proceeded to the internal exam with a vague eagerness for Willet's fragmentation, for the disarticulation of that sadness in his natural form. He grasped Willet by the jaw and took up the post-mortem knife. He sank its point beneath the chin and began the long, gently sawing incision that opened Willet from throat to groin.

In the painstaking separation of the body's laminae Dr. Winters found absorption and pleasure. And yet throughout he felt, marginal but insistent, the movement of a stream of irrelevant images. These were of the building that contained him, and of the night containing it. As from outside, he saw the plant—bleached planks, iron roofing—and the trees crowding it, all in starlight, a ghost-town image. And he saw the refrigerator vault beyond the wall as from within, feeling the stillness of murdered men in a cold, yellow light. And at length a question formed itself, darting in and out of the weave of his concentration as the images did: Why did he still feel, like some stir of the air, that sense of mute vigilance surrounding his action, furtively touching his nerves with its inquiry as he worked? He shrugged, overtly angry now. Who else was attending but Death? Wasn't he Death's hireling, and this Death's place? Then let the master look on.

Peeling back Willet's cover of hemorrhage-stippled skin, Dr. Winters read the corpse with an increasing dispassion, a mortuary text. He confined his inspection to the lungs and mediastinum and found there unequivocal testimony to Willet's asphyxial death. The pleurae of the lungs exhibited the expected ecchymoses—bruised spots in the glassy, enveloping membrane. Beneath, the polyhedral surface lobules of the lungs themselves were bubbled and blistered—the expected interstitial emphysema. The lungs, on section, were intensely and bloodily congested. The left half of the heart he found contracted and empty, while the right was over-distended and engorged with dark blood, as were the large veins of the upper mediastinum. It was a classic picture of death by suffocation, and at length the doctor, with needle and suture, closed up the text again.

He returned the corpse to the gurney and draped one of his mortuary bags over it in the manner of a shroud. When he had help in the morning, he would weigh the bodies on a platform scale the office contained and afterwards bag them properly. He came to the refrigerator door, and hesitated. He stared at the door, not moving, not understanding why.

Run. Get out, now.

The thought was his own, but it came to him so urgently he turned around as if someone behind him had spoken. Across the room a thin man in smock and gloves, his eyes shadows, glared at the doctor from the black windows. Behind the man was a shrouded cart; behind that, a wide metal door.

Quietly, wonderingly, the doctor asked, "Run from what?" The eyele ʒ man in the glass was still half-crouched, afraid.

Then, a moment later, the man straightened, threw back his head, and laughed. The doctor walked to the desk and sat down shoulder to shoulder with him. He pulled out the bottle and they had a drink together, regarding each other with identical bemused smiles. Then the doctor said, "Let me pour you another. You need it, old fellow. It makes a man himself again."

Nevertheless his re-entry of the vault was difficult, toilsome, each step seeming to require a new summoning of the will to move. In the freezing half-light all movement felt like defiance. His body lagged behind his craving to be quick, to be done with this molestation of the gathered dead. He returned Willet to his pallet and took his neighbor. The name on the tag wired to his boot was Ed Moses. Dr. Winters wheeled him back to the office and closed the big door behind him.

With Moses his work gained momentum. He expected to perform no further internal necropsies. He thought of his employer, rejoicing now in his seeming-submission to Waddleton's ultimatum. The impact would be dire. He pictured the coroner in shock, a sheaf of Pathologist's Reports in one hand, and smiled.

Waddleton could probably make a plausible case for incomplete examination. Still, a pathologist's discretionary powers were not well-defined. Many good ones would approve the adequacy of the doctor's method, given his working conditions. The inevitable litigation with a coalition of compensation claimants would be strenuous and protracted. Win or lose, Waddleton's venal devotion to the insurance company's interest would be abundantly displayed. Further, immediately on his dismissal the doctor would formally disclose its occult cause to the press. A libel action would ensue which he would have as little cause to fear as he had to fear his firing. Both his savings and the lawsuit would long outlast his life.

Externally, Ed Moses exhibited a condition as typically asphyxial as Willet's had been, with no slightest mark of fragment entry. The doctor finished his report and returned Moses to the vault, his movements brisk and precise. His unease was all but gone. That queasy stirring of the air—had he really felt it? It had been, perhaps, some new reverberation of the death at work in him, a psychic shudder of response to the cancer's stealthy probing for his life. He brought out the body next to Moses in the line.

Walter Lou Jackson was big, 6' 2" from heel to crown, and would surely weigh out at more than two hundred pounds. He had writhed mightily against his million-ton coffin with an agonal strength that had torn his face and hands. Death had mauled him like a lion. The doctor set to work.

His hands were fully themselves now—fleet, exact, intricately testing the corpse's character as other fingers might explore a keyboard for its latent melodies. And the doctor watched them with an old pleasure, one of the few that had never failed him, his mind at one remove from their busy intelligence. All the hard deaths! A worldful of them, time without end. Lives wrenched kicking from their snug meat-frames. Walter Lou Jackson had died very hard. Joe Allen brought this on you, Mr. Jackson. We think it was part of his attempt to escape the law.

But what a botched flight! The unreason of it—more than baffling—was eerie in its colossal futility. Beyond question, Allen had been cunning. A ghoul with a psychopath's social finesse. A good old boy who could make a tavernful of men laugh with delight while he cut his victim from their midst, make them applaud his exit with the prey, who stepped jovially into the darkness with murder at his side clapping him on the shoulder. Intelligent, certainly, with a strange technical sophistication as well, suggested by the sphere. Then what of the lunacy yet more strongly suggested by the same object? In the sphere was concentrated all the lethal mystery of Bailey's long nightmare.

Why the explosion? Its location implied an ambush for Allen's pursuers, a purposeful detonation. Had he aimed at a limited cave-in from which he schemed some inconceivable escape? Folly enough in this—far more if, as seemed sure, Allen had made the bomb himself, for then he would have to know its power was grossly inordinate to the need.

But if it was not a bomb, had a different function and only incidentally an explosive potential, Allen might underestimate the blast. It appeared the object was somehow remotely monitored by him, for the timing of events showed he had gone straight for it the instant he emerged from the shaft—shunned the bus waiting to take his shift back to town and made a beeline across the compound for a patrol car that was hidden from his view by the office building. This suggested something more complex than a mere explosive device, something, perhaps, whose destruction was itself more Allen's aim than the explosion produced thereby.

The fact that he risked the sphere's retrieval at all pointed to this interpretation. For the moment he sensed its presence at the mine, he must have guessed that the murder investigation had led to its discovery and removal from his room. But then, knowing himself already liable to the extreme penalty, why should Allen go to such lengths to recapture evidence incriminatory of a lesser offense, possession of an explosive device?

Then grant that the sphere was something more, something instrumental to his murders that could guarantee a conviction he might otherwise evade. Still, his gambit made no sense. Since the sphere—and thus the lawmen he could assume to have taken it—were already at the mine office, he must expect the compound to be sealed at any moment. Meanwhile, the gate was open, escape into the mountains a strong possibility for a man capable of stalking and destroying two experienced and well-armed woodsmen lying in ambush for him. Why had he all but insured his capture to weaken a case against himself that his escape would have rendered irrelevant? Dr. Winters saw his fingers, like a hunting pack round a covert, converge on a small puncture wound below Walter Lou Jackson's xiphoid process, between the eighth ribs.

His left hand touched its borders, the fingers' inquiry quick and tender. The right hand introduced a probe, and both together eased it into the wound. It inched unobstructed deep into the body, curving upwards through the diaphragm towards the heart. The doctor's own heart accelerated. He watched his hands move to record the observation, watched them pause, watched them return to their survey of the corpse, leaving pen and page untouched.

Inspection revealed no further anomaly. All else he observed the doctor recorded faithfully, wondering throughout at the distress he felt. When he had finished, he understood it. Its cause was not the discovery of an entry wound that might bolster Waddleton's case. For the find had, within moments, revealed to him that, should he encounter anything he thought to be a mark of fragment penetration, he was going to ignore it. The damage Joe Allen had done was going to end here, with this last grand slaughter, and would not extend to the impoverishment of his victims' survivors. No more internals. The externals will-they nill-they, would from now on explicitly contraindicate the need for them.

The problem was that he did not believe the puncture in Jackson's thorax *was* a mark of fragment entry. Why? And, finding no answer to this question, why was he, once again, afraid? Slowly, he signed the report on Jackson, set it aside, and took up the post-mortem knife.

First the long, sawing slice, unzippering the mortal overcoat. Next, two great, square flaps of flesh reflected, scrolled laterally to the armpits' line, disrobing the chest: one hand grasping the flap's skirt, the other sweeping beneath it with the knife, flensing through the glassy tissue that joined it to the chest-wall, and shaving all muscles from their anchorages to bone and cartilage beneath. Then the dismantling of the strong-box within. Rib-shears —so frank and forward a tool, like a gardener's. The steel beak bit through each rib's gristle anchor to the sternum's centerplate. At the sternum's crownpiece the collarbones' ends were knifed, pried, and sprung free from their sockets. The coffer unhasped, unhinged, a knife teased beneath the lid and levered it off.

Some minutes later the doctor straightened up and stepped back from his subject. He moved almost drunkenly, and his age seemed scored more deeply in his face. With loathing haste he stripped his gloves off. He went to the desk, sat down, and poured another drink. If there was something like horror in his face, there was also a hardening in his mouth's line, and the muscles of his jaw. He spoke to his glass: "So be it, your Excellency. Something new for your humble servant. Testing my nerve?"

Jackson's pericardium, the shapely capsule containing his heart, should have been all but hidden between the big, blood-fat loaves of his lungs. The doctor had found it fully exposed, the lungs flanking it wrinkled lumps less than a third their natural bulk. Not only they, but the left heart and the superior mediastinal veins—all the regions that should have been grossly engorged with blood—were utterly drained of it.

The doctor swallowed his drink and got out the photographs again. He found that Jackson had died on his stomach across the body of another worker, with the upper part of a third trapped between them. Neither these two subjacent corpses nor the surrounding earth showed any stain of a blood loss that must have amounted to two liters.

Possibly the pictures, by some trick of shadow, had failed to pick it up. He turned to the Investigator's Report, where Craven would surely have mentioned any significant amounts of bloody earth uncovered during the disinterment. The sheriff recorded nothing of the kind. Dr. Winters returned to the pictures.

Ronald Pollock, Jackson's most intimate associate in the grave, had died on his back, beneath and slightly askew of Jackson, placing most of their torsos in contact, save where the head and shoulder of the third interposed. It seemed inconceivable Pollock's clothing should lack any trace of such massive drainage from a death mate thus embraced.

The doctor rose abruptly, pulled on fresh gloves, and returned to Jackson. His hands showed a more brutal speed now, closing the great incision temporarily with a few widely spaced sutures. He replaced him in the vault and brought out Pollock, striding, heaving hard at the dead shapes in the shifting of them, thrusting always—so it seemed to him—just a step ahead of urgent thoughts he did not want to have, deformities that whispered at his back, emitting faint, chill gusts of putrid breath. He shook his head— denying, delaying—and pushed the new corpse onto the worktable. The scissors undressed Pollock in greedy bites.

But at length, when he had scanned each scrap of fabric and found nothing like the stain of blood, he came to rest again, relinquishing that simplest, desired resolution he had made such haste to reach. He stood at the instrument table, not seeing it, submitting to the approach of the half-formed things at his mind's periphery.

The revelation of Jackson's shriveled lungs had been more than a shock. He felt a stab of panic too, in fact that same curiously explicit terror of this place that had urged him to flee earlier. He acknowledged now that the germ of that quickly suppressed terror had been a premonition of this failure to find any trace of the missing blood. Whence the premonition? It had to do with a problem he had steadfastly refused to consider: the mechanics of so complete a drainage of the lungs' densely reticulated vascular structure. Could the earth's crude pressure by itself work so thoroughly, given only a single vent both slender and strangely curved? And then the photograph he had studied. It frightened him now to recall the image—some covert meaning stirred within it, struggling to be seen. Dr. Winters picked the probe up from the table and turned again to the corpse. As surely and exactly as if he had already ascertained the wound's presence, he leaned forward and touched it: a small, neat puncture, just beneath the xiphoid process. He introduced the probe. The wound received it deeply, in a familiar direction.

The doctor went to the desk, and took up the photograph again. Pollock's and Jackson's wounded areas were not in contact. The third man's head was sandwiched between their bodies at just that point. He searched out another picture, in which this third man was more central, and found his name inked in below his image: Joe Allen.

Dreamingly, Dr. Winters went to the wide metal door, shoved it aside, entered the vault. He did not search, but went straight to the trestle where his friend had paused some hours before, and found the same name on its tag.

The body, beneath decay's spurious obesity, was trim and well-muscled. The face was square-cut, shelf-browed, with a vulpine nose skewed by an old fracture. The swollen tongue lay behind the teeth, and the bulge of decomposition did not obscure what the man's initial impact must have been—handsome and open, his now-waxen black eyes sly and convivial. Say, good buddy, got a minute? I see you comin' on the swing shift every day, don't I? Yeah, Joe Allen. Look, I know it's late, you want to get home, tell the wife you ain't been in there drinkin' since you got off, right? Oh, yeah, I heard that. But this damn disappearance thing's got me so edgy, and I'd swear to God just as I was coming here I seen someone moving around back of that frame house up the street. See how the trees thin out a little down back of the yard, where the moonlight gets in? That's right. Well, I got me this little popper here. Oh, yeah, that's a beauty, we'll have it covered between us. I knew I could spot a man ready for some trouble—couldn't find a patrol car anywhere on the street. Yeah, just down in here now, to that clump of pine. Step careful, you can barely see. That's right. . . .

The doctor's face ran with sweat. He turned on his heel and walked out of the vault, heaving the door shut behind him. In the office's greater warmth he felt the perspiration soaking his shirt under the smock. His stomach rasped with steady oscillations of pain, but he scarcely attended it. He went to Pollock and seized up the post-mortem knife.

The work was done with surreal speed, the laminae of flesh and bone recoiling smoothly beneath his desperate but unerring hands, until the thoracic cavity lay exposed, and in it, the vampire-stricken lungs, two gnarled lumps of grey tissue.

He searched no deeper, knowing what the heart and veins would show. He returned to sit at the desk, weakly drooping, the knife, forgotten, still in his left hand. He looked at the window, and it seemed his thoughts originated with that fainter, more tenuous Dr. Winters hanging like a ghost outside.

What was this world he lived in? Surely, in a lifetime, he had not begun to guess. To feed in such a way! There was horror enough in this alone. But to feed thus *in his own grave.* How had he accomplished it—leaving aside how he had fought suffocation long enough to do anything at all? How was it to be comprehended, a greed that raged so hotly it would glut itself at the very threshold of its own destruction? That last feast was surely in his stomach still.

Dr. Winters looked at the photograph, at Allen's head snugged into the others' middles like a hungry suckling nuzzling to the sow. Then he looked at the knife in his hand. The hand felt empty of all technique. Its one impulse was to slash, cleave, obliterate the remains of this gluttonous thing, this Joe Allen. He must do this, or flee it utterly. There was no course between. He did not move.

"I *will* examine him," said the ghost in the glass, and did not move. Inside the refrigerator vault, there was a slight noise.

No. It had been some hitch in the generator's murmur. Nothing in there could move. There was another noise, a brief friction against the vault's inner wall. The two old men shook their heads at one another. A catch clicked and the metal door slid open. Behind the staring image of his own amazement, the doctor saw that a filthy shape stood in the doorway and raised its arms towards him in a gesture of supplication. The doctor turned in his chair. From the shape came a whistling groan, the decayed fragment of a human voice.

Pleadingly, Joe Allen worked his jaw and spread his purple hands. As if speech were a maggot struggling to emerge from his mouth, the blue, tumescent face toiled, the huge tongue wallowed helplessly between the viscid lips.

The doctor reached for the telephone, lifted the receiver. Its deadness to his ear meant nothing—he could not have spoken. The thing confronting him, with each least movement that it made, destroyed the very frame of sanity in which words might have meaning, reduced the world itself around him to a waste of dark and silence, a starlit ruin where already, everywhere, the alien and unimaginable was awakening to its new dominion. The corpse raised and reached out one hand as if to stay him—turned, and walked towards the instrument table. Its legs were leaden, it rocked its shoulders like a swimmer, fighting to make its passage through gravity's dense medium. It reached the table and grasped it exhaustedly. The doctor found himself on his feet, crouched slightly, weightlessly still. The knife in his hand was the only part of himself he clearly felt, and it was like a tongue of fire, a crematory flame. Joe Allen's corpse thrust one hand among the instruments. The thick fingers, with a queer, simian ineptitude, brought up a scalpel. Both hands clasped the little handle and plunged the blade between the lips, as a thirsty child might a popsicle, then jerked it out again, slashing the tongue. Turbid fluid splashed down to the floor. The jaw worked stiffly, the mouth brought out words in a wet, ragged hiss:

"Please. Help me. Trapped in *this*." One dead hand struck the dead chest. "Starving."

"What are you?"

"Traveler. Not of earth."

"An eater of human flesh. A drinker of human blood."

"No. No. Hiding only. Am small. Shape hideous to you. Feared death."

"You brought death." The doctor spoke with the calm of perfect disbelief, himself as incredible to him as the thing he spoke with. It shook its head, the dull, popped eyes glaring with an agony of thwarted expression.

"Killed none. Hid in this. Hid in this not to be killed. Five days now. Drowning in decay. Free me. Please."

"No. You have come to feed on us, you are not hiding in fear. We are your food, your meat and drink. You fed on those two men within your grave. *Their* grave. For you, a delay. In fact, a diversion that has ended the hunt for you."

"No! No! Used men already dead. For me, five days, starvation. Even less. Fed only from necessity. Horrible necessity!"

The spoiled vocal instrument made a mangled gasp of the last word—an inhuman, snakepit noise the doctor felt as a cold flicker of ophidian tongues within his ears—while the dead arms moved in a sodden approximation of the body language that swears truth.

"No," the doctor said. "You killed them all. Including your . . . tool—this man. *What are you?*" Panic erupted in the question which he tried to bury by answering himself instantly. "Resolute, yes. That surely. You used death for an escape route. You need no oxygen perhaps."

"Extracted more than my need from gasses of decay. A lesser component of our metabolism."

The voice was gaining distinctness, developing makeshifts for tones lost in the agonal rupturing of the valves and stops of speech, more effectively wrestling vowel and consonant from the putrid tongue and lips. At the same time the body's crudity of movement did not quite obscure a subtle, incessant experimentation. Fingers flexed and stirred, testing the give of tendons, groping the palm for the old points of purchase and counter-pressure there. The knees, with cautious repetitions, assessed the new limits of their articulation.

"What was the sphere?"

"My ship. Its destruction our first duty facing discovery." (Fear touched the doctor, like a slug climbing his neck; he had seen, as it spoke, a sharp, spastic activity of the tongue, a pleating and shrinkage of its bulk as at the tug of some inward adjustment.) "No chance to re-enter. Leaving this take far too long. Not even time to set for destruct—must extrude a cilium, chemical key to broach hull shield. In shaft my only chance to halt host."

The right arm tested the wrist, and the scalpel the hand still held cut white sparks from the air, while the word "host" seemed itself a little knife-prick, a teasing abandonment of fiction—though the dead mask showed no irony—preliminary to attack.

But he found that fear had gone from him. The impossibility with which he conversed, and was about to struggle, was working in him an overwhelming amplification of his life's long helpless rage at death. He found his parochial pity for earth alone stretched to the trans-stellar scope this traveler commanded, to the whole cosmic trashyard with its bulldozed multitudes of corpses; galactic wheels of carnage—stars, planets with their most majestic generations—all trash, cracked bones and foul rags that pooled, settled, reconcatenated in futile symmetries gravid with new multitudes of briefly animate trash.

And this, standing before him now, was the death it was given him particularly to deal—his mite was being called in by the universal Treasury of death, and Dr. Winters found himself, an old healer, on fire to pay. His own, more lethal, blade tugged at his hand with its own sharp appetite. He felt entirely the Examiner once more, knew the precise cuts he would make, swiftly and without error. *Very soon now,* he thought and cooly probed for some further insight before its onslaught:

"Why must your ship be destroyed, even at the cost of your host's life?"

"We must not be understood."

"The livestock must not understand what is devouring them."

"Yes, doctor. Not all at once. But one by one. You will understand what is devouring you. That is essential to my feast."

The doctor shook his head. "You are in your grave already, Traveler. That body will be your coffin. You will be buried in it a second time, for all time."

The thing came one step nearer and opened its mouth. The flabby throat wrestled as with speech, but what sprang out was a slender white filament, more than whip-fast. Dr. Winters saw only the first flicker of its eruption, and then his brain nova-ed, thinning out at light-speed to a white nullity.

When the doctor came to himself, it was in fact to a part of himself only. Before he had opened his eyes he found that his wakened mind had repossessed proprioceptively only a bizarre truncation of his body. His head, neck, left shoulder, arm and hand declared themselves—the rest was silence.

When he opened his eyes, he found that he lay supine on the gurney, and naked. Something propped his head. A strap bound his left elbow to the gurney's edge, a strap he could feel. His chest was also anchored by a strap, and this he could not feel. Indeed, save for its active remnant, his entire body might have been bound in a block of ice, so numb was it, and so powerless was he to compel the slightest movement from the least part of it.

The room was empty, but from the open door of the vault there came slight sounds: the creak and soft frictions of heavy tarpaulin shifted to accommodate some business involving small clicking and kissing noises.

Tears of fury filled the doctor's eyes. Clenching his one fist at the starry engine of creation that he could not see, he ground his teeth and whispered in the hot breath of strangled weeping:

"Take it back, this dirty little shred of life! I throw it off gladly like the filth it is." The slow knock of bootsoles loudened from within the vault, and he turned his head. From the vault door Joe Allen's corpse approached him.

It moved with new energy, though its gait was grotesque, a ducking, hitching progress, jerky with circumventions of decayed muscle, while above this galvanized, struggling frame, the bruise-colored face hung inanimate, an image of detachment. With terrible clarity it revealed the thing for what it was—a damaged hand-puppet vigorously worked from within. And when that frozen face was brought to hang above the doctor, the reeking hands, with the light, solicitous touch of friends at sickbeds, rested on his naked thigh.

The absence of sensation made the touch more dreadful than if felt. It showed him that the nightmare he still desperately denied at heart had annexed his body while he—holding head and arm free—had already more than half-drowned in its mortal paralysis. There lay his nightmare part, a nothingness freely possessed by an unspeakability. The corpse said:

"Rotten blood. Thin nourishment. Only one hour alone before you came. Fed from neighbor to my left—barely had strength to extend siphon. Fed from the right while you worked. Tricky going—you are alert. Expected Dr. Parsons. Energy needs of animating this"—one hand left the doctor's thigh and smote the dusty overalls—"and of host-transfer, very high. Once I have you synapsed, will be near starvation again."

A sequence of unbearable images unfolded in the doctor's mind, even as the robot carrion turned from the gurney and walked to the instrument table: the sheriff's arrival just after dawn, alone of course, since Craven always took thought for his deputies' rest and because on this errand he would want privacy to consider any indiscretion on behalf of the miners' survivors that the situation might call for; his finding his old friend, supine and alarmingly weak; his hurrying over, his leaning near. Then, somewhat later, a police car containing a rack of still wet bones might plunge off the highway above some deep spot in the gorge.

The corpse took an evidence box from the table and put the scalpel in it. Then it turned and retrieved the mortuary knife from the floor and put that in as well, saying as it did so, without turning, "The sheriff will come in the morning. You spoke like close friends. He will probably come alone."

The coincidence with his thoughts had to be accident, but the intent to terrify and appall him was clear. The tone and timing of that patched-up voice were unmistakably deliberate—sly probes that sought his anguish specifically, sought his mind's personal center. He watched the corpse—back at the table—dipping an apish but accurate hand and plucking up rib shears, scissors, clamps, adding all to the box. He stared, momentarily emptied by shock of all but the will to know finally the full extent of the horror that had appropriated his life. Joe Allen's body carried the box to the worktable beside the gurney, and the expressionless eyes met the doctor's.

"I have gambled. A grave gamble. But now I have won. At risk of personal discovery we are obliged to disconnect, contract, hide as well as possible in host body. Suicide in effect. I disregarded situational imperatives, despite starvation before disinterment and subsequent autopsy all but certain. I caught up with crew, tackled Pollock and Jackson microseconds before blast. Computed five days' survival from this cache, could disconnect at limit of strength to do so, but otherwise would chance autopsy, knowing doctor was alcoholic incompetent. And now see my gain. You are a prize host, can feed with near impunity even when killing too dangerous. Safe meals delivered to you still warm."

The corpse had painstakingly aligned the gurney parallel to the worktable but offset, the table's foot extending past the gurney's, and separated from it by a distance somewhat less than the reach of Joe Allen's right arm. Now the dead hands distributed the implements along the right edge of the table, save for the scissors and the box. These the corpse took to the table's foot, where it set down the box and slid the scissors' jaws round one strap of its overalls. It began to speak again, and as it did, the scissors dismembered its cerements in unhesitating strokes.

"The cut must be medical, forensically right, though a smaller one easier. Must be careful of the pectoral muscles or arms will not convey me. I am no larva anymore—over fifteen hundred grams."

To ease the nightmare's suffocating pressure, to thrust out some flicker of his own will against its engulfment, the doctor flung a question, his voice more cracked than the other's now was:

"Why is my arm free?"

"The last, fine neural splicing needs a sensory-motor standard, to perfect my brain's fit to yours. Lacking this eye-hand coordinating check, much coarser motor control of host. This done, I flush out the paralytic, unbind us, and we are free together."

The grave-clothes had fallen in a puzzle of fragments, and the cadaver stood naked, its dark, gas-rounded contours making it seem some sleek marine creature, ruddered with the black-veined, gas-distended sex. Again the voice had teased for his fear, had uttered the last word with a savoring protraction, and now the doctor's cup of anguish brimmed over; horror and outrage wrenched his spirit in brutal alternation as if trying to tear it naked from its captive frame. He rolled his head in this deadlock, his mouth beginning to split with the slow birth of a mind-emptying outcry.

The corpse watched this, giving a single nod that might have been approbation. Then it mounted the worktable and, with the concentrated caution of some practiced convalescent reentering his bed, lay on its back. The dead eyes again sought the living and found the doctor staring back, grinning insanely.

"Clever corpse!" the doctor cried. "Clever, carnivorous corpse! Able alien! Please don't think I'm criticizing. Who am I to criticize? A mere arm and shoulder, a talking head, just a small piece of a pathologist. But I'm confused." He paused, savoring the monster's attentive silence and his own buoyancy in the hysterical levity that had unexpectedly liberated him. "You're going to use your puppet there to pluck you out of itself and put you on me. But once he's pulled you from your driver's seat, won't he go dead, so to speak, and drop you? You could get a nasty knock. Why not set a plank between the tables—the puppet opens the door, and you scuttle, ooze, lurch, flop, slither, as the case may be, across the bridge. No messy spills. And in any case, isn't this an odd, rather clumsy way to get around among your cattle? Shouldn't you at least carry your own scalpels when you travel? There's always the risk you'll run across that one host in a million that isn't carrying one with him."

He knew his gibes would be answered to his own despair. He exulted, but solely in the momentary bafflement of the predator—in having, for just a moment, mocked its gloating assurance to silence and marred its feast.

Its right hand picked up the post-mortem knife beside it, and the left wedged a roll of gauze beneath Allen's neck, lifting the throat to a more prominent arch. The mouth told the ceiling:

"We retain larval form till entry of the host. As larvae we have locomotor structures, and sense-buds usable outside our ships' sensory amplifiers. I waited coiled round Ed Sykes' bed leg till night, entered by his mouth as he slept." Allen's hand lifted the knife, held it high above the dull, quick eyes, turning it in the light. "Once lodged, we have three instars to adult form," the voice continued absently—the knife might have been a mirror from which the corpse read its features. "Larvally we have only a sketch of our full neural tap. Our metamorphosis is cued and determined by the host's endosomatic ecology. I matured in three days." Allen's wrist flexed, tipping the knife's point downmost. "Most supreme adaptations are purchased at the cost of inessential capacities." The elbow pronated and slowly flexed, hooking the knife body-wards. "Our hosts are all sentients, eco-dominants, are already carrying the baggage of coping structures for the planetary environment. Limbs, sensory portals"—the fist planted the fang of its tool under the chin, tilted it and rode it smoothly down the throat, the voice proceeding unmarred from under the furrow that the steel ploughed—"somatic envelopes, instrumentalities"—down the sternum, diaphragm, abdomen the stainless blade painted its stripe of gaping, muddy tissue—"with a host's brain we inherit all these, the mastery of any planet, netted in its dominant's cerebral nexus. Thus our genetic codings are now all but disencumbered of such provisions."

So swiftly the doctor flinched, Joe Allen's hand slashed four lateral cuts from the great wound's axis. The seeming butchery left two flawlessly drawn thoracic flaps cleanly outlined. The left hand raised the left flap's hem, and the right coaxed the knife into the aperture, deepening it with small stabs and slices. The posture was a man's who searches a breast pocket, with the dead eyes studying the slow recoil of flesh. The voice, when it resumed, had geared up to an intenser pitch:

"Galactically, the chordate nerve/brain paradigm abounds, and the neural labyrinth is our dominion. Are we to make plank bridges and worm across them to our food? Are cockroaches greater than we for having legs to run up walls and antennae to grope their way! All the quaint, hinged crutches that life sports! The stilts, fins, fans, springs, stalks, flippers and feathers, all in turn so variously terminating in hooks, clamps, suckers, scissors, forks or little cages of digits! And besides all the gadgets it concocts for wrestling through its worlds, it is all knobbed, whiskered, crested, plumed, vented, spiked or measeled over with perceptual gear for combing pittances of noise or color from the environing plentitude."

Invincibly calm and sure, the hands traded tool and tasks. The right flap eased back, revealing ropes of ingeniously spared muscle while promising a genuine appearance once sutured back in place. Helplessly the doctor felt his delirious defiance bleed away and a bleak fascination rebind him.

"We are the taps and relays that share the host's aggregate of afferent nerve-impulse precisely at its nodes of integration. We are the brains that peruse these integrations, integrate them with our existing banks of host-specific data, and, lastly, let their consequences flow down the motor pathway—either the consequences they seek spontaneously, or those we wish to graft upon them. We are besides a streamlined alimentary/circulatory system and a reproductive apparatus. And more than this we need not be."

The corpse had spread its bloody vest, and the feculent hands now took up the rib shears. The voice's sinister coloration of pitch and stress grew yet more marked—the phrases slid from the tongue with a cobra's seeking sway, winding their liquid rhythms round the doctor till a gap in his resistance should let them pour through to slaughter the little courage left him.

"For in this form we have inhabited the densest brainweb of three hundred races, lain intricately snug within them like thriving vine on trelliswork. We've looked out from too many variously windowed masks to regret our own vestigial senses. None read their worlds definitely. Far better then, our nomad's range and choice, than an unvarying tenancy of one poor set of structures. Far better to slip on as we do whole living beings and wear at once all of their limbs and organs, memories and powers—wear all as tightly congruent to our wills as a glove is to the hand that fills it."

The shears clipped through the gristle, stolid, bloody jaws monotonously feeding, stopping short of the sterno-clavicular joint in the manubrium where the muscles of the pectoral girdle have an important anchorage.

"No consciousness of the chordate type that we have found has been impermeable to our finesse—no dendritic pattern so elaborate we could not read its stitchwork and thread ourselves to match, precisely map its each synaptic seam till we could loosen it and re-tailor all to suit ourselves. We have strutted costumed in the bodies of planetary autarchs, venerable manikins of moral fashion, but cut of the universal cloth: the weave of fleet electric filaments of experience which we easily re-shuttled to the warp of our wishes. Whereafter—newly hemmed and gathered—their living fabric hung obedient to our bias, investing us with honor and influence unlimited."

The tricky verbal melody, through the corpse's deft, unfaltering self-dismemberment—the sheer neuromuscular orchestration of the compound activity—struck Dr. Winters with the detached enthrallment great keyboard performers could bring him. He glimpsed the alien's perspective—a Gulliver waiting in a brobdingnagian grave, then marshaling a dead giant against a living, like a dwarf in a huge mechanical crane, feverishly programming combat on a battery of levers and pedals, waiting for the robot arms' enactments, the remote, titanic impact of the foes—and he marveled, filled with a bleak wonder at life's infinite strategy and plasticity. Joe Allen's hands reached into his half-opened abdominal cavity, reached deep below the uncut anterior muscle that was exposed by the shallow, spurious incision of the epidermis, till by external measure they were extended far enough to be touching his thighs. The voice was still as the forearms advertised a delicate rummaging with the buried fingers. The shoulders drew back. As the steady withdrawal brought the wrists into view, the dead legs tremored and quaked with diffuse spasms.

"You called your kind our food and drink, doctor. If you were merely that, an elementary usurpation of your motor tracts alone would satisfy us, give us perfect cattle-control—for what rarest word or subtlest behavior is more than a flurry of varied muscles? That trifling skill was ours long ago. It is not mere blood that feeds this lust I feel now to tenant you, this craving for an intimacy that years will not stale. My truest feast lies in compelling you to feed in that way and in the utter deformation of your will this will involve. Had gross nourishment been my prime need, then my gravemates—Pollock and Jackson—could have eked out two weeks of life for me or more. But I scorned a cowardly parsimony in the face of death. I reinvested more than half the energy that their blood gave me in fabricating chemicals to keep their brains alive, and fluid-bathed with oxygenated nutriment."

Out of the chasmed midriff the smeared hands dragged two long tresses of silvery filament that writhed and sparkled with a million simultaneous coilings and contractions. The legs jittered with faint, chaotic pulses throughout their musculature, until the bright, vermiculate tresses had gathered into two spheric masses which the hands laid carefully within the incision. Then the legs lay still as death.

"I had accessory neural taps only to spare, but I could access much memory, and all of their cognitive responses, and having in my banks all the organ of Corti's electrochemical conversions of English words, I could whisper anything to them directly into the eighth cranial nerve. Those are our true feast, doctor, such bodiless electric storms of impotent cognition as I tickled up in those two little bone globes. I was forced to drain them yesterday, just before disinterment. They lived till then and understood everything—*everything* I did to them."

When the voice paused, the dead and living eyes were locked together. They remained so a moment, and then the dead face smiled.

It recapitulated all the horror of Allen's first resurrection—this waking of expressive soul from those grave-mound contours. And it was a demon-soul the doctor saw awaken: the smile was barbed with fine, sharp hooks of cruelty at the corners of the mouth, while the barbed eyes beamed fond, languorous anticipation of his pain. Remotely, Dr. Winters heard the flat sound of his own voice asking:

"And Eddie Sykes?"

"Oh, yes, doctor. He is with us now, has been throughout. I grieve to abandon so rare a host! He is a true hermit-philosopher, well-read in four languages. He is writing a translation of Marcus Aurelius—he was, I mean, in his free time. . . ."

Long minutes succeeded of the voice accompanying the surreal self-autopsy, but the doctor lay stilled, emptied of reactive power. Still, the full understanding of his fate reverberated in his mind—an empty room through which the voice, not heard exactly but somehow implanted directly as in the subterranean torture it had just described, sent aftershocks of realization, amplifications of the Unspeakable.

The parasite had traced and tapped the complex interface between cortical integration of input and the consequent neural output shaping response. It had interposed its brain between, sharing consciousness while solely commanding the pathways of reaction. The host, the bottled personality, was mute and limbless for any least expression of its own will, while hellishly articulate and agile in the service of the parasite's. It was the host's own hands that bound and wrenched the life half out of his prey, his own loins that experienced the repeated orgasms crowning his other despoliations of their bodies. And when they lay, bound and shrieking still, ready for the consummation, it was his own strength that hauled the smoking entrails from them, and his own intimate tongue and guzzling mouth he plunged into the rank, palpitating feast.

And the doctor had glimpses of the history behind this predation, that of a race so far advanced in the essentializing, the inexorable abstraction of their own mental fabric that through scientific commitment and genetic self-cultivation they had come to embody their own model of perfected consciousness, streamlined to permit the entry of other beings and the direct acquisition of their experiential worlds. All strictest scholarship at first, until there matured in the disembodied scholars their long-germinal and now blazing, jealous hatred for all "lesser" minds rooted and clothed in the soil and sunlight of solid, particular worlds. The parasite spoke of the "cerebral music," the "symphonies of agonized paradox" that were its invasion's chief plunder. The doctor felt the truth behind this grandiloquence: its actual harvest from the systematic violation of encoffined personalities was the experience of a barren supremacy of means over lives more primitive, perhaps, but vastly wealthier in the vividness and passionate concern with which life for them was imbued.

Joe Allen's hands had scooped up the bunched skeins of alien nerve, with the wrinkled brain-node couched admidst them, and for some time had waited the slow retraction of a last major trunkline which seemingly had followed the spine's axis. At last, when only a slender subfiber of this remained implanted, the corpse, smiling once more, held up for him to view its reconcatenated master. The doctor looked into its eyes then and spoke—not to their controller, but to the captive who shared them with it, and who now, the doctor knew, neared his final death.

"Goodbye, Joe Allen. Eddie Sykes. You are guiltless. Peace be with you at last."

The demon smile remained fixed, the right hand reached its viscid cargo across the gap and over the doctor's groin. He watched the hand set the glittering medusa's head—his new self—upon his flesh, return to the table, take up the scalpel, and reach back to cut in his groin a four-inch incision—all in eerie absence of tactile stimulus. The line that had remained plunged into the corpse suddenly whipped free of the mediastinal crevice, retracted across the gap and shortened to a taut stub on the seething organism atop the doctor.

Joe Allen's body collapsed, emptied, all slack. He was a corpse again entirely, but with one anomalous feature to his posture. His right arm had not dropped to the nearly vertical hang that would have been natural. At the instant of the alien's unplugging, the shoulder had given a fierce shrug and wrenching of its angle, flinging the arm upward as it died so that it now lay in the orientation of an arm that reaches up for a ladder's next rung. The slightest tremor would unfix the joints and dump the arm back into the gravitational bias; it would also serve to dump the scalpel from the proferred, upturned palm that implement still precariously occupied.

The man had repossessed himself one microsecond before his end. The doctor's heart stirred, woke, and sang within him, for he saw that the scalpel was just in reach of his fingers at his forearm's fullest stretch from the bound elbow. The horror crouched on him and, even now slowly feeding its trunkline into his groin incision, at first stopped the doctor's hand with a pang of terror. Then he reminded himself that, until implanted, the enemy was a senseless mass, bristling with plugs, with input jacks for senses, but, until installed in the physical amplifiers of eyes and ears, an utterly deaf, blind monad that waited in a perfect solipsism between two captive sensory envelopes.

He saw his straining fingers above the bright tool of freedom, thought with an insane smile of God and Adam on the Sistine ceiling, and then, with a lifespan of surgeon's fine control, plucked up the scalpel. The arm fell and hung.

"Sleep," the doctor said. "Sleep revenged."

But he found his retaliation harshly reined-in by the alien's careful provisions. His elbow had been fixed with his upper arm almost at right angles to his body's long axis; his forearm could reach his hand inward and present it closely to the face, suiting the parasite's need of an eye-hand coordinative check, but could not, even with the scalpel's added reach, bring its point within four inches of his groin. Steadily the parasite fed in its tapline. It would usurp motor control in three or four minutes at most, to judge by the time its extrication from Allen had taken.

Frantically the doctor bent his wrist inwards to its limit, trying to pick through the strap where it crossed his inner elbow. Sufficient pressure was impossible, and the hold so awkward that even feeble attempts threatened the loss of the scalpel. Smoothly the root of alien control sank into him. It was a defenseless thing of jelly against which he lay lethally armed, and he was still doomed—a preview of all his thrall's impotence-to-be.

But of course there was a way. Not to survive. But to escape, and to have vengeance. For a moment he stared at his captor, hardening his mettle in the blaze of hate it lit in him. Then, swiftly, he determined the order of his moves, and began.

He reached the scalpel to his neck and opened his superior thyroid vein—his inkwell. He laid the scalpel by his ear, dipped his finger in his blood, and began to write on the metal surface of the gurney, beginning by his thigh and moving towards his armpit. Oddly, the incision of his neck, though this was muscularly awake, had been painless, which gave him hopes that raised his courage for what remained to do. His neat, sparing strokes scribed with ghastly legibility.

When he had done the message read:

MIND PARASITE
FM ALLEN IN ME
CUT *all* TILL FIND
1500 GM MASS
NERVE FIBRE

He wanted to write goodbye to his friend, but the alien had begun to pay out smaller, auxiliary filaments collaterally with the main one, and all now lay in speed.

He took up the scalpel, rolled his head to the left, and plunged the blade deep in his ear.

Miracle! Last, accidental mercy! It was painless. Some procedural, highly specific anesthetic was in effect. With careful plunges, he obliterated the right inner ear and then thrust silence, with equal thoroughness, into the left. The slashing of the vocal cords followed, then the tendons in the back of the neck that hold it erect. He wished he were free to unstring knees and elbows too, but it could not be. But blinded, with centers of balance lost, with only rough motor control—all these conditions should fetter the alien's escape, should it in the first place manage the reanimation of a bloodless corpse in which it had not yet achieved a fine-tuned interweave. Before he extinguished his eyes, he paused, the scalpel poised above his face, and blinked them to clear his aim of tears. The right, then the left, both retinas meticulously carved away, the yolk of vision quite scooped out of them. The scalpel's last task, once it had tilted the head sideways to guide the bloodflow absolutely clear of possible effacement of the message, was to slash the external carotid artery.

When this was done the old man sighed with relief and laid his scalpel down. Even as he did so, he felt the deep, inward prickle of an alien energy—something that flared, crackled, flared, *groped for* but did not quite find its purchase. And inwardly, as the doctor sank towards sleep—cerebrally, as a voiceless man must speak—he spoke to the parasite these carefully chosen words:

"Welcome to your new house. I'm afraid there's been some vandalism—the lights don't work, and the plumbing has a very bad leak. There are some other things wrong as well—the neighborhood is perhaps a little *too* quiet, and you may find it hard to get around very easily. But it's been a lovely home to me for fifty-seven years, and somehow I think you'll stay. . . ."

The face, turned towards the body of Joe Allen, seemed to weep scarlet tears, but its last movement before death was to smile.

E. Nesbit

John Charrington's Wedding

Edith Nesbit is a dominant figure in children's literature, but her horror and supernatural fiction is less well known. "John Charrington's Wedding" seems at first just a little romantic fantasy about love conquering all, but there is more than a touch of Le Fanu's "Schalken the Painter" and Ivan Turgenev's "Clara Militch" in this short piece by a woman who was at the center of the intellectual movements of her era.

No one ever thought that May Forster would marry John Charrington; but he thought differently, and things which John Charrington intended had a queer way of coming to pass. He asked her to marry him before he went up to Oxford. She laughed and refused him. He asked her again next time he came home. Again she laughed, tossed her dainty blonde head, and again refused. A third time he asked her; she said it was becoming a confirmed bad habit, and laughed at him more than ever.

John was not the only man who wanted to marry her: She was the belle of our village coterie, and we were all in love with her more or less; it was a sort of fashion, like heliotrope ties or Inverness capes. Therefore we were as much annoyed as surprised when John Charrington walked into our little local Club—we held it in a loft over the saddler's, I remember—and invited us all to his wedding.

"Your wedding?"

"You don't mean it?"

"Who's the happy fair? When's it to be?"

John Charrington filled his pipe and lighted it before he replied. Then he said, "I'm sorry to deprive you fellows of your only joke—but Miss Forster and I are to be married in September."

"You don't meant it?"

"He's got the boot again, and it's turned his head."

"No," I said, rising, "I see it's true. Lend me a pistol someone—or a first-class fare to the other end of Nowhere. Charrington has bewitched the only pretty girl in our twenty-mile radius. Was it mesmerism, or a love potion, Jack?"

"Neither, sir, but a gift you'll never have—perseverance—and the best luck a man ever had in this world."

There was something in his voice that silenced me, and all the chaff of the other fellows failed to draw him further.

The queer thing about it was that when we congratulated Miss Forster, she

203

blushed and smiled and dimpled, for all the world as though she were in love with him, and had been in love with him all the time. Upon my word, I think she had. Women are strange creatures.

We were all asked to the wedding. In Brixham everyone who was anybody knew everybody else who was anyone. My sisters were, I truly believe, more interested in the trousseau than the bride herself, and I was to be best man. The coming marriage was much canvassed at afternoon tea-tables, and at our little Club over the saddler's, and the question was always asked: "Does she care for him?"

I used to ask that question myself in the early days of their engagement, but after a certain evening in August I never asked it again. I was coming home from the Club through the churchyard. Our church is on a thyme-grown hill, and the turf about it is so thick and soft that one's footsteps are noiseless.

I made no sound as I vaulted the low lichened wall and threaded my way between the tombstones. It was at the same instant that I heard John Charrington's voice, and saw her. May was sitting on a low flat gravestone, her face turned towards the full splendor of the western sun. Its expression ended, at once and for ever, any question of love for him; it was transfigured to a beauty I should not have believed possible, even to that beautiful little face.

John lay at her feet, and it was his voice that broke the stillness of the golden August evening. "My dear, my dear, I believe I should come back from the dead if you wanted me!"

I coughed at once to indicate my presence, and passed on into the shadow, fully enlightened.

The wedding was to be early in September. Two days before I had to run up to town on business. The train was late, of course, for we are on the South-eastern, and as I stood grumbling with my watch in my hand, whom should I see but John Charrington and May Forster. They were walking up and down the unfrequented end of the platform, arm in arm, looking into each other's eyes, careless of the sympathetic interest of the porters.

Of course I knew better than to hesitate a moment before burying myself in the booking-office, and it was not till the train drew up at the platform, that I obtrusively passed the pair with my suitcase and took the corner in a first-class smoking-carriage. I did this with as good an air of not seeing them as I could assume. I pride myself on my discretion, but if John was travelling alone I wanted his company. I had it.

"Hullo, old man," came his cheery voice as he swung his bag into my carriage. "Here's luck; I was expecting a dull journey!"

"Where are you off to?" I asked, discretion still bidding me turn my eyes away, though I felt, without looking, that hers were red-rimmed.

"To old Branbridge's," he answered, shutting the door and leaning out for a last word with his sweetheart.

"Oh, I wish you wouldn't go, John," she was saying in a low, earnest voice. "I feel certain something will happen."

"Do you think I should let anything happen to keep me, and the day after tomorrow our wedding-day?"

"Don't go," she answered, with a pleading intensity which would have sent my suitcase onto the platform and me after it. But she wasn't speaking to me. John Charrington was made differently; he rarely changed his opinions, never his resolutions.

He only stroked the little ungloved hands that lay on the carriage door.

"I must, May. The old boy's been awfully good to me, and now he's dying I must go and see him, but I shall come home in time for—" The rest of the parting was lost in a whisper and in the rattling lurch of the starting train.

She spoke as the train moved: "You're sure to come?"

"Nothing shall keep me," he answered; and we steamed out. After he had seen the last of the little figure on the platform, he leaned back in his corner and kept silence for a minute.

When he spoke it was to explain to me that his godfather, whose heir he was, lay dying at Peasmarsh Place, some fifty miles away, and had sent for John, and John had felt bound to go.

"I shall surely be back tomorrow," he said, "or, if not, the day after, in heaps of time. Thank Heaven, one hasn't to get up in the middle of the night to get married nowadays!"

"And suppose Mr. Branbridge dies?"

"Alive or dead I mean to be married on Thursday!" John answered, lighting a cigar and unfolding *The Times.*

At Peasmarsh station we said good-bye, and he got out, and I saw him ride off; I went on to London, where I stayed the night.

When I got home the next afternoon, a very wet one, by the way, my sister Fanny greeted me with: "Where's Mr. Charrington?"

"Goodness knows," I answered testily. Every man, since Cain, has resented that kind of question.

"I thought you might have heard from him," she went on, "as you're to give him away tomorrow."

"Isn't he back?" I asked, for I had confidently expected to find him at home.

"No, Geoffrey"—my sister Fanny always had a way of jumping to conclusions, especially such conclusions as were least favorable to her fellow-creatures—"he has not returned, and, what is more, you may depend upon it he won't. You mark my words, there'll be no wedding tomorrow."

My sister Fanny has a power of annoying me which no other human being possesses.

"*You* mark *my* words," I retorted with asperity, "you had better give up making such a thundering idiot of yourself. There'll be more wedding tomorrow than ever you'll take the first part in." A prophecy which, by the way, came true.

But though I could snarl confidently to my sister, I did not feel so comfortable when late that night, I, standing on the doorstep of John's house, heard that he had not returned. I went home gloomily through the rain. Next morning brought a brilliant blue sky, gold sun, and all such softness of air and beauty of cloud as go to make up a perfect day. I woke with a vague feeling of having gone to bed anxious, and of being rather averse to facing that anxiety in the light of full wakefulness.

But with my shaving-water came a note from John which relieved my mind and sent me up to the Forsters' with a light heart.

May was in the garden. I saw her blue gown through the hollyhocks as the lodge gates swung to behind me. So I did not go up to the house, but turned aside down the turfed path.

"He's written to you too," she said, without preliminary greeting, when I reached her side.

"Yes, I'm to meet him at the station at three and come straight on to the church."

Her face looked pale, but there was a brightness in her eyes, and a tender quiver about the mouth that spoke of renewed happiness.

"Mr. Branbridge begged him so to stay another night that he had not the heart to refuse," she went on. "He is so kind, but I wish he hadn't stayed."

I was at the station at half past two. I felt rather annoyed with John. It seemed a sort of slight to the beautiful girl who loved him that he should come, as it were, out of breath, and with the dust of travel upon him, to take her hand, which some of us would have given the best years of our lives to take.

But when the three o'clock train glided in, and glided out again having brought no passengers to our little station, I was more than annoyed. There was no other train for thirty-five minutes; I calculated that, with much hurry, we might just get to the church in time for the ceremony; but, oh, what a fool to have missed that first train! What other man could have done it?

That thirty-five minutes seemed a year as I wandered around the station reading the advertisements and the time-tables, and the company's by-laws, and getting more and more angry with John Charrington. This confidence in his own power of getting everything he wanted the minute he wanted it was leading him too far. I hate waiting. Everyone does, but I believe I hate it more than anyone else. The three thirty-five was late, of course.

I ground my pipe between my teeth and stamped with impatience as I watched the signals. *Click.* The signal went down. Five minutes later I flung myself into the carriage that I had brought for John.

"Drive to the church!" I said as someone shut the door. "Mr. Charrington hasn't come by this train."

Anxiety now replaced anger. What had become of the man? Could he have been taken ill suddenly? I had never known him have a day's illness in his life. And even so he might have telegraphed. Some awful accident must have happened to him. The thought that he had played her false never—no, not for a moment—entered my head. Yes, something terrible had happened to him, and on me lay the task of telling his bride. I almost wished the carriage would upset and break my head so that someone else might tell her, not I, who— But that's nothing to do with this story.

It was five minutes to four as we drew up to the churchyard gate. A double row of eager onlookers lined the path from lych-gate to porch. I sprang from the carriage and passed up between them. Our gardener had a good place near the front door. I stopped.

"Are they waiting still, Byles?" I asked simply to gain time, for of course I knew they were by the waiting crowd's attentive attitude.

"Waiting, sir? No, no, sir; why, it must be over by now."

"Over! Then Mr. Charrington's come?"

"To the minute, sir; must have missed you somehow, and I say, sir," lowering his voice, "I never seen Mr. John the least bit so afore, but my opinion is he's been drinking pretty free. His clothes was all dusty and his face like a sheet. I tell you I didn't like the looks of him at all, and the folks inside are saying all sorts of things. You'll see, something's gone very wrong with Mr. John, and he's tried liquor. He looked like a ghost, and in he went with his eyes straight before him, with never a look or a word for none of us, him that was always such a gentleman!"

I had never heard Byles make so long a speech. The crowd in the churchyard were talking in whispers and getting ready rice and slippers to throw at the bride and bridegroom. The ringers were ready with their hands on the ropes to ring out the merry peal as the bride and bridegroom should come out.

A murmur from the church announced them; out they came. Byles was right. John Charrington did not look himself. There was dust on his coat, his hair was disarranged. He seemed to have been in some row, for there was a black mark above his eyebrow. He was deathly pale. But his pallor was not greater than that of the bride, who might have been carved in ivory—dress, veil, orange blossoms, face and all.

As they passed, the ringers stopped—there were six of them—and then, on the ears expecting the gay wedding peal, came the slow tolling of the passing bell.

A thrill of horror at so foolish a jest from the ringers passed through us all. But the ringers themselves dropped the ropes and fled like rabbits out of the church into the sunlight. The bride shuddered, and grey shadows came about her mouth, but the bridegroom led her on down the path where the people stood with the handfuls of rice; but the handfuls were never thrown, and the wedding-bells never rang. In vain the ringers were urged to remedy their mistake: They protested with many whispered expletives that they would see themselves further first.

In a hush like the hush in the chamber of death, the bridal pair passed into their carriage and its door slammed behind them.

Then the tongues were loosed. A babel of anger, wonder, and conjecture from the guests and the spectators.

"If I'd seen his condition, sir," said old Forster to me as we drove off, "I would have stretched him on the floor of the church, sir, by Heaven I would, before I'd have let him marry my daughter!"

Then he put his head out of the window.

"Drive like hell," he cried to the coachman. "Don't spare the horses."

He was obeyed. We passed the bride's carriage. I forbore to look at it, and old Forster turned his head away and swore. We reached home before it.

We stood in the hall doorway, in the blazing afternoon sun, and in about half a minute we heard wheels crunching the gravel. When the carriage stopped in front of the steps, old Forster and I ran down.

"Great Heaven, the carriage is empty! And yet—"

I had the door opened in a minute, and this is what I saw—no sign of John Charrington; only May, his wife, a huddled heap of white satin lying half on the floor of the carriage and half on the seat.

"I drove straight here, sir," said the coachman, as the bride's father lifted her out; "and I'll swear no one got out of the carriage."

We carried her into the house in her bridal dress and drew back her veil. I saw her face. Shall I ever forget it? White, white and drawn with agony and horror, bearing such a look of terror as I have never seen since except in dreams. And her hair, her radiant blonde hair, I tell you it was white as snow.

As we stood, her father and I, half mad with the horror and mystery of it, a boy came up the avenue—a telegraph boy. He brought the orange envelope to me. I tore it open.

Mr. Charrington was thrown from the dog-cart on his way to the station at half past one. Killed on the spot!

And he was married to May Forster in our parish church at *half past three*, in the presence of half the parish.

"Alive or dead I mean to be married!"

What had passed in that carriage on the homeward drive? No one knows—no one will ever know. Oh, May! Oh, my dear!

Before a week was over, they laid her beside her husband in our little churchyard on the thyme-covered hill—the churchyard where they had kept their love-trysts.

Thus was accomplished John Charrington's wedding.

Karl Edward Wagner

Sticks

Karl Edward Wagner is a young writer committed to the tradition of modern horror and dark fantasy. His mentor was Manly Wade Wellman but his influences range throughout contemporary horror. "Sticks" is generally regarded as his finest work to date. It is based upon an anecdote of the great horror artist, Lee Brown Coye, who told of strange, weird artifacts and drawings found in an abandoned farmhouse in upstate New York and around it. Although Wagner's story is overtly a Lovecraftian story of historical and cosmic evil, a forbidden knowledge piece, it is also structured to awaken in the reader imaginative possibilities deeply embedded in the human subconscious. Wagner is a forceful personality in the contemporary field and editor of the annual volume, *The Year's Best Horror Stories*, as well as the small-press publisher of Carcosa House books.

1

The lashed-together framework of sticks jutted from a small cairn alongside the stream. Colin Leverett studied it in perplexment—half a dozen odd lengths of branch, wired together at cross angles for no fathomable purpose. It reminded him unpleasantly of some bizarre crucifix, and he wondered what might lie beneath the cairn.

It was the spring of 1942—the kind of day to make the war seem distant and unreal, although the draft notice waited on his desk. In a few days Leverett would lock his rural studio, wonder if he would see it again—be able to use its pens and brushes and carving tools when he did return. It was good-by to the woods and streams of upstate New York, too. No fly rods, no tramps through the countryside in Hitler's Europe. No point in putting off fishing that troutstream he had driven past once, exploring back roads of the Otselic Valley.

Mann Brook—so it was marked on the old Geological Survey map—ran southeast of DeRuyter. The unfrequented country road crossed over a stone bridge old before the first horseless carriage, but Leverett's Ford eased across and onto the shoulder. Taking fly rod and tackle, he included pocket flask and tied an iron skillet to his belt. He'd work his way downstream a few miles. By afternoon he'd lunch on fresh trout, maybe some bullfrog-legs.

It was a fine clear stream, though difficult to fish as dense bushes hung out

209

from the bank, broken with stretches of open water hard to work without being seen. But the trout rose boldly to his fly, and Leverett was in fine spirits.

From the bridge the valley along Mann Brook began as fairly open pasture, but half a mile downstream the land had fallen into disuse and was thick with second growth evergreens and scrub-apple trees. Another mile, and the scrub merged with dense forest, which continued unbroken. The land here, he had learned, had been taken over by the state many years back.

As Leverett followed the stream he noted the remains of an old railroad embankment. No vestige of tracks or ties—only the embankment itself, overgrown with large trees. The artist rejoiced in the beautiful dry-wall culverts spanning the stream as it wound through the valley. To his mind it seemed eerie, this forgotten railroad running straight and true through virtual wilderness.

He could imagine an old wood-burner with its conical stack, steaming along through the valley dragging two or three wooden coaches. It must be a branch of the old Oswego Midland Rail Road, he decided, abandoned rather suddenly in the 1870's. Leverett, who had a memory for detail, knew of it from a story his grandfather told of riding the line in 1871 from Otselic to DeRuyter on his honeymoon. The engine had so labored up the steep grade over Crumb Hill that he got off to walk alongside. Probably that sharp grade was the reason for the line's abandonment.

When he came across a scrap of board nailed to several sticks set into a stone wall, his darkest thought was that it might read "No Trespassing." Curiously, though the board was weathered featureless, the nails seemed quite new. Leverett scarcely gave it much thought, until a short distance beyond he came upon another such contrivance. And another.

Now he scratched at the day's stubble on his long jaw. This didn't make sense. A prank? But on whom? A child's game? No, the arrangement was far too sophisticated. As an artist, Leverett appreciated the craftsmanship of the work—the calculated angles and lengths, the designed intricacy of the maddeningly inexplicable devices. There was something distinctly uncomfortable about their effect.

Leverett reminded himself that he had come here to fish and continued downstream. But as he worked around a thicket he again stopped in puzzlement.

Here was a small open space with more of the stick lattices and an arrangement of flat stones laid out on the ground. The stones—likely taken from one of the many dry-wall culverts—made a pattern maybe twenty by fifteen feet, that at first glance resembled a ground plan for a house. Intrigued, Leverett quickly saw that this was not so. If the ground plan were for anything, it would have to be for a small maze.

The bizarre lattice structures were all around. Sticks from trees and bits of board nailed together in fantastic array. They defied description; no two seemed alike. Some were only one or two sticks lashed together in parallel or at angles. Others were worked into complicated lattices of dozens of sticks and boards. One could have been a child's tree house—it was built in three planes, but was so abstract and useless that it could be nothing more than an insane conglomeration of sticks and wire. Sometimes the contrivances were stuck in a pile of stones or a wall, maybe thrust into the railroad embankment or nailed to a tree.

It should have been ridiculous. It wasn't. Instead it seemed somehow sinister—these utterly inexplicable, meticulously constructed stick lattices spread through a wilderness where only a tree-grown embankment or a forgotten stone wall gave evidence that man had ever passed through. Leverett forgot about trout and frog-legs, instead dug into his pockets for a notebook and stub of pencil. Busily he began to sketch the more intricate structures. Perhaps someone could explain them; perhaps there was something to their insane complexity that warranted closer study for his own work.

Leverett was roughly two miles from the bridge when he came upon the ruins of a house. It was an unlovely colonial farmhouse, box-shaped and gambrel-roofed, fast falling into the ground. Windows were dark and empty; the chimneys on either end looked ready to topple. Rafters showed through open spaces in the room, and the weathered boards of the walls had in places rotted away to reveal hewn timber beams. The foundation was stone and disproportionately massive. From the size of the unmortared stone blocks, its builder had intended the foundation to stand forever.

The house was nearly swallowed up by undergrowth and rampant lilac bushes, but Leverett could distinguish what had been a lawn with imposing shade trees. Farther back were gnarled and sickly apple trees and an overgrown garden where a few lost flowers still bloomed—wan and serpentine from years in the wild. The stick lattices were everywhere—the lawn, the trees, even the house were covered with the uncanny structures. They reminded Leverett of a hundred misshapen spider webs—grouped so closely together as to almost ensnare the entire house and clearing. Wondering, he sketched page on page of them, as he cautiously approached the abandoned house.

He wasn't certain just what he expected to find inside. The aspect of the farmhouse was frankly menacing, standing as it did in gloomy desolation where the forest had devoured the works of man—where the only sign that man had been here in this century were these insanely wrought latticeworks of sticks and board. Some might have turned back at this point. Leverett, whose fascination for the macabre was evident in his art, instead was intrigued. He drew a rough sketch of the farmhouse and the grounds, overrun with the enigmatic devices, with thickets of hedges and distorted flowers. He regretted that it might be years before he could capture the eeriness of this place on scratchboard or canvas.

The door was off its hinges, and Leverett gingerly stepped within, hoping that the flooring remained sound enough to bear even his sparse frame. The afternoon sun pierced the empty windows, mottling the decaying floorboards with great blotches of light. Dust drifted in the sunlight. The house was empty—stripped of furnishings other than indistinct tangles of rubble mounded over with decay and the drifted leaves of many seasons.

Someone had been here, and recently. Someone who had literally covered the mildewed walls with diagrams of the mysterious lattice structures. The drawings were applied directly to the walls, crisscrossing the rotting wallpaper and crumbling plaster in bold black lines. Some of vertiginous complexity covered an entire wall like a mad mural. Others were small, only a few crossed lines, and reminded Leverett of cuneiform glyphics.

His pencil hurried over the pages of his notebook. Leverett noted with fascination that a number of the drawings were recognizable as schematics of lattices he had earlier sketched. Was this then the planning room for the madman or educated idiot who had built these structures? The gouges etched by the charcoal into the soft plaster appeared fresh—done days or months ago, perhaps.

A darkened doorway opened into the cellar. Were there drawings there as well? And what else? Leverett wondered if he should dare it. Except for streamers of light that crept through cracks in the flooring, the cellar was in darkness.

"Hello?" he called. "Anyone here?" It didn't seem silly just then. These stick lattices hardly seemed the work of a rational mind. Leverett wasn't enthusiastic with the prospect of encountering such a person in this dark cellar. It occurred to him that virtually anything might transpire here, and no one in the world of 1942 would ever know.

And that in itself was too great a fascination for one of Leverett's temperament. Carefully he started down the cellar stairs. They were stone and thus solid, but treacherous with moss and debris.

The cellar was enormous—even more so in the darkness. Leverett reached the foot of the steps and paused for his eyes to adjust to the damp gloom. An earlier impression recurred to him. The cellar was too big for the house. Had another dwelling stood here originally—perhaps destroyed and rebuilt by one of lesser fortune? He examined the stonework. Here were great blocks of gneiss that might support a castle. On closer look they reminded him of a fortress—for the dry-wall technique was startlingly Mycenaean.

Like the house above, the cellar appeared to be empty, although without light Leverett could not be certain what the shadows hid. There seemed to be darker areas of shadow along sections of the foundation wall, suggesting openings to chambers beyond. Leverett began to feel uneasy in spite of himself.

There was something here—a large tablelike bulk in the center of the cellar. Where a few ghosts of sunlight drifted down to touch its edges, it seemed to be of stone. Cautiously he crossed the stone paving to where it loomed—waist-high, maybe eight feet long and less wide. A roughly shaped slab of gneiss, he judged, and supported by pillars of unmortared stone. In the darkness he could only get a vague conception of the object. He ran his hand along the slab. It seemed to have a groove along its edge.

His groping fingers encountered fabric, something cold and leathery and yielding. Mildewed harness, he guessed in distaste.

Something closed on his wrist, set icy nails into his flesh.

Leverett screamed and lunged away with frantic strength. He was held fast, but the object on the stone slab pulled upward.

A sickly beam of sunlight came down to touch one end of the slab. It was enough. As Leverett struggled backward and the thing that held him heaved up from the stone table, its face passed through the beam of light.

It was a lich's face—desiccated flesh tight over its skull. Filthy strands of hair were matted over its scalp, tattered lips were drawn away from broken yellowed teeth, and, sunken in their sockets, eyes that should be dead were bright with hideous life.

Leverett screamed again, desperate with fear. His free hand clawed the iron skillet tied to his belt. Ripping it loose, he smashed at the nightmarish face with all his strength.

For one frozen instant of horror the sunlight let him see the skillet crush through the mould-eaten forehead like an axe—cleaving the dry flesh and brittle bone. The grip on his wrist failed. The cadaverous face fell away, and the sight of its caved-in forehead and unblinking eyes from between which thick blood had begun to ooze would awaken Leverett from nightmare on countless nights.

But now Leverett tore free and fled. And when his aching legs faltered as he plunged headlong through the scrub-growth, he was spurred to desperate energy by the memory of the footsteps that had stumbled up the cellar stairs behind him.

2

When Colin Leverett returned from the war, his friends marked him a changed man. He had aged. There were streaks of gray in his hair; his springy step had slowed. The athletic leanness of his body had withered to an unhealthy gauntness. There were indelible lines to his face, and his eyes were haunted.

More disturbing was an alteration of temperament. A mordant cynicism had eroded his earlier air of whimsical asceticism. His fascination with the macabre had assumed a darker mood, a morbid obsession that his old acquaintances found disquieting. But it had been that kind of a war, especially for those who had fought through the Apennines.

Leverett might have told them otherwise, had he cared to discuss his nightmarish experience on Mann Brook. But Leverett kept his own counsel, and when he grimly recalled that creature he had struggled with in the abandoned cellar, he usually convinced himself it had only been a derelict— a crazy hermit whose appearance had been distorted by the poor light and his own imagination. Nor had his blow more than glanced off the man's forehead, he reasoned, since the other had recovered quickly enough to give chase. It was best not to dwell upon such matters, and this rational explanation helped restore sanity when he awoke from nightmares of that face.

Thus Colin Leverett returned to his studio, and once more plied his pens and brushes and carving knives. The pulp magazines, where fans had acclaimed his work before the war, welcomed him back with long lists of assignments. There were commissions from galleries and collectors, unfinished sculptures and wooden models. Leverett busied himself.

There were problems now. *Short Stories* returned a cover painting as "too grotesque." The publishers of a new anthology of horror stories sent back a pair of his interior drawings—"too gruesome, especially the rotted, bloated faces of those hanged men." A customer returned a silver figurine, complaining that the martyred saint was too thoroughly martyred. Even *Weird Tales,* after heralding his return to its ghoul-haunted pages, began returning illustrations they considered "too strong, even for our readers."

Leverett tried half-heartedly to tone things down, found the results vapid and uninspired. Eventually the assignments stopped trickling in. Leverett, becoming more the recluse as years went by, dismissed the pulp days from his mind. Working quietly in his isolated studio, he found a living doing occasional commissioned pieces and gallery work, from time to time selling a painting or sculpture to major museums. Critics had much praise for his bizarre abstract sculptures.

3

The war was twenty-five years history when Colin Leverett received a letter from a good friend of the pulp days—Prescott Brandon, now editor-publisher of Gothic House, a small press that specialized in books of the weird-fantasy genre. Despite a lapse in correspondence of many years, Brandon's letter began in his typically direct style:

> *The Eyrie/Salem, Mass./Aug. 2*
> *To the Macabre Hermit of the Midlands:*
>   *Colin, I'm putting together a deluxe three-volume collection of H. Kenneth Allard's horror stories. I well recall that Kent's stories were personal favorites of yours. How about shambling forth from retirement and illustrating these for me? Will need two-color jackets and a dozen line interiors each. Would hope that you can startle fandom with some especially ghastly drawings for these—something different from the hackneyed skulls and bats and werewolves carting off half-dressed ladies.*
>   *Interested? I'll send you the materials and details, and you can have a free hand. Let us hear—Scotty.*

Leverett was delighted. He felt some nostalgia for the pulp days, and he had always admired Allard's genius in transforming visions of cosmic horror into convincing prose. He wrote Brandon an enthusiastic reply.

He spent hours rereading the stories for inclusion, making notes and preliminary sketches. No squeamish subeditors to offend here; Scotty meant what he said. Leverett bent to his task with maniacal relish.

Something different, Scotty had asked. A free hand. Leverett studied his pencil sketches critically. The figures seemed headed in the right direction, but the drawings needed something more—something that would inject the mood of sinister evil that pervaded Allard's work. Grinning skulls and leathery bats? Trite. Allard demanded more.

The idea had inexorably taken hold of him. Perhaps because Allard's tales evoked that same sense of horror; perhaps because Allard's visions of crumbling Yankee farmhouses and their depraved secrets so reminded him of that spring afternoon at Mann Brook . . .

Although he had refused to look at it since the day he had staggered in, half-dead from terror and exhaustion, Leverett perfectly recalled where he had flung his notebook. He retrieved it from the back of a seldom used file, thumbed through the wrinkled pages thoughtfully. These hasty sketches reawakened the sense of foreboding evil, the charnel horror of that day. Studying the bizarre lattice patterns, it seemed impossible to Leverett that others would not share his feeling of horror that the stick structures evoked in him.

He began to sketch bits of stick latticework into his pencil roughs. The sneering faces of Allard's degenerate creatures took on an added shadow of menace. Leverett nodded, pleased with the effect.

4

Some months afterward a letter from Brandon informed Leverett he had received the last of the Allard drawings and was enormously pleased with the work. Brandon added a postcript:

> For God's sake Colin—What is it *with these insane sticks you've got poking up everywhere in the illos! The damn things get really creepy after awhile. How on earth did you get onto this?*

Leverett supposed he owed Brandon some explanation. Dutifully he wrote a lengthy letter, setting down the circumstances of his experience at Mann Brook—omitting only the horror that had seized his wrist in the cellar. Let Brandon think him eccentric, but not madman and murderer.

Brandon's reply was immediate:

> Colin—*Your account of the Mann Brook episode is fascinating— and incredible! It reads like the start of one of Allard's stories! I have taken the liberty of forwarding your letter to Alexander Stefroi in Pelham. Dr. Stefroi is an earnest scholar of this region's history—as you may already know. I'm certain your account will interest him, and he may have some light to shed on the uncanny affair.*
>
> *Expect 1st volume,* Voices from the Shadow, *to be ready from the binder next month. The proofs looked great. Best—Scotty.*

The following week brought a letter postmarked Pelham, Massachusetts:

> *A mutual friend, Prescott Brandon, forwarded your fascinating account of discovering curious sticks and stone artifacts on an*

abandoned farm in upstate New York. I found this most intriguing, and wonder if you recall further details? Can you relocate the exact site after thirty years? If possible, I'd like to examine the foundations this spring, as they call to mind similar megalithic sites of this region. Several of us are interested in locating what we believe are remains of megalithic constructions dating back to the Bronze Age, and to determine their possible use in rituals of black magic in colonial days.

Present archaeological evidence indicates that ca. 1700–2000 B.C. there was an influx of Bronze Age peoples into the Northeast from Europe. We know that the Bronze Age saw the rise of an extremely advanced culture, and that as seafarers they were to have no peers until the Vikings. Remains of a megalithic culture originating in the Mediterranean can be seen in the Lion Gate in Mycenae, in the Stonehenge, and in dolmens, passage graves and barrow mounds throughout Europe. Moreover, this seems to have represented far more than a style of architecture peculiar to the era. Rather, it appears to have been a religious cult whose adherents worshipped a sort of Earth-mother, served her with fertility rituals and sacrifices, and believed that immortality of the soul could be secured through interment in megalithic tombs.

That this culture came to America cannot be doubted from the hundreds of megalithic remnants found—and now recognized—in our region. The most important site to date is Mystery Hill in N.H., comprising a great many walls and dolmens of megalithic construction—most notably the Y Cavern barrow mound and the Sacrificial Table (see postcard). Less spectacular megalithic sites include the group of cairns and carved stones at Mineral Mt., subterranean chambers with stone passageways such as at Petersham and Shutesbury, and uncounted shaped megaliths and buried "monks' cells" throughout this region.

Of further interest, these sites seem to have retained their mystic aura for the early colonials, and numerous megalithic sites show evidence of having been used for sinister purposes by colonial sorcerers and alchemists. This became particularly true after the witchcraft persecutions drove many practitioners into the western wilderness—explaining why upstate New York and western Mass. have seen the emergence of so many cultist groups in later years.

Of particular interest here is Shadrach Ireland's "Brethren of the New Light," who believed that the world was soon to be destroyed by sinister "Powers from Outside" and that they, the elect, would then attain physical immortality. The elect who died beforehand were to have their bodies preserved on tables of stone until the "Old Ones" came forth to return them to life. We have definitely linked the megalithic sites at Shutesbury to later unwholesome practices of the New Light cult. They were absorbed in 1781 by Mother Ann Lee's Shakers, and Ireland's putrescent corpse was hauled from the stone table in his cellar and buried.

Thus I think it probable that your farmhouse may have figured in similar hidden practices. At Mystery Hill a farmhouse was built in 1826 that incorporated one dolmen in its foundations. The house burned down ca. 1848–55, and there were some unsavory local stories as to what took place there. My guess is that your farmhouse had been built over or incorporated a similar megalithic site—and that your "sticks" indicate some unknown cult still survived there. I can recall certain vague references to lattice devices figuring in secret ceremonies, but can pinpoint nothing definite. Possibly they represent a development of occult symbols to be used in certain conjurations, but this is just a guess. I suggest you consult Waite's Ceremonial Magic *or such to see if you can recognize similar magical symbols.*

Hope this is of some use to you. Please let me hear back.

Sincerely, Alexander Stefroi.

There was a postcard enclosed—a photograph of a four-and-a-half-ton slab, ringed by a deep groove with a spout, identified as the Sacrificial Table at Mystery Hill. On the back Stefroi had written:

You must have found something similar to this. They are not rare—we have one in Pelham removed from a site now beneath Quabbin Reservoir. They were used for sacrifice—animal and human—and the groove is to channel blood into a bowl, presumably.

Leverett dropped the card and shuddered. Stefroi's letter reawakened the old horror, and he wished now he had let the matter lie forgotten in his files. Of course, it couldn't be forgotten—even after thirty years.

He wrote Stefroi a careful letter, thanking him for his information and adding a few minor details to his account. This spring, he promised, wondering if he would keep that promise, he would try to relocate the farmhouse on Mann Brook.

5

Spring was late that year, and it was not until early June that Colin Leverett found time to return to Mann Brook. On the surface, very little had changed in three decades. The ancient stone bridge yet stood, nor had the country lane been paved. Leverett wondered whether anyone had driven past since his terror-sped flight.

He found the old railroad grade easily as he started downstream. Thirty years, he told himself—but the chill inside him only tightened. The going was far more difficult than before. The day was unbearably hot and humid.

Wading through the rank underbrush raised clouds of black flies that savagely bit him.

Evidently the stream had seen severe flooding in the past years, judging from piled logs and debris that blocked his path. Stretches were scooped out to barren rocks and gravel. Elsewhere gigantic barriers of uprooted trees and debris looked like ancient and mouldering fortifications. As he worked his way down the valley, he realized that his search would yield nothing. So intense had been the force of the long-ago flood that even the course of the stream had changed. Many of the dry-wall culverts no longer spanned the brook, but sat lost and alone far back from its present banks. Others had been knocked flat and swept away, or were buried beneath tons of rotting logs.

At one point Leverett found remnants of an apple orchard groping through weeds and bushes. He thought that the house must be close by, but here the flooding had been particularly severe, and evidently even those ponderous stone foundations had been toppled over and buried beneath debris.

Leverett finally turned back to his car. His step was lighter.

A few weeks later he received a response from Stefroi to his reported failure:

> *Forgive my tardy reply to your letter of 13 June. I have recently been pursuing inquiries which may, I hope, lead to the discovery of a previously unreported megalithic site of major significance. Naturally I am disappointed that no traces remained of the Mann Brook site. While I tried not to get my hopes up, it did seem likely that the foundations would have survived. In searching through regional data, I note that there were particularly severe flashfloods in the Otselic area in July 1942 and again in May 1946. Very probably your old farmhouse with its enigmatic devices was utterly destroyed not very long after your discovery of the site. This is weird and wild country, and doubtless there is much we shall never know.*
>
> *I write this with a profound sense of personal loss over the death two nights ago of Prescott Brandon. This was a severe blow to me—as I am sure it was to you and to all who knew him. I only hope the police will catch the vicious killers who did this senseless act—evidently thieves surprised while ransacking his office. Police believe the killers were high on drugs from the mindless brutality of their crime.*
>
> *I had just received a copy of the third Allard volume,* Unhallowed Places. *A superbly designed book, and this tragedy becomes all the more insuperable with the realization that Scotty will give the world no more such treasures. In Sorrow, Alexander Stefroi.*

Leverett stared at the letter in shock. He had not received news of Brandon's death—had only a few days before opened a parcel from the publisher containing a first copy of *Unhallowed Places.* A line in Brandon's last letter recurred to him—a line that seemed amusing to him at the time:

> *Your sticks have bewildered a good many fans, Colin, and I've worn out a ribbon answering inquiries. One fellow in particular—a Major George Leonard—has pressed me for details, and I'm afraid that I told him too much. He has written several times for your address, but knowing how you value your privacy I told him simply to permit me to forward any correspondence. He wants to see your original sketches, I gather, but these overbearing occult types give me a pain. Frankly, I wouldn't care to meet the man myself.*

6

"Mr. Colin Leverett?"

Leverett studied the tall lean man who stood smiling at the doorway of his studio. The sports car he had driven up in was black and looked expensive. The same held for the turtleneck and leather slacks he wore, and the sleek briefcase he carried. The blackness made his thin face deathly pale. Leverett guessed his age to be late forty by the thinning of his hair. Dark glasses hid his eyes, black driving gloves his hands.

"Scotty Brandon told me where to find you," the stranger said.

"Scotty?" Leverett's voice was wary.

"Yes, we lost a mutual friend, I regret to say. I'd been talking with him just before. . . . But I see by your expression that Scotty never had time to write."

He fumbled awkwardly. "I'm Dana Allard."

"Allard?"

His visitor seemed embarrassed. "Yes—H. Kenneth Allard was my uncle."

"I hadn't realized Allard left a family," mused Leverett, shaking the extended hand. He had never met the writer personally, but there was a strong resemblance to the few photographs he had seen. And Scotty had been paying royalty checks to an estate of some sort, he recalled.

"My father was Kent's half-brother. He later took his father's name, but there was no marriage, if you follow."

"Of course." Leverett was abashed. "Please find a place to sit down. And what brings you here?"

Dana Allard tapped his briefcase. "Something I'd been discussing with Scotty. Just recently I turned up a stack of my uncle's unpublished manuscripts." He unlatched the briefcase and handed Leverett a sheaf of yellowed paper. "Father collected Kent's personal effects from the state hospital as next-of-kin. He never thought much of my uncle, or his writing. He stuffed this away in our attic and forgot about it. Scotty was quite excited when I told him of my discovery."

Leverett was glancing through the manuscript—page on page of cramped handwriting, with revisions pieced throughout like an indecipherable puzzle. He had seen photographs of Allard manuscripts. There was no mistaking this.

Or the prose. Leverett read a few passages with rapt absorption. It was authentic—and brilliant.

"Uncle's mind seems to have taken an especially morbid turn as his illness drew on," Dana hazarded. "I admire his work very greatly but I find these last few pieces . . . well, a bit *too* horrible. Especially his translation of his mythical *Book of Elders."*

It appealed to Leverett perfectly. He barely noticed his guest as he pored over the brittle pages. Allard was describing a megalithic structure his doomed narrator had encountered in the crypts beneath an ancient church-yard. There were references to "elder glyphics" that resembled his lattice devices.

"Look here," pointed Dana. "These incantations he records here from Alorri-Zrokros's forbidden tome: 'Yogth-Yugth-Sut-Hyrath-Yogng'—hell, I can't pronounce them. And he has pages of them."

"This is incredible!" Leverett protested. He tried to mouth the alien syllables. It could be done. He even detected a rhythm.

"Well, I'm relieved that you approve. I'd feared these last few stories and fragments might prove a little too much for Kent's fans."

"Then you're going to have them published?"

Dana nodded. "Scotty was going to. I just hope those thieves weren't searching for this—a collector would pay a fortune. But Scotty said he was going to keep this secret until he was ready for announcement." His thin face was sad.

"So now I'm going to publish it myself—in a deluxe edition. And I want you to illustrate it."

"I'd feel honored!" vowed Leverett, unable to believe it.

"I really liked those drawings you did for the trilogy. I'd like to see more like those—as many as you feel like doing. I mean to spare no expense in publishing this. And those stick things . . ."

"Yes?"

"Scotty told me the story on those. Fascinating! And you have a whole notebook of them? May I see it?"

Leverett hurriedly dug the notebook from his file, returned to the manuscript.

Dana paged through the book in awe. "These things are totally bizarre—and there are references to such things in the manuscript, to make it even more fantastic. Can you reproduce them all for the book?"

"All I can remember," Leverett assured him. "And I have a good memory. But won't that be overdoing it?"

"Not at all! They fit into the book. And they're utterly unique. No, put everything you've got into this book. I'm going to entitle it *Dwellers in the Earth,* after the longest piece. I've already arranged for its printing, so we begin as soon as you can have the art ready. And I know you'll give it your all."

7

He was floating in space. Objects drifted past him. Stars, he first thought. The objects drifted closer.

Sticks. Stick lattices of all configurations. And then he was drifting among them, and he saw that they were not sticks—not of wood. The lattice designs were of dead-pale substance, like streaks of frozen starlight. They reminded him of glyphics of some unearthly alphabet—complex, enigmatic symbols arranged to spell . . . what? And there *was* an arrangement—a three-dimensional pattern. A maze of utterly baffling intricacy . . .

Then somehow he was in a tunnel. A cramped, stone-lined tunnel through which he must crawl on his belly. The dank, moss-slimed stones pressed close about his wriggling form, evoking shrill whispers of claustrophobic dread.

And after an indefinite space of crawling through this and other stone-lined burrows, and sometimes through passages whose angles hurt his eyes, he would creep forth into a subterranean chamber. Great slabs of granite a dozen feet across formed the walls and ceiling of this buried chamber, and between the slabs other burrows pierced the earth. Altarlike, a gigantic slab of gneiss waited in the center of the chamber. A spring welled darkly between the stone pillars that supported the table. Its outer edge was encircled by a groove, sickeningly stained by the substance that clotted in the stone bowl beneath its collecting spout.

Others were emerging from the darkened burrows that ringed the chamber —slouched figures only dimly glimpsed and vaguely human. And a figure in a tattered cloak came toward him from the shadow—stretched out a clawlike hand to seize his wrist and draw him toward the sacrificial table. He followed unresistingly, knowing that something was expected of him.

They reached the altar and in the glow from the cuneiform lattices chiseled into the gneiss slab he could see the guide's face. A mouldering corpse-face, the rotten bone of its forehead smashed inward upon the foulness that oozed forth . . .

And Leverett would awaken to the echo of his screams . . .

He'd been working too hard, he told himself, stumbling about in the darkness, getting dressed because he was too shaken to return to sleep. The nightmares had been coming every night. No wonder he was exhausted.

But in his studio his work awaited him. Almost fifty drawings finished now, and he planned another score. No wonder the nightmares.

It was a grueling pace, but Dana Allard was ecstatic with the work he had done. And *Dwellers in the Earth* was waiting. Despite problems with typesetting, with getting the special paper Dana wanted—the book only waited on him.

Though his bones ached with fatigue, Leverett determinedly trudged through the graying night. Certain features of the nightmare would be interesting to portray.

8

The last of the drawings had gone off to Dana Allard in Petersham, and Leverett, fifteen pounds lighter and gut-weary, converted part of the bonus check into a case of good whiskey. Dana had the offset presses rolling as soon as the plates were shot from the drawings. Despite his precise planning, presses had broken down, one printer quit for reasons not stated, there had been a bad accident at the new printer—seemingly innumerable problems, and Dana had been furious at each delay. But the production pushed along quickly for all that. Leverett wrote that the book was cursed, but Dana responded that a week would see it ready.

Leverett amused himself in his studio constructing stick lattices and trying to catch up on his sleep. He was expecting a copy of the book when he received a letter from Stefroi:

> *Have tried to reach you by phone last few days, but no answer at your house. I'm pushed for time just now, so must be brief. I have indeed uncovered an unsuspected megalithic site of enormous importance. It's located on the estate of a long-prominent Mass. family—and as I cannot receive authorization to visit it, I will not say where. Have investigated secretly (and quite illegally) for a short time one night and was nearly caught. Came across reference to the place in collection of seventeenth century letters and papers in a divinity school library. Writer denouncing the family as a brood of sorcerers and witches, references to alchemical activities and other less savory rumors—and describes underground stone chambers, megalithic artifacts, etc. which are put to "foul usage and diabolic praktise." Just got a quick glimpse but his description was not exaggerated. And Colin—in creeping through the woods to get to the site, I came across dozens of your mysterious "sticks"! Brought a small one back and have it here to show you. Recently constructed and exactly like your drawings. With luck, I'll gain admittance and find out their significance—undoubtedly they have significance— though these cultists can be stubborn about sharing their secrets. Will explain my interest is scientific, no exposure to ridicule—and see what they say. Will get a closer look one way or another. And so—I'm off! Sincerely, Alexander Stefroi.*

Leverett's bushy brows rose. Allard had intimated certain dark rituals in which the stick lattices figured. But Allard had written over thirty years ago, and Leverett assumed the writer had stumbled onto something similar to the Mann Brook site. Stefroi was writing about something current.

He rather hoped Stefroi would discover nothing more than an inane hoax.

* * *

The nightmares haunted him still—familiar now, for all that its scenes and phantasms were visited by him only in dream. Familiar. The terror that they evoked was undiminished.

Now he was walking through forest—a section of hills that seemed to be close by. A huge slab of granite had been dragged aside, and a pit yawned where it had lain. He entered the pit without hesitation, and the rounded steps that led downward were known to his tread. A buried stone chamber, and leading from it stone-lined burrows. He knew which one to crawl into.

And again the underground room with its sacrificial altar and its dark spring beneath, and the gathering circle of poorly glimpsed figures. A knot of them clustered about the stone table, and as he stepped toward them he saw they pinned a frantically writhing man.

It was a stoutly built man, white hair disheveled, flesh gouged and filthy. Recognition seemed to burst over the contorted features, and he wondered if he should know the man. But now the lich with the caved-in skull was whispering in his ear, and he tried not to think of the unclean things that peered from that cloven brow, and instead took the bronze knife from the skeletal hand, and raised the knife high, and because he could not scream and awaken, did with the knife as the tattered priest had whispered . . .

And when after an interval of unholy madness, he at last did awaken, the stickiness that covered him was not cold sweat, nor was it nightmare the half-devoured heart he clutched in one fist.

9

Leverett somehow found sanity enough to dispose of the shredded lump of flesh. He stood under the shower all morning, scrubbing his skin raw. He wished he could vomit.

There was a news item on the radio. The crushed body of noted archaeologist, Dr. Alexander Stefroi, had been discovered beneath a fallen granite slab near Whately. Police speculated the gigantic slab had shifted with the scientist's excavations at its base. Identification was made through personal effects.

When his hands stopped shaking enough to drive, Leverett fled to Petersham—reaching Dana Allard's old stone house about dark. Allard was slow to answer his frantic knock.

"Why, good evening, Colin! What a coincidence your coming here just now! The books are ready. The bindery just delivered them."

Leverett brushed past him. "We've got to destroy them!" he blurted. He'd thought a lot since morning.

"Destroy them?"

"There's something none of us figured on. Those stick lattices—there's a cult, some damnable cult. The lattices have some significance in their rituals. Stefroi hinted once they might be glyphics of some sort, I don't know. But the cult is still alive. They killed Scotty . . . they killed Stefroi. They're onto me—I don't know what they intend. They'll kill you to stop you from releasing this book!"

Dana's frown was worried, but Leverett knew he hadn't impressed him the right way. "Colin, this sounds insane. You really have been overextending yourself, you know. Look, I'll show you the books. They're in the cellar."

Leverett let his host lead him downstairs. The cellar was quite large, flagstoned and dry. A mountain of brown-wrapped bundles awaited them.

"Put them down here where they wouldn't knock the floor out," Dana explained. "They start going out to distributors tomorrow. Here, I'll sign your copy."

Distractedly Leverett opened a copy of *Dwellers in the Earth*. He gazed at his lovingly rendered drawings of rotting creatures and buried stone chambers and stained altars—and everywhere the enigmatic latticework structures. He shuddered.

"Here." Dana Allard handed Leverett the book he had signed. "And to answer your question, they *are* elder glyphics."

But Leverett was staring at the inscription in its unmistakable handwriting: "For Colin Leverett, Without whom this work could not have seen completion—H. Kenneth Allard."

Allard was speaking. Leverett saw places where the hastily applied flesh-toned make-up didn't quite conceal what lay beneath. "Glyphics symbolic of alien dimensions—inexplicable to the human mind, but essential fragments of an evocation so unthinkably vast that the 'pentagram' (if you will) is miles across. Once before we tried—but your iron weapon destroyed part of Althol's brain. He erred at the last instant—almost annihilating us all. Althol had been formulating the evocation since he fled the advance of iron four millennia past.

"Then you reappeared, Colin Leverett—you with your artist's knowledge and diagrams of Althol's symbols. And now a thousand new minds will read the evocation you have returned to us, unite with our minds as we stand in the Hidden Places. And the Great Old Ones will come forth from the earth, and we, the dead who have steadfastly served them, shall be masters of the living."

Leverett turned to run, but now they were creeping forth from the shadows of the cellar, as massive flagstones slid back to reveal the tunnels beyond. He began to scream as Althol came to lead him away, but he could not awaken, could only follow.

Robert Aickman

Larger Than Oneself

Robert Aickman was the great English master of the ghost story of the second half of this century. Editor, theoretician and writer, he never attained the recognition or popularity his immense contributions deserved, although he did win a World Fantasy Award in the decade before his death. A significant portion of his fiction remained unpublished in the U.S. at the time of his death. "Larger Than Oneself" is an ironic reinterpretation of the moral tale for our era. Mrs. Iblis spends the weekend at a convention of people interested in the supernatural, the metaphysical and the occult, and finds it uniquely disturbing. One might compare the story to Joyce Carol Oates' treatment of similar matter in "Nightside." "Larger Than Oneself" is an interesting example of the blend of all three major streams of horror fiction.

Upon the death of his father, Vincent Coner got out of mine owning, which had always been the family business, and invested heavily in popular journalism with himself as editor in chief. It is hard to believe that in any other place or time, past or future, his publications would have found many readers; but as it was, the thing most needed by his generation seemed to be the recipe he offered: the sweet things of life (the more obvious of them) smeared and contaminated with envious guilt.

A typical man of his time, Coner throve exceedingly. While at Cambridge, he edited a symposium of modern philosophy, which attracted considerable attention; and he soon became known for his advocacy of a synthesis between the best of this world and the best of the next. Already he was giving parties: his thin figure, precociously bald, wove in and out pouring gin while others talked. Occasionally he would bring the uproar back to the point as he conceived it. He developed an exceptional eye for the view which would prevail.

With increasing popular success, easily acquired, Coner's main business in life became more and more an almost paranoiac pursuit of self-integration. He read Berdyaev, Maritain, and C. S. Lewis, and even the first thirty pages of Ouspensky. Almost he believed what he read. Kierkegaard and Leopardi, rebound by a refugee craftsman, always attended his bedside (he had married a nightclub singer named Eileen); and Pascal he constantly rediscovered with new understanding, gorging on the insane root as he passed class-conscious photographs for the press. At the time Mrs. Iblis entered his life, he was greatly interested in several of the newer spiritual movements competing to offer a deadbeat world metaphysical immunization against its

225

own shadow. He had decided to ask the different leaders to Bunhill for the weekend in order that they might have the chance to exchange views on neutral ground. A symposium for *Roundabout* might emerge, a real chance to give a lead.

Mrs. Iblis entered Coner's life in the usual way through the front door. While waiting for the bell to be answered, she was joined on the large white step by two other visitors, who introduced themselves as David Stillman and Ruth. Ruth was not Mr. Stillman's daughter, but Mrs. Iblis was unable to catch her other name, nor did she ever learn it. Mr. Stillman appeared to be a prosperous businessman. He arrived in a large car, which, when he had alighted, immediately drove away. He was well preserved and had excellent manners, but Mrs. Iblis had had little contact with Jews. Ruth was a highly strung voluble creature, little more than a girl in appearance, small and thin, with tousled hair, a round face, and restless hands. She wore red corduroy trousers, a shapeless jumper, and sandals. Mrs. Iblis had been speaking to Mr. Stillman when she appeared, presumably from the dense bushes which closely lined the drive, but carrying a bulging reticule with two handles. Mrs. Iblis had a suitcase; Mr. Stillman a dressing case of a type which Mrs. Iblis had thought obsolete.

Presumably the din inside the house made it difficult for the servant to hear the bell, so, at Mr. Stillman's suggestion, Mrs. Iblis rang again. Ruth maintained an intermittent flow of observations about the difficulty of reaching Bunhill (or indeed anywhere) by train and her own trials with the timetable.

"I do hope you've not been kept waiting." The door had been opened by Mrs. Coner, wearing a long tight dress of blue-bottle green and smoking a cigarette from which the ash needed removing. "My husband's sent all the servants to a Domestic Science Congress at Littlehampton, and we're entirely in the hands of the caterers this weekend. Do come in."

Immediately inside stood a large figure in evening dress, with drink written all over him.

"Your names, please." He prepared to tick them off on a list with an indelible pencil.

"Mrs. Iblis."

He crawled slowly through the list, stopping at each name with the pencil. Three raw youths in dinner jackets had seized the visitors' luggage and were standing at the ready.

"Could you spell it?"

"I–B–L–I–S."

He repeated the search, then turned with irritation to Mrs. Coner.

In the meantime, the masterful figure of Coner had appeared from the crowd within. "Ruth, my darling. How lovely to see you." He kissed her mouth violently but dispassionately. "Did we ask you this weekend, or have you just dropped from heaven?"

"Surely you asked me, Vincent."

"It's wonderful to see you anyhow. Do come and join in right away. It will be really valuable to have the orthodox point of view."

"Could I have a sandwich first?"

"Have everything there is. Haven't you lunched?"

"I left London at half past ten."

"If we'd known, we'd have sent a car. It only takes half an hour by road. But come on and eat." Gripping her round the waist, he dragged her towards the hubbub.

"Vincent." His wife had clutched him by the other sleeve of his beautifully made gray suit. He stopped.

"What is it, Eileen?"

"Why do we have to have that damned list?"

"I've told you more than once. The people we've asked this weekend have all been carefully picked by me for the contribution they can make. As I've hardly met any of them before, we must have a list and keep to it. What's gone wrong?"

"Two people have arrived. They are not on the list. They both say they were told to arrive at three. I can hardly send them away."

"All the people this weekend were told to arrive for breakfast if they could. Who are they?"

"Mrs. Iblis and Mr. Stillman. They don't seem like the others." The suspect guests could be seen in the still open door miserably awaiting their fate.

"Mavis!" Coner bawled at the top of his voice. "Forgive me a moment, Ruth." With a violent squeeze, he released her.

A tall, bony, off-blonde, ageless woman strode forward. Coner succinctly outlined the crisis.

"I'll have a look in the invitations book, Mr. Coner." She departed.

Coner addressed his wife. "I leave it to you, my dear. But whoever they are, we don't want them unless they harmonize. Come on, Ruth." Resuming his python hold round Ruth's narrow waist, he propelled her forward.

Mavis returned with a huge folio volume of the minute book type. It must have contained five hundred pages. It was ruled into dates and packed with thousands of names in Mavis's small clear writing.

Almost at once Mavis had the answer. "They're left over from the lot we asked before Mr. Coner decided on the Forum. Haven't they had their postponement letters?"

"I'd better let them in. They'll have to share rooms with someone."

"Everyone's doing that this weekend, Mrs. Coner."

"Can you take over, Mavis?"

Explaining the situation about the rooms in a few courteous but emotionless words, Mavis was simultaneously scanning the hired butler's list of guests and their accommodation. "So I do hope you don't mind sharing," she concluded. "This weekend is rather a special occasion."

Mr. Stillman smiled acquiescence, though he did not look too happy. Mrs. Iblis said: "Please do not go to any trouble about me."

"No trouble at all." Then Mavis decided. "Mr. Stillman can have the Louise Room. I doubt Rabbi Morocco will come at all now. And perhaps Mrs. Iblis won't mind sleeping with Sister Nuper? Our House Sister, you know."

"Is part of the house used as a hospital?"

"Oh no. It's just in case of sudden or serious illness. And Sister Nuper advises us on our diet and on questions of personal hygiene as well. You'll find her a delightful person. Really, you couldn't find anyone better to room with."

The youth who had seized Ruth's piece of luggage had long ago departed with it, presumably to her room. Now the other two youths constituted themselves escorts to Mr. Stillman and Mrs. Iblis.

"The lift's through 'ere." They held back heavy, dark brown velvet curtains.

The lift, a Waywood-Otis installation capacious enough for twelve at a hoist, was descending. When it reached the ground floor, there emerged two apparently identical Negroes in clerical dress. Small, compact, and beautifully polished, they looked like marionettes. They smiled and bowed in unison to the new arrivals, then walked off in step, conversing enthusiastically in some African tongue.

At the first-floor landing (Mrs. Iblis felt that it would have been quicker to have walked it), Mr. Stillman was at once shown into an enormous room which even through the door Mrs. Iblis could see contained at least two canopied beds. Mrs. Iblis was led away down a long passage, not too well proportioned, decorated in goose gray and lined with modern religious paintings, ascending on occasion as high in the scale as Vanessa Bell, and even Rouault. (Mrs. Iblis could not be sure, however, that they were not merely good reproductions.) From the opposite direction advanced an extremely good-looking woman of bold proportions; she was wearing a heavy black brassière, black-and-white striped knickers, and huge furry slippers. She made no acknowledgment of Mrs. Iblis's presence, still less of the luggage carrier's, and in the end, having passed the lift, vanished round the corner beyond the Louise Room, as Mrs. Iblis was unable to resist turning to see.

Sister Nuper's room was beautifully light and filled with built-in cupboards. There was a large, double divan-bed with silk sheets. Above the bed was a ghastly and lurid cartoon of the Crucifixion by Edward Burra. Mrs. Iblis was unable to make up her mind whether the artist was in favor of religion or against it. A satinwood bookcase, which had been scraped and painted white like the other furniture, proved to contain mainly volumes of the more popular nursing and home medical journals (bound by Coner's refugee craftsman). A French window and small balcony overlooked a garden of about an acre, from which rose a smell of intensive composting. A figure in a boiler suit could be seen at the dark work now.

Mrs. Iblis peered into one of the built-in cupboards. It was stuffed with evening dresses, depending from a thick chromium-plated rail and each in a transparent envelope made of plastic.

Not caring to unpack without consulting Sister Nuper, Mrs. Iblis nonetheless changed into the other dress she had brought. Looking for an ashtray, she noticed the Sister's bedside book: entitled *Bowel Discipline*, it was a lesser work by a well-known member of the Labor party. A realistic colored drawing on the jacket depicted the alimentary system surrounded by a luminous radiation.

For some time after Mrs. Iblis had descended (by the stairs) into the mêlée below, no one took any notice of her. The Forum, about fifty strong, were surging and wheeling between the drawing room, the dining room, and the large hall. Most of them, of course, were shouting at the tops of their voices, or reasoning at the full stretch of their intellects; but some, Mrs. Iblis noticed, sat or even stood perfectly silent and ignored. She had read an article in the *Evening News* of the previous night upon the value in a bustling noisy life of regular periods of meditation, and gazed at these mute figures with interest and awe. Press photographers moved about the throng. In the end Mrs. Iblis's eye lighted upon Ruth eating a strawberry ice cream. This being the only person present to whom she had ever spoken (there was no sign of Mr. Stillman), Mrs. Iblis advanced.

"Hullo. I'm afraid I know no one else here but you. Can you tell me who some of these people are?"

"Don't know. I'm strictly orthodox."

"How interesting! In what way?"

"Full Anglican. I accept the Thirty-Nine Articles. Unconditionally." Ruth looked round for somewhere to deposit the ice cream glass.

"Well, so do I, I suppose."

"What's Article Thirty-three?"

"I can hardly recall the exact words."

"Then you're not an Anglican, are you?" Ruth was reduced to laying the receptacle in much jeopardy on the floor.

"Can *you* recite Article Thirty-three?" This feeble rejoinder was the best Mrs. Iblis could muster. It was so long since one had been at school.

"That person which by open denunciation of the Church is rightly cut off from the unity of the Church and excommunicated ought to be taken of the whole multitude of the faithful as a Heathen and Publican until he be openly reconciled by penance and received into the Church by a Judge that hath authority there-unto."

"Not a very Christian sentiment surely?" Mrs. Iblis inquired almost involuntarily.

"Why not?"

"More like the Church of Rome. Excommunication and penance, you know."

"I do penance daily." Ruth's voice was dreamy, her eyes blank.

"You can hardly be as wicked as that!" But Mrs. Iblis's mind recalled the alarming figure she had seen upstairs in the passage, and was instantly less sure.

"Not wicked. Sinful."

"Is there any difference?"

"Sin is a sense of something larger than oneself."

"Ah, now I understand you." Mrs. Iblis began to glance about for some sign of tea, surely overdue. "I think that is something we all feel."

But Ruth ignored her. "To merge," she cried in her soft, light voice. "To break through the barrier and become One. For a single infinitely small person to meet the infinitely vast. The end of every pilgrimage must be orthodoxy." Her eye lighted upon a fellow guest the other side of the room. "You see that man to the left of the big 'Annunciation'?"

"The red-haired one in tweeds?"

"He's a Lewisite. He's misplaced, like me."

"I thought lewisite was a kind of explosive."

Ruth merely said in the most casual way, "Have you read *Arrival and Departure*?"

"No."

"I'm going to look for another ice."

Before she had disappeared, Mrs. Iblis had time to ask: "Do you know what time we get tea?"

Ruth replied: "Any time you like. Ask at the buffet in the billiard room." And she was gone before Mrs. Iblis had completed the horrifying realization that at Bunhill there were no regular meals.

The better to face the situation, Mrs. Iblis opened her handbag and produced a compact. Peering into the little mirror, she failed to notice that two strange men now stood before her.

"Permit me to introduce my friend, Professor Dr. Borgia, principal of the Demokratischereligion Gesellschaft of Zürich." The speaker was a rotund young man of highly educated accent and masterful demeanor.

"How do you do? I suppose you must be used to people asking whether you are really one of the Borgias?"

"But *natürlich* I am one of the Borgias." The professor had the strongest of Teutonic accents. He was a slight, worn, Semitic-looking figure, with large fanatical eyes. "The Borgias were a great *aristocratische* family of old Spain. My family."

The rotund young man said: "I am sure you will both have much to say. Will you excuse me if I seek a word with Dr. Spade?" He was gone.

Professor Borgia rolled his eyes. "Have you found spiritual proficiency, *gnädige Frau*? You see I come straight from the point."

Mrs. Iblis considered carefully. "Well, actually, not yet, I think."

"Mine is the shortest way to truth." His diction had much of the charm of the German classical actor, the aptitude for making the most commonplace words profound and stirring. "I am in a sense a commercial traveler for God." This was uttered in a tone which recalled Manfred confronting the abyss. "You have first to sign your name only." He was holding out a quite fat booklet closely printed in a way which reminded Mrs. Iblis of Dutch seed catalogues.

"Thank you very much. I shall look forward to reading it."

"Reading alone will not avail. Words reach only the mind. It is the spirit, the *Geist,* we grope for, *nicht wahr*?"

"I suppose so." Mrs. Iblis was beginning to feel cowed and upset, unequal to life.

"Do you come much to Switzerland?" He pronounced the English name so elaborately that Mrs. Iblis had difficulty in following him.

"Only for the winter sports, I'm afraid. And that not for some years now."

"*Ach, so*? But no matter. We are starting an *Enfiedelei* in London this very winter. There will be your rebirth."

At this point it dawned on Mrs. Iblis that quite possibly the rotund young man had merely intended to unload upon her a bigger than ordinary bore, a person recognized to be such even in this company.

Excusing herself, she began firmly to look for the billiard room. The professor stood quite still, smiling after her retreating figure.

En route she passed a particularly frenzied group, at the center of which a man was saying, "Now can't we reduce our differences to a few simple points which we could talk over?" This, though Mrs. Iblis did not know it, was her host.

"What is the use of words if the spirit is wrong?" screamed out a woman whose style of looks Mrs. Iblis considered obsolete, and who wore a complex, black tea gown. For people who set so little store by words, they seemed to Mrs. Iblis remarkably dependent on them.

There were only ten or eleven people at the buffet, eating and drinking not being primary interests of the present gathering (unlike some at Bunhill). The billiard room also contained two tables, on one of which a couple of young waiters were playing half-hearted snooker. Above the dark brown mantelpiece was a huge vague-colored drawing of a Universal City designed by Patrick Geddes. A new strip-lighting system had been installed; but something had gone wrong with it and instead of giving better than daylight, it emitted a depressing yellow red glare as dusk descended outside.

As Mrs. Iblis stood drinking Indian tea and nibbling a maid of honor, a massive figure approached her, wearing enormous highly polished shoes.

"And what do *you* make of it all?" The accent was transatlantic.

"I'm afraid I know very little about it. I'm not really a member of the Forum."

"Nor I, ma'am. I just dropped in to see that Coner's on the right lines."

"And is he?" There seemed nothing else to say.

"Well now, I'm a Canadian. I'm also a businessman and editor, like Coner. But that doesn't mean I'm impervious to spiritual values. Quite the contrary. The one thing the whole world needs, the one thing every man's heart is sighing for—*and* every woman's—is a big spiritual revival. And what I say is, it's up to us servants of the public to get things rolling."

"I always think the press could be such an influence for good," said Mrs. Iblis, selecting an éclair. "After all, it's foolish not to take things as we find them."

"Sure, sure. Those are wise words, ma'am. I swear to you that not a copy goes out of a single journal in my group without it contains both a passage from the good book and some words of cheer by one of a panel of leading ministers."

"That must be very nice for your readers." Mrs. Iblis wished she had a larger handkerchief on which to deposit some of the sticky chocolate now coating her fingers. Nonetheless, she took a second éclair.

"You should see the thankful letters. Never less than sixty a day and often above the century. I tell you they make me a humble man. But I'm not a narrow man either, and I tell you something more is needed."

"Yes?" said Mrs. Iblis.

"After all, what are sects? What are denominations, creeds, dogmas, rituals? Aren't we all the same where it really matters—in our hearts? What are the little orthodoxies besides the great universal need, man's eternal quest for something larger than his puny self? That's what I'm doing here this very afternoon. Watching Coner pull the old country's socks up." His somewhat inflexible features almost beamed upon Mrs. Iblis.

"You think all this will really lead to something useful?" She turned to the buffet. The waiter was at the other end, and Mrs. Iblis raised her voice: "Could I have another cup of tea, please?"

"Sure, sure. There's just nothing that can't be had if you'll give your soul for it." Mrs. Iblis turned back to him with some surprise; but now he had seized the sleeve of a cadaverous, academic-looking young man with an enormous Wellingtonian nose. "And you, sir. What do you think?"

The young man merely snatched away his sleeve without a word or even a glance. He was like a preoccupied child. In ardent tones, he addressed his friend: "You know, Neville, I've found that much of the best modern thought, the really deep stuff, now comes from inside the Salvation Army."

"I still remain faithful to the dear old Hibbert Journal. That and my Karma Research Group. Let's have a cup of char, then I'll tell you about a new technique we're working on to accelerate the ecstasy." His voice had hushed almost to inaudibility. They glanced at one another, conscious of secrets shared.

The Canadian was now conversing with an enormously fat woman in a cassock. About her neck, on the end of a brass chain, hung an object which Mrs. Iblis fancied was called an *ankh*. Or was it a *crux ansata*?

At this point an exceedingly attractive woman entered the billiard room accompanied by a positive throng of unusually handsome young men. She wore a gray nurse's uniform made of silk, like the nurse's uniforms worn by film stars in the early silent days, and a high white collar. Mrs. Iblis had been about to leave the billiard room but, supposing that this might be Sister Nuper, remained for a moment.

The posse advanced upon the buffet, laughing and calling loudly for refreshments, which seemed to be brought to them with more alacrity than had attended the service of the other guests. They stood in a group exchanging merry commonplaces, carefree, exuberant. They were totally unlike the rest of the Forum, but no one other than Mrs. Iblis and the waiter seemed to be taking any particular notice of them. To Mrs. Iblis, however, they seemed in the end even to be engaged in parodying the transactions around them.

"And what faith are you, my pretty maid?" cried out an Apollo-like young man.

And Sister Nuper (if she it was) instantly replied in a cooing, but perfectly clear, voice: "I worship St. Nicholas, sir," she said.

At this all the young men laughed very loudly. The group made Mrs. Iblis feel a wild girl again. But the billiard room was emptying and the waiter beginning to assemble supper dishes and bottles of beer. Mrs. Iblis felt she could not stay longer without becoming conspicuous, possibly a butt, not for any sort of unkindness (the group did not seem unkind), but simply for witty remarks calling for witty answers which she had never been able to provide, even long after the need. Before she left, she noticed through the line of long windows that the lurid light in the billiard room seemed to have its counterpart in a livid autumnal glare outside. Was it something to do with the equinox, she wondered.

"Shall I find you a chair?" The speaker was a shaggy, elderly, paternal figure.

"That would be very kind of you. Such tiring weather."

He guided her gently forward by the arm. They reached a small sofa. He seated himself beside her. This was not exactly what she wanted.

"Permit me to introduce myself. O'Rorke: founder of the New Vision Movement, small for the present, it is true, but a veritable seed of mustard, if I may quote from an anachronistic scripture."

"How do you do? My name is Iblis. Mrs. Iblis."

"Ah yes." He seemed abstracted. "I think I have convinced Mr. Coner. I think I have moved his heart to see that a new world demands a new faith and will not be put off." The speaker appeared to be at least seventy-five.

"There have indeed been many changes."

"But still we worship the old false gods! Still we prostrate ourselves before the concepts of medieval anthropomorphism." He looked exactly like a cathedral figure of St. Peter.

"Life is not easy," said Mrs. Iblis.

"But need we therefore rend ourselves like vultures? Can we not seek the truth each in his own way? Or, of course, hers? After all, in every heart is an unimaginable arcana: must we sell out to the money changers of the temple? Evil is, after all, so very small."

Mrs. Iblis looked up. "Is it?"

"Indeed it is. In how many mythologies the Devil is represented as a little fellow, as Mannikin or Peterkin, and how rightly! It is only the sophisticated theologians who make him vast and roaring and terrible: in order that we may be afraid of him and in their power. But pluck up your heart, Mrs.—er—" He stumbled for the name. "Only God is vast and great: that is to say, Good; for they are one and the same."

"How convincingly you put it!" Mrs. Iblis said this without the slightest irony. It was merely that the lowering weather was giving her a headache. Even as she passed her hand across her brow, there was a distant roll of thunder, too faint to be generally heard above the many voices, the diversities of business.

"It is God who speaks through me," said the patriarch modestly. "Or rather Good, the life spirit of the universe, to which it is within all of us to hearken."

Mrs. Iblis wondered whether Sister Nuper could produce some aspirin. Somehow it seemed improbable. It also seemed almost impossible to ask her.

Suddenly, however, the chic but world-worn figure of Mrs. Coner leaned over the back of the sofa and spoke in Mrs. Iblis's ear.

"Mavis tells me that you are unfortunately not feeling too good." Mrs. Iblis had not consciously set eyes on Mavis since her arrival.

"I *have* a slight headache, I'm afraid. It is foolish of me. The weather, I think."

"Take my advice and have a rest on your bed. Mavis is mixing you a draught."

With relief, Mrs. Iblis rose to her feet. "You are very kind." She addressed the patriarch: "Please excuse me. I'm not feeling very well, I'm afraid. I am going to rest for a little. I expect we shall meet again later."

He grasped her hand and held it. "Hold on to the spirit, Mrs.—er—I shall confidently await your return—purged and splendid." It was not quite what was usually said in such circumstances.

Mrs. Coner came with her upstairs. As they passed the door to the Louise Room, Mrs. Coner said: "We've been having some trouble there, I'm afraid. Mavis thought that Rabbi Morocco and your friend Mr. Stillman would have a lot in common. Anyway, she didn't expect Rabbi Morocco to turn up at all. But he has. And he and Mr. Stillman seem to be somehow different *kinds* of Jews. I don't really get it. They always seem to cause some sort of trouble, don't they?" She and Mrs. Iblis exchanged glances.

Lying on Sister Nuper's double bed was a girl in her underclothes and black silk stockings. Her thick black hair was drawn into a ballet dancer's bun, and she was reading a tome by Karl Barth.

"Sorry, Mrs. Coner. I thought Sister Nuper wouldn't mind." She sat up, staring at Mrs. Iblis.

"I am sure she won't, Patacake. But haven't we given you a room?"

"Can't stop. Have to get back to the Shelter."

"Oh." Mrs. Coner didn't seem to like her very much. But she did her duty as hostess. "This is Mrs. Iblis. Lady Cecilia Capulet."

"How do you do?" said Mrs. Iblis. "Please don't move." But her head was splitting, and she very much hoped that Lady Cecilia would move.

"I must go anyway." With great elegance she crossed to the window and looked out between the bright Gordon Russel curtains. "Oh God, it's raining."

Mavis appeared, bearing a large graduated glass filled to the brim with a blue green liquor, seething and opaque.

"Vincent's special," said Mrs. Coner. "Drink it down."

"You're really very kind," said Mrs. Iblis weakly. She sipped. Mavis, she noticed, had changed her dress and now wore a flame-colored model, very out of key with her apparent general temperament. Lady Cecilia was washing her hands and forearms with great thoroughness.

"It's almost pure peptomycin," said Mavis encouragingly.

The beverage tasted of liquid candle-grease gone flat with the years.

"Down the hatch," said Mrs. Coner, displaying for the first time the slightest hint of impatience.

There was a terrific crash of thunder. The four women looked at one another momentarily. Mrs. Iblis felt quite frightened.

"Christ!" ejaculated Lady Cecilia. "Can you lend me a mack, Mavis?"

"Of course, Patacake—if you'll give me five minutes." Mavis collected the now empty glass (a sticky bright yellow sediment occupied the last inch of it), said "Thank you" to Mrs. Iblis, and departed. It was now thundering briskly.

"Well now," said Mrs. Coner, once more sensibly sympathetic. "Lie down with your feet up so that the vapors can rise, and get some sleep. When you're better, come down again. The Forum will carry on most of the night, I expect, so you needn't rush things." She dragged out the bolster from the head of the bed and put it under Mrs. Iblis's feet. Mrs. Iblis had cast off her shoes but did not care to remove her dress, being conscious that her underclothes compared unfavorably with Lady Cecilia's. Lady Cecilia was now carefully rubbing under her arms with (presumably) Sister Nuper's Arrid.

"Bye-bye," said Mrs. Coner in the idiom of her former avocation. She went, shutting the door which Mavis had left open.

"These clothes do make one stink." Lady Cecilia was putting on a plain navy blue skirt. Mrs. Iblis only wished she would go. Then Lady Cecilia put on a matching tunic, and Mrs. Iblis realized.

"I've never actually met a Salvation Army lassie before."

"It gives one a standing," said Lady Cecilia. "At places like this and times like the present. Major Barbara was on to something." She had buttoned the tunic to the neck. "It's a damned fetching outfit, you know." She extended one black silk leg. "The number it fetches might surprise you."

"Are you making it your career?"

"Until they chuck me out." There was a tap on the door. It was Mavis with an emerald-colored silk mackintosh. "How frightfully sweet of you! I'll be back immediately the Shelter shuts."

"Hurry. The Forum will give out if you don't keep their glands working."

"Your book!" cried Mrs. Iblis. It had obviously been forgotten.

"You read it," said Lady Cecilia. *"Auf Wiedersehen."*

Mrs. Iblis had hoped to see Patacake put on her bonnet; but she was gone with no sign of the object.

"Shall I lock you in?" inquired Mavis. "It might be quieter for you, and there's a bell."

"Thank you very much," said Mrs. Iblis. "But no."

When Mrs. Iblis awoke, she felt extremely hungry. Used to four reasonable meals a day, she had had nothing of the kind since an early and rushed luncheon at the London railway terminus. She had turned out the light but could see by the illuminated dial of her wristwatch that it was half past eleven. Despite Mrs. Coner's words, surely the party below might be over? Panic seized Mrs. Iblis, confronted with a foodless night. Switching on the bedside light, she rose, tried to smooth her dress, and put on her shoes. If the party were over, then Sister Nuper would have been with her by now. The thunder and rain seemed to have stopped, though Mrs. Iblis did not give the time to making sure. She felt once more in vigorous health, considering the hour. Mrs. Iblis did what she could with her hair and hastened downstairs.

There was still a great crowd, but the atmosphere had changed. There was very little light (Bunhill was supplied by two separate circuits, one of which had been affected by the thunderstorm) and astonishingly little noise. People were sitting about in small groups, often on the floor: and the general conversational level rose little above a mutter. Mrs. Iblis recalled a number of the faces, but none in the hall (to her relief) belonged to anyone with whom she had spoken.

To reach the billiard room, it was necessary to pass through the drawing room and take a passage leading off between the drawing room and the dining room. In the murky drawing room (decorated with neutral-colored abstractions screwed in pale frames to the walls) Mrs. Iblis noticed the unmistakable figure of Ruth. She was lying on the antique-shop chaise-lounge, with an entirely blank expression on her round face and clasped frankly and ruthlessly in the arms of a man whose back was turned to Mrs. Iblis, but who was wearing a black suit. Ruth's moplike hair was in worse disarray than ever. Mrs. Iblis could not help wondering if Ruth were happy.

From off the passage led an apartment known as the music room, which Mrs. Iblis had not so far entered. The door of this room was open, and from it came a loud and cheerful noise, contrasting with the subdued, almost dead tone which ruled elsewhere. When Mrs. Iblis reached the door, she could not but look in. Seated on top of a vast black concert grand was the woman she had supposed to be Sister Nuper, in her silken nurse's dress and tall stiff collar. She appeared to be administering some kind of light-hearted "quiz" to her group of young men, now apparently increased in number, who were gathered round her on the floor. They had mostly placed themselves very close to her. The prevailing attitude among them was far from one of relaxation; on the contrary, most of them were kneeling and leaning eagerly forward. Though the distance from the door was not great, Mrs. Iblis was unable to hear the question asked in Sister Nuper's soft cooing voice; but a number of the young men appeared to answer in unison. Sister Nuper's position, dangling her beautifully shaped legs in gray silk stockings from the piano, enabled Mrs. Iblis to see that, unlike most tenders of the sick, she was wearing shoes with enormously high heels. In the back row of the cluster of men, one figure, Mrs. Iblis noticed, seemed almost hysterically eager to answer the question or to answer it first. As Sister Nuper asked another question, Mrs. Iblis passed on. She was far from sure that she agreed with Mavis's view that no better person than Sister Nuper could be found with whom to share her bedroom.

The billiard room, still illuminated from the defective strip, looked exactly as before, except that there was now only one surviving waiter, the toiler behind the buffet, the other two having cut the cloth to bits and then gone back to London together, leaving the damaged table littered with colored balls and cubes of chalk. As before, there were about a dozen guests eating and drinking. The tone of their hushed conversations suggested that they were complaining of one another to confidential friends.

Mrs. Iblis asked what there was to eat. Little seemed visible on the buffet but débris.

"There's only lobster salad." The waiter had had enough.

It was not at all what Mrs. Iblis wanted. "That will be delicious." She recognized that it was late.

The waiter shoved up from under the buffet a plateful assembled many hours earlier.

"Cider? No beer."

"I'd love a glass of cider."

It was drawn from a plywood cask and was a product of a local industries group which Coner fostered. The smell and flavor were unusual, but Mrs. Iblis almost at once recognized that the brew was potent.

She was so hungry that the lobster salad was soon gone, though normally she avoided tinned shellfish.

"There's some cake."

"Thank you. I'd love some cake." Again, however, she felt that there were at the moment more desirable foods.

The waiter gave her two large pieces, as the buffet was soon to close. The plate was too small for its load, but the cake was cake, not good, not bad, not indifferent.

This time no one came near Mrs. Iblis, or enforced conversation. This time she would almost have been glad for someone to do so (though not, for choice, any single one of the day's previous new acquaintances).

"Could I possibly have some coffee if there's any left?" She had not yet finished the cider.

The waiter glared at her, then went to the other end of the buffet, produced a full cup from under it, and returned to her without a word. He had slopped much of the contents into the saucer. The coffee was far from hot and contained insufficient sugar. When it was finished, Mrs. Iblis was unsure what to do next. She stood sipping the remains of the peculiar amateur cider. To the waiter she might not have existed. To her fellow guests, as they finished their scraps of food and drink, she might have been a hostile object.

In the end she was almost alone and contemplating a return to bed, when Coner entered. Mrs. Iblis identified him at once as the overanxious figure in the back row round Sister Nuper. He advanced upon the buffet. His face was strained and his gait slightly shambling.

"Got any Scotch?"

"Only cider left, Mr. Coner."

Encountering her host thus for the first time, Mrs. Iblis wondered whether good manners enjoined that she should speak to him. On the whole, she thought it would be simpler to do nothing. Coner, however, took the initiative. Glancing round the room before departing to unlock his spirit store, his eye lighted upon her isolated figure, still holding the glass. He stared at her for several moments, then advanced.

"Who are *you*?"

"I'm Mrs. Iblis. I've no business here, really. My invitation was postponed on account of the Forum. But your wife asked me to stay as I didn't get the letter of postponement."

"I'm glad she did." Coner was still staring hard. The flesh on his face was like a loose mask covering another face beneath. "I hope they're looking after you properly."

"Perfectly, thank you. I'm having a lovely time."

"What d'you think of the Forum? We've got pretty well everyone who carries weight, don't you think?"

"I'm afraid some of it's rather above my head."

Though continuing to stare at her in a way which Mrs. Iblis was beginning to find odd, Coner seemed hardly to be attending.

"No real synthesis has emerged," he said. "Nothing beyond the separate individual arguments and experiences." He spoke like a defeated general referring to reinforcements. "Pity about Rabbi Morocco having to go home. He could have helped a lot."

"How?" Mrs. Iblis wanted to enter into the spirit of it.

"The A. G. S. is making headway all the time, you know."

"I'm sure I've no business not to know, but what is the A. G. S.?"

"The Avant Garde Synagogue. Something entirely new. It's a great mistake to ignore what the Jews are doing."

"I am told that the Salvation Army are doing a lot too," said Mrs. Iblis, greatly venturing.

"Of course Patacake's utterly irreplaceable. One just wouldn't try." His eyes were now wandering up and down her body in a way to which she was unaccustomed; but he sank into silence.

"Will you be writing about the Forum in your papers?" inquired Mrs. Iblis, in order to say something.

"The whole of the next issue in each case except for a slaughterhouse feature in *Roundabout*. But I doubt whether we really reach them." He seemed in the last stages of gloom.

"Oh, I'm sure you do," said Mrs. Iblis comfortingly. "All those millions of copies. Power like that over people's minds must be a rather terrible thing." She was conscious that the very strong cider had reached her very weak head from her very empty stomach.

The pupils of Coner's eyes seemed to perform a complete halfcircle. Then he said: "You should wear nothing but black. Cut rather low. The sort of style young girls can't manage." He had placed his hand firmly on Mrs. Iblis's thorax to indicate precisely how low. Mrs. Iblis withdrew slightly with a distinct shudder.

"Thank you for the advice."

He stepped toward her again. "I find something quite remarkably charming about you. Even in pale blue."

Without the cider, Mrs. Iblis would probably have blushed and felt flattered. As it was, she answered: "Nonsense, Mr. Coner. I'm not quite so silly as that."

The waiter had just drawn a greasy overcoat from the hidden recess which had earlier evicted lobster salad. He departed, worming his way into the garment.

"Shall I leave the lights, Mr. Coner?"

"Yes. I'll put them out."

The last guests having also withdrawn, Mrs. Iblis was alone in the billiard room with her host and a dish filled with sliced cake.

"What's your name?"

"Iblis. I–B–L–I–S."

"How much do you know about me?"

"Very little more than I've read in the papers and so forth. Only what everyone knows."

"Shall we sit down?"

Mrs. Iblis wanted few things less. However, they sat in the depressing yellow glare on blue basketwork chairs brought in for use by frequenters of the buffet. It was not even very warm.

"It's close." Coner passed his handkerchief round the inside of his collar. "But never mind that. Now where shall I begin?" This question was for answer by the speaker himself. Clearly he was about to tell his life story.

"I expect you'll soon have to join your other guests, so I mustn't keep you too long."

"Oh God," said Coner, "the world's weight! The terror of one's own littleness." He was even whiter and had begun to weep profusely. His head dropped onto his hands, so that they covered his face. A cataract of tears fell through his fingers onto his gray trousers, which became as if spattered with ink.

Mrs. Iblis, who had never seen a man behave like this before (and hardly even a woman), was completely at a loss. After all the events of that day, Coner's demonstration was too much for her. Her body was insufficiently nourished, her mind awash in homemade cider. She too began gaspingly to weep. The scene in the billiard room was as if the two of them had just forsaken the last childhood's illusions.

Coner seemed quite lost to the world. Tears flooded his clothing. His body shook. His mind might have ceased to function.

Mrs. Iblis was less collapsed. The tears raced down her face, but she scrabbled through her handbag for a handkerchief and after a few minutes had somewhat pulled herself together.

"Please forgive me, Mr. Coner," she said. "Is there anything I can do to help?"

Coner went on sobbing and shivering like a man whose heart was long since broken and for whom such episodes as this were regular occurrences.

"Please, Mr. Coner." She extended her own rather unsteady hand and touched his shoulder. "What can I do?" Afraid, like most women, to go too far in sympathy lest the sympathy be misinterpreted, she had never in her life gone further than this.

Coner began to babble distressingly of his littleness and inadequacy; his responsibilities; his uncertainties; his health troubles. "The human mind is such a minnow," he spluttered out. "If only one could find some all-embracing pattern to guide one."

"The human mind is a whale." The speaker was Mr. Stillman, who had entered the large murky room unnoticed. It was the first time Mrs. Iblis had seen him since her arrival. He looked businesslike and prosperous in his well-cut dark suit. He carried a copy of the *Jewish Monthly*.

"The human mind is a whale," said Mr. Stillman again. "It's all there inside you, enormous unknown things, difficult to reach. And woe betide the man who looks outside himself for what he can only find inside. That is surely one thing which modern psychology has made clearer than ever. The subconscious mind, you know. So much larger than the conscious. The sublimal self." He paused. His eye was traveling along the buffet. "Ah, cake. There are hungry people in the house. Do you mind if I take the cake?"

Coner was staring at him, his face like an idiot's.

Mrs. Iblis replied: "I am sure that will be all right."

"Thank you," said Mr. Stillman, picked up the large white dish in his free hand, and left.

Coner now partially came to. "That's what we're all trying to do," he said. "To find ourselves."

"I gather not," rejoined Mrs. Iblis, with what might almost have been acerbity. "You're all trying to find something larger than yourselves."

She rose and left the billiard room, leaving Coner recumbent like a drenched tea cloth.

Everybody was eating cake and seemed more cheerful. It was like the miracle of the loaves, until Mrs. Iblis realized that volunteers had scoured the house for food and had stumbled upon a cache in the little pantry allotted to the caterers for their supplies. Also in the pantry were traces of proteinous foodstuffs which the hired staff had withheld and taken home to sell. The discovery had diverted much of the conversation to questions of supply and then rapidly to politics. Altogether, though disagreeing with many of the views expressed, Mrs. Iblis had never felt so much at home at Bunhill as now. Even Professor Borgia made comparatively agreeable company when discoursing upon the complexities of Swiss dietetics. Mrs. Iblis took another piece of cake herself, though it was long past her hour. After the last crumb went down, Sister Nuper emerged from the music room at the head of her young men. Idly curious, Mrs. Iblis counted them. They numbered no less than twelve, each as radiantly good-looking as the rest. Would Sister Nuper, her pleasant evening over, now proceed to bed? Apparently not: Sister Nuper went directly to the front door, opened it, and led the way out into the chilly night, closely attended as ever by her faithful followers. The door banged loudly behind the last of them, shaking the house.

Mrs. Iblis now dared to ask questions. "Where are they going at this hour?"

Her neighbor, a metaphysical daredevil who had recently been the youngest Ph.D. of his year, became suddenly reserved, almost aggressive. "They've gone for a walk," he replied rudely, as if it were no business of hers.

Mrs. Iblis did not care to invite another snub from these strange people by pursuing the matter further. Despite the welcome loosening up of the talk, she had the irritating feeling that she alone (or almost alone) was excluded from a general and advantageous secret. Of course, she reflected, she had not been really intended to be present that weekend.

Nonetheless, she felt piqued. She decided to go to bed and went. One or two of her fellow guests to whom she said good night (there was no sign of

Coner or Mrs. Coner, or even Mr. Stillman) seemed surprised, but only faintly.

Mrs. Iblis turned out the light and drew back the curtains, glad to stand for a moment in the cool darkness. Though the storm was long since over, the sky was not clear. There appeared, on the contrary, to be a dense ceiling of low cloud obscuring the stars but tinged with a radiance towards the east, which Mrs. Iblis supposed to come from the moon.

In the comfortable bed Mrs. Iblis soon fell asleep once more, despite the uncertainties relating to Sister Nuper's movements. After a dreamless span of uncertain length, she was awakened by a knocking on the door, at once purposeful and agitated.

"Come in, come in," said Mrs. Iblis rather peevishly. She switched on the bedside light.

She supposed it to be Sister Nuper (in who knows what condition?); but, in fact, it was Mavis. She wore saffron silk pajamas and no dressing gown. Her face was covered with unpleasing traces of what Mrs. Iblis presumed to be a "pack."

"I'm sorry, but there's something wrong. I'm frightened." Mavis was shivering noticeably.

Mrs. Iblis felt none too helpful. "You should have put something on."

"Yes. I suppose I should." Mavis vaguely clasped her pajamas about her.

"Have my dressing gown?"

"Thank you." Rather halfheartedly, she donned it. "Forgive my coming to you. Mrs. Coner's right out."

"Out?"

"Stuff she takes to make her sleep. She's never *compos mentis* till midday."

"What about the other guests? Not that I don't want to help," Mrs. Iblis added. Still, she did feel that this was the last straw.

"That's just it. They're not in their rooms. I'm frightened," repeated Mavis. "It's bloody awful."

Mrs. Iblis was now sitting up in bed and herself feeling none too warm. "Tell me exactly what's the matter."

"There's a queer light." Mavis crossed to the window and slightly drew back one of the curtains. "Look!"

"It's the moon."

"There's no moon."

"How do you know?"

"We compost the garden. You need to know for that. It's left to me, like most other things. I do know."

"Do you think it's a fire?"

"No." Mavis further withdrew the curtain. "Do you?"

A white radiance filled the air.

"It was beginning when I went to bed. I thought it was the moon. Are you quite sure?"

"Quite sure. It comes from the other side of the house."

"Searchlights?"

"It's not in beams. It's everywhere."

Mrs. Iblis felt no particular eagerness to leave her bed and investigate further.

"Have you *looked* on the other side of the house?"

"No. I wanted some moral support. Things go on here, you know." Mavis looked around the room so as to seem in part to localize her reference in a way which Mrs. Iblis found rather unpleasant. "I went to Ruth's room and it was empty. Then I went to several other rooms. They are all empty."

"So then you thought of Sister Nuper?"

"No. I thought of you. Will you come down with me?"

"Yes, of course, if you wish it." Mrs. Iblis got out of bed. "But why do we have to go down? Is that the first thing?"

"They're all in the hall. I can hear them."

Mrs. Iblis was reduced to putting on her overcoat. "Well now, let's see."

In what was precisely a half-light, the house did seem to Mrs. Iblis somewhat eerie. A life-sized figure of Buddha stood on the half landing, serenely menacing.

Through the thick brown curtains below and up the stairwell ascended a wavering hubbub. Then, just as Mrs. Iblis and her companion reached the bottom, a woman screamed sharply. She controlled herself almost at once.

The scene in the hall was certainly the strangest Mrs. Iblis had yet seen. The entire Forum (or so it seemed) were packed in, like refugees from some catastrophe. All appeared to be in their nightclothes, and there were the usual contrasts, comic and revealing. Professor Borgia's friend, the rotund young man, Mrs. Iblis noticed, was wearing a rich Oriental dressing gown. The leader of the New Vision Movement was wearing a nightshirt. Mrs. Iblis looked at once for Coner but could not see him.

In the poor light the throng appeared all to be gazing at the front door. They were now quite silent. Ruth, in the loose sweater and trousers she had worn by day, was elbowing her way forward, her face like that of St. Joan en route to the stake. Mrs. Iblis realized that she was going to open the door and deduced that someone had screamed when Ruth had made clear this intention.

All their faces were wrung in a conflict between a dreadful curiosity and the instinct to flee. A grim figure of the Kingsley Martin type collapsed upon his knees and, sinking his tortured face in his hands, began to pray. The rotund young man glanced at him and smiled faintly. A tall woman in an ulsterlike garment began to emit crooning sounds. Her face was stony with dread. Mrs. Iblis suspected that it had been she who had screamed.

Ruth had now struggled through to the door. With a final self-dedicatory gesture she lugged it open.

The strange luminosity fell upon her martyr's face. The doorway was filled with light. Behind could be seen a huge luminous shape. The light filled this shape and seemed to go towering upwards. The shape recalled in Mrs. Iblis's mind some common quotation: something about the feet of the gods on the mountains.

The Forum began to creep out into the garden, silently like snails under the moon.

"Come away," said a voice quietly to Mrs. Iblis. "Come upstairs." Mr.

Stillman, in white silk pajamas and a black dressing gown, had gently touched her arm. He still carried a copy of the *Jewish Monthly*, his finger between the pages. Round his neck was a scarf with the colors of some good club.

Mrs. Iblis glanced at Mavis.

"You come too," said Mr. Stillman.

"I wonder what's become of Mr. Coner?"

"He's in good hands," said Mr. Stillman; and Mavis seemed willing to leave it at that.

The trio ascended to the first floor. There Mrs. Iblis had expected them to stop. But Mr. Stillman said: "We're going on the roof."

They went up two more stories; then by a Slingsby ladder to the roof, which Coner had laid out for sunbathing and deck games. Inflatable rubber objects lay about, once bright and crude, now discolored. Every now and then one stumbled over a quoit. The house was L-shaped, so that, by looking over the rail, Mrs. Iblis could see the Forum still issuing slowly from the front door. The light kept burning all night in Mrs. Coner's bedroom could also be seen.

Once outside, members of the Forum seemed to lose initiative and to accumulate in a mass against the wall of the house. The entire atmosphere was filled with the strange light, but Mrs. Iblis began to realize that the light nonetheless had a distinct source, a source independent of the general air. It was like the concentration and narrowing of the perceptions which often follow emergence from an anesthetic. The cause of the confusion was simply the vastness of the source. Up here it looked as if the air was alight: but in fact it was a vast shining figure which filled the entire visible earth and sky. As each member of the Forum realized this fact, he or she drew back into the company of the other members against the wall.

Although the members of the Forum might have been frightened, Mrs. Iblis found the scale of the occurrence simply too large for fright. She quite consciously rehearsed this fact over to herself in her mind. Mavis, however, was shaking more than ever and looked about to faint. Mrs. Iblis drew forward a striped deck chair and seated Mavis upon it, whispering some comforting words to her. She noticed that the strange light drew all the strong color from Mavis's pajamas. Mr. Stillman was looking on at these particular workings of the universe with apparently complete equipoise. The paper in his hand might have been a program of events.

The light suddenly increased around and upon the Forum huddled against the wall to the left of the front door. It was as if an immense spotlight picked out a group of the opposition about to be laid low with machine-gun fire. But in fact it was that the vast figure was looking downwards from the empyrean.

Mr. Stillman had placed his forearms on the railing round the roof. Mavis had sunk her head between her knees. It was only Mrs. Iblis who looked upwards, and what she saw nearly finished her.

When Mrs. Iblis came round, the radiance in the air was much diminished. Mavis and Mr. Stillman had lifted her into Mavis's deck chair. It was cold.

Mrs. Iblis peered through the railings. There was no one in sight. Only the light in Mrs. Coner's bedroom burned reddish through the glimmer.

"Where are they?"

"They have merged," said Mr. Stillman. "They are at one." He was rubbing her left wrist. Mavis, now apparently much recovered, was rubbing her right.

"Where have they gone to?"

Mavis made a slight gesture away from the house. "We shan't see *them* any more."

Mrs. Iblis hardly dared to follow with her eyes. Then she saw that the radiance had entirely faded. It was a starry, moonless night without a cloud in the sky.

"I no longer feel frightened."

"Nor I," said Mavis. "Only cold. Why don't we?"

"Why should you?" said Mr. Stillman. "They've got what they wanted. As everyone does." He retied the cord of his dressing gown. "Shall we go down?" He led the way.

"I must look for Mr. Coner," said Mavis as they descended. Mrs. Iblis realized that she had not noticed her host among the group in the garden.

They found him sitting in the empty hall. He was drunk and still drinking. The key of his private spirit store was gripped tightly in his hand. The hall looked as if recently swept by a cyclone.

Mr. Stillman shut the open front door.

"Please God," said Coner in weak and sozzled accents, "please God give me something larger than myself."

He dropped into stupor, knocking a full glass to the floor. The disordered room began to reek of whiskey.

"Let me give you a hand," said Mr. Stillman to Mavis. They began to ease Coner toward the lift. "I think *you'd* better get some sleep," said Mr. Stillman to Mrs. Iblis. "Good night. See you in the morning." Mavis merely smiled at her.

Just as the cortège had passed through the brown curtains, the front door burst open once more. It was Sister Nuper and her friends. Their clothes seemed much damaged and covered with mud. It was as if they had been riding to hounds. But they all seemed as cheerful and gay as ever.

Mrs. Iblis had withdrawn into the shadows. She rather gathered that the revelers were contemplating final drinks.

Sister Nuper, graceful even in fatigue, dropped into the armchair just vacated by her employer. The bad light fell upon her beautiful features. Her face was glistening in a way Mrs. Iblis did not like. Her eyes were filled with such happiness that Mrs. Iblis was thoroughly scared all over again.

Unnoticed by the group of companions, Mrs. Iblis slipped away. Rather than pass what was left of the night with such a happy woman, she hastened to that room with the painted Crucifixion in it, she stuffed her possessions into her suitcase, and she left the house by a window at the back which had been carelessly left open by the hired staff.

Fritz Leiber

Belsen Express

Fritz Leiber was a correspondent of H. P. Lovecraft and an admirer of Robert E. Howard, the great dark fantasist of the pulps and inventor of the "heroic fantasy" genre (typified in his Conan the Barbarian stories). Leiber's first stories appeared in *Unknown* magazine and *Astounding*—he was a Campbell writer who later became the standard bearer of 1950s SF with revolutionary stories in *Galaxy* magazine. But his early triumphs were in the horror mode: the classic novel *Conjure Wife*, and the stories collected in his first book, *Night's Black Agents* (Arkham House, 1949). His stories of urban horrors were a key factor in establishing the new horror mode of *Unknown* magazine. Now an elder statesman of his field, he continues to produce a tale or two a year over the past decade, including this World Fantasy Award–winner, "Belsen Express," a classic examination of the most egregious of horrors of the century, an understated contrast to the city horrors of Ellison or Bradbury.

George Simister watched the blue flames writhe beautifully in the grate, like dancing girls drenched with alcohol and set afire, and congratulated himself on having survived well through the middle of the Twentieth Century without getting involved in military service, world-saving, or any activities that interfered with the earning and enjoyment of money.

Outside rain dripped, a storm snarled at the city from the outskirts, and sudden gusts of wind produced in the chimney a sound like the mourning of doves. Simister shimmied himself a fraction of an inch deeper in his easy chair and took a slow sip of diluted scotch—he was sensitive to most cheaper liquors. Simister's physiology was on the delicate side; during his childhood certain tastes and odors, playing on an elusive heart weakness, had been known to make him faint.

The outspread newspaper started to slip from his knee. He detained it, let his glance rove across the next page, noted a headline about an uprising in Prague like that in Hungary in 1956 and murmured, "Damn Slavs," noted another about border fighting around Israel and muttered, "Damn Jews," and let the paper go. He took another sip of his drink, yawned, and watched a virginal blue flame flutter frightenedly the length of the log before it turned to a white smoke ghost. There was a sharp *knock-knock*.

Simister jumped and then got up and hurried tight-lipped to the front door. Lately some of the neighborhood children had been trying to annoy him probably because his was the most respectable and best-kept house on the block. Doorbell ringing, obscene sprayed scrawls, that sort of thing. And

245

hardly children—young rowdies rather, who needed rough handling and a trip to the police station. He was really angry by the time he reached the door and swung it wide. There was nothing but a big wet empty darkness. A chilly draft spattered a couple of cold drops on him. Maybe the noise had come from the fire. He shut the door and started back to the living room, but a small pile of books untidily nested in wrapping paper on the hall table caught his eye and he grimaced.

They constituted a blotchily addressed parcel which the postman had delivered by mistake a few mornings ago. Simister could probably have deciphered the address, for it was clearly on this street, and rectified the postman's error, but he did not choose to abet the activities of illiterates with leaky pens. And the delivery must have been a mistake for the top book was titled *The Scourge of the Swastika* and the other two had similar titles, and Simister had an acute distaste for books that insisted on digging up that satisfactorily buried historical incident known as Nazi Germany.

The reason for this distaste was a deeply hidden fear that George Simister shared with millions, but that he had never revealed even to his wife. It was a quite unrealistic and now completely anachronistic fear of the Gestapo.

It had begun years before the Second World War, with the first small reports from Germany of minority persecutions and organized hoodlumism —the sense of something reaching out across the dark Atlantic to threaten his life, his security, and his confidence that he would never have to suffer pain except in a hospital.

Of course it had never got at all close to Simister, but it had exercised an evil tyranny over his imagination. There was one nightmarish series of scenes that had slowly grown in his mind and then had kept bothering him for a long time. It began with a thunderous knocking, of boots and rifle butts rather than fists, and a shouted demand: "Open up! It's the Gestapo." Next he would find himself in a stream of frantic people being driven toward a portal where a division was made between those reprieved and those slated for immediate extinction. Last he would be inside a closed motor van jammed so tightly with people that it was impossible to move. After a long time the van would stop, but the motor would keep running, and from the floor, leisurely seeking the crevices between the packed bodies, the entrapped exhaust fumes would begin to mount.

Now in the shadowy hall the same horrid movie had a belated showing. Simister shook his head sharply, as if he could shake the scenes out, reminding himself that the Gestapo was dead and done with for more than ten years. He felt the angry impulse to throw in the fire the books responsible for the return of his waking nightmare. But he remembered that books are hard to burn. He stared at them uneasily, excited by thoughts of torture and confinement, concentration and death camps, but knowing the nasty aftermath they left in his mind. Again he felt a sudden impulse, this time to bundle the books together and throw them in the trash can. But that would mean getting wet, it could wait until tomorrow. He put the screen in front of the fire, which had died and was smoking like a crematory, and went up to bed.

Some hours later he waked with the memory of a thunderous knocking.

He started up, exclaiming, "Those damned kids!" The drawn shades seemed abnormally dark—probably they'd thrown a stone through the street lamp.

He put one foot on the chilly floor. It was now profoundly still. The storm had gone off like a roving cat. Simister strained his ears. Beside him his wife breathed with irritating evenness. He wanted to wake her and explain about the young delinquents. It was criminal that they were permitted to roam the streets at this hour. Girls with them too, likely as not.

The knocking was not repeated. Simister listened for footsteps going away, or for the creaking of boards that would betray a lurking presence on the porch.

After awhile he began to wonder if the knocking might not have been part of a dream, or perhaps a final rumble of actual thunder. He lay down and pulled the blankets up to his neck. Eventually his muscles relaxed and he got to sleep.

At breakfast he told his wife about it.

"George, it may have been burglars," she said.

"Don't be stupid, Joan. Burglars don't knock. If it was anything it was those damned kids."

"Whatever it was, I wish you'd put a bigger bolt on the front door."

"Nonsense. If I'd known you were going to act this way I wouldn't have said anything. I told you it was probably just the thunder."

But next night at about the same hour it happened again.

This time there could be little question of dreaming. The knocking still reverberated in his ears. And there had been words mixed with it, some sort of yapping in a foreign language. Probably the children of some of those European refugees who had settled in the neighborhood.

Last night they'd fooled him by keeping perfectly still after banging on the door, but tonight he knew what to do. He tiptoed across the bedroom and went down the stairs rapidly, but quietly because of his bare feet. In the hall he snatched up something to hit them with, then in one motion unlocked and jerked open the door.

There was no one.

He stood looking at the darkness. He was puzzled as to how they could have got away so quickly and silently. He shut the door and switched on the light. Then he felt the thing in his hand. It was one of the books. With a feeling of disgust he dropped it on the others. He must remember to throw them out first thing tomorrow.

But he overslept and had to rush. The feeling of disgust or annoyance, or something akin, must have lingered, however, for he found himself sensitive to things he wouldn't ordinarily have noticed. People especially. The swollen-handed man seemed deliberately surly as he counted Simister's pennies and handed him the paper. The tight-lipped woman at the gate hesitated suspiciously, as if he were trying to pass off a last month's ticket.

And when he was hurrying up the stairs in response to an approaching rumble, he brushed against a little man in an oversize coat and received in return a glance that gave him a positive shock.

Simister vaguely remembered having seen the little man several times before. He had the thin nose, narrow-set eyes and receding chin that is by a stretch of the imagination described as "rat-faced." In the movies he'd have played a stool pigeon. The flapping overcoat was rather comic.

But there seemed to be something at once so venomous and sly, so time-bidingly vindictive, in the glance he gave Simister that the latter was taken aback and almost missed the train.

He just managed to squeeze through the automatically closing door of the smoker after the barest squint at the sign to assure himself that the train was an express. His heart was pounding in a way that another time would have worried him, but now he was immersed in a savage pleasure at having thwarted the man in the oversize coat. The latter hadn't hurried fast enough and Simister had made no effort to hold open the door for him.

As a smooth surge of electric power sent them sliding away from the station Simister pushed his way from the vestibule into the car and snagged a strap. From the next one already swayed his chief commuting acquaintance, a beefy, suspiciously red-nosed, irritating man named Holstrom, now reading a folded newspaper one-handed. He shoved a headline in Simister's face. The latter knew what to expect.

"Atomic Weapons for West Germany," he read tonelessly. Holstrom was always trying to get him into outworn arguments about totalitarianism, Nazi Germany, racial prejudice and the like. "Well, what about it?"

Holstrom shrugged. "It's a natural enough step, I suppose, but it started me thinking about the top Nazis and whether we really got all of them."

"Of course," Simister snapped.

"I'm not so sure," Holstrom said. "I imagine quite a few of them got away and are still hiding out somewhere."

But Simister refused the bait. The question bored him. Who talked about the Nazis any more? For that matter, the whole trip this morning was boring; the smoker was overcrowded; and when they finally piled out at the downtown terminus, the rude jostling increased his irritation.

The crowd was approaching an iron fence that arbitrarily split the stream of hurrying people into two sections which reunited a few steps farther on. Beside the fence a new guard was standing, or perhaps Simister hadn't noticed him before. A cocky-looking young fellow with close-cropped blond hair and cold blue eyes.

Suddenly it occurred to Simister that he habitually passed to the right of the fence, but that this morning he was being edged over toward the left. This trifling circumstance, coming on top of everything else, made him boil. He deliberately pushed across the stream, despite angry murmurs and the hard stare of the guard.

He had intended to walk the rest of the way, but his anger made him forgetful and before he realized it he had climbed aboard a bus. He soon regretted it. The bus was even more crowded than the smoker and the standees were morose and lumpy in their heavy overcoats. He was tempted to get off and waste his fare, but he was trapped in the extreme rear and moreover shrank from giving the impression of a man who didn't know his own mind.

Soon another annoyance was added to the ones already plaguing him—a trace of exhaust fumes was seeping up from the motor at the rear. He immediately began to feel ill. He looked around indignantly, but the others did not seem to notice the odor, or else accepted it fatalistically.

In a couple of blocks the fumes had become so bad that Simister decided he must get off at the next stop. But as he started to push past her, a fat woman beside him gave him such a strangely apathetic stare that Simister, whose mind was perhaps a little clouded by nausea, felt almost hypnotized by it, so that it was several seconds before he recalled and carried out his intention.

Ridiculous, but the woman's face stuck in his mind all day.

In the evening he stopped at a hardware store. After supper his wife noticed him working in the front hall.

"Oh, you're putting on a bolt," she said.

"Well, you asked me to, didn't you?"

"Yes, but I didn't think you'd do it."

"I decided I might as well." He gave the screw a final turn and stepped back to survey the job. "Anything to give you a feeling of security."

Then he remembered the stuff he had been meaning to throw out that morning. The hall table was bare.

"What did you do with them?" he asked.

"What?"

"Those fool books."

"Oh, those. I wrapped them up again and gave them to the postman."

"Now why did you do that? There wasn't any return address and I might have wanted to look at them."

"But you said they weren't addressed to us and you hate all that war stuff."

"I know, but—" he said and then stopped, hopeless of making her understand why he particularly wanted to feel he had got rid of that package himself, and by throwing it in the trash can. For that matter, he didn't quite understand his feelings himself. He began to poke around the hall.

"I did return the package," his wife said sharply. "I'm not losing my memory."

"Oh, all right!" he said and started for bed.

That night no knocking awakened him, but rather a loud crashing and rending of wood along with a harsh metallic *ping* like a lock giving.

In a moment he was out of bed, his sleep-sodden nerves jangling with anger. Those hoodlums! Rowdy pranks were perhaps one thing, deliberate destruction of property certainly another. He was halfway down the stairs before it occurred to him that the sound he had heard had a distinctly menacing aspect. Juvenile delinquents who broke down doors would hardly panic at the appearance of an unarmed householder.

But just then he saw that the front door was intact.

Considerably puzzled and apprehensive, he searched the first floor and even ventured into the basement, racking his brains as to just what could have caused such a noise. The water heater? Weight of the coal bursting a side of the bin? Those objects were intact. But perhaps the porch trellis giving way?

That last notion kept him peering out of the front window several moments. When he turned around there was someone behind him.

"I didn't mean to startle you," his wife said. "What's the matter, George?"

"I don't know. I thought I heard a sound. Something being smashed."

He expected that would send her into one of her burglar panics, but instead she kept looking at him.

"Don't stand there all night," he said. "Come on to bed."

"George, is something worrying you? Something you haven't told me about?"

"Of course not. Come on."

Next morning Holstrom was on the platform when Simister got there and they exchanged guesses as to whether the dark rainclouds would burst before they got downtown. Simister noticed the man in the oversize coat loitering about, but he paid no attention to him.

Since it was a bank holiday there were empty seats in the smoker and he and Holstrom secured one. As usual the latter had his newspaper. Simister waited for him to start his ideological sniping—a little uneasily for once; usually he was secure in his prejudices, but this morning he felt strangely vulnerable.

It came. Holstrom shook his head. "That's a bad business in Czechoslovakia. Maybe we were a little too hard on the Nazis."

To his surprise Simister found himself replying with both nervous hypocrisy and uncharacteristic vehemence. "Don't be ridiculous! Those rats deserved a lot worse than they got!"

As Holstrom turned toward him saying, "Oh, so you've changed your mind about the Nazis," Simister thought he heard someone just behind him say at the same time in a low, distinct, pitiless voice: "I heard you."

He glanced around quickly. Leaning forward a little, but with his face turned sharply away as if he had just become interested in something passing the window, was the man in the oversize coat.

"What's wrong?" Holstrom asked.

"What do you mean?"

"You've turned pale. You look sick."

"I don't feel that way."

"Sure? You know, at our age we've got to begin to watch out. Didn't you once tell me something about your heart?"

Simister managed to laugh that off, but when they parted just outside the train he was conscious that Holstrom was still eying him rather closely.

As he slowly walked through the terminus his face began to assume an abstracted look. In fact he was lost in thought to such a degree that when he approached the iron fence, he started to pass it on the left. Luckily the crowd was thin and he was able to cut across to the right without difficulty. The blond young guard looked at him closely—perhaps he remembered yesterday morning.

Simister had told himself that he wouldn't again under any circumstances take the bus, but when he got outside it was raining torrents. After a moment's hesitation he climbed aboard. It seemed even more crowded than yesterday, if that were possible, with more of the same miserable people, and the damp air made the exhaust odor particularly offensive.

The abstracted look clung to his face all day long. His secretary noticed, but did not comment. His wife did, however, when she found him poking around in the hall after supper.

"Are you still looking for that package, George?" Her tone was flat.

"Of course not," he said quickly, shutting the table drawer he'd opened.

She waited. "Are you sure you didn't order those books?"

"What gave you that idea?" he demanded. "You know I didn't."

"I'm glad," she said. "I looked through them. There were pictures. They were nasty."

"You think I'm the sort of person who'd buy books for the sake of nasty pictures?"

"Of course not, dear, but I thought you might have seen them and they were what had depressed you."

"Have I been depressed?"

"Yes. Your heart hasn't been bothering you, has it?"

"No."

"Well, what is it then?"

"I don't know." Then with considerable effort he said, "I've been thinking about war and things."

"War! No wonder you're depressed. You shouldn't think about things you don't like, especially when they aren't happening. What started you?"

"Oh, Holstrom keeps talking to me on the train."

"Well, don't listen to him."

"I won't."

"Well, cheer up then."

"I will."

"And don't let anyone make you look at morbid pictures. There was one of some people who had been gassed in a motor van and then laid out—"

"Please, Joan! Is it any better to tell me about them than to have me look at them?"

"Of course not, dear. That was silly of me. But do cheer up."

"Yes."

The puzzled, uneasy look was still in her eyes as she watched him go down the front walk next morning. It was foolish, but she had the feeling that his gray suit was really black—and he had whimpered in his sleep. With a shiver at her fancy she stepped inside.

That morning George Simister created a minor disturbance in the smoker, it was remembered afterwards, though Holstrom did not witness the beginning of it. It seems that Simister had run to catch the express and had almost missed it, due to a collision with a small man in a large overcoat. Someone recalled that trifling prelude because of the amusing circumstance that the small man, although he had been thrown to his knees and the collision was chiefly Simister's fault, was still anxiously begging Simister's pardon after the latter had dashed on.

Simister just managed to squeeze through the closing door while taking a quick squint at the sign. It was then that his queer behavior started. He instantly turned around and unsuccessfully tried to force his way out again, even inserting his hands in the crevice between the door frame and the rubber edge of the sliding door and yanking violently.

Apparently as soon as he noticed the train was in motion, he turned away from the door, his face pale and set, and roughly pushed his way into the interior of the car.

There he made a beeline for the little box in the wall containing the identifying signs of the train and the miniature window which showed in reverse the one now in use, which read simply EXPRESS. He stared at it as if he couldn't believe his eyes and then started to turn the crank, exposing in turn all the other white signs on the roll of black cloth. He scanned each one intently, oblivious to the puzzled or outraged looks of those around him.

He had been through all the signs once and was starting through them again before the conductor noticed what was happening and came hurrying. Ignoring his expostulations, Simister asked him loudly if this was really the express. Upon receiving a curt affirmative, Simister went on to assert that he had in the moment of squeezing aboard glimpsed another sign in the window—and he mentioned a strange name. He seemed both very positive and very agitated about it, the conductor said. The latter asked Simister to spell the name. Simister haltingly complied: "B . . . E . . . L . . . S . . . E . . . N . . ." The conductor shook his head, then his eyes widened and he demanded, "Say, are you trying to kid me? That was one of those Nazi death camps." Simister slunk toward the other end of the car.

It was there that Holstrom saw him, looking "as if he'd just got a terrible shock." Holstrom was alarmed—and as it happened felt a special private guilt—but could hardly get a word out of him, though he made several attempts to start a conversation, choosing uncharacteristically neutral topics. Once, he remembered, Simister looked up and said, "Do you suppose there are some things a man simply can't escape, no matter how quietly he lives or how carefully he plans?" But his face immediately showed he had realized there was at least one very obvious answer to this question, and Holstrom didn't know what to say. Another time he suddenly remarked, "I wish we were like the British and didn't have standing in buses," but he subsided as quickly. As they neared the downtown terminus Simister seemed to brace up a little, but Holstrom was still worried about him to such a degree that he went out of his way to follow him through the terminus. "I was afraid something would happen to him, I don't know what," Holstrom said. "I would have stayed right beside him except he seemed to resent my presence."

Holstrom's private guilt, which intensified his anxiety and doubtless accounted for his feeling that Simister resented him, was due to the fact that ten days ago, cumulatively irritated by Simister's smug prejudices and blinkered narrow-mindedness, he had anonymously mailed him three books recounting with uncompromising realism and documentation some of the least pleasant aspects of the Nazi tyranny. Now he couldn't but feel they might have helped to shake Simister up in a way he hadn't intended, and he was ashamedly glad that he had been in such a condition when he sent the package that it had been addressed in a drunken scrawl. He never discussed this matter afterwards, except occasionally to make strangely feelingful remarks about "what little things can unseat a spring in a man's clockworks!"

So, continuing Holstrom's story, he followed Simister at a distance as the latter dejectedly shuffled across the busy terminus. "Terminus?" Holstrom once interrupted his story to remark. "He's a god of endings, isn't he?—and of human rights. Does that mean anything?"

When Simister was nearing an iron fence a puzzling episode occurred. He was about to pass it to the right, when someone just ahead of him lurched or stumbled. Simister almost fell himself, veering toward the fence. A nearby guard reached out and in steadying him pulled him around the fence to the left.

Then, Holstrom maintains, Simister turned for a moment and Holstrom caught a glimpse of his face. There must have been something peculiarly frightening about that backward look, something perhaps that Holstrom cannot adequately describe, for he instantly forgot any idea of surveillance at a distance and made every effort to catch up.

But the crowd from another commuters' express enveloped Holstrom. When he got outside the terminus it was some moments before he spotted Simister in the midst of a group jamming their way aboard an already crowded bus across the street. This perplexed Holstrom, for he knew Simister didn't have to take the bus and he recalled his recent complaint.

Heavy traffic kept Holstrom from crossing. He says he shouted, but Simister did not seem to hear him. He got the impression that Simister was making feeble efforts to get out of the crowd that was forcing him onto the bus, but, "They were all jammed together like cattle."

The best testimony to Holstrom's anxiety about Simister is that as soon as the traffic thinned a trifle he darted across the street, skipping between the cars. But by then the bus had started. He was in time only for a whiff of particularly obnoxious exhaust fumes.

As soon as he got to his office he phoned Simister. He got Simister's secretary and what she had to say relieved his worries, which is ironic in view of what happened a little later.

What happened a little later is best described by the same girl. She said, "I never saw him come in looking so cheerful, the old grouch—excuse me. But anyway he came in all smiles, like he'd just got some bad news about somebody else, and right away he started to talk and kid with everyone, so that it was awfully funny when that man called up worried about him. I guess maybe, now I think back, he did seem a bit shaken underneath, like a person who's just had a narrow squeak and is very thankful to be alive.

"Well, he kept it up all morning. Then just as he was throwing his head back to laugh at one of his own jokes, he grabbed his chest, let out an awful scream, doubled up and fell on the floor. Afterwards I couldn't believe he was dead, because his lips stayed so red and there were bright spots of color on his cheeks, like rouge. Of course it was his heart, though you can't believe what a scare that stupid first doctor gave us when he came in and looked at him."

Of course, as she said, it must have been Simister's heart, one way or the other. And it is undeniable that the doctor in question was an ancient, possibly incompetent dispenser of penicillin, morphine and snap diagnoses swifter than Charcot's. They only called him because his office was in the same building. When Simister's own doctor arrived and pronounced it heart failure, which was what they'd thought all along, everyone was much relieved and inclined to be severely critical of the first doctor for having said something that sent them all scurrying to open the windows.

For when the first doctor had come in, he had taken one look at Simister and rasped, "Heart failure? Nonsense! Look at the color of his face. Cherry red. That man died of carbon monoxide poisoning."

Robert Bloch

Yours Truly, Jack the Ripper

Robert Bloch was a correspondent of Lovecraft and became a supernatural horror writer for *Weird Tales*, a science fiction writer, a mystery writer, then a film writer. "Bloch epitomizes the horror dimension of today's pop culture," says one major reference book. His novel, *Psycho*, appears on Stephen King's ten-best list and the film made by Alfred Hitchcock is a classic. He has published more than a dozen story collections principally horrific. His earliest stories, such as "The Shambler From the Stars," are Lovecraftian but his characteristic work has as its hallmark abnormal psychology and absurd irony. He is a master of the pun. "Yours Truly, Jack the Ripper" is arguably his best story, an ironic blend of psychology and the supernatural, a monster story, a story that reinforces our belief in supernatural evil and connects it cleverly to evil in the real world. While later Bloch is often psychological horror (some of his best effects occur in mystery novels such as *The Scarf*), this story suggests the same moral universe as Harlan Ellison's "The Whimper of Whipped Dogs." Bloch was the first winner of the Grand Master Award for Life Achievement at the first World Fantasy Convention in 1975.

1

I looked at the stage Englishman. He looked at me.

"Sir Guy Hollis?" I asked.

"Indeed. Have I the pleasure of addressing John Carmody, the psychiatrist?"

I nodded. My eyes swept over the figure of my distinguished visitor. Tall, lean, sandy-haired—with the traditional tufted moustache. And the tweeds. I suspected a monocle concealed in a vest pocket, and wondered if he'd left his umbrella in the outer office.

But more than that, I wondered what the devil had impelled Sir Guy Hollis of the British Embassy to seek out a total stranger here in Chicago.

Sir Guy didn't help matters any as he sat down. He cleared his throat, glanced around nervously, tapped his pipe against the side of the desk. Then he opened his mouth.

"Mr. Carmody," he said, "have you ever heard of—Jack the Ripper?"

"The murderer?" I asked.

"Exactly. The greatest monster of them all. Worse than Springheel Jack or Crippen. Jack the Ripper. Red Jack."

"I've heard of him," I said.

"Do you know his history?"

"I don't think we'll get any place swapping old wives' tales about famous crimes of history."

He took a deep breath.

"This is no old wives' tale. It's a matter of life or death."

He was so wrapped up in his obsession he even talked that way. Well—I was willing to listen. We psychiatrists get paid for listening.

"Go ahead," I told him. "Let's have the story."

Sir Guy lit a cigarette and began to talk.

"London, 1888," he began. "Late summer and early fall. That was the time. Out of nowhere came the shadowy figure of Jack the Ripper—a stalking shadow with a knife, prowling through London's East End. Haunting the squalid dives of Whitechapel, Spitalfields. Where he came from no one knew. But he brought death. Death in a knife.

"Six times that knife descended to slash the throats and bodies of London's women. Drabs and alley sluts. August 7th was the date of the first butchery. They found her lying there with thirty-nine stab wounds. A ghastly murder. On August 31st, another victim. The press became interested. The slum inhabitants were more deeply interested still.

"Who was this unknown killer who prowled in their midst and struck at will in the deserted alleyways of nighttown? And what was more important —when would he strike again?

"September 8th was the date. Scotland Yard assigned special deputies. Rumors ran rampant. The atrocious nature of the slayings was the subject for shocking speculation.

"The killer used a knife—expertly. He cut throats and removed—certain portions—of the bodies after death. He chose victims and settings with a fiendish deliberation. No one saw him or heard him. But watchmen making their gray rounds in the dawn would stumble across the hacked and horrid thing that was the Ripper's handiwork.

"Who was he? What was he? A mad surgeon? A butcher? An insane scientist? A pathological degenerate escaped from an asylum? A deranged nobleman? A member of the London police?

"Then the poem appeared in the newspapers. The anonymous poem, designed to put a stop to speculations—but which only aroused public interest to a further frenzy. A mocking little stanza:

> I'm not a butcher, I'm not a Yid
> Nor yet a foreign skipper,
> But I'm your own true loving friend,
> Yours truly—Jack the Ripper.

"And on September 30th, two more throats were slashed open. There was silence, then, in London for a time. Silence, and a nameless fear. When would Red Jack strike again? They waited through October. Every figment of fog concealed his phantom presence. Concealed it well—for nothing was learned of the Ripper's identity, or his purpose. The drabs of London shivered in the raw wind of early November. Shivered, and were thankful for the coming of each morning's sun.

"November 9th. They found her in her room. She lay there very quietly, limbs neatly arranged. And beside her, with equal neatness, were laid her breasts and heart. The Ripper had outdone himself in execution.

"Then, panic. But needless panic. For though press, police, and populace alike waited in sick dread, Jack the Ripper did not strike again.

"Months passed. A year. The immediate interest died, but not the memory. They said Jack had skipped to America. That he had committed suicide. They said—and they wrote. They've written ever since. But to this day no one knows who Jack the Ripper was. Or why he killed. Or why he stopped killing."

Sir Guy was silent. Obviously he expected some comment from me.

"You tell the story well," I remarked. "Though with a slight emotional bias."

"I suppose you want to know why I'm interested?" he snapped.

"Yes. That's exactly what I'd like to know."

"Because," said Sir Guy Hollis, "I am on the trail of Jack the Ripper now. I think he's here—in Chicago!"

"Say that again."

"Jack the Ripper is alive, in Chicago, and I'm out to find him."

He wasn't smiling. It wasn't a joke.

"See here," I said. "What was the date of these murders?"

"August to November, 1888."

"1888? But if Jack the Ripper was an able-bodied man in 1888, he'd surely be dead today! Why look, man—if he were merely born in that year, he'd be fifty-seven years old today!"

"Would he?" smiled Sir Guy Hollis. "Or should I say, 'Would she?' Because Jack the Ripper may have been a woman. Or any number of things."

"Sir Guy," I said. "You came to the right person when you looked me up. You definitely need the services of a psychiatrist."

"Perhaps. Tell me, Mr. Carmody, do you think I'm crazy?"

I looked at him and shrugged. But I had to give him a truthful answer.

"Frankly—no."

"Then you might listen to the reasons I believe Jack the Ripper is alive today."

"I might."

"I've studied these cases for thirty years. Been over the actual ground. Talked to officials. Talked to friends and acquaintances of the poor drabs who were killed. Visited with men and women in the neighborhood. Collected an entire library of material touching on Jack the Ripper. Studied all the wild theories or crazy notions.

"I learned a little. Not much, but a little. I won't bore you with my conclusions. But there was another branch of inquiry that yielded more fruitful return. I have studied unsolved crimes. Murders.

"I could show you clippings from the papers of half the world's greatest cities. San Francisco. Shanghai. Calcutta. Omsk. Paris. Berlin. Pretoria. Cairo. Milan. Adelaide.

"The trail is there, the pattern. Unsolved crimes. Slashed throats of women. With the peculiar disfigurations and removals. Yes, I've followed a trail of blood. From New York westward across the continent. Then to the Pacific. From there to Africa. During the World War of 1914–18 it was Europe. After that, South America. And since 1930, the United States again. Eighty-seven such murders—and to the trained criminologist, all bear the stigma of the Ripper's handiwork.

"Recently there were the so-called Cleveland torso slayings. Remember? A shocking series. And finally, two recent deaths in Chicago. Within the past six months. One out on South Dearborn. The other somewhere up in Halsted. Same type of crime, same technique. I tell you, there are unmistakable indications in all these affairs—indications of the work of Jack the Ripper!"

"A very tight theory," I said. "I'll not question your evidence at all, or the deductions you draw. You're the criminologist, and I'll take your word for it. Just one thing remains to be explained. A minor point, perhaps, but worth mentioning."

"And what is that?" asked Sir Guy.

"Just how could a man of, let us say, eighty-five years commit these crimes? For if Jack the Ripper was around thirty in 1888 and lived, he'd be eighty-five today."

"Suppose he didn't get any older?" whispered Sir Guy.

"What's that?"

"Suppose Jack the Ripper didn't grow old? Suppose he is still a young man today?

"It's a crazy theory, I grant you," he said. "All the theories about the Ripper are crazy. The idea that he was a doctor. Or a maniac. Or a woman. The reasons advanced for such beliefs are flimsy enough. There's nothing to go by. So why should my notion be any worse?"

"Because people grow older," I reasoned with him. "Doctors, maniacs and women alike."

"What about—*sorcerers*?"

"Sorcerers?"

"Necromancers. Wizards. Practicers of Black Magic."

"What's the point?"

"I studied," said Sir Guy. "I studied everything. After a while I began to study the dates of the murders. The pattern those dates formed. The rhythm. The solar, lunar, stellar rhythm. The sidereal aspect. The astrological significance.

"Suppose Jack the Ripper didn't murder for murder's sake alone? Suppose he wanted to make—a sacrifice?"

"What kind of a sacrifice?"

Sir Guy shrugged. "It is said that if you offer blood to the dark gods they grant boons. Yes, if a blood offering is made at the proper time—when the moon and the stars are right—and with the proper ceremonies—they grant boons. Boons of youth. Eternal youth."

"But that's nonsense!"

"No. That's—Jack the Ripper."

I stood up. "A most interesting theory," I told him. "But why do you come here and tell it to me? I'm not an authority on witchcraft. I'm not a police official or criminologist. I'm a practicing psychiatrist. What's the connection?"

Sir Guy smiled.

"You are interested, then?"

"Well, yes. There must be some point."

"There is. But I wished to be assured of your interest first. Now I can tell you my plan."

"And just what is that plan?"

Sir Guy gave me a long look.

"John Carmody," he said, "you and I are going to capture Jack the Ripper."

2

That's the way it happened. I've given the gist of that first interview in all its intricate and somewhat boring detail, because I think it's important. It helps to throw some light on Sir Guy's character and attitude. And in view of what happened after that—

But I'm coming to those matters.

Sir Guy's thought was simple. It wasn't even a thought. Just a hunch.

"You know the people here," he told me. "I've inquired. That's why I came to you as the ideal man for my purpose. You number amongst your acquaintances many writers, painters, poets. The so-called intelligentsia. The lunatic fringe from the near north side.

"For certain reasons—never mind what they are—my clues lead me to infer that Jack the Ripper is a member of that element. He chooses to pose as an eccentric. I've a feeling that with you to take me around and introduce me to your set, I might hit upon the right person."

"It's all right with me," I said. "But just how are you going to look for him? As you say, he might be anybody, anywhere. And you have no idea what he looks like. He might be young or old. Jack the Ripper—a Jack of all trades? Rich man, poor man, beggar man, thief, doctor, lawyer—how will you know?"

"We shall see." Sir Guy sighed heavily. "But I must find him. At once."

"Why the hurry?"

Sir Guy sighed again. "Because in two days he will kill again."

"Are you sure?"

"Sure as the stars. I've plotted this chart, you see. All of the murders correspond to certain astrological rhythm patterns. If, as I suspect, he makes a blood sacrifice to renew his youth, he must murder within two days. Notice the pattern of his first crimes in London. August 7th. Then August 31st. September 8th. September 30th. November 9th. Intervals of twenty-four days, nine days, twenty-two days—he killed two this time—and then forty days. Of course there were crimes in between. There had to be. But they weren't discovered and pinned on him.

"At any rate, I've worked out a pattern for him, based on all my data. And I say that within the next two days he kills. So I must seek him out, somehow, before then."

"And I'm still asking you what you want me to do."

"Take me out," said Sir Guy. "Introduce me to your friends. Take me to parties."

"But where do I begin? As far as I know, my artistic friends, despite their eccentricities, are all normal people."

"So is the Ripper. Perfectly normal. Except on certain nights." Again that faraway look in Sir Guy's eyes. "Then he becomes an ageless pathological monster, crouching to kill."

"All right," I said. "All right. I'll take you."

We made our plans. And that evening I took him over to Lester Baston's studio.

As we ascended to the penthouse roof in the elevator I took the opportunity to warn Sir Guy.

"Baston's a real screwball," I cautioned him. "So are his guests. Be prepared for anything and everything."

"I am." Sir Guy Hollis was perfectly serious. He put his hand in his trousers pocket and pulled out a gun.

"What the—" I began.

"If I see him I'll be ready," Sir Guy said. He didn't smile, either.

"But you can't go running around at a party with a loaded revolver in your pocket, man!"

"Don't worry, I won't behave foolishly."

I wondered. Sir Guy Hollis was not, to my way of thinking, a normal man.

We stepped out of the elevator, went toward Baston's apartment door.

"By the way," I murmured, "just how do you wish to be introduced? Shall I tell them who you are and what you are looking for?"

"I don't care. Perhaps it would be best to be frank."

"But don't you think that the Ripper—if by some miracle he or she is present—will immediately get the wind up and take cover?"

"I think the shock of the announcement that I am hunting the Ripper would provoke some kind of betraying gesture on his part," said Sir Guy.

"It's a fine theory. But I warn you, you're going to be in for a lot of ribbing. This is a wild bunch."

Sir Guy smiled.

"I'm ready," he announced. "I have a little plan of my own. Don't be shocked at anything I do."

I nodded and knocked on the door.

Baston opened it and poured out into the hall. His eyes were as red as the maraschino cherries in his Manhattan. He teetered back and forth regarding us very gravely. He squinted at my square-cut homburg hat and Sir Guy's moustache.

"Aha," he intoned. "The Walrus and the Carpenter."

I introduced Sir Guy.

"Welcome," said Baston, gesturing us inside with over-elaborate courtesy.

He stumbled after us into the garish parlor.

I stared at the crowd that moved restlessly through the fog of cigarette smoke.

It was the shank of the evening for this mob. Every hand held a drink. Every face held a slightly hectic flush. Over in one corner the piano was going full blast, but the imperious strains of the *March* from *The Love for Three Oranges* couldn't drown out the profanity from the crap game in the other corner.

Prokofieff had no chance against African polo, and one set of ivories rattled louder than the other.

Sir Guy got a monocle-full right away. He saw LaVerne Gonnister, the poetess, hit Hymie Kralik in the eye. He saw Hymie sit down on the floor and cry until Dick Pool accidentally stepped on his stomach as he walked through to the dining room for a drink.

He heard Nadia Vilinoff, the commercial artist, tell Johnny Odcutt that she thought his tattooing was in dreadful taste, and he saw Barclay Melton crawl under the dining room table with Johnny Odcutt's wife.

His zoological observations might have continued indefinitely if Lester Baston hadn't stepped to the center of the room and called for silence by dropping a vase on the floor.

"We have distinguished visitors in our midst," bawled Lester, waving his empty glass in our direction. "None other than the Walrus and the Carpenter. The Walrus is Sir Guy Hollis, a something-or-other from the British Embassy. The Carpenter, as you all know, is our own John Carmody, the prominent dispenser of libido liniment."

He turned and grabbed Sir Guy by the arm, dragging him to the middle of the carpet. For a moment I thought Hollis might object, but a quick wink reassured me. He was prepared for this.

"It is our custom, Sir Guy," said Baston, loudly, "to subject our new friends to a little cross-examination. Just a little formality at these very formal gatherings, you understand. Are you prepared to answer questions?"

Sir Guy nodded and grinned.

"Very well," Baston muttered. "Friends—I give you this bundle from Britain. Your witness."

Then the ribbing started. I meant to listen, but at that moment Lydia Dare saw me and dragged me off into the vestibule for one of those Darling-I-waited-for-your-call-all-day routines.

By the time I got rid of her and went back, the impromptu quiz session was in full swing. From the attitude of the crowd, I gathered that Sir Guy was doing all right for himself.

Then Baston himself interjected a question that upset the apple-cart.

"And what, may I ask, brings you to our midst tonight? What is your mission, oh Walrus?"

"I'm looking for Jack the Ripper."

Nobody laughed.

Perhaps it struck them all the way it did me. I glanced at my neighbors and began to *wonder*.

LaVerne Gonnister. Hymie Kralik. Harmless. Dick Pool. Nadia Vilinoff.

Johnny Odcutt and his wife. Barclay Melton. Lydia Dare. All harmless.

But what a forced smile on Dick Pool's face! And that sly, self-conscious smirk that Barclay Melton wore!

Oh, it was absurd, I grant you. But for the first time I saw these people in a new light. I wondered about their lives—their secret lives beyond the scenes of parties.

How many of them were playing a part, concealing something?

Who here would worship Hecate and grant that horrid goddess the dark boon of blood?

Even Lester Baston might be masquerading.

The mood was upon us all, for a moment. I saw questions flicker in the circle of eyes around the room.

Sir Guy stood there, and I could swear he was fully conscious of the situation he'd created, and enjoyed it.

I wondered idly just what was *really* wrong with him. Why he had this odd fixation concerning Jack the Ripper. Maybe he was hiding secrets, too. . . .

Baston, as usual, broke the mood. He burlesqued it.

"The Walrus isn't kidding, friends," he said. He slapped Sir Guy on the back and put his arm around him as he orated. "Our English cousin is really on the trail of the fabulous Jack the Ripper. You all remember Jack the Ripper, I presume? Quite a cut-up in the old days, as I recall. Really had some ripping good times when he went out on a tear.

"The Walrus has some idea that the Ripper is still alive, probably prowling around Chicago with a Boy Scout knife. In fact—" Baston paused impressively and shot it out in a rasping stage whisper—"in fact, he has reason to believe that Jack the Ripper might even be right here in our midst tonight."

There was the expected reaction of giggles and grins. Baston eyed Lydia Dare reprovingly. "You girls needn't laugh," he smirked. "Jack the Ripper might be a woman, too, you know. Sort of a Jill the Ripper."

"You mean you actually suspect one of us?" shrieked LaVerne Gonnister, simpering up to Sir Guy. "But that Jack the Ripper person disappeared ages ago, didn't he? In 1888?"

"Aha!" interrupted Baston. "How do you know so much about it, young lady? Sounds suspicious! Watch her, Sir Guy—she may not be as young as she appears. These lady poets have dark pasts."

The tension was gone, the mood was shattered, and the whole thing was beginning to degenerate into a trivial party joke. The man who had played the *March* was eyeing the piano with a *scherzo* gleam in his eye that augured ill for Prokofieff. Lydia Dare was glancing at the kitchen, waiting to make a break for another drink.

Then Baston caught it.

"Guess what?" he yelled. "The Walrus has a gun."

His embracing arm had slipped and encountered the hard outline of the gun in Sir Guy's pocket. He snatched it out before Hollis had the opportunity to protest.

I stared hard at Sir Guy, wondering if this thing had carried far enough.

But he flicked a wink my way and I remembered he had told me not to be alarmed.

So I waited as Baston broached a drunken inspiration.

"Let's play fair with our friend the Walrus," he cried. "He came all the way from England to our party on this mission. If none of you is willing to confess, I suggest we give him a chance to find out—the hard way."

"What's up?" asked Johnny Odcutt.

"I'll turn out the lights for one minute. Sir Guy can stand here with his gun. If anyone in this room is the Ripper he can either run for it or take the opportunity to—well, eradicate his pursuer. Fair enough?"

It was even sillier than it sounds, but it caught the popular fancy. Sir Guy's protests went unheard in the ensuing babble. And before I could stride over and put in my two cents' worth, Lester Baston had reached the light switch.

"Don't anybody move," he announced, with fake solemnity. "For one minute we will remain in darkness—perhaps at the mercy of a killer. At the end of that time, I'll turn up the lights again and look for bodies. Choose your partners, ladies and gentlemen."

The lights went out.

Somebody giggled.

I heard footsteps in the darkness. Mutterings.

A hand brushed my face.

The watch on my wrist ticked violently. But even louder, rising above it, I heard another thumping. The beating of my heart.

Absurd. Standing in the dark with a group of tipsy fools. And yet there was real terror lurking here, rustling through the velvet blackness.

Jack the Ripper prowled in darkness like this. And Jack the Ripper had a knife. Jack the Ripper had a madman's brain and a madman's purpose.

But Jack the Ripper was dead, dead and dust these many years—by every human law.

Only there are no human laws when you feel yourself in the darkness, when the darkness hides and protects and the outer mask slips off your face and you feel something welling up within you, a brooding shapeless purpose that is brother to the blackness.

Sir Guy Hollis shrieked.

There was a grisly thud.

Baston put the lights on.

Everybody screamed.

Sir Guy Hollis lay sprawled on the floor in the center of the room. The gun was still clutched in his hand.

I glanced at the faces, marveling at the variety of expressions human beings can assume when confronting horror.

All the faces were present in the circle. Nobody had fled. And yet Sir Guy Hollis lay there.

LaVerne Gonnister was wailing and hiding her face.

"All right."

Sir Guy rolled over and jumped to his feet. He was smiling.

"Just an experiment, eh? If Jack the Ripper *were* among those present, and thought I had been murdered, he would have betrayed himself in some way when the lights went on and he saw me lying there.

"I am convinced of your individual and collective innocence. Just a gentle spoof, my friends."

Hollis stared at the goggling Baston and the rest of them crowding in behind him.

"Shall we leave, John?" he called to me. "It's getting late, I think."

Turning, he headed for the closet. I followed him. Nobody said a word.

It was a pretty dull party after that.

3

I met Sir Guy the following evening as we agreed, on the corner of Twenty-Ninth and South Halsted.

After what had happened the night before, I was prepared for almost anything. But Sir Guy seemed matter-of-fact enough as he stood huddled against a grimy doorway and waited for me to appear.

"Boo!" I said, jumping out suddenly. He smiled. Only the betraying gesture of his left hand indicated that he'd instinctively reached for his gun when I startled him.

"All ready for our wild-goose chase?" I asked.

"Yes." He nodded. "I'm glad that you agreed to meet me without asking questions," he told me. "It shows you trust my judgment." He took my arm and edged me along the street slowly.

"It's foggy tonight, John," said Sir Guy Hollis. "Like London."

I nodded.

"Cold, too, for November."

I nodded again and half-shivered my agreement.

"Curious," mused Sir Guy. "London fog and November. The place and the time of the Ripper murders."

I grinned through darkness. "Let me remind you, Sir Guy, that this isn't London, but Chicago. And it isn't November, 1888. It's over fifty years later."

Sir Guy returned my grin, but without mirth. "I'm not so sure, at that," he murmured. "Look about you. Those tangled alleys and twisted streets. They're like the East End. Mitre Square. And surely they are as ancient as fifty years, at least."

"You're in the black neighborhood of South Clark Street," I said shortly. "And why you dragged me down here I still don't know."

"It's a hunch," Sir Guy admitted. "Just a hunch on my part, John. I want to wander around down here. There's the same geographical conformation in these streets as in those courts where the Ripper roamed and slew. That's where we'll find him, John. Not in the bright lights, but down here in the darkness. The darkness where he waits and crouches."

"Isn't that why you brought a gun?" I asked. I was unable to keep a trace of sarcastic nervousness from my voice. All this talk, this incessant obsession with Jack the Ripper, got on my nerves more than I cared to admit.

"We may need a gun," said Sir Guy, gravely. "After all, tonight is the appointed night."

I sighed. We wandered on through the foggy, deserted streets. Here and there a dim light burned above a gin-mill doorway. Otherwise, all was darkness and shadow. Deep, gaping alleyways loomed as we proceeded down a slanting side street.

We crawled through that fog, alone and silent, like two tiny maggots floundering within a shroud.

"Can't you see there's not a soul around these streets?" I said.

"He's bound to come," said Sir Guy. "He'll be drawn here. This is what I've been looking for. A *genius loci*. An evil spot that attracts evil. Always, when he slays, it's in the slums.

"You see, that must be one of his weaknesses. He has a fascination for squalor. Besides, the women he needs for sacrifice are more easily found in the dives and stewpots of a great city."

"Well, let's go into one of the dives or stewpots," I suggested. "I'm cold. Need a drink. This damned fog gets into your bones. You Britishers can stand it, but I like warmth and dry heat."

We emerged from our sidestreet and stood upon the threshold of an alley.

Through the white clouds of mist ahead, I discerned a dim blue light, a naked bulb dangling from a beer sign above an alley tavern.

"Let's take a chance," I said. "I'm beginning to shiver."

"Lead the way," said Sir Guy. I led him down the alley passage. We halted before the door of the dive.

"What are you waiting for?" he asked.

"Just looking in," I told him. "This is a rough neighborhood, Sir Guy. Never know what you're liable to run into. And I'd prefer we didn't get into the wrong company. Some of these places resent white customers."

"Good idea, John."

I finished my inspection through the doorway. "Looks deserted," I murmured. "Let's try it."

We entered a dingy bar. A feeble light flickered above the counter and railing, but failed to penetrate the further gloom of the back booths.

A gigantic black lolled across the bar. He scarcely stirred as we came in, but his eyes flicked open quite suddenly and I knew he noted our presence and was judging us.

"Evening," I said.

He took his time before replying. Still sizing us up. Then, he grinned.

"Evening, gents. What's your pleasure?"

"Gin," I said. "Two gins. It's a cold night."

"That's right, gents."

He poured, I paid, and took the glasses over to one of the booths. We wasted no time in emptying them.

I went over to the bar and got the bottle. Sir Guy and I poured ourselves another drink. The big man went back into his doze, with one wary eye half-open against any sudden activity.

The clock over the bar ticked on. The wind was rising outside, tearing the shroud of fog to ragged shreds. Sir Guy and I sat in the warm booth and drank our gin.

He began to talk, and the shadows crept up about us to listen.

He rambled a great deal. He went over everything he'd said in the office when I met him, just as though I hadn't heard it before. The poor devils with obsessions are like that.

I listened very patiently. I poured Sir Guy another drink. And another.

But the liquor only made him more talkative. How he did run on! About ritual killings and prolonging the life unnaturally—the whole fantastic tale came out again. And of course, he maintained his unyielding conviction that the Ripper was abroad tonight.

I suppose I was guilty of goading him.

"Very well," I said, unable to keep the impatience from my voice. "Let us say that your theory is correct—even though we must overlook every natural law and swallow a lot of superstition to give it any credence.

"But let us say, for the sake of argument, that you are right. Jack the Ripper was a man who discovered how to prolong his own life through making human sacrifices. He did travel around the world as you believe. He is in Chicago now and is planning to kill. In other words, let us suppose that everything you claim is gospel truth. So what?"

"What do you mean, 'so what'?" said Sir Guy.

"I mean—so what?" I answered him. "If all this is true, it still doesn't prove that by sitting down in a dingy gin-mill on the South Side, Jack the Ripper is going to walk in here and let you kill him, or turn him over to the police. And come to think of it, I don't even know now just what you intend to *do* with him if you ever did find him."

Sir Guy gulped his gin. "I'd capture the bloody swine," he said. "Capture him and turn him over to the government, together with all the papers and documentary evidence I've collected against him over a period of many years. I've spent a fortune investigating this affair, I tell you, a fortune! His capture will mean the solution of hundreds of unsolved crimes, of that I am convinced."

In vino veritas. Or was all this babbling the result of too much gin? It didn't matter. Sir Guy Hollis had another. I sat there and wondered what to do with him. The man was rapidly working up to a climax of hysterical drunkenness.

"That's enough," I said, putting out my hand as Sir Guy reached for the half-emptied bottle again. "Let's call a cab and get out of here. It's getting late and it doesn't look as though your elusive friend is going to put in his appearance. Tomorrow, if I were you, I'd plan to turn all those papers and documents over to the FBI. If you're so convinced of the truth of your theory, they are competent to make a very thorough investigation, and find your man."

"No." Sir Guy was drunkenly obstinate. "No cab."

"But let's get out of here anyway," I said, glancing at my watch. "It's past midnight."

He sighed, shrugged, and rose unsteadily. As he started for the door, he tugged the gun free from his pocket.

"Here, give me that!" I whispered. "You can't walk around the street brandishing that thing."

I took the gun and slipped it inside my coat. Then I got hold of his right arm and steered him out of the door. The black man didn't look up as we departed.

We stood shivering in the alleyway. The fog had increased. I couldn't see either end of the alley from where we stood. It was cold. Damp. Dark. Fog or no fog, a little wind was whispering secrets to the shadows at our backs.

Sir Guy, despite his incapacity, still stared apprehensively at the alley, as though he expected to see a figure approaching.

Disgust got the better of me.

"Childish foolishness," I snorted. "Jack the Ripper, indeed! I call this carrying a hobby too far."

"Hobby?" He faced me. Through the fog I could see his distorted face. "You call this a hobby?"

"Well, what is it?" I grumbled. "Just why else are you so interested in tracking down this mythical killer?"

My arm held his. But his stare held me.

"In London," he whispered. "In 1888 . . . one of those nameless drabs the Ripper slew . . . was my mother."

"What?"

"Later I was recognized by my father, and legitimatized. We swore to give our lives to find the Ripper. My father was the first to search. He died in Hollywood in 1926—on the trail of the Ripper. They said he was stabbed by an unknown assailant in a brawl. But I knew who that assailant was.

"So I've taken up his work, do you see, John? I've carried on. And I will carry on until I do find him and kill him with my own hands."

I believed him then. He wouldn't give up. He wasn't just a drunken babbler any more. He was as fanatical, as determined, as relentless as the Ripper himself.

Tomorrow he'd be sober. He'd continue the search. Perhaps he'd turn those papers over to the FBI. Sooner or later, with such persistence—and with his motive—he'd be successful. I'd always known he had a motive.

"Let's go," I said, steering him down the alley.

"Wait a minute," said Sir Guy. "Give me back my gun." He lurched a little. "I'd feel better with the gun on me."

He pressed me into the dark shadows of a little recess.

I tried to shrug him off, but he was insistent.

"Let me carry the gun, now, John," he mumbled.

"All right," I said.

I reached into my coat, brought my hand out.

"But that's not a gun," he protested. "That's a knife."

"I know."

I bore down on him swiftly.

"John!" he screamed.

"Never mind the 'John,'" I whispered, raising the knife. "Just call me . . . Jack."

Charles L. Grant

If Damon Comes

Charles L. Grant is the most important anthologist of horror fiction since August Derleth in the U.S., principally for his reprint works and for his original series, *Shadows*, annually nominated for the World Fantasy Award as best collection of the year (and often the winner, or the source of the short fiction winner). Grant is a prolific novelist and short story writer of the company of Ramsey Campbell and Stephen King and a popular figure among fans of horror fiction for his novels and stories of Oxrun Station, an imaginary Connecticut town (based to a certain extent upon Lovecraft's Dunwich and Arkham, from the Cthulhu mythos stories). "If Damon Comes" is one of the finest Oxrun stories. Grant is at his best in the short form, as here, and is a salient example of the traditional horror writer of his generation, initially influenced by Bradbury (primarily . . . then Bloch and Leiber and Matheson— all short fiction writers), then in the mid-seventies breaking into the novel form during the great commercial boom in horror.

Fog, nightbreath of the river, luring without whispering in the thick crown of an elm, huddling without creaking around the base of a chimney; it drifted past porch lights, and in passing blurred them, dropped over the streetlights, and in dropping grayed them. It crept in with midnight to stay until dawn, and there was no wind to bring the light out of hiding.

Frank shivered and drew his raincoat's collar closer around his neck, held it closed with one hand while the other wiped at the pricks of moisture that clung to his cheeks, his short dark hair. He whistled once, loudly, but in listening heard nothing, not even an echo. He stamped his feet against the November cold and moved to the nearest corner, squinted and saw nothing. He knew the cat was gone, had known it from the moment he had seen the saucer still brimming with milk on the back porch. Damon had been sitting beside it, hands folded, knees pressed tightly together, elbows tucked into his sides. He was cold, but refused to acknowledge it, and Frank had only tousled his son's softly brown hair, squeezed his shoulder once and went inside to say good-bye to his wife.

And now . . . now he walked, through the streets of Oxrun Station, looking for an animal he had seen only once—a half-breed Siamese with a milk white face—whistling like a fool afraid of the dark, searching for the note that would bring the animal running.

And in walking, he was unpleasantly reminded of a night the year before, when he had had one drink too many at someone's party, made one amorous boast too many in someone's ear, and had ended up on a street corner with a woman he knew only vaguely. They had kissed once and long, and once broken, he had turned around to see Damon staring up at him. The boy had turned, had fled, and Frank had stayed away most of the night, not knowing what Susan had heard, fearing more what Damon had thought.

It had been worse than horrid facing the boy again, but Damon had acted as though nothing had happened; and the guilt passed as the months passed, and the wondering why his son had been out in the first place.

He whistled. Crouched and snapped his fingers at the dark of some shrubbery. Then he straightened and blew out a deeply held breath. There was no cat, there were no cars, and he finally gave in to his aching feet and sore back and headed for home. Quickly. Watching the fog tease the road before him, cut it sharply off behind.

It wasn't fair, he thought, his hands shoved in his pockets, his shoulders hunched as though expecting a blow. Damon, in his short eight years, had lost two dogs already to speeders, a canary to some disease he couldn't even pronounce, and two brothers stillborn—it was getting to be a problem. *He* was getting to be a problem, fighting each day that he had to go to school, whining and weeping whenever vacations came around and trips were planned.

He'd asked Doc Simpson about it when Damon turned seven. Dependency, he was told; clinging to the only three things left in his life—his short, short life—that he still believed to be constant: his home, his mother . . . and Frank.

And Frank had kissed a woman on a corner and Damon had seen him.

Frank shuddered and shook his head quickly, remembering how the boy had come to the office at least once a day for the next three weeks, saying nothing, just standing on the sidewalk looking in through the window. Just for a moment. Long enough to be sure that his father was still there.

Once home, then, Frank shed his coat and hung it on the rack by the front door. A call, a muffled reply, and he took the stairs two at a time and trotted down the hall to Damon's room set over the kitchen.

"Sorry, old pal," he said with a shrug as he made himself a place on the edge of the mattress. "I guess he went home."

Damon, small beneath the flowered quilt, innocent from behind long curling lashes, shook his head sharply. "No," he said. "This is home. It is, Dad, it really is."

Frank scratched at the back of his neck. "Well, I guess he didn't think of it quite that way."

"Maybe he got lost, huh? It's awfully spooky out there. Maybe he's afraid to come out of where he's hiding."

"A cat's never—" He stopped as soon as he saw the expression on the boy's thin face. Then he nodded and broke out a rueful smile, "Well, maybe you're right, pal. Maybe the fog messed him up a little." Damon's hand crept into his, and he squeezed it while thinking that the boy was too thin by far; it made his head look ungainly. "In the morning," he promised. "In the morning. If he's not back by then, I'll take the day off and we'll hunt him together."

Damon nodded solemnly, withdrew the hand and pulled the quilt up to his chin. "When's mom coming home?"

"In a while. It's Friday, you know. She's always late on Fridays. And Saturdays." And, he thought, Wednesdays and Thursdays, too.

Damon nodded again. And, as Frank reached the door and switched off the light: "Dad, does she sing pretty?"

"Like a bird, pal," he said, grinning. "Like a bird."

The voice was small in the dark: "I love you, dad."

Frank swallowed hard, and nodded before he realized the boy couldn't see him. "Well, pal, it seems I love you, too. Now you'd better get some rest."

"I thought you were going to get lost in the fog."

Frank stopped the move to close the door. He'd better get some rest himself, he thought; that sounded like a threat.

"Not me," he finally said. "You'd always come for me, right?"

"Right, dad."

Frank grinned, closed the door, and wandered through the small house for nearly half an hour before finding himself in the kitchen, his hands waving at his sides for something to do. Coffee. No. He'd already had too much of that today. But the walk had chilled him, made his bones seem brittle. Warm milk, maybe, and he opened the refrigerator, stared, then took out a container and poured half its contents into a pot. He stood by the stove, every few seconds stirring a finger through the milk to check its progress. Stupid cat, he thought; there ought to be a law against doing something like that to a small boy that never hurt anyone, never had anyone to hurt.

He poured himself a glass, smiling when he didn't spill a drop, but he refused to turn around and look up at the clock; instead, he stared at the flames as he finished the second glass, wondering what it would be like to stick his finger into the fires. He read somewhere . . . he thought he'd read somewhere that the blue near the center was the hottest part and it wasn't so bad elsewhere. His hand wavered, but he changed his mind, not wanting to risk a burn on something he only thought he had read; besides, he decided as he headed into the living room, the way things were going these days, he probably had it backward.

He sat in an armchair flanking the television, took out a magazine from the rack at his side and had just found the table of contents when he heard a car door slam in the drive. He waited, looked up and smiled when the front door swung open and Susan rushed in. She blew him a distant kiss, mouthed *I'll be back in a second*, and ran up the stairs. She was much shorter than he, her hair waist-long black and left free to fan in the wind of her own making. She'd been taking vocal lessons for several years now, and when they'd moved to the Station when Damon was five, she had landed a job singing at the Chancellor Inn. Torch songs, love songs, slow songs, sinner songs; she was liked well enough to be asked to stay on after the first night, but she began so late that Damon had never heard her. And for the last six months, the two-nights-a-week became four, and Frank became adept at cooking supper.

When she returned, her make-up was gone and she was in a shimmering green robe. She flopped on the sofa opposite him and rubbed her knees, her thighs, her upper arms. "If that creep drummer tries to pinch me again, so help me I'll castrate him."

"That is hardly the way for a lady to talk," he said, smiling. "If you're not careful, I'll have to punish you. Whips at thirty paces."

In the old days—the very old days, he thought—she would have laughed and entered a game that would last for nearly an hour. Lately, however, and tonight, she only frowned at him as though she were dealing with a dense, unlettered child. He ignored it, and listened politely as she detailed her evening, the customers, the compliments, the raise she was looking for so she could buy her own car.

"You don't need a car," he said without thinking.

"But aren't you tired of walking home every night?"

He closed the magazine and dropped it on the floor. "Lawyers, my dear, are a sedentary breed. I could use the exercise."

"If you didn't work so late on those damned briefs," she said without looking at him, "and came to bed on time, I'd give you all the exercise you need."

He looked at his watch. It was going on two.

"The cat's gone."

"Oh no," she said. "No wonder you look so tired. You go out after him?"

He nodded, and she rolled herself suddenly into a sitting position. "Not with Damon."

"No. He was in bed when I came home."

She said nothing more, only examined her nails. He watched her closely, the play of her hair falling over her face, the squint that told him her contact lenses were still on her dresser. And he knew she meant: *did you take Damon with you?* She was asking if Damon had followed him. Like the night in the fog, with the woman; like the times at the office; like the dozens of other instances when the boy just happened to show up at the courthouse, in the park while Frank was eating lunch under a tree, at a nearby friend's house late one evening, claiming to have had a nightmare and the sitter wouldn't help him.

Like a shadow.

Like a conscience.

"Are you going to replace it?" He blinked. "The cat, stupid. Are you going to get him a new cat?"

He shook his head. "We've had too much bad luck with animals. I don't think he could take it again."

She swung herself off the sofa and stood in front of him, her hands on her hips, her lips taut, her eyes narrowed. "You don't care about him, do you?"

"What?"

"He follows you around like a goddamn pet because he's afraid of losing you, and you won't even buy him a lousy puppy or something. You're something else again, Frank, you really are. I work my tail trying to help—"

"My salary is plenty good enough," he said quickly.

"—this family and you're even trying to get me to stop that, too."

He shoved himself to his feet, his chest brushing against hers and forcing her back. "Listen," he said tightly. "I don't care if you sing your heart out a million times a week, lady, but when it starts to interfere with your duties here—"

"My *duties*?"

"—then yes, I'll do everything I can to make sure you stay home when you're supposed to."

"You're raising your voice. You'll wake Damon."

The argument was familiar, and old, and so was the rage he felt stiffening his muscles. But this time she wouldn't stop when she saw his anger. She kept on, and on, and he didn't even realize it when his hand lifted and struck her across the cheek. She stumbled back a step, whirled to run out of the room, and stopped.

Damon was standing at the foot of the stairs.

He was sucking his thumb.

He was staring at his father.

"Go to bed, son," Frank said quietly. "Everything's all right."

For the next week the tension in the house was proverbially knife-cutting thick. Damon stayed up as late as he could, sitting by his father as they watched television together or read from the boy's favorite books. Susan remained close, but not touching, humming to herself and playing with her son whenever he left—for the moment—his father's side; each time, however, her smile was more forced, her laughter more strained, and it was apparent to Frank that Damon was merely tolerating her, nothing more. That puzzled him. It was he who had struck her, not the other way around, and the boy's loyalty should have been thrown into his mother's camp. Yet it hadn't. And it was apparent that Susan was growing more resentful of the fact each day. Each hour. Each time Damon walked silently to Frank's side and slid his hand around the man's waist, or into his palm, or into his hip pocket.

He began showing up at the office again, until one afternoon when Susan skidded the car to a halt at the curb and ran out, grabbed the boy and practically threw him, arms and legs thrashing, into the front seat. Frank raced from his desk and out the front door, leaned over and rapped at the window until Susan lowered it.

"What the hell are you doing?" he whispered, with a glance to the boy.

"You hit me, or had you forgotten," she whispered back. "And there's my son's alienation of affection."

He almost straightened. "That's lawyer talk, Susan," he said.

"Not here," she answered. "Not in front of the boy."

He stepped back quickly as the car growled away from the curb, walked in a daze to his desk and sat there, chin in one palm, staring out the window as the afternoon darkened and a faint drizzle began to fall. His secretary muttered something about a court case the following morning, and Frank nodded until she stared at him, gathered her purse and raincoat and left hurriedly. He continued to nod, not knowing the movement, trying to understand what he had done, what both of them had done to bring themselves to this moment. Ambition, surely. A conflict of generations where women were homebodies and women had careers; where men tried to adjust when they couldn't have both. But he had tried, he told himself . . . or he thought he had, until the dishes began to pile up and the dust stayed on the furniture and Damon said *does she sing pretty?*

It's always the children who get hurt, he thought angrily.

Held that idea in early December when the separation papers had been prepared and he stood on the front porch watching his car, his wife, and his son drive away from Oxrun Station south toward the city. Damon's face was in the rear window, nose flat, palms flat, hair pressed down over his forehead. He waved, and Frank answered.

I love you, dad.

Frank wiped a hand under his nose and went back inside, searched the house for some liquor and, in failing, went straight to bed where he watched the moonshadows make monsters of the curtains.

"Dad," the boy said, "do I have to go with mommy?"

"I'm afraid so. The judge . . . well, he knows better, believe it or not, what's best right now. Don't worry, pal. I'll see you at Christmas. It won't be forever."

"I don't like it, dad. I'll run away."

"No! You'll do what your mother tells you, you hear me? You behave yourself and go to school every day, and I'll . . . call you whenever I can."

"The city doesn't like me, dad. I want to stay at the Station."

Frank said nothing.

"It's because of the lady, isn't it?"

He had stared, but Susan's back was turned, bent over a suitcase that would not close once it had sprung open again by the front door.

"What are you talking about?" he'd said harshly.

"I told," Damon said as though it were nothing. "You weren't supposed to do that."

When Susan straightened, her smile was grotesque.

And when they had driven away, Damon had said *I love you, dad.*

Frank woke early, made himself breakfast and stood at the back door, looking out into the yard. There was a fog again, nothing unusual as the Connecticut weather fought to stabilize into winter. But as he sipped at his coffee, thinking how large the house had become, how large and how empty, he saw a movement beside the cherry tree in the middle of the yard. The fog swirled, but he was sure . . .

He yanked open the door and shouted: "Damon!"

The fog closed, and he shook his head. Easy, pal, he told himself; you're not cracking up yet.

Days.

Nights.

He called Susan regularly, twice a week at preappointed times. But as Christmas came and Christmas went, she became more terse, and his son more sullen.

"He's getting fine grades, Frank, I'm seeing to that."

"He sounds terrible."

"He's losing a little weight, that's all. Picks up colds easily. It takes a while, Frank, to get used to the city."

"He doesn't like the city."

"It's his home. He will."

In mid-January Susan did not answer the phone and finally, in desperation, he called the school, was told that Damon had been in the hospital for nearly a week. The nurse thought it was something like pneumonia.

When he arrived that night, the waiting room was crowded with drab bundles of scarves and overcoats, whispers and moans and a few muffled sobs. Susan was standing by the window, looking out at the lights far colder than stars. She didn't turn when she heard him, didn't answer when he demanded to know why she had not contacted him. He grabbed her shoulder and spun her around; her eyes were dull, her face pinched with red hints of cold.

"All right," she said. "All right, Frank, it's because I didn't want you to upset him."

"What the hell are you talking about?"

"He would have seen you and he would have wanted to go back to Oxrun." Her eyes narrowed. "This is his home, Frank! He's got to learn to live with it."

"I'll get a lawyer."

She smiled. "Do that. You do that, Frank."

He didn't have to. He saw Damon a few minutes later and could not stay more than a moment. The boy was in dim light and almost invisible, too thin to be real beneath the clear plastic tent and the tubes and the monitors . . . too frail, the doctor said in professional conciliation, too frail for too long, and Frank remembered the day on the porch with the saucer of milk when he had thought the same thing and had thought nothing of it.

He returned after the funeral, all anger gone. He had accused Susan of murder, knowing at the time how foolish it had been, but feeling better for it in his own absolution. He had apologized. Had been, for the moment, forgiven.

Had stepped off the train, had wept, had taken a deep breath and decided to live on.

Returned to the office the following day, piled folders onto his desk and hid behind them for most of the morning. He looked up only once, when his secretary tried to explain about a new client's interest, and saw around her waist the indistinct form of his son peering through the window.

"Damon," he muttered, brushed the woman to one side and ran out to the sidewalk. A fog encased the road whitely, but he could see nothing, not even a car, not even the blinking amber light at the nearest intersection.

Immediately after lunch he dialed Susan's number, stared at the receiver when there was no answer and returned it to the cradle. Wondering.

"You look pale," his secretary said softly. She pointed with a pencil at his desk. "You've already done a full day's work. Why don't you go home and lie down? I can lock up. I don't mind."

He smiled, turned as she held his coat for him, touched her cheek . . . and froze.

Damon was in the window.

No, he told himself . . . and Damon was gone.

He rested for two days, returned to work and lost himself in a battle over a will probated by a judge he thought nothing less than senile, to be charitable. He tried calling Susan again, and again received no answer.

And Damon would not leave him alone.

When there was fog, rain, clouds, wind . . . he would be there by the window, there by the cherry tree, there in the darkest corner of the porch.

He knew it was guilt, for not fighting hard enough to keep his son with him, thinking that if he had the boy might still be alive; seeing his face everywhere and the accusations that if the boy loved him, why wasn't he loved just as much in return?

By February's end he decided it was time to make a friendly call on a fellow professional, a doctor who shared the office building with him. It wasn't so much the faces that he saw—he had grown somewhat accustomed to them and assumed they would vanish in time—but that morning there had been snow on the ground; and in the snow by the cherry tree the footprints of a small boy. When he brought the doctor to the yard to show him, they were gone.

"You're quite right, Frank. You're feeling guilty. But not because of the boy in and of himself. The law and the leanings of most judges are quite clear—you couldn't be expected to keep him at his age. You're still worrying yourself about that woman you kissed and the fact that Damon saw you; and the fact that you think you could have saved his life somehow, even if the doctors couldn't; and lastly, the fact that you weren't able to give him things like pets, like that cat. None of it is your fault, really. It's merely something unpleasant you'll have to face up to. Now."

Though he didn't feel all that much better, Frank appreciated the calm that swept over him when the talk was done and they had parted. He worked hard for the rest of the day, for the rest of the week, but he knew that it was not guilt and it was not his imagination and it was not anything the doctor would be able to explain away when he opened his door on Saturday morning and found, lying carefully atop his newspaper, the white-faced Siamese. Dead. Its neck broken.

He stumbled back over the threshold, whirled around and raced into the downstairs bathroom where he fell onto his knees beside the bowl and lost his breakfast. The tears were acid, the sobs like blows to his lungs and stomach, and by the time he had pulled himself together, he knew what was happening.

The doctor, the secretary, even his wife . . . they were all wrong.

There was no guilt.

There was only . . . Damon.

A little boy with large brown eyes who loved his father. Who loved his father so much that he would never leave him. Who loved his father so much that he was going to make sure, absolutely sure, that he would never be alone.

You've been a bad boy, daddy.

Frank stumbled to his feet, into the kitchen, leaned against the back door.

There was a figure by the cherry tree dark and formless; but he knew there was no use running outside. The figure would vanish.

You never did like that cat, daddy. Or the dogs. Or mommy.

The telephone rang. He took his time getting to it, stared at it dumbly for several moments before lifting the receiver. He could see straight down the hall and into the kitchen. He had not turned on the overhead light and, as a consequence, could see through the small panes of the back door to the yard beyond. The air outside was heavy with impending snow. Gray. Almost lifeless.

"Frank? Frank, it's Susan. Frank, I've been thinking . . . about you and me . . . and what happened."

He kept his eyes on the door. "It's done, Sue. Done."

"Frank, I don't know what happened. Honest to God, I was trying, really I was. He was getting the best grades in school, had lots of friends. . . . I even bought him a little dog, a poodle, two weeks before he . . . I don't know what happened, Frank! I woke up this morning and all of a sudden I was so damned *alone*. Frank, I'm frightened. Can . . . can I come home?"

The gray darkened. There was a shadow on the porch, much longer now than the shadow in the yard.

"No," he said.

"He thought about you all the damned time," she said, her voice rising into hysteria. "He tried to run away once, to get back to you."

The shadow filled the panes, the windows on either side, and suddenly there was static on the line and Susan's voice vanished. He dropped the receiver and turned around.

In the front.

Shadows.

He heard the furnace humming, but the house was growing cold.

The lamp in the living room flickered, died, shone brightly for a moment before the bulb shattered.

He was . . . wrong.

God, he was wrong!

Damon . . . Damon didn't love him.

Not since the night on the corner in the fog; not since the night he had not really tried to locate a cat with a milk white face.

Damon knew.

And Damon didn't love him.

He dropped to his hands and knees and searched in the darkness for the receiver, found it and nearly threw it away when the bitterly cold plastic threatened to burn through his fingers.

"Susan!" he shouted. "Susan, dammit, can you hear me?"

A bad boy, daddy.

There was static, but he thought he could hear her crying into the wind.

"Susan . . . Susan, this is crazy, I've no time to explain, but you've got to help me. You've got to do something for me."

Daddy.

"Susan, please . . . he'll be back, I know he will. Don't ask me how, but I know! Listen, you've got to do something for me. Susan, dammit, can you hear me?"

Daddy, I'm—

"For God's sake, Susan, if Damon comes, tell him I'm sorry!"

home.

Manly Wade Wellman

Vandy, Vandy

Manly Wade Wellman was a prolific writer for the pulp magazines in the 1930s and 1940s whose work appeared in many genres. Today he is remembered for that portion of his work, principally from *Weird Tales* magazine, that is horror fiction, and for a series of regional horror tales published in the 1950s in *The Magazine of Fantasy and Science Fiction* (alongside Shirley Jackson's stories and the works of Matheson, Sturgeon and most of the other masters of that decade). Now called the "Silver John" stories and novels, these supernatural tales of an itinerant, John, whose guitar is strung with silver strings, are rich in Southern U.S. folklore and settings. John meets a variety of supernatural evils but perhaps the most typical, and one of Wellman's finest achievements, is the historic warlock of "Vandy, Vandy." Wellman's best stories are collected in *Worse Things Waiting* (1973) and *Who Fears the Devil?* (1963).

N ary name that valley had. Such outside folks as knew about it just said, "Back in yonder," and folks inside said, "Here." The mail truck would drop a few letters in a hollow tree next to a ridge where the trail went up and over and down. Three-four times a year bearded men in homemade clothes and shoes fetched out their makings—clay dishes and pots, mostly—for dealers to sell to the touristers. They toted back coffee, salt, gunpowder, a few nails. Stuff like that.

It was a day's scramble along that ridge trail. I vow, even with my long legs and no load but my silver-strung guitar. The thick, big old trees had never been cut, for lumber nor yet for cleared land. I found a stream, quenched my thirst, and followed it down. Near sunset time, I heard music a-jangling, and headed for that.

Fire shone out through an open cabin door, to where folks sat on a stoop log and front-yard rocks. One had a banjo, another fiddled, and the rest slapped hands so a boy about ten or twelve could jig. Then they spied me and fell quiet. They looked at me, but they didn't know me.

"That was right pretty, ladies and gentlemen," I said, walking in, but nobody remarked.

A long-bearded old man with one suspender and no shoes held the fiddle on his knee. I reckoned he was the grandsire. A younger, shorter-bearded man with the banjo might could be his son. There was a dry old mother, there was the son's plump wife, there was a young yellow-haired girl, and there was that dancing little grandboy.

278

"What can we do for you, young sir?" the old man asked. Not that he sounded like doing aught—mountain folks say that even to the government man who comes hunting a still on their place.

"Why," I said, "I sort of want a place to sleep."

"Right much land to stretch out on down the hollow a piece," said the banjo man.

I tried again. "I was hearing you folks play first part of *Fire in the Mountains.*"

"Is they two parts?" That was the boy, before anyone could silence him.

"Sure enough, son," I said. "I'll play you the second part."

The old man opened his beard, like enough to say wait till I was asked, but I strummed my guitar into second part, best I knew how. Then I played the first part through, and, "You sure God can pick that," said the short-bearded one. "Do it again."

I did it again. When I reached the second part, the fiddle and banjo joined me in. We went round *Fire in the Mountains* one time more, and the lady-folks clapped hands and the boy jigged. When we stopped, the old man made me a nod.

"Sit on that there rock," he said. "What might we call you?"

"My name's John."

"I'm Tewk Millen. Mother, I reckon John's a-tired, coming from outside. Might be he'd relish a gourd of cold water."

"We're just before having a bite," the old lady said to me. "Ain't but just smoke meat and beans, but you're welcome."

"I'm sure enough honored, Mrs. Millen," I said. "But I don't wish to be a trouble to you."

"No trouble," said Mr. Tewk Millen. "Let me make you known to my son Heber and his wife Jill, and this here is their boy Calder."

"Proud to know you, John," they said.

"And my girl Vandy," said Mr. Tewk.

I looked on her hair like yellow corn silk and her eyes like purple violets. "Miss Vandy," I said.

Shy, she dimpled at me. "I know that's a scarce name, Mr. John. I never heard it anywhere but among my kinfolks."

"I have," I said. "It's what brought me here."

Mr. Tewk Millen looked funny above his whiskers. "Thought you was a young stranger-man."

"I heard the name outside, in a song, sir. Somebody allowed the song's known here. I'm a singer, I go a far piece after a good song." I looked around. "Do you folks know that Vandy song?"

"Yes, sir," said little Calder, but the others studied a minute. Mr. Tewk rubbed up a leaf of tobacco into his pipe.

"Calder," he said, "go in and fetch me a chunk of fire to light up with. John, you certain sure you never met my girl Vandy?"

"Sure as can be," I replied him. "Only I can figure how any young fellow might come long miles to meet her."

She stared down at her hands in her lap. "We learnt the song from papa," she half-whispered, "and he learnt it from his papa."

"And my papa learnt it from his," finished Mr. Tewk for her. "I reckon that song goes long years back."

"I'd relish hearing it," I said.

"After you learnt it yourself," said Mr. Tewk, "what would you do then?"

"Go back outside," I said, "and sing it some."

He enjoyed to hear me say that. "Heber," he told his son, "you pick out and I'll scrape this fiddle, and Calder and Vandy can sing it for John."

They played the tune through once without words. The notes came together lonesomely, in what schooled folks call minors. But other folks, better schooled yet, say such tunes come out strange and lonesome because in the ancient times folks had another note-scale from our do-re-mi-fa today. Little Calder piped up, high and young but strong:

> "Vandy, Vandy, I've come to court you,
> Be you rich or be you poor,
> And if you'll kindly entertain me,
> I will love you forever more.
>
> "Vandy, Vandy, I've gold and silver,
> Vandy, Vandy, I've a house and land,
> Vandy, Vandy, I've a world of pleasure,
> I would make you a handsome man. . . ."

He sang that far for the fellow come courting, and Vandy sang back the reply, sweet as a bird:

> "I love a man who's in the army,
> He's been there for seven long years,
> And if he's there for seven years longer,
> I won't court no other dear.
>
> "What care I for your gold and silver,
> What care I for—"

She stopped, and the fiddle and banjo stopped, and it was like the sudden death of sound. The leaves didn't rustle in the trees, nor the fire didn't stir on the hearth inside. They all looked with their mouths half open, where somebody stood with his hands crossed on the gold knob of a black cane and grinned all on one side of his toothy mouth.

Maybe he'd come down the stream trail, maybe he'd dropped from a tree like a possum. He was built slim and spry, with a long coat buttoned to his pointed chin, and brown pants tucked into elastic-sided boots, like what your grand-sire wore. His hands on the cane looked slim and strong. His face, bar its crooked smile, might could be called handsome. His dark brown hair curled like buffalo wool, and his eyes were as shiny pale gray as a new knife. Their gaze crawled all over us, and he laughed a slow, soft laugh.

"I thought I'd stop by," he crooned out, "if I haven't worn out my welcome."

"Oh, *no*, sir!" said Mr. Tewk, quick standing up on his two bare feet, fiddle in hand. "No, sir, Mr. Loden, we're right proud to have you," he jabber-squawked, like a rooster caught by the leg. "You sit down, sir, make yourself easy."

Mr. Loden sat down on the rock Mr. Tewk had got up from, and Mr. Tewk found a place on the stoop log by his wife, nervous as a boy caught stealing apples.

"Your servant, Mrs. Millen," said Mr. Loden. "Heber, you look well, and your good wife. Calder, I brought you candy."

His slim hand offered a bright striped stick, red and yellow. You'd think a country child would snatch it. But Calder took it slow and scared, as he'd take a poison snake. You'd know he'd decline if only he dared, but he didn't dare.

"For you, Mr. Tewk," went on Mr. Loden, "I fetched some of my tobacco, an excellent weed." He handed out a soft brown leather pouch. "Empty your pipe and fill it with this."

"Thank you kindly," said Mr. Tewk, and sighed, and began to do as he'd been ordered.

"Miss Vandy." Mr. Loden's crooning voice petted her name. "I wouldn't venture here without hoping you'd receive a trifle at my hands."

He dangled it from a chain, a gold thing the size of his pink thumbnail. In it shone a white jewel that grabbed the firelight and twinkled red.

"Do me the honor, Miss Vandy, to let it rest on your heart, that I may envy it."

She took the thing and sat with it between her soft little hands. Mr. Loden's eye-knives turned on me.

"Now," he said, "we come round to the stranger within your gates."

"We come around to me," I agreed him, hugging my guitar on my knees. "My name's John, sir."

"Where are you from, John?" It was sudden, almost fierce, like a lawyer in court.

"From nowhere," I said.

"Meaning, from everywhere," he supplied me. "What do you do?"

"I wander," I said. "I sing songs. I mind my business and watch my manners."

"Touché!" he cried out in a foreign tongue, and smiled on that one side of his mouth. "My duties and apologies, John, if my country ways seem rude to a world traveler. No offense meant."

"None taken," I said, and didn't add that country ways are most times polite ways.

"Mr. Loden," put in Mr. Tewk again, "I make bold to offer you what poor rations my old woman's made for us—"

"They're good enough for the best man living," Mr. Loden broke him off. "I'll help Mrs. Millen prepare them. After you, ma'am."

She walked in, and he followed. What he said there was what happened.

"Miss Vandy," he said over his shoulder, "you might help."

She went in, too. Dishes clattered. Through the doorway I saw Mr. Loden fling a tweak of powder in the skillet. The menfolks sat outside and said naught. They might have been nailed down, with stones in their mouths. I studied what might could make a proud, honorable mountain family so scared of a guest, and knew it wouldn't be a natural thing. It would be a thing beyond nature or the world.

Finally little Calder said, "Maybe we'll finish the singing after while," and his voice was a weak young voice now.

"I recollect another song from around here," I said. "About the fair and blooming wife."

Those closed mouths all snapped open, then shut again. Touching the silver strings, I began:

> "There was a fair and blooming wife
>   And of children she had three,
>   She sent them to a Northern school
>   To study gramarie.

> "But the King's men came upon that school,
>   And when sword and rope had done,
>   Of the children three she sent away,
>   Returned to her but one. . . ."

"Supper's made," said Mrs. Millen from inside.

We went in to where there was a trestle table and a clean home-woven cloth and clay dishes set out. Mr. Loden, by the pots at the fire, waved for Mrs. Millen and Vandy to dish up the food.

It wasn't smoke meat and beans I saw on my plate. Whatever it might be, it wasn't that. They all looked at their helps of food, but not even Calder took any till Mr. Loden sat down.

"Why," said Mr. Loden, "one would think you feared poison."

Then Mr. Tewk forked up a bit and put it into his beard. Calder did likewise, and the others. I took a mouthful; sure enough, it tasted good.

"Let me honor your cooking, sir," I told Mr. Loden. "It's like witch magic."

His eyes came on me, and he laughed, short and sharp.

"John, you were singing about the blooming wife," he said. "She had three children who went North to study gramarie. Do you know what gramarie means?"

"Grammar," spoke up Calder. "The right way to talk."

"Hush," whispered his father, and he hushed.

"Why," I replied. "Mr. Loden, I've heard that gramarie is witch stuff, witch knowledge and power. That Northern school could have been at only one place."

"What place, John?" he almost sang under his breath.

"A Massachusetts Yankee town called Salem. Around three hundred years back—"

"Not by so much," said Mr. Loden. "In 1692, John."

Everybody was staring above those steaming plates.

"A preacher-man named Cotton Mather found them teaching the witch stuff to children," I said. "I hear tell they killed twenty folks, mostly the wrong ones, but two-three were sure enough witches."

"George Burroughs," said Mr. Loden, half to himself. "Martha Carrier. And Bridget Bishop. They were real. But others got safe away, and one young child of the three. Somebody owed that child the two young lost lives of his brothers, John."

"I call something else to mind," I said. "They scare young folks with the tale. The one child lived to be a hundred, and his son likewise and a hundred years of life, and his son's son a hundred more. Maybe that's why I thought the witch school at Salem was three hundred years back."

"Not by so much, John," he said again. "Even give that child that got away the age of Calder there, it would be only about two hundred and eighty years, or thereabouts."

He was daring any of Mr. Tewk Millen's family to speak or even breathe heavy, and none took the dare.

"From three hundred, that would leave twenty," I reckoned. "A lot can be done in twenty years, Mr. Loden."

"That's the naked truth," he said, the knives of his eyes on Vandy's young face, and he got up and bowed all round. "I thank you all for your hospitality. I'll come again if I may."

"Yes, sir," said Mr. Tewk in a hurry, but Mr. Loden looked at Vandy and waited.

"Yes, sir," she told him, as if it would choke her.

He took his gold-headed cane, and gazed a hard gaze at me. Then I did a rude thing, but it was all I could think of.

"I don't feel right, Mrs. Millen, not paying for what you gave me," I allowed, getting up myself. From my dungaree pocket I took a silver quarter and dropped it on the table, right in front of Mr. Loden.

"Take it away!" he squeaked, high as a bat, and out of the house he was gone, bat-quick and bat-sudden.

The others gopped after him. Outside the night had fallen, thick as black wool round the cabin. Mr. Tewk cleared his throat.

"John, I hope you're better raised than that," he said. "We don't take money from nobody we bid to our table. Pick it up."

"Yes, sir, I ask pardon."

Putting away the quarter, I felt a mite better. I'd done that one other time with a silver quarter, I'd scared Mr. Onselm almost out of the black art. So Mr. Loden was a witch man, too, and could be scared the same way. I reckon I was foolish for the lack of sense to think it would be as easy as that.

I walked outside, leaving Mrs. Millen and Vandy to do the dishes. The firelight showed me the stoop log to sit on. I touched my guitar strings and began to pick out the *Vandy, Vandy* tune, soft and gentle. After while, Calder came out and sat beside me and sang the words. I liked best the last verse:

"Wake up, wake up! The dawn is breaking.
Wake up, wake up! It's almost day.

"Open up your doors and your divers windows,
See my true love march away. . . ."

"Mr. John," said Calder, "I never made sure what divers windows is."

"That's an old-timey word," I said. "It means different kinds of windows. Another thing proves it's a right old song. A man seven years in the army must have gone to the first war with the English. It lasted longer here in the South than other places—from 1775 to 1782. How old are you, Calder?"

"Rising onto ten."

"Big for your age. A boy your years in 1692 would be a hundred if he lived to 1782, when the English war was near done and somebody or other had been seven years in the army."

"Washington's army," said Calder. "King Washington."

"King who?" I asked.

"Mr. Loden calls him King Washington—the man that hell-drove the English soldiers and rules in his own name town."

So that's what they thought in that valley. I never said that Washington was no king but a president, and that he'd died and gone to his rest when his work was done and his country safe. I kept thinking about somebody a hundred years old in 1782, trying to court a girl whose true love was seven years marched off in the army.

"Calder," I said, "does the *Vandy, Vandy* song tell about your own folks?"

He looked into the cabin. Nobody listened. I struck a chord on the silver strings. He said, "I've heard tell so, Mr. John."

I hushed the strings with my hand, and he talked on:

"I reckon you've heard some about it. That witch child that lived to be a hundred—he come courting a girl named Vandy, but she was a good girl."

"Bad folks sometimes try to court good ones," I said.

"She wouldn't have him, not with all his land and money. And when he pressed her, her soldier man come home, and in his hand was his discharge-writing, and on it King Washington's name. He was free from the war. He was Hosea Tewk, my grandsire some few times removed. And my own grandsire's mother was Vandy Tewk, and my sister is Vandy Millen."

"What about the hundred-year-old witch man?"

Calder looked round again. Then he said, "I reckon he got him some other girl to birth him a son, and we think that son married at another hundred years, and his son is Mr. Loden, the grandson of the first witch man."

"Your grandsire's mother, Vandy Tewk—how old would she be, Calder?"

"She's dead and gone, but she was born the first year her pa was off fighting the Yankees."

Eighteen sixty-one, then. In 1882, end of the second hundred years, she'd have been ripe for courting. "And she married a Millen," I said.

"Yes, sir. Even when the Mr. Loden that lived then tried to court her. But she married Mr. Washington Millen. That was my great-grandsire. He wasn't feared of aught. He was like King Washington."

I picked a silver string. "No witch man got the first Vandy," I reminded him. "Nor yet the second Vandy."

"A witch man wants the Vandy that's here now," said Calder. "Mr. John, I wish you'd steal her away from him."

I got up. "Tell your folks I've gone for a night walk."

"Not to Mr. Loden's." His face was pale beside me. "He won't let you come."

The night was more than black then, it was solid. No sound in it. No life. I won't say I couldn't have stepped off into it, but I didn't. I sat down again. Mr. Tewk spoke my name, then Vandy.

We sat in front of the cabin and spoke about weather and crops. Vandy was at my one side, Calder at the other. We sang—*Dream True*, I recollect, and *The Rebel Soldier*. Vandy sang the sweetest I'd ever heard, but while I played I felt that somebody harked in the blackness. If it was on Yandro Mountain and not in the valley, I'd have feared the Behinder sneaking close, or the Flat under our feet. But Vandy's violet eyes looked happy at me, her rose lips smiled.

Finally Vandy and Mrs. Millen said good night and went into a back room. Heber and his wife and Calder laddered up into the loft. Mr. Tewk offered to make me a pallet bed by the fire.

"I'll sleep at the door," I told him.

He looked at me, at the door. And: "Have it your way," he said.

I pulled off my shoes. I said a prayer and stretched out on the quilt he gave me. But long after the others must have been sleeping, I lay and listened.

Hours afterward, the sound came. The fire was just only a coal ember, red light was soft in the cabin when I heard the snicker. Mr. Loden stooped over me at the door sill.

"I won't let you come in," I said to him.

"Oh, you're awake," he said. "The others are asleep, by my doing. And you can't move, any more than they can."

It was true. I couldn't sit up. I might have been dried into clay, like a frog or a lizard that must wait for the rain.

"Bind," he said above me. "Bind, bind. Unless you can count the stars or the ocean drops, be bound."

It was a spell saying. "From the *Long-Lost Friend*?" I asked.

"Albertus Magnus. The book they say he wrote."

"I've seen the book."

"You'll lie where you are till sunrise. Then—"

I tried to get up. It was no use.

"See this?" He held it to my face. It was my picture, drawn true to how I looked. He had the drawing gift. "At sunrise I'll strike it with this."

He laid the picture on the ground. Then he brought forward his gold-headed cane. He twisted the handle, and out of the cane's inside he drew a blade of pale iron, thin and mean as a snake. There was writing on it, but I couldn't read in that darkness.

"I'll touch my point to your picture," he said. "Then you'll bother Vandy and me no more. I should have done that to Hosea Tewk."

"Hosea Tewk," I said after him, "or Washington Millen."

The tip of his blade stirred in front of my eyes. "Don't say that name, John."

"Washington Millen," I said it again. "Named for George Washington. Did you hate Washington when you knew him?"

He took a long, mean breath, as if cold rain fell on him. "You've guessed what these folks haven't guessed, John."

"I've guessed you're not a witch man's grandson, but a witch woman's son," I said. "You got free from that Salem school in 1692. You've lived near three hundred years, and when they're over, you know where you'll go and burn, forever amen."

His blade hung over my throat, like a wasp over a ripe peach. Then he drew it back. "No," he told himself. "The Millens would know I'd stabbed you. Let them think you died in your sleep."

"You knew Washington," I said again. "Maybe—"

"Maybe I offered him help, and he was foolish enough to refuse it. Maybe—"

"Maybe Washington scared you off from him," I broke in the way he had, "and won his war without your witch magic. And maybe that was bad for you, because the one who'd given you three hundred years expected pay—good hearts turned into bad ones. Then you tried to win Vandy for yourself, the first Vandy."

"A little for myself," he half sang, "but mostly for—"

"Mostly for who gave you three hundred years," I finished for him.

I was tightening and swelling my muscles, trying to pull a-loose from what held me down. I might as well have tried to wear my way through solid rock.

"Vandy," Mr. Loden's voice touched her name. "The third Vandy, the sweetest and the best. She's like a spring day and like a summer night. When I see her with a bucket at the spring or a basket in the garden, my eyes swim, John. It's as if I see a spirit walking past."

"A good spirit," I said. "Your time's short. You want to win her from good ways to bad ways."

"Her voice is like a lark's," he crooned, the blade low in his hand. "It's like wind over a bank of roses and violets. It's like the light of stars turned into music."

"And you want to lead her down into hell," I said.

"Maybe we won't go to hell, or to heaven either. Maybe we'll live and live. Why don't you say something about that, John?"

"I'm thinking," I made answer, and I was. I was trying to remember what I had to remember.

It's in the third part of the Albertus Magnus book Mr. Loden had mentioned, the third part full of holy names he sure enough would never read. I'd seen it, as I'd told him. If the words would come back to me—

Something sent part of them.

"The cross in my right hand," I said, too soft for him to hear, "that I may travel the open land. . . ."

"Maybe three hundred years more," said Mr. Loden, "without anyone like Hosea Tewk, or Washington Millen, or you, John, to stop us. Three hundred years with Vandy, and she'll know the things I know, do the things I do."

I'd been able to twist my right forefinger over my middle one, for the cross in my right hand. I said more words as I remembered:

". . . So must I be loosed and blessed, as the cup and the holy bread. . . ."

Now my left hand could creep along my side, as far as my belt. But it couldn't lift up just yet, because I couldn't think of the rest of the charm.

"The night's black just before dawn," Mr. Loden was saying. "I'll make my fire. When I've done what I'll do, I can step over your dead body, and Vandy's mine."

"Don't you fear Washington?" I asked him, and my left fingertips were in my dungaree pocket.

"Can he come from the place to which he's gone? Washington has forgotten me and our old falling-out."

"Where he is, he remembers you," I said.

Mr. Loden was on his knee. His blade point scratched a circle round him on the ground. The circle held him and the paper with my picture. Then he took a sack from inside his coat, and poured powder along the scratched circle. He stood up, and golden-brown fire jumped up around him.

"Now we begin," he said.

He sketched in the air with his blade. He put his boot toe on my picture. He looked into the golden-brown fire.

"I made my wish before this," he spaced out the words. "I make it now. There was no day when I have not seen my wish fulfilled."

Paler than the fire shone his eyes.

"No son to follow John. No daughter to mourn him."

My fingers in my pocket touched something round and thin. The quarter he'd been scared by, that Mr. Tewk Millen had made me take back.

Mr. Loden spoke names I didn't like to hear. "Haade," he said. "Mikaded. Rakeben. Rika. Tasarith. Modeka."

My hand worried out, and in it the quarter.

"Truth," said Mr. Loden. "Tumch. Here with this image I slay—"

I lifted my left hand three inches and flung the quarter. My heart went rotten with sick sorrow, for it didn't hit Mr. Loden—it fell into the fire—

Then in one place up there shot white smoke, like a steam puff from an engine, and the fire died down everywhere else. Mr. Loden stopped his spell-speaking and wavered back. I saw the glow of his goggling eyes and of his open mouth.

Where the steamy smoke had puffed, it was making a shape.

Taller than a man. Taller than Mr. Loden or me. Wide-shouldered, long-legged, with a dark tail coat and high boots and hair tied back behind the head. It turned, and I saw the brave face, the big, big nose—

"King Washington!" screamed out Mr. Loden, and tried to stab.

But a long hand like a tongs caught his wrist, and I heard the bones break like dry sticks, and Mr. Loden whinnied like a horse that's been bad hurt. That was the grip of the man who'd been America's strongest, who could jump twenty-four feet broad or throw a dollar across the Rappahannock River or wrestle down his biggest soldier.

The other hand came across, flat and stiff, to strike. It sounded like a door a-slamming in a high wind, and Mr. Loden never needed to be struck the second time. His head sagged over widewise. When the grip left his broken wrist, he fell at the booted feet.

I sat up, and stood up. The big nose turned to me, just a second. The head nodded. Friendly. Then it was gone back into steam, into nothing.

I'd said the truth. Where George Washington had been, he'd remembered Mr. Loden. And the silver quarter, with his picture on it, had struck the fire just when Mr. Loden was conjuring with a picture he was making real. And then there had happened what had happened.

A pale streak went up the back sky for the first dawn. There was no fire left, and of the quarter was just a spatter of melted silver. And there was no Mr. Loden, only a mouldy little heap like a rotted-out stump or a hammock or loam or what might could be left of a man that death had caught up with after two hundred years. I picked up the iron blade and broke it on my knee and flung it away into the trees. Then I picked up the paper with my drawn picture. It wasn't hurt a bit, and it looked a right much like me.

Inside the door I put that picture, on the quilt where I'd lain. Maybe the Millens would keep it to remember me by, after they found I was gone and that Mr. Loden came round no more to try to court Vandy. Then I started away, carrying my guitar. If I made good time, I'd be out of the valley by high noon.

As I went, pots started to rattle. Somebody was awake in the cabin. And it was hard, hard, not to turn back when Vandy sang to herself, not thinking what she sang:

> "Wake up, wake up! The dawn is breaking.
> Wake up, wake up! It's almost day.
> Open up your doors and your divers windows,
> See my true love march away. . . ."

PART II

The Medusa in the Shield

Robert Aickman

The Swords

Robert Aickman is surely one of the masters in this century of the ghost story and the horror story in the psychological metaphor strain. Characteristically Aickman uses not monstrosity but the fantastic to achieve his effects, as in "The Swords," a story of male sexual initiation in which the overt is transformed into the absurd and the surreal, a fantastic language. The effect is unusually powerful and horrifying, complex and devastating, and darkly humorous, because the reader is aware of so much more than the character. Aickman's work is perhaps best called symbolist. "The good ghost story gives form and symbol to themes from enormous areas of our own minds which we cannot directly discern, but which totally govern us," Aickman said. He categorized his own work as "strange stories," a general term that represents something close to Freud's "unheimlich." "Aickman's entire body of short fiction expresses a coherent vision," says the critic Gary Crawford. "Man is trapped in a vortex of subtle, symbolic terror, a victim of forces within himself over which he has no control." One might add that external reality is quite strange and literally, if not symbolically, uncontrollable. Aickman is, in Russell Kirk's opinion, "the greatest of all writers of the uncanny," and Fritz Leiber called him "a weatherman of the unconscious."

Corazón malherido
Por cinco espadas

FEDERICO GARCIA LORCA

My first experience?
My first experience was far more of a test than anything that has ever happened to me since in that line. Not more agreeable, but certainly more testing. I have noticed several times that it is to beginners that strange things happen, and often, I think, to beginners only. When you know about a thing, there's just nothing to it. This kind of thing included—anyway, in most cases. After the first six women, say, or seven, or eight, the rest come much of a muchness.

I was a beginner all right; raw as a spring onion. What's more, I was a real mother's boy: scared stiff of life, and crass ignorant. Not that I want to sound disrespectful to my old mother. She's as good as they come, and I still hit it off better with her than with most other females.

She had a brother, my Uncle Elias. I should have said that we're all supposed to be descended from one of the big pottery families, but I don't know how true it is. My gran had little bits of pot to prove it, but it's always hard to be sure. After my dad was killed in an accident, my mother asked my Uncle Elias to take me into his business. He was a grocery salesman in a moderate way—and nothing but cheap lines. He said I must first learn the ropes by going out on the road. My mother was thoroughly upset because of my dad having died in a smash, and because she thought I was bound to be in moral danger, but there was nothing she could do about it, and on the road I went.

It was true enough about the moral danger, but I was too simple and too scared to involve myself. As far as I could, I steered clear even of the other chaps I met who were on the road with me. I was pretty certain they would be bad influences, and I was always bound to be the baby of the party anyway. I was dead rotten at selling and I was utterly lonely—not just in a manner of speaking, but truly lonely. I hated the life but Uncle Elias had promised to see me all right and I couldn't think of what else to do. I stuck it on the road for more than two years, and then I heard of my present job with the building society—read about it, actually, in the local paper—so that I was able to tell Uncle Elias what he could do with his cheap groceries.

For most of the time we stopped in small hotels—some of them weren't bad either, both the room and the grub—but in a few towns there were special lodgings known to Uncle Elias, where I and Uncle Elias's regular traveller, a sad chap called Bantock, were ordered by Uncle Elias to go. To this day I don't know exactly why. At the time I was quite sure that there was some kickback for my uncle in it, which was the obvious thing to suppose, but I've come since to wonder if the old girls who kept the lodgings might not have been my uncle's fancy women in the more or less distant past. At least once, I got as far as asking Bantock about it, but he merely said he didn't know what the answer was. There was very little that Bantock admitted to knowing about anything beyond the current prices of soapflakes and Scotch. He had been 42 years on the road for my uncle when one day he dropped dead of a thrombosis in Rochdale. Mrs. Bantock, at least, had been one of my uncle's women off and on for years. That was something everyone knew.

These women who kept the lodgings certainly behaved as if what I've said was true. You've never seen or heard such dives. Noises all night so that it was impossible to sleep properly, and often half-dressed tarts beating on your door and screaming that they'd been swindled or strangled. Some of the travellers even brought in boys, which is something I have never been able to understand. You read about it and hear about it, and I've often seen it happen, as I say, but I still don't understand it. And there was I in the middle of it all, pure and unspotted. The woman who kept the place often cheeked me for it. I don't know how old Bantock got on. I never found myself in one of these places at the same time as he was there. But the funny part was that my mother thought I was extra safe in one of these special lodgings, because they were all particularly guaranteed by her brother, who made Bantock and me go to them for our own good.

Of course it was only on some of the nights on the road. But always it was when I was quite alone. I noticed that at the time when Bantock was providing me with a few introductions and openings, they were always in towns where we could stay in commercial hotels. All the same, Bantock had to go to these special places when the need arose, just as much as I did, even though he never would talk about them.

One of the towns where there was a place on Uncle Elias's list was Wolverhampton. I fetched up there for the first time, after I had been on the job for perhaps four or five months. It was by no means my first of these lodgings, but for that very reason my heart sank all the more as I set eyes on the place and was let in by the usual bleary-eyed cow in curlers and a dirty overall.

There was absolutely nothing to do. Nowhere even to sit and watch the telly. All you could think of was to go out and get drunk, or bring someone in with you from the pictures. Neither idea appealed very much to me, and I found myself just wandering about the town. It must have been late spring or early summer, because it was pleasantly warm, though not too hot, and still only dusk when I had finished my tea, which I had to find in a café, because the lodging did not even provide tea.

I was strolling about the streets of Wolverhampton, with all the girls giggling at me, or so it seemed, when I came upon a sort of small fair. Not knowing the town at all, I had drifted into the rundown area up by the old canal. The main streets were quite wide, but they had been laid out for daytime traffic to the different works and railway yards, and were now quiet and empty, except for the occasional lorry and the boys and girls playing around at some of the corners. The narrow streets running off contained lines of small houses, but a lot of the houses were empty, with windows broken or boarded up, and holes in the roof. I should have turned back, but for the sound made by the fair; not pop songs on the amplifiers, and not the pounding of the old steam organs, but more a sort of high tinkling, which somehow fitted in with the warm evening and the rosy twilight. I couldn't at first make out what the noise was, but I had nothing else to do, very much not, and I looked around the empty back streets, until I could find what was going on.

It proved to be a very small fair indeed; just half a dozen stalls, where a few kids were throwing rings or shooting off toy rifles, two or three covered booths, and, in the middle, one very small roundabout. It was this that made the tinkling music. The roundabout *looked* pretty too; with snow-queen and icing sugar effects in the centre, and different coloured sleighs going round, each just big enough for two, and each, as I remember, with a coloured light high up at the peak. And in the middle was a very pretty, blonde girl dressed as some kind of pierrette. Anyway she seemed very pretty at that time to me. Her job was to collect the money from the people riding in the sleighs, but the trouble was that there weren't any. Not a single one. There weren't many people about at all, and inevitably the girl caught my eye. I felt I looked a

Charley as I had no one to ride with, and I just turned away. I shouldn't have dared to ask the girl herself to ride with me, and I imagine she wouldn't have been allowed to in any case. Unless, perhaps, it was her roundabout.

The fair had been set up on a plot of land which was empty simply because the houses which had stood on it had been demolished or just fallen down. Tall, blank factory walls towered up on two sides of it, and the ground was so rough and uneven that it was like walking on lumpy rocks at the seaside. There was nothing in the least permanent about the fair. It was very much here today and gone tomorrow. I should not have wondered if it had had no real business to have set up there at all. I doubted very much if it had come to any kind of agreement for the use of the land. I thought at once that the life must be a hard one for those who owned the fair. You could see why fairs like that have so largely died out from what things used to be in my gran's day, who was always talking about the wonderful fairs and circuses when she was a girl. Such customers as there were, were almost all mere kids, even though kids do have most of the money nowadays. These kids were doing a lot of their spending at a tiny stall where a drab-looking woman was selling ice-cream and toffee-apples. I thought it would have been much simpler and more profitable to concentrate on that, and enter the catering business rather than trying to provide entertainment for people who prefer to get it in their houses. But very probably I was in a gloomy frame of mind that evening. The fair was pretty and old-fashioned, but no one could say it cheered you up.

The girl on the roundabout could still see me, and I was sure was looking at me reproachfully—and probably contemptuously as well. With that layout, she was in the middle of things and impossible to get away from. I should just have mooched off, especially since the people running the different stalls were all beginning to shout at me, as pretty well the only full adult in sight, when, going round, I saw a booth in more or less the farthest corner, where the high factory walls made an angle. It was a square tent of very dirty red and white striped canvas, and over the crumpled entrance flap was a rough-edged, dark painted, horizontal board, with written on it in faint gold capital letters THE SWORDS. That was all there was. Night was coming on fast, but there was no light outside the tent and none shining through from inside. You might have thought it was a store of some kind.

For some reason, I put out my hand and touched the hanging flap. I am sure I should never have dared actually to draw it aside and peep in. But a touch was enough. The flap was pulled back at once, and a young man stood there, sloping his head to one side so as to draw me in. I could see at once that some kind of show was going on. I did not really want to watch it, but felt that I should look a complete imbecile if I just ran away across the fairground, small though it was.

"Two bob," said the young man, dropping the dirty flap, and sticking out his other hand, which was equally dirty. He wore a green sweater, mended but still with holes, grimy grey trousers, and grimier sandshoes. Sheer dirt was so much my first impression of the place that I might well have fled after all, had I felt it possible. I had not noticed this kind of griminess about the rest of the fair.

Running away, however, wasn't on. There were so few people inside. Dotted about the bare, bumpy ground, with bricks and broken glass sticking out from the hard earth, were 20 or 30 wooden chairs, none of them seeming to match, most of them broken or defective in one way or another, all of them chipped and off-colour. Scattered among these hard chairs was an audience of seven. I know it was seven, because I had no difficulty in counting, and because soon it mattered. I made the eighth. All of them were in single units and all were men: this time men and not boys. I think that I was the youngest among them, by quite a long way.

And the show was something I have never seen or heard of since. Nor even read of. Not exactly.

There was a sort of low platform of dark and discoloured wood up against the back of the tent—probably right on to the factory walls outside. There was a burly chap standing on it, giving the spiel, in a pretty rough delivery. He had tight yellow curls, the colour of cheap lemonade but turning grey, and a big red face, with a splay nose, and very dark red lips. He also had small eyes and ears. The ears didn't seem exactly opposite one another, if you know what I mean. He wasn't much to look at, though I felt he was very strong, and could probably have taken on all of us in the tent single-handed and come out well on top. I couldn't decide how old he was—either then or later. (Yes, I did see him again—twice.) I should imagine he was nearing 50, and he didn't look in particularly good condition, but it seemed as though he had just been made with more thew and muscle than most people are. He was dressed like the youth at the door, except that the sweater of the chap on the platform was not green but dark blue, as if he were a seaman, or perhaps acting one. He wore the same dirty grey trousers and sandshoes as the other man. You might almost have thought the place was some kind of boxing booth.

But it wasn't. On the chap's left (and straight ahead of where I sat at the edge of things and in the back row) a girl lay sprawled out facing us in an upright canvas chair, as faded and battered as everything else in the outfit. She was dressed up like a French chorus, in a tight and shiny black thing, cut low, and black fishnet stockings, and those shiny black shoes with super high heels that many men go for in such a big way. But the total effect was not particularly sexy, all the same. The different bits of costume had all seen better days, like everything else, and the girl herself looked more sick than spicy. Under other conditions, I thought to begin with, she might have been pretty enough, but she had made herself up with green powder, actually choosing it apparently, or having it chosen for her, and her hair, done in a tight bun, like a ballet dancer's, was not so much mousy as plain colourless. On top of all this, she was lying over the chair, rather than sitting in it, just as if she was feeling faint or about to be ill. Certainly she was doing nothing at all to lead the chaps on. Not that I myself should have wanted to be led. Or so I thought at the start.

And in front of her, at the angle of the platform, was this pile of swords. They were stacked criss-cross, like cheese-straws, on top of a low stool, square and black, the sort of thing they make in Sedgeley and Wednesfield and sell as Japanese, though this specimen was quite plain and undecorated, even though more than a bit chipped. There must have been 30 or 40 swords, as the pile had four corners to it, where the hilts of the swords were set diagonally above one another. It struck me later that perhaps there was one sword for each seat, in case there was ever a full house in the tent.

If I had not seen the notice outside, I might not have realized they *were* swords, or not at first. There was nothing gleaming about them, and nothing decorative. The blades were a dull grey, and the hilts were made of some black stuff, possibly even plastic. They looked thoroughly mass-produced and industrial, and I could not think where they might have been got. They were not fencing foils but something much solider, and the demand for real swords nowadays must be mainly ceremonial, and less and less even of that. Possibly these swords came from suppliers for the stage, though I doubt that too. Anyway, they were thoroughly dingy swords, no credit at all to the regiment.

I do not know how long the show had been going on before I arrived, or if the man in the seaman's sweater had offered any explanations. Almost the first thing I heard was him saying, "And now, gentlemen, which of you is going to be the first?"

There was no movement or response of any kind. Of course there never is.

"Come *on*," said the seaman, not very politely. I felt that he was so accustomed to the backwardness of his audiences that he was no longer prepared to pander to it. He did not strike me as a man of many words, even though speaking appeared to be his job. He had a strong accent, which I took to be Black Country, though I wasn't in a position properly to be sure at that time of my life, and being myself a Londoner.

Nothing happened.

"What you think you've paid your money for?" cried the seaman, more truculent, I thought, than sarcastic.

"You tell us," said one of the men on the chairs. He happened to be the man nearest to me, though in front of me.

It was not a very clever thing to say, and the seaman turned it to account.

"You," he shouted, sticking out his thick, red forefinger at the man who had cheeked him. "Come along up. We've got to start somewhere."

The man did not move. I became frightened by my own nearness to him. I might be picked on next, and I did not even know what was expected of me, if I responded.

The situation was saved by the appearance of a volunteer. At the other side of the tent, a man stood up and said, "I'll do it."

The only light in the tent came from a single Tilley lamp hissing away (none too safely, I thought) from the crosspiece of the roof, but the volunteer looked to me exactly like everyone else.

"At last," said the seaman, still rather rudely. "Come on then."

The volunteer stumbled across the rough ground, stepped on to my side of the small platform, and stood right in front of the girl. The girl seemed to make no movement. Her head was thrown so far back that, as she was some distance in front of me, I could not see her eyes at all clearly. I could not even be certain whether they were open or closed.

"Pick up a sword," said the seaman sharply.

The volunteer did so, in a rather gingerly way. It looked like the first time he had ever had his hand on such a thing, and, of course, I never had either. The volunteer stood there with the sword in his hand, looking an utter fool. His skin looked grey by the light of the Tilley, he was very thin, and his hair was failing badly.

The seaman seemed to let him stand there for quite a while, as if out of devilry, or perhaps resentment at the way he had to make a living. To me the atmosphere in the dirty tent seemed full of tension and unpleasantness, but the other men in the audience were still lying about on their hard chairs looking merely bored.

After quite a while, the seaman, who had been facing the audience, and speaking to the volunteer out of the corner of his mouth, half-turned on his heel, and still not looking right at the volunteer, snapped out: "What are you waiting for? There are others to come, though we could do with more."

At this, another member of the audience began to whistle "Why are we waiting?" I felt he was getting at the seaman or showman, or whatever he should be called, rather than at the volunteer.

"Go on," shouted the seaman, almost in the tone of a drill instructor. "Stick it in."

And then it happened, this extraordinary thing.

The volunteer seemed to me to tremble for a moment, and then plunged the sword right into the girl on the chair. As he was standing between me and her, I could not see where the sword entered, but I could see that the man seemed to press it right in, because almost the whole length of it seemed to disappear. What I could have no doubt about at all was the noise the sword made. A curious thing was that we are so used to at least the idea of people being stuck through with swords, that, even though, naturally, I had never before seen anything of the kind, I had no doubt at all of what the man had done. The noise of the sword tearing through the flesh was only what I should have expected. But it was quite distinct even above the hissing of the Tilley. And quite long drawn out too. And horrible.

I could sense the other men in the audience gathering themselves together on the instant and suddenly coming to life. I could still see little of what precisely had happened.

"Pull it out," said the seaman, quite casually, but as if speaking to a moron. He was still only half-turned towards the volunteer, and still looking straight in front of him. He was not looking at anything; just holding himself in control while getting through a familiar routine.

The volunteer pulled out the sword. I could again hear that unmistakable sound.

The volunteer still stood facing the girl, but with the tip of the sword resting on the platform. I could see no blood. Of course I thought I had made some complete misinterpretation, been fooled like a kid. Obviously it was some kind of conjuring.

"Kiss her if you want to," said the seaman. "It's included in what you've paid."

And the man did, even though I could only see his back. With the sword drooping from his hand, he leaned forwards and downwards. I think it was a slow and loving kiss, not a smacking and public kiss, because this time I could hear nothing.

The seaman gave the volunteer all the time in the world for it, and, for some odd reason, there was no whistling or catcalling from the rest of us; but in the end, the volunteer slowly straightened up.

"Please put back the sword," said the seaman, sarcastically polite.

The volunteer carefully returned it to the heap, going to some trouble to make it lie as before.

I could now see the girl. She was sitting up. Her hands were pressed together against her left side, where, presumably, the sword had gone in. But there was still no sign of blood, though it was hard to be certain in the bad light. And the strangest thing was that she now looked not only happy, with her eyes very wide open and a little smile on her lips, but, in spite of that green powder, beautiful too, which I was far from having thought in the first place.

The volunteer passed between the girl and me in order to get back to his seat. Even though the tent was almost empty, he returned to his original place religiously. I got a slightly better look at him. He still looked just like everyone else.

"Next," said the seaman, again like a sergeant numbering off.

This time there was no hanging back. Three men rose to their feet immediately, and the seaman had to make a choice.

"You then," he said, jabbing out his thick finger towards the centre of the tent.

The man picked was elderly, bald, plump, respectable-looking, and wearing a dark suit. He might have been a retired railway foreman or electricity inspector. He had a slight limp, probably taken in the way of his work.

The course of events was very much the same, but the second comer was readier and in less need of prompting, including about the kiss. His kiss was as slow and quiet as the first man's had been: paternal perhaps. When the elderly man stepped away, I saw that the girl was holding her two hands against the centre of her stomach. It made me squirm to look.

And then came the third man. When he went back to his seat, the girl's hands were to her throat.

The fourth man, on the face of it a rougher type, with a cloth cap (which, while on the platform, he never took off) and a sports jacket as filthy and worn out as the tent, apparently drove the sword into the girl's left thigh, straight through the fishnet stocking. When he stepped off the platform, she was clasping her leg, but looking so pleased that you'd have thought a great favour had been done her. And still I could see no blood.

I did not really know whether or not I wanted to see more of the details. Raw as I was, it would have been difficult for me to decide.

I didn't have to decide, because I dared not shift in any case to a seat with a better view. I considered that a move like that would quite probably result in my being the next man the seaman called up. And one thing I knew for certain was that whatever exactly was being done, I was not going to be one who did it. Whether it was conjuring, or something different that I knew nothing about, I was not going to get involved.

And, of course, if I stayed, my turn must be coming close in any case.

Still, the fifth man called was not me. He was a tall, lanky, perfectly black Negro. I had not especially spotted him as such before. He appeared to drive the sword in with all the force you might expect of a black man, even though he was so slight, then threw it on the floor of the platform with a clatter, which no one else had done before him, and actually drew the girl to her feet when kissing her. When he stepped back, his foot struck the sword. He paused for a second, gazing at the girl, then carefully put the sword back on the heap.

The girl was still standing, and it passed across my mind that the Negro might try to kiss her again. But he didn't. He went quietly back to his place. Behind the scenes of it all, there appeared to be some rules, which all the other men knew about. They behaved almost as though they came quite often to the show, if a show was what it was.

Sinking down once more into her dilapidated canvas chair, the girl kept her eyes fixed on mine. I could not even tell what colour her eyes were, but the fact of the matter is that they turned my heart right over. I was so simple and inexperienced that nothing like that had ever happened to me before in my whole life. The incredible green powder made no difference. Nothing that had just been happening made any difference. I wanted that girl more than I had ever wanted anything. And I don't mean I just wanted her body. That comes later in life. I wanted to love her and tousle her and all the other, better things we want before the time comes when we know that however much we want them, we're not going to get them.

But, in justice to myself, I must say that I did not want to take my place in a queue for her.

That was about the last thing I wanted. And it was one chance in three that I should be next to be called. I drew a deep breath and managed to scuttle out. I can't pretend it was difficult. I was sitting near the back of the tent, as I've said, and no one tried to stop me. The lad at the entrance merely gaped at me like a fish. No doubt he was quite accustomed to the occasional patron leaving early. I fancied that the bruiser on the platform was in the act of turning to me at the very instant I got up, but I knew it was probably imagination on my part. I don't think he spoke, nor did any of the other men react. Most men at shows of that kind prefer to behave as if they were invisible. I did get mixed up in the greasy tent flap, and the lad in the green sweater did nothing to help, but that was all. I streaked across the fairground, still almost deserted, and still with the roundabout tinkling away, all for nothing, but very prettily. I tore back to my nasty bedroom, and locked myself in.

On and off, there was the usual fuss and schemozzle in the house, and right through the hours of darkness. I know, because I couldn't sleep. I couldn't have slept that night if I'd been lying between damask sheets in the Hilton Hotel. The girl on the platform had got deep under my skin, green face and all: the girl and the show too, of course. I think I can truly say that what I experienced that night altered my whole angle on life, and it had nothing to do with the rows that broke out in the other bedrooms, or the cackling and bashing on the staircase, or the constant pulling the plug, which must have been the noisiest in the Midlands, especially as it took six or seven pulls or more for each flush. That night I really grasped the fact that most of the time we have no notion of what we really want, or we lose sight of it. And the even more important fact that what we really want just doesn't fit in with life as a whole, or very seldom. Most folk learn slowly, and never altogether learn at all. I seemed to learn all at once.

Or perhaps not quite, because there was very much more to come.

The next morning I had calls to make, but well before the time arrived for the first of them I had sneaked back to that tiny, battered, little fairground. I even skipped breakfast, but breakfast in Uncle Elias's special lodging was very poor anyway, though a surprising number turned up for it each day. You wondered where so many had been hiding away all night. I don't know what I expected to find at the fair. Perhaps I wasn't sure I should find the fair there at all.

But I did. In full daylight, it looked smaller, sadder, and more utterly hopeless for making a living even than the night before. The weather was absolutely beautiful, and so many of the houses in the immediate area were empty, to say nothing of the factories, that there were very few people around. The fair itself was completely empty, which took me by surprise. I had expected some sort of gypsy scene and had failed to realize that there was nowhere on the lot for even gypsies to sleep. The people who worked the fair must have gone to bed at home, like the rest of the world. The plot of land was surrounded by a wire-mesh fence, put up by the owner to keep out tramps and meth-drinkers, but by now the fence wasn't up to much, as you would expect, and, after looking round, I had no difficulty in scrambling through a hole in it, which the lads of the village had carved out for fun and from having nothing better to do. I walked over to the dingy booth in the far corner, and tried to lift the flap.

It proved to have been tied up at several places and apparently from the inside. I could not see how the person doing the tying had got out of the tent when he had finished, but that was the sort of trick of the trade you would expect of fairground folk. I found it impossible to see inside the tent at all without using my pocketknife, which I should have hesitated to do at the best of times, but while I was fiddling around, I heard a voice just behind me.

"What's up with you?"

There was a very small, old man standing at my back. I had certainly not heard him come up, even though the ground was so rough and lumpy. He was hardly more than a dwarf, he was as brown as a horse-chestnut or very nearly, and there was not a hair on his head.

"I wondered what was inside," I said feebly.

"A great big python, two miles long, that don't even pay its rent," said the little man.

"How's that?" I asked. "Hasn't it a following?"

"Old-fashioned," said the little man. "Old-fashioned and out of date. Doesn't appeal to the women. The women don't like the big snakes. But the women have the money these times, *and* the power and the glory too." He changed his tone. "You're trespassing."

"Sorry, old man," I said. "I couldn't hold myself back on a lovely morning like this."

"I'm the watchman," said the little man. "I used to have snakes too. Little ones, dozens and dozens of them. All over me, and every one more poisonous than the next. Eyes darting, tongues flicking, scales shimmering: then *in*, right home, then back, then in again, then back. Still in the end, it wasn't a go. There's a time and a span for all things. But I like to keep around. So now I'm the watchman. While the job lasts. While anything lasts. Move on then. Move on."

I hesitated.

"This big snake you talk of," I began, "this python——"

But he interrupted quite shrilly.

"There's no more to be said. Not to the likes of you, any road. Off the ground you go, and sharply. Or I'll call the police constable. He and I work hand in glove. I take care to keep it that way. You may not have heard that trespass is a breach of the peace. Stay here and you'll be sorry for the rest of your life."

The little man was actually squaring up to me, even thought the top of his brown skull (not shiny, by the way, but matt and patchy, as if he had some trouble with it) rose hardly above my waist. Clearly, he was daft.

As I had every kind of reason for going, I went. I did not even ask the little man about the times of performances that evening, or if there were any. Inside myself, I had no idea whether I should be back, even if there were performances, as there probably were.

I set about my calls. I'd had no sleep, and, since last night's tea, no food, and my head was spinning like a top, but I won't say I did my business any worse than usual. I probably felt at the time that I did, but now I doubt it. Private troubles, I have since noticed, make very little difference to the way most of us meet the outside world, and as for food and sleep, they don't matter at all until weeks and months have passed.

I pushed on then, more or less in the customary way (though, in my case, the customary way, at that job, wasn't up to very much at the best of times), and all the while mulling over and around what had happened to me, until the time came for dinner. I had planned to eat in the café where I had eaten the night before, but I found myself in a different part of the city, which, of course, I didn't know at all, and, feeling rather faint and queer, fell instead into the first place there was.

And there, in the middle of the floor, believe it or not, sitting at a Formica-topped table, was my girl with the green powder, and, beside her, the seaman or showman, looking more than ever like a run-down boxer.

I had not seriously expected ever to set eyes on the girl again. It was not, I thought, the kind of thing that happens. At the very most I might have gone again to the queer show, but I don't think I really would have done, when I came to think out what it involved.

The girl had wiped off the green powder, and was wearing a black coat and skirt and a white blouse, a costume you might perhaps have thought rather too old for her, and the same fishnet stockings. The man was dressed exactly as he had been the night before, except that he wore heavy boots instead of dirty sandshoes, heavy and mud-caked, as if he had been walking through fields.

Although it was the dinner-hour, the place was almost empty, with a dozen unoccupied tables, and these two sitting in the centre. I must almost have passed out.

But I wasn't really given time. The man in the jersey recognized me at once. He stood up and beckoned to me with his thick arm. "Come and join us." The girl had stood up too.

There was nothing else I could do but what he said.

The man actually drew back a chair for me (they were all painted in different, bright colours, and had been reseated in new leatherette), and even the girl waited until I had sat down before sitting down herself.

"Sorry you missed the end of last night's show," said the man.

"I had to get back to my lodgings, I suddenly realized." I made it up quite swiftly. "I'm new to the town," I added.

"It can be difficult when you're new," said the man. "What'll you have?"

He spoke as if we were on licensed premises, but it was pretty obvious we weren't, and I hesitated.

"Tea or coffee?"

"Tea, please," I said.

"Another tea, Berth," called out the man. I saw that the two of them were both drinking coffee, but I didn't like the look of it, any more than I usually do.

"I'd like something to eat as well," I said, when the waitress brought the tea. "Thank you very much," I said to the man.

"Sandwiches: York ham, salt beef, or luncheon meat. Pies. Sausage rolls," said the waitress. She had a very bad stye on her left lower eyelid.

"I'll have a pie," I said, and, in due course, she brought one, with some salad on the plate, and the bottle of sauce. I really required something hot, but there it was.

"Come again tonight," said the man.

"I'm not sure I'll be able to."

I was finding it difficult even to drink my tea properly, as my hands were shaking so badly, and I couldn't think how I should cope with a cold pie.

"Come on the house, if you like. As you missed your turn last night."

The girl, who had so far left the talking to the other, smiled at me very sweetly and personally, as if there was something quite particular between us. Her white blouse was open very low, so that I saw more than I really should, even though things are quite different today from what they once were. Even without the green powder, she was a very pale girl, and her body looked as if it might be even whiter than her face, almost as white as her blouse. Also I could now see the colour of her eyes. They were green. Somehow I had known it all along.

"In any case," went on the man, "it won't make much difference with business like it is now."

The girl glanced at him as if she were surprised at his letting out something private, then looked at me again and said, "Do come." She said it in the friendliest, meltingest way, as if she really cared. What's more, she seemed to have some kind of foreign accent, which made her even more fascinating, if that were possible. She took a small sip of coffee.

"It's only that I might have another engagement that I couldn't get out of. I don't know right now."

"We mustn't make you break another engagement," said the girl, in her foreign accent, but sounding as if she meant just the opposite.

I managed a bit more candour. "I might get out of my engagement," I said, "but the truth is, if you don't mind my saying so, that I didn't greatly care for some of the others in the audience last night."

"I don't blame you," said the man very dryly, and rather to my relief, as you can imagine. "What would you say to a private show? A show just for you?" He spoke quite quietly, suggesting it as if it had been the most normal thing in the world, or as if I had been Charles Clore.

I was so taken by surprise that I blurted out, "What! Just me in the tent?"

"In your own home, I meant," said the man, still absolutely casually, and taking a noisy pull on his pink earthenware cup. As the man spoke, the girl shot a quick, devastating glance. It was exactly as if she softened everything inside me to water. And, absurdly enough, it was then that my silly pie arrived, with the bit of green salad, and the sauce. I had been a fool to ask for anything at all to eat, however much I might have needed it in theory.

"With or without the swords," continued the man, lighting a cheap-looking cigarette. "Madonna has been trained to do anything else you want. Anything you may happen to think of." The girl was gazing into her teacup.

I dared to speak directly to her. "Is your name really Madonna? It's nice."

"No," she said, speaking rather low. "Not really. It's my working name." She turned her head for a moment, and again our eyes met.

"There's no harm in it. We're not Catholics," said the man, "though Madonna was once."

"I like it," I said. I was wondering what to do about the pie. I could not possibly eat.

"Of course a private show would cost a bit more than two bob," said the man. "But it would be all to yourself, and, under those conditions, Madonna will do anything you feel like." I noticed that he was speaking just as he had spoken in the tent: looking not at me or at anyone else, but straight ahead into the distance, and as if he were repeating words he had used again and again and was fed up with but compelled to make use of.

I was about to tell him I had no money, which was more or less the case, but didn't.

"When could it be?" I said.

"Tonight, if you like," said the man. "Immediately after the regular show, and that won't be very late, as we don't do a ten or eleven o'clock house at a date like this. Madonna could be with you at a quarter to ten, easy. And she wouldn't necessarily have to hurry away either, not when there's no late-night matinée. There'd be time for her to do a lot of her novelties if you'd care to see them. Items from her repertoire, as we call them. Got a good place for it, by the way? Madonna doesn't need much. Just a room with a lock on the door to keep out the non-paying patrons, and somewhere to wash her hands."

"Yes," I said. "As a matter of fact, the place I'm stopping at should be quite suitable, though I wish it was brighter, and a bit quieter too."

Madonna flashed another of her indescribably sweet glances at me. "I shan't mind," she said softly.

I wrote down the address on the corner of a paper I had found on my seat, and tore it off.

"Shall we call it ten pounds?" said the man, turning to look at me with his small eyes. "I usually ask twenty and sometimes fifty, but this is Wolverhampton not the Costa Brava, and you belong to the refined type."

"What makes you say that?" I asked; mainly in order to gain time for thinking what I could do about the money.

"I could tell by where you sat last night. At pretty well every show there's someone who picks that seat. It's a special seat for the refined types. I've learnt better now than to call them up, because it's not what they want. They're too refined to be called up, and I respect them for it. They often leave before the end, as you did. But I'm glad to have them in at any time. They raise the standard. Besides, they're the ones who are often interested in a private show, as you are, and willing to pay for it. I have to watch the business of the thing too."

"I haven't got ten pounds ready in spare cash," I said, "but I expect I can find it, even if I have to fiddle it."

"It's what you often have to do in this world," said the man. "Leastways if you like nice things."

"You've still got most of the day," said the girl, smiling encouragingly.

"Have another cup of tea?" said the man.

"No thanks very much."

"Sure?"

"Sure."

"Then we must move. We've an afternoon show, though it'll probably be only for a few kids. I'll tell Madonna to save herself as much as she can until the private affair tonight."

As they were going through the door on to the street, the girl looked back to throw me a glance over her shoulder, warm and secret. But when she was moving about, her clothes looked much too big for her, the skirt too long, the jacket and blouse too loose and droopy, as if they were not really her clothes at all. On top of everything else, I felt sorry for her. Whatever the explanation of last night, her life could not be an easy one.

They'd both been too polite to mention my pie. I stuffed it into my attaché case, of course without the salad, paid for it, and dragged off to my next call, which proved to be right across the town once more.

I didn't have to do anything dishonest to get the money.

It was hardly to be expected that my mind would be much on my work that afternoon, but I stuck to it as best I could, feeling that my life was getting into deep waters and that I had better keep land of some kind within sight, while it was still possible. It was as well that I did continue on my proper round of calls, because at one of the shops my immediate problem was solved for me without my having to lift a finger. The owner of the shop was a nice old gentleman with white hair, named Mr. Edis, who seemed to take to me immediately I went through the door. He said at one point that I made a change from old Bantock with his attacks of asthma (I don't think I've so far mentioned Bantock's asthma, but I knew all about it), and that I seemed a good lad, with a light in my eyes. Those were his words, and I'm not likely to make a mistake about them just yet, seeing what he went on to. He asked me if I had anything to do that evening. Rather pleased with myself, because it was not an answer I should have been able to make often before, not if I had been speaking the truth, I told him Yes, I had a date with a girl.

"Do you mean with a Wolverhampton girl?" asked Mr. Edis.

"Yes. I've only met her since I've been in the town." I shouldn't have admitted that to most people, but there was something about Mr. Edis that led me on and made me want to justify his good opinion of me.

"What's she like?" asked Mr. Edis, half closing his eyes, so that I could see the red all round the edges of them.

"Gorgeous." It was the sort of thing people said, and my real feelings couldn't possibly have been put into words.

"Got enough small change to treat her properly?"

I had to think quickly, being taken so much by surprise, but Mr. Edis went on before I had time to speak.

"So that you can cuddle her as you want?"

I could see that he was getting more and more excited.

"Well, Mr. Edis," I said, "as a matter of fact, not quite enough. I'm still a beginner in my job, as you know."

I thought I might get a pound out of him, and quite likely only as a loan, the Midlands people being what we all know they are.

But on the instant he produced a whole fiver. He flapped it in front of my nose like a kipper.

"It's yours on one condition."

"I'll fit in if I can, Mr. Edis."

"Come back tomorrow morning after my wife's gone out—she works as a traffic warden, and can't hardly get enough of it—come back here and tell me all about what happens."

I didn't care for the idea at all, but I supposed that I could make up some lies, or even break my word and not go back at all, and I didn't seem to have much alternative.

"Why, of course, Mr. Edis. Nothing to it."

He handed over the fiver at once.

"Good boy," he said. "Get what you're paying for out of her, and think of me while you're doing it, though I don't expect you will."

As for the other five pounds, I could probably manage to wangle it out of what I had, by scraping a bit over the next week or two, and cooking the cash

book a trifle if necessary, as we all do. Anyway, and being the age I was, I
hated all this talk about money. I hated the talk about it much more than I
hated the job of having to find it. I did not see Madonna in that sort of way at
all, and I should have despised myself if I had. Nor, to judge by how she
spoke, did it seem the way in which she saw me. I could not really think of
any other way in which she would be likely to see me, but I settled that one
by trying not to think about the question at all.

My Uncle Elias's special lodging in Wolverhampton was not the kind of
place where visitors just rang the bell and waited to be admitted by the
footman. You had to know the form a bit, if you were to get in at all, not
being a resident, and still more if, once inside, you were going to find the
exact person you were looking for. At about half past nine I thought it best to
start lounging around in the street outside. Not right on top of the house
door, because that might have led to misunderstanding and trouble of some
kind, but moving up and down the street, keeping both eyes open and an ear
cocked for the patter of tiny feet on the pavement. It was almost dark, of
course, but not quite. There weren't many people about but that was partly
because it was raining gently, as it does in the Midlands: a soft, slow rain that
you can hardly see, but extra wetting, or so it always feels. I am quite sure I
should have taken up my position earlier if it hadn't been for the rain.
Needless to say, I was like a cat on hot bricks. I had managed to get the pie
inside me between calls during the afternoon. I struggled through it on a
bench just as the rain was beginning. And at about half past six I'd had a cup
of tea and some beans in the café I'd been to the night before. I didn't want
any of it. I just felt that I ought to eat something in view of what lay ahead of
me. Though, of course, I had precious little idea of what that was. When it's
truly your first experience, you haven't; no matter how much you've been
told and managed to pick up. I'd have been in a bad state if it had been any
woman that was supposed to be coming, let alone my lovely Madonna.

And there she was, on the dot, or even a little early. She was dressed in the
same clothes as she had worn that morning. Too big for her and too old for
her; and she had no umbrella and no raincoat and no hat.

"You'll be wet," I said.

She didn't speak, but her eyes looked, I fancied, as if she were glad to see
me. If she had set out in that green powder of hers, it had all washed off.

I thought she might be carrying something, but she wasn't, not even a
handbag.

"Come in," I said.

Those staying in the house were lent a key (with a deposit to pay on it),
and, thank God, we got through the hall and up the stairs without meeting
anyone, or hearing anything out of the way, even though my room was at the
top of the building.

She sat down on my bed and looked at the door. After what had been said,
I knew what to do and turned the key. It came quite naturally. It was the sort
of place where you turned the key as a matter of course. I took off my
raincoat and let it lie in a corner. I had not turned on the light. I was not
proud of my room.

"You must be soaked through," I said. The distance from the fairground was not all that great, but the rain was of the specially wetting kind, as I've remarked.

She got up and took off her outsize black jacket. She stood there holding it until I took it and hung it on the door. I can't say it actually dripped, but it was saturated, and I could see a wet patch on the eiderdown where she had been sitting. She had still not spoken a word. I had to admit that there seemed to have been no call for her to do so.

The rain had soaked through to her white blouse. Even with almost no light in the room I could see that. The shoulders were sodden and clinging to her, one more than the other. Without the jacket, the blouse looked quainter than ever. Not only was it loose and shapeless, but it had sleeves that were so long as to droop down beyond her hands when her jacket was off. In my mind I had a glimpse of the sort of woman the blouse was made for, big and stout, not my type at all.

"Better take that off too," I said, though I don't now know how I got the words out. I imagine that instinct looks after you even the first time, provided it is given a chance. Madonna did give me a chance, or I felt that she did. Life was sweeter for a minute or two than I had ever thought possible.

Without a word, she took off her blouse and I hung it over the back of the single bedroom chair.

I had seen in the café that under it she had been wearing something black, but I had not realized until now that it was the same tight, shiny sheath that she wore in the show, and that made her look so French.

She took off her wet skirt. The best I could do was to drape it over the seat of the chair. And there she was, super high heels and all. She looked ready to go on stage right away, but that I found rather disappointing.

She stood waiting, as if for me to tell her what to do.

I could see that the black sheath was soaking wet, anyway in patches, but this time I didn't dare to suggest that she take it off.

At last Madonna opened her mouth. "What would you like me to begin with?"

Her voice was so beautiful, and the question she asked so tempting, that something got hold of me and, before I could stop myself, I had put my arms round her. I had never done anything like it before in my whole life, whatever I might have felt.

She made no movement, so that I supposed at once I had done the wrong thing. After all, it was scarcely surprising, considering how inexperienced I was.

But I thought too that something else was wrong. As I say, I wasn't exactly accustomed to the feel of a half-naked woman, and I myself was still more or less fully dressed, but all the same I thought at once that the feel of her was disappointing. It came as a bit of a shock. Quite a bad one, in fact. As often, when facts replace fancies. Suddenly it had all become rather like a nightmare.

I stepped back.

"I'm sorry," I said.

She smiled in her same sweet way. "I don't mind," she said.

It was nice of her, but I no longer felt quite the same about her. You know how, at the best, a tiny thing can make all the difference in your feeling about a woman, and I was far from sure that this thing was tiny at all. What I was wondering was whether I wasn't proving not to be properly equipped for life. I had been called backward before now, and perhaps here was the reason.

Then I realized that it might all be something to do with the act she put on, the swords. She might be some kind of freak, or possibly the man in the blue jersey did something funny to her, hypnotized her, in some way.

"Tell me what you'd like," she said, looking down at the scruffy bit of rug on the floor.

I was a fool, I thought, and merely showing my ignorance.

"Take that thing off," I replied. "It's wet. Get into bed. You'll be warmer there."

I began taking off my own clothes.

She did what I said, squirmed out of the black sheath, took her feet gently out of the sexy shoes, rolled off her long stockings. Before me for a moment was my first woman, even though I could hardly see her. I was still unable to face the idea of love by that single, dim electric light, which only made the draggled room look more draggled.

Obediently, Madonna climbed into my bed and I joined her there as quickly as I could.

Obediently, she did everything I asked, just as the man in the blue sweater had promised. To me she still felt queer and disappointing—flabby might almost be the word—and certainly quite different from what I had always fancied a woman's body would feel like if ever I found myself close enough to it. But she gave me my first experience none the less, the thing we're concerned with now. I will say one thing for her: from first to last she never spoke an unnecessary word. It's not always like that, of course.

But everything had gone wrong. For example, we had not even started by kissing. I had been cram full of romantic ideas about Madonna, but I felt that she was not being much help in that direction, for all her sweet and beautiful smiles and her soft voice and the gentle things she said. She was making herself almost too available, and not bringing out the best in me. It was as if I had simply acquired new information, however important, but without any exertion of my feelings. You often feel like that, of course, about one thing or another, but it seemed dreadful to feel it about this particular thing, especially when I had felt so differently about it only a little while before.

"Come on," I said to her. "Wake up."

It wasn't fair, but I was bitterly disappointed, and all the more because I couldn't properly make out why. I only felt that everything in my life might be at stake.

She moaned a little.

I heaved up from on top of her in the bed and threw back the bedclothes behind me. She lay there flat in front of me, all grey—anyway in the dim twilight. Even her hair was colourless, in fact pretty well invisible.

I did what I suppose was rather a wretched thing. I caught hold of her left arm by putting both my hands round her wrist, and tried to lug her up towards me, so that I could feel her thrown against me, and could cover her neck and front with kisses, if only she would make me want to. I suppose I might under any circumstances have hurt her by dragging at her like that, and that I shouldn't have done it. Still no one could have said it was very terrible. It was quite a usual sort of thing to do, I should say.

But what actually happened was very terrible indeed. So simple and so terrible that people won't always believe me. I gave this great, bad-tempered, disappointed pull at Madonna. She came up towards me and then fell back again with a sort of wail. I was still holding on to her hand and wrist with my two hands, and it took me quite some time to realize what had happened. What had happened was that I had pulled her left hand and wrist right off.

On the instant, she twisted out of the bed and began to wriggle back into her clothes. I was aware that even in the almost nonexistent light she was somehow managing to move very swiftly. I had a frightful sensation of her beating round in my room with only one hand, and wondered in terror how she could possibly manage. All the time, she was weeping to herself, or wailing might be the word. The noise she made was very soft, so soft that but for what was happening, I might have thought it was inside my own head.

I got my feet on to the floor with the notion of turning on the light. The only switch was of course by the door. I had the idea that with some light on the scene, there might be certain explanations. But I found that I couldn't get to the switch. In the first place, I couldn't bear the thought of touching Madonna, even accidentally. In the second place, I discovered that my legs would go no farther. I was too utterly scared to move at all. Scared, repelled, and that mixed-up something else connected with disappointed sex for which there is no exact word.

So I just sat there, on the edge of the bed, while Madonna got back into her things, crying all the while, in that awful, heart-breaking way which I shall never forget. Not that it went on for long. As I've said, Madonna was amazingly quick. I couldn't think of anything to say or do. Especially with so little time for it.

When she had put on her clothes, she made a single appallingly significant snatch in my direction, caught something up, almost as if she, at least, could see in the dark. Then she had unlocked the door and bolted.

She had left the door flapping open off the dark landing (we had time-switches, of course), and I could hear her pat-patting down the staircase, and so easily and quietly through the front door that you might have thought she lived in the place. It was still a little too early for the regulars to be much in evidence.

What I felt now was physically sick. But I had the use of my legs once more. I got off the bed, shut and locked the door, and turned on the light.

There was nothing in particular to be seen. Nothing but my own clothes lying about, my sodden-looking raincoat in the corner, and the upheaved bed. The bed looked as if some huge monster had risen through it, but nowhere in the room was there blood. It was all just like the swords.

As I thought about it, and about what I had done, I suddenly vomited. They were not rooms with hot and cold running water, and I half-filled the old-fashioned washbowl, with its faded flowers at the bottom and big thumbnail chippings round the rim, before I had finished.

I lay down on the crumpled bed, too fagged to empty the basin, to put out the light, even to draw something over me, though I was still naked and the night getting colder.

I heard the usual sounds beginning on the stairs and in the other rooms. Then, there was an unexpected, businesslike rapping at my own door.

It was not the sort of house where it was much use first asking who was there. I got to my feet again, this time frozen stiff, and, not having a dressing-gown with me, put on my wet raincoat, as I had to put on something and get the door open, or there would be more knocking, and then complaints, which could be most unpleasant.

It was the chap in the blue sweater; the seaman or showman or whatever he was. Somehow I had known it might be.

I can't have looked up to much, as I stood there shaking, in only the wet raincoat, especially as all the time you could hear people yelling and beating it up generally in the other rooms. And of course I hadn't the slightest idea what line the chap might choose to take.

I needn't have worried. Not at least about that.

"Show pass off all right?" was all he asked; and looking straight into the distance as if he were on his platform, not at anyone or anything in particular, but sounding quite friendly notwithstanding, provided everyone responded in the right kind of way.

"I think so," I replied.

I daresay I didn't appear very cordial, but he seemed not to mind much.

"In that case, could I have the fee? I'm sorry to disturb your beauty sleep, but we're moving on early."

I had not known in what way I should be expected to pay, so had carefully got the ten pounds into a pile, Mr. Edis's fiver and five single pounds of my own, and put it into the corner of a drawer, before I had gone out into the rain to meet Madonna.

I gave it to him.

"Thanks," he said, counting it, and putting it into his trousers pocket. I noticed that even his trousers seemed to be seaman's trousers, now that I could see them close to, with him standing just in front of me. "Everything all right then?"

"I think so," I said again. I was taking care not to commit myself too far in any direction I could think of.

I saw that now he was looking at me, his small eyes deep-sunk.

At that exact moment, there was a wild shriek from one of the floors below. It was about the loudest human cry I had heard until then, even in one of those lodgings.

But the man took no notice.

"All right then," he said.

For some reason, he hesitated a moment, then he held out his hand. I took it. He was very strong, but there was nothing else remarkable about his hand.

"We'll meet again." he said. "Don't worry."

Then he turned away and pressed the black time-switch for the staircase light. I did not stop to watch him go. I was sick and freezing.

And so far, despite what he said, our paths have not recrossed.

Thomas M. Disch

The Roaches

Poet, reviewer and novelist, Thomas M. Disch has produced a variety of short fiction of uniformly high quality over three decades, often in the horror mode. Like Shirley Jackson, Peter Straub, Joyce Carol Oates and Theodore Sturgeon, his domain is literature in the broadest sense and his works increase the cross-fertilization of categories that has proven so broadening to horror literature since the 1930s. Telepathy has ordinarily been the domain of science fiction—in "The Roaches," it becomes the basis for a particularly ironic drama of abnormal psychology, one which might be compared to Stephen King's *Carrie*, as an example of horror in a science fiction frame. At the same time the absurd humor of this piece helps to give it its Dischean charm, just a few steps short of parody.

Miss Marcia Kenwell had a perfect horror of cockroaches. It was an altogether different horror than the one which she felt, for instance, toward the color puce. Marcia Kenwell loathed the little things. She couldn't see one without wanting to scream. Her revulsion was so extreme that she could not bear to crush them under the soles of her shoes. No, that would be too awful. She would run, instead, for the spray can of Black Flag and inundate the little beast with poison until it ceased to move or got out of reach into one of the cracks where they all seemed to live. It was horrible, unspeakably horrible, to think of them nestling in the walls, under the linoleum, only waiting for the lights to be turned off, and then . . . No, it was best not to think about it.

Every week she looked through the *Times* hoping to find another apartment, but either the rents were prohibitive (this *was* Manhattan, and Marcia's wage was a mere $62.50 a week, gross) or the building was obviously infested. She could always tell: there would be husks of dead roaches scattered about in the dust beneath the sink, stuck to the greasy backside of the stove, lining the out-of-reach cupboard shelves like the rice on the church steps after a wedding. She left such rooms in a passion of disgust, unable even to think till she reached her own apartment, where the air would be thick with the wholesome odors of Black Flag, Roach-It, and the toxic pastes that were spread on slices of potato and hidden in a hundred cracks which only she and the roaches knew about.

At least, she thought, *I keep my apartment clean.* And truly, the linoleum under the sink, the backside and underside of the stove, and the white contact paper lining her cupboards were immaculate. She could not under-

312

stand how other people could let these matters get so entirely out-of-hand. *They must be Puerto Ricans,* she decided—and shivered again with horror, remembering that litter of empty husks, the filth and the disease.

Such extreme antipathy toward insects—toward one particular insect—may seem excessive, but Marcia Kenwell was not really exceptional in this. There are many women, bachelor women like Marcia chiefly, who share this feeling though one may hope, for sweet charity's sake, that they escape Marcia's peculiar fate.

Marcia's phobia was, as in most such cases, hereditary in origin. That is to say, she inherited it from her mother, who had a morbid fear of anything that crawled or skittered or lived in tiny holes. Mice, frogs, snakes, worms, bugs—all could send Mrs. Kenwell into hysterics, and it would indeed have been a wonder, if little Marcia had not taken after her. It was rather strange, though, that her fear had become so particular, and stranger still that it should particularly be cockroaches that captured her fancy, for Marcia had never seen a single cockroach, didn't know what they were. (The Kenwells were a Minnesota family, and Minnesota families simply don't have cockroaches.) In fact, the subject did not arise until Marcia was nineteen and setting out (armed with nothing but a high school diploma and pluck, for she was not, you see, a very attractive girl) to conquer New York.

On the day of her departure, her favorite and only surviving aunt came with her to the Greyhound Terminal (her parents being deceased) and gave her this parting advice: "Watch out for the roaches, Marcia darling. New York City is full of cockroaches." At that time (at almost any time really) Marcia hardly paid attention to her aunt, who had opposed the trip from the start and given a hundred or more reasons why Marcia had better not go, not till she was older at least.

Her aunt had been proven right on all counts: Marcia after five years and fifteen employment agency fees could find nothing in New York but dull jobs at mediocre wages; she had no more friends than when she lived on West 16th; and, except for its view (the Chock Full O'Nuts warehouse and a patch of sky), her present apartment on lower Thompson Street was not a great improvement on its predecessor.

The city was full of promises, but they had all been pledged to other people. The city Marcia knew was sinful, indifferent, dirty, and dangerous. Every day she read accounts of women attacked in subway stations, raped in the streets, knifed in their own beds. A hundred people looked on curiously all the while and offered no assistance. And on top of everything else there were the roaches!

There were roaches everywhere, but Marcia didn't see them until she'd been in New York a month. They came to her—or she to them—at Silversmith's on Nassau Street, a stationery shop where she had been working for three days. It was the first job she'd been able to find. Alone or helped by a pimply stockboy (in all fairness it must be noted that Marcia was not without an acne problem of her own), she wandered down rows of rasp-edged metal shelves in the musty basement, making an inventory of the sheaves and piles and boxes of bond paper, leatherette-bound diaries, pins and clips, and carbon paper. The basement was dirty and so dim that she needed a flashlight for the lowest shelves. In the obscurest corner, a faucet leaked perpetually into a gray sink: she had been resting near this sink, sipping a cup of tepid coffee (saturated, in the New York manner, with sugar and drowned in milk), thinking, probably, of how she could afford several things she simply couldn't afford, when she noticed the dark spots moving on the side of the sink. At first she thought they might be no more than motes floating in the jelly of her eyes, or the giddy dots that one sees after over-exertion on a hot day. But they persisted too long to be illusory, and Marcia drew nearer, feeling compelled to bear witness. *How do I know they are insects?* she thought.

How are we to explain the fact that what repels us most can be at times—at the same time—inordinately attractive? Why is the cobra poised to strike so beautiful? The fascination of the abomination is something that . . . Something which we would rather not account for. The subject borders on the obscene, and there is no need to deal with it here, except to note the breathless wonder with which Marcia observed these first roaches of hers. Her chair was drawn so close to the sink that she could see the mottling of their oval, unsegmented bodies, the quick scuttering of their thin legs, and the quicker flutter of their antennae. They moved randomly, proceeding nowhere, centered nowhere. They seemed greatly disturbed over nothing. *Perhaps,* Marcia thought, *my presence has a morbid effect on them?*

Only then did she become aware, aware fully, that these were the cockroaches of which she had been warned. Repulsion took hold; her flesh curdled on her bones. She screamed and fell back in her chair, almost upsetting a shelf of oddlots. Simultaneously the roaches disappeared over the edge of the sink and into the drain.

Mr. Silversmith, coming downstairs to inquire the source of Marcia's alarm, found her supine and unconscious. He sprinkled her face with tapwater, and she awoke with a shudder of nausea. She refused to explain why she had screamed and insisted that she must leave Mr. Silversmith's employ immediately. He, supposing that the pimply stockboy (who was his son) had made a pass at Marcia, paid her for the three days she had worked and let her go without regrets. From that moment on, cockroaches were to be a regular feature of Marcia's existence.

On Thompson Street Marcia was able to reach a sort of stalemate with the cockroaches. She settled into a comfortable routine of pastes and powders, scrubbing and waxing, prevention (she never had even a cup of coffee without washing and drying cup and coffeepot immediately afterward) and ruthless extermination. The only roaches who trespassed upon her two cozy rooms came up from the apartment below, and they did not stay long, you may be sure. Marcia would have complained to the landlady, except that it was the landlady's apartment and her roaches. She had been inside, for a glass of wine on Christmas Eve, and she had to admit that it wasn't exceptionally dirty. It was, in fact, more than commonly clean—but *that* was not enough in New York. *If everyone,* Marcia thought, *took as much care as I, there would soon be no cockroaches in New York City.*

* * *

Then (it was March and Marcia was halfway through her sixth year in the city) the Shchapalovs moved in next door. There were three of them—two men and a woman—and they were old, though exactly how old it was hard to say: they had been aged by more than time. Perhaps they weren't more than forty. The woman, for instance, though she still had brown hair, had a face wrinkly as a prune and was missing several teeth. She would stop Marcia in the hallway or on the street, grabbing hold of her coatsleeve, and talk to her—always a simple lament about the weather, which was too hot or too cold or too wet or too dry. Marcia never knew half of what the old woman was saying, she mumbled so. Then she'd totter off to the grocery with her bagful of empties.

The Shchapalovs, you see, drank. Marcia, who had a rather exaggerated idea of the cost of alcohol (the cheapest thing she could imagine was vodka), wondered where they got the money for all the drinking they did. She knew they didn't work, for on days when Marcia was home with the flu she could hear the three Shchapalovs through the thin wall between their kitchen and hers screaming at each other to exercise their adrenal glands. *They're on welfare,* Marcia decided. Or perhaps the man with only one eye was a veteran on pension.

She didn't so much mind the noise of their arguments (she was seldom home in the afternoon), but she couldn't stand their singing. Early in the evening they'd start in, singing along with the radio stations. Everything they listened to sounded like Guy Lombardo. Later, about eight o'clock they sang *a cappella*. Strange, soulless noises rose and fell like Civil Defense sirens; there were bellowings, bayings, and cries. Marcia had heard something like it once on a Folkways record of Czechoslovakian wedding chants. She was quite beside herself whenever the awful noise started up and had to leave the house till they were done. A complaint would do no good: the Shchapalovs had a right to sing at that hour.

Besides, one of the men was said to be related by marriage to the landlady. That's how they got the apartment, which had been used as a storage space until they'd moved in. Marcia couldn't understand how the three of them could fit into such a little space—just a room-and-a-half with a narrow window opening onto the air shaft. (Marcia had discovered that she could see their entire living space through a hole that had been broken through the wall when the plumbers had installed a sink for the Shchapalovs.)

But if their singing distressed her, *what* was she to do about the roaches? The Shchapalov woman, who was the sister of one man and married to the other—or else the men were brothers and she was the wife of one of them (sometimes, it seemed to Marcia, from the words that came through the walls, that she was married to neither of them—or to both), was a bad housekeeper, and the Shchapalov apartment was soon swarming with roaches. Since Marcia's sink and the Shchapalovs' were fed by the same pipes and emptied into a common drain, a steady overflow of roaches was disgorged into Marcia's immaculate kitchen. She could spray and lay out more poisoned potatoes; she could scrub and dust and stuff Kleenex tissues into holes where the pipes passed through the wall: it was all to no avail. The Shchapalov roaches could always lay another million eggs in the garbage bags rotting beneath the Shchapalov sink. In a few days they would be swarming through the pipes and cracks and into Marcia's cupboards. She would lay in bed and watch them (this was possible because Marcia kept a nightlight burning in each room) advancing across the floor and up the walls, trailing the Shchapalovs' filth and disease everywhere they went.

One such evening the roaches were especially bad, and Marcia was trying to muster the resolution to get out of her warm bed and attack them with Roach-It. She had left the windows open from the conviction that cockroaches do not like the cold, but she found that she liked it much less. When she swallowed, it hurt, and she knew she was coming down with a cold. And all because of *them*!

"Oh go away!" she begged. *"Go away! Go away! Get out of my apartment."*
She addressed the roaches with the same desperate intensity with which she sometimes (though not often in recent years) addressed prayers to the Almighty. Once she had prayed all night long to get rid of her acne, but in the morning it was worse than ever. People in intolerable circumstances will pray to anything. Truly, there are no atheists in foxholes: the men there pray to the bombs that they may land somewhere else.

The only strange thing in Marcia's case is that her prayers were answered. The cockroaches fled from her apartment as quickly as their little legs could carry them—and in straight lines, too. Had they heard her? Had they understood?

Marcia could still see one cockroach coming down from the cupboard. *"Stop!"* she commanded. And it stopped.

At Marcia's spoken command, the cockroach would march up and down, to the left and to the right. Suspecting that her phobia had matured into madness, Marcia left her warm bed, turned on the light, and cautiously approached the roach, which remained motionless, as she had bidden it. *"Wiggle your antennas,"* she commanded. The cockroach wiggled its antennae.

She wondered if they would *all* obey her and found, within the next few days, that they all would. They would do anything she told them to. They would eat poison out of her hand. Well, not exactly out of her hand, but it amounted to the same thing. They were devoted to her. Slavishly.

It is the end, she though, *of my roach problem.* But of course it was only the beginning.

Marcia did not question too closely the *reason* the roaches obeyed her. She had never much troubled herself with abstract problems. After expending so much time and attention on them, it seemed only natural that she should exercise a certain power over them. However, she was wise enough never to speak of this power to anyone else—even to Miss Bismuth at the insurance office. Miss Bismuth read the horoscope magazines and claimed to be able to communicate with her mother, aged sixty-eight, telepathically. Her mother lived in Ohio. But what would Marcia have said: that *she* could communicate telepathically with cockroaches? Impossible.

Nor did Marcia use her power for any other purpose than keeping the cockroaches out of her own apartment. Whenever she saw one, she simply commanded it to go to the Shchapalov apartment and stay there. It was surprising then that there were always more roaches coming back through the pipes. Marcia assumed that they were younger generations. Cockroaches are known to breed fast. But it was easy enough to send them to the Shchapalovs.

"Into their beds," she added as an afterthought. *"Go into their beds."* Disgusting as it was, the idea gave her a queer thrill of pleasure.

The next morning, the Shchapalov woman, smelling a little worse than usual (Whatever was it, Marcia wondered, that they drank?), was waiting at the open door of her apartment. She wanted to speak to Marcia before she left for work. Her housedress was mired from an attempt at scrubbing the floor, and while she sat there talking, she tried to wring out the scrubwater.

"No idea!" she exclaimed. "You ain't got no idea how bad! 'S terrible!"

"What?" Marcia asked, knowing perfectly well what.

"The boogs! Oh, the boogs are just everywhere. Don't you have 'em, sweetheart? I don't know what to do. I try to keep a decent house, God knows—" She lifted her rheumy eyes to heaven, testifying. "—but I don't know what to do." She leaned forward, confidingly. "You won't believe this, sweetheart, but last night . . ." A cockroach began to climb out of the limp strands of hair straggling down into the woman's eyes. ". . . they got into bed with us! Would you believe it? There must have been a hundred of 'em. I said to Osip, I said—What's wrong, sweetheart?"

Marcia, speechless with horror, pointed at the roach, which had almost reached the bridge of the woman's nose. "Yech!" the woman agreed, smashing it and wiping her dirtied thumb on her dirtied dress. "Goddam boogs! I hate 'em, I swear to God. But what's a person gonna do? Now, what I wanted to ask, sweetheart, is do you have a problem with the boogs? Being as how you're right next door, I thought—" She smiled a confidential smile, as though to say this is just between us ladies. Marcia almost expected a roach to skitter out between her gapped teeth.

"No," she said. "No, I use Black Flag." She backed away from the doorway toward the safety of the stairwell. "Black Flag," she said again, louder. "Black Flag," she shouted from the foot of the stairs. Her knees trembled so, that she had to hold onto the metal banister for support.

At the insurance office that day, Marcia couldn't keep her mind on her work five minutes at a time. (Her work in the Actuarial Dividends department consisted of adding up long rows of two-digit numbers on a Burroughs adding machine and checking the similar additions of her co-workers for errors.) She kept thinking of the cockroaches in the tangled hair of the Shchapalov woman, of her bed teeming with roaches, and of other, less concrete horrors on the periphery of consciousness. The numbers swam and swarmed before her eyes, and twice she had to go to the Ladies' Room, but each time it was a false alarm. Nevertheless, lunchtime found her with no appetite. Instead of going down to the employee cafeteria she went out into the fresh April air and strolled along 23rd Street. Despite the spring, it all seemed to bespeak a sordidness, a festering corruption. The stones of the Flatiron Building oozed damp blackness; the gutters were heaped with soft decay; the smell of burning grease hung in the air outside the cheap restaurants like cigarette smoke in a close room.

The afternoon was worse. Her fingers would not touch the correct numbers on the machine unless she looked at them. One silly phrase kept running through her head: "Something must be done. Something must be done." She had quite forgotten that she had sent the roaches into the Shchapalovs' bed in the first place.

That night, instead of going home immediately, she went to a double feature on 42nd Street. She couldn't afford the better movies. Susan Hayward's little boy almost drowned in quicksand. That was the only thing she remembered afterward.

She did something then that she had never done before. She had a drink in a bar. She had two drinks. Nobody bothered her; nobody even looked in her direction. She took a taxi to Thompson Street (the subways weren't safe at that hour) and arrived at her door by eleven o'clock. She didn't have anything left for a tip. The taxi driver said he understood.

There was a light on under the Shchapalovs' door, and they were singing. It was eleven o'clock. "Something must be done," Marcia whispered to herself earnestly. "Something must be *done*."

Without turning on her own light, without even taking off her new spring jacket from Ohrbach's, Marcia got down on her knees and crawled under the sink. She tore out the Kleenexes she had stuffed into the cracks around the pipes.

There they were, the three of them, the Shchapalovs, drinking, the woman plumped on the lap of the one-eyed man, and the other man, in a dirty undershirt, stamping his foot on the floor to accompany the loud discords of their song. Horrible. They were drinking of course, she might have known it, and now the woman pressed her roachy mouth against the mouth of the one-eyed man—kiss, kiss. Horrible, horrible. Marcia's hands knotted into her mouse-colored hair, and she thought: *The filth, the disease!* Why, they hadn't learned a thing from last night!

Some time later (Marcia had lost track of time) the overhead light in the Shchapalovs' apartment was turned off. Marcia waited till they made no more noise. "Now," Marcia said, "all of you.

"All of you in this building, all of you that can hear me, gather around the bed, but wait a little while yet. Patience. All of you . . ." The words of her command fell apart into little fragments, which she told like the beads of a rosary—little brown ovoid wooden beads. ". . . gather round . . . wait a little while yet . . . all of you . . . patience . . . gather round . . ." Her hand stroked the cold water pipes rhythmically, and it seemed that she could hear them—gathering, scuttering up through the walls, coming out of the cupboards, the garbage bags—a host, an army, and she was their absolute queen.

"Now!" she said. "Mount them! Cover them! Devour them!"

There was no doubt that she could hear them now. She heard them quite palpably. Their sound was like grass in the wind, like the first stirrings of gravel dumped from a truck. Then there was the Shchapalov woman's scream, and curses from the men, such terrible curses that Marcia could hardly bear to listen.

A light went on, and Marcia could see them, the roaches, everywhere. Every surface, the walls, the doors, the shabby sticks of furniture, was motley thick with *Blattelae Germanicae.* There was more than a single thickness.

The Shchapalov woman, standing up in her bed, screamed monotonously. Her pink rayon nightgown was speckled with brown-black dots. Her knobby fingers tried to brush bugs out of her hair, off her face. The man in the undershirt who a few minutes before had been stomping his feet to the music stomped now more urgently, one hand still holding onto the lightcord. Soon the floor was slimy with crushed roaches, and he slipped. The light went out. The woman's scream took on a rather choked quality, as though . . .

But Marcia wouldn't think of that. "Enough," she whispered. "No more. Stop."

She crawled away from the sink, across the room on to her bed, which tried, with a few tawdry cushions, to dissemble itself as a couch for the daytime. Her breathing came hard, and there was a curious constriction in her throat. She was sweating incontinently.

From the Shchapalovs' room came scuffling sounds, a door banged, running feet, and then a louder, muffled noise, perhaps a body falling downstairs. The landlady's voice: "What the hell do you think you're—" Other voices overriding hers. Incoherences, and footsteps returning up the stairs. Once more, the landlady: "There ain't no *boogs* here, for heaven's sake. The boogs is in your heads. You've got the d.t.'s, that's what. And it wouldn't be any wonder, if there were boogs. The place is filthy. Look at that crap on the floor. Filth! I've stood just about enough from you. Tomorrow you move out, hear? This *used* to be a decent building."

The Shchapalovs did not protest their eviction. Indeed, they did not wait for the morrow to leave. They quitted their apartment with only a suitcase, a laundry bag, and an electric toaster. Marcia watched them go down the steps through her half-open door. *It's done,* she thought. It's all *over.*

With a sigh of almost sensual pleasure, she turned on the lamp beside the bed, then the other lamps. The room gleamed immaculately. Deciding to celebrate her victory, she went to the cupboard, where she kept a bottle of *crème de menthe.*

The cupboard was full of roaches.

She had not told them where to go, where *not* to go, when they left the Shchapalov apartment. It was her own fault.

The great silent mass of roaches regarded Marcia calmly, and it seemed to the distracted girl that she could read *their* thoughts, their thought rather, for they had but a single thought. She could read it as clearly as she could read the illuminated billboard for Chock Full O'Nuts outside her window. It was delicate music issuing from a thousand tiny pipes. It was an ancient music box open after centuries of silence: "We love you we love you we love you we love you."

Something strange happened inside Marcia then, something unprecedented: she responded.

"I love you too," she replied. "Oh, I love you. Come to me, all of you. Come to me. I love you. Come to me. I love you. Come to me."

From every corner of Manhattan, from the crumbling walls of Harlem, from restaurants on 56th Street, from warehouses along the river, from sewers and from orange peels moldering in garbage cans, the loving roaches came forth and began to crawl toward their mistress.

Theodore Sturgeon

Bright Segment

Theodore Sturgeon's fiction was published in the science fiction field throughout his distinguished career, although it encompassed a wide variety of genres. He was one of the American masters of the short story form and generally considered the greatest conscious artist working in the field of SF and fantasy from the 1940s to the 1970s. His early stories were published in John W. Campbell's *Astounding* and *Unknown* magazines, but his greatest impact was achieved in the fantastic fictions in *Unknown,* a significant proportion of them horror. He was a model for the young Ray Bradbury, who contributed an enthusiastic introduction to Sturgeon's first collection, *Without Sorcery* (1949). But it was in the 1950s, especially in such works as *Some of Your Blood* and "And Now the News," that Sturgeon reached the heights of his powers. "Bright Segment" was published in 1955 and is a classic of horror fiction representative of Sturgeon's mastery of penetrating psychological insight. His contributions to fantasy and horror were recognized by a Life Achievement award from the World Fantasy Convention.

He had never held a girl before. He was not terrified; he had used that up earlier when he had carried her in and kicked the door shut behind him and had heard the steady drip of blood from her soaked skirt, and before that, when he had thought her dead there on the curb, and again when she made that sound, that sigh or whispered moan. He had brought her in and when he saw all that blood he had turned left, turned right, put her down on the floor, his brains all clabbered and churned and his temples athump with the unaccustomed exercise. All he could act on was *Don't get blood on the bedspread.* He turned on the overhead light and stood for a moment blinking and breathing hard; suddenly he leaped for the window to lower the blind against the street light staring in and all other eyes. He saw his hands reach for the blind and checked himself; they were red and ready to paint anything he touched. He made a sound, a detached part of his mind recognizing it as the exact duplicate of that agonized whisper she had uttered out there on the dark, wet street, and leapt to the light switch, seeing the one red smudge already there, knowing as he swept his hand over it he was leaving another. He stumbled to the sink in the corner and washed his hands, washed them again, every few seconds looking over his shoulder at the girl's body and the thick flat finger of blood which crept curling toward him over the linoleum.

He had his breath now, and moved more carefully to the window. He

321

drew down the blind and pulled the curtains and looked at the sides and the bottom to see that there were no crevices. In pitch blackness he felt his way back to the opposite wall, going around the edges of the linoleum, and turned on the light again. The finger of blood was a tentacle now, fumbling toward the soft, stain-starved floorboards. From the enamel table beside the stove he snatched a plastic sponge and dropped it on the tentacle's seeking tip and was pleased, it was a reaching thing no more, it was only something spilled that could be mopped up.

He took off the bedspread and hung it over the brass headrail. From the drawer of the china closet and from the gate leg table he took his two plastic table cloths. He covered the bed with them, leaving plenty of overlap, then stood a moment rocking with worry and pulling out his lower lip with a thumb and forefinger. *Fix it right,* he told himself firmly. So she'll die before you fix it, never mind, fix it, right.

He expelled air from his nostrils and got books from the shelf in the china closet—a six-year-old World Almanac, a half-dozen paperbacked novels, a heavy catalog of jewelry findings. He pulled the bed away from the wall and put books one by one under two of the legs so that the bed was tilted slightly down to the foot and slightly to one side. He got a blanket and rolled it and slipped it under the plastic so that it formed a sort of fence down the high side. He got a six-quart aluminum pot from under the sink and set it on the floor by the lowest corner of the bed and pushed the trailing end of plastic down into it. *So bleed now,* he told the girl silently, with satisfaction.

He bent over her and grunted, lifting her by the armpits. Her head fell back as if she had no bones in her neck and he almost dropped her. He dragged her to the bed, leaving a wide red swath as her skirt trailed through the scarlet puddle she had lain in. He lifted her clear of the floor, settled his feet, and leaned over the bed with her in his arms. It took an unexpected effort to do it. He realized only then how drained, how tired he was, and how old. He put her down clumsily, almost dropping her in an effort to leave the carefully arranged tablecloths undisturbed, and he very nearly fell into the bed with her. He levered himself away with rubbery arms and stood panting. Around the soggy hem of her skirt blood began to gather, and as he watched, began to find its way lazily to the low corner. *So much, so much blood in a person,* he marveled, and *stop it, how to make it stop if it won't stop?*

He glanced at the locked door, the blinded window, the clock. He listened. It was raining harder now, drumming and hissing in the darkest hours. Otherwise nothing; the house was asleep and the street, dead. He was alone with his problem.

He pulled at his lip, then snatched his hand away as he tasted her blood. He coughed and ran to the sink and spat, and washed his mouth and then his hands.

So all right, go call up. . . .

Call up? Call what, the hospital they should call the cops? Might as well call the cops altogether. *Stupid.* What could I tell them, she's my sister, she's hit by a car, they going to believe me? Tell them the truth, a block away I see somebody push her out of a car, drive off, no lights, I bring her in out of the rain, only inside I find she is bleeding like this, they believe me? *Stupid.* What's the matter with you, mind your own business why don't you.

He thought he would pick her up now and put her back in the rain. Yes and somebody sees you, *stupid.*

He saw that the wide, streaked patch of blood on the linoleum was losing gloss where it lay thin, drying and soaking in. He picked up the sponge, two-thirds red now and the rest its original baby-blue except at one end where it looked like bread drawn with a sharp red pencil. He turned it over so it wouldn't drip while he carried it and took it to the sink and rinsed it, wringing it over and over in the running water. *Stupid,* call up somebody and get help.

Call who?

He thought of the department store where for eighteen years he had waxed floors and vacuumed rugs at night. The neighborhood, where he knew the grocery and the butcher. Closed up, asleep, everybody gone; names, numbers he didn't know and anyway, who to trust? *My God in fifty-three years you haven't got a friend?*

He took the clean sponge and sank to his knees on the linoleum, and just then the band of blood creeping down the bed reached the corner and turned to a sharp streak; *ponk* it went into the pan, and *pitti-pittipitti* in a rush, then drip-drip-drip-drip, three to the second and not stopping. He knew then with absolute and belated certainty that this bleeding was not going to stop by itself. He whimpered softly and then got up and went to the bed. "*Don't be dead,*" he said aloud, and the way his voice sounded, it frightened him. He put out his hand to her chest, but drew it back when he saw her blouse was torn and blood came from there too.

He swallowed hard and then began fumbling with her clothes. Flat ballet slippers, worn, soggy, thin like paper and little silken things he had never seen before, like just the foot of a stocking. More blood on—but no, that was peeled and chipped enamel on her cold white toes. The skirt had a button at the side and a zipper which baffled him for a moment, but he got it down and tugged the skirt off in an interminable series of jerks from the hem, one side and the other, while she rolled slightly and limply to the motion. Small silken pants, completely soaked and so badly cut on the left side that he snapped them apart easily between his fingers; but the other side was surprisingly strong and he had to get his scissors to cut them away. The blouse buttoned up the front and was no problem; under it was a brassiere which was cut right in two near the front. He lifted it away but had to cut one of the straps with his scissors to free it altogether.

He ran to the sink with his sponge, washed it and wrung it out, filled a saucepan with warm water and ran back. He sponged the body down; it looked firm but too thin, with its shadow-ladder of ribs down each side and the sharp protrusion of the hip-bones. Under the left breast was a long cut, starting on the ribs in front and curving upward almost to the nipple. It seemed deep but the blood merely welled out. The other cut, though, in her groin, released blood brightly in regular gouts, one after the other, eager but weakly. He had seen the like before, the time Garber pinched his arm off in the elevator cable-room, but then the blood squirted a foot away. Maybe this did, too, he thought suddenly, but now it's slowing up, now it's going to stop, yes, and you, stupid, you have a dead body you can tell stories to the police.

He wrung out the sponge in the water and mopped the wound. Before it could fill up again he spread the sides of the cut and looked down into it. He could clearly see the femoral artery, looking like an end of spaghetti and cut almost through; and then there was nothing but blood again.

He squatted back on his heels, pulling heedlessly at his lip with his bloody hand and trying to think. *Pinch, shut, squeeze. Squeezers. Tweezers!* He ran to his toolbox and clawed it open. Years ago he had learned to make fine chains out of square silver wire, and he used to pass the time away by making link after tiny link, soldering each one closed with an alcohol torch and a needle-tipped iron. He picked up the tweezers and dropped them in favor of the small spring clamp which he used for holding the link while he worked on it. He ran to the sink and washed the clamp and came back to the bed. Again he sponged away the little lake of blood, and quickly reached down and got the fine jaws of the clamp on the artery near its cut. Immediately there was another gush of blood. Again he sponged it away, and in a blaze of inspiration, released the clamp, moved it to the other side of the cut, and clamped it again.

Blood still oozed from the inside of the wound, but that terrible pulsing gush was gone. He sat back on his heels and painfully released a breath he must have held for two minutes. His eyes ached from the strain, and his brain was still whirling, but with these was a feeling, a new feeling almost like an ache or a pain, but it was nowhere and everywhere inside him; it wanted him to laugh but at the same time his eyes stung and hot salt squeezed out through holes too small for it.

After a time he recovered, blinking away his exhaustion, and sprang up, overwhelmed by urgency. *Got to fix everything.* He went to the medicine cabinet over the sink. Adhesive tape, pack of gauze pads. Maybe not big enough; okay tape together, fix right. New tube this sulfa-thia-dia-whatchamacall-um, fix anything, time I got vacuum-cleaner grit in cut hand, infection. Fixed boils too.

He filled a kettle and his saucepan with clean water and put them on the stove. Sew up, yes. He found needles, white thread, dumped them into the water. He went back to the bed and stood musing for a long time, looking at the oozing gash under the girl's breast. He sponged out the femoral wound again and stared pensively into it until the blood slowly covered the clamped artery. He could not be positive, but he had a vague recollection of something about tourniquets, they should be opened up every once in a while or there is trouble; same for an artery, maybe? Better he should sew up the artery; it was only opened, not cut through. If he could find out how to do it and still let it be like a pipe, not like a darned sock.

So into the pot went the tweezers, a small pair of needle-nose pliers, and, after some more thought, a dozen silver broach-pins out of his jewelry kit. Waiting for the water to boil, he inspected the wounds again. He pulled on his lip, frowning, then got another fine needle, held it with pliers in the gas flame until it was red, and with another of his set of pliers bent it around in a small semi-circle and dropped it into the water. From the sponge he cut a number of small flat slabs and dropped them in too.

He glanced at the clock, and then for ten minutes he scrubbed the white enamel table-top with cleanser. He tipped it into the sink, rinsed it at the faucet, and then slowly poured the contents of the kettle over it. He took it to the stove, held it with one hand while he fished in the boiling saucepan with a silver knife until he had the pliers resting with their handles out of the water. He grasped them gingerly with a clean washcloth and carefully, one by one, transferred everything from saucepan to table. By the time he had found the last of the needles and the elusive silver pins, sweat was running into his eyes and the arm that held the table-top threatened to drop right off. But he set his stumpy yellow teeth and kept at it.

Carrying the table-top, he kicked a wooden chair bit by bit across the room until it rested by the bed, and set his burden down on its seat. *This no hospital,* he thought, *but I fix everything.*

Hospital! Yes, in the movies—

He went to a drawer and got a clean white handkerchief and tried to tie it over his mouth and nose like in the movies. His knobby face and square head were too much for one handkerchief; it took three before he got it right, with a great white tassel hanging down the back like in an airplane picture.

He looked helplessly at his hands, then shrugged; so no rubber globes, what the hell. I wash good. His hands were already pink and wrinkled from his labors, but he went back to the sink and scratched a bar of soap until his horny nails were packed with it, then cleaned them with a file until they hurt, and washed and cleaned them again. And at last he knelt by the bed, holding his shriven hands up in a careful salaam. Almost, he reached for his lip to pull it, but not quite.

He squeezed out two globs of the sulfa ointment onto the table-top and, with the pliers, squashed two slabs of sponge until the creamy stuff was through and through them. He mopped out the femoral wound and placed a medicated sponge on each side of the wound, leaving the artery exposed at the bottom. Using tweezers and pliers, he laboriously threaded the curved needle while quelling the urge to stick the end of the thread into his mouth.

He managed to get four tiny stitches into the artery below the break, out of it above the break. Each one he knotted with exquisite care so that the thread would not cut the tissue but still would draw the severed edges together. Then he squatted back on his heels to rest, his shoulders afire with tension, his eyes misted. Then, taking a deep breath, he removed the clamp.

Blood filled the wound and soaked the sponges. But it came slowly, without spurting. He shrugged grimly. So what's to do, use a tire patch? He mopped the blood out once more, and quickly filled the incision with ointment, slapping a piece of gauze over it more to hide it than to help it.

He wiped his eyebrows first with one shoulder, then the other, and fixed his eyes on the opposite wall the way he used to do when he worked on his little silver chains. When the mist went away he turned his attention to the long cut on the underside of the breast. He didn't know how to stitch one this size, but he could cook and he knew how to skewer up a chicken. Biting his tongue, he stuck the first of his silver pins into the flesh at right angles to the cut, pressing it across the wound and out the other side. He started the next pin not quite an inch away, and the same with the third. The fourth grated on something in the wound; it startled him like a door slamming and he bit his tongue painfully. He backed the pin out and probed carefully with his tweezers. Yes, something hard in there. He probed deeper with both points of the tweezers, feeling them enter uncut tissue with a soft crunching that only a fearful fingertip could hear. He conquered a shudder and glanced up at the girl's face. He resolved not to look up there again. It was a very dead face.

Stupid! but the self-insult was lost in concentration even as it was born. The tweezers closed on something hard, slippery and stubborn. He worked it gently back and forth, feeling a puzzled annoyance at this unfamiliar flesh that yielded as he moved. Gradually, very gradually, a sharp angular corner of *something* appeared. He kept at it until there was enough to grasp with his fingers; then he set his tweezers aside and gently worked it loose. Blood began to flow freely before it was half out, but he did not stop until he could draw it free. The light glinted on the strip of hollow-ground steel and its shattered margins; he turned it over twice before it came to him that it was a piece of straight razor. He set it down on his enamel table, thinking of what the police might have said to him if he had turned her over to them with that story about a car accident.

He stanched the blood, pulled the wound as wide apart as he could. The nipple writhed under his fingers, its pink halo shrunken and wrinkled; he grunted, thinking that a bug had crawled under his hand, and then aware that whatever the thing meant, it couldn't mean death, not yet anyway. He had to go back and start over, stanching the cut and spreading it, and quickly squeezing in as much ointment as it would hold. Then he went on with his insertion of the silver pins, until there was a little ladder of twelve of them from one end of the wound to the other. He took his thread, doubled it, put the loop around the topmost pin and drew the two parts of the thread underneath. Holding them both in one hand, he gently pinched the edges of the wound together at the pin. Then he drew the loop tight without cutting, crossed the threads and put them under the next pin, and again closed the wound. He continued this all the way down, lacing the cut closed around the ladder of pins. At the bottom he tied the thread off and cut it. There was blood and ointment all over his handiwork, but when he mopped up it looked good to him.

He stood up and let sensation flow agonizingly into his numb feet. He was sopping wet; he could feel perspiration searching its way down through the hairs of his legs; like a migration of bedbugs. He looked down at himself; wrinkles and water and blood. He looked across at the wavery mirror, and saw a bandaged goblin with brow-ridges like a shelf and sunken eyes with a cast to them, with grizzled hair which could be scrubbed only to the color of grime, and with a great gout of blood where the mouth hid behind the bandage. He snatched it down and looked again. *More better you cover your face, no matter what.* He turned away, not from his face, but with it, in the pained patience of a burro with saddle sores.

Wearily he carried his enameled table-top to the sink. He washed his hands and forearms and took off the handkerchiefs from around his neck and washed his face. Then he got what was left of his sponge and a pan of warm soapy water and came back to the bed.

It took him hours. He sponged the tablecloths on which she lay, shifted her gently so as to put no strain on the wounds, and washed and dried where she had lain. He washed her from head to toe, going back for clean water, and then had to dry the bed again afterward. When he lifted her head he found her hair matted and tacky with rain and drying blood, and fresh blood with it, so he propped up her shoulders with a big pillow under the plastic and tipped her head back and washed and dried her hair, and found an ugly lump and a bleeding contusion on the back of her head. He combed the hair away from it on each side and put cold water on it, and it stopped bleeding, but there was a lump the size of a plum. He separated half a dozen of the gauze pads and packed them around the lump so that it need not take the pressure off her head; he dared not turn her over.

When her hair was wet and fouled it was only a dark mat, but cleaned and combed, it was the darkest of auburns, perfectly straight. There was a broad lustrous band of it on the bed on each side of her face, which was radiant with pallor, cold as a moon. He covered her with the bedspread, and for a long while stood over her, full of that strange nowhere-everywhere almost-pain, not liking it but afraid to turn away from it . . . maybe he would never have it again.

He sighed, a thing that came from his marrow and his years, and doggedly set to work scrubbing the floor. When he had finished, and the needles and thread were put away, the bit of tape which he had not used, the wrappers of the gauze pads and the pan of blood from the end of the bed disposed of, and all the tools cleaned and back in their box, the night was over and daylight pressed weakly against the drawn blind. He turned out the light and stood without breathing, listening with all his mind, wanting to know from where he stood if she still lived. To bend close and find out she was gone—oh no. He wanted to know from here.

But a truck went by, and a woman called a child, and someone laughed; so he went and knelt by the bed and closed his eyes and slowly put his hand on her throat. It was cool—please, not cold!—and quiet as a lost glove.

Then the hairs on the back of his hand stirred to her breath, and again, the faintest of motions. The stinging came to his eyes and through and through him came the fiery urge to *do*: make some soup, buy some medicine, maybe, for her, a ribbon or a watch; clean the house, run to the store . . . and while doing all these things, all at once, to shout and shout great shaking wordless bellows to tell himself over and over again, so he could hear for sure, that she was alive. At the very peak of this explosion of urges, there was a funny little side-slip and he was fast asleep.

He dreamed someone was sewing his legs together with a big curved sail needle, and at the same time drawing the thread from his belly; he could feel the spool inside spinning and emptying. He groaned and opened his eyes, and knew instantly where he was and what had happened, and hated himself for the noise he made. He lifted his hand and churned his fingers to be sure they could feel, and lowered them gently to her throat. It was warm—no, hot, too hot. He pushed back from the bed and scrabbled half-across the floor on his knuckles and his numb, rubbery legs. Cursing silently he made a long lunge and caught the wooden chair to him, and used it to climb to his feet. He dared not let it go, so clumped softly with it over to the corner, where he twisted and hung gasping to the edge of the sink, while boiling acid ate downward through his legs. When he could, he splashed cold water on his face and neck and, still drying himself on a towel, stumbled across to the bed. He flung the bedspread off and *stupid!* he almost screamed as it plucked at his fingers on the way; it had adhered to the wound in her groin and he was sure he had ripped it to shreds, torn a whole section out of the clumsily patched artery. And he couldn't see; it must be getting dark outside; how long had he crouched there? He ran to the light switch, leaped back. Yes, bleeding, it was bleeding again—

But a little, only a very little. The gauze was turned up perhaps halfway, and though the exposed wound was wet with blood, blood was not running. It had, while he was asleep, but hardly enough to find its way to the mattress. He lifted the loose corner of the gauze very gently, and found it stuck fast. But the sponges, the little sponges to put on the sulfa-whatchama, they were still in the wound. He'd meant to take them out after a couple of hours, not let the whole clot form around them!

He ran for warm water, his big sponge. Soap in it, yes. He squatted beside the bed, though his legs still protested noisily, and began to bathe the gauze with tiny, gentle touches.

Something made him look up. She had her eyes open, and was looking down at him. Her face and her eyes were utterly without expression. He watched them close slowly and slowly open again, lackluster and uninterested. "All right, all right," he said harshly, "I fix everything." She just kept on looking. He nodded violently, it was all that soothes, all that encourages, hope for her and a total promise for her, but it was only a rapid bobbing of his big ugly head. Annoyed as he always was at his own speechlessness, he went back to work. He got the gauze off and began soaking the edge of one of the sponges. When he thought it was ready to come, he tugged gently at it.

In a high, whispery soprano, "Ho-o-o-o . . . ?" she said; it was like a question and a sob. Slowly she turned her head to the left. "Ho-o-o-o?" She turned her head again and slipped back to unconsciousness.

"I," he said loudly, excitedly, and "I—" and that was all; she wouldn't hear him anyway. He held still until his hands stopped trembling, and went on with the job.

The wound looked wonderfully clean, though the skin all around it was dry and hot.

Down inside the cut he could see the artery in a nest of wet jelly; that was probably right—he didn't know, but it looked all right, he wouldn't disturb it. He packed the opening full of ointment, pressed the edges gently together, and put on a piece of tape. It promptly came unstuck, so he discarded it and dried the flesh all around the wound, put on gauze first, then the tape, and this time it held.

The other cut was quite closed, though more so where the pins were than between them. It too was surrounded by hot, dry, red flesh.

The scrape on the back of her head had not bled, but the lump was bigger than ever. Her face and neck were dry and very warm, though the rest of her body seemed cool. He went for a cold cloth and put it across her eyes and pressed it down on her cheeks, and she sighed. When he took it away she was looking at him again.

"You all right?" he asked her, and inanely, "You all right," he told her. A small frown flickered for a moment and then her eyes closed. He knew somehow that she was asleep. He touched her cheeks with the backs of his fingers. "Very hot," he muttered.

He turned out the light and in the dimness changed his clothes. From the bottom of a drawer he took a child's exercise book, and from it a piece of paper with a telephone number in large black penciled script. "I come back," he said to the darkness. She didn't say anything. He went out, locking the door behind him.

Laboriously he called the office from the big drugstore, referring to his paper for each digit and for each, holding the dial against the stop for a full three or four seconds as if to be sure the number would stick. He got the big boss Mr. Laddie first of all, which was acutely embarrassing; he had not spoken to him in a dozen years. At the top of his bull voice he collided with Laddie's third impatient "Hello?" with "Sick! I—uh, *sick*!" He heard the phone say "—in God's name . . . ?" and Mr. Wismer's laughter, and "Gimme the phone, that's got to be that orangutan of mine," and right in his ear, "Hello?"

"Sick tonight," he shouted.

"What's the matter with you?"

He swallowed. "I can't," he yelled.

"That's just old age," said Mr. Wismer. He heard Mr. Laddie laughing too. Mr. Wismer said, "How many nights you had off in the last fifteen years?"

He thought about it. "No!" he roared. Anyway, it was eighteen years.

"You know, that's right," said Mr. Wismer, speaking to Mr. Laddie without trying to cover his phone, "fifteen years and never asked for a night off before."

"So who needs him? Give him all his nights off."

"Not at those prices," said Mr. Wismer, and to his phone, "Sure, dummy, take off. Don't work no con games." The phone clicked off on laughter, and he waited there in the booth until he was sure nothing else would be said. Then he hung up his receiver and emerged into the big drugstore where everyone all over was looking at him. Well, they always did. That didn't bother him. Only one thing bothered him, and that was Mr. Laddie's voice saying over and over in his head, "So who needs him?" He knew he would have to stop and face those words and let them and all that went with them go through his mind. But not now, please not now.

He kept them away by being busy; he bought tape and gauze and ointment and a canvas cot and three icebags and, after some thought, aspirin, because someone had told him once . . . and then to the supermarket where he bought enough to feed a family of nine for nine days. And for all his bundles, he still had a thick arm and a wide shoulder for a twenty-five-pound cake of ice.

He got the door open and the ice in the box, and went out in the hall and picked up the bundles and brought those in, and then went to her. She was burning up, and her breathing was like the way seabirds fly into the wind, a small beat, a small beat, and a long wait, balancing. He cracked a corner off the ice-cake, wrapped it in a dishtowel and whacked it angrily against the sink. He crowded the crushed ice into one of the bags and put it on her head. She sighed but did not open her eyes. He filled the other bags and put one on her breast and one on her groin. He wrung his hands uselessly over her until it came to him *she has to eat, losing blood like that.*

So he cooked, tremendously, watching her every second minute. He made minestrone and baked cabbage and mashed potatoes and veal cutlets. He cut a pie and warmed cinnamon buns, and he had hot coffee with ice cream ready to spoon into it. She didn't eat it, any of it, nor did she drink a drop. She lay there and occasionally let her head fall to the side, so he had to run and pick up the icebag and replace it. Once again she sighed, and once he thought she opened her eyes, but couldn't be sure.

On the second day she ate nothing and drank nothing, and her fever was unbelievable. During the night, crouched on the floor beside her, he awoke once with the echoes of weeping still in the room, but he may have dreamed it.

Once he cut the tenderest, juiciest piece of veal he could find on a cutlet, and put it between her lips. Three hours later he pressed them apart to put in another piece, but the first one was still there. The same thing happened with aspirin, little white crumbs on a dry tongue.

And the time soon came when he had busied himself out of things to do, and fretted himself into a worry-reflex that operated by itself, and the very act of thinking new thoughts trapped him into facing the old ones, and then of course there was nothing to do but let them run on through, with all the ache and humiliation they carried with them. He was trying to think a new thing about what would happen if he called a doctor, and the doctor would want to take her to a hospital; he would say, "She needs treatment, old man, she doesn't need you," and there it was in his mind, ready to run, so:

Be eleven years old, bulky and strong and shy, standing in the kitchen doorway, holding your wooden box by its string and trying to shape your mouth so that the reluctant words can press out properly; and there's Mama hunched over a gin bottle like a cat over a half-eaten bird, peering; watch her lipless wide mouth twitch and say, "Don't stand there clackin' and slurpin'! Speak up, boy! What are you tryin' to say, you're leaving?"

So nod, it's easier, and she'll say, "Leave, then, leave, who needs you?" and you go:

And be a squat, powerful sixteen and go to the recruiting station and watch the sergeant with the presses and creases asking "Whadda *you* want?" and you try, you try and you can't say it so you nod your head at the poster with the pointing finger, UNCLE SAM NEEDS YOU; and the sergeant glances at it and at you, and suddenly his pointing finger is half an inch away from your nose; crosseyed you watch it while he barks, "Well, Uncle don't need *you*!" and you wait, watching the finger that way, not moving until you understand; you understand things real good, it's just that you hear slowly. So there you hang crosseyed and they all laugh.

Or 'way back, you're eight years old and in school, that Phyllis with the row of springy brown sausage-curls flying when she tosses her head, pink and clean and so pretty; you have the chocolates wrapped in gold paper tied in gold-string mesh; you go up the aisle to her desk and put the chocolates down and run back; she comes down the aisle and throws them so hard the mesh breaks on your desk and she says, loud, "I don't need these and I don't need you, and you know what, you got snot on your face," and you put up your hand and sure enough you have.

That's all. Only every time anyone says "Who needs him?" or the like, you have to go through all of them, every one. Sooner or later, however much you put it off, you've got to do it all.

I get doctor, you don't need me.

You die, you don't need me.

Please . . .

Far back in her throat, a scraping hiss, and her lips moved. She held his eyes with hers, and her lips moved silently, and a little late for the lips, the hiss came again. He didn't know how he guessed right, but he did and brought water, dribbling it slowly on her mouth. She licked at it greedily, lifting her head up. He put a hand under it, being careful of the lump, and helped her. After a while she slumped back and smiled weakly at the cup. Then she looked up into his face and though the smile disappeared, he felt much better. He ran to the icebox and the stove, and got glasses and straws—one each of orange juice, chocolate milk, plain milk, consommé from a can, and ice water. He lined them up on the chair-seat by the bed and watched them and her eagerly, like a circus seal waiting to play "America" on the bulb-horns. She did smile this time, faintly, briefly, but right at him, and he tried the consommé. She drank almost half of it through the straw without stopping and fell asleep.

Later, when he checked to see if there was any bleeding, the plastic sheet was wet, but not with blood. *Stupid!* he raged at himself, and stamped out and bought a bedpan.

She slept a lot now, and ate often but lightly. She began to watch him as he moved about; sometimes when he thought she was asleep, he would turn and meet her eyes. Mostly, it was his hands she watched, those next two days. He washed and ironed her clothes, and sat and mended them with straight small stitches; he hung by his elbows to the edge of the enameled table and worked his silver wire, making her a broach like a flower on a fan, and a pendant on a silver chain, and a bracelet to match them. She watched his hands while he cooked; he made his own spaghetti—tagliatelli, really—rolling and rolling the dough until it was a huge tough sheet, winding it up like a jelly-roll only tight, slicing it in quick, accurate flickers of a paring-knife so it came out like yellow-white flat shoelaces. He had hands which had never learned their limitations, because he had never thought to limit them. Nothing else in life cared for this man but his hands, and since they did everything, they could do anything.

But when he changed her dressings or washed her, or helped with the bedpan, she never looked at his hands. She would lie perfectly still and watch his face.

She was very weak at first and could move nothing but her head. He was glad because her stitches were healing nicely. When he withdrew the pins it must have hurt, but she made not a sound; twelve flickers of her smooth brow, one for each pin as it came out.

"Hurts," he rumbled.

Faintly, she nodded. It was the first communication between them, except for those mute, crowded eyes following him about. She smiled too, as she nodded, and he turned his back and ground his knuckles into his eyes and felt wonderful.

He went back to work on the sixth night, having puttered and fussed over her all day to keep her from sleeping until he was ready to leave, then not leaving until he was sure she was fast asleep. He would lock her in and hurry to work, warm inside and ready to do three men's work; and home again in the dark early hours as fast as his bandy legs would carry him, bringing her a present—a little radio, a scarf, something special to eat—every single day. He would lock the door firmly and then hurry to her, touching her forehead and check to see what her temperature was, straightening the bed gently so she wouldn't wake. Then he would go out of her sight, away back by the sink, and undress and change to the long drawers he slept in, and come back and curl up on the camp cot. For perhaps an hour and a half he would sleep like a stone, but after that the slightest rustle of her sheet, the smallest catch of breath, would bring him to her in a bound, croaking, "You all right?" and hanging over her tensely, frantically trying to divine what she might need, what he might do or get for her.

And when the daylight came he would give her warm milk with an egg beaten in it, and then he would bathe her and change her dressings and comb her hair, and when there was nothing left to do for her he would clean the room, scrub the floor, wash clothes and dishes and, interminably, cook. In the afternoon he shopped, moving everywhere at a half-trot, running home again as soon as he could to show her what he had bought, what he had planned for her dinner. All these days, and then these weeks, he glowed inwardly, hugging the glow while he was away from her, fanning it with her presence when they were together.

He found her crying one afternoon late in the second week, staring at the little radio with the tears streaking her face. He made a harsh cooing syllable and wiped her cheeks with a dry washcloth and stood back with torture on his animal face. She patted his hand weakly, and made a series of faint gestures which utterly baffled him. He sat on the bedside chair and put his face close to hers as if he could tear the meaning out of her with his eyes. There was something different about her; she had watched him, up to now, with the fascinated, uncomprehending attention of a kitten watching a tankful of tropical fish; but now there was something more in her gaze, in the way she moved and in what she did.

"You hurt?" he rasped.

She shook her head. Her mouth moved, and she pointed to it and began to cry again.

"Oh, you hungry. I fix, fix good." He rose but she caught his wrist, shaking her head and crying, but smiling too. He sat down, torn apart by his perplexity. Again she moved her mouth, pointing to it, shaking her head.

"No talk," he said. She was breathing so hard it frightened him, but when he said that she gasped and half sat up; he caught her shoulders and put her down, but she was nodding urgently. "You can't talk!" he said.

Yes, yes! she nodded.

He looked at her for a long time. The music on the radio stopped and someone began to sell used cars in a crackling baritone. She glanced at it and her eyes filled with tears again. He leaned across her and shut the set off. After a profound effort he formed his mouth in the right shape and released a disdainful snort: "Ha! What you want talk? Don't talk. I fix everything, no talk I—" He ran out of words, so instead slapped himself powerfully on the chest and nodded at her, the stove, the bedpan, the tray of bandages. He said again, "What you want talk?"

She looked up at him, overwhelmed by his violence, and shrank down. He tenderly wiped her cheeks again, mumbling, "I fix everything."

He came home in the dark one morning, and after seeing that she was comfortable according to his iron standards, went to bed. The smell of bacon and fresh coffee was, of course, part of a dream; what else could it be? And the faint sounds of movement around the room had to be his weary imagination.

He opened his eyes on the dream and closed them again, laughing at himself for a crazy stupid. Then he went still inside, and slowly opened his eyes again.

Beside his cot was the bedside chair, and on it was a plate of fried eggs and crisp bacon, a cup of strong black coffee, toast with the gold of butter disappearing into its older gold. He stared at these things in total disbelief, and then looked up.

She was sitting on the end of the bed, where it formed an eight-inch corridor between itself and the cot. She wore her pressed and mended blouse and her skirt. Her shoulders sagged with weariness and she seemed to have some difficulty in holding her head up; her hands hung limply between her knees. But her face was suffused with delight and anticipation as she watched him waking up to his breakfast.

His mouth writhed and he bared his blunt yellow teeth, and ground them together while he uttered a howl of fury. It was a strangled, rasping sound and she scuttled away from it as if it had burned her, and crouched in the middle of the bed with her eyes huge and her mouth slack. He advanced on her with his arms raised and his big fists clenched; she dropped her face on the bed and covered the back of her neck with both hands and lay there trembling. For a long moment he hung over her, then slowly dropped his arms. He tugged at the skirt. "Take off," he grated. He tugged it again, harder.

She peeped up at him and then slowly turned over. She fumbled weakly at the button. He helped her. He pulled the skirt away and tossed it on the cot, and gestured sternly at the blouse. She unbuttoned it and he lifted it from her shoulders. He pulled down the sheet, taking it right out from under her. He took her ankles gently in his powerful hands and pulled them down until she was straightened out on the bed, and then covered her carefully. He was breathing hard. She watched him in terror.

In a frightening quiet he turned back to his cot and the laden chair beside it. Slowly he picked up the cup of coffee and smashed it on the floor. Steadily as the beat of a woodman's axe the saucer followed, the plate of toast, the plate of eggs. China and yolk squirted and sprayed over the floor and on the walls. When he had finished he turned back to her. "I fix everything," he said hoarsely. He emphasized each syllable with a thick forefinger as he said again, "*I* fix everything."

She whipped over on her stomach and buried her face in the pillow, and began to sob so hard he could feel the bed shaking the floor through the soles of his feet. He turned angrily away from her and got a pan and a scrub-brush and a broom and dustpan, and laboriously, methodically, cleaned up the mess.

Two hours later he approached her where she lay, still on her stomach, stiff and motionless. He had had a long time to think of what to say: "Look, you see, you *sick* . . . you see?" He said it, as gently as he could. He put his hand on her shoulder but she twitched violently, flinging it away. Hurt and baffled, he backed away and sat down on the couch, watching her miserably.

She wouldn't eat any lunch.

She wouldn't eat any dinner.

As the time approached for him to go to work, she turned over. He still sat on the cot in his long johns, utter misery on his face and in every line of his ugly body. She looked at him and her eyes filled with tears. He met her gaze but did not move. She sighed suddenly and held out her hand. He leaped to it and pulled it to his forehead, knelt, bowed over it and began to cry. She patted his wiry hair until the storm passed, which it did abruptly, at its height. He sprang away from her and clattered pans on the stove, and in a few minutes brought her some bread and gravy and a parboiled artichoke, rich with olive oil and basil. She smiled wanly and took the plate, and slowly ate while he watched each mouthful and radiated what could only be gratitude. Then he changed his clothes and went to work.

He brought her a red housecoat when she began to sit up, though he would not let her out of bed. He brought her a glass globe in which a flower would keep, submerged in water, for a week, and two live turtles in a plastic bowl and a pale-blue toy rabbit with a music box in it that played "Rock-a-bye Baby" and a blinding vermilion lipstick. She remained obedient and more watchful than ever; when his fussing and puttering were over and he took up his crouch on the cot, waiting for whatever need in her he could divine next, their eyes would meet, and increasingly, his would drop. She would hold the blue rabbit tight to her and watch him unblinkingly, or smile suddenly, parting her lips as if something vitally important and deeply happy was about to escape them. Sometimes she seemed inexpressibly sad, and sometimes she was so restless that he would go to her and stroke her hair until she fell asleep, or seemed to. It occurred to him that he had not seen her wounds for almost two days, and that perhaps they were bothering her during one of these restless spells, and so he pressed her gently down and uncovered her. He touched the scar carefully and she suddenly thrust his hand away and grasped her own flesh firmly, kneading it, slapping it stingingly. Shocked, he looked at her face and saw she was smiling, nodding. "Hurt?" She shook her head. He said, proudly, as he covered her, "I fix. I fix good." She nodded and caught his hand briefly between her chin and her shoulder.

It was that night, after he had fallen into that heavy first sleep on his return from the store, that he felt the warm firm length of her tight up against him on the cot. He lay still for a moment, somnolent, uncomprehending, while quick fingers plucked at the buttons of his long johns. He brought his hands up and trapped her wrists. She was immediately still, though her breath came swiftly and her heart pounded his chest like an angry little knuckle. He made a labored, inquisitive syllable, "Wh-wha . . . ?" and she moved against him and then stopped, trembling. He held her wrists for more than a minute, trying to think this out, and at last sat up. He put one arm around her shoulders and the other under her knees. He stood up. She clung to him and the breath hissed in her nostrils. He moved to the side of her bed and bent slowly and put her down. He had to reach back and detach her arms from around his neck before he could straighten up. "You sleep," he said. He fumbled for the sheet and pulled it over her and tucked it around her. She lay absolutely motionless, and he touched her hair and went back to his cot. He lay down and after a long time fell into a troubled sleep. But something woke him; he lay and listened, hearing nothing. He remembered suddenly and vividly the night she had balanced between life and death, and he had awakened to the echo of a sob which was not repeated; in sudden fright he jumped up and went to her, bent down and touched her head. She was lying face down. "You cry?" he whispered, and she shook her head rapidly. He grunted and went back to bed.

It was the ninth week and it was raining; he plodded homeward through the black, shining streets, and when he turned into his own block and saw the dead, slick river stretching between him and the streetlight in front of his house, he experienced a moment of fantasy, of dreamlike disorientation; it seemed to him for a second that none of this had happened, that in a moment the car would flash by him and dip toward the curb momentarily while a limp body tumbled out, and he must run to it and take it indoors, and it would bleed, it would bleed, it might die. . . . He shook himself like a big dog and put his head down against the rain, saying *Stupid!* to his inner self. Nothing could be wrong, now. He had found a way to live, and live that way he would, and he would abide no change in it.

But there was a change, and he knew it before he entered the house; his window, facing the street, had a dull orange glow which could not have been given it by the street light alone. But maybe she was reading one of those paperback novels he had inherited with the apartment; maybe she had to use the bedpan or was just looking at the clock . . . but the thoughts did not comfort him; he was sick with an unaccountable fear as he unlocked the hall door. His own entrance showed light through the crack at the bottom; he dropped his keys as he fumbled with them, and at last opened the door.

He gasped as if he had been struck in the solar plexus. The bed was made, flat, neat, and she was not in it. He spun around; his frantic gaze saw her and passed her before he could believe his eyes. Tall, queenly in her red housecoat, she stood at the other end of the room, by the sink.

He stared at her in amazement. She came to him, and as he filled his lungs for one of his grating yells, she put a finger on her lips and, lightly, her other hand across his mouth. Neither of these gestures, both even, would have been enough to quiet him ordinarily, but there was something else about her, something which did not wait for what he might do and would not quail before him if he did it. He was instantly confused, and silent. He stared after her as, without breaking stride, she passed him and gently closed the door. She took his hand, but the keys were in the way; she drew them from his fingers and tossed them on the table and then took his hand again, firmly. She was sure, decisive; she was one who had thought things out and weighed and discarded, and now knew what to do. But she was triumphant in some way, too; she had the poise of a victor and the radiance of the witness to a miracle. He could cope with her helplessness, of any kind, to any degree, but this—he had to think, and she gave him no time to think.

She led him to the bed and put her hands on his shoulders, turning him and making him sit down. She sat close to him, her face alight, and when again he filled his lungs, "Shh!" she hissed, sharply, and smilingly covered his mouth with her hand. She took his shoulders again and looked straight into his eyes, and said clearly, "I can talk now, I can talk!"

Numbly he gaped at her.

"Three days already, it was a secret, it was a surprise." Her voice was husky, hoarse even, but very clear and deeper than her slight body indicated. "I been practicing, to be sure. I'm all right again, I'm all right. You fix everything!" she said, and laughed.

Hearing that laugh, seeing the pride and joy in her face, he could take nothing away from her. "Ahh . . ." he said, wonderingly.

She laughed again. "I can go, I can go!" she sang. She leapt up suddenly and pirouetted, and leaned over him laughing. He gazed up at her and her flying hair, and squinted his eyes as he would looking into the sun. "Go?" he blared, the pressure of his confusion forcing the syllable out as an explosive shout.

She sobered immediately, and sat down again close to him. "Oh, honey, don't, *don't* look as if you was knifed or something. You know I can't camp on you, live off you, just for*ever*!"

"No, no you stay," he blurted, anguish in his face.

"Now look," she said, speaking simply and slowly as to a child. "I'm all well again, I can talk now. It wouldn't be right, me staying, locked up here, that bedpan and all. Now wait, wait," she said quickly before he could form a word, "I don't mean I'm not grateful, you been . . . you been, well, I just can't tell you. Look, nobody in my life ever did anything like this, I mean, I had to run away when I was thirteen, I done all sorts of bad things. And I got treated . . . I mean, nobody else . . . look, here's what I mean, up to now I'd steal, I'd rob anybody, what the hell. What I mean, why not, you see?" She shook him gently to make him see; then, recognizing the blankness and misery of his expression, she wet her lips and started over. "What I'm trying to say is, you been so kind, all this—" She waved her hand at the blue rabbit, the turtle tank, everything in the room— "I can't take any more. I mean, not a thing, not breakfast. If I could pay you back some way, no matter what, I would, you know I would." There was a tinge of bitterness in her husky voice. "Nobody can pay you anything. You don't need anything or anybody. I can't give you anything you need, or do anything for you that needs doing, you do it all yourself. If there was something you wanted from me—" She curled her hands inward and placed her fingertips between her breasts, inclining her head with a strange submissiveness that made him ache. "But no, you fix everything," she mimicked. There was no mockery in it.

"No, no, you don't go," he whispered harshly.

She patted his cheek, and her eyes loved him. "I do go," she said, smiling. Then the smile disappeared. "I got to explain to you, those hoods who cut me, I asked for that. I goofed. I was doing something real bad—well, I'll tell you. I was a runner, know what I mean? I mean dope, I was selling it."

He looked at her blankly. He was not catching one word in ten; he was biting and biting only on emptiness and uselessness, aloneness, and the terrible truth of this room without her or the blue rabbit or anything else but what it had contained all these years—linoleum with the design scrubbed off, six novels he couldn't read, a stove waiting for someone to cook for, grime and regularity and who needs you?

She misunderstood his expression. "Honey, honey, don't look at me like that, I'll never do it again. I only did it because I didn't care, I used to get glad when people hurt themselves; yeah, I mean that. I never knew someone could be kind, like you; I always thought that was sort of a lie, like the movies. Nice but not real, not for me.

"But I have to tell you, I swiped a cache, my God, twenty, twenty-two G's worth. I had it all of forty minutes, they caught up with me." Her eyes widened and saw things not in the room. "With a razor, he went to hit me with it so hard he broke it on top of the car door. He hit me here *down* and here *up,* I guess he was going to gut me but the razor was busted." She expelled air from her nostrils, and her gaze came back into the room. "I guess I got the lump on the head when they threw me out of the car. I guess that's why I couldn't talk, I heard of that. Oh *honey*! Don't look like that, you're tearing me apart!"

He looked at her dolefully and wagged his big head helplessly from side to side. She knelt before him suddenly and took both his hands. "Listen, you *got* to understand. I was going to slide out while you were working but I stayed just so I could make you understand. After all you done. . . . See, I'm well, I can't stay cooped up in one room forever. If I could, I'd get work some place near here and see you all the time, honest I would. But my life isn't worth a rubber dime in this town. I got to leave here and that means I got to leave town. I'll be all right, honey. I'll write to you; I'll never forget you, how could I?"

She was far ahead of him. He had grasped that she wanted to leave him; the next thing he understood was that she wanted to leave town too.

"You don't go," he choked. "You need me."

"You don't need me," she said fondly, "and I don't need you. It comes to that, honey; it's the way you fixed it. It's the right way; can't you see that?"

Right in there was the third thing he understood.

He stood up slowly, feeling her hands slide from his, from his knees to the floor as he stepped away from her. "Oh God!" she cried from the floor where she knelt, "you're killing me, taking it this way! Can't you be happy for me?"

He stumbled across the room and caught himself on the lower shelf of the china closet. He looked back and forward along the dark, echoing corridor of his years, stretching so far and drearily, and he looked at this short bright segment slipping away from him. . . . He heard her quick footsteps behind him and when he turned he had the flatiron in his hand. She never saw it. She came to him bright-faced, pleading, and he put out his arms and she ran inside, and the iron curved around and crashed into the back of her head.

He lowered her gently down on the linoleum and stood for a long time over her, crying quietly.

Then he put the iron away and filled the kettle and a saucepan with water, and in the saucepan he put needles and a clamp and thread and little slabs of sponge and a knife and pliers. From the gateleg table and from a drawer he got his two plastic tablecloths and began arranging them on the bed.

"I fix everything," he murmured as he worked, "fix it right."

Clive Barker

Dread

Clive Barker is the only horror writer of the 1980s to catapult to prominence and popularity on the basis of his short fiction, the six stunning volumes called *The Books of Blood*. His work has been called the wave of the future in horror by Ramsey Campbell and Stephen King, among others. Nothing could illustrate the profound changes in horror fiction over the past decade more clearly than that Barker is the *only* major writer to emerge through short fiction, while others are primarily novelists. Fashion and economic pressure have moved him recently toward the novel form in *The Damnation Game* (1985), but his success in the short story form has created manifest excitement among other short story writers and has pointed out new directions for a new generation in horror. Rarely fully polished, the stories in *The Books of Blood* have a raw power that is undeniable, especially for the audience built for horror by the generally crudely executed novels of the previous decade. And, significantly, Barker's influences do not include a majority of the classics of horror from the past except, perhaps, King and Ellison—but rather the graphic horror of the famous E.C. comics of the 1950s, horror films and those same novels of the seventies mentioned above. A new hybrid tradition seems in the process of formation. "Dread" is one of the best stories from the six collections, moving at first in the direction of an examination of the nature of reality, then turning toward psychological monstrosities and heightened *grand guignol* violence. For Barker, powerful impact is all.

There is no delight the equal of dread. If it were possible to sit, invisible, between two people on any train, in any waiting room or office, the conversation overheard would time and again circle on that subject. Certainly the debate might appear to be about something entirely different; the state of the nation, idle chat about death on the roads, the rising price of dental care; but strip away the metaphor, the innuendo, and there, nestling at the heart of the discourse, is dread. While the nature of God and the possibility of eternal life go undiscussed, we happily chew over the minutiae of misery. The syndrome recognizes no boundaries; in bath-house and seminar-room alike, the same ritual is repeated. With the inevitability of a tongue returning to probe a painful tooth, we come back and back and back again to our fears, sitting to talk them over with the eagerness of a hungry man before a full and steaming plate.

* * *

While he was still at university, and afraid to speak, Stephen Grace was taught to speak of why he was afraid. In fact not simply to talk about it, but to analyze and dissect his every nerve-ending, looking for tiny terrors.

In this investigation, he had a teacher: Quaid.

It was an age of gurus; it was their season. In universities up and down England young men and women were looking east and west for people to follow like lambs; Steve Grace was just one of many. It was his bad luck that Quaid was the Messiah he found.

They'd met in the Student Common Room.

"The name's Quaid," said the man at Steve's elbow at the bar.

"Oh."

"You're—?"

"Steve Grace."

"Yes. You're in the Ethics class, right?"

"Right."

"I don't see you in any of the other Philosophy seminars or lectures."

"It's my extra subject for the year. I'm on the English Literature course. I just couldn't bear the idea of a year in the Old Norse classes."

"So you plumped for Ethics."

"Yes."

Quaid ordered a double brandy. He didn't look that well off, and a double brandy would have just about crippled Steve's finances for the next week. Quaid downed it quickly, and ordered another.

"What are you having?"

Steve was nursing half a pint of luke-warm lager, determined to make it last an hour.

"Nothing for me."

"Yes you will."

"I'm fine."

"Another brandy and a pint of lager for my friend."

Steve didn't resist Quaid's generosity. A pint and a half of lager in his unfed system would help no end in dulling the tedium of his oncoming seminars on "Charles Dickens as a Social Analyst." He yawned just to think of it.

"Somebody ought to write a thesis on drinking as a social activity."

Quaid studied his brandy a moment, then downed it.

"Or as oblivion," he said.

Steve looked at the man. Perhaps five years older than Steve's twenty. The mixture of clothes he wore was confusing. Tattered running shoes, cords, a grey-white shirt that had seen better days: and over it a very expensive black leather jacket that hung badly on his tall, thin frame. The face was long and unremarkable; the eyes milky-blue, and so pale that the color seemed to seep into the whites, leaving just the pin-pricks of his irises visible behind his heavy glasses. Lips full, like a Jagger, but pale, dry and unsensual. Hair, a dirty blond.

Quaid, Steve decided, could have passed for a Dutch dope-pusher.

He wore no badges. They were the common currency of a student's obsessions, and Quaid looked naked without something to imply how he took his pleasures. Was he a gay, feminist, save-the-whale campaigner; or a fascist vegetarian? What was he into, for God's sake?

"You should have been doing Old Norse," said Quaid.

"Why?"

"They don't even bother to mark the papers on that course," said Quaid. Steve hadn't heard about this. Quaid droned on.

"They just throw them all up into the air. Face up, an A. Face down, a B."

Oh, it was a joke. Quaid was being witty. Steve attempted a laugh, but Quaid's face remained unmoved by his own attempt at humor.

"You should be in Old Norse," he said again. "Who needs Bishop Berkeley anyhow. Or Plato. Or—"

"Or?"

"It's all shit."

"Yes."

"I've watched you, in the Philosophy Class—"

Steve began to wonder about Quaid.

"—You never take notes, do you?"

"No."

"I thought you were either sublimely confident, or you simply couldn't care less."

"Neither. I'm just completely lost."

Quaid grunted, and pulled out a pack of cheap cigarettes. Again, that was not the done thing. You either smoked Gauloises, Camel or nothing at all.

"It's not true philosophy they teach you here," said Quaid, with unmistakable contempt.

"Oh?"

"We get spoonfed a bit of Plato, or a bit of Bentham—no real analysis. It's got all the right markings of course. It looks like the beast: it even smells a bit like the beast to the uninitiated."

"What beast?"

"Philosophy. *True* Philosophy. It's a beast, Stephen. Don't you think?"

"I hadn't—"

"It's wild. It bites."

He grinned, suddenly vulpine.

"Yes. It bites," he replied.

Oh, that pleased him. Again, for luck: "Bites."

Stephen nodded. The metaphor was beyond him.

"I think we should feel mauled by our subject." Quaid was warming to the whole subject of mutilation by education. "We should be frightened to juggle the ideas we should talk about."

"Why?"

"Because if we were philosophers worth we wouldn't be exchanging academic pleasantries. We wouldn't be talking semantics; using linguistic trickery to cover the real concerns."

"What would we be doing?"

Steve was beginning to feel like Quaid's straight-man. Except that Quaid wasn't in a joking mood. His face was set: his pin-prick irises had closed down to tiny dots.

"We should be walking close to the beast, Steve, don't you think? Reaching out to stroke, pet it, milk it—"

"What . . . er . . . what is the beast?"

Quaid was clearly a little exasperated by the pragmatism of the enquiry.

"It's the subject of any worthwhile philosophy, Stephen. It's the things we fear, because we don't understand them. It's the dark behind the door."

Steve thought of a door. Thought of the dark. He began to see what Quaid was driving at in his labyrinthine fashion. Philosophy was a way to talk about fear.

"We should discuss what's intimate to our psyches," said Quaid. "If we don't . . . we risk . . ."

Quaid's loquaciousness deserted him suddenly.

"What?"

Quaid was staring at his empty brandy glass, seeming to will it to be full again.

"Want another?" said Steve, praying that the answer would be no.

"What do we risk?" Quaid repeated the question. "Well, I think if we don't go out and find the beast—"

Steve could see the punchline coming.

"—sooner or later the beast will come and find us."

There is no delight the equal of dread. As long as it's someone else's.

Casually, in the following week or two, Steve made some enquiries about the curious Mr. Quaid.

Nobody knew his first name.

Nobody was certain of his age; but one of the secretaries thought he was over thirty, which came as a surprise.

His parents, Cheryl had heard him say, were dead. Killed, she thought.

That appeared to be the sum of human knowledge where Quaid was concerned.

"I owe you a drink," said Steve, touching Quaid on the shoulder.

He looked as though he'd been bitten.

"Brandy?"

"Thank you."

Steve ordered the drinks.

"Did I startle you?"

"I was thinking."

"No philosopher should be without one."

"One what?"

"Brain."

They fell to talking. Steve didn't know why he'd approached Quaid again. The man was ten years his senior and in a different intellectual league. He probably intimidated Steve, if he was to be honest about it. Quaid's relentless talk of beasts confused him. Yet he wanted more of the same: more metaphors: more of that humorless voice telling him how useless the tutors were, how weak the students.

In Quaid's world there were no certainties. He had no secular gurus and certainly no religion. He seemed incapable of viewing any system, whether it was political or philosophical, without cynicism.

Though he seldom laughed out loud, Steve knew there was a bitter humor in his vision of the world. People were lambs and sheep, all looking for shepherds. Of course these shepherds were fictions, in Quaid's opinion. All that existed, in the darkness outside the sheep-fold, were the fears that fixed on the innocent mutton: waiting, patient as stone, for their moment.

Everything was to be doubted, but the fact that dread existed.

Quaid's intellectual arrogance was exhilarating. Steve soon came to love the iconoclastic ease with which he demolished belief after belief. Sometimes it was painful when Quaid formulated a water-tight argument against one of Steve's dogmas. But after a few weeks, even the sound of the demolition seemed to excite. Quaid was clearing the undergrowth, felling the trees, razing the stubble. Steve felt free.

Nation, family, Church, law. All ash. All useless. All cheats, and chains and suffocation.

There was only dread.

"I fear, you fear, we fear," Quaid was fond of saying. "He, she or it fears. There's no conscious thing on the face of the world that doesn't know dread more intimately than its own heartbeat."

One of Quaid's favorite baiting-victims was another Philosophy and Eng. Lit. student, Cheryl Fromm. She would rise to his more outrageous remarks like fish to rain, and while the two of them took knives to each other's arguments Steve would sit back and watch the spectacle. Cheryl was, in Quaid's phrase, a pathological optimist.

"And you're full of shit," she'd say when the debate had warmed up a little. "So who cares if you're afraid of your own shadow? I'm not. I feel fine."

She certainly looked it. Cheryl Fromm was wet dream material, but too bright for anyone to try making a move on her.

"We all taste dread once in a while," Quaid would reply to her, and his milky eyes would study her face intently, watching for her reaction, trying, Steve knew, to find a flaw in her conviction.

"I don't."

"No fears? No nightmares?"

"No way. I've got a good family; I don't have any skeletons in my closet. I don't even eat meat, so I don't feel bad when I drive past a slaughterhouse. I don't have any shit to put on show. Does that mean I'm not real?"

"It means," Quaid's eyes were snake-slits, "it means your confidence has something big to cover."

"Back to nightmares."

"Big nightmares."

"Be specific: define your terms."

"I can't tell you what you fear."

"Tell me what you fear then."

Quaid hesitated. "Finally," he said, "it's beyond analysis."

"Beyond analysis, my ass!"

That brought an involuntary smile to Steve's lips. Cheryl's ass was indeed beyond analysis. The only response was to kneel down and worship.

Quaid was back on his soap-box.

"What I fear is personal to me. It makes no sense in a larger context. The signs of my dread, the images my brain uses, if you like, to *illustrate* my fear, those signs are mild stuff by comparison with the real horror that's at the root of my personality."

"I've got images," said Steve. "Pictures from childhood that make me think of—" He stopped, regretting this confessional already.

"What?" said Cheryl. "You mean things to do with bad experiences? Falling off your bike, or something like that?"

"Perhaps," Steve said. "I find myself, sometimes, thinking of those pictures. Not deliberately, just when my concentration's idling. It's almost as though my mind went to them automatically."

Quaid gave a little grunt of satisfaction. "Precisely," he said.

"Freud writes on that," said Cheryl.

"What?"

"Freud," Cheryl repeated, this time making a performance of it, as though she were speaking to a child. "Sigmund Freud: you may have heard of him."

Quaid's lip curled with unrestrained contempt. "Mother fixations don't answer the problem. The real terrors in me, in all of us, are pre-personality. Dread's there before we have any notion of ourselves as individuals. The thumb-nail, curled up on itself in the womb, feels fear."

"You remember, do you?" said Cheryl.

"Maybe," Quaid replied, deadly serious.

"The womb?"

Quaid gave a sort of half-smile. Steve thought the smile said: "I have knowledge you don't."

It was a weird, unpleasant smile; one Steve wanted to wash off his eyes.

"You're a liar," said Cheryl, getting up from her seat, and looking down her nose at Quaid.

"Perhaps I am," he said, suddenly the perfect gentleman.

After that the debates stopped.

No more talking about nightmares, no more debating the things that go bump in the night. Steve saw Quaid irregularly for the next month, and when he did Quaid was invariably in the company of Cheryl Fromm. Quaid was polite with her, even deferential. He no longer wore his leather jacket, because she hated the smell of dead animal matter. This sudden change in their relationship confounded Stephen; but he put it down to his primitive understanding of sexual matters. He wasn't a virgin, but women were still a mystery to him: contradictory and puzzling.

He was also jealous, though he wouldn't entirely admit that to himself. He resented the fact that the wet dream genius was taking up so much of Quaid's time.

There was another feeling; a curious sense he had that Quaid was courting Cheryl for his own strange reasons. Sex was not Quaid's motive, he felt sure. Nor was it respect for Cheryl's intelligence that made him so attentive. No, he was cornering her somehow; that was Steve's instinct. Cheryl Fromm was being rounded up for the kill.

Then, after a month, Quaid let a remark about Cheryl drop in conversation.

"She's a vegetarian," he said.

"Cheryl?"

"Of course, Cheryl."

"I know. She mentioned it before."

"Yes, but it isn't a fad with her. She's passionate about it. Can't even bear to look in a butcher's window. She won't touch meat, smell meat—"

"Oh." Steve was stumped. Where was this leading?

"Dread, Steve."

"Of meat?"

"The signs are different from person to person. *She fears meat.* She says she's so healthy, so balanced. Shit! I'll find it—"

"Find what?"

"The fear, Steve."

"You're not going to . . . ?" Steve didn't know how to voice his anxiety without sounding accusatory.

"Harm her?" said Quaid. "No, I'm not going to harm her in any way. Any damage done to her will be strictly self-inflicted."

Quaid was staring at him almost hypnotically.

"It's about time we learned to trust one another," Quaid went on. He leaned closer. "Between the two of us—"

"Listen, I don't think I want to hear."

"We have to touch the beast, Stephen."

"Damn the beast! I don't want to hear!"

Steve got up, as much to break the oppression of Quaid's stare as to finish the conversation.

"We're friends, Stephen."

"Yes . . ."

"Then respect that."

"What?"

"Silence. Not a word."

Steve nodded. That wasn't a difficult promise to keep. There was nobody he could tell his anxieties to without being laughed at.

Quaid looked satisfied. He hurried away, leaving Steve feeling as though he had unwillingly joined some secret society, for what purpose he couldn't begin to tell. Quaid had made a pact with him and it was unnerving.

For the next week he cut all his lectures and most of his seminars. Notes went uncopied, books unread, essays unwritten. On the two occasions he actually went into the university building he crept around like a cautious mouse, praying he wouldn't collide with Quaid.

He needn't have feared. The one occasion he did see Quaid's stooping shoulders across the quadrangle he was involved in a smiling exchange with Cheryl Fromm. She laughed, musically, her pleasure echoing off the wall of the History Department. The jealousy had left Steve altogether. He wouldn't have been paid to be so near to Quaid, so intimate with him.

The time he spent alone, away from the bustle of lectures and overfull corridors, gave Steve's mind time to idle. His thoughts returned, like tongue to tooth, like fingernail to scab, to his fears.

And so to his childhood.

At the age of six, Steve had been struck by a car. The injuries were not particularly bad, but concussion left him partially deaf. It was a profoundly distressing experience for him; not understanding why he was suddenly cut off from the world. It was an inexplicable torment, and the child assumed it was eternal.

One moment his life had been real, full of shouts and laughter. The next he was cut off from it, and the external world became an aquarium, full of gaping fish with grotesque smiles. Worse still, there were times when he suffered what the doctors called tinnitus, a roaring or ringing sound in the ears. His head would fill with the most outlandish noises, whoops and whistlings, that played like sound-effects to the flailings of the outside world. At those times his stomach would churn, and a band of iron would be wrapped around his forehead, crushing his thoughts into fragments, dissociating head from hand, intention from practice. He would be swept away in a tide of panic, completely unable to make sense of the world while his head sang and rattled.

But at night came the worst terrors. He would wake, sometimes, in what had been (before the accident) the reassuring womb of his bedroom, to find the ringing had begun in his sleep.

His eyes would jerk open. His body would be wet with sweat. His mind would be filled with the most raucous din, which he was locked in with, beyond hope of reprieve. Nothing could silence his head, and nothing, it seemed, could bring the world, the speaking, laughing, crying, world, back to him.

He was alone.

That was the beginning, middle and end of the dread. He was absolutely alone with his cacophony. Locked in this house, in this room, in this body, in this head, a prisoner of deaf, blind flesh.

It was almost unbearable. In the night the boy would sometimes cry out, not knowing he was making any sound, and the fish who had been his parents would turn on the light and come to try and help him, bending over his bed making faces, their soundless mouths forming ugly shapes in their attempts to help. Their touches would calm him at last; with time his mother learned the trick of soothing away the panic that swept over him.

A week before his seventh birthday his hearing returned, not perfectly, but well enough for it to seem like a miracle. The world snapped back into focus; and life began afresh.

It took several months for the boy to trust his senses again. He would still wake in the night, half-anticipating the head-noises.

But though his ears would ring at the slightest volume of sound, preventing Steve from going to rock concerts with the rest of the students, he now scarcely ever noticed his slight deafness.

He remembered, of course. Very well. He could bring back the taste of his panic; the feel of the iron band around his head. And there was a residue of fear there; of the dark, of being alone.

But then, wasn't everyone afraid to be alone? To be utterly alone.

Steve had another fear now, far more difficult to pin down.

Quaid.

In a drunken revelation session he had told Quaid about his childhood, about the deafness, about the night terrors.

Quaid knew about his weakness: the clear route into the heart of Steve's dread. He had a weapon, a stick to beat Steve with, should it ever come to that. Maybe that was why he chose not to speak to Cheryl (warn her, was that what he wanted to do?) and certainly that was why he avoided Quaid.

The man had a look, in certain moods, of malice. Nothing more or less. He looked like a man with malice deep, deep in him.

Maybe those four months of watching people with the sound turned down had sensitized Steve to the tiny glances, sneers and smiles that flit across people's faces. He knew Quaid's life was a labyrinth; a map of its complexities was etched on his face in a thousand tiny expressions.

The next phase of Steve's initiation into Quaid's secret world didn't come for almost three and a half months. The university broke for the summer recess, and the students went their ways. Steve took his usual vacation job at his father's printing works; it was long hours, and physically exhausting, but an undeniable relief for him. Academe had overstuffed his mind, he felt force-fed with words and ideas. The print work sweated all of that out of him rapidly, sorting out the jumble in his mind.

It was a good time: he scarcely thought of Quaid at all.

He returned to campus in the late September. The students were still thin on the ground. Most of the courses didn't start for another week; and there was a melancholy air about the place without its usual mêlée of complaining, flirting, arguing kids.

Steve was in the library, cornering a few important books before others on his course had their hands on them. Books were pure gold at the beginning of term, with reading lists to be checked off, and the university book shop forever claiming the necessary titles were on order. They would invariably arrive, those vital books, two days after the seminar in which the author was to be discussed. This final year Steve was determined to be ahead of the rush for the few copies of seminal works the library possessed.

The familiar voice spoke.

"Early to work."

Steve looked up to meet Quaid's pin-prick eyes.

"I'm impressed, Steve."

"What with?"

"Your enthusiasm for the job."

"Oh."

Quaid smiled. "What are you looking for?"

"Something on Bentham."

"I've got 'Principles of Morals and Legislation.' Will that do?"

It was a trap. No: that was absurd. He was offering a book; how could that simple gesture be construed as a trap?

"Come to think of it," the smile broadened, "I think it's the library copy I've got. I'll give it to you."

"Thanks."

"Good holiday?"

"Yes. Thank you. You?"

"Very rewarding."

The smile had decayed into a thin line beneath his—

"You've grown a moustache."

It was an unhealthy example of the species. Thin, patchy, and dirty-blond, it wandered back and forth under Quaid's nose as if looking for a way off his face. Quaid looked faintly embarrassed.

"Was it for Cheryl?"

He was definitely embarrassed now.

"Well . . ."

"Sounds like you had a good vacation."

The embarrassment was surmounted by something else.

"I've got some wonderful photographs," Quaid said.

"What of?"

"Holiday snaps."

Steve couldn't believe his ears. Had C. Fromm tamed the Quaid? Holiday snaps?

"You won't believe some of them."

There was something of the Arab selling dirty postcards about Quaid's manner. What the hell were these photographs? Split beaver shots of Cheryl, caught reading Kant?

"I don't think of you as being a photographer."

"It's become a passion of mine."

He grinned as he said "passion." There was a barely-suppressed excitement in his manner. He was positively gleaming with pleasure.

"You've got to come and see them."

"I—"

"Tonight. And pick up the Bentham at the same time."

"Thanks."

"I've got a house for myself these days. Round the corner from the Maternity Hospital, in Pilgrim Street. Number sixty-four. Some time after nine?"

"Right. Thanks. Pilgrim Street."

Quaid nodded.

"I didn't know there were any inhabitable houses in Pilgrim Street."

"Number sixty-four."

* * *

Pilgrim Street was on its knees. Most of the houses were already rubble. A few were in the process of being knocked down. Their inside walls were unnaturally exposed; pink and pale green wallpapers, fireplaces on upper stories hanging over chasms of smoking brick. Stairs leading from nowhere to nowhere, and back again.

Number sixty-four stood on its own. The houses in the terrace to either side had been demolished and bulldozed away, leaving a desert of impacted brick-dust which a few hardy, and foolhardy, weeds had tried to populate.

A three-legged white dog was patrolling its territory along the side of sixty-four, leaving little piss-marks at regular intervals as signs of its ownership.

Quaid's house, though scarcely palatial, was more welcoming than the surrounding wasteland.

They drank some bad red wine together, which Steve had brought with him, and they smoked some grass. Quaid was far more mellow than Steve had ever seen him before, quite happy to talk trivia instead of dread; laughing occasionally; even telling a dirty joke. The interior of the house was bare to the point of being spartan. No pictures on the walls; no decoration of any kind. Quaid's books, and there were literally hundreds of them, were piled on the floor in no particular sequence that Steve could make out. The kitchen and bathroom were primitive. The whole atmosphere was almost monastic.

After a couple of easy hours, Steve's curiosity got the better of him.

"Where's the holiday snaps, then?" he said, aware that he was slurring his words a little, and no longer giving a shit.

"Oh yes. My experiment."

"Experiment?"

"Tell you the truth, Steve, I'm not so sure I should show them to you."

"Why not?"

"I'm into serious stuff, Steve."

"And I'm not ready for serious stuff, is that what you're saying?"

Steve could feel Quaid's technique working on him, even though it was transparently obvious what he was doing.

"I didn't say you weren't ready—"

"What the hell is this stuff?"

"Pictures."

"Of?"

"You remember Cheryl."

Pictures of Cheryl. Ha.

"How could I forget?"

"She won't be coming back this term."

"Oh."

"She had a revelation."

Quaid's stare was basilisk-like.

"What do you mean?"

"She was always so calm, wasn't she?" Quaid was talking about her as though she were dead. "Calm, cool, and collected."

"Yes, I suppose she was."

"Poor bitch. All she wanted was a good fuck."

Steve smirked like a kid at Quaid's dirty talk. It was a little shocking; like seeing teacher with his dick hanging out of his trousers.

"She spent some of the vacation here."

"Here?"

"In this house."

"You like her then?"

"She's an ignorant cow. She's pretentious, she's weak, she's stupid. But she wouldn't *give*, she wouldn't give a fucking thing."

"You mean she wouldn't screw?"

"Oh no, she'd strip off her knickers soon as look at you. It was her fears she wouldn't give—"

Same old song.

"But I persuaded her, in the fullness of time."

Quaid pulled out a box from behind a pile of philosophy books. In it was a sheaf of black and white photographs, blown up to twice postcard size. He passed the first one of the series over to Steve.

"I locked her away you see, Steve." Quaid was as unemotional as a newsreader. "To see if I could needle her into showing her dread a little bit."

"What do you mean, locked her away?"

"Upstairs."

Steve felt strange. He could hear his ears singing, very quietly. Bad wine always made his head ring.

"I locked her away upstairs," Quaid said again, "as an experiment. That's why I took this house. No neighbors to hear."

No neighbors to hear what?

Steve looked at the grainy image in his hand.

"Concealed camera," said Quaid, "she never knew I was photographing her."

Photograph One was of a small, featureless room. A little plain furniture.

"That's the room. Top of the house. Warm. A bit stuffy even. No noise."

No noise.

Quaid proffered Photograph Two.

Same room. Now most of the furniture had been removed. A sleeping bag was laid along one wall. A table. A chair. A bare light bulb.

"That's how I laid it out for her."

"It looks like a cell."

Quaid grunted.

Photograph Three. The same room. On the table a jug of water. In the corner of the room, a bucket, roughly covered with a towel.

"What's the bucket for?"

"She had to piss."

"Yes."

"All amenities provided," said Quaid. "I didn't intend to reduce her to an animal."

Even in his drunken state, Steve took Quaid's inference. He didn't *intend* to reduce her to an animal. However . . .

Photograph Four. On the table, on an unpatterned plate, a slab of meat. A bone sticks out from it.

"Beef," said Quaid.

"But she's a vegetarian."

"So she is. It's slightly salted, well-cooked, good beef."

Photograph Five. The same. Cheryl is in the room. The door is closed. She is kicking the door, her foot and fist and face a blur of fury.

"I put her in the room about five in the morning. She was sleeping: I carried her over the threshold myself. Very romantic. She didn't know what the hell was going on."

"You locked her in there?"

"Of course. An experiment."

"She knew nothing about it?"

"We'd talked about dread, you know me. She knew what I wanted to discover. Knew I wanted guinea-pigs. She soon caught on. Once she realized what I was up to she calmed down."

Photograph Six. Cheryl sits in the corner of the room, thinking.

"I think she believed she could out-wait me."

Photograph Seven. Cheryl looks at the leg of beef, glancing at it on the table.

"Nice photo, don't you think? Look at the expression of disgust on her face. She hated even the smell of cooked meat. She wasn't hungry then, of course."

Eight: she sleeps.

Nine: she pisses. Steve felt uncomfortable, watching the girl squatting on the bucket, knickers round her ankles. Tearstains on her face.

Ten: she drinks water from the jug.

Eleven: she sleeps again, back to the room, curled up like a fetus.

"How long has she been in the room?"

"This was only fourteen hours in. She lost orientation as to time very quickly. No light change, you see. Her body-clock was fucked up pretty soon."

"How long was she in here?"

"Till the point was proved."

Twelve: Awake, she cruises the meat on the table, caught surreptitiously glancing down at it.

"This was taken the following morning. I was asleep: the camera just took pictures every quarter hour. Look at her eyes . . ."

Steve peered more closely at the photograph. There was a certain desperation on Cheryl's face: a haggard, wild look. The way she stared at the beef she could have been trying to hypnotize it.

"She looks sick."

"She's tired, that's all. She slept a lot, as it happened, but it seemed just to make her more exhausted than ever. She doesn't know now if it's day or night. And she's hungry of course. It's been a day and a half. She's more than a little peckish."

Thirteen: she sleeps again, curled into an even tighter ball, as though she wanted to swallow herself.

Fourteen: she drinks more water.

"I replaced the jug when she was asleep. She slept deeply: I could have done a jig in there and it wouldn't have woken her. Lost to the world."

He grinned. Mad, thought Steve, the man's mad.

"God, it stank in there. You know how women smell sometimes; it's not sweat, it's something else. Heavy odor: meaty. Bloody. She came on towards the end of her time. Hadn't planned it that way."

Fifteen: she touches the meat.

"This is where the cracks begin to show," said Quaid, with quiet triumph in his voice. "This is where the dread begins."

Steve studied the photograph closely. The grain of the print blurred the detail, but the cool mama was in pain, that was for sure. Her face was knotted up, half in desire, half in repulsion, as she touched the food.

Sixteen: she was at the door again, throwing herself at it, every part of her body flailing. Her mouth a black blur of angst, screaming at the blank door.

"She always ended up haranguing me, whenever she'd had a confrontation with the meat."

"How long is this?"

"Coming up for three days. You're looking at a hungry woman."

It wasn't difficult to see that. The next photo she stood still in the middle of the room, averting her eyes from the temptation of the food, her entire body tensed with the dilemma.

"You're starving her."

"She can go ten days without eating quite easily. Fasts are common in any civilized country, Steve. Sixty percent of the British population is clinically obese at any one time. She was too fat anyhow."

Eighteen: she sits, the fat girl, in her corner of the room, weeping.

"About now she began to hallucinate. Just little mental ticks. She thought she felt something in her hair, or on the back of her hand. I'd see her staring into mid-air sometimes watching nothing."

Nineteen: she washes herself. She is stripped to the waist, her breasts are heavy, her face is drained of expression. The meat is a darker tone than in the previous photographs.

"She washed herself regularly. Never let twelve hours go by without washing from head to toe."

"The meat looks . . ."

"Ripe?"

"Dark."

"It's quite warm in her little room; and there's a few flies in there with her. They've found the meat: laid their eggs. Yes, it's ripening up quite nicely."

"Is that part of the plan?"

"Sure. If the meat revolted when it was fresh, what about her disgust at rotted meat? That's the crux of her dilemma, isn't it? The longer she waits to eat, the more disgusted she becomes with what she's been given to feed on. She's trapped with her own horror of meat on the one hand, and her dread of dying on the other. Which is going to give first?"

Steve was no less trapped now.

On the one hand this joke had already gone too far, and Quaid's experiment had become an exercise in sadism. On the other hand he wanted to know how far this story ended. There was an undeniable fascination in watching the woman suffer.

The next seven photographs—twenty, twenty-one, -two, -three, -four, -five and -six—pictured the same circular routine. Sleeping, washing, pissing, meat-watching. Sleeping, washing, pissing—

Then twenty-seven.

"See?"

She picks up the meat.

Yes, she picks it up, her face full of horror. The haunch of the beef looks well-ripened now, speckled with flies' eggs. Gross.

"She bites it."

The next photograph, and her face is buried in the meat.

Steve seemed to taste the rotten flesh in the back of his throat. His mind found a stench to imagine, and created a gravy of putrescence to run over his tongue. How could she do it?

Twenty-nine: she is vomiting in the bucket in the corner of the room.

Thirty: she is sitting looking at the table. It is empty. The water-jug has been thrown against the wall. The plate has been smashed. The beef lies on the floor in a slime of degeneration.

Thirty-one: she sleeps. Her head is lost in a tangle of arms.

Thirty-two: she is standing up. She is looking at the meat again, defying it. The hunger she feels is plain on her face. So is the disgust.

Thirty-three. She sleeps.

"How long now?" asked Steve.

"Five days. No, six."

Six days.

Thirty-four. She is a blurred figure, apparently flinging herself against a wall. Perhaps beating her head against it, Steve couldn't be sure. He was past asking. Part of him didn't want to know.

Thirty-five: she is again sleeping, this time beneath the table. The sleeping bag has been torn to pieces, shredded cloth and pieces of stuffing littering the room.

Thirty-six: she speaks to the door, through the door, knowing she will get no answer.

Thirty-seven: she eats the rancid meat.

Calmly she sits under the table, like a primitive in her cave, and pulls at the meat with her incisors. Her face is again expressionless; all her energy is bent to the purpose of the moment. To eat. To eat 'til the hunger disappears, 'til the agony in her belly and the sickness in her head disappear.

Steve stared at the photograph.

"It startled me," said Quaid, "how suddenly she gave in. One moment she seemed to have as much resistance as ever. The monologue at the door was the same mixture of threats and apologies as she'd delivered day in, day out.

Then she broke. Just like that. Squatted under the table and ate the beef down to the bone, as though it were a choice cut."

Thirty-eight: she sleeps. The door is open. Light pours in.

Thirty-nine: the room is empty.

"Where did she go?"

"She wandered downstairs. She came into the kitchen, drank several glasses of water, and sat in a chair for three or four hours without saying a word."

"Did you speak to her?"

"Eventually. When she started to come out of her fugue state. The experiment was over. I didn't want to hurt her."

"What did she say?"

"Nothing."

"Nothing?"

"Nothing at all. For a long time I don't believe she was even aware of my presence in the room. Then I cooked some potatoes, which she ate."

"She didn't try and call the police?"

"No."

"No violence?"

"No. She knew what I'd done, and why I'd done it. It wasn't pre-planned, but we'd talked about such experiments, in abstract conversations. She hadn't come to any harm, you see. She'd lost a bit of weight perhaps, but that was about all."

"Where is she now?"

"She left the day after. I don't know where she went."

"And what did it all prove?"

"Nothing at all, perhaps. But it made an interesting start to my investigations."

"Start? This was only a start?"

There was plain disgust for Quaid in Steve's voice.

"Stephen—"

"You could have killed her!"

"No."

"She could have lost her mind. Unbalanced her permanently."

"Possibly. But unlikely. She was a strong-willed woman."

"But you broke her."

"Yes. It was a journey she was ready to take. We'd talked of going to face her fear. So here was I, arranging for Cheryl to do just that. Nothing much really."

"You forced her to do it. She wouldn't have gone otherwise."

"True. It was an education for her."

"So now you're a teacher?"

Steve wished he'd been able to keep the sarcasm out of his voice. But it was there. Sarcasm; anger; and a little fear.

"Yes, I'm a teacher," Quaid replied, looking at Steve obliquely, his eyes not focussed. "I'm teaching people dread."

Steve stared at the floor. "Are you satisfied with what you've taught?"

"And learned, Steve. I've learned too. It's a very exciting prospect: a world of fears to investigate. Especially with intelligent subjects. Even in the face of rationalization—"

Steve stood up. "I don't want to hear any more."

"Oh? OK."

"I've got classes early tomorrow."

"No."

"What?"

A beat, faltering.

"No. Don't go yet."

"Why?" His heart was racing. He feared Quaid, he'd never realized how profoundly.

"I've got some more books to give you."

Steve felt his face flush. Slightly. What had he thought in that moment? That Quaid was going to bring him down with a rugby tackle and start experimenting on his fears?

No. Idiot thoughts.

"I've got a book on Kierkegaard you'll like. Upstairs. I'll be two minutes."

Smiling, Quaid left the room.

Steve squatted on his haunches and began to sheaf through the photographs again. It was the moment when Cheryl first picked up the rotting meat that fascinated him most. Her face wore an expression completely uncharacteristic of the woman he had known. Doubt was written there, and confusion, and deep—

"en."

Dread.

It was Quaid's word. A dirty word. An obscene word, associated from this night on with Quaid's torture of an innocent girl.

For a moment Steve thought of the expression on his own face, as he stared down at the photograph. Was there not some of the same confusion on his face? And perhaps some of the dread too, waiting for release.

He heard a sound behind him, too soft to be Quaid.

Unless he was creeping.

Oh, God, unless he was—

A pad of chloroformed cloth was clamped over Steve's mouth and his nostrils. Involuntarily, he inhaled and the vapors stung his sinuses, made his eyes water.

A blob of blackness appeared at the corner of the world, just out of sight, and it started to grow, this stain, pulsing to the rhythm of his quickening heart.

In the center of Steve's head he could see Quaid's voice as a veil. It said his name.

"Stephen."

Again.

"—ephen."

"—phen."

"—hen."

"en."

The stain was the world. The world was dark, gone away. Out of sight, out of mind.

Steve fell clumsily amongst the photographs.

When he woke up he was unaware of his consciousness. There was darkness everywhere, on all sides. He lay awake for an hour with his eyes wide before he realized they were open.

Experimentally, he moved first his arms and his legs, then his head. He wasn't bound as he'd expected, except by his ankle. There was definitely a chain or something similar around his left ankle. It chafed his skin when he tried to move too far.

The floor beneath him was very uncomfortable, and when he investigated it more closely with the palm of his hand he realized he was lying on a huge grille or grid of some kind. It was metal, and its regular surface spread in every direction as far as his arms would reach. When he poked his arm down through the holes in this lattice he touched nothing. Just empty air falling away beneath him.

The first infra-red photographs Quaid took of Stephen's confinement pictured his exploration. As Quaid had expected the subject was being quite rational about his situation. No hysterics. No curses. No tears. That was the challenge of this particular subject. He knew precisely what was going on; and he would respond logically to his fears. That would surely make a more difficult mind to break than Cheryl's.

But how much more rewarding the results would be when he did crack. Would his soul not open up then, for Quaid to see and touch? There was so much there, in the man's interior, he wanted to study.

Gradually Steve's eyes became accustomed to the darkness.

He was imprisoned in what appeared to be some kind of shaft. It was, he estimated, about twenty feet wide, and completely round. Was it some kind of air-shaft, for a tunnel, or an underground factory? Steve's mind mapped the area around Pilgrim Street, trying to pinpoint the most likely place for Quaid to have taken him. He could think of nowhere.

Nowhere.

He was lost in a place he couldn't fix or recognize. The shaft had no corners to focus his eyes on; and the walls offered no crack or hole to hide his consciousness in.

Worse, he was lying spreadeagled on a grid that hung over this shaft. His eyes could make no impression on the darkness beneath him: it seemed that the shaft might be bottomless. And there was only the thin network of the grille, and the fragile chain that shackled his ankle to it, between him and falling.

He pictured himself poised under an empty black sky, and over an infinite darkness. The air was warm and stale. It dried up the tears that had suddenly sprung to his eyes, leaving them gummy. When he began to shout for help, which he did after the tears had passed, the darkness ate his words easily.

Having yelled himself hoarse, he lay back on the lattice. He couldn't help but imagine that beyond his frail bed, the darkness went on forever. It was absurd, of course. Nothing goes on forever, he said aloud.

Nothing goes on forever.

And yet, he'd never know. If he fell in the absolute blackness beneath him, he'd fall and fall and fall and not see the bottom of the shaft coming. Though he tried to think of brighter, more positive, images, his mind conjured his body cascading down this horrible shaft, with the bottom a foot from his hurtling body and his eyes not seeing it, his brain not predicting it.

Until he hit.

Would he see light as his head was dashed open on impact? Would he understand, in the moment that his body became offal, why he'd lived and died?

Then he thought: Quaid wouldn't dare. "Wouldn't dare!" he screeched. "Wouldn't dare!"

The dark was a glutton for words. As soon as he'd yelled into it, it was as though he'd never made a sound.

And then another thought: a real baddie. Suppose Quaid had found this circular hell to put him in because it would *never* be found, *never* be investigated? Maybe he wanted to take his experiment to the limits.

To the limits. Death was at the limits. And wouldn't that be the ultimate experiment for Quaid? Watching a man die: watching the fear of death, the motherlode of dread, approach. Sartre had written that no man could ever know his own death. But to know the deaths of others, intimately—to watch the acrobatics that the mind would surely perform to avoid the bitter truth—that was a clue to death's nature, wasn't it? That might, in some small way, prepare a man for his own death. To live another's dread vicariously was the safest, cleverest way to touch the beast.

Yes, he thought, Quaid might kill me; out of his own terror.

Steve took a sour satisfaction in that thought. That Quaid, the impartial experimenter, the would-be educator, was obsessed with terrors because his own dread ran deepest.

That was why he had to watch others deal with their fears. He needed a solution, a way out for himself.

Thinking all this through took hours. In the darkness Steve's mind was quick-silver, but uncontrollable. He found it difficult to keep one train of argument for very long. His thoughts were like fish, small, fast fish, wriggling out of his grasp as soon as he took a hold of them.

But underlying every twist of thought was the knowledge that he must out-play Quaid. That was certain. He must be calm; prove himself a useless subject for Quaid's analysis.

The photographs of these hours showed Stephen lying with his eyes closed on the grid, with a slight frown on his face. Occasionally, paradoxically, a smile would flit across his lips. Sometimes it was impossible to know if he was sleeping or waking, thinking or dreaming.

Quaid waited.

Eventually Steve's eyes began to flicker under his lids, the unmistakable sign of dreaming. It was time, while the subject slept, to turn the wheel of the rack—

Steve woke with his hands cuffed together. He could see a bowl of water on a plate beside him; and a second bowl, full of luke-warm unsalted porridge, beside it. He ate and drank thankfully.

As he ate, two things registered. First, that the noise of his eating seemed very loud in his head; and second, that he felt a constriction, a tightness, around his temples.

The photographs show Stephen clumsily reaching up to his head. A harness is strapped on to him, and locked in place. It clamps plugs deep into his ears, preventing any sound from getting in.

The photographs show puzzlement. Then anger. Then fear.

Steve was deaf.

All he could hear were the noises in his head. The clicking of his teeth. The slush and swallow of his palate. The sounds boomed between his ears like guns.

Tears sprang to his eyes. He kicked at the grid, not hearing the clatter of his heels on the metal bars. He screamed until his throat felt as if it was bleeding. He heard none of his cries.

Panic began in him.

The photographs showed its birth. His face was flushed. His eyes were wide, his teeth and gums exposed in a grimace.

He looked like a frightened monkey.

All the familiar, childhood feelings swept over him. He remembered them like the faces of old enemies; the chittering limbs, the sweat, the nausea. In desperation he picked up the bowl of water and upturned it over his face. The shock of the cold water diverted his mind momentarily from the panic-ladder it was climbing. He lay back down on the grid, his body a board, and told himself to breathe deeply and evenly.

Relax, relax, relax, he said aloud.

In his head, he could hear his tongue clicking. He could hear his mucus too, moving sluggishly in the panic-constricted passages of his nose, blocking and unblocking in his ears. Now he could detect the low, soft hiss that waited under all the other noises. The sound of his mind—

It was like the white noise between stations on the radio, this was the same whine that came to fetch him under anesthetic, the same noise that would sound in his ears on the borders of sleep.

His limbs still twitched nervously, and he was only half-aware of the way he wrestled with his handcuffs, indifferent to their edges scouring the skin at his wrists.

The photographs recorded all these reactions precisely. His war with hysteria: his pathetic attempts to keep the fears from resurfacing. His tears. His bloody wrists.

Eventually, exhaustion won over panic; as it had so often as a child. How many times had he fallen asleep with the salt-taste of tears in his nose and mouth, unable to fight any longer?

The exertion had heightened the pitch of his head-noises. Now, instead of a lullaby, his brain whistled and whooped him to sleep.

Oblivion was good.

Quaid was disappointed. It was clear from the speed of his response that Stephen Grace was going to break very soon indeed. In fact, he was as good as broken, only a few hours into the experiment. And Quaid had been relying on Stephen. After months of preparing the ground, it seemed that this subject was going to lose his mind without giving up a single clue.

One word, one miserable word, was all Quaid needed. A little sign as to the nature of the experience. Or better still, something to suggest a solution, a healing totem, a prayer even. Surely some Savior comes to the lips, as the personality is swept away in madness? There must be *something*.

Quaid waited like a carrion bird at the site of some atrocity, counting the minutes left to the expiring soul, hoping for a morsel.

Steve woke face down on the grid. The air was much staler now, and the metal bars bit into the flesh of his cheek. He was hot and uncomfortable.

He lay still, letting his eyes become accustomed to his surroundings again. The lines of the grid ran off in perfect perspective to meet the wall of the shaft. The simple network of criss-crossed bars struck him as pretty. Yes, pretty. He traced the lines back and forth, 'til he tired of the game. Bored, he rolled over onto his back, feeling the grid vibrate under his body. Was it less stable now? It seemed to rock a little as he moved.

Hot and sweaty, Steve unbuttoned his shirt. There was sleep-spittle on his chin but he didn't care to wipe it off. What if he drooled? Who was to see?

He half pulled off his shirt, and using one foot, kicked his shoe off the other.

Shoe: lattice: fall. Sluggishly, his mind made the connection. He sat up. Oh poor shoe. His shoe would fall. It would slip between the bars and be lost. But no. It was finely balanced across two sides of a lattice-hole; he could still save it if he tried.

He reached for his poor, poor shoe, and his movement shifted the grid.

The shoe began to slip.

"Please," he begged it, "don't fall." He didn't want to lose his nice shoe, his pretty shoe. It mustn't fall. It mustn't fall.

As he stretched to snatch it, the shoe tipped, heel down, through the grid and fell into the darkness.

He let out a cry of loss that he couldn't hear.

Oh, if only he could listen to the shoe falling; to count the seconds of its descent. To hear it thud home at the bottom of the shaft. At least then he'd know how far he had to fall to his death.

He couldn't endure it any longer. He rolled over on to his stomach and thrust both arms through the grid, screaming:

"I'll go too! I'll go too!"

He couldn't bear waiting to fall, in the dark, in the whining silence, he just wanted to follow his shoe down, down, down the dark shaft to extinction, and have the whole game finished once and for all.

"I'll go! I'll go! I'll go!" he shrieked. He pleaded with gravity.

Beneath him, the grid moved.

Something had broken. A pin, a chain, a rope that held the grid in position had snapped. He was no longer horizontal; already he was sliding across the bars as they tipped him off into the dark.

With shock he realized his limbs were no longer chained.

He would fall.

The man wanted him to fall. The bad man—what was his name? Quake? Quail? Quarrel—

Automatically he seized the grid with both hands as it tipped even further over. Maybe he didn't want to fall after his shoe, after all? Maybe life, a little moment more of life, was worth holding on to—

The dark beyond the edge of the grid was so deep; and who could guess what lurked in it?

In his head the noises of his panic multiplied. The thumping of his bloody heart, the stutter of his mucus, the dry rasp of his palate. His palms, slick with sweat, were losing their grip. Gravity wanted him. It demanded its rights of his body's bulk: demanded that he fall. For a moment, glancing over his shoulder at the mouth that opened under him, he thought he saw monsters stirring below him. Ridiculous, loony things, crudely drawn, dark on dark. Vile graffiti leered up from his childhood and uncurled their claws to snatch at his legs.

"Mama," he said, as his hands failed him, and he was delivered into dread.

"*Mama.*"

That was the word. Quaid heard it plainly, in all its banality.

"Mama!"

By the time Steve hit the bottom of the shaft, he was past judging how far he'd fallen. The moment his hands let go of the grid, and he knew the dark would have him, his mind snapped. The animal self survived to relax his body, saving him all but minor injury on impact. The rest of his life, all but the simplest responses, were shattered, the pieces flung into the recesses of his memory.

When the light came, at last, he looked up at the person in the Mickey Mouse mask at the door, and smiled at him. It was a child's smile, one of thankfulness for his comical rescuer. He let the man take him by the ankles and haul him out of the big round room in which he was lying. His pants were wet, and he knew he'd dirtied himself in his sleep. Still, the Funny Mouse would kiss him better.

His head lolled on his shoulders as he was dragged out of the torture-chamber. On the floor beside his head was a shoe. And seven or eight feet above him was the grid from which he had fallen.

It meant nothing at all.

He let the Mouse sit him down in a bright room. He let the Mouse give him his ears back, though he didn't really want them. It was funny watching the world without sound, it made him laugh.

He drank some water, and ate some sweet cake.

He was tired. He wanted to sleep. He wanted his Mama. But the Mouse didn't seem to understand, so he cried, and kicked the table and threw the plates and cups on the floor. Then he ran into the next room, and threw all the papers he could find in the air. It was nice watching them flutter up and flutter down. Some of them fell face down, some face up. Some were covered with writing. Some were pictures. Horrid pictures. Pictures that made him feel very strange.

They were all pictures of dead people, every one of them. Some of the pictures were of little children, others were of grown-up children. They were lying down, or half-sitting, and there were big cuts in their faces and their bodies, cuts that showed a mess underneath, a mish-mash of shiny bits and oozy bits. And all around the dead people: black paint. Not in neat puddles, but splashed all around, and finger-marked, and hand-printed and very messy.

In three or four of the pictures the thing that made the cuts was still there. He knew the word for it.

Axe.

There was an axe in a lady's face buried almost to the handle. There was an axe in a man's leg, and another lying on the floor of a kitchen beside a dead baby.

This man collected pictures of dead people and axes, which Stevie thought was strange.

That was his last thought before the too-familiar scent of chloroform filled his head and he lost consciousness.

The sordid doorway smelt of old urine and fresh vomit. It was his own vomit; it was all over the front of his shirt. He tried to stand up, but his legs felt wobbly. It was very cold. His throat hurt.

Then he heard footsteps. It sounded like the Mouse was coming back. Maybe he'd take him home.

"Get up, son."

It wasn't the Mouse. It was a policeman.

"What are you doing down there? I said get up."

Bracing himself against the crumbling brick of the doorway Steve got to his feet. The policeman shone his torch at him.

"Jesus Christ," said the policeman, disgust written over his face. "You're in a right fucking state. Where do you live?"

Steve shook his head, staring down at his vomit-soaked shirt like a shamed schoolboy.

"What's your name?"

He couldn't quite remember.

"Name, lad?"

He was trying. If only the policeman wouldn't shout.

"Come on, take a hold of yourself."

The words didn't make much sense. Steve could feel tears pricking the backs of his eyes.

"Home."

Now he was blubbering, sniffling snot, feeling utterly forsaken. He wanted to die: he wanted to lie down and die.

The policeman shook him.

"You high on something?" he demanded, pulling Steve into the glare of the streetlights and staring at his tear-stained face.

"You'd better move on."

"Mama," said Steve, "I want my Mama."

The words changed the encounter entirely.

Suddenly the policeman found the spectacle more than disgusting; more than pitiful. This little bastard, with his bloodshot eyes and his dinner down his shirt, was really getting on his nerves. Too much money, too much dirt in his veins, too little discipline.

"Mama" was the last straw. He punched Steve in the stomach, a neat, sharp, functional blow. Steve doubled up, whimpering.

"Shut up, son."

Another blow finished the job of crippling the child, and then he took a fistful of Steve's hair and pulled the little druggy's face up to meet his.

"You want to be a derelict, is that it?"

"No. No."

Steve didn't know what a derelict was; he just wanted to make the policeman like him.

"Please," he said, tears coming again, "take me home."

The policeman seemed confused. The kid hadn't started fighting back and calling for civil rights, the way most of them did. That was the way they usually ended up: on the ground, bloody-nosed, calling for a social worker. This one just wept. The policeman began to get a bad feeling about the kid. Like he was mental or something. And he'd beaten the shit out of the little snot. Fuck it. Now he felt responsible. He took hold of Steve by the arm and bundled him across the road to his car.

"Get in."

"Take me—"

"I'll take you home, son. I'll take you home."

At the Night Hostel they searched Steve's clothes for some kind of identification, found none, then scoured his body for fleas, his hair for nits. The policeman left him then, which Steve was relieved about. He hadn't liked the man.

The people at the Hostel talked about him as though he wasn't in the room. Talked about how young he was; discussed his mental-age; his clothes; his appearance. Then they gave him a bar of soap and showed him the showers. He stood under the cold water for ten minutes and dried himself with a stained towel. He didn't shave, though they'd lent him a razor. He'd forgotten how to do it.

Then they gave him some old clothes, which he liked. They weren't such bad people, even if they did talk about him as though he wasn't there. One of them even smiled at him; a burly man with a grizzled beard. Smiled as he would at a dog.

They were odd clothes he was given. Either too big or too small. All colors: yellow socks, dirty white shirt, pin-stripe trousers that had been made for a glutton, a thread-bare sweater, heavy boots. He liked dressing up, putting on two vests and two pairs of socks when they weren't looking. He felt assured with several thicknesses of cotton and wool wrapped around him.

Then they left him with a ticket for his bed in his hand, to wait for the dormitories to be unlocked. He was not impatient, like some of the men in the corridors with him. They yelled incoherently, many of them, their accusations laced with obscenities, and they spat at each other. It frightened him. All he wanted was to sleep. To lie down and sleep.

At eleven o'clock one of the warders unlocked the gate to the dormitory, and all the lost men filed through to find themselves an iron bed for the night. The dormitory, which was large and badly lit, stank of disinfectant and old people.

Avoiding the eyes and the flailing arms of the other derelicts, Steve found himself an ill-made bed, with one thin blanket tossed across it, and lay down to sleep. All around him men were coughing and muttering and weeping. One was saying his prayers as he lay, staring at the ceiling, on his grey pillow. Steve thought that was a good idea. So he said his own child's prayer.

"Gentle Jesus, meek and mild,
Look upon this little child,
Pity my—
What was the word?
Pity my—*simplicity*,
Suffer me to come to thee."
That made him feel better; and the sleep, a balm, was blue and deep.

Quaid sat in darkness. The terror was on him again, worse than ever. His body was rigid with fear; so much so that he couldn't even get out of bed and snap on the light. Besides, what if this time, this time of all times, the terror was true? What if the axe-man was at the door in flesh and blood? Grinning like a loon at him, dancing like the devil at the top of the stairs, as Quaid had seen him, in dreams, dancing and grinning, grinning and dancing.

Nothing moved. No creak of the stair, no giggle in the shadows. It wasn't him, after all. Quaid would live 'til morning.

His body had relaxed a little now. He swung his legs out of bed and switched on the light. The room was indeed empty. The house was silent. Through the open door he could see the top of the stairs. There was no axe-man, of course.

Steve woke to shouting. It was still dark. He didn't know how long he'd been asleep, but his limbs no longer ached so badly. Elbows on his pillow, he half-sat up and stared down the dormitory to see what all the commotion was about. Four bed-rows down from his, two men were fighting. The bone of contention was by no means clear. They just grappled with each other like girls (it made Steve laugh to watch them), screeching and pulling each other's hair. By moonlight the blood on their faces and hands was black: One of them, the older of the two, was thrust back across his bed, screaming: "I will not go to the Finchley Road! You will not make me. Don't strike me! I'm not your man! I'm not!"

The other was beyond listening; he was too stupid, or too mad, to understand that the old man was begging to be left alone. Urged on by spectators on every side, the old man's assailant had taken off his shoe and was belaboring his victim with it. Steve could hear the crack, crack of his blows: heel on head. There were cheers accompanying each strike, and lessening cries from the old man.

Suddenly, the applause faltered, as somebody came into the dormitory. Steve couldn't see who it was; the mass of men crowded around the fight were between him and the door.

He did see the victor toss his shoe into the air however, with a final shout of "Fucker!"

The shoe.

Steve couldn't take his eyes off the shoe. It rose in the air, turning as it rose, then plummeted to the bare boards like a shot bird. Steve saw it clearly, more clearly than he'd seen anything in many days.

It landed not far from him.

It landed with a loud thud.

It landed on its side. As his shoe had landed. His shoe. The one he kicked off. On the grid. In the room. In the house. In Pilgrim Street.

Quaid woke with the same dream. Always the stairway. Always him looking down the tunnel of the stairs, while that ridiculous sight, half-joke, half-horror, tip-toed up towards him, a laugh on every step.

He'd never dreamt twice in one night before. He swung his hand out over the edge of the bed and fumbled for the bottle he kept there. In the dark he swigged from it, deeply.

Steve walked past the knot of angry men, not caring about their shouts or the old man's groans and curses. The warders were having a hard time dealing with the disturbance. It was the last time Old Man Crowley would be let in: he always invited violence. This had all the marks of a near-riot; it would take hours to settle them down again.

Nobody questioned Steve as he wandered down the corridor, through the gate, and into the vestibule of the Night Hostel. The swing doors were closed, but the night air, bitter before dawn, smelt refreshing as it seeped in.

The pokey reception office was empty, and through the door Steve could see the fire-extinguisher hanging on the wall. It was red and bright. Beside it was a long black hose, curled up on a red drum like a sleeping snake. Beside that, sitting in two brackets on the wall, was an axe.

A very pretty axe.

Stephen walked into the office. A little distance away he heard running feet, shouts, a whistle. But nobody came to interrupt Steve, as he made friends with the axe.

First he smiled at it.

The curve of the blade of the axe smiled back.

Then he touched it.

The axe seemed to like being touched. It was dusty, and hadn't been used in a long while. Too long. It wanted to be picked up, and stroked, and smiled at. Steve took it out of its brackets very gently, and slid it under his jacket to keep warm. Then he walked back out of the reception office, through the swing-doors and out to find his other shoe.

Quaid woke again.

It took Steve a very short time to orient himself. There was a spring in his step as he began to make his way to Pilgrim Street. He felt like a clown, dressed in so many bright colors, in such floppy trousers, such silly boots. He was a comical fellow, wasn't he? He made himself laugh, he was so comical.

The wind began to get into him, whipping him up into a frenzy as it scooted through his hair and made his eyeballs as cold as two lumps of ice in his sockets.

He began to run, skip, dance, cavort through the streets, white under the lights, dark in between. Now you see me, now you don't. Now you see me, now you—

Quaid hadn't been woken by the dream this time. This time he had heard a noise. Definitely a noise.

The moon had risen high enough to throw its beams through the window, through the door and on to the top of the stairs. There was no need to put on the light. All he needed to see, he could see. The top of the stairs were empty, as ever.

Then the bottom stair creaked, a tiny noise as though a breath had landed on it.

Quaid knew dread then.

Another creak, as it came up the stairs towards him, the ridiculous dream. It had to be a dream. After all, he knew no clowns, no axe-killers. So how could that absurd image, the same image that woke him night after night, be anything but a dream?

Yet, perhaps there were some dreams so preposterous they could only be true.

No clowns, he said to himself, as he stood watching the door, and the stairway, and the spotlight of the moon. Quaid knew only fragile minds, so weak they couldn't give him a clue to the nature, to the origin, or to the cure for the panic that now held him in thrall. All they did was break, crumble into dust, when faced with the slightest sign of the dread at the heart of life.

He knew no clowns, never had, never would.

Then it appeared; the face of a fool. Pale to whiteness in the light of the moon, its young features bruised, unshaven and puffy, its smile open like a child's smile. It had bitten its lip in its excitement. Blood was smeared across its lower jaw, and its gums were almost black with blood. Still it was a clown. Indisputably a clown even to its ill-fitting clothes, so incongruous, so pathetic.

Only the axe didn't quite match the smile.

It caught the moonlight as the maniac made small, chopping motions with it, his tiny black eyes glinting with anticipation of the fun ahead.

Almost at the top of the stairs, he stopped, his smile not faltering for a moment as he gazed at Quaid's terror.

Quaid's legs gave out, and he stumbled to his knees.

The clown climbed another stair, skipping as he did so, his glittering eyes fixed on Quaid, filled with a sort of benign malice. The axe rocked back and forth in his white hands, in a petite version of the killing stroke.

Quaid knew him.

It was his pupil: his guinea-pig, transformed into the image of his own dread.

Him. Of all men. Him. The deaf boy.

The skipping was bigger now, and the clown was making a deep-throated noise, like the call of some fantastical bird. The axe was describing wider and wider sweeps in the air, each more lethal than the last.

"Stephen," said Quaid.

The name meant nothing to Steve. All he saw was the mouth opening. The mouth closing. Perhaps a sound came out: perhaps not. It was irrelevant to him.

The throat of the clown gave out a screech, and the axe swung up over his head, two-handed. At the same moment the merry little dance became a run, as the axe-man leapt the last two stairs and ran into the bedroom, full into the spotlight.

Quaid's body half turned to avoid the killing blow, but not quickly or elegantly enough. The blade slit the air and sliced through the back of Quaid's arm, sheering off most of his triceps, shattering his humerus and opening the flesh of his lower arm in a gash that just missed his artery.

Quaid's scream could have been heard ten houses away, except that those houses were rubble. There was nobody to hear. Nobody to come and drag the clown off him.

The axe, eager to be about its business, was hacking at Quaid's thigh now, as though it was chopping a log. Yawning wounds four or five inches deep exposed the shiny steak of the philosopher's muscle, the bone, the marrow. With each stroke the clown would tug at the axe to pull it out, and Quaid's body would jerk like a puppet.

Quaid screamed. Quaid begged. Quaid cajoled.

The clown didn't hear a word.

All he heard was the noise in his head: the whistles, the whoops, the howls, the hums. He had taken refuge where no rational argument, no threat, would ever fetch him out again. Where the thump of his heart was law, and the whine of his blood was music.

How he danced, this deaf-boy, danced like a loon to see his tormentor gaping like a fish, the depravity of his intellect silenced forever. How the blood spurted! How it gushed and fountained!

The little clown laughed to see such fun. There was a night's entertainment to be had here, he thought. The axe was his friend forever, keen and wise. It would cut, and cross-cut, it could slice and amputate, yet still they could keep this man alive, if they were cunning enough, alive for a long, long while.

Steve was happy as a lamb. They had the rest of the night ahead of them, and all the music he could possibly want was sounding in his head.

And Quaid knew, meeting the clown's vacant stare through an air turned bloody, that there was worse in the world than dread. Worse than death itself.

There was pain without hope of healing. There was life that refused to end, long after the mind had begged the body to cease. And worst, there were dreams come true.

Edgar Allan Poe

The Fall of the House of Usher

The greatest and most influential of all horror writers, Edgar Allan Poe is the primary transition figure between the Gothic and the modern. He is responsible for the transformation of Gothic paraphrenalia into useful devices for the investigation of human psychology (used consciously) and for symbolism. He characteristically used abnormal situations and characters for dramatic effect and characteristically wrote horror. His critical writing, as well as his fiction, has given instruction to generations of short story writers ever since, and influenced the entire course of the development and evolution of the short story . . . including the entire genres of mystery fiction and science fiction, which grow significantly out of his stories. Nearly a dozen of his stories are classics of nineteenth-century literature and of these, half are horror. "The Fall of the House of Usher" is printed here as representative. It is one of the foundations of the haunted house story (prior to Poe it was usually the haunted castle of the Gothic), provocative, symbolic, psychologically intricate. "In Poe's work a thing is never merely a 'thing'; it is a language," says the Poe-scholar Benjamin Franklin Fisher IV. Poe's horror stories invent the language of horror, give meaning to the idea of the fantastic as a language.

> Son coeur est un luth suspendu;
> Sitôt qu'on le touche il résonne.
> —*De Béranger*

During the whole of a dull, dark, and soundless day in the autumn of the year, when the clouds hung oppressively low in the heavens, I had been passing alone, on horseback, through a singularly dreary tract of country, and at length found myself, as the shades of the evening drew on, within view of the melancholy House of Usher. I know not how it was—but, with the first glimpse of the building, a sense of insufferable gloom pervaded my spirit. I say insufferable; for the feeling was unrelieved by any of that half-pleasurable, because poetic, sentiment with which the mind usually received even the sternest natural images of the desolate or terrible. I looked upon the scene before me—upon the mere house, and the simple landscape features of the domain—upon the bleak walls—upon the vacant eye-like windows—upon a few rank sedges—and upon a few white trunks of decayed trees—with an utter depression of soul which I can compare to no earthly sensation more properly than to the after-dream of the reveller upon opium—the bitter lapse into every-day life—the hideous dropping off of the veil. There was an iciness, a sinking, a sickening of the heart—an unredeemed dreariness of thought which no goading of the imagination could torture into aught of the sublime. What was it—I paused to think—what was it that so unnerved me in the contemplation of the House of Usher? It was a mystery all insoluble; nor could I grapple with the shadowy fancies that crowded upon me as I pondered. I was forced to fall back upon the unsatisfactory conclusion, that while, beyond doubt, there *are* combinations of very simple natural objects which have the power of thus affecting us, still the analysis of this power lies among considerations beyond our depth. It was possible, I reflected, that a mere different arrangement of the particulars of the scene, of the details of the picture, would be sufficient to modify, or perhaps to annihilate its capacity for sorrowful impression; and, acting upon this idea, I reined my horse to the precipitous brink of a black and lurid tarn that lay in unruffled lustre by the dwelling, and gazed down—but with a shudder even more thrilling than before—upon the remodelled and inverted images of the gray sedge, and the ghastly tree-stems, and the vacant and eye-like windows.

Nevertheless, in this mansion of gloom I now proposed to myself a sojourn of some weeks. Its proprietor, Roderick Usher, had been one of my boon companions in boyhood; but many years had elapsed since our last meeting. A letter, however, had lately reached me in a distant part of the country—a letter from him—which, in its wildly importunate nature, had admitted of no other than a personal reply. The MS. gave evidence of nervous agitation. The writer spoke of acute bodily illness—of a mental disorder which oppressed him—and of an earnest desire to see me, as his best and indeed his only personal friend, with a view of attempting, by the cheerfulness of my society, some alleviation of his malady. It was the manner in which all this, and much more, was said—it was the apparent *heart* that went with his request—which allowed me no room for hesitation; and I accordingly obeyed forthwith what I still considered a very singular summons.

Although, as boys, we had been even intimate associates, yet I really knew little of my friend. His reserve had been always excessive and habitual. I was aware, however, that his very ancient family had been noted, time out of mind, for a peculiar sensibility of temperament, displaying itself, through long ages, in many works of exalted art, and manifested, of late, in repeated deeds of munificent yet unobtrusive charity, as well as in a passionate devotion to the intricacies, perhaps even more than to the orthodox and easily recognizable beauties, of musical science. I had learned, too, the very remarkable fact, that the stem of the Usher race, all time-honored as it was, had put forth, at no period, any enduring branch; in other words, that the entire family lay in the direct line of descent, and had always, with very trifling and very temporary variation, so lain. It was this deficiency, I considered, while running over in thought the perfect keeping of the character of the premises with the accredited character of the people, and while speculating upon the possible influence which the one, in the long lapse of centuries, might have exercised upon the other—it was this deficiency, perhaps, of collateral issue, and the consequent undeviating transmission, from sire to son, of the patrimony with the name, which had, at length, so identified the two as to merge the original title of the estate in the quaint and equivocal appellation of the "House of Usher"—an appellation which seemed to include, in the minds of the peasantry who used it, both the family and the family mansion.

I have said that the sole effect of my somewhat childish experiment—that of looking down within the tarn—had been to deepen the first singular impression. There can be no doubt that the consciousness of the rapid increase of my superstition—for why should I not so term it?—served mainly to accelerate the increase itself. Such, I have long known, is the paradoxical law of all sentiments having terror as a basis. And it might have been for this reason only, that, when I again uplifted my eyes to the house itself, from its image in the pool, there grew in my mind a strange fancy—a fancy so ridiculous, indeed, that I but mention it to show the vivid force of the sensations which oppressed me. I had so worked upon my imagination as really to believe that about the whole mansion and domain there hung an atmosphere peculiar to themselves and their immediate vicinity—an atmosphere which had no affinity with the air of heaven, but which had reeked up from the decayed trees, and the gray wall, and the silent tarn—a pestilent and mystic vapor, dull, sluggish, faintly discernible, and leaden-hued.

Shaking off from my spirit what *must* have been a dream, I scanned more narrowly the real aspect of the building. Its principal feature seemed to be that of an excessive antiquity. The discoloration of ages had been great. Minute fungi overspread the whole exterior, hanging in a fine tangled web-work from the eaves. Yet all this was apart from any extraordinary dilapidation. No portion of the masonry had fallen; and there appeared to be a wild inconsistency between its still perfect adaptation of parts, and the crumbling condition of the individual stones. In this there was much that reminded me of the specious totality of old wood-work which has rotted for long years in some neglected vault, with no disturbance from the breath of the external air. Beyond this indication of extensive decay, however, the fabric gave little token of instability. Perhaps the eye of a scrutinizing observer might have discovered a barely perceptible fissure, which, extending from the roof of the building in front, made its way down the wall in a zigzag direction, until it became lost in the sullen waters of the tarn.

Noticing these things, I rode over a short causeway to the house. A servant in waiting took my horse, and I entered the Gothic archway of the hall. A valet, of stealthy step, thence conducted me, in silence, through many dark and intricate passages in my progress to the *studio* of his master. Much that I encountered on the way contributed, I know not how, to heighten the vague sentiments of which I have already spoken. While the objects around me—while the carvings of the ceilings, the sombre tapestries of the walls, the ebon blackness of the floors, and the phantasmagoric armorial trophies which rattled as I strode, were but matters to which, or to such as which, I had been accustomed from my infancy—while I hesitated not to acknowledge how familiar was all this—I still wondered to find how unfamiliar were the fancies which ordinary images were stirring up. On one of the staircases,

I met the physician of the family. His countenance, I thought, wore a mingled expression of low cunning and perplexity. He accosted me with trepidation and passed on. The valet now threw open a door and ushered me into the presence of his master.

The room in which I found myself was very large and lofty. The windows were long, narrow, and pointed, and at so vast a distance from the black oaken floor as to be altogether inaccessible from within. Feeble gleams of encrimsoned light made their way through the trellissed panes, and served to render sufficiently distinct the more prominent objects around; the eye, however, struggled in vain to reach the remoter angles of the chamber, or the recesses of the vaulted and fretted ceiling. Dark draperies hung upon the walls. The general furniture was profuse, comfortless, antique, and tattered. Many books and musical instruments lay scattered about, but failed to give any vitality to the scene. I felt that I breathed an atmosphere of sorrow. An air of stern, deep, and irredeemable gloom hung over and pervaded all.

Upon my entrance, Usher arose from a sofa on which he had been lying at full length, and greeted me with a vivacious warmth which had much in it, I at first thought, of an overdone cordiality—of the constrained effort of the *ennuyé* man of the world. A glance, however, at his countenance convinced me of his perfect sincerity. We sat down; and for some moments, while he spoke not, I gazed upon him with a feeling half of pity, half of awe. Surely, man had never before so terribly altered, in so brief a period, as had Roderick Usher! It was with difficulty that I could bring myself to admit the identity of the wan being before me with the companion of my early boyhood. Yet the character of his face had been at all times remarkable. A cadaverousness of complexion; an eye large, liquid, and luminous beyond comparison; lips somewhat thin and very pallid, but of a surpassingly beautiful curve; a nose of a delicate Hebrew model, but with a breadth of nostril unusual in similar formations; a finely moulded chin, speaking, in its want of prominence, of a want of moral energy; hair of a more than web-like softness and tenuity;—these features, with an inordinate expansion above the regions of the temple, made up altogether a countenance not easily to be forgotten. And now in the mere exaggeration of the prevailing character of these features, and of the expression they were wont to convey, lay so much of change that I doubted to whom I spoke. The now ghastly pallor of the skin, and the now miraculous lustre of the eye, above all things startled and even awed me. The silken hair, too, had been suffered to grow all unheeded, and as, in its wild gossamer texture, it floated rather than fell about the face, I could not, even with effort, connect its Arabesque expression with any idea of simple humanity.

In the manner of my friend I was at once struck with an incoherence—an inconsistency; and I soon found this to arise from a series of feeble and futile struggles to overcome an habitual trepidancy—an excessive nervous agitation. For something of this nature I had indeed been prepared, no less by his letter, than by reminiscences of certain boyish traits, and by conclusions deduced from his peculiar physical confirmation and temperament. His action was alternately vivacious and sullen. His voice varied rapidly from a tremulous indecision (when the animal spirits seemed utterly in abeyance) to that species of energetic concision—that abrupt, weighty, unhurried, and hollow-sounding enunciation—that leaden, self-balanced, and perfectly modulated guttural utterance, which may be observed in the lost drunkard, or the irreclaimable eater of opium, during the periods of his most intense excitement.

It was thus that he spoke of the object of my visit, of his earnest desire to see me, and of the solace he expected me to afford him. He entered, at some length, into what he conceived to be the nature of his malady. It was, he said, a constitutional and a family evil, and one for which he despaired to find a remedy—a mere nervous affection, he immediately added, which would undoubtedly soon pass off. It displayed itself in a host of unnatural sensations. Some of these, as he detailed them, interested and bewildered me; although, perhaps, the terms and the general manner of their narration had their weight. He suffered much from a morbid acuteness of the senses; the most insipid food was alone endurable; he could wear only garments of certain texture; the odors of all flowers were oppressive; his eyes were tortured by even a faint light; and there were but peculiar sounds, and these from stringed instruments, which did not inspire him with horror.

To an anomalous species of terror I found him a bounden slave. "I shall perish," said he, "I *must* perish in this deplorable folly. Thus, thus, and not otherwise, shall I be lost. I dread the events of the future, not in themselves, but in their results. I shudder at the thought of any, even the most trivial, incident, which may operate upon this intolerable agitation of soul. I have, indeed, no abhorrence of danger, except in its absolute effect—in terror. In this unnerved, in this pitiable, condition I feel that the period will sooner or later arrive when I must abandon life and reason together, in some struggle with the grim phantasm, FEAR."

I learned, moreover, at intervals, and through broken and equivocal hints, another singular feature of his mental condition. He was enchained by certain superstitious impressions in regard to the dwelling which he tenanted, and whence, for many years, he had never ventured forth—in regard to an influence whose suppositious force was conveyed in terms too shadowy here to be re-stated—an influence which some peculiarities in the mere form and substance of his family mansion had, by dint of long sufferance, he said, obtained over his spirit—an effect which the *physique* of the gray walls and turrets, and of the dim tarn into which they all looked down, had, at length, brought about upon the *morale* of his existence.

He admitted, however, although with hesitation, that much of the peculiar gloom which thus afflicted him could be traced to a more natural and far more palpable origin—to the severe and long-continued illness—indeed to the evidently approaching dissolution—of a tenderly beloved sister, his sole companion for long years, his last and only relative on earth. "Her decease," he said, with a bitterness which I can never forget, "would leave him (him, the hopeless and the frail) the last of the ancient race of the Ushers." While he spoke, the lady Madeline (for so was she called) passed through a remote portion of the apartment, and, without having noticed my presence, disappeared. I regarded her with an utter astonishment not unmingled with dread; and yet I found it impossible to account for such feelings. A sensation of stupor oppressed me as my eyes followed her retreating steps. When a door, at length, closed upon her, my glance sought instinctively and eagerly the countenance of the brother; but he had buried his face in his hands, and I could only perceive that a far more than ordinary wanness had overspread the emaciated fingers through which trickled many passionate tears.

The disease of the lady Madeline had long baffled the skill of her physicians. A settled apathy, a gradual wasting away of the person, and frequent although transient affections of a partially cataleptical character were the unusual diagnosis. Hitherto she had steadily borne up against the pressure of her malady, and had not betaken herself finally to bed; but on the closing in of the evening of my arrival at the house, she succumbed (as her brother told me at night with inexpressible agitation) to the prostrating power of the destroyer; and I learned that the glimpse I had obtained of her person would thus probably be the last I should obtain—that the lady, at least while living, would be seen by me no more.

For several days ensuing, her name was unmentioned by either Usher or myself; and during this period I was busied in earnest endeavors to alleviate the melancholy of my friend. We painted and read together, or I listened, as if in a dream, to the wild improvisations of his speaking guitar. And thus, as a closer and still closer intimacy admitted me more unreservedly into the recesses of his spirit, the more bitterly did I perceive the futility of all attempts at cheering a mind from which darkness, as if an inherent positive quality, poured forth upon all objects of the moral and physical universe in one unceasing radiation of gloom.

I shall ever bear about me a memory of the many solemn hours I thus spent alone with the master of the House of Usher. Yet I should fail in any attempt to convey an idea of the exact character of the studies, or of the occupations, in which he involved me, or led me the way. An excited and highly distempered ideality threw a sulphureous lustre over all. His long improvised dirges will ring forever in my ears. Among other things, I hold painfully in mind a certain singular perversion and amplification of the wild air of the last waltz of Von Weber. From the paintings over which his elaborate fancy brooded, and which grew, touch by touch, into vaguenesses at which I shuddered the more thrillingly, because I shuddered knowing not why—from these paintings (vivid as their images now are before me) I would in vain endeavor to educe more than a small portion which should lie within the compass of merely written words. By the utter simplicity, by the nakedness of his designs, he arrested and overawed attention. If ever mortal painted an idea, that mortal was Roderick Usher. For me at least, in the circumstances then surrounding me, there arose out of the pure abstractions which the hypochondriac contrived to throw upon his canvas, an intensity of intolerable awe, no shadow of which felt I ever yet in the contemplation of the certainly glowing yet too concrete reveries of Fuseli.

One of the phantasmagoric conceptions of my friend, partaking not so rigidly of the spirit of abstraction, may be shadowed forth, although feebly, in words. A small picture presented the interior of an immensely long and rectangular vault or tunnel, with low walls, smooth, white, and without interruption or device. Certain accessory points of the design served well to convey the idea that this excavation lay at an exceeding depth below the surface of the earth. No outlet was observed in any portion of its vast extent, and no torch or other artificial source of light was discernible; yet a flood of intense rays rolled throughout, and bathed the whole in a ghastly and inappropriate splendor.

I have just spoken of that morbid condition of the auditory nerve which rendered all music intolerable to the sufferer, with the exception of certain effects of stringed instruments. It was, perhaps, the narrow limits to which he thus confined himself upon the guitar which gave birth, in great measure, to the fantastic character of his performances. But the fervid *facility* of his *impromptus* could not be so accounted for. They must have been, and were, in the notes, as well as in the words of his wild fantasies (for he not unfrequently accompanied himself with rhymed verbal improvisations), the result of that intense mental collectedness and concentration to which I have previously alluded as observable only in particular moments of the highest artificial excitement. The words of one of these rhapsodies I have easily remembered. I was, perhaps, the more forcibly impressed with it as he gave it, because, in the under or mystic current of its meaning, I fancied that I perceived, and for the first time, a full consciousness on the part of Usher of the tottering of his lofty reason upon her throne. The verses, which were entitled "The Haunted Palace," ran very nearly, if not accurately, thus:—

I

In the greenest of our valleys,
　　By good angels tenanted,
Once a fair and stately palace—
　　Radiant palace—reared its head.
In the monarch Thought's dominion—
　　It stood there!
Never seraph spread a pinion
　　Over fabric half so fair.

II

Banners yellow, glorious, golden,
　　On its roof did float and flow
(This—all this—was in the olden
　　Time long ago);
And every gentle air that dallied,
　　In that sweet day,
Along the ramparts plumed and pallid,
　　A winged odor went away.

III

Wanderers in that happy valley
  Through two luminous windows saw
Spirits moving musically
  To a lute's well-tuned law;
Round about a throne, where sitting
  (Porphyrogene!)
In state his glory well befitting,
  The ruler of the realm was seen.

IV

And all with pearl and ruby glowing
  Was the fair palace door,
Through which came flowing, flowing, flowing
  And sparkling evermore,
A troop of Echoes whose sweet duty
  Was but to sing,
In voices of surpassing beauty,
  The wit and wisdom of their king.

V

But evil things, in robes of sorrow,
  Assailed the monarch's high estate;
(Ah, let us mourn, for never morrow
  Shall dawn upon him, desolate!)
And, round about his home, the glory
  That blushed and bloomed
Is but a dim-remembered story
  Of the old time entombed.

VI

And travellers now within that valley,
  Through the red-litten windows see
Vast forms that move fantastically
  To a discordant melody;
While, like a rapid ghastly river,
  Through the pale door;
A hideous throng rush out forever,
  And laugh—but smile no more.

I well remember that suggestions arising from this ballad led us into a train of thought wherein there became manifest an opinion of Usher's which I mention not so much on account of its novelty (for other men[1] have thought thus), as on account of the pertinacity with which he maintained it. This opinion, in its general form, was that of the sentience of all vegetable things. But, in his disordered fancy, the idea had assumed a more daring character, and trespassed, under certain conditions, upon the kingdom of inorganization. I lack words to express the full extent, or the earnest *abandon* of his persuasion. The belief, however, was connected (as I have previously hinted) with the gray stones of the home of his forefathers. The conditions of the sentence had been here, he imagined, fulfilled in the method of collocation of these stones—in the order of their arrangement, as well as in that of the many *fungi* which overspread them, and of the decayed trees which stood around—above all, in the long undisturbed endurance of this arrangement, and in its reduplication in the still waters of the tarn. Its evidence—the evidence of the sentience—was to be seen, he said (and I here started as he spoke), in the gradual yet certain condensation of an atmosphere of their own about the waters and the walls. The result was discoverable, he added, in that silent yet importunate and terrible influence which for centuries had moulded the destinies of his family, and which made *him* what I now saw him— what he was. Such opinions need no comment, and I will make none.

Our books—the books which, for years, had formed no small portion of the mental existence of the invalid—were, as might be supposed, in strict keeping with this character of phantasm. We pored together over such works as the "Ververt et Chartreuse" of Gresset; the "Belphegor" of Machiavelli; the "Heaven and Hell" of Swedenborg; the "Subterranean Voyage of Nicholas Klimm" of Holberg; the "Chiromancy" of Robert Flud, of Jean D'Indaginé, and of Dela Chambre; the "Journey into the Blue Distance" of Tieck; and the "City of the Sun" of Campanella. One favorite volume was a small octavo edition of the "Directorium Inquisitorium," by the Dominican Eymeric de Gironne; and there were passages in Pomponius Mela, about the old African Satyrs and Œgipans, over which Usher would sit dreaming for hours. His chief delight, however, was found in the perusal of an exceedingly rare and curious book in quarto Gothic—the manual of a forgotten church—the *Vigiliæ Mortuorum Secundum Chorum Ecclesiæ Maguntinæ*.

I could not help thinking of the wild ritual of this work, and of its probable influence upon the hypochondriac, when, one evening, having informed me abruptly that the lady Madeline was no more, he stated his intention of preserving her corpse for a fortnight (previously to its final interment), in one of the numerous vaults within the main walls of the building. The worldly reason, however, assigned for this singular proceeding, was one

---

[1] Watson, Dr. Percival, Spallanzani, and especially the Bishop of Landaff.—See "Chemical Essays," vol. v.

which I did not feel at liberty to dispute. The brother had been led to his resolution (so he told me) by consideration of the unusual character of the malady of the deceased, of certain obtrusive and eager inquiries on the part of her medical men, and of the remote and exposed situation of the burial-ground of the family. I will not deny that when I called to mind the sinister countenance of the person whom I met upon the staircase, on the day of my arrival at the house, I had no desire to oppose what I regarded as at best but a harmless, and by no means an unnatural, precaution.

At the request of Usher, I personally aided him in the arrangements for the temporary entombment. The body having been encoffined, we two alone bore it to its rest. The vault in which we placed it (and which had been so long unopened that our torches, half smothered in its oppressive atmosphere, gave us little opportunity for investigation) was small, damp, and entirely without means of admission for light; lying, at great depth, immediately beneath that portion of the building in which was my own sleeping apartment. It had been used, apparently, in remote feudal times, for the worst purposes of a donjon-keep, and, in later days, as a place of deposit for powder, or some other highly combustible substance, as a portion of its floor, and the whole interior of a long archway through which we reached it, were carefully sheathed with copper. The door, of massive iron, had been, also, similarly protected. Its immense weight caused an unusually sharp, grating sound, as it moved upon its hinges.

Having deposited our mournful burden upon tressels within this region of horror, we partially turned aside the yet unscrewed lid of the coffin, and looked upon the face of the tenant. A striking similitude between the brother and sister now first arrested my attention; and Usher, divining, perhaps, my thoughts, murmured out some few words from which I learned that the deceased and himself had been twins, and that sympathies of a scarcely intelligible nature had always existed between them. Our glances, however, rested not long upon the dead—for we could not regard her unawed. The disease which had thus entombed the lady in the maturity of youth, had left, as usual in all maladies of a strictly cataleptical character, the mockery of a faint blush upon the bosom and the face, and that suspiciously lingering smile upon the lip which is so terrible in death. We replaced and screwed down the lid, and, having secured the door of iron, made our way, with toil, into the scarcely less gloomy apartments of the upper portion of the house.

And now, some days of bitter grief having elapsed, an observable change came over the features of the mental disorder of my friend. His ordinary manner had vanished. His ordinary occupations were neglected or forgotten. He roamed from chamber to chamber with hurried, unequal, and objectless step. The pallor of his countenance had assumed, if possible, a more ghastly hue—but the luminousness of his eye had utterly gone out. The once occasional huskiness of his tone was heard no more; and a tremendous quaver, as if of extreme terror, habitually characterized his utterance. There were times, indeed, when I thought his unceasingly agitated mind was laboring with some oppressive secret, to divulge which he struggled for the necessary courage. At times, again, I was obliged to resolve all into the mere inexplicable vagaries of madness, for I beheld him gazing upon vacancy for long hours, in an attitude of the profoundest attention, as if listening to some imaginary sound. It was no wonder that his condition terrified—that it infected me. I felt creeping upon me, by slow yet certain degrees, the wild influences of his own fantastic yet impressive superstitions.

It was, especially, upon retiring to bed late in the night of the seventh or eighth day after the placing of the lady Madeline within the donjon, that I experienced the full power of such feelings. Sleep came not near my couch—while the hours waned and waned away. I struggled to reason off the nervousness which had dominion over me. I endeavored to believe that much, if not all of what I felt, was due to the bewildering influence of the gloomy furniture of the room—of the dark and tattered draperies, which, tortured into motion by the breath of a rising tempest, swayed fitfully to and fro upon the walls, and rustled uneasily about the decorations of the bed. But my efforts were fruitless. An irrepressible tremor gradually pervaded my frame; and, at length, there sat upon my very heart an incubus of utterly causeless alarm. Shaking this off with a gasp and a struggle, I uplifted myself upon the pillows, and, peering earnestly within the intense darkness of the chamber, hearkened—I know not why, except that an instinctive spirit prompted me—to certain low and indefinite sounds which came, through the pauses of the storm, at long intervals, I knew not whence. Overpowered by an intense sentiment of horror, unaccountable yet unendurable, I threw on my clothes with haste (for I felt that I should sleep no more during the night), and endeavored to arouse myself from the pitiable condition into which I had fallen, by pacing rapidly to and fro through the apartment.

I had taken but few turns in this manner, when a light step on an adjoining staircase arrested my attention. I presently recognized it as that of Usher. In an instant afterward he rapped, with a gentle touch, at my door, and entered, bearing a lamp. His countenance was, as usual, cadaverously wan—but, moreover, there was a species of mad hilarity in his eyes—an evidently restrained *hysteria* in his whole demeanor. His air appalled me—but any thing was preferable to the solitude which I had so long endured, and I even welcomed his presence as a relief.

"And you have not seen it?" he said abruptly, after having stared about him for some moments in silence—"you have not then seen it?—but, stay! you shall." Thus speaking, and having carefully shaded his lamp, he hurried to one of the casements, and threw it freely open to the storm.

The impetuous fury of the entering gust nearly lifted us from our feet. It was, indeed, a tempestuous yet sternly beautiful night, and one wildly singular in its terror and its beauty. A whirlwind had apparently collected its force in our vicinity; for there were frequent and violent alterations in the direction of the wind; and the exceeding density of the clouds (which hung so low as to press upon the turrets of the house) did not prevent our perceiving the life-like velocity with which they flew careering from all points against each other, without passing away into the distance. I say that even their exceeding density did not prevent our perceiving this—yet we had no glimpse of the moon or stars, nor was there any flashing forth of the lightning. But the under surfaces of the huge masses of agitated vapor, as well as all terrestrial objects immediately around us, were glowing in the unnatural light of a faintly luminous and distinctly visible gaseous exhalation which hung about and enshrouded the mansion.

"You must not—you shall not behold this!" said I, shuddering, to Usher, as I led him, with a gentle violence, from the window to a seat. "These appearances, which bewilder you, are merely electrical phenomena not uncommon—or it may be that they have their ghastly origin in the rank miasma of the tarn. Let us close this casement;—the air is chilling and dangerous to your frame. Here is one of your favorite romances. I will read, and you shall listen:—and so we will pass away this terrible night together."

The antique volume which I had taken up was the "Mad Trist" of Sir Launcelot Canning; but I had called it a favorite of Usher's more in sad jest than in earnest; for, in truth, there is little in its uncouth and unimaginative prolixity which could have had interest for the lofty and spiritual ideality of my friend. It was, however, the only book immediately at hand; and I indulged a vague hope that the excitement which now agitated the hypochondriac, might find relief (for the history of mental disorder is full of similar anomalies) even in the extremeness of the folly which I should read. Could I have judged, indeed, by the wildly overstrained air of vivacity with which he hearkened, or apparently hearkened, to the words of the tale, I might well have congratulated myself upon the success of my design.

I had arrived at that well-known portion of the story where Ethelred, the hero of the Trist, having sought in vain for peaceable admission into the dwelling of the hermit, proceeds to make good an entrance by force. Here, it will be remembered, the words of the narrative run thus:

"And Ethelred, who was by nature of a doughty heart, and who was now mighty withal, on account of the powerfulness of the wine which he had drunken, waited no longer to hold parley with the hermit, who, in sooth, was of an obstinate and maliceful turn, but, feeling the rain upon his shoulders, and fearing the rising of the tempest, uplifted his mace outright, and, with blows, made quickly room in the plankings of the door for his gauntleted hand; and now pulling therewith sturdily, he so cracked, and ripped, and tore all asunder, that the noise of the dry and hollow-sounding wood alarumed and reverberated throughout the forest."

At the termination of this sentence I started and, for a moment, paused; for it appeared to me (although I at once concluded that my excited fancy had deceived me)—it appeared to me that, from some very remote portion of the mansion, there came, indistinctly to my ears, what might have been, in its exact similarity of character, the echo (but a stifled and dull one certainly) of the very cracking and ripping sound which Sir Launcelot had so particularly described. It was, beyond doubt, the coincidence alone which had arrested my attention; for, amid the rattling of the sashes of the casements, and the ordinary commingled noises of the still increasing storm, the sound, in itself, had nothing, surely, which should have interested or disturbed me. I continued the story:

"But the good champion Ethelred, now entering within the door, was sore enraged and amazed to perceive no signal of the maliceful hermit; but, in the stead thereof, a dragon of a scaly and prodigious demeanor, and of a fiery tongue, which sate in guard before a palace of gold, with a floor of silver; and upon the wall there hung a shield of shining brass with this legend enwritten—

> Who entereth herein, a conqueror hath bin;
> Who slayeth the dragon, the shield he shall win.

And Ethelred uplifted his mace, and struck upon the head of the dragon, which fell before him, and gave up his pesty breath, with a shriek so horrid and harsh, and withal so piercing, that Ethelred had fain to close his ears with his hands against the dreadful noise of it, the like whereof was never before heard."

Here again I paused abruptly, and now with a feeling of wild amazement —for there could be no doubt whatever that, in this instance, I did actually hear (although from what direction it proceeded I found it impossible to say) a low and apparently distant, but harsh, protracted, and most unusual screaming or grating sound—the exact counterpart of what my fancy had already conjured up for the dragon's unnatural shriek as described by the romancer.

Oppressed, as I certainly was, upon the occurrence of this second and most extraordinary coincidence, by a thousand conflicting sensations, in which wonder and extreme terror were predominant, I still retained sufficient presence of mind to avoid exciting, by any observation, the sensitive nervousness of my companion. I was by no means certain that he had noticed the sounds in question; although, assuredly, a strange alteration had, during the last few minutes, taken place in his demeanor. From a position fronting my own, he had gradually brought round his chair, so as to sit with his face to the door of the chamber; and thus I could but partially perceive his features, although I saw that his lips trembled as if he were murmuring inaudibly. His head had dropped upon his breast—yet I knew that he was not asleep, from the wide and rigid opening of the eye as I caught a glimpse of it in profile. The motion of his body, too, was at variance with this idea—for he rocked from side to side with a gentle yet constant and uniform sway. Having rapidly taken notice of all this, I resumed the narrative of Sir Launcelot, which thus proceeded:

"And now, the champion, having escaped from the terrible fury of the dragon, bethinking himself of the brazen shield, and of the breaking up of the enchantment which was upon it, removed the carcass from out of the way before him, and approached valorously over the silver pavement of the castle to where the shield was upon the wall; which in sooth tarried not for his full coming, but fell down at his feet upon the silver floor, with a mighty great and terrible ringing sound."

No sooner had these syllables passed my lips, than—as if a shield of brass had indeed, at the moment, fallen heavily upon a floor of silver—I became aware of a distinct, hollow, metallic, and clangorous, yet apparently muffled, reverberation. Completely unnerved, I leaped to my feet; but the measured rocking movement of Usher was undisturbed. I rushed to the chair in which he sat. His eyes were bent fixedly before him, and throughout his whole countenance there reigned a stony rigidity. But, as I placed my hand upon his shoulder, there came a strong shudder over his whole person; a sickly smile quivered about his lips; and I saw that he spoke in a low, hurried, and gibbering murmur, as if unconscious of my presence. Bending closely over him, I at length drank in the hideous import of his words.

"Now hear it?—yes, I hear it, and *have* heard it. Long—long—long— many minutes, many hours, many days, have I heard it—yet I dared not—oh, pity me, miserable wretch that I am!—I dared not—I *dared* not speak! *We have put her living in the tomb!* Said I not that my senses were acute? I *now* tell you that I heard her first feeble movements in the hollow coffin. I heard them—many, many days ago—yet I dared not—*I dared not speak!* And now—to-night—Ethelred—ha! ha!—the breaking of the hermit's door, and the death-cry of the dragon, and the clangor of the shield—say, rather, the rending of her coffin, and the grating of the iron hinges of her prison, and her struggles within the coppered archway of the vault! Oh! whither shall I fly? Will she not be here anon? Is she not hurrying to upbraid me for my haste? Have I not heard her footstep on the stair? Do I not distinguish that heavy and horrible beating of her heart? Madman!"— here he sprang furiously to his feet, and shrieked out his syllables, as if in the effort he were giving up his soul—*"Madman! I tell you that she now stands without the door!"*

As if in the superhuman energy of his utterance there had been found the potency of a spell, the huge antique panels to which the speaker pointed threw slowly back, upon the instant, their ponderous and ebony jaws. It was the work of the rushing gust—but then without those doors there *did* stand the lofty and enshrouded figure of the lady Madeline of Usher. There was blood upon her white robes, and the evidence of some bitter struggle upon every portion of her emaciated frame. For a moment she remained trembling and reeling to and fro upon the threshold—then, with a low moaning cry, fell heavily inward upon the person of her brother, and in her violent and now final death-agonies, bore him to the floor a corpse, and a victim to the terrors he had anticipated.

From that chamber, and from that mansion, I fled aghast. The storm was still abroad in all its wrath as I found myself crossing the old causeway. Suddenly there shot along the path a wild light, and I turned to see whence a gleam so unusual could have issued; for the vast house and its shadows were alone behind me. The radiance was that of the full, setting, and blood-red mood, which now shone vividly through that once barely discernible fissure, of which I have before spoken as extending from the roof of the building, in a zigzag direction, to the base. While I gazed, this fissure rapidly widened—there came a fierce breath of the whirlwind—the entire orb of the satellite burst at once upon my sight—my brain reeled as I saw the mighty walls rushing asunder—there was a long tumultuous shouting sound like the voice of a thousand waters—and the deep and dank tarn at my feet closed sullenly and silently over the fragments of the *"House of Usher."*

Stephen King

The Monkey

Stephen King often writes in the mode of psychological horror, most often in the monster story. "The Raft" and "The Crate" come to mind, but particularly "The Monkey." Using the forms of the story of generational haunting, King draws on the Ray Bradbury-esque device of the evil toy, a moral symbol of some complexity. Shadows of the dark ironies of Robert Bloch and Richard Matheson, and the graphic depictions of E. C. comics, make this one of King's most successful stories at integrating and interweaving the strands of contemporary horror. Yet in spite of its central concern with psychological horror, the story retains the characteristic moral concerns that elevate King's major work. One of King's most salient influences on the horror story is the extent to which he is synthesizing and mutating, from his voluminous reading in horror, the entire historical development of the field. As Dickens regenerated the Christmas ghost story, so King has accomplished a wholesale regeneration of horror traditions in the contemporary field.

When Hal Shelburn saw it, when his son Dennis pulled it out of a mouldering Ralston-Purina carton that had been pushed far back under one attic eave, such a feeling of horror and dismay rose in him that for one moment he thought he surely must scream. He put one fist to his mouth, as if to cram it back . . . and then merely coughed into his fist. Neither Terry nor Dennis noticed, but Petey looked around, momentarily curious.

"Hey, neat," Dennis said respectfully. It was a tone Hal rarely got from the boy anymore himself. Dennis was twelve.

"What is it?" Petey asked. He glanced at his father again before his eyes were dragged back to the thing his big brother had found. "What is it, Daddy?"

"It's a monkey, fartbrains," Dennis said. "Haven't you ever seen a monkey before?"

"Don't call your brother fartbrains," Terry said automatically, and began to examine a box of curtains. The curtains were slimy with mildew and she dropped them quickly. "Uck."

"Can I have it, Daddy?" Petey asked. He was nine.

"What do you mean?" Dennis cried. "*I* found it!"

"Boys, please," Terry said. "I'm getting a headache."

Hal barely heard them—any of them. The monkey glimmered up at him from his older son's hands, grinning its old familiar grin. The same grin that had haunted his nightmares as a child, haunted them until he had————

Outside a cold gust of wind rose, and for a moment lips with no flesh blew a long note through the old, rusty gutter outside. Petey stepped closer to his father, eyes moving uneasily to the rough attic roof through which nailheads poked.

"What was that, Daddy?" he asked as the whistle died to a guttural buzz.

"Just the wind," Hal said, still looking at the monkey. Its cymbals, crescents of brass rather than full circles in the weak light of the one naked bulb, were moveless, perhaps a foot apart, and he added automatically, "Wind can whistle, but it can't carry a tune." Then he realized that was a saying of his Uncle Will's, and a goose ran over his grave.

The long note came again, the wind coming off Crystal Lake in a long, droning swoop and then wavering in the gutter. Half a dozen small drafts puffed cold October air into Hal's face—God, this place was so much like the back closet of the house in Hartford that they might all have been transported thirty years back in time.

I won't think about that.

But the thought wouldn't be denied.

In the back closet where I found that goddammed monkey in that same box.

Terry had moved away to examine a wooden crate filled with knick-knacks, duck-walking because the pitch of the eave was so sharp.

"I don't like it," Petey said, and felt for Hal's hand. "Dennis c'n have it if he wants. Can we go, Daddy?"

"Worried about ghosts, chickenguts?" Dennis inquired.

"Dennis, you stop it," Terry said absently. She picked up a wafer-thin cup with a Chinese pattern. "This is nice. This————"

Hal saw that Dennis had found the wind-up key in the monkey's back. Terror flew through him on dark wings.

"Don't do that!"

It came out more sharply than he had intended, and he had snatched the monkey out of Dennis's hands before he was really aware he had done it. Dennis looked around at him, startled. Terry had also glanced back over her shoulder, and Petey looked up. For a moment they were all silent, and the wind whistled again, very low this time, like an unpleasant invitation.

"I mean, it's probably broken," Hal said.

It used to be broken . . . except when it wanted to be fixed.

"Well you didn't have to *grab*," Dennis said.

"Dennis, shut up."

Dennis blinked at him and for a moment looked almost uneasy. Hal hadn't spoken to him so sharply in a long time. Not since he had lost his job with National Aerodyne in California two years before and they had moved to Texas. Dennis decided not to push it . . . for now. He turned back to the Ralston-Purina carton and began to root through it again, but the other stuff was nothing but shit. Broken toys bleeding springs and stuffings.

The wind was louder now, hooting instead of whistling. The attic began to creak softly, making a noise like footsteps.

"Please, Daddy?" Petey asked, only loud enough for his father to hear.

"Yeah," he said. "Terry, let's go."

"I'm not through with this————"

"I said let's *go*."

It was her turn to look startled.

They had taken two adjoining rooms in a motel. By ten that night the boys were asleep in their room and Terry was asleep in the adults' room. She had taken two Valium on the ride back from the home place in Casco. To keep her nerves from giving her a migraine. Just lately she took a lot of Valium. It had started around the time National Aerodyne had laid Hal off. For the last two years he had been working for Texas Instruments—it was $4,000 less a year, but it was work. He told Terry they were lucky. She agreed. There were plenty of software architects drawing unemployment, he said. She agreed. The company housing in Arnette was every bit as good as the place in Fresno, he said. She agreed, but he thought her agreement was a lie.

And he had been losing Dennis. He could feel the kid going, achieving a premature escape velocity, so long, Dennis, bye-bye stranger, it was nice sharing this train with you. Terry said she thought the boy was smoking reefer. She smelled it sometimes. You have to talk to him, Hal. And *he* agreed, but so far he had not.

The boys were asleep. Terry was asleep. Hal went into the bathroom and locked the door and sat down on the closed lid of the john and looked at the monkey.

He hated the way it felt, that soft brown nappy fur, worn bald in spots. He hated its grin—*that monkey grins just like a nigger*, Uncle Will had said once, but it didn't grin like a nigger, or like anything human. Its grin was all teeth, and if you wound up the key, the lips would move, the teeth would seem to get bigger, to become vampire teeth, the lips would writhe and the cymbals would bang, stupid monkey, stupid clockwork monkey, stupid, stupid———

He dropped it. His hands were shaking and he dropped it.

The key clicked on the bathroom tile as it struck the floor. The sound seemed very loud in the stillness. It grinned at him with its murky amber eyes, doll's eyes, filled with idiot glee, its brass cymbals poised as if to strike up a march for some black band from hell, and on the bottom the words MADE IN HONG KONG were stamped.

"You can't be here," he whispered. "I threw you down the well when I was nine."

The monkey grinned up at him.

Hal Shelburn shuddered.

Outside in the night, a black capful of wind shook the motel.

Hal's brother Bill and Bill's wife Collette met them at Uncle Will's and Aunt Ida's the next day. "Did it ever cross your mind that a death in the family is a really lousy way to renew the family connection?" Bill asked him with a bit of a grin. He had been named for Uncle Will. Will and Bill, champions of the rodayo, Uncle Will used to say, and ruffle Bill's hair. It was one of his sayings . . . like the wind can whistle but it can't carry a tune. Uncle Will had died six years before, and Aunt Ida had lived on here alone, until a stroke had taken her just the previous week. Very sudden, Bill had said when he called long distance to give Hal the news. As if he could know; as if anyone could know. She had died alone.

"Yeah," Hal said. "The thought crossed my mind."

They looked at the place together, the home place where they had finished growing up. Their father, a merchant mariner, had simply disappeared as if from the very face of the earth when they were young; Bill claimed to remember him vaguely, but Hal had no memories of him at all. Their mother had died when Bill was ten and Hal eight. They had come to Uncle Will's and Aunt Ida's from Hartford, and they had been raised here, and gone to college here. Bill had stayed and now had a healthy law practice in Portland.

Hal saw that Petey had wandered off toward the blackberry tangles that lay on the eastern side of the house in a mad jumble. "Stay away from there, Petey," he called.

Petey looked back, questioning. Hal felt simple love for the boy rush him . . . and he suddenly thought of the monkey again.

"Why, Dad?"

"The old well's in there someplace," Bill said. "But I'll be damned if I remember just where. Your dad's right, Petey—those blackberry tangles are a good place to stay away from. Thorns'll do a job on you. Right, Hal?"

"Right," Hal said automatically. Pete moved away, not looking back, and then started down the embankment toward the small shingle of beach where Dennis was skipping stones over the water. Hal felt something in his chest loosen a little.

Bill might have forgotten where the old well had been, but late that afternoon Hal went to it unerringly, shouldering his way through the brambles that tore at his old flannel jacket and hunted for his eyes. He reached it and stood there, breathing hard, looking at the rotted, warped boards that covered it. After a moment's debate, he knelt (his knees fired twin pistol shots) and moved two of the boards aside.

From the bottom of that wet, rock-lined throat a face stared up at him, wide eyes, grimacing mouth, and a moan escaped him. It was not loud, except in his heart. There it had been very loud.

It was his own face, reflected up from dark water.

Not the monkey's. For a moment he had thought it was the monkey's.

He was shaking. Shaking all over.

I threw it down the well. I threw it down the well, please God don't let me be crazy. I threw it down the well.

The well had gone dry the summer Johnny McCabe died, the year after Bill and Hal came to stay at the home place with Uncle Will and Aunt Ida. Uncle Will had borrowed money from the bank to have an artesian well sunk, and the blackberry tangles had grown up around the old dug well. The dry well.

Except the water had come back. Like the monkey.

This time the memory would not be denied. Hal sat there helplessly, letting it come, trying to do with it, to ride it like a surfer riding a monster wave that will crush him if he falls off his board, just trying to get through it so it would be gone again.

He had crept out here with the monkey late that summer, and the blackberries had been out, the smell of them thick and cloying. No one came in here to pick, although Aunt Ida would sometimes stand at the edge of the tangles and pick a cupful of berries into her apron. In here the blackberries had gone past ripe to overripe, some of them were rotting, sweating a thick white fluid like pus, and the crickets sang maddeningly in the high grass underfoot, their endless cry: *Reeeeeeee—*

The thorns tore at him, brought dots of blood onto his bare arms. He made no effort to avoid their sting. He had been blind with terror—so blind that he had come within inches of stumbling onto the boards that covered the well, perhaps within inches of crashing thirty feet to the well's muddy bottom. He had pinwheeled his arms for balance, and more thorns had branded his forearms. It was that memory that had caused him to call Petey back sharply.

That was the day Johnny McCabe had died—his best friend. Johnny had been climbing the rungs up to his treehouse in his back yard. The two of them had spent many hours up there that summer, playing pirate, seeing make-believe galleons out on the lake, unlimbering the cannons, preparing to board. Johnny had been climbing up to the treehouse as he had done a thousand times before, and the rung just below the trap door in the bottom of the treehouse had snapped off in his hands and Johnny had fallen thirty feet to the ground and had broken his neck and it was the monkey's fault, the monkey, the goddam hateful monkey. When the phone rang, when Aunt Ida's mouth dropped open and then formed an O of horror as her friend Milly from down the road told her the news, when Aunt Ida said, "Come out on the porch, Hal, I have to tell you some bad news—," he had thought with sick horror, *The monkey! What's the monkey done now?*

There had been no reflection of his face trapped at the bottom of the well that day, only the stone cobbles going down into the darkness and the smell of wet mud. He had looked at the monkey lying there on the wiry grass that grew between the blackberry tangles, its cymbals poised, its grinning teeth huge between its splayed lips, its fur, rubbed away in balding, mangy patches here and there, its glazed eyes.

"I hate you," he had hissed at it. He wrapped his hand around its loathsome body, feeling the nappy fur crinkle. It grinned at him as he held it up in front of his face. "Go on!" he dared it, beginning to cry for the first time that day. He shook it. The poised cymbals trembled minutely. It spoiled everything good. Everything. "Go on, clap them! Clap them!"

The monkey only grinned.

"Go on and clap them!" His voice rose hysterically. "Fraidy-cat, fraidy-cat, go on and clap them! I dare you!"

Its brownish-yellow eyes. Its huge and gleeful teeth.

He threw it down the well then, mad with grief and terror. He saw it turn over once on its way down, a simian acrobat doing a trick, and the sun glinted one last time on those cymbals. It struck the bottom with a thud, and that must have jogged its clockwork, for suddenly the cymbals *did* begin to beat. Their steady, deliberate, and tinny banging rose to his ears, echoing and fey in the stone throat of the dead well: *jang-jang-jang-jang—*

Hal clapped his hands over his mouth, and for a moment he could see it down there, perhaps only in the eye of imagination . . . lying there in the mud, eyes glaring up at the small circle of his boy's face peering over the lip of the well (as if marking its shape forever), lips expanding and contracting around those grinning teeth, cymbals clapping, funny wind-up monkey.

Jang-jang-jang-jang, who's dead? *Jang-jang-jang-jang*, is it Johnny McCabe, falling with his eyes wide, doing his own acrobatic somersault as he falls through the bright summer vacation air with the splintered rung still held in his hands to strike the ground with a single bitter snapping sound? Is it Johnny, Hal? Or is it you?

Moaning, Hal had shoved the boards across the hole, getting splinters in his hands, not caring, not even aware of them until later. And still he could hear it, even through the boards, muffled now and somehow all the worse for that: it was down there in stone-faced dark, clapping its cymbals and jerking its repulsive body, the sounding coming up like the sound of a prematurely buried man scrabbling for a way out.

Jang-jang-jang-jang, who's dead this time?

He fought and battered his way back through the blackberry creepers. Thorns stitched fresh lines of welling blood briskly across his face and burdocks caught in the cuffs of his jeans, and he fell full-length once, his ears still jangling, as if it had followed him. Uncle Will found him later, sitting on an old tire in the garage and sobbing, and he had thought Hal was crying for his dead friend. So he had been; but he had also cried in the aftermath of terror.

He had thrown the monkey down the well in the afternoon. That evening, as twilight crept in through a shimmering mantle of ground-fog, a car moving too fast for the reduced visibility had run down Aunt Ida's manx cat in the road and gone right on. There had been guts everywhere, Bill had thrown up, but Hal had only turned his face away, his pale, still face, hearing Aunt Ida's sobbing (this on top of the news about the McCabe boy had caused a fit of weeping that was almost hysterics, and it was almost two hours before Uncle Will could calm her completely) as if from miles away. In his heart there was a cold and exultant joy. It hadn't been his turn. It had been Aunt Ida's manx, not him, not his brother Bill or his Uncle Will (just two champions of the rodayo). And now the monkey was gone, it was down the well, and one scruffy manx cat with ear mites was not too great a price to pay. If the monkey wanted to clap its hellish cymbals now, let it. It could clap and clash them for the crawling bugs and beetles, the dark things that made their home in the well's stone gullet. It would rot down there in the darkness and its loathsome cogs and wheels and springs would rust in darkness. It would die down there. In the mud and the darkness. Spiders would spin it a shroud.

But . . . it had come back.

Slowly, Hal covered the well again, as he had on that day, and in his ears he heard the phantom echo of the monkey's cymbals: *Jang-jang-jang-jang, who's dead, Hal? Is it Terry? Dennis? Is it Petey, Hal? He's your favorite, isn't he? Is it him? Jang-jang-jang—*

"Put that *down!*"

Petey flinched and dropped the monkey, and for one nightmare moment Hal thought that would do it, that the jolt would jog its machinery and the cymbals would begin to beat and clash.

"Daddy, you scared me."

"I'm sorry. I just . . . I don't want you to play with that."

The others had gone to see a movie, and he had thought he would beat them back to the motel. But he had stayed at the home place longer than he would have guessed; the old, hateful memories seemed to move in their own eternal time zone.

Terry was sitting near Dennis, watching "The Beverly Hillbillies." She watched the old, grainy print with a steady, bemused concentration that spoke of a recent Valium pop. Dennis was reading a rock magazine with the group Styx on the cover. Petey had been sitting cross-legged on the carpet, goofing with the monkey.

"It doesn't work anyway," Petey said. *Which explains why Dennis let him have it,* Hal thought, and then felt ashamed and angry at himself. He seemed to have no control over the hostility he felt toward Dennis more and more often, but in the aftermath he felt demeaned and tacky . . . helpless.

"No," he said. "It's old. I'm going to throw it away. Give it to me."

He held out his hand and Petey, looking troubled, handed it over.

Dennis said to his mother, "Pop's turning into a friggin schizophrenic."

Hal was across the room even before he knew he was going, the monkey in one hand, grinning as if in approbation. He hauled Dennis out of his chair by the shirt. There was a purring sound as a seam came adrift somewhere. Dennis looked almost comically shocked. His copy of *Tiger Beat* fell to the floor.

"Hey!"

"You come with me," Hal said grimly, pulling his son toward the door to the connecting room.

"Hal!" Terry nearly screamed. Petey just goggled.

Hal pulled Dennis through. He slammed the door and then slammed Dennis against the door. Dennis was starting to look scared. "You're getting a mouth problem," Hal said.

"Let *go* of me! You tore my shirt, you————"

Hal slammed the boy against the door again. "Yes," he said. "A real mouth problem. Did you learn that in school? Or back in the smoking area?"

Dennis flushed, his face momentarily ugly with guilt. "I wouldn't be in that shitty school if you didn't get canned!" he burst out.

Hal slammed Dennis against the door again. "I didn't get canned, I got laid off, you know it, and I don't need any of your shit about it. You have problems? Welcome to the world, Dennis. Just don't you lay off all your problems on me. You're eating. Your ass is covered. At eleven, I don't . . . need any . . . shit from you." He punctuated each phrase by pulling the boy forward until their noses were almost touching and then slamming him back into the door. It was not hard enough to hurt, but Dennis was scared—his father had not laid a hand on him since they moved to Texas—and now he began to cry with a young boy's loud, braying, healthy sobs.

"Go ahead, beat me up!" he yelled at Hal, his face twisted and blotchy. "Beat me up if you want, I know how much you fucking hate me!"

"I don't hate you. I love you a lot, Dennis. But I'm your dad and you're going to show me respect or I'm going to bust you for it."

Dennis tried to pull away. Hal pulled the boy to him and hugged him. Dennis fought for a moment and then put his face against Hal's chest and wept as if exhausted. It was the sort of cry Hal hadn't heard from either of his children in years. He closed his eyes, realizing that he felt exhausted himself.

Terry began to hammer on the other side of the door. "Stop it, Hal! Whatever you're doing to him, stop it!"

"I'm not killing him," Hal said. "Go away, Terry."

"Don't you————"

"It's all right, Mom," Dennis said, muffled against Hal's chest.

He could feel her perplexed silence for a moment, and then she went. Hal looked at his son again.

"I'm sorry I badmouthed you, Dad," Dennis said reluctantly.

"When we get home next week, I'm going to wait two or three days and then I'm going to go through all your drawers, Dennis. If there's something in them you don't want me to see, you better get rid of it."

That flash of guilt again. Dennis lowered his eyes and wiped away snot with the back of his hand.

"Can I go now?" He sounded sullen once more.

"Sure," Hal said, and let him go. *Got to take him camping in the spring, just the two of us. Do some fishing, like Uncle Will used to do with Bill and me. Got to get close to him. Got to try.*

He sat down on the bed in the empty room and looked at the monkey. *You'll never be close to him again, Hal,* its grin seemed to say. *Never again. Never again.*

Just looking at the monkey made him feel tired. He laid it aside and put a hand over his eyes.

That night Hal stood in the bathroom, brushing his teeth, and thought: *It was in the same box. How could it be in the same box?*

The toothbrush jabbed upward, hurting his gums. He winced.

He had been four, Bill six, the first time he saw the monkey. Their missing father had bought a house in Hartford, and it had been theirs, free and clear, before he died or disappeared or whatever it had been. Their mother worked as a secretary at Holmes Aircraft, the helicopter plant out in Westville, and a series of sitters came in to stay with the boys, except by then it was just Hal that the sitters had to mind through the day—Bill was in first grade, big school. None of the babysitters stayed for long. They got pregnant and married their boyfriends or got work at Holmes, or Mrs. Shelburn would discover they had been at the cooking sherry or her bottle of brandy which was kept in the sideboard for special occasions. Most of them were stupid girls who seemed only to want to eat or sleep. None of them wanted to read to Hal as his mother would do.

The sitter that long winter was a huge, sleek black girl named Beulah. She fawned over Hal when Hal's mother was around and sometimes pinched him when she wasn't. Still, Hal had some liking for Beulah, who once in awhile would read him a lurid tale from one of her confession or true-detective magazines ("Death Came for the Voluptuous Redhead," Beulah would intone ominously in the dozey daytime silence of the living room, and pop another Reese's Peanut Butter Cup into her mouth while Hal solemnly studied the grainy tabloid pictures and drank his milk from his Wish-Cup). And the liking made what happened worse.

He found the monkey on a cold, cloudy day in March. Sleet ticked sporadically off the windows, and Beulah was asleep on the couch, a copy of *My Story* tented open on her admirable bosom.

So Hal went into the back closet to look at his father's things.

The back closet was a storage space that ran the length of the second floor on the left side, extra space that had never been finished off. One got into the back closet by using a small door—a down-the-rabbit-hole sort of door—on Bill's side of the boy's bedroom. They both liked to go in there, even though it was chilly in winter and hot enough in summer to wring a bucketful of sweat out of your pores. Long and narrow and somehow snug, the back closet was full of fascinating junk. No matter how much stuff you looked at, you never seemed to be able to look at it all. He and Bill had spent whole Saturday afternoons up here, barely speaking to each other, taking things out of boxes, examining them, turning them over and over so their hands could absorb each unique reality, putting them back. Now Hal wondered if he and Bill hadn't been trying, as best they could, to somehow make contact with their vanished father.

He had been a merchant mariner with a navigator's certificate, and there were stacks of charts back there, some marked with neat circles (and the dimple of the compass' swing-point in the center of each). There were twenty volumes of something called *Barron's Guide to Navigation*. A set of cockeyed binoculars that made your eyes feel hot and funny if you looked through them too long. There were touristy things from a dozen ports of call—rubber hula-hula dolls, a black cardboard bowler with a torn band that said YOU PICK A GIRL AND I'LL PICCADILLY, a glass globe with a tiny Eiffel Tower inside—and there were also envelopes with foreign stamps tucked carefully away inside, and foreign coins; there were rock samples from the Hawaiian island of Maui, a glassy Black—heavy and somehow ominous, and funny records in foreign languages.

That day, with the sleet ticking hypnotically off the roof just above his head, Hal worked his way all the way down to the far end of the back closet, moved a box aside, and saw another box behind it—a Ralston-Purina box. Looking over the top was a pair of glassy hazel eyes. They gave him a start and he skittered back for a moment, heart thumping, as if he had discovered a deadly pygmy. Then he saw its silence, the glaze in those eyes, and realized it was some sort of toy. He moved forward again and lifted it carefully from the box.

It grinned its ageless, toothy grin in the yellow light, its cymbals held apart.

Delighted, Hal had turned it this way and that, feeling the crinkle of its nappy fur. Its funny grin pleased him. Yet hadn't there been something else? An almost instinctive feeling of disgust that had come and gone almost before he was aware of it? Perhaps it was so, but with an old, old memory like this one, you had to be careful not to believe too much. Old memories could lie. But . . . hadn't he seen that same expression on Petey's face, in the attic of the home place?

He had seen the key set into the small of its back, and turned it. It had turned far too easily; there were no winding-up clicks. Broken, then. Broken, but still neat.

He took it out to play with it.

"Whatchoo got, Hal?" Beulah asked, waking from her nap.

"Nothing," Hal said. "I found it."

He put it up on the shelf on his side of the bedroom. It stood atop his Lassie coloring books, grinning, staring into space, cymbals poised. It was broken, but it grinned nonetheless. That night Hal awakened from some uneasy dream, bladder full, and got up to use the bathroom in the hall. Bill was a breathing lump of covers across the room.

Hal came back, almost asleep again . . . and suddenly the monkey began to beat its cymbals together in the darkness.

Jang-jang-jang-jang—

He came fully awake, as if snapped in the face with a cold, wet towel. His heart gave a staggering leap of surprise, and a tiny, mouselike squeak escaped his throat. He stared at the monkey, eyes wide, lips trembling.

Jang-jang-jang-jang—

Its body rocked and humped on the shelf. Its lips spread and closed, spread and closed, hideously gleeful, revealing huge and carnivorous teeth.

"Stop," Hal whispered.

His brother turned over and uttered a loud, single snore. All else was silent . . . except for the monkey. The cymbals clapped and clashed, and surely it would wake his brother, his mother, the world. It would wake the dead.

Jang-jang-jang-jang—

Hal moved toward it, meaning to stop it somehow, perhaps put his hand between its cymbals until it ran down (*but it was broken, wasn't it?*), and then it stopped on its own. The cymbals came together one last time—*Jang!*— and then spread slowly apart to their original position. The brass glimmered in the shadows. The monkey's dirty yellowish teeth grinned their improbable grin.

The house was silent again. His mother turned over in her bed and echoed Bill's single snore. Hal got back into his bed and pulled the covers up, his heart still beating fast, and he thought: *I'll put it back in the closet again tomorrow. I don't want it.*

But the next morning he forgot all about putting the monkey back because his mother didn't go to work. Beulah was dead. Their mother wouldn't tell them exactly what happened. "It was an accident, just a terrible accident" was all she would say. But that afternoon Bill bought a newspaper on his way home from school and smuggled page four up to their room under his shirt (TWO KILLED IN APARTMENT SHOOT-OUT, the headline read) and read the article haltingly to Hal, following along with his finger, while their mother cooked supper in the kitchen. Beulah McCaffery, 19, and Sally Tremont, 20, had been shot by Miss McCaffery's boyfriend, Leonard White, 25, following an argument over who was to go out and pick up an order of Chinese food. Miss Tremont had expired at Hartford Receiving; Beulah McCaffery had been pronounced dead at the scene.

It was like Beulah just disappeared into one of her own detective magazines, Hal Shelburn thought, and felt a cold chill race up his spine and then circle his heart. And then he realized the shootings had occurred about the same time the monkey————

"Hal?" It was Terry's voice, sleepy. "Coming to bed?"

He spat toothpaste into the sink and rinsed his mouth. "Yes," he said.

He had put the monkey in his suitcase earlier, and locked it up. They were flying back to Texas in two or three days. But before they went, he would get rid of the damned thing for good.

Somehow.

"You were pretty rough on Dennis this afternoon," Terry said in the dark.

"Dennis has needed somebody to start being rough on him for quite a while now, I think. He's been drifting. I just don't want him to start falling."

"Psychologically, beating the boy isn't a very productive————"

"I didn't *beat* him, Terry—for Christ's sake!"

"—way to assert parental authority————"

"Oh, don't give me any of that encounter-group shit," Hal said angrily.

"I can see you don't want to discuss this." Her voice was cold.

"I told him to get the dope out of the house, too."

"You did?" Now she sounded apprehensive. "How did he take it? What did he say?"

"Come on, Terry! What *could* he say? 'You're fired'?"

"Hal, what's the *matter* with you? You're not like this—what's *wrong*?"

"Nothing," he said, thinking of the monkey locked away in his Samsonite. Would he hear it if it began to clap its cymbals? Yes, he surely would. Muffled, but audible. Clapping doom for someone, as it had for Beulah, Johnny McCabe, Uncle Will's dog Daisy. *Jang-jang-jang*, is it you, Hal? "I've just been under a strain."

"I *hope* that's all it is. Because I don't like you this way."

"No?" And the words escaped before he could stop them; he didn't even want to stop them. "So pop a few Valium and everything will look okay again, right?"

He heard her draw breath in and let it out shakily. She began to cry then. He could have comforted her (maybe), but there seemed to be no comfort in him. There was too much terror. It would be better when the monkey was gone again, gone for good. Please God, gone for good.

He lay wakeful until very late, until morning began to gray the air outside. But he thought he knew what to do.

* * *

Bill had found the monkey the second time.

That was about a year and a half after Beulah McCaffery had been pronounced dead at the scene. It was summer. Hal had just finished kindergarten.

He came in from playing with Stevie Arlingen and his mother called, "Wash your hands, Hal, you're filthy like a pig." She was on the porch, drinking an iced tea and reading a book. It was her vacation; she had two weeks.

Hal gave his hands a token pass under cold water and printed dirt on the hand-towel. "Where's Bill?"

"Upstairs. You tell him to clean his side of the room. It's a mess."

Hal, who enjoyed being the messenger of unpleasant news in such matters, rushed up. Bill was sitting on the floor. The small down-the-rabbit-hole door leading to the back closet was ajar. He had the monkey in his hands.

"That don't work," Hal said immediately. "It's busted."

He was apprehensive, although he barely remembered coming back from the bathroom that night, and the monkey suddenly beginning to clap its cymbals. A week or so after that, he had had a bad dream about the monkey and Beulah—he couldn't remember exactly what—and had awakened screaming, thinking for a moment that the soft weight on his chest was the monkey, that he would open his eyes and see it grinning down at him. But of course the soft weight had only been his pillow, clutched with panicky tightness. His mother came in to soothe him with a drink of water and two chalky-orange baby aspirins, those Valium for childhood's troubled times. She thought it was the fact of Beulah's death that had caused the nightmare. So it was, but not in the way she thought.

He barely remembered any of this now, but the monkey still scared him, particularly its cymbals. And its teeth.

"I know that," Bill said, and tossed the monkey aside. "It's stupid." It landed on Bill's bed, staring up at the ceiling, cymbals poised. Hal did not like to see it there. "You want to go down to Teddy's and get Popsicles?"

"I spent my allowance already," Hal said. "Besides, Mom says you got to clean up your side of the room."

"I can do that later," Bill said. "And I'll loan you a nickel, if you want." Bill was not above giving Hal an Indian rope burn sometimes, and would occasionally trip him up or punch him for no particular reason, but mostly he was okay.

"Sure," Hal said gratefully. "I'll just put that busted monkey back in the closet first, okay?"

"Nah," Bill said, getting up. "Let's go-go-go."

Hal went. Bill's moods were changeable, and if he paused to put the monkey away, he might lose his Popsicle. They went down to Teddy's and got them, then down to the Rec where some kids were getting up a baseball game. Hal was too small to play, but he sat far out in foul territory, sucking his root beer Popsicle and chasing what the big kids called "Chinese home runs." They didn't get home until almost dark, and their mother whacked Hal for getting the hand-towel dirty and whacked Bill for not cleaning up his side of the room, and after supper there was TV, and by the time all of that had happened, Hal had forgotten all about the monkey. It somehow found its way up onto *Bill's* shelf, where it stood right next to Bill's autographed picture of Bill Boyd. And there it stayed for nearly two years.

By the time Hal was seven, babysitters had become an extravagance, and Mrs. Shelburn's last word to the two of them each morning was, "Bill, look after your brother."

That day, however, Bill had to stay after school for a Safety Patrol Boy meeting and Hal came home alone, stopping at each corner until he could see absolutely no traffic coming in either direction and then skittering across, shoulders hunched, like a doughboy crossing no man's land. He let himself into the house with the key under the mat and went immediately to the refrigerator for a glass of milk. He got the bottle, and then it slipped through his fingers and crashed to smithereens on the floor, the pieces of glass flying everywhere, as the monkey suddenly began to beat its cymbals together upstairs.

Jang-jang-jang-jang, on and on.

He stood there immobile, looking down at the broken glass and the puddle of milk, full of a terror he could not name or understand. It was simply there, seeming to ooze from his pores.

He turned and rushed upstairs to their room. The monkey stood on Bill's shelf, seeming to stare at him. He had knocked the autographed picture of Bill Boyd face-down onto Bill's bed. The monkey rocked and grinned and beat its cymbals together. Hal approached it slowly, not wanting to, not able to stay away. Its cymbals jerked apart and crashed together and jerked apart again. As he got closer, he could hear the clockwork running in the monkey's guts.

Abruptly, uttering a cry of revulsion and terror, he swatted it from the shelf as one might swat a large, loathsome bug. It struck Bill's pillow and then fell on the floor, cymbals still beating together, *jang-jang-jang*, lips flexing and closing as it lay there on its back in a patch of late April sunshine.

Then, suddenly, he remembered Beulah. The monkey had clapped its cymbals that night, too.

Hal kicked it with one Buster Brown shoe, kicked it as hard as he could, and this time the cry that escaped him was one of fury. The clockwork monkey skittered across the floor, bounced off the wall, and lay still. Hal stood staring at it, fists bunched, heart pounding. It grinned saucily back at him, the sun a burning pinpoint in one glass eye. *Kick me all you want*, it seemed to tell him. *I'm nothing but cogs and clockwork and a worm-gear or two, kick me all you feel like, I'm not real, just a funny clockwork monkey is all I am, and who's dead? There's been an explosion at the helicopter plant! What's that rising up into the sky like a big bloody bowling ball with eyes where the finger-holes should be? Is it your mother's head, Hal? Down at Brook Street Corner! The car was going too fast! The driver was drunk! There's one Patrol Boy less! Could you hear the crunching sound when the wheels ran over Bill's skull and his brains squirted out of his ears? Yes? No? Maybe? Don't ask me, I don't know, I can't know, all I know how to do is beat these cymbals together jang-jang-jang, and who's dead, Hal? Your mother?*

Your brother? Or is it you, Hal? Is it you?

He rushed at it again, meaning to stomp on it, smash its loathsome body, jump on it until cogs and gears flew and its horrible glass eyes rolled across the floor. But just as he reached it its cymbals came together once more, very softly . . . (*jang*) . . . as a spring somewhere inside expanded one final, minute notch . . . and a sliver of ice seemed to whisper its way through the walls of his heart, impaling it, stilling its fury and leaving him sick with terror again. The monkey almost seemed to know—how gleeful its grin seemed!

He picked it up, tweezing one of its arms between the thumb and first finger of his right hand, mouth drawn down in a bow of loathing, as if it were a corpse he held. Its mangy fake fur seemed hot and fevered against his skin. He fumbled open the tiny door that led to the back closet and turned on the bulb. The monkey grinned at him as he crawled down the length of the storage area between boxes piled on top of boxes, past the set of navigation books and the photograph albums with their fume of old chemicals and the souvenirs and the old clothes, and Hal thought: *If it begins to clap its cymbals together now and move in my hand, I'll scream, and if I scream, it'll do more than grin, it'll start to laugh, to laugh at me, and then I'll go crazy and they'll find me in here, drooling and laughing, crazy, I'll be crazy, oh please dear God, please dear Jesus, don't let me go crazy—*

He reached the far end and clawed two boxes aside, spilling one of them, and jammed the monkey back into the Ralston-Purina box in the farthest corner. And it leaned in there, comfortably, as if home at last, cymbals poised, grinning its simian grin, as if the joke were still on Hal. Hal crawled backward, sweating, hot and cold, all fire and ice, waiting for the cymbals to begin, and when they began, the monkey would leap from its box and scurry beetlelike toward him, clockwork whirring, cymbals clashing madly, and———

—and none of that happened. He turned off the light and slammed the small down-the-rabbit-hole door and leaned on it, panting. At last he began to feel a little better. He went downstairs on rubbery legs, got an empty bag, and began carefully to pick up the jagged shards and splinters of the broken milk bottle, wondering if he was going to cut himself and bleed to death, if that was what the clapping cymbals had meant. But that didn't happen, either. He got a towel and wiped up the milk and then sat down to see if his mother and brother would come home.

His mother came first, asking, "Where's Bill?"

In a low, colorless voice, now sure that Bill must be dead, Hal started to explain about the Patrol Boy meeting, knowing that, even given a very long meeting, Bill should have been home half an hour ago.

His mother looked at him curiously, started to ask what was wrong, and then the door opened and Bill came in—only it was not Bill at all, not really. This was a ghost-Bill, pale and silent.

"What's wrong?" Mrs. Shelburn exclaimed. "Bill, what's wrong?"

Bill began to cry and they got the story through his tears. There had been a car, he said. He and his friend Charlie Silverman were walking home together after the meeting and the car came around Brook Street Corner too fast and Charlie had frozen, Bill had tugged Charlie's hand once but had lost his grip and the car————

Bill began to bray out loud, hysterical sobs, and his mother hugged him to her, rocking him, and Hal looked out on the porch and saw two policemen standing there. The squad car in which they had conveyed Bill home was at the curb. Then he began to cry himself . . . but his tears were tears of relief.

It was Bill's turn to have nightmares now—dreams in which Charlie Silverman died over and over again, knocked out of his Red Ryder cowboy boots, and flipped onto the hood of the old Hudson Hornet the drunk driver had been driving. Charlie Silverman's head and the Hudson's windshield had met with an explosive noise, and both had shattered. The drunk driver, who owned a candy store in Milford, suffered a heart attack shortly after being taken into custody (perhaps it was the sight of Charlie Silverman's brains drying on his pants), and his lawyer was quite successful at the trial with his "this man has been punished enough" theme. The drunk was given sixty days (suspended) and lost his privilege to operate a motor vehicle in the state of Connecticut for five years . . . which was about as long as Bill Shelburn's nightmares lasted. The monkey was hidden away again in the back closet. Bill never noticed it was gone from his shelf . . . or if he did, he never said.

Hal felt safe for a while. He even began to forget about the monkey again, or to believe it had only been a bad dream. But when he came home from school on the afternoon his mother died, it was back on his shelf, cymbals poised, grinning down at him.

He approached it slowly as if from outside himself—as if his own body had been turned into a wind-up toy at the sight of the monkey. He saw his hand reach out and take it down. He felt the nappy fur crinkle under his hand, but the feeling was muffled, mere pressure, as if someone had shot him full of Novocaine. He could hear his breathing, quick and dry, like the rattle of wind through straw.

He turned it over and grasped the key and years later he would think that his drugged fascination was like that of a man who puts a six-shooter with one loaded chamber against a closed and jittering eyelid and pulls the trigger.

No don't—let it alone throw it away don't touch it————

He turned the key and in the silence he heard a perfect tiny series of winding-up clicks. When he let the key go, the monkey began to clap its cymbals together and he could feel its body jerking, bend-and-*jerk*, bend-and-*jerk*, as if it were live, it *was* alive, writhing in his hand like some loathsome pygmy, and the vibration he felt through its balding brown fur was not that of turning cogs but the beating of its black and cindered heart.

With a groan, Hal dropped the monkey and backed away, fingernails digging into the flesh under his eyes, palms pressed to his mouth. He stumbled over something and nearly lost his balance (then he would have been right down on the floor with it, his bulging blue eyes looking into its glassy hazel ones). He scrambled toward the door, backed through it, slammed it, and leaned against it. Suddenly he bolted for the bathroom and vomited.

It was Mrs. Stukey from the helicopter plant who brought the news and stayed with them those first two endless nights, until Aunt Ida got down from Maine. Their mother had died of a brain embolism in the middle of the afternoon. She had been standing at the water cooler with a cup of water in one hand and had crumpled as if shot, still holding the paper cup in one hand. With the other she had clawed at the water cooler and had pulled the great glass bottle of Poland water down with her. It had shattered . . . but the plant doctor, who came on the run, said later that he believed Mrs. Shelburn was dead before the water had soaked through her dress and her under-clothes to wet her skin. The boys were never told any of this, but Hal knew anyway. He dreamed it again and again on the long nights following his mother's death. *You still have trouble gettin to sleep, little brother?* Bill had asked him, and Hal supposed Bill thought all the thrashing and bad dreams had to do with their mother dying so suddenly, and that was right . . . but only partly right. There was the guilt: the certain, deadly knowledge that he had killed his mother by winding the monkey up on that sunny after-school afternoon.

When Hal finally fell asleep, his sleep must have been deep. When he awoke, it was nearly noon. Petey was sitting cross-legged in a chair across the room, methodically eating an orange section by section and watching a game show on TV.

Hal swung his legs out of bed, feeling as if someone had punched him down into sleep . . . and then punched him back out of it. His head throbbed. "Where's your mom, Petey?"

Petey glanced around. "She and Dennis went shopping. I said I'd stay here with you. Do you always talk in your sleep, Dad?"

Hal looked at his son cautiously. "No, I don't think so. What did I say?"

"It was all muttering. I couldn't make it out. It scared me, a little."

"Well, here I am in my right mind again," Hal said, and managed a small grin. Petey grinned back, and Hal felt simple love for the boy again, an emotion that was bright and strong and uncomplicated. He wondered why he had always been able to feel so good about Petey, to feel he understood Petey and could help him, and why Dennis seemed a window too dark to look through, a mystery in his ways and habits, the sort of boy he could not understand because he had never been that sort of boy. It was too easy to say that the move from California had changed Dennis, or that————

His thoughts froze. The monkey. The monkey was sitting on the window-sill, cymbals poised. Hal felt his heart stop dead in his chest and then suddenly begin to gallop. His vision wavered, and his throbbing head began to ache ferociously.

It had escaped from the suitcase and now stood on the windowsill, grinning at him. *Thought you got rid of me, didn't you? But you've thought that before, haven't you?*

Yes, he thought sickly. Yes, I have.

"Pete, did you take that monkey out of my suitcase?" he asked, knowing the answer already. He had locked the suitcase and had put the key in his overcoat pocket.

Petey glanced at the monkey, and something—Hal thought it was unease—passed over his face. "No," he said. "Mom put it there."

"Mom did?"

"Yeah. She took it from you. She laughed."

"Took it from me? What are you talking about?"

"You had it in bed with you. I was brushing my teeth, but Dennis saw. He laughed, too. He said you looked like a baby with a teddy bear."

Hal looked at the monkey. His mouth was too dry to swallow. He'd had it in *bed* with him? In *bed*? That loathsome fur against his cheek, maybe against his *mouth*, those glass eyes staring into his sleeping face, those grinning teeth near his neck? Dear *God*.

He turned abruptly and went to the closet. The Samsonite was there, still locked. The key was still in his overcoat pocket.

Behind him, the TV snapped off. He came out of the closet slowly. Petey was looking at him soberly. "Daddy, I don't like that monkey," he said, his voice almost too low to hear.

"Nor do I," Hal said.

Petey looked at him closely, to see if he was joking, and saw that he was not. He came to his father and hugged him tight. Hal could feel him trembling.

Petey spoke into his ear, then, very rapidly, as if afraid he might not have courage enough to say it again . . . or that the monkey might overhear.

"It's like it looks at you. Like it looks at you no matter where you are in the room. And if you go into the other room, it's like it's looking through the wall at you. I kept feeling like it . . . like it wanted me for something."

Petey shuddered. Hal held him tight.

"Like it wanted you to wind it up," Hal said.

Pete nodded violently. "It isn't really broken, is it, Dad?"

"Sometimes it is," Hal said, looking over his son's shoulder at the monkey. "But sometimes it still works."

"I kept wanting to go over there and wind it up. It was so quiet, and I thought, I can't, it'll wake up Daddy, but I still wanted to, and I went over and I . . . I *touched* it and I hate the way it feels . . . but I liked it, too . . . and it was like it was saying, Wind me up, Petey, we'll play, your father isn't going to wake up, he's never going to wake up at all, wind me up, wind me up. . . ."

The boy suddenly burst into tears.

"It's bad, I know it is. There's something wrong with it. Can't we throw it out, Daddy? Please?"

The monkey grinned its endless grin at Hal. He could feel Petey's tears between them. Late morning sun glinted off the monkey's brass cymbals— the light reflected upward and put sunstreaks on the motel's plain white stucco ceiling.

"What time did your mother think she and Dennis would be back, Petey?"

"Around one." He swiped at his red eyes with his shirt-sleeve, looking embarrassed at his tears. But he wouldn't look at the monkey. "I turned on the TV," he whispered. "And I turned it up loud."

"That was all right, Petey."

"I had a crazy idea," Petey said. "I had this idea that if I wound that monkey up, you . . . you would have just died there in bed. In your sleep. Wasn't that a crazy idea, Daddy?" His voice had dropped again, and it trembled helplessly.

How would it have happened? Hal wondered. *Heart attack? An embolism, like my mother? What? It doesn't really matter, does it?*

And on the heels of that, another, colder thought: *Get rid of it, he says. Throw it out. But can it be gotten rid of? Ever?*

The monkey grinned mockingly at him, its cymbals held a foot apart. Did it suddenly come to life on the night Aunt Ida died? he wondered suddenly. Was that the last sound she heard, the muffled *jang-jang-jang* of the monkey beating its cymbals together up in the black attic while the wind whistled along the drainpipe?

"Maybe not so crazy," Hal said slowly to his son. "Go get your flight bag, Petey."

Petey looked at him uncertainly. "What are we going to do?"

Maybe it can be got rid of. Maybe permanently, maybe just for a while . . . a long while or a short while. Maybe it's just going to come back and come back and that's what all this is about . . . but maybe I—we—can say good-bye to it for a long time. It took twenty years to come back this time. It took twenty years to get out of the well. . . .

"We're going to go for a ride," Hal said. He felt fairly calm, but somehow too heavy inside his skin. Even his eyeballs seemed to have gained weight. "But first I want you to take your flight bag out there by the edge of the parking lot and find three or four good-sized rocks. Put them inside the bag and bring it back to me. Got it?"

Understanding flickered in Petey's eyes. "All right, Daddy."

Hal glanced at his watch. It was nearly 12:15. "Hurry. I want to be gone before your mother gets back."

"Where are we going?"

"To Uncle Will's and Aunt Ida's," Hal said. "To the home place."

Hal went into the bathroom, looked behind the toilet, and got the bowl brush leaning there. He took it back to the window and stood there with it in his hand like a cut-rate magic wand. He looked out at Petey in his melton shirt-jacket, crossing the parking lot with his flight bag, DELTA showing clearly in white letters against a blue field. A fly bumbled in an upper corner of the window, slow and stupid with the end of the warm season. Hal knew how it felt.

He watched Petey hunt up three good-sized rocks and then start back across the parking lot. A car came around the corner of the motel, a car that was moving too fast, much too fast, and without thinking, reaching with the kind of reflex a good short-stop shows going to his right, his hand flashed down, as if in a karate chop . . . and stopped.

The cymbals closed soundlessly on his intervening hand, and he felt something in the air. Something like rage.

The car's brakes screamed. Petey flinched back. The driver motioned to

him impatiently, as if what had almost happened was Petey's fault, and
Petey ran across the parking lot with his collar flapping and into the motel's
rear entrance.

Sweat was running down Hal's chest; he felt it on his forehead like a
drizzle of oily rain. The cymbals pressed coldly against his hand, numbing it.

Go on, he thought grimly. *Go on, I can wait all day. Until hell freezes over,
if that's what it takes.*

The cymbals drew apart and came to rest. Hal heard one faint *click!* from
inside the monkey. He withdrew his hand and looked at it. On both the back
and the palm there were grayish semicircles printed into the skin, as if he had
been frostbitten.

The fly bumbled and buzzed, trying to find the cold October sunshine that
seemed so close.

Petey came bursting in, breathing quickly, cheeks rosy. "I got three good
ones, Dad, I—" He broke off. "Are you all right, Daddy?"

"Fine," Hal said. "Bring the bag over."

Hal hooked the table by the sofa over to the window with his foot, so it
stood below the sill, and put the flight bag on it. He spread its mouth open
like lips. He could see the stones Petey had collected glimmering inside. He
used the toilet-bowl brush to hook the monkey forward. It teetered for a
moment and then fell into the bag. There was a faint *jing!* as one of its
cymbals struck one of the rocks.

"Dad? Daddy?" Petey sounded frightened. Hal looked around at him.
Something was different; something had changed. What was it?

Then he saw the direction of Petey's gaze and he knew. The buzzing of the
fly had stopped. It lay dead on the windowsill.

"Did the monkey do that?" Petey whispered.

"Come on," Hal said, zipping the bag shut. "I'll tell you while we ride out
to the home place."

"How can we go? Mom and Dennis took the car."

"I'll get us there," Hal said, and ruffled Petey's hair.

He showed the desk clerk his driver's license and a twenty-dollar bill. After
taking Hal's Texas Instruments digital watch as further collateral, the clerk
handed Hal the keys to his own car—a battered AMC Gremlin. As they
drove east on Route 302 toward Casco, Hal began to talk, haltingly at first,
then a little faster. He began by telling Petey that his father had probably
brought the monkey home with him from overseas, as a gift for his sons. It
wasn't a particularly unique toy; there was nothing strange or valuable about
it. There must have been hundreds of thousands of wind-up monkeys in the
world, some made in Hong Kong, some in Taiwan, some in Korea. But
somewhere along the line—perhaps even in the dark back closet of the house
in Connecticut where the two boys had begun their growing up—something
had happened to the monkey. Something bad, evil. It might be, Hal told
Petey as he tried to coax the clerk's Gremlin up past forty (he was very aware
of the zipped-up flight bag on the back seat, and Petey kept glancing around
at it), that some evil—maybe even most evil—isn't even sentient and aware
of what it is. It might be that most evil is very much like a monkey full of

clockwork that you wind up; the clockwork turns, the cymbals begin to beat, the teeth grin, the stupid glass eyes laugh . . . or appear to laugh. . . .

He told Petey about finding the monkey, but he found himself skipping over large chunks of the story, not wanting to terrify his already scared boy any more than he was already. The story thus became disjointed, not really clear, but Petey asked no questions; perhaps he was filling in the blanks for himself, Hal thought, in much the same way that he had dreamed his mother's death over and over, although he had not been there.

Uncle Will and Aunt Ida had both been there for the funeral. Afterward, Uncle Will had gone back to Maine—it was harvest-time—and Aunt Ida had stayed on for two weeks with the boys to neaten up her sister's affairs. But more than that, she spent the time making herself known to the boys, who were so stunned by their mother's sudden death that they were nearly sleepwalking. When they couldn't sleep, she was there with warm milk; when Hal woke at three in the morning with nightmares (nightmares in which his mother approached the water cooler without seeing the monkey that floated and bobbed in its cool sapphire depths, grinning and clapping its cymbals, each converging pair of sweeps leaving trails of bubbles behind); she was there when Bill came down with first a fever and then a rash of painful mouth sores and then hives three days after the funeral; she was there. She made herself known to the boys, and before they rode the New England Flyer from Hartford to Portland with her, both Bill and Hal had come to her separately and wept on her lap while she held them and rocked them, and the bonding began.

The day before they left Connecticut for good to go "down Maine" (as it was called in those days), the rag-man came in his great old rattly truck and picked up the huge pile of useless stuff that Bill and Hal had carried out to the sidewalk from the back closet. When all the junk had been set out by the curb for pick-up, Aunt Ida had asked them to go through the back closet again and pick out any souvenirs or remembrances they wanted specially to keep. We just don't have room for it all, boys, she told them, and Hal supposed Bill had taken her at her word and had gone through all those fascinating boxes their father had left behind one final time. Hal did not join his older brother. Hal had lost his taste for the back closet. A terrible idea had come to him during those first two weeks of mourning: perhaps his father hadn't just disappeared, or run away because he had an itchy foot and had discovered marriage wasn't for him.

Maybe the monkey had gotten him.

When he heard the rag-man's truck roaring and farting and backfiring its way down the block, Hal nerved himself, snatched the scruffy wind-up monkey from his shelf where it had been since the day his mother died (he had not dared to touch it until then, not even to throw it back into the closet), and ran downstairs with it. Neither Bill nor Aunt Ida saw him. Sitting on top of a barrel filled with broken souvenirs and mouldy books was the Ralston-Purina carton, filled with similar junk. Hal had slammed the monkey back into the box it had originally come out of, hysterically daring it to begin clapping its cymbals *(go on, go on, I dare you, dare you, DARE YOU),* but the monkey only waited there, leaning back nonchalantly, as if expecting a bus, grinning its awful, knowing grin.

Hal stood by, a small boy in old corduroy pants and scuffed Buster Browns, as the rag-man, an Italian gent who wore a crucifix and whistled through the space in his teeth, began loading boxes and barrels into his ancient truck with the high wooden sides. Hal watched as he lifted both the barrel and the Ralston-Purina box balanced atop it; he watched the monkey disappear into the maw of the truck; he watched as the rag-man climbed back into the cab, blew his nose mightily into the palm of his hand, wiped his hand with a huge red handkerchief, and started the truck's engine with a mighty roar and a stinking blast of oily blue smoke; he watched the truck draw away. And a great weight had dropped away from his heart—he actually felt it go. He had jumped up and down twice, as high as he could jump, his arms spread, palms held out, and if any of the neighbors had seen him, they would have thought it odd almost to the point of blasphemy, perhaps—*why is that boy jumping for joy* (for that was surely what it was; a jump for joy can hardly be disguised) *with his mother not even a month in her grave?*

He was jumping for joy because the monkey was gone, gone forever. Gone forever, but not three months later Aunt Ida had sent him up into the attic to get the boxes of Christmas decorations, and as he crawled around looking for them, getting the knees of his pants dusty, he had suddenly come face to face with it again, and his wonder and terror had been so great that he had to bite sharply into the side of his hand to keep from screaming . . . or fainting dead away. There it was, grinning its toothy grin, cymbals poised a foot apart and ready to clap, leaning nonchalantly back against one corner of a Ralston-Purina carton as if waiting for a bus, seeming to say: *Thought you got rid of me, didn't you? But I'm not that easy to get rid of, Hal. I like you, Hal. We were made for each other, just a boy and his pet monkey, a couple of good old buddies. And somewhere south of here there's a stupid old Italian rag-man lying in a claw-foot tub with his eyeballs bulging and his dentures half-popped out of his mouth, his screaming mouth, a rag-man who smells like a burned-out Exide battery. He was saving me for his grandson, Hal, he put me on the shelf with his soap and his razor and his Burma-Shave and the Philco radio he listened to the Brooklyn Dodgers on, and I started to clap, and one of my cymbals hit that old radio and into the tub it went, and then I came to you, Hal, I worked my way along country roads at night and the moonlight shone off my teeth at three in the morning and I left death in my wake, Hal, I came to you, I'm your Christmas present, Hal, wind me up, who's dead? Is it Bill? Is it Uncle Will? Is it you, Hal? Is it* you?

Hal had backed away, grimacing madly, eyes rolling, and nearly fell going downstairs. He told Aunt Ida he hadn't been able to find the Christmas decorations—it was the first lie he had ever told her, and she had seen the lie on his face but had not asked him why he had told it, thank God—and later when Bill came in she asked him to look and he brought the Christmas decorations down. Later, when they were alone, Bill hissed at him that he was a dummy who couldn't find his own ass with both hands and a flashlight. Hal said nothing. Hal was pale and silent, only picking at his supper. And that night he dreamed of the monkey again, one of its cymbals striking the Philco radio as it babbled out Dean Martin singing Whenna da moon hitta you eye like a big pizza pie *ats-a moray*, the radio tumbling into the bathtub as the monkey grinned and beat its cymbals together with a *JANG* and a *JANG* and a *JANG*; only it wasn't the Italian rag-man who was in the tub when the water turned electric.

It was him.

Hal and his son scrambled down the embankment behind the home place to the boathouse that jutted out over the water on its old pilings. Hal had the flight bag in his right hand. His throat was dry, his ears were attuned to an unnaturally keen pitch. The bag seemed very heavy.

"What's down here, Daddy?" Petey asked.

Hal didn't answer. He set down the flight bag. "Don't touch that," he said, and Petey backed away from it. Hal felt in his pocket for the ring of keys Bill had given him and found one neatly labeled B'HOUSE on a scrap of adhesive tape.

The day was clear and cold, windy, the sky a brilliant blue. The leaves of the trees that crowded up to the verge of the lake had gone every bright fall shade from blood red to sneering yellow. They rattled and talked in the wind. Leaves swirled around Petey's sneakers as he stood anxiously by, and Hal could smell November on the wind, with winter crowding close behind it.

The key turned in the padlock and he pulled the swing doors open. Memory was strong; he didn't even have to look to kick down the wooden block that held the door open. The smell in here was all summer: canvas and bright wood, a lingering, musty warmth.

Uncle Will's rowboat was still here, the oars neatly shipped as if he had last loaded it with his fishing tackle and two six-packs of Black Label on ice yesterday afternoon. Bill and Hal had both gone out fishing with Uncle Will many times, but never together; Uncle Will maintained the boat was too small for three. The red trim, which Uncle Will had touched up each spring, was now faded and peeling, though, and spiders had spun their silk in the boat's bow.

Hal laid hold of it and pulled it down the ramp to the little shingle of beach. The fishing trips had been one of the best parts of his childhood with Uncle Will and Aunt Ida. He had a feeling that Bill felt much the same. Uncle Will was ordinarily the most taciturn of men, but once he had the boat positioned to his liking, some sixty or seventy yards offshore, lines set and bobbers floating on the water, he would crack a beer for himself and one for Hal (who rarely drank more than half of the one can Uncle Will would allow, always with the ritual admonition from Uncle Will that Aunt Ida must never be told because "she'd shoot me for a stranger if she knew I was givin you boys beer, don't you know"), and wax expansive. He would tell stories, answer questions, rebait Hal's hook when it needed rebaiting; and the boat would drift where the wind and the mild current wanted it to be.

"How come you never go right out to the middle, Uncle Will?" Hal had asked once.

"Look over the side there, Hal," Uncle Will had answered.

Hal did. He saw blue water and his fish line going down into black.

"You're looking into the deepest part of Crystal Lake," Uncle Will said, crunching his empty beer can in one hand and selecting a fresh one with the other. "A hundred feet if she's an inch. Amos Culligan's old Studebaker is down there somewhere. Damn fool took it out on the lake one early December, before the ice was made. Lucky to get out of it alive, he was. They'll never get that Studebaker out, nor see it until Judgment Trump blows. Lake's one deep son of a whore right here, it is. Big ones are right here, Hal. No need to go out no further. Let's see how your worm looks. Reel that son of a whore right in."

Hal did, and while Uncle Will put a fresh crawler from the old Crisco tin that served as his bait box on his hook, he stared into the water, fascinated, trying to see Amos Culligan's old Studebaker all rust and waterweed drifting out of the open driver's side window through which Amos had escaped at the absolute last moment, waterweed festooning the steering wheel like a rotting necklace, waterweed dangling from the rearview mirror and drifting back and forth in the currents like some strange rosary. But he could see only blue shading to black, and there was the shape of Uncle Will's night-crawler, the hook hidden inside its knots, hung up there in the middle of things, its own sun-shafted version of reality. Hal had a brief, dizzying vision of being suspended over a mighty gulf, and he had closed his eyes for a moment until the vertigo passed. That day, he seemed to recollect, he had drunk his entire can of beer.

. . . the deepest part of Crystal Lake . . . a hundred feet if she's an inch.

He paused a moment, panting, and looked up at Petey, still watching anxiously. "You want some help, Daddy?"

"In a minute."

He had his breath again, and now he pulled the rowboat across the narrow strip of sand to the water, leaving a groove. The paint had peeled, but the boat had been kept under cover and it looked sound.

When he and Uncle Will went out, Uncle Will would pull the boat down the ramp, and when the bow was afloat, he would clamber in, grab an oar to push with, and say: "Push me off, Hal . . . this is where you earn your truss!"

"Hand that bag in, Petey, and then give me a push," he said. And smiling a little, he added: "This is where you earn your truss."

Petey didn't smile back. "Am I coming, Daddy?"

"Not this time. Another time I'll take you out fishing, but . . . not this time."

Petey hesitated. The wind tumbled his brown hair and a few yellow leaves, crisp and dry, wheeled past his shoulders and landed at the edge of the water, bobbing like boats themselves.

"You should have muffled them," he said, low.

"What?" But he thought he understood what Petey had meant.

"Put cotton over the cymbals. Taped it on. So it couldn't . . . make that noise."

Hal suddenly remembered Daisy coming toward him—not walking but lurching—and how, quite suddenly, blood had burst from both of Daisy's eyes in a flood that soaked her ruff and pattered down on the floor of the barn, how she had collapsed on her forepaws . . . and on that still, rainy spring air of that day he had heard the sound, not muffled but curiously clear, coming from the attic of the house fifty feet away: *Jang-jang-jang-jang!*

He began to scream hysterically, dropping the armload of wood he had been getting for the fire. He ran for the kitchen to get Uncle Will, who was eating scrambled eggs and toast, his suspenders not even up over his shoulders yet.

She was an old dog, Hal, Uncle Will had said, his face haggard and unhappy—he looked old himself. *She was twelve, and that's old for a dog. You mustn't take on, now—old Daisy wouldn't like that.*

Old, the vet had echoed, but he had looked troubled all the same, because dogs don't die of explosive brain hemorrhages, even at twelve ("like as if someone had stuck a firecracker in his head," Hal overheard the vet saying to Uncle Will as Uncle Will dug a hole in back of the barn not far from the place where he had buried Daisy's mother in 1950; "I never seen the beat of it, Will").

And later, terrified almost out of his mind but unable to help himself, Hal had crept up to the attic.

Hello, Hal, how you doing? the monkey grinned from its shadowy corner. Its cymbals were poised, a foot or so apart. The sofa cushion Hal had stood on end between them was now all the way across the attic. Something— some force—had thrown it hard enough to split its cover, and stuffing foamed out of it. *Don't worry about Daisy,* the monkey whispered inside his head, its glassy hazel eyes fixed on Hal Shelburn's wide blue ones. *Don't worry about Daisy, she was old, old, Hal, even the vet said so, and by the way, did you see the blood coming out of her eyes, Hal? Wind me up, Hal. Wind me up, let's play, and who's dead, Hal? Is it you?*

And when he came back to himself he had been crawling toward the monkey as if hypnotized. One hand had been outstretched to grasp the key. He scrambled backward then, and almost fell down the attic stairs in his haste—probably would have if the stairwell had not been so narrow. A little whining noise had been coming from his throat.

Now he sat in the boat, looking at Petey. "Muffling the cymbals doesn't work," he said. "I tried it once."

Petey cast a nervous glance at the flight bag. "What happened, Daddy?"

"Nothing I want to talk about now," Hal said, "and nothing you want to hear about. Come on and give me a push."

Petey bent to it, and the stern of the boat grated along the sand. Hal dug in with an oar, and suddenly that feeling of being tied to the earth was gone and the boat was moving lightly, its own thing again after years in the dark boathouse, rocking on the light waves. Hal unshipped the oars one at a time and clicked the oarlocks shut.

"Be careful, Daddy," Petey said. His face was pale.

"This won't take long," Hal promised, but he looked at the flight bag and wondered.

He began to row, bending to the work. The old, familiar ache in the small of his back and between his shoulder blades began. The shore receded. Petey was magically eight again, six, a four-year-old standing at the edge of the water. He shaded his eyes with one infant hand.

Hal glanced casually at the shore but would not allow himself to actually study it. It had been nearly fifteen years, and if he studied the shoreline carefully, he would see the changes rather than the similarities and become lost. The sun beat on his neck, and he began to sweat. He looked at the flight bag, and for a moment he lost the bend-and-pull rhythm. The flight bag seemed . . . seemed to be bulging. He began to row faster.

The wind gusted, drying the sweat and cooling his skin. The boat rose and the bow slapped water to either side when it came down. Hadn't the wind freshened, just in the last minute or so? And was Petey calling something? Yes. Hal couldn't make out what it was over the wind. It didn't matter. Getting rid of the monkey for another twenty years—or maybe forever (please God, forever)—that was what mattered.

The boat reared and came down. He glanced left and saw baby whitecaps. He looked shoreward again and saw Hunter's Point and a collapsed wreck that must have been the Burdon's boathouse when he and Bill were kids. Almost there, then. Almost over the spot where Amos Culligan's Studebaker had plunged through the ice one long-ago December. Almost over the deepest part of the lake.

Petey was screaming something; screaming and pointing. Hal still couldn't hear. The rowboat rocked and bucked, flatting off clouds of thin spray to either side of its peeling bow. A tiny rainbow glowed in one, was pulled apart. Sunlight and shadow raced across the lake in shutters and the waves were not mild now; the whitecaps had grown up. His sweat had dried to gooseflesh, and spray had soaked the back of his jacket. He rowed grimly, eyes alternating between the shoreline and the flight bag. The boat rose again, this time so high that for a moment the left oar pawed at air instead of water.

Petey was pointing at the sky, his screams now only a faint, bright runner of sound.

Hal looked over his shoulder.

The lake was a frenzy of waves. It had gone a deadly dark shade of blue sewn with white seams. A shadow raced across the water toward the boat and something in its shape was familiar, so terribly familiar, that Hal looked up and then the scream was there, struggling in his tight throat.

The sun was behind the cloud, turning it into a hunched working shape with two gold-edged crescents held apart. Two holes were torn in one end of the cloud, and sunshine poured through in two shafts.

As the cloud crossed over the boat, the monkey's cymbals, barely muffled by the flight bag, began to beat. *Jang-jang-jang-jang, it's you. Hal, it's finally you, you're over the deepest part of the lake now and it's your turn, your turn, your turn—*

All the necessary shoreline elements had clicked into their places. The rotting bones of Amos Culligan's Studebaker lay somewhere below, this was where the big ones were, this was the place.

Hal shipped the oars to the locks in one quick jerk, leaned forward unmindful of the wildly rocking boat, and snatched the flight bag. The cymbals made their wild, pagan music; the bag's sides bellowed as if with tenebrous respiration.

"Right here, you sonofabitch!" Hal screamed. *"RIGHT HERE!"*

He threw the bag over the side.

It sank fast. For a moment he could see it going down, sides moving, and for that endless moment *he could still hear the cymbals beating.* And for a moment the black waters seemed to clear and he could see down into that terrible gulf of waters to where the big ones lay; there was Amos Culligan's Studebaker, and Hal's mother was behind its slimy wheel, a grinning skeleton with a lake bass staring coldly from the skull's nasal cavity. Uncle Will and Aunt Ida lolled beside her, and Aunt Ida's gray hair trailed upward as the bag fell, turning over and over, a few silver bubbles trailing up: *jang-jang-jang-jang . . .*

Hal slammed the oars back into the water, scraping blood from his knuckles *(and ah God the back of Amos Culligan's Studebaker had been full of dead children! Charlie Silverman . . . Johnny McCabe . . .),* and began to bring the boat about.

There was a dry pistol-shot crack between his feet, and suddenly clear water was welling up between two boards. The boat was old; the wood had shrunk a bit, no doubt; it was just a small leak. But it hadn't been there when he rowed out. He would have sworn to it.

The shore and lake changed places in his view. Petey was at his back now. Overhead, that awful, simian cloud was breaking up. Hal began to row. Twenty seconds was enough to convince him he was rowing for his life. He was only a so-so swimmer, and even a great one would have been put to the test in this suddenly angry water.

Two more boards suddenly shrank apart with that pistol-shot sound. More water poured into the boat, dousing his shoes. There were tiny metallic snapping sounds that he realized were nails breaking. One of the oarlocks snapped and flew off into the water—would the swivel itself go next?

The wind now came from his back, as if trying to slow him down or even to drive him into the middle of the lake. He was terrified, but he felt a crazy kind of exhilaration through the terror. The monkey was gone for good this time. He knew it somehow. Whatever happened to him, the monkey would not be back to draw a shadow over Dennis's life, or Petey's. The monkey was gone, perhaps resting on the roof or the hood of Amos Culligan's Studebaker at the bottom of Crystal Lake. Gone for good.

He rowed, bending forward and rocking back. That cracking, crimping sound came again, and now the rusty old bait can that had been lying in the bow of the boat was floating in three inches of water. Spray blew in Hal's face. There was a louder snapping sound, and the bow seat fell in two pieces and floated next to the bait box. A board tore off the left side of the boat, and then another, this one at the waterline, tore off at the right. Hal rowed. Breath rasped in his mouth, hot and dry, and his throat swelled with the coppery taste of exhaustion. His sweaty hair flew.

Now a crack ran directly up the bottom of the rowboat, zigzagged between his feet, and ran up to the bow. Water gushed in; he was in water up to his ankles, then to the swell of calf. He rowed, but the boat's shoreward movement was sludgy now. He didn't dare look behind him to see how close he was getting.

Another board tore loose. The crack running up the center of the boat grew branches, like a tree. Water flooded in.

Hal began to make the oars sprint, breathing in great, failing gasps. He pulled once . . . twice . . . and on the third pull both oar swivels snapped off. He lost one oar, held onto the other. He rose to his feet and began to flail at the water with it. The boat rocked, almost capsized, and spilled him back onto his seat with a thump.

Moments later more boards tore loose, the seat collapsed, and he was lying in the water which filled the bottom of the boat, astounded at its coldness. He tried to get on his knees, desperately thinking: *Petey must not see this, must not see his father drown right in front of his eyes, you're going to swim, dog-paddle if you have to, but do, do something—*

There was another splintering crack—almost a crash—and he was in the water, swimming for the shore as he never had swum in his life . . . and the shore was amazingly close. A minute later he was standing waist-deep in water, not five yards from the beach.

Petey splashed toward him, arms out, screaming and crying and laughing. Hal started toward him and floundered. Petey, chest-deep, floundered.

They caught each other.

Hal, breathing in great, winded gasps, nevertheless hoisted the boy into his arms and carried him up to the beach where both of them sprawled, panting.

"Daddy? Is it really gone? That monkey?"

"Yes. I think it's really gone."

"The boat fell apart. It just . . . fell apart all around you."

Disintegrated, Hal thought, and looked at the boards floating loose on the water forty feet out. They bore no resemblance to the tight, handmade rowboat he had pulled out of the boathouse.

"It's all right now," Hal said, leaning back on his elbows. He shut his eyes and let the sun warm his face.

"Did you see the cloud?" Petey whispered.

"Yes. But I don't see it now . . . do you?"

They looked at the sky. There were scattered white puffs here and there, but no large dark cloud. It was gone, as he had said.

Hal pulled Petey to his feet. "There'll be towels up at the house. Come on." But he paused, looking at his son. "You were crazy, running out there like that."

Petey looked at him solemnly. "You were brave, Daddy."

"Was I?" The thought of bravery had never crossed his mind. Only his fear. The fear had been too big to see anything else. If anything else had indeed been there. "Come on, Pete."

"What are we going to tell Mom?"

Hal smiled. "I dunno, big guy. We'll think of something."

He paused a moment longer, looking at the boards floating on the water. The lake was calm again, sparkling with small wavelets. Suddenly Hal thought of summer people he didn't even know—a man and his son, perhaps, fishing for the big one. *I've got something Dad!* the boy screams.

Well reel it up and let's see, the father says, and coming up from the depths, weeds draggling from its cymbals, grinning its terrible, welcoming grin . . . the monkey.

He shuddered—but those were only things that might be.

"Come on," he said to Petey again, and they walked up the path through the flaming October woods toward the home place.

From the Bridgton News
October 24, 1980:

MYSTERY
OF THE DEAD FISH
By betsy moriarty

HUNDREDS of dead fish were found floating belly-up on Crystal Lake in the neighboring township of Casco late last week. The largest numbers appeared to have died in the vicinity of Hunter's Point, although the lake's currents make this a bit difficult to determine. The dead fish included all types commonly found in these waters—bluegills, pickerel, sunnies, carp, brown and rainbow trout, even one landlocked salmon. Fish and Game authorities say they are mystified, and caution fishermen and women not to eat any sort of fish from Crystal Lake until tests have determined . . .

Michael Bishop

Within the Walls of Tyre

Michael Bishop is one of the most distinguished SF writers of contemporary times. On occasion he ventures into horror, with such success that Arkham House released a collection of his dark fantasy, *One Winter in Eden* (1983). "Within the Walls of Tyre" is among his strongest and most effective pieces, with echoes of William Faulkner and Flannery O'Connor underpinning an ironic Christmas ghost story without a ghost . . . perhaps. The Southern Gothic tradition underlies this disturbing contemporary cityscape wherein Marilyn Odau maintains the illusion of psychological control. Bishop's ability to examine character and his exquisite control of imagery and detail make his small body of work in horror a significant contribution to the field.

As she eased her Nova into the lane permitting access to the perimeter highway, Marilyn Odau reflected that the hardest time of year for her was the Christmas season. From late November to well into January her nerves were invariably as taut as harp strings. The traffic on the expressway —lane-jumping vans and pickups, sleek sports cars, tailgating semis, and all the blurred, indistinguishable others—was no help, either. Even though she could see her hands on the wheel, trembling inside beige, leather-tooled gloves, her Nova seemed hardly to be under her control; instead, it was a piece of machinery given all its impetus and direction by an invisible slot in the concrete beneath it. Her illusion of control was exactly that—an illusion.

Looking quickly over her left shoulder, Marilyn Odau had to laugh at herself as she yanked the automobile around a bearded young man on a motorcycle. If your car's in someone else's control, why is it so damn hard to steer?

Nerves; balky Yuletide nerves.

Marilyn Odau was fifty-five; she had lived in this city—*her* city—ever since leaving Greenville during the first days of World War II to begin her own life and to take a job clerking at Satterwhite's. Ten minutes ago, before reaching the perimeter highway, she had passed through the heart of the city and driven beneath the great, grey, cracking backside of Satterwhite's (which was now a temporary warehouse for an electronics firm located in a suburban industrial complex). Like the heart of the city itself, Satterwhite's was dead—its great silver escalators, its pneumatic message tubes, its elevator bell tones, and its perfume-scented mezzanines as surely things of the past as . . . well, as Tojo, Tarawa Atoll, and a young marine named Jordan Burk. That was why, particularly at this time of year, Marilyn never

410

glanced at the old department store as she drove beneath it on her way to Summerstone.

For the past two years she had been the manager of the Creighton's Corner Boutique at Summerstone Mall, the largest self-contained shopping facility in the five-county metropolitan area. Business had been shifting steadily, for well over a decade, from downtown to suburban and even quasi-rural commercial centers. And when a position had opened up for her at the new tri-level mecca bewilderingly dubbed Summerstone, Marilyn had shifted too, moving from Creighton's original franchise near Capitol Square to a second-level shop in an acre-square monolith sixteen miles to the city's northwest—a building more like a starship hangar than a shopping center.

Soon, she supposed, she ought also to shift residences. There were town houses closer to Summerstone, after all, with names just as ersatz-elegant as that of the Brookmist complex in which she now lived: Chateau Royale, Springhaven, Tivoli, Smoke Glade, Eden Manor, Sussex Wood . . . *There,* she told herself, glancing sidelong at the Matterhorn Heights complex nestled below the highway to her left, its cheesebox-and-cardboard-shingle chalets distorted by a teepee of glaring window panes on a glass truck cruising abreast of her.

Living at Matterhorn Heights would have put Marilyn fifteen minutes closer to her job, but it would have meant enduring a gaudier lapse of taste than she had opted for at Brookmist. There were degrees of artificiality, she knew, and each person found his own level. . . . Above her, a green and white highway sign indicated the Willowglen and Summerstone exits. Surprised as always by its sudden appearance, she wrestled the Nova into an off-ramp lane and heard behind her the inevitable blaring of horns.

Pack it in, she told the driver on her bumper—an expression she had learned from Jane Sidney, one of her employees at the boutique. Pack it in, laddie.

Intent on the traffic light at the end of the off-ramp, conscious too of the wetness under the arms of her pantsuit jacket, Marilyn managed to giggle at the incongruous *feel* of these words. In her rearview mirror she could see the angry features of a modishly long-haired young man squinting at her over the hood of a Le Mans—and it was impossible to imagine herself confronting him, outside their automobiles, with the imperative, "Pack it in, laddie!" Absolutely impossible. All she could do was giggle at the thought and jab nervously at her clutch and brake pedals. Morning traffic—Christmas traffic—was bearable only if you remembered that impatience was a self-punishing sin.

At 8:50 she reached Summerstone and found a parking place near a battery of army-green trash bins. A security guard was passing in mall employees through a second-tier entrance near Montgomery-Ward's: and when Marilyn showed him her ID card, he said almost by way of ritual shibboleth, "Have a good day, Miss Odau." Then, with a host of people to whom she never spoke, she was on the enclosed promenade of machined wooden beams and open carpeted shops. As always, the hour could have been high noon or twelve midnight—there was no way to tell. The season was identifiable only because of the winter merchandise on display and the

Christmas decorations suspended overhead or twining like tinfoil helixes through the central shaft of the mall. The smells of ammonia, confectionery goods, and perfumes commingled piquantly, even at this early hour, but Marilyn scarcely noticed.

Managing Creighton's Corner had become her life, the enterprise for which she lived; and because Summerstone contained Creighton's Corner, she went into it daily with less philosophical scrutiny than a coal miner gives his mine. Such speculation, Marilyn knew from thirty-five years on her own, was worse than useless—it imprisoned you in doubts and misapprehensions largely of your own devising. She was glad to be but a few short steps from Creighton's, glad to feel her funk disintegrating beneath the prospect of an efficient day at work. . . .

"Good morning, Ms. Odau," Jane Sidney said as she entered Creighton's.

"Good morning. You look nice today."

The girl was wearing a green and gold jersey, a kind of gaucho skirt of imitation leather, and suede boots. Her hair was not much longer than a military cadet's. She always pronounced "Ms." as a muted buzz—either out of feminist conviction or, more likely, her fear that "Miss" would betray her more-than-middle-aged superior as unmarried . . . as if that were a shameful thing in one of Marilyn's generation. Only Cissy Campbell of the three girls who worked in the boutique could address her as "Miss Odau" without looking flustered. Or maybe Marilyn imagined this. She didn't try to plumb the personal feelings of her employees, and they in turn didn't try to cast her in the role of a mother confessor. They liked her well enough, though. Everyone got along.

"I'm working for Cissy until three, Ms. Odau. We've traded shifts. Is that all right?" Jane followed her toward her office.

"Of course it is. What about Terri?"

The walls were mercury-colored mirrors; there were mirrors overhead. Racks of swirl-patterned jerseys, erotically tailored jumpsuits, and flamboyant scarves were reiterated around them like the refrain of a toothpaste or cola jingle. Macrame baskets with plastic flowers and exotic bath soaps hung from the ceiling. Black-light and pop-art posters went in and out of the walls, even though they never moved—and looking up at one of them, Marilyn had a vision of Satterwhite's during the austere days of 1942-43, when the war had begun to put money in people's pockets for the first time since the twenties but it was unpatriotic to spend it. She remembered the Office of Price Administration and ration-stamp booklets. Because of leather shortages, you couldn't have more than two pairs of shoes a year. . . .

Jane was looking at her fixedly.

"I'm sorry, Jane. I didn't hear you."

"I said Terri'll be here at twelve, but she wants to work all day tomorrow too, if that's okay. There aren't any Tuesday classes at City College, and she wants to get in as many hours at she can before final exams come up." Terri was still relatively new to the boutique.

"Of course, that's fine. Won't you be here too?"

"Yes, ma'am. In the afternoon."

"Okay, good. . . . I've got some order forms to look over and a letter or two to write." She excused herself and went behind a tie-dyed curtain into an office as plain and practical as Creighton's decor was peacockish and orgiastic. She sat down to a small metal filing cabinet with an audible moan—a moan at odds with the satisfaction she felt in getting down to work. What was wrong with her? She knew, she knew, dear God wasn't she perfectly aware. . . . Marilyn pulled her gloves off. As her fingers went to the onion-skin order forms and bills of lading in her files, she was surprised by the deep oxblood color of her nails. Why? She had worn this polish for a week, since well before Thanksgiving. . . .

The answer of course was Maggie Hood. During the war Marilyn and Maggie had roomed together in a clapboard house not far from Satterwhite's, a house with two poplars in the small front yard but not a single blade of grass. Maggie had worked for the telephone company (an irony, since they had no phone in their house) and she always wore oxblood nail polish. Several months before the Axis surrender, Maggie married a 4-F telephone-company official and moved to Mobile. The little house on Greenbriar Street was torn down during the mid-fifties to make way for an office building. Maggie Hood and oxblood nail polish—

Recollections that skirted the heart of the matter, Marilyn knew. She shook them off and got down to business.

Tasteful rock was playing in the boutique, something from Stevie Wonder's *Songs in the Key of Life*—Jane had flipped the music on. Through it, Marilyn could hear the morning herds passing along the concourses and interior bridges of Summerstone. Sometimes it seemed that half the population of the state was out there. Twice the previous Christmas season the structural vibrations had become so worrisome that security guards were ordered to keep new shoppers out until enough people had left to avert the danger of collapse. That was the rumor, anyway, and Marilyn almost believed it. Summerstone's several owners, on the other hand, claimed that the doors had been locked simply to minimize crowding. But how many times did sane business people turn away customers solely to "minimize crowding?"

Marilyn helped Jane wait on shoppers until noon. Then Terri Bready arrived, and she went back to her office. Instead of eating she checked outstanding accounts and sought to square away records. She kept her mind wholly occupied with the minutiae of running her business for its semi-retired owners, Charlie and Agnes Creighton. It didn't bother her at all that they were ten years younger than she, absentee landlords with a condominium apartment on the gulf coast. She did a good job for them, working evenings as well as lunch hours, and the Creightons were smart enough to realize her worth. They trusted her completely and paid her well.

At one o'clock Terri Bready stepped through Marilyn's curtain and made an apologetic noise in her throat.

"Hey, Terri. What is it?"

"There's a salesman out here who'd like to see you." Bending a business card between her thumb and forefinger, the girl gave an odd baritone chuckle. Tawny-haired and lean, she was a freshman drama major who made the most fashionable clothes look like off-the-racks from a Salvation Army outlet. But she was sweet—so sweet that Marilyn had been embarrassed to hear her discussing with Cissy Campbell the boy with whom she was living.

"Is he someone we regularly buy from, Terri?"

"I don't know. I don't know who we buy from."

"Is that his card?"

"Yeah, it is."

"Why don't you let me see it, then?"

"Oh. Okay. Sorry, Ms. Odau. Here." Trying to hand it over, the girl popped the card out of her fingers; it struck Marilyn's chest and fluttered into her lap. "Sorry again. Sheesh, I really am." Terri chuckled her baritone chuckle, and Marilyn, smiling briefly, retrieved the card.

It said: *Nicholas Anson/Products Consultant & Sales Representative/ Latter-Day Novelties/Los Angeles, California.* Also on the card were two telephone numbers and a zip code.

Terri Bready wet her lips and her tongue. "He's a hunk, Ms. Odau, I'm not kidding you—he's as pretty as a naked Swede."

"Is that right? How old?"

"Oh, he's too old for me. He's got to be in his thirties at least."

"Decrepit, dear."

"Oh, he's not decrepit, any. But I'm out of the market. You know."

"Off the auction block?"

"Yes, ma'am. Yeah."

"What's he selling? We don't often work through independent dealers— the Creightons don't, that is—and I've never heard of this firm."

"Jane says she thinks he's been hitting the stores up and down the mall for the last couple of days. Don't know what he's pushing. He's got a samples case, though—and really the most incredible kiss-me eyes."

"If he's been here two days, I'm surprised he hasn't already sold those."

"Do you want me to send him back? He's too polite to burst in. He's been calling Jane and me 'Ms. Sidney' and 'Ms. Bready,' like that."

"Don't send him back yet." Marilyn had a premonition, almost a fear. "Let me take a look at him first."

Terri Bready barked a laugh and had to cover her mouth. "Hey, Ms. Odau, I wouldn't talk him up like Robert Redford and then send you a bald frog. I mean, why would I?"

"Go on, Terri. I'll talk to him in a couple of minutes."

"Yeah. Okay." The girl was quickly gone, and at the curtain's edge Marilyn looked out. Jane was waiting on a heavyset woman in a fire-engine-red pantsuit, and just inside the boutique's open threshold the man named Nicholas Anson was watching the crowds and countercrowds work through each other like grim armies.

Anson's hair was modishly long, and he reminded Marilyn a bit of the man who had grimaced at her on the off-ramp. Then, however, the sun had been ricocheting off windshields, grilles, and hood ornaments, and any real identification of the man in the Le Mans with this composed sales representative was impossible, if not downright pointless. A person in an automobile was not the same person you met on common ground. . . . Now Terri was approaching this Anson fellow, and he was turning toward the girl.

Marilyn Odau felt her fingers tighten on the curtain. Already she had taken in the man's navy blue leisure jacket and, beneath it, his silky shirt the color and pattern of a cumulus-filled sky. Already she had noted the length and the sun-flecked blondness of his hair, the etched-out quality of his profile. . . . But when he turned, the only thing apparent to her was Anson's resemblance to a dead marine named Jordan Burk, even though he was older than Jordan had lived to be. Ten or twelve years older, at the very least. Jordan Burk had died at twenty-four taking an amphibious tractor ashore at Betio, a tiny island near Tarawa Atoll in the Gilbert Islands. Nicholas Anson, however, had crow's-feet at the corners of his eyes and glints of silver in his sideburns. These things didn't matter much—the resemblance was still a heartbreaking one, and Marilyn found that she was staring at Anson like a starstruck teenager. She let the curtain fall.

This has happened before, she told herself. In a world of four billion people, over a period of thirty-five years, it isn't surprising that you should encounter two or more young men who look like each other. For God's sake, Odau, don't go to pieces over the sight of still another man who reminds you of Jordan—a stranger from Los Angeles who in just a couple of years is going to be old enough to be the *father* of your forever-twenty-four Jordan darling.

It's the season, Marilyn protested, answering her relentlessly rational self. It's especially cruel that this should happen now.

It happens all the time. You're just more susceptible at this time of year. Odau, you haven't outgrown what amounts to a basically childish syndrome, and it's beginning to look as if you never will.

Old enough in just a couple of years to be Jordan's father? He's old enough right now to be Jordan's and my child. *Our* child.

Marilyn could feel tears welling up from some ancient spring; susceptible, she had an unexpected mental glimpse of the upstairs bedroom in her Brookmist town house, the bedroom next to hers, the bedroom she had made a sort of shrine. In its corner, a white wicker bassinet—

That's enough, Odau!

"That's enough!" she said aloud, clenching a fist at her throat.

The curtain drew back, and she was again face to face with Terri Bready. "I'm sorry, Ms. Odau. You talkin' to me?"

"No, Terri. To myself."

"He's a neat fella, really. Says he played drums for a rock band in Haight-Ashbury once upon a time. Says he was one of the original hippies. He's been straight since Nixon resigned, he says—his faith was restored. . . . Whyn't you talk to him, Ms. Odau? Even if you don't place an order wtih him, he's an interesting person to talk to. Really. He says he's heard good things about you from the other managers on the mall. He thinks our place is just the sort of place to handle one of his products."

"I bet he does. You certainly got a lot out of him in the short time he's been here."

"Yeah. All my doing, too. I thought maybe, being from Los Angeles, he knew somebody in Hollywood. I sorta told him I was a drama major. You know. . . . Let me send him back, okay?"

"All right. Send him back."

Marilyn sat down at her desk. Almost immediately Nicholas Anson came through the curtain with his samples case. They exchanged polite greetings, and she was struck again by his resemblance to Jordan. Seeing him at close range didn't dispel the illusion of an older Jordan Burk, but intensified it. This was the reverse of the way it usually happened, and when he put his case on her desk, she had to resist a real urge to reach out and touch his hand.

No wonder Terri had been snowed. Anson's presence was a mature and amiable one, faintly sexual in its undertones. Haight-Ashbury? No, that was wrong. Marilyn couldn't imagine this man among Jesus freaks and flower children, begging small change, the ankles of his grubby blue jeans frayed above a pair of falling-to-pieces sandals. Altogether wrong. Thank God, he had found his calling. He seemed born to move gracefully among boutiques and front-line department stores, making recommendations, giving of his smile. Was it possible that he had once turned his gaunt young face upward to the beacon of a strobe and howled his heart out to the rhythms of his own acid drumming? Probably. A great many things had changed since the sixties. . . .

"You're quite far afield," Marilyn said, to be saying something. "I've never heard of Latter-Day Novelties."

"It's a consortium of independent business people and manufacturers," Anson responded. "We're trying to expand our markets, go nation-wide. I'm not really used to acting as—what does it say on my card?—a sales representative. My first job—my real love—is being a products consultant. If your company is a novelties company, it has to have novelties, products that are new and appealing and unusual. Prior to coming East on this trip, my principal responsibility was making product suggestions. That seems to be my forte, and that's what I really like to do."

"Well, I think you'll be an able enough sales representative too."

"Thank you, Miss Odau. Still, I always feel a little hesitation opening this case and going to bat for what it contains. There's an element of egotism in going out and pushing your own brainchildren on the world."

"There's an element of egotism in almost every human enterprise. I don't think you need to worry."

"I suppose not."

"Why don't you show me what you have?"

Nicholas Anson undid the catches on his case. "I've only brought you a single product. It was my judgment you wouldn't be interested in celebrity T-shirts, cartoon-character paperweights—products of that nature. Have I judged fairly, Miss Odau?"

"We've sold novelty T-shirts and jerseys, Mr. Anson, but the others sound like gift-shop gim-cracks and we don't ordinarily stock that sort of thing. Clothing, cosmetics, toiletries, a few handicraft or decorator items if they correlate well with the Creightons' image of their franchise."

"Okay." Anson removed a glossy cardboard package from his case and handed it across the desk to Marilyn. The kit was blue and white, with two triangular windows in the cardboard. Elegant longhand lettering on the package spelled out the words *Liquid Sheers.* Through one of the triangular windows she could see a bottle of mahogany-colored liquid, a small foil tray, and a short bristled brush with a grip on its back; through the other window was visible an array of colored pencils.

"Liquid Sheers?"

"Yes, ma'am. The idea struck me only about a month ago, I drew up a marketing prospectus, and the Latter-Day consortium rushed the concept into production so quickly that the product's already selling quite well in a number of West Coast boutiques. Speed is one of the keynotes of our company's early success. By cutting down the elapsed time between concept-visualization and actual manufacture of the product, we've been able to stay ahead of most of our California competitors. . . . If you like Liquid Sheers, we have the means to keep you in a good supply."

Marilyn was reading the instructions on the kit. Her attention refused to stay fixed on the words and they kept slipping away from her. Anson's matter-of-fact monologue about his company's business practices didn't help her concentration. She gave up and set the package down.

"But what are . . . these Liquid Sheers?"

"They're a novel substitute—a decorator substitute—for pantyhose or nylons, Miss Odau. A woman mixes a small amount of the Liquid Sheer solution with water and rubs or paints it on her legs. The pencils can be used to draw on seams or color in some of the applicator designs we've included in the kit—butterflies, flowers, that sort of thing. Placement's up to the individual. . . . We have kits for dark- as well as light-complexioned women, and the application process takes much less time than you might expect. It's fun too, some of our products-testers have told us. Several boutiques have even reported increased sales of shorts, abbreviated skirts, and short culotte outfits once they began stocking Liquid Sheers. This, I ought to add, right here at the beginning of winter." Anson stopped, his spiel dutifully completed and his smile expectant.

"They're bottled stockings," Marilyn said.

"Yes, ma'am. I suppose you could phrase it that way."

"We sold something very like this at Satterwhite's during the war," Marilyn went on, careful not to look at Anson. "Without the design doodads and the different colored pencils, at any rate. Women painted on their stockings and set the seams with mascara pencils."

Anson laughed. "To tell you the truth, Miss Odau, that's where I got part of my original idea. I rummage old mail-order catalogues and the ads in old magazines. Of course, Liquid Sheers also derive a little from the body-painting fad of the sixties—but in our advertising we plan to lay heavy stress on their affinity to the World War era."

"Why?"

"Nostalgia sells. Girls who don't know World War II from the Peloponnesian War—girls who've worn seamless stockings all their lives, if they've worn stockings at all—are painting on Liquid Sheers and setting grease-pencil seams because they've seen Lauren Bacall and Ann Sheridan in Bogart film revivals and it makes them feel vaguely heroic. It's amazing, Miss Odau. In the last few years we've had sales and entertainment booms featuring nostalgia for the twenties, the thirties, the fifties, and the sixties. The forties—if you except Bogart—have been pretty much bypassed, and Liquid Sheers purposely play to that era while recalling some of the art-deco creations of the Beatles period too."

Marilyn met Anson's gaze and refused to fall back from it. "Maybe the forties have been 'pretty much bypassed' because it's hard to recall World War II with unfettered joy."

"I don't really buy that," Anson replied, earnest and undismayed. "The twenties gave us Harding and Coolidge, the thirties the Great Depression, the fifties the Cold War, and the sixties Vietnam. There's no accounting what people are going to remember with fondness—but I can assure you that Liquid Sheers are doing well in California."

Marilyn pushed her chair back on its coasters and stood up. "I sold bottled stockings, Mr. Anson. I painted them on my legs. You couldn't *pay* me to use a product like that again—even with colored pencils and butterflies thrown in gratis."

Seemingly out of deference to her Anson also stood. "Oh, no, Miss Odau—I wouldn't expect you to. This is a product aimed at adolescent girls and post-adolescent young women. We fully realize it's a fad product. We expect booming sales for a year and then a rapid tapering off. But it won't matter—our overhead on Liquid Sheers is low and when sales have bottomed out we'll drop 'em and move on to something else. You understand the transience of items like this."

"Mr. Anson, do you know why bottled stockings existed at all during the Second World War?"

"Yes, ma'am. There was a nylon shortage."

"The nylon went into the war effort—parachutes, I don't know what else." She shook her head, trying to remember. "All I know is that you didn't see them as often as you'd been used to. They were an important commodity on the domestic black market, just like alcohol and gasoline and shoes."

Anson's smile was sympathetic, but he seemed to know he was defeated. "I guess you're not interested in Liquid Sheers?"

"I don't see how I could have them on my shelves, Mr. Anson."

He reached across her desk, picked up the kit he had given her, and dropped it in his samples case. When he snapped its lid down, the reports of the catches were like distant gunshot. "Maybe you'll let me try you with something else, another time."

"You don't have anything else with you?"

"To tell you the truth, I was so certain you'd like these I didn't bring another product along. I've placed Liquid Sheers with another boutique on the first level, though, and sold a few things to gift and novelty stores. Not a complete loss, this trip." He paused at the curtain. "Nice doing business with you, Miss Odau."

"I'll walk you to the front."

Together they stolled through an aisleway of clothes racks and toiletry shelves over a mulberry carpet. Jane and Terri were busy with customers. . . . Why am I being so solicitous? Marilyn asked herself. Anson didn't look a bit broken by her refusal, and Liquid Sheers were definitely offensive to her—she wanted nothing to do with them. Still, any rejection was an intimation of failure, and Marilyn knew how this young man must feel. It was a shame her visitor would have to plunge himself back into the mall's motivelessly surging bodies on a note, however small, of defeat. He would be lost to her, borne to oblivion on the tide. . . .

"I'm sorry, Jordan," she said. "Please do try us again with something else."

The man beside her flinched and cocked his head. "You called me Jordan, Miss Odau."

Marilyn covered the lower portion of her face with her hand. She spread her fingers and spoke through them. "Forgive me." She dropped her hand. "Actually, I'm surprised it didn't happen before now. You look very much like someone I once knew. The resemblance is uncanny."

"You did say Jordan, didn't you?"

"Yes, I guess I did—that was his name."

"Ah." Anson seemed on the verge of some further comment but all he came out with was, "Goodbye, Miss Odau. Hope you have a good Christmas season," after which he set himself adrift and disappeared in the crowd.

The tinfoil decorations in the mall's central shaft were like columns of a strange scarlet coral, and Marilyn studied them intently until Terri Bready spoke her name and returned her to the present. She didn't leave the boutique until ten that evening.

Tuesday, ten minutes before noon.

He wore the same navy blue leisure jacket, with an open collar shirt of gentle beige and bold indigo. He carried no samples case, and speaking with Cissy Campbell and then Terri, he seemed from the vantage of Marilyn's office, her curtain partially drawn back, less certain of his ground. Marilyn knew a similar uncertainty—Anson's presence seemed ominous, a challenge. She put a hand to her hair, then rose and went through the shop to meet him.

"You didn't bring me something else to look at, did you?"

"No; no, I didn't." He revealed his empty hand. "I didn't come on business at all . . . unless. . . ." He let his voice trail away. "You haven't changed your mind about Liquid Sheers, have you?"

This surprised her. Marilyn could hear the stiffness in her voice. "I'm afraid I haven't."

Anson waved a hand. "Please forget that. I shouldn't have brought it up—because I *didn't* come on business." He raised his palm, like a Boy

Scout pledging his honor. "I was hoping you'd have lunch with me."

"Why?"

"Because you seem *simpático*—that's the Spanish word for the quality you have. And it would be nice to sit down and talk with someone congenial about something other than Latter-Day Novelties. I've been on the road a week."

Out of the corner of her eye she could see Terri Bready straining to interpret her response to this proposal. Cissy Campbell, Marilyn's black clerk, had stopped racking a new supply of puff-sleeved blouses, and Marilyn had a glimpse of orange eyeliner and irridescent lipstick—the girl's face was that of an alert and self-confident panther.

"I don't usually eat lunch, Mr. Anson."

"Make an exception today. Not a word about business, I promise you."

"Go with him," Terri urged from the cash computer. "Cissy and I can take care of things here, Ms. Odau." Then she chuckled.

"Excellent advice," Anson said. "If I were you, I'd take it."

"Okay," Marilyn agreed. "So long as we don't leave Summerstone and don't stay gone too long. Let me get my bag."

Inevitably, they ended up at the McDonald's downstairs—yellow and orange wall paneling, trash bins covered with wood-grained contact paper, rows of people six and seven deep at the shiny metal counters. Marilyn found a table for two and eased herself into one of the attached, scoop-shaped plastic chairs. It took Anson almost fifteen minutes to return with two cheeseburgers and a couple of soft-drinks, which he nearly spilled squeezing his way out of the crowd to their tiny table.

"Thank God for plastic tops. Is it always like this?"

"Worse at Christmas. Aren't there any McDonald's in Los Angeles?"

"Nothing but. But it's three whole weeks till Christmas. Have these people no piety?"

"None."

"It's the same in Los Angeles."

They ate. While they were eating, Anson asked that she use his first name and she in turn felt obligated to tell him hers. Now they were Marilyn and Nicholas, mother and son on an outing to McDonald's. Except that his attention to her wasn't filial—it was warm and direct, with a wooer's deliberately restrained urgency. His manner reminded her again of Jordan Burk, and at one point she realized that she had heard nothing at all he'd said for the last several minutes. Listen to this man, she cautioned herself. Come back to the here and now. After that, she managed better.

He told her that he'd been born in the East, raised singlehandedly by his mother until her remarriage in the late forties, and after his new family's removal to Encino, educated entirely on the West Coast. He told her of his abortive career as a rock drummer, his early resistance to the war in Southeast Asia, and his difficulties with the United States military.

"I had no direction at all until my thirty-second birthday, Marilyn. Then I discovered where my talent lay and I haven't looked back since. I tell you, if I had the sixties to do over again—well, I'd gladly do them. I'd finagle myself a place in an Army reserve unit, be a weekend soldier, and get right down to products-consulting on a full-time basis. If I'd done that in '65, I'd probably be retired by now."

"You have plenty of time. You're still young."

"I've just turned thirty-six."

"You look less."

"But not much. Thanks anyway, though—it's nice to hear."

"Did you fight in Vietnam?" Marilyn asked on impulse.

"I *went* there in '68. I don't think you could say I fought. I was one of the oldest enlisted men in my unit, with a history of anti-war activity and draft-card burning. I'm going to tell you something, though—once I got home and turned myself around, I wept when Saigon fell. That's the truth—I wept. Saigon was some city, if you looked at it right."

Mentally counting back, Marilyn realized that Nicholas was the right age to be her and Jordan's child. Exactly. In early December, 1942, she and Jordan had made their last farewells in the little house on Greenbriar Street. . . . She attached no shame to his memory, had no regrets about it. The shame had come twenty-six years later—the same year, strangely enough, that Nicholas Anson was reluctantly pulling a tour of duty in Vietnam. The white wicker bassinet in her upstairs shrine was a perpetual reminder of this shame, of her secret monstrousness, and yet she could not dispose of the evidence branding her a freak, if only to herself, for the simple reason that she loved it. She loved it because she had once loved Jordan Burk. . . . Marilyn put her cheeseburger down. There was no way—no way at all—that she was going to be able to finish eating.

"Are you all right?"

"I need to get back to the boutique."

"Let me take you out to dinner this evening. You can hardly call this a relaxed and unhurried get-together. I'd like to take you somewhere nice. I'd like to buy you a snifter of brandy and a nice rare cut of prime rib."

"Why?"

"You use that word like a stiletto, Marilyn. Why not?"

"Because I don't go out. My work keeps me busy. And there's a discrepancy in our ages that embarrasses me. I don't know whether your motives are commercial, innocently social, or. . . . Go ahead, then—laugh." She was wadding up the wrapper from her cheeseburger, squeezing the paper tighter and tighter, and she could tell that her face was crimsoning.

"I'm not laughing," Nicholas said. "I don't either—know what my motives are, I mean. Except that they're not blameworthy or unnatural."

"I'd better go." She eased herself out of the underslung plastic chair and draped her bag over her shoulder.

"When can I see you?" His eyes were full of remonstrance and appeal. "The company wants me here another week or so—problems with a delivery. I don't know anyone in this city. I'm living out of a suitcase. And I've never in my life been married, if that's worrying you."

"Maybe I should worry because you haven't."

Nicholas smiled at her, a self-effacing charmer's smile. "When?"

"Wednesdays and Sundays are the only nights I don't work. And tomorrow's Wednesday."

"What time?"

"I don't know," she said distractedly. "Call me. Or come by the boutique. Or don't. Whatever you want."

She stepped into the aisle beside their table and quickly worked her way through the crowd to the capsule-lift outside McDonald's. Her thoughts were jumbled, and she hoped feebly—willing the hope—that Nicholas Anson would simply disappear from her life.

The next morning, before any customers had been admitted to the mall, Marilyn Odau went down to Summerstone's first level and walked past the boutique whose owner had elected to sell Nicholas' Liquid Sheers. The kits were on display in two colorful pyramids just inside the shop's entrance.

That afternoon a leggy, dark-haired girl came into Creighton's Corner to browse, and when she let her fur-trimmed coat fall open Marilyn saw a small magenta rose above her right knee. The girl's winter tan had been rubbed or brushed on, and there were magenta seams going up the backs of her legs. Marilyn didn't like the effect, but she understood that others might not find it unattractive.

At six o'clock Nicholas Anson showed up in sports clothes and an expensive deerskin coat. Jane Sidney and Cissy Campbell left, and Marilyn had a mall attendant draw the shop's movable grating across its entrance. Despite the early Wednesday closing time, people were still milling about as shopkeepers transacted last-minute business or sought to shoo away their last heel-dragging customers. This was the last Wednesday evening before Christmas that Summerstone would be closed.

Marilyn began walking, and Nicholas fell in beside her like an assigned escort at a military ball. "Did you think I wasn't coming?"

"I didn't know. What now?"

"Dinner."

"I'd like to go home first. To freshen up."

"I'll drive you."

"I have a car."

"Lock it and let it sit. This place is about as well guarded as Fort Knox. I've rented a car from the service at the airport."

Marilyn didn't want to see Nicholas Anson's rental car. "Let *yours* sit. You can drive me home in mine." He started to protest. "It's either that or an early goodbye. I worry about my car."

So he drove her to Brookmist in her '68 Nova. The perimeter highway was yellow-grey under its ghostly lamps and the traffic was bewilderingly swift. Twilight had already edged over into evening—a dreary winter evening. The Nova's gears rattled even when Nicholas wasn't touching the stick on the steering column.

"I'm surprised you don't have a newer car. Surely you can afford one."

"I could, I suppose, but I like this one. It's easy on gas, and during the oil embargo I felt quite smart. . . . What's the matter with it?"

"Nothing. It's just that I'd imagined you in a bigger or a sportier one. I shouldn't have said anything." He banged his temple with the heel of his right hand. "I'm sorry, Marilyn."

"Don't apologize. Jane Sidney asked me the same thing one day. I told her that my parents were dirt-poor during the Depression and that as soon as I was able to sock any money away for them, that's what I did. It's a habit I haven't been able to break—even today, with my family dead and no real financial worries."

They rode in silence beneath the haloed lamps on the overpass and the looming grey shadow of Satterwhite's.

"A girl came into the boutique this afternoon wearing Liquid Sheers," Marilyn said. "It does seem your product's selling."

"Hooo," Nicholas replied, laughing mirthlessly. "Just remember that *I* didn't bring that up, okay?"

They left the expressway and drove down several elm-lined residential streets. The Brookmist complex of town houses came into the Nova's headlights like a photographic image emerging from a wash of chemicals, everything gauzy and indistinct at first. Marilyn directed Nicholas to the community carport against a brick wall behind one of the rows of houses, and he parked the car. They walked hunch-shouldered in the cold to a tall redwood fence enclosing a concrete patio not much bigger than a phone booth. Marilyn pushed the gate aside, let the latch fall behind them, and put her key into the lock on the kitchen door. Two or three flower pots with drooping, unrecognizable plants in them sat on a peeling windowsill beside the door.

"I suppose you think I could afford a nicer place to live, too."

"No, but you do give yourself a long drive to work."

"This place is paid for, Nicholas. It's mine."

She left him sitting under a table lamp with several old copies of *McCall's* and *Cosmopolitan* in front of him on her stonework coffee table and went upstairs to change clothes. She came back down wearing a long-sleeved black jumpsuit with a peach-colored sweater and a single polished-stone pendant at her throat. The heat had kicked on, and the downstairs was cozily warm.

Nicholas stood up. "You've set things up so that I'm going to have to drive your car and you're going to have to navigate. I hope you'll let me buy the gas."

"Why couldn't I drive and you just sit back and enjoy the ride?" Her voice was tight again, with uneasiness and mild disdain. For a products consultant Nicholas didn't seem quite as imaginative as he ought. Liquid Sheers were a rip-off of an idea born out of necessity during World War II, and the "novelties" he'd mentioned in his spiel on Monday were for the most part variations on the standard fare of gift shops and bookstores. He wasn't even able to envision her doing the driving while he relaxed and played the role of a passenger. And *he* was the one who'd come to maturity during the sixties, that fabled decade of egalitarian upheaval and heightened social awareness. . . .

"The real point, Marilyn, is that I wanted to do something for *you*. But you've taken the evening out of my hands."

All right, she could see that. She relented. "Nicholas, I'm not trying to stage-manage this—this *date*, if that's what it is. I was surprised that you came by the shop. I wasn't ready. And I'm not ready to go out this evening, either—I'm cold and I'm tired. I have a pair of steaks and a bottle of cold duck in the refrigerator, and enough fixings for a salad. Let me make dinner."

"A *pair* of steaks?"

"There's a grocery store off the perimeter highway that stays open night and day. I stopped there last night after work."

"But you didn't think I'd come by today?"

"No. Not really. And despite buying the steaks, I'm not sure I really wanted you to. I know that sounds backwards somehow but it's the truth."

Nicholas ignored this. "But you'll have to cook. I wanted to spare you that. I wanted to do something *for* you."

"Spare me another trip down the highway in my car and the agony of waiting for service in one of this city's snooty night spots."

He gave in, and she felt kindlier toward him. They ate at the coffee table in the living room, sitting on the floor in their stocking feet and listening to an FM radio station. They talked cursorily about sports and politics and movies, which neither of them was particularly interested in anymore; and then, because they had both staked their lives to it, Marilyn lifted the taboo that Nicholas had promised to observe and they talked business. They didn't talk about Liquid Sheers or profit margins or tax shelters, they talked about the involvement of their feelings with what they were doing and the sense of satisfaction that they derived from their work. That was common ground, and the evening passed—as Jane Sidney might have put it—"like sixty."

They were finishing the bottle of cold duck. Nicholas shifted positions, catching his knees with his right arm and rocking back a little.

"Marilyn?"

"Mmm?"

"You would never have let me drive you over here if I hadn't reminded you of this fellow you once knew, would you? This fellow named Jordan? Tell me the truth. No bet-hedging."

Her uneasiness returned. "I don't know."

"Yes, you do. Your answer won't hurt my feelings. I'd like to think that now that you know me a little better my resemblance to this person doesn't matter anymore—that you like me for myself." He waited.

"Okay, then. You're right."

"I'm right," he echoed her dubiously.

"I wouldn't have let you bring me home if you hadn't looked like Jordan. But now that I know you a little better it doesn't make any difference."

Not much, Marilyn told herself. At least I've stopped putting you in a marine uniform and trimming back the hair over your ears. . . . She felt a quiet tenderness for both men, the dead Jordan and the boyish Nicholas Anson who in many ways seemed younger than Jordan ever had. . . . That's because Jordan was almost three years older than you, Odau, and Nicholas is almost twenty years younger. Think a little.

The young man who resembled Jordan Burk drained his glass and hoisted himself nimbly off the floor.

"I'm staying at the Holiday Inn near the airport," he said. "Let me call a cab so you won't have to get out again."

"Cabs aren't very good about answering night calls anymore. The drivers are afraid to come."

"I hate for you to have to drive me, Marilyn." His look was expectant, and she hated to disappoint him.

"Why don't you just spend the night here?" she said.

They went upstairs together, and she was careful to close the door to the bedroom containing the wicker bassinet before following him into her own. They undressed in the greenish light sifting through the curtains from the arc lamp in the elm trees. Her heart raced. Then his body covered its beating, and afterwards she lay staring wide-eyed and bemused at her acoustic ceiling panels as he slept beside her with a hand on her hip. Then she fell asleep too, and woke when her sleeping mind noted that his hand was gone, and sat up to discover that Nicholas was no longer there. The wind in the leafless elms was making a noise like angry surf.

"Nick!" she called.

He didn't answer.

She swung her feet to the carpet, put on her gown, and found him standing in a pair of plaid boxer shorts beside the wicker bassinet. He had put on a desk lamp, and its glow made a pool of light that contained and illuminated everything in that corner of the room. There was no doubt that he had discovered the proof of her monstrousness there, even if he didn't know what it meant.

Instead of screaming or flying at him like a drunken doxy, she sank to the floor in the billow of her dressing gown, shamefully conscious of her restraint and too well satisfied by Nicholas' snooping to be shocked by it. If she hadn't wanted this to happen, she would never have let him come. Or she would have murdered Nicholas in the numb sleep of his fulfillment. Any number of things. But this was what she had wanted.

Confession and surcease.

"I was looking for the bathroom," Nicholas said. "I didn't know where the upstairs bathroom was. But when I saw the baby bed. . . . well, I didn't know why you'd have a baby bed and—" He broke off.

"Don't explain, Nicholas." She gave him an up-from-under look and wondered what her own appearance must suggest. Age, promiscuousness, dissolution? You grew old, that you couldn't stop. But the others . . . those were lies. She wanted confession and surcease, that was all, and he was too intent on the bassinet to escape giving them to her, too intent to see how downright *old* she could look at two in the morning. Consumed by years. Consumed by that which life itself is nourished by. Just one of a world of consumer goods.

Nicholas lifted something from the bassinet. He held it in the palm of one hand. "What is this?" he asked. "Marilyn . . . ?"

"Lithopedion," she said numbly. "The medical term is lithopedion. And lithopedion is the word I use when I want to put myself at a distance from it. With you here, that's what I think I want to do—put myself at a distance from it. I don't know. Do you understand?"

He stared at her blankly.

"It means stone child, Nicholas. I was delivered of it during the first week of December, 1968. A petrified fetus."

"Delivered of it?"

"That's wrong. I don't know why I say that. It was removed surgically, cut from my abdominal cavity. Lithopedion." Finally she began to cry. "Bring him to me."

The unfamiliar man across from her didn't move. He held the stone child questioningly on his naked palm.

"Damn it, Nicholas, I asked you to bring him to me! He's mine! Bring him here!"

She put a fist to one of her eyes and drew it away to find black makeup on the back of her hand. Anson brought her the lithopedion, and she cradled it against the flimsy bodice of her dressing gown. A male child, calcified, with a tiny hand to the side of its face and its eyes forever shut; a fossil before it had ever really begun to live.

"This is Jordan's son," Marilyn told Anson, who was still standing over her. "Jordan's and mine."

"But how could that be? He died during the Pacific campaign."

Marilyn took no notice of either the disbelief in Anson's voice or his unaccountable knowledge of the circumstances of Jordan's death. "We had a honeymoon in the house on Greenbriar while Maggie was off for Christmas," she said, cradling her son. "Then Jordan had to return to his Division. In late March of '43 I collapsed while I was clerking at Satterwhite's. I was stricken with terrible cramps and I collapsed. Maggie drove me home to Greenville, and I was treated for intestinal flu. That was the diagnosis of a local doctor. I was in a coma for a while. I had to be forcibly fed. But after a while I got well again, and the manager of the notions department at Satterwhite's let me have my job back. I came back to the city."

"And twenty-five years later you had your baby?"

Even the nastiness that Anson imparted to this question failed to dismay her. "Yes. It was an ectopic pregnancy. The fetus grew not in my womb, you see, but in the right Fallopian tube—where there isn't much room for it to grow. I didn't know, I didn't suspect anything. There were no signs."

"Until you collapsed at Satterwhite's?"

"Dr. Rule says that was the fetus bursting the Fallopian tube and escaping into the abdominal cavity. I didn't know. I was twenty years old. It was diagnosed as flu, and they put me to bed. I had a terrible time. I almost died. Later in the year, just before Thanksgiving, Jordan was killed at Tarawa, and I wished that I had died before him."

"He never lived to see his son," Anson said bitterly.

"No. I was frightened of doctors. I'm still frightened by them. But in 1965 I went to work for the Creightons at Capitol Square, and when I began having severe pains in my side a couple of years later, they *made* me go to Dr. Rule. They told me I'd have to give up my job if I didn't go." Marilyn brought a fold of her nightgown around the calcified infant in her arms. "He discovered what was wrong. He delivered my baby. A lithopedion, he said. . . . Do you know that there've been only a few hundred of them in all recorded history? That makes me a freak, all my love at the beck and call of a father and son who'll never be able to hear me." Marilyn's shoulders began to heave and her mouth fell slack to let the sounds of her grief work clear. "A freak," she repeated, sobbing.

"No more a freak than that thing's father."

She caught Anson's tone and turned her eyes up to see his face through a blur of tears.

"Its father was Jordan Burk," Anson told her. "My father was Jordan Burk. He even went so far as to *marry* my mother, Miss Odau. But when he discovered she was pregnant, he deserted her to enlist in a Division bound for combat. And he came here first and found another pretty piece to slip it to before he left. You."

"No," Marilyn said, her sobs suddenly stilled.

"Yes. My mother found Burk in this city and asked him to come back to her. He pleaded his overmastering love for another woman and refused. *I* was no enticement at all—I was an argument for remaining with you. Once during her futile visit here Burk took my mother into Satterwhite's by a side-street entrance and pointed you out to her from one of the mezzanines. The 'other woman' was prettier than she was, my mother said. She gave up and returned home. She permitted Burk to divorce her without alimony while he was in the Pacific. Don't ask me why. I don't know. Later my mother married a man named Samuel Anson and we moved with him to California. . . . That thing in your arms, Miss Odau, is my half-brother."

It was impossible to cry now. Marilyn could hear her voice growing shrill and accusative. "That's why you asked me to lunch yesterday, isn't it? And why you asked me to dinner this evening. A chance for revenge. A chance to defile a memory you could have easily left untouched." She slapped Anson across the thigh, harmlessly. "I didn't know anything about your mother or you! I never suspected and I wasn't responsible! I'm not that kind of freak! Why have you set out to destroy both me and one of the few things in my life I've truly been able to cherish? Why do you turn on me with a nasty 'truth' that doesn't have any significance for me and never can? What kind of vindictive jackal are you?"

Anson looked bewildered. He dropped onto his knees in front of her and tried to grip her shoulders. She shook his hands away.

"Marilyn, I'm sorry. I asked you to lunch because you called me Jordan, just like you let me drive you home because I resembled him."

" 'Marilyn?' What happened to 'Miss Odau?' "

"Never mind that." He tried to grip her shoulders again, and she shook him off. "Is my crime greater than yours? If I've spoiled your memory of the man who fathered me, it's because of the bitterness I've carried against him for as long as I can remember. My intention wasn't to hurt you. The 'other woman' that my mother always used to talk about, even after she married Anson, has always been an abstract to me. Revenge wasn't my motive. Curiosity, maybe. But not revenge. Please believe me."

"You have no imagination, Nicholas."

He looked at her searchingly. "What does that mean?"

"It means that if you'd only. . . . Why should I explain this to you? I want you to get dressed and take my car and drive back to your motel. You can drop it off at Summerstone tomorrow when you come to get your rental car. Give the keys to one of the girls, I don't want to see you."

"Out into the cold, huh?"

"Please go, Nicholas. I might resort to screaming if you don't."

He rose, went into the other room, and a few minutes later descended the carpeted stairs without saying a word. Marilyn heard the flaring of her Nova's engine and a faint grinding of gears. After that, she heard nothing but the wind in the skeletal elm trees.

Without rising from the floor in her second upstairs bedroom, she sang a lullaby to the fossil child in her arms. "Dapples and greys," she crooned. "Pintos and bays,/All the pretty little horses. . . ."

It was almost seven o'clock of the following evening before Anson returned her key case to Cissy Campbell at the cash computer up front. Marilyn didn't hear him or see him, and she was happy that she had been in her office when he at last came by. The episode was over. She hoped that she never saw Anson again, even if he was truly Jordan's son—and she believed that Anson understood her wishes.

Four hours later she pulled into the carport at Brookmist and crossed the parking lot to her small patio. The redwood gate was standing open. She pulled it shut behind her and set its latch. Then, inside, she felt briefly on the verge of swooning because there was an odor in the air like that of a man's cologne, a fragrance Anson had worn. For a moment she considered running back onto the patio and shouting for assistance. If Anson was upstairs waiting for her, she'd be a fool to go up there alone. She'd be a fool to go up there at all. Who could read the mind of an enigma like Anson?

He's not up there waiting for you, Marilyn told herself. He's been here and gone.

But why?

Your baby, Marilyn—see to your baby. Who knows what Anson might have done for spite? Who knows what sick destruction he might have—

"Oh, God!" Marilyn cried aloud. She ran up the stairs unmindful of the intensifying smell of cologne and threw the door to her second bedroom open. The wicker bassinet was not in its corner but in the very center of the room. She ran to it and clutched its side, very nearly tipping it over.

Unharmed, her and Jordan's tiny child lay on the satin bolster she had made for him.

Marilyn stood over the baby trying to catch her breath. Then she moved his bed back into the corner where it belonged. Not until the following morning was the smell of that musky cologne dissipated enough for her to forget that Anson—or someone—had been in her house. Because she had no evidence of theft, she rationalized that the odor had drifted into her apartment through the ventilation system from the town house next to hers.

The fact that the bassinet had been moved she conveniently put out of her mind.

Two weeks passed. Business at Creighton's Corner Boutique was brisk, and if Marilyn thought of Nicholas Anson at all, it was to console herself with the thought that by now he was back in Los Angeles. A continent away. But on the last weekend before Christmas, Jane Sidney told Marilyn that she thought she had seen Anson going through the center of one of Summerstone's largest department stores carrying his samples case. He looked tan and happy, Jane said.

"Good. But if he shows up here, I'm not in. If I'm waiting on a customer and he comes by, you or Terri will have to take over for me. Do you understand?"

"Yes, ma'am."

But later that afternoon the telephone in her office rang, and when she answered it, the voice coming through the receiver was Anson's.

"Don't hang up, Miss Odau. I knew you wouldn't see me in person, so I've been reduced to telephoning."

"What do you want?"

"Take a walk down the mall toward Davner's. Take a walk down the mall and meet me there."

"Why should I do that? I thought that's why you phoned."

Anson hung up.

You can wait forever, then, she told him. The phone didn't ring again, and she busied herself with the onionskin order forms and bills of lading. It was hard to pay attention to them, though.

At last she got up and told Jane she was going to stroll down the mall to stretch her legs. The crowd was shoulder to shoulder. She saw old people being pushed along in wheelchairs and, as if they were dogs or monkeys, small children in leather harnesses. There were girls whose legs had been painted with Liquid Sheers, and young men in Russian hats and low-heeled shoes who made no secret of their appreciation of these girls' legs. The benches lining the shaft at the center of the promenade were all occupied, and the people sitting on them looked fatigued and irritable.

A hundred or so yards ahead of her, in front of the jewelry store called Davner's, there was a Santa Claus and a live reindeer.

She kept walking.

An odd display caught Marilyn's eye. She did a double-take and halted amid the traffic surging in both directions around her.

"Hey," a man said. He shoved past.

The shop window to her right was lined with eight or ten chalk-white effigies not much longer than her hand. They were eyeless. A small light played on them like the revolving blue strobe on a police vehicle. A sign in the window said: *Stone Children for Christmas, from Latter-Day Novelties.* Marilyn put a hand to her mouth and made a gagging sound that no one else on the mall paid any mind. She spun around. It seemed that Summerstone itself was swaying under her. Across from the gift shop, on one of the display cases of the bookstore located there, were a dozen more of these minute statuettes. Tiny figures, tiny feet, tiny eyeless faces. She looked down the collapsing mall and saw still another window displaying replicas of her and Jordan's baby. And in the windows that they weren't displayed, they were endlessly reflected.

Tiny fingers, tiny feet, tiny eyeless faces.

"Anson!" Marilyn shouted hoarsely, trying to find something to hang on to. "Anson, God damn you! God *damn* you!" She rushed on the gift-shop window and broke it with her fists. Then, not knowing what else to do, she withdrew her hands—with their worn oxblood nail polish—and held them bleeding above her head. A woman screamed, and the crowd fell back from her aghast.

In front of Davner's, only three or four stores away now, Nicholas Anson was stroking the head of the live reindeer. When he saw Marilyn, he gave her a friendly boyish smile.

H. P. Lovecraft

The Rats in the Walls

As Barton L. St. Armand pointed out in his extraordinary study of Lovecraft *(The Roots of Horror),* although Lovecraft overtly rejected contemporary psychoanalytic theory, "The Rats in the Walls" is a masterpiece of psychological structure, precisely paralleling a famous dream of C. G. Jung. This is a compelling story of psychological devolution and, at the same time, one of the most unusual of haunted house stories. Only traces, herein, can one find of the cosmic Lovecraftian strain—and "The Rats in the Walls" is in structure, it seems to me, more comparable to M. R. James' "The Ash-Tree" than has been heretofore noted. In Lovecraft's own work this story is an interesting contrast to "The Shunned House," his other, and very different, house story in the antiquarian vein.

On July 16, 1923, I moved into Exham Priory after the last workman had finished his labours. The restoration had been a stupendous task, for little had remained of the deserted pile but a shell-like ruin; yet because it had been the seat of my ancestors I let no expense deter me. The place had not been inhabited since the reign of James the First, when a tragedy of intensely hideous, though largely unexplained, nature had struck down the master, five of his children, and several servants; and driven forth under a cloud of suspicion and terror the third son, my lineal progenitor and the only survivor of the abhorred line. With this sole heir denounced as a murderer, the estate had reverted to the crown, nor had the accused man made any attempt to exculpate himself or regain his property. Shaken by some horror greater than that of conscience or the law, and expressing only a frantic wish to exclude the ancient edifice from his sight and memory, Walter de la Poer, eleventh Baron Exham, fled to Virginia and there founded the family which by the next century had become known as Delapore.

Exham Priory had remained untenanted, though later allotted to the estates of the Norrys family and much studied because of its peculiarly composite architecture; an architecture involving Gothic towers resting on a Saxon or Romanesque substructure, whose foundation in turn was of a still earlier order or blend of orders—Roman, and even Druidic or native Cymric, if legends speak truly. This foundation was a very singular thing, being merged on one side with the solid limestone of the precipice from whose brink the priory overlooked a desolate valley three miles west of the village of Anchester. Architects and antiquarians loved to examine this strange relic of forgotten centuries, but the country folk hated it. They had

431

hated it hundreds of years before, when my ancestors lived there, and they hated it now, with the moss and mould of abandonment on it. I had not been a day in Anchester before I knew I came of an accursed house. And this week workmen have blown up Exham Priory, and are busy obliterating the traces of its foundations.

The bare statistics of my ancestry I had always known, together with the fact that my first American forbear had come to the colonies under a strange cloud. Of details, however, I had been kept wholly ignorant through the policy of reticence always maintained by the Delapores. Unlike our planter neighbours, we seldom boasted of crusading ancestors or other mediaeval and Renaissance heroes; nor was any kind of tradition handed down except what may have been recorded in the sealed envelope left before the Civil War by every squire to his eldest son for posthumous opening. The glories we cherished were those achieved since the migration; the glories of a proud and honourable, if somewhat reserved and unsocial Virginia line.

During the war our fortunes were extinguished and our whole existence changed by the burning of Carfax, our home on the banks of the James. My grandfather, advanced in years, had perished in that incendiary outrage, and with him the envelope that bound us all to the past. I can recall that fire today as I saw it then at the age of seven, with the Federal soldiers shouting, the women screaming, and the negroes howling and praying. My father was in the army, defending Richmond, and after many formalities my mother and I were passed through the lines to join him. When the war ended we all moved north, whence my mother had come; and I grew to manhood, middle age, and ultimate wealth as a stolid Yankee. Neither my father nor I ever knew what our hereditary envelope had contained, and as I merged into the greyness of Massachusetts business life I lost all interest in the mysteries which evidently lurked far back in my family tree. Had I suspected their nature, how gladly I would have left Exham Priory to its moss, bats, and cobwebs!

My father died in 1904, but without any message to leave to me, or to my only child, Alfred, a motherless boy of ten. It was this boy who reversed the order of family information; for although I could give him only jesting conjectures about the past, he wrote me of some very interesting ancestral legends when the late war took him to England in 1917 as an aviation officer. Apparently the Delapores had a colourful and perhaps sinister history, for a friend of my son's, Capt. Edward Norrys of the Royal Flying Corps, dwelt near the family seat at Anchester and related some peasant superstitions which few novelists could equal for wildness and incredibility. Norrys himself, of course, did not take them seriously; but they amused my son and made good material for his letters to me. It was this legendry which definitely turned my attention to my transatlantic heritage, and made me resolve to purchase and restore the family seat which Norrys shewed to Alfred in its picturesque desertion, and offered to get for him at a surprisingly reasonable figure, since his own uncle was the present owner.

I bought Exham Priory in 1918, but was almost immediately distracted from my plans of restoration by the return of my son as a maimed invalid.

During the two years that he lived I thought of nothing but his care, having even placed my business under the direction of partners. In 1921, as I found myself bereaved and aimless, a retired manufacturer no longer young, I resolved to divert my remaining years with my new possession. Visiting Anchester in December, I was entertained by Capt. Norrys, a plump, amiable young man who had thought much of my son, and secured his assistance in gathering plans and anecdotes to guide in the coming restoration. Exham Priory itself I saw without emotion, a jumble of tottering mediaeval ruins covered with lichens and honeycombed with rooks' nests, perched perilously upon a precipice, and denuded of floors or other interior features save the stone walls of the separate towers.

As I gradually recovered the image of the edifice as it had been when my ancestors left it over three centuries before, I began to hire workmen for the reconstruction. In every case I was forced to go outside the immediate locality, for the Anchester villagers had an almost unbelievable fear and hatred of the place. This sentiment was so great that it was sometimes communicated to the outside labourers, causing numerous desertions; whilst its scope appeared to include both the priory and its ancient family.

My son had told me that he was somewhat avoided during his visits because he was a de la Poer, and I now found myself subtly ostracised for a like reason until I convinced the peasants how little I knew of my heritage. Even then they sullenly disliked me, so that I had to collect most of the village traditions through the mediation of Norrys. What the people could not forgive, perhaps, was that I had come to restore a symbol so abhorrent to them; for, rationally or not, they viewed Exham Priory as nothing less than a haunt of fiends and werewolves.

Piecing together the tales which Norrys collected for me, and supplementing them with the accounts of several savants who had studied the ruins, I deduced that Exham Priory stood on the site of a prehistoric temple; a Druidical or ante-Druidical thing which must have been contemporary with Stonehenge. That indescribable rites had been celebrated there, few doubted; and there were unpleasant tales of the transference of these rites into the Cybele-worship which the Romans had introduced. Inscriptions still visible in the sub-cellar bore such unmistakable letters as "DIV . . . OPS . . . MAGNA. MAT . . ." sign of the Magna Mater whose dark worship was once vainly forbidden to Roman citizens. Anchester had been the camp of the third Augustan legion, as many remains attest, and it was said that the temple of Cybele was splendid and thronged with worshippers who performed nameless ceremonies at the bidding of a Phrygian priest. Tales added that the fall of the old religion did not end the orgies at the temple, but that the priests lived on in the new faith without real change. Likewise was it said that the rites did not vanish with the Roman power, and that certain among the Saxons added to what remained of the temple, and gave it the essential outline it subsequently preserved, making it the centre of a cult feared through half the heptarchy. About 1000 A. D. the place is mentioned in a chronicle as being a substantial stone priory housing a strange and powerful monastic order and surrounded by extensive gardens which needed no walls to exclude a frightened populace. It was never destroyed by the Danes, though after the Norman Conquest it must have declined tremendously; since there was no impediment when Henry the Third granted the site to my ancestor, Gilbert de la Poer, First Baron Exham, in 1261.

Of my family before this date there is no evil report, but something strange must have happened then. In one chronicle there is a reference to a de la Poer as "cursed of God" in 1307, whilst village legendry had nothing but evil and frantic fear to tell of the castle that went up on the foundations of the old temple and priory. The fireside tales were of the most grisly description, all the ghastlier because of their frightened reticence and cloudy evasiveness. They represented my ancestors as a race of hereditary daemons beside whom Gilles de Retz and the Marquis de Sade would seem the veriest tyros, and hinted whisperingly at their responsibility for the occasional disappearances of villagers through several generations.

The worst characters, apparently, were the barons and their direct heirs; at least, most was whispered about these. If of healthier inclinations, it was said, an heir would early and mysteriously die to make way for another more typical scion. There seemed to be an inner cult in the family, presided over by the head of the house, and sometimes closed except to a few members. Temperament rather than ancestry was evidently the basis of this cult, for it was entered by several who married into the family. Lady Margaret Trevor from Cornwall, wife of Godfrey, the second son of the fifth baron, became a favourite bane of children all over the countryside, and the daemon heroine of a particularly horrible old ballad not yet extinct near the Welsh border. Preserved in balladry, too, though not illustrating the same point, is the hideous tale of Lady Mary de la Poer, who shortly after her marriage to the Earl of Shrewsfield was killed by him and his mother, both of the slayers being absolved and blessed by the priest to whom they confessed what they dared not repeat to the world.

These myths and ballads, typical as they were of crude superstition, repelled me greatly. Their persistence, and their application to so long a line of my ancestors, were especially annoying; whilst the imputations of monstrous habits proved unpleasantly reminiscent of the one known scandal of my immediate forbears—the case of my cousin, young Randolph Delapore of Carfax, who went among the negroes and became a voodoo priest after he returned from the Mexican War.

I was much less disturbed by the vaguer tales of wails and howlings in the barren, windswept valley beneath the limestone cliff; of the graveyard stenches after the spring rains; of the floundering, squealing white thing on which Sir John Clave's horse had trod one night in a lonely field; and of the servant who had gone mad at what he saw in the priory in the full light of day. These things were hackneyed spectral lore, and I was at that time a pronounced sceptic. The accounts of vanished peasants were less to be dismissed, though not especially significant in view of mediaeval custom. Prying curiosity meant death, and more than one severed head had been publicly shewn on the bastions—now effaced—around Exham Priory.

A few of the tales were exceedingly picturesque, and made me wish I had learnt more of comparative mythology in my youth. There was, for instance, the belief that a legion of bat-winged devils kept Witches' Sabbath each night

at the priory—a legion whose sustenance might explain the disprop
abundance of coarse vegetables harvested in the vast gardens. A
vivid of all, there was the dramatic epic of the rats—the scamperin
obscene vermin which had burst forth from the castle three months
tragedy that doomed it to desertion—the lean, filthy, ravenous arr
had swept all before it and devoured fowl, cats, dogs, hogs, sheep,
two hapless human beings before its fury was spent. Around that un
ble rodent army a whole separate cycle of myths revolves, for it
among the village homes and brought curses and horrors in its tra

Such was the lore that assailed me as I pushed to completion
elderly obstinacy, the work of restoring my ancestral home. It mu
imagined for a moment that these tales formed my principal psyc
environment. On the other hand, I was constantly praised and en
by Capt. Norrys and the antiquarians who surrounded and aided n
the task was done, over two years after its commencement, I viewed
rooms, wainscotted walls, vaulted ceilings, mullioned windows, a
staircases with a pride which fully compensated for the prodigious
of the restoration. Every attribute of the Middle Ages was c
reproduced, and the new parts blended perfectly with the original
foundations. The seat of my fathers was complete, and I looked fc
redeeming at last the local fame of the line which ended in me.
reside here permanently, and prove that a de la Poer (for I had adop
the original spelling of the name) need not be a fiend. My con
perhaps augmented by the fact that, although Exham Priory was
vally fitted, its interior was in truth wholly new and free from ol
and old ghosts alike.

As I have said, I moved in on July 16, 1923. My household con
seven servants and nine cats, of which latter species I am particula
My eldest cat, "Nigger-Man", was seven years old and had come
from my home in Bolton, Massachusetts; the others I had accu
whilst living with Capt. Norrys' family during the restoration of th
For five days our routine proceeded with the utmost placidity, my ti
spent mostly in the codification of old family data. I had now obtain
very circumstantial accounts of the final tragedy and flight of Wal
Poer, which I conceived to be the probable contents of the heredita
lost in the fire at Carfax. It appeared that my ancestor was accu
much reason of having killed all the other members of his household
four servant confederates, in their sleep, about two weeks after a
discovery which changed his whole demeanour, but which, ex
implication, he disclosed to no one save perhaps the servants who
him and afterward fled beyond reach.

This deliberate slaughter, which included a father, three brothers,
sisters, was largely condoned by the villagers, and so slackly treate
law that its perpetrator escaped honoured, unharmed, and undisg
Virginia; the general whispered sentiment being that he had purged
of an immemorial curse. What discovery had prompted an act so te
could scarcely even conjecture. Walter de la Poer must have known
the sinister tales about his family, so that this material could have gi

no fresh impulse. Had he, then, witnessed some appalling ancient rite, or stumbled upon some frightful and revealing symbol in the priory or its vicinity? He was reputed to have been a shy, gentle youth in England. In Virginia he seemed not so much hard or bitter as harassed and apprehensive. He was spoken of in the diary of another gentleman-adventurer, Francis Harley of Bellview, as a man of unexampled justice, honour, and delicacy.

On July 22 occurred the first incident which, though lightly dismissed at the time, takes on a preternatural significance in relation to later events. It was so simple as to be almost negligible, and could not possibly have been noticed under the circumstances; for it must be recalled that since I was in a building practically fresh and new except for the walls, and surrounded by a well-balanced staff of servitors, apprehension would have been absurd despite the locality. What I afterward remembered is merely this—that my old black cat, whose moods I know so well, was undoubtedly alert and anxious to an extent wholly out of keeping with his natural character. He roved from room to room, restless and disturbed, and sniffed constantly about the walls which formed part of the old Gothic structure. I realize how trite this sounds—like the inevitable dog in the ghost story, which always growls before his master sees the sheeted figure—yet I cannot consistently suppress it.

The following day a servant complained of restlessness among all the cats in the house. He came to me in my study, a lofty west room on the second story, with groined arches, black oak panelling, and a triple Gothic window overlooking the limestone cliff and desolate valley; and even as he spoke I saw the jetty form of Nigger-Man creeping along the west wall and scratching at the new panels which overlaid the ancient stone. I told the man that there must be some singular odour or emanation from the old stonework, imperceptible to human senses, but affecting the delicate organs of cats even through the new woodwork. This I truly believed, and when the fellow suggested the presence of mice or rats, I mentioned that there had been no rats there for three hundred years, and that even the field mice of the surrounding country could hardly be found in these high walls, where they had never been known to stray. That afternoon I called on Capt. Norrys, and he assured me that it would be quite incredible for field mice to infest the priory in such a sudden and unprecedented fashion.

That night, dispensing as usual with a valet, I retired in the west tower chamber which I had chosen as my own, reached from the study by a stone staircase and short gallery—the former partly ancient, the latter entirely restored. This room was circular, very high, and without wainscotting, being hung with arras which I had myself chosen in London. Seeing that Nigger-Man was with me, I shut the heavy Gothic door and retired by the light of the electric bulbs which so cleverly counterfeited candles, finally switching off the light and sinking on the carved and canopied four-poster, with the venerable cat in his accustomed place across my feet. I did not draw the curtains, but gazed out at the narrow north window which I faced. There was a suspicion of aurora in the sky, and the delicate traceries of the window were pleasantly silhouetted.

At some time I must have fallen quietly asleep, for I recall a distinct sense of leaving strange dreams, when the cat started violently from his placid position. I saw him in the faint auroral glow, head strained forward, fore feet on my ankles, and hind feet stretched behind. He was looking intensely at a point on the wall somewhat west of the window, a point which to my eye had nothing to mark it, but toward which all my attention was now directed. And as I watched, I knew that Nigger-Man was not vainly excited. Whether the arras actually moved I cannot say. I think it did, very slightly. But what I can swear to is that behind it I heard a low, distinct scurrying as of rats or mice. In a moment the cat had jumped bodily on the screening tapestry, bringing the affected section to the floor with his weight, and exposing a damp, ancient wall of stone; patched here and there by the restorers, and devoid of any trace of rodent prowlers. Nigger-Man raced up and down the floor by this part of the wall, clawing the fallen arras and seemingly trying at times to insert a paw between the wall and the oaken floor. He found nothing, and after a time returned wearily to his place across my feet. I had not moved, but I did not sleep again that night.

In the morning I questioned all the servants, and found that none of them had noticed anything unusual, save that the cook remembered the actions of a cat which had rested on her windowsill. This cat had howled at some unknown hour of the night, awaking the cook in time for her to see him dart purposefully out of the open door down the stairs. I drowsed away the noontime, and in the afternoon called again on Capt. Norrys, who became exceedingly interested in what I told him. The odd incidents—so slight yet so curious—appealed to his sense of the picturesque, and elicited from him a number of reminiscences of local ghostly lore. We were genuinely perplexed at the presence of rats, and Norrys lent me some traps and Paris green, which I had the servants place in strategic localities when I returned.

I retired early, being very sleepy, but was harassed by dreams of the most horrible sort. I seemed to be looking down from an immense height upon a twilit grotto, knee-deep with filth, where a white-bearded daemon swineherd drove about with his staff a flock of fungous, flabby beasts whose appearance filled me with unutterable loathing. Then, as the swineherd paused and nodded over his task, a mighty swarm of rats rained down on the stinking abyss and fell to devouring beasts and man alike.

From this terrific vision I was abruptly awaked by the motions of Nigger-Man, who had been sleeping as usual across my feet. This time I did not have to question the source of his snarls and hisses, and of the fear which made him sink his claws into my ankle, unconscious of their effect; for on every side of the chamber the walls were alive with nauseous sound—the verminous slithering of ravenous, gigantic rats. There was now no aurora to shew the state of the arras—the fallen section of which had been replaced—but I was not too frightened to switch on the light.

As the bulbs leapt into radiance I saw a hideous shaking all over the tapestry, causing the somewhat peculiar designs to execute a singular dance of death. This motion disappeared almost at once, and the sound with it. Springing out of bed, I poked at the arras with the long handle of a warming-pan that rested near, and lifted one section to see what lay beneath. There was nothing but the patched stone wall, and even the cat had lost his tense realization of abnormal presences. When I examined the circular trap that had been placed in the room, I found all of the openings sprung, though no trace remained of what had been caught and had escaped.

Further sleep was out of the question, so, lighting a candle, I opened the door and went out in the gallery toward the stairs to my study, Nigger-Man following at my heels. Before we had reached the stone steps, however, the cat darted ahead of me and vanished down the ancient flight. As I descended the stairs myself, I became suddenly aware of sounds in the great room below; sounds of a nature which could not be mistaken. The oak-panelled walls were alive with rats, scampering and milling, whilst Nigger-Man was racing about with the fury of a baffled hunter. Reaching the bottom, I switched on the light, which did not this time cause the noise to subside. The rats continued their riot, stampeding with such force and distinctness that I could finally assign to their motions a definite direction. These creatures, in numbers apparently inexhaustible, were engaged in one stupendous migration from inconceivable heights to some depth conceivably, or inconceivably, below.

I now heard steps in the corridor, and in another moment two servants pushed open the massive door. They were searching the house for some unknown source of disturbance which had thrown all the cats into a snarling panic and caused them to plunge precipitately down several flights of stairs and squat, yowling, before the closed door to the sub-cellar. I asked them if they had heard the rats, but they replied in the negative. And when I turned to call their attention to the sounds in the panels, I realized that the noise had ceased. With the two men, I went down to the door of the sub-cellar, but found the cats already dispersed. Later I resolved to explore the crypt below, but for the present I merely made a round of the traps. All were sprung, yet all were tenantless. Satisfying myself that no one had heard the rats save the felines and me, I sat in my study till morning; thinking profoundly, and recalling every scrap of legend I had unearthed concerning the building I inhabited.

I slept some in the forenoon, leaning back in the one comfortable library chair which my mediaeval plan of furnishing could not banish. Later I telephoned to Capt. Norrys, who came over and helped me explore the sub-cellar. Absolutely nothing untoward was found, although we could not repress a thrill at the knowledge that this vault was built by Roman hands. Every low arch and massive pillar was Roman—not the debased Romanesque of the bungling Saxons, but the severe and harmonious classicism of the age of the Caesars; indeed, the walls abounded with inscriptions familiar to the antiquarians who had repeatedly explored the place—things like "P.GETAE.PROP . . . TEMP . . . DONA . . ." and "L.PRAEC . . . VS . . . PONTIFI . . . ATYS. . . ."

The reference to Atys made me shiver, for I had read Catullus and knew something of the hideous rites of the Eastern god, whose worship was so mixed with that of Cybele. Norrys and I, by the light of lanterns, tried to interpret the odd and nearly effaced designs on certain irregularly rectangular blocks of stone generally held to be altars, but could make nothing of them. We remembered that one pattern, a sort of rayed sun, was held by students to imply a non-Roman origin, suggesting that these altars had merely been adopted by the Roman priests from some older and perhaps aboriginal temple on the same site. On one of these blocks were some brown stains which made me wonder. The largest, in the center of the room, had certain features on the upper surface which indicated its connexion with fire—probably burnt offerings.

Such were the sights in that crypt before whose door the cats had howled, and where Norrys and I now determined to pass the night. Couches were brought down by the servants, who were told not to mind any nocturnal actions of the cats, and Nigger-Man was admitted as much for help as for companionship. We decided to keep the great oak door—a modern replica with slits for ventilation—tightly closed; and, with this attended to, we retired with lanterns still burning to await whatever might occur.

The vault was very deep in the foundations of the priory, and undoubtedly far down on the face of the beetling limestone cliff overlooking the waste valley. That it had been the goal of the scuffling and unexplainable rats I could not doubt, though why, I could not tell. As we lay there expectantly, I found my vigil occasionally mixed with half-formed dreams from which the uneasy motions of the cat across my feet would rouse me. These dreams were not wholesome, but horribly like the one I had had the night before. I saw again the twilit grotto, and the swineherd with his unmentionable fungous beasts wallowing in filth, and as I looked at these things they seemed nearer and more distinct—so distinct that I could almost observe their features. Then I did observe the flabby features of one of them—and awaked with such a scream that Nigger-Man started up, whilst Capt. Norrys, who had not slept, laughed considerably. Norrys might have laughed more—or perhaps less—had he known what it was that made me scream. But I did not remember myself till later. Ultimate horror often paralyses memory in a merciful way.

Norrys waked me when the phenomena began. Out of the same frightful dream I was called by his gentle shaking and his urging to listen to the cats. Indeed, there was much to listen to, for beyond the closed door at the head of the stone steps was a veritable nightmare of feline yelling and clawing, whilst Nigger-Man, unmindful of his kindred outside, was running excitedly around the bare stone walls, in which I heard the same babel of scurrying rats that had troubled me the night before.

An acute terror now rose within me, for here were anomalies which nothing normal could well explain. These rats, if not the creatures of a madness which I shared with the cats alone, must be burrowing and sliding in Roman walls I had thought to be of solid limestone blocks . . . unless perhaps the action of water through more than seventeen centuries had eaten winding tunnels which rodent bodies had worn clear and ample. . . . But even so, the spectral horror was no less; for if these were living vermin why did not Norrys hear their disgusting commotion? Why did he urge me to watch Nigger-Man and listen to the cats outside, and why did he guess wildly and vaguely at what could have aroused them?

By the time I had managed to tell him, as rationally as I could, what I thought I was hearing, my ears gave me the last fading impression of the scurrying; which had retreated *still downward*, far underneath this deepest of sub-cellars till it seemed as if the whole cliff below were riddled with questing rats. Norrys was not as skeptical as I had anticipated, but instead seemed profoundly moved. He motioned to me to notice that the cats at the door had ceased their clamour, as if giving up the rats for lost; whilst Nigger-Man had a burst of renewed restlessness, and was clawing frantically around the bottom of the large stone altar in the centre of the room, which was nearer Norrys' couch than mine.

My fear of the unknown was at this point very great. Something astounding had occurred, and I saw that Capt. Norrys, a younger, stouter, and presumably more naturally materialistic man, was affected fully as much as myself—perhaps because of his lifelong and intimate familiarity with local legend. We could for the moment do nothing but watch the old black cat as he pawed with decreasing fervour at the base of the altar, occasionally looking up and mewing to me in that persuasive manner which he used when he wished me to perform some favour for him.

Norrys now took a lantern close to the altar and examined the place where Nigger-Man was pawing; silently kneeling and scraping away the lichens of centuries which joined the massive pre-Roman block to the tessellated floor. He did not find anything, and was about to abandon his efforts when I noticed a trivial circumstance which made me shudder, even though it implied nothing more than I had already imagined. I told him of it, and we both looked at its almost imperceptible manifestation with the fixedness of fascinated discovery and acknowledgment. It was only this—that the flame of the lantern set down near the altar was slightly but certainly flickering from a draught of air which it had not before received, and which came indubitably from the crevice between floor and altar where Norrys was scraping away the lichens.

We spent the rest of the night in the brilliantly lighted study, nervously discussing what we should do next. The discovery that some vault deeper than the deepest known masonry of the Romans underlay this accursed pile—some vault unsuspected by the curious antiquarians of three centuries —would have been sufficient to excite us without any background of the sinister. As it was, the fascination became twofold; and we paused in doubt whether to abandon our search and quit the priory forever in superstitious caution, or to gratify our sense of adventure and brave whatever horrors might await us in the unknown depths. By morning we had compromised, and decided to go to London to gather a group of archaeologists and scientific men fit to cope with the mystery. It should be mentioned that before leaving the sub-cellar we had vainly tried to move the central altar which we now recognized as the gate to a new pit of nameless fear. What secret would open the gate, wiser men than we would have to find.

During many days in London Capt. Norrys and I presented our facts, conjectures, and legendary ancedotes to five eminent authorities, all men who could be trusted to respect any family disclosures which future explorations might develop. We found most of them little disposed to scoff, but instead intensely interested and sincerely sympathetic. It is hardly necessary to name them all, but I may say that they included Sir William

Brinton, whose excavations in the Troad excited most of the world in their day. As we all took the train for Anchester I felt myself poised on the brink of frightful revelations, a sensation symbolized by the air of mourning among the many Americans at the unexpected death of the President on the other side of the world.

On the evening of August 7th we reached Exham Priory, where the servants assured me that nothing unusual had occurred. The cats, even old Nigger-Man, had been perfectly placid; and not a trap in the house had been sprung. We were to begin exploring on the following day, awaiting which I assigned well-appointed rooms to all my guests. I myself retired in my own tower chamber, with Nigger-Man across my feet. Sleep came quickly, but hideous dreams assailed me. There was a vision of a Roman feast like that of Trimalchio, with a horror in a covered platter. Then came that damnable, recurrent thing about the swineherd and his filthy drove in the twilit grotto. Yet when I awoke it was full daylight, with normal sounds in the house below. The rats, living or spectral, had not troubled me; and Nigger-Man was still quietly asleep. On going down, I found that the same tranquility had prevailed elsewhere; a condition which one of the assembled savants—a fellow named Thornton, devoted to the psychic—rather absurdly laid to the fact that I had now been shewn the thing which certain forces had wished to shew me.

All was now ready, and at 11 a.m. our entire group of seven men, bearing powerful electric searchlights and implements of excavation, went down to the sub-cellar and bolted the door behind us. Nigger-Man was with us, for the investigators found no occasion to despise his excitability, and were indeed anxious that he be present in case of obscure rodent manifestations. We noted the Roman inscriptions and unknown altar designs only briefly, for three of the savants had already seen them, and all knew their characteristics. Prime attention was paid to the momentous central altar, and within an hour Sir William Brinton had caused it to tilt backward, balanced by some unknown species of counterweight.

There now lay revealed such a horror as would have overwhelmed us had we not been prepared. Through a nearly square opening in the tiled floor, sprawling on a flight of stone steps so prodigiously worn that it was little more than an inclined plane at the centre, was a ghastly array of human or semi-human bones. Those which retained their collocation as skeletons shrewd attitudes of panic fear, and over all were the marks of rodent gnawing. The skulls denoted nothing short of utter idiocy, cretinism, or primitive semi-apedom. Above the hellishly littered steps arched a descending passage seemingly chiselled from the solid rock, and conducting a current of air. This current was not a sudden and noxious rush as from a closed vault, but a cool breeze with something of freshness in it. We did not pause long, but shiveringly began to clear a passage down the steps. It was then that Sir William, examining the hewn walls, made the odd observations that the passage, according to the direction of the strokes, must have been chiselled *from beneath.*

I must be very deliberate now, and choose my words.

After ploughing down a few steps amidst the gnawed bones we saw that there was light ahead; not any mystic phosphorescence, but a filtered daylight which could not come except from unknown fissures in the cliff that overlooked the waste valley. That such fissures had escaped notice from outside was hardly remarkable, for not only is the valley wholly uninhabited, but the cliff is so high and beetling that only an aëronaut could study its face in detail. A few steps more, and our breaths were literally snatched from us by what we saw; so literally that Thornton, the psychic investigator, actually fainted in the arms of the dazed man who stood behind him. Norrys, his plump face utterly white and flabby, simply cried out inarticulately; whilst I think that what I did was to gasp or hiss, and cover my eyes. The man behind me—the only one of the party older than I—croaked the hackneyed "My God!" in the most cracked voice I ever heard. Of seven cultivated men, only Sir William Brinton retained his composure; a thing the more to his credit because he led the party and must have seen the sight first.

It was a twilit grotto of enormous height, stretching away farther than any eye could see; a subterraneous world of limitless mystery and horrible suggestion. There were buildings and other architectural remains—in one terrified glance I saw a weird pattern of tumuli, a savage circle of monoliths, a low-domed Roman ruin, a sprawling Saxon pile, and an early English edifice of wood—but all these were dwarfed by the ghoulish spectacle presented by the general surface of the ground. For yards about the steps extended an insane tangle of human bones, or bones at least as human as those on the steps. Like a foamy sea they stretched, some fallen apart, but others wholly or partly articulated as skeletons; these latter invariably in postures of daemoniac frenzy, either fighting off some menace or clutching other forms with cannibal intent.

When Dr. Trask, the anthropologist, stooped to classify the skulls, he found a degraded mixture which utterly baffled him. They were mostly lower than the Piltdown man in the scale of evolution, but in every case definitely human. Many were of higher grade, and a very few were the skulls of supremely and sensitively developed types. All the bones were gnawed, mostly by rats, but somewhat by others of the half-human drove. Mixed with them were many tiny bones of rats—fallen members of the lethal army which closed the ancient epic.

I wonder that any man among us lived and kept his sanity through that hideous day of discovery. Not Hoffmann or Huysmans could conceive a scene more wildly incredible, more frenetically repellent, or more Gothically grotesque than the twilit grotto through which we seven staggered; each stumbling on revelation after revelation, and trying to keep for the nonce from thinking of the events which must have taken place there three hundred, or a thousand, or two thousand, or ten thousand years ago. It was the antechamber of hell, and poor Thornton fainted again when Trask told him that some of the skeleton things must have descended as quadrupeds through the last twenty or more generations.

Horror piled on horror as we began to interpret the architectural remains. The quadruped things—with their occasional recruits from the biped class—had been kept in stone pens, out of which they must have broken in their last delirium of hunger or rat-fear. There had been great herds of them, evidently fattened on the coarse vegetables whose remains could be found as a sort of poisonous ensilage at the bottom of huge stone bins older than Rome. I knew now why my ancestors had had such excessive gardens— would to heaven I could forget! The purpose of the herds I did not have to ask.

Sir William, standing with his searchlight in the Roman ruin, translated aloud the most shocking ritual I have ever known; and told of the diet of the antediluvian cult which the priests of Cybele found and mingled with their own. Norrys, used as he was to the trenches, could not walk straight when he came out of the English building. It was a butcher shop and kitchen—he had expected that—but it was too much to see familiar English implements in such a place, and to read familiar English *graffiti* there, some as recent as 1610. I could not go in that building—that building whose daemon activities were stopped only by the dagger of my ancestor Walter de la Poer.

What I did venture to enter was the low Saxon building, whose oaken door had fallen, and there I found a terrible row of ten stone cells with rusty bars. Three had tenants, all skeletons of high grade, and on the bony forefinger of one I found a seal ring with my own coat-of-arms. Sir William found a vault with far older cells below the Roman chapel, but these cells were empty. Below them was a low crypt with cases of formally arranged bones, some of them bearing terrible parallel inscriptions carved in Latin, Greek, and the tongue of Phrygia. Meanwhile, Dr. Trask had opened one of the prehistoric tumuli, and brought to light skulls which were slightly more human than a gorilla's, and which bore indescribable ideographic carvings. Through all this horror my cat stalked unperturbed. Once I saw him monstrously perched atop a mountain of bones, and wondered at the secrets that might lie behind his yellow eyes.

Having grasped to some slight degree the frightful revelations of this twilit area—an area so hideously foreshadowed by my recurrent dream—we turned to that apparently boundless depth of midnight cavern where no ray of light from the cliff could penetrate. We shall never know what sightless Stygian worlds yawn beyond the little distance we went, for it was decided that such secrets are not good for mankind. But there was plenty to engross us close at hand, for we had not gone far before the searchlights shewed that accursed infinity of pits in which the rats had feasted, and whose sudden lack of replenishment had driven the ravenous rodent army first to turn on the living herds of starving things, and then to burst forth from the priory in that historic orgy of devastation which the peasants will never forget.

God! those carrion black pits of sawed, picked bones and opened skulls! Those nightmare chasms choked with the pithecanthropoid, Celtic, Roman, and English bones of countless unhallowed centuries! Some of them were full, and none can say how deep they had once been. Others were still bottomless to our searchlights, and peopled by unnamable fancies. What, I thought, of the hapless rats that stumbled into such traps amidst the blackness of their quests in this grisly Tartarus?

Once my foot slipped near a horribly yawning brink, and I had a moment of ecstatic fear. I must have been musing a long time, for I could not see any of the party but the plump Capt. Norrys. Then there came a sound from that inky, boundless, farther distance that I thought I knew; and I saw my old black cat dart past me like a winged Egyptian god, straight into the illimitable gulf of the unknown. But I was not far behind, for there was no doubt after another second. It was the eldritch scurrying of those fiend-born rats, always questing for new horrors, and determined to lead me on even unto those grinning caverns of earth's centre where Nyarlathotep, the mad faceless god, howls blindly in the darkness to the piping of two amorphous idiot flute-players.

My searchlight expired, but still I ran. I heard voices, and yowls, and echoes, but above all there gently rose that impious, insidious scurrying; gently rising, rising, as a stiff bloated corpse gently rises above an oily river that flows under endless onyx bridges to a black, putrid sea. Something bumped into me—something soft and plump. It must have been the rats; the viscous, gelatinous, ravenous army that feast on the dead and the living. . . . Why shouldn't rats eat a de la Poer as a de la Poer eats forbidden things? . . . The war ate my boy, damn them all . . . and the Yanks ate Carfax with flames and burnt Grandsire Delapore and the secret . . . No, no, I tell you, I am *not* that daemon swineherd in the twilit grotto! It was *not* Edward Norrys' fat face on that flabby, fungous thing! Who says I am a de la Poer? He lived, but my boy died! . . . Shall a Norrys hold the lands of a de la Poer? . . . It's voodoo, I tell you . . . that spotted snake . . . Curse you, Thornton, I'll teach you to faint at what my family do! . . . 'Sblood, thou stinkard, I'll learn ye how to gust . . . wolde ye swynke me thilke wys? . . . *Magna Mater! Magna Mater!* . . . *Atys* . . . *Dia ad aghaidh's ad aodann . . . agus bas dunach ort! Dhonas 's dholas ort, agus leat-sa!* . . . *Ungl . . . ungl . . . rrrlh . . . chchch . . .*

That is what they say I said when they found me in the blackness after three hours; found me crouching in the blackness over the plump, half-eaten body of Capt. Norrys, with my own cat leaping and tearing at my throat. Now they have blown up Exham Priory, taken my Nigger-Man away from me, and shut me into this barred room at Hanwell with fearful whispers about my heredity and experiences. Thornton is in the next room, but they prevent me from talking to him. They are trying, too, to suppress most of the facts concerning the priory. When I speak of poor Norrys they accuse me of a hideous thing, but they must know that I did not do it. They must know it was the rats; the slithering, scurrying rats whose scampering will never let me sleep; the daemon rats that race behind the padding in this room and beckon me down to greater horrors than I have ever known; the rats they can never hear; the rats, the rats in the walls.

J. Sheridan Le Fanu

Schalken the Painter

At the historical moment when the short story and the horror story were being invented, Poe and Le Fanu introduced psychological metaphor into the center of concern in many of their major fictions, de-emphasizing the moral didacticism of, say, Dickens, and influencing the later development of all short fiction in English in the direction of psychological investigation. "Schalken the Painter" (1839) is an historical tale with quite modern concerns: an innocent woman is married to a supernatural monster and no one can do anything about it. This tale is a direct ancestor of Charlotte Perkins Gilman's masterpiece, "The Yellow Wallpaper," and the horror derives in part from the impotence of the good man and the irrelevance of virtue in the face of quotidian but extraordinary evil. Allegorical interpretation is not to the point. Le Fanu's fantastic world in "Schalken the Painter" has more in common with Kafka and Joseph Conrad than with his contemporaries.

"For he is not a man as I am that we should come together; neither is there any that might lay his hand upon us both. Let him, therefore, take his rod away from me, and let not his fear terrify me."

There exists, at this moment, in good preservation a remarkable work of Schalken's. The curious management of its lights constitutes, as usual in his pieces, the chief apparent merit of the picture. I say *apparent*, for in its subject, and not in its handling, however exquisite, consists its real value. The picture represents the interior of what might be a chamber in some antique religious building; and its foreground is occupied by a female figure, in a species of white robe, part of which is arranged so as to form a veil. The dress, however, is not that of any religious order. In her hand the figure bears a lamp, by which alone her figure and face are illuminated; and her features wear such an arch smile, as well becomes a pretty woman when practising some prankish roguery; in the background, and, excepting where the dim red light of an expiring fire serves to define the form, in total shadow, stands the figure of a man dressed in the old Flemish fashion, in an attitude of alarm, his hand being placed upon the hilt of his sword, which he appears to be in the act of drawing.

There are some pictures, which impress one, I know not how, with a conviction that they represent not the mere ideal shapes and combinations which have floated through the imagination of the artist, but scenes, faces,

445

and situations which have actually existed. There is in that strange picture, something that stamps it as the representation of a reality.

And such in truth it is, for it faithfully records a remarkable and mysterious occurrence, and perpetuates, in the face of the female figure, which occupies the most prominent place in the design, an accurate portrait of Rose Velderkaust, the niece of Gerard Douw, the first, and I believe, the only love of Godfrey Schalken. My great grandfather knew the painter well; and from Schalken himself he learned the fearful story of the painting, and from him too he ultimately received the picture itself as a bequest. The story and the picture have become heirlooms in my family, and having described the latter, I shall, if you please, attempt to relate the tradition which has descended with the canvas.

There are few forms on which the mantle of romance hangs more ungracefully than upon that of the uncouth Schalken—the boorish but most cunning worker in oils, whose pieces delight the critics of our day almost as much as his manners disgusted the refined of his own; and yet this man, so rude, so dogged, so slovenly, in the midst of his celebrity, had in his obscure, but happier days, played the hero in a wild romance of mystery and passion.

When Schalken studied under the immortal Gerard Douw, he was a very young man; and in spite of his phlegmatic temperament, he at once fell over head and ears in love with the beautiful niece of his wealthy master. Rose Velderkaust was still younger than he, having not yet attained her seventeenth year, and, if tradition speaks truth, possessed all the soft and dimpling charms of the fair, light-haired Flemish maidens. The young painter loved honestly and fervently. His frank adoration was rewarded. He declared his love, and extracted a faltering confession in return. He was the happiest and proudest painter in all Christendom. But there was somewhat to dash his elation; he was poor and undistinguished. He dared not ask old Gerard for the hand of his sweet ward. He must first win a reputation and a competence.

There were, therefore, many dread uncertainties and cold days before him; he had to fight his way against sore odds. But he had won the heart of dear Rose Velderkaust, and that was half the battle. It is needless to say his exertions were redoubled, and his lasting celebrity proves that his industry was not unrewarded by success.

These ardent labours, and worse still, the hopes that elevated and beguiled them, were however, destined to experience a sudden interruption—of a character so strange and mysterious as to baffle all inquiry and to throw over the events themselves a shadow of preternatural horror.

Schalken had one evening outstayed all his fellow-pupils, and still pursued his work in the deserted room. As the daylight was fast falling, he laid aside his colours, and applied himself to the completion of a sketch on which he had expressed extraordinary pains. It was a religious composition, and represented the temptations of a pot-bellied Saint Anthony. The young artist, however destitute of elevation, had, nevertheless, discernment enough to be dissatisfied with his own work, and many were the patient erasures and improvements which saint and devil underwent, yet all in vain. The large, old-fashioned room was silent, and, with the exception of himself, quite emptied of its usual inmates. An hour had thus passed away, nearly two, without any improved result. Daylight had already declined, and twilight was deepening into the darkness of night. The patience of the young painter was exhausted, and he stood before his unfinished production, angry and mortified, one hand buried in the folds of his long hair, and the other holding the piece of charcoal which had so ill-performed its office, and which he now rubbed, without much regard to the sable streaks it produced, with irritable pressure upon his ample Flemish inexpressibles. "Curse the subject!" said the young man aloud; "curse the picture, the devils, the saint—"

At this moment a short, sudden sniff uttered close behind him made the artist turn sharply round, and he now, for the first time, became aware that his labours had been overlooked by a stranger. Within about a yard and half, and rather behind him, there stood the figure of an elderly man in a cloak and broad-brimmed, conical hat; in his hand, which was protected with a heavy gauntlet-shaped glove, he carried a long ebony walking-stick, surmounted with what appeared, as it glittered dimly in the twilight, to be a massive head of gold, and upon his breast, through the folds of the cloak, there shone the links of a rich chain of the same metal. The room was so obscure that nothing further of the appearance of the figure could be ascertained, and his hat threw his features into profound shadow. It would not have been easy to conjecture the age of the intruder; but a quantity of dark hair escaping from beneath his sombre hat, as well as his firm and upright carriage served to indicate that his years could not yet exceed threescore, or thereabouts. There was an air of gravity and importance about the garb of the person, and something indescribably odd, I might say awful, in the perfect, stone-like stillness of the figure, that effectually checked the testy comment which had at once risen to the lips of the irritated artist. He, therefore, as soon as he had sufficiently recovered his surprise, asked the stranger, civilly, to be seated, and desired to know if he had any message to leave for his master.

"Tell Gerard Douw," said the unknown, without altering his attitude in the smallest degree, "that Minheer Vanderhausen, of Rotterdam, desires to speak with him on tomorrow evening at this hour, and if he please, in this room, upon matters of weight; that is all."

The stranger, having finished this message, turned abruptly, and, with a quick, but silent step quitted the room, before Schalken had time to say a word in reply. The young man felt a curiosity to see in what direction the burgher of Rotterdam would turn, on quitting the *studio*, and for that purpose he went directly to the window which commanded the door. A lobby of considerable extent intervened between the inner door of the painter's room and the street entrance, so that Schalken occupied the post of observation before the old man could possibly have reached the street. He watched in vain, however. There was no other mode of exit. Had the queer old man vanished, or was he lurking about the recesses of the lobby for some sinister purpose? This last suggestion filled the mind of Schalken with a vague uneasiness, which was so unaccountably intense as to make him alike afraid to remain in the room alone, and reluctant to pass through the lobby. However, with an effort which appeared very disproportioned to the occasion, he summoned resolution to leave the room, and, having locked the door and thrust the key in his pocket, without looking to the right or left, he traversed the passage which had so recently, perhaps still, contained the person of his mysterious visitant, scarcely venturing to breathe till he had arrived in the open street.

"Minheer Vanderhausen!" said Gerard Douw within himself, as the appointed hour approached, "Minheer Vanderhausen, of Rotterdam! I never heard of the man till yesterday. What can he want of me? A portrait, perhaps, to be painted; or a poor relation to be apprenticed; or a collection to be valued; or—pshaw! there's no one in Rotterdam to leave me a legacy. Well, whatever the business may be, we shall soon know it all."

It was now the close of day, and again every easel, except that of Schalken, was deserted. Gerard Douw was pacing the apartment with the restless step of impatient expectation, sometimes pausing to glance over the work of one of his absent pupils, but more frequently placing himself at the window, from whence he might observe the passengers who threaded the obscure by-street in which his studio was placed.

"Said you not, Godfrey," exclaimed Douw, after a long and fruitful gaze from his post of observation, and turning to Schalken, "that the hour he appointed was about seven by the clock of the Stadhouse?"

"It had just told seven when I first saw him, sir," answered the student.

"The hour is close at hand, then," said the master, consulting a horologe as large and as round as an orange. "Minheer Vanderhausen from Rotterdam —is it not so?

"Such was the name."

"And an elderly man, richly clad?" pursued Douw, musingly.

"As well as I might see," replied his pupil; "he could not be young, nor yet very old, neither; and his dress was rich and grave, as might become a citizen of wealth and consideration."

At this moment the sonorous boom of the Stadhouse clock told, stroke after stroke, the hour of seven; the eyes of both master and student were directed to the door; and it was not until the last peal of the bell had ceased to vibrate, that Douw exclaimed—

"So, so; we shall have his worship presently, that is, if he means to keep his hour; if not, you may wait for him, Godfrey, if you court his acquaintance. But what, after all, if it should prove but a mummery got up by Vankarp, or some such wag? I wish you had run all risks, and cudgelled the old burgomaster soundly. I'd wager a dozen of Rhenish, his worship would have unmasked, and pleaded old acquaintance in a trice."

"Here he comes, sir," said Schalken, in a low monitory tone; and instantly, upon turning towards the door, Gerard Douw observed the same figure which had, on the day before, so unexpectedly greeted his pupil Schalken.

There was something in the air of the figure which at once satisfied the painter that there was no masquerading in the case, and that he really stood in the presence of a man of worship; and so, without hesitation, he doffed his cap, and courteously saluting the stranger, requested him to be seated. The visitor waved his hand slightly, as if in acknowledgment of the courtesy, but remained standing.

"I have the honour to see Minheer Vanderhausen of Rotterdam?" said Gerard Douw.

"The same," was the laconic reply of his visitor.

"I understand your worship desires to speak with me," continued Douw, "and I am here by appointment to wait your commands."

"Is that a man of trust?" said Vanderhausen, turning towards Schalken, who stood at a little distance behind his master.

"Certainly," replied Gerard.

"Then let him take this box, and get the nearest jeweller or goldsmith to value its contents, and let him return hither with a certificate of the valuation."

At the same time, he placed a small case about nine inches square in the hands of Gerard Douw, who was as much amazed at its weight as at the strange abruptness with which it was handed to him. In accordance with the wishes of the stranger, he delivered it into the hands of Schalken, and repeating his direction, despatched him upon the mission.

Schalken disposed his precious charge securely beneath the folds of his cloak, and rapidly traversing two or three narrow streets, he stopped at a corner house, the lower part of which was then occupied by the shop of a Jewish goldsmith. He entered the shop, and calling the little Hebrew into the obscurity of its back recesses, he proceeded to lay before him Vanderhausen's casket. On being examined by the light of a lamp, it appeared entirely cased with lead, the outer surface of which was much scraped and soiled, and nearly white with age. This having been partially removed, there appeared beneath a box of some hard wood; which also they forced open and after the removal of two or three folds of linen, they discovered its contents to be a mass of golden ingots, closely packed, and, as the Jew declared, of the most perfect quality. Every ingot underwent the scrutiny of the little Jew, who seemed to feel an epicurean delight in touching and testing these morsels of the glorious metal; and each one of them was replaced in its berth with the exclamation: "*Mein Gott,* how very perfect! not one grain of alloy— beautiful, beautiful!" The task was at length finished, and the Jew certified under his hand the value of the ingots submitted to his examination, to amount to many thousand rix-dollars. With the desired document in his pocket, and the rich box of gold carefully pressed under his arm, and concealed by his cloak, he retraced his way, and entering the studio, found his master and the stranger in close conference. Schalken had no sooner left the room, in order to execute the commission he had taken in charge, than Vanderhausen addressed Gerard Douw in the following terms:—

"I cannot tarry with you tonight more than a few minutes, and so I shall shortly tell you the matter upon which I come. You visited the town of Rotterdam some four months ago, and then I saw in the church of St. Lawrence your niece, Rose Velderkaust. I desire to marry her; and if I satisfy you that I am wealthier than any husband you can dream of for her, I expect that you will forward my suit with your authority. If you approve my proposal, you must close with it here and now, for I cannot wait for calculations and delays."

Gerard Douw was hugely astonished by the nature of Minheer Vanderhausen's communication, but he did not venture to express surprise; for besides the motives supplied by prudence and politeness, the painter experienced a kind of chill and oppression like that which is said to intervene when one is placed in unconscious proximity with the object of a natural antipathy—an undefined but overpowering sensation, while standing in the presence of the eccentric stranger, which made him very unwilling to say anything which might reasonably offend him.

"I have no doubt," said Gerard, after two or three prefatory hems, "that the alliance which you propose would prove alike advantageous and honourable to my niece; but you must be aware that she has a will of her own, and may not acquiesce in what *we* may design for her advantage."

"Do not seek to deceive me, sir painter," said Vanderhausen; "you are her guardian—she is your ward—she is mine if *you* like to make her so."

The man of Rotterdam moved forward a little as he spoke, and Gerard Douw, he scarce knew why, inwardly prayed for the speedy return of Schalken.

"I desire," said the mysterious gentleman, "to place in your hands at once an evidence of my wealth, and a security for my liberal dealing with your niece. The lad will return in a minute or two with a sum in value five times the fortune which she has a right to expect from her husband. This shall lie in your hands, together with her dowry, and you may apply the united sum as suits her interest best; it shall be all exclusively hers while she lives: is that liberal?"

Douw assented, and inwardly acknowledged that fortune had been extraordinarily kind to his niece; the stranger, he thought, must be both wealthy and generous, and such an offer was not to be despised, though made by a humourist, and one of no very prepossessing presence. Rose had no very high pretensions for she had but a modest dowry, which she owed entirely to the generosity of her uncle; neither had she any right to raise exceptions on the score of birth, for her own origin was far from splendid, and as the other objections, Gerard resolved, and indeed, by the usages of the time, was warranted in resolving, not to listen to them for a moment.

"Sir," said he, addressing the stranger, "your offer is liberal, and whatever hesitation I may feel in closing with it immediately, arises solely from my not having the honour of knowing anything of your family or station. Upon these points you can, of course, satisfy me without difficulty?"

"As to my respectability," said the stranger, drily, "you must take that for granted at present; pester me with no inquiries; you can discover nothing more about me than I choose to make known. You shall have sufficient security for my respectability—my word, if you are honourable: if you are sordid, my gold."

"A testy old gentleman," thought Douw, "he must have his own way; but, all things considered, I am not justified to declining his offer. I will not pledge myself unnecessarily, however."

"You will not pledge yourself unnecessarily," said Vanderhausen, strangely uttering the very words which had just floated through the mind of his companion; "but you will do so if it *is* necessary, I presume; and I will show you that I consider it indispensable. If the gold I mean to leave in your hands satisfy you, and if you don't wish my proposal to be at once withdrawn, you must, before I leave this room, write your name to this engagement."

Having thus spoken, he placed a paper in the hands of the master, the contents of which expressed an engagement entered into by Gerard Douw, to give to Wilken Vanderhausen of Rotterdam, in marriage, Rose Velderkaust, and so forth, within one week of the date thereof. While the painter was employed in reading this covenant, by the light of a twinkling oil lamp in the far wall of the room, Schalken, as we have stated, entered the studio, and having delivered the box and the valuation of the Jew, into the hands of the stranger, he was about to retire, when Vanderhausen called to him to wait; and, presenting the case and the certificate to Gerard Douw, he paused in silence until he had satisfied himself, by an inspection of both, respecting the value of the pledge left in his hands. At length he said—

"Are you content?"

The painter said he would fain have another day to consider.

"Not an hour," said the suitor, apathetically.

"Well then," said Douw, with a sore effort, "I *am* content, it is a bargain."

"Then sign at once," said Vanderhausen, "for I am weary."

At the same time he produced a small case of writing materials, and Gerard signed the important document.

"Let this youth witness the covenant," said the old man; and Godfrey Schalken unconsciously attested the instrument which for ever bereft him of his dear Rose Velderkaust.

The compact being thus completed, the strange visitor folded up the paper, and stowed it safely in an inner pocket.

"I will visit you tomorrow night at nine o'clock, at your own house, Gerard Douw, and will see the object of our contract;" and so saying Wilken Vanderhausen moved stiffly, but rapidly, out of the room.

Schalken, eager to resolve his doubts, had placed himself by the window, in order to watch the street entrance; but the experiment served only to support his suspicions, for the old man did not issue from the door. This was *very* strange, odd, nay fearful. He and his master returned together, and talked but little on the way, for each had his own subjects of reflection, of anxiety, and of hope. Schalken, however, did not know the ruin which menaced his dearest projects.

Gerard Douw knew nothing of the attachment which had sprung up between his pupil and his niece; and even if he had, it is doubtful whether he would have regarded its existence as any serious obstruction to the wishes of Minheer Vanderhausen. Marriages were then and there matters of traffic and calculation; and it would have appeared as absurd in the eyes of the guardian to make a mutual attachment an essential element in a contract of the sort, as it would have been to draw up his bonds and receipts in the language of romance.

The painter, however, did not communicate to his niece the important step which he had taken in her behalf, a forebearance caused not by any anticipated opposition on her part, but solely by a ludicrous consciousness that if she were to ask him for a description of her destined bridegroom, he would be forced to confess that he had not once seen his face, and if called upon, would find it absolutely impossible to identify him. Upon the next day, Gerard Douw, after dinner, called his niece to him and having scanned her person with an air of satisfaction, he took her hand, and looking upon her pretty innocent face with a smile of kindness, he said:—

"Rose, my girl, that face of yours will make your fortune." Rose blushed and smiled. "Such faces and such tempers seldom go together, and when they do, the compound is a love charm, few heads or hearts can resist; trust me, you will soon be a bride, girl. But this is trifling, and I am pressed for time, so make ready the large room by eight o'clock tonight, and give directions for supper at nine. I expect a friend; and observe me, child, do you trick yourself out handsomely. I will not have him think us poor or sluttish."

With these words he left her, and took his way to the room in which his pupils worked.

When the evening closed in, Gerard called Schalken, who was about to take his departure to his own obscure and comfortless lodgings, and asked him to come home and sup with Rose and Vanderhausen. The invitation was, of course, accepted and Gerard Douw and his pupil soon found themselves in the handsome and, even then, antique chamber, which had been prepared for the reception of the stranger. A cheerful wood fire blazed in the hearth, a little at one side of which an old-fashioned table, which shone in the fire-light like burnished gold, was awaiting the supper, for which preparations were going forward; and ranged with exact regularity, stood the tall-backed chairs, whose ungracefulness was more than compensated by their comfort. The little party, consisting of Rose, her uncle, and the artist, awaited the arrival of the expected visitor with considerable impatience. Nine o'clock at length came, and with it a summons at the street door, which being speedily answered, was followed by a slow and emphatic tread upon the staircase; the steps moved heavily across the lobby, the door of the room in which the party we have described were assembled slowly opened, and there entered a figure which startled, almost appalled, the phlegmatic Dutchmen, and nearly made Rose scream with terror. It was the form, and arrayed in the garb of Minheer Vanderhausen; the air, the gait, the height were the same, but the features had never been seen by any of the party before. The stranger stopped at the door of the room, and displayed his form and face completely. He wore a dark-coloured cloth cloak, which was short and full, not falling quite to his knees; his legs were cased in dark purple silk stockings, and his shoes were adorned with roses of the same colour. The opening of the cloak in front showed the under-suit to consist of some very dark, perhaps sable material, and his hands were enclosed in a pair of heavy leather gloves, which ran up considerably above the wrist, in the manner of a gauntlet. In one hand he carried his walking-stick and his hat, which he had removed, and the other hung heavily by his side. A quantity of grizzled hair descended in long tresses from his head, and rested upon the plaits of a stiff ruff, which effectually concealed his neck. So far all was well; but the face!—all the flesh of the face was coloured with the bluish leaden hue, which is sometimes produced by metallic medicines, administered in excessive quantities; the eyes showed an undue proportion of muddy white, and had a certain indefinable character of insanity; the hue of the lips bearing the usual relation to that of the face, was, consequently, nearly black; and the entire character of the face was sensual, malignant, and even satanic. It was remarkable that the worshipful stranger suffered as little as possible of his flesh to appear, and that during his visit he did not once remove his gloves. Having stood for some moments at the door, Gerard Douw at length found breath and collectedness to bid him welcome, and with a mute inclination of the head, the stranger stepped forward into the room. There was something indescribably odd, even horrible, about all his motions, something undefinable, that was unnatural, unhuman; it was as if the limbs were guided and directed by a spirit unused to the management of bodily machinery. The stranger spoke hardly at all during his visit, which did not exceed half an hour; and the host himself could scarcely muster courage enough to utter the few necessary salutations and courtesies; and, indeed, such was the nervous terror which the presence of Vanderhausen inspired, that very little would have made all his entertainers fly in downright panic from the room. They had not so far lost all self-possession, however, as to fail to observe two strange peculiarities of their visitor. During his stay his eyelids did not once close, or, indeed, move in the slightest degree; and farther, there was a deathlike stillness in his whole person, owing to the absence of the heaving motion of the chest, caused by the process of respiration. These two peculiarities, though when told they may appear trifling, produced a very striking and unpleasant effect when seen and observed. Vanderhausen at length relieved the painter of Leyden of his inauspicious presence; and with no trifling sense of relief the little party heard the street door close after him.

"Dear uncle," said Rose, "what a frightful man! I would not see him again for the wealth of the States."

"Tush, foolish girl," said Douw, whose sensations were anything but comfortable. "A man may be as ugly as the devil, and yet, if his heart and actions are good, he is worth all the pretty-faced perfumed puppies that walk the Mall. Rose, my girl, it is very true he has not thy pretty face, but I know him to be wealthy and liberal; and were he ten times more ugly, these two virtues would be enough to counter balance all his deformity, and if not sufficient actually to alter the shape and hue of his features, at least enough to prevent one thinking them so much amiss."

"Do you know, uncle," said Rose, "when I saw him standing at the door, I could not get it out of my head that I saw the old painted wooden figure that used to frighten me so much in the Church of St. Laurence at Rotterdam."

Gerard laughed, though he could not help inwardly acknowledging the justness of the comparison. He was resolved, however, as far as he could, to check his niece's disposition to dilate upon the ugliness of her intended bridegroom, although he was not a little pleased, as well as puzzled, to observe that she appeared totally exempt from that mysterious dread of the stranger which, he could not disguise it from himself, considerably affected him, as also his pupil Godfrey Schalken.

Early on the next day there arrived, from various quarters of the town, rich presents of silks, velvets, jewellery, and so forth, for Rose; and also a packet directed to Gerard Douw, which on being opened, was found to contain a contract of marriage, formally drawn up, between Wilken Vanderhausen of the *Boom-quay*, in Rotterdam, and Rose Velderkaust of Leyden, niece to Gerard Douw, master in the art of painting, also of the same city; and containing engagements on the part of Vanderhausen to make settlements upon his bride, far more splendid than he had before led her guardian to believe likely, and which were to be secured to her use in the most unexceptionable manner possible—the money being placed in the hand of Gerard Douw himself.

I have no sentimental scenes to describe, no cruelty of guardians, no magnanimity of wards, no agonies, or transport of lovers. The record I have to make is one of sordidness, levity, and heartlessness. In less than a week after the first interview which we have just described, the contract of marriage was fulfilled, and Schalken saw the prize which he would have risked existence to secure, carried off in solemn pomp by his repulsive rival. For two or three days he absented himself from the school; he then returned and worked, if with less cheerfulness, with far more dogged resolution than before; the stimulus of love had given place to that of ambition. Months passed away, and, contrary to his expectation, and, indeed, to the direct promise of the parties, Gerard Douw heard nothing of his niece or her worshipful spouse. The interest of the money, which was to have been demanded in quarterly sums, lay unclaimed in his hands.

He began to grow extremely uneasy. Minheer Vanderhausen's direction in Rotterdam he was fully possessed of; after some irresolution he finally determined to journey thither—a trifling undertaking, and easily accomplished—and thus to satisfy himself of the safety and comfort of his ward, for whom he entertained an honest and strong affection. His search was in vain, however; no one in Rotterdam had ever heard of Minheer Vanderhausen. Gerard Douw left not a house in the Boom-quay untried, but all in vain. No one could give him any information whatever touching the object of his inquiry, and he was obliged to return to Leyden nothing wiser and far more anxious, than when he had left it.

On his arrival he hastened to the establishment from which Vanderhausen had hired the lumbering, though, considering the times, most luxurious vehicle, which the bridal party had employed to convey them to Rotterdam. From the driver of this machine he learned, that having proceeded by slow stages, they had late in the evening approached Rotterdam; but that before they entered the city, and while yet nearly a mile from it, a small party of men, soberly clad, and after the old fashion, with peaked beards and moustaches, standing in the centre of the road, obstructed the further progress of the carriage. The driver reined in his horses, much fearing, from the obscurity of the hour, and the loneliness, of the road, that some mischief was intended. His fears were, however, somewhat allayed by his observing that these strange men carried a large litter, of an antique shape, and which they immediately set down upon the pavement, whereupon the bridegroom, having opened the coach-door from within, descended, and having assisted his bride to do likewise, led her, weeping bitterly, and wringing her hands, to the litter, which they both entered. It was then raised by the men who surrounded it, and speedily carried towards the city, and before it had proceeded very far, the darkness concealed it from the view of the Dutch coachman. In the inside of the vehicle he found a purse, whose contents more than thrice paid the hire of the carriage and man. He saw and could tell nothing more of Minheer Vanderhausen and his beautiful lady.

This mystery was a source of profound anxiety and even grief to Gerard Douw. There was evidently fraud in the dealing of Vanderhausen with him, though for what purpose committed he could not imagine. He greatly doubted how far it was possible for a man possessing such a countenance to be anything but a villain, and every day that passed without his hearing from or of his niece, instead of inducing him to forget his fears, on the contrary tended more and more to aggravate them. The loss of her cheerful society tended also to depress his spirits; and in order to dispel the gloom, which often crept upon his mind after his daily occupations were over, he was wont frequently to ask Schalken to accompany him home, and share his otherwise solitary supper.

One evening, the painter and his pupil were sitting by the fire, having accomplished a comfortable meal, and had yielded to the silent and delicious melancholy of digestion, when their ruminations were disturbed by a loud sound at the street door, as if occasioned by some person rushing and scrambling vehemently against it. A domestic had run without delay to ascertain the cause of the disturbance, and they heard him twice or thrice interrogate the applicant for admission, but without eliciting any other answer but a sustained reiteration of sounds. They heard him then open the hall-door, and immediately there followed a light and rapid tread on the staircase. Schalken advanced towards the door. It opened before he reached it, and Rose rushed into the room. She looked wild, fierce and haggard with terror and exhaustion, but her dress surprised them as much as even her unexpected appearance. It consisted of a kind of white woollen wrapper, made close about the neck, and descending to the very ground. It was much deranged and travel-soiled. The poor creature had hardly entered the chamber when she fell senseless on the floor. With some difficulty they succeeded in reviving her, and on recovering her senses, she instantly exclaimed, in a tone of terror rather than mere impatience:—

"Wine! wine! quickly, or I'm lost!"

Astonished and almost scared at the strange agitation in which the call was made, they at once administered to her wishes, and she drank some wine with a haste and eagerness which surprised them. She had hardly swallowed it, when she exclaimed, with the same urgency:

"Food, for God's sake, food, at once, or I perish."

A considerable fragment of a roast joint was upon the table, and Schalken immediately began to cut some, but he was anticipated, for no sooner did she see it than she caught it, a more than mortal image of famine, and with her hands, and even with her teeth, she tore off the flesh, and swallowed it.

When the paroxysm of hunger had been a little appeased, she appeared on a sudden overcome with shame, or it may have been that other more agitating thoughts overpowered and scared her, for she began to weep bitterly and to wring her hands.

"Oh, send for a minister of God," said she; "I am not safe till he comes; send for him speedily."

Gerard Douw despatched a messenger instantly, and prevailed on his niece to allow him to surrender his bed chamber to her use. He also persuaded her to retire to it at once to rest; her consent was extorted upon the condition that they would not leave her for a moment.

"Oh that the holy man were here," she said; "he can deliver me: the dead and the living can never be one: God has forbidden it."

With these mysterious words she surrendered herself to their guidance, and they proceeded to the chamber which Gerard Douw had assigned to her use.

"Do not, do not leave me for a moment," said she; "I am lost forever if you do."

Gerard Douw's chamber was approached through a spacious apartment, which they were now about to enter. He and Schalken each carried a candle, so that a sufficiency of light was cast upon all surrounding objects. They were now entering the large chamber, which as I have said, communicated with Douw's apartment, when Rose suddenly stopped, and, in a whisper which thrilled them both with horror, she said:—

"Oh, God! he is here! he is here! See, see! there he goes!"

She pointed towards the door of the inner room, and Schalken thought he saw a shadowy and ill-defined form gliding into that apartment. He drew his sword, and, raising the candle so as to throw its light with increased distinctness upon the objects in the room, he entered the chamber into which the shadow had glided. No figure was there—nothing but the furniture which belonged to the room, and yet he could not be deceived as to the fact that something had moved before them into the chamber. A sickening dread came upon him, and the cold perspiration broke out in heavy drops upon his forehead; nor was he more composed, when he heard the increased urgency and agony of entreaty, with which Rose implored them not to leave her for a moment.

"I saw him," said she; "he's here. I cannot be deceived; I know him; he's by me; he is with me; he's in the room. Then, for God's sake, as you would save me, do not stir from beside me."

They at length prevailed upon her to lie down upon the bed, where she continued to urge them to stay by her. She frequently uttered incoherent sentences, repeating, again and again, "the dead and the living cannot be one: God has forbidden it." And then again, "Rest to the wakeful—sleep to the sleep-walkers." These and such mysterious and broken sentences, she continued to utter until the clergyman arrived. Gerard Douw began to fear, naturally enough, that terror or ill-treatment, had unsettled the poor girl's intellect, and he half suspected, by the suddenness of her appearance, the unseasonableness of the hour, and above all, from the wildness and terror of her manner, that she had made her escape from some place of confinement for lunatics, and was in imminent fear of pursuit. He resolved to summon medical advice as soon as the mind of his niece had been in some measure set at rest by the offices of the clergyman whose attendance she had so earnestly desired; and until this object had been attained, he did not venture to put any questions to her, which might possibly, by reviving painful or horrible recollections, increase her agitation. The clergyman soon arrived— a man of ascetic countenance and venerable age—one whom Gerard Douw respected very much, forasmuch as he was a veteran polemic, though one perhaps more dreaded as a combatant than beloved as a Christian—of pure morality, subtle brain, and frozen heart. He entered the chamber which communicated with that in which Rose reclined and immediately on his arrival, she requested him to pray for her, as for one who lay in the hands of Satan, and who could hope for deliverance only from heaven.

That you may distinctly understand all the circumstances of the event which I am going to describe, it is necessary to state the relative position of the parties who were engaged in it. The old clergyman and Schalken were in the anteroom of which I have already spoken; Rose lay in the inner chamber, the door of which was open; and by the side of the bed, at her urgent desire, stood her guardian; a candle burned in the bedchamber, and three were lighted in the outer apartment. The old man now cleared his voice as if about to commence, but before he had time to begin, a sudden gust of air blew out the candle which served to illuminate the room in which the poor girl lay, and she, with hurried alarm, exclaimed:—

"Godfrey, bring in another candle; the darkness is unsafe."

Gerard Douw forgetting for the moment her repeated injunctions, in the immediate impulse, stepped from the bedchamber into the other, in order to supply what she desired.

"Oh God! do not go, dear uncle," shrieked the unhappy girl—and at the same time she sprung from the bed, and darted after him, in order, by her grasp, to detain him. But the warning came too late, for scarcely had he passed the threshold, and hardly had his niece had time to utter the startling exclamation, when the door which divided the two rooms closed violently after him, as if swung by a strong blast of wind. Schalken and he both rushed to the door, but their united and desperate efforts could not avail so much as to shake it. Shriek after shriek burst from the inner chamber, with all the piercing loudness of despairing terror. Schalken and Douw applied every nerve to force open the door; but all in vain. There was no sound of struggling from within, but the screams seemed to increase in loudness, and at the same time they heard the bolts of the latticed window withdrawn, and the window itself grated upon the sill as if thrown open. One *last* shriek, so long and piercing and agonized as to be scarcely human, swelled from the room, and suddenly there followed a death-like silence. A light step was heard crossing the floor, as if from the bed to the window; and almost at the same instant the door gave way, and, yielding to the pressure of the external applicants, nearly precipitated them into the room. It was empty. The window was open, and Schalken sprung to a chair and gazed out upon the street and canal below. He saw no form, but he saw, or thought he saw, the waters of the broad canal beneath settling ring after ring in heavy circles, as if a moment before disturbed by the submission of some ponderous body.

No trace of Rose was ever after found, nor was anything certain respecting her mysterious wooer discovered or even suspected—no clue whereby to trace the intricacies of the labyrinth and to arrive at its solution, presented itself. But an incident occurred, which, though it will not be received by our rational readers in lieu of evidence, produced nevertheless a strong and a lasting impression upon the mind of Schalken. Many years after the events which we have detailed, Schalken, then residing far away received an intimation of his father's death, and of his intended burial upon a fixed day in the church of Rotterdam. It was necessary that a very considerable journey should be performed by the funeral procession, which as it will be readily believed, was not very numerously attended. Schalken with difficulty arrived in Rotterdam late in the day upon which the funeral was appointed to take place. It had not then arrived. Evening closed in, and still it did not appear.

Schalken strolled down to the church; he found it open; notice of the arrival of the funeral had been given, and the vault in which the body was to be laid had been opened. The sexton, on seeing a well-dressed gentleman, whose object was to attend the expected obsequies, pacing the aisle of the church, hospitably invited him to share with him the comforts of a blazing fire, which, as was his custom in winter time upon such occasions, he had kindled in the hearth of a chamber in which he was accustomed to await the arrival of such grisly guests and which communicated, by a flight of steps, with the vault below. In this chamber, Schalken and his entertainer seated themselves; and the sexton, after some fruitless attempts to engage his guest in conversation, was obliged to apply himself to his tobacco-pipe and can, to solace his solitude. In spite of his grief and cares, the fatigues of a rapid journey of nearly forty hours gradually overcame the mind and body of Godfrey Schalken, and he sank into a deep sleep, from which he awakened by someone's shaking him gently by the shoulder. He first thought that the old sexton had called him, but *he* was no longer in the room. He roused himself, and as soon as he could clearly see what was around him, he perceived a female form, clothed in a kind of light robe of white, part of which was so disposed as to form a veil, and in her hand she carried a lamp. She was moving rather away from him, in the direction of the flight of steps which conducted towards the vaults. Schalken felt a vague alarm at the sight of this figure and at the same time an irresistible impulse to follow its guidance. He followed it towards the vaults, but when it reached the head of the stairs, he paused; the figure paused also, and, turning gently round, displayed, by the light of the lamp it carried, the face and features of his first love, Rose Velderkaust. There was nothing horrible, or even sad, in the countenance. On the contrary, it wore the same arch smile which used to enchant the artist long before in his happy days. A feeling of awe and interest, too intense to be resisted, prompted him to follow the spectre, if spectre it were. She descended the stairs—he followed—and turning to the left, through a narrow passage, she led him, to his infinite surprise, into what appeared to be an old-fashioned Dutch apartment, such as the pictures of

Gerard Douw have served to immortalize. Abundance of costly antique furniture was disposed about the room, and in one corner stood a four-post bed, with heavy black cloth curtains around it; the figure frequently turned towards him with the same arch smile; and when she came to the side of the bed, she drew the curtains, and, by the light of the lamp, which she held towards its contents, she disclosed to the horror-stricken painter, sitting bolt upright in the bed, the livid and demoniac form of Vanderhausen. Schalken had hardly seen him, when he fell senseless upon the floor, where he lay until discovered, on the next morning, by persons employed in closing the passages into the vaults. He was lying in a cell of considerable size, which had not been disturbed for a long time, and he had fallen beside a large coffin, which was supported upon small pillars, a security against the attacks of vermin.

To his dying day Schalken was satisfied of the reality of the vision which he had witnessed, and he has left behind him a curious evidence of the impression which it wrought upon his fancy, in a painting executed shortly after the event I have narrated, and which is valuable as exhibiting not only the peculiarities which have made Schalken's pictures sought after, but even more so as presenting a portrait of his early love, Rose Velderkaust, whose mysterious fate must always remain matter of speculation.

Charlotte Perkins Gilman

The Yellow Wallpaper

Charlotte Perkins Gilman, feminist and reformer, wrote only one horror story and that one such an outstanding masterpiece that it has seldom been equalled in this century, only, perhaps, in the work of Shirley Jackson and Joanna Russ. "The Yellow Wallpaper" is either a haunted house story or a story of insanity, but in either case it is a monument of feminist horror, pointing out subtly and effectively all the restrictions which bring the central character to the moment of the story. This is the classic response to the story of male guilt and horror at how badly a woman has been treated, making the case for all time that the horror story need not be conservative.

It is very seldom that mere ordinary people like John and myself secure ancestral halls for the summer.

A colonial mansion, a hereditary estate, I would say a haunted house, and reach the height of romantic felicity—but that would be asking too much of fate!

Still I will proudly declare that there is something queer about it.

Else, why should it be let so cheaply? And why have stood so long untenanted?

John laughs at me, of course, but one expects that in marriage.

John is practical in the extreme. He has no patience with faith, an intense horror of superstition, and he scoffs openly at any talk of things not to be felt and seen and put down in figures.

John is a physician, and *perhaps*—(I would not say it to a living soul, of course, but this is dead paper and a great relief to my mind)—*perhaps* that is one reason I do not get well faster.

You see he does not believe I am sick!

And what can one do?

If a physician of high standing, and one's own husband, assures friends and relatives that there is really nothing the matter with one but temporary nervous depression—a slight hysterical tendency—what is one to do?

My brother is also a physician, and also of high standing, and he says the same thing.

So I take phosphates or phospites—whichever it is, and tonics, and journeys, and air, and exercise, and am absolutely forbidden to "work" until I am well again.

Personally, I disagree with their ideas.

Personally, I believe that congenial work, with excitement and change, would do me good.

But what is one to do?

I did write for a while in spite of them; but it *does* exhaust me a good deal—having to be so sly about it, or else meet with heavy opposition.

I sometimes fancy that in my condition if I had less opposition and more society and stimulus—but John says the very worst thing I can do is to think about my condition, and I confess it always makes me feel bad.

So I will let it alone and talk about the house.

The most beautiful place! It is quite alone, standing well back from the road, quite three miles from the village. It makes me think of English places that you read about, for there are hedges and walls and gates that lock, and lots of separate little houses for the gardeners and people.

There is a *delicious* garden! I never saw such a garden—large and shady, full of box-bordered paths, and lined with long grape-covered arbors with seats under them.

There were greenhouses, too, but they are all broken now.

There was some legal trouble, I believe, something about the heirs and coheirs; anyhow, the place has been empty for years.

That spoils my ghostliness, I am afraid, but I don't care—there is something strange about the house—I can feel it.

I even said so to John one moonlight evening, but he said what I felt was a *draught*, and shut the window.

I get unreasonably angry with John sometimes. I'm sure I never used to be so sensitive. I think it is due to this nervous condition.

But John says if I feel so, I shall neglect proper self-control; so I take pains to control myself—before him, at least, and that makes me very tired.

I don't like our room a bit. I wanted one downstairs that opened on the piazza and had roses all over the window, and such pretty old-fashioned chintz hangings! but John would not hear of it.

He said there was only one window and not room for two beds, and no near room for him if he took another.

He is very careful and loving, and hardly lets me stir without special direction.

I have a schedule prescription for each hour in the day; he takes all care from me, and so I feel basely ungrateful not to value it more.

He said we came here solely on my account, that I was to have perfect rest and all the air I could get. "Your exercise depends on your strength, my dear," said he, "and your food somewhat on your appetite; but air you can absorb all the time." So we took the nursery at the top of the house.

It is a big, airy room, the whole floor nearly, with windows that look all ways, and air and sunshine galore. It was nursery first and then playroom and gymnasium, I should judge; for the windows are barred for little children, and there are rings and things in the walls.

The paint and paper look as if a boys' school had used it. It is stripped off—the paper—in great patches all around the head of my bed, about as far as I can reach, and in a great place on the other side of the room low down. I never saw a worse paper in my life.

One of those sprawling flamboyant patterns committing every artistic sin.

It is dull enough to confuse the eye in following, pronounced enough to constantly irritate and provoke study, and when you follow the lame uncertain curves for a little distance they suddenly commit suicide—plunge off at outrageous angles, destroy themselves in unheard of contradictions.

The color is repellent, almost revolting; a smouldering unclean yellow, strangely faded by the slow-turning sunlight.

It is a dull yet lurid orange in some places, a sickly sulphur tint in others.

No wonder the children hated it! I should hate it myself if I had to live in this room long.

There comes John, and I must put this away,—he hates to have me write a word.

We have been here two weeks, and I haven't felt like writing before, since that first day.

I am sitting by the window now, up in this atrocious nursery, and there is nothing to hinder my writing as much as I please, save lack of strength.

John is away all day, and even some nights when his cases are serious.

I am glad my case is not serious!

But these nervous troubles are dreadfully depressing.

John does not know how much I really suffer. He knows there is no *reason* to suffer, and that satisfies him.

Of course it is only nervousness. It does weigh on me so not to do my duty in any way!

I meant to be such a help to John, such a real rest and comfort, and here I am a comparative burden already!

Nobody would believe what an effort it is to do what little I am able,—to dress and entertain, and order things.

It is fortunate Mary is so good with the baby. Such a dear baby!

And yet I *cannot* be with him, it makes me so nervous.

I suppose John never was nervous in his life. He laughs at me so about this wall-paper!

At first he meant to repaper the room, but afterwards he said that I was letting it get the better of me, and that nothing was worse for a nervous patient than to give way to such fancies.

He said that after the wall-paper was changed it would be the heavy bedstead, and then the barred windows, and then that gate at the head of the stairs, and so on.

"You know the place is doing you good," he said, "and really, dear, I don't care to renovate the house just for a three months' rental."

"Then do let us go downstairs," I said, "there are such pretty rooms there."

Then he took me in his arms and called me a blessed little goose, and said he would go down to the cellar, if I wished, and have it whitewashed into the bargain.

But he is right enough about the beds and windows and things.

It is an airy and comfortable room as any one need wish, and, of course, I would not be so silly as to make him uncomfortable just for a whim.

I'm really getting quite fond of the big room, all but that horrid paper.

Out of one window I can see the garden, those mysterious deepshaded arbors, the riotous old-fashioned flowers, and bushes and gnarly trees.

Out of another I get a lovely view of the bay and a little private wharf belonging to the estate. There is a beautiful shaded lane that runs down there from the house. I always fancy I see people walking in these numerous paths and arbors, but John has cautioned me not to give way to fancy in the least. He says that with my imaginative power and habit of story-making, a nervous weakness like mine is sure to lead to all manner of excited fancies, and that I ought to use my will and good sense to check the tendency. So I try.

I think sometimes that if I were only well enough to write a little it would relieve the press of ideas and rest me.

But I find I get pretty tired when I try.

It is so discouraging not to have any advice and companionship about my work. When I get really well, John says we will ask Cousin Henry and Julia down for a long visit; but he says he would as soon put fireworks in my pillow-case as to let me have those stimulating people about now.

I wish I could get well faster.

But I must not think about that. This paper looks to me as if it *knew* what a vicious influence it had!

There is a recurrent spot where the pattern lolls like a broken neck and two bulbous eyes stare at you upside down.

I get positively angry with the impertinence of it and the everlastingness. Up and down and sideways they crawl, and those absurd, unblinking eyes are everywhere. There is one place where two breaths didn't match, and the eyes go all up and down the line, one a little higher than the other.

I never saw so much expression in an inanimate thing before, and we all know how much expression they have! I used to lie awake as a child and get more entertainment and terror out of blank walls and plain furniture than most children could find in a toy-store.

I remember what a kindly wink the knobs of our big, old bureau used to have, and there was one chair that always seemed like a strong friend.

I used to feel that if any of the other things looked too fierce I could always hop into that chair and be safe.

The furniture in this room is no worse than inharmonious, however, for we had to bring it all from downstairs. I suppose when this was used as a playroom they had to take the nursery things out, and no wonder! I never saw such ravages as the children have made here.

The wall-paper, as I said before, is torn off in spots, and it sticketh closer than a brother—they must have had perseverance as well as hatred.

Then the floor is scratched and gouged and splintered, the plaster itself is dug out here and there, and this great heavy bed which is all we found in the room, looks as if it had been through the wars.

But I don't mind it a bit—only the paper.

There comes John's sister. Such a dear girl as she is, and so careful of me! I must not let her find me writing.

She is a perfect and enthusiastic housekeeper, and hopes for no better profession. I verily believe she thinks it is the writing which made me sick!

But I can write when she is out, and see her a long way off from these windows.

There is one that commands the road, a lovely shaded winding road, and one that just looks off over the country. A lovely country, too, full of great elms and velvet meadows.

This wall-paper has a kind of sub-pattern in a different shade, a particularly irritating one, for you can only see it in certain lights, and not clearly then.

But in the places where it isn't faded and where the sun is just so—I can see a strange, provoking, formless sort of figure, that seems to skulk about behind that silly and conspicuous front design.

There's sister on the stairs!

Well, the Fourth of July is over! The people are all gone and I am tired out. John thought it might do me good to see a little company, so we just had mother and Nellie and the children down for a week.

Of course I didn't do a thing. Jennie sees to everything now.

But it tired me all the same.

John says if I don't pick up faster he shall send me to Weir Mitchell in the fall.

But I don't want to go there at all. I had a friend who was in his hands once, and she says he is just like John and my brother, only more so!

Besides, it is such an undertaking to go so far.

I don't feel as if it was worth while to turn my hand over for anything, and I'm getting dreadfully fretful and querulous.

I cry at nothing, and cry most of the time.

Of course I don't when John is here, or anybody else, but when I am alone.

And I am alone a good deal just now. John is kept in town very often by serious cases, and Jennie is good and lets me alone when I want her to.

So I walk a little in the garden or down that lovely lane, sit on the porch under the roses, and lie down up here a good deal.

I'm getting really fond of the room in spite of the wall-paper. Perhaps *because* of the wall-paper.

It dwells in my mind so!

I lie here on this great immovable bed—it is nailed down, I believe—and follow that pattern about by the hour. It is as good as gymnastics, I assure you. I start, we'll say, at the bottom, down in the corner over there where it has not been touched, and I determine for the thousandth time that I *will* follow that pointless pattern to some sort of a conclusion.

I know a little of the principle of design, and I know this thing was not arranged on any laws of radiation, or alternation, or repetition, or symmetry, or anything else that I ever heard of.

It is repeated, of course, by the breadths, but not otherwise.

Looked at in one way each breadth stands alone, the bloated curves and flourishes—a kind of "debased Romanesque" with *delirium tremens*—go waddling up and down in isolated columns of fatuity.

But, on the other hand, they connect diagonally, and the sprawling outlines run off in great slanting waves of optic horror, like a lot of wallowing seaweeds in full chase.

The whole thing goes horizontally, too, at least it seems so, and I exhaust myself in trying to distinguish the order of its going in that direction.

They have used a horizontal breadth for a frieze, and that adds wonderfully to the confusion.

There is one end of the room where it is almost intact, and there, when the crosslights fade and the low sun shines directly upon it, I can almost fancy radiation after all,—the interminable grotesques seem to form around a common centre and rush off in headlong plunges of equal distraction.

It makes me tired to follow it. I will take a nap I guess.

I don't know why I should write this.

I don't want to.

I don't feel able.

And I know John would think it absurd. But I *must* say what I feel and think in some way—it is such a relief!

But the effort is getting to be greater than the relief.

Half the time now I am awfully lazy, and lie down ever so much.

John says I mustn't lose my strength, and has me take cod liver oil and lots of tonics and things, to say nothing of ale and wine and rare meat.

Dear John! He loves me very dearly, and hates to have me sick. I tried to have a real earnest reasonable talk with him the other day, and tell him how I wish he would let me go and make a visit to Cousin Henry and Julia.

But he said I wasn't able to go, nor able to stand it after I got there; and I did not make out a very good case for myself, for I was crying before I had finished.

It is getting to be a great effort for me to think straight. Just this nervous weakness I suppose.

And dear John gathered me up in his arms, and just carried me upstairs and laid me on the bed, and sat by me and read to me till it tired my head.

He said I was his darling and his comfort and all he had, and that I must take care of myself for his sake, and keep well.

He says no one but myself can help me out of it, that I must use my will and self-control and not let any silly fancies run away with me.

There's one comfort, the baby is well and happy, and does not have to occupy this nursery with the horrid wall-paper.

If we had not used it, that blessed child would have! What a fortunate escape! Why, I wouldn't have a child of mine, an impressionable little thing, live in such a room for worlds.

I never thought of it before, but it is lucky that John kept me here after all, I can stand it so much easier than a baby, you see.

Of course I never mention it to them any more—I am too wise,—but I keep watch of it all the same.

There are things in that paper that nobody knows but me, or ever will. Behind that outside pattern the dim shapes get clearer every day.

It is always the same shape, only very numerous.

And it is like a woman stooping down and creeping about behind that pattern. I don't like it a bit. I wonder—I begin to think—I wish John would take me away from here!

It is so hard to talk with John about my case, because he is so wise, and because he loves me so.

But I tried it last night.

It was moonlight. The moon shines in all around just as the sun does.

I hate to see it sometimes, it creeps so slowly, and always comes in by one window or another.

John was asleep and I hated to waken him, so I kept still and watched the moonlight on that undulating wall-paper till I felt creepy.

The faint figure behind seemed to shake the pattern, just as if she wanted to get out.

I got up softly and went to feel and see if the paper *did* move, and when I came back John was awake.

"What is it, little girl?" he said. "Don't go walking about like that—you'll get cold."

I thought it was a good time to talk, so I told him that I really was not gaining here, and that I wished he would take me away.

"Why darling!" said he, "our lease will be up in three weeks, and I can't see how to leave before.

"The repairs are not done at home, and I cannot possibly leave town just now. Of course if you were in any danger, I could and would, but you really are better, dear, whether you can see it or not. I am a doctor, dear, and I know. You are gaining flesh and color, your appetite is better, I feel really much easier about you."

"I don't weigh a bit more," said I, "nor as much; and my appetite may be better in the evening when you are here, but it is worse in the morning when you are away!"

"Bless her little heart!" said he with a big hug, "she shall be as sick as she pleases! But now let's improve the shining hours by going to sleep, and talk about it in the morning!"

"And you won't go away?" I asked gloomily.

"Why, how can I, dear? It is only three weeks more and then we will take a nice little trip of a few days while Jennie is getting the house ready. Really dear you are better!"

"Better in body perhaps—" I began, and stopped short, for he sat up straight and looked at me with such a stern, reproachful look that I could not say another word.

"My darling," said he, "I beg of you, for my sake and for our child's sake, as well as for your own, that you will never for one instant let that idea enter your mind! There is nothing so dangerous, so fascinating, to a temperament like yours. It is a false and foolish fancy. Can you not trust me as a physician when I tell you so?"

So of course I said no more on that score, and we went to sleep before long.

He thought I was asleep first, but I wasn't, and lay there for hours trying to decide whether that front pattern and the back pattern really did move together or separately.

On a pattern like this, by daylight, there is a lack of sequence, a defiance of law, that is a constant irritant to a normal mind.

The color is hideous enough, and unreliable enough, and infuriating enough, but the pattern is torturing.

You think you have mastered it, but just as you get well underway in following, it turns a backsomersault and there you are. It slaps you in the face, knocks you down, and tramples upon you. It is like a bad dream.

The outside pattern is a florid arabesque, reminding one of a fungus. If you can imagine a toadstool in joints, an interminable string of toadstools, budding and sprouting in endless convolutions—why, that is something like it.

That is, sometimes!

There is one marked peculiarity about this paper, a thing nobody seems to notice but myself, and that is that it changes as the light changes.

When the sun shoots in through the east window—I always watch for that first long, straight ray—it changes so quickly that I never can quite believe it.

That is why I watch it always.

By moonlight—the moon shines in all night when there is a moon—I wouldn't know it was the same paper.

At night in any kind of light, in twilight, candle light, lamplight, and worst of all by moonlight, it becomes bars! The outside pattern I mean, and the woman behind it is as plain as can be.

I didn't realize for a long time what the thing was that showed behind, that dim sub-pattern, but now I am quite sure it is a woman.

By daylight she is subdued, quiet. I fancy it is the pattern that keeps her so still. It is so puzzling. It keeps me quiet by the hour.

I lie down ever so much now. John says it is good for me, and to sleep all I can.

Indeed he started the habit by making me lie down for an hour after each meal.

It is a very bad habit I am convinced, for you see I don't sleep.

And that cultivates deceit, for I don't tell them I'm awake—O no!

The fact is I am getting a little afraid of John.

He seems very queer sometimes, and even Jennie has an inexplicable look.

It strikes me occasionally, just as a scientific hypothesis,—that perhaps it is the paper!

I have watched John when he did not know I was looking, and come into the room suddenly on the most innocent excuses, and I've caught him several times *looking at the paper*! And Jennie too. I caught Jennie with her hand on it once.

She didn't know I was in the room, and when I asked her in a quiet, a very quiet voice, with the most restrained manner possible, what she was doing with the paper—she turned around as if she had been caught stealing, and looked quite angry—asked me why I should frighten her so!

Then she said that the paper stained everything it touched, that she had found yellow smooches on all my clothes and John's, and she wished we would be more careful!

Did not that sound innocent? But I know she was studying that pattern, and I am determined that nobody shall find it out but myself!

Life is very much more exciting now than it used to be. You see I have something more to expect, to look forward to, to watch. I really do eat better, and am more quiet than I was.

John is so pleased to see me improve! He laughed a little the other day, and said I seemed to be flourishing in spite of my wall-paper.

I turned it off with a laugh. I had no intention of telling him it was *because* of the wall-paper—he would make fun of me. He might even want to take me away.

I don't want to leave now until I have found it out. There is a week more, and I think that will be enough.

I'm feeling ever so much better! I don't sleep much at night, for it is so interesting to watch developments; but I sleep a good deal in the daytime.

In the daytime it is tiresome and perplexing.

There are always new shoots on the fungus, and new shades of yellow all over it. I cannot keep count of them, though I have tried conscientiously.

It is the strangest yellow, that wall-paper! It makes me think of all the yellow things I ever saw—not beautiful ones like buttercups, but old foul, bad yellow things.

But there is something else about that paper—the smell! I noticed it the moment we came into the room, but with so much air and sun it was not bad. Now we have had a week of fog and rain, and whether the windows are open or not, the smell is here.

It creeps all over the house.

I find it hovering in the dining-room, skulking in the parlor, hiding in the hall, lying in wait for me on the stairs.

It gets into my hair.

Even when I go to ride, if I turn my head suddenly and surprise it—there is that smell!

Such a peculiar odor, too! I have spent hours in trying to analyze it, to find what it smelled like.

It is not bad—at first, and very gentle, but quite the subtlest, most enduring odor I ever met.

In this damp weather it is awful, I wake up in the night and find it hanging over me.

It used to disturb me at first. I thought seriously of burning the house—to reach the smell.

But now I am used to it. The only thing I can think of that it is like is the *color* of the paper! A yellow smell.

There is a very funny mark on this wall, low down, near the mopboard. A streak that runs round the room. It goes behind every piece of furniture, except the bed, a long, straight, even *smooch*, as if it had been rubbed over and over.

I wonder how it was done and who did it, and what they did it for. Round and round and round—round and round and round—it makes me dizzy!

I really have discovered something at last.

Through watching so much at night, when it changes so, I have finally found out.

The front pattern *does* move—and no wonder! The woman behind shakes it!

Sometimes I think there are a great many women behind, and sometimes only one, and she crawls around fast, and her crawling shakes it all over.

Then in the very bright spots she keeps still, and in the very shady spots she just takes hold of the bars and shakes them hard.

And she is all the time trying to climb through. But nobody could climb through that pattern—it strangles so; I think that is why it has so many heads.

They get through, and then the pattern strangles them off and turns them upside down, and makes their eyes white!

If those heads were covered or taken off it would not be half so bad.

I think that woman gets out in the daytime!

And I'll tell you why—privately—I've seen her!

I can see her out of every one of my windows!

It is the same woman, I know, for she is always creeping, and most women do not creep by daylight.

I see her on that long road under the trees, creeping along, and when a carriage comes she hides under the blackberry vines.

I don't blame her a bit. It must be very humiliating to be caught creeping by daylight!

I always lock the door when I creep by daylight. I can't do it at night, for I know John would suspect something at once.

And John is so queer now, that I don't want to irritate him. I wish he would take another room! Besides, I don't want anybody to get that woman out at night but myself.

I often wonder if I could see her out of all the windows at once.

But, turn as fast as I can, I can only see out of one at one time.

And though I always see her, she *may* be able to creep faster than I can turn!

I have watched her sometimes away off in the open country, creeping as fast as a cloud shadow in a high wind.

If only that top pattern could be gotten off from the under one! I mean to try it, little by little.

I have found out another funny thing, but I shan't tell it this time! It does not do to trust people too much.

There are only two more days to get this paper off, and I believe John is beginning to notice. I don't like the look in his eyes.

And I heard him ask Jennie a lot of professional questions about me. She had a very good report to give.

She said I slept a good deal in the daytime.

John knows I don't sleep very well at night, for all I'm so quiet!

He asked me all sorts of questions, too, and pretended to be very loving and kind.

As if I couldn't see through him!

Still, I don't wonder he acts so, sleeping under this paper for three months.

It only interests me, but I feel sure John and Jennie are secretly affected by it.

Hurrah! This is the last day, but it is enough. John to stay in town over night, and won't be out until this evening.

Jennie wanted to sleep with me—the sly thing! but I told her I should undoubtedly rest better for a night all alone.

That was clever, for really I wasn't alone a bit! As soon as it was moonlight and that poor thing began to crawl and shake the pattern, I got up and ran to help her.

I pulled and she shook, I shook and she pulled, and before morning we had peeled off yards of that paper.

A strip about as high as my head and half around the room.

And then when the sun came and that awful pattern began to laugh at me, I declared I would finish it to-day!

We go away to-morrow, and they are moving all my furniture down again to leave things as they were before.

Jennie looked at the wall in amazement, but I told her merrily that I did it out of pure spite at the vicious thing.

She laughed and said she wouldn't mind doing it herself, but I must not get tired.

How she betrayed herself that time!

But I am here, and no person touches this paper but me,—not *alive!*

She tried to get me out of the room—it was too patent! But I said it was so quiet and empty and clean now that I believed I would lie down again and sleep all I could; and not to wake me even for dinner—I would call when I woke.

So now she is gone, and the servants are gone, and the things are gone, and there is nothing left but that great bedstead nailed down, with the canvas mattress we found on it.

We shall sleep downstairs to-night, and take the boat home to-morrow.

I quite enjoy the room, now it is bare again.

How those children did tear about here!

This bedstead is fairly gnawed!

But I must get to work.

I have locked the door and thrown the key down into the front path.

I don't want to go out, and I don't want to have anybody come in, till John comes.

I want to astonish him.

I've got a rope up here that even Jennie did not find. If that woman does get out, and tries to get away, I can tie her!

But I forgot I could not reach far without anything to stand on!

This bed will *not* move!

I tried to lift and push it until I was lame, and then I got so angry I bit off a little piece at one corner—but it hurt my teeth.

Then I peeled off all the paper I could reach standing on the floor. It sticks horribly and the pattern just enjoys it! All those strangled heads and bulbous eyes and waddling fungus growths just shriek with derision!

I am getting angry enough to do something desperate. To jump out of the window would be admirable exercise, but the bars are too strong even to try.

Besides I wouldn't do it. Of course not. I know well enough that a step like that is improper and might be misconstrued.

I don't like to *look* out of the windows even—there are so many of those creeping women, and they creep so fast.

I wonder if they all come out of that wall-paper as I did?

But I am securely fastened now by my well-hidden rope—you don't get *me* out in the road there!

I suppose I shall have to get back behind the pattern when it comes night, and that is hard!

It is so pleasant to be out in this great room and creep around as I please!

I don't want to go outside. I won't, even if Jennie asks me to.

For outside you have to creep on the ground, and everything is green instead of yellow.

But here I can creep smoothly on the floor, and my shoulder just fits in that long smooch around the wall, so I cannot lose my way.

Why there's John at the door!

It is no use, young man, you can't open it!

How he does call and pound!

Now he's crying for an axe.

It would be a shame to break down that beautiful door!

"John dear!" said I in the gentlest voice, "the key is down by the front steps, under a plantain leaf!"

That silenced him for a few moments.

Then he said—very quietly indeed, "Open the door, my darling!"

"I can't," said I. "The key is down by the front door under a plantain leaf!"

And then I said it again, several times, very gently and slowly, and said it so often that he had to go and see, and he got it of course, and came in. He stopped short by the door.

"What is the matter?" he cried. "For God's sake, what are you doing!"

I kept on creeping just the same, but I looked at him over my shoulder.

"I've got out at last," said I, "in spite of you and Jane. And I've pulled off most of the paper, so you can't put me back!"

Now why should that man have fainted? But he did, and right across my path by the wall, so that I had to creep over him every time!

William Faulkner

A Rose for Emily

Psychological investigation in the Gothic mode is a characteristic of Faulkner's major work. One thinks of the central chapter of *As I Lay Dying* (the interior monologue of a corpse) or the brutal horrors of *Sanctuary*. But the precision and clarity and quiet monstrosity of "A Rose for Emily" represents his central contribution to horror fiction, in the period of transition from supernatural to psychological horror as the major mode of the literature, when D. H. Lawrence and Conrad Aiken and many others were investigating the abnormal in some of the major short fiction of the period. Often reprinted, "A Rose for Emily" is one of the most perfect and enduring classics of the century.

I

When Miss Emily Grierson died, our whole town went to her funeral: the men through a sort of respectful affection for a fallen monument, the women mostly out of curiosity to see the inside of her house, which no one save an old man-servant—a combined gardener and cook—had seen in at least ten years.

It was a big, squarish frame house that had once been white, decorated with cupolas and spires and scrolled balconies in the heavily lightsome style of the Seventies, set on what had once been our most select street. But garages and cotton gins had encroached and obliterated even the august names of that neighborhood; only Miss Emily's house was left, lifting its stubborn and coquettish decay above the cotton wagons and the gasoline pumps—an eyesore among eyesores. And now Miss Emily had gone to join the representatives of those august names where they lay in the cedar-bemused cemetery among the ranked and anonymous graves of Union and Confederate soldiers who fell at the battle of Jefferson.

Alive, Miss Emily had been a tradition, a duty, and a care; a sort of hereditary obligation upon the town, dating from that day in 1891 when Colonel Sartoris, the mayor—he who fathered the edict that no Negro woman should appear on the streets without an apron—remitted her taxes, the dispensation dating from the death of her father on into perpetuity. Not that Miss Emily would have accepted charity. Colonel Sartoris invented an involved tale to the effect that Miss Emily's father had loaned money to the town, which the town, as a matter of business, preferred this way of repaying.

Only a man of Colonel Sartoris' generation and thought could have invented it, and only a woman could have believed it.

When the next generation, with its more modern ideas, became mayors and aldermen, this arrangement created some little dissatisfaction. On the first of the year they mailed her a tax notice. February came, and there was no reply. They wrote her a formal letter, asking her to call at the sheriff's office at her convenience. A week later the mayor wrote her himself, offering to call or to send his car for her, and received in reply a note on paper of an archaic shape, in a thin, flowing calligraphy in faded ink, to the effect that she no longer went out at all. The tax notice was also enclosed, without comment.

They called a special meeting of the Board of Aldermen. A deputation waited upon her, knocked at the door through which no visitor had passed since she ceased giving china-painting lessons eight or ten years earlier. They were admitted by the old Negro into a dim hall from which a stairway mounted into still more shadow. It smelled of dust and disuse—a close, dank smell. The Negro led them into the parlor. It was furnished in heavy, leather-covered furniture. When the Negro opened the blinds of one window, they could see that the leather was cracked; and when they sat down, a faint dust rose sluggishly about their thighs, spinning with slow motes in the single sun-ray. On a tarnished gilt easel before the fireplace stood a crayon portrait of Miss Emily's father.

They rose when she entered—a small, fat woman in black, with a thin gold chain descending to her waist and vanishing into her belt, leaning on an ebony cane with a tarnished gold head. Her skeleton was small and spare; perhaps that was why what would have been merely plumpness in another was obesity in her. She looked bloated, like a body long submerged in motionless water, and of that pallid hue. Her eyes, lost in the fatty ridges of her face, looked like two small pieces of coal pressed into a lump of dough as they moved from one face to another while the visitors stated their errand.

She did not ask them to sit. She just stood in the door and listened quietly until the spokesman came to a stumbling halt. Then they could hear the invisible watch ticking at the end of the gold chain.

Her voice was dry and cold. "I have no taxes in Jefferson. Colonel Sartoris explained it to me. Perhaps one of you can gain access to the city records and satisfy yourselves."

"But we have. We are the city authorities, Miss Emily. Didn't you get a notice from the sheriff, signed by him?"

"I received a paper, yes," Miss Emily said. "Perhaps he considers himself the sheriff . . . I have no taxes in Jefferson."

"But there is nothing on the books to show that, you see. We must go by the—"

"See Colonel Sartoris. I have no taxes in Jefferson."

"But, Miss Emily—"

"See Colonel Sartoris." (Colonel Sartoris had been dead almost ten years.) "I have no taxes in Jefferson. Tobe!" The Negro appeared. "Show these gentlemen out."

II

So she vanquished them, horse and foot, just as she had vanquished their
fathers thirty years before about the smell. That was two years after her
father's death and a short time after her sweetheart—the one we believed
would marry her—had deserted her. After her father's death she went out
very little; after her sweetheart went away, people hardly saw her at all. A few
of the ladies had the temerity to call, but were not received, and the only sign
of life about the place was the Negro man—a young man then—going in and
out with a market basket.

"Just as if a man—any man—could keep a kitchen properly," the ladies
said; so they were not surprised when the smell developed. It was another
link between the gross, teeming world and the high and mighty Griersons.

A neighbor, a woman, complained to the mayor, Judge Stevens, eighty
years old.

"But what will you have me do about it, madam?" he said.

"Why, send her word to stop it," the woman said. "Isn't there a law?"

"I'm sure that won't be necessary," Judge Stevens said. "It's probably just
a snake or a rat that nigger of hers killed in the yard. I'll speak to him about
it."

The next day he received two more complaints, one from a man who came
in diffident deprecation. "We really must do something about it, Judge. I'd
be the last one in the world to bother Miss Emily, but we've got to do
something." That night the Board of Aldermen met—three graybeards and
one younger man, a member of the rising generation.

"It's simple enough," he said. "Send her word to have her place cleaned
up. Give her a certain time to do it in, and if she don't . . ."

"Dammit, sir," Judge Stevens said, "will you accuse a lady to her face of
smelling bad?"

So the next night, after midnight, four men crossed Miss Emily's lawn and
slunk about the house like burglars, sniffing along the base of the brickwork
and at the cellar openings while one of them performed a regular sowing
motion with his hand out of a sack slung from his shoulder. They broke open
the cellar door and sprinkled lime there, and in all the outbuildings. As they
recrossed the lawn, a window that had been dark was lighted and Miss Emily
sat in it, the light behind her, and her upright torso motionless as that of an
idol. They crept quietly across the lawn and into the shadow of the locusts
that lined the street. After a week or two the smell went away.

That was when people had begun to feel really sorry for her. People in our
town, remembering how Old Lady Wyatt, her great-aunt, had gone completely crazy at last, believed that the Griersons held themselves a little too
high for what they really were. None of the young men was quite good
enough to Miss Emily and such. We had long thought of them as a tableau:
Miss Emily a slender figure in white in the background, her father a
spraddled silhouette in the foreground, his back to her and clutching a

horsewhip, the two of them framed by the back-flung front door. So when she got to be thirty and was still single, we were not pleased exactly, but vindicated; even with insanity in the family she wouldn't have turned down all of her chances if they had really materialized.

When her father died, it got about that the house was all that was left to her; and in a way, people were glad. At last they could pity Miss Emily. Being left alone, and a pauper, she had become humanized. Now she too would know the old thrill and the old despair of a penny more or less.

The day after his death all the ladies prepared to call at the house and offer condolence and aid, as is our custom. Miss Emily met them at the door, dressed as usual and with no trace of grief on her face. She told them that her father was not dead. She did that for three days, with the ministers calling on her, and the doctors, trying to persuade her to let them dispose of the body. Just as they were about to resort to law and force, she broke down, and they buried her father quickly.

We did not say she was crazy then. We believed she had to do that. We remembered all the young men her father had driven away, and we knew that with nothing left, she would have to cling to that which had robbed her, as people will.

III

She was sick for a long time. When we saw her again, her hair was cut short, making her look like a girl, with a vague resemblance to those angels in colored church windows—sort of tragic and serene.

The town had just let the contracts for paving the sidewalks, and in the summer after her father's death they began the work. The construction company came with niggers and mules and machinery, and a foreman named Homer Barron, a Yankee—a big, dark, ready man, with a big voice and eyes lighter than his face. The little boys would follow in groups to hear him cuss the niggers, and the niggers singing in time to the rise and fall of picks. Pretty soon he knew everybody in town. Whenever you heard a lot of laughing anywhere about the square, Homer Barron would be in the center of the group. Presently we began to see him and Miss Emily on Sunday afternoons driving in the yellow-wheeled buggy and the matched team of bays from the livery stable.

At first we were glad that Miss Emily would have an interest, because the ladies all said, "Of course a Grierson would not think seriously of a Northerner, a day laborer." But there were still others, older people, who said that even grief could not cause a real lady to forget *noblesse oblige*—without calling it *noblesse oblige*. They just said, "Poor Emily. Her kinsfolk should come to her." She had some kin in Alabama; but years ago her father had fallen out with them over the estate of Old Lady Wyatt, the crazy woman, and there was no communication between the two families. They had not even been represented at the funeral.

And as soon as the old people said, "Poor Emily," the whispering began.

"Do you suppose it's really so?" they said to one another. "Of course it is. What else could . . ." This behind their hands; rustling of craned silk and satin behind jalousies closed upon the sun of Sunday afternoon as the thin, swift clop-clop-clop of the matched team passed: "Poor Emily."

She carried her head high enough—even when we believed that she was fallen. It was as if she demanded more than ever the recognition of her dignity as the last Grierson; as if it had wanted that touch of earthiness to reaffirm her imperviousness. Like when she bought the rat poison, the arsenic. That was over a year after they had begun to say "Poor Emily," and while the two female cousins were visiting her.

"I want some poison," she said to the druggist. She was over thirty then, still a slight woman, though thinner than usual, with cold, haughty black eyes in a face the flesh of which was strained across the temples and about the eye-sockets as you imagine a lighthouse-keeper's face ought to look. "I want some poison," she said.

"Yes, Miss Emily. What kind? For rats and such? I'd recom—"

"I want the best you have. I don't care what kind."

The druggist named several. "They'll kill anything up to an elephant. But what you want is—"

"Arsenic," Miss Emily said. "Is that a good one?"

"Is . . . arsenic? Yes, ma'am. But what you want—"

"I want arsenic."

The druggist looked down at her. She looked back at him, erect, her face like a strained flag. "Why, of course," the druggist said. "If that's what you want. But the law requires you to tell what you are going to use it for."

Miss Emily just stared at him, her head tilted back in order to look him eye for eye, until he looked away and went and got the arsenic and wrapped it up. The Negro delivery boy brought her the package; the druggist didn't come back. When she opened the package at home there was written on the box, under the skull and bones: "For rats."

IV

So the next day we all said, "She will kill herself"; and we said it would be the best thing. When she had first begun to be seen with Homer Barron, we had said, "She will marry him." Then we said, "She will persuade him yet," because Homer himself had remarked—he liked men, and it was known that he drank with the younger men in the Elks' Club—that he was not a marrying man. Later we said, "Poor Emily" behind the jalousies as they passed on Sunday afternoon in the glittering buggy, Miss Emily with her head high and Homer Barron with his hat cocked and a cigar in his teeth, reins and whip in a yellow glove.

Then some of the ladies began to say that it was a disgrace to the town and a bad example to the young people. The men did not want to interfere, but at last the ladies forced the Baptist minister—Miss Emily's people were Episcopal—to call upon her. He would never divulge what happened during that interview, but he refused to go back again. The next Sunday they again drove about the streets, and the following day the minister's wife wrote to Miss Emily's relations in Alabama.

So she had blood-kin under her roof again and we sat back to watch developments. At first nothing happened. Then we were sure that they were to be married. We learned that Miss Emily had been to the jeweler's and ordered a man's toilet set in silver, with the letters H.B. on each piece. Two days later we learned that she had bought a complete outfit of men's clothing, including a nightshirt, and we said, "They are married." We were really glad. We were glad because the two female cousins were even more Grierson than Miss Emily had ever been.

So we were not surprised when Homer Barron—the streets had been finished some time since—was gone. We were a little disappointed that there was not a public blowing-off, but we believed that he had gone on to prepare for Miss Emily's coming, or to give her a chance to get rid of the cousins. (By that time it was a cabal, and we were all Miss Emily's allies to help circumvent the cousins.) Sure enough, after another week they departed. And, as we had expected all along, within three days Homer Barron was back in town. A neighbor saw the Negro man admit him at the kitchen door at dusk one evening.

And that was the last we saw of Homer Barron. And of Miss Emily for some time. The Negro man went in and out with the market basket, but the front door remained closed. Now and then we would see her at a window for a moment, as the men did that night when they sprinkled the lime, but for almost six months she did not appear on the streets. Then we knew that this was to be expected too; as if that quality of her father which had thwarted her woman's life so many times had been too virulent and too furious to die.

When we next saw Miss Emily, she had grown fat and her hair was turning gray. During the next few years it grew grayer and grayer until it attained an even pepper-and-salt iron-gray, when it ceased turning. Up to the day of her death at seventy-four it was still that vigorous iron-gray, like the hair of an active man.

From that time on her front door remained closed, save for a period of six or seven years, when she was about forty, during which she gave lessons in china-painting. She fitted up a studio in one of the downstairs rooms, where the daughters and granddaughters of Colonel Sartoris' contemporaries were sent to her with the same regularity and in the same spirit that they were sent to church on Sundays with a twenty-five-cent piece for the collection plate. Meanwhile her taxes had been remitted.

Then the newer generation became the backbone and the spirit of the town, and the painting pupils grew up and fell away and did not send their children to her with boxes of color and tedious brushes and pictures cut from the ladies' magazines. The front door closed upon the last one and remained closed for good. When the town got free postal delivery, Miss Emily alone refused to let them fasten the metal numbers above her door and attach a mailbox to it. She would not listen to them.

Daily, monthly, yearly we watched the Negro grow grayer and more stooped, going in and out with the market basket. Each December we sent her a tax notice, which would be returned by the post office a week later, unclaimed. Now and then we would see her in one of the downstairs windows—she had evidently shut up the top floor of the house—like the carven torso of an idol in a niche, looking or not looking at us, we could never tell which. Thus she passed from generation to generation—dear, inescapable, impervious, tranquil, and perverse.

And so she died. Fell ill in the house filled with dust and shadows, with only a doddering Negro man to wait on her. We did not even know she was sick; we had long since given up trying to get any information from the Negro. He talked to no one, probably not even to her, for his voice had grown harsh and rusty, as if from disuse.

She died in one of the downstairs rooms, in a heavy walnut bed with a curtain, her gray head propped on a pillow yellow and moldy with age and lack of sunlight.

V

The Negro met the first of the ladies at the front door and let them in, with their hushed, sibilant voices and their quick, curious glances, and then he disappeared. He walked right through the house and out the back and was not seen again.

The two female cousins came at once. They held the funeral on the second day, with the town coming to look at Miss Emily beneath a mass of bought flowers, with the crayon face of her father musing profoundly above the bier and the ladies sibilant and macabre; and the very old men—some in their brushed Confederate uniforms—on the porch and the lawn, talking of Miss Emily as if she had been a contemporary of theirs, believing that they had danced with her and courted her perhaps, confusing time with its mathematical progression, as the old do, to whom all the past is not a diminishing road but, instead, a huge meadow which no winter ever quite touches, divided from them now by the narrow bottle-neck of the most recent decade of years.

Already we knew that there was one room in that region above stairs which no one had seen in forty years, and which would have to be forced. They waited until Miss Emily was decently in the ground before they opened it.

The violence of breaking down the door seemed to fill this room with pervading dust. A thin, acrid pall as of the tomb seemed to lie everywhere upon this room decked and furnished as for a bridal: upon the valence curtains of faded rose color, upon the rose-shaded lights, upon the dressing table, upon the delicate array of crystal and the man's toilet things backed with tarnished silver, silver so tarnished that the monogram was obscured. Among them lay a collar and tie, as if they had just been removed, which, lifted, left upon the surface a pale crescent in the dust. Upon a chair hung the suit, carefully folded; beneath it the two mute shoes and the discarded socks.

The man himself lay in the bed.

For a long while we just stood there, looking down at the profound and fleshless grin. The body had apparently once lain in the attitude of an embrace, but now the long sleep that outlasts love, that conquers even the grimace of love, had cuckolded him. What was left of him, rotted beneath what was left of the nightshirt, had become inextricable from the bed in which he lay; and upon him and upon the pillow beside him lay that even coating of the patient and biding dust.

Then we noticed that in the second pillow was the indentation of a head. One of us lifted something from it, and leaning forward, that faint and invisible dust dry and acrid in the nostrils, we saw a long strand of iron-gray hair.

Robert Hichens

How Love Came to Professor Guildea

Hichens' masterpiece is one of the greatest of all horror stories, successful both as a moral investigation and as psychological anatomy, but it is in the latter area that it excels, rising above its contemporaries to stand beside Oliver Onions' "The Beckoning Fair One" and Le Fanu's "Carmilla" and Henry James' "The Turn of the Screw" as one of the landmarks of the novella form. It is a deconstruction of Victorian Christian morality under the guise of a moral tale that provides provocative contrasts on the one hand to Lucy Clifford's "The New Mother" and on the other to Oliver Onions' "The Beckoning Fair One." Onions alters the structure further by replacing Father Murchison's narrative view with that of an independent woman reporter, showing a break in horror and supernatural fiction of the period from the overt moral center to progressive interest in psychological investigation. Onions leads us toward the nonsupernatural and feminist consciousness of Gilman, and later, Russ.

I

Dull people often wondered how it came about that Father Murchison and Professor Frederic Guildea were intimate friends. The one was all faith, the other all scepticism. The nature of the Father was based on love. He viewed the world with an almost childlike tenderness above his long, black cassock; and his mild, yet perfectly fearless, blue eyes seemed always to be watching the goodness that exists in humanity, and rejoicing at what they saw. The Professor, on the other hand, had a hard face like a hatchet, tipped with an aggressive black goatee beard. His eyes were quick, piercing and irreverent. The lines about his small, thin-lipped mouth were almost cruel. His voice was harsh and dry, sometimes, when he grew energetic, almost soprano. It fired off words with a sharp and clipping utterance. His habitual manner was one of distrust and investigation. It was impossible to suppose that, in his busy life, he found any time for love, either of humanity in general or of an individual.

Yet his days were spent in scientific investigations which conferred immense benefits upon the world.

Both men were celibates. Father Murchison was a member of an Anglican order which forbade him to marry. Professor Guildea had a poor opinion of most things, but especially of women. He had formerly held a post as lecturer at Birmingham. But when his fame as a discoverer grew, he removed

to London. There, at a lecture he gave in the East End, he first met Father
Murchison. They spoke a few words. Perhaps the bright intelligence of the
priest appealed to the man of science, who was inclined, as a rule, to regard
the clergy with some contempt. Perhaps the transparent sincerity of this
devotee, full of common sense, attracted him. As he was leaving the hall he
abruptly asked the Father to call on him at his house in Hyde Park Place.
And the Father, who seldom went into the West End, except to preach,
accepted the invitation.

"When will you come?" said Guildea.

He was folding up the blue paper on which his notes were written in a tiny,
clear hand. The leaves rustled drily in accompaniment to his sharp, dry
voice.

"On Sunday week I am preaching in the evening at St. Saviour's, not far
off," said the Father.

"I don't go to church."

"No," said the Father, without any accent of surprise or condemnation.

"Come to supper afterwards?"

"Thank you, I will."

"What time will you come?"

The Father smiled.

"As soon as I have finished my sermon. The service is at six-thirty."

"About eight then, I suppose. Don't make the sermon too long. My
number in Hyde Park Place is 100. Good-night to you."

He snapped an elastic band round his papers and strode off without
shaking hands.

On the appointed Sunday, Father Murchison preached to a densely
crowded congregation at St. Saviour's. The subject of his sermon was
sympathy, and the comparative uselessness of man in the world unless he
can learn to love his neighbour as himself. The sermon was rather long, and
when the preacher, in his flowing, black cloak, and his hard, round hat, with
a straight brim over which hung the ends of a black cord, made his way
towards the Professor's house, the hands of the illuminated clock disc at the
Marble Arch pointed to twenty minutes past eight.

The Father hurried on, pushing his way through the crowd of standing
soldiers, chattering women and giggling street boys in their Sunday best. It
was a warm April night, and, when he reached number 100, Hyde Park
Place, he found the Professor bareheaded on his doorstep, gazing out
towards the Park railings, and enjoying the soft, moist air, in front of his
lighted passage.

"Ha, a long sermon!" he exclaimed. "Come in."

"I fear it was," said the Father, obeying the invitation. "I am that
dangerous thing—an extempore preacher."

"More attractive to speak without notes, if you can do it. Hang your hat
and coat—oh, cloak—here. We'll have supper at once. This is the dining
room."

He opened a door on the right and they entered a long, narrow room, with
a gold paper and a black ceiling, from which hung an electric lamp with a
gold-coloured shade. In the room stood a small oval table with covers laid

for two. The Professor rang the bell. Then he said:

"People seem to talk better at an oval table than at a square one."

"Really? Is that so?"

"Well, I've had precisely the same party twice, once at a square table, once at an oval table. The first dinner was a dull failure, the second a brilliant success. Sit down, won't you?"

"How d'you account for the difference?" said the Father, sitting down, and pulling the tail of his cassock well under him.

"H'm. I know how you'd account for it."

"Indeed. How then?"

"At an oval table, since there are no corners, the chain of human sympathy—the electric current, is much more complete. Eh! Let me give you some soup."

"Thank you."

The Father took it, and, as he did so, turned his beaming blue eyes on his host. Then he smiled.

"What!" he said, in his pleasant, light tenor voice. "You do go to church sometimes, then?"

"To-night is the first time for ages. And, mind you, I was tremendously bored."

The Father still smiled, and his blue eyes gently twinkled.

"Dear, dear!" he said, "what a pity!"

"But not by the sermon," Guildea added. "I don't pay a compliment. I state a fact. The sermon didn't bore me. If it had, I should have said so, or said nothing."

"And which would you have done?"

The Professor smiled almost genially.

"Don't know," he said. "What wine d'you drink?"

"None, thank you. I'm a teetotaller. In my profession and *milieu* it is necessary to be one. Yes, I will have some soda water. I think you would have done the first."

"Very likely, and very wrongly. You wouldn't have minded much."

"I don't think I should."

They were intimate already. The Father felt most pleasantly at home under the black ceiling. He drank some soda water and seemed to enjoy it more than the Professor enjoyed his claret.

"You smile at the theory of the chain of human sympathy, I see," said the Father. "Then what is your explanation of the failure of your square party with corners, the success of your oval party without them?"

"Probably on the first occasion the wit of the assembly had a chill on his liver, while on the second he was in perfect health. Yet, you see, I stick to the oval table."

"And that means—"

"Very little. By the way, your omission of any allusion to the notorious part liver plays in love was a serious one to-night."

"Your omission of any desire for close human sympathy in your life is a more serious one."

"How can you be sure I have no such desire?"

"I divine it. Your look, your manner, tell me it is so. You were disagreeing with my sermon all the time I was preaching. Weren't you?"

"Part of the time."

The servant changed the plates. He was a middle-aged, blond, thin man, with a stony white face, pale, prominent eyes, and an accomplished manner of service. When he had left the room the Professor continued.

"Your remarks interested me, but I thought them exaggerated."

"For instance?"

"Let me play the egoist for a moment. I spend most of my time in hard work, very hard work. The results of this work, you will allow, benefit humanity."

"Enormously," assented the Father, thinking of more than one of Guildea's discoveries.

"And the benefit conferred by this work, undertaken merely for its own sake, is just as great as if it were undertaken because I loved my fellow man, and sentimentally desired to see him more comfortable than he is at present. I'm as useful precisely in my present condition of—in my present non-affectional condition—as I should be if I were as full of gush as the sentimentalists who want to get murderers out of prison, or to put a premium on tyranny—like Tolstoi—by preventing the punishment of tyrants."

"One may do great harm with affection; great good without it. Yes, that is true. Even *le bon motif* is not everything, I know. Still I contend that, given your powers, you would be far more useful in the world with sympathy, affection for your kind, added to them than as you are. I believe even that you would do still more splendid work."

The Professor poured himself another glass of claret.

"You noticed my butler?" he said.

"I did."

"He's a perfect servant. He makes me perfectly comfortable. Yet he has no feeling of liking for me. I treat him civilly. I pay him well. But I never think about him, or concern myself with him as a human being. I know nothing of his character except what I read of it in his last master's letter. There are, you may say, no truly human relations between us. You would affirm that his work would be better done if I had made him personally like me as a man—of any class—can like a man—of any other class?"

"I should, decidedly."

"I contend that he couldn't do his work better than he does it at present."

"But if any crisis occurred?"

"What?"

"Any crisis, change in your condition. If you needed his help, not only as a man and a butler, but as a man and a brother? He'd fail you then, probably. You would never get from your servant that finest service which can only be prompted by an honest affection."

"You have finished?"

"Quite."

"Let us go upstairs then. Yes, those are good prints. I picked them up in Birmingham when I was living there. This is my workroom."

They came to a double room lined entirely with books, and brilliantly, rather hardly, lit by electricity. The windows at one end looked on to the Park, at the other on to the garden of a neighbouring house. The door by which they entered was concealed from the inner and smaller room by the jutting wall of the outer room, in which stood a huge writing table loaded with letters, pamphlets and manuscripts. Between the two windows of the inner room was a cage in which a large, grey parrot was clambering, using both beak and claws to assist him in his slow and meditative peregrinations.

"You have a pet," said the Father, surprised.

"I possess a parrot," the Professor answered drily. "I got him for a purpose when I was making a study of the imitative powers of birds, and I have never got rid of him. A cigar?"

"Thank you."

They sat down. Father Murchison glanced at the parrot. It had paused in its journey, and, clinging to the bars of its cage, was regarding them with attentive round eyes that looked deliberately intelligent, but by no means sympathetic. He looked away from it to Guildea, who was smoking, with his head thrown back, his sharp, pointed chin, on which the small black beard bristled, upturned. He was moving his under lip up and down rapidly. This action caused the beard to stir and look peculiarly aggressive. The Father suddenly chuckled softly.

"Why's that?" cried Guildea, letting his chin drop down on his breast and looking at his guest sharply.

"I was thinking it would have to be a crisis indeed that could make you cling to your butler's affection for assistance."

Guildea smiled too.

"You're right. It would. Here he comes."

The man entered with coffee. He offered it gently, and retired like a shadow retreating on a wall.

"Splendid, inhuman fellow," remarked Guildea.

"I prefer the East End lad who does my errands in Bird Street," said the Father. "I know all his worries. He knows some of mine. We are friends. He's more noisy than your man. He even breathes hard when he is especially solicitous, but he would do more for me than put the coals on my fire, or black my square-toed boots."

"Men are differently made. To me the watchful eye of affection would be abominable."

"What about that bird?"

The Father pointed to the parrot. It had got up on its perch and, with one foot uplifted in an impressive, almost benedictory, manner, was gazing steadily at the Professor.

"That's the watchful eye of imitation, with a mind at the back of it, desirous of reproducing the peculiarities of others. No, I thought your sermon to-night very fresh, very clever. But I have no wish for affection. Reasonable liking, of course, one desires"—he tugged sharply at his beard, as if to warn himself against sentimentality—"but anything more would be most irksome, and would push me, I feel sure, towards cruelty. It would also hamper one's work."

"I don't think so."

"The sort of work I do. I shall continue to benefit the world without loving it, and it will continue to accept the benefits without loving me. That's all as it should be."

He drank his coffee. Then he added rather aggressively:

"I have neither time nor inclination for sentimentality."

When Guildea let Father Murchison out, he followed the Father on to the doorstep and stood there for a moment. The Father glanced across the damp road into the Park.

"I see you've got a gate just opposite you," he said idly.

"Yes. I often slip across for a stroll to clear my brain. Good-night to you. Come again some day."

"With pleasure. Good-night."

The Priest strode away, leaving Guildea standing on the step.

Father Murchison came many times again to number 100, Hyde Park Place. He had a feeling of liking for most men and women whom he knew, and of tenderness for all, whether he knew them or not, but he grew to have a special sentiment towards Guildea. Strangely enough, it was a sentiment of pity. He pitied this hard-working, eminently successful man of big brain and bold heart, who never seemed depressed, who never wanted assistance, who never complained of the twisted skein of life or faltered in his progress along its way. The Father pitied Guildea, in fact, because Guildea wanted so little. He had told him so, for the intercourse of the two men, from the beginning, had been singularly frank.

One evening, when they were talking together, the Father happened to speak of one of the oddities of life, the fact that those who do not want things often get them, while those who seek them vehemently are disappointed in their search.

"Then I ought to have affection poured upon me," said Guildea, smiling rather grimly. "For I hate it."

"Perhaps some day you will."

"I hope not, most sincerely."

Father Murchison said nothing for a moment. He was drawing together the ends of the broad band round his cassock. When he spoke he seemed to be answering someone.

"Yes," he said slowly, "yes, that *is* my feeling—pity."

"For whom?" said the Professor.

Then, suddenly, he understood. He did not say that he understood, but Father Murchison felt, and saw, that it was quite unnecessary to answer his friend's question. So Guildea, strangely enough, found himself closely acquainted with a man—his opposite in all ways—who pitied him.

The fact that he did not mind this, and scarcely ever thought about it, shows perhaps as clearly as anything could, the peculiar indifference of his nature.

II

One Autumn evening, a year and a half after Father Murchison and the Professor had first met, the Father called in Hyde Park Place and enquired of the blond and stony butler—his name was Pitting—whether his master was at home.

"Yes, sir," replied Pitting. "Will you please come this way?"

He moved noiselessly up the rather narrow stairs, followed by the Father, tenderly opened the library door, and in his soft, cold voice, announced:

"Father Murchison."

Guildea was sitting in an armchair, before a small fire. His thin, long-fingered hands lay outstretched upon his knees, his head was sunk down on his chest. He appeared to be pondering deeply. Pitting very slightly raised his voice.

"Father Murchison to see you, sir," he repeated.

The Professor jumped up rather suddenly and turned sharply round as the Father came in.

"Oh," he said. "It's you, is it? Glad to see you. Come to the fire."

The Father glanced at him and thought him looking unusually fatigued.

"You don't look well tonight," the Father said.

"No?"

"You must be working too hard. That lecture you are going to give in Paris is bothering you?"

"Not a bit. It's all arranged. I could deliver it to you at this moment verbatim. Well, sit down."

The Father did so, and Guildea sank once more into his chair and stared hard into the fire without another word. He seemed to be thinking profoundly. His friend did not interrupt him, but quietly lit a pipe and began to smoke reflectively. The eyes of Guildea were fixed upon the fire. The Father glanced about the room, at the walls of soberly bound books, at the crowded writing-table, at the windows, before which hung heavy, dark-blue curtains of old brocade, at the cage, which stood between them. A green baize covering was thrown over it. The Father wondered why. He had never seen Napoleon—so the parrot was named—covered up at night before. While he was looking at the baize, Guildea suddenly jerked up his head, and, taking his hands from his knees and clasping them, said abruptly:

"D'you think I'm an attractive man?"

Father Murchison jumped. Such a question coming from such a man astounded him.

"Bless me!" he ejaculated. "What makes you ask? Do you mean attractive to the opposite sex?"

"That's what I don't know," said the Professor gloomily, and staring again into the fire. "That's what I don't know."

The Father grew more astonished.

"Don't know!" he exclaimed.

And he laid down his pipe.

"Let's say—d'you think I'm attractive, that there's anything about me which might draw a—a human being, or an animal irresistibly to me?"

"Whether you desired it or not?"

"Exactly—or—no, let us say definitely—if I did not desire it."

Father Murchison pursed up his rather full, cherubic lips, and little wrinkles appeared about the corners of his blue eyes.

"There might be, of course," he said, after a pause. "Human nature is weak, engagingly weak, Guildea. And you're inclined to flout it. I could understand a certain class of lady—the lion-hunting, the intellectual lady, seeking you. Your reputation, your great name—"

"Yes, yes," Guildea interrupted, rather irritably—"I know all that, I know."

He twisted his long hands together, bending the palms outwards till his thin, pointed fingers cracked. His forehead was wrinkled in a frown.

"I imagine," he said—he stopped and coughed drily, almost shrilly—"I imagine it would be very disagreeable to be liked, to be run after—that is the usual expression, isn't it—by anything one objected to."

And now he half turned in his chair, crossed his legs one over the other, and looked at his guest with an unusual, almost piercing interrogation.

"Anything?" said the Father.

"Well—well, anyone. I imagine nothing could be more unpleasant."

"To you—no," answered the Father. "But—forgive me, Guildea, I cannot conceive your permitting such intrusion. You don't encourage adoration."

Guildea nodded his head gloomily.

"I don't," he said, "I don't. That's just it. That's the curious part of it, that I—"

He broke off deliberately, got up and stretched.

"I'll have a pipe, too," he said.

He went over to the mantelpiece, got his pipe, filled it and lighted it. As he held the match to the tobacco, bending forward with an enquiring expression, his eyes fell upon the green baize that covered Napoleon's cage. He threw the match into the grate, and puffed at the pipe as he walked forward to the cage. When he reached it he put out his hand, took hold of the baize and began to pull it away. Then suddenly he pushed it back over the cage.

"No," he said, as if to himself, "no."

He returned rather hastily to the fire and threw himself once more into his armchair.

"You're wondering," he said to Father Murchison. "So am I. I don't know at all what to make of it. I'll just tell you the facts and you must tell me what you think of them. The night before last, after a day of hard work—but no harder than usual—I went to the front door to get a breath of air. You know I often do that."

"Yes, I found you on the doorstep when I first came here."

"Just so. I didn't put on hat or coat. I just stood on the step as I was. My mind, I remember, was still full of my work. It was rather a dark night, not very dark. The hour was about eleven, or a quarter past. I was staring at the Park, and presently I found that my eyes were directed towards somebody who was sitting, back to me, on one of the benches. I saw the person—if it was a person—through the railings."

"If it was a person!" said the Father. "What do you mean by that?"

"Wait a minute. I say that because it was too dark for me to know. I merely saw some blackish object on the bench, rising into view above the level of the back of the seat. I couldn't say it was man, woman or child. But something there was, and I found that I was looking at it."

"I understand."

"Gradually, I also found that my thoughts were becoming fixed upon this thing or person. I began to wonder, first, what it was doing there; next, what it was thinking; lastly, what it was like."

"Some poor creature without a home, I suppose," said the Father.

"I said that to myself. Still, I was taken with an extraordinary interest about this object, so great an interest that I got my hat and crossed the road to go into the Park. As you know, there's an entrance almost opposite to my house. Well, Murchison, I crossed the road, passed through the gate in the railings, went up to the seat, and found that there was—nothing on it."

"Were you looking at it as you walked?"

"Part of the time. But I removed my eyes from it just as I passed through the gate, because there was a row going on a little way off, and I turned for an instant in that direction. When I saw that the seat was vacant I was seized by a most absurd sensation of disappointment, almost of anger. I stopped and looked about me to see if anything was moving away, but I could see nothing. It was a cold night and misty, and there were few people about. Feeling, as I say, foolishly and unnaturally disappointed, I retraced my steps to this house. When I got here I discovered that during my short absence I had left the hall door open—half open."

"Rather imprudent in London."

"Yes. I had no idea, of course, that I had done so, till I got back. However, I was only away three minutes or so."

"Yes."

"It was not likely that anybody had gone in."

"I suppose not."

"Was it?"

"Why do you ask me that, Guildea?"

"Well, well!"

"Besides, if anybody had gone in, on your return you'd have caught him, surely."

Guildea coughed again. The Father, surprised, could not fail to recognise that he was nervous and that his nervousness was affecting him physically.

"I must have caught cold that night," he said, as if he had read his friend's thought and hastened to contradict it. Then he went on:

"I entered the hall, or passage, rather."

He paused again. His uneasiness was becoming very apparent.

"And you did catch somebody?" said the Father.

Guildea cleared his throat.

"That's just it," he said, "now we come to it. I'm not imaginative, as you know."

"You certainly are not."

"No, but hardly had I stepped into the passage before I felt certain that somebody had got into the house during my absence. I felt convinced of it, and not only that, I also felt convinced that the intruder was the very person I had dimly seen sitting upon the seat in the Park. What d'you say to that?"

"I begin to think you are imaginative."

"H'm! It seemed to me that the person—the occupant of the seat—and I had simultaneously formed the project of interviewing each other, had simultaneously set out to put that project into execution. I became so certain of this that I walked hastily upstairs into this room, expecting to find the visitor awaiting me. But there was no one. I then came down again and went into the dining-room. No one. I was actually astonished. Isn't that odd?"

"Very," said the Father, quite gravely.

The Professor's chill and gloomy manner, and uncomfortable, constrained appearance kept away the humour that might well have lurked round the steps of such a discourse.

"I went upstairs again," he continued, "sat down and thought the matter over. I resolved to forget it, and took up a book. I might perhaps have been able to read, but suddenly I thought I noticed—"

He stopped abruptly. Father Murchison observed that he was staring towards the green baize that covered the parrot's cage.

"But that's nothing," he said. "Enough that I couldn't read. I resolved to explore the house. You know how small it is, how easily one can go all over it. I went all over it. I went into every room without exception. To the servants, who were having supper, I made some excuse. They were surprised at my advent, no doubt."

"And Pitting?"

"Oh, he got up politely when I came in, stood while I was there, but never said a word. I muttered 'don't disturb yourselves,' or something of the sort, and came out. Murchison, I found nobody new in the house—yet I returned to this room entirely convinced that somebody had entered while I was in the Park."

"And gone out again before you came back?"

"No, had stayed, and was still in the house."

"But, my dear Guildea," began the Father, now in great astonishment. "Surely—"

"I know what you want to say—what I should want to say in your place. Now, do wait. I am also convinced that this visitor has not left the house and is at this moment in it."

He spoke with evident sincerity, with extreme gravity. Father Murchison looked him full in the face, and met his quick, keen eyes.

"No," he said, as if in reply to an uttered question: "I'm perfectly sane, I assure you. The whole matter seems almost as incredible to me as it must to you. But, as you know, I never quarrel with facts, however strange. I merely try to examine into them thoroughly. I have already consulted a doctor and been pronounced in perfect bodily health."

He paused, as if expecting the Father to say something.

"Go on, Guildea," he said, "you haven't finished."

"No. I felt that night positive that somebody had entered the house, and remained in it, and my conviction grew. I went to bed as usual, and, contrary to my expectation, slept as well as I generally do. Yet directly I woke up yesterday morning, I knew that my household had been increased by one."

"May I interrupt you for one moment? How did you know it?"

"By my mental sensation. I can only say that I was perfectly conscious of a new presence within my house, close to me."

"How very strange," said the Father. "And you feel absolutely certain that you are not overworked? Your brain does not feel tired? Your head is quite clear?"

"Quite. I was never better. When I came down to breakfast that morning I looked sharply into Pitting's face. He was as coldly placid and inexpressive as usual. It was evident to me that his mind was in no way distressed. After breakfast I sat down to work, all the time ceaselessly conscious of the fact of this intruder upon my privacy. Nevertheless, I laboured for several hours, waiting for any development that might occur to clear away the mysterious obscurity of this event. I lunched. About half-past two I was obliged to go out to attend a lecture. I therefore took my coat and hat, opened my door, and stepped on to the pavement. I was instantly aware that I was no longer intruded upon, and this although I was now in the street, surrounded by people. Consequently, I felt certain that the thing in my house must be thinking of me, perhaps even spying upon me."

"Wait a moment," interrupted the Father. "What was your sensation? Was it one of fear?"

"Oh, dear no. I was entirely puzzled—as I am now—and keenly interested, but not in any way alarmed. I delivered my lecture with my usual ease and returned home in the evening. On entering the house again I was perfectly conscious that the intruder was still there. Last night I dined alone and spent the hours after dinner in reading a scientific work in which I was deeply interested. While I read, however, I never for one moment lost the knowledge that some mind—very attentive to me—was within hail of mine. I will say more than this—the sensation constantly increased, and, by the time I got up to go to bed, I had come to a very strange conclusion."

"What? What was it?"

"That whoever—or whatever—had entered my house during my short absence in the Park was more than interested in me."

"More than interested in you?"

"Was fond, or was becoming fond, of me."

"Oh!" exclaimed the Father. "Now I understand why you asked me just now whether I thought there was anything about you that might draw a human being or an animal irresistibly to you."

"Precisely. Since I came to this conclusion, Murchison, I will confess that my feeling of strong curiosity has become tinged with another feeling."

"Of fear?"

"No, of dislike, or irritation. No—not fear, not fear."

As Guildea repeated unnecessarily this asseveration he looked again towards the parrot's cage.

"What is there to be afraid of in such a matter?" he added. "I am not a child to tremble before bogies."

In saying the last words he raised his voice sharply; then he walked quickly to the cage, and, with an abrupt movement, pulled the baize covering from it. Napoleon was disclosed, apparently dozing upon his perch with his head held slightly on one side. As the light reached him, he moved, ruffled the feathers about his neck, blinked his eyes, and began slowly to sidle to and fro, thrusting his head forward and drawing it back with an air of complacent, though rather unmeaning, energy. Guildea stood by the cage, looking at him closely, and indeed with an attention that was so intense as to be remarkable, almost unnatural.

"How absurd these birds are!" he said at length, coming back to the fire.

"You have no more to tell me?" asked the Father.

"No. I am still aware of the presence of something in my house. I am still conscious of its close attention to me. I am still irritated, seriously annoyed—I confess it—by that attention."

"You say you are aware of the presence of something at this moment?"

"At this moment—yes."

"Do you mean in this room, with us, now?"

"I should say so—at any rate, quite near us."

Again he glanced quickly, almost suspiciously, towards the cage of the parrot. The bird was sitting still on its perch now. Its head was bent down and cocked sideways, and it appeared to be listening attentively to something.

"That bird will have the intonations of my voice more correctly than ever by to-morrow morning," said the Father, watching Guildea closely with his mild blue eyes. "And it has always imitated me very cleverly."

The Professor started slightly.

"Yes," he said. "Yes, no doubt. Well, what do you make of this affair?"

"Nothing at all. It is absolutely inexplicable. I can speak quite frankly to you, I feel sure."

"Of course. That's why I have told you the whole thing."

"I think you must be over-worked, over-strained, without knowing it."

"And that the doctor was mistaken when he said I was all right?"

"Yes."

Guildea knocked his pipe out against the chimney piece.

"It may be so," he said. "I will not be so unreasonable as to deny the possibility, although I feel as well as I ever did in my life. What do you advise then?"

"A week of complete rest away from London, in good air."

"The usual prescription. I'll take it. I'll go to-morrow to Westgate and leave Napoleon to keep house in my absence."

For some reason, which he could not explain to himself, the pleasure which Father Murchison felt in hearing the first part of his friend's final remark was lessened, was almost destroyed, by the last sentence.

He walked towards the City that night, deep in thought, remembering and carefully considering the first interview he had with Guildea in the latter's house a year and a half before.

On the following morning Guildea left London.

III

Father Murchison was so busy a man that he had little time for brooding over the affairs of others. During Guildea's week at the sea, however, the Father thought about him a great deal, with much wonder and some dismay. This dismay was soon banished, for the mild-eyed priest was quick to discern weakness in himself, quicker still to drive it forth as a most undesirable inmate of the soul. But the wonder remained. It was destined to a crescendo. Guildea had left London on a Thursday. On a Thursday he returned, having previously sent a note to Father Murchison to mention that he was leaving Westgate at a certain time. When his train ran into Victoria Station, at five o'clock in the evening, he was surprised to see the cloaked figure of his friend standing upon the grey platform behind a line of porters.

"What, Murchison!" he said. "You here! Have you seceded from your order that you are taking this holiday?"

They shook hands.

"No," said the Father. "It happened that I had to be in this neighbourhood to-day, visiting a sick person. So I thought I would meet you."

"And see if I were still a sick person, eh?"

The Professor glanced at him kindly, but with a dry little laugh.

"Are you?" replied the Father gently, looking at him with interest. "No, I think not. You appear very well."

The sea air had, in fact, put some brownish red into Guildea's always thin cheeks. His keen eyes were shining with life and energy, and he walked forward in his loose grey suit and fluttering overcoat with a vigour that was noticeable, carrying easily in his left hand his well-filled Gladstone bag.

The Father felt completely reassured.

"I never saw you look better," he said.

"I never was better. Have you an hour to spare?"

"Two."

"Good. I'll send my bag up by cab, and we'll walk across the Park to my house and have a cup of tea there. What d'you say?"

"I shall enjoy it."

They walked out of the station yard, past the flower girls and newspaper sellers towards Grosvenor Place.

"And you have had a pleasant time?" the Father said.

"Pleasant enough, and lonely. I left my companion behind me in the passage at number 100, you know."

"And you'll not find him there now, I feel sure."

"H'm!" ejaculated Guildea. "What a precious weakling you think me, Murchison."

As he spoke he strode forward more quickly, as if moved to emphasise his sensation of bodily vigour.

"A weakling—no. But anyone who uses his brain as persistently as you do yours must require an occasional holiday."

"And I required one very badly, eh?"

"You required one, I believe."

"Well, I've had it. And now we'll see."

The evening was closing in rapidly. They crossed the road at Hyde Park Corner, and entered the Park, in which were a number of people going home from work; men in corduroy trousers, caked with dried mud, and carrying tin cans slung over their shoulders, and flat panniers, in which lay their tools. Some of the younger ones talked loudly or whistled shrilly as they walked.

"Until the evening," murmured Father Murchison to himself.

"What?" asked Guildea.

"I was only quoting the last words of the text which seems written upon life, especially upon the life of pleasure: 'Man goeth forth to his work, and to his labour.'"

"Ah, those fellows are not half bad fellows to have in an audience. There were a lot of them at the lecture I gave when I first met you, I remember. One of them tried to heckle me. He had a red beard. Chaps with red beards are always hecklers. I laid him low on that occasion. Well, Murchison, and now we're going to see."

"What?"

"Whether my companion has departed."

"Tell me—do you feel any expectation of—well—of again thinking something is there?"

"How carefully you choose language. No, I merely wonder."

"You have no apprehension?"

"Not a scrap. But I confess to feeling curious."

"Then the sea air hasn't taught you to recognise that the whole thing came from overstrain?"

"No," said Guildea, very drily.

He walked on in silence for a minute. Then he added:

"You thought it would?"

"I certainly thought it might."

"Make me realise that I had a sickly, morbid, rotten imagination—eh? Come now, Murchison, why not say frankly that you packed me off to Westgate to get rid of what you considered an acute form of hysteria?"

The Father was quite unmoved by this attack.

"Come now, Guildea," he retorted, "what did you expect me to think? I saw no indication of hysteria in you. I never have. One would suppose you the last man likely to have such a malady. But which is more natural—for me to believe in your hysteria or in the truth of such a story as you told me?"

"You have me there. No, I mustn't complain. Well, there's no hysteria about me now, at any rate."

"And no stranger in your house, I hope."

Father Murchison spoke the last words with earnest gravity, dropping the half-bantering tone—which they had both assumed.

"You take the matter very seriously, I believe," said Guildea, also speaking more gravely.

"How else can I take it? You wouldn't have me laugh at it when you tell it to me seriously?"

"No. If we find my visitor still in the house, I may even call upon you to exorcise it. But first I must do one thing."

"And that is?"

"Prove to you, as well as to myself, that it is still there."

"That might be difficult," said the Father, considerably surprised by Guildea's matter-of-fact tone.

"I don't know. If it has remained in my house I think I can find a means. And I shall not be at all surprised if it is still there—despite the Westgate air."

In saying the last words the Professor relapsed into his former tone of dry chaff. The Father could not quite make up his mind whether Guildea was feeling unusually grave or unusually gay. As the two men drew near to Hyde Park Place their conversation died away and they walked forward silently in the gathering darkness.

"Here we are!" said Guildea at last.

He thrust his key into the door, opened it and let Father Murchison into the passage, following him closely, and banging the door.

"Here we are!" he repeated in a louder voice.

The electric light was turned on in anticipation of his arrival. He stood still and looked round.

"We'll have some tea at once," he said. "Ah, Pitting!"

The pale butler, who had heard the door bang, moved gently forward from the top of the stairs that led to the kitchen, greeted his master respectfully, took his coat and Father Murchison's cloak, and hung them on two pegs against the wall.

"All's right, Pitting? All's as usual?" said Guildea.

"Quite so, sir."

"Bring us up some tea to the library."

"Yes, sir."

Pitting retreated. Guildea waited till he had disappeared, then opened the dining-room door, put his head into the room and kept it there for a moment, standing perfectly still. Presently he drew back into the passage, shut the door, and said:

"Let's go upstairs."

Father Murchison looked at him enquiringly, but made no remark. They ascended the stairs and came into the library. Guildea glanced rather sharply round. A fire was burning on the hearth. The blue curtains were drawn. The bright gleam of the strong electric light fell on the long rows of books, on the writing table—very orderly in consequence of Guildea's holiday—and on the uncovered cage of the parrot. Guildea went up to the cage. Napoleon was sitting humped up on his perch with his feathers ruffled. His long toes, which looked as if they were covered with crocodile skin, clung to the bar. His round and blinking eyes were filmy, like old eyes. Guildea stared at the bird very hard, and then clucked with his tongue against his teeth. Napoleon shook himself, lifted one foot, extended his toes, sidled along the perch to the bars nearest to the Professor and thrust his head against them. Guildea scratched it with his forefinger two or three times, still gazing attentively at the parrot; then he returned to the fire just as Pitting entered with the tea-tray.

Father Murchison was already sitting in an armchair on one side of the fire. Guildea took another chair and began to pour out tea, as Pitting left the room, closing the door gently behind him. The Father sipped his tea, found it hot, and set the cup down on a little table at his side.

"You're fond of that parrot, aren't you?" he asked his friend.

"Not particularly. It's interesting to study sometimes. The parrot mind and nature are peculiar."

"How long have you had him?"

"About four years. I nearly got rid of him just before I made your acquaintance. I'm very glad now I kept him."

"Are you? Why is that?"

"I shall probably tell you in a day or two."

The Father took his cup again. He did not press Guildea for an immediate explanation, but when they had both finished their tea he said:

"Well, has the sea-air had the desired effect?"

"No," said Guildea.

The Father brushed some crumbs from the front of his cassock and sat up higher in his chair.

"Your visitor is still here?" he asked, and his blue eyes became almost ungentle and piercing as he gazed at his friend.

"Yes," answered Guildea, calmly.

"How do you know it, when did you know it—when you looked into the dining room just now?"

"No. Not until I came into this room. It welcomed me here."

"Welcomed you! In what way?"

"Simply by being here, by making me feel that it is here, as I might feel that a man was if I came into the room when it was dark."

He spoke quietly, with perfect composure in his usual dry manner.

"Very well," the Father said, "I shall not try to contend against your sensation, or to explain it away. Naturally, I am in amazement."

"So am I. Never has anything in my life surprised me so much. Murchison, of course I cannot expect you to believe more than that I honestly—imagine, if you like—that there is some intruder here, of what kind I am totally unaware. I cannot expect you to believe that there really is anything. If you were in my place, I in yours, I should certainly consider you the victim of some nervous delusion. I could not do otherwise. But—wait. Don't condemn me as a hysteria patient, or as a madman, for two or three days. I feel convinced that—unless I am indeed unwell, a mental invalid, which I don't think is possible—I shall be able very shortly to give you some proof that there is a newcomer in my house."

"You don't tell me what kind of proof?"

"Not yet. Things must go a little farther first. But, perhaps even to-morrow I may be able to explain myself more fully. In the meanwhile, I'll say this, that if, eventually, I can't bring any kind of proof that I'm not dreaming, I'll let you take me to any doctor you like, and I'll resolutely try to adopt your present view—that I'm suffering from an absurd delusion. That is your view, of course?"

Father Murchison was silent for a moment. Then he said, rather doubtfully:

"It ought to be."

"But isn't it?" asked Guildea, surprised.

"Well, you know, your manner is enormously convincing. Still, of course, I doubt. How can I do otherwise? The whole thing must be fancy."

The Father spoke as if he were trying to recoil from a mental position he was being forced to take up.

"It must be fancy," he repeated.

"I'll convince you by more than my manner, or I'll not try to convince you at all," said Guildea.

When they parted that evening, he said:

"I'll write to you in a day or two probably. I think the proof I am going to give you has been accumulating during my absence. But I shall soon know."

Father Murchison was extremely puzzled as he sat on the top of the omnibus going homeward.

IV

In two days' time he received a note from Guildea asking him to call, if possible, the same evening. This he was unable to do as he had an engagement to fulfil at some East End gathering. The following day was Sunday. He wrote saying he would come on the Monday, and got a wire shortly afterwards: "Yes Monday come to dinner seven-thirty Guildea." At half-past seven he stood on the doorstep of number 100.

Pitting let him in.

"Is the Professor quite well, Pitting?" the Father enquired as he took off his cloak.

"I believe so, sir. He has not made any complaint," the butler formally replied. "Will you come upstairs, sir?"

Guildea met them at the door of the library. He was very pale and sombre, and shook hands carelessly with his friend.

"Give us dinner," he said to Pitting.

As the butler retired, Guildea shut the door rather cautiously. Father Murchison had never before seen him look so disturbed.

"You're worried, Guildea," the Father said. "Seriously worried."

"Yes, I am. This business is beginning to tell on me a good deal."

"Your belief in the presence of something here continues then?"

"Oh, dear, yes. There's no sort of doubt about the matter. The night I went across the road into the Park something got into the house, though what the devil it is I can't yet find out. But now, before we go down to dinner, I'll just tell you something about that proof I promised you. You remember?"

"Naturally."

"Can't you imagine what it might be?"

Father Murchison moved his head to express a negative reply.

"Look about the room," said Guildea. "What do you see?"

The Father glanced around the room, slowly and carefully.

"Nothing unusual. You do not mean to tell me there is any appearance of—"

"Oh, no, no, there's no conventional, white-robed, cloud-like figure. Bless my soul, no! I haven't fallen so low as that."

He spoke with considerable irritation.

"Look again."

Father Murchison looked at him, turned in the direction of his fixed eyes and saw the grey parrot clambering in its cage, slowly and persistently.

"What?" he said, quickly. "Will the proof come from there?"

The Professor nodded.

"I believe so," he said. "Now let's go down to dinner. I want some food badly."

They descended to the dining room. While they ate and Pitting waited upon them, the Professor talked about birds, their habits, their curiosities, their fears and their powers of imitation. He had evidently studied this subject with the thoroughness that was characteristic of him in all that he did.

"Parrots," he said presently, "are extraordinarily observant. It is a pity that their means of reproducing what they see are so limited. If it were not so, I have little doubt that their echo of gesture would be as remarkable as their echo of voice often is."

"But hands are missing."

"Yes. They do many things with their heads, however. I once knew an old woman near Goring on the Thames. She was afflicted with the palsy. She held her head perpetually sideways and it trembled, moving from right to left. Her sailor son brought her home a parrot from one of his voyages. It used to reproduce the old woman's palsied movement of the head exactly. Those grey parrots are always on the watch."

Guildea said the last sentence slowly and deliberately, glancing sharply over his wine at Father Murchison, and, when he had spoken it, a sudden light of comprehension dawned in the priest's mind. He opened his lips to make a swift remark. Guildea turned his bright eyes towards Pitting, who at the moment was tenderly bearing a cheese meringue from the lift that connected the dining room with the lower regions. The Father closed his lips again. But presently, when the butler had placed some apples on the table, had meticulously arranged the decanters, brushed away the crumbs and evaporated, he said, quickly:

"I begin to understand. You think Napoleon is aware of the intruder?"

"I know it. He has been watching my visitant ever since the night of that visitant's arrival."

Another flash of light came to the priest.

"That was why you covered him with green baize one evening?"

"Exactly. An act of cowardice. His behaviour was beginning to grate upon my nerves."

Guildea pursed up his thin lips and drew his brows down, giving to his face a look of sudden pain.

"But now I intend to follow his investigations," he added, straightening his features. "The week I wasted at Westgate was not wasted by him in London, I can assure you. Have an apple."

"No, thank you; no, thank you."

The Father repeated the words without knowing that he did so. Guildea pushed away his glass.

"Let us come upstairs, then."

"No, thank you," reiterated the Father.

"Eh?"

"What am I saying?" exclaimed the Father, getting up. "I was thinking over this extraordinary affair."

"Ah, you're beginning to forget the hysteria theory?"

They walked out into the passage.

"Well, you are so very practical about the whole matter."

"Why not? Here's something very strange and abnormal come into my life. What should I do but investigate it closely and calmly?"

"What, indeed?"

The Father began to feel rather bewildered, under a sort of compulsion which seemed laid upon him to give earnest attention to a matter that ought to strike him—so he felt—as entirely absurd. When they came into the library his eyes immediately turned, with profound curiosity, towards the parrot's cage. A slight smile curled the Professor's lips. He recognised the effect he was producing upon his friend. The Father saw the smile.

"Oh, I'm not won over yet," he said in answer to it.

"I know. Perhaps you may be before the evening is over. Here comes the coffee. After we have drunk it we'll proceed to our experiment. Leave the coffee, Pitting, and don't disturb us again."

"No, sir."

"I won't have it black to-night," said the Father; "plenty of milk, please. I don't want my nerves played upon."

"Suppose we don't take coffee at all?" said Guildea. "If we do, you may trot out the theory that we are not in a perfectly normal condition. I know you, Murchison, devout priest and devout sceptic."

The Father laughed and pushed away his cup.

"Very well, then. No coffee."

"One cigarette, and then to business."

The grey-blue smoke curled up.

"What are we going to do?" said the Father.

He was sitting bolt upright as if ready for action. Indeed there was no suggestion of repose in the attitudes of either of the men.

"Hide ourselves, and watch Napoleon. By the way—that reminds me."

He got up, went to a corner of the room, picked up a piece of green baize and threw it over the cage.

"I'll pull that off when we are hidden."

"And tell me first if you have had any manifestation of this supposed presence during the last few days?"

"Merely an increasingly intense sensation of something here, perpetually watching me, perpetually attending to all my doings."

"Do you feel that it follows you about?"

"Not always. It was in this room when you arrived. It is here now—I feel. But, in going down to dinner, we seemed to get away from it. The conclusion is that it remained here. Don't let us talk about it just now."

They spoke of other things till their cigarettes were finished. Then, as they threw away the smouldering ends, Guildea said:

"Now, Murchison, for the sake of this experiment, I suggest that we should conceal ourselves behind the curtains on either side of the cage, so that the bird's attention may not be drawn towards us and so distracted from that which we want to know more about. I will pull away the green baize when we are hidden. Keep perfectly still, watch the bird's proceedings, and tell me afterwards how you feel about them, how you explain them. Tread softly."

The Father obeyed, and they stole towards the curtains that fell before the two windows. The Father concealed himself behind those on the left of the cage, the Professor behind those on the right. The latter, as soon as they were hidden, stretched out his arm, drew the baize down from the cage, and let it fall on the floor.

The parrot, which had evidently fallen asleep in the warm darkness, moved on its perch as the light shone upon it, ruffled the feathers round its throat, and lifted first one foot and then the other. It turned its head round on its supple, and apparently elastic, neck, and, diving its beak into the down upon its back, made some searching investigations with, as it seemed, a satisfactory result, for it soon lifted its head again, glanced around its cage, and began to address itself to a nut which had been fixed between the bars for its refreshment. With its curved beak it felt and tapped the nut, at first gently, then with severity. Finally it plucked the nut from the bars, seized it with its rough, grey toes, and, holding it down firmly on the perch, cracked it and pecked out its contents, scattering some on the floor of the cage and letting the fractured shell fall into the china bath that was fixed against the bars. This accomplished, the bird paused meditatively, extended one leg backwards, and went through an elaborate process of wing-stretching that made it look as if it were lopsided and deformed. With its head reversed, it again applied itself to a subtle and exhaustive search among the feathers of its wing. This time its investigation seemed interminable, and Father Murchison had time to realise the absurdity of the whole position, and to wonder why he had lent himself to it. Yet he did not find his sense of humour laughing at it. On the contrary, he was smitten by a sudden gust of horror. When he was talking to his friend and watching him, the Professor's manner, generally so calm, even so prosaic, vouched for the truth of his story and the well-adjusted balance of his mind. But when he was hidden this was not so. And Father Murchison, standing behind his curtain, with his eyes upon the unconcerned Napoleon, began to whisper to himself the word—madness, with a quickening sensation of pity and of dread.

The parrot sharply contracted one wing, ruffled the feathers around its throat again, then extended its other leg backwards, and proceeded to the cleaning of its other wing. In the still room the dry sound of the feathers being spread was distinctly audible. Father Murchison saw the blue curtains behind which Guildea stood tremble slightly, as if a breath of wind had come through the window they shrouded. The clock in the far room chimed, and a coal dropped into the grate, making a noise like dead leaves stirring abruptly on hard ground. And again a gust of pity and of dread swept over the Father. It seemed to him that he had behaved very foolishly, if not wrongly, in encouraging what must surely be the strange dementia of his friend. He ought to have declined to lend himself to a proceeding that, ludicrous, even childish in itself, might well be dangerous in the encouragement it gave to a diseased expectation. Napoleon's protruding leg, extended wing and twisted neck, his busy and unconscious devotion to the arrangement of his person, his evident sensation of complete loneliness and most comfortable solitude, brought home with vehemence to the Father the undignified buffoonery of his conduct, the more piteous buffoonery of his friend. He seized the curtains with his hand and was about to thrust them aside and issue forth, when an abrupt movement of the parrot stopped him. The bird, as if sharply attracted by something, paused in its pecking, and, with its head still bent backward and twisted sideways on its neck, seemed to listen intently. Its round eye looked glistening and strained, like the eye of a disturbed pigeon. Contracting its wing, it lifted its head and sat for a moment erect on its perch, shifting its feet mechanically up and down, as if a dawning excitement produced in it an uncontrollable desire of movement. Then it thrust its head forward in the direction of the further room and remained perfectly still. Its attitude so strongly suggested the concentration of its attention on something immediately before it, that Father Murchison instinctively stared about the room, half expecting to see Pitting advance softly, having entered through the hidden door. He did not come, and there was no sound in the chamber. Nevertheless, the parrot was obviously getting excited and increasingly attentive. It bent its head lower and lower, stretching out its neck until, almost falling from the perch, it half extended its wings, raising them slightly from its back, as if about to take flight, and fluttering them rapidly up and down. It continued this fluttering movement for what seemed to the Father an immense time. At length, raising its wings as far as possible, it dropped them slowly and deliberately down to its back, caught hold of the edge of its bath with its beak, hoisted itself on to the floor of the cage, waddled to the bars, thrust its head against them, and stood quite still in the exact attitude it always assumed when its head was being scratched by the Professor. So complete was the suggestion of this delight conveyed by the bird, that Father Murchison felt as if he saw a white finger gently pushed among the soft feathers of its head, and he was seized by a most strong conviction that something, unseen by him but seen and welcomed by

Napoleon, stood immediately before the cage.

The parrot presently withdrew its head, as if the coaxing finger had been lifted from it, and its pronounced air of acute physical enjoyment faded into one of marked attention and alert curiosity. Pulling itself up by the bars it climbed again upon its perch, sidled to the left side of the cage, and began apparently to watch something with profound interest. It bowed its head oddly, paused for a moment, then bowed its head again. Father Murchison found himself conceiving—from this elaborate movement of the head—a distinct idea of a personality. The bird's proceedings suggested extreme sentimentality combined with that sort of weak determination which is often the most persistent. Such weak determination is a very common attribute of persons who are partially idiotic. Father Murchison was moved to think of these poor creatures who will often, so strangely and unreasonably, attach themselves with persistence to those who love them least. Like many priests, he had had some experience of them, for the amorous idiot is peculiarly sensitive to the attraction of preachers. This bowing movement of the parrot recalled to his memory a terrible, pale woman who for a time haunted all churches in which he ministered, who was perpetually endeavouring to catch his eye, and who always bent her head with an obsequious and cunningly conscious smile when she did so. The parrot went on bowing, making a short pause between each genuflection, as if it waited for a signal to be given that called into play its imitative faculty.

"Yes, yes, it's imitating an idiot," Father Murchison caught himself saying as he watched.

And he looked again about the room, but saw nothing; except the furniture, the dancing fire, and the serried ranks of the books. Presently the parrot ceased from bowing, and assumed the concentrated and stretched attitude of one listening very keenly. He opened his beak, showing his black tongue, shut it, then opened it again. The Father thought he was going to speak, but he remained silent, although it was obvious that he was trying to bring out something. He bowed again two or three times, paused, and then, again opening his beak, made some remark. The Father could not distinguish any words, but the voice was sickly and disagreeable, a cooing and, at the same time, querulous voice, like a woman's, he thought. And he put his ear nearer to the curtain, listening with almost feverish attention. The bowing was resumed, but this time Napoleon added to it a sidling movement, affectionate and affected, like the movement of a silly and eager thing, nestling up to someone, or giving someone a gentle and furtive nudge. Again the Father thought of that terrible, pale woman who had haunted churches. Several times he had come upon her waiting for him after evening services. Once she had hung her head smiling, and lolled out her tongue and pushed against him sideways in the dark. He remembered how his flesh had shrunk from the poor thing, the sick loathing of her that he could not banish by remembering that her mind was all astray. The parrot paused, listened, opened his beak, and again said something in the same dove-like, amorous voice, full of sickly suggestion and yet hard, even dangerous, in its intonation. A loathsome voice, the Father thought it. But this time, although he heard the voice more distinctly than before, he could not make up his mind whether it was like a woman's voice or a man's—or perhaps a child's. It seemed to be a human voice, and yet oddly sexless. In order to resolve his doubt he withdrew into the darkness of the curtains, ceased to watch Napoleon and simply listened with keen attention, striving to forget that he was listening to a bird, and to imagine that he was overhearing a human being in conversation. After two or three minutes' silence the voice spoke again, and at some length, apparently repeating several times an affectionate series of ejaculations with a cooing emphasis that was unutterably mawkish and offensive. The sickliness of the voice, its falling intonations and its strange indelicacy, combined with a die-away softness and meretricious refinement, made the Father's flesh creep. Yet he could not distinguish any words, nor could he decide on the voice's sex or age. One thing alone he was certain of as he stood still in the darkness—that such a sound could only proceed from something peculiarly loathsome, could only express a personality unendurably abominable to him, if not to everybody. The voice presently failed, in a sort of husky gasp, and there was a prolonged silence. It was broken by the Professor, who suddenly pulled away the curtains that hid the Father and said to him:

"Come out now, and look."

The Father came into the light, blinking, glanced towards the cage, and saw Napoleon poised motionless on one foot with his head under his wing. He appeared to be asleep. The Professor was pale, and his mobile lips were drawn into an expression of supreme disgust.

"Faugh!" he said.

He walked to the windows of the further room, pulled aside the curtains and pushed the glass up, letting in the air. The bare trees were visible in the grey gloom outside. Guildea leaned out for a minute drawing the night air into his lungs. Presently he turned round to the Father, and exclaimed abruptly:

"Pestilent! Isn't it?"

"Yes—most pestilent."

"Ever hear anything like it?"

"Not exactly."

"Nor I. It gives me nausea, Murchison, absolute physical nausea."

He closed the window and walked uneasily about the room.

"What d'you make of it?" he asked, over his shoulder.

"How d'you mean exactly?"

"Is it man's, woman's, or child's voice?"

"I can't tell, I can't make up my mind."

"Nor I."

"Have you heard it often?"

"Yes, since I returned from Westgate. There are never any words that I can distinguish. What a voice!"

He spat into the fire.

"Forgive me," he said, throwing himself down in a chair. "It turns my stomach—literally."

"And mine," said the Father truly.

"The worst of it is," continued Guildea, with a high, nervous accent, "that there's no brain with it, none at all—only the cunning of idiocy."

The Father started at this exact expression of his own conviction by another.

"Why d'you start like that?" said Guildea, with a quick suspicion which showed the unnatural condition of his nerves.

"Well, the very same idea had occurred to me."

"What?"

"That I was listening to the voice of something idiotic."

"Ah! That's the devil of it, you know, to a man like me. I could fight against brain—but this!"

He sprang up again, poked the fire violently, then stood on the hearth-rug with his back to it, and his hands thrust into the high pockets of his trousers.

"That's the voice of the thing that's got into my house," he said. "Pleasant, isn't it?"

And now there was really horror in his eyes and his voice.

"I must get it out," he exclaimed. "I must get it out. But how?"

He tugged at his short black beard with a quivering hand.

"How?" he continued. "For what is it? Where is it?"

"You feel it's here—now?"

"Undoubtedly. But I couldn't tell you in what part of the room."

He stared about, glancing rapidly at everything.

"Then you consider yourself haunted?" said Father Murchison. He, too, was much moved and disturbed, although he was not conscious of the presence of anything near them in the room.

"I have never believed in any nonsense of that kind, as you know," Guildea answered. "I simply state a fact, which I cannot understand, and which is beginning to be very painful to me. There is something here. But whereas most so-called hauntings have been described to me as inimical, what I am conscious of is that I am admired, loved, desired. This is distinctly horrible to me, Murchison, distinctly horrible."

Father Murchison suddenly remembered the first evening he had spent with Guildea, and the latter's expression almost of disgust at the idea of receiving warm affection from anyone. In the light of that long-ago conversation, the present event seemed supremely strange, and almost like a punishment for an offence committed by the Professor against humanity. But, looking up at his friend's twitching face, the Father resolved not to be caught in the net of his hideous belief.

"There can be nothing here," he said. "It's impossible."

"What does that bird imitate, then?"

"The voice of someone who has been here."

"Within the last week then. For it never spoke like that before, and mind, I noticed that it was watching and striving to imitate something before I went away, since the night that I went into the Park, only since then."

"Somebody with a voice like that must have been here while you were away," Father Murchison repeated, with a gentle obstinacy.

"I'll soon find out."

Guildea pressed the bell. Pitting stole in almost immediately.

"Pitting," said the Professor, speaking in a high, sharp voice, "did anyone come into this room during my absence at the sea?"

"Certainly not, sir, except the maids—and me, sir."

"Not a soul? You are certain?"

"Perfectly certain, sir."

The cold voice of the butler sounded surprised, almost resentful. The Professor flung out his hand towards the cage.

"Has the bird been here the whole time?"

"Yes, sir."

"He was not moved, taken elsewhere, even for a moment?"

Pitting's pale face began to look almost expressive, and his lips were pursed.

"Certainly not, sir."

"Thank you. That will do."

The butler retired, moving with a sort of ostentatious rectitude. When he had reached the door, and was just going out, his master called:

"Wait a minute, Pitting."

The butler paused. Guildea bit his lips, tugged at his beard uneasily two or three times, and then said:

"Have you noticed—er—the parrot talking lately in a—a very peculiar, very disagreeable voice?"

"Yes, sir—a soft voice like, sir."

"Ha! Since when?"

"Since you went away, sir. He's always at it."

"Exactly. Well, and what did you think of it?"

"Beg pardon, sir?"

"What do you think about his talking in this voice?"

"Oh, that it's only his play, sir."

"I see. That's all, Pitting."

The butler disappeared and closed the door noiselessly behind him.

Guildea turned his eyes on his friend.

"There, you see!" he ejaculated.

"It's certainly very odd," said the Father. "Very odd indeed. You are certain you have no maid who talks at all like that?"

"My dear Murchison! Would you keep a servant with such a voice about you for two days?"

"No."

"My housemaid has been with me for five years, my cook for seven. You've heard Pitting speak. The three of them make up my entire household. A parrot never speaks in a voice it has not heard. Where has it heard that voice?"

"But we hear nothing?"

"No. Nor do we see anything. But it does. It feels something too. Didn't you observe it presenting its head to be scratched?"

"Certainly it seemed to be doing so."

"It was doing so."

Father Murchison said nothing. He was full of increasing discomfort that almost amounted to apprehension.

"Are you convinced?" said Guildea, rather irritably.

"No. The whole matter is very strange. But till I hear, see or feel—as you do—the presence of something, I cannot believe."

"You mean that you will not?"

"Perhaps. Well, it is time I went."

Guildea did not try to detain him, but said, as he let him out:

"Do me a favour, come again tomorrow night."

The Father had an engagement. He hesitated, looked into the Professor's face and said:

"I will. At nine I'll be with you. Good-night."

When he was on the pavement he felt relieved. He turned round, saw Guildea stepping into his passage, and shivered.

V

Father Murchison walked all the way home to Bird Street that night. He required exercise after the strange and disagreeable evening he had spent, an evening upon which he looked back already as a man looks back upon a nightmare. In his ears, as he walked, sounded the gentle and intolerable voice. Even the memory of it caused him physical discomfort. He tried to put it from him, and to consider the whole matter calmly. The Professor had offered his proof that there was some strange presence in his house. Could any reasonable man accept such proof? Father Murchison told himself that no reasonable man could accept it. The parrot's proceedings were, no doubt, extraordinary. The bird had succeeded in producing an extraordinary illusion of an invisible presence in the room. But that there really was such a presence the Father insisted on denying to himself. The devoutly religious, those who believe implicitly in the miracles recorded in the Bible, and who regulate their lives by the messages they suppose themselves to receive directly from the Great Ruler of a hidden World, are seldom inclined to accept any notion of supernatural intrusion into the affairs of daily life. They put it from them with anxious determination. They regard it fixedly as hocus-pocus, childish if not wicked.

Father Murchison inclined to the normal view of the devoted churchman. He was determined to incline to it. He could not—so he now told himself—accept the idea that his friend was being supernaturally punished for his lack of humanity, his deficiency in affection, by being obliged to endure the love of some horrible thing, which could not be seen, heard, or handled. Nevertheless, retribution did certainly seem to wait upon Guildea's condition. That which he had unnaturally dreaded and shrunk from in his thought he seemed to be now forced unnaturally to suffer. The Father prayed for his friend that night before the little, humble altar in the barely furnished, cell-like chamber where he slept.

On the following evening, when he called in Hyde Park Place, the door was opened by the housemaid, and Father Murchison mounted the stairs, wondering what had become of Pitting. He was met at the library door by Guildea and was painfully struck by the alteration in his appearance. His face was ashen in hue, and there were lines beneath his eyes. The eyes themselves looked excited and horribly forlorn. His hair and dress were disordered and his lips twitched continually, as if he were shaken by some acute nervous apprehension.

"What has become of Pitting?" asked the Father, grasping Guildea's hot and feverish hand.

"He has left my service."

"Left your service!" exclaimed the Father in utter amazement.

"Yes, this afternoon."

"May one ask why?"

"I'm going to tell you. It's all part and parcel of this—this most odious business. You remember once discussing the relations men ought to have with their servants?"

"Ah!" cried the Father, with a flash of inspiration. "The crisis has occurred?"

"Exactly," said the Professor, with a bitter smile. "The crisis has occurred. I called upon Pitting to be a man and a brother. He responded by declining the invitation. I upbraided him. He gave me warning. I paid him his wages and told him he could go at once. And he has gone. What are you looking at me like that for?"

"I didn't know," said Father Murchison, hastily dropping his eyes, and looking away. "Why," he added, "Napoleon is gone too."

"I sold him today to one of those shops in Shaftesbury Avenue."

"Why?"

"He sickened me with his abominable imitation of—his intercourse with—well, you know what he was at last night. Besides, I have no further need of his proof to tell me I am not dreaming. And, being convinced as I now am, that all I have thought to have happened has actually happened, I care very little about convincing others. Forgive me for saying so, Murchison, but I am now certain that my anxiety to make you believe in the presence of something here really arose from some faint doubt on that subject—within myself. All doubt has now vanished."

"Tell me why."

"I will."

Both men were standing by the fire. They continued to stand while Guildea went on:

"Last night I felt it."

"What?" cried the Father.

"I say that last night, as I was going upstairs to bed, I felt something accompanying me and nestling up against me."

"How horrible!" exclaimed the Father, involuntarily.

Guildea smiled drearily.

"I will not deny the horror of it. I cannot, since I was compelled to call on Pitting for assistance."

"But—tell me—what was it, at least what did it seem to be?"

"It seemed to be a human being. It seemed, I say; and what I mean exactly is that the effect upon me was rather that of human contact than of anything else. But I could see nothing, hear nothing. Only, three times, I felt this gentle, but determined, push against me, as if to coax me and to attract my attention. The first time it happened I was on the landing outside this room, with my foot on the first stair. I will confess to you, Murchison, that I bounded upstairs like one pursued. That is the shameful truth. Just as I was about to enter my bedroom, however, I felt the thing entering with me, and, as I have said, squeezing, with loathsome, sickening tenderness, against my side. Then—"

He paused, turned towards the fire and leaned his head on his arm. The Father was greatly moved by the strange helplessness and despair of the attitude. He laid his hand affectionately on Guildea's shoulder.

"Then?"

Guildea lifted his head. He looked painfully abashed.

"Then, Murchison, I am ashamed to say, I broke down, suddenly, unaccountably, in a way I should have thought wholly impossible to me. I struck out with my hands to thrust the thing away. It pressed more closely to me. The pressure, the contact became unbearable to me. I shouted out for Pitting. I—I believe I must have cried—'Help.' "

"He came, of course?"

"Yes, with his usual soft, unemotional quiet. His calm—its opposition to my excitement of disgust and horror—must, I suppose, have irritated me. I was not myself, no, no!"

He stopped abruptly. Then—

"But I need hardly tell you that," he added, with most piteous irony.

"And what did you say to Pitting?"

"I said that he should have been quicker. He begged my pardon. His cold voice really maddened me, and I burst out into some foolish, contemptible diatribe, called him a machine, taunted him, then—as I felt that loathsome thing nestling once more to me—begged him to assist me, to stay with me, not to leave me alone—I meant in the company of my tormentor. Whether he was frightened, or whether he was angry at my unjust and violent manner and speech a moment before, I don't know. In any case he answered that he was engaged as a butler, and not to sit up all night with people. I suspect he thought I had taken too much to drink. No doubt that was it. I believe I swore at him as a coward—I! This morning he said he wished to leave my service. I gave him a month's wages, a good character as a butler, and sent him off at once."

"But the night? How did you pass it?"

"I sat up all night."

"Where? In your bedroom?"

"Yes—with the door open—to let it go."

"You felt that it stayed?"

"It never left me for a moment, but it did not touch me again. When it was light I took a bath, lay down for a little while, but did not close my eyes. After breakfast I had the explanation with Pitting and paid him. Then I came up here. My nerves were in a very shattered condition. Well, I sat down, tried to write, to think. But the silence was broken in the most abominable manner."

"How?"

"By the murmur of that appalling voice, that voice of a lovesick idiot, sickly but determined. Ugh!"

He shuddered in every limb. Then he pulled himself together, assumed, with a self-conscious effort, his most determined, most aggressive, manner, and added:

"I couldn't stand that. I had come to the end of my tether; so I sprang up, ordered a cab to be called, seized the cage and drove with it to a bird shop in Shaftesbury Avenue. There I sold the parrot for a trifle. I think, Murchison, that I must have been nearly mad then, for, as I came out of the wretched shop, and stood for an instant on the pavement among the cages of rabbits, guinea-pigs, and puppy dogs, I laughed aloud. I felt as if a load was lifted from my shoulders, as if in selling that voice I had sold the cursed thing that torments me. But when I got back to the house it was here. It's here now. I suppose it will always be here."

He shuffled his feet on the rug in front of the fire.

"What on earth am I to do?" he said. "I'm ashamed of myself, Murchison, but—but I suppose there are things in the world that certain men simply can't endure. Well, I can't endure this, and there's an end of the matter."

He ceased. The Father was silent. In presence of this extraordinary distress he did not know what to say. He recognised the uselessness of attempting to comfort Guildea, and he sat with his eyes turned, almost moodily, to the ground. And while he sat there he tried to give himself to the influences within the room, to feel all that was within it. He even, half-unconsciously, tried to force his imagination to play tricks with him. But he remained totally unaware of any third person with them. At length he said:

"Guildea, I cannot pretend to doubt the reality of your misery here. You must go away, and at once. When is your Paris lecture?"

"Next week. In nine days from now."

"Go to Paris tomorrow then; you say you have never had any consciousness that this—this thing pursued you beyond your own front door?"

"Never—hitherto."

"Go tomorrow morning. Stay away till after your lecture. And then let us see if the affair is at an end. Hope, my dear friend, hope."

He had stood up. Now he clasped the Professor's hand.

"See all your friends in Paris. Seek distractions. I would ask you also to seek—other help."

He said the last words with a gentle, earnest gravity and simplicity that touched Guildea, who returned his handclasp almost warmly.

"I'll go," he said. "I'll catch the ten o'clock train, and tonight I'll sleep at an hotel, at the Grosvenor—that's close to the station. It will be more convenient for the train."

As Father Murchison went home that night he kept thinking of that sentence: "It will be more convenient for the train." The weakness in Guildea that had prompted its utterance appalled him.

VI

No letter came to Father Murchison from the Professor during the next few days, and this silence reassured him, for it seemed to betoken that all was well. The day of the lecture dawned, and passed. On the following morning, the Father eagerly opened the *Times,* and scanned its pages to see if there were any report of the great meeting of scientific men which Guildea had addressed. He glanced up and down the columns with anxious eyes, then suddenly his hands stiffened as they held the sheets. He had come upon the following paragraph:

"We regret to announce that Professor Frederic Guildea was suddenly seized with severe illness yesterday evening while addressing a scientific meeting in Paris. It was observed that he looked very pale and nervous when he rose to his feet. Nevertheless, he spoke in French fluently for about a quarter of an hour. Then he appeared to become uneasy. He faltered and glanced about like a man apprehensive, or in severe distress. He even stopped once or twice, and seemed unable to go on, to remember what he wished to say. But, pulling himself together with an obvious effort, he continued to address the audience. Suddenly, however, he paused again, edged furtively along the platform, as if pursued by something which he feared, struck out with his hands, uttered a loud, harsh cry and fainted. The sensation in the hall was indescribable. People rose from their seats. Women screamed, and, for a moment, there was a veritable panic. It is feared that the Professor's mind must have temporarily given way owing to overwork. We understand that he will return to England as soon as possible, and we sincerely hope that necessary rest and quiet will soon have the desired effect, and that he will be completely restored to health and enabled to prosecute further the investigations which have already so benefited the world."

The Father dropped the paper, hurried out into Bird Street, sent a wire of inquiry to Paris, and received the same day the following reply: "Returning tomorrow. Please call evening. Guildea." On that evening the Father called in Hyde Park Place, was at once admitted, and found Guildea sitting by the fire in the library, ghastly pale, with a heavy rug over his knees. He looked like a man emaciated by a long and severe illness, and in his wide open eyes there was an expression of fixed horror. The Father started at the sight of him, and could scarcely refrain from crying out. He was beginning to express his sympathy when Guildea stopped him with a trembling gesture.

"I know all that," Guildea said, "I know. This Paris affair—" He faltered and stopped.

"You ought never to have gone," said the Father. "I was wrong. I ought not

509

to have advised your going. You were not fit."

"I was perfectly fit," he answered, with the irritability of sickness. "But I was—I was accompanied by that abominable thing."

He glanced hastily round him, shifted his chair and pulled the rug higher over his knees. The Father wondered why he was thus wrapped up. For the fire was bright and red and the night was not very cold.

"I was accompanied to Paris," he continued, pressing his upper teeth upon his lower lip.

He paused again, obviously striving to control himself. But the effort was vain. There was no resistance in the man. He writhed in his chair and suddenly burst forth in a tone of hopeless lamentation.

"Murchison, this being, thing—whatever it is—no longer leaves me even for a moment. It will not stay here unless I am here, for it loves me, persistently, idiotically. It accompanied me to Paris, stayed with me there, pursued me to the lecture hall, pressed against me, caressed me while I was speaking. It has returned with me here. It is here now"—he uttered a sharp cry—"now, as I sit here with you. It is nestling up to me, fawning upon me, touching my hands. Man, man, can't you feel that it is here?"

"No," the Father answered truly.

"I try to protect myself from its loathsome contact," Guildea continued, with fierce excitement, clutching the thick rug with both hands. "But nothing is of any avail against it. Nothing. What is it? What can it be? Why should it have come to me that night?"

"Perhaps as a punishment," said the Father, with a quick softness.

"For what?"

"You hated affection. You put human feeling aside with contempt. You had, you desired to have, no love for anyone. Nor did you desire to receive any love from anything. Perhaps this is a punishment."

Guildea stared into his face.

"D'you believe that?" he cried.

"I don't know," said the Father. "But it may be so. Try to endure it, even to welcome it. Possibly then the persecution will cease."

"I know it means me no harm," Guildea exclaimed, "it seeks me out of affection. It was led to me by some amazing attraction which I exercise over it ignorantly. I know that. But to a man of my nature that is the ghastly part of the matter. If it would hate me, I could bear it. If it would attack me, if it would try to do me some dreadful harm, I should become a man again. I should be braced to fight against it. But this gentleness, this abominable solicitude, this brainless worship of an idiot, persistent, sickly, horribly physical, I cannot endure. What does it want of me? What would it demand of me? It nestles to me. It leans against me. I feel its touch, like the touch of a feather, trembling about my heart, as if it sought to number my pulsations, to find out the inmost secrets of my impulses and desires. No privacy is left to me." He sprang up excitedly. "I cannot withdraw," he cried, "I cannot be alone, untouched, unworshipped, unwatched for even one-half second. Murchison, I am dying of this, I am dying."

He sank down again in his chair, staring apprehensively on all sides, with the passion of some blind man, deluded in the belief that by his furious and continued effort he will attain sight. The Father knew well that he sought to pierce the veil of the invisible, and have knowledge of the thing that loved him.

"Guildea," the Father said, with insistent earnestness, "try to endure this—do more—try to give this thing what it seeks."

"But it seeks my love."

"Learn to give it your love and it may go, having received what it came for."

"T'sh! You talk like a priest. Suffer your persecutors. Do good to them that despitefully use you. You talk as a priest."

"As a friend I spoke naturally, indeed, right out of my heart. The idea suddenly came to me that all this—truth or seeming, it doesn't matter which—may be some strange form of lesson. I have had lessons—painful ones. I shall have many more. If you could welcome—"

"I can't! I can't!" Guildea cried fiercely. "Hatred! I can give it that—always that, nothing but that—hatred, hatred."

He raised his voice, glared into the emptiness of the room, and repeated, "Hatred!"

As he spoke the waxen pallor of his cheeks increased, until he looked like a corpse with living eyes. The Father feared that he was going to collapse and faint, but suddenly he raised himself upon his chair and said, in a high and keen voice, full of suppressed excitement:

"Murchison, Murchison!"

"Yes. What is it?"

An amazing ecstasy shone in Guildea's eyes.

"It wants to leave me," he cried. "It wants to go! Don't lose a moment! Let it out! The window—the window!"

The Father, wondering, went to the near window, drew aside the curtains and pushed it open. The branches of the trees in the garden creaked drily in the light wind. Guildea leaned forward on the arms of his chair. There was silence for a moment. Then Guildea, speaking in a rapid whisper, said:

"No, no. Open this door—open the hall door. I feel—I feel that it will return the way it came. Make haste—ah, go!"

The Father obeyed—to soothe him, hurried to the door and opened it wide. Then he glanced back to Guildea. He was standing up, bent forward. His eyes were glaring with eager expectation, and, as the Father turned, he made a furious gesture towards the passage with his thin hands.

The Father hastened out and down the stairs. As he descended in the twilight he fancied he heard a slight cry from the room behind him, but he did not pause. He flung the hall door open, standing back against the wall. After waiting a moment—to satisfy Guildea, he was about to close the door again, and had his hand on it, when he was attracted irresistibly to look forth towards the park. The night was lit by a young moon, and, gazing through the railings, his eyes fell upon a bench beyond them.

Upon the bench something was sitting, huddled together very strangely.

The Father remembered instantly Guildea's description of that former night, that night of Advent, and a sensation of horror-stricken curiosity stole through him.

Was there then really something that had indeed come to the Professor? And had it finished its work, fulfilled its desire and gone back to its former existence?

The Father hesitated a moment in the doorway. Then he stepped out resolutely and crossed the road, keeping his eyes fixed upon this black or dark object that leaned so strangely upon the bench. He could not tell yet what it was like, but he fancied it was unlike anything with which his eyes were acquainted. He reached the opposite path, and was about to pass through the gate in the railings, when his arm was brusquely grasped. He started, turned round, and saw a policeman eyeing him suspiciously.

"What are you up to?" said the policeman.

The Father was suddenly aware that he had no hat upon his head, and that his appearance, as he stole forward in his cassock, with his eyes intently fixed upon the bench in the park, was probably unusual enough to excite suspicion.

"It's all right, policeman," he answered quickly, thrusting some money into the constable's hand.

Then, breaking from him, the Father hurried towards the bench, bitterly vexed at the interruption. When he reached it, nothing was there. Guildea's experience had been almost exactly repeated and, filled with unreasonable disappointment, the Father returned to the house, entered it, shut the door and hastened up the narrow stairway into the library.

On the hearthrug, close to the fire, he found Guildea lying with his head lolled against the armchair from which he had recently risen. There was a shocking expression of terror on his convulsed face. On examining him the Father found that he was dead.

The doctor, who was called in, said that the cause of death was failure of the heart.

When Father Murchison was told this, he murmured:

"Failure of the heart! It was that then!"

He turned to the doctor and said:

"Could it have been prevented?"

The doctor drew on his gloves and answered:

"Possibly, if it had been taken in time. Weakness of the heart requires a great deal of care. The Professor was too much absorbed in his work. He should have lived very differently."

The Father nodded.

"Yes, yes," he said, sadly.

Richard Matheson

Born of Man and Woman

Richard Matheson, one of the great contemporary fantasists, burst upon the scene in 1950 with the publication of "Born of Man and Woman," which later became the title story for his first collection. He was one of the most prolific and important voices in horror in that decade, producing two of the most important horror novels of the contemporary period, *I Am Legend* (1954) and *The Shrinking Man,* (1956) both in the science fiction genre, before going to Hollywood to pursue a successful film-writing career. "Born of Man and Woman" is the contemporary monster story par excellence: concise, chilling, psychologically disturbing. The child is abused and is going to get even. And the world in which such a child exists is not our own, but the world of fantastic horror.

X—This day when it had light mother called me a retch. You retch she said. I saw in her eyes the anger. I wonder what it is a retch.

This day it had water falling from upstairs. It fell all around. I saw that. The ground of the back I watched from the little window. The ground it sucked up the water like thirsty lips. It drank too much and it got sick and runny brown. I didn't like it.

Mother is a pretty I know. In my bed place with cold walls around I have a paper thing that was behind the furnace. It says on it SCREEN-STARS. I see in the pictures faces like of mother and father. Father says they are pretty. Once he said it.

And also mother he said. Mother so pretty and me decent enough. Look at you he said and didn't have the nice face. I touched his arm and said it is alright father. He shook and pulled away where I couldn't reach.

Today mother let me off the chain a little so I could look out the little window. That's how I saw the water falling from upstairs.

XX—This day it had goldness in the upstairs. As I know, when I looked at it my eyes hurt. After I look at it the cellar is red.

I think this was church. They leave the upstairs. The big machine swallows them and rolls out past and is gone. In the back part is the *little* mother. She is much small than me. I am big. It is a secret but I have pulled the chain out of the wall. I can see out the little window all I like.

In this day when it got dark I had eat my food and some bugs. I hear laughs upstairs. I like to know why there are laughs for. I took the chain from the

513

wall and wrapped it around me. I walked squish to the stairs. They creak when I walk on them. My legs slip on them because I don't walk on stairs. My feet stick to the wood.

I went up and opened a door. It was a white place. White as white jewels that come from upstairs sometime. I went in and stood quiet. I hear the laughing some more. I walk to the sound and look through to the people. More people than I thought was. I thought I should laugh with them.

Mother came out and pushed the door in. It hit me and hurt. I fell back on the smooth floor and the chain made noise. I cried. She made a hissing noise into her and put her hand on her mouth. Her eyes got big.

She looked at me. I heard father call. What fell he called. She said a iron board. Come help pick it up she said. He came and said now is *that* so heavy you need. He saw me and grew big. The anger came in his eyes. He hit me. I spilled some of the drip on the floor from one arm. It was not nice. It made ugly green on the floor.

Father told me to go to the cellar. I had to go. The light it hurt some now in my eyes. It is not so like that in the cellar.

Father tied my legs and arms up. He put me on my bed. Upstairs I heard laughing while I was quiet there looking on a black spider that was swinging down to me. I thought what father said. Ohgod he said. And only eight.

XXX—This day father hit in the chain again before it had light. I have to try pull it out again. He said I was bad to come upstairs. He said never do that again or he would beat me hard. That hurts.

I hurt. I slept the day and rested my head against the cold wall. I thought of the white place upstairs.

XXXX—I got the chain from the wall out. Mother was upstairs. I heard little laughs very high. I looked out the window. I saw all little people like the little mother and little fathers too. They are pretty.

They were making nice noise and jumping around the ground. Their legs was moving hard. They are like mother and father. Mother says all right people look like they do.

One of the little fathers saw me. He pointed at the window. I let go and slid down the wall in the dark. I curled up as they would not see. I heard their talks by the window and foots running. Upstairs there was a door hitting. I heard the little mother call upstairs. I heard heavy steps and I rushed to my bed place. I hit the chain in the wall and lay down on my front.

I heard mother come down. Have you been at the window she said. I heard the anger. *Stay* away from the window. You have pulled the chain out again.

She took the stick and hit me with it. I didn't cry. I can't do that. But the drip ran all over the bed. She saw it and twisted away and made a noise. Oh mygod mygod she said why have you *done* this to me? I heard the stick go bounce on the stone floor. She ran upstairs. I slept the day.

XXXXX—This day it had water again. When mother was upstairs I heard the little one come slow down the steps. I hidded myself in the coal bin for mother would have anger if the little mother saw me.

She had a little live thing with her. It walked on the arms and had pointy ears. She said things to it.

It was all right except the live thing smelled me. It ran up the coal and looked down at me. The hairs stood up. In the throat it made an angry noise. I hissed but it jumped on me.

I didn't want to hurt it. I got fear because it bit me harder than the rat does. I hurt and the little mother screamed. I grabbed the live thing tight. It made sounds I never heard. I pushed it all together. It was all lumpy and red on the black coal.

I hid there when mother called. I was afraid of the stick. She left. I crept over the coal with the thing. I hid it under my pillow and rested on it. I put the chain in the wall again.

X—This is another times. Father chained me tight. I hurt because he beat me. This time I hit the stick out of his hands and made noise. He went away and his face was white. He ran out of my bed place and locked the door.

I am not so glad. All day it is cold in here. The chain comes slow out of the wall. And I have a bad anger with mother and father. I will show them. I will do what I did that once.

I will screech and laugh loud. I will run on the walls. Last I will hang head down by all my legs and laugh and drip green all over until they are sorry they didn't be nice to me.

If they try to beat me again I'll hurt them. I will.

Joanna Russ

My Dear Emily

Joanna Russ is best known for her award-winning science fiction and her notable feminist criticism, but throughout her career she has been a persistent investigator of psychological horrors and has produced a small number of extraordinary tales of the highest quality in that mode. "My Dear Emily" is one of the finest vampire stories since Le Fanu's "Carmilla," monstrous and subversive in its conscious use of psychological metaphor. It is a love story that discovers transcendence through horror. Russ' short fiction is collected in *The Zanzibar Cat* (Arkham House, 1983). Recently in the last decade the vampire story has staged a major comeback in the novels of Ann Rice, Chelsea Quinn Yarbro and Suzy McKee Charnas, Les Daniels and Stephen King. "My Dear Emily" is a nearly lone example from the previous decade and surpasses all but the best of them.

San Francisco, 188-
 I am so looking forward to seeing my dear Emily at last, now she is grown, a woman, although I'm sure I will hardly recognize her. She must not be proud (as if she could be!) but will remember her friends, I know, and have patience with her dear Will who cannot help but remember the girl she was, and the sweet influence she had in her old home. I talk to your father about you every day, dear, and he longs to see you as I do. Think! a learned lady in our circle! But I know you have not changed . . .

Emily came home from school in April with her bosom friend Charlotte. They had loved each other in school, but they didn't speak much on the train. While Emily read Mr. Emerson's poems, Charlotte examined the scenery through opera-glasses. She expressed her wish to see "savages."

"That's foolish," says Emily promptly.

"If we were carried off," says Charlotte, "I don't think you would notice it in time to disapprove."

"That's very foolish," says Emily, touching her round lace collar with one hand. She looks up from Mr. Emerson to stare Charlotte out of countenance, properly, morally, and matter-of-course young lady. It has always been her style.

"The New England look," Charlotte snaps resentfully. She makes her opera-glasses slap shut.

"I should like to be carried off," she proposes; "but then I don't have an

516

engagement to look forward to. A delicate affair."

"You mustn't make fun," says Emily. Mr. Emerson drops into her lap. She stares unseeing at Charlotte's opera-glasses.

"Why do they close?" she asks helplessly.

"I beg your pardon?" blankly, from Charlotte.

"Nothing. You're much nicer than I am," says Emily.

"Look," urges Charlotte kindly, pressing the toy into her friend's hand.

"For savages?"

Charlotte nods, Emily pushes the spring that will open the little machine, and a moment later drops them into her lap where they fall on Mr. Emerson. There is a cut across one of her fingers and a blue pinch darkening the other.

"They hurt me," she says without expression, and as Charlotte takes the glasses up quickly, Emily looks with curious sad passivity at the blood from her little wound, which has bled an incongruous passionate drop on Mr. Emerson's clothbound poems. To her friend's surprise (and her own, too) she begins to cry, heavily, silently, and totally without reason.

He wakes up slowly, mistily, dizzily, with a vague memory of having fallen asleep on plush. He is intensely miserable, bound down to his bed with hoops of steel, and the memory adds nausea to his misery, solidifying ticklishly around his bare hands and the back of his neck as he drifts towards wakefulness. His stomach turns over with the dry brushy filthiness of it. With the caution of the chronically ill, he opens his eyelids, careful not to move, careful even to keep from focusing his gaze until—he thinks to himself—his bed stops holding him with the force of Hell and this intense miserable sickness goes down, settles . . . Darkness. No breath. A glimmer of light, a stone wall. He thinks: *I'm dead and buried, dead and buried, dead and*—With infinite care he attempts to breathe, sure that this time it will be easy; he'll be patient, discreet, sensible, he won't do it all at once—

He gags. Spasmodically, he gulps, cries out, and gags again, springing convulsively to his knees and throwing himself over the low wall by his bed, laboring as if he were breathing sand. He starts to sweat. His heartbeat comes back, then pulse, then seeing, hearing, swallowing . . . High in the wall a window glimmers, a star is out, the sky is pale evening blue. Trembling with nausea, he rises to his feet, sways a little in the gloom, then puts out one arm and steadies himself against the stone wall. He sees the window, sees the door ahead of him. In his tearing eyes the star suddenly blazes and lengthens like a knife; his head is whirling, his heart painful as a man's; he throws his hands over his face, longing for life and strength to come back, the overwhelming flow of force that will crest at sunrise, leaving him raging at the world and ready to kill anyone, utterly proud and contemptuous, driven to sleep as the last resort of a balked assassin. But it's difficult to stand, difficult to breathe: *I wish I were dead and buried, dead and buried, dead and buried—But there!* he whispers to himself like a charm, *There, it's going, it's going away.* He smiles slyly round at his companionable, merciful stone walls. With an involuntarily silent, gliding gait he moves towards the door, opens the iron gate, and goes outside. Life is coming back. The trees are black against the sky, which yet holds some light; far away in the West lie the radiant memories of a vanished sun. An always vanished sun.

"Alive!" he cries, in triumph. It is—as usual—his first word of the day.

Dear Emily, sweet Emily, met Martin Guevara three days after she arrived home. She had been shown the plants in the garden and the house plants in stands and had praised them; she had been shown the sun-pictures and had praised *them;* she had fingered antimacassars, promised to knit, exclaimed at gaslights, and passed two evenings at home, doing nothing. Then in the hall that led to the pantry sweet Will had taken her hand and she had dropped her eyes because you were supposed to and that was her style. Charlotte (who slept in the same room as her friend) embraced her at bedtime, wept over the handtaking, and then Emily said to her dear, dear friend (without thinking):

"Sweet William."

Charlotte laughed.

"It's not a joke!"

"It's so funny."

"I love Will dearly." She wondered if God would strike her dead for a hypocrite. Charlotte was looking at her oddly, and smiling.

"You mustn't be full of levity," said Emily, peeved. It was then that sweet William came in and told them of tomorrow's garden-party, which was to be composed of her father's congregation. They were lucky, he said, to have acquaintances of such position and character. Charlotte slipped out on purpose and Will, seeing they were alone, attempted to take Emily's hand again.

"Leave me alone!" Emily said angrily. He stared.

"I said leave me alone!"

And she gave him such a look of angry pride that, in fact, he did.

Emily sees Guevara across the parlor by the abominable cherry-red sofa, talking animatedly and carelessly. In repose he is slight, undistinguished, and plain, but no one will ever see him in repose; Emily realizes this. His strategy is never to rest, to bewilder, he would (she thinks) slap you if only to confuse you, and when he can't he's always out of the way and attacking, making one look ridiculous. She knows nobody and is bored; she starts for the door to the garden.

At the door his hand closes over her wrist; he has somehow gotten there ahead of her.

"The lady of the house," he says.

"I'm back from school."

"And you've learned—?"

"Let me go, please."

"Never." He drops her hand and stands in the doorway. She says:

"I want to go outside."

"Never."

"I'll call my father."

"Do." She tries and can't talk; I wouldn't *bother,* she thinks to herself, loftily. She goes out into the garden with him. Under the trees his plainness vanishes like smoke.

"You want lemonade," he says.

"I'm not going to talk to you," she responds. "I'll talk to Will. Yes! I'll make him—"

"In trouble," says Mr. Guevara, returning silently with lemonade in a glass cup.

"No thank you."

"She wants to get away," says Martin Guevara. "I know."

"If I had your trick of walking like a cat," she says, "I could get out of anything."

"I *can* get out of anything," says the gentleman, handing Emily her punch, "Out of an engagement, a difficulty. I can even get *you* out of anything."

"I loathe you," whispers Emily suddenly. "You walk like a cat. You're ugly."

"Not out here," he remarks.

"Who has to be afraid of lights?" cries Emily energetically. He stands away from the paper lanterns strung between the trees, handsome, comfortable and collected, watching Emily's cut-glass cup shake in her hand.

"I can't move," she says miserably.

"Try." She takes a step towards him. "See; you can."

"But I wanted to go *away!*" With sudden hysteria she flings the lemonade (cup and all) into his face, but he is no longer there.

"What are you doing at a church supper, you hypocrite!" she shouts tearfully at the vacancy.

Sweet William has to lead her in to bed.

"You thought better of it," remarks Martin, head framed in an evening window, sounds of footsteps outside, ladies' heels clicking in the streets.

"I don't know you," she says miserably, "I just don't." He takes her light shawl, a pattern in India cashmere.

"That will come," he says, smiling. He sits again, takes her hand, and squeezes the skin on the wrist.

"Let me go, please?" she says like a child.

"I don't know."

"You talk like the smart young gentlemen at Andover; they were all fools."

"Perhaps you overawed them." He leans forward and puts his hand around the back of her neck for a moment. "Come on, dear."

"What are you talking about!" Emily cries.

"San Francisco is a lovely city. I had ancestors here three hundred years ago."

"Don't think that because I came here—"

"She doesn't," he whispers, grasping her shoulder, "She doesn't know a thing."

"God damn you!"

He blinks and sits back. Emily is weeping. The confusion of the room—an over-stuffed, over-draped hotel room—has gotten on her nerves. She snatches for her shawl, which is still in his grasp, but he holds it out of her reach, darting his handsome, unnaturally young face from side to side as she tries to reach round him. She falls across his lap and lies there, breathless with terror.

"You're cold," she whispers horrified, "you're cold as a corpse." The shawl descends lightly over her head and shoulders. His frozen hands help her to her feet. He is delighted; he bares his teeth in a smile.

"I think," he says, tasting it, "that I'm going to visit your family."

"But you don't—" she stumbles—"you don't want to . . . sleep with me. I know it."

"I can be a suitor like anyone else," he says.

That night Emily tells it all to Charlotte, who, afraid of the roué, stays up and reads a French novel as the light drains from the windows and the true black dark takes its place. It is towards dawn and Charlotte has been dozing, when Emily shakes her friend awake, kneeling by the bed with innocent blue eyes reflecting the dying night.

"I had a terrible dream," she complains.

"Hmmmm?"

"I dreamed," says Emily tiredly. "I had a nightmare. I dreamed I was walking by the beach and I decided to go swimming and then a . . . a thing, I don't know . . . it took me by the neck."

"Is that all?" says Charlotte peevishly.

"I'm sick," says Emily with childish satisfaction. She pushes Charlotte over in the bed and climbs in with her. "I won't have to see that man again if I'm sick."

"Pooh, why not?" mumbles Charlotte.

"Because I'll have to stay home."

"He'll visit you."

"William won't let him."

"Sick?" says Charlotte then, suddenly waking up. She moves away from her friend, for she has read more bad fiction than Emily and less moral poetry.

"Yes, I feel awful," says Emily simply, resting her head on her knees. She pulls away in tired irritation when her friend reaches for the collar of her nightdress. Charlotte looks and jumps out of bed.

"Oh," says Charlotte. "Oh—goodness—oh—" holding out her hands.

"What on earth's the matter with you?"

"He's—" whispers Charlotte in horror, "He's—"

In the dim light her hands are black with blood.

"You've come," he says. He is lying on his hotel sofa, reading a newspaper, his feet over one arm and a hand trailing on the rug.

"Yes," she answers, trembling with resolution.

"I never thought this place would have such a good use. But I never know when I'll manage to pick up money—"

With a blow of her hand, she makes a fountain of the newspaper; he lies on the sofa, mildly amused.

"Nobody knows I came," she says rapidly. "But I'm going to finish you off. I know how." She hunts feverishly in her bag.

"I wouldn't," he remarks quietly.

"Ah!" Hauling out her baby cross (silver), she confronts him with it like

Joan of Arc. He is still amused, still mildly surprised.

"In your hands?" he says delicately. Her fingers are loosening, her face pitiful.

"My dear, the significance is in the feeling, the faith, not the symbol. You use that the way you would use a hypodermic needle. Now in your father's hands—"

"I dropped it," she says in a little voice. He picks it up and hands it to her.

"You can touch—" she says, her face screwing up for tears.

"I can."

"Oh my God!" she cries in despair.

"My dear." He puts one arm around her, holding her against him, a very strong man for she pushes frantically to free herself. "How many times have *I* said that! But you'll learn. Do I sound like the silly boys at Andover?" Emily's eyes are fixed and her throat contracts; he forces her head between her knees. "The way you go on, you'd think I was bad luck."

"I—I—"

"And you without the plentiful lack of brains that characterizes your friend. She'll be somebody's short work and I think I know whose."

Emily turns white again.

"I'll send her around to you afterwards. Good God! What do you think will happen to her?"

"She'll die," says Emily clearly. He grasps her by the shoulders.

"Ah!" he says with immense satisfaction. "And after that? Who lives forever after that? Did you know that?"

"Yes, people like you don't die," whispers Emily. "But you're not people—"

"No," he says intently, "No. We're not." He stands Emily on her feet. "We're a passion!" Smiling triumphantly, he puts his hands on each side of her head, flattening the pretty curls, digging his fingers into the hair, in a grip Emily can no more break than she could break a vise.

"We're passion," he whispers, amused. "Life is passion. Desire makes life."

"Ah, let me go," says Emily.

He smiles ecstatically at the sick girl.

"Desire," he says dreamily, "lives; *that* lives when nothing else does, and we're desire made purely, desire walking the Earth. Can a dead man walk? Ah! If you want, want, want . . ."

He throws his arms around her, pressing her head to his chest and nearly suffocating her, ruining her elaborate coiffure and crushing the lace at her throat. Emily breathes in the deadness about him, the queer absence of odor, or heat, or presence; her mouth is pressed against the cloth of his fashionable suit, expensive stuff, a good dollar a yard, gotten by—what? But his hands are strong enough to get anything.

"You see," he says gently, "I enjoy someone with intelligence, even with morals; it adds a certain—And besides—" here he releases her and holds her face up to his—"we like souls that come to us; these visits to the bedrooms of unconscious citizens are rather like frequenting a public brothel."

"I abhor you," manages Emily. He laughs. He's delighted.

"Yes, yes, dear," he says, "But don't imagine we're callous parasites. Followers of the Marquis de Sade, perhaps—you see Frisco has evening hours for its bookstores!—but sensitive souls, really, and apt to long for a little conscious partnership." Emily shuts her eyes. "I said," he goes on, with a touch of hardness, "that I am a genuine seducer. I flatter myself that I'm not an animal."

"You're a monster," says Emily, with utter conviction. Keeping one hand on her shoulder, he steps back a pace.

"Go." She stands, unable to believe her luck, then makes what seems to her a rush for the door; it carries her into his arms.

"You see?" He's pleased; he's proved a point.

"I can't," she says, with wide eyes and wrinkled forehead . . .

"You will." He reaches for her and she faints.

Down in the dark where love and some other things make their hiding-place, Emily drifts aimlessly, quite alone, quite cold, like a dead woman without a passion in her soul to make her come back to life.

She opens her eyes and finds herself looking at his face in the dark, as if the man carried his own light with him.

"I'll die," she says softly.

"Not for a while," he drawls, sleek and content.

"You've killed me."

"I've loved."

"Love!"

"Say 'taken' then, if you insist."

"I do! I do!" she cried bitterly.

"You decided to faint."

"Oh the hell with you!" she shouts.

"Good girl!" And as she collapses, weeping hysterically, "Now, now, come here, dear . . ." nuzzling her abused little neck. He kisses it in the tenderest fashion with an exaggerated, mocking sigh; she twists away, but is pulled closer and as his lips open over the teeth of inhuman, dead desire, his victim finds—to her surprise—that there is no pain. She braces herself and then, unexpectedly, shivers from head to foot.

"Stop it!" she whispers, horrified. "Stop it! Stop it!"

But a vampire who has found a soul-mate (even a temporary one) will be immoderate. There's no stopping them.

Charlotte's books have not prepared her for *this*.

"You're to stay in the house, my dear, because you're ill."

"I'm not," Emily says, pulling the sheet up to her chin.

"Of course you are." The Reverend beams at her, under the portrait of Emily's dead mother which hangs in Emily's bedroom. "You've had a severe chill."

"But I have to get out!" says Emily, sitting up. "Because I have an appointment, you see."

"Not now," says the Reverend.

"But I *can't* have a severe chill in the *summer*!"

"You look so like your mother," says the Reverend, musing. After he has gone away, Charlotte comes in.

"I have to stay in the damned bed," says Emily forcefully, wiggling her toes under the sheet. Charlotte, who has been carrying a tray with tea and a posy on it, drops it on the washstand.

"Why, Emily!"

"I have to stay in the damned bed the whole damned day," Emily adds.

"Dear, why do you use those words?"

"Because the whole world's damned!"

After the duties of his employment were completed at six o'clock on a Wednesday, William came to the house with a doctor and introduced him to the Reverend and Emily's bosom friend. The street lamps would not be lit for an hour but the sun was just down and the little party congregated in the garden under remains of Japanese paper lanterns. No one ever worried that these might set themselves on fire. Lucy brought tea—they were one of the few civilized circles in Frisco—and over the tea, in the darkening garden, to the accompaniment of sugar-tongs and plopping cream (very musical) they talked.

"Do you think," says the Reverend, very worried, "that it might be consumption?"

"Perhaps the lungs are affected," says the doctor.

"She's always been such a robust girl." This is William, putting down the teapot which has a knitted tube about the handle, for insulation. Charlotte is stirring her tea with a spoon.

"It's very strange," says the doctor serenely, and he repeats "It's very strange" as shadows advance in the garden. "But young ladies, you know—especially at twenty—young ladies often take strange ideas into their heads; they do, they often do; they droop; they worry." His eyes are mild, his back sags, he hears the pleasant gurgle of more tea. A quiet consultation, good people, good solid people, a little illness, nothing serious—

"No," says Charlotte. Nobody hears her.

"I knew a young lady once—" ventures the doctor mildly.

"No," says Charlotte, more loudly. Everyone turns to her, and Lucy, taking the opportunity, insinuates a plate of small-sized muffins in front of Charlotte.

"I can tell you all about it," mutters Charlotte, glancing up from under her eyebrows. "But you'll *laugh*."

"Now, dear—" says the Reverend.

"Now, miss—" says the doctor.

"As a friend—" says William.

Charlotte begins to sob.

"Oh," she says, "I'll—I'll tell you about it."

Emily meets Mr. Guevara at the Mansion House at seven, having recovered an appearance of health (through self-denial) and a good solid record of spending the evenings at home (through self-control). She stands at the hotel's wrought-iron gateway, her back rigid as a stick, drawing on white gloves. Martin materializes out of the blue evening shadows and takes her arm.

"I shall like living forever," says Emily, thoughtfully.

"God deliver me from Puritans," says Mr. Guevara.

"What?"

"You're a lady. You'll swallow me up."

"I'll do anything I please," remarks Emily severely, with a glint of teeth.

"Ah."

"I will." They walk through the gateway. "You don't care two pins for me."

"Unfortunately," says he, bowing.

"It's not unfortunate as long as *I* care for me," says Emily, smiling with great energy. "Damn them all."

"You proper girls would overturn the world." Along they walk in the evening, in a quiet, respectable rustle of clothes. Halfway to the restaurant she stops and says breathlessly:

"Let's go—somewhere else!"

"My dear, you'll ruin your health!"

"You know better. Three weeks ago I was sick as a dog and much you cared; I haven't slept for days and I'm fine."

"You look fine."

"Ah! You mean I'm beginning to look dead, like you." She tightens her hold on his arm, to bring him closer.

"Dead?" says he, slipping his arm around her.

"Fixed. Bright-eyed. Always at the same heat and not a moment's rest."

"It agrees with you."

"I adore you," she says.

When Emily gets home, there's a reckoning. The Reverend stands in the doorway and sad William, too, but not Charlotte, for she is on the parlor sofa, having had hysterics.

"Dear Emily," says the Reverend. "We don't know how to tell you this—"

"Why, Daddy, *what*?" exclaims Emily, making wide-eyes at him.

"Your little friend told us—"

"Has something happened to Charlotte?" cries Emily. "Oh tell me, tell me, what happened to Charlotte?" And before they can stop her she has flown into the parlor and is kneeling beside her friend, wondering if she dares pinch her under cover of her shawl. William, quick as a flash, kneels on one side of her and Daddy on the other.

"Dear Emily!" cries William with fervor.

"Oh sweetheart!" says Charlotte, reaching down and putting her arms around her friend.

"You're well!" shouts Emily, sobbing over Charlotte's hand and thinking perhaps to bite her. But the Reverend's arms lift her up.

"My dear," says he, "you came home unaccompanied. You were not at the Society."

"But," says Emily, smiling dazzlingly, "two of the girls took all my hospital sewing to their house because we must finish it right away and I have not—"

"You have been lying to us," the Reverend says. *Now*, thinks Emily, *sweet William will cover his face*. Charlotte sobs.

"She can't help it," says Charlotte brokenly. "It's the spell."

"Why, I think everyone's gone out of their minds," says Emily, frowning. Sweet William takes her from Daddy, leading her away from Charlotte.

"Weren't you with a gentleman tonight?" says Sweet Will firmly. Emily backs away.

"For shame!"

"She doesn't remember it," explains Charlotte; "it's part of his spell."

"I think you ought to get a doctor for *her*," observes Emily.

"You were with a gentleman named Guevara," says Will, showing less tenderness than Emily expects. "Weren't you? Well—weren't you?"

"Bad cess to you if I was!" snaps Emily, surprised at herself. The other three gasp. "I won't be questioned," she goes on, "and I won't be spied upon. And I think you'd better take some of Charlotte's books away from her; she's getting downright silly."

"You have too much color," says Will, catching her hands. "You're ill but you don't sleep. You stay awake all night. You don't eat. But look at you!"

"I don't understand you. Do you want me to be ugly?" says Emily, trying to be pitiful. Will softens; she sees him do it.

"My dear Emily," he says. "My dear girl—we're afraid for you."

"Me?" says Emily, enjoying herself.

"We'd better put you to bed," says the Reverend kindly.

"You're so kind," whispers Emily, blinking as if she held back tears.

"That's a good girl," says Will, approving. "We know you don't understand. But we'll take care of you, Em."

"*Will* you?"

"Yes, dear. You've been near very grave danger, but luckily we found out in time, and we found out what to do; we'll make you well, we'll keep you safe, we'll—"

"Not with *that* you won't," says Emily suddenly, rooting herself to the spot, for what William takes out of his vest pocket (where he usually keeps his watch) is a broad-leaved, prickle-faced dock called wolfsbane; it must distress any vampire of sense to be so enslaved to pure superstition. But enslaved they are, nonetheless.

"Oh, no!" says Emily swiftly. "That's silly, perfectly silly!"

"Common sense must give way in such a crisis," remarks the Reverend gravely.

"You bastard!" shouts Emily, turning red, attempting to tear the charm out of her fiance's hand and jump up and down on it. But the Reverend holds one arm and Charlotte the other and between them they pry her fingers apart and William puts his property gently in his vest-pocket again.

"She's far gone," says the Reverend fearfully, at his angry daughter. Emily is scowling, Charlotte stroking her hair.

"Ssssh" says Will with great seriousness. "We must get her to bed," and between them they half-carry Emily up the stairs and put her, dressed as she is, in the big double bed with the plush headboard that she has shared so far with Charlotte. Daddy and fiance confer in the room across the long, low rambling hall, and Charlotte sits by her rebellious friend's bed and attempts to hold her hand.

"I won't permit it; you're a damned fool!" says Emily.

"Oh, Emmy!"

"Bosh."

"It's true!"

"Is it?" With extraordinary swiftness, Emily turns round in the bed and rises to her knees. "Do you know anything about it?"

"I know it's horrid, I—"

"Silly!" Playfully Emily puts her hands on Charlotte's shoulders. Her eyes are narrowed, her nostrils widened to breathe; she parts her lips a little and looks archly at her friend. "You don't know anything about it," she says insinuatingly.

"I'll call your father," says Charlotte quickly.

Emily throws an arm around her friend's neck.

"Not yet! Dear Charlotte!"

"We'll save you," says Charlotte doubtfully.

"Sweet Charrie; you're my friend, aren't you?"

Charlotte begins to sob again.

"Give me those awful things, those leaves."

"Why, Emily, I *couldn't*!"

"But he'll come for me and I have to protect myself, don't I?"

"I'll call your father," says Charlotte firmly.

"No, I'm *afraid*." And Emily wrinkles her forehead sadly.

"Well—"

"Sometimes I—I—" falters Emily. "I can't move or run away and everything looks so—so strange and *horrible*—"

"Oh, here!" Covering her face with one hand, Charlotte holds out her precious dock leaves in the other.

"Dear, dear! Oh, sweet! Oh thank you! Don't be afraid. He isn't after you."

"I hope not," says the bosom friend.

"Oh no, he told me. It's me he's after."

"How awful," says Charlotte, sincerely.

"Yes," says Emily. "Look." And she pulls down the collar of her dress to show the ugly marks, white dots unnaturally healed up, like the pockmarks of a drug addict.

"Don't!" chokes Charlotte.

Emily smiles mournfully. "We really ought to put the lights out," she says.

"Out!"

"Yes, you can see him better that way. If the lights are on, he could sneak in without being seen; he doesn't mind lights, you know."

"I don't know, dear—"

"I do." (Emily is dropping the dock leaves into the washstand, under cover of her skirt.) "I'm afraid. Please."

"Well—"

"Oh, you must!" And leaping to her feet, she turns down the gas to a dim glow; Charlotte's face fades into the obscurity of the deepening shadows.

"So. The lights are out," says Emily quietly.

"I'll ask Will—" Charlotte begins . . .

"No, dear."

"But, Emily—"

"He's coming, dear."

"You mean Will is coming."

"No, not Will."

"Emily, you're a—"

"I'm a sneak," says Emily, chuckling. "Sssssh!" And, while her friend sits paralyzed, one of the windows swings open in the night breeze, a lead-paned window that opens on a hinge, for the Reverend is fond of culture and old architecture. Charlotte lets out a little noise in her throat; and then—with the smash of a pistol shot—the gaslight shatters and the flame goes out. Gas hisses into the air, quietly, insinuatingly, as if explaining the same thing over and over. Charlotte screams with her whole heart. In the dark a hand clamps like a vise on Emily's wrist. A moment passes.

"Charlotte?" she whispers.

"Dead," says Guevara.

Emily has spent most of the day asleep in the rubble, with his coat rolled under her head where he threw it the moment before sunrise, the moment before he staggered to his place and plunged into sleep. She has watched the dawn come up behind the rusty barred gate, and then drifted into sleep herself with his face before her closed eyes—his face burning with a rigid, constricted, unwasting vitality. Now she wakes aching and bruised, with the sun of late afternoon in her face. Sitting against the stone wall, she sneezes twice and tries, ineffectually, to shake the dust from her silk skirt.

Oh, how—she thinks vaguely—*how messy.* She gets to her feet. *There's something I have to do.* The iron gate swings open at a touch. *Trees and gravestones tilted every which way. What did he say? Nothing would disturb it but a Historical Society.*

Having tidied herself as best she can, with his coat over her arm and the address of his tailor in her pocket, she trudges among the erupted stones, which tilt crazily to all sides as if in an earthquake. Blood (Charlotte's, whom she does not think about) has spread thinly on to her hair and the hem of her dress, but her hair is done up with fine feeling, despite the absence of a mirror, and her dress is dark gray; the spot looks like a spot of dusk. She folds the coat into a neat package and uses it to wipe the dust off her shoes, then lightens her step past the cemetery entrance, trying to look healthy and respectable. She aches all over from sleeping on the ground.

Once in town and having ascertained from a shop window that she will pass muster in a crowd, Emily trudges up hills and down hills to the tailor, the evidence over her arm. She stops at other windows, to look or to admire herself; thinks smugly of her improved coloring; shifts the parcel on her arm to show off her waist. In one window there is a display of religious objects—beads and crosses, books with fringed gilt bookmarks, a colored chromo of Madonna and Child. In this window Emily admires herself.

"It's Emily, dear!"

A Mrs. L———appears in the window beside her, with Constantia, Mrs. L———'s twelve-year-old offspring.

"Why, dear, whatever happened to you?" says Mrs. L———, noticing no hat, no gloves, and no veil.

"Nothing; whatever happened to you?" says Emily cockily. Constantia's eyes grow wide with astonishment at the fine, free audacity of it.

"Why, you look as if you'd been—"

"Picknicking," says Emily, promptly. "One of the gentlemen spilled beer on his coat." And she's in the shop now and hanging over the counter, flushed, counting the coral and amber beads strung around a crucifix.

Mrs. L———knocks doubtfully on the window-glass.

Emily waves and smiles.

Your father—form Mrs. L———'s lips in the glass.

Emily nods and waves cheerfully.

They do go away, finally.

"A fine gentleman," says the tailor earnestly, "a very fine man." He lisps a little.

"Oh very fine," agrees Emily, sitting on a stool and kicking the rungs with her feet. "Monstrous fine."

"But very careless," says the tailor fretfully, pulling Martin's coat nearer the window so he can see it, for the shop is a hole-in-the-wall and dark. "He shouldn't send a lady to this part of the town."

"I was a lady once," says Emily.

"Mmmmm."

"It's fruit stains—something awful, don't you think?"

"I cannot have this ready by tonight," looking up.

"Well, you must, that's all," says Emily calmly. "You always have and he has a lot of confidence in you, you know. He'd be awfully angry if he found out."

"Found out?" sharply.

"That you can't have it ready by tonight."

The tailor ponders.

"I'll positively stay in the shop while you work," says Emily flatteringly.

"Why, Reverend, I saw her on King Street as dirty as a gypsy, with her hair loose and the wildest eyes and I *tried* to talk to her, but she dashed into a shop—"

The sun goes down in a broad belt of gold, goes down over the ocean, over the hills and the beaches, makes shadows lengthen in the street near the quays where a lisping tailor smooths and alters, working against the sun (and very uncomfortable he is, too), watched by a pair of unwinking eyes that glitter a little in the dusk inside the stuffy shop. (*I think I've changed,* meditates Emily.)

He finishes, finally, with relief, and sits with an *ouf!* handing her the coat,

the new and beautiful coat that will be worn as soon as the eccentric
gentleman comes out to take the evening air. The eccentric gentleman, says
Emily incautiously, will do so in an hour by the Mansion House when the
last traces of light have faded from the sky.

"Then, my dear Miss," says the tailor unctuously, "I think a little matter
of pay—"

"You don't think," says Emily softly, "or you wouldn't have gotten
yourself into such a mess as to be this eccentric gentleman's tailor." And out
she goes.

Now nobody can see the stains on Emily's skirt or in her hair; street lamps
are being lit, there are no more carriages, and the number of people in the
streets grows—San Francisco making the most of the short summer nights.
It is perhaps fifteen minutes back to the fashionable part of the town where
Emily's hatless, shawlless state will be looked on with disdain; here nobody
notices. Emily dawdles through the streets, fingering her throat, yawning,
looking at the sky, thinking: I love, I love, I love—

She has fasted for the day but she feels fine; she feels busy, busy inside as if
the life inside her is flowering and bestirring itself, populated as the streets.
She remembers—

*I love you. I hate you. You enchantment, you degrading necessity, you foul
and filthy life, you promise of endless love and endless time . . .*

What words to say with Charlotte sleeping in the same room, no, the same
bed, with her hands folded under her face! Innocent sweetheart, whose state
must now be rather different.

Up the hills she goes, where the view becomes wider and wider, and the
lights spread out like sparkles on a cake, out of the section which is too
dangerous, too low, and too furtive to bother with a lady (or is it something
in her eyes?), into the broader by-streets where shore-leave sailors try to
make her acquaintance by falling into step and seizing her elbow; she snakes
away with unbounded strength, darts into shadows, laughs in their faces:
"I've got what I want!"

"Not like me!"

"Better!"

This is the Barbary Coast, only beginning to become a tourist attraction;
there are barkers outside the restaurants advertising pretty waiter girls,
dance halls, spangled posters twice the height of a man, crowds upon crowds
of people, one or two guides with tickets in their hats, and Emily—who
keeps to the shadows. She nearly chokes with laughter: *What a field of ripe
wheat!* One of the barkers hoists her by the waist onto his platform.

"Do you see this little lady? Do you see this—"

"Let me go, God damn you!" she cries indignantly.

"This angry little lady—" pushing her chin with one sunburned hand to
make her face the crowd. "This—" But here Emily hurts him, slashing his
palm with her teeth, quite pleased with herself, but surprised, too, for the
man was holding his hand cupped and the whole thing seemed to happen of
itself. She escapes instantly into the crowd and continues up through the
Coast, through the old Tenderloin, drunk with self-confidence, slipping like a
shadow through the now genteel streets and arriving at the Mansion House

gate having seen no family spies and convinced that none has seen her.

But nobody is there.

Ten by the clock, and no one is there, either; eleven by the clock and still no one. *Why didn't I leave this life when I had the chance!* Only one thing consoles Emily, that by some alchemy or nearness to the state she longs for, no one bothers or questions her and even the policemen pass her by as if in her little corner of the gate there is nothing but a shadow. Midnight and no one, half-past and she dozes; perhaps three hours later, perhaps four, she is startled awake by the sound of footsteps. She wakes: nothing. She sleeps again and in her dream hears them for the second time, then she wakes to find herself looking into the face of a lady who wears a veil.

"What!" Emily's startled whisper.

The lady gestures vaguely, as if trying to speak.

"What is it?"

"Don't—" and the lady speaks with feeling but, it seems, with difficulty also—"don't go home."

"Home?" echoes Emily, stupefied, and the stranger nods, saying:

"In danger."

"Who?" Emily is horrified.

"He's in danger." Behind her veil her face seems almost to emit a faint light of its own.

"You're one of them," says Emily. "Aren't you?" and when the woman nods, adds desperately, "Then you must save him!"

The lady smiles pitifully; that much of her face can be seen as the light breeze plays with her net veil.

"But you must!" exclaims Emily, "You know how; I don't; you've got to!"

"I don't dare," very softly. Then the veiled woman turns to go, but Emily—quite hysterical now—seizes her hand, saying:

"Who are you? Who are you?"

The lady gestures vaguely and shakes her head.

"Who are you!" repeats Emily with more energy. "You tell me, do you hear?"

Somberly the lady raises her veil and stares at her friend with a tragic, dignified, pitiful gaze. In the darkness her face burns with unnatural and beautiful color.

It is Charlotte.

Dawn comes with a pellucid quickening, glassy and ghostly. Slowly, shapes emerge from darkness and the blue pours back into the world—twilight turned backwards and the natural order reversed. Destruction, which is simple, logical, and easy, finds a kind of mocking parody in the morning's creation. Light has no business coming back, but light does.

Emily reaches the cemetery just as the caldron in the east overflows, just as the birds (idiots! she thinks) begin a tentative cheeping and chirping. She sits at the gate for a minute to regain her strength, for the night's walking and worry have tried her severely. In front of her the stones lie on graves, almost completely hard and real, waiting for the rising of the sun to finish them off and make complete masterpieces of them. Emily rises and trudges up the hill, slower and slower as the ground rises to its topmost swell, where three hundred years of peaceful Guevaras fertilize the grass and do their best to discredit the one wild shoot that lives on, the only disrespectful member of the family. Weeping a little to herself, Emily lags up the hill, raising her skirts to keep them off the weeds, and murderously hating in her heart the increasing light and the happier celebrating of the birds. She rounds the last hillock of ground and raises her eyes to the Guevaras' eternal mansion, expecting to see nobody again. There is the corner of the building, the low iron gate—

In front of it stands Martin Guevara between her father and sweet sweet Will, captived by both arms, his face pale and beautiful between two gold crosses that are just beginning to sparkle in the light of day.

"We are caught," says Guevara, seeing her, directing at her his fixed, white smile.

"You let him go," says Emily—very reasonably.

"You're safe, my Emily!" cries sweet Will.

"Let him go!" She runs to them, stops, look at them, perplexed to the bottom of her soul.

"Let him go," she says. "Let him go, let him go!"

Between the two bits of jewelry, Emily's life and hope and only pleasure smiles painfully at her, the color drained out of his face, desperate eyes fixed on the east.

"You don't understand," says Emily, inventing. "He isn't dangerous now. If you let him go, he'll run inside and then you can come back any time during the day and finish him off. I'm sick. You—"

The words die in her throat. All around them, from every tree and hedge, from boughs that have sheltered the graveyard for a hundred years, the birds begin their morning noise. A great hallelujah rises; after all, the birds have nothing to worry about. Numb, with legs like sticks, Emily sees sunlight touch the top of the stone mausoleum, sunlight slide down its face, sunlight reach the level of a standing man—

"I adore you," says Martin to her. With the slow bending over of a drowning man, he doubles up, like a man stuck with a knife in a dream; he doubles up, falls—

And Emily screams; What a scream! as if her soul were being haled out through her throat; and she is running down the other side of the little hill to regions as yet untouched by the sun, crying inwardly: I need help! help! help!—She knows where she can get it. Three hundred feet down the hill in a valley, a wooded protected valley sunk below the touch of the rising sun, there she runs through the trees, past the fence that separates the old graveyard from the new, expensive, polished granite—Charlotte is her friend, she loves her: Charlotte in her new home will make room for her.

Dennis Etchison

You Can Go Now

Dennis Etchison is an anthologist and writer whose occasional short stories have established a respectable following in the past fifteen years. The title story of his first collection, *The Dark Country*, won the World Fantasy Award for best short fiction (1982). He is an indefatigable supporter of horror fiction, especially in his anthology series, *The Cutting Edge* (1987), promoting new and different fiction. "You Can Go Now" is characteristic of his surreal psychological short fiction: intense, shifting, suggestive. What happens, happens offstage . . . the horror is internal, in the central character's mind at the moment of realization, which is the story. The maltreatment of women by men is a common theme in contemporary horror, nowhere more pointedly represented than in "You Can Go Now."

1

The receiver purred in his hand.

He glanced around the bedroom, feeling as if he had just awakened from a long, dreamless sleep.

A click, then recorded music. He had been placed on hold.

There was something he was trying to remember. Everything seemed to be ready, but—

"Thank-you-for-waiting-good-afternoon-Pacific-Southwest-Airlines-may--I-help-you?"

He told the voice about his reservation; he was sure he had one. Would she—

Yes. Confirmed.

He thanked her and hung up.

Wait. What was the flight number? He must have written it down—yes. It was probably in his wallet.

He bent over the coat on the bed, feeling for the slim leather billfold. There, in the breast pocket. He fumbled through business cards, odd papers, credit plates.

No.

But no matter. He would find out when he got there.

Still, there was *something*.

He pulled out the drawer in the nightstand, under the phone, and started poking around, not even sure of what he was looking for.

He found a long, unmarked envelope, near the bottom. He took it and held it tightly as he slipped the coat on, then put it into the inside pocket while he felt with his other hand for the keys. He patted his outer pockets, but they were not there.

Head down, he left the room.

His bags were stacked neatly by the wall of the foyer, but the keys were not there. He paced through the living room, the kitchen, checking the tables.

He went back to the bedroom, eyes down.

There.

By the door. The key ring was wedged by the bottom edge, between the door and the pile of the carpet, as though it had been flung or kicked there.

He picked it up, walked to the front door, lifted his bags, and went out to the car.

It was still early afternoon, so the freeway would be a clear shot most of the way.

He switched off the air conditioning—who had left it on?—and rolled down the window, stretching out. The seat was adjusted wrong again, damn it, so he had to grope for the lever and push with his feet, struggling to seat the runner back another notch.

He connected through to the San Diego Freeway, made the turn and tried to unwind the rest of the way. He sampled the radio, but it was only more of the same: back scratchings about love or the lack of it and the pleasure or the pain it brought or might bring; maybe, could be, possibly, for sure, always, never, too soon, not soon enough, in the wrong rain or the wrong style. *Wrong, wrong.* He flicked it off.

The airport turnoff would be coming up.

He flexed his arm, checking his watch. But it had stopped. The face was spattered with dry, flaking paint, so it would have been hard to read the numbers, anyway.

He toed the accelerator until he was moving five miles over the speed limit, then ten.

He was glad to have made such good time; a few extra minutes would mean a drink first, maybe two—

It was funny. The car ahead, at the foot of the ramp. The back-up lights were on, but not the brake lights. He did not slow, because it meant that the signal at the intersection would be—

Headlights. They were headlights.

Headed directly at him.

You can go now, said a voice.

He leaned on the horn, but then there was the heavy, bonesnapping impact and everything was driven into him with such force that the horn stayed on, bleating like a siren, whether or not he would have wanted it to or would even have thought of it or of anything, of anything else at all.

2

He was late getting to LAX, so he swung at once into the western parking lot, hoofed it over to the PSA building and sloughed his bags through the metal detector without stopping at the flight information desk. A couple of quick questions later, a hostess in a Halloween-colored uniform was pointing him toward the boarding tunnel, and then another was ushering him onto the plane and back to the smoking section.

He stashed his bags and found himself in a seat on the aisle, next to a pregnant woman and two drugged-looking hyperactive children. They continued to squirm, but slowly, as though underwater, as he tugged at the seat belt, trying to dislodge the oversized buckle from beneath his buttocks.

A double vodka and two cigarettes later, he was halfway to Oakland and swinging inland away from the silvery tilt of the sea. He drained the ice against his teeth and snared the elbow of a stewardess.

Another?

Well, the bottles were all put away, but—yes. Of course.

Of course.

The smaller child was busy on the floor in front of the seat, trying to tear out the pages of a washable cloth picture book about animals who wore gloves and had one-syllable names. The child had already stripped the airline coloring book, the oxygen mask instruction card and the air sickness bag into piles of ragged chits. Now, however, he dropped his work and wobbled to his feet, straining to clamber up the seat and under his mother's smock.

But the mother was absorbed in the counting and recounting of empty punch cups—one, two, three, see? one, two three—over and over, for the older child, who was working with all his might to slide out from under his seat belt. He would flatten like a limbo dancer until his shoes touched the floor and his knees buckled; then the mother would reach down, hoist him back up and begin counting the cups for him again.

"One, two, three, see? Why don't you try, Joshua?"

Ignored, the smaller child twisted like a bendable rubber doll and, sucking the ink off two fingers, watched the man across from him.

Who looked away. He was, mercifully, beginning to feel something from the double: a familiar ease, faint but unmistakable. He folded his hands, cold against each other, and tried to unwind while there was still time. He caught a glimpse out the window of farmlands sectioned like the layers of a surgical operation, beyond the flashing tip of the wing.

The child followed his eyes. "Break-ing," the child announced.

Idly he watched the wing swaying slowly as it knifed through the air currents. He remembered seeing the wing moving up and down like that on his first flight, how he worried that it might break off until someone had explained to him about expansion and contraction and allowances for stress.

"What's breaking?" said the mother. "Nothing's breaking, Jeremiah. Look, look what Mommy's . . ."

The stewardess reappeared. She rattled the plastic serving tray, bending over his lap with the drink.

He reached into his back pocket for his wallet.

"Want more punch!" said the older child.

"More punch?" asked the stewardess.

The wallet wasn't there. He remembered. He reached inside his coat.

He felt a long envelope, and the billfold. He removed both, peeled off two bills and laid them on the tray.

"Break-ing!" said the smaller child.

At that moment a shadow passed over the tray and the stewardess's wet fingers. He glanced up.

Outside, heavy strands of mist had begun to drift above the wings, temporarily blocking the sun. Looking down, he saw the black outline of the plane passing over the manicured rectangles of land.

Suddenly, sharply, the plane dropped like an elevator falling between floors. Then just as suddenly it stopped.

"Looks like we might be hitting some turbulence," he said. "Sure you've got a pilot up there?"

His attention returned to the window. Now darker clouds clotted the view, turning the window opaque so that he saw a reflection of his own face within the thick glass.

He heard a voice say something he did not understand.

"What?" he said.

"I said, that's funny," said the stewardess, "like an open grave."

A flash of brilliant light struck outside, penetrating the cloud bank. She stopped pouring the drink. He looked up at her, then at the tray. He noticed that her hands were shaking.

Then a dull, muffled sound from the back of the plane. Then a series of jolts that rattled the bottle against the lip of the glass. He thought he heard a distant crackling, like ants crawling over aluminum foil. Then the quick, shocking smell of smoke wafted up the aisle.

"Oh my God," whispered the stewardess hoarsely, "we've been—"

"I know," he said, strangely calm, "I know," *with tears of blood I tell you I know.*

The tray, ice and drink went flying, and then they were falling, everything falling inward and children, pillows, oxygen masks, bottles, the envelope he still clutched stupidly in his hand, the whole thing, the plane and the entire world were falling, falling and would not, could not be stopped.

It was dusk as he drove into the delta, and the river, washed over with the memory of the dying red eye of the sun, seemed to be reflecting a gradual darkening of the world.

He wound down the windows of the rented car, cranking back the wind wings so that he could feel the air. The smell of seed crops and of the rich, silted undergrowth of the banks blew around him, bathing him in the special dark parturience of the Sacramento Valley.

He had been away too long.

And soon he would be back, away for a time from the practices of the city, which he had come to think of more and more lately as the art of doing natural things in an unnatural way—something he was afraid he had learned all too well. But now, very soon, he would be back on the houseboat; for a while, at least.

He did not know how long.

He would anchor somewhere near The Meadows. He would tie up to that same tree in the deep, still water, near the striped bass hole, hearing the lowing of cattle from behind the clutch of wild blackberry bushes on shore . . .

And this time, he dared himself, he might not go back at all. Not, at least, for a long, long time.

He drove past the weathered, century-old mansions left from the gold days, past the dirt roads marked only by rural mailboxes, past the fanning rows of shadowy, pungent trees, past the collapsing wooden walkways of the abandoned settlement towns, past the broad landmark barn and the whitewash message fading on its doors, one he had never understood:

HIARA PERU RESH.

He geared down and took the last, unpaved mile in a growing rush of anticipation. Rocks and eucalyptus pods rained up under the car, the wheel jerking in his hands, the shocks and the leaf springs groaning and creaking.

Then he saw a curl of smoke beyond the next grove and caught the warm smell of catfish frying over open coals. And he knew, at last, that he was nearing the inlet, the diner and the dock.

He braked in the gravel and walked down the path to the riverbank. He heard the lapping of the tide and the low, heavy knocking of hulls against splintered pilings. Finally he saw the long pier, the planks glistening, the light and dark prows of cabin cruisers rocking in their berths, the dinghies tied up to battered cleats, their slack, frayed ropes swollen where they dipped into the water, the buoys bobbing slowly, the running lights of a smaller, rented houseboat chugging away around the bend, toward Wimpy's Landing.

The boards moved underfoot as he counted the steps, head down, and he smiled, reminding himself that it would take a few hours to regain his sea legs. He reached the spot, a few yards from the end of the docking area, where he knew the *Shelley Ann* would be waiting.

He tried to remember how long it had been. Since the spring. Yes, that was right, Memorial Day weekend. Sometimes friends rode him about paying for the year-round space—why, when he used her only a few times each year? Even Shelley had begun talking that way in the last few weeks. *Cut your losses on that albatross!* She had actually said that. But at times like this, coming to her after so many months, he forgot it all. It felt like coming home. It always did.

He looked up.

The space was empty.

His eyes darted around the landing, but she was nowhere that he could see.

Unless—of course. She had been moved. That was it. But why? His boat had never been assigned any other stall for as long as he had owned her. Something had happened, then. But there had been no long distance call, no word in the mail; Old John would not be one to hide anything as serious as an accident. Would he?

He took a few steps, his hands in his back pockets, scanning the river in both directions.

He could just make out the diner/office/tackle shop through the trees. A dim light was burning behind the peeling wooden panes.

Yes. Old John would know. Old John would be able to tell him the story, whatever it was.

Which was the trouble. Knowing him, it would take an hour, two. A beer, three beers, maybe even dinner. The lonely old man would not let him go with a simple explanation, of that he was sure.

And now he found he could think only of the *Shelley Ann*. He had waited and he had planned and he had come all this way, and at the moment nothing else seemed to matter. He needed to feel her swaying under him, rocking him. Now, right now.

Then. Everything. Would be. All right.

He stepped off the end to the bank, peering under the covered section of the landing, even though he knew that his boat would have been too large to clear the drooping canvas overhang.

He crouched at the edge, feeling suddenly very alone. The river smelled like dead stars. He watched the water purl gently around the floats and echo back and forth over the fine sand. A few small bubbles rode the surface, and a thin patina of oil shone with mirror-like luminescence under the dimming sky, reflecting a dark, swirling rainbow.

No stars were visible yet. In fact, the sky above the trees grew more steely as he watched.

He looked again at the water. He fingered a chip of gravel and tossed it. It made a plunking sound and settled quickly, and as it disappeared he found that he was straining to follow it with his eyes all the way down to the bottom.

He reached into his coat for a cigarette. His hands were still cold, and growing colder.

He felt the cigarette case and drew it out, along with something else.

He pushed a cigarette into his lips and stared at the envelope. It had no name and address on it. He couldn't remember—

He opened it, slipped out a neatly folded sheet of bond paper, unfolded it.

The leaves of the trees near him rustled, and then a light breeze strafed the water, tipping it with silver.

Still crouching, he fired up the lighter, lit the cigarette and squinted, trying to make out the words. It was written in careful longhand, a letter or—no. Something else.

He read the title.

The paper began to make a tapping sound. He held out his hand. Rain had started to fall, a light rain that danced on the river and left it glittering. As he blinked down at the paper, more drops hit the page. The ink began to run, blurring before his eyes.

The lighter became too hot to hold. He snapped it shut and stood. He heard the rain talking in the trees, on the canvas tarpaulin, on the struts of the rotting pier.

His legs were cramped. He made a staggering step forward. His shoes sloshed the water. He stepped still further, led by the swinging arc of his cigarette tip in the darkness, until the rain found the cigarette and extinguished it.

He dropped it and moved forward, ankle-deep in the river. Is she really there? he thought.

Then he waded out into the low tide, the rain striking around him with a sound like musical notes, the melting paper still gripped in his hand, trailing the water.

4

Dazed, he glanced around the bedroom.

The receiver was in his hand. By now the plastic had become quite warm against his palm. He stared at it for a moment, then returned it to his ear.

He heard recorded music.

Click.

"Thank-you-for-waiting-good-afternoon-Pacific-Southwest-Airlines-may–I-help-you?"

There was something he wanted to tell her. He had been trying hard to remember, but—

His eyes continued to roam the lower half of the room. Then he spotted the keys, the car keys, wedged between the bottom edge of the door and the pile of the carpet, as though they had been flung or kicked there with great force.

It started to come back to him. Shelley had done it. She had thrown the key ring with all her strength, a while ago. Yes. That had happened.

He raised his head at last, rubbed his neck.

And saw her, there on the other side of the bed.

She lay with eyes closed, hands at her sides, fingers clutching the bedspread.

He didn't want to disturb her. He modulated his voice, cupping the mouthpiece with his hand.

He told the maddeningly cheerful voice on the phone—it reminded him of a Nichiren Shoshu recruiter who had buttonholed him on the street once—to cancel one reservation. His wife was not ready, would not be ready on time.

Yes. Only one. That's right. Thank you.

He hung up.

He lifted the phone and replaced it on the nightstand.

On the bed, where the phone had been, was an envelope.

He picked it up.

It was empty.

There was a sheet of paper on the floor, where Shelley had crumpled and thrown it. That was right, wasn't it?

He smoothed it out on his knee.

It was written in a very careful, painstaking longhand, much more legible than his own. He started to read it.

At the end of the first stanza he paused.

Yes, it was something Shelley had found—no, she had had it all along, saved (hidden?) in her drawer in the nightstand. She had taken it out earlier this morning, or perhaps it had been last night, and had shown it to him, and one of them had become angry and crumpled it onto the floor. That was how it had started.

He read it again, this time to the end.

(1)
brown hair
curling smile
shadowed eyes
the line of your lips . . .
hair tangled
over me

(2)
warm skin
tender breasts
your mouth and
sweet throat . . .
hair moist
under me

(3)
there will be more
my eyes tell your eyes

than love of touch
face lost in my face . . .
do you know what lives
between our breathing palms?

(4)
twisted hair
seashell ear
soft sounds
stopped by my chest . . .
dark eyes sleep
while I speak to your heart

He turned to his wife.

It was true; she was beautiful. Whoever had written those words had loved her. He studied her intently until he began to feel an odd sense of dislocation, as if he were seeing her for the first time.

He looked again at the paper.

At the bottom of the page, following the last stanza, there was a name.

It was his own.

And in the corner, a date: almost fifteen years ago.

Quietly, almost imperceptibly, he began to cry.

For so much had changed over the years, much more than handwriting. He did not love her now, not in any traditional sense; instead, he thought, there was merely a sense of loving that seemed to exist somewhere between her and his mind.

As he sat there, he forced his eyes to trace the lines of her body, her face: the shrug of her shoulders, the sweep of her long, slender neck, the surprisingly full jaw and yet the almost weak point of the chin, the slight lips, the sad curve at the corners of her mouth, the smooth, even shade of her skin, the narrow nose, the nearly parallel lines that formed the sides of her small face, the close-set eyes, the thin and almond-shaped lids and delicately sketched lashes, the worried cast of her forehead and the baby-fine wisps at the hairline, the soft down that grew near her temples, the fuller curls that filled out a nimbus around her head, the hair bunched behind her neck, the ends hard and stiff now where the dried brown web had trickled out, just a spot at first but soon spreading onto the pillow after he had lain her down so gently. He had not meant it. He had not meant anything like it. He did not even remember what he had meant, and that was the truth. He had tried to tell her that, practically at the moment it had happened, but then it was too late. And it was too late now. It would always be too late.

He lowered his head.

When he opened his eyes again, he was looking at the paper.

At the top of the page, perfectly centered, was the title. It said:

YOU CAN GO NOW.

D. H. Lawrence

The Rocking-horse Winner

D. H. Lawrence, the great critic, poet, novelist and short story writer, made only this one landmark contribution to the evolution of the horror story, a small masterpiece of Modern literature. During the era when the Modernists had for the most part assumed the death of the supernatural tale in the mainstream of literature, the investigation of abnormal human psychology remained nevertheless at the center of much fiction. So one of the mainstreams of horror, became prominent in such fiction as "The Rocking-horse Winner," a story of monstrosity using the form of the "possessed child" story but without supernatural paraphrenalia. The child is haunted, possessed, but the most overt interpretation is Freudian, not moral, allegory.

There was a woman who was beautiful, who started with all the advantages, yet she had no luck. She married for love, and the love turned to dust. She had bonny children, yet she felt they had been thrust upon her, and she could not love them. They looked at her coldly, as if they were finding fault with her. And hurriedly she felt she must cover up some fault in herself. Yet what it was that she must cover up she never knew. Nevertheless, when her children were present, she always felt the centre of her heart go hard. This troubled her, and in her manner, she was all the more gentle and anxious for her children, as if she loved them very much. Only she herself knew that at the centre of her heart was a hard little place that could not feel love, no, not for anybody. Everybody else said of her. "She is such a good mother. She adores her children." Only she herself, and her children themselves, knew it was not so. They read it in each other's eyes.

There was a boy and two little girls. They lived in a pleasant house, with a garden, and they had discreet servants, and felt themselves superior to anyone in the neighbourhood.

Although they lived in style, they felt always an anxiety in the house. There was never enough money. The mother had a small income, and the father had a small income, but not nearly enough for the social position which they had to keep up. The father went into town to some office. But though he had good prospects, these prospects never materialized. There was always the grinding sense of the shortage of money, though the style was always kept up.

At last the mother said, "I will see if *I* can't make something." But she did not know where to begin. She racked her brains, and tried this thing and the other, but could not find anything successful. The failure made deep lines come into her face. Her children were growing up, they would have to go to

541

school. There must be more money, there must be more money. The father, who was always very handsome and expensive in his tastes, seemed as if he never *would* be able to do anything worth doing. And the mother, who had a great belief in herself, did not succeed any better, and her tastes were just as expensive.

And so the house came to be haunted by the unspoken phrase: *There must be more money! There must be more money!* The children could hear it all the time, though nobody said it aloud. They heard it at Christmas, when the expensive and splendid toys filled the nursery. Behind the shining modern rocking-horse, behind the smart doll's-house, a voice would start whispering, "There *must* be more money! There *must* be more money!" And the children would stop playing, to listen for a moment. They would look into each other's eyes, to see if they had all heard. And each one saw in the eyes of the other two that they too had heard. "There *must* be more money! There *must* be more money!"

It came whispering from the springs of the still-swaying rocking-horse, and even the horse, bending his wooden, champing head, heard it. The big doll, sitting so pink and smirking in her new pram, could hear it quite plainly, and seemed to be smirking all the more self-consciously because of it. The foolish puppy too, that took the place of the teddy-bear, he was looking so extraordinarily foolish for no other reason but that he heard the secret whisper all over the house. "There *must* be more money."

Yet nobody ever said it aloud. The whisper was everywhere, and therefore no one spoke it. Just as no one ever says: "We are breathing!" in spite of the fact that breath is coming and going all the time.

"Mother!" said the boy Paul one day. "Why don't we keep a car of our own? Why do we always use uncle's or else a taxi?"

"Because we're the poor members of the family," said the mother.

"But *why* are we, Mother?"

"Well—I suppose," she said slowly and bitterly, "it's because your father has no luck."

The boy was silent for some time.

"Is luck money, Mother?" he asked, rather timidly.

"No, Paul! Not quite. It's what causes you to have money."

"Oh!" said Paul vaguely. "I thought when Uncle Oscar said *filthy lucker*, it meant money."

"*Filthy lucre* does mean money," said the mother. "But it's lucre, not luck."

"Oh!" said the boy. "Then what *is* luck, Mother?"

"It's what causes you to have money. If you're lucky you have money. That's why it's better to be born lucky than rich. If you're rich, you may lose your money. But if you're lucky, you will always get more money."

"Oh! Will you! And is Father not lucky?"

"Very unlucky, I should say," she said, bitterly.

The boy watched her with unsure eyes.

"Why?" he asked.

"I don't know. Nobody ever knows why one person is lucky and another unlucky."

"Don't they? Nobody at all? Does *nobody* know?"

"Perhaps God! But He never tells."

"He ought to, then. And aren't you lucky either, Mother?"

"I can't be, if I married an unlucky husband."

"But by yourself, aren't you?"

"I used to think I was, before I married. Now I think I am very unlucky indeed."

"Why?"

"Well—never mind! Perhaps I'm not really," she said.

The child looked at her, to see if she meant it. But he saw, by the lines of her mouth, that she was only trying to hide something from him.

"Well, anyhow," he said stoutly. "I'm a lucky person."

"Why?" said his mother, with a sudden laugh.

He stared at her. He didn't even know why he had said it.

"God told me," he asserted, brazening it out.

"I hope He did, dear!" she said, again with a laugh, but rather bitter.

"He did, Mother!"

"Excellent!" said the mother, using one of her husband's exclamations.

The boy saw she did not believe him; or rather, that she paid no attention to his assertion. This angered him somewhere, and made him want to compel her attention.

He went off by himself, vaguely, in a childish way, seeking for the clue to "luck." Absorbed, taking no heed of other people, he went about with a sort of stealth, seeking inwardly for luck. He wanted luck, he wanted it, he wanted it. When the two girls were playing dolls, in the nursery, he would sit on his big rocking-horse, charging madly into space, with a frenzy that made the little girls peer at him uneasily. Wildly the horse careered, the waving dark hair of the boy tossed, his eyes had a strange glare in them. The little girls dared not speak to him.

When he had ridden to the end of his mad little journey, he climbed down and stood in front of his rocking-horse, staring fixedly into its lowered face. Its red mouth was slightly open, its big eye was wide and glassy bright.

"Now!" he would silently command the snorting steed. "Now take me where there is luck! Now take me!"

And he would slash the horse on the neck with the little whip he had asked Uncle Oscar for. He *knew* the horse could take him to where there was luck, if only he forced it. So he would mount again, and start on his furious ride, hoping at last to get there. He knew he could get there.

"You'll break your horse, Paul!" said the nurse.

"He's always riding like that! I wish he'd leave off!" said his elder sister Joan.

But he only glared down on them in silence. Nurse gave him up. She could make nothing of him. Anyhow he was growing beyond her.

One day his mother and his Uncle Oscar came in when he was on one of his furious rides. He did not speak to them.

"Hallo! you young jockey! Riding a winner?" said his uncle.

"Aren't you growing too big for a rocking-horse? You're not a very little boy any longer, you know," said his mother.

But Paul only gave a blue glare from his big, rather close-set eyes. He would speak to nobody when he was in full tilt. His mother watched him with an anxious expression on her face.

At last he suddenly stopped forcing his horse into the mechanical gallop, and slid down.

"Well, I got there!" he announced fiercely, his blue eyes still flaring, and his sturdy long legs straddling apart.

"Where did you get to?" asked his mother.

"Where I wanted to go to," he flared back at her.

"That's right, son!" said Uncle Oscar. "Don't you stop till you get there. What's the horse's name?"

"He doesn't have a name," said the boy.

"Gets on without all right?" asked the uncle.

"Well, he has different names. He was called Sansovino last week."

"Sansovino, eh? Won the Ascot. How did you know his name?"

"He always talks about horse-races with Bassett," said Joan.

The uncle was delighted to find that his small nephew was posted with all the racing news. Bassett, the young gardener who had been wounded in the left foot in the war, and had got his present job through Oscar Cresswell, whose batman he had been, was a perfect blade of the "turf." He lived in the racing events, and the small boy lived with him.

Oscar Cresswell got it all from Bassett.

"Master Paul comes and askes me, so I can't do more than tell him, sir," said Bassett, his face terribly serious, as if he were speaking of religious matters.

"And does he ever put anything on a horse he fancies?"

"Well—I don't want to give him away—he's a young sport, a fine sport, sir. Would you mind asking him himself? He sort of takes a pleasure in it, and perhaps he'd feel I was giving him away, sir, if you don't mind."

Bassett was serious as a church.

The uncle went back to his nephew, and took him off for a ride in the car.

"Say, Paul, old man, do you ever put anything on a horse?" the uncle asked.

The boy watched the handsome man closely.

"Why, do you think I oughtn't to?" he parried.

"Not a bit of it! I thought perhaps you might give me a tip for the Lincoln."

The car sped on into the country, going down to Uncle Oscar's place in Hampshire.

"Honour bright?" said the nephew.

"Honour bright, son!" said the uncle.

"Well, then, Daffodil."

"Daffodil! I doubt it, sonny. What about Mirza?"

"I only know the winner," said the boy. "That's Daffodil!"

"Daffodil, eh?"

There was a pause. Daffodil was an obscure horse, comparatively.

"Uncle!"

"Yes, son?"

"You won't let it go any further, will you? I promised Bassett."

"Bassett be damned, old man! What's he got to do with it?"

"We're partners! We've been partners from the first! Uncle, he lent me my first five shillings, which I lost. I promised him, honour bright, it was only between me and him: only you gave me that ten-shilling note I started winning with, so I thought you were lucky. You won't let it go any further, will you?"

The boy gazed at his uncle from those big, hot, blue eyes, set rather close together. The uncle stirred and laughed uneasily.

"Right you are, son! I'll keep your tip private. Daffodil, eh! How much are you putting on him?"

"All except twenty pounds," said the boy. "I keep that in reserve."

The uncle thought it was a joke.

"You keep twenty pounds in reserve, do you, you young romancer? What are you betting, then?"

"I'm betting three hundred," said the boy gravely. "But it's between you and me, Uncle Oscar! Honour bright?"

The uncle burst into a roar of laughter.

"It's between you and me all right, you young Nat Gould," he said, laughing. "But where's your three hundred?"

"Bassett keeps it for me. We're partners."

"You are, are you! And what is Bassett putting on Daffodil?"

"He won't go quite as high as I do, I expect. Perhaps he'll go a hundred and fifty."

"What, pennies?" laughed the uncle.

"Pounds," said the child, with a surprised look at his uncle. "Bassett keeps a bigger reserve than I do."

Between wonder and amusement, Uncle Oscar was silent. He pursued the matter no further, but he determined to take his nephew with him to the Lincoln races.

"Now, son," he said. "I'm putting twenty on Mirza, and I'll put five for you on any horse you fancy. What's your pick?"

"Daffodil, uncle!"

"No, not the fiver on Daffodil!"

"I should if it was my own fiver," said the child.

"Good! Good! Right you are! A fiver for me and a fiver for you on Daffodil."

The child had never been to a race-meeting before, and his eyes were blue fire. He pursed his mouth tight, and watched. A Frenchman just in front had put his money on Lancelot. Wild with excitement, he flared his arms up and down, yelling "*Lancelot! Lancelot!*" in his French accent.

Daffodil came in first, Lancelot second, Mirza third. The child, flushed and with eyes blazing, was curiously serene. His uncle brought him five five-pound notes: four to one.

"What am I to do with these?" he cried, waving them before the boy's eyes.

"I suppose we'll talk to Bassett," said the boy. "I expect I have fifteen hundred now: and twenty in reserve: and this twenty."

His uncle studied him for some moments.

"Look here, son!" he said. "You're not serious about Bassett and that fifteen hundred, are you?"

"Yes, I am. But it's between you and me, uncle! Honour bright!"

"Honour bright, all right, son! But I must talk to Bassett."

"If you'd like to be a partner, uncle, with Bassett and me, we could all be partners. Only you'd have to promise, honour bright, uncle, not to let it go beyond us three. Bassett and I are lucky, and you must be lucky, because it was your ten shillings I started winning with . . ."

Uncle Oscar took both Bassett and Paul into Richmond Park for an afternoon, and there they talked.

"It's like this, you see, sir," Bassett said. "Master Paul would get me talking about racing events, spinning yarns, you know, sir. And he was always keen on knowing if I'd made or if I'd lost. It's about a year since, now, that I put five shillings on Blush of Dawn for him: and we lost. Then the luck turned, with that ten shillings he had from you: that we put on Singhalese. And since that time, it's been pretty steady, all things considering. What do you say, Master Paul?"

"We're all right when we're *sure*," said Paul. "It's when we're not quite sure that we go down."

"Oh, but we're careful then," said Bassett.

"But when are your *sure*?" smiled Uncle Oscar.

"It's Master Paul, sir," said Bassett, in a secret, religious voice. "It's as if he had it from heaven. Like Daffodil, now, for the Lincoln. That was as sure as eggs."

"Did you put anything on Daffodil?" asked Oscar Cresswell.

"Yes, sir. I made my bit."

"And my nephew?"

Bassett was obstinately silent, looking at Paul.

"I made twelve hundred, didn't I, Bassett? I told uncle I was putting three hundred on Daffodil."

"That's right," said Bassett, nodding.

"But where's the money?" asked the uncle.

"I keep it safe locked up, sir. Master Paul, he can have it any minute he likes to ask for it."

"What, fifteen hundred pounds?"

"And twenty! And *forty*, that is, with the twenty he made on the course."

"It's amazing," said the uncle.

"If Master Paul offers you to be partners, sir, I would, if I were you: if you'll excuse me," said Bassett.

Oscar Cresswell thought about it.

"I'll see the money," he said.

They drove home again, and sure enough, Bassett came round to the garden-house with fifteen hundred pounds in notes. The twenty pounds reserve was left with Joe Glee, in the Turf Commission deposit.

"You see, it's all right, uncle, when I'm *sure!* Then we go strong, for all we're worth. Don't we, Bassett?"

"We do that, Master Paul."

"And when are you sure?" said the uncle, laughing.

"Oh well, sometimes I'm absolutely sure, like about Daffodil," said the boy; "and sometimes I have an idea; and sometimes I haven't an idea, have I, Bassett? Then we're careful, because we mostly go down."

"You do, do you! And when you're sure, like about Daffodil, what makes you sure, sonny?"

"Oh, well, I don't know," said the boy uneasily. "I'm sure, you know, uncle; that's all."

"It's as if he had it from heaven, sir," Bassett reiterated.

"I should say so!" said the uncle.

But he became a partner. And when the Leger was coming on, Paul was "sure" about Lively Spark, which was a quite inconsiderable horse. The boy insisted on putting a thousand on the horse, Bassett went for five hundred, and Oscar Cresswell two hundred. Lively Spark came in first and the betting had been ten to one against him. Paul had made ten thousand.

"You see," he said, "I was absolutely sure of him."

Even Oscar Cresswell had cleared two thousand.

"Look here, son," he said, "this sort of thing makes me nervous."

"It needn't, uncle! Perhaps I shan't be sure again for a long time."

"But what are you going to do with your money?" asked the uncle.

"Of course," said the boy, "I started it for Mother. She said she had no luck, because Father is unlucky, so I thought if I was lucky, it might stop whispering."

"What might stop whispering?"

"Our house! I *hate* our house for whispering."

"What does it whisper?"

"Why—why"—the boy fidgeted—"why I don't know! But it's always short of money, you know, uncle."

"I know it, son, I know it."

"You know people send Mother writs, don't you uncle?"

"I'm afraid I do," said the uncle.

"And then the house whispers like people laughing at you behind your back. It's awful, that is! I thought if I was lucky—"

"You might stop it," added the uncle.

The boy watched him with big blue eyes, that had an uncanny cold fire in them, and he said never a word.

"Well, then!" said the uncle. "What are we doing?"

"I shouldn't like Mother to know I was lucky," said the boy.

"Why not, son?"

"She'd stop me."

"I don't think she would."

"Oh!"—and the boy writhed in an odd way—"I *don't* want her to know, uncle."

"All right, son! We'll manage it without her knowing."

They managed it very easily. Paul, at the other's suggestion, handed over five thousand pounds to his uncle, who deposited it with the family lawyer, who was then to inform Paul's mother that a relative had put five thousand pounds into his hands, which sum was to be paid out a thousand pounds at a time, on the mother's birthday, for the next five years.

"So she'll have a birthday present of a thousand pounds for five successive years," said Uncle Oscar.

"I hope it won't make it all the harder for her later."

Paul's mother had her birthday in November. The house had been "whispering" worse than ever lately, and even in spite of his luck, Paul could not bear up against it. He was very anxious to see the effect of the birthday letter, telling his mother about the thousand pounds.

When there were no visitors, Paul now took his meals with his parents, as he was beyond the nursery control. His mother went into town nearly every day. She had discovered that she had an odd knack of sketching furs and dress materials, so she worked secretly in the studio of a friend who was the chief "artist" for the leading drapers. She drew the figures of ladies in furs and ladies in silk and sequins for the newspaper advertisements. This young woman artist earned several thousand pounds a year, but Paul's mother only made several hundreds, and she was again dissatisfied. She so wanted to be first in something, and she did not succeed, even in making sketches for drapery advertisements.

She was down to breakfast on the morning of her birthday. Paul watched her face as she read her letters. He knew the lawyer's letter. As his mother read it, her face hardened and became more expressionless. Then a cold, determined look came on her mouth. She hid the letter under the pile of others, and said not a word about it.

"Didn't you have anything nice in the post for your birthday, Mother?" said Paul.

"Quite moderately nice," she said, her voice cold and absent.

She went away to town without saying more.

But in the afternoon Uncle Oscar appeared. He said Paul's mother had had a long interview with the lawyer, asking if the whole five thousand could not be advanced at once, as she was in debt.

"What do you think, uncle?" said the boy.

"I leave it to you, son."

"Oh, let her have it, then! We can get some more with the other," said the boy.

"A bird in the hand is worth two in the bush, laddie!" said Uncle Oscar.

"But I'm sure to *know* for the Grand National; or the Lincolnshire; or else the Derby. I'm sure to know for *one* of them," said Paul.

So Uncle Oscar signed the agreement, and Paul's mother touched the whole five thousand. Then something very curious happened. The voices in the house suddenly went mad, like a chorus of frogs on a spring evening. There were certain new furnishings, and Paul had a tutor. He was *really* going to Eton, his father's school, in the following autumn. There were flowers in the winter, and a blossoming of the luxury Paul's mother had been used to. And yet the voices in the house, behind the sprays of mimosa and almond-blossom, and from under the piles of iridescent cushions, simply trilled and screamed in a sort of ecstasy: "There *must* be more money! Oh-h-h! There *must* be more money! Oh, now, now-w! now-w-w—there *must* be more money!—more than ever! More than ever!"

It frightened Paul terribly. He studied away at his Latin and Greek with his tutors. But his intense hours were spent with Bassett. The Grand National had gone by; he had not "known," and had lost a hundred pounds. Summer was at hand. He was in agony for the Lincoln. But even for the Lincoln he didn't "know," and he lost fifty pounds. He became wild-eyed and strange, as if something were going to explode in him.

"Let it alone, son! Don't you bother about it!" urged Uncle Oscar. But it was as if the boy couldn't really hear what his uncle was saying.

"I've got to know for the Derby! I've *got* to know for the Derby!" the child reiterated, his big blue eyes blazing with a sort of madness.

His mother noticed how overwrought he was.

"You'd better go to the seaside. Wouldn't you like to go now to the seaside, instead of waiting? I think you'd better," she said, looking down at him anxiously, her heart curiously heavy because of him.

But the child lifted his uncanny blue eyes.

"I couldn't possibly go before the Derby, Mother!" he said. "I couldn't possibly!"

"Why not?" she said, her voice becoming heavy when she was opposed. "Why not? You can still go from the seaside to see the Derby with your Uncle Oscar if that's what you wish. No need for you to wait here. Besides, I think you care too much about these races. It's a bad sign. My family has been a gambling family, and you won't know till you grow up how much damage it has done. But it has done damage. I shall have to send Bassett away and ask Uncle Oscar not to talk racing to you, unless you promise to be reasonable about it; go away to the seaside and forget it. You're all nerves!"

"I'll do what you like, Mother, so long as you don't send me away till after the Derby," the boy said.

"Send you away from where? Just from this house?"

"Yes," he said, gazing at her.

"Why, you curious child, what makes you care about this house so much, suddenly? I never knew you loved it!"

He gazed at her without speaking. He had a secret within a secret, something he had not divulged, even to Bassett or to his Uncle Oscar.

But his mother, after standing undecided and a little bit sullen for some moments, said:

"Very well, then! Don't go to the seaside till after the Derby, if you don't wish it. But promise me you won't let your nerves go to pieces! Promise you won't think so much about horse-racing and *events*, as you call them!"

"Oh no!" said the boy, casually. "I won't think much about them, Mother. You needn't worry. I wouldn't worry, Mother, if I were you."

"If you were me and I were you," said his mother, "I wonder what we *should* do!"

"But you know you needn't worry, Mother, don't you?" the boy repeated.

"I should be awfully glad to know it," she said wearily.

"Oh, well, you can, you know. I mean you ought to know you needn't worry!" he insisted.

"Ought I? Then I'll see about it," she said.

Paul's secret of secrets was his wooden horse, that which had no name. Since he was emancipated from a nurse and a nursery governess, he had had his rocking-horse removed to his own bedroom at the top of the house.

"Surely you're too big for a rocking-horse," his mother had remonstrated.

"Well, you see, Mother, till I can have a *real* horse, I like to have *some* sort of animal about," had been his quaint answer.

"Do you feel he keeps you company?" she laughed.

"Oh yes! He's very good, he always keeps me company, when I'm there," said Paul.

So the horse, rather shabby, stood in an arrested prance in the boy's bedroom.

The Derby was drawing near, and the boy grew more and more tense. He hardly heard what was spoken to him, he was very frail, and his eyes were really uncanny. His mother had sudden strange seizures of uneasiness about him. Sometimes, for half an hour, she would feel a sudden anxiety about him that was almost anguish. She wanted to rush to him at once, and know he was safe.

Two nights before the Derby, she was at a big party in town, when one of her rushes of anxiety about her boy, her first-born, gripped her heart till she could hardly speak. She fought with the feeling, might and main, for she believed in common-sense. But it was too strong. She had to leave the dance and go downstairs to telephone to the country. The children's nursery governess was terribly surprised and startled at being rung up in the night.

"Are the children all right, Miss Wilmot?"

"Oh yes, they are quite all right."

"Master Paul? Is he all right?"

"He went to bed as right as a trivet. Shall I run up and look at him?"

"No!" said Paul's mother reluctantly. "No! Don't trouble. It's all right. Don't sit up. We shall be home fairly soon." She did not want her son's privacy intruded upon.

"Very good," said the governess.

It was about one o'clock when Paul's mother and father drove up to their house. All was still. Paul's mother went to her room and slipped off her white fur cloak. She had told the maid not to wait up for her. She heard her husband downstairs, mixing a whisky-and-soda.

And then, because of the strange anxiety at her heart, she stole upstairs to her son's room. Noiselessly, she went along the upper corridor. Was there a faint noise? What was it?

She stood, with arrested muscles, outside his door, listening. There was a strange, heavy, and yet not loud noise. Her heart stood still. It was a soundless noise, yet rushing and powerful. Something huge, in violent, hushed motion. What was it? What in God's Name was it? She ought to know. She felt she *knew* the noise. She knew what it was.

Yet she could not place it. She couldn't say what it was. And on and on it went, like a madness.

Softly, frozen with anxiety and fear, she turned the door-handle.

The room was dark. Yet in the space near the window, she heard and saw something plunging to and fro. She gazed in fear and amazement.

Then suddenly she switched on the light, and saw her son, in his green pyjamas, madly surging on his rocking-horse. The blaze of light suddenly lit him up, as he urged the wooden horse, and lit her up, as she stood, blonde, in her dress of pale green and crystal, in the doorway.

"Paul!" she cried. "Whatever are you doing?"

"It's Malabar!" he screamed, in a powerful, strange voice. "It's Malabar!"

His eyes blazed at her for one strange and senseless second, as he ceased urging his wooden horse. Then he fell with a crash to the ground, and she, all her tormented motherhood flooding upon her, rushed to gather him up.

But he was unconscious, and unconscious he remained, with some brain-fever. He talked and tossed, and his mother sat stonily by his side.

"Malabar! It's Malabar! Bassett, Bassett, I *know*: it's Malabar!"

So the child cried, trying to get up and urge the rocking-horse that gave him his inspiration.

"What does he mean by Malabar?" she asked her brother Oscar.

"It's one of the horses running for the Derby," was the answer.

And, in spite of himself Oscar Cresswell spoke to Bassett, and himself put a thousand on Malabar: at fourteen to one.

The third day of the illness was critical: they were watching for a change. The boy, with his rather long, curly hair, was tossing ceaselessly on the pillow. He neither slept nor regained consciousness, and his eyes were like blue stones. His mother sat, feeling her heart had gone, turned actually into a stone.

In the evening, Oscar Cresswell did not come, but Bassett sent a message, saying could he come up for one moment, just one moment? Paul's mother was very angry at the intrusion, but on second thoughts she agreed. The boy was the same. Perhaps Bassett might bring him to consciousness.

The gardener, a shortish fellow with a little brown moustache and sharp little brown eyes, tiptoed into the room, touched his imaginary cap to Paul's mother, and stole to the bedside, staring with glittering, smallish eyes at the tossing, dying child.

"Master Paul!" he whispered. "Master Paul! Malabar came in first all right, a clean win. I did as you told me. You've made over seventy thousand pounds, you have; you've got over eighty thousand. Malabar came in all right, Master Paul."

"Malabar! Malabar! Did I say Malabar, Mother? Did I say Malabar! Do you think I'm lucky, Mother? I knew Malabar, didn't I? Over eighty thousand pounds! I call that lucky, don't you, Mother? Over eighty thousand pounds! I knew, didn't I know I knew? Malabar came in all right. If I ride my horse till I'm sure, then I tell you, Bassett, you can go as high as you like. Did you go for all you were worth, Bassett?"

"I went a thousand on it, Master Paul."

"I never told you, Mother, that if I can ride my horse, and *get there*, then

I'm absolutely sure—oh, absolutely! Mother, did I ever tell you? I *am* lucky!"

"No, you never did," said the mother.

But the boy died in the night.

And even as he lay dead, his mother heard her brother's voice saying to her: "My God, Hester, you're eighty-odd thousand to the good, and a poor devil of a son to the bad. But, poor devil, poor devil, he's best gone out of a life where he rides his rocking-horse to find a winner."

Tanith Lee

Three Days

Tanith Lee, a popular and prolific author of fantastic novels and stories, often works in the horror mode in short fiction, although her principal reputation is as a genre fantasy writer. Her range is impressive, her effects dramatic, her imagery vivid. The principal focus in her fiction is often psycho-sexual, overtly or metaphorically. "Three Days" is one of her lesser known stories but one of her best. It is overtly a melodramatic romance in the historical genre, with overt reference to Poe, then a story of reincarnation, the occult rationalized, then undercut. Lee gives the essence of the horror story: "I went over the bridge with the strangest feeling imaginable. I find no name for it even now. It seemed for a moment I had glimpsed the rickety facade of all things and the boundless, restless, terrible truth beyond. But it faded, and I was glad of it." The self-consciously antiquated manner of the telling is an interesting comparison to Joyce Carol Oates' "Nightside."

The house was tall, impressive, peeling, and seemed old before its time. The only attractive thing about it, to my eyes, was the dark-lidded glance of an attic, looking out of the slope of the roof, which such houses sometimes have. The attic eye seemed to say: "There is something beautiful here, after all. Or, there *could* be something beautiful, if such a thing were allowed."

Below and before, a green haze of young chestnut trees lined the street, which gave on the Bois Palais. Behind, rising above the walled gardens, were the stepped roads and blue slate caps of distant Montmoulin over the river, with, as their apparent apex, the white dome of the Sacré. All this was of course very pleasant. Yet I never come into the area now without a sense of misgiving. That is due to the house, and to what took place there.

One felt nothing extravagant could ever have issued from such a proper dwelling. And one would have been wrong. My friend (I use the term indiscriminately) Charles Laurent had issued from it. He was at that season making something of a star of himself in the legal profession, and also by way of a series of books—fictionalized, witty, rather brilliant studies of past trials and case histories. It was in the latter capacity, the literary side, that our paths crossed. I took to him, it was difficult not to. Handsome and informed was Laurent, an easy companion, and a very entertaining one. I suppose too the best of us may agree it is no bad thing to be on good terms with a clever lawyer. I was at this time also attempting to become engaged, and the girl's father had suddenly begun to make my way stony. After a

553

stormy, possibly hysterical scene, worthy of the opera, my love and I had agreed we should put some physical distance between us for a while, allowing Papa's temper to cool, and relying on letters and the connivance of the mother—who liked me, and was no less than an angel—to save our hopes and prevent our mutually going mad. It is a shabby thing for a young man to be in love with one he may not have. It puts an end to a number of solaces, without replacing them. In short, life was not at its nicest. To take up with a Charles Laurent was the ideal solution.

To say our relationship was superficial would be a perfect description; its superficiality was the shining crown of it. We knew just enough of each other as might be helpful. For the rest—food, drink, music, the arts—such as these were ably sufficient to carry us across whole continents of hours into the small ones before dawn. So it was with slight surprise that I found one day he had invited me to dine at his home.

"And well your face may fall," he said. "Believe me, it will be a hideous evening, I can promise you that. I'm asking you selfishly, to relieve the tedium and horror. Not that anyone conceivably could."

Not unnaturally, I inquired after details. He told me with swift disdain that his father observed yearly the anniversary of his mother's death.

"I'm a stranger," I said. "At such a function I could hardly be welcome."

"We are *all* strangers. He hates everyone of us. My brother, my sister. He hated my mother, too." He spoke frivolously. That did not stop a slight frisson of interest from going over me. "Now I have you, I see," said Charles. "The writer has been woken up and is scenting the air."

"Not at all. But you never mentioned a brother, or a sister."

"Semery won't be there. He never comes near the house on such occasions. Honorine lives there, as I do, and has no choice."

"Honorine, your sister?"

"My sister. Poor plain pitiful creation of an unjust God."

I confess I did not like his way of referring to her. If it were true, I felt he should have protected, not slandered her, with that able tongue of his, to loose acquaintances such as I. He saw me frowning and said, "Don't be afraid, my friend. We shan't try to marry her off to you. I recall too well la bonne Anette."

I frankly thought the entire dialogue would be forgotten, but not so. The next morning an embossed invitation was delivered. A couple of nights later I found myself under the chestnut trees before that tall, unprepossessing house, and presently inside, for good or ill.

I was uneasy—that was the least of it—but also, I confess, extremely curious. Charles had hit home with that remark about the writer in me waking up. What was I about to see at this annual wake? Images of the American writer Mr. Poe trooped across my mind: an embalmed corpse, black wreaths, a vault, a creaking black-clad aristo with long tapering hands. . . . Even the daughter had assumed some importance. I think I toyed with the picture of her playing an eastern harp.

Naturally, I was far out. The family, what there was of it, seemed familiarly normal. Monsieur Laurent was a wine-faced, portly *maître d'affaires.* He looked me up and down, found me wanting (of course), greeted me, and let me pass. He reminded me but too well of that other father I had to do with, Anette's, four miles to the west, and I felt an instant depression. There was also an uncle on the premises, who stammered and was not well dressed, two deaf and shortsighted old ladies whose connection I did not quite resolve, and a florid, limping servant. I began to feel I had come among a collection of the deaf, the dumb, the halt, and the lame. Charles, obviously, was not to be numbered among these. Like a firework, he had exploded from the dull genetic sink, as sometimes happens. The younger brother, Semery, who after all attended, was also an exception. Good-looking, he had a makeshift air; Charles and he hailed each other heartily, as rival bandits meeting unarmed in the hills. Semery was the ne'er-do-well with which so many families attempt to equip themselves. Some twist of fortune, some strain of energy, had denied the role to Charles who, I felt, might have handled it better.

The sister came down late. She did not have a harp about her, but alas, everything Charles had said seemed a fact.

The sons perhaps had taken their looks from the dead mother we were supposed to be celebrating. Poor Honorine did not even favor her father. She was that sad combination of small bones and heavy flesh that seems to indicate some mistake has been made in assembly. She ate very little, and one knew instinctively that her dumpy form and puffy features were not the results of gluttony, or even appetite. She was not ugly, but that is all that can be said. Indeed, had she been ugly, she would have possessed a greater advantage than she did. For she was unmemorable. Her small eyes, whose color I truly do, God forgive me, forget, were downcast. Her thin hair, drawn back into a false chignon that did not exactly match, made me actually miserable. We writers sometimes postulate future states of freedom for both sexes, regardless of physical advantage. Never had one seemed so necessary. Poor wretched girl.

That her father detested her was obvious, but—as Charles had told me—Monsieur Laurent cared little for any of them. The dire lucklessness of it was that, while his sons escaped or absconded, the daughter was trapped. She had no option but to wait out, as how many do, the death of the tyrant. He was hale and hearty. It would be a long wait. How did she propose to spend it? How did she spend her days as it was?

No doubt my remarks on Monsieur Laurent sound unduly callous. Patently, they are colored by hindsight, but I took against him immediately, and he against me, I am sure. Yes, he resembled my own reluctant intended father-in-law, but there was more to it than that. Lest I do myself greater injustice than I must, I will hastily reproduce some of the conversation and the events of that first, really most unglittering, dinner party.

To begin with there was some sherry, or something rather like it, but very little talk. Monsieur Laurent maintained guard across the fireplace. Aside from snapping rudely a couple of times at the old ladies and the limping servant, he only stood eyeing us all, as if we were a squadron of raw troops foisted on him at the very eve of important hostilities. Annoyance, contempt, and actual exasperation were mingled in that glance, which generously included us all. I found it irritating. He knew nothing of me, as yet, to warrant such an opinion. In the case of Charles, most fathers would have been proud. We were meanwhile talking sotto voice and Charles said, as if reading my thoughts, "You can see what he thinks of me, go on, can't you?" "I assume," I said, "that his expression is misleading." "Not at all. When I won my first case, he looked at me just that way. When I foolishly spoke of it, the old wretch said to me, "The stupidity of other men doesn't make *you* clever." As for the first book—well, it was a success, and I recall we met on the stairs and he had a copy. I was stunned he'd even looked at it, and said so. At which he put the book in my hand as if I'd demanded it and replied, "I suppose you'll sell this rubbish, since the majority of the populace is dustbin-brained.' "

Just then the food was ready and our host marched before us into the dining salon. No pretense was made of escort or invitation. Charles conducted the two elderly ladies. Semery idled through. I looked round to offer my arm to Mademoiselle Honorine, but she was making a great fuss over the discarded sherry goblets. I sensed too exactly the dreadful embarrassment of the unlovely, and left well alone.

Needless to say, I wondered how on earth, and why on earth, Charles had procured me a place at this specter's feast. I could only conclude that Monsieur Laurent's utter disgust with humanity en masse did not deign to distinguish between absence and arrival. Come or go as we would, we were a source of displeasure. Perhaps even, new specimens of the loathsome breed momentarily satisfied him, bringing him as they must the unassailable proof that nothing had altered, he was still quite right about us all.

"*Sit*," rapped Monsieur Laurent, glaring around him.

Obedient as dogs, we sat.

Some kind of entrée was served and a vintage inspected. Monsieur Laurent then looked directly at me. "The wine isn't so good, but I expect you'll put up with it." This, as if I were some destitute who had scrounged a place at the board. A number of retorts bolted into my mind, but I curbed them, smiled politely, and had thereafter a schoolboy urge to kick Charles' shins under the table.

Whether the wine was good or not good, after a glass or two, the demon father began noticeably to brighten. I was struck by the flash of his eye, and realized that generalized contempt was about to flower into malice. I am afraid only two thoughts occurred to me at that moment. One was, I regret, that this was very intriguing. The other was concerned with wondering what *I* would do if he grossly insulted me. For I could sense, the way animals scent a coming storm, how the thunder was getting up. I reasoned though I was safe, being not such fun to attack as his own. He had not had time to learn my weaknesses and wants. While the rest of them—they had been his playground from birth.

Honorine—there was no attempt at fashionable order—sat three seats away from me, with Semery and an empty chair between. Behind Honorine, above the mahogany sideboard, a large framed photograph with black ribbon on it seemed to depict the dead wife and mother. My current angle prevented any perusal of this, but to it Monsieur Laurent now ordered our attention.

"That woman," he said, "was a very great nuisance while she lived. I drink, as you see, to her departure. Ah, what a nasty, wicked sentiment. Correction, an honest one. Besides, she has taken her revenge. Look what she saddled me with. All of you." There was a concerted dismal rustle round the table. One of the old ladies dabbed her face with a handkerchief, but one saw it was a sort of reflex. It was plainly not the only occasion all this had been voiced. I looked surreptitiously at Charles. He was a perfect blank, composed and cool. Small wonder he could keep his head in a courtroom after being raised to the tune of this!

Beside me, however, Semery either deliberately, or uncontrollably, acted out the role of foil by snarling: "Cher Papa. Can't you leave anything in decent peace?"

"Ah, my little Semery," said Cher Papa, smiling at him now. "You have toiled up from the slime of your slum to say this? And how is the painting going? Sell well, do you, my boy? You came to ask . . . now what was it for? Ah, yes. For money. And I told you I would think about it, but after all, what use is it to give you cash?" (Semery had gone white. I could hardly believe what I was hearing or that Semery could have given such a faultless cue for his own public castigation. It was as if he had *had* to do it.) "You squander everything. And have such slender talent. No, I really think after all you must do without. Tighten your belt. Or, you could return and live here. My doors are always open to you."

"I'd rather die in the gutter," shouted Semery.

"No you wouldn't. Or why are you here?"

"Not to ask anything from *you*, as you well know."

"Begging from your brother Charles then. This afternoon's most touching scene. Such a pity I disturbed you. But Charles isn't a fool with his money if he's a fool with everything else. You won't get it from him. And I promise you, you won't get it from me."

Semery rose. An amazing change reshaped the monster's face. It grew rock-hard, petrified. But the eyes were filled by potent electricity. "Down," rasped the father. The room seemed to shake at the command. Semery sank back into his chair and his trembling hands knocked over his wineglass. Seldom have I witnessed such a display of the casual, absolute power one mortal thing may obtain over another. I felt myself as if I had received a blow in the stomach, and yet what had actually happened? To set it out here does not convey anything.

"Yes, Semery," Monsieur Laurent now said, "you should return under my roof, and make your name painting portraits of this beautiful sister of yours."

Having leveled one gun emplacement with his unerring cannon, the warmonger had turned his fire from the rout of the wounded to the demolition of the totally helpless. I could not prevent myself glancing at her, in horrid fascination, to see how she took it. Of course, she too was well used to such treatment. She cowered, her eyes down, her terrible, unmatched chignon shuddering. Yet the pose was native to her. It seemed almost comfortable. Her body sagged in the lines of abjection so readily, easily.

"Compliment your coiffeur, Honorine," said Monsieur Laurent. "These enemies of yours have succeeded in making of you, yet again, a fright. Heaven hurry the day," he added, drinking his wine in greedy little sips, "when this pretense at having hair is done. A daughter who is completely bald will be a novelty. All this scraping and combing and messing. Fate intended you as a catastrophe, my child. You should accept the part. Look at you, my dear, graceless lump—" At this point I put out my hand and picked up my own glass. I believe I had every intention of throwing it at his head, anything to make him stop. But thank God Charles interrupted with a (perhaps faked) gargantuan sneeze. The father turned slowly, fire duly drawn. "And you," he said to the recovering Charles, "our own moneylender, the wealthy gigolo of the bookstalls. What have you to say for yourself?"

Charles shrugged. "What I always say for myself. And what you also have just said. I've a private income and you don't frighten me. You could put me out on the street tomorrow—"

"I put none of my own tribe onto the street. They put themselves there. As for your books—what are they? You plagiarize and you steal, you botch and bungle—"

"And *livres* pour into my hands," said Charles.

My God, I thought, at last the razor of the father's tongue was going into a block of cork. Naturally, the confounded devil knew it. This means of hurting pride no longer worked, it seemed, or at least without evidence. Talented, loved, an egoist, and lucky, Charles was not a happy target. Unerringly, the father retraced his aim.

"A pity," he said, "your sister has taken to reading your works. Filling her hairless skull with more predigested idiocy than is already in there. She puts her hat on her bald head and goes puttering off to the bookshop to discuss your successes. And so has fallen into the clutches of madwomen."

Strangely, Honorine was moved by this to murmur quickly, "No, Father, no, you mustn't say they are—"

"*Mustn't?* Mustn't I? You keep your mouth closed, my fat, balding daughter. I say what I know. Your great friends are lunatics, and I'm considering whether or not I shall approach the police—"

"Father!" The cry now was anguished.

"What? You think they're friends of yours, hah? You, with a friend? How should you have friends, you overweighted slug? Do you think they're captivated by your prettiness and charm? Eh? It's my money they like the idea of, and your insane acquaintances from the bookshop are a fine example of a certain animal known as a charlatan."

"I won't go there ever again," said Honorine.

This startled me. Her voice was altered when she spoke. It had grown deeper, it was definite. By agreeing with him she had, albeit temporarily, removed the bludgeon from his grasp.

At the time, the business of the "charlatan madwomen" and the bookshop were only a facet of an astonishing whole. I paid no particular attention. Nor do I think much more needs to be said of the dinner. Dishes came in and were taken away, and those with the heart to eat (they were few) did so. There were many and various further sallies from the indefatigable Monsieur Laurent. None were aimed at me, though I was now primed and eager for them and, I imagine, slightly drunk. In my confusion, even as I sat there, I was already mentally composing a letter to Anette, telling her everything, word for word, of this unspeakable affair. (It is from the same letter, penned fresh and with the vivid recall of insomniac indignation at two that morning, that I am able to quote fairly accurately what I have just set down.) I also wished him dead at least twenty times. I backed the big heavy body and the thick red face for an apoplexy, yet they looked more like ebullient good health.

As soon as I could, without augmenting the casualties of that war zone of a table by slamming out halfway through the meal, I left. I bade Charles a brisk adieu and walked by myself beside the river until well past midnight, powerlessly on the boil. As I told Anette, my entertaining friend was out of favor now completely. I reckoned never to see him again, for it was not simple, after the fact, to forgive him this exposure to alien filial strife. I even in a wild moment suspected some joke at my expense.

However, my having ignored two notes and a subsequent attempted visit, he finally caught me up in the gardens of the Palais. There was an argument, at least on my side, but Charles was not to be fought with if he had no mind for it.

"I can only apologize," he said, in broken accents. "What more can I say?"

"Why in God's name did you make me a party to the bloody affair?"

"Well, frankly, my friend, because—though you'll find it hard to credit—he is kinder to us when there is some stranger present."

I fell silent at that, moodily staring away between the green groves of trees. Now and then, Anette and I had contrived a meeting here, and the gardens filled me always with a piercing sweet sadness that tended to override other emotions. I looked at Charles, who seemed genuinely contrite, and acknowledged there might be some logic in his statement. Although the idea of Monsieur Laurent *un*kind, if such was a version of his restraint, filled one with laughing horror.

So, if you will, ends the first act.

The second act commences with a scene or two going on offstage. There had been an improvement in my own fortunes, to wit, Anette's father deeming it necessary, in the way of business, to travel to England. This brought an unexpected luster to the summer. It also meant that I saw very little of Charles Laurent.

Then one morning, strolling through the covered market near the cathedral, I literally bumped into Semery and, after the usual exchanges, was invited to an apartment above a chandler's, on the left bank of the river.

Here is the area of the Montmoulin, the medieval hill of the windmill, the namesake of which is long since gone. One hears the place referred to frequently as being of a "picturesque, quaint squalor." Certainly, the poor do live here, and the fallen angels of the bourgeoisie perch in the garrets and studios above the twisting cobbled lanes. The smell of cabbage soup and the good coffee even the poverty-stricken sometimes manage to get hold of, hang in the air, along with the marvelous inexpressible smell of the scarlet geraniums that explode over balconies and on walls above narrow stairways, and against a sky tangled with washing and pigeons.

We got up into a suitable attic studio and found a table already laid with cheese and bread and fruit and wine, and a fawn cat at play with an apple. A very pretty girl came from behind a curtain. She ran to kiss Semery and, her arms still around him, turned to beam at me in just the way women in love so often do when another man comes on the scene. Even in her loose blouse, I could tell she was carrying a child. Little doubt of the father, though her hand was ringless. I remembered, with a fleeting embarrassment, Semery's supposed request for money from his brother, or Monsieur Laurent. Here might be the excuse.

There were pictures, naturally, everywhere—on the walls, on easels, stacked up, or even horizontal on the floor for the cat to sit on.

"Courage," said Semery, seeing me glance around, "I won't try to sell anything to you. Not at all." This in turn reflected Charles' avowal, on first inviting me to the gruesome dinner party, that they would not try to marry Honorine off to me. It was a little thing, but it made me conscious of some strange defensiveness inherent, and probably engendered in them by their disgusting father. "But," added Semery, "look, if you like." "Of course he will like," said the girl mischievously. "How nice the table is, Miou," said Semery. "Let's have some wine."

A very pleasant couple of hours ensued. Semery was acting at least as fine a companion as Charles; I was charmed by Miou, and by the cat, and the simple luncheon was appetizing. As for the art—I am no critic, but suppose I have some slight knowledge. While not being in that first startling rank of original genius, Semery's work seemed bright with talent. It had enormous energy, was attractive, sometimes lush, yet never too easy. Particularly, I liked two or three unusual night scenes of the city, one astonishingly lit by a flight of birds escaping from some baskets and streaming over a lamp-strung bridge.

"Yes," he said, coming to my side, "I call that one *Honorine*." I was at a loss to reply. "I don't mean to make you uncomfortable," he said. "But you've been blooded, after all. You were there just the last time I was."

"Hush, Semery," said Miou, who was rocking the cat in an armchair, practicing for her baby. "Talking of *him* makes you sick and gives you migraine."

"True," said Semery. He refilled our glasses with wine. "But I can talk of Honorine? Yes? No? But I must. That poor little sack of sadness. If there were any money, I'd take her in with me, though God knows she bores me to despair. Our dear father, you understand, has stamped and trampled all the life from her. She can no longer talk. She only answers questions. So you say to her, 'Would you care to do this?' And you get in return, 'Oh yes, if *you* wish.' And she drops things. And she stumbles when she walks even when there's nothing to stumble over. However," he said, with a boy's fierceness, "there was one service I think I did her. I first took her to the bookshop on the Rue Danton. And so introduced her to the three witches."

Miou began to sing a street song, quietly but firmly disowning us.

"That's the bookshop your father objected to? And the witches?"

"Well, three old ladies, in particular one, very gray and thin, read the tarot there in the backroom. And sometimes, when the moon is full, work the planchette of a Ouija board."

"And Honorine . . ."

"Honorine attended a session or two. She wouldn't reveal the results, but you could tell she enjoyed every moment. When you saw her after, her cheeks would be flushed, her eyes had a light in them. Unfortunately, that limping gargoyle who serves *mon père* found out about it all and duly informed. Now Honorine's one poor, pitiful pleasure is ended. Unless she can somehow evade the spies, and our confounded father—"

"*Sur la chatte, le chat,/Et sur la reine le roi . . .*" naughtily sang Miou to the cat-baby.

"On the other hand," Semery added, now with great nonchalance, "I did visit the shop today, and one of the eldritch sisters—good lord, I must paint them—no rush, they're each about three hundred years old and will outlive us all—well, Miou-who-has-stopped-singing-and-is-all-ears-and-eyes, well, one of them gave me a note to give to Honorine. Something the spirit guides had revealed that my sister apparently desired to know." And from his jacket Semery produced a piece of paper, unsealed, merely folded in the middle, which he held aloft quizzically. "I wonder what it can be?"

"You shouldn't have brought it here," said Miou. She crossed herself between fawn paws. "Magic. Ghosts."

"Where else then? Papa is out tomorrow afternoon and I can take it to the house. But I could hardly do so today, could I now? One foot on the threshold, and he'd have seized me in his jaws."

"Well," said Miou. "Put it away somewhere."

"Don't you think I should read it? Secret communications to my little sister . . ." He looked back at me. "Actually, I did. Here, what do you make of this?"

And he opened the paper and put it in my hand.

I admit I was curious. There seemed no harm in it, and I have always had a quiet disrespect for "supernatural" things.

On the paper from the mysterious bookshop were these words as follows:

> As we have told you, she is to be found as a minor character in some of the history books, and there has also been at least one novel written about her. The name is correct, Lucie Belmains. She did indeed die as a result of hanging herself. The date of her death is the morning of the eighth April, 1760.

"Fascinating, isn't it," said Semery. "What does it mean? Who is Lucie Belmains?"

Miou and the cat were already peering between our shoulders at the paper.

"Lucie Belmains," said Miou, "was a minor aristocrat, very beautiful and very wicked. She would drink and ride a horse and swear better—or worse—than a man. She was the mistress of several princes and dukes. She once dressed as a bandit and waylaid the king on some road, and was his mistress too perhaps, till she became bored with all the riches he lavished on her. Then she fell in love with a man five years her junior. He loved her too, to distraction, and when he was killed in a duel over her, Lucie gave a great party, like a Roman empress, and in the morning she hanged herself like Antigone from a crimson cord."

Semery and I stood amazed until Miou stopped, breathless and in triumph.

"It seems," said Semery then, "there is indeed one novel, and you have read it."

"Yes. When I was a little girl," said Miou, all of seventeen now. "I remember my sister and I read the book aloud to each other when we were supposed to be asleep. And how we giggled. And we dressed up in lace curtains and our mother's hats and raised glasses of water pretending they were champagne and said, 'I am Lucie and you are my slave!' And fought like cats because neither of us would *be* the slave. And then one day Adèle hung her doll up by the neck from a red ribbon and we had a funeral party. Maman found us and we were both beaten."

"Quite right. These are most corrupting activities for a future wife of France's leading painter, and the mother of his heir." At which Miou smiled and laid her head on his shoulder. "But even so," said Semery, stroking her hair, "what has all this got to do with Honorine?"

I said, "She's making a study of this woman, or the period?"

"No. She has no interests anymore."

Later, toward evening, we strolled along the riverbank. The leveling rays of the sun flashed over the water. I had arranged to buy the picture of the escaping birds for Anette. I knew she would like it, as indeed she did—we have it still, and since Semery's name is now not unknown, it is worth rather a deal more than I paid for it. But there was some argument with Semery at the time, who thought I was patronizing him, or trying to pay for my luncheon. Thank God, all that had been settled, however, by the hour we emerged on the street, Miou in her light shawl and straw bonnet with cherries. When we reached the Pont Nouveau and I was about to cross over, Semery said to me, "You see, that business with the paper—belle Lucie Belmains. Something about it worries me. Perhaps I shouldn't let Honorine have it. Would that be dishonorable?"

"Yes."

"Or prudent?"

"Maybe that too. But as you don't know—"

"I think perhaps I do. The purpose of the witches' Ouija has often to do with reincarnation—the passage of the soul through many lives and many bodies."

We had all paused in mutual revelation.

"Do you mean your sister is being told she lived a previous life in which—"

"In which she was beautiful and notorious, kings slobbered at her feet, and duels were organized for her favors."

We looked at the river, the womb and fount of the city, glittering with sun, all sequins, which on the dark days of winter seems like lead.

"Well," Semery said at last, "why not? If it makes her happy for a moment. If it gives her something nice to think about. There's nothing now. What has she got? What can she hope to have? If she can say to herself, just one time in every day, *once* I was beautiful, *once* I was free, and crazy and lavish and adored, and loved."

I looked at him. His eyes were wet, and he was pale, as if at the onset of a headache. Impulsively, I clasped his hand.

"Why not?" I said. "Yes, Semery, why *not?*"

Miou let me kiss her blossomy cheek as a reward.

I went over the bridge with the strangest feeling imaginable. I find no name for it even now. It seemed for a moment I had glimpsed the rickety facade of all things and the boundless, restless, terrible truth beyond. But it faded, and I was glad of it.

As the glorious summer drew to its close, intimations of winter and discontent appeared. The birds and golden leaves began to be displaced by emptiness in the trees of the Bois; Anette's father returned, foul-tempered, and shut his house like a castle under siege against all comers, particularly one.

It was nearly three months since my chance meeting with Semery. We had met deliberately a couple of times since; I had even been invited to his wedding, the thought of which now made me rather melancholy. As for Charles Laurent, I was sitting at a café table one morning, curiously enough reading a review of his latest book—as usual a success—when I happened to look up and saw two women seating themselves a few tables away. I was struck at once by a sense of confusion, such as comes when one is accosted by an old acquaintance whose name one forgets. But it was not that a name had been forgotten, for frankly I was not familiar with either of these women. It must be, then, that they put me in mind of others with whom I was. Because of this I studied them surreptitiously over my newspaper.

The nearer woman, with her back to me now, was apparently a maid or companion, and a withered specimen at that. She seemed ill at ease, full of humble, insistent protestation. No, I did not know her at all. The other, who sat facing me, was not particularly remarkable. Not tall, quite slim, and plainly dressed, her fine brown hair had been cut daringly short and she was hatless. Two little silver earrings flickered attractively in her earlobes. That was all. Her skin was sallow, her features ordinary. Then the waiter came and I was struck again, this time by a quality of fearlessness, *boldness*, out of all proportion to what she did, which was merely to order a pot of chocolate. There was something gallant in this minor action, such as you sometimes find in invalids taking their first convalescent stroll, or the blind listening to music.

Quite suddenly, I realized who she was. It was the graceful bravery, though I had never seen her exhibit it previously, that gave her away. Honorine, of course.

I resolved immediately I would not go over. I had no real wish to, heaven knows. Memories of her wounded social clumsiness did not inspire me. I could only be a ghastly reminder of a hideous event. Let her enjoy her chocolate in peace, while I stayed here, keeping stealthy watch from my covert of newspaper.

So I kept watch, true to my profession, taking rapid mental notes the while. Surely, she was not as I recalled. It was small wonder I had not recognized her at once. She had lost a great deal of weight, yet here she sat eating gateau, drinking chocolate, with the accustomed appetite of a famished child. And there truly was about her a gracefulness—of gesture, of attitude. And a strange air of laughter, mischievous and essentially womanly, that despite myself began to entice me to her vicinity. In the end I gave in, rose, walked across and stood before her.

"Mademoiselle Laurent. Can I hope you remember me?"

Her eyes came up. Those eyes not large nor bright—but they were altered. They shone, they were alive. The oddest thing happened now. The loud blush of shyness, which one might have expected, rushed over her face. It was the order of blush well known to the adolescent, which makes physically uncomfortable with its heat, the drumming in the ears, the feeling the brain may explode under its pressure. All is instant panic and surrender to panic. What is there to be said or done when such a mark of shame is branded on one's forehead? But the eyes of Honorine Laurent did not fall. She drew in a long breath and said, calmly, as if blood and body did not belong to each other, "Why, monsieur, of course I remember you. My brother's friend. Please, will you sit down? We have greedily eaten all the cake, but there's some chocolate left." And she smiled. As she did so, the red blush went out, defeated. Her smile was open, friendly, not afraid—nor false. And her eyes sparkled so they were pretty, just as the smile was pretty. One writes of auras. Honorine had just such an aura. I knew in that moment that I was in the presence of a woman who found her own lack of beauty no disadvantage, who therefore would not use pain or sullenness as a weapon, who believed that in the end she herself was all that she required, although others were quietly welcomed should they come close to warm themselves in the light. In short, the look of a confident woman, a woman who has known great love, and awaits, without impatience or aggression, some future, unhurried, certain joy.

As if I had been hypnotized, I drew out a chair and sat down. I had only just breakfasted, but I drank the chocolate that was poured for me in a daze. Presently, the withered lady companion, fretting like a horse for hay, was thankfully dispatched to collect some cotton, and arm in arm, Mademoiselle Honorine and I turned toward the graveled paths of the Bois Palais. I had offered to see her to her door, and she had said, "Yes, do. Charles is home in a filthy temper—one bad review, I think, of his excellent book. He'll be delighted to see you. And my father is . . . out." And there was that mischief again. She did not then hate Monsieur Laurent, this elfin woman with her slim hand so lightly through my arm. She did not hate me for being witness to his humiliation of her. And she was used to escorts, she was used to friends.

I recall she asked me about Anette, very graciously and tactfully, and abruptly all my cares came flooding out in a torrent of words that astonished me, so in the end we sat down by the fountain with the nymphs as I made my complaints to life and heaven. Sometimes Honorine patted my arm gently. "Oh, yes," she said, "ah, no?" with such unflurried kindness and sympathy —*she* with all her woes, so tender toward mine—and at the finish I remember too she said, "You have a sound literary reputation and I would say your prospects are fine. Besides, you and she love each other. Could you perhaps," and those eyes of hers flashed like her earrings, like the summer river, "run away together?" I realized, even at the time, that this last piece of advice came straight from the idiomatic guide book of Lucie Belmains.

For that, naturally, was who I had beside me, there on that bench: Lucie Belmains, who had died on the eighth of April, 1760. Lucie Belmains, but at her softest, sweetest—who knew love, and love's fulfillment, and touched my hand from her greater knowledge, ready to listen, and to reassure me. Even to suggest a madcap means of how to win the age-old game. The means *she*, more daring than I, might have taken.

Why not? Semery had said. Why not let that poor little dumpy bundle of a sister, that sack of sadness, creation of an unjust God, think of some better chance she had been given, once, if it could make her glad? And, *Why not?* I had magnanimously echoed. My God, why not indeed, if this exquisite person was to be the result . . . No, I did not believe in her reincarnation. But her *alteration*—*this* I believed. How could I avoid belief? The living proof sat with limpid laughing eyes beside me. As tyrants are changed by faith to flawless saints, so faith of her own kind had changed this human failure to a glowing being. There was a loveliness about her—yes, loveliness. Some latent charm, extant in her brothers, formerly lost in her, had evolved and possessed her perfectly. And that smile, those eyes. And her walk. Her carriage. Years have gone by since that day, to dim the vista. I loved Anette then, I love her still, and no woman in the world, in my eyes, can equal Anette. And yet I look back to this Honorine I had the happiness to find that far-off morning, and I must set down the truth as it seemed to me then, and seems to me now, older, wiser, and less innocent as I am. I have never, save for my wife, met any woman who enchanted me so thoroughly. For she was beautiful. Her beauty lay all around us on the air. And even if I did not credit the transference of the soul, yet the soul I did credit. And it was the soul of Honorine that brought the loveliness and the beauty and the enchantment. For you see, she was then completely those things so few of us ever are, and if we are, so briefly: at peace, joyful, *sure*.

We reached the house, that dire house, and even this seemed less awful by her light. She was no longer afraid of it. She went up the steps and beckoned me in as if I might be comfortable there, and so I, too, felt no foreboding.

Charles was in the drawing room and jumped up when he saw me out of a snowfall of papers. Having brought us together, she was gone. I stared after her and then at the closed door. Presently, Charles left off talking of his book and said, "Well, what do you think of *her*?"

She had made me skittish too. I said, no doubt rudely, "This is not the same sister."

Charles nodded vigorously. "It can't be, can it? Isn't she a jewel?" He was proud of her. "If she keeps this up, we'll get her married to a rich potentate in half a year. You've seen Semery and know the cause, I understand?"

"Yes."

He gazed at me and said mock-seriously, "Of course, it's a form of madness. If she killed someone, I could get her off on a plea of this. My client reckons she is actually a lady who is dead."

"Surely she reckons she has *been*, not is, Lucie Belmains."

"Hairsplitting worthy of the bar. But it's a miracle. If she's gone a little mad, so nicely, why not?"

And thus the third culpable party added his careless *why not*? to Semery's and mine.

"But does she," I said, "know that you—"

"She knows Semery and I—though not you, *cher ami*—are in on it. But she doesn't review the matter with us, nor we with her. Then again, considering the extravagance of the idea, not to mention results, she's very serene about it all. I don't think she's even read anything, no history of this woman. Save the smallest outline in some encyclopedia. On the other hand, I suspect her of writing about her feelings. I gather a diary has been started. But she only revealed that to me because I caught sight of the article on her vanité. She's said nothing else. After all, she knows we're a bunch of vile skeptics. As for father—well, no whisper must reach *his* ears. And you can guess, all this of hers has thrown him off balance. She eats more and grows more slight, she cuts off her hair and buys earrings. But you should see her with him. Stay and lunch with us and you will."

The prospect of encountering Monsieur Laurent again brought me to with a jolt.

"Unfortunately, I must be elsewhere."

"And anywhere but here? Well, you'll be missing a treat. And by the way, have you seen what this devil in the *Journal* has the wretched audacity to say about my book . . . ?"

Half an hour later, just as I got out into the hall, the limping servant hobbled by me and flung open the street door. And there stood Monsieur Laurent, his horrible puce face thrust forward, seeing me at once, before Charles and all things else. I felt like a seven-year-old boy caught stealing fruit in someone's orchard. I had been so determined to avoid the monster. Nor had I heard any summons to warn me of this collision; the sinister limper seemed to have known of his master's arrival by telepathic means alone.

"Good day," said the *maître* to me, advancing into his domain. "Hoping for lunch?"

I writhed to utter as I wanted, but did not.

"No, monsieur. I am lunching with friends."

"I thought my plagiarist son was your friend. Or have you grown wise to him, seen through him? I note," he added, directing his attention now to Charles, "one critic at least has had the wit to penetrate your sham nonsense. I must send him my congratulations."

Charles, touchy over the review (for which his father must truly have scoured the journals) was plainly for once caught on the raw spot. Without looking at him, I saw his anger reflected in the momentary pleasure of Monsieur Laurent's little eyes.

"And where's your beauteous sister? I've some news for her."

"Here I am," said a voice from the stairs.

Monsieur Laurent gave vent to that toneless, noisy amusement generally called a guffaw. "Yes, there you are. What plenteous abundance of hair! Where is it? Have I gone blind? Do you still go out on the street like that and make yourself a laughingstock?"

Turned to stone, my eyes only on the shut front door, I waited. And I heard her gentle voice say casually, light as down, "Yes, Papa, I'm afraid I do."

"You silly sheep. Look at you. Well, I suppose it's generous of you to give everyone, complete strangers, such a good laugh. But do I permit you to draw money to buy earrings and make yourself resemble a circus monkey?"

"No, Papa, the earrings were purchased from the small allowance Mother left me. But if they worry you, I'll take them off."

"Worry me? *You* worry me. You brainless thing, flapping about the house, scribbling, mooning. What's wrong with you?"

"I am very well, thank you, Papa."

"That damnable fool, your female parent, what a curse she left me. A sniveling, profligate dunce and a literary jackal for sons. An idiot daughter."

She was down the stairs now; I heard the rustle of her gown. She seemed to bring a coolness with her, a freshness, like open air, escape from the trap.

She said, "Come and see the new sherry, Papa. I took your advice on the business of wines and have been trying to improve my knowledge. I'd like you to taste this latest bottle and see what you think."

"If you chose the stuff, it must be worthless muck," said this charming father.

"Not necessarily," replied Honorine, for all the world as if she were talking to a sane and rational human being instead of to a thing from the Pit. "I've tried, in my choice, to apply all you told me the other day. But if you think the sherry is poor and I'm mistaken again, of course I shall want you to correct me. How can I benefit from your superior understanding in these matters if you're lenient?"

What could he say, the beast? She had him, as seldom have I heard any so had. What had gone on? I can only conclude she had begun to take an interest in the ordering of the cellar, as la Belmains would certainly have done, and Monsieur, true to himself as always, had insulted her and attempted to belittle her over it, as over all else. Whereupon she must have assumed the attitude that she was being given an altruistic lesson for her own benefit, which notion she here continued. I have done just as you said, she informed him now. But if I am wrong—for naturally, I do not for a moment deny you are more clever than I am—you must let me know. And *do* be as harsh, as discourteous as you can be. I shall regard it as a mark of your concern and patronage. My God! I nearly laughed aloud. Whatever revolting abuse he threw at her now came with her awarded license. She would sit meekly before him, nodding as he ranted, presently thanking him for the tutorial. I was, despite everything, after all tempted to stay for lunch.

I compromised then, and indicated to Charles I would remain long enough to try the new sherry. And when the monster eyed me and made some remark about there being no luckier club for a minor writer than the free one of somebody else's house, I snatched a leaf from her book, grinned wildly at him, and cried, "And such an entertaining club, too."

It goes without saying he hated the sherry, which was a discerning one. But he said not much about it, save it was ditchwater. Honorine promised to bear this in mind. It was at this point that he recollected the news he wanted to tell her.

"Your hags of the tarot have gone," he said. "Did you know? An end to clandestine sorties to the bookshop and table tappings at my expense. Perhaps an end to the silliness you've been parading these last months, eh?"

"Ever since you showed such displeasure," said Honorine placidly, "I've not visited the shop."

"No. But things have come here from there. From your faker parasites. Bits of paper brought by your ugly maid. Or by dear Semery when I'm out—you thought I wasn't aware? There's not much I miss. I've read some of these secret notes, *billets doux*. Let me see. What did they say?"

We had all turned very silent. Honorine was pale and she put down her glass. From the erratic glitter of those delightful earrings of hers I could learn the quick, erratic motion of her pulse.

Monsieur Laurent made a great drama over recalling. He, like the soulless evil he was, had sound instincts for a victim's shrinking and fear. Yet, if he had got hold of any communications from Honorine's three witches, it seemed to me they would probably mean nothing to him. His was a sly mind, but not an intellectual slyness. He pulled the wings from insects to agonize them and prevent their flight, not to study the complexity of their pain and flightlessness. But the information of the Ouija board, ridiculous as it might be, was also intensely personal. He had, no doubt, always been in the habit of opening his children's private correspondence and taunting them with its closest passages.

Eventually, his head tilted back in a sort of cold, dry ecstasy, he announced: "'Lucie Belmains. Born at Troy-la-Dianne in April 1729. Hanged dead on April 8, 1760.' Now do I quote that as it should be? Hah? And do I have *this* right—that you, my dollop of dough, unlovely, loveless, hopeless wreck that you are, are the reborn Lucie, so beautiful, kings paid ransoms for her company, and duels were fought to the death?"

There was a long terrible pause, with no noises in it save a patter of leafy rain on the road outside.

I did not look at her. I do not know how she seemed, but I can conjure it. Who needs to be told? This was her sacrament, holy, and hidden. And now he had it in his fangs, mauling and maiming it before us all. He had only been waiting, only *seeming* muzzled. But how could he be? All the servants were in his thrall. And her diary, maybe he had even got a grip on that, this savage, rabid dog. Yes, so he must have done, to come at the roots of her dream, the beautiful, abnormal structure that had made bearable her life. But it was not to be bearable. *He* could not bear that. She should not spring up from the crushing. He would pile on another weight.

I suppose seconds went by, no more, while I thought this, and suffered for her, and yearned again to kill him.

Then she spoke, and my head cleared of the black cloud, because her voice was steady, self-possessed. She had made a virtue of passivity. She gave no resistance now, since it would only lead the torturer on. She said, "Yes, Papa. Isn't it absurd? For me to imagine, even for an instant, I might have been such a person. But you seem to have discovered that I do imagine it. And I do. While, truly, thinking it every bit as unlikely and preposterous as you do yourself."

The cold ecstasy left him at that. Temper came instead. For a moment I thought he would strike her, but physical blows were not what he enjoyed.

"And what gives you to think such errant twaddle? This salivatory drivel from what? A *Ouija board*? Fakers and schemers—they take your money—*my* money—and tell you anything you like to hear."

"No, Father. They never asked a sou from me."

"So you say. You *say*. But no doubt you make donations? Eh? And you've done their dubious reputation good, I expect, babbling to those you know of the *accomplishments* of this hocus-pocus. Lucie Belmains. *Lucie Belmains*. Does she even exist? Tell me that, you dunce. You'd swallow anything to make you out not the clod you are."

I could hold myself no longer. I regret it, but I think in the long term it made no difference. He was on the trail, this bloody dog. He would have found it all at length, whatever was done or said or omitted.

"Monsieur. Lucie Belmains most decidedly did exist. I'm surprised, sir, with your exceptional bent for knowing everything and missing nothing, that you've never heard of her."

"*Ah*," he said, turning his gaze on me. "So we're to be paid for our sherry with information. This is not," he said, "your concern. You may leave my house." And he smiled.

"I can think of nowhere, offhand, I could leave with greater pleasure."

"Brave words for a sponger," he said. "Or did you steal something while my back was turned?"

"In the sight of God!" shouted Charles.

But I, at the reckless, heedless spur of immaturity, answered, "Steal from you, monsieur? I'd be more fastidious."

"Would you?" he said. "From Anette Dupleys then, that fine, plump dowry of hers and her property in the south that goes with it. Indeed, a much juicier theft than anything the poor Laurents could offer you."

It seems he had done me the honor of finding out something about my circumstances also. And what he had found out, of course, was the thing set to cut me to the bone. I forget what I said or anything at all, until I got out, burning as if in flames and in an icy sweat, onto the street. Unfortunately, whatever I did in my passion, I did not seize a fire iron and murder him.

Charles came flying after me and grabbed my shoulder as I reached the Bois.

"In God's name—what can I say? Oh my God—forgive me."

I had chilled in the fire-following ice by then and said stiffly, "There's nothing to forgive you. I stayed when I was aware I should not. As for Anette's money, who doesn't know? That is all the argument between her father and myself. I am a fortune hunter. Naturally."

We quarreled about all this for a while, aimless and appalled. Finally, I accused him of leaving Honorine to face horror alone. "No, no," he said, "it was she sent me after you. She was quite calm still. He hasn't broken her. I thought he had. But she's talking to him so delicately, saying yes, she agrees with everything he says, but there it is."

I thought of her grey face. I said, "Now he has the name of her hopes in front of him, he'll go on until he has destroyed them all."

"How? She believes exactly what her witch ladies told her. He can't touch that."

"He'll find some way," I said.

As I walked alone back along the leaf-lit paths I had traveled with Honorine, through the somber dusk of a coming storm, I knew my premonition was a true one.

The week before Semery's wedding to Miou, the two brothers and I dined in a good restaurant on the Boulevard du Pays. Charles seemed vaguely troubled at the outset, but he neither explained nor made a burden of it, the wine flowed, and soon enough there were no troubles in the world.

I judge it was about midnight when a written message was brought to Charles at the table. He read it and went very white.

"What?" said Semery. But a sense of dread and dismay had passed unsounded between them, not by any mystical means, but from old habit, a boyhood terror that came back whenever some dark shadow proceeded from their father.

I put down my glass and sat in silence.

Presently, Charles covered his eyes with his hand.

"We must go to the house," he said.

"Very well," said Semery, his bright tipsiness all gone. "But why?"

Charles took his hand from his eyes. He looked at me.

"This isn't your affair. There's no need for you to be caught up in it."

"If you prefer," I said. It had had echoes of his father's words in showing me the door.

"No, no, I don't mean to offend you. Oh my God, my God." He stumbled to his feet and the chair chattered over. He did not even seem to see the obstacle as he avoided it.

In a few minutes we were out in the autumn night, still without an answer. Only a pall of black disaster hung about us, sure as the smell of death. It needed no name. In some degree, each of us knew.

I think he told us on the way to the house. I am not positive. It may have been on the very threshold. Or perhaps he did not tell us at all, was not required to. It seems to me now he never did say, in words. Yet I remember later, when we were in a room downstairs, lighted only by a lamp, and cold, he took up the open book left lying on a table and directed me to the place. I remember I read it and for a moment it made no sense, and then I fathomed the sense and my heart sank through me, leaden and afraid, for her sake.

To piece it together now will, perhaps, be better. What use is there, after all, to hesitate? As I had known, Monsieur Laurent must destroy her dream, and so he had, by the very simple expedient of doing what she had not. Honorine had taken her enlightenment almost solely from her ladies of the bookshop. What she had already read of Lucie Belmains had not been, presumably, specific in the matter of dates.

Honorine had trusted her mediums implicitly. She had believed what she had been told. Every fragment of it. But every fragment rested on every other. It was not a house of stone, not even of cards, but of glass, that whole, harmless, shining, starry edifice, and it shattered at a tiny mortal blow. How gratified he must have been, that demon, the weapon so easily come by, and so sharp.

They had told her—I had myself witnessed it—that Honorine's former self, her belle Lucie, had hanged herself, and died on the eighth of April, 1760. But if they were wrong in this, then the entire codex must be mistaken, a lie. And so it was proved. For this date was in error. Lucie Belmains, as history has recorded, as that very book Charles handed to me had recorded, had hanged herself on the morning of the fifth of April and, being cut down, was buried on the evening of the seventh, for the summer was forward that year. Of the eighth of April there was, and needed to be, no mention.

Three days out. Only that. Three days.

Monsieur Laurent had been at pains to tell her, and to show her, no doubt. I can envisage the scene that passed between them, father and daughter, there in that dank, fireless room, as *we* dined on the Boulevard du Pays. I have seen it often in my mind's eye, and listened to it over and over in those half dreams that come between sleep and waking when one is unhappy or very tired.

So she was rid of her fantasy and her madness. So he gave her back the single and only life she had, that dreary, pointless, loathing life, and her own former self, he gave her that, too. He widowed her of beauty and of love, love which had been, love which might yet come, if not as Honorine then in some future when she might be born once more another Lucie. And worse than all that, he throttled the sweet dignity and charm of what she was becoming, had become. God damn him. I do not ask for lives, but for a hell of fire and shrieking where he may burn and scream for all eternity.

After he had instructed her, Monsieur Laurent went out to his own gentleman's club. And Honorine, climbing up to that attic room whose window I had first admired, swallowed a dose of some poison kept for rats. She died in convulsions about an hour after we arrived.

She had written none of those parting notes so common in such cases. I do not think her wish was to instill in anyone feelings of guilt. In her father, the prime offender, it would have been impossible. I gather, though I never met him again, that his attitude remained consistent toward her, even after her death. She was a fool who had always displeased him, and displeased him only a fraction more by dying so violently under his roof. He used to say, I believe, that if she had desired an end so greatly, she should have drowned herself in the river and thereby saved them all the fuss and the expense her domestic suicide entailed. And of course, there was fuss and expense. The newspapers carried the story in a riot. This did Charles no good, but it was the shocking death itself, I am sure, which wore him down and eventually changed the pattern of his life, as is generally reckoned to its detriment. He left the bar less than a year after. His elegant and carefree wit, which had long deserted him, began to return in a strange little lay community attached to a monastery of the Languedoc. Occasionally, we correspond; I do not presume to understand his present existence, or to approve or disapprove of it, but he apparently does some good for himself and for those around him. Other than these messages to me or to Semery, he writes nothing now.

Semery himself, who in his way had already broken off the chains of a false life, was not fundamentally altered, but his grief and his remorse were awesome. Though the marriage went forward on the day assigned, he faltered through it all barely coherent and blind with tears. Later, I gather, he made some attempt to destroy his canvases, but fortunately, friends arrived and prevented it. Miou helped as only she could, by her persevering tenderness, until in the end some care of her and of their approaching child brought him to his senses.

But none of us was untouched.

Honorine, as I said, surely did not intend this torrent of guilt. That guilt should be experienced was unavoidable. Yet she, she was in that last hour so isolate, I would say she thought of no other, either to long for their comfort or to wish them ill. She must have climbed those stairs up through the house in an utter darkness of heart and mind, and soulless too, for her soul had been wrenched from her, as in the myths it is, by the devil. Her imaginings, or rather the black void within her—one shrinks from its contemplation.

However, though she left no concrete parting gift of bitterness in the form of a letter, there is that journal of hers, which Semery now possesses, and which he has allowed me to see. She wrote nothing in it of despair. It was all joy from start to finish. The finish being where she had left it off in the midst of a sentence, probably because she had been told her father required her downstairs. It is the joy, of course, which is unbearable. It is the unfinished sentence that fills one with terror, as if reading theorder for an execution. What breaks the heart is the motto she has written just inside the cover: *Je suis parce que j'ai été.**

For none of us were untouched.

At six o'clock on the morning after her death, not having slept or shaved, nor completely in my right mind, I hurried westward across the city. The dawn was beginning to wash stealthily in along the dry riverbeds of the streets, and I remember I met a flock of sheep being ushered into the Faubourg St. Marie. When I reached the house of the Dupleys, I woke it, and its neighbors, by hammering on the door.

*I am because I was.

What was said and performed was madness, and I can recollect only fragments of it now, that to this day have the power to embarrass me, or sometimes to make me laugh. Suffice it to relate, I fought my way by means of shouted threats through several servants and eventually through Anette's father himself (who thought me dangerously insane), all the way to Anette's mother (who thought much as he did, but with more compassion). And so to Anette herself, who, whatever she thought, did not love me less. There in a corner of a room, her good, kind mother outside the door as our protector, the father in the hall roaring that the police should be called, I said nothing of what had happened, only perpetrated yet one more scene worthy of the opera, crying in Anette's arms and then seizing her hands and asking her to get dressed and come away with me at once. There was the briefest addendum to this plea. It concerned her trusting me, it concerned our being married by the quickest means the law allowed, it concerned my ability to support her, that she was of age but would lose all her money and inheritance. That maybe we should live without pecuniary margin forever. That she should bring warm clothing and whatever else she might need, and her pet kitten. And that I could not swear not to attack her father if he interfered any further. To all of which she listened gravely, then said that I must go away at once, and that she would then meet me, with her mother's help, complete with one small valise and the kitten, in an hour's time in the Bois Palais. At first I argued. Not because I thought she was putting me off—wretch that I was I had every right to think that she might be—but simply because I was so shaken and wild I could not bear to leave her. Nevertheless, in the end she persuaded me. I went, while Monsieur Dupleys, standing on his steps in his dressing gown, with the manservant, waved a purportedly loaded pistol at my back. And in just over an hour mother, daughter, and kitten appeared in the Bois, and we and the fountains wept, and the little cat wailed in astonishment, and God alone knows what the early strollers made of it all.

As it turned out, there was a later reconciliation, and Anette lost nothing by her elopement. We were, though, a year married by then, and my own financial prospects had taken a soaring turn toward fortune. I like to suppose that even if they had not, we could still have possessed the great happiness we had from the commencement, and still share together. I am now received by Monsieur Dupleys, who pompously and placatingly, and also out of a need to make me uncomfortable, sometimes refers to that tempestuous morning, as if it were some game we all played. But it was nothing of the sort. Or, if so, it was Honorine's—Lucie's.

For it was because of Honorine that I risked, as I did, our chances. This I have since explained to my wife. Not only through the upheaval of that ghastly suicide. No, more because of those ephemeral moments of a woman's *life*, in which I had participated. I had been trying, desperately, to make at least one iota of the dream be true. *Could you perhaps run away together?* she had said to me. Lucie's scheme—brave, beautiful, reckless Lucie. Lucie gracious enough to assume Anette's money meant nothing to me, in which assumption she and Anette have been, probably, quite alone. And so I honored Lucie. I went to my love and asked her to run away with me, and she consented. I shall be grateful for that, to Honorine, until the day of my death.

The last act is now concluded, and yet there remains something in the way of an epilogue. I have said I have no leanings to superstition, or to esoteric occult ideas, and part of me clamors here to leave well alone. After all, if, as I believe, it proves nothing, then the circumstances I have outlined turn only darker, and they are surely dark enough. On the other hand, the inveterate storyteller finds it hard to reject such a gem. For gem it is, of a sort.

Some years had passed; the great-grandchildren of Anette's first cat were playing with two children of our own across the floors of our house. Researching in an area that had nothing whatever to do with Lucie Belmains, I suddenly came across a strange reference to her. It dealt, as did the rest of the rather obscure material I was examining, with the negligence, connivance, and ineptitude of some doctors when presented with various classic but misleading symptoms. There was, for instance, a case of hysteria amusingly and dreadfully diagnosed as *la rage*, and a nastier affair of the same rabid condition, genuine, thought to be lycanthropy. Then came an interim paragraph, and next a name (Lucie's) that caught me unawares and made me start. Some wounds, though they heal, retain a lifelong capacity for hurt.

"Lucie Belmains," my material went on after a token biography, "having slain herself on the morning of the fifth of April, was medically certified as mortal, and buried swiftly, due to the extreme and unusual heat of the season. Readers who have scanned the novel *La Prise En Geste* will be familiar with the following quotation from it." The quotation does indeed follow, but I will omit it here. It was from a flowery work, the very one I am sure Miou and her sister had giggled over under the covers, and as a result of which their poor doll was hanged on a ribbon. The substance of the quotation was this: That on the sixth of April, one of Lucie's living admirers, having entered the bedroom where the body was laid out, and kneeling by the bed in a transport of grief, was abruptly terrified to see the dead woman's left hand flutter as if beckoning to him. Hastening to uncover her face, however, he found only the discoloration and popping eyes such a corpse would exhibit and, running out of the room, he fainted.

"What is not widely known," the material went on, "is that this incident is a fact, and not merely a flight of fancy on the part of a romantic author. There are two other facts, even more slenderly recorded, and not utilized by the writer of *La Prise En Geste*. Firstly, that Belmains' maid, on the evening of the seventh, the actual night of burial, found disturbed the veil which covered the cadaver's face, it being partly pushed or drawn in between the lips. Secondly, that several comments were made on the suppleness of the limbs. This was put down to the hot weather. While the whole affair was meanwhile thought so scandalous, its sequels were largely rushed and overall camouflaged, to the point that for several years even the Duc de M——, who had been for so long the lady's intimate protector, thought she had died from accidental choking."

The conclusion my material evolved from all this is a fairly obvious one.

That though Lucie had sufficiently strangled herself as to induce a kind of catalepsy, she was not dead, and did not die until the injury of a mainly collapsed windpipe was augmented by the disadvantages of the grave. Not the material but I myself venture to suggest she could not, in this state, have lingered very much longer. No doubt only until the morning of the eighth of April.

Flannery O'Connor

Good Country People

Flannery O'Connor is one of the finest American writers of the latter half of this century, an ironist in the Southern tradition of William Faulkner and Eudora Welty. She was not in any sense a category writer, but her contributions to horror literature place her beside Shirley Jackson and Joyce Carol Oates. A number of her stories of bleak, black humor show horrific insight into human psychology, of which "Good Country People" is a prime example. It forms an interesting couplet with Robert Aickman's "The Swords" as a story of sexual initiation dealing with body parts, and shows the strength of the nonsupernatural strain in American psychological horror fiction.

Besides the neutral expression that she wore when she was alone, Mrs. Freeman had two others, forward and reverse, that she used for all her human dealings. Her forward expression was steady and driving like the advance of a heavy truck. Her eyes never swerved to left or right but turned as the story turned as if they followed a yellow line down the center of it. She seldom used the other expression because it was not often necessary for her to retract a statement, but when she did, her face came to a complete stop, there was an almost imperceptible movement of her black eyes, during which they seemed to be receding, and then the observer would see that Mrs. Freeman, though she might stand there as real as several grain sacks thrown on top of each other, was no longer there in spirit. As for getting anything across to her when this was the case, Mrs. Hopewell had given it up. She might talk her head off. Mrs. Freeman could never be brought to admit herself wrong on any point. She would stand there and if she could be brought to say anything, it was something like, "Well, I wouldn't of said it was and I wouldn't of said it wasn't," or letting her gaze range over the top kitchen shelf where there was an assortment of dusty bottles, she might remark, "I see you ain't ate many of them figs you put up last summer."

They carried on their most important business in the kitchen at breakfast. Every morning Mrs. Hopewell got up at seven o'clock and lit her gas heater and Joy's. Joy was her daughter, a large blonde girl who had an artificial leg. Mrs. Hopewell thought of her as a child though she was thirty-two years old and highly educated. Joy would get up while her mother was eating and lumber into the bathroom and slam the door, and before long, Mrs. Freeman would arrive at the back door. Joy would hear her mother call, "Come on in," and then they would talk for a while in low voices that were indistinguishable in the bathroom. By the time Joy came in, they had usually finished the weather report and were on one or the other of Mrs. Freeman's daughters, Glynese or Carramae. Joy called them Glycerin and Caramel. Glynese, a redhead, was eighteen and had many admirers; Carramae, a blonde, was only fifteen but already married and pregnant. She could not keep anything on her stomach. Every morning Mrs. Freeman told Mrs. Hopewell how many times she had vomited since the last report.

Mrs. Hopewell liked to tell people that Glynese and Carramae were two of the finest girls she knew and that Mrs. Freeman was a *lady* and that she was never ashamed to take her anywhere or introduce her to anybody they might meet. Then she would tell how she had happened to hire the Freemans in the first place and how they were a godsend to her and how she had had them four years. The reason for her keeping them so long was that they were not trash. They were good country people. She had telephoned the man whose name they had given as a reference and he had told her that Mr. Freeman was a good farmer but that his wife was the nosiest woman ever to walk the earth. "She's got to be into everything," the man said. "If she don't get there before the dust settles, you can bet she's dead, that's all. She'll want to know all your business. I can stand him real good," he had said, "but me nor my wife neither could have stood that woman one more minute on this place." That had put Mrs. Hopewell off for a few days.

She had hired them in the end because there were no other applicants but she had made up her mind beforehand exactly how she would handle the woman.Since she was the type who had to be into everything, then, Mrs. Hopewell had decided, she would not only let her be into everything, she would *see to it* that she was into everything—she would give her the responsibility of everything, she would put her in charge. Mrs. Hopewell had no bad qualities of her own but she was able to use other people's in such a constructive way that she never felt the lack. She had hired the Freemans and she had kept them four years.

Nothing is perfect. This was one of Mrs. Hopewell's favorite sayings. Another was: that is life! And still another, the most important, was: well, other people have their opinions too. She would make these statements, usually at the table, in a tone of gentle insistence as if no one held them but her, and the large hulking Joy, whose constant outrage had obliterated every expression from her face, would stare just a little to the side of her, her eyes icy blue, with the look of someone who has achieved blindness by an act of will and means to keep it.

When Mrs. Hopewell said to Mrs. Freeman that life was like that, Mrs. Freeman would say, "I always said so myself." Nothing had been arrived at by anyone that had not first been arrived at by her. She was quicker than Mr. Freeman. When Mrs. Hopewell said to her after they had been on the place a while, "You know, you're the wheel behind the wheel," and winked, Mrs. Freeman had said, "I know it. I've always been quick. It's some that are quicker than others."

"Everybody is different," Mrs. Hopewell said.

"Yes, most people is," Mrs. Freeman said.

"It takes all kinds to make the world."

"I always said it did myself."

The girl was used to this kind of dialogue for breakfast and more of it for dinner; sometimes they had it for supper too. When they had no guest they ate in the kitchen because that was easier. Mrs. Freeman always managed to arrive at some point during the meal and to watch them finish it. She would stand in the doorway if it were summer but in the winter she would stand with one elbow on top of the refrigerator and look down on them, or she would stand by the gas heater, lifting the back of her skirt slightly. Occasionally she would stand against the wall and roll her head from side to side. At no time was she in any hurry to leave. All this was very trying on Mrs. Hopewell but she was a woman of great patience. She realized that nothing is perfect and that in the Freemans she had good country people and that if, in this day and age, you get good country people, you had better hang onto them.

She had had plenty of experience with trash. Before the Freemans she had averaged one tenant family a year. The wives of these farmers were not the kind you would want to be around you for very long. Mrs. Hopewell, who had divorced her husband long ago, needed someone to walk over the fields with her; and when Joy had to be impressed for these services, her remarks were usually so ugly and her face so glum that Mrs. Hopewell would say, "If you can't come pleasantly, I don't want you at all," to which the girl, standing square and rigid-shouldered with her neck thrust slightly forward, would reply, "If you want me, here I am—LIKE I AM."

Mrs. Hopewell excused this attitude because of the leg (which had been shot off in a hunting accident when Joy was ten). It was hard for Mrs. Hopewell to realize that her child was thirty-two now and that for more than twenty years she had had only one leg. She thought of her still as a child because it tore her heart to think instead of the poor stout girl in her thirties who had never danced a step or had any *normal* good times. Her name was really Joy but as soon as she was twenty-one and away from home, she had had it legally changed. Mrs. Hopewell was certain that she had thought and thought until she had hit upon the ugliest name in any language. Then she had gone and had the beautiful name, Joy, changed without telling her mother until after she had done it. Her legal name was Hulga.

When Mrs. Hopewell thought the name, Hulga, she thought of the broad blank hull of a battleship. She would not use it. She continued to call her Joy to which the girl responded but in a purely mechanical way.

Hulga had learned to tolerate Mrs. Freeman who saved her from taking walks with her mother. Even Glynese and Carramae were useful when they occupied attention that might otherwise have been directed at her. At first she had thought she could not stand Mrs. Freeman for she had found that it was not possible to be rude to her. Mrs. Freeman would take on strange resentments and for days together she would be sullen but the source of her displeasure was always obscure; a direct attack, a positive leer, blatant ugliness to her face—these never touched her. And without warning one day, she began calling her Hulga.

She did not call her that in front of Mrs. Hopewell who would have been incensed but when she and the girl happened to be out of the house together, she would say something and add the name Hulga to the end of it, and the big spectacled Joy-Hulga would scowl and redden as if her privacy had been intruded upon. She considered the name her personal affair. She had arrived at it first purely on the basis of its ugly sound and then the full genius of its fitness had struck her. She had a vision of the name working like the ugly sweating Vulcan who stayed in the furnace and to whom, presumably, the goddess had to come when called. She saw it as the name of her highest creative act. One of her major triumphs was that her mother had not been able to turn her dust into Joy, but the greater one was that she had been able to turn it herself into Hulga. However, Mrs. Freeman's relish for using the name only irritated her. It was as if Mrs. Freeman's beady steelpointed eyes had penetrated far enough behind her face to reach some secret fact. Something about her seemed to fascinate Mrs. Freeman and then one day Hulga realized that it was the artificial leg. Mrs. Freeman had a special fondness for the details of secret infections, hidden deformities, assaults upon children. Of diseases, she preferred the lingering or incurable. Hulga had heard Mrs. Hopewell give her the details of the hunting accident, how the leg had been literally blasted off, how she had never lost consciousness. Mrs. Freeman could listen to it any time as if it had happened an hour ago.

When Hulga stumped into the kitchen in the morning (she could walk without making the awful noise but she made it—Mrs. Hopewell was certain—because it was ugly-sounding), she glanced at them and did not speak. Mrs. Hopewell would be in her red kimono with her hair tied around her head in rags. She would be sitting at the table, finishing her breakfast and Mrs. Freeman would be hanging by her elbow outward from the refrigerator, looking down at the table. Hulga always put her eggs on the stove to boil and then stood over them with her arms folded, and Mrs. Hopewell would look at her—a kind of indirect gaze divided between her and Mrs. Freeman—and would think that if she would only keep herself up a little, she wouldn't be so bad looking. There was nothing wrong with her face that a pleasant expression wouldn't help. Mrs. Hopewell said that people who looked on the bright side of things would be beautiful even if they were not.

Whenever she looked at Joy this way, she could not help but feel that it would have been better if the child had not taken the Ph.D. It had certainly not brought her out any and now that she had it, there was no more excuse for her to go to school again. Mrs. Hopewell thought it was nice for girls to go to school to have a good time but Joy had "gone through." Anyhow, she would not have been strong enough to go again. The doctors had told Mrs. Hopewell that with the best of care, Joy might see forty-five. She had a weak heart. Joy had made it plain that if it had not been for this condition, she would be far from these red hills and good country people. She would be in a university lecturing to people who knew what she was talking about. And Mrs. Hopewell could very well picture her there, looking like a scarecrow and lecturing to more of the same. Here she went about all day in a six-year-old skirt and a yellow sweat shirt with a faded cowboy on a horse embossed on it. She thought this was funny; Mrs. Hopewell thought it was idiotic and showed simply that she was still a child. She was brilliant but she didn't have a grain of sense. It seemed to Mrs. Hopewell that every year she grew less like other people and more like herself—bloated, rude, and squint-eyed. And she said such strange things! To her own mother she had said—without warning, without excuse, standing up in the middle of a meal with her face purple and her mouth half full—"Woman! do you ever look inside? Do you ever look inside and see what you are *not*? God!" she had cried sinking down again and staring at her plate, "Malebranche was right: we are not our own light. We are not our own light!" Mrs. Hopewell had no idea to this day what brought that on. She had only made the remark, hoping Joy would take it in, that a smile never hurt anyone.

The girl had taken the Ph.D. in philosophy and this left Mrs. Hopewell at a complete loss. You could say, "My daughter is a nurse," or "My daughter is a school teacher," or even, "My daughter is a chemical engineer." You could not say, "My daughter is a philosopher." That was something that had ended with the Greeks and Romans. All day Joy sat on her neck in a deep chair, reading. Sometimes she went for walks but she didn't like dogs or cats or birds or flowers or nature or nice young men. She looked at nice young men as if she could smell their stupidity.

One day Mrs. Hopewell had picked up one of the books the girl had just put down and opening it at random, she read, "Science, on the other hand, has to assert its soberness and seriousness afresh and declare that it is concerned solely with what-is. Nothing—how can it be for science anything but a horror and a phantasm? If science is right, then one thing stands firm: science wishes to know nothing of nothing. Such is after all the strictly scientific approach to Nothing. We know it by wishing to know nothing of Nothing." These words had been underlined with a blue pencil and they worked on Mrs. Hopewell like some evil incantation in gibberish. She shut the book quickly and went out of the room as if she were having a chill.

This morning when the girl came in, Mrs. Freeman was on Carramae. "She thrown up four times after supper," she said, "and was up twict in the night after three o'clock. Yesterday she didn't do nothing but ramble in the bureau drawer. All she did. Stand up there and see what she could run up on."

"She's got to eat," Mrs. Hopewell muttered, sipping her coffee, while she watched Joy's back at the stove. She was wondering what the child had said to the Bible salesman. She could not imagine what kind of a conversation she could possibly have had with him.

He was a tall gaunt hatless youth who had called yesterday to sell them a Bible. He had appeared at the door, carrying a large black suitcase that weighted him so heavily on one side that he had to brace himself against the door facing. He seemed on the point of collapse but he said in a cheerful voice, "Good morning, Mrs. Cedars!" and set the suitcase down on the mat. He was not a bad-looking young man though he had on a bright blue suit and yellow socks that were not pulled up far enough. He had prominent face bones and a streak of sticky-looking brown hair falling across his forehead.

"I'm Mrs. Hopewell," she said.

"Oh!" he said, pretending to look puzzled but with his eyes sparkling, "I

saw it said 'The Cedars,' on the mailbox so I thought you was Mrs. Cedars!"
and he burst out in a pleasant laugh. He picked up the satchel and under
cover of a pant, he fell forward into her hall. It was rather as if the suitcase
had moved first, jerking him after it. "Mrs. Hopewell!" he said and grabbed
her hand. "I hope you are well!" and he laughed again and then all at once
his face sobered completely. He paused and gave her a straight earnest look
and said, "Lady, I've come to speak of serious things."

"Well, come in," she muttered, none too pleased because her dinner was
almost ready. He came into the parlor and sat down on the edge of a straight
chair and put the suitcase between his feet and glanced around the room as if
he were sizing her up by it. Her silver gleamed on the two sideboards; she
decided he had never been in a room as elegant as this.

"Mrs. Hopewell," he began, using her name in a way that sounded almost
intimate, "I know you believe in Chrustian service."

"Well yes," she murmured.

"I know," he said and paused, looking very wise with his head cocked on
one side, "that you're a good woman. Friends have told me."

Mrs. Hopewell never liked to be taken for a fool. "What are you selling?"
she asked.

"Bibles," the young man said and his eye raced around the room before he
added, "I see you have no family Bible in your parlor, I see that is the one
lack you got!"

Mrs. Hopewell could not say, "My daughter is an atheist and won't let me
keep the Bible in the parlor." She said, stiffening slightly, "I keep my Bible by
my bedside." This was not the truth. It was in the attic somewhere.

"Lady," he said, "the word of God ought to be in the parlor."

"Well, I think that's a matter of taste," she began. "I think . . ."

"Lady," he said, "for a Chrustian, the word of God ought to be in every
room in the house besides in his heart. I know you're a Chrustian because I
can see it in every line of your face."

She stood up and said, "Well, young man, I don't want to buy a Bible and I
smell my dinner burning."

He didn't get up. He began to twist his hands and looking down at them,
he said softly, "Well lady, I'll tell you the truth—not many people want to
buy one nowadays and besides, I know I'm real simple. I don't know how to
say a thing but to say it. I'm just a country boy." He glanced up into her
unfriendly face. "People like you don't like to fool with country people like
me!"

"Why!" she cried, "good country people are the salt of the earth! Besides,
we all have different ways of doing, it takes all kinds to make the world go
'round. That's life!"

"You said a mouthful," he said.

"Why, I think there aren't enough good country people in the world!" she
said, stirred. "I think that's what's wrong with it!"

His face had brightened. "I didn't inraduce myself," he said. "I'm Manley
Pointer from out in the country around Willohobie, not even from a place,
just from near a place."

"You wait a minute," she said. "I have to see about my dinner." She went out to the kitchen and found Joy standing near the door where she had been listening.

"Get rid of the salt of the earth," she said, "and let's eat."

Mrs. Hopewell gave her a pained look and turned the heat down under the vegetables. "*I* can't be rude to anybody," she murmured and went back into the parlor.

He had opened the suitcase and was sitting with a Bible on each knee.

"You might as well put those up," she told him. "I don't want one."

"I appreciate your honesty," he said. "You don't see any more real honest people unless you go way out in the country."

"I know," she said, "real genuine folks!" Through the crack in the door she heard a groan.

"I guess a lot of boys come telling you they're working their way through college," he said, "but I'm not going to tell you that. Somehow," he said, "I don't want to go to college. I want to devote my life to Chrustian service. See," he said, lowering his voice, "I got this heart condition. I may not live long. When you know it's something wrong with you and you may not live long, well then, lady . . ." He paused, with his mouth open, and stared at her.

He and Joy had the same condition! She knew that her eyes were filling with tears but she collected herself quickly and murmured, "Won't you stay for dinner? We'd love to have you!" and was sorry the instant she heard herself say it.

"Yes mam," he said in an abashed voice, "I would sher love to do that!"

Joy had given him one look on being introduced to him and then throughout the meal had not glanced at him again. He had addressed several remarks to her, which she had pretended not to hear. Mrs. Hopewell could not understand deliberate rudeness, although she lived with it, and she felt she had always to overflow with hospitality to make up for Joy's lack of courtesy. She urged him to talk about himself and he did. He said he was the seventh child of twelve and that his father had been crushed under a tree when he himself was eight year old. He had been crushed very badly, in fact, almost cut in two and was practically not recognizable. His mother had got along the best she could by hard working and she had always seen that her children went to Sunday School and that they read the Bible every evening. He was now nineteen year old and he had been selling Bibles for four months. In that time he had sold seventy-seven Bibles and had the promise of two more sales. He wanted to become a missionary because he thought that was the way you could do most for people. "He who losest his life shall find it," he said simply and he was so sincere, so genuine and earnest that Mrs. Hopewell would not for the world have smiled. He prevented his peas from sliding onto the table by blocking them with a piece of bread which he later cleaned his plate with. She could see Joy observing sidewise how he handled his knife and fork and she saw too that every few minutes, the boy would dart a keen appraising glance at the girl as if he were trying to attract her attention.

After dinner Joy cleared the dishes off the table and disappeared and Mrs. Hopewell was left to talk with him. He told her again about his childhood and his father's accident and about various things that had happened to him. Every five minutes or so she would stifle a yawn. He sat for two hours until finally she told him she must go because she had an appointment in town. He packed his Bibles and thanked her and prepared to leave, but in the doorway he stopped and wrung her hand and said that not on any of his trips had he met a lady as nice as her and he asked if he could come again. She had said she would always be happy to see him.

Joy had been standing in the road, apparently looking at something in the distance, when he came down the steps toward her, bent to the side with his heavy valise. He stopped where she was standing and confronted her directly. Mrs. Hopewell could not hear what he said but she trembled to think what Joy would say to him. She could see that after a minute Joy said something and that then the boy began to speak again, making an excited gesture with his free hand. After a minute Joy said something else at which the boy began to speak once more. Then to her amazement, Mrs. Hopewell saw the two of them walk off together, toward the gate. Joy had walked all the way to the gate with him and Mrs. Hopewell could not imagine what they had said to each other, and she had not yet dared to ask.

Mrs. Freeman was insisting upon her attention. She had moved from the refrigerator to the heater so that Mrs. Hopewell had to turn and face her in order to seem to be listening. "Glynese gone out with Harvey Hill again last night," she said. "She had this sty."

"Hill," Mrs. Hopewell said absently, "is that the one who works in the garage?"

"Nome, he's the one that goes to chiropracter school," Mrs. Freeman said. "She had this sty. Been had it two days. So she says when he brought her in the other night he says, 'Lemme get rid of that sty for you,' and she says, 'How?' and he says, 'You just lay yourself down acrost the seat of that car and I'll show you.' So she done it and he popped her neck. Kept on a-popping it several times until she made him quit. This morning," Mrs. Freeman said, "she ain't got no sty. She ain't got no traces of a sty."

"I never heard of that before," Mrs. Hopewell said.

"He ast her to marry him before the Ordinary," Mrs. Freeman went on, "and she told him she wasn't going to be married in no *office*."

"Well, Glynese is a fine girl," Mrs. Hopewell said. "Glynese and Carramae are both fine girls."

"Carramae said when her and Lyman was married Lyman said it sure felt sacred to him. She said he said he wouldn't take five hundred dollars for being married by a preacher."

"How much would he take?" the girl asked from the stove.

"He said he wouldn't take five hundred dollars," Mrs. Freeman repeated.

"Well we all have work to do," Mrs. Hopewell said.

"Lyman said it just felt more sacred to him," Mrs. Freeman said. "The doctor wants Carramae to eat prunes. Says instead of medicine. Says them cramps is coming from pressure. You know where I think it is?"

"She'll be better in a few weeks," Mrs. Hopewell said.

"In the tube," Mrs. Freeman said. "Else she wouldn't be as sick as she is."

Hulga had cracked her two eggs into a saucer and was bringing them to the table along with a cup of coffee that she had filled too full. She sat down carefully and began to eat, meaning to keep Mrs. Freeman there by questions if for any reason she showed an inclination to leave. She could perceive her mother's eye on her. The first round-about question would be about the Bible salesman and she did not wish to bring it on. "How did he pop her neck?" she asked.

Mrs. Freeman went into a description of how he had popped her neck. She said he owned a '55 Mercury but that Glynese said she would rather marry a man with only a '36 Plymouth who would be married by a preacher. The girl asked what if he had a '32 Plymouth and Mrs. Freeman said what Glynese had said was a '36 Plymouth.

Mrs. Hopewell said there were not many girls with Glynese's common sense. She said what she admired in those girls was their common sense. She said that reminded her that they had had a nice visitor yesterday, a young man selling Bibles. "Lord," she said, "he bored me to death but he was so sincere and genuine I couldn't be rude to him. He was just good country people, you know," she said, "—just the salt of the earth."

"I seen him walk up," Mrs. Freeman said, "and then later—I seen him walk off," and Hulga could feel the slight shift in her voice, the slight insinuation, that he had not walked off alone, had he? Her face remained expressionless but the color rose into her neck and she seemed to swallow it down with the next spoonful of egg. Mrs. Freeman was looking at her as if they had a secret together.

"Well, it takes all kinds of people to make the world go 'round," Mrs. Hopewell said. "It's very good we aren't all alike."

"Some people are more alike than others," Mrs. Freeman said.

Hulga got up and stumped, with about twice the noise that was necessary, into her room and locked the door. She was to meet the Bible salesman at ten o'clock at the gate. She had thought about it half the night. She had started thinking of it as a great joke and then she had begun to see profound implications in it. She had lain in bed imagining dialogues for them that were insane on the surface but that reached below to depths that no Bible salesman would be aware of. Their conversation yesterday had been of this kind.

He had stopped in front of her and had simply stood there. His face was bony and sweaty and bright, with a little pointed nose in the center of it, and his look was different from what it had been at the dinner table. He was gazing at her with open curiosity, with fascination, like a child watching a new fantastic animal at the zoo, and he was breathing as if he had run a great distance to reach her. His gaze seemed somehow familiar but she could not think where she had been regarded with it before. For almost a minute he didn't say anything. Then on what seemed an insuck of breath, he whispered, "You ever ate a chicken that was two days old?"

The girl looked at him stonily. He might have just put this question up for consideration at the meeting of a philosophical association. "Yes," she presently replied as if she had considered it from all angles.

"It must have been mighty small!" he said triumphantly and shook all over with little nervous giggles, getting very red in the face, and subsiding finally into his gaze of complete admiration, while the girl's expression remained exactly the same.

"How old are you?" he asked softly.

She waited some time before she answered. Then in a flat voice she said, "Seventeen."

His smiles came in succession like waves breaking on the surface of a little lake. "I see you got a wooden leg," he said. "I think you're real brave. I think you're real sweet."

The girl stood blank and solid and silent.

"Walk to the gate with me," he said. "You're a brave sweet little thing and I liked you the minute I seen you walk in the door."

Hulga began to move forward.

"What's your name?" he asked, smiling down on the top of her head.

"Hulga," she said.

"Hulga," he murmured, "Hulga. Hulga. I never heard of anybody name Hulga before. You're shy, aren't you, Hulga?" he asked.

She nodded, watching his large red hand on the handle of the giant valise.

"I like girls that wear glasses," he said. "I think a lot. I'm not like these people that a serious thought don't ever enter their heads. It's because I may die."

"I may die too," she said suddenly and looked up at him. His eyes were very small and brown, glittering feverishly.

"Listen," he said, "don't you think some people was meant to meet on account of what all they got in common and all? Like they both think serious thoughts and all?" He shifted the valise to his other hand so that the hand nearest her was free. He caught hold of her elbow and shook it a little. "I don't work on Saturday," he said. "I like to walk in the woods and see what Mother Nature is wearing. O'er the hills and far away. Pic-nics and things. Couldn't we go on a pic-nic tomorrow? Say yes, Hulga," he said and gave her a dying look as if he felt his insides about to drop out of him. He had even seemed to sway slightly toward her.

During the night she had imagined that she seduced him. She imagined that the two of them walked on the place until they came to the storage barn beyond the two back fields and there, she imagined, that things came to such a pass that she very easily seduced him and that then, of course, she had to reckon with his remorse. True genius can get an idea across even to an inferior mind. She imagined that she took his remorse in hand and changed it into a deeper understanding of life. She took all his shame away and turned it into something useful.

She set off for the gate at exactly ten o'clock, escaping without drawing Mrs. Hopewell's attention. She didn't take anything to eat, forgetting that food is usually taken on a picnic. She wore a pair of slacks and a dirty white shirt, and as an afterthought, she had put some Vapex on the collar of it since she did not own any perfume. When she reached the gate no one was there.

She looked up and down the empty highway and had the furious feeling that she had been tricked, that he had only meant to make her walk to the gate after the idea of him. Then suddenly he stood up, very tall, from behind a bush on the opposite embankment. Smiling, he lifted his hat which was new and wide-brimmed. He had not worn it yesterday and she wondered if he had bought it for the occasion. It was toast-colored with a red and white band around it and was slightly too large for him. He stepped from behind the bush still carrying the black valise. He had on the same suit and the same yellow socks sucked down in his shoes from walking. He crossed the highway and said, "I knew you'd come!"

The girl wondered acidly how he had known this. She pointed to the valise and asked, "Why did you bring your Bibles?"

He took her elbow, smiling down on her as if he could not stop. "You can never tell when you'll need the word of God, Hulga," he said. She had a moment in which she doubted that this was actually happening and then they began to climb the embankment. They went down into the pasture toward the woods. The boy walked lightly by her side, bouncing on his toes. The valise did not seem to be heavy today; he even swung it. They crossed half the pasture without saying anything and then, putting his hand easily on the small of her back, he asked softly, "Where does your wooden leg join on?"

She turned an ugly red and glared at him and for an instant the boy looked abashed. "I didn't mean you no harm," he said. "I only meant you're so brave and all. I guess God takes care of you."

"No," she said, looking forward and walking fast, "I don't even believe in God."

At this he stopped and whistled. "No!" he exclaimed as if he were too astonished to say anything else.

She walked on and in a second he was bouncing at her side, fanning with his hat. "That's very unusual for a girl," he remarked, watching her out of the corner of his eye. When they reached the edge of the wood, he put his hand on her back again and drew her against him without a word and kissed her heavily.

The kiss, which had more pressure than feeling behind it, produced that extra surge of adrenalin in the girl that enables one to carry a packed trunk out of a burning house, but in her, the power went at once to the brain. Even before he released her, her mind, clear and detached and ironic anyway, was regarding him from a great distance, with amusement but with pity. She had never been kissed before and she was pleased to discover that it was an unexceptional experience and all a matter of the mind's control. Some people might enjoy drain water if they were told it was vodka. When the boy, looking expectant but uncertain, pushed her gently away, she turned and walked on, saying nothing as if such business, for her, were common enough.

He came along panting at her side, trying to help her when he saw a root that she might trip over. He caught and held back the long swaying blades of thorn vine until she had passed beyond them. She led the way and he came breathing heavily behind her. Then they came out on a sunlit hillside, sloping softly into another one a little smaller. Beyond, they could see the rusted top of the old barn where the extra hay was stored.

The hill was sprinkled with small pink weeds. "Then you ain't saved?" he asked suddenly, stopping.

The girl smiled. It was the first time she had smiled at him at all. "In my economy," she said, "I'm saved and you are damned but I told you I didn't believe in God."

Nothing seemed to destroy the boy's look of admiration. He gazed at her now as if the fantastic animal at the zoo had put its paw through the bars and given him a loving poke. She thought he looked as if he wanted to kiss her again and she walked on before he had the chance.

"Ain't there somewheres we can sit down sometime?" he murmured, his voice softening toward the end of the sentence.

"In that barn," she said.

They made for it rapidly as if it might slide away like a train. It was a large two-story barn, cool and dark inside. The boy pointed up the ladder that led into the loft and said, "It's too bad we can't go up there."

"Why can't we?" she asked.

"Yer leg," he said reverently.

The girl gave him a contemptuous look and putting both hands on the ladder, she climbed it while he stood below, apparently awestruck. She pulled herself expertly through the opening and then looked down at him and said, "Well, come on if you're coming," and he began to climb the ladder, awkwardly bringing the suitcase with him.

"We won't need the Bible," she observed.

"You never can tell," he said, panting. After he had got into the loft, he was a few seconds catching his breath. She had sat down in a pile of straw. A wide sheath of sunlight, filled with dust particles, slanted over her. She lay back against a bale, her face turned away, looking out the front opening of the barn where hay was thrown from a wagon into the loft. The two pink-speckled hillsides lay back against a dark ridge of woods. The sky was cloudless and cold blue. The boy dropped down by her side and put one arm under her and the other over her and began methodically kissing her face, making little noises like a fish. He did not remove his hat but it was pushed far enough back not to interfere. When her glasses got in his way, he took them off of her and slipped them into his pocket.

The girl at first did not return any of the kisses but presently she began to and after she had put several on his cheek, she reached his lips and remained there, kissing him again and again as if she were trying to draw all the breath out of him. His breath was clear and sweet like a child's and the kisses were sticky like a child's. He mumbled about loving her and about knowing when he first seen her that he loved her, but the mumbling was like the sleepy fretting of a child being put to sleep by his mother. Her mind, throughout this, never stopped or lost itself for a second to her feelings. "You ain't said you loved me none," he whispered finally, pulling back from her. "You got to say that."

She looked away from him off into the hollow sky and then down at a black ridge and then down farther into what appeared to be two green swelling lakes. She didn't realize he had taken her glasses but this landscape could not seem exceptional to her for she seldom paid any close attention to her surroundings.

"You got to say it," he repeated. "You got to say you love me."

She was always careful how she committed herself. "In a sense," she began, "if you use the word loosely, you might say that. But it's not a word I use. I don't have illusions. I'm one of those people who see *through* to nothing."

The boy was frowning. "You got to say it. I said it and you got to say it," he said.

The girl looked at him almost tenderly. "You poor baby," she murmured. "It's just as well you don't understand," and she pulled him by the neck, face-down, against her. "We are all damned," she said, "but some of us have taken off our blindfolds and see that there's nothing to see. It's a kind of salvation."

The boy's astonished eyes looked blankly through the ends of her hair. "Okay," he almost whined, "but do you love me or don'tcher?"

"Yes," she said and added, "in a sense. But I must tell you something. There mustn't be anything dishonest between us." She lifted his head and looked him in the eye. "I am thirty years old," she said. "I have a number of degrees."

The boy's look was irritated but dogged. "I don't care," he said. "I don't care a thing about what all you done. I just want to know if you love me or don'tcher?" and he caught her to him and wildly planted her face with kisses until she said, "Yes, yes."

"Okay then," he said, letting her go. "Prove it."

She smiled, looking dreamily out on the shifty landscape. She had seduced him without even making up her mind to try. "How?" she asked, feeling that he should be delayed a little.

He leaned over and put his lips to her ear. "Show me where your wooden leg joins on," he whispered.

The girl uttered a sharp little cry and her face instantly drained of color. The obscenity of the suggestion was not what shocked her. As a child she had sometimes been subject to feelings of shame but education had removed the last traces of that as a good surgeon scrapes for cancer; she would no more have felt it over what he was asking than she would have believed in his Bible. But she was as sensitive about the artificial leg as a peacock about his tail. No one ever touched it but her. She took care of it as someone else would his soul, in private and almost with her own eyes turned away. "No," she said.

"I known it," he muttered, sitting up. "You're just playing me for a sucker."

"Oh no no!" she cried. "It joins on at the knee. Only at the knee. Why do you want to see it?"

The boy gave her a long penetrating look. "Because," he said, "it's what makes you different. You ain't like anybody else."

She sat staring at him. There was nothing about her face or her round freezing-blue eyes to indicate that this had moved her; but she felt as if her heart had stopped and left her mind to pump her blood. She decided that for the first time in her life she was face to face with real innocence. This boy, with an instinct that came from beyond wisdom, had touched the truth about her. When after a minute, she said in a hoarse high voice, "All right," it was like surrendering to him completely. It was like losing her own life and finding it again, miraculously, in his.

Very gently he began to roll the slack leg up. The artificial limb, in a white sock and brown flat shoe, was bound in a heavy material like canvas and ended in an ugly jointure where it was attached to the stump. The boy's face and his voice were entirely reverent as he uncovered it and said, "Now show me how to take it off and on."

She took it off for him and put it back on again and then he took it off himself, handling it as tenderly as if it were a real one. "See!" he said with a delighted child's face. "Now I can do it myself!"

"Put it back on," she said. She was thinking that she would run away with him and that every night he would take the leg off and every morning put it back on again. "Put it back on," she said.

"Not yet," he murmured, setting it on its foot out of her reach. "Leave it off for a while. You got me instead."

She gave a little cry of alarm but he pushed her down and began to kiss her again. Without the leg she felt entirely dependent on him. Her brain seemed to have stopped thinking altogether and to be about some other function that it was not very good at. Different expressions raced back and forth over her face. Every now and then the boy, his eyes like two steel spikes, would glance behind him where the leg stood. Finally she pushed him off and said, "Put it back on me now."

"Wait," he said. He leaned the other way and pulled the valise toward him and opened it. It had a pale blue spotted lining and there were only two Bibles in it. He took one of these out and opened the cover of it. It was hollow and contained a pocket flask of whiskey, a pack of cards, and a small blue box with printing on it. He laid these out in front of her one at a time in an evenly-spaced row, like one presenting offerings at the shrine of a goddess. He put the blue box in her hand. THIS PRODUCT TO BE USED ONLY FOR THE PREVENTION OF DISEASE, she read, and dropped it. The boy was unscrewing the top of the flask. He stopped and pointed, with a smile, to the deck of cards. It was not an ordinary deck but one with an obscene picture on the back of each card. "Take a swig," he said, offering her the bottle first. He held it in front of her, but like one mesmerized, she did not move.

Her voice when she spoke had an almost pleading sound. "Aren't you," she murmured, "aren't you just good country people?"

The boy cocked his head. He looked as if he were just beginning to understand that she might be trying to insult him. "Yeah," he said, curling his lip slightly, "but it ain't held me back none. I'm as good as you any day in the week."

"Give me my leg," she said.

He pushed it farther away with his foot. "Come on now, let's begin to have us a good time," he said coaxingly. "We ain't got to know one another good yet."

"Give me my leg!" she screamed and tried to lunge for it but he pushed her down easily.

"What's the matter with you all of a sudden?" he asked, frowning as he screwed the top on the flask and put it quickly back inside the Bible. "You just a while ago said you didn't believe in nothing. I thought you was some girl!"

Her face was almost purple. "You're a Christian!" she hissed. "You're a fine Christian! You're just like them all—say one thing and do another. You're a perfect Christian, you're . . ."

The boy's mouth was set angrily. "I hope you don't think," he said in a lofty indignant tone, "that I believe in that crap! I may sell Bibles but I know which end is up and I wasn't born yesterday and I know where I'm going!"

"Give me my leg!" she screeched. He jumped up so quickly that she barely saw him sweep the cards and the blue box back into the Bible and throw the Bible into the valise. She saw him grab the leg and then she saw it for an instant slanted forlornly across the inside of the suitcase with a Bible at either side of its opposite ends. He slammed the lid shut and snatched up the valise and swung it down the hole and then stepped through himself.

When all of him had passed but his head, he turned and regarded her with a look that no longer had any admiration in it. "I've gotten a lot of interesting things," he said. "One time I got a woman's glass eye this way. And you needn't to think you'll catch me because Pointer ain't really my name. I use a different name at every house I call at and don't stay nowhere long. And I'll tell you another thing, Hulga," he said, using the name as if he didn't think much of it, "you ain't so smart. I been believing in nothing ever since I was born!" and then the toast-colored hat disappeared down the hole and the girl was left, sitting on the straw in the dusty sunlight. When she turned her churning face toward the opening, she saw his blue figure struggling successfully over the green speckled lake.

Mrs. Hopewell and Mrs. Freeman, who were in the back pasture, digging up onions, saw him emerge a little later from the woods and head across the meadow toward the highway. "Why, that looks like that nice dull young man that tried to sell me a Bible yesterday," Mrs. Hopewell said, squinting. "He must have been selling them to the Negroes back in there. He was so simple," she said, "but I guess the world would be better off if we were all that simple."

Mrs. Freeman's gaze drove forward and just touched him before he disappeared under the hill. Then she returned her attention to the evil-smelling onion shoot she was lifting from the ground. "Some can't be that simple," she said. "I know I never could."

Ramsey Campbell

Mackintosh Willy

Ramsey Campbell is perhaps the most important living writer in the horror fiction field. Jack Sullivan (in his excellent scholarly anthology, *Lost Souls*) calls Campbell "the most sophisticated stylist in current supernatural fiction," and goes on to praise his images, "which dwell on the disorderliness of middle- and lower-class life, have a jagged, contemporary edge," and continues on to credit him with "bringing the supernatural tale up to date without sacrificing the literary standards." He works consciously in the horror tradition and has consistently experimented with all the varied modes of the contemporary horror story, from the Lovecraftian to the Aickmanesque. He is in addition a devotee of pop culture horror in films, comics, and is an acute critic. Campbell is one of the leading figures in the development of the long form horror novel, along with Peter Straub and Stephen King and others. His novel, *The Face That Must Die*, is one of the contemporary masterpieces of the long form, and he is constantly working to extend his range. "Mackintosh Willy" is among his finest efforts in the psychological mode, a disturbing story of male sexual innocence comparable in effect to Robert Aickman's "The Swords." It won the World Fantasy Award for best short fiction in 1980.

To start with, he wasn't called Mackintosh Willy. I never knew who gave him that name. Was it one of those nicknames that seem to proceed from a group subconscious, names recognized by every member of the group yet apparently originated by none? One has to call one's fears something, if only to gain the illusion of control. Still, sometimes I wonder how much of his monstrousness we created. Wondering helps me not to ponder my responsibility for what happened at the end.

When I was ten I thought his name was written inside the shelter in the park. I saw it only from a distance; I wasn't one of those who made a game of braving the shelter. At ten I wasn't afraid to be timid—that came later, with adolescence.

Yet if you had walked past Newsham Park you might have wondered what there was to fear: why were children advancing, bold but wary, on the red-brick shelter by the twilit pool? Surely there could be no danger in the shallow shed, which might have held a couple of dozen bicycles. By now the fishermen and the model boats would have left the pool alone and still; lamps on the park road would have begun to dangle luminous tails in the water. The only sounds would be the whispering of children, the murmur of trees around the pool, perhaps a savage incomprehensible muttering whose source you would be unable to locate. Only a game, you might reassure yourself.

And of course it was: a game to conquer fear. If you had waited long enough you might have heard shapeless movement in the shelter, and a snarling. You might have glimpsed him as he came scuttling lopsidedly out of the shelter, like an injured spider from its lair. In the gathering darkness, how much of your glimpse would you believe? The unnerving swiftness of the obese limping shape? The head which seemed to belong to another, far smaller, body, and which was almost invisible within a gray balaclava cap, except for the small eyes which glared through the loose hole?

All of that made us hate him. We were too young for tolerance—and besides, he was intolerant of us. Ever since we could remember he had been there, guarding his territory and his bottle of red biddy. If anyone ventured too close he would start muttering. Sometimes you could hear some of the words: "Damn bastard prying interfering snooper . . . thieving bastard layabout . . . think you're clever, eh? . . . I'll give you something clever . . ."

We never saw him until it was growing dark: that was what made him into a monster. Perhaps during the day he joined his cronies elsewhere—on the steps of ruined churches in the center of Liverpool, or lying on the grass in St. John's Gardens, or crowding the benches opposite Edge Hill Public Library, whose stopped clock no doubt helped their draining of time. But if anything of this occurred to us, we dismissed it as irrelevant. He was a creature of the dark.

Shouldn't this have meant that the first time I saw him in daylight was the end? In fact, it was only the beginning.

It was a blazing day at the height of summer, my tenth. It was too hot to think of games to while away my school holidays. All I could do was walk errands for my parents, grumbling a little.

They owned a small newsagent's on West Derby Road. That day they were expecting promised copies of the *Tuebrook Bugle*. Even when he disagreed with them, my father always supported the independent newspapers—the *Bugle*, the *Liverpool Free Press*: at least they hadn't been swallowed or destroyed by a monopoly. The lateness of the *Bugle* worried him; had the paper given in? He sent me to find out.

I ran across West Derby Road just as the traffic lights at the top of the hill released a flood of cars. Only girls used the pedestrian subway so far as I was concerned; besides, it was flooded again. I strolled past the concrete police station into the park, to take the long way round. It was too hot to go anywhere quickly or even directly.

The park was crowded with games of football, parked prams, sunbathers draped over the greens. Patients sat outside the hospital on Orphan Drive beside the park. Around the lake, fishermen sat by transistor radios and whipped the air with hooks. Beyond the lake, model boats snarled across the shallow circular pool. I stopped to watch their patterns on the water, and caught sight of an object in the shelter.

At first I thought it was an old gray sack that someone had dumped on the bench. Perhaps it held rubbish—sticks which gave parts of it an angular look. Then I saw that the sack was an indeterminate stained garment, which might have been a mackintosh or raincoat of some kind. What I had vaguely assumed to be an ancient shopping bag, resting next to the sack, displayed a ragged patch of flesh and the dull gleam of an eye.

Exposed to daylight, he looked even more dismaying: so huge and still, less stupefied than dormant. The presence of the boatmen with their remote-control boxes reassured me. I ambled past the allotments to Pringle Street, where a terraced house was the editorial office of the *Bugle*.

Our copies were on the way, said Chrissie Maher the editor, and insisted on making me a cup of tea. She seemed a little upset when, having gulped the tea, I hurried out into the sudden rain. Perhaps it was rude of me not to wait until the rain had stopped—but on this parched day I wanted to make the most of it, to bathe my face and my bare arms in the onslaught, gasping almost hysterically.

By the time I had passed the allotments, where cabbages rattled like toy machine-guns, the downpour was too heavy even for me. The park provided little cover; the trees let fall their own belated storms, miniature but drenching. The nearest shelter was by the pool, which had been abandoned to its web of ripples. I ran down the slippery tarmac hill, splashing through puddles, trying to blink away rain, hoping there would be room in the shelter.

There was plenty of room, both because the rain reached easily into the depths of the brick shed and because the shelter was not entirely empty. He lay as I had seen him, face upturned within the sodden balaclava. Had the boatmen avoided looking closely at him? Raindrops struck his unblinking eyes and trickled over the patch of flesh.

I hadn't seen death before. I stood shivering and fascinated in the rain. I needn't be scared of him now. He'd stuffed himself into the gray coat until it split in several places; through the rents I glimpsed what might have been dark cloth or discolored hairy flesh. Above him, on the shelter, were graffiti which at last I saw were not his name at all, but the names of three boys: MACK TOSH WILLY. They were partly erased, which no doubt was why one's mind tended to fill the gap.

I had to keep glancing at him. He grew more and more difficult to ignore; his presence was intensifying. His shapelessness, the rents in his coat, made me think of an old bag of washing, decayed and moldy. His hand lurked in his sleeve; beside it, amid a scattering of Coca-Cola caps, lay fragments of the bottle whose contents had perhaps killed him. Rain roared on the dull green roof of the shelter; his staring eyes glistened and dripped. Suddenly I was frightened. I ran blindly home.

"There's someone dead in the park," I gasped. "The man who chases everyone."

"Look at you!" my mother cried. "Do you want pneumonia? Just you get out of those wet things this instant!"

Eventually I had a chance to repeat my news. By this time the rain had stopped. "Well, don't be telling us," my father said. "Tell the police. They're just across the road."

Did he think I had exaggerated a drunk into a corpse? He looked surprised when I hurried to the police station. But I couldn't miss the chance to venture in there—I believed that elder brothers of some of my schoolmates had been taken into the station and hadn't come out for years.

Beside a window which might have belonged to a ticket office was a bell which you rang to make the window's partition slide back and display a policeman. He frowned down at me. What was my name? What had I been doing in the park? Who had I been with? When a second head appeared beside him he said reluctantly, "He thinks someone's passed out in the park."

A blue-and-white Mini called for me at the police station, like a taxi; on the roof a red sign said POLICE. People glanced in at me as though I were on the way to prison. Perhaps I was: suppose Mackintosh Willy had woken up and gone? How long a sentence did you get for lying? False diamonds sparkled on the grass and in the trees. I wished I'd persuaded my father to tell the police.

As the car halted, I saw the gray bulk in the shelter. The driver strode, stiff with dignity, to peer at it. "My God," I heard him say in disgust.

Did he know Mackintosh Willy? Perhaps, but that wasn't the point. "Look at this," he said to his colleague. "Ever see a corpse with pennies on the eyes? Just look at this, then. See what someone thought was a joke."

He looked shocked, sickened. He was blocking my view as he demanded, "Did you do this?"

His white-faced anger, and my incomprehension, made me speechless. But his colleague said, "It wouldn't be him. He wouldn't come and tell us afterward, would he?"

As I tried to peer past them he said, "Go on home, now. Go on." His gentleness seemed threatening. Suddenly frightened, I ran home through the park.

For a while I avoided the shelter. I had no reason to go near, except on the way home from school. Sometimes I'd used to see schoolmates tormenting Mackintosh Willy; sometimes, at a distance, I had joined them. Now the shelter yawned emptily, baring its dim bench. The dark pool stirred, disturbing the green beards of the stone margin. My main reason for avoiding the park was that there was nobody with whom to go.

Living on a main road was the trouble. I belonged to none of the side streets, where they played football among parked cars or chased through the back alleys. I was never invited to street parties. I felt like an outsider, particularly when I had to pass the groups of teenagers who sat on the railings above the pedestrian subway, lazily swinging their legs, waiting to pounce. I stayed at home, in the flat above the newsagent's, when I could, and read everything in the shop. But I grew frustrated: I did enough reading at school. All this was why I welcomed Mark. He could save me from my isolation.

Not that we became friends immediately. He was my parents' latest paper boy. For several days we examined each other warily. He was taller than me, which was intimidating, but seemed unsure how to arrange his lankiness. Eventually he said, "What're you reading?"

He sounded as though reading was a waste of time. "A book," I retorted.

At last, when I'd let him see that it was Mickey Spillane, he said, "Can I read it after you?"

"It isn't mine. It's the shop's."

"All right, so I'll buy it." He did so at once, paying my father. He was certainly wealthier than me. When my resentment of his gesture had cooled somewhat, I realized that he was letting me finish what was now his book. I dawdled over it to make him complain, but he never did. Perhaps he might be worth knowing.

My instinct was accurate: he proved to be generous—not only with money, though his father made plenty of that in home improvements, but also in introducing me to his friends. Quite soon I had my place in the tribe at the top of the pedestrian subway, though secretly I was glad that we never exchanged more than ritual insults with the other gangs. Perhaps the police station, looming in the background, restrained hostilities.

Mark was generous too with his ideas. Although Ben, a burly lad, was nominal leader of the gang, it was Mark who suggested most of our activities. Had he taken to delivering papers to save himself from boredom—or, as I wondered afterward, to distract himself from his thoughts? It was Mark who brought his skates so that we could brave the slope of the pedestrian subway, who let us ride his bicycle around the side streets, who found ways into derelict houses, who brought his transistor radio so that we could hear the first Beatles records as the traffic passed unheeding on West Derby Road. But was all this a means of distracting us from the park?

No doubt it was inevitable that Ben resented his supremacy. Perhaps he deduced, in his slow and stolid way, that Mark disliked the park. Certainly he hit upon the ideal method to challenge him.

It was a hot summer evening. By then I was thirteen. Dust and fumes drifted in the wakes of cars; wagons clattered repetitively across the railway bridge. We lolled about the pavement, kicking Coca-Cola caps. Suddenly Ben said, "I know something we can do."

We trooped after him, dodging an aggressive gang of taxis, toward the police station. He might have meant us to play some trick there; when he swaggered past, I'm sure everyone was relieved—everyone except Mark, for Ben was leading us onto Orphan Drive.

Heat shivered above the tarmac. Beside us in the park, twilight gathered beneath the trees, which stirred stealthily. The island in the lake creaked with ducks; swollen litter drifted sluggishly, or tried to climb the bank. I could sense Mark's nervousness. He had turned his radio louder; a misshapen Elvis Presley blundered out of the static, then sank back into incoherence as a neighboring wave band seeped into his voice. Why was Mark on edge? I could see only the dimming sky, trees on the far side of the lake diluted by haze, the gleam of bottle caps like eyes atop a floating mound of litter, the glittering of broken bottles in the lawns.

We passed the locked ice-cream kiosk. Ben was heading for the circular pool, whose margin was surrounded by a fluorescent orange tape tied between iron poles, a makeshift fence. I felt Mark's hesitation, as though he were a scared dog dragged by a lead. The lead was pride: he couldn't show fear, especially when none of us knew Ben's plan.

A new concrete path had been laid around the pool. "We'll write our names in that," Ben said.

The dark pool swayed, as though trying to douse reflected lights. Black clouds spread over the sky and loomed in the pool; the threat of a storm lurked behind us. The brick shelter was very dim, and looked cavernous. I strode to the orange fence, not wanting to be last, and poked the concrete with my toe. "We can't," I said; for some reason, I felt relieved. "It's set."

Someone had been there before us, before the concrete had hardened. Footprints led from the dark shelter toward us. As they advanced, they faded, no doubt because the concrete had been setting. They looked as though the man had suffered from a limp.

When I pointed them out, Mark flinched, for we heard the radio swing wide of comprehensibility. "What's up with you?" Ben demanded.

"Nothing."

"It's getting dark," I said, not as an answer but to coax everyone back toward the main road. But my remark inspired Ben; contempt grew in his eyes. "I know what it is," he said, gesturing at Mark. "This is where he used to be scared."

"Who was scared? I wasn't bloody scared."

"Not much you weren't. You didn't look it," Ben scoffed, and told us, "Old Willy used to chase him all round the pool. He used to hate him, did old Willy. Mark used to run away from him. I never. *I* wasn't scared."

"You watch who you're calling scared. If you'd seen what I did to that old bastard—"

Perhaps the movements around us silenced him. Our surroundings were crowded with dark shifting: the sky unfurled darkness, muddy shapes rushed at us in the pool, a shadow huddled restlessly in one corner of the shelter. But Ben wasn't impressed by the drooping boast. "Go on," he sneered. "You're scared now. Bet you wouldn't dare go in his shelter."

"Who wouldn't? You watch it, you!"

"Go on, then. Let's see you do it."

We must all have been aware of Mark's fear. His whole body was stiff as a puppet's. I was ready to intervene—to say, lying, that I thought the police were near—when he gave a shrug of despair and stepped forward. Climbing gingerly over the tape as though it were electrified, he advanced onto the concrete.

He strode toward the shelter. He had turned the radio full on; I could hear nothing else, only watch the shifting of dim shapes deep in the reflected sky, watch Mark stepping in the footprints for bravado. They swallowed his feet. He was nearly at the shelter when I saw him glance at the radio.

The song had slipped awry again; another wave band seeped in, a blurred muttering. I thought it must be Mark's infectious nervousness which made me hear it forming into words. "Come on, son. Let's have a look at you." But why shouldn't the words have been real, fragments of a radio play?

Mark was still walking, his gaze held by the radio. He seemed almost hypnotized; otherwise he would surely have flinched back from the huddled shadow which surged forward from the corner by the bench, even though it must have been the shadow of a cloud.

As his foot touched the shelter I called nervously, "Come on, Mark. Let's go and skate." I felt as though I'd saved him. But when he came hurrying back, he refused to look at me or at anyone else.

For the next few days he hardly spoke to me. Perhaps he thought of avoiding my parents' shop. Certainly he stayed away from the gang—which turned out to be all to the good, for Ben, robbed of Mark's ideas, could think only of shoplifting. They were soon caught, for they weren't very skillful. After that my father had doubts about Mark, but Mark had always been scrupulously honest in deliveries; after some reflection, my father kept him on. Eventually Mark began to talk to me again, though not about the park.

That was frustrating: I wanted to tell him how the shelter looked now. I still passed it on my way home, though from a different school. Someone had been scrawling on the shelter. That was hardly unusual—graffiti filled the pedestrian subway, and even claimed the ends of streets—but the words were odd, to say the least: like the scribbles on the walls of a psychotic's cell, or the gibberish of an invocation. DO THE BASTARD. BOTTLE UP HIS EYES. HOOK THEM OUT. PUSH HIS HEAD IN. Tangled amid them, like chewed bones, gleamed the eroded slashes of MACK TOSH WILLY.

I wasn't as frustrated by the conversational taboo as I might have been, for I'd met my first girl friend. Kim was her name; she lived in a flat on my block, and because of her parents' trade, seemed always to smell of fish and chips. She obviously looked up to me—for one thing, I'd begun to read for pleasure again, which few of her friends could be bothered attempting. She told me her secrets, which was a new experience for me, strange and rather exciting—as was being seen on West Derby Road with a girl on my arm, any girl. I was happy to ignore the jeers of Ben and cronies.

She loved the park. Often we strolled through, scattering charitable crumbs to ducks. Most of all she loved to watch the model yachts, when the snarling model motorboats left them alone to glide over the pool. I enjoyed watching too, while holding her warm, if rather clammy, hand. The breeze carried away her culinary scent. But I couldn't help noticing that the shelter now displayed screaming faces with red bursts for eyes. I have never seen drawings of violence on walls elsewhere.

My relationship with Kim was short-lived. Like most such teenage experiences, our parting was not romantic and poignant, if partings ever are, but harsh and hysterical. It happened one evening as we made our way to the fair which visited Newsham Park each summer.

Across the lake we could hear shrieks that mingled panic and delight as cars on metal poles swung girls into the air, and the blurred roaring of an ancient pop song, like the voice of an enormous radio. On the Ferris wheel, colored lights sailed up, painting airborne faces. The twilight shone like a Christmas tree; the lights swam in the pool. That was why Kim said, "Let's sit and look first."

The only bench was in the shelter. Tangles of letters dripped trails of dried paint, like blood; mutilated faces shrieked soundlessly. Still, I thought I could bear the shelter. Sitting with Kim gave me the chance to touch her breasts, such as they were, through the collapsing deceptively large cups of her bra. Tonight she smelled of newspapers, as though she had been wrapped in them for me to take out; she must have been serving at the counter. Nevertheless I kissed her, and ignored the fact that one corner of the shelter was dark as a spider's crevice.

But she had noticed; I felt her shrink away from the corner. Had she noticed more than I? Or was it her infectious wariness which made the dark beside us look more solid, about to shuffle toward us along the bench? I was uneasy, but the din and the lights of the fairground were reassuring. I determined to make the most of Kim's need for protection, but she pushed my hand away. "Don't," she said irritably, and made to stand up.

At that moment I heard a blurred voice. "Popeye," it muttered as if to itself; it sounded gleeful. "Popeye." Was it part of the fair? It might have been a stallholder's voice, distorted by the uproar, for it said, "I've got something for you."

The struggles of Kim's hand in mine excited me. "Let me go," she was wailing. Because I managed not to be afraid, I was more pleased than dismayed by her fear—and I was eager to let my imagination flourish, for it was better than reading a ghost story. I peered into the dark corner to see what horrors I could imagine.

Then Kim wrenched herself free and ran around the pool. Disappointed and angry, I pursued her. "Go away," she cried. "You're horrible. I never want to speak to you again." For a while I chased her along the dim paths, but once I began to plead I grew furious with myself. She wasn't worth the embarrassment. I let her go, and returned to the fair, to wander desultorily for a while. When I'd stayed long enough to prevent my parents from wondering why I was home early, I walked home.

I meant to sit in the shelter for a while, to see if anything happened, but someone was already there. I couldn't make out much about him, and didn't like to go closer. He must have been wearing spectacles, for his eyes seemed perfectly circular and gleamed like metal, not like eyes at all.

I quickly forgot that glimpse, for I discovered Kim hadn't been exaggerating: she refused to speak to me. I stalked off to buy fish and chips elsewhere. I decided that I hadn't liked her anyway. My one lingering disappointment, I found glumly, was that I had nobody with whom to go to the fairground. Eventually, when the fair and the school holidays were approaching their end, I said to Mark, "Shall we go to the fair tonight?"

He hesitated, but didn't seem especially wary. "All right," he said with the indifference we were beginning to affect about everything.

At sunset the horizon looked like a furnace, and that was how the park felt. Couples rambled sluggishly along the paths; panting dogs splashed in the lake. Between the trees the lights of the fairground shimmered and twinkled, cheap multicolored stars. As we passed the pool, I noticed that the air was quivering above the footprints in the concrete, and looked darkened, perhaps by dust. Impulsively I said, "What did you do to old Willy?"

"Shut up." I'd never heard Mark so savage or withdrawn. "I wish I hadn't done it."

I might have retorted to his rudeness, but instead I let myself be captured by the fairground, by the glade of light amid the balding rutted green. Couples and gangs roamed, harangued a shade halfheartedly by stallholders.

Young children hid their faces in pink candy floss. A siren thin as a Christmas party hooter set the Dodgems running. Mark and I rode a tilting bucket above the fuzzy clamor of music, the splashes of glaring light, the cramped crowd. Secretly I felt a little sick, but the ride seemed to help Mark regain his confidence. Shortly, as we were playing a pinball machine with senile flippers, he said, "Look, there's Lorna and what's-her-name."

It took me a while to be sure where he was pointing: at a tall, bosomy girl, who probably looked several years older than she was, and a girl of about my height and age, her small bright face sketched with makeup. By this time I was following him eagerly.

The tall girl was Lorna; her friend's name was Carol. We strolled for a while, picking our way over power cables, and Carol and I began to like each other; her scent was sweet, if rather overpowering. As the fair began to close, Mark easily won trinkets at a shooting gallery and presented them to the girls, which helped us persuade them to meet us on Saturday night. By now Mark never looked toward the shelter—I think not from wariness but because it had ceased to worry him, at least for the moment. I glanced across, and could just distinguish someone pacing unevenly round the pool, as if impatient for a delayed meeting.

If Mark had noticed, would it have made any difference? Not in the long run, I try to believe. But however I rationalize, I know that some of the blame was mine.

We were to meet Lorna and Carol on our side of the park in order to take them to the Carlton cinema, nearby. We arrived late, having taken our time over sprucing ourselves; we didn't want to seem too eager to meet them. Beside the police station, at the entrance to the park, a triangular island of pavement, large enough to contain a spinney of trees, divided the road. The girls were meant to be waiting at the nearest point of the triangle. But the island was deserted except for the caged darkness beneath the trees.

We waited. Shop windows on West Derby Road glared fluorescent green. Behind us trees whispered, creaking. We kept glancing into the park, but the only figure I could distinguish on the dark paths was alone. Eventually, for something to do, we strolled desultorily around the island.

It was I who saw the message first, large letters scrawled on the corner nearest the park. Was it Lorna's or Carol's handwriting? It rather shocked me, for it looked semiliterate. But she must have had to use a stone as a pencil, which couldn't have helped; indeed, some letters had had to be dug out of the moss which coated stretches of the pavement. MARK SEE YOU AT SHELTER, the message said.

I felt him withdraw a little. "Which shelter?" he muttered.

"I expect they mean the one near the kiosk," I said, to reassure him.

We hurried along Orphan Drive. Above the lamps, patches of foliage shone harshly. Before we reached the pool we crossed the bridge, from which in daylight manna rained down to the ducks, and entered the park. The fair had gone into hibernation; the paths, and the mazes of tree trunks, were silent and very dark. Occasional dim movements made me think that we were passing the girls, but the figure that was wandering a nearby path looked far too bulky.

The shelter was at the edge of the main green, near the football pitch. Beyond the green, tower blocks loomed in glaring auras. Each of the four sides of the shelter was an alcove housing a bench. As we peered into each, jeers or curses challenged us.

"I know where they'll be," Mark said. "In the one by the bowling green. That's near where they live."

But we were closer to the shelter by the pool. Nevertheless I followed him onto the park road. As we turned toward the bowling green I glanced toward the pool, but the streetlamps dazzled me. I followed him along a narrow path between hedges to the green, and almost tripped over his ankles as he stopped short. The shelter was empty, alone with its view of the decaying Georgian houses on the far side of the bowling green.

To my surprise and annoyance, he still didn't head for the pool. Instead, we made for the disused bandstand hidden in a ring of bushes. Its only tune now was the clink of broken bricks. I was sure that the girls wouldn't have called it a shelter, and of course it was deserted. Obese dim bushes hemmed us in. "Come on," I said, "or we'll miss them. They must be by the pool."

"They won't be there," he said—stupidly, I thought.

Did I realize how nervous he suddenly was? Perhaps, but it only annoyed me. After all, how else could I meet Carol again? I didn't know her address. "Oh, all right," I scoffed, "if you want us to miss them."

I saw him stiffen. Perhaps my contempt hurt him more than Ben's had; for one thing, he was older. Before I knew what he intended he was striding toward the pool, so rapidly that I would have had to run to keep up with him—which, given the hostility that had flared between us, I refused to do. I strolled after him rather disdainfully. That was how I came to glimpse movement in one of the islands of dimness between the lamps of the park road. I glanced toward it and saw, several hundred yards away, the girls.

After a pause they responded to my waving—somewhat timidly, I thought. "There they are," I called to Mark. He must have been at the pool by now, but I had difficulty in glimpsing him beyond the glare of the lamps. I was beckoning the girls to hurry when I heard his radio blur into speech.

At first I was reminded of a sailor's parrot. "Aye aye," it was croaking. The distorted voice sounded cracked, uneven, almost too old to speak. "You know what I mean, son?" it grated triumphantly. "Aye aye." I was growing uneasy, for my mind had begun to interpret the words as "Eye eye"—when suddenly, dreadfully, I realized Mark hadn't brought his radio.

There might be someone in the shelter with a radio. But I was terrified, I wasn't sure why. I ran toward the pool, calling, "Come on, Mark, they're here!" The lamps dazzled me; everything swayed with my running—which was why I couldn't be sure what I saw.

I know I saw Mark at the shelter. He stood just within, confronting darkness. Before I could discern whether anyone else was there, Mark staggered out blindly, hands covering his face, and collapsed into the pool.

Did he drag something with him? Certainly by the time I reached the margin of the light he appeared to be tangled in something, and to be struggling feebly. He was drifting, or being dragged, toward the center of the pool by a half-submerged heap of litter. At the end of the heap nearest

Mark's face was a pale ragged patch in which gleamed two round objects—bottle caps? I could see all this because I was standing helpless, screaming at the girls, "Quick, for Christ's sake! He's drowning!" He was drowning, and I couldn't swim.

"Don't be stupid," I heard Lorna say. That enraged me so much that I turned from the pool. "What do you mean?" I cried. "What do you mean, you stupid bitch?"

"Oh, be like that," she said haughtily, and refused to say more. But Carol took pity on my hysteria, and explained, "It's only three feet deep. He'll never drown in there."

I wasn't sure that she knew what she was talking about, but that was no excuse for me not to try to rescue him. When I turned to the pool I gasped miserably, for he had vanished—sunk. I could only wade into the muddy water, which engulfed my legs and closed around my waist like ice, ponderously hindering me.

The floor of the pool was fattened with slimy litter. I slithered, terrified of losing my balance. Intuition urged me to head for the center of the pool. And it was there I found him, as my sluggish kick collided with his ribs.

When I tried to raise him, I discovered that he was pinned down. I had to grope blindly over him in the chill water, feeling how still he was. Something like a swollen cloth bag, very large, lay over his face. I couldn't bear to touch it again, for its contents felt soft and fat. Instead I seized Mark's ankles and managed at last to drag him free. Then I struggled toward the edge of the pool, heaving him by his shoulders, lifting his head above water. His weight was dismaying. Eventually the girls waded out to help me.

But we were too late. When we dumped him on the concrete, his face stayed agape with horror; water lay stagnant in his mouth. I could see nothing wrong with his eyes. Carol grew hysterical, and it was Lorna who ran to the hospital, perhaps in order to get away from the sight of him. I only made Carol worse by demanding why they hadn't waited for us at the shelter; I wanted to feel they were to blame. But she denied they had written the message, and grew more hysterical when I asked why they hadn't waited at the island. The question, or the memory, seemed to frighten her.

I never saw her again. The few newspapers that bothered to report Mark's death gave the verdict "by misadventure." The police took a dislike to me after I insisted that there might be somebody else in the pool, for the draining revealed nobody. At least, I thought, whatever was there had gone away. Perhaps I could take some credit for that, at least.

But perhaps I was too eager for reassurance. The last time I ventured near the shelter was years ago, one winter night on the way home from school. I had caught sight of a gleam in the depths of the shelter. As I went close, nervously watching both the shelter and the pool, I saw two discs glaring at me from the darkness beside the bench. They were Coca-Cola caps, not eyes at all, and it must have been a wind that set the pool slopping and sent the caps scuttling toward me. What frightened me most as I fled through the dark was that I wouldn't be able to see where I was running if, as I desperately wanted to, I put up my hands to protect my eyes.

Henry James

The Jolly Corner

"The Turn of the Screw" by Henry James is arguably the best of all novellas written to date in the horror mode. It is certainly the most argued-over. James' fiction sits like the tallest skyscraper casting a shadow over all of twentieth-century fiction, fanatically polished and detailed and ultimately unfathomable because it is consistently interpretable on many levels, no one of which exhausts the potential meaning. He is devoted to the inner life of characters of intricate complexity who, in his supernatural stories, are confronted with questions as to the nature of reality. These supernatural tales show a direct line of influence through Walter de la Mare and Edith Wharton to the works of Robert Aickman and others. "The Jolly Corner" is his finest ghost story in the short story form, a masterpiece of delicate horror in which the central character confronts the possibilities of his own ghostly doppelganger, evoking awe and wonder. The story occupies the border territory between the second and third streams of horror.

I

"Every one asks me what I 'think' of everything," said Spencer Brydon; "and I make answer as I can—begging or dodging the question, putting them off with any nonsense. It wouldn't matter to any of them really," he went on, "for, even were it possible to meet in that stand-and-deliver way so silly a demand on so big a subject, my 'thoughts' would still be almost altogether about something that concerns only myself." He was talking to Miss Staverton, with whom for a couple of months now he had availed himself of every possible occasion to talk; this disposition and this resource, this comfort and support, as the situation in fact presented itself, having promptly enough taken the first place in the considerable array of rather unattenuated surprises attending his so strangely belated return to America. Everything was somehow a surprise; and that might be natural when one had so long and so consistently neglected everything, taken pains to give surprises so much margin for play. He had given them more than thirty years—thirty-three, to be exact; and they now seemed to him to have organised their performance quite on the scale of that licence. He had been twenty-three on leaving New York—he was fifty-six today: unless indeed he were to reckon as he had sometimes, since his repatriation, found himself feeling; in which case he would have lived longer than is often allotted to man. It would have taken a century, he repeatedly said to himself, and said also to Alice Staverton, it would have taken a longer absence and a more averted mind than those even of which he had been guilty, to pile up the differences, the newnesses, the queernesses, above all the bignesses, for the better or the worse, that at present assaulted his vision wherever he looked.

The great fact all the while however had been the incalculability; since he *had* supposed himself, from decade to decade, to be allowing, and in the most liberal and intelligent manner, for brilliancy of change. He actually saw that he had allowed for nothing; he missed what he would have been sure of finding, he found what he would never have imagined. Proportions and values were upside-down; the ugly things he had expected, the ugly things of his far-away youth, when he had too promptly waked up to a sense of the ugly—these uncanny phenomena placed him rather, as it happened, under the charm; whereas the "swagger" things, the modern, the monstrous, the famous things, those he had more particularly, like thousands of ingenuous inquirers every year, come over to see, were exactly his sources of dismay. They were as so many set traps for displeasure, above all for reaction, of which his restless tread was constantly pressing the spring. It was interesting, doubtless, the whole show, but it would have been too disconcerting hadn't a certain finer truth saved the situation. He had distinctly not, in this steadier light, come over *all* for the monstrosities; he had come, not only in the last analysis but quite on the face of the act, under an impulse with which they had nothing to do. He had come—putting the thing pompously—to look at his "property," which he had thus for a third of a century not been within four thousand miles of; or, expressing it less sordidly, he had yielded to the humour of seeing again his house on the jolly corner, as he usually, and quite fondly, described it—the one in which he had first seen the light, in which various members of his family had lived and died, in which the holidays of his overschooled boyhood had been passed and the few social flowers of his chilled adolescence gathered, and which, alienated then for so long a period, had, through the successive deaths of his two brothers and the termination of old arrangements, come wholly into his hands. He was the owner of another, not quite so "good"—the jolly corner having been, from far back, superlatively extended and consecrated; and the value of the pair represented his main capital, with an income consisting, in these later years, of their respective rents which (thanks precisely to their original excellent type) had never been depressingly low. He could live in "Europe," as he had been in the habit of living, on the product of these flourishing New York leases, and all the better since, that of the second structure, the mere number in its long row, having within a twelvemonth fallen in, renovation at a high advance had proved beautifully possible.

These were items of property indeed, but he had found himself since his arrival distinguishing more than ever between them. The house within the street, two bristling blocks westward, was already in course of reconstruction as a tall mass of flats; he had acceded, some time before, to overtures for this conversion—in which, now that it was going forward, it had been not the least of his astonishments to find himself able, on the spot, and though without a previous ounce of such experience, to participate with a certain intelligence, almost with a certain authority. He had lived his life with his back so turned to such concerns and his face addressed to those of so different an order that he scarce knew what to make of this lively stir, in a compartment of his mind never yet penetrated, of a capacity for business and a sense for construction. These virtues, so common all round him now, had been dormant in his own organism—where it might be said of them perhaps that they had slept the sleep of the just. At present, in the splendid autumn weather—the autumn at least was a pure boon in the terrible place—he loafed about his "work" undeterred, secretly agitated; not in the least "minding" that the whole proposition, as they said, was vulgar and sordid, and ready to climb ladders, to walk the plank, to handle materials and look wise about them, to ask questions, in fine, and challenge explanations and really "go into" figures.

It amused, it verily quite charmed him; and, by the same stroke, it amused, and even more, Alice Staverton, though perhaps charming her perceptibly less. She wasn't however going to be better-off for it, as *he* was—and so astonishingly much: nothing was now likely, he knew, ever to make her better-off than she found herself, in the afternoon of life, as the delicately frugal possessor and tenant of the small house in Irving Place to which she had subtly managed to cling through her almost unbroken New York career. If he knew the way to it now better than to any other address among the dreadful multiplied numberings which seemed to him to reduce the whole place to some vast ledger-page, overgrown, fantastic, of ruled and criss-crossed lines and figures—if he had formed, for his consolation, that habit, it was really not a little because of the charm of his having encountered and recognised, in the vast wilderness of the wholesale, breaking through the mere gross generalisation of wealth and force and success, a small still scene where items and shades, all delicate things, kept the sharpness of the notes of a high voice perfectly trained, and where economy hung about like the scent of a garden. His old friend lived with one maid and herself dusted her relics and trimmed her lamps and polished her silver; she stood off, in the awful modern crush, when she could, but she sallied forth and did battle when the challenge was really to "spirit," the spirit she after all confessed to, proudly and a little shyly, as to that of the better time, that of *their* common, their quite far-away and antediluvian social period and order. She made use of the streetcars when need be, the terrible things that people scrambled for as the panic-stricken at sea scramble for the boats; she affronted, inscrutably, under stress, all the public concussions and ordeals; and yet, with that slim mystifying grace of her appearance, which defied you to say if she were a fair young woman who looked older through trouble, or a fine smooth older one who looked young through successful indifference; with her precious reference, above all, to memories and histories into which he could enter, she was as exquisite for him as some pale pressed flower (a rarity to begin with), and, failing other sweetnesses, she was a sufficient reward of his effort. They had communities of knowledge, "their" knowledge (this discriminating possessive was always on her lips) of presences of the other age, presences all overlaid, in his case, by the experience of a man and the freedom of a wanderer, overlaid by pleasure, by infidelity, by passages of life that were strange and dim to her, just by "Europe" in short, but still unobscured, still exposed and cherished, under that pious visitation of the spirit from which she had never been diverted.

She had come with him one day to see how his "apartment-house" was rising; he had helped her over gaps and explained to her plans, and while they were there had happened to have, before her, a brief but lively discussion with the man in charge, the representative of the building-firm that had undertaken his work. He had found himself quite "standing-up" to this personage over a failure on the latter's part to observe some detail of one of their noted conditions, and had so lucidly argued his case that, besides ever so prettily flushing, at the time, for sympathy in his triumph, she had afterwards said to him (though to a slightly greater effect of irony) that he had clearly for too many years neglected a real gift. If he had but stayed at home he would have anticipated the inventor of the sky-scraper. If he had but stayed at home he would have discovered his genius in time really to start some new variety of awful architectural hare and run it till it burrowed in a gold-mine. He was to remember these words, while the weeks elapsed, for the small silver ring they had sounded over the queerest and deepest of his own lately most disguised and most muffled vibrations.

It had begun to be present to him after the first fortnight, it had broken out with the oddest abruptness, this particular wanton wonderment: it met him there—and this was the image under which he himself judged the matter, or at least, not a little, thrilled and flushed with it—very much as he might have been met by some strange figure, some unexpected occupant, at a turn of one of the dim passages of an empty house. The quaint analogy quite hauntingly remained with him, when he didn't indeed rather improve it by a still intenser form: that of his opening a door behind which he would have made sure of finding nothing, a door into a room shuttered and void, and yet so coming, with a great suppressed start, on some quite erect confronting presence, something planted in the middle of the place and facing him through the dusk. After that visit to the house in construction he walked with his companion to see the other and always so much the better one, which in the eastward direction formed one of the corners, the "jolly" one precisely, of the street now so generally dishonoured and disfigured in its westward reaches, and of the comparatively conservative Avenue. The Avenue still had pretensions, as Miss Staverton said, to decency; the old people had mostly gone, the old names were unknown, and here and there an old association seemed to stray, all vaguely, like some very aged person, out too late, whom you might meet and feel the impulse to watch or follow, in kindness, for safe restoration to shelter.

They went in together, our friends; he admitted himself with his key, as he kept no one there, he explained, preferring, for his reasons, to leave the place empty, under a simple arrangement with a good woman living in the neighborhood and who came for a daily hour to open windows and dust and sweep. Spencer Brydon had his reasons and was growingly aware of them; they seemed to him better each time he was there, though he didn't name them all to his companion, any more than he told her as yet how often, how quite absurdly often, he himself came. He only let her see for the present, while they walked through the great blank rooms, that absolute vacancy reigned and that, from top to bottom, there was nothing but Mrs. Muldoon's broomstick, in a corner, to tempt the burglar. Mrs. Muldoon was then on the premises, and she loquaciously attended the visitors, preceding them from room to room and pushing back shutters and throwing up sashes—all to show them, as she remarked, how little there was to see. There was little indeed to see in the great gaunt shell where the main dispositions and the general apportionment of space, the style of an age of ampler allowances, had nevertheless for its master their honest pleading message, affecting him as some good old servant's, some lifelong retainer's appeal for a character, or even for a retiring-pension; yet it was also a remark of Mrs. Muldoon's that, glad as she was to oblige him by her noonday round, there was a request she greatly hoped he would never make of her. If he should wish her for any reason to come in after dark she would just tell him, if he "plased," that he must ask it of somebody else.

The fact that there was nothing to see didn't militate for the worthy woman against what one *might* see, and she put it frankly to Miss Staverton that no lady could be expected to like, could she? "craping up to thim top storeys in the ayvil hours." The gas and the electric light were off the house, and she fairly evoked a gruesome vision of her march through the great grey rooms—so many of them as there were too!—with her glimmering taper. Miss Staverton met her honest glare with a smile and the profession that she herself certainly would recoil from such an adventure. Spencer Brydon meanwhile held his peace—for the moment; the question of the "evil" hours in his old home had already become too grave for him. He had begun some time since to "crape," and he knew just why a packet of candles addressed to that pursuit had been stowed by his own hand, three weeks before, at the back of a drawer of the fine old sideboard that occupied, as a "fixture," the deep recess in the dining-room. Just now he laughed at his companions— quickly however changing the subject; for the reason that, in the first place, his laugh struck him even at that moment as starting the odd echo, the conscious human resonance (he scarce knew how to qualify it) that sounds made while he was there alone sent back to his ear or his fancy; and that, in the second, he imagined Alice Staverton for the instant on the point of asking him, with a divination, if he ever so prowled. There were divinations he was unprepared for, and he had at all events averted inquiry by the time Mrs. Muldoon had left them, passing on to other parts.

There was happily enough to say, on so consecrated a spot, that could be said freely and fairly; so that a whole train of declarations was precipitated by his friend's having herself broken out, after a yearning look round: "But I hope you don't mean they want you to pull *this* to pieces!" His answer came, promptly, with his reawakened wrath: it was of course exactly what they wanted, and what they were "at" him for, daily, with the iteration of people who couldn't for their life understand a man's liability to decent feelings. He had found the place, just as it stood and beyond what he could express, an interest and a joy. There were values other than the beastly rent-values, and in short, in short——! But it was thus Miss Staverton took him up. "In short you're to make so good a thing of your sky-scraper that, living in luxury on *those* ill-gotten gains, you can afford for a while to be sentimental here!" Her smile had for him, with the words, the particular mild irony with which he found half her talk suffused; an irony without bitterness and that came, exactly, from her having so much imagination—not, like the cheap sarcasms with which one heard most people, about the world of "society," bid for the reputation of cleverness, from nobody's really having any. It was agreeable to him at this very moment to be sure that when he had answered, after a brief demur, "Well yes: so, precisely, you may put it!" her imagination would still do him justice. He explained that even if never a dollar were to come to him from the other house he would nevertheless cherish this one; and he dwelt, further, while they lingered and wandered, on the fact of the stupefaction he was already exciting, the positive mystification he felt himself create.

He spoke of the value of all he read into it, into the mere sight of the walls, mere shapes of the rooms, mere sound of the floors, mere feel, in his hand, of the old silver-plated knobs of the several mahogany doors, which suggested the pressure of the palms of the dead; the seventy years of the past in fine that these things represented, the annals of nearly three generations, counting his grandfather's, the one that had ended there, and the impalpable ashes of his long-extinct youth, afloat in the very air like microscopic motes. She listened to everything; she was a woman who answered intimately but who utterly didn't chatter. She scattered abroad therefore no cloud of words; she could assent, she could agree, above all she could encourage, without doing that. Only at the last she went a little further than he had done himself. "And then how do you know? You may still, after all, want to live here." It rather indeed pulled him up, for it wasn't what he had been thinking, at least in her sense of the words. "You mean I may decide to stay on for the sake of it?"

"Well, *with* such a home——!" But, quite beautifully, she had too much tact to dot so monstrous an *i*, and it was precisely an illustration of the way she didn't rattle. How could any one—of any wit—insist on any one else's "wanting" to live in New York?

"Oh," he said, "I *might* have lived here (since I had my opportunity early in life); I might have put in here all these years. Then everything would have been different enough—and, I daresay, 'funny' enough. But that's another matter. And then the beauty of it—I mean of my perversity, of my refusal to agree to a 'deal'—is just in the total absence of a reason. Don't you see that if I had a reason about the matter at all it would *have* to be the other way, and would then be inevitably a reason of dollars? There are no reasons here *but* of dollars. Let us therefore have none whatever—not the ghost of one."

They were back in the hall then for departure, but from where they stood the vista was large, through an open door, into the great square main saloon, with its almost antique felicity of brave spaces between windows. Her eyes came back from that reach and met his own a moment. "Are you very sure the 'ghost' of one doesn't, much rather, serve——?"

He had a positive sense of turning pale. But it was as near as they were then to come. For he made answer, he believed, between a glare and a grin: "Oh ghosts—of course the place must swarm with them! I should be ashamed of it if it didn't. Poor Mrs. Muldoon's right, and it's why I haven't asked her to do more than look in."

Miss Staverton's gaze again lost itself; and things she didn't utter, it was clear, came and went in her mind. She might even for the minute, off there in the fine room, have imagined some element dimly gathering. Simplified like the death-mask of a hand, some face, it perhaps produced for her just then an effect akin to the stir of an expression in the "set" commemorative plaster. Yet whatever her impression may have been she produced instead a vague platitude. "Well, if it were only furnished and lived in——!"

She appeared to imply that in case of its being still furnished he might have been a little less opposed to the idea of a return. But she passed straight into the vestibule, as if to leave her words behind her, and the next moment he had opened the house-door and was standing with her on the steps. He closed the door and, while he re-pocketed his key, looking up and down, they took in the comparatively harsh actuality of the Avenue, which reminded him of the assault of the outer light of the Desert on the traveller emerging from an Egyptian tomb. But he risked before they stepped into the street his gathered answer to her speech. "For me it *is* lived in. For me it *is* furnished." At which it was easy for her to sigh "Ah yes——!" all vaguely and discreetly; since his parents and his favourite sister, to say nothing of other kin, in numbers, had run their course and met their end there. That represented, within the walls, ineffaceable life.

It was a few days after this that, during an hour passed with her again, he had expressed his impatience of the too flattering curiosity—among the people he met—about his appreciation of New York. He had arrived at none at all that was socially producible, and as for that matter of his "thinking" (thinking the better or the worse of anything there) he has wholly taken up with one subject of thought. It was mere vain egoism, and it was moreover, if she liked, a morbid obsession. He found all things come back to the question of what he personally might have been, how he might have led his life and "turned out," if he had not so, at the outset, given it up. And confessing for the first time to the intensity within him of his absurd speculation—which but proved also, no doubt, the habit of too selfishly thinking—he affirmed the impotence there of any other source of interest, any other native appeal. "What would it have made of me, what would it have made of me? I keep for ever wondering, all idiotically; as if I could possibly know! I see what it has made of dozens of others, those I meet, and it positively aches within me, to the point of exasperation, that it would have made something of me as well. Only I can't make out *what,* and the worry of it, the small rage of curiosity never to be satisfied, brings back what I remember to have felt, once or twice, after judging best, for reasons, to burn some important letter unopened. I've been sorry, I've hated it—I've never known what was in the letter. You may of course say it's a trifle——!"

"I don't say it's a trifle," Miss Staverton gravely interrupted.

She was seated by her fire, and before her, on his feet and restless, he turned to and fro between this intensity of his idea and a fitful and unseeing inspection, through his single eye-glass, of the dear little old objects on her chimney-piece. Her interruption made him for an instant look at her harder.

"I shouldn't care if you did!" he laughed, however; "and it's only a figure, at any rate, for the way I now feel. *Not* to have followed my perverse young course—and almost in the teeth of my father's curse, as I may say; not to have kept it up, so, 'over there,' from that day to this, without a doubt or a pang; not, above all, to have liked it, to have loved it, so much, loved it, no doubt, with such an abysmal conceit of my own preference: some variation from *that*, I say, must have produced some different effect for my life and for my 'form.' I should have stuck here—if it had been possible; and I was too young, at twenty-three, to judge, *pour deux sons,* whether it *were* possible. If I had waited I might have seen it was, and then I might have been, by staying here, something nearer to one of these types who have been hammered so hard and made so keen by their conditions. It isn't that I admire them so much—the question of any charm in them, or of any charm, beyond that of the rank money-passion, exerted by their conditions *for* them, has nothing to do with the matter: it's only a question of what fantastic, yet perfectly possible, development of my own nature I mayn't have missed. It comes over me that I had then a strange *alter ego* deep down somewhere within me, as the full-blown flower is in the small tight bud, and that I just took the course, I just transferred him to the climate, that blighted him for once and for ever."

"And you wonder about the flower," Miss Staverton said. "So do I, if you want to know; and so I've been wondering these several weeks. I believe in the flower," she continued, "I feel it would have been quite splendid, quite huge and monstrous."

"Monstrous above all!" her visitor echoed; "and I imagine, by the same stroke, quite hideous and offensive."

"You don't believe that," she returned; "if you did you wouldn't wonder. You'd know, and that would be enough for you. What you feel—and what I feel *for* you—is that you'd have had power."

"You'd have liked me that way?" he asked.

She barely hung fire. "How should I not have liked you?"

"I see. You'd have liked me, have preferred me, a billionaire!"

"How should I not have liked you?" she simply again asked.

He stood before her still—her question kept him motionless. He took it in, so much there was of it; and indeed his not otherwise meeting it testified to that. "I know at least what I am," he simply went on; "the other side of the medal's clear enough. I've not been edifying—I believe I'm thought in a hundred quarters to have been barely decent. I've followed strange paths and worshipped strange gods; it must have come to you again and again—in fact you've admitted to me as much—that I was leading, at any time these thirty years, a selfish frivolous scandalous life. And you see what it has made of me."

She just waited, smiling at him. "You see what it has made of *me*."

"Oh you're a person whom nothing can have altered. You were born to be what you are, anywhere, anyway: you've the perfection nothing else could have blighted. And don't you see how, without my exile, I shouldn't have been waiting till now——?" But he pulled up for the strange pang.

"The great thing to see," she presently said, "seems to me to be that it has spoiled nothing. It hasn't spoiled your being here at last. It hasn't spoiled this. It hasn't spoiled your speaking——" She also however faltered.

He wondered at everything her controlled emotion might mean. "Do you believe then—too dreadfully!—that I *am* as good as I might ever have been?"

"Oh no! Far from it!" With which she got up from her chair and was nearer to him. "But I don't care," she smiled.

"You mean I'm good enough?"

She considered a little. "Will you believe it if I say so? I mean will you let that settle your question for you?" And then as if making out in his face that he drew back from this, that he had some idea which, however absurd, he couldn't yet bargain away: "Oh you don't care either—but very differently: you don't care for anything but yourself."

Spencer Brydon recognized it—it was in fact what he had absolutely professed. Yet he importantly qualified. "*He* isn't myself. He's the just so totally other person. But I do want to see him," he added. "And I can. And I shall."

Their eyes met for a minute while he guessed from something in hers that she divined his strange sense. But neither of them otherwise expressed it, and her apparent understanding, with no protesting shock, no easy derision, touched him more deeply than anything yet, constituting for his stifled perversity, on the spot, an element that was like breatheable air. What she said however was unexpected. "Well, *I've* seen him."

"You——?"

"I've seen him in a dream."

"Oh a 'dream'——!" It let him down.

"But twice over," she continued. "I saw him as I see you now."

"You've dreamed the same dream——?"

"Twice over," she repeated. "The very same."

This did somehow a little speak to him, as it also gratified him. "You dream about me at that rate?"

"Ah about *him*!" she smiled.

His eyes again sounded her. "Then you know all about him." And as she said nothing more: "What's the wretch like?"

She hesitated, and it was as if he were pressing her so hard that, resisting for reasons of her own, she had to turn away. "I'll tell you some other time!"

II

It was after this that there was most of a virtue for him, most of a cultivated charm, most of a preposterous secret thrill, in the particular form of surrender to his obsession and of address to what he more and more believed to be his privilege. It was what in these weeks he was living for—since he really felt life to begin but after Mrs. Muldoon had retired from the scene and, visiting the ample house from attic to cellar, making sure he was alone, he knew himself in safe possession and, as he tacitly expressed it, let himself go. He sometimes came twice in the twenty-four hours; the moments he liked best were those of gathering dusk, of the short autumn twilight; this was the time of which, again and again, he found himself hoping most. Then he could, as seemed to him, most intimately wander and wait, linger and listen, feel his fine attention, never in his life before so fine, on the pulse of the great vague place: he preferred the lampless hour and only wished he might have prolonged each day the deep crepuscular spell. Later—rarely much before midnight, but then for a considerable vigil—he watched with his glimmering light; moving slowly, holding it high, playing it far, rejoicing above all, as much as he might, in open vistas, reaches of communication between rooms and by passages; the long straight chance or show, as he would have called it, for the revelation he pretended to invite. It was a practice he found he could perfectly "work" without exciting remark; no one was in the least the wiser for it; even Alice Staverton, who was moreover a well of discretion, didn't quite fully imagine.

He let himself in and let himself out with the assurance of calm proprietorship; and accident so far favoured him that, if a fat Avenue "officer" had happened on occasion to see him entering at eleven-thirty, he had never yet, to the best of his belief, been noticed as emerging at two. He walked there on the crisp November nights, arrived regularly at the evening's end; it was as easy to do this after dining out as to take his way to a club or to his hotel. When he left his club, if he hadn't been dining out, it was ostensibly to go to his hotel; and when he left his hotel, if he had spent a part of the evening there, it was ostensibly to go to his club. Everything was easy in fine; everything conspired and promoted: there was truly even in the strain of his experience something that glossed over, something that salved and simplified, all the rest of consciousness. He circulated, talked, renewed, loosely and pleasantly, old relations—met indeed, so far as he could, new expectations and seemed to make out on the whole that in spite of the career, of such different contacts, which he had spoken of to Miss Staverton as ministering so little, for those who might have watched it, to edification, he was positively rather liked than not. He was a dim secondary social success—and all with people who had truly not an idea of him. It was all mere surface sound, this murmur of their welcome, this popping of their corks—just as his gestures of response were the extravagant shadows, emphatic in proportion as they meant little, of some game of *ombres chinoises.* He projected himself all day, in thought, straight over the bristling line of hard unconscious heads and into the other, the real, the waiting life; the life that, as soon as he had heard behind him the click of his great house-door, began for him, on the jolly corner, as beguilingly as the slow opening bars of some rich music follows the tap of the conductor's wand.

He always caught the first effect of the steel point of his stick on the old marble of the hall pavement, large black-and-white squares that he remembered as the admiration of his childhood and that had then made in him, as he now saw, for the growth of an early conception of style. This effect was the dim reverberating tinkle as of some far-off bell hung who should say where?—in the depths of the house, of the past, of that mystical other world that might have flourished for him had he not, for weal or woe, abandoned it. On this impression he did ever the same thing; he put his stick noiselessly away in a corner—feeling the place once more in the likeness of some great glass bowl, all precious concave crystal, set delicately humming by the play of a moist finger round its edge. The concave crystal held, as it were, this mystical other world, and the indescribably fine murmur of its rim was the sigh there, the scarce audible pathetic wail to his strained ear, of all the old baffled forsworn possibilities. What he did therefore by this appeal of his hushed presence was to wake them into such measure of ghostly life as they might still enjoy. They were shy, all but unappeasably shy, but they weren't really sinister; at least they weren't as he had hitherto felt them—before they had taken the Form he so yearned to make them take, the Form he at moments saw himself in the light of fairly hunting on tiptoe, the points of his evening-shoes, from room to room and from storey to storey.

That was the essence of his vision—which was all rank folly, if one would, while he was out of the house and otherwise occupied, but which took on the last verisimilitude as soon as he was placed and posted. He knew what he meant and what he wanted; it was as clear as the figure on a cheque presented in demand for cash. His *alter ego* "walked"—that was the note of his image of him, while his image of his motive for his own odd pastime was the desire to waylay him and meet him. He roamed, slowly, warily, but all restlessly, he himself did—Mrs. Muldoon had been right, absolutely, with her figure of their "craping"; and the presence he watched for would roam restlessly too. But it would be as cautious and as shifty; the conviction of its probable, in fact its already quite sensible, quite audible evasion of pursuit grew for him from night to night, laying on him finally a rigour to which nothing in his life had been comparable. It had been the theory of many superficially-judging persons, he knew, that he was wasting that life in a surrender to sensations, but he had tasted of no pleasure so fine as his actual tension, had been introduced to no sport that demanded at once the patience and the nerve of this stalking of a creature more subtle, yet at bay perhaps more formidable, than any beast of the forest. The terms, the comparisons, the very practices of the chase positively came again into play; there were even moments when passages of his occasional experience as a sportsman, stirred memories, from his younger time, of moor and mountain and desert, revived for him—and to the increase of his keenness—by the tremendous force of analogy. He found himself at moments—once he had placed his single light on some mantel-shelf or in some recess—stepping back into shelter or shade, effacing himself behind a door or in an embrasure, as he had sought of old the vantage of rock and tree; he found himself holding his breath and living in the joy of the instant, the supreme suspense created by big game alone.

He wasn't afraid (though putting himself the question as he believed gentlemen on Bengal tiger-shoots or in close quarters with the great bear of the Rockies had been known to confess to having put it); and this indeed—since here at least he might be frank!—because of the impression, so intimate and so strange, that he himself produced as yet a dread, produced certainly a strain, beyond the liveliest he was likely to feel. They fell for him into categories, they fairly became familiar, the signs, for his own perception, of the alarm his presence and his vigilance created; though leaving him always to remark, portentously, on his probably having formed a relation, his probably enjoying a consciousness, unique in the experience of man. People enough, first and last, had been in terror of apparitions, but who had ever before so turned the tables and become himself, in the apparitional world, an incalculable terror? He might have found this sublime had he quite dared to think of it; but he didn't too much insist, truly, on that side of his privilege. With habit and repetition he gained to an extraordinary degree the power to penetrate the dusk of distances and the darkness of corners, to resolve back into their innocence the treacheries of uncertain light, the evil-looking forms taken in the gloom by mere shadows, by accidents of the air, by shifting effects of perspective; putting down his dim luminary he could still wander on without it, pass into other rooms and, only knowing it was there behind him in case of need, see his way about, visually project for his purpose a comparative clearness. It made him feel, this acquired faculty, like some monstrous stealthy cat; he wondered if he would have glared at these moments with large shining yellow eyes, and what it mightn't verily be, for the poor hard-pressed *alter ego*, to be confronted with such a type.

He liked however the open shutters; he opened everywhere those Mrs. Muldoon had closed, closing them as carefully afterwards, so that she shouldn't notice: he liked—oh this he did like, and above all in the upper rooms!—the sense of the hard silver of the autumn stars through the window-panes, and scarcely less the flare of the street-lamps below, the white electric lustre which it would have taken curtains to keep out. This was human actual social; this was of the world he had lived in, and he was more at his ease certainly for the countenance, coldly general and impersonal, that all the while and in spite of his detachment it seemed to give him. He had support of course mostly in the rooms at the wide front and the prolonged side; it failed him considerably in the central shades and the parts at the back. But if he sometimes, on his rounds, was glad of his optical reach, so none the less often the rear of the house affected him as the very jungle of his prey. The place was there more subdivided; a large "extension" in particular, where small rooms for servants had been multiplied, abounded in nooks and corners, in closets and passages, in the ramifications especially of an ample back staircase over which he leaned, many a time, to look far down—not deterred from his gravity even while aware that he might, for a spectator, have figured some solemn simpleton playing at hide-and-seek. Outside in fact he might himself make that ironic *rapprochement*; but within the walls, and in spite of the clear windows, his consistency was proof against the cynical light of New York.

It had belonged to that idea of the exasperated consciousness of his victim to become a real test for him; since he had quite put it to himself from the first that, oh distinctly! he could "cultivate" his whole perception. He had felt it as above all open to cultivation—which indeed was but another name for his manner of spending his time. He was bringing it on, bringing it to perfection, by practice; in consequence of which it had grown so fine that he was now aware of impressions, attestations of his general postulate, that couldn't have broken upon him at once. This was the case more specifically with a phenomenon at last quite frequent for him in the upper rooms, the recognition—absolutely unmistakable, and by a turn dating from a particular hour, his resumption of his campaign after a diplomatic drop, a calculated absence of three nights—of his being definitely followed, tracked at a distance carefully taken and to the express end that he should the less confidently, less arrogantly, appear to himself merely to pursue. It worried, it finally broke him up, for it proved, of all the conceivable impressions, the one least suited to his book. He was kept in sight while remaining himself—as regards the essence of his position—sightless, and his only recourse then was in abrupt turns, rapid recoveries of ground. He wheeled about, retracing his steps, as if he might so catch in his face at least the stirred air of some other quick revolution. It was indeed true that his fully dislocalised thought of these manoeuvres recalled to him Pantaloon, at the Christmas farce, buffeted and tricked from behind by ubiquitous Harlequin; but it left intact the influence of the conditions themselves each time he was re-exposed to them, so that in fact this association, had he suffered it to become constant, would on a certain side have but ministered to his intenser gravity. He had made, as I have said, to create on the premises the baseless sense of a reprieve, his three absences; and the result of the third was to confirm the after-effect of the second.

On his return, that night—the night succeeding his last intermission—he stood in the hall and looked up the staircase with a certainty more intimate than any he had yet known. "He's *there*, at the top, and waiting—not, as in general, falling back for disappearance. He's holding his ground, and it's the first time—which is a proof, isn't it? that something has happened for him." So Brydon argued with his hand on the banister and his foot on the lowest stair; in which position he felt as never before the air chilled by his logic. He himself turned cold in it, for he seemed of a sudden to know what now was involved. "Harder pressed?—yes, he takes it in, with its thus making clear to him that I've come, as they say, 'to stay.' He finally doesn't like and can't bear it, in the sense, I mean, that his wrath, his menaced interest, now balances with his dread. I've hunted him till he has 'turned': that, up there, is what has happened—he's the fanged or the antlered animal brought at last to bay." There came to him, as I say—but determined by an influence beyond my notation!—the acuteness of this certainty; under which, however, the next moment he had broken into a sweat that he would as little have consented to attribute to fear as he would have dared immediately to act upon it for enterprise. It marked none the less a prodigious thrill, a thrill that represented sudden dismay, no doubt, but also represented, and with the selfsame throb, the strangest, the most joyous, possibly the next minute almost the proudest, duplication of consciousness.

"He has been dodging, retreating, hiding, but now, worked up to anger, he'll fight!"—this intense impression made a single mouthful, as it were, of terror and applause. But what was wondrous was that the applause, for the felt fact, was so eager, since, if it was his other self he was running to earth, this ineffable identity was thus in the last resort not unworthy of him. It bristled there—somewhere near at hand, however unseen still—as the hunted thing, even as the trodden worm of the adage *must* at last bristle; and Brydon at this instant tasted probably of a sensation more complex than had ever before found itself consistent with sanity. It was as if it would have shamed him that a character so associated with his own should triumphantly succeed in just skulking, should to the end not risk the open; so that the drop of this danger was, on the spot, a great lift of the whole situation. Yet with another rare shift of the same subtlety he was already trying to measure by how much more he himself might now be in peril of fear; so rejoicing that he could, in another form, actively inspire that fear, and simultaneously quaking for the form in which he might passively know it.

The apprehension of knowing it must after a little have grown in him, and the strangest moment of his adventure perhaps, the most memorable or really most interesting, afterwards, of his crisis, was the lapse of certain instants of concentrated conscious *combat*, the sense of a need to hold on to something, even after the manner of a man slipping and slipping on some awful incline; the vivid impulse, above all, to move, to act, to charge, somehow and upon something—to show himself, in a word, that he wasn't afraid. The state of "holding-on" was thus the state to which he was momentarily reduced; if there had been anything, in the great vacancy, to seize, he would presently have been aware of having clutched it as he might under a shock at home have clutched the nearest chair-back. He had been surprised at any rate—of this he *was* aware—into something unprecedented since his original appropriation of the place; he had closed his eyes, held them tight, for a long minute, as with that instinct of dismay and that terror of vision. When he opened them the room, the other contiguous rooms, extraordinarily, seemed lighter—so light, almost, that at first he took the change for day. He stood firm, however that might be, just where he had paused; his resistance had helped him—it was as if there were something he had tided over. He knew after a little what this was—it had been in the imminent danger of flight. He had stiffened his will against going; without this he would have made for the stairs, and it seemed to him that, still with his eyes closed, he would have descended them, would have known how, straight and swiftly, to the bottom.

Well, as he had held out, here he was—still at the top, among the more intricate upper rooms and with the gauntlet of the others, of all the rest of the house, still to run when it should be his time to go. He would go at his time—only at his time: didn't he go every night very much at the same hour? He took out his watch—there was light for that: it was scarcely a quarter past one, and he had never withdrawn so soon. He reached his lodgings for the most part at two—with his walk of a quarter of an hour. He would wait for the last quarter—he wouldn't stir till then; and he kept his watch there with his eyes on it, reflecting while he held it that this deliberate wait, a wait with an effort, which he recognised, would serve perfectly for the attestation he desired to make. It would prove his courage—unless indeed the latter might most be proved by his budging at last from his place. What he mainly felt now was that, since he hadn't originally scuttled, he had his dignities—

which had never in his life seemed so many—all to preserve and to carry aloft. This was before him in truth as a physical image, an image almost worthy of an age of greater romance. That remark indeed glimmered for him only to glow the next instant with a finer light; since what age of romance, after all, could have matched either the state of his mind or, "objectively," as they said, the wonder of his situation? The only difference would have been that, brandishing his dignities over his head as in a parchment scroll, he might then—that is in the heroic time—have proceeded downstairs with a drawn sword in his other grasp.

At present, really, the light he had set down on the mantel of the next room would have to figure his sword; which utensil, in the course of a minute, he had taken the requisite number of steps to possess himself of. The door between the rooms was open, and from the second another door opened to a third. These rooms, as he remembered, gave all three upon a common corridor as well, but there was a fourth, beyond them, without issue save through the preceding. To have moved, to have heard his step again, was appreciably a help; though even in recognising this he lingered once more a little by the chimney-piece on which his light had rested. When he next moved, just hesitating where to turn, he found himself considering a circumstance that, after his first and comparatively vague apprehension of it, produced in him the start that often attends some pang of recollection, the violent shock of having ceased happily to forget. He had come into sight of the door in which the brief chain of communication ended and which he now surveyed from the nearer threshold, the one not directly facing it. Placed at some distance to the left of this point, it would have admitted him to the last room of the four, the room without other approach or egress, had it not, to his intimate conviction, been closed *since* his former visitation, the matter probably of a quarter of an hour before. He stared with all his eyes at the wonder of the fact, arrested again where he stood and again holding his breath while he sounded its sense. Surely it had been *subsequently* closed—that is it had been on his previous passage indubitably open!

He took it full in the face that something had happened between—that he couldn't not have noticed before (by which he meant on his original tour of all the rooms that evening) that such a barrier had exceptionally presented itself. He had indeed since that moment undergone an agitation so extraordinary that it might have muddled for him any earlier view; and he tried to convince himself that he might perhaps then have gone into the room and, inadvertently, automatically, on coming out, have drawn the door after him. The difficulty was that this exactly was what he never did; it was against his whole policy, as he might have said, the essence of which was to keep vistas clear. He had them from the first, as he was well aware, quite on the brain: the strange apparition, at the far end of one of them, of his baffled "prey" (which had become by so sharp an irony so little the term now to apply!) was the form of success his imagination had most cherished, projecting into it always a refinement of beauty. He had known fifty times the start of perception that had afterwards dropped; had fifty times gasped to himself "There!" under some fond brief hallucination. The house, as the case stood, admirably lent itself; he might wonder at the taste, the native architecture of

the particular time, which could rejoice so in the multiplication of doors—
the opposite extreme to the modern, the actual almost complete proscription
of them; but it had fairly contributed to provoke this obsession of the
presence encountered telescopically, as he might say, focussed and studied in
diminishing perspective and as by a rest for the elbow.

It was with these considerations that his present attention was charged—
they perfectly availed to make what he saw portentous. He *couldn't*, by any
lapse, have blocked that aperture; and if he hadn't, if it was unthinkable, why
what else was clear but that there had been another agent? Another
agent?—he had been catching, as he felt, a moment back, the very breath of
him; but when he had been so close as in this simple, this logical, this
completely personal act? It was so logical, that is, that one might have *taken*
it for personal; yet for what did Brydon take it, he asked himself, while, softly
panting, he felt his eyes almost leave their sockets. Ah this time at last they
were, the two, the opposed projections of him, in presence; and this time, as
much as one would, the question of danger loomed. With it rose, as not
before, the question of courage—for what he knew the blank face of the door
to say to him was "Show us how much you have!" It stared, it glared back at
him with that challenge; it put to him the two alternatives: should he just
push it open or not? Oh to have this consciousness was to *think*—and to
think, Brydon knew, as he stood there, was, with the lapsing moments, not
to have acted! Not to have acted—that was the misery and the pang—was
even still not to act; was in fact *all* to feel the thing in another, in a new and
terrible way. How long did he pause and how long did he debate? There was
presently nothing to measure it; for his vibration had already changed—as
just by the effect of its intensity. Shut up there, at bay, defiant, and with the
prodigy of the thing palpably, provably *done*, thus giving notice like some
stark signboard—under that accession of accent the situation itself had
turned; and Brydon at last remarkably made up his mind on what it had
turned to.

It had turned altogether to a different admonition; to a supreme hint, for
him, of the value of Discretion! This slowly dawned, no doubt—for it could
take its time; so perfectly, on his threshold, had he been stayed, so little as yet
had he either advanced or retreated. It was the strangest of all things that
now when, by his taking ten steps and applying his hand to a latch, or even
his shoulder and his knee, if necessary, to a panel, all the hunger of his prime
need might have been met, his high curiosity crowned, his unrest assuaged—
it was amazing, but it was also exquisite and rare, that insistence should
have, at a touch, quite dropped from him. Discretion—he jumped at that;
and yet not, verily, at such a pitch, because it saved his nerves or his skin,
but because, much more valuably, it saved the situation. When I say
he "jumped" at it I feel the consonance of this term with the fact
that—at the end indeed of I know not how long—he did move again, he
crossed straight to the door. He wouldn't touch it—it seemed now that he
might *if* he would: he would only just wait there a little, to show, to prove,
that he wouldn't. He had thus another station, close to the thin partition by which revelation was denied him; but with his eyes bent and his
hands held off in a mere intensity of stillness. He listened as if there

had been something to hear, but this attitude, while it lasted, was his own communication. "If you won't then—good: I spare you and I give up. You affect me as by the appeal positively for pity: you convince me that for reasons rigid and sublime—what do I know?—we both of us should have suffered. I respect them then, and, though moved and privileged as, I believe, it has never been given to man, I retire, I renounce—never, on my honour, to try again. So rest for ever—and let *me!*"

That, for Brydon was the deep sense of this last demonstration—solemn, measured, directed, as he felt it to be. He brought it to a close, he turned away; and now verily he knew how deeply he had been stirred. He retraced his steps, taking up his candle, burnt, he observed, well-nigh to the socket, and marking again, lighten it as he would, the distinctness of his footfall; after which, in a moment, he knew himself at the other side of the house. He did here what he had not yet done at these hours—he opened half a casement, one of those in the front, and let in the air of the night; a thing he would have taken at any time previous for a sharp rupture of his spell. His spell was broken now, and it didn't matter—broken by his concession and his surrender, which made it idle henceforth that he should ever come back. The empty street—its other life so marked even by the great lamplit vacancy—was within call, within touch; he stayed there as to be in it again, high above it though he was still perched; he watched as for some comforting common fact, some vulgar human note, the passage of a scavenger or a thief, some night-bird however base. He would have blessed that sign of life; he would have welcomed positively the slow approach of his friend the policeman, whom he had hitherto only sought to avoid, and was not sure that if the patrol had come into sight he mightn't have felt the impulse to get into relation with it, to hail it, on some pretext, from his fourth floor.

The pretext that wouldn't have been too silly or too compromising, the explanation that would have saved his dignity and kept his name, in such a case, out of the papers, was not definite to him: he was so occupied with the thought of recording his Discretion—as an effect of the vow he had just uttered to his intimate adversary—that the importance of this loomed large and something had overtaken all ironically his sense of proportion. If there had been a ladder applied to the front of the house, even one of the vertiginous perpendiculars employed by painters and roofers and sometimes left standing overnight, he would have managed somehow, astride of the window-sill, to compass by outstretched leg and arm that mode of descent. If there had been some such uncanny thing as he had found in his room at hotels, a workable fire-escape in the form of notched cable or a canvas shoot, he would have availed himself of it as a proof—well, of his present delicacy. He nursed that sentiment, as the question stood, a little in vain, and even—at the end of he scarce knew, once more, how long—found it, as by the action on his mind of the failure of response of the outer world, sinking back to vague anguish. It seemed to him he had waited an age for some stir of the great grim hush; the life of the town was itself under a spell—so unnaturally, up and down the whole prospect of known and rather ugly objects, the blankness and the silence lasted. Had they ever, he asked himself, the hard-faced houses, which had begun to look livid in the dim dawn, had they ever spoken so little to any need of his spirit? Great builded voids, great crowded stillnesses put on, often, in the heart of cities, for the small hours, a sort of sinister mask, and it was of this large collective negation that Brydon presently became conscious—all the more that the break of day was, almost incredibly, now at hand, proving to him what a night he had made of it.

He looked again at his watch, saw what had become of his time-values (he had taken hours for minutes—not, as in other tense situations, minutes for hours) and the strange air of the streets was but the weak, the sullen flush of a dawn in which everything was still locked up. His choked appeal from his own open window had been the sole note of life, and he could but break off at last as for a worse despair. Yet while so deeply demoralised he was capable again of an impulse denoting—at least by his present measure— extraordinary resolution; of retracing his steps to the spot where he had turned cold with the extinction of his last pulse of doubt as to there being in the place another presence than his own. This required an effort strong enough to sicken him; but he had his reason, which overmastered for the moment everything else. There was the whole of the rest of the house to traverse, and how should he screw himself to that if the door he had seen closed were at present open? He could hold to the idea that the closing had practically been for him an act of mercy, a chance offered him to descend, depart, get off the ground and never again profane it. This conception held together, it worked; but what it meant for him depended now clearly on the amount of forbearance his recent action, or rather his recent inaction, had engendered. The image of the "presence," whatever it was, waiting there for him to go—this image had not yet been so concrete for his nerves as when he stopped short of the point at which certainty would have come to him. For, with all his resolution, or more exactly with all his dread, he did stop short—he hung back from really seeing. The risk was too great and his fear too definite: it took at this moment an awful specific form.

He knew—yes, as he had never known anything—that, *should* he see the door open, it would all too abjectly be the end of him. It would mean that the agent of his shame—for his shame was the deep abjection—was once more at large and in general possession; and what glared him thus in the face was the act that this would determine for him. It would send him straight about to the window he had left open, and by that window, be long ladder and dangling rope as absent as they would, he saw himself uncontrollably insanely fatally take his way to the street. The hideous chance of this he at least could avert; but he could only avert it by recoiling in time from assurance. He had the whole house to deal with, this fact was still there; only he now knew that uncertainty alone could start him. He stole back from where he had checked himself—merely to do so was suddenly like safety— and, making blindly for the greater staircase, left gaping rooms and sounding passages behind. Here was the top of the stairs, with a fine large dim descent and three spacious landings to mark off. His instinct was all for mildness, but his feet were harsh on the floors, and, strangely, when he had in a couple of minutes become aware of this, it counted somehow for help. He couldn't have spoken, the tone of his voice would have scared him, and the common conceit or resource of "whistling in the dark" (whether literally or figuratively) have appeared basely vulgar; yet he liked none the less to hear himself go, and when he had reached his first landing—taking it all with no rush, but quite steadily—that stage of success drew from him a gasp of relief.

The house, withal, seemed immense, the scale of space again inordinate; the open rooms, to no one of which his eyes deflected, gloomed in their shuttered state like mouths of caverns; only the high skylight that formed the crown of the deep well created for him a medium in which he could advance, but which might have been, for queerness of colour, some watery underworld. He tried to think of something noble, as that his property was really grand, a splendid possession; but this nobleness took the form too of the clear delight with which he was finally to sacrifice it. They might come in now, the builders, the destroyers—they might come as soon as they would. At the end of two flights he had dropped to another zone, and from the middle of the third, with only one more left, he recognised the influence of the lower windows, of half-drawn blinds, of the occasional gleam of streetlamps, of the glazed spaces of the vestibule. This was the bottom of the sea, which showed an illumination of its own and which he even saw paved—when at a given moment he drew up to sink a long look over the banisters—with the marble squares of his childhood. By that time indubitably he felt, as he might have said in a commoner cause, better; it had allowed him to stop and draw breath, and the ease increased with the sight of the old black-and-white slabs. But what he most felt was that now surely, with the element of impunity pulling him as by hard firm hands, the case was settled for what he might have seen above had he dared that last look. The closed door, blessedly remote now, was still closed—and he had only in short to reach that of the house.

He came down further, he crossed the passage forming the access to the last flight; and if here again he stopped an instant it was almost for the sharpness of the thrill of assured escape. It made him shut his eyes—which opened again to the straight slope of the remainder of the stairs. Here was impunity still, but impunity almost excessive; inasmuch as the sidelights and the high fan-tracery of the entrance were glimmering straight into the hall; an appearance produced, he the next instant saw, by the fact that the vestibule gaped wide, that the hinged halves of the inner door had been thrown far back. Out of that again the *question* sprang at him, making his eyes, as he felt, half-start from his head, as they had done, at the top of the house, before the sign of the other door. If he had left that one open, hadn't he left this one closed, and wasn't he now in *most* immediate presence of some inconceivable occult activity? It was as sharp, the question, as a knife in his side, but the answer hung fire still and seemed to lose itself in the vague darkness to which the thin admitted dawn, glimmering archwise over the whole outer door, made a semicircular margin, a cold silvery nimbus that seemed to play a little as he looked—to shift and expand and contract.

It was as if there had been something within it, protected by indistinctness and corresponding in extent with the opaque surface behind, the painted panels of the last barrier to his escape, of which the key was in his pocket.

The indistinctness mocked him even while he stared, affected him as somehow shrouding or challenging certitude, so that after faltering an instant on his step he let himself go with the sense that here *was* at last something to meet, to touch, to take, to know—something all unnatural and dreadful, but to advance upon which was the condition for him either of liberation or of supreme defeat. The penumbra, dense and dark, was the virtual screen of a figure which stood in it as still as some image erect in a niche or as some black-vizored sentinel guarding a treasure. Brydon was to know afterwards, was to recall and make out, the particular thing he had believed during the rest of his descent. He saw, in its great grey glimmering margin, the central vagueness diminish, and he felt it to be taking the very form toward which, for so many days, the passion of his curiosity had yearned. It gloomed, it loomed, it was something, it was somebody, the prodigy of a personal presence.

Rigid and conscious, spectral yet human, a man of his own substance and stature waited there to measure himself with his power to dismay. This only could it be—this only till he recognised, with his advance, that what made the face dim was the pair of raised hands that covered it and in which, so far from being offered in defiance, it was buried as for dark deprecation. So Brydon, before him, took him in; with every fact of him now, in the higher light, hard and acute—his planted stillness, his vivid truth, his grizzled bent head and white masking hands, his queer actuality of evening-dress, of dangling double eye-glass, of gleaming silk lappet and white linen, of pearl button and gold watch-guard and polished shoe. No portrait by a great modern master could have presented him with more intensity, thrust him out of his frame with more art, as if there had been "treatment," of the consummate sort, in his every shade and salience. The revulsion, for our friend, had become, before he knew it, immense—this drop, in the act of apprehension, to the sense of his adversary's inscrutable manoeuvre. That meaning at least, while he gaped, it offered him; for he could but gape at his other self in this other anguish, gape as a proof that *he*, standing there for the achieved, the enjoyed, the triumphant life, couldn't be faced in his triumph. Wasn't the proof in the splendid covering hands, strong and completely spread?—so spread and so intentional that, in spite of a special verity that surpassed every other, the fact that one of these hands had lost two fingers, which were reduced to stumps, as if accidentally shot away, the face was effectually guarded and saved.

"Saved," though, *would* it be?—Brydon breathed his wonder till the very impunity of his attitude and the very insistence of his eyes produced, as he felt, a sudden stir which showed the next instant as a deeper portent, while the head raised itself, the betrayal of a braver purpose. The hands, as he looked, began to move, to open; then, as if deciding in a flash, dropped from the face and left it uncovered and presented. Horror, with the sight, had leaped into Brydon's throat, gasping there in a sound he couldn't utter; for the bared identity was too hideous as *his*, and his glare was the passion of his protest. The face, *that* face, Spencer Brydon's?—he searched it still, but looking away from it in dismay and denial, falling straight from his height of sublimity. It was unknown, inconceivable, awful, disconnected from any possibility——! He had been "sold," he inwardly moaned, stalking such game as this: the presence before him was a presence, the horror within him a horror, but the waste of his nights had been only grotesque and the success of his adventure an irony. Such an identity fitted his at *no* point, made its alternative monstrous. A thousand times yes, as it came upon him nearer now—the face was the face of a stranger. It came upon him nearer now, quite as one of those expanding fantastic images projected by the magic lantern of childhood; for the stranger, whoever he might be, evil, odious, blatant, vulgar, had advanced as for aggression, and he knew himself give ground. Then harder pressed still, sick with the force of his shock, and falling back as under the hot breath and the roused passion of a life larger than his own, a rage of personality before which his own collapsed, he felt the whole vision turn to darkness and his very feet give way. His head went round; he was going; he had gone.

III

What had next brought him back, clearly—though after how long?—was Mrs. Muldoon's voice, coming to him from quite near, from so near that he seemed presently to see her as kneeling on the ground before him while he lay looking up at her; himself not wholly on the ground, but half-raised and upheld—conscious, yes, of tenderness of support and, more particularly, of a head pillowed in extraordinary softness and fainly refreshing fragrance. He considered, he wondered, his wit but half at his service; then another face intervened, bending more directly over him, and he finally knew that Alice Staverton had made her lap an ample and perfect cushion to him, and that she had to this end seated herself on the lowest degree of the staircase, the rest of his long person remaining stretched on his old black-and-white slabs. They were cold, these marble squares of his youth; but *he* somehow was not, in this rich return of consciousness—the most wonderful hour, little by little, that he had ever known, leaving him, as it did, so gratefully, so abysmally passive, and yet as with a treasure of intelligence waiting all round him for quiet appropriation; dissolved, he might call it, in the air of the place and producing the golden glow of a late autumn afternoon. He had come back, yes—come back from further away than any man but himself had ever travelled; but it was strange how with this sense what he had come back *to* seemed really the great thing, and as if his prodigious journey had been all for the sake of it. Slowly but surely his consciousness grew, his vision of his state thus completing itself: he had been miraculously *carried* back—lifted and carefully borne as from where he had been picked up, the uttermost end of an interminable grey passage. Even with this he was suffered to rest, and what had now brought him to knowledge was the break in the long mild motion.

It had brought him to knowledge, to knowledge—yes, this was the beauty of his state; which came to resemble more and more that of a man who has gone to sleep on some news of a great inheritance, and then, after dreaming it away, after profaning it with matters strange to it, has waked up again to serenity of certitude and has only to lie and watch it grow. This was the drift of his patience—that he had only to let it shine on him. He must moreover, with intermissions, still have been lifted and borne; since why and how else should he have known himself, later on, with the afternoon glow intenser, no longer at the foot of his stairs—situated as these now seemed at that dark other end of his tunnel—but on a deep window-bench of his high saloon, over which had been spread, couch-fashion, a mantle of soft stuff lined with grey fur that was familiar to his eyes and that one of his hands kept fondly feeling as for its pledge of truth. Mrs. Muldoon's face had gone, but the other, the second he had recognised, hung over him in a way that showed how he was still propped and pillowed. He took it all in, and the more he took it the more it seemed to suffice: he was as much at peace as if he had had food and drink. It was the two women who had found him, on Mrs. Muldoon's having plied, at her usual hour, her latch-key—and on her having above all arrived while Miss Staverton still lingered near the house. She had been turning away, all anxiety, from worrying the vain bell-handle—her calculation having been of the hour of the good woman's visit; but the latter, blessedly, had come up while she was still there, and they had entered together. He had then lain, beyond the vestibule, very much as he was lying now—quite, that is, as he appeared to have fallen, but all so wondrously without bruise or gash; only in a depth of stupor. What he most took in, however, at present, with the steadier clearance, was that Alice Staverton had for a long unspeakable moment not doubted he was dead.

"It must have been that I *was*." He made it out as she held him. "Yes—I can only have died. You brought me literally to life. Only," he wondered, his eyes rising to her, "only, in the name of all the benedictions, how?"

It took her but an instant to bend her face and kiss him, and something in the manner of it, and in the way her hands clasped and locked his head while he felt the cool charity and virtue of her lips, something in all this beatitude somehow answered everything. "And now I keep you," she said.

"Oh keep me, keep me!" he pleaded while her face still hung over him: in response to which it dropped again and stayed close, clingingly close. It was the seal of their situation—of which he tasted the impress for a long blissful moment in silence. But he came back. "Yet how did you know——?"

"I was uneasy. You were to have come, you remember—and you had sent no word."

"Yes, I remember—I was to have gone to you at one to-day." It caught on to their "old" life and relation—which were so near and so far. "I was still out there in my strange darkness—where was it, what was it? I must have stayed there so long." He could but wonder at the depth and the duration of his swoon.

"Since last night?" she asked with a shade of fear for her possible indiscretion.

"Since this morning—it must have been: the cold dim dawn of to-day. Where have I been," he vaguely wailed, "where have I been?" He felt her hold him close, and it was as if this helped him now to make in all security his mild moan. "What a long dark day!"

All in her tenderness she had waited a moment. "In the cold dim dawn?" she quavered.

But he had already gone on piecing together the parts of the whole prodigy. "As I didn't turn up you came straight——?"

She barely cast about. "I went first to your hotel—where they told me of your absence. You had dined out last evening and hadn't been back since. But they appeared to know you had been at your club."

"So you had the idea of *this*——?"

"Of what?" she asked in a moment.

"Well—of what has happened."

"I believed at least you'd have been here. I've known, all along," she said, "that you've been coming."

"'Known' it——?"

"Well, I've believed it. I said nothing to you after that talk we had a month ago—but I felt sure. I knew you *would*," she declared.

"That I'd persist, you mean?"

"That you'd see him."

"Ah but I didn't!" cried Brydon with his long wail. "There's somebody—an awful beast; whom I brought, too horribly, to bay. But it's not me."

At this she bent over him again, and her eyes were in his eyes. "No—it's not you." And it was as if, while her face hovered, he might have made out in it, hadn't it been so near, some particular meaning blurred by a smile. "No, thank heaven," she repeated—"it's not you! Of course it wasn't to have been."

"Ah but it *was,*" he gently insisted. And he stared before him now as he had been staring for so many weeks. "I was to have known myself."

"You couldn't!" she returned consolingly. And then reverting, and as if to account further for what she had herself done, "But it wasn't only *that,* that you hadn't been at home," she went on. "I waited till the hour at which we had found Mrs. Muldoon that day of my going with you; and she arrived, as I've told you, while, failing to bring any one to the door, I lingered in my despair on the steps. After a little, if she hadn't come, by such a mercy, I should have found means to hunt her up. But it wasn't," said Alice Staverton, as if once more with her fine intention—"it wasn't only that."

His eyes, as he lay, turned back to her. "What more then?"

She met it, the wonder she had stirred. "In the cold dim dawn, you say? Well, in the cold dim dawn of this morning I too saw you."

"Saw *me*——?"

"Saw *him,*" said Alice Staverton. "It must have been at the same moment."

He lay an instant taking it in—as if he wished to be quite reasonable. "At the same moment?"

"Yes—in my dream again, the same one I've named to you. He came back to me. Then I knew it for a sign. He had come to you."

At this Brydon raised himself; he had to see her better. She helped him when she understood his movement, and he sat up, steadying himself beside her there on the window-bench and with his right hand grasping her left. "*He* didn't come to me."

"You came to yourself," she beautifully smiled.

"Ah I've come to myself now—thanks to you, dearest. But this brute, with his awful face—this brute's a black stranger. He's none of *me,* even as I *might* have been," Brydon sturdily declared.

But she kept the clearness that was like the breath of infallibility. "Isn't the whole point that you'd have been different?"

He almost scowled for it. "As different as *that*——?"

Her look again was more beautiful to him than the things of this world. "Haven't you exactly wanted to know *how* different? So this morning," she said, "you appeared to me."

"Like *him?*"

"A black stranger!"

"Then how did you know it was I?"

"Because, as I told you weeks ago, my mind, my imagination, had worked so over what you might, what you mightn't have been—to show you, you see, how I've thought of you. In the midst of that you came to me—that my wonder might be answered. So I knew," she went on; "and believed that, since the question held you too so fast, as you told me that day, you too would see for yourself. And when this morning I again saw I knew it would be because you had—and also then, from the first moment, because you somehow wanted me. *He* seemed to tell me of that. So why," she strangely smiled, "shouldn't I like him?"

It brought Spencer Brydon to his feet. "You 'like' that horror—?"

"I *could* have liked him. And to me," she said, "he was no horror. I had accepted him."

"'Accepted'——?" Brydon oddly sounded.

"Before, for the interest of his difference—yes. And as *I* didn't disown him, as *I* knew him—which you at last, confronted with him in his difference, so cruelly didn't, my dear—well, he must have been, you see, less dreadful to me. And it may have pleased him that I pitied him."

She was beside him on her feet, but still holding his hand—still with her arm supporting him. But though it all brought for him thus a dim light, "You 'pitied' him?" he grudgingly, resentfully asked.

"He has been unhappy, he has been ravaged," she said.

"And haven't I been unhappy? Am not I—you've only to look at me!—ravaged?"

"Ah I don't say I like him *better,*" she granted after a thought. "But he's grim, he's worn—and things have happened to him. He doesn't make shift, for sight, with your charming monocle."

"No"—it struck Brydon: "I couldn't have sported mine 'downtown.' They'd have guyed me there."

"His great convex pince-nez—I saw it, I recognised the kind—is for his poor ruined sight. And his poor right hand——!"

"Ah!" Brydon winced—whether for his proved identity or for his lost fingers. Then, "He has a million a year," he lucidly added. "But he hasn't you."

"And he isn't—no, he isn't—*you!*" she murmured as he drew her to his breast.

PART III

A Fabulous Formless Darkness

Fritz Leiber

Smoke Ghost

Fritz Leiber's most famous short story of the 1940s is the urban horror piece, "Smoke Ghost." The impact of this story on horror writing in the U.S. can scarcely be overestimated. It is a revolutionary ghost story that rethinks the entire tradition and re-imagines the supernatural in our time. Leiber uses the traditional device of the ghost in an aggressively new way—as a projection of the group unconscious of civilized and rational humanity that alters the nature of reality—that must be worshipped. Combining the moral and psychological traditions, Leiber transforms them into an ambiguous and unsettling other reality. Perhaps a descendent of the stories of other dimensions such as Blackwood's "The Willows" or Bierce's "The Damned Thing" or Frank Belknap Long's "The Hounds of Tindalos," "Smoke Ghost" influences the field from Bradbury to Ramsey Campbell and is representative of the transition from old to new styles in horror fiction influenced by *Unknown* magazine. Leiber was the recipient of the Grand Master Award for life achievement at the World Fantasy Convention in 1976.

Miss Millick wondered just what had happened to Mr. Wran. He kept making the strangest remarks when she took dictation. Just this morning he had quickly turned around and asked, "Have you ever seen a ghost, Miss Millick?" And she had tittered nervously and replied, "When I was a girl there was a thing in white that used to come out of the closet in the attic bedroom when I slept there, and moan. Of course it was just my imagination. I was frightened of lots of things." And he had said, "I don't mean that kind of ghost. I mean a ghost from the world today, with the soot of the factories on its face and the pounding of machinery in its soul. The kind that would haunt coal yards and slip around at night through deserted office buildings like this one. A real ghost. Not something out of books." And she hadn't known what to say.

He'd never been like this before. Of course he might be joking, but it didn't sound that way. Vaguely Miss Millick wondered whether he mightn't be seeking some sort of sympathy from her. Of course, Mr. Wran was married and had a little child, but that didn't prevent her from having daydreams. The daydreams were not very exciting, still they helped fill up her mind. But now he was asking her another of those unprecedented questions.

"Have you ever thought what a ghost of our times would look like, Miss Millick? Just picture it. A smoky composite face with the hungry anxiety of the unemployed, the neurotic restlessness of the person without purpose, the jerky tension of the high-pressure metropolitan worker, the uneasy resentment of the striker, the callous opportunism of the scab, the aggressive whine of the panhandler, the inhibited terror of the bombed civilian, and a thousand other twisted emotional patterns. Each one overlying and yet blending with the other, like a pile of semi-transparent masks?"

Miss Millick gave a little self-conscious shiver and said, "That would be terrible. What an awful thing to think of."

She peered furtively across the desk. She remembered having heard that there had been something impressively abnormal about Mr. Wran's childhood, but she couldn't recall what it was. If only she could do something—laugh at his mood or ask him what was really wrong. She shifted the extra pencils in her left hand and mechanically traced over some of the shorthand curlicues in her notebook.

"Yet, that's just what such a ghost or vitalized projection would look like, Miss Millick," he continued, smiling in a tight way. "It would grow out of the real world. It would reflect the tangled, sordid, vicious things. All the loose ends. And it would be very grimy. I don't think it would seem white or wispy, or favor graveyards. It wouldn't moan. But it would mutter unintelligibly, and twitch at your sleeve. Like a sick, surly ape. What would such a thing want from a person, Miss Millick? Sacrifice? Worship? Or just fear? What could you do to stop it from troubling you?"

Miss Millick giggled nervously. There was an expression beyond her powers of definition in Mr. Wran's ordinary, flat-cheeked, thirtyish face, silhouetted against the dusty window. He turned away and stared out into the gray downtown atmosphere that rolled in from the railroad yards and the mills. When he spoke again his voice sounded far away.

"Of course, being immaterial, it couldn't hurt you physically—at first. You'd have to be peculiarly sensitive to see it, or be aware of it at all. But it would begin to influence your actions. Make you do this. Stop you from doing that. Although only a projection, it would gradually get its hooks into the world of things as they are. Might even get control of suitably vacuous minds. Then it could hurt whomever it wanted."

Miss Millick squirmed and read back her shorthand, like the books said you should do when there was a pause. She became aware of the failing light and wished Mr. Wran would ask her to turn on the overhead. She felt scratchy, as if soot were sifting down on to her skin.

"It's a rotten world, Miss Millick," said Mr. Wran, talking at the window. "Fit for another morbid growth of superstition. It's time the ghosts, or whatever you call them, took over and began a rule of fear. They'd be no worse than men."

"But"—Miss Millick's diaphragm jerked, making her titter inanely—"of course, there aren't any such things as ghosts."

Mr. Wran turned around.

"Of course there aren't, Miss Millick," he said in a loud, patronizing voice, as if she had been doing the talking rather than he. "Science and common sense and psychiatry all go to prove it."

She hung her head and might even have blushed if she hadn't felt so all at sea. Her leg muscles twitched, making her stand up, although she hadn't intended to. She aimlessly rubbed her hand along the edge of the desk.

"Why, Mr. Wran, look what I got off your desk," she said, showing him a heavy smudge. There was a note of clumsily playful reproof in her voice. "No wonder the copy I bring you always gets so black. Somebody ought to talk to those scrubwomen. They're skimping on your room."

She wished he would make some normal joking reply. But instead he drew back and his face hardened.

"Well, to get back," he rapped out harshly, and began to dictate.

When she was gone, he jumped up, dabbed his finger experimentally at the smudged part of the desk, frowned worriedly at the almost inky smears. He jerked open a drawer, snatched out a rag, hastily swabbed off the desk, crumpled the rag into a ball and tossed it back. There were three or four other rags in the drawer, each impregnated with soot.

Then he went over to the window and peered out anxiously through the dusk, his eyes searching the panorama of roofs, fixing on each chimney and water tank.

"It's a neurosis. Must be. Compulsions. Hallucinations," he muttered to himself in a tired, distraught voice that would have made Miss Millick gasp. "It's that damned mental abnormality cropping up in a new form. Can't be any other explanation. But it's so damned real. Even the soot. Good thing I'm seeing the psychiatrist. I don't think I could force myself to get on the elevated tonight." His voice trailed off, he rubbed his eyes, and his memory automatically started to grind.

It had all begun on the elevated. There was a particular little sea of roofs he had grown into the habit of glancing at just as the packed car carrying him homeward lurched around a turn. A dingy, melancholy little world of tar-paper, tarred gravel, and smoky brick. Rusty tin chimneys with odd conical hats suggested abandoned listening posts. There was a washed-out advertisement of some ancient patent medicine on the nearest wall. Superficially it was like ten thousand other drab city roofs. But he always saw it around dusk, either in the smoky half-light, or tinged with red by the flat rays of a dirty sunset, or covered by ghostly windblown white sheets of rain-splash, or patched with blackish snow; and it seemed unusually bleak and suggestive; almost beautifully ugly though in no sense picturesque; dreary, but meaningful. Unconsciously it came to symbolize for Catesby Wran certain disagreeable aspects of the frustrated, frightened century in which he lived, the jangled century of hate and heavy industry and total wars. The quick daily glance into the half darkness became an integral part of his life. Oddly, he never saw it in the morning, for it was then his habit to sit on the other side of the car, his head buried in the paper.

One evening toward winter he noticed what seemed to be a shapeless black sack lying on the third roof from the tracks. He did not think about it. It merely registered as an addition to the well-known scene and his memory stored away the impression for further reference. Next evening, however, he decided he had been mistaken in one detail. The object was a roof nearer than he had thought. Its color and texture, and the grimy stains around it, suggested that it was filled with coal dust, which was hardly reasonable.

Then, too, the following evening it seemed to have been blown against a rusty ventilator by the wind—which could hardly have happened if it were at all heavy. Perhaps it was filled with leaves. Catesby was surprised to find himself anticipating his next daily glance with a minor note of apprehension. There was something unwholesome in the posture of the thing that stuck in his mind—a bulge in the sacking that suggested a misshaped head peering around the ventilator. And his apprehension was justified, for that evening the thing was on the nearest roof, though on the farther side, looking as if it had just flopped down over the low brick parapet.

Next evening the sack was gone. Catesby was annoyed at the momentary feeling of relief that went through him, because the whole matter seemed too unimportant to warrant feelings of any sort. What difference did it make if his imagination had played tricks on him, and he'd fancied that the object was slowly crawling and hitching itself closer across the roofs? That was the way any normal imagination worked. He deliberately chose to disregard the fact that there were reasons for thinking his imagination was by no means a normal one. As he walked home from the elevated, however, he found himself wondering whether the sack was really gone. He seemed to recall a vague, smudgy trail leading across the gravel to the nearer side of the roof, which was masked by a parapet. For an instant an unpleasant picture formed in his mind—that of an inky, humped creature crouched behind the parapet, waiting.

The next time he felt the familiar grating lurch of the car, he caught himself trying not to look out. That angered him. He turned his head quickly. When he turned it back, his compact face was definitely pale. There had been only time for a fleeting rearward glance at the escaping roof. Had he actually seen in silhouette the upper part of a head of some sort peering over the parapet? Nonsense, he told himself. And even if he had seen something, there were a thousand explanations which did not involve the supernatural or even true hallucination. Tomorrow he would take a good look and clear up the whole matter. If necessary, he would visit the roof personally, though he hardly knew where to find it and disliked in any case the idea of pampering a silly fear.

He did not relish the walk home from the elevated that evening, and visions of the thing disturbed his dreams, and were in and out of his mind all next day at the office. It was then that he first began to relieve his nerves by making jokingly serious remarks about the supernatural to Miss Millick, who seemed properly mystified. It was on the same day, too, that he became aware of a growing antipathy to grime and soot. Everything he touched seemed gritty, and he found himself mopping and wiping at his desk like an old lady with a morbid fear of germs. He reasoned that there was no real change in his office, and that he'd just now become sensitive to the dirt that had always been there, but there was no denying an increasing nervousness. Long before the car reached the curve, he was straining his eyes through the murky twilight, determined to take in every detail.

Afterward he realized he must have given a muffled cry of some sort, for the man beside him looked at him curiously, and the woman ahead gave him an unfavorable stare. Conscious of his own pallor and uncontrollable trembling, he stared back at them hungrily, trying to regain the feeling of security he had completely lost. They were the usual reassuringly wooden-faced people everyone rides home with on the elevated. But suppose he had pointed out to one of them what he had seen—that sodden, distorted face of sacking and coal dust, that boneless paw which waved back and forth, unmistakably in his direction, as if reminding him of a future appointment —he involuntarily shut his eyes tight. His thoughts were racing ahead to tomorrow evening. He pictured this same windowed oblong of light and packed humanity surging around the curve—then an opaque monstrous form leaping out from the roof in a parabolic swoop—an unmentionable face pressed close against the window, smearing it with wet coal dust—huge paws fumbling sloppily at the glass—

Somehow he managed to turn off his wife's anxious inquiries. Next morning he reached a decision and made an appointment for that evening with a psychiatrist a friend had told him about. It cost him a considerable effort, for Catesby had a well-grounded distaste for anything dealing with psychological abnormality. Visiting a psychiatrist meant raking up an episode in his past which he had never fully described even to his wife. Once he had made the decision, however, he felt considerably relieved. The psychiatrist, he told himself, would clear everything up. He could almost fancy him saying, "Merely a bad case of nerves. However, you must consult the oculist whose name I'm writing down for you, and you must take two of these pills in water every four hours," and so on. It was almost comforting, and made the coming revelation he would have to make seem less painful.

But as the smoky dusk rolled in, his nervousness had returned and he had let his joking mystification of Miss Millick run away with him until he had realized he wasn't frightening anyone but himself.

He would have to keep his imagination under better control, he told himself, as he continued to peer out restlessly at the massive, murky shapes of the downtown office buildings. Why, he had spent the whole afternoon building up a kind of neo-medieval cosmology of superstition. It wouldn't do. He realized then that he had been standing at the window much longer than he'd thought, for the glass panel in the door was dark and there was no noise coming from the outer office. Miss Millick and the rest must have gone home.

It was then he made the discovery that there would have been no special reason for dreading the swing around the curve that night. It was, as it happened, a horrible discovery. For, on the shadowed roof across the street and four stories below, he saw the thing huddle and roll across the gravel and, after one upward look of recognition, merge into the blackness beneath the water tank.

As he hurriedly collected his things and made for the elevator, fighting the panicky impulse to run, he began to think of hallucination and mild psychosis as very desirable conditions. For better or for worse, he pinned all his hopes on the psychiatrist.

"So you find yourself growing nervous and . . . er . . . jumpy, as you put it," said Dr. Trevethick, smiling with dignified geniality. "Do you notice any more definite physical symptoms? Pain? Headache? Indigestion?"

Catesby shook his head and wet his lips. "I'm especially nervous while riding in the elevated," he murmured swiftly.

"I see. We'll discuss that more fully. But I'd like you first to tell me about something you mentioned earlier. You said there was something about your childhood that might predispose you to nervous ailments. As you know, the early years are critical ones in the development of an individual's behavior pattern."

Catesby studied the yellow reflections of frosted globes in the dark surface of the desk. The palm of his left hand aimlessly rubbed the thick nap of the armchair. After a while he raised his head and looked straight into the doctor's small brown eyes.

"From perhaps my third to my ninth year," he began, choosing the words with care, "I was what you might call a sensory prodigy."

The doctor's expression did not change. "Yes?" he inquired politely.

"What I mean is that I was supposed to be able to see through walls, read letters through envelopes and books through their covers, fence and play ping-pong blindfolded, find things that were buried, read thoughts." The words tumbled out.

"And could you?" The doctor's voice was toneless.

"I don't know. I don't suppose so," answered Catesby, long-lost emotions flooding back into his voice. "It's all confused now. I thought I could, but then they were always encouraging me. My mother . . . was . . . well . . . interested in psychic phenomena. I was . . . exhibited. I seem to remember seeing things other people couldn't. As if most opaque objects were transparent. But I was very young. I didn't have any scientific criteria for judgment."

He was reliving it now. The darkened rooms. The earnest assemblages of gawking, prying adults. Himself alone on a little platform, lost in a straight-backed wooden chair. The black silk handkerchief over his eyes. His mother's coaxing, insistent questions. The whispers. The gasps. His own hate of the whole business, mixed with hunger for the adulation of adults. Then the scientists from the university, the experiments, the big test. The reality of those memories engulfed him and momentarily made him forget the reason why he was disclosing them to a stranger.

"Do I understand that your mother tried to make use of you as a medium for communicating with the . . . er . . . other world?"

Catesby nodded eagerly.

"She tried to, but she couldn't. When it came to getting in touch with the dead, I was a complete failure. All I could do—or thought I could do—was see real, existing, three-dimensional objects beyond the vision of normal people. Objects anyone could have seen except for distance, obstruction, or darkness. It was always a disappointment to mother."

He could hear her sweetish, patient voice saying, "Try again, dear, just this once. Katie was your aunt. She loved you. Try to hear what she's saying." And he had answered, "I can see a woman in a blue dress standing on the other side of Dick's house." And she had replied, "Yes, I know, dear. But that's not Katie. Katie's a spirit. Try again. Just this once, dear." The doctor's voice gently jarred him back into the softly gleaming office.

"You mentioned scientific criteria for judgment, Mr. Wran. As far as you know, did anyone ever try to apply them to you?"

Catesby's nod was emphatic.

"They did. When I was eight, two young psychologists from the university got interested in me. I guess they did it for a joke at first, and I remember being very determined to show them I amounted to something. Even now I seem to recall how the note of polite superiority and amused sarcasm drained out of their voices. I suppose they decided at first that it was very clever trickery, but somehow persuaded mother to let them try me out under controlled conditions. There were lots of tests that seemed very businesslike after mother's slipshod little exhibitions. They found I was clairvoyant—or so they thought. I got worked up and on edge. They were going to demonstrate my supernormal sensory powers to the university psychology faculty. For the first time I began to worry about whether I'd come through. Perhaps they kept me going at too hard a pace, I don't know. At any rate, when the test came, I couldn't do a thing. Everything became opaque. I got desperate and made things up out of my imagination. I lied. In the end I failed utterly, and I believe the two young psychologists got into a lot of hot water as a result."

He could hear the brusque, bearded man saying, "You've been taken in by a child, Flaxman, a mere child. I'm greatly disturbed. You've put yourself on the same plane as common charlatans. Gentlemen, I ask you to banish from your minds this whole sorry episode. It must never be referred to." He winced at the recollection of his feeling of guilt. But at the same time he was beginning to feel exhilarated and almost light-hearted. Unburdening his long-repressed memories had altered his whole viewpoint. The episodes on the elevated began to take on what seemed their proper proportions as merely the bizarre workings of overwrought nerves and an overly suggestible mind. The doctor, he anticipated confidently, would disentangle the obscure subconscious causes, whatever they might be. And the whole business would be finished off quickly, just as his childhood experience— which was beginning to seem a little ridiculous now—had been finished off.

"From that day on," he continued, "I never exhibited a trace of my supposed powers. My mother was frantic and tried to sue the university. I had something like a nervous breakdown. Then the divorce was granted, and my father got custody of me. He did his best to make me forget it. We went on long outdoor vacations and did a lot of athletics, associated with normal matter-of-fact people. I went to business college eventually. I'm in advertising now. But," Catesby paused, "now that I'm having nervous symptoms, I've wondered if there mightn't be a connection. It's not a question of whether I was really clairvoyant or not. Very likely my mother taught me a lot of unconscious deceptions, good enough to fool even young psychology instructors. But don't you think it may have some important bearing on my present condition?"

For several moments the doctor regarded him with a professional frown. Then he said quietly, "And is there some . . . er . . . more specific connection between your experiences then and now? Do you by any chance find that you are once again beginning to . . . er . . . see things?"

Catesby swallowed. He had felt an increasing eagerness to unburden himself of his fears, but it was not easy to make a beginning, and the doctor's shrewd question rattled him. He forced himself to concentrate. The thing he thought he had seen on the roof loomed up before his inner eye with unexpected vividness. Yet it did not frighten him. He groped for words.

Then he saw that the doctor was not looking at him but over his shoulder. Color was draining out of the doctor's face and his eyes did not seem so small. Then the doctor sprang to his feet, walked past Catesby, threw up the window and peered into the darkness.

As Catesby rose, the doctor slammed down the window and said in a voice whose smoothness was marred by a slight, persistent gasping, "I hope I haven't alarmed you. I saw the face of . . . er . . . a Negro prowler on the fire escape. I must have frightened him, for he seems to have gotten out of sight in a hurry. Don't give it another thought. Doctors are frequently bothered by *voyeurs* . . . er . . . Peeping Toms."

"A Negro?" asked Catesby, moistening his lips.

The doctor laughed nervously. "I imagine so, though my first odd impression was that it was a white man in blackface. You see, the color didn't seem to have any brown in it. It was dead-black."

Catesby moved toward the window. There were smudges on the glass. "It's quite all right, Mr. Wran." The doctor's voice had acquired a sharp note of impatience, as if he were trying hard to reassume his professional authority. "Let's continue our conversation. I was asking you if you were"—he made a face—"seeing things."

Catesby's whirling thoughts slowed down and locked into place. "No, I'm not seeing anything that other people don't see, too. And I think I'd better go now. I've been keeping you too long." He disregarded the doctor's half-hearted gesture of denial. "I'll phone you about the physical examination. In a way you've already taken a big load off my mind." He smiled woodenly. "Goodnight, Dr. Trevethick."

Catesby Wran's mental state was a peculiar one. His eyes searched every angular shadow, he glanced sideways down each chasm-like alley and barren basement passageway, and kept stealing looks at the irregular line of the roofs, yet he was hardly conscious of where he was going. He pushed away the thoughts that came into his mind, and kept moving. He became aware of a slight sense of security as he turned into a lighted street where there were people and high buildings and blinking signs. After a while he found himself in the dim lobby of the structure that housed his office. Then he realized why he couldn't go home, why he daren't go home—after what had happened at the office of Dr. Trevethick.

"Hello, Mr. Wran," said the night elevator man, a burly figure in overalls, sliding open the grille-work door to the old-fashioned cage. "I didn't know you were working nights now, too."

Catesby stepped in automatically. "Sudden rush of orders," he murmured inanely. "Some stuff that has to be gotten out."

The cage creaked to a stop at the top floor. "Be working very late, Mr. Wran?"

He nodded vaguely, watched the car slide out of sight, found his keys, swiftly crossed the outer office, and entered his own. His hand went out to the light switch, but then the thought occurred to him that the two lighted windows, standing out against the dark bulk of the building, would indicate his whereabouts and serve as a goal toward which something could crawl and climb. He moved his chair so that the back was against the wall and sat down in the semidarkness. He did not remove his overcoat.

For a long time he sat there motionless, listening to his own breathing and the faraway sounds from the streets below: the thin metallic surge of the crosstown streetcar, the farther one of the elevated, faint lonely cries and honkings, indistinct rumblings. Words he had spoken to Miss Millick in nervous jest came back to him with the bitter taste of truth. He found himself unable to reason critically or connectedly, but by their own volition thoughts rose up into his mind and gyrated slowly and rearranged themselves with the inevitable movement of planets.

Gradually his mental picture of the world was transformed. No longer a world of material atoms and empty space, but a world in which the bodiless existed and moved according to its own obscure laws or unpredictable impulses. The new picture illuminated with dreadful clarity certain general facts which had always bewildered and troubled him and from which he had tried to hide: the inevitability of hate and war, the diabolically timed mischances which wreck the best of human intentions, the walls of willful misunderstanding that divide one man from another, the eternal vitality of cruelty and ignorance and greed. They seemed appropriate now, necessary parts of the picture. And superstition only a kind of wisdom.

Then his thoughts returned to himself and the question he had asked Miss Millick, "What would such a thing want from a person? Sacrifices? Worship, Or just fear? What could you do to stop it from troubling you?" It had become a practical question.

With an explosive jangle, the phone began to ring. "Cate, I've been trying everywhere to get you," said his wife. "I never thought you'd be at the office. What are you doing? I've been worried."

He said something about work.

"You'll be home right away?" came the faint anxious question. "I'm a little frightened. Ronny just had a scare. It woke him up. He kept pointing to the window saying, 'Black man, black man.' Of course it's something he dreamed. But I'm frightened. You will be home? What's that, dear? Can't you hear me?"

"I will. Right away," he said. Then he was out of the office, buzzing the night bell and peering down the shaft.

He saw it peering up the shaft at him from the deep shadows three floors below, the sacking face pressed against the iron grille-work. It started up the stair at a shockingly swift, shambling gait, vanishing temporarily from sight as it swung into the second corridor below.

Catesby clawed at the door to the office, realized he had not locked it, pushed it in, slammed and locked it behind him, retreated to the other side of the room, cowered between the filing cases and the wall. His teeth were clicking. He heard the groan of the rising cage. A silhouette darkened the frosted glass of the door, blotting out part of the grotesque reverse of the company name. After a little the door opened.

The big-globed overhead light flared on and, standing inside the door, her hand on the switch, was Miss Millick.

"Why, Mr. Wran," she stammered vacuously, "I didn't know you were here. I'd just come in to do some extra typing after the movie. I didn't . . . but the lights weren't on. What were you—"

He stared at her. He wanted to shout in relief, grab hold of her, talk rapidly. He realized he was grinning hysterically.

"Why, Mr. Wran, what's happened to you?" she asked embarrassedly, ending with a stupid titter. "Are you feeling sick? Isn't there something I can do for you?"

He shook his head jerkily and managed to say, "No, I'm just leaving. I was doing some extra work myself."

"But you *look* sick," she insisted, and walked over toward him. He inconsequentially realized she must have stepped in mud, for her high-heeled shoes left neat black prints.

"Yes, I'm sure you must be sick. You're so terribly pale." She sounded like an enthusiastic, incompetent nurse. Her face brightened with a sudden inspiration. "I've got something in my bag, that'll fix you up right away," she said. "It's for indigestion."

She fumbled at her stuffed oblong purse. He noticed that she was absent-mindedly holding it shut with one hand while she tried to open it with the other. Then, under his very eyes, he saw her bend back the thick prongs of metal locking the purse as if they were tinfoil, or as if her fingers had become a pair of steel pliers.

Instantly his memory recited the words he had spoken to Miss Millick that afternoon. "It couldn't hurt you physically—at first . . . gradually get its hooks into the world . . . might even get control of suitably vacuous minds. Then it could hurt whomever it wanted." A sickish, cold feeling grew inside him. He began to edge toward the door.

But Miss Millick hurried ahead of him.

"You don't have to wait, Fred," she called. "Mr. Wran's decided to stay a while longer."

The door to the cage shut with a mechanical rattle. The cage creaked. Then she turned around in the door.

"Why, Mr. Wran," she gurgled reproachfully, "I just couldn't think of letting you go home now. I'm sure you're terribly unwell. Why, you might collapse in the street. You've just got to stay here until you feel different."

The creaking died away. He stood in the center of the office, motionless. His eyes traced the coal-black course of Miss Millick's footprints to where she stood blocking the door. Then a sound that was almost a scream was wrenched out of him, for it seemed to him that the blackness was creeping up her legs under the thin stockings.

"Why, Mr. Wran," she said, "you're acting as if you were crazy. You must lie down for a while. Here, I'll help you off with your coat."

The nauseously idiotic and rasping note was the same; only it had been intensified. As she came toward him he turned and ran through the storeroom, clattered a key desperately at the lock of the second door to the corridor.

"Why, Mr. Wran," he heard her call, "are you having some kind of a fit? You must let me help you."

The door came open and he plunged out into the corridor and up the stairs immediately ahead. It was only when he reached the top that he realized the heavy steel door in front of him led to the roof. He jerked up the catch.

"Why, Mr. Wran, you mustn't run away. I'm coming after you."

Then he was out on the gritty gravel of the roof. The night sky was clouded and murky, with a faint pinkish glow from the neon signs. From the distant mills rose a ghostly spurt of flame. He ran to the edge. The street lights glared dizzily upward. Two men were tiny round blobs of hat and shoulders. He swung around.

The thing was in the doorway. The voice was no longer solicitous but moronically playful, each sentence ending in a titter.

"Why, Mr. Wran, why have you come up here? We're all alone. Just think, I might push you off."

The thing came slowly toward him. He moved backward until his heels touched the low parapet. Without knowing why, or what he was going to do, he dropped to his knees. He dared not look at the face as it came nearer, a focus for the worst in the world, a gathering point for poisons from everywhere. Then the lucidity of terror took possession of his mind, and words formed on his lips.

"I will obey you. You are my god," he said. "You have supreme power over man and his animals and his machines. You rule this city and all others. I recognize that."

Again the titter, closer. "Why, Mr. Wran, you never talked like this before. Do you mean it?"

"The world is yours to do with as you will, save or tear to pieces," he answered fawningly, the words automatically fitting themselves together in vaguely liturgical patterns. "I recognize that. I will praise, I will sacrifice. In smoke and soot I will worship you for ever."

The voice did not answer. He looked up. There was only Miss Millick, deathly pale and swaying drunkenly. Her eyes were closed. He caught her as she wobbled toward him. His knees gave way under the added weight and they sank down together on the edge of the roof.

After a while she began to twitch. Small noises came from her throat and her eyelids edged open.

"Come on, we'll go downstairs," he murmured jerkily, trying to draw her up. "You're feeling bad."

"I'm terribly dizzy," she whispered. "I must have fainted, I didn't eat enough. And then I'm so nervous lately, about the war and everything, I guess. Why, we're on the roof! Did you bring me up here to get some air? Or did I come up without knowing it? I'm awfully foolish. I used to walk in my sleep, my mother said."

As he helped her down the stairs, she turned and looked at him. "Why, Mr. Wran," she said, faintly, "you've got a big black smudge on your forehead. Here, let me get it off for you." Weakly she rubbed at it with her handkerchief. She started to sway again and he steadied her.

"No, I'll be all right," she said. "Only I feel cold. What happened, Mr. Wran? Did I have some sort of fainting spell?"

He told her it was something like that.

Later, riding home in the empty elevated car, he wondered how long he would be safe from the thing. It was a purely practical problem. He had no way of knowing, but instinct told him he had satisfied the brute for some time. Would it want more when it came again? Time enough to answer that question when it arose. It might be hard, he realized, to keep out of an insane asylum. With Helen and Ronny to protect, as well as himself, he would have to be careful and tight-lipped. He began to speculate as to how many other men and women had seen the thing or things like it.

The elevated slowed and lurched in a familiar fashion. He looked at the roofs near the curve. They seemed very ordinary, as if what made them impressive had gone away for a while.

Gene Wolfe

Seven American Nights

Gene Wolfe is the finest writer in the contemporary science fiction field and is reviewed as a major American writer. His works range throughout the varieties of the fantastic to stories and novels of contemporary life. "Seven American Nights" is a masterpiece of SF by a former fan of *Weird Tales,* a complex and horrifying vision of the future: strange, elusive, ambiguous. It is a direct descendent of Poe's "Mellonta Tauta" and J. Leslie Mitchell's *The Last American,* classic satires set in the future; the humor is subtle and ironic. Overtly a simple story, in the end it is a Poesian cryptogram. The theme of drug-induced hallucination is an old one in the literature of the fantastic, never more gracefully or effectively handled than in "Seven American Nights."

ESTEEMED AND LEARNED MADAME:

As I last wrote you, it appears to me likely that your son Nadan (may Allah preserve him!) has left the old capital and traveled—of his own will or another's—north into the region about the Bay of Delaware. My conjecture is now confirmed by the discovery in those regions of the notebook I enclose. It is not of American manufacture, as you see; and though it holds only the records of a single week, several suggestive items therein provide us new reason to hope.

I have photocopied the contents to guide me in my investigations; but I am alert to the probability that you, Madame, with your superior knowledge of the young man we seek, may discover implications I have overlooked. Should that be the case, I urge you to write me at once.

Though I hesitate to mention it in connection with so encouraging a finding, your most recently due remission has not yet arrived. I assume that this tardiness results from the procrastination of the mails, which is here truly abominable. I must warn you, however, that I shall be forced to discontinue the search unless funds sufficient for my expenses are forthcoming before the advent of winter.

With inexpressible respect,
HASSAN KERBELAI

Here I am at last! After twelve mortal days aboard the *Princess Fatimah*—twelve days of cold and ennui—twelve days of bad food and throbbing engines—the joy of being on land again is like the delight a condemned man must feel when a letter from the shah snatches him from beneath the very blade of death. America! America! Dull days are no more! They say that everyone who comes here either loves or hates you, America— by Allah I love you now!

Having begun this record at last, I find I do not know where to begin. I had been reading travel diaries before I left home; and so when I saw you, O Book, lying so square and thick in your stall in the bazaar—why should I not have adventures too, and write a book like Osman Aga's? Few come to this sad country at the world's edge after all, and most who do land farther up the coast.

And that gives me the clue I was looking for—how to begin. America began for me as colored water. When I went out on deck yesterday morning, the ocean had changed from green to yellow. I had never heard of such a thing before, neither in my reading, nor in my talks with Uncle Mirza, who was here thirty years ago. I am afraid I behaved like the greatest fool imaginable, running about the ship babbling, and looking over the side every few minutes to make certain the rich mustard color was still there and would not vanish the way things do in dreams when we try to point them out to someone else. The steward told me he knew. Golam Gassem the grain merchant (whom I had tried to avoid meeting for the entire trip until that moment) said, "Yes, yes," and turned away in a fashion that showed he had been avoiding me too, and that it was going to take more of a miracle than yellow water to change his feelings.

One of the few native Americans in first class came out just then: Mister—as the style is here—Tallman, husband of the lovely Madam Tallman, who really deserves such a tall man as myself. (Whether her husband chose that name in self-derision, or in the hope that it would erase others' memory of his infirmity; or whether it was his father's, and is merely one of the countless ironies of fate, I do not know. There was something wrong with his back.) As if I had not made enough spectacle of myself already, I took this Mr. Tallman by the sleeve and told him to look over the side, explaining that the sea had turned yellow. I am afraid Mr. Tallman turned white himself instead, and turned something else too—his back— looking as though he would have struck me if he dared. It was comic enough, I suppose—I heard some of the other passengers chuckling about it afterward—but I don't believe I have seen such hatred in a human face before. Just then the captain came strolling up, and I—considerably deflated but not flattened yet, and thinking that he had not overheard Mr. Tallman and me—mentioned for the final time that day that the water had turned yellow. "I know," the captain said. "It's his country"—there he jerked his head in the direction of the pitiful Mr. Tallman—"bleeding to death."

*   *   *

Here it is evening again, and I see that I stopped writing last night before I had so much as described my first sight of the coast. Well, so be it. At home it is midnight, or nearly, and the life of the cafés is at its height. How I wish that I were there now, with you, Yasmin, not webbed among these red- and purple-clad strangers, who mob their own streets like an invading army, and duck into their houses like rats into their holes. But you, Yasmin, or Mother, or whoever may read this, will want to know of my day—only you are sometimes to think of me as I am now, bent over an old, scarred table in a decayed room with two beds, listening to the hastening feet in the streets outside.

I slept late this morning; I suppose I was more tired from the voyage than I realized. By the time I woke, the whole of the city was alive around me, with vendors crying fish and fruits under my shuttered window, and the great wooden wains the Americans call *trucks* rumbling over the broken concrete on their wide iron wheels, bringing up goods from the ships in the Potomac anchorage. One sees very odd teams here, Yasmin. When I went to get my breakfast (one must go outside to reach the lobby and dining room in these American hotels, which I would think would be very inconvenient in bad weather) I saw one of these *trucks* with two oxen, a horse, and a mule in the traces, which would have made you laugh. The drivers crack their whips all the time.

The first impression one gets of America is that it is not as poor as one has been told. It is only later that it becomes apparent how much has been handed down from the previous century. The streets here are paved, but they are old and broken. There are fine, though decayed, buildings everywhere (this hotel is one—the Inn of Holidays, it is called), more modern in appearance than the ones we see at home, where for so long traditional architecture was enforced by law. We are on Maine Street, and when I had finished my breakfast (it was very good, and very cheap by our standards, though I am told it is impossible to get anything out of season here), I asked the manager where I should go to see the sights of the city. He is a short and phenomenally ugly man, something of a hunchback, as so many of them are. "There are no tours," he said. "Not any more."

I told him that I simply wanted to wander about by myself, and perhaps sketch a bit.

"You can do that. North for the buildings, south for the theater, west for the park. Do you plan to go to the park, Mr. Jaffarzadeh?"

"I haven't decided yet."

"You should hire at least two securities if you go to the park—I can recommend an agency."

"I have my pistol."

"You'll need more than that, sir."

Naturally, I decided then and there that I would go to the park, and alone. But I have determined not to spend this, the sole, small coin of adventure this land has provided me so far, before I discover what else it may offer to enrich my existence.

Accordingly, I set off for the north when I left the hotel. I have not, thus far, seen this city, or any American city, by night. What they might be like if these people thronged the streets then, as we do, I cannot imagine. Even by clearest day, there is the impression of carnival, of some mad circus whose performance began a hundred or more years ago and has not ended yet.

At first it seemed that only every fourth or fifth person suffered some trace of the genetic damage that destroyed the old America, but as I grew more accustomed to the streets, and thus less quick to dismiss as Americans and no more the unhappy old woman who wanted me to buy flowers and the boy who dashed shrieking between the wheels of a *truck,* and began instead to look at them as human beings—in other words, just as I would look at some chance-met person on one of our own streets—I saw that there was hardly a soul not marked in some way. These deformities, though they are individually hideous, in combination with the bright, ragged clothing so common here, give the meanest assemblage the character of a pageant. I sauntered along, hardly out of earshot of one group of street musicians before encountering another, and in a few strides passed a man so tall that he was taller seated on a low step than I standing; a bearded dwarf with a withered arm; and a woman whose face had been divided by some devil into halves, one large-eyed and idiotically despairing, the other squinting and sneering.

There can be no question about it—Yasmin must not read this. I have been sitting here for an hour at least, staring at the flame of the candle. Sitting and listening to something that from time to time beats against the steel shutters that close the window of this room. The truth is that I am paralyzed by a fear that entered me—I do not know from where—yesterday, and has been growing ever since.

Everyone knows that these Americans were once the most skilled creators of consciousness-altering substances the world has ever seen. The same knowledge that permitted them to forge the chemicals that destroyed them, so that they might have bread that never staled, innumerable poisons for vermin, and a host of unnatural materials for every purpose, also contrived synthetic alkaloids that produced endless feverish imaginings.

Surely some, at least, of these skills remain. Or if they do not, then some of the substances themselves, preserved for eighty or a hundred years in hidden cabinets, and no doubt growing more dangerous as the world forgets them. I think that someone on the ship may have administered some such drug to me.

That is out at last! I felt so much better at having written it—it took a great deal of effort—that I took several turns about this room. Now that I have written it down, I do not believe it at all.

Still, last night I dreamed of that bread, of which I first read in the little schoolroom of Uncle Mirza's country house. It was no complex, towering "literary" dream such as I have sometimes had, and embroidered, and boasted of afterward over coffee. Just the vision of a loaf of soft white bread lying on a plate in the center of a small table: bread that retained the fragrance of the oven (surely one of the most delicious in the world) though it was smeared with gray mold. Why would the Americans wish such a thing? Yet all the historians agree that they did, just as they wished their own corpses to appear living forever.

It is only this country, with its colorful, fetid streets, deformed people, and harsh, alien language, that makes me feel as drugged and dreaming as I do. Praise Allah that I can speak Farsi to you, O Book. Will you believe that I have taken out every article of clothing I have, just to read the makers' labels? Will *I* believe it, for that matter, when I read this at home?

The public buildings to the north—once the great center, as I understand it, of political activity—offer a severe contrast to the streets of the still-occupied areas. In the latter, the old buildings are in the last stages of decay, or have been repaired by makeshift and inappropriate means; but they seethe with the life of those who depend upon such commercial activity as the port yet provides, and with those who depend on them, and so on. The monumental buildings, because they were constructed of the most imperishable materials, appear almost whole, though there are a few fallen columns and sagging porticos, and in several places small trees (mostly the sad *carpinus caroliniana,* I believe) have rooted in the crevices of walls. Still, if it is true, as has been written, that Time's beard is gray not with the passage of years but with the dust of ruined cities, it is here that he trails it. These imposing shells are no more than that. They were built, it would seem, to be cooled and ventilated by machinery. Many are windowless, their interiors now no more than sunless caves, reeking of decay; into these I did not venture. Others had had fixed windows that once were mere walls of glass; and a few of these remained, so that I was able to sketch their construction. Most, however, are destroyed. Time's beard has swept away their very shards.

Though these old buildings (with one or two exceptions) are deserted, I encountered several beggars. They seemed to be Americans whose deformities preclude their doing useful work, and one cannot help but feel sorry for them, though their appearance is often as distasteful as their importunities. They offered to show me the former residence of their Padshah, and as an excuse to give them a few coins I accompanied them, making them first pledge to leave me when I had seen it.

The structure they pointed out to me was situated at the end of a long avenue lined with impressive buildings; so I suppose they must have been correct in thinking it once important. Hardly more than the foundation, some rubble, and one ruined wing remain now, and it cannot have been originally of an enduring construction. No doubt it was actually a summer palace or something of that kind. The beggars have now forgotten its very name, and call it merely "the white house."

When they had guided me to this relic, I pretended that I wanted to make drawings, and they left as they had promised. In five or ten minutes, however, one particularly enterprising fellow returned. He had no lower jaw, so that I had quite a bit of difficulty in understanding him at first; but after we had shouted back and forth a good deal—I telling him to depart and threatening to kill him on the spot, and he protesting—I realized that he was forced to make the sound of *d* for *b, n* for *m,* and *t* for *p;* and after that we got along better.

I will not attempt to render his speech phonetically, but he said that since I had been so generous, he wished to show me a great secret—something foreigners like myself did not even realize existed.

"Clean water," I suggested.

"No, no. A great, great secret, Captain. You think all this is dead." He waved a misshapen hand at the desolated structures that surrounded us.

"Indeed I do."

"One still lives. You would like to see it? I will guide. Don't worry about the others—they're afraid of me. I will drive them away."

"If you are leading me into some kind of ambush, I warn you, you will be the first to suffer."

He looked at me very seriously for a moment, and a man seemed to stare from the eyes in that ruined face, so that I felt a twinge of real sympathy. "See there? The big building to the south, on Pennsylvania? Captain, my father's father's father was chief of a department" ("detartnent") "there. I would not betray you."

From what I have read of this country's policies in the days of his father's father's father, that was little enough reassurance, but I followed him.

We went diagonally across several blocks, passing through two ruined buildings. There were human bones in both, and remembering his boast, I asked him if they had belonged to the workers there.

"No, no." He tapped his chest again—a habitual gesture, I suppose—and scooping up a skull from the floor, held it beside his own head so that I could see that it exhibited cranial deformities much like his own. "We sleep here, to be shut behind strong walls from the things that come at night. We die here, mostly in wintertime. No one buries us."

"You should bury each other," I said.

He tossed down the skull, which shattered on the terrazzo floor, waking a thousand dismal echoes. "No shovel, and few are strong. But come with me."

At first sight the building to which he led me looked more decayed than many of the ruins. One of its spires had fallen, and the bricks lay in the street. Yet when I looked again, I saw that there must be something in what he said. The broken windows had been closed with ironwork at least as well made as the shutters that protect my room here; and the door, though old and weathered, was tightly shut, and looked strong.

"This is the museum," my guide told me. "The only part left, almost, of the Silent City that still lives in the old way. Would you like to see inside?"

I told him that I doubted that we would be able to enter.

"Wonderful machines." He pulled at my sleeve. "You *see* in, Captain. Come."

We followed the building's walls around several corners, and at last entered a sort of alcove at the rear. Here there was a grill set in the weed-grown ground, and the beggar gestured toward it proudly. I made him

Here it is evening again, and I see that I stopped writing last night before I had so much as described my first sight of the coast. Well, so be it. At home it is midnight, or nearly, and the life of the cafés is at its height. How I wish that I were there now, with you, Yasmin, not webbed among these red- and purple-clad strangers, who mob their own streets like an invading army, and duck into their houses like rats into their holes. But you, Yasmin, or Mother, or whoever may read this, will want to know of my day—only you are sometimes to think of me as I am now, bent over an old, scarred table in a decayed room with two beds, listening to the hastening feet in the streets outside.

I slept late this morning; I suppose I was more tired from the voyage than I realized. By the time I woke, the whole of the city was alive around me, with vendors crying fish and fruits under my shuttered window, and the great wooden wains the Americans call *trucks* rumbling over the broken concrete on their wide iron wheels, bringing up goods from the ships in the Potomac anchorage. One sees very odd teams here, Yasmin. When I went to get my breakfast (one must go outside to reach the lobby and dining room in these American hotels, which I would think would be very inconvenient in bad weather) I saw one of these *trucks* with two oxen, a horse, and a mule in the traces, which would have made you laugh. The drivers crack their whips all the time.

The first impression one gets of America is that it is not as poor as one has been told. It is only later that it becomes apparent how much has been handed down from the previous century. The streets here are paved, but they are old and broken. There are fine, though decayed, buildings everywhere (this hotel is one—the Inn of Holidays, it is called), more modern in appearance than the ones we see at home, where for so long traditional architecture was enforced by law. We are on Maine Street, and when I had finished my breakfast (it was very good, and very cheap by our standards, though I am told it is impossible to get anything out of season here), I asked the manager where I should go to see the sights of the city. He is a short and phenomenally ugly man, something of a hunchback, as so many of them are. "There are no tours," he said. "Not any more."

I told him that I simply wanted to wander about by myself, and perhaps sketch a bit.

"You can do that. North for the buildings, south for the theater, west for the park. Do you plan to go to the park, Mr. Jaffarzadeh?"

"I haven't decided yet."

"You should hire at least two securities if you go to the park—I can recommend an agency."

"I have my pistol."

"You'll need more than that, sir."

Naturally, I decided then and there that I would go to the park, and alone. But I have determined not to spend this, the sole, small coin of adventure this land has provided me so far, before I discover what else it may offer to enrich my existence.

Accordingly, I set off for the north when I left the hotel. I have not, thus

far, seen this city, or any American city, by night. What they might be like if
these people thronged the streets then, as we do, I cannot imagine. Even by
clearest day, there is the impression of carnival, of some mad circus whose
performance began a hundred or more years ago and has not ended yet.

At first it seemed that only every fourth or fifth person suffered some trace
of the genetic damage that destroyed the old America, but as I grew more
accustomed to the streets, and thus less quick to dismiss as Americans and
no more the unhappy old woman who wanted me to buy flowers and the boy
who dashed shrieking between the wheels of a *truck,* and began instead to
look at them as human beings—in other words, just as I would look at some
chance-met person on one of our own streets—I saw that there was hardly a
soul not marked in some way. These deformities, though they are individually hideous, in combination with the bright, ragged clothing so common here,
give the meanest assemblage the character of a pageant. I sauntered along,
hardly out of earshot of one group of street musicians before encountering
another, and in a few strides passed a man so tall that he was taller seated on
a low step than I standing; a bearded dwarf with a withered arm; and a
woman whose face had been divided by some devil into halves, one
large-eyed and idiotically despairing, the other squinting and sneering.

There can be no question about it—Yasmin must not read this. I have
been sitting here for an hour at least, staring at the flame of the candle.
Sitting and listening to something that from time to time beats against the
steel shutters that close the window of this room. The truth is that I am
paralyzed by a fear that entered me—I do not know from where—yesterday,
and has been growing ever since.

Everyone knows that these Americans were once the most skilled creators
of consciousness-altering substances the world has ever seen. The same
knowledge that permitted them to forge the chemicals that destroyed them,
so that they might have bread that never staled, innumerable poisons for
vermin, and a host of unnatural materials for every purpose, also contrived
synthetic alkaloids that produced endless feverish imaginings.

Surely some, at least, of these skills remain. Or if they do not, then some of
the substances themselves, preserved for eighty or a hundred years in hidden
cabinets, and no doubt growing more dangerous as the world forgets them. I
think that someone on the ship may have administered some such drug to
me.

That is out at last! I felt so much better at having written it—it took a great
deal of effort—that I took several turns about this room. Now that I have
written it down, I do not believe it at all.

Still, last night I dreamed of that bread, of which I first read in the little
schoolroom of Uncle Mirza's country house. It was no complex, towering
"literary" dream such as I have sometimes had, and embroidered, and
boasted of afterward over coffee. Just the vision of a loaf of soft white bread
lying on a plate in the center of a small table: bread that retained the
fragrance of the oven (surely one of the most delicious in the world) though it

stand some distance off, then knelt as he had indicated to look through the grill.

There was a window of unshattered glass beyond the grill. It was very soiled now, but I could see through into the basement of the building, and there, just as the beggar had said, stood an orderly array of complex mechanisms.

I stared for some time, trying to gain some notion of their purpose; and at length an old American appeared among them, peering at one and then another, and whisking the shining bars and gears with a rag.

The beggar had crept closer as I watched. He pointed at the old man, and said, "Still come from north and south to study here. Someday we are great again." Then I thought of my own lovely country, whose eclipse—though without genetic damage—lasted twenty-three hundred years. And I gave him money, and told him that, yes, I was certain America would be great again someday, and left him, and returned here.

I have opened the shutters so that I can look across the city to the obelisk and catch the light of the dying sun. Its fields and valleys of fire do not seem more alien to me, or more threatening, than this strange, despondent land. Yet I know that we are all one—the beggar, the old man moving among the machines of a dead age, those machines themselves, the sun, and I. A century ago, when this was a thriving city, the philosophers used to speculate on the reason that each neutron and proton and electron exhibited the same mass as all the others of its kind. Now we know that there is only one particle of each variety, moving backward and forward in time, an electron when it travels as we do, a positron when its temporal displacement is retrograde, the same few particles appearing billions of billions of times to make up a single object, and the same few particles forming all the objects, so that we are all the sketches, as it were, of the same set of pastels.

I have gone out to eat. There is a good restaurant not far from the hotel, better even than the dining room here. When I came back the manager told me that there is to be a play tonight at the theater, and assured me that because it is so close to his hotel (in truth, he is very proud of this theater, and no doubt its proximity to his hotel is the only circumstance that permits the hotel to remain open) I will be in no danger if I go without an escort. To tell the truth, I am a little ashamed that I did not hire a boat today to take me across the channel to the park; so now I will attend the play, and dare the night streets.

Here I am again, returned to this too-large, too-bare, uncarpeted room, which is already beginning to seem a second home, with no adventures to retail from the dangerous benighted streets. The truth is that the theater is hardly more than a hundred paces to the south. I kept my hand on the butt of my pistol and walked along with a great many other people (mostly Americans) who were also going to the theater, and felt something of a fool.

The building is as old as those in the Silent City, I should think; but it has been kept in some repair. There was more of a feeling of gaiety (though to me it was largely an alien gaiety) among the audience than we have at home, and less of the atmosphere of what I may call the sacredness of Art. By that I knew that the drama really is sacred here, as the colorful clothes of the populace make clear in any case. An exaggerated and solemn respect always indicates a loss of faith.

Having recently come from my dinner, I ignored the stands in the lobby at which the Americans—who seem to eat constantly when they can afford it—were selecting various cold meats and pastries, and took my place in the theater proper. I was hardly in my seat before a pipe-puffing old gentleman, an American, desired me to move in order that he might reach his own. I stood up gladly, of course, and greeted him as "Grandfather," as our own politeness (if not theirs) demands. But while he was settling himself and I was still standing beside him, I caught a glimpse of his face from the exact angle at which I had seen it this afternoon, and recognized him as the old man I had watched through the grill.

Here was a difficult situation. I wanted very much to draw him into conversation, but I could not well confess that I had been spying on him. I puzzled over the question until the lights were extinguished and the play began.

It was Vidal's *Visit to a Small Planet,* one of the classics of the old American theater, a play I have often read about but never (until now) seen performed. I would have liked it much better if it had been done with the costumes and settings of its proper period; unhappily, the director had chosen to "modernize" the entire affair, just as we sometimes present *Rustam Beg* as if Rustam had been a hero of the war just past. General Powers was a contemporary American soldier with the mannerisms of a cowardly bandit, Spelding a publisher of libelous broadsheets, and so on. The only characters that gave me much pleasure were the limping spaceman, Kreton, and the ingenue, Ellen Spelding, played as and by a radiantly beautiful American blonde.

All through the first act my mind had been returning (particularly during Spelding's speeches) to the problem of the old man beside me. By the time the curtain fell, I had decided that the best way to start a conversation might be to offer to fetch him a kebab—or whatever he might want—from the lobby, since his thread-bare appearance suggested that he might be ready enough to be treated, and the weakness of his legs would provide an admirable excuse. I tried the gambit as soon as the flambeaux were relit, and it worked as well as I could have wished. When I returned with a paper tray of sandwiches and bitter drinks, he remarked to me quite spontaneously that he had noticed me flexing my right hand during the performance.

"Yes," I said, "I had been writing a good deal before I came here."

That set him off, and he began to discourse, frequently with a great deal more detail than I could comprehend, on the topic of writing machines. At last I halted the flow with some question that must have revealed that I knew less of the subject than he had supposed. "Have you ever," he asked me, "carved a letter in a potato, and moistened it with a stamp pad, and used it to imprint paper?"

"As a child, yes. We use a turnip, but no doubt the principle is the same."

"Exactly; and the principle is that of extended abstraction. I ask you—on the lowest level, what is communication?"

"Talking, I suppose."

His shrill laugh rose above the hubbub of the audience. "Not at all! Smell"—here he gripped my arm—"smell is the essence of communication. Look at that word *essence* itself. When you smell another human being, you take chemicals from his body into your own, analyze them, and from the analysis you accurately deduce his emotional state. You do it so constantly and so automatically that you are largely unconscious of it, and say simply, 'He seemed frightened,' or 'He was angry.' You see?"

I nodded, interested in spite of myself.

"When you speak, you are telling another how you would smell if you smelled as you should and if he could smell you properly from where he stands. It is almost certain that speech was not developed until the glaciations that terminated the Pliocene stimulated mankind to develop fire, and the frequent inhalation of wood smoke had dulled the olfactory organs."

"I see."

"No, you hear—unless you are by chance reading my lips, which in this din would be a useful accomplishment." He took an enormous bite of his sandwich, spilling pink meat that had surely come from no natural animal. "When you write, you are telling the other how you would speak if he could hear you, and when you print with your turnip, you are telling him how you would write. You will notice that we have already reached the third level of abstraction."

I nodded again.

"It used to be believed that only a limited number K of levels of abstraction were possible before the original matter disappeared altogether —some very interesting mathematical work was done about seventy years ago in an attempt to derive a generalized expression for K for various systems. Now we know that the number can be infinite if the array represents an open curve, and that closed curves are also possible."

"I don't understand."

"You are young and handsome—very fine looking, with your wide shoulders and black mustache; let us suppose a young woman loves you. If you and I and she were crouched now on the limb of a tree, you would scent her desire. Today, perhaps she tells you of that desire. But it is also possible, is it not, that she may write you of her desire?"

Remembering Yasmin's letters, I assented.

"But suppose those letters are perfumed—a musky, sweet perfume. You understand? A closed curve—the perfume is not the odor of her body, but an artificial simulation of it. It may not be what she feels, but it is what she tells you she feels. Your real love is for a whale, a male deer, and a bed of roses."

He was about to say more, but the curtain went up for the second act.

I found that act both more enjoyable, and more painful, than the first. The opening scene, in which Kreton (soon joined by Ellen) reads the mind of the family cat, was exceptionally effective. The concealed orchestra furnished music to indicate cat thoughts; I wish I knew the identity of the composer, but my playbill does not provide the information. The bedroom wall became a shadow screen, where we saw silhouettes of cats catching birds, and then, when Ellen tickled the real cat's belly, making love. As I have said, Kreton and Ellen were the play's best characters. The juxtaposition of Ellen's willowy beauty and high-spirited naïveté and Kreton's clear desire for her illuminated perfectly the Paphian difficulties that would confront a powerful telepath, were such persons to exist.

On the other hand, Kreton's summoning of the presidents, which closes the act, was as objectionable as it could possibly have been made. The foreign ruler conjured up by error was played as a Turk, and as broadly as possible. I confess to feeling some prejudice against that bloodthirsty race myself, but what was done was indefensible. When the president of the World Council appeared, he was portrayed as an American.

By the end of that scene I was in no very good mood. I think that I have not yet shaken off the fatigues of the crossing; and they, combined with a fairly strenuous day spent prowling around the ruins of the Silent City, had left me now in that state in which the smallest irritation takes on the dimensions of a mortal insult. The old curator beside me discerned my irascibility, but mistook the reason for it, and began to apologize for the state of the American stage, saying that all the performers of talent emigrated as soon as they gained recognition, and returned only when they had failed on the eastern shore of the Atlantic.

"No, no," I said. "Kreton and the girl are very fine, and the rest of the cast is at least adequate."

He seemed not to have heard me. "They pick them up wherever they can—they choose them for their faces. When they have appeared in three plays, they call themselves actors. At the Smithsonian—I am employed there, perhaps I've already mentioned it—we have tapes of real theater: Laurence Olivier, Orson Welles, Katharine Cornell. Spelding is a barber, or at least he was. He used to put his chair under the old Kennedy statue and shave the passers-by. Ellen is a trollop, and Powers a drayman. That lame fellow Kreton used to snare sailors for a singing house on Portland Street."

His disparagement of his own national culture embarrassed me, though it put me in a better mood. (I have noticed that the two often go together—perhaps I am secretly humiliated to find that people of no great importance can affect my interior state with a few words or some mean service.) I took my leave of him and went to the confectioner's stand in the lobby. The Americans have a very pretty custom of duplicating the speckled eggs of wild birds in marzipan, and I bought a box of these—not only because I wanted to try them myself, but because I felt certain they would prove a treat for the old man, who must seldom have enough money to afford luxuries of that kind. I was quite correct—he ate them eagerly. But when I sampled one, I found its odor (as though I were eating artificial violets) so unpleasant that I did not take another.

"We were speaking of writing," the old man said. "The closed curve and the open curve. I did not have time to make the point that both could be achieved mechanically; but the monograph I am now developing turns upon that very question, and it happens that I have examples with me. First the closed curve. In the days when our president was among the world's ten most powerful men—the reality of the Paul Laurent you see on the stage there—each president received hundreds of requests every day for his signature. To have granted them would have taken hours of his time. To have refused them would have raised a brigade of enemies."

"What did they do?"

"They called upon the resources of science. That science devised the machine that wrote this."

From within his clean, worn coat he drew a folded sheet of paper. I opened it and saw that it was covered with the text of what appeared to be a public address, written in a childish scrawl. Mentally attempting to review the list of the American presidents I had seen in some digest of world history long ago, I asked whose hand it was.

"The machine's. Whose hand is being imitated here is one of the things I am attempting to discover."

In the dim light of the theater it was almost impossible to make out the faded script, but I caught the word *Sardinia.* "Surely, by correlating the contents to historical events it should be possible to date it quite accurately."

The old man shook his head. "The text itself was composed by another machine to achieve some national psychological effect. It is not probable that it bears any real relationship to the issues of its day. But now look here." He drew out a second sheet, and unfolded it for me. So far as I could see, it was completely blank. I was still staring at it when the curtain went up.

As Kreton moved his toy aircraft across the stage, the old man took a final egg and turned away to watch the play. There was still half a carton left, and I, thinking that he might want more later, and afraid that they might be spilled from my lap and lost underfoot, closed the box and slipped it into the side pocket of my jacket.

The special effects for the landing of the second spaceship were well done; but there was something else in the third act that gave me as much pleasure as the cat scene in the second. The final curtain hinges on the device our poets call *the Peri's asphodel,* a trick so shopworn now that it is acceptable only if it can be presented in some new light. The one used here was to have John—Ellen's lover—find Kreton's handkerchief and, remarking that it seemed perfumed, bury his nose in it. For an instant, the shadow wall used at the beginning of the second act was illuminated again to graphically (or I should say, pornographically) present Ellen's desire, conveying to the audience that John had, for that moment, shared the telepathic abilities of Kreton, whom all of them had now entirely forgotten.

The device was extremely effective, and left me feeling that I had by no means wasted my evening. I joined the general applause as the cast appeared to take their bows; then, as I was turning to leave, I noticed that the old man appeared very ill. I asked if he were all right, and he confessed ruefully that he had eaten too much, and thanked me again for my kindness—which must at that time have taken a great deal of resolution.

I helped him out of the theater, and when I saw that he had no transportation but his feet, told him I would take him home. He thanked me again, and informed me that he had a room at the museum.

Thus the half-block walk from the theater to my hotel was transformed into a journey of three or four kilometers, taken by moonlight, much of it through rubble-strewn avenues of the deserted parts of the city.

During the day I had hardly glanced at the stark skeleton of the old highway. Tonight, when we walked beneath its ruined overpasses, they seemed inexpressibly ancient and sinister. It occurred to me then that there may be a time-flaw, such as astronomers report from space, somewhere in the Atlantic. How is it that this western shore is more antiquated in the remains of a civilization not yet a century dead than we are in the shadow of Darius? May it not be that every ship that plows that sea moves through ten thousand years?

For the past hour—I find I cannot sleep—I have been debating whether to make this entry. But what good is a travel journal, if one does not enter everything? I will revise it on the trip home, and present a cleansed copy for my mother and Yasmin to read.

It appears that the scholars at the museum have no income but that derived from the sale of treasures gleaned from the past; and I bought a vial of what is supposed to be the greatest creation of the old hallucinatory chemists from the woman who helped me get the old man into bed. It is—it was—about half the height of my smallest finger. Very probably it was alcohol and nothing more, though I paid a substantial price.

I was sorry I had bought it before I left, and still more sorry when I arrived here; but at the time it seemed that this would be my only opportunity, and I could think of nothing but to seize the adventure. After I have swallowed the drug I will be able to speak with authority about these things for the remainder of my life.

Here is what I have done. I have soaked the porous sugar of one of the eggs with the fluid. The moisture will soon dry up. The drug—if there is a drug—will remain. Then I will rattle the eggs together in an empty drawer, and each day, beginning tomorrow night, I will eat one egg.

I am writing today before I go down to breakfast, partly because I suspect that the hotel does not serve so early. Today I intend to visit the park on the other side of the channel. If it is as dangerous as they say, it is very likely I will not return to make an entry tonight. If I do return—well, I will plan for that when I am here again.

After I had blown out my candle last night I could not sleep, though I was tired to the bone. Perhaps it was only the excitement of the long walk back from the museum; but I could not free my mind from the image of Ellen. My wandering thoughts associated her with the eggs, and I imagined myself Kreton, sitting up in bed with the cat on my lap. In my daydream (I was not asleep) Ellen brought me my breakfast on a tray, and the breakfast consisted of the six candy eggs.

When my mind had exhausted itself with this kind of imagery, I decided to have the manager procure a girl for me so that I could rid myself of the accumulated tensions of the voyage. After about an hour, during which I sat up reading, he arrived with three; and when he had given me a glimpse of them through the half-open door, he slipped inside and shut it behind him, leaving them standing in the corridor. I told him I had only asked for one.

"I know, Mr. Jaffarzadeh, I know. But I thought you might like to have a choice."

None of them—from the glimpse I had had—resembled Ellen; but I thanked him for his thoughtfulness and suggested that he bring them in.

"I wanted to tell you first, sir, that you must allow me to set the price with them—I can get them for much less than you, sir, because they know they cannot deceive me, and they must depend on me to bring them to my guests in the future." He named a sum that was in fact quite trivial.

"That will be fine," I said. "Bring them in."

He bowed and smiled, making his pinched and miserly face as pleasant as possible and reminding me very much of a picture I had once seen of an imp summoned before the court of Suleiman. "But first, sir, I wished to inform you that if you would like all three—together—you may have them for the price of two. And should you desire only two of the three, you may have them for one and one-half the price of one. All are very lovely, and I thought you might want to consider it."

"Very well, I have considered it. Show them in."

"I will light another candle," he said, bustling about the room. "There is no charge, sir, for candles at the rate you're paying. I can put the girls on your bill as well. They'll be down as room service—you understand, I'm sure."

When the second candle was burning and he had positioned it to his liking on the nightstand between the two beds, he opened the door and waved in the girls, saying, "I'll go now. Take what you like and send out the others." (I feel certain this was a stratagem—he felt I would have difficulty in getting any to leave, and so would have to pay for all three.)

Yasmin must never see this—that is decided. It is not just that this entire incident would disturb her greatly, but because of what happened next. I was sitting on the bed nearest the door, hoping to decide quickly which of the three most resembled the girl who had played Ellen. The first was too short, with a wan, pinched face. The second was tall and blonde, but plump. The third, who seemed to stumble as she entered, exactly resembled Yasmin.

For a few seconds I actually believed it was she. Science has so accustomed us to devising and accepting theories to account for the facts we observe, however fantastic, that our minds must begin their manufacture before we are aware of it. Yasmin had grown lonely for me. She had booked passage a few days after my own departure, or perhaps had flown, daring the notorious American landing facilities. Arriving here, she had made inquiries at the consulate, and was approaching my door as the manager lit his candle, and not knowing what was taking place had entered with prostitutes he had engaged.

It was all moonshine, of course. I jumped to my feet and held up the candle, and saw that the third girl, though she had Yasmin's large, dark eyes and rounded little chin, was not she. For all her night-black hair and delicate features, she was indisputably an American; and as she came toward me (encouraged, no doubt, because she had attracted my attention) I saw that like Kreton in the play she had a club foot.

As you see, I returned alive from the park after all. Tonight before I retire I will eat an egg; but first I will briefly set down my experiences.

The park lies on the opposite side of the Washington Channel, between the city and the river. It can be reached by land only at the north end. Not choosing to walk so far and return, I hired a little boat with a tattered red sail to carry me to the southern tip, which is called Hains Point. Here there was a fountain, I am told, in the old times; but nothing remains of it now.

We had clear, sunny spring weather, and made our way over exhilarating swells of wave with nothing of the deadly wallowing that oppressed me so much aboard the *Princess Fatimah*. I sat in the bow and watched the rolling greenery of the park on one side of the channel and the ruins of the old fort on the other, while an elderly man handled the tiller, and his thin, sun-browned granddaughter, aged about eleven, worked the sail.

When we rounded the point, the old man told me that for very little more he would take me across to Arlington to see the remains of what is supposed to be the largest building of the country's antiquity. I refused, determined to save that experience for another time, and we landed where a part of the ancient concrete coping remained intact.

The tracks of old roads run up either shore; but I decided to avoid them, and made my way up the center, keeping to the highest ground in so far as I could. Once, no doubt, the whole area was devoted to pleasure. Very little remains, however, of the pavilions and statuary that must have dotted the ground. There are little, worn-away hills that may once have been rockeries but are now covered with soil, and many stagnant pools. In a score of places I saw the burrows of the famous giant American rats, though I never saw the animals themselves. To judge from the holes, their size has not been exaggerated—there were several I could have entered with ease.

The wild dogs, against which I had been warned by both the hotel manager and the old boatman, began to follow me after I had walked about a kilometer north. They are short-haired, and typically blotched with black and brown flecked with white. I would say their average weight was about twenty-five kilos. With their erect ears and alert, intelligent faces they did not seem particularly dangerous; but I soon noticed that whichever way I turned, the ones in back of me edged nearer. I sat on a stone with my back to a pool and made several quick sketches of them, then decided to try my pistol. They did not seem to know what it was, so I was able to center the red aiming laser very nicely on one big fellow's chest before I pressed the stud for a high energy pulse.

For a long time afterward, I heard the melancholy howling of these dogs behind me. Perhaps they were mourning their fallen leader. Twice I came across rusting machines that may have been used to take invalids through the gardens in such fair weather as I myself experienced today. Uncle Mirza says I am a good colorist, but I despair of ever matching the green-haunted blacks with which the declining sun painted the park.

I met no one until I had almost reached the piers of the abandoned railway bridge. Then four or five Americans who pretended to beg surrounded me. The dogs, who as I understand it live mostly upon the refuse cast up by the river, were more honest in their intentions and cleaner in their persons. If these people had been like the pitiful creatures I had met in the Silent City, I would have thrown them a few coins; but they were more or less able-bodied men and women who could have worked, and chose instead to rob. I told them that I had been forced to kill a fellow countryman of theirs (not mentioning that he was a dog) who had assaulted me; and asked where I could report the matter to the police. At that they backed off, and permitted me to walk around the northern end of the channel in peace, though not without a thousand savage looks. I returned here without further incident, tired and very well satisfied with my day.

I have eaten one of the eggs! I confess I found it difficult to take the first taste; but marshaling my resolution was like pushing at a wall of glass—all at once the resistance snapped, and I picked the thing up and swallowed it in a few bites. It was piercingly sweet, but there was no other flavor. Now we will see. This is more frightening than the park by far.

Nothing seemed to be happening, so I went out to dinner. It was twilight, and the carnival spirit of the streets was more marked than ever—colored lights above all the shops, and music from the rooftops where the wealthier natives have private gardens. I have been eating mostly at the hotel, but was told of a "good" American-style restaurant not too far south on Maine Street.

It was just as described—people sitting on padded benches in alcoves. The tabletops are of a substance like fine-grained, greasy, artificial stone. They looked very old. I had the Number One Dinner—buff-colored fish soup with the pasty American bread on the side, followed by a sandwich of ground meat and raw vegetables doused with a tomato sauce and served on a soft, oily roll. To tell the truth, I did not much enjoy the meal; but it seems a sort of duty to sample more of the American food than I have thus far.

I am very tempted to end the account of my day here, and in fact I laid down this pen when I had written *thus far,* and made myself ready for bed. Still, what good is a dishonest record? I will let no one see this—just keep it to read over after I get home.

Returning to the hotel from the restaurant, I passed the theater. The thought of seeing Ellen again was irresistible; I bought a ticket and went inside. It was not until I was in my seat that I realized that the bill had changed.

The new play was *Mary Rose.* I saw it done by an English company several years ago, with great authenticity; and it struck me that (like Mary herself) it had far outlived its time. The American production was as inauthentic as the other had been correct. For that reason, it retained—or I should have said it had acquired—a good deal of interest.

Americans are superstitious about the interior of their country, not its coasts, so Mary Rose's island had been shifted to one of the huge central lakes. The highlander, Cameron, had accordingly become a Canadian, played by General Powers' former aide. The Speldings had become the

Morelands, and the Morelands had become Americans. Kreton was Harry, the knife-throwing wounded soldier; and my Ellen had become Mary Rose.

The role suited her so well that I imagined the play had been selected as a vehicle for her. Her height emphasized the character's unnatural immaturity, and her slenderness, and the vulnerability of her pale complexion, would have told us, I think, if the play had not, that she had been victimized unaware. More important than any of these things was a wild and innocent affinity for the supernatural, which she projected to perfection. It was that quality alone (as I now understood) that had made us believe on the preceding night that Kreton's spaceship might land in the Speldings' rose garden—he would have been drawn to Ellen, though he had never seen her. Now it made Mary Rose's disappearances and reappearances plausible and even likely; it was as likely that unseen spirits lusted for Mary Rose as that Lieutenant Blake (previously John Randolf) loved her.

Indeed, it was more likely. And I had no sooner realized that than the whole mystery of *Mary Rose*—which had seemed at once inexplicable and banal when I had seen it well played in Teheran—lay clear before me. We of the audience were the envious and greedy spirits. If the Morelands could not see that one wall of their comfortable drawing room was but a sea of dark faces, if Cameron had never noticed that we were the backdrop of his island, the fault was theirs. By rights then, Mary Rose should have been drawn to us when she vanished. At the end of the second act I began to look for her, and in the beginning of the third I found her, standing silent and unobserved behind the last row of seats. I was only four rows from the stage, but I slipped out of my place as unobtrusively as I could, and crept up the aisle toward her.

I was too late. Before I had gone halfway, it was nearly time for her entrance at the end of the scene. I watched the rest of the play from the back of the theater, but she never returned.

Same night. I am having a good deal of trouble sleeping, though while I was on the ship I slept nine hours a night, and was off as soon as my head touched the pillow.

The truth is that while I lay in bed tonight I recalled the old curator's remark that the actresses were all prostitutes. If it is true and not simply an expression of hatred for younger people whose bodies are still attractive, then I have been a fool to moan over the thought of Mary Rose and Ellen when I might have had the girl herself.

Her name is Ardis Dahl—I just looked it up in the playbill. I am going to the manager's office to consult the city directory there.

Writing before breakfast. Found the manager's office locked last night. It was after two. I put my shoulder against the door and got it open easily enough. (There was no metal socket for the bolt such as we have at home—just a hole mortised in the frame.) The directory listed several Dahls in the city, but since it was nearly eight years out of date it did not inspire a great deal of confidence. I reflected, however, that in a backwater like this people were not likely to move about so much as we do at home, and that if it were not still of some utility, the manager would not be likely to retain it; so I selected the one that appeared from its address to be nearest the theater, and set out.

The streets were completely deserted. I remember thinking that I was now doing what I had previously been so afraid to do, having been frightened of the city by reading. How ridiculous to suppose that robbers would be afoot now, when no one else was. What would they do, stand for hours at the empty corners?

The moon was full and high in the southern sky, showering the street with the lambent white fluid of its light. If it had not been for the sharp, unclean odor so characteristic of American residential areas, I might have thought myself walking through an illustration from some old book of wonder tales, or an actor in a children's pantomime, so bewitched by the scenery that he has forgotten the audience.

(In writing that—which to tell the truth I did not think of at the time, but only now, as I sat here at my table—I realized that that is in fact what must happen to the American girl I have been in the habit of calling Ellen but must now learn to call Ardis. She could never perform as she does if it were not that in some part of her mind her stage became her reality.)

The shadows about my feet were a century old, tracing faithfully the courses they had determined long before New Tabriz came to jewel the lunar face with its sapphire. Webbed with thoughts of her—my Ellen, my Mary Rose, my Ardis!—and with the magic of that pale light that commands all the tides, I was elevated to a degree I cannot well describe.

Then I was seized by the thought that everything I felt might be no more than the effect of the drug.

At once, like someone who falls from a tower and clutches at the very wisps of air, I tried to return myself to reality. I bit the interiors of my cheeks until the blood filled my mouth, and struck the unfeeling wall of the nearest building with my fist. In a moment the pain sobered me. For a quarter hour or more I stood at the curbside, spitting into the gutter and trying to clean and bandage my knuckles with strips torn from my handkerchief. A thousand times I thought what a sight I would be if I did in fact succeed in seeing Ellen, and I comforted myself with the thought that if she were indeed a prostitute it would not matter to her—I could afford her a few additional rials and all would be well.

Yet that thought was not really much comfort. Even when a woman sells her body, a man flatters himself that she would not do so quite so readily were he not who he is. At the very moment I drooled blood into the street, I was congratulating myself on the strong, square face so many have admired; and wondering how I should apologize if in kissing her I smeared her mouth with red.

Perhaps it was some faint sound that brought me to myself; perhaps it was only the consciousness of being watched. I drew my pistol and turned this way and that, but saw nothing.

Yet the feeling endured. I began to walk again; and if there was any sense of unreality remaining, it was no longer the unearthly exultation I had felt earlier. After a few steps I stopped and listened. A dry sound of rattling and scraping had followed me. It too stopped now.

I was nearing the address I had taken from the directory. I confess my mind was filled with fancies in which I was rescued by Ellen herself, who in the end should be more frightened than I, but who would risk her lovely person to save mine. Yet I knew these *were* but fancies, and the thing pursuing me was not, though it crossed my mind more than once that it might be, some *druj* made to seem visible and palpable to me.

Another block, and I had reached the address. It was a house no different from those on either side—built of the rubble of buildings that were older still, three-storied, heavy-doored, and almost without windows. There was a bookshop on the ground floor (to judge by an old sign) with living quarters above it. I crossed the street to see it better, and stood, wrapped again in my dreams, staring at the single thread of yellow light that showed between the shutters of a gable window.

As I watched that light, the feeling of being watched myself grew upon me. Time passed, slipping through the waist of the universe's great hourglass like the eroded soil of this continent slipping down her rivers to the seas. At last my fear and desire—desire for Ellen, fear of whatever it was that glared at me with invisible eyes—drove me to the door of the house. I hammered the wood with the butt of my pistol, though I knew how unlikely it was that any American would answer a knock at such a time of night, and when I had knocked several times, I heard slow steps from within.

The door creaked open until it was caught by a chain. I saw a gray-haired man, fully dressed, holding an old-fashioned long-barreled gun. Behind him a woman lifted a stub of smoking candle to let him see; and though she was clearly much older than Ellen, and was marked, moreover, by the deformities so prevalent here, there was a certain nobility in her features and a certain beauty as well, so that I was reminded of the fallen statue that is said to have stood on an island farther north, and which I have seen pictured.

I told the man that I was a traveler—true enough!—and that I had just arrived by boat from Arlington and had no place to stay, and so had walked into the city until I had noticed the light of his window. I would pay, I said, a silver rial if they would only give me a bed for the night and breakfast in the morning, and I showed them the coin. My plan was to become a guest in the house so that I might discover whether Ellen was indeed one of the inhabitants; if she were, it would have been an easy matter to prolong my stay.

The woman tried to whisper in her husband's ear, but save for a look of nervous irritation he ignored her. "I don't dare let a stranger in." From his voice I might have been a lion, and his gun a trainer's chair. "Not with no one here but my wife and myself."

"I see," I told him. "I quite understand your position."

"You might try the house on the corner," he said, shutting the door, "but don't tell them Dahl sent you." I heard the heavy bar dropped into place at the final word.

I turned away—and then by the mercy of Allah who is indeed compassionate happened to glance back one last time at the thread of yellow between the shutters of that high window. A flicker of scarlet higher still caught my attention, perhaps only because the light of the setting moon now bathed the rooftop from a new angle. I think the creature I glimpsed there had been waiting to leap upon me from behind, but when our eyes met it launched itself toward me. I had barely time to lift my pistol before it struck me and slammed me to the broken pavement of the street.

For a brief period I think I lost consciousness. If my shot had not killed the thing as it fell, I would not be sitting here writing this journal this morning. After half a minute or so I came to myself enough to thrust its weight away, stand up, and rub my bruises. No one had come to my aid; but neither had anyone rushed from the surrounding houses to kill and rob me. I was as alone with the creature that lay dead at my feet as I had been when I only stood watching the window in the house from which it had sprung.

After I found my pistol and assured myself that it was still in working order, I dragged the thing to a spot of moonlight. When I glimpsed it on the roof, it had seemed a feral dog, like the one I had shot in the park. When it lay dead before me, I had thought it a human being. In the moonlight I saw it was neither, or perhaps both. There was a blunt muzzle; and the height of the skull above the eyes, which anthropologists say is the surest badge of humanity and speech, had been stunted until it was not greater than I have seen in a macaque. Yet the arms and shoulders and pelvis—even a few filthy rags of clothing—all bespoke mankind. It was a female, with small, flattened breasts still apparent on either side of the burn channel.

At least ten years ago I read about such things in Osman Aga's *Mystery Beyond the Sun's Setting;* but it was very different to stand shivering on a deserted street corner of the old capital and examine the thing in the flesh. By Osman Aga's account (which no one, I think, but a few old women has ever believed) these creatures were in truth human beings—or at least the descendants of human beings. In the last century, when the famine gripped their country and the irreversible damage done to the chromosomal structures of the people had already become apparent, some few turned to the eating of human flesh. No doubt the corpses of the famine supplied their food at first; and no doubt those who ate of them congratulated themselves that by so doing they had escaped the effects of the enzymes that were then still used to bring slaughter animals to maturity in a matter of months. What they failed to realize was that the bodies of the human beings they ate had accumulated far more of these unnatural substances than were ever found in the flesh of the short-lived cattle. From them, according to *Mystery Beyond the Sun's Setting,* rose such creatures as the thing I had killed.

But Osman Aga has never been believed. So far as I know, he is a mere popular writer, with a reputation for glorifying Caspian resorts in recompense for free lodging, and for indulging in absurd expeditions to breed more books and publicize the ones he has already written—crossing the desert on a camel and the Alps on an elephant—and no one else has ever, to my knowledge, reported such things from this continent. The ruined cities filled with rats and rabid bats, and the terrible whirling dust storms of the interior, have been enough for other travel writers. Now I am sorry I did not contrive a way to cut off the thing's head; I feel sure its skull would have been of interest to science.

* * *

As soon as I had written the preceding paragraph, I realized that there might still be a chance to do what I had failed to do last night. I went to the kitchen, and for a small bribe was able to secure a large, sharp knife, which I concealed beneath my jacket.

It was still early as I ran down the street, and for a few minutes I had high hopes that the thing's body might still be lying where I had left it; but my efforts were all for nothing. It was gone, and there was no sign of its presence—no blood, no scar from my beam on the house. I poked into alleys and waste cans. Nothing. At last I came back to the hotel for breakfast, and I have now (it is mid-morning) returned to my room to make my plans for the day.

Very well. I failed to meet Ellen last night—I shall not fail today. I am going to buy another ticket for the play, and tonight I will not take my seat, but wait behind the last row where I saw her standing. If she comes to watch at the end of the second act as she did last night, I will be there to compliment her on her performance and present her with some gift. If she does not come, I will make my way backstage—from what I have seen of these Americans, a quarter rial should get me anywhere, but I am willing to loosen a few teeth if I must.

What absurd creatures we are! I have just reread what I wrote this morning, and I might as well have been writing of the philosophic speculations of the Congress of Birds or the affairs of the demons in Domdaniel, or any other subject on which neither I nor anyone else knows or can know a thing. O Book, you have heard what I supposed would occur, now let me tell you what actually took place.

I set out as I had planned to procure a gift for Ellen. On the advice of the hotel manager, I followed Maine Street north until I reached the wide avenue that passes close by the obelisk. Around the base of this still imposing monument is held a perpetual fair in which the merchants use the stone blocks fallen from the upper part of the structure as tables. What remains of the shaft is still, I should say, upwards of one hundred meters high; but it is said to have formerly stood three or four times that height. Much of the fallen material has been carted away to build private homes.

There seems to be no logic to the prices in this country, save for the general rule that foodstuffs are cheap and imported machinery—cameras and the like—costly. Textiles are expensive, which no doubt explains why so many of the people wear ragged clothes that they mend and dye in an effort to make them look new. Certain kinds of jewelry are quite reasonable; others sell for much higher prices than they would in Teheran. Rings of silver or white gold set, usually, with a single modest diamond, may be had in great numbers for such low prices that I was tempted into buying a few to take home as an investment. Yet I saw bracelets that would have sold at home for no more than half a rial, for which the seller asked ten times that much. There were many interesting antiques, all of which are alleged to have been dug from the ruined cities of the interior at the cost of someone's life. When I had talked to five or six vendors of such items, I was able to believe that I knew how the country was depopulated.

After a good deal of this pleasant, wordy shopping, during which I spent very little, I selected a bracelet made of old coins—many of them silver—as my gift to Ellen. I reasoned that women always like jewelry, and that such a showy piece might be of service to an actress in playing some part or other, and that the coins must have a good deal of intrinsic value. Whether she will like it or not—if she ever receives it—I do not know; it is still in the pocket of my jacket.

When the shadow of the obelisk had grown long, I returned here to the hotel and had a good dinner of lamb and rice, and retired to groom myself for the evening. The five remaining candy eggs stood staring at me from the top of my dresser. I remembered my resolve, and took one. Quite suddenly I was struck by the conviction that the demon I believed I had killed the night before had been no more than a phantom engendered by the action of the drug.

What if I had been firing my pistol at mere empty air? That seemed a terrible thought—indeed, it seems so to me still. A worse one is that the drug really may have rendered visible—as some say those ancient preparations were intended to—a real but spiritual being. If such things in fact walk what we take to be unoccupied rooms and rooftops, and the empty streets of night, it would explain many sudden deaths and diseases, and perhaps the sudden changes for the worse we sometimes see in others and others in us, and even the birth of evil men. This morning I called the thing a *druj;* it may be true.

Yet if the drug had been in the egg I ate last night, then the egg I held was harmless. Concentrating on that thought, I forced myself to eat it all, then stretched myself upon the bed to wait.

Very briefly I slept and dreamed. Ellen was bending over me, caressing me with a soft, long-fingered hand. It was only for an instant, but sufficient to make me hope that dreams are prophecies.

If the drug was in the egg I consumed, that dream was its only result. I got up and washed, and changed my clothes, sprinkling my fresh shirt liberally with our Pamir rosewater, which I have observed the Americans hold in high regard. Making certain my ticket and pistol were both in place, I left for the theater.

The play was still *Mary Rose.* I intentionally entered late (after Harry and Mrs. Otery had been talking for several minutes), then lingered at the back of the last row as though I were too polite to disturb the audience by taking my seat. Mrs. Otery made her exit; Harry pulled his knife from the wood of the packing case and threw it again, and when the mists of the past had marched across the stage, Harry was gone, and Moreland and the parson were chatting to the tune of Mrs. Moreland's knitting needles. Mary Rose would be on stage soon. My hope that she would come out to watch the opening scene had come to nothing; I would have to wait until she vanished at the end of Act II before I could expect to see her.

I was looking for a vacant seat when I became conscious of someone standing near me. In the dim light I could tell little except that he was rather slender, and a few centimeters shorter than I.

Finding no seat, I moved back a step or two. The newcomer touched my arm and asked in a whisper if I could light his cigarette. I had already seen that it was customary to smoke in the theaters here, and I had fallen into the habit of carrying matches to light the candles in my room. The flare of the flame showed the narrow eyes and high cheekbones of Harry—or as I preferred to think of him, Kreton. Taken somewhat aback, I murmured some inane remark about the excellence of his performance.

"Did you like it? It is the least of all parts—I pull the curtain to open the show, then pull it again to tell everyone it's time to go home."

Several people in the audience were looking angrily at us, so we retreated to a point at the head of the aisle that was at least legally in the lobby, where I told him I had seen him in *Visit to a Small Planet* as well.

"Now *there* is a play. The character—as I am sure you saw—is good and bad at once. He is benign, he is mischievous, he is hellish."

"You carried it off wonderfully well, I thought."

"Thank you. This turkey here—do you know how many roles it has?"

"Well, there's yourself, Mrs. Otery, Mr. Amy—"

"No, no." He touched my arm to stop me. "I mean *roles,* parts that require real acting. There's one—the girl. She gets to skip about the stage as an eighteen-year-old whose brain atrophied at ten; and at least half what she does is wasted on the audience because they don't realize what's wrong with her until Act I is almost over."

"She's wonderful," I said. "I mean Mlle. Dahl."

Kreton nodded and drew on his cigarette. "She is a very competent ingenue, though it would be better if she weren't quite so tall."

"Do you think there's any chance that she might come out here—as you did?"

"Ah," he said, and looked me up and down.

For a moment I could have sworn that the telepathic ability he was credited with in *Visit to a Small Planet* was no fiction; nevertheless, I repeated my question: "Is it probable or not?"

"There's no reason to get angry—no, it's not likely. Is that enough payment for your match?"

"She vanishes at the end of the second act, and doesn't come on stage again until near the close of the third."

Kreton smiled. "You've read the play?"

"I was here last night. She must be off for nearly forty minutes, including the intermission."

"That's right. But she won't be here. It's true she goes out front sometimes—as I did myself tonight—but I happen to know she has company backstage."

"Might I ask who?"

"You might. It's even possible I might answer. You're Moslem, I suppose —do you drink?"

"I'm not a *strict* Moslem; but no, I don't. I'll buy you a drink gladly though, if you want one, and have coffee with you while you drink it."

We left by a side door and elbowed our way through the crowd in the street. A flight of narrow and dirty steps descending from the sidewalk led us to a cellar tavern that had all the atmosphere of a private club. There was a bar with a picture (now much dimmed by dirt and smoke) of the cast of a play I did not recognize behind it, three tables, and a few alcoves. Kreton and I slipped into one of these and ordered from a barman with a misshapen head. I suppose I must have stared at him, because Kreton said, "I sprained my ankle stepping out of a saucer, and now I am a convalescent soldier. Should we make up something for him, too? Can't we just say the potter is angry sometimes?"

"The potter?" I asked.

" 'None answered this; but after Silence spake/A Vessel of a more ungainly Make:/They sneer at me for leaning all awry;/What! Did the Hand then of the Potter shake?' "

I shook my head. "I've never heard that; but you're right, he looks as though his head had been shaped in clay, then knocked in on one side while it was still wet."

"This is a republic of hideousness, as you have no doubt already seen. Our national symbol is supposed to be an extinct eagle; it is in fact the nightmare."

"I find it a very beautiful country," I said. "Though I confess that many of your people are unsightly. Still, there are the ruins, and you have such skies as we never see at home."

"Our chimneys have been filled with wind for a long time."

"That may be for the best. Blue skies are better than most of the things made in factories."

"And not all our people are unsightly," Kreton murmured.

"Oh, no. Mlle. Dahl—"

"I had myself in mind."

I saw that he was baiting me, but I said, "No, you aren't hideous—in fact, I would call you handsome in an exotic way. Unfortunately, my tastes run more toward Mlle. Dahl."

"Call her Ardis—she won't mind."

The barman brought Kreton a glass of green liqueur, and me a cup of the weak, bitter American coffee.

"You were going to tell me who she is entertaining."

"Behind the scenes." Kreton smiled. "I just thought of that—I've used the phrase a thousand times, as I suppose everyone has. This time it happens to be literally correct, and its birth is suddenly made plain, like Oedipus's. No, I don't think I promised I would tell you that—though I suppose I said I might. Aren't there other things you would really rather know? The secret hidden beneath Mount Rushmore, or how you might meet her yourself?"

"I will give you twenty rials to introduce me to her, with some assurance that something will come of the introduction. No one need ever find out."

Kreton laughed. "Believe me, I would be more likely to boast of my profit than keep it secret—though I would probably have to divide my fee with the lady to fulfill the guarantee."

"You'll do it then?"

He shook his head, still laughing. "I only pretend to be corrupt; it goes with this face. Come backstage after the show tonight, and I'll see that you meet Ardis. You're very wealthy, I presume, and if you're not, we'll say you are anyway. What are you doing here?"

"Studying your art and architecture."

"Great reputation in your own country, no doubt?"

"I am a pupil of Akhon Mirza Ahmak; he has a great reputation, surely. He even came here, thirty years ago, to examine the miniatures in your National Gallery of Art."

"Pupil of Akhon Mirza Ahmak, pupil of Akhon Mirza Ahmak," Kreton muttered to himself. "That is very good—I must remember it. But now"—he glanced at the old clock behind the bar—"it's time we got back. I'll have to freshen my makeup before I go on in the last act. Would you prefer to wait in the theater, or just come around to the stage door when the play's over? I'll give you a card that will get you in."

"I'll wait in the theater," I said, feeling that would offer less chance for mishap; also because I wanted to see Ellen play the ghost again.

"Come along then—I have a key for that side door."

I rose to go with him, and he threw an arm about my shoulder that I felt it would be impolite to thrust away. I could feel his hand, as cold as a dead man's, through my clothing, and was reminded unpleasantly of the twisted hands of the beggar in the Silent City.

We were going up the narrow stairs when I felt a gentle touch inside my jacket. My first thought was that he had seen the outline of my pistol, and meant to take it and shoot me. I gripped his wrist and shouted something—I do not remember what. Bound together and struggling, we staggered up the steps and into the street.

In a few seconds we were the center of a mob—some taking his side, some mine, most only urging us to fight, or asking each other what the disturbance was. My pocket sketchpad, which he must have thought held money, fell to the ground between us. Just then the American police arrived—not by air as the police would have come at home, but astride shaggy, hulking horses, and swinging whips. The crowd scattered at the first crackling arc from the lashes, and in a few seconds they had beaten Kreton to the ground. Even at the time I could not help thinking what a terrible thing it must be to be one of these people, whose police are so quick to prefer any prosperous-looking foreigner to one of their own citizens.

They asked me what had happened (my questioner even dismounted to show his respect for me), and I explained that Kreton had tried to rob me, but that I did not want him punished. The truth was that seeing him sprawled unconscious with a burn across his face had put an end to any resentment I might have felt toward him; out of pity, I would gladly have given him the few rials I carried. They told me that if he had attempted to rob me he must be charged, and that if I would not accuse him they would do so themselves.

I then said that Kreton was a friend; and that on reflection I felt certain that what he had attempted had been intended as a prank. (In maintaining this I was considerably handicapped by not knowing his real name, which I had read on the playbill but forgotten, so that I was forced to refer to him as "this poor man.")

At last the policeman said, "We can't leave him in the street, so we'll have to bring him in. How will it look if there's no complaint?"

Then I understood that they were afraid of what their superiors might say if it became known that they had beaten him unconscious when no charge was made against him; and when I became aware that if I would not press charges, the charges they would bring themselves would be far more serious—assault or attempted murder—I agreed to do what they wished, and signed a form alleging the theft of my sketchbook.

When they had gone at last, carrying the unfortunate Kreton across a saddlebow, I tried to reenter the theater. The side door through which we had left was locked, and though I would gladly have paid the price of another ticket, the box office was closed. Seeing that there was nothing further to be done, I returned here, telling myself that my introduction to Ellen, if it ever came, would have to wait for another day.

Very truly it is written that we walk by paths that are always turning. In recording these several pages I have managed to restrain my enthusiasm, though when I described my waiting at the back of the theater for Ardis, and again when I recounted how Kreton had promised to introduce me to her, I was forced for minutes at a time to lay down my pen and walk about the room singing and whistling, and—to reveal everything—jumping over the beds! But now I can conceal no longer. I have seen her! I have touched her hand; I am to see her again tomorrow; and there is every hope that she will become my mistress!

I had undressed and laid myself on the bed (thinking to bring this journal up to date in the morning) and had even fallen into the first doze of sleep when there was a knock at the door. I slipped into my robe and pressed the release.

It was the only time in my life that for even an instant I thought I might be dreaming—actually asleep—when in truth I was up and awake.

How feeble it is to write that she is more beautiful in person than she appears on the stage. It is true, and yet it is a supreme irrelevance. I have seen more beautiful women—indeed, Yasmin is, I suppose, by the formal standards of art, more lovely. It is not Ardis' beauty that draws me to her—the hair like gold, the translucent skin that then still showed traces of the bluish makeup she had worn as a ghost, the flashing eyes like the clear, clean skies of America. It is something deeper than that; something that would remain if all that were somehow taken away. No doubt she has habits that would disgust me in someone else, and the vanity that is said to be so common in her profession, and yet I would do anything to possess her.

Enough of this. What is it but empty boasting, now that I am on the point of winning her?

She stood in my doorway. I have been trying to think how I can express what I felt then. It was as though some tall flower, a lily perhaps, had left the garden and come to tap at my door, a thing that had never happened before in all the history of the world, and would never happen again.

"You are Nadan Jaffarzadeh?"

I admitted that I was, and shamefacedly, twenty seconds too late, moved out of her way.

She entered, but instead of taking the chair I indicated, turned to face me; her blue eyes seemed as large as the colored eggs on the dresser, and they were filled with a melting hope. "You are the man, then, that Bobby O'Keene tried to rob tonight."

I nodded.

"I know you—I mean, I know your face. This is insane. You came to *Visit* on the last night and brought your father, and then to *Mary Rose* on the first night, and sat in the third or fourth row. I thought you were an American, and when the police told me your name, I imagined some greasy fat man with gestures. Why on earth would Bobby want to steal from *you?*"

"Perhaps he needed the money."

She threw back her head and laughed. I had heard her laugh in *Mary Rose* when Simon was asking her father for her hand; but that had held a note of childishness that (however well suited to the part) detracted from its beauty. This laugh was the merriment of houris sliding down a rainbow. "I'm sure he did. He always needs money. You're sure, though, that he meant to rob you? You couldn't have . . ."

She saw my expression and let the question trail away. The truth is that I was disappointed that I could not oblige her, and at last I said, "If you want me to be mistaken, Ardis, then I was mistaken. He only bumped against me on the steps, perhaps, and tried to catch my sketchbook when it fell."

She smiled, and her face was the sun smiling upon roses. "You would say that for me? And you know my name?"

"From the program. I came to the theater to see you—and that was not my father, who it grieves me to say is long dead, but only an old man, an American, whom I had met that day."

"You brought him sandwiches at the first intermission—I was watching you through the peephole in the curtain. You must be a very thoughtful person."

"Do you watch everyone in the audience so carefully?"

She blushed at that, and for a moment could not meet my eyes.

"But you will forgive Bobby, and tell the police that you want them to let him go? You must love the theater, Mr. Jef—Jaff—"

"You've forgotten my name already. It is Jaffarzadeh, a very common-place name in my country."

"I hadn't forgotten it—only how to pronounce it. You see, when I came here I had learned it without knowing who you were, and so I had no trouble with it. Now you're a real person to me and I can't say it as an actress should." She seemed to notice the chair behind her for the first time, and sat down.

I sat opposite her. "I'm afraid I know very little about the theater."

"We are trying to keep it alive here, Mr. Jaffar, and—"

"Jaffarzadeh. Call me Nadan—then you won't have so many syllables to trip over."

She took my hand in hers, and I knew quite well that the gesture was as studied as a salaam and that she felt she was playing me like a fish; but I was beside myself with delight. To be played by *her!* To have *her* eager to cultivate my affection! And the fish will pull her in yet—wait and see!

"I will," she said, "Nadan. And though you may know little of the theater, you feel as I do—as we do—or you would not come. It has been such a long struggle; all the history of the stage is a struggle, the gasping of a beautiful child born at the point of death. The moralists, censorship and oppression, technology, and now poverty have all tried to destroy her. Only we, the actors and audiences, have kept her alive. We have been doing well here in Washington, Nadan."

"Very well indeed," I said. "Both the productions I have seen have been excellent."

"But only for the past two seasons. When I joined the company it had nearly fallen apart. We revived it—Bobby and Paul and I. We could do it because we cared, and because we were able to find a few naturally talented people who can take direction. Bobby is the best of us—he can walk away with any part that calls for a touch of the sinister . . ."

She seemed to run out of breath. I said, "I don't think there will be any trouble about getting him free."

"Thank God. We're getting the theater on its feet again now. We're attracting new people, and we've built up a following—people who come to see every production. There's even some money ahead at last. But *Mary Rose* is supposed to run another two weeks, and after that we're doing *Faust,* with Bobby as Mephistopheles. We've simply no one who can take his place, no one who can come close to him."

"I'm sure the police will release him if I ask them to."

"They *must.* We have to have him tomorrow night. Bill—someone you don't know—tried to go on for him in the third act tonight. It was just ghastly. In Iran you're very polite; that's what I've heard."

"We enjoy thinking so."

"We're not. We never were; and as . . ."

Her voice trailed away, but a wave of one slender arm evoked everything —the cracked plaster walls became as air, and the decayed city, the ruined continent, entered the room with us. "I understand," I said.

"They—we—were betrayed. In our souls we have never been sure by whom. When we feel cheated we are ready to kill; and maybe we feel cheated all the time."

She slumped in her chair, and I realized, as I should have long before, how exhausted she was. She had given a performance that had ended in disaster, then had been forced to plead with the police for my name and address, and at last had come here from the station house, very probably on foot. I asked when I could obtain O'Keene's release.

"We can go tomorrow morning, if you'll do it."

"You wish to come too?"

She nodded, smoothed her skirt, and stood. "I'll have to know. I'll come for you about nine, if that's all right."

"If you'll wait outside for me to dress, I'll take you home."

"That's not necessary."

"It will only take a moment," I said.

The blue eyes held something pleading again. "You're going to come in with me—that's what you're thinking, I know. You have two beds here— bigger, cleaner beds than the one I have in my little apartment; if I were to ask you to push them together, would you still take me home afterward?"

It was as though I were dreaming indeed: a dream in which everything I wanted—the cosmos purified—delivered itself to me. I said, "You won't have to leave at all—you can spend the night with me. Then we can breakfast together before we go to release your friend."

She laughed again, lifting that exquisite head. "There are a hundred things at home I need. Do you think I'd have breakfast with you without my cosmetics, and in these dirty clothes?"

"Then I will take you home—yes, though you lived in Kazvin. Or on Mount Kaf."

She smiled. "Get dressed, then. I'll wait outside, and I'll show you my apartment; perhaps you won't want to come back here afterward."

She went out, her wooden-soled American shoes clicking on the bare floor, and I threw on trousers, shirt, and jacket, and jammed my feet into my boots. When I opened the door, she was gone. I rushed to the barred window at the end of the corridor, and was in time to see her disappear down a side street. A last swirl of her skirt in a gust of night wind, and she had vanished into the velvet dark.

For a long time I stood there looking out over the ruinous buildings. I was not angry—I do not think I could be angry with her. I was, though here it is hard to tell the truth, in some way glad. Not because I feared the embrace of love—I have no doubt of my ability to suffice any woman who can be sated by man—but because an easy exchange of my cooperation for her person would have failed to satisfy my need for romance, for adventure of a certain type, in which danger and love are twined like coupling serpents. Ardis, my Ellen, will provide that, surely, as neither Yasmin nor the pitiful wanton who was her double could. I sense that the world is opening for me only now; that I am being born; that that corridor was the birth canal, and that Ardis in leaving me was drawing me out toward her.

When I returned to my own door, I noticed a bit of paper on the floor before it. I transcribe it exactly here, though I cannot transmit its scent of lilacs.

> You are a most attractive man and I want very much to stretch the truth and tell you you can have me freely when Bobby is free but I won't sell myself etc. Really I *will* sell myself for Bobby but I have other fish to fry tonight. I'll see you in the morning and if you can get Bobby out or even try hard you'll have (real) love from the vanishing
>
> Mary Rose

Morning. Woke early and ate here at the hotel as usual, finishing about eight. Writing this journal will give me something to do while I wait for Ardis. Had an American breakfast today, the first time I have risked one. Flakes of pastry dough toasted crisp and drenched with cream, and with it strudel and the usual American coffee. Most natives have spiced pork in one form or another, which I cannot bring myself to try; but several of the people around me were having egg dishes and oven-warmed bread, which I will sample tomorrow.

I had a very unpleasant dream last night; I have been trying to put it out of my mind ever since I woke. It was dark, and I was under an open sky with Ardis, walking over ground much rougher than anything I saw in the park on the farther side of the channel. One of the hideous creatures I shot night before last was pursuing us—or rather, lurking about us, for it appeared first to the left of us, then to the right, silhouetted against the night sky. Each time we saw it, Ardis grasped my arm and urged me to shoot, but the little indicator light on my pistol was glowing red to show that there was not enough charge left for a shot. All very silly, of course, but I am going to buy a fresh powerpack as soon as I have the opportunity.

It is late afternoon—after six—but we have not had dinner yet. I am just out of the tub, and sit here naked, with today's candy egg laid (pinker even than I) beside this book on my table. Ardis and I had a sorry, weary time of it, and I have come back here to make myself presentable. At seven we will meet for dinner; the curtain goes up at eight, so it can't be a long one, but I am going backstage to watch the play from the wings, where I will be able to talk to her when she isn't performing.

I just took a bite of the egg—no unusual taste, nothing but an unpleasant sweetness. The more I reflect on it, the more inclined I am to believe that the drug was in the first I ate. No doubt the monster I saw had been lurking in my brain since I read *Mysteries,* and the drug freed it. True, there were bloodstains on my clothes (the Peri's asphodel!) but they could as easily have come from my cheek, which is still sore. I have had my experience, and all I have left is my candy. I am almost tempted to throw out the rest. Another bite.

Still twenty minutes before I must dress and go for Ardis—she showed me where she lives, only a few doors from the theater. To work then.

Ardis was a trifle late this morning, but came as she had promised. I asked where we were to go to free Kreton, and when she told me—a still-living building at the eastern end of the Silent City—I hired one of the rickety American caleches to drive us there. Like most of them, it was drawn by a starved horse; but we made good time.

The American police are organized on a peculiar system. The national secret police (officially, the Federated Enquiry Divisions) are in a tutorial position to all the others, having power to review their decisions, promote, demote, and discipline, and as the ultimate reward, enroll personnel from the other organizations. In addition they maintain a uniformed force of their own. Thus when an American has been arrested by uniformed police, his friends can seldom learn whether he has been taken by the local police, by the F.E.D. uniformed national force, or by members of the F.E.D. secret police posing as either of the foregoing.

Since I had known nothing of these distinctions previously, I had no way of guessing which of the three had O'Keene; but the local police to whom Ardis had spoken the night before had given her to understand that he had been taken by them. She explained all this to me as we rattled along, then added that we were now going to the F.E.D. Building to secure his release. I must have looked as confused as I felt at this, because she added, "Part of it is a station for the Washington Police Department—they rent the space from the F.E.D."

My own impression (when we arrived) was that they did no such thing—that the entire apparatus was no more real than one of the scenes in Ardis's theater, and that all the men and women to whom we spoke were in fact agents of the secret police, wielding ten times the authority they pretended to possess, and going through a solemn ritual of deception. As Ardis and I moved from office to office, explaining our simple errand, I came to think that she felt as I did, and that she had refrained from expressing these feelings to me in the cab not only because of the danger, the fear that I might betray her or the driver be a spy, but because she was ashamed of her nation, and eager to make it appear to me, a foreigner, that her government was less devious and meretricious than is actually the case.

If this is so—and in that windowless warren of stone I was certain it was—then the very explanation she proffered in the cab (which I have given in its proper place) differentiating clearly between local police, uniformed F.E.D. police, and secret police, was no more than a children's fable, concealing an actuality less forthright and more convoluted.

Our questioners were courteous to me, much less so to Ardis, and (so it seemed to me) obsessed by the idea that something more lay behind the simple incident we described over and over again—so much so in fact that I came to believe it myself. I have neither time nor patience enough to describe all these interviews, but I will attempt to give a sample of one.

We went into a small, windowless office crowded between two others that appeared empty. A middle-aged American woman was seated behind a metal desk. She appeared normal and reasonably attractive until she spoke; then her scarred gums showed that she had once had two or three times the proper number of teeth—forty or fifty, I suppose, in each jaw—and that the dental surgeon who had extracted the supernumerary ones had not always, perhaps, selected those he suffered to remain as wisely as he might. She asked, "How is it outside? The weather? You see, I don't know, sitting in here all day."

Ardis said, "Very nice."

"Do you like it, *Hajji?* Have you had a pleasant stay in our great country?"

"I don't think it has rained since I've been here."

She seemed to take the remark as a covert accusation. "You came too late for the rains, I'm afraid. This is a very fertile area, however. Some of our oldest coins show heads of wheat. Have you seen them?" She pushed a small copper coin across the desk, and I pretended to examine it. There are one or two like it in the bracelet I bought for Ardis, and which I still have not presented to her. "I must apologize on behalf of the District for what happened to you," the woman continued. "We are making every effort to control crime. You have not been victimized before this?"

I shook my head, half suffocated in that airless office, and said I had not been.

"And now you are here." She shuffled the papers she held, then pretended to read from one of them. "You are here to secure the release of the thief who assaulted you. A very commendable act of magnanimity. May I ask why you brought this young woman with you? She does not seem to be mentioned in any of these reports."

I explained that Ardis was a coworker of O'Keene's, and that she had interceded for him.

"Then it is you, Ms. Dahl, who are really interested in securing this prisoner's release. Are you related to him?"

And so on.

At the conclusion of each interview we were told either that the matter was completely out of the hands of the person to whom we had just spent half an hour or an hour talking, that it was necessary to obtain a clearance from someone else, or that an additional deposition had to be made. About two o'clock we were sent to the other side of the river—into what my guidebooks insist is an entirely different jurisdiction—to visit a penal facility. There we were forced to look for Kreton among five hundred or so miserable prisoners, all of whom stank and had lice. Not finding him, we returned to the F.E.D. Building past the half-overturned and yet still brooding figure called the Seated Man, and the ruins and beggars of the Silent City, for another round of interrogations. By five, when we were told to leave, we were both exhausted, though Ardis seemed surprisingly hopeful. When I left her at the door of her building a few minutes ago, I asked her what they would do tonight without Kreton.

"Without Harry, you mean." She smiled. "The best we can, I suppose, if we must. At least Paul will have someone ready to stand in for him tonight."

We shall see how well it goes.

I have picked up this pen and replaced it on the table ten times at least. It seems very likely that I should destroy this journal instead of continuing with it, were I wise; but I have discovered a hiding place for it which I think will be secure.

When I came back from Ardis's apartment tonight there were only two candy eggs remaining. I am certain—absolutely certain—that three were left when I went to meet Ardis. I am almost equally sure that after I had finished making the entry in this book, I put it, as I always do, at the left side of the drawer. It was on the right side.

It is possible that all this is merely the doing of the maid who cleans the room. She might easily have supposed that a single candy egg would not be missed, and have shifted this book while cleaning the drawer, or peeped inside out of curiosity.

I will assume the worst, however. An agent sent to investigate my room might be equipped to photograph these pages—but he might not, and it is not likely that he himself would have a reading knowledge of Farsi. Now I have gone through the book and eliminated all the passages relating to my reason for visiting this leprous country. Before I leave this room tomorrow I will arrange indicators—hairs and other objects whose positions I shall carefully record—that will tell me if the room has been searched again.

Now I may as well set down the events of the evening, which were truly extraordinary enough.

I met Ardis as we had planned, and she directed me to a small restaurant not far from her apartment. We had no sooner seated ourselves than two heavy-looking men entered. At no time could I see plainly the face of either, but it appeared to me that one was the American I had met aboard the *Princess Fatimah* and that the other was the grain dealer I had so assiduously avoided there, Golam Gassem. It is impossible, I think, for my divine Ardis ever to look less than beautiful; but she came as near to it then as the laws of nature permit—the blood drained from her face, her mouth opened slightly, and for a moment she appeared to be a lovely corpse. I began to ask what the trouble was, but before I could utter a word she touched my lips to silence me, and then, having somewhat regained her composure, said, "They have not seen us. I am leaving now. Follow me as though we were finished eating." She stood, feigned to pat her lips with a napkin (so that the lower half of her face was hidden) and walked out into the street.

I followed her, and found her laughing not three doors away from the entrance to the restaurant. The change in her could not have been more startling if she had been released from an enchantment. "It is so funny," she said. "Though it wasn't then. Come on, we'd better go; you can feed me after the show."

I asked her what those men were to her.

"Friends," she said, still laughing.

"If they are friends, why were you so anxious that they not see you? Were you afraid they would make us late?" I knew that such a trivial explanation could not be true, but I wanted to leave her a means of evading the question if she did not want to confide in me.

She shook her head. "No, no. I didn't want either to think I did not trust him. I'll tell you more later, if you want to involve yourself in our little charade."

"With all my heart."

She smiled at that—that sun-drenched smile for which I would gladly have entered a lion pit. In a few more steps we were at the rear entrance to the theater, and there was no time to say more. She opened the door, and I heard Kreton arguing with a woman I later learned was the wardrobe mistress. "You are free," I said, and he turned to look at me.

"Yes. Thanks to you, I think. And I do thank you."

Ardis gazed on him as though he were a child saved from drowning. "Poor Bobby. Was it very bad?"

"It was frightening, that's all. I was afraid I'd never get out. Do you know Terry is gone?"

She shook her head, and said, "What do you mean?" but I was certain—and here I am not exaggerating or coloring the facts, though I confess I have occasionally done so elsewhere in this chronicle—that she had known it before he spoke.

"He simply isn't here. Paul is running around like a lunatic. I hear you missed me last night."

"God, yes," Ardis said, and darted off too swiftly for me to follow.

Kreton took my arm. I expected him to apologize for having tried to rob me, but he said, "You've met her, I see."

"She persuaded me to drop the charges against you."

"Whatever it was you offered me—twenty rials? I'm morally entitled to it, but I won't claim it. Come and see me when you're ready for something more wholesome—and meanwhile, how do you like her?"

"That is something for me to tell her," I said, "not you."

Ardis returned as I spoke, bringing with her a balding black man with a mustache. "Paul, this is Nadan. His English is very good—not so British as most of them. He'll do, don't you think?"

"He'll have to—you're sure he'll do it?"

"He'll love it," Ardis said positively, and disappeared again.

It seemed that "Terry" was the actor who played Mary Rose's husband and lover, Simon; and I—who had never acted in so much as a school play—was to be pressed into the part. It was about half an hour before curtain time, so I had all of fifty minutes to learn my lines before my entrance at the end of the first act.

Paul, the director, warned me that if my name were used, the audience would be hostile; and since the character (in the version of the play they were presenting) was supposed to be an American, they would see errors where none existed. A moment later, while I was still in frantic rehearsal, I heard him saying, "The part of Simon Blake will be taken by Ned Jefferson."

The act of stepping onto the stage for the first time was really the worst part of the entire affair. Fortunately I had the advantage of playing a nervous young man come to ask for the hand of his sweetheart, so that my shaky laughter and stammer became "acting."

My second scene—with Mary Rose and Cameron on the magic island— ought by rights to have been much more difficult than the first. I had had only the intermission in which to study my lines, and the scene called for pessimistic apprehension rather than mere anxiety. But all the speeches were short, and Paul had been able by that time to get them lettered on large sheets of paper, which he and the stage manager held up in the wings. Several times I was forced to extemporize, but though I forgot the playwright's words, I never lost my sense of the *trend* of the play, and was always able to contrive something to which Ardis and Cameron could adapt their replies.

In comparison to the first and second acts, my brief appearance in the third was a holiday; yet I have seldom been so exhausted as I was tonight when the stage darkened for Ardis's final confrontation with Kreton, and Cameron and I, and the middle-aged people who had played the Morelands were able to creep away.

We had to remain in costume until we had taken our bows, and it was nearly midnight before Ardis and I got something to eat at the same small, dirty bar outside which Kreton had tried to rob me. Over the steaming plates she asked me if I had enjoyed acting, and I had to nod.

"I thought you would. Under all that solidity you're a very dramatic person, I think."

I admitted it was true, and tried to explain why I feel that what I call *the romance of life* is the only thing worth seeking. She did not understand me, and so I passed it off as the result of having been brought up on the *Shah Namah,* of which I found she had never heard.

We went to her apartment. I was determined to take her by force if necessary—not because I would have enjoyed brutalizing her, but because I felt she would inevitably think my love far less than it was if I permitted her to put me off a second time. She showed me about her quarters (two small rooms in great disorder), then, after we had lifted into place the heavy bar that is the sigil of every American dwelling, put her arms about me. Her breath was fragrant with the arrack I had bought for her a few minutes before. I feel sure now that for the rest of my life that scent will recall this evening to me.

When we parted, I began to unloose the laces that closed her blouse, and she at once pinched out the candle. I pleaded that she was thus depriving me of half the joy I might have had of her love; but she would not permit me to relight it, and our caresses and the embraces of our couplings were exchanged in perfect darkness. I was in ecstasy. To have seen her, I would have blinded myself; yet nothing could have increased my delight.

When we separated for the last time, both spent utterly, and she left to wash, I sought for matches. First in the drawer of the unsteady little table beside the bed, then among the disorder of my own clothes, which I had dropped to the floor and we had kicked about. I found some eventually, but could not find the candle—Ardis, I think, had hidden it. I struck a match; but she had covered herself with a robe. I said, "Am I never to see you?"

"You will see me tomorrow. You're going to take me boating, and we'll picnic by the water, under the cherry trees. Tomorrow night the theater will be closed for Easter, and you can take me to a party. But now you are going home, and I am going to go to sleep." When I was dressed and standing in her doorway, I asked her if she loved me; but she stopped my mouth with a kiss.

I have already written about the rest—returning to find two eggs instead of three, and this book moved. I will not write of that again. But I have just—between this paragraph and the last—read over what I wrote earlier tonight, and it seems to me that one sentence should have had more weight than I gave it: when I said that in my role as Simon I never lost the *trend* of the play.

What the fabled secret buried by the old Americans beneath their carved mountain may be I do not know; but I believe that if it is some key to the world of human life, it must be some form of that. Every great man, I am sure, consciously or not, in those terms or others, has grasped that secret—save that in the play that is our life we can grapple that trend and draw it to left or right if we have the will.

So I am doing now. If the taking of the egg was not significant, yet I will make it so—indeed I already have when I infused one egg with the drug. If the scheme in which Ardis is entangled—with Golam Gassem and Mr. Tallman if it be they—is not some affair of statecraft and dark treasure, yet I will make it so before the end. If our love is not a great love, destined to live forever in the hearts of the young and the mouths of the poets, it will be so before the end.

Once again I am here; and in all truth I am beginning to wonder if I do not write this journal only to read it. No man was ever happier than I am now—so happy, indeed, that I was sorely tempted not to taste either of the two eggs that remain. What if the drug, in place of hallucination, self-knowledge, and euphoria, brings permanent and despairing madness? Yet I have eaten it nonetheless, swallowing the whole sweet lump in a few bites. I would rather risk whatever may come than think myself a coward. With equanimity I await the effects.

The fact is that I am too happy for all the Faustian determination I penned last night. (How odd that *Faust* will be the company's next production. Kreton will be Mephistopheles, of course—Ardis said as much, and it would be certain in any case. Ardis herself will be Margaret. But who will play the Doctor?) Yet now, when all the teeth-gritting, table-pounding determination is gone, I know that I will carry out the essentials of the *plan* more surely than ever—with the ease, in fact, of an accomplished violinist sawing out some simple tune while his mind roves elsewhere. I have been looking at the ruins of the Jeff (as they call it), and it has turned my mind again to the fate of the old Americans. How often they, who chose their leaders for superficial appearances of strength, wisdom, and resolution, must have elected them only because they were as fatigued as I was last night.

I had meant to buy a hamper of delicacies, and call for Ardis about one, but she came for me at eleven with a little basket already packed. We walked north along the bank of the channel until we reached the ruins of the old tomb to which I have already referred, and the nearly circular artificial lake the Americans call the Basin. It is rimmed with flowering trees—old and gnarled, but very beautiful in their robes of white blossom. For some little American coin we were given command of a bright blue boat with a sail twice or three times the size of my handkerchief, in which to dare the halcyon waters of the lake.

When we were well away from the people on shore, Ardis asked me, rather suddenly, if I intended to spend all my time in America here in Washington.

I told her that my original plan had been to stay here no more than a week, then make my way up the coast to Philadelphia and the other ancient cities before I returned home; but that now that I had met her I would stay here forever if she wished it.

"Haven't you ever wanted to see the interior? This strip of beach we live on is kept half alive by the ocean and the trade that crosses it; but a hundred miles inland lies the wreck of our entire civilization, waiting to be plundered."

"Then why doesn't someone plunder it?" I asked.

"They do. A year never passes without someone bringing some great prize out—but it is so large . . ." I could see her looking beyond the lake and the fragrant trees. "So large that whole cities are lost in it. There was an arch of gold at the entrance to St. Louis—no one knows what became of it. Denver, the Mile-High City, was nested in silver mines; no one can find them now."

"Many of the old maps must still be in existence."

Ardis nodded slowly, and I sensed that she wanted to say more than she had. For a few seconds there was no sound but the water lapping against the side of the boat.

"I remember having seen some in the museum in Teheran—not only our maps, but some of your own from a hundred years ago."

"The courses of the rivers have changed," she said. "And when they have not, no one can be sure of it."

"Many buildings must still be standing, as they are here, in the Silent City."

"That was built of stone—more solidly than anything else in the country. But yes, some, many, are still there."

"Then it would be possible to fly in, land somewhere, and pillage them."

"There are many dangers, and so much rubble to look through that anyone might search for a lifetime and only scratch the surface."

I saw that talking of all this only made her unhappy, and tried to change the subject. "Didn't you say that I could escort you to a party tonight? What will that be like?"

"Nadan, I have to trust someone. You've never met my father, but he lives close to the hotel where you are staying, and has a shop where he sells old books and maps." (So I had visited the right house—almost—after all!) "When he was younger, he wanted to go into the interior. He made three or four trips, but never got farther than the Appalachian foothills. Eventually he married my mother and didn't feel any longer that he could take the risks . . ."

"I understand."

"The things he had sought to guide him to the wealth of the past became his stock in trade. Even today, people who live farther inland bring him old papers; he buys them and resells them. Some of those people are only a step better than the ones who dig up the cemeteries for the wedding rings of the dead women."

I recalled the rings I had bought in the shadow of the broken obelisk, and shuddered, though I do not believe Ardis observed it.

"I said that some of them were hardly better than the grave robbers. The truth is that some are worse—there are people in the interior who are no longer people. Our bodies are poisoned—you know that, don't you? All of us Americans. They have adapted—that's what Father says—but they are no longer human. He made his peace with them long ago, and he trades with them still."

"You don't have to tell me this."

"Yes, I do—I must. Would you go into the interior, if I went with you? The government will try to stop us if they learn of it, and to confiscate anything we find."

I assured her with every oath I could remember that with her beside me I would cross the continent on foot if need be.

"I told you about my father. I said that he sells the maps and records they bring him. What I did not tell you is that he reads them first. He has never given up, you see, in his heart."

"He has made a discovery?" I asked.

"He's made many—hundreds. Bobby and I have used them. You remember those men in the restaurant? Bobby went to each of them with a map and some of the old letters. He's persuaded them to help finance an expedition into the interior, and made each of them believe that we'll help him cheat the other—that keeps them from combining to cheat us, you see."

"And you want me to go with you?" I was beside myself with joy.

"We weren't going to go at all—Bobby was going to take the money, and go to Baghdad or Marrakesh, and take me with him. But, Nadan"—here she leaned forward, I remember, and took my hands in hers—"there really is a secret. There are many, but one better—more likely to be true, more likely to yield truly immense wealth than all the others. I know you would share fairly with me. We'll divide everything, and I'll go back to Teheran with you."

I know that I have never been more happy in my life than I was then, in that silly boat. We sat together in the stern, nearly sinking it, under the combined shade of the tiny sail and Ardis's big straw hat, and kissed and stroked one another until we would have been pilloried a dozen times in Iran.

At last, when I could bear no more unconsummated love, we ate the sandwiches Ardis had brought, and drank some warmish, fruit-flavored beverage, and returned to shore.

When I took her home a few minutes ago, I very strongly urged her to let me come upstairs with her; I was on fire for her, sick to impale her upon my own flesh and pour myself into her as some mad god before the coming of the Prophet might have poured his golden blood into the sea. She would not permit it—I think because she feared that her apartment could not be darkened enough to suit her modesty. I am determined that I will yet see her.

I have bathed and shaved to be ready for the party, and as there is still time I will insert here a description of the procession we passed on the way back from the lake. As you see, I have not yet completely abandoned the thought of a book of travels.

A very old man—I suppose a priest—carried a cross on a long pole, using it as a staff, and almost as a crutch. A much younger one, fat and sweating, walked backward before him swinging a smoking censer. Two robed boys carrying large candles preceded them, and they were followed by more robed children, singing, who fought with nudges and pinches when they felt the fat man was not watching them.

Like everyone else, I have seen this kind of thing done much better in Rome; but I was more affected by what I saw here. When the old priest was born, the greatness of America must have been a thing of such recent memory that few can have realized it had passed forever; and the entire procession—from the flickering candles in clear sunshine, to the dead leader lifted up, to his inattentive, bickering followers behind—seemed to me to incarnate the philosophy and the dilemma of these people. So I felt, at least, until I saw that they watched it as uncomprehendingly as they might if they themselves were only travelers abroad, and I realized that its ritualized plea for life renewed was more foreign to them than to me.

It is very late—three, my watch says.

I resolved again not to write in this book. To burn it or tear it to pieces, or to give it to some beggar; but now I am writing once again because I cannot sleep. The room reeks of my vomit, though I have thrown open the shutters and let in the night.

How could I have loved that? (And yet a few moments ago, when I tried to sleep, visions of Ellen pursued me back to wakefulness.)

The party was a masque, and Ardis had obtained a costume for me—a fantastic gilded armor from the wardrobe of the theater. She wore the robes of an Egyptian princess, and a domino. At midnight we lifted our masks and kissed, and in my heart I swore that tonight the mask of darkness would be lifted too.

When we left, I carried with me the bottle we had brought, still nearly half full; and before she pinched out the candle I persuaded her to pour out a final drink for us to share when the first frenzy of our desire was past. She—it—did as I asked, and set it on the little table near the bed. A long time afterward, when we lay gasping side by side, I found my pistol with one groping hand and fired the beam into the wide-bellied glass. Instantly it filled with a blue fire from the burning alcohol. Ardis screamed, and sprang up.

I ask myself now how I could have loved; but then, how could I in one week have come so near to loving this corpse-country? Its eagle is dead— Ardis is the proper symbol of its rule.

One hope, one very small hope remains. It is possible that what I saw tonight was only an illusion, induced by the egg. I know now that the thing I killed before Ardis's father's house was real, and between this paragraph and the last I have eaten the last egg. If hallucinations now begin, I will know that what I saw by the light of the blazing arrack was in truth a thing with which I have lain, and in one way or another will see to it that I never return to corrupt the clean wombs of the women of our enduring race. I might seek to claim the miniatures of our heritage after all, and allow the guards to kill me—but what if I were to succeed? I am not fit to touch them. Perhaps the best end for me would be to travel alone into this maggot-riddled continent; in that way I will die at fit hands.

Later. Kreton is walking in the hall outside my door, and the tread of his twisted black shoe jars the building like an earthquake. I heard the word *police* as though it were thunder. My dead Ardis, very small and bright, has stepped out of the candle-flame, and there is a hairy face coming through the window.

> The old woman closed the notebook. The younger woman, who had been reading over her shoulder, moved to the other side of the small table and seated herself on a cushion, her feet politely positioned so that the soles could not be seen. "He is alive then," she said.
>
> The older woman remained silent, her gray head bowed over the notebook, which she held in both hands.
>
> "He is certainly imprisoned, or ill, otherwise he would have been in touch with us." The younger woman paused, smoothing the

fabric of her *chador* with her right hand, while the left toyed with the gem simulator she wore on a thin chain. "It is possible that he has already tried, but his letters have miscarried."

"You think this is his writing?" the older woman asked, opening the notebook at random. When the younger did not answer, she added, "Perhaps. Perhaps."

Charles Dickens

The Signal-Man

Charles Dickens is the most important force in the popularity of the ghost story in the nineteenth century. Dickens gave the ghost story a traditional home in the Christmas issues of the influential magazines he edited, and wrote the most enduring classic in the Christmas ghost sub-genre himself, "A Christmas Carol." He solidified the scattered tradition of telling ghost stories of all types during the Christmas season into a cultural ritual as not only the most popular writer in English of his era but also as one of the most powerful editors. His active career extends from the 1830s to the 1870s and by the end of that career, Dickens had brought into print some of the finest horror stories of the century and made them fashionable. Dickens' own short fiction was nearly always sentimental and in the moral allegory mode . . . certainly all of his once famous Christmas stories are. But "The Signal-Man" is something else entirely, a penetrating psychological story and a disturbingly ambiguous questioning of the nature of reality, a story of "nameless horror." It is perhaps Dickens' best horror story.

"**H**alloa! Below there!"

When he heard a voice thus calling to him, he was standing at the door of his box, with a flag in his hand, furled round its short pole. One would have thought, considering the nature of the ground, that he could not have doubted from what quarter the voice came; but instead of looking up to where I stood on the top of the steep cutting nearly over his head, he turned himself about, and looked down the Line. There was something remarkable in his manner of doing so, though I could not have said for my life what. But I know it was remarkable enough to attract my notice, even though his figure was foreshortened and shadowed, down in the deep trench, and mine was high above him, so steeped in the glow of an angry sunset, that I had shaded my eyes with my hand before I saw him at all.

"Halloa! Below!"

From looking down the Line, he turned himself about again, and, raising his eyes, saw my figure high above him.

"Is there any path by which I can come down and speak to you?"

He looked up at me without replying, and I looked down at him without pressing him too soon with a repetition of my idle question. Just then there came a vague vibration in the earth and air, quickly changing into a violent pulsation, and an oncoming rush that caused me to start back, as though it had force to draw me down. When such vapour as rose to my height from this rapid train had passed me, and was skimming away over the landscape, I looked down again, and saw him refurling the flag he had shown while the train went by.

I repeated my inquiry. After a pause, during which he seemed to regard me with fixed attention, he motioned with his rolled-up flag towards a point on my level, some two or three hundred yards distant. I called down to him, "All right!" and made for that point. There, by dint of looking closely about me, I found a rough zigzag descending path notched out, which I followed.

The cutting was extremely deep and unusually precipitous. It was made through a clammy stone, that became oozier and wetter as I went down. For these reasons, I found the way long enough to give me time to recall a singular air of reluctance or compulsion with which he had pointed out the path.

When I came down low enough upon the zigzag descent to see him again, I saw that he was standing between the rails on the way by which the train had lately passed, in an attitude as if he were waiting for me to appear. He had his left hand at his chin, and that left elbow rested on his right hand, crossed over his breast. His attitude was one of such expectation and watchfulness that I stopped a moment, wondering at it.

I resumed my downward way, and stepping out upon the level of the railroad, and drawing nearer to him, saw that he was a dark, sallow man, with a dark beard and rather heavy eyebrows. His post was in as solitary and dismal a place as ever I saw. On either side a dripping-wet wall of jagged stone, excluding all view but a strip of sky; the perspective one way only a crooked prolongation of this great dungeon; the shorter perspective in the other direction terminating in a gloomy red light, and the gloomier entrance to a black tunnel, in whose massive architecture there was a barbarous, depressing, and forbidding air. So little sunlight ever found its way to this spot that it had an earthy, deadly smell; and so much cold wind rushed through it that it struck chill to me, as if I had left the natural world.

Before he stirred, I was near enough to him to have touched him. Not even then removing his eyes from mine, he stepped back one step, and lifted his hand.

This was a lonesome post to occupy (I said), and it had riveted my attention when I looked down from up yonder. A visitor was a rarity, I should suppose; not an unwelcome rarity, I hoped? In me he merely saw a man who had been shut up within narrow limits all his life, and who, being at last set free, had a newly-awakened interest in these great works. To such purpose I spoke to him; but I am far from sure of the terms I used, for, besides that I am not happy in opening any conversation, there was something in the man that daunted me.

He directed a most curious look towards the red light near the tunnel's mouth, and looked all about it, as if something were missing from it, and then looked at me.

That light was part of his charge, was it not?

He answered in a low voice, "Don't you know it is?"

The monstrous thought came into my mind, as I perused the fixed eyes and the saturnine face, that this was a spirit, not a man. I have speculated since whether there may have been infection in his mind.

In my turn I stepped back. But in making the action, I detected in his eyes some latent fear of me. This put the monstrous thought to flight.

"You look at me," I said, forcing a smile, "as if you had a dread of me."

"I was doubtful," he returned, "whether I had seen you before."

"Where?"

He pointed to the red light he had looked at.

"There?" I said.

Intently watchful of me, he replied (but without sound), "Yes."

"My good fellow, what should I do there? However, be that as it may, I never was there, you may swear."

"I think I may," he rejoined. "Yes; I am sure I may."

His manner cleared, like my own. He replied to my remarks with readiness, and in well-chosen words. Had he much to do there? Yes—that was to say, he had enough responsibility to bear; but exactness and watchfulness were what was required of him, and of actual work—manual labour—he had next to none. To change that signal, to trim those lights, and to turn this iron handle now and then, was all he had to do under that head. Regarding those many long and lonely hours of which I seemed to make so much, he could only say that the routine of his life had shaped itself into that form, and he had grown used to it. He had taught himself a language down here—if only to know it by sight, and to have formed his own crude ideas of its pronunciation, could be called learning it. He had also worked at fractions and decimals, and tried a little algebra; but he was, and had been as a boy, a poor hand at figures. Was it necessary for him when on duty always to remain in that channel of damp air, and could he never rise into the sunshine from between those high stone walls? Why that depended upon times and circumstances. Under some conditions there would be less upon the Line than under others; and the same held good as to certain hours of the day and night. In bright weather, he did choose occasions for getting a little above these lower shadows; but, being at all times liable to be called by his electric bell, and at such times listening for it with redoubled anxiety, the relief was less than I would suppose.

He took me into his box, where there was a fire, a desk for an official book in which he had to make certain entries, a telegraphic instrument with its dial, face, and needles, and the little bell of which he had spoken. On my trusting that he would excuse the remark that he had been well educated, and (I hoped I might say without offence) perhaps educated above that station, he observed that instances of slight incongruity in such wise would rarely be found wanting among large bodies of men; that he had heard it was so in workhouses, in the police force, even in that last desperate resource the army; and that he knew it was so, more or less, in any great railway staff. He had been, when young (if I could believe it, sitting in that hut—he scarcely could), a student of natural philosophy, and had attended lectures; but he had run wild, misused his opportunities, gone down, and never risen again. He had no complaint to offer about that. He had made his bed, and he lay upon it. It was far too late to make another.

All that I have here condensed he said in a quiet manner, with his grave dark regards divided between me and the fire. He threw in the word "Sir" from time to time, and especially when he referred to his youth—as though to request me to understand that he claimed to be nothing but what I found him. He was several times interrupted by the little bell, and had to read off messages, and send replies. Once he had to stand without the door, and display a flag as a train passed, and make some verbal communication to the driver. In the discharge of his duties, I observed him to be remarkably exact and vigilant, breaking off his discourse at a syllable, and remaining silent until what he had to do was done.

In a word, I should have set this man down as one of the safest of men to be employed in that capacity, but for the circumstance that while he was speaking to me he twice broke off with a fallen colour, turned his face towards the little bell when it did NOT ring, opened the door of the hut (which was kept shut to exclude the unhealthy damp), and looked out towards the red light near the mouth of the tunnel. On both of those occasions, he came back to the fire with the inexplicable air upon him which I had remarked, without being able to define, when we were so far asunder.

Said I, when I rose to leave him, "You almost make me think that I have met with a contented man."

(I am afraid I must acknowledge that I said it to lead him on.)

"I believe I used to be so," he rejoined, in the low voice in which he had first spoken; "but I am troubled, sir, I am troubled."

He would have recalled the words if he could. He had said them, however, and I took them up quickly.

"With what? What is your trouble?"

"It is very difficult to impart, sir. It is very, very difficult to speak of. If ever you make me another visit, I will try to tell you."

"But I expressly intend to make you another visit. Say, when shall it be?"

"I go off early in the morning, and I shall be on again at ten tomorrow night, sir."

"I will come at eleven."

He thanked me, and went out at the door with me. "I'll show my white light, sir," he said, in his peculiar low voice, "till you have found the way up. When you have found it, don't call out! And when you are at the top, don't call out!"

His manner seemed to make the place strike colder to me, but I said no more than, "Very well."

"And when you come down to-morrow night, don't call out! Let me ask you a parting question. What made you cry, 'Halloa! Below there!' to-night?"

"Heaven knows," said I. "I cried something to that effect—"

"Not to that effect, sir. Those were the very words. I know them well."

"Admit those were the very words. I said them, no doubt, because I saw you below."

"For no other reason?"

"What other reason could I possibly have?"

"You had no feeling that they were conveyed to you in any supernatural way?"

"No."

He wished me good-night, and held up his light. I walked by the side of the down Line of rails (with a very disagreeable sensation of a train coming behind me) until I found the path. It was easier to mount than to descend, and I got back to my inn without any adventure.

Punctual to my appointment, I placed my foot on the first notch of the zigzag next night, as the distant clocks were striking eleven. He was waiting for me at the bottom, with his white light on. "I have not called out," I said, when we came close together; "may I speak now?" "By all means, sir." "Good-night, then, and here's my hand." "Good-night, sir, and here's mine." With that we walked side by side to his box, entered it, closed the door, and sat down by the fire.

"I have made up my mind, sir," he began, bending forward as soon as we were seated, and speaking in a tone but a little above a whisper, "that you shall not have to ask me twice what troubles me. I took you for some one else yesterday evening. That troubles me."

"That mistake?"

"No. That Some one else."

"Who is it?"

"I don't know."

"Like me?"

"I don't know. I never saw the face. The left arm is across the face, and the right arm is waved—violently waved. This way."

I followed his action with my eyes, and it was the action of an arm gesticulating, with the utmost passion and vehemence, "For God's sake, clear the way!"

"One moonlight night," said the man, "I was sitting here, when I heard a voice cry, 'Halloa! Below there!' I started up, looked from that door, and saw this Some one else standing by the red light near the tunnel, waving as I just now showed you. The voice seemed hoarse with shouting, and it cried, 'Look out! Look out!' And then again, 'Halloa! Below there! Look out!' I caught up my lamp, turned it on red, and ran towards the figure, calling, 'What's wrong? What has happened? Where?' It stood just outside the blackness of the tunnel. I advanced so close upon it that I wondered at its keeping the sleeve across its eyes. I ran right up at it, and had my hand stretched out to pull the sleeve away, when it was gone."

"Into the tunnel?" said I.

"No. I ran on into the tunnel, five hundred yards. I stopped, and held my lamp above my head, and saw the figures of the measured distance, and saw the wet stains stealing down the walls and trickling through the arch. I ran out again faster than I had run in (for I had a mortal abhorrence of the place upon me), and I looked all round the red light with my own red light, and I went up the iron ladder to the gallery atop of it, and I came down again, and ran back here. I telegraphed both ways, 'An alarm has been given. Is anything wrong?' The answer came back, both ways, 'All well.'"

Resisting the slow touch of a frozen finger tracing out my spine, I showed him how that this figure must be a deception of his sense of sight; and how that figures, originating in disease of the delicate nerves that minister to the functions of the eye, were known to have often troubled patients, some of whom had become conscious of the nature of their affliction, and had even proved it by experiments upon themselves. "As to an imaginary cry," said I, "do but listen for a moment to the wind in this unnatural valley while we speak so low, and to the wild harp it makes of the telegraph wires."

That was all very well, he returned, after we had sat listening for a while, and he ought to know something of the wind and the wires—he who so often passed long winter nights there, alone and watching. But he would beg to remark that he had not finished.

I asked his pardon, and he slowly added these words, touching my arm,—

"Within six hours after the Appearance, the memorable accident on this Line happened, and within ten hours the dead and wounded were brought along through the tunnel over the spot where the figure had stood."

A disagreeable shudder crept over me, but I did my best against it. It was not to be denied, I rejoined, that this was a remarkable coincidence, calculated deeply to impress his mind. But it was unquestionable that remarkable coincidences did continually occur, and they must be taken into account in dealing with such a subject. Though to be sure I must admit, I added (for I thought I saw that he was going to bring the objection to bear upon me), men of common sense did not allow much for coincidences in making the ordinary calculations of life.

He again begged to remark that he had not finished.

I again begged his pardon for being betrayed into interruptions.

"This," he said, again laying his hand upon my arm, and glancing over his shoulder with hollow eyes, "was just a year ago. Six or seven months passed, and I had recovered from the surprise and shock, when one morning, as the day was breaking, I, standing at the door, looked towards the red light, and saw the spectre again." He stopped, with a fixed look at me.

"Did it cry out?"

"No. It was silent."

"Did it wave its arm?"

"No. It leaned against the shaft of the light, with both hands before the face. Like this."

Once more I followed his action with my eyes. It was an action of mourning. I have seen such an attitude in stone figures on tombs.

"Did you go up to it?"

"I came in and sat down, partly to collect my thoughts, partly because it had turned me faint. When I went to the door again, daylight was above me, and the ghost was gone."

"But nothing followed? Nothing came of this?"

He touched me on the arm with his forefinger twice or thrice, giving a ghastly nod each time:—

"That very day, as a train came out of the tunnel, I noticed, at a carriage window on my side, what looked like a confusion of hands and heads, and something waved. I saw it just in time to signal the driver, Stop! He shut off, and put his brake on; but the train drifted past here a hundred and fifty yards or more. I ran after it, and, as I went along, heard terrible screams and cries.

A beautiful young lady had died instantaneously in one of the compartments, and was brought in here, and laid down on this floor between us."

Involuntarily I pushed my chair back, as I looked from the boards at which he pointed to himself.

"True, sir. True. Precisely as it happened, so I tell it you."

I could think of nothing to say, to any purpose, and my mouth was very dry. The wind and the wires took up the story with a long lamenting wail.

He resumed. "Now, sir, mark this, and judge how my mind is troubled. The spectre came back a week ago. Ever since, it has been there, now and again, by fits and starts."

"At the light?"

"At the Danger-light."

"What does it seem to do?"

He repeated, if possible with increased passion and vehemence, that former gesticulation of, "For God's sake, clear the way!"

Then he went on: "I have no peace or rest for it. It calls to me, for many minutes together, in an agonized manner, 'Below there! Look out! Look out!' It stands waving to me. It rings my little bell——"

I caught at that. "Did it ring your bell yesterday evening when I was here, and you went to the door?"

"Twice."

"Why, see," said I, "how your imagination misleads you. My eyes were on the bell, and my ears were open to the bell, and if I am a living man, it did NOT ring at those times. No, nor at any other time, except when it was rung in the natural course of physical things by the station communicating with you."

He shook his head. "I have never made a mistake as to that yet, sir. I have never confused the spectre's ring with the man's. The ghost's ring is a strange vibration in the bell that it derives from nothing else, and I have not asserted that the bell stirs to the eye. I don't wonder that you failed to hear it. But *I* heard it."

"And did the spectre seem to be there when you looked out?"

"It WAS there."

"Both times?"

He repeated firmly, "Both times."

"Will you come to the door with me and look for it now?"

He bit his under lip, as though he were somewhat unwilling, but arose. I opened the door, and stood on the step, while he stood in the doorway. There was the Danger-light. There was the dismal mouth of the tunnel. There were the high, wet stone walls of the cutting. There were the stars above them.

"Do you see it?" I asked him, taking particular note of his face. His eyes were prominent and strained, but not very much more so, perhaps, than my own had been when I had directed them earnestly towards the same spot.

"No," he answered. "It is not there."

"Agreed," said I.

We went in again, shut the door, and resumed our seats. I was thinking how best to improve this advantage, if it might be called one, when he took up the conversation in such a matter-of-course way, so assuming that there could be no serious question of fact between us, that I felt myself placed in the weakest of positions.

"By this time you will fully understand, sir," he said, "that what troubles me so dreadfully is the question, What does the spectre mean?"

I was not sure, I told him, that I did fully understand.

"What is its warning against?" he said, ruminating, with his eyes on the fire, and only by times turning them on me. "What is the danger? Where is the danger? There is danger overhanging somewhere on the Line. Some dreadful calamity will happen. It is not to be doubted this third time, after what has gone before. But surely this is a cruel haunting of *me*. What can *I* do?"

He pulled out his handkerchief, and wiped the drops from his heated forehead.

"If I telegraph Danger, on either side of me, or on both, I can give no reason for it," he went on, wiping the palms of his hands. "I should get into trouble, and do no good. They would think I was mad. This is the way it would work:—Message: 'Danger! Take care!' Answer: 'What Danger? Where?' Message: 'Don't know. But, for God's sake, take care!' They would displace me. What else could they do?"

His pain of mind was most pitiable to see. It was the mental torture of a conscientious man, oppressed beyond endurance by an unintelligible responsibility involving life.

"When it first stood under the Danger-light," he went on, putting his dark hair back from his head, and drawing his hands outward across his temples in an extremity of feverish distress, "why not tell me where that accident was to happen—if it must happen? Why not tell me how it could be averted—if it could have been averted? When on its second coming it hid its face, why not tell me, instead, 'She is going to die. Let them keep her at home'? If it came, on those two occasions, only to show me that its warnings were true, and so to prepare me for the third, why not warn me plainly now? And I, Lord help me! A mere poor signal-man on this solitary station! Why not go to somebody with credit to be believed, and power to act?"

When I saw him in this state, I saw that for the poor man's sake, as well as for the public safety, what I had to do for the time was to compose his mind. Therefore, setting aside all question of reality or unreality between us, I represented to him that whoever thoroughly discharged his duty must do well, and that at least it was his comfort that he understood his duty, though he did not understand these confounding Appearances. In this effort I succeeded far better than in the attempt to reason him out of his conviction. He became calm; the occupations incidental to his post as the night advanced began to make larger demands on his attention; and I left him at two in the morning. I had offered to stay through the night, but he would not hear of it.

That I more than once looked back at the red light as I ascended the pathway, that I did not like the red light, and that I should have slept but poorly if my bed had been under it, I see no reason to conceal. Nor did I like the two sequences of the accident and the dead girl. I see no reason to conceal that either.

But what ran most in my thoughts was the consideration how ought I to act, having become the recipient of this disclosure? I had proved the man to be intelligent, vigilant, painstaking, and exact; but how long might he remain so, in his state of mind? Though in a subordinate position, still he held a most important trust; and would I (for instance) like to stake my own life on the chances of his continuing to execute it with precision?

Unable to overcome a feeling that there would be something treacherous in my communicating what he had told me to his superiors in the Company, without first being plain with himself and proposing a middle course to him, I ultimately resolved to offer to accompany him (otherwise keeping his secret for the present) to the wisest medical practitioner we could hear of in those parts, and to take his opinion. A change in his time of duty would come round next night, he had apprised me, and he would be off an hour or two after sunrise, and on again soon after sunset. I had appointed to return accordingly.

Next evening was a lovely evening, and I walked out early to enjoy it. The sun was not yet quite down when I traversed the field-path near the top of the deep cutting. I would extend my walk for an hour, I said to myself, half an hour on and half an hour back, and it would then be time to go to my signal-man's box.

Before pursuing my stroll, I stepped to the brink, and mechanically looked down from the point from which I had first seen him. I cannot describe the thrill that seized upon me when, close at the mouth of the tunnel, I saw the appearance of a man, with his left sleeve across his eyes, passionately waving his right arm.

The nameless horror that oppressed me passed in a moment, for in a moment I saw that this appearance of a man was a man indeed, and that there was a little group of other men, standing at a short distance, to whom he seemed to be rehearsing the gesture he made. The Danger-light was not yet lighted. Against its shaft, a little low hut, entirely new to me, had been made of some wooden supports and tarpaulin. It looked no bigger than a bed.

With an irresistible sense that something was wrong—with a flashing self-reproachful fear that fatal mischief had come of my leaving the man there, and causing no one to be sent to overlook or correct what he did—I descended the notched path with all the speed I could make.

"What is the matter?" I asked the men.

"Signal-man killed this morning, sir."

"Not the man belonging to that box?"

"Yes, sir."

"Not the man I know?"

"You will recognize him, sir, if you knew him," said the man who spoke for the others, solemnly uncovering his own head, and raising an end of the tarpaulin, "for his face is quite composed."

"Oh, how did this happen—how did this happen?" I asked, turning from one to another as the hut closed in again.

"He was cut down by an engine, sir. No man in England knew his work better. But somehow he was not clear of the outer rail. It was just at broad day. He had struck the light, and had the lamp in his hand. As the engine came out of the tunnel, his back was towards her, and she cut him down. That man drove her, and was showing how it happened. "Show the gentleman, Tom.""

The man who wore a rough dark dress, stepped back to his former place at the mouth of the tunnel.

"Coming round the curve in the tunnel, sir," he said, "I saw him at the end, like as if I saw him down a perspective-glass. There was no time to check speed, and I knew him to be very careful. As he didn't seem to take heed of the whistle, I shut it off when we were running down upon him, and called to him as loud as I could call."

"What did you say?"

"I said, "Below there! Look out! Look out! For God's sake, clear the way!""

I started.

"Ah! it was a dreadful time, sir. I never left off calling to him. I put this arm before my eyes not to see, and I waved this arm to the last; but it was no use."

Without prolonging the narrative to dwell on any one of its curious circumstances more than on any other, I may, in closing it, point out the coincidence that the warning of the Engine-Driver included, not only the words which the unfortunate Signal-man had repeated to me as haunting him, but also the words which I myself—not he—had attached, and that only in my own mind, to the gesticulation he had imitated.

Stephen King

Crouch End

It is a tribute to King's range of talent that he, like Dickens, can work outside his ordinary métier upon occasion. He is in fact the Dickens of the contemporary horror field: his unparallelled popularity and moral stance, his irrevocable commitment to popular culture and commerce, his flair for storytelling and entertainment, his seemingly tireless energy, his rejection by the majority of the guardians of high art. While Stephen King's "The Mist" is the premier example to date in his works of a story concerned with shifting realities, "Crouch End," King's Lovecraftian Cthulhu mythos story, occupies a more borderline position. This story is the closest King approaches, except in the odd, surreal "Big Wheels," and perhaps in "Mrs. Todd's Shortcut" to a concern with alterations in base or consensus reality. And he does so here only by adopting the borrowed posture of "The Call of Cthulhu," that the elder gods are real, distinguishing his own approach by maintaining that they are real in an other or alternate universe connected to ours only at spots such as Crouch End in London. In Lovecraft there is only one reality, cosmic and evilly inhuman. At this writing King is just past forty and already a phenomenal worldwide success, and the evolution of the horror novel has been advanced more by his works than those of any writer in the history of the genre. And he is so exceedingly generous in his support of the work of other writers that his name stands behind (or on the paperback cover) of many books every year by others. He is a one-man boom in the publishing of horror in our time.

By the time the woman had finally gone, it was nearly two-thirty in the morning. Outside the Crouch End police station, Tottenham Lane was a small dead river. London was asleep—but of course, London never sleeps deeply, and its dreams are uneasy.

PC Vetter closed his notebook, which he'd almost filled as the American woman's strange frenzied story had poured out. He looked at the typewriter and the stack of blank forms on the shelf beside it.

"This one'll look odd come the morning light," PC Vetter said.

PC Farnham was drinking a Coke. He didn't speak for a long time. "She was an American woman," he said finally, as if that might explain the story she had told.

"It'll go in the back file," Vetter agreed, and looked around for a cigarette. "But I wonder . . ."

Farnham laughed. "You don't mean you believe any part of it?"

"Didn't say that, did I? No. But you're new here."

PC Farnham sat a little straighter. He was twenty-seven, and it was hardly his fault that he had been posted here from Muswell Hill to the north, or that Vetter, who was nearly twice his age, had spent his entire uneventful career in the quiet London backwater of Crouch End.

"Perhaps so, sir," he said, "but, respectfully, I still think I know a piece of whole cloth when I see one . . . or hear one."

"Give us a fag, Farnham," Vetter said, looking a little amused. "There's a good boy." He lit it with a wooden match from a bright red railway box, shook it out, and tossed the match stub into Farnham's ashtray. He peered at Farnham through a haze of drifting smoke. His face was deeply lined and his nose was a map of broken veins—he liked his six cans of Harp a night, did PC Vetter.

"You think Crouch End's a very quiet place, don't you?"

Farnham shrugged. He thought Crouch End was suburban and, tell the truth, dull as dishwater. "Quiet, yes."

"And you're right. It is. Goes to sleep by eleven, most nights. But I've seen a lot of strange things in Crouch End. If you're here half as long as I've been, you'll see your share, too. There are more strange things happen right here in this quiet six or eight blocks than anywhere else in London, I'll take my oath. And that's saying a lot. It scares me. So I have my lager, and then I'm not so scared. You look at Sergeant Gordon sometime, Farnham, and ask yourself why his hair is dead white at forty. Or I'd say take a look at Petty, but you can't very well, can you? Petty committed suicide in the summer of 1976. Our hot summer. It was . . ." Vetter seemed to consider his words. "It was quite bad that summer. Quite bad. There were a lot of us who were afraid . . . they might break through."

"Who might break through what?" Farnham asked. He felt a contemptuous smile turning up the corners of his mouth, knew it was far from politic, but was unable to stop it. In his way, Vetter was raving as badly as the American woman had. He had always been a bit queer. The booze, probably. Then he saw Vetter was smiling right back at him.

"You think I'm dotty," he said.

"Not at all," Farnham protested, groaning inwardly.

"You're a good boy," Vetter said. "Won't be riding a desk here in the station when you're my age. Not if you stick on the force. D'you plan to stick it, Farnham?"

"Yes," Farnham said firmly. It was true. He meant to stick it even though Sheila wanted him off the police force and somewhere she could count on him. The Ford assembly line, perhaps. The thought of it curdled his stomach.

"I thought you did," Vetter said, crushing his smoke. "Gets in your blood, doesn't it? And you could go far. And it'll not be Crouch End you finish up in, either. Still, you don't know everything. Crouch End is . . . strange. You ought to look in the back file sometime, Farnham. Oh, a lot of it's the usual . . . girls and boys run away from home to be hippies . . . punks, they call themselves now . . . men who went out for a pack of fags and just never came back . . . and when you clap an eye to their wives you understand why . . . unsolved arsons . . . purse-snatching . . . all of that. But in between, there's enough stories to curdle your blood. And some to sick your stomach."

"Is that true?" Farnham demanded suddenly.

Vetter didn't seem offended by the question. He just nodded. "Stories very much like the one that poor American girl told us. She'll not see her husband no more, that girl won't." He looked at Farnham and shrugged. "Believe me, believe me not. It's all one, isn't it? The file's there. We call it the open file because it's more polite than the back file or the unsolved file. Study it up, Farnham. Study it up."

Farnham said nothing, but he intended to study it up. The idea that there might be a whole series of stories such as the one the American woman had told was . . . was disturbing.

"Sometimes," Vetter said, stealing another of Farnham's Silk Cut cigarettes, "I wonder about Dimensions. Science fiction writers are always going on about Dimensions, aren't they? Ever read science fiction, Farnham?"

"No," Farnham said. He had decided this was some sort of elaborate leg-pull.

"Ever read Lovecraft?"

"Never heard of him."

"Well, this fellow Lovecraft was always writing about Dimensions," Vetter said, producing his box of railway matches. "Dimensions close to ours. Full of these immortal monsters that would drive a man mad at one look. Frightful rubbish, what? Except, whenever one of these people straggles in, I think it all might just be true. I say to myself then—when it's quiet and late at night, like it is now—that our whole world, everything we think of as nice and normal and sane, is like a big leather ball filled with air. Only in some places, the leather's scuffed almost down to nothing. Places where . . . where the barriers are thinner. Do you get me?"

"Yes," Farnham said. He did not get PC Vetter at all.

"And then I think, Crouch End's one of those thin places. Highgate's mostly all right, it's just as thick as you'd want between us and the Dimensions in Muswell Hill and Highgate, but now you take Archway and Finsbury Park. They border on Crouch End, too. I've got friends in both places, and they know of my . . . my interest in certain things that don't seem to be any way rational. Certain things related, we'll say, by people with nothing to gain by making up a crazy story. Did you ask yourself, Farnham, why the woman would have told us the things she did if they weren't true?" He struck a match and looked at Farnham over it. "Pretty young woman, twenty-six, two kiddies back at her hotel, husband's a young lawyer doing well in Milwaukee or someplace? What's to gain by coming in here and raving about monsters?"

"I don't know," Farnham said stiffly. "But there may be an ex—"

"So I say to myself," Vetter overrode him, "that if there were such things as 'thin spots,' this one would begin at Archway and Finsbury Park . . . but the real thin place is here at Crouch End. And I say to myself, wouldn't it be a day if whatever was left just . . . rubbed away? Wouldn't it be a day if even half of what that woman told us was true?"

Farnham was silent. He had decided that PC Vetter probably also believed in palmistry and phrenology and the Rosicrucians.

"Read the back file," Vetter said, getting up. There was a crackling sound as he put his hands in the small of his back and stretched. "I'm going out to get some fresh air."

He strolled out. Farnham looked after him with a mixture of amusement and resentment. Vetter was dotty, all right. He was also a bloody fag-mooch. Fags didn't come cheap in this brave new world of socialism and the welfare state. He picked up Vetter's notebook and began leafing through the girl's story again.

And, yes, he would go through the back file.

He would do it for laughs.

The girl—the young woman—had burst into the station at quarter past ten the previous evening, her hair in damp strings around her face, her eyes bulging. She was dragging her purse by the strap.

"Lonnie," she said. "Oh, my God, you've got to find Lonnie."

"Well, we'll do our best, won't we?" Vetter said. "But you've got to tell us who Lonnie is."

"He's dead," the young woman said. "I know he is." She began to cry. Then she began to laugh—to cackle, really. She dropped her purse in front of her. She was hysterical.

The station was fairly deserted at that hour on a weeknight. Sergeant Raymond was listening to a Pakistani woman tell, with almost unearthly calm, how her purse had been nicked on Hillfield Avenue. He half rose, and PC Farnham came in from the anteroom, where he had been taking down old posters (HAVE YOU ROOM IN YOUR HEART FOR AN UNWANTED CHILD?) and putting up new ones (SIX RULES FOR SAFE NIGHT-CYCLING).

Vetter nodded for Farnham and waved Sergeant Raymond back. Raymond, who liked to break pickpockets' fingers for them, was not the man for a hysterical woman.

"Lonnie!" she shrieked. "Oh, my God, Lonnie, they've got him—!"

The Pakistani woman turned the steady brown moon of her face toward the young American woman, studied her for a moment, and then turned back to Sergeant Raymond, her calm unbroken. Farnham came forward.

"Miss—" PC Farnham began.

"What's going on out there?" she whispered. Her breath was coming in quick pants. Farnham noticed there was a slight scratch on her left cheek. She was a pretty thing with auburn hair. Her clothes were moderately expensive. The heel had come off one of her shoes.

"What's going on out there?" she repeated, and then she said it for the first time: "Monsters—"

The Pakistani woman looked over again . . . and smiled. Her teeth were rotten. The smile was gone like a conjurer's trick, and she was looking at the lost/stolen property form Raymond had handed her.

"Get the lady a cup of coffee and bring it down to room three," Vetter said. "Could you do with a cup of coffee, mum?"

"Lonnie," she whispered. "I know he's dead."

"Now, you just come with old Ted Vetter and we'll see what this is about," he said, and helped her to her feet. She was still talking in a low moaning voice when he led her away, one arm around her. She was rocking unsteadily because of the broken shoe.

Farnham got the coffee and brought it into room three, a plain white cubicle furnished with a scarred table, four chairs, and a water cooler in the corner. He put the coffee in front of her.

"Here, mum," he said, "this'll do you good. I've got sugars if—"

"I can't drink it," she said. "I couldn't—" And then she clutched the porcelain cup—someone's long-forgotten souvenir of Blackpool—in her hands as if for warmth. Her hands were shaking quite badly, and Farnham wanted to tell her to put it down before she slopped the coffee and burned herself.

"I couldn't," she said again, and then drank, still holding the cup two-handed, the way a child will hold his cup of broth. And when she looked at them, it was a child's look—simple, exhausted, appealing . . . and at bay. It was as if whatever had happened had somehow made her roughly young; as if some invisible hand had swooped down from the sky and roughly slapped the last twenty years from her, leaving a child in grown-up American clothes in this small white interrogation room in Crouch End. Yes, it had been like that.

"Lonnie," she said. "The monsters," she said. "Will you help me? Will you please help me? Maybe he isn't dead. Maybe . . . I'm an American citizen!" she cried out suddenly, and then, as if she had said something deeply shameful, she began to sob.

Vetter patted her shoulder. "There, mum. I think we can help find your Lonnie. Your husband, is he?"

Still sobbing, she nodded. "Danny and Norma are back at the hotel . . . with the sitter . . . they'll be sleeping . . . expecting him to kiss them when he comes in . . ."

"Now if you could just relax and tell us what happened—"

"And where it happened," Farnham added. Vetter looked up at him swiftly, frowning.

"But that's just it!" she cried. "I don't know *where* it happened! I'm not even sure what happened, except that it was h-h-hor—"

Vetter had taken out his notebook. "What's your name, mum?"

"My name is Doris Freeman. My husband is Leonard Freeman. We're staying at the Hotel Inter-Continental. We're American citizens." This recital seemed to steady her a little. She sipped her coffee and put the mug down. Farnham saw that the palms of her hands were quite red.

Vetter was writing all of this down in his notebook. Now he looked momentarily at PC Farnham, just an unobtrusive flick of the eyes.

"Are you on holiday?" he asked.

"Yes . . . two weeks here and one week in Spain. We were supposed to have a week in Spain . . . but this isn't helping find Lonnie! Why are you asking me these stupid questions?"

"Just trying to get the background, Mrs. Freeman," Farnham said. Without really thinking about it, both of them had adopted low soothing voices. "Now you go ahead and tell us what happened. Tell it in your own words."

"Why is it so hard to get a taxi in London?" she asked abruptly.

Farnham hardly knew what to say, but Vetter responded as if the question was utterly germane to the discussion.

"Hard to say, mum. The tourists, maybe. And it can be specially hard around five o'clock. That's when they start changing drivers, you know. Day shift goes off, night shift comes on. Why? Did you have a problem getting someone who'd take you from in town out here to Crouch End?"

"Yes," she said, and looked at him gratefully. "We left the hotel at three and came down to Foyle's Bookshop. Is that Cambridge Circus?"

"Near there," Vetter agreed. "Lovely big bookshop, mum, isn't it?"

"We had no trouble getting a cab from the Inter-Continental . . . they were lined up outside. But when we came out of Foyle's, it was like you said. They went by, but their lights on top were always off and when the first one did stop, when Lonnie said Crouch End, the driver just laughed and shook his head. Said it wasn't his cab."

"Aye, that's right," Farnham said.

"He even refused a pound tip," Doris Freeman said, and a very American perplexity had crept into her tone. "We waited for almost half an hour before we got a driver who said he'd take us out. It was five-thirty by then, or maybe quarter of six. And that was when Lonnie discovered he'd lost the address . . ."

She clutched the mug again.

"Who were you going to see?" Vetter asked.

"A colleague of my husband's. A lawyer named John Squales. My husband had never met him, but their two firms were—" She gestured vaguely.

"Affiliated?"

"Yes, that's right. And over the last four years Lonnie and Mr. Squales have had a lot of correspondence back and forth. And when Mr. Squales found out we were going to be in London on vacation, he invited us to his home for dinner. Lonnie had always written him at his office, of course, but he had Mr. Squales's home address on a slip of paper. After we got in the cab, he discovered he'd lost it. And all he could remember was that it was in Crouch End."

She looked at them.

"Crouch End. That's an ugly name."

Vetter said, "So what did you do then?"

She began to talk. By the time she finished, her first cup of coffee and another one were gone, and PC Vetter had filled up several pages in his notebook with his blocky, sprawling script . . .

Lonnie Freeman was a big man, and hunched forward in the roomy back seat of the black London cab so he could talk to the driver, he looked to her amazingly as he had looked when she had first seen him at a college basketball game in their senior year—sitting on the bench, his knees somewhere up around his ears, his hands on their big wrists dangling between his legs. Only then he had been wearing basketball shorts and a towel around his neck, and now he was in a business suit and tie. He had never gotten in many games, she remembered fondly, because he just wasn't that good. And he lost addresses.

The cabby listened indulgently to the tale of the lost address after all of Lonnie's pockets had been duly investigated. He was an elderly man impeccably turned out in a grey summer-weight suit, the antithesis of the slouching New York cab driver. Only the checked wool cap on the driver's head clashed, but it was an agreeable clash; it lent him a touch of rakish charm. Outside, the traffic flowed endlessly past on Cambridge Circus; the theater nearby announced that *Jesus Christ Superstar* was entering its eighth year of continuous performances.

"Well, I tell you what, guv," the cabby said. "I'll take you out to Crouch End, but I'm not going to just put yer down there. Because Crouch End's a big place, en't it?"

And Lonnie, who had never been in Crouch End—or out of the United States, for that matter—in his life, nodded sagely.

"Yes, it is," the cabby agreed with himself. "So I take yer there, and we'll stop at a call box, and you check your friend's address, and off we go, right to the door."

"That's wonderful," Doris said, really meaning it. They had been in London six days now, and she could not recall ever having been in a place where the people were more polite, kinder, or . . . or more civilized.

"Thank you," Lonnie said, and sat back. He put his arm around Doris and smiled. "See? No problem."

"No thanks to you," she mock-growled, and threw a light punch at his midsection. There was plenty of room for even a tall man like Lonnie to stretch out; the black London cabs were roomier than the New York Checkers, too.

"Right," the cabby said. "Off we go, then. Heigh-ho for Crouch End."

It was late August, and a steady hot wind rattled the trash across the roads and whipped at the coats and skirts of the men and women going home from work. The sun had settled below the tops of the buildings, but when it shone between them, Doris saw that it was beginning to take on the reddish cast of evening. The cabby hummed. She relaxed with Lonnie's arm around her—she had seen more of him in the last six days than she had all year, it seemed, and she was very pleased to discover that she liked it. She had never been out of America before, either, and she had to keep reminding herself that she was in England, she was in *London*, thousands should be so lucky.

Very quickly she had lost any sense of direction. Cab rides in London did that to you, she had discovered. The city was a great sprawling warren of Roads and Mews and Hills and Closes (and even Inns), and she couldn't understand how anyone could get around. When she had mentioned it to Lonnie the day before, he had replied that they got around very carefully . . . hadn't she noticed that they all kept the *London Streetfinder* tucked cozily away beneath the dash?

This was the longest cab ride they had taken. The fashionable section of town dropped behind them (in spite of that perverse going-around-in-circles feeling). They passed through an area of monolithic housing developments that might have been utterly deserted for all the signs of life they showed (no, she corrected herself to Vetter and Farnham in the small white room; she had seen one small boy sitting on the curb, striking matches), then an area of small, rather tatty-looking shops and fruit stalls, and then—no wonder driving in London seemed to produce such a disorienting round-and-round feeling—they seemed to have driven smack into the fashionable section again.

"There was even a McDonald's hamburger place," she told Vetter and Farnham, in a tone of voice usually reserved for the Sphinx and the Hanging Gardens.

"Was there?" Vetter replied, being properly amazed and respectful—she had achieved a kind of total recall, and he wanted nothing to break that mood, at least until she had told them everything she could.

The fashionable section with the McDonald's as its centerpiece dropped behind. Now the sun was a solid orange ball sitting above the horizon, washing the streets with a strange clear light that nevertheless made all the pedestrians look as if their faces were aflame.

"It was then that things began to . . . to change," she said. Her voice had dropped a little. Her hands were trembling again.

Vetter leaned forward, intent. "Changed? How? How did things change, Mrs. Freeman?"

They had passed a newsagent's window, she remembered, and the signboard outside had read SIXTY LOST IN UNDERGROUND HORROR.

"Lonnie, look at that!"

"What?" He craned around, but the newsagent's was already behind them.

"It said, 'Sixty Lost in Underground Horror.' Isn't that what they call the subways?"

"Yes," Lonnie said, "the underground or the tubes. Was it a crash?"

"I don't know." She leaned forward. "Driver, do you know what that was about? Was there a subway crash?"

"A collision, mum? Not that I know of."

"Do you have a radio?"

"Not in me cab, mum."

"Lonnie?"

"Hmm?"

But she could see that Lonnie had lost interest. He was going through his pockets again (and because he was wearing his three-piece suit, there were a lot of them to go through), having another hunt for the scrap of paper with John Squales's address written on it.

The message chalked on the board played over and over in her mind. SIXTY KILLED IN TUBE CRASH, it should have read. SIXTY KILLED AS UNDERGROUND TRAINS COLLIDE, it should have read. But . . . SIXTY LOST IN UNDERGROUND HORROR. It made her uneasy. It didn't say "killed," it said "lost" . . . the way sailors were referred to when they drowned at sea.

UNDERGROUND HORROR.

She didn't like it. It made her think of graveyards, sewers, and flabby-pale, noisome things swarming suddenly out of the tubes themselves, wrapping their arms (tentacles, maybe) around the hapless commuters on the platforms, dragging them away to darkness . . .

They turned right. Standing on the corner beside their parked motorcycles were three boys in leathers. They looked up at the cab and for a moment—the setting sun was almost full in her face from this angle—it seemed that the bikers did not have human heads at all. For that one moment she was nastily sure that the sleek, flat, and sloping heads of rats sat atop those black leather jackets, rats with beady black eyes staring at the cab. Then the light shifted just a tiny bit and she saw of course she had been mistaken; there were only three boys in their late teens there, smoking cigarettes and standing in front of the British version of the American candy store.

"Here we go," Lonnie said, giving up the search and pointing out the window. They were passing a sign which read "Crouch Hill Road." Elderly brick houses like sleepy dowagers had closed in, seeming to look down at the cab from their blank windows. A few kids passed back and forth, riding bikes or trikes. Two others were trying to ride a skateboard with no notable success. Fathers home from work sat together, smoking and talking and watching the children. It all looked reassuringly normal.

The cab drew up in front of a dismal-looking restaurant with a small spotted sign in the corner of the window reading FULLY LICENSED and a much larger one in the center which informed that within one could purchase curries to take away. On the inner ledge there slept a gigantic grey cat. Beside the restaurant was a call box.

"Here you are, guv," the cab driver said. "You find your friend's address and I'll track him down."

"Fair enough," Lonnie said, and got out.

Doris sat in the cab for a moment and then also emerged, feeling like stretching her legs. The hot wind was still blowing. It whipped her skirt around her knees and then plastered an old ice-cream wrapper to her shin. She removed it with a grimace of disgust. When she looked up, she was staring directly through the plate-glass window at the big grey tom. It stared back at her, one-eyed. The rest of its face had been clawed away in some long-ago but gigantic battle, and all that remained was a twisted pinkish mass of scar tissue, one milky cataract, and a few tufts of fur.

It miaowed at her, silently through the glass.

Feeling a surge of disgust, she went to the call box and peered in through one of the dirty panes. Lonnie made a circle at her with his thumb and forefinger and winked. Then he pushed tenpence into the slot and talked with someone. He laughed—soundlessly through the glass. Like the cat. She looked over, but now the window was empty. In the dimness beyond she could see chairs up on tables and an old man pushing a broom. When she looked back, she saw that Lonnie was jotting something down. He put his pen away, held the paper in his hand—she could see an address was jotted on it—said one or two other things, then hung up and came out.

He waggled the address at her in mild triumph. "Okay, that's th—" His eyes went past her shoulder and he frowned. "Where's the cab gone?"

She turned around. The taxi had vanished. Where it had stood there was only curbing and a few papers blowing lazily up the gutter. Across the street, two kids were clutching at each other and giggling. Doris noticed that one of them had a hand that was deformed into something like a claw—she had thought the National Health was supposed to take care of things like that. The children looked across the street, saw her observing them, and fell into each others' arms, giggling again.

"Well . . . I don't know," Doris said. She felt disoriented and a little stupid. The heat, the wind that seemed to blow constantly with no gusts or drops, like the draft from a furnace, the almost painted quality of the light . . .

("What time was it then?" Farnham asked suddenly.

("I don't know," Doris Freeman said, startled out of her recital. "Six, I suppose. No later than twenty past."

("I see, go on," Farnham said, knowing perfectly well that in August the setting of the sun would not have begun—even by the loosest standards—until seven o'clock or after.)

"Don't know?" Lonnie repeated. "What did he do, just pick up and leave?"

"Maybe when you put your hand up," Doris said, raising her own hand and making the thumb-and-forefinger circle Lonnie had made in the call box, "maybe when you did that he thought you were waving him on."

"I'd have to wave a long time to send him on with two pounds-five on the meter," Lonnie grunted, and walked over to the curb. On the other side of Crouch Hill Road, the two small children were still giggling. "Hey!" Lonnie called. "You kids!"

"You an American, sir?" one of them called back. It was the boy with the claw hand.

"Yes," Lonnie said, smiling. "Did you see a cab over here? Did the driver pull away up the road?"

The two children seemed to consider the question. The boy's companion was a girl of about five with an untidy tangle of brown hair. She stepped forward to the opposite curb, formed her hands into a megaphone, and still smiling—she screamed it through her megaphoned hands and her smile—she cried at them: "*Fuck you, Joe!*"

Lonnie's mouth dropped open.

"*Sir! Sir! Sir!*" the boy screeched, and made an obscene gesture with his deformed hand. Then the two of them took to their heels and fled around the corner and out of sight, leaving only their laughter to echo back.

Lonnie looked at Doris, dumbstruck.

"I . . . I guess they don't like Americans," he said lamely.

She looked around nervously. The street appeared totally deserted.

He slipped an arm around her. "Well, kid, looks like we hike it."

"I'm not sure I want to, Lonnie," she said. "Those two might have gone to get their big brothers." She laughed to show it was a joke, but there was a shrill quality to it she didn't like. Come to think of it, the evening had taken on a decidely surreal quality she didn't much like. She wished they had stayed at the hotel.

"Not much else we can do," he said. "The street's not exactly overflowing with taxis, is it?"

"Lonnie, why would he do that? Just—what do they say?—just scarper like that."

"I don't have the slightest idea. But John gave me good directions for the taxi driver. He lives in a street called Brass End, which is a very minor dead-end street, and he said it wasn't in the *Streetfinder*." As he talked he was moving her away from the call box, from the restaurant that sold curries to take away, from the now-empty curb. They were walking up Crouch Hill Road again. "We take a right onto Hillfield Avenue, a left halfway down, then our first right . . . or was it left? Anyway, onto Petrie Street. Second left is Brass End."

"Can you remember all that?"

"Try me," he said bravely, and she just had to laugh. Lonnie had a way of making things seem better.

There was a map of the Crouch End area on the wall. Farnham approached it and studied it with his hands stuffed into his pockets. The station seemed very quiet, now. Vetter was still outside—clearing some of the witchmoss from his brains, one hoped—and Raymond had finished with the woman who'd had her purse nicked.

Farnham put his finger on the spot where the cabby had most likely let them off (if anything about the woman's story was to be believed, that was). Yes, their route to the lawyer's house looked pretty straightforward. Crouch Hill Road to Hillfield Avenue, a left onto Vickers Lane, left onto Petrie Street, from Petrie Street into Brass End, which was no more than six or eight houses long. No more than a mile all told. Ought to have been able to do that walking on their hands.

"Raymond!" he called. "You still here?"

Raymond came in. He had changed into street clothes and was zipping up a light poplin windcheater. "Only just, my beardless darling."

"Cut it," Farnham said, smiling all the same. Raymond frightened him a little. He was one of those people you could take one look at and know they were standing close to the law-and-order fence . . . on one side or the other. There was a twisted white line of scar running down from the left corner of Raymond's mouth almost all the way to his Adam's apple. He claimed a pickpocket had once nearly cut his throat with a jagged bit of bottle. Claimed that's why he broke their fingers for them. Farnham thought that was shit. He thought Raymond broke their fingers because he liked to break them.

"Got a cig?" Raymond asked.

Farnham sighed and gave him one. His pack was becoming rapidly depleted. As he lit Raymond's smoke he said, "Is there a curry shop on Crouch Hill Road?"

"Not to my knowledge, love," Raymond said.

"That's what I thought."

"Has my poppet got a problem?"

"No," Farnham said, a little too sharply, remembering Doris Freeman's clotted hair and staring eyes.

Near the top of Crouch Hill Road, Doris and Lonnie turned onto Hillfield Avenue, which was lined with imposing and gracious-looking homes—nothing but shells, she thought, probably cut up into apartments and bed-sitters inside with surgical precision.

"So far, so good," Lonnie said.

"Yes, it's—" she began, and that was when the low moaning arose.

They both stopped. The moaning was coming almost directly from their right, where a high hedge ran around a small yard. Lonnie started toward the sound, and she grasped his arm. "Lonnie, no—"

"What do you mean, no?" he said. "Someone's hurt."

She stepped after him nervously. The hedge was high but thin. He was able to brush it aside and reveal a small square of lawn outlined with flowers. The lawn was very green. In the center of it was a black, smoking patch—or at least that was her first impression. When she peered around Lonnie's shoulder again—his shoulder was too high for her to peer over—she saw it was a hole, vaguely man-shaped. The tendrils of smoke were emanating from it.

SIXTY LOST IN UNDERGROUND HORROR, she thought abruptly.

The moaning was coming from the hole, and Lonnie began to force himself through the hedge toward it.

"Lonnie," she said. "No, don't."

"Someone's hurt," he said, and pushed himself the rest of the way through with a bristly tearing sound. She saw him going toward the hole, and then the hedge snapped back, leaving her nothing but a vague impression of his shape as he went toward it. She tried to push through after him and was scratched by the short, stiff branches of the hedge for her trouble. She was wearing a sleeveless blouse.

"Lonnie?" she called, suddenly very afraid. "Lonnie, come back!"

"Just a minute, hon—"

The house looked at her impassively over the top of the hedge.

The moaning sounds continued, but now they sounded lower—guttural and somehow gleeful. Couldn't Lonnie *hear* that?

"Hey, is somebody down there?" she heard Lonnie ask. "Is there—oh! Hey! Jesus!" And suddenly Lonnie screamed. She had never heard him scream before, and it was a terrible sound. Her legs seemed to turn to waterbags. She looked wildly for the entrance path through the hedge and couldn't see it. Anywhere. Images swirled before her eyes—the bikies who had looked like large sleek-headed rats for a moment, the cat with the pink chewed face, the small boy with the claw hand.

Lonnie! She tried to scream, but no words came out.

Now there were sounds of struggle. The moaning had stopped. But there were sounds—wet, sloshing sounds—from the other side of the hedge. Then, suddenly, Lonnie came flying back through the hedge as if he had been given a tremendous push. The left arm of his suit-coat was torn, and the entire suit was splattered with runnels of black stuff that seemed to be smoking, as the pit in the lawn had been smoking.

"Doris, run!"

"Lonnie, what—"

"Run!" His face was totally devoid of color.

Doris looked around wildly, for a cop or anyone else. But Hillfield Avenue might have been a part of some great deserted city for all the life or movement she saw. Then she glanced back at the hedge and saw something else was moving behind there, something that was more than black; it seemed ebony, the antithesis of all light.

And it was sloshing.

A moment later, the short, stiff branches of the hedge began to rustle. She stared, hypnotized with dreadful fascination. She might have stood there forever (so she told Vetter and Farnham) if Lonnie hadn't grabbed her arm roughly and shrieked at her—yes, Lonnie, who never even raised his voice at the kids, had *shrieked*—she might have been standing there yet. Standing there, or . . .

But they ran.

Where? Farnham had asked her.

She didn't know. Lonnie was totally undone. He was in a hysteria of panic and revulsion. He didn't talk. His fingers clamped over her wrist like a handcuff. They ran away from the house looming over the hedge, they ran away from the smoking hole in the lawn. She knew those things for sure; all the rest was vague impressions.

At first it had been hard to run, and then it got easier because they were going downhill. They turned, then turned again. Houses stared at them, grey houses with high stoops and drawn green shades. She remembered Lonnie pulling off his jacket, which had been splattered with that black goo, and throwing it away. Then they had come to a wider street.

"Stop," she panted. "Lonnie . . . stop . . . I can't . . ." Her free hand was pressed to her side. There seemed to be a red-hot spike planted in there.

And he did stop. They had come out of the residential area and were standing at the corner of Crouch Lane and Norris Road. A sign on the far side of Norris Road proclaimed that they were but one mile from Slaughter Towen. Town? Vetter suggested. No, Doris Freeman said. Slaughter *Towen*, with an "e."

Raymond crushed out the cigarette he had "borrowed" from Farnham. "I'm off," he announced, and then looked more closely at Farnham. "My poppet should take better care of himself. He's got big dark circles under his eyes. Any hair on your palms, poppet?" He laughed uproariously.

"Ever hear of a Crouch Lane?" Farnham asked.

"Crouch Hill Road, you mean."

"No, I mean Crouch Lane."

"Never heard of it."

"What about Norris Road?"

"There's a Norris Road cuts off from the high street in Basingstoke—"

"No, here."

"Not by me, poppet."

For some reason he couldn't understand—the woman was obviously crackers—Farnham persisted. "What about Slaughter Towen?"

"Towen, you said? Not Town?"

"Yes, that's right."

"Never heard of it, poppet, but if I do, I believe I'll steer clear."

"Why's that?"

"Because in the old Druidic lingo, a touen or towen was a place for ritual sacrifice. That's where they took out your liver and lights. Sleep tight, love." And, zipping his windcheater up to the chin, Raymond glided out.

Farnham looked after him uneasily. He made that last up, he told himself. What a hard copper like Sid Raymond knows about the druids you could carve on the head of a pin and still have room for the Lord's Prayer. Right. And even if he had picked up a piece of information like that, it didn't change the fact that the woman was . . .

"Must be going crazy," Lonnie said, and laughed shakily.

Doris had looked at her watch earlier and saw that somehow it had gotten to be quarter of eight. The light had changed; from a clear orange it had gone to a thick and murky red that glared off the windows of the shops in Norris Road and seemed to face a church steeple across the way in fresh-clotted blood. The sun itself sat on the horizon now, an oblate sphere.

"What happened back there?" Doris asked. "What was it, Lonnie?"

"Lost my jacket, too. Hell of a note."

"You didn't lose it, you took it off. It was covered with . . ."

"Don't be foolish!" he snapped at her. But his eyes were not snappish; they were soft, shocked, wandering. "I lost it, that's all."

"Lonnie, what happened when you went through the hedge?"

"Nothing," he said briskly. "Let's not talk about it. Where are we?"

"Lonnie—"

"I can't remember," he said softly, looking at her. "It's all a blank. We were there . . . we heard a sound . . . then I was running. That's all I can remember." And then he added in a frighteningly childish voice: "Did I throw my jacket away? I liked that one. It matched the pants." He laughed suddenly, idiotically.

This was something new to be frightened of. Whatever he had seen beyond the hedge seemed to have partially unhinged him. She was not sure the same wouldn't have happened to her . . . if she had seen. It didn't matter. They had to get out of here. Get back to the hotel with the kids.

"Let's get a cab. I want to go home."

"But John—"

"Never mind John!" she said, and now she was shrill herself. "It's wrong, everything's wrong, we're getting a cab and going home!"

"Yes, all right. Okay." Lonnie passed a shaking hand across his forehead. "But there aren't any."

There was, in fact, no traffic at all on Norris Road, which was wide and cobbled. Directly down the center of it ran a set of old tram-tracks. On the other side, in front of a flower shop, an old and rusty three-wheeled D-car was parked. Farther down on their own side, a Yamaha bike stood aslant on its kickstand. That was all. They could *hear* cars, but the sound was faraway, diffuse.

"Maybe the street's closed for repairs," he muttered, and then Lonnie had done a strange thing . . . strange, at least, for him; he was always so easy and self-assured. He looked back over his shoulder as if afraid they had been followed.

"We'll walk," she said.

"Where?"

"Anywhere. Away from Crouch End. We can get a taxi if we get away from here." She was suddenly positive of that, if nothing else.

"All right." Now he seemed perfectly willing to entrust the leadership of the whole matter over to her.

They began walking toward the setting sun along Norris Road. The faraway hum of the traffic remained constant, not seeming to diminish, but not seeming to grow any, either. The desertion was beginning to get on her nerves. She felt they were being watched, tried to dismiss the feeling, and found that she couldn't. The sound of their footfalls

(SIXTY LOST IN UNDERGROUND HORROR)

echoed back to them. The business at the hedge played on her mind more and more, and finally she had to ask again.

"Lonnie, what *was* it?"

He answered simply: "I don't remember, Doris. And I don't want to."

They passed a market that was closed—a pile of coconuts like shrunken heads seen back-to were piled in the window. They passed a laundromat where white machines had been pulled from the washed-out pink plasterboard walls like square teeth from dying gums—the image made her feel queasy. They passed a soap-streaked show window with an old SHOP TO LEASE sign in the front. Something moved behind the soap streaks, and Doris saw, peering out at her, the pink and tufted battle-scarred face of the cat.

She consulted the workings and tickings of her body and discovered that she was in a state of slowly building terror. It felt as if her intestines had begun to crawl slightly inside her. Her mouth had a sharp unpleasant taste, almost as if she had dosed with a strong mouthwash. The cobbles of Norris Road bled fresh blood in the sunset.

They were approaching an underpass. And it was dark under there. *I can't,* her mind informed her in a matter-of-fact sort of way. *I can't go under there, anything might be under there. Don't ask me because I just can't.*

Another part of her mind asked if she could bear to retrace their steps . . . past the empty shop with the cat in it (how had he gotten there from the restaurant by the call box? best not to think about that), the somehow oral shambles of the laundromat, the market of severed shrunken heads. She didn't think she could.

They had drawn closer to the underpass now. A six-car train lunged over it with startling suddenness, a crazy bride rushing to meet her groom with unseemly rapaciousness, trailing a train of sparks. They both leaped back involuntarily, but it was Lonnie who cried out aloud. She looked at him and saw that he had aged and turned into someone she didn't think she knew in the last hour . . . had it been an hour? She didn't know. But she did know that his hair looked somehow greyer, and while she told herself firmly—as firmly as she could—that it was just a trick of the light, it decided her. Lonnie was in no shape to go back. Therefore, the underpass.

"Doris—" he said, pulling back a little.

"Come on," she said, and took his hand. She took it brusquely so he would not feel it trembling. She walked forward and he followed docilely.

They were almost out—it was a very short underpass, she thought with ridiculous relief—when the hand grasped her upper arm.

She didn't scream. Her lungs seemed to have collapsed like small crumpled paper sacks. Her mind wanted to leave her body behind and just . . . just fly. Lonnie's hand parted from her own. He seemed unaware. He walked out on the other side—she saw him for just one moment silhouetted, tall and lanky, against the bloody, furious colors of the sunset, and then he was gone. She had not seen him again since.

The hand grasping her upper arm was hairy, like an ape's hand. It turned her remorselessly toward a heavy slumped shape leaning against the sooty concrete wall. It leaned there in the double shadow of two concrete supporting pillars, and the shape was all she could make out . . . the shape, and two luminous green eyes.

"Got a cigarette, love?" a husky cockney voice asked her, and she smelled raw meat and deep-fat-fried chips and something sweet and awful, like the residue at the bottom of garbage cans.

Those green eyes were cat's eyes. And suddenly she became sure, horribly sure, that if the big slumped shape stepped out of the shadows, she would see the milky cataract of eye, the pink ridges of scar tissue, the tufts of ginger hair.

She tore free, backed up, and felt something part the air near her . . . a hand? Claws? A spitting, hissing sound—

Another train charged overhead. The roar was huge, brainrattling. Soot sifted down like black snow. She fled in blind panic, for the second time that evening not knowing where . . . or for how long.

What brought her back to herself was the realization that Lonnie was gone. She had half collapsed against a dirty brick wall, breathing in great tearing gasps. She was still in Norris Road (at least she believed herself to be, she told the two constables; the wide way was still cobbled, and the tram tracks still ran directly down the center of the road), but the deserted, decaying shops had given way to deserted, decaying warehouses. DAWGLISH & SONS read the soot-begrimed signboard on one. A second had the name ALHAZRED emblazoned across ancient and peeling green paint. Below the name was a series of Arabian pothooks and dashes.

"Lonnie!" she called. There was no echo, no carrying in spite of the silence (no, not complete silence, she told them; there was still the sound of traffic, and it might have been closer . . . but not much). The word that stood for her husband seemed to drop from her mouth and fall dead at her feet. The blood of sunset had been replaced by the cool grey ashes of twilight. For the first time it occurred to her that night might fall upon her here in Crouch

End—if she was still indeed in Crouch End—and that thought brought fresh terror.

She told Vetter and Farnham that there had been absolutely no reflection on her part during that unknowable length of time between being dropped off at the call box and the final horror. She had reacted like a frightened animal. Stimulus was applied; they fled. And now she was alone. She wanted Lonnie, her husband. She was aware of that. But it did not occur to her to wonder much—if at all—about why this area, which must surely lie within five miles of Cambridge Circus, should be utterly deserted. It did not occur to her to wonder how the disfigured cat could have gotten from the restaurant to the shop-to-let. She did not even wonder much about the inexplicable pit in the lawn of that house, except as it bore on Lonnie. Those questions came later, when it was too late, and they would (she said) haunt her for the rest of her life.

Doris Freeman set off walking, calling for Lonnie. Her voice did not echo, but her footfalls seemed to. The shadows began to fill Norris Road. Overhead, the sky was now purple. It might have been some distorting effect of the twilight, or her own exhaustion, but the warehouses seemed to lean over the road now. The windows, caked with the dirt of decades—of centuries, perhaps—seemed to be staring at her. And the names on the signboards (she said) became progressively stranger, lunatic, and certainly unpronounceable. The vowels were in the wrong places, and consonants had been strung together in a way that would make it impossible for any human tongue to get around them. CTHULU KRYON read one, with more of those Arabian pothooks beneath it. YOGSOGGOTH read another. R'YELEH said yet another. There was one that she remembered particularly: NRTESN NYARLA-HOTEP.

("How could you remember such gibberish?" Farnham asked her.)

(And Doris Freeman had shook her head, slowly and tiredly. "I don't know. I really don't know.")

Norris Road seemed to stretch on into infinity, cobbled, split by tram tracks. And although she continued to walk—she wouldn't have believed she could run, although later, she said, she did—she no longer called for Lonnie. She was now in the grip of the greatest fear she had ever known, a fear she would not have believed a human being could endure without going mad or dropping stone dead. Yet it was impossible for her to articulate her fear except in one way, and even this, although concrete, was not satisfactory.

She said it was as if she was no longer on earth. As if she was on a different planet, a place so alien that the human mind could not even begin to comprehend it. The *angles* seemed different, she said. The *colors* seemed different. The . . . but it was hopeless.

She could only walk under a sky that seemed twisted and strange between the dark bulking buildings, and hope that it would end.

And it did.

She became aware of two figures standing on the sidewalk ahead of her. It was the two children—the boy with the deformed claw hand and the little girl. Her hair was in braids.

"It's the American woman," the boy said.

"She's lost," said the girl.
"Lost her husband."
"Lost her way."
"Found the darker way."
"Found the way into the funnel."
"Lost her hope."
"Found the Whistler from the Stars—"
"—Eater of Dimensions—"
"—the Blind Piper who is not named for a thousand years—"

Faster and faster their words came, a breathless liturgy, a flashing loom. Her head spun with them. The buildings leaned. The stars were out, but they were not *her* stars, the ones she had wished on as a girl or courted under as a young woman, these were crazed stars in lunatic constellations, and her hands went to her ears and her hands did not shut out the sounds and finally she screamed at them:

"Where's my husband? Where's Lonnie? What have you done to him?"

There was silence. And then the girl said: "He's gone beneath."

The boy: "Gone to Him Who Waits."

The girl smiled—a malicious smile full of evil innocence. "He couldn't well not go, could he? The mark was on him. And you'll go. You'll go now."

"Lonnie! *What have you done with—*"

The boy raised his hand and chanted in a high fluting language that she could not understand—but the sound of the words drove Doris Freeman nearly mad with fear.

"The street began to move then," she told Vetter and Farnham. "The cobbles began to . . . to undulate like a carpet. They rose and fell, rose and fell. The tram tracks came loose and flew into the air—I remember that, I remember the starlight shining on them—and then the cobbles themselves began to come loose, one by one at first, and then in bunches. They just flew off into the darkness. There was a tearing sound when they came loose. A grinding, tearing sound . . . the way an earthquake must sound. And— something started to come through—"

"What?" Vetter asked. He was hunched forward, his eyes boring into Doris Freeman. "What did you see? What was it?"

"Tentacles," she said, slowly and haltingly. "I think . . . I think it was tentacles. But they were as thick as old banyan trees, as if each of them was made up of a thousand squirming smaller tentacles . . . and there were pink things like suckers . . . but sometimes they looked like faces . . . like Lonnie's face, some of them, some like other faces, all of them in agony . . . screaming in agony . . . but below them, in the darkness under the street . . . in the darkness *beneath* . . . there was something else. Something like great . . . great *eyes* . . . ."

At that point she had broken down, unable to go on for some time.

And as it turned out, there was really no more to tell. She had no coherent memory of what had happened after that. The next thing she remembered was cowering in the doorway of a closed newsagent's shop. She might be there yet, she had told them, except that she had seen cars passing back and forth, and the reassuring glow of arc-sodium streetlights. Two people had passed in front of her, and Doris had cringed farther back into the shadows, afraid of the two evil children. But these were not children, she saw; they were a teenage boy and girl walking hand in hand. The boy was saying something about the new Francis Coppola film.

She had come out onto the sidewalk warily, ready to dart back into the convenient bolthole the newsagent's doorway made—but there was no need. Fifty yards up on her left was a moderately busy intersection, with cars and lorries standing at a stop-and-go light. Across the way was a jeweler's shop with a large lighted clock in the show window. A steel accordion grille had been drawn across the window, but she could still make out the time. It was five minutes of ten.

She had walked up to the intersection then, and despite the streetlights and the comforting rumble of traffic, she had kept shooting terrified glances over her shoulder. She ached all over. She was limping on one broken heel. Somehow she had kept her purse. She had pulled muscles in her belly and both legs—her right leg was particularly bad, as if she had strained something in it.

At the intersection she saw that somehow she had come around to Hillfield Avenue and Tottenham Road. A woman of about sixty with her greying hair escaping from the rag it was done up in was talking to a man of about the same age under a streetlamp. They both looked at Doris as she approached them as if she were some sort of dreadful apparition.

"Police," Doris Freeman had croaked. "Where's the police station? I . . . I'm an American citizen and . . . I've lost my husband . . . and I need the police."

"What's happened, then, love?" the woman asked, not unkindly. "You look like you've been through the wringer, you do."

"Car accident?" her companion asked.

"No," she managed. "Please . . . is there a police station somewhere near?"

"Right up Tottenham Road," the man said. He took a package of Players from his pocket. "Like a cigarette? You look like you could use one, mum."

"Thank you," she said, and took the cigarette although she had quit nearly four years ago. The elderly man had to follow the jittering tip of it with his lighted match to get it going for her.

He glanced at the woman with her hair bound up in the rag. "I'll just take a little stroll up with her, Evvie. Make sure she gets there all right."

"I'll come along as well, then, won't I?" Evvie said, and put an arm around Doris's shoulders. "Now what is it, love? Did someone try to mug you?"

"No," Doris said. "It . . . I . . . I . . . the street . . . there was a cat with only one eye . . . the street . . . the street opened up . . . I saw it . . . He Who Waits, they called it . . . Lonnie . . . I've got to find Lonnie . . ."

She was aware that she was speaking incoherencies, but she seemed helpless to be any clearer. And at any rate, she told Vetter and Farnham, she hadn't been all *that* incoherent, because the man and woman had drawn away from her, as if, when Evvie asked what the matter was, Doris had told her it was bubonic plague.

The man said something then, and Doris thought it was: "Happened again."

The woman pointed. "Station house is right up there. Globes hanging in front. You'll see it." And very quickly the two of them began to walk away . . . but now they were the ones glancing back over their shoulders.

Doris took two steps toward them. "Don't you come near!" Evvie called shrilly . . . and forked the sign of the evil eye at Doris, simultaneously cringing against the man, who put an arm about her. "Don't you come near, if you've been to Crouch End Towen!"

And with that, the two of them had disappeared into the night.

Now PC Farnham stood leaning in the doorway between the common room and the main filing room—the back files Vetter had spoken of were certainly not kept here. Farnham had made himself a fresh cup of tea and was smoking the last cigarette in his pack—the woman had also bummed several—smoking op's, he believed they called it in the States.

The woman had gone back to her hotel, in the company of the nurse Vetter had called—the nurse would be staying with her tonight, and would make a judgment in the morning as to whether the woman would need to go in hospital. The children made that difficult, Farnham supposed, and where the woman was an American national (as she kept proclaiming), it became that much more complicated. And what was she going to tell the kiddies when they woke up? That the big bad monster of Crouch End Town

(Towen)

had eaten up daddy?

Farnham grimaced and put down his teacup. It wasn't his problem, none of it. For good or for ill, Mrs. Doris Freeman had become sandwiched between the National State and the American Embassy in the great waltz of governments. It was none of his affair; he was only a PC who wanted to forget the whole thing. And he intended to let Vetter write the report. It was Vetter's baby. Vetter could afford to put his name to such a bouquet of lunacy; he was an old man, used up. He would still be a PC on the night shift when he got his gold watch, his pension, and his council flat. Farnham, on the other hand, had ambitions of making sergeant soon, and that meant he had to watch every little thing.

And speaking of Vetter, where was he? He'd been taking the night air for quite a while now.

Farnham crossed the common room and went out. He stood between the two lighted globes and stared across Tottenham Road. Vetter was nowhere in sight. It was past three A.M., and silence lay thick and even, like a shroud. What was that line from Wordsworth? "All that great heart lying still," something like that.

He went down the steps and stood on the sidewalk. He felt a trickle of unease now. It was silly, of course it was. He was angry with himself, angry that the woman's mad story should have had even this slight effect on him. Perhaps he deserved to be afraid of a hard copper like Sid Raymond.

Farnham walked slowly up to the corner, thinking he would meet Vetter coming back from his night stroll. But he would go no farther than the corner; if the station was left empty even for a few moments, there would be hell to pay—if it was discovered.

He went up to the corner and looked around. It was funny, but all the arc-sodiums seemed to have gone out up here. The entire street looked different without them. Would it have to be reported, he wondered? And where was Vetter?

He would take a little walk up, he decided, and see just what was what. But not far. It wouldn't do to leave the station unattended, that would be a sure and simple way of assuring an end like Vetter's, an old man on the night shift in a quiet part of town, mostly concerned with kids congregating on the corners after midnight . . . and crazy American women.

He would walk up just a little way.

Not far.

Vetter came in less than five minutes after Farnham had left. Farnham had gone in the opposite direction, and if Vetter had come along a minute earlier, he would have seen the young constable stand at the corner for a moment and then disappear from sight.

"Farnham?" he called.

There was no answer but the buzz of the clock on the wall.

"Farnham?" he called again, and wiped his mouth with the palm of his hand.

Lonnie Freeman was never found. Eventually his wife—who had begun to grey around the temples—flew back to America with her children. They went on the Concorde. A month later she attempted suicide. She spent a year in a rest home. She came out much improved.

PC Robert Farnham was never seen or heard from again. He left a wife and a two-year-old set of twin girls. His wife wrote a series of angry letters to her MP, insisting that something was going on, something was being covered up, that her Bob had been enticed into taking some dangerous sort of undercover assignment or other, like that fellow Hackett on the BBC. He would have done anything to make sergeant, she told the MP repeatedly. Eventually, the MP stopped answering her letters, and at about the same time that Doris Freeman was coming out of the rest home, her hair almost entirely white now, Sheila Farnham moved back to Sussex, where her parents lived. Eventually she married a man in a steadier line of work than that of policing London—Frank Hobbs worked on the Ford assembly line. It had been necessary to get a divorce from her Bob first on grounds of desertion, but that was no problem.

Vetter took early retirement about four months after Doris Freeman had stumbled her way into the station in Tottenham Road in Crouch End. He did indeed move into council housing, a two-above-the-shops in the town of Frimley. Six months later he was found dead of a heart attack, a can of Harp Lager in his hand.

The hot end-of-summer night when Doris Freeman told her tale was August 19, 1974. Better than three and a half years have passed since then.

And Doris's Lonnie and Sheila's Bob are together.

Vetter would have known where.

By the entirely democratic and accidental process of alphabetical order, they are together in the back file, the place where unsolved cases and tales too wild to bear any credence are kept.

FARNHAM, ROBERT is written on the tab of one thin folder. FREEMAN, LEONARD is written on the tab of the folder directly behind. Both folders contain a single page—a badly typed report by the investigating officer. In both cases, the signature is Vetter's.

And in Crouch End, which is really a quiet suburb of London, strange things still happen. From time to time.

Joyce Carol Oates

Night-Side

Joyce Carol Oates is one of the major talents in contemporary American literature, a poet, novelist, essayist and short story writer of the first rank. Her contributions to horror literature include many stories in the Gothic mold of William Faulkner and Flannery O'Connor, but she sometimes writes more nearly in the tradition of Shirley Jackson, as in "Night-Side," which is perhaps her finest horror story. It is the title piece of one of her many short story collections, the one that contains a large part of her significant work in the horror mode. In this story, she deals with the occult directly, in an uncharacteristic (for her) fashion most comparable to, say, Robert Aickman, or Edith Wharton. She is in the main tradition of horror in American literature in this century, though she works outside category boundaries. If there is such a thing as supernatural mainstream, Henry James, Edith Wharton, Shirley Jackson, Joyce Carol Oates and Peter Straub define it.

6 February 1887. Quincy, Massachusetts. Montague House.

Disturbing experience at Mrs. A——'s home yesterday evening. Few theatrics—comfortable though rather pathetically shabby surroundings—an only mildly sinister atmosphere (especially in contrast to the Walpurgis Night presented by that shameless charlatan in Portsmouth: the Dwarf Eustace who presumed to introduce me to Swedenborg himself, under the erroneous impression that I am a member of the Church of the New Jerusalem—*I!*) Nevertheless I came away disturbed, and my conversation with Dr. Moore afterward, at dinner, though dispassionate and even, at times, a bit flippant, did not settle my mind. Perry Moore is of course a hearty materialist, an Aristotelian-Spencerian with a love of good food and drink, and an appreciation of the more nonsensical vagaries of life; when in his company I tend to support that general view, as I do at the University as well—for there is a terrific pull in my nature toward the gregarious that I cannot resist. (That I do not wish to resist.) Once I am alone with my thoughts, however, I am accursed with doubts about my own position and nothing seems more precarious than my intellectual "convictions."

The more hardened members of our Society, like Perry Moore, are apt to put the issue bluntly: Is Mrs. A——of Quincy a conscious or unconscious fraud? The conscious frauds are relatively easy to deal with; once discovered, they prefer to erase themselves from further consideration. The unconscious frauds are not, in a sense, "frauds" at all. It would certainly be difficult to prove criminal intention. Mrs. A——, for instance, does not accept money or gifts so far as we have been able to determine, and both Perry Moore and I

712

noted her courteous but firm refusal of the Judge's offer to send her and her husband (presumably ailing?) on holiday to England in the spring. She is a mild, self-effacing, rather stocky woman in her mid-fifties who wears her hair parted in the center, like several of my maiden aunts, and whose sole item of adornment was an old-fashioned cameo brooch; her black dress had the appearance of having been homemade, though it was attractive enough, and freshly ironed. According to the Society's records she has been a practicing medium now for six years. Yet she lives, still, in an undistinguished section of Quincy, in a neighborhood of modest frame dwellings. The A——s' house is in fairly good condition, especially considering the damage routinely done by our winters, and the only room we saw, the parlor, is quite ordinary, with overstuffed chairs and the usual cushions and a monstrous horsehair sofa and, of course, the oaken table; the atmosphere would have been so conventional as to have seemed disappointing had not Mrs. A——made an attempt to brighten it, or perhaps to give it a glamourously occult air, by hanging certain watercolors about the room. (She claims that the watercolors were "done" by one of her contact spirits, a young Iroquois girl who died in the seventeen seventies of smallpox. They are touchingly garish—mandalas and triangles and stylized eyeballs and even a transparent Cosmic Man with Indian-black hair.)

At last night's sitting there were only three persons in addition to Mrs. A——. Judge T——of the New York State Supreme Court (now retired); Dr. Moore; and I, Jarvis Williams. Dr. Moore and I came out from Cambridge under the aegis of the Society for Psychical Research in order to make a preliminary study of the kind of mediumship Mrs. A——affects. We did not bring a stenographer along this time though Mrs. A——indicated her willingness to have the sitting transcribed; she struck me as being rather warmly cooperative, and even interested in our formal procedures, though Perry Moore remarked afterward at dinner that she had struck him as "noticeably reluctant." She was, however, flustered at the start of the séance and for a while it seemed as if we and the Judge might have made the trip for nothing. (She kept waving her plump hands about like an embarrassed hostess, apologizing for the fact that the spirits were evidently in a "perverse uncommunicative mood tonight.")

She did go into trance eventually, however. The four of us were seated about the heavy round table from approximately 6:50 P.M. to 9 P.M. For nearly forty-five minutes Mrs. A—— made abortive attempts to contact her Chief Communicator and then slipped abruptly into trance (dramatically, in fact: her eyes rolled back in her head in a manner that alarmed me at first), and a personality named Webley appeared. "Webley's" voice appeared to be coming from several directions during the course of the sitting. At all times it was a least three yards from Mrs. A——; despite the semi-dark of the parlor I believe I could see the woman's mouth and throat clearly enough, and I could not detect any obvious signs of ventriloquism. (Perry Moore, who is more experienced than I in psychical research, and rather more casual about the whole phenomenon, claims he has witnessed feats of ventriloquism that would make poor Mrs. A——look quite shabby in comparison.) "Webley's" voice was raw, singsong, peculiarly disturbing. At times it was shrill and at

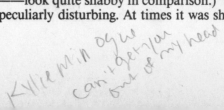

other times so faint as to be nearly inaudible. Something brattish about it. Exasperating. "Webley" took care to pronounce his final *g*'s in a self-conscious manner, quite unlike Mrs. A——. (Which could be, of course, a deliberate ploy.)

This Webley is one of Mrs. A——'s most frequent manifesting spirits, though he is not the most reliable. Her Chief Communicator is a Scots patriarch who lived "in the time of Merlin" and who is evidently very wise; unfortunately he did not choose to appear yesterday evening. Instead, Webley presided. He is supposed to have died some seventy-five years ago at the age of nineteen in a house just up the street from the A——s'. He was either a butcher's helper or an apprentice tailor. He died in a fire—or by a "slow dreadful crippling disease"—or beneath a horse's hooves, in a freakish accident; during the course of the sitting he alluded self-pityingly to his death but seemed to have forgotten the exact details. At the very end of the evening he addressed me directly as Dr. Williams of Harvard University, saying that since I had influential friends in Boston I could help him with his career—it turned out he had written hundreds of songs and poems and parables but none had been published; would I please find a publisher for his work? Life had treated him so unfairly. His talent—his genius—had been lost to humanity. I had it within my power to help him, he claimed, was I not *obliged* to help him . . .? He then sang one of his songs, which sounded to me like an old ballad; many of the words were so shrill as to be unintelligible, but he sang it just the same, repeating the verses in a haphazard order:

> This ae nighte, this ae nighte,
> —Every nighte and alle,
> Fire and fleet and candle-lighte,
> And Christe receive thy saule.

> When thou from hence away art past,
> —Every nighte and alle,
> To Whinny-muir thou com'st at last:
> And Christe receive thy saule.

> From Brig o' Dread when thou may'st pass,
> —Every nighte and alle,
> The whinnes sall prick thee to the bare bane:
> And Christe receive thy saule.

The elderly Judge T—— had come up from New York City in order, as he earnestly put it, to "speak directly to his deceased wife as he was never able to do while she was living"; but Webley treated the old gentleman in a high-handed, cavalier manner, as if the occasion were not at all serious. He kept saying, "Who is there tonight? *Who* is there? Let them introduce themselves again—I don't *like* strangers! I tell you I don't *like* strangers!" Though Mrs. A—— had informed us beforehand that we would witness no physical phenomena, there were, from time to time, glimmerings of light in the darkened room, hardly more than the tiny pulsations of light made by fireflies; and both Perry Moore and I felt the table vibrating beneath our fingers. At about the time when Webley gave way to the spirit of Judge T——'s wife, the temperature in the room seemed to drop suddenly and I remember being gripped by a sensation of panic—but it lasted only an instant and I was soon myself again. (Dr. Moore claimed not to have noticed any drop in temperature and Judge T——was so rattled after the sitting that it would have been pointless to question him.)

The séance proper was similar to others I have attended. A spirit—or a voice—laid claim to being the late Mrs. T——; this spirit addressed the survivor in a peculiarly intense, urgent manner, so that it was rather embarrassing to be present. Judge T——was soon weeping. His deeply creased face glistened with tears like a child's.

"Why Darrie! *Darrie*! Don't cry! Oh don't cry!" the spirit said. "No one is dead, Darrie. There is no death. No death! . . . Can you hear me, Darrie? Why are you so frightened? So upset? No need, Darrie, no need! Grandfather and Lucy and I are together here—happy together. Darrie, look up! Be brave, my dear! My poor frightened dear! We never knew each other, did we? My poor dear! My love! . . . I saw you in a great transparent house, a great burning house; poor Darrie, they told me you were ill, you were weak with fever; all the rooms of the house were aflame and the staircase was burnt to cinders, but there were figures walking up and down, Darrie, great numbers of them, and you were among them, dear, stumbling in your fright—so clumsy! Look up, dear, and shade your eyes, and you will see me. Grandfather helped me—did you know? Did I call out his name at the end? My dear, my darling, it all happened so quickly—we never knew each other, did we? Don't be hard on Annie! Don't be cruel! Darrie? Why are you crying?" And gradually the spirit voice grew fainter; or perhaps something went wrong and the channels of communication were no longer clear. There were repetitions, garbled phrases, meaningless queries of "Dear? Dear?" that the Judge's replies did not seem to placate. The spirit spoke of her gravesite, and of a trip to Italy taken many years before, and of a dead or unborn baby, and again of Annie—evidently Judge T——'s daughter; but the jumble of words did not always make sense and it was a great relief when Mrs. A——suddenly woke from her trance.

Judge T——rose from the table, greatly agitated. He wanted to call the spirit back; he had not asked her certain crucial questions; he had been overcome by emotion and had found it difficult to speak, to interrupt the spirit's monologue. But Mrs. A——(who looked shockingly tired) told him the spirit would not return again that night and they must not make any attempt to call it back.

"The other world obeys its own laws," Mrs. A——said in her small, rather reedy voice.

We left Mrs. A——'s home shortly after 9:00 P.M. I too was exhausted; I had not realized how absorbed I had been in the proceedings.

*   *   *

Judge T——is also staying at Montague House, but he was too upset after the sitting to join us for dinner. He assured us, though, that the spirit was authentic—the voice had been his wife's, he was certain of it, he would stake his life on it. She had never called him "Darrie" during her lifetime, wasn't it odd that she called him "Darrie" now?—and was so concerned for him, so loving?—and concerned for their daughter as well? He was very moved. He had a great deal to think about. (Yes, he'd had a fever some weeks ago—a severe attack of bronchitis and a fever; in fact, he had not completely recovered.) What was extraordinary about the entire experience was the wisdom revealed: There is no death.

There is no death.

Dr. Moore and I dined heartily on roast crown of lamb, spring potatoes with peas, and buttered cabbage. We were served two kinds of bread— German rye and sour-cream rolls; the hotel's butter was superb; the wine excellent; the dessert—crepes with cream and toasted almonds—looked marvelous, though I had not any appetite for it. Dr. Moore was ravenously hungry. He talked as he ate, often punctuating his remarks with rich bursts of laughter. It was his opinion, of course, that the medium was a fraud—and not a very skillful fraud, either. In his fifteen years of amateur, intermittent investigations he had encountered far more skillful mediums. Even the notorious Eustace with his levitating tables and hobgoblin chimes and shrieks was cleverer than Mrs. A——; one knew of course that Eustace was a cheat, but one was hard pressed to explain his method. Whereas Mrs. A——was quite transparent.

Dr. Moore spoke for some time in his amiable, dogmatic way. He ordered brandy for both of us, though it was nearly midnight when we finished our dinner and I was anxious to get to bed. (I hoped to rise early and work on a lecture dealing with Kant's approach to the problem of Free Will, which I would be delivering in a few days.) But Dr. Moore enjoyed talking and seemed to have been invigorated by our experience at Mrs. A——'s.

At the age of forty-three Perry Moore is only four years my senior, but he has the air, in my presence at least, of being considerably older. He is a second cousin of my mother, a very successful physician with a bachelor's flat and office in Louisburg Square; his failure to marry, or his refusal, is one of Boston's perennial mysteries. Everyone agrees that he is learned, witty, charming, and extraordinarily intelligent. Striking rather than conventionally handsome, with a dark, lustrous beard and darkly bright eyes, he is an excellent amateur violinist, an enthusiastic sailor, and a lover of literature— his favorite writers are Fielding, Shakespeare, Horace, and Dante. He is, of course, the perfect investigator in spiritualist matters since he is detached from the phenomena he observes and yet he is indefatigably curious; he has a positive love, a mania, for facts. Like the true scientist he seeks facts that, assembled, may possibly give rise to hypotheses: he does not set out with a hypothesis in mind, like a sort of basket into which certain facts may be tossed, helter-skelter, while others are conveniently ignored. In all things he is an empiricist who accepts nothing on faith.

"If the woman is a fraud, then," I say hesitantly, "you believe she is a self-deluded fraud? And her spirits' information is gained by means of telepathy?"

"Telepathy indeed. There can be no other explanation," Dr. Moore says emphatically. "By some means not yet known to science . . . by some uncanny means she suppresses her conscious personality . . . and thereby releases other, secondary personalities that have the power of seizing upon others' thoughts and memories. It's done in a way not understood by science at the present time. But it will be understood eventually. Our investigations into the unconscious powers of the human mind are just beginning; we're on the threshold, really, of a new era."

"So she simply picks out of her clients' minds whatever they want to hear," I say slowly. "And from time to time she can even tease them a little—insult them, even: she can unloose a creature like that obnoxious Webley upon a person like Judge T——without fear of being discovered. Telepathy. . . . Yes, that would explain a great deal. Very nearly everything we witnessed tonight."

"*Everything*, I should say," Dr. Moore says.

In the coach returning to Cambridge I set aside Kant and my lecture notes and read Sir Thomas Browne: *Light that makes all things seen, makes some things invisible. The greatest mystery of Religion is expressed by adumbration.*

19 March 1887. Cambridge. 11 P.M.

Walked ten miles this evening; must clear cobwebs from mind.

Unhealthy atmosphere. Claustrophobic. Last night's sitting in Quincy—a most unpleasant experience.

(Did not tell my wife what happened. Why is she so curious about the Spirit World?—about Perry Moore?)

My body craves more violent physical activity. In the summer, thank God, I will be able to swim in the ocean: the most strenuous and challenging of exercises.

Jotting down notes re the Quincy experience:

I. Fraud

Mrs. A————, possibly with accomplices, conspires to deceive; she does research into her clients' lives beforehand, possibly bribes servants. She is either a very skillful ventriloquist or works with someone who is. (Husband? Son? The husband is a retired cabinet-maker said to be in poor health; possibly consumptive. The son, married, lives in Waterbury.)

Her stated wish to avoid publicity and her declining of payment may simply be ploys; she may intend to make a great deal of money at some future time.

(Possibility of blackmail?—might be likely in cases similar to Perry Moore's.)

II. Non-fraud

Naturalistic

1. Telepathy. She reads minds of clients.
2. "Multiple personality" of medium. Aspects of her own buried psyche are released as her conscious personality is suppressed. These secondary beings are in mysterious rapport with the "secondary" personalities of the clients.

Spiritualistic

1. The controls are genuine communicators, intermediaries between our world and the world of the dead. These spirits give way to other spirits, who then speak through the medium; or
2. These spirits *influence* the medium, who relays their messages using her own vocabulary. Their personalities are then filtered through and limited by hers.
3. The spirits are not those of the deceased; they are perverse, willful spirits. (Perhaps demons? But there are no demons.)

III. Alternative hypothesis

Madness: the medium is mad, the clients are mad, even the detached, rationalist investigators are mad.

Yesterday evening at Mrs. A——'s home, the second sitting Perry Moore and I observed together, along with Miss Bradley, a stenographer from the Society, and two legitimate clients—a Brookline widow, Mrs. P——, and her daughter Clara, a handsome young woman in her early twenties. Mrs. A——exactly as she appeared to us in February; possibly a little stouter. Wore black dress and cameo brooch. Served Lapsang tea, tiny sandwiches, and biscuits when we arrived shortly after 6 P.M. Seemed quite friendly to Perry, Miss Bradley, and me; fussed over us, like any hostess; chattered a bit about the cold spell. Mrs. P——and her daughter arrived at six-thirty and the sitting began shortly thereafter.

Jarring from the very first. A babble of spirit voices. Mrs. A——in trance, head flung back, mouth gaping, eyes rolled upward. Queer. Unnerving. I glanced at Dr. Moore but he seemed unperturbed, as always. The widow and her daughter, however, looked as frightened as I felt.

Why are we here, sitting around this table?

What do we believe we will discover?

What are the risks we face . . .?

"Webley" appeared and disappeared in a matter of minutes. His shrill, raw, aggrieved voice was supplanted by that of a creature of indeterminate sex who babbled in Gaelic. This creature in turn was supplanted by a hoarse German, a man who identified himself as Felix; he spoke a curiously ungrammatical German. For some minutes he and two or three other spirits quarreled. (Each declared himself Mrs. A——'s Chief Communicator for the evening.) Small lights flickered in the semi-dark of the parlor and the table quivered beneath my fingers and I felt, or believed I felt, something

brushing against me, touching the back of my head. I shuddered violently but regained my composure at once. An unidentified voice proclaimed in English that the Spirit of our Age was Mars: there would be a catastrophic war shortly and most of the world's population would be destroyed. All atheists would be destroyed. Mrs. A——shook her head from side to side as if trying to wake. Webley appeared, crying "Hello? Hello? I can't see anyone! Who is there? Who has called me?" but was again supplanted by another spirit who shouted long strings of words in a foreign language. [Note: I discovered a few days later that this language was Walachian, a Romanian dialect. Of course Mrs. A——, whose ancestors are English, could not possibly have known Walachian, and I rather doubt that the woman has even heard of the Walachian people.]

The sitting continued in this chaotic way for some minutes. Mrs. P——must have been quite disappointed, since she had wanted to be put in contact with her deceased husband. (She needed advice on whether or not to sell certain pieces of property.) Spirits babbled freely in English, German, Gaelic, French, even in Latin, and at one point Dr. Moore queried a spirit in Greek, but the spirit retreated at once as if not equal to Dr. Moore's wit. The atmosphere was alarming but at the same time rather maniac; almost jocular. I found myself suppressing laughter. Something touched the back of my head and I shivered violently and broke into perspiration, but the experience was not altogether unpleasant; it would be very difficult for me to characterize it.

And then—

And then, suddenly, everything changed. There was complete calm. A spirit voice spoke gently out of a corner of the room, addressing Perry Moore by his first name in a slow, tentative, groping way. "Perry? Perry . . .?" Dr. Moore jerked about in his seat. He was astonished; I could see by his expression that the voice belonged to someone he knew.

"Perry . . .? This is Brandon. I've waited so long for you, Perry, how could you be so selfish? I forgave you. Long ago. You couldn't help your cruelty and I couldn't help my innocence. Perry? My glasses have been broken—I can't see. I've been afraid for so long, Perry, please have mercy on me! I can't bear it any longer. I didn't *know* what it would be like. There are crowds of people here, but we can't see one another, we don't know one another, we're strangers, there is a universe of strangers—I can't see anyone clearly—I've been lost for twenty years, Perry, I've been waiting for you for twenty years! You don't dare turn away again, Perry! Not again! Not after so long!"

Dr. Moore stumbled to his feet, knocking his chair aside.

"No—Is it—I don't believe—"

"Perry? Perry? Don't abandon me again, Perry! Not again!"

"What is this?" Dr. Moore cried.

He was on his feet now; Mrs. A——woke from her trance with a groan. The women from Brookline were very upset and I must admit that I was in a mild state of terror, my shirt and my underclothes drenched with perspiration.

The sitting was over. It was only seven-thirty.

"Brandon?" Dr. Moore cried. "Wait. Where are—? Brandon? Can you hear me? Where are you? Why did you do it, Brandon? Wait! Don't leave! Can't anyone call him back— Can't anyone help me—"

Mrs. A——rose unsteadily. She tried to take Dr. Moore's hands in hers but he was too agitated.

"I heard only the very last words," she said. "They're always that way—so confused, so broken—the poor things— Oh, what a pity! It wasn't murder, was it? Not murder! Suicide—? I believe suicide is even worse for them! The poor broken things, they wake in the other world and are utterly, utterly lost—they have no guides, you see—no help in crossing over— They are completely alone for eternity—"

"Can't you call him back?" Dr. Moore asked wildly. He was peering into a corner of the parlor, slightly stooped, his face distorted as if he were staring into the sun. "Can't someone help me? . . . Brandon? Are you here? Are you here somewhere? For God's sake can't someone help!"

"Dr. Moore, please, the spirits are gone—the sitting is over for tonight—"

"You foolish old woman, leave me alone! Can't you see I—I—I must not lose him—Call him back, will you? I insist! I insist!"

"Dr. Moore, please—You mustn't shout—"

"I said call him back! At once! *Call him back!*"

Then he burst into tears. He stumbled against the table and hid his face in his hands and wept like a child; he wept as if his heart had been broken.

And so today I have been reliving the séance. Taking notes, trying to determine what happened. A brisk windy walk of ten miles. Head buzzing with ideas. Fraud? Deceit? Telepathy? Madness?

What a spectacle! Dr. Perry Moore calling after a spirit, begging it to return—and then crying, afterward, in front of four astonished witnesses.

Dr. Perry Moore of all people.

My dilemma: whether I should report last night's incident to Dr. Rowe, the president of the Society, or whether I should say nothing about it and request that Miss Bradley say nothing. It would be tragic if Perry's professional reputation were to be damaged by a single evening's misadventure; and before long all of Boston would be talking.

In his present state, however, he is likely to tell everyone about it himself.

At Montague House the poor man was unable to sleep. He would have kept me up all night had I had the stamina to endure his excitement.

There *are* spirits! There have always been spirits!

His entire life up to the present time has been misspent!

And of course, most important of all—there is no death!

He paced about my hotel room, pulling at his beard nervously. At times there were tears in his eyes. He seemed to want a response of some kind from me but whenever I started to speak he interrupted; he was not really listening.

"Now at last I know. I can't undo my knowledge," he said in a queer hoarse voice. "Amazing, isn't it, after so many years . . . so many wasted years . . . Ignorance has been my lot, darkness . . . and a hideous complacency. My God, when I consider my deluded smugness! I am so ashamed, so ashamed. All along people like Mrs. A——have been in contact with a world of such power . . . and people like me have been toiling in ignorance, accumulating material achievements, expending our energies in idiotic transient things . . . But all that is changed now. Now I know. I *know*. There is no death, as the Spiritualists have always told us."

"But, Perry, don't you think—Isn't it possible that—"

"I *know*," he said quietly. "It's as clear to me as if I had crossed over into that other world myself. Poor Brandon! He's no older now than he was *then*. The poor boy, the poor tragic soul! To think that he's still living after so many years . . . Extraordinary. . . . It makes my head spin," he said slowly. For a moment he stood without speaking. He pulled at his beard, then absently touched his lips with his fingers, then wiped at his eyes. He seemed to have forgotten me. When he spoke again his voice was hollow, rather ghastly. He sounded drugged. "I . . . I had been thinking of him as . . . as dead, you know. As dead. Twenty years. Dead. And now, tonight, to be forced to realize that . . . that he isn't dead after all . . . It was laudanum he took. I found him. His rooms on the third floor of Weld Hall. I found him, I had no real idea, none at all, not until I read the note . . . and of course I destroyed the note . . . I had to, you see: for his sake. For his sake more than mine. It was because he realized there could be no . . . no hope. . . . Yet he called me cruel! You heard him, Jarvis, didn't you? Cruel! I suppose I was. Was I? I don't know what to think. I must talk with him again. I . . . I don't know what to . . . what to think. I. . . ."

"You look awfully tired, Perry. It might be a good idea to go to bed," I said weakly.

". . . recognized his voice at once. Oh at once: no doubt. None. What a revelation! And my life so misspent. . . . Treating people's *bodies*. Absurd. I know now that nothing matters except that other world . . . nothing matters except our dead, our beloved dead . . . who are *not dead*. What a colossal revelation. . . . ! Why, it will change the entire course of history. It will alter men's minds throughout the world. You were there, Jarvis, so you understand. You were a witness. . . ."

"But—"

"You'll bear witness to the truth of what I am saying?"

He stared at me, smiling. His eyes were bright and threaded with blood.

I tried to explain to him as courteously and sympathetically as possible that his experience at Mrs. A——'s was not substantially different from the experiences many people have had at séances. "And always in the past psychical researchers have taken the position—"

"You were *there*," he said angrily. "You heard Brandon's voice as clearly as I did. Don't deny it!"

"—have taken the position that—that the phenomenon can be partly explained by the telepathic powers of the medium—"

"That was Brandon's *voice*," Perry said. "I felt his presence, I tell you! *His*. Mrs. A——had nothing to do with it—nothing at all. I feel as if . . . as if I could call Brandon back by myself. . . . I feel his presence even now. Close about me. He isn't dead, you see; no one is dead, there's a universe of . . . of people who are not dead. . . . Parents, grandparents, sisters, brothers, everyone . . . everyone. . . . How can you deny, Jarvis, the evidence of your own senses? You were there with me tonight and you know as well as I do. . . ."

"Perry, I don't *know*. I did hear a voice, yes, but we've heard voices before at other sittings, haven't we? There are always voices. There are always 'spirits.' The Society has taken the position that the spirits could be real, of course, but that there are other hypotheses that are perhaps more likely—"

"Other hypotheses indeed!" Perry said irritably. "You're like a man with his eyes shut tight who refuses to open them out of sheer cowardice. Like the cardinals refusing to look through Galileo's telescope! And you have pretensions of being a man of learning, of science. . . . Why, we've got to destroy all the records we've made so far; they're a slander on the world of the spirits. Thank God we didn't file a report yet on Mrs. A——! It would be so embarrassing to be forced to call it back. . . ."

"Perry, please. Don't be angry. I want only to remind you of the fact that we've been present at other sittings, haven't we?—and we've witnessed others responding emotionally to certain phenomena. Judge T——, for instance. He was convinced he'd spoken with his wife. But you must remember, don't you, that you and I were not at all convinced . . . ? It seemed to us more likely that Mrs. A——is able, through extrasensory powers we don't quite understand, to read the minds of her clients, and then to project certain voices out into the room so that it sounds as if they are coming from other people. . . . You even said, Perry, that she wasn't a very skillful ventriloquist. You said—"

"What does it matter what, in my ignorance, I said?" he cried. "Isn't it enough that I've been humiliated? That my entire life has been turned about? Must you insult me as well—sitting there so smugly and insulting *me*? I think I can make claim to being someone whom you might respect."

And so I assured him that I did respect him. And he walked about the room, wiping at his eyes, greatly agitated. He spoke again of his friend, Brandon Gould, and of his own ignorance, and of the important mission we must undertake to inform men and women of the true state of affairs. I tried to talk with him, to reason with him, but it was hopeless. He scarcely listened to me.

". . . must inform the world . . . crucial truth. . . . There is no death, you see. Never was. Changes civilization, changes the course of history. Jarvis?" he said groggily. "You see? *There is no death.*"

25 March 1887. Cambridge.

Disquieting rumors re Perry Moore. Heard today at the University that one of Dr. Moore's patients (a brother-in-law of Dean Barker) was extremely offended by his behavior during a consultation last week. Talk of his having been drunk—which I find incredible. If the poor man appeared to be excitable and not his customary self, it was not because he was *drunk*, surely.

Another far-fetched tale told me by my wife, who heard it from her sister Maude: Perry Moore went to church (St. Aidan's Episcopal Church on Mount Street) for the first time in a decade, sat alone, began muttering and laughing during the sermon, and finally got to his feet and walked out, creating quite a stir. *What delusions*! What delusions!—he was said to have muttered.

I fear for the poor man's sanity.

31 March 1887. Cambridge. 4 A.M.

Sleepless night. Dreamed of swimming . . . swimming in the ocean . . . enjoying myself as usual when suddenly the water turns thick . . . turns to mud. Hideous! Indescribably awful. I was swimming nude in the ocean, by moonlight, I believe, ecstatically happy, entirely alone, when the water turned to mud. . . . Vile, disgusting mud; faintly warm; sucking at my body. Legs, thighs, torso, arms. Horrible. Woke in terror. Drenched with perspiration: pajamas wet. One of the most frightening nightmares of my adulthood.

A message from Perry Moore came yesterday just before dinner. Would I like to join him in visiting Mrs. A——sometime soon, in early April perhaps, on a noninvestigative basis . . .? He is uncertain now of the morality of our "investigating" Mrs. A——or any other medium.

4 April 1887. Cambridge.

Spent the afternoon from two to five at William James's home on Irving Street, talking with Professor James of the inexplicable phenomenon of consciousness. He is robust as always, rather irreverent, supremely confident in a way I find enviable; rather like Perry Moore before his conversion (Extraordinary eyes—so piercing, quick, playful; a graying beard liberally threaded with white; close-cropped graying hair; a large, curving, impressive forehead; a manner intelligent and graceful and at the same time rough-edged, as if he anticipates or perhaps even hopes for recalcitration in his listeners.) We both find conclusive the ideas set forth in Binét's *Alterations of Personality* . . . unsettling as these ideas may be to the rationalist position. James speaks of a *peculiarity* in the constitution of human nature: that is, the fact that we inhabit not only our ego-consciousness but a wide field of psychological experience (most clearly represented by the phenomenon of memory, which no one can adequately explain) over which we have no control whatsoever. In fact, we are not generally aware of this field of consciousness.

We inhabit a lighted sphere, then; and about us is a vast penumbra of memories, reflections, feelings, and stray uncoordinated thoughts that "belong" to us theoretically, but that do not seem to be part of our conscious identity. (I was too timid to ask Professor James whether it might be the case that we do not inevitably own these aspects of the personality—that such phenomena belong as much to the objective world as to our subjective selves.) It is quite possible that there is an element of some indeterminate kind: oceanic, timeless, and living, against which the individual being constructs temporary barriers as part of an ongoing process of unique, particularized survival; like the ocean itself, which appears to separate islands that are in fact not "islands" at all, but aspects of the earth firmly joined together below the surface of the water. Our lives, then, resemble these islands. . . . All this is no more than a possibility, Professor James and I agreed.

James is acquainted, of course, with Perry Moore. But he declined to speak on the subject of the poor man's increasingly eccentric behavior when I alluded to it. (It may be that he knows even more about the situation than I do—he enjoys a multitude of acquaintances in Cambridge and Boston.) I brought our conversation round several times to the possibility of the *naturalness* of the conversion experience in terms of the individual's evolution of self, no matter how his family, his colleagues, and society in general viewed it, and Professor James appeared to agree; at least he did not emphatically disagree. He maintains a healthy skepticism, of course, regarding Spiritualist claims, and all evangelical and enthusiastic religious movements, though he is, at the same time, a highly articulate foe of the "rationalist" position and he believes that psychical research of the kind some of us are attempting will eventually unearth riches—revealing aspects of the human psyche otherwise closed to our scrutiny.

"The fearful thing," James said, "is that we are at all times vulnerable to incursions from the 'other side' of the personality. . . . We cannot determine the nature of the total personality simply because much of it, perhaps most, is hidden from us. . . . When we are invaded, then, we are overwhelmed and surrender immediately. Emotionally charged intuitions, hunches, guesses, even ideas may be the least aggressive of these incursions; but there are visual and auditory hallucinations, and forms of automatic behavior not controlled by the conscious mind. . . . Ah, you're thinking I am simply describing insanity?"

I stared at him, quite surprised.

"No. Not at all. Not at all," I said at once.

Reading through my grandfather's journals, begun in East Anglia many years before my birth. Another world then. Another language, now lost to us. *Man is sinful by nature. God's justice takes precedence over His mercy.* The dogma of Original Sin: something brutish about the innocence of that belief. And yet consoling. . . .

Fearful of sleep since my dreams are so troubled now. The voices of impudent spirits (Immanuel Kant himself come to chide me for having made too much of his categories—!), stray shouts and whispers I cannot decipher, the faces of my own beloved dead hovering near, like carnival masks, insubstantial and possibly fraudulent. Impatient with my wife, who questions me too closely on these personal matters; annoyed from time to time, in the evenings especially, by the silliness of the children. (The eldest is twelve now and should know better.) Dreading to receive another lengthy letter—sermon, really—from Perry Moore re his "new position," and yet perversely hoping one will come soon.

I must know.

(Must know what . . .?)
I must know.

10 April 1887. Boston. St. Aidan's Episcopal Church.

Funeral service this morning for Perry Moore; dead at forty-three.

17 April 1887. Seven Hills, New Hampshire.

A weekend retreat. No talk. No need to think.

Visiting with a former associate, author of numerous books. Cartesian specialist. Elderly. Partly deaf. Extraordinarily kind to me. (Did not ask about the Department or about my work.) Intensely interested in animal behavior now, in observation primarily; fascinated with the phenomenon of hibernation.

He leaves me alone for hours. He sees something in my face I cannot see myself.

The old consolations of a cruel but just God: ludicrous today.

In the nineteenth century we live free of God. We live in the illusion of freedom-of-God.

Dozing off in the guest room of this old farmhouse and then waking abruptly. *Is someone here? Is someone here?* My voice queer, hushed, childlike. *Please: is someone here?*

Silence.

Query: Is the penumbra outside consciousness all that was ever meant by "God"?

Query: Is inevitability all that was ever meant by "God"?

God—the body of fate we inhabit, then; no more and no less.

God pulled Perry down into the body of fate: into Himself. (Or Itself.) As Professor James might say, Dr. Moore was "vulnerable" to an assault from the other side.

At any rate he is dead. They buried him last Saturday.

25 April 1887. Cambridge.

Shelves of books. The sanctity of books. Kant, Plato, Schopenhauer, Descartes, Hume, Hegel, Spinoza. The others. All. Nietzsche, Spencer, Leibnitz (on whom I did a torturous Master's thesis). Plotinus. Swedenborg. *The Transactions of the American Society for Psychical Research.* Voltaire. Locke. Rousseau. And Berkeley: the good Bishop adrift in a dream.

An etching by Halbrech above my desk, The Thames 1801. Water too black. Inky-black. Thick with mud . . .? Filthy water in any case.

Perry's essay, forty-five scribbled pages. "The Challenge of the Future." Given to me several weeks ago by Dr. Rowe, who feared rejecting it for the *Transactions* but could not, of course, accept it. I can read only a few pages at a time, then push it aside, too moved to continue. Frightened also.

The man had gone insane.

Died insane.

Personality broken: broken bits of intellect.

His argument passionate and disjointed, with no pretense of objectivity. Where some weeks ago he had taken the stand that it was immoral to investigate the Spirit World, now he took the stand that it was imperative we do so. We are on the brink of a new age . . . new knowledge of the universe . . . comparable to the stormy transitional period between the Ptolemaic and the Copernican theories of the universe. . . . More experiments required. Money. Donations. Subsidies by private institutions. All psychological research must be channeled into a systematic study of the Spirit World and the ways by which we can communicate with that world. Mediums like Mrs. A——must be brought to centers of learning like Harvard and treated with the respect their genius deserves. Their value to civilization is, after all, beyond estimation. They must be rescued from arduous and routine lives where their genius is drained off into vulgar pursuits . . . they must be rescued from a clientele that is mainly concerned with being put into contact with deceased relatives for utterly trivial, self-serving reasons. Men of learning must realize the gravity of the situation. Otherwise we will fail, we will stagger beneath the burden, we will be defeated, ignobly, and it will remain for the twentieth century to discover the existence of the Spirit Universe that surrounds the Material Universe, and to determine the exact ways by which one world is related to another.

Perry Moore died of a stroke on the eighth of April; died instantaneously on the steps of the Bedford Club shortly after 2 P.M. Passers-by saw a very excited, red-faced gentleman with an open collar push his way through a small gathering at the top of the steps—and then suddenly fall, as if shot down.

In death he looked like quite another person: his features sharp, the nose especially pointed. Hardly the handsome Perry Moore everyone had known.

He had come to a meeting of the Society, though it was suggested by Dr. Rowe and by others (including myself) that he stay away. Of course he came to argue. To present his "new position." To insult the other members. (He was contemptuous of a rather poorly organized paper on the medium Miss E——of Salem, a young woman who works with objects like rings, articles of clothing, locks of hair, et cetera; and quite angry with the evidence presented by a young geologist that would seem to discredit, once and for all, the claims of Eustace of Portsmouth. He interrupted a third paper, calling the reader a "bigot" and an "ignorant fool.")

Fortunately the incident did not find its way into any of the papers. The press, misunderstanding (deliberately and maliciously) the Society's attitude toward Spiritualism, delights in ridiculing our efforts.

There were respectful obituaries. A fine eulogy prepared by Reverend Tyler of St. Aidan's. Other tributes. *A tragic loss. . . . Mourned by all who knew him. . . .* (I stammered and could not speak. I cannot speak of him, of it, even now. Am I mourning, am I aggrieved? Or merely shocked? Terrified?) Relatives and friends and associates glossed over his behavior these past few months and settled upon an earlier Perry Moore, eminently sane, a distinguished physician and man of letters. I did not disagree, I merely acquiesced; I could not make any claim to have really known the man.

And so he has died, and so he is dead. . . .

Shortly after the funeral I went away to New Hampshire for a few days. But I can barely remember that period of time now. I sleep poorly, I yearn for summer, for a drastic change of climate, of scene. It was unwise for me to take up the responsibility of psychical research, fascinated though I am by it; my classes and lectures at the University demand most of my energy.

How quickly he died, and so young: so relatively young.

No history of high blood pressure, it is said.

At the end he was arguing with everyone, however. His personality had completely changed. He was rude, impetuous, even rather profane; even poorly groomed. (Rising to challenge the first of the papers, he revealed a shirtfront that appeared to be stained.) Some claimed he had been drinking all along, for years. Was it possible . . .? (He had clearly enjoyed the wine and brandy in Quincy that evening, but I would not have said he was intemperate.) Rumors, fanciful tales, outright lies, slander. . . . It is painful, the vulnerability death brings.

Bigots, he called us. Ignorant fools. Unbelievers—atheists—traitors to the Spirit World—heretics. Heretics! I believe he looked directly at me as he pushed his way out of the meeting room: his eyes glaring, his face dangerously flushed, no recognition in his stare.

After his death, it is said, books continue to arrive at his home from England and Europe. He spent a small fortune on obscure, out-of-print volumes—commentaries on the Kabbala, on Plotinus, medieval alchemical texts, books on astrology, witchcraft, the metaphysics of death. Occult cosmologies. Egyptian, Indian, and Chinese "wisdom." Blake, Swedenborg, Cozad. *The Tibetan Book of the Dead.* Datsky's *Lunar Mysteries.* His estate is in chaos because he left not one but several wills, the most recent made out only a day before his death, merely a few lines scribbled on scrap paper, without witnesses. The family will contest, of course. Since in this will he left his money and property to an obscure woman living in Quincy, Massachusetts, and since he was obviously not in his right mind at the time, they would be foolish indeed not to contest.

Days have passed since his sudden death. Days continue to pass. At times I am seized by a sort of quick, cold panic; at other times I am inclined to think the entire situation has been exaggerated. In one mood I vow to myself that I will never again pursue psychical research because it is simply too dangerous. In another mood I vow I will never again pursue it because it is a waste of time and my own work, my own career, must come first.

Heretics, he called us. Looking straight at me.
Still, he was mad. And is not to be blamed for the vagaries of madness.

19 June 1887. Boston.

Luncheon with Dr. Rowe, Miss Madeleine van der Post, young Lucas Matthewson; turned over my personal records and notes re the mediums Dr. Moore and I visited. (Destroyed jottings of a private nature.) Miss van der Post and Matthewson will be taking over my responsibilities. Both are young, quick-witted, alert, with a certain ironic play about their features; rather like Dr. Moore in his prime. Matthewson is a former seminary student now teaching physics at the Boston University. They questioned me about Perry Moore, but I avoided answering frankly. Asked if we were close, I said *No*. Asked if I had heard a bizarre tale making the rounds of Boston salons—that a spirit claiming to be Perry Moore has intruded upon a number of séances in the area—I said honestly that I had not; and I did not care to hear about it.

Spinoza: *I will analyze the actions and appetites of men as if it were a question of lines, of planes, and of solids.*
It is in this direction, I believe, that we must move. Away from the phantasmal, the vaporous, the unclear; toward lines, planes, and solids.
Sanity.

8 July 1887. Mount Desert Island, Maine.

Very early this morning, before dawn, dreamed of Perry Moore: a babbling gesticulating spirit, bearded, bright-eyed, obviously mad. Jarvis? Jarvis? Don't deny me! he cried. I am so . . . so bereft. . . .
Paralyzed, I faced him: neither awake nor asleep. His words were not really *words* so much as unvoiced thoughts. I heard them in my own voice; a terrible raw itching at the back of my throat yearned to articulate the man's grief.
Perry?
You don't dare deny me! Not now!
He drew near and I could not escape. The dream shifted, lost its clarity. Someone was shouting at me. Very angry, he was, and baffled—as if drunk—or ill—or injured.
Perry? I can't hear you—
—our dinner at Montague House, do you remember? Lamb, it was. And crepes with almonds for dessert. You remember! You remember! You can't deny me! We were both nonbelievers then, both abysmally ignorant—you can't deny me!
(I was mute with fear or with cunning.)
—that idiot Rowe, how humiliated he will be! All of them! All of you! The

entire rationalist bias, the—the conspiracy of—of fools—bigots— In a few years—In a few short years—Jarvis, where are you? Why can't I see you? Where have you gone?—My eyes can't focus: will someone help me? I seem to have lost my way. Who is here? Who am I talking with? You remember me, don't you?

(He brushed near me, blinking helplessly. His mouth was a hole torn into his pale ravaged flesh.)

Where are you? Where is everyone? I thought it would be crowded here but—but there's no one—I am forgetting so much! My name—what was my name? Can't see. Can't remember. Something very important—something very important I must accomplish—can't remember—Why is there no God? No one here? No one in control? We drift this way and that way, we come to no rest, there are no landmarks—no way of judging—everything is confused—disjointed—Is someone listening? Would you read to me, please? Would you read to me?—anything!—that speech of Hamlet's—*To be or not*—a sonnet of Shakespeare's—any sonnet, anything—*That time of year thou may in me behold*—is that it?—is that how it begins? *Bare ruin'd choirs where the sweet birds once sang.* How does it go? Won't you tell me? I'm lost—there's nothing here to see, to touch—isn't anyone listening? I thought there was someone nearby, a friend: isn't anyone here?

(I stood paralyzed, mute with caution: he passed by.)

—*When in the chronicle of wasted time—the wide world dreaming of things to come*—is anyone listening?—can anyone help?—I am forgetting so much—my name, my life—my life's work—to penetrate the mysteries—the veil—to do justice to the universe of—of what—what had I intended?—am I in my place of repose now, have I come home? Why is it so empty here? Why is no one in control? My eyes—my head—mind broken and blown about—slivers—shards—annihilating all that's made to a—a green thought —a green shade—Shakespeare? Plato? Pascal? Will someone read me Pascal again? I seem to have lost my way—I am being blown about—Jarvis, was it? My dear young friend Jarvis? But I've forgotten your last name—I've forgotten so much—

(I wanted to reach out to touch him—but could not move, could not wake. The back of my throat ached with sorrow. Silent! Silent! I could not utter a word.)

—my papers, my journal—twenty years—a key somewhere hidden—where?—ah yes: the bottom drawer of my desk—do you hear?—my desk—house—Louisburg Square—the key is hidden there—wrapped in a linen handkerchief—the strongbox is—the locked box is—hidden—my brother Edward's house—attic—trunk—steamer trunk—initials R. W. M. —Father's trunk, you see—strongbox hidden inside—my secret journals— life's work—physical and spiritual wisdom—must not be lost—are you listening?—is anyone listening? I am forgetting so much, my mind is in shreds—but if you could locate the journal and read it to me—if you could salvage it—me—I would be so very grateful—I would forgive you anything, all of you—Is anyone there? Jarvis? Brandon? No one?—My journal, my soul: will you salvage it? Will—

(He stumbled away and I was alone again.)
Perry—?
But it was too late: I awoke drenched with perspiration.

Nightmare.
Must forget.

Best to rise early, before the others. Mount Desert Island lovely in July. Our lodge on a hill above the beach. No spirits here: wind from the northeast, perpetual fresh air, perpetual waves. Best to rise early and run along the beach and plunge into the chilly water.

Clear the cobwebs from one's mind.

How beautiful the sky, the ocean, the sunrise!

No spirits here on Mount Desert Island. Swimming: skillful exertion of arms and legs. Head turned this way, that way. Eyes half shut. The surprise of the cold rough waves. One yearns almost to slip out of one's human skin at such times . . . ! Crude blatant beauty of Maine. Ocean. Muscular exertion of body. How alive I am, how living, how invulnerable; what a triumph in my every breath. . . .

Everything slips from my mind except the present moment. I am living, I am alive, I am immortal. Must not weaken: must not sink. Drowning? No. Impossible. Life is the only reality. It is not extinction that awaits but a hideous dreamlike state, a perpetual groping, blundering—far worse than extinction—incomprehensible: so it is life we must cling to, arm over arm, swimming, conquering the element that sustains us.

Jarvis? someone cried. *Please hear me—*

How exquisite life is, the turbulent joy of life contained in flesh! I heard nothing except the triumphant waves splashing about me. I swam for nearly an hour. Was reluctant to come ashore for breakfast, though our breakfast's are always pleasant rowdy sessions: my wife and my brother's wife and our seven children thrown together for the month of July. Three boys, four girls: noise, bustle, health, no shadows, no spirits. No time to think. Again and again I shall emerge from the surf, face and hair and body streaming water, exhausted but jubilant, triumphant. Again and again the children will call out to me, excited, from the dayside of the world that they inhabit.

I will not investigate Dr. Moore's strongbox and his secret journal; I will not even think about doing so. The wind blows words away. The surf is hypnotic. I will not remember this morning's dream once I sit down to breakfast with the family. I will not clutch my wife's wrist and say *We must not die! We dare not die!*—for that would only frighten and offend her.

Jarvis? she is calling at this very moment.

And I say *Yes—? Yes, I'll be there at once.*

Walter de la Mare

Seaton's Aunt

Walter de la Mare, after Henry James, until Robert Aickman, is the master of dreadful uncertainty in the horror story. His finest tales most often suggest the supernatural without confirming it, which method Aickman later raised to a primary aesthetic principle of the ghost story. He has an excellent and refined style and a thorough, Jamesian attitude toward the buildup of detail and the psychological rounding of character. He is a major figure in the literature of the fantastic, one who has fallen out of fashion as the popularity of the overtly monstrous and the overtly moral horror story has risen since the 1930s. "Seaton's Aunt" is one of his most famous pieces and, with "Out of the Deep," often considered his best by connoisseurs and commentators. The slow accretion of effect does not give the audience looking for immediate thrills satisfaction; de la Mare is for that category of readers whom Stephen King alluded to as "human beings who read to think." "Seaton's Aunt" is an example of the twentieth-century development of the fantastic as the third major mode of horror. "De la Mare was happy to live with uncertainties, conscious of the infinite possibilities created by the imagination but exclusively committed to none of them," says the scholar Julia Briggs. His purpose was to awaken his readers to the life of the imagination. Horror was often his primary tool.

I had heard rumors of Seaton's aunt long before I actually encountered her. Seaton, in the hush of confidence, or at any little show of toleration on our part, would remark, "My aunt," or "My old aunt, you know," as if his relative might be a kind of cement to an *entente cordiale.*

He had an unusual quantity of pocket-money; or, at any rate, it was bestowed on him in unusually large amounts; and he spent it freely, though none of us would have described him as an "awfully generous chap." "Hullo, Seaton," we would say, "the old Begum?" At the beginning of term, too, he used to bring back surprising and exotic dainties in a box with a trick padlock that accompanied him from his first appearance at Gummidge's in a billycock hat to the rather abrupt conclusion of his schooldays.

From a boy's point of view he looked distastefully foreign with his yellowish skin, slow chocolate-coloured eyes, and lean weak figure. Merely for his looks he was treated by most of us true-blue Englishmen with condescension, hostility, or contempt. We used to call him "Pongo," but without any much better excuse for the nickname than his skin. He was, that

731

is, in one sense of the term what he assuredly was not in the other sense, a sport.

Seaton and I, as I may say, were never in any sense intimate at school; our orbits only intersected in class. I kept deliberately aloof from him. I felt vaguely he was a sneak, and remained quite unmollified by advances on his side, which, in a boy's barbarous fashion, unless it suited me to be magnanimous, I haughtily ignored.

We were both of us quick-footed, and at Prisoner's Base used occasionally to hide together. And so I best remember Seaton—his narrow watchful face in the dusk of a summer evening; his peculiar crouch, and his inarticulate whisperings and mumblings. Otherwise he played all games slackly and limply; used to stand and feed at his locker with a crony or two until his "tuck" gave out; or waste his money on some outlandish fancy or other. He bought, for instance, a silver bangle, which he wore above his left elbow, until some of the fellows showed their masterly contempt of the practice by dropping it nearly red-hot down his neck.

It needed, therefore, a rather peculiar taste, and a rather rare kind of schoolboy courage and indifference to criticism, to be much associated with him. And I had neither the taste nor, probably, the courage. None the less, he did make advances, and on one memorable occasion went to the length of bestowing on me a whole pot of some outlandish mulberry-coloured jelly that had been duplicated in his term's supplies. In the exuberance of my gratitude I promised to spend the next half-term holiday with him at his aunt's house.

I had clean forgotten my promise when, two or three days before the holiday, he came up and triumphantly reminded me of it.

"Well, to tell you the honest truth, Seaton, old chap—" I began graciously: but he cut me short.

"My aunt expects you," he said; "she is very glad you are coming. She's sure to be quite decent to *you*, Withers."

I looked at him in sheer astonishment; the emphasis was so uncalled for. It seemed to suggest an aunt not hitherto hinted at, and a friendly feeling on Seaton's side that was far more disconcerting than welcome.

We reached his aunt's house partly by train, partly by a lift in an empty farm-cart, and partly by walking. It was a whole-day holiday, and we were to sleep the night; he lent me extraordinary night-gear, I remember. The village street was unusually wide, and was fed from a green by two converging roads, with an inn, and a high green sign at the corner. About a hundred yards down the street was a chemist's shop—a Mr. Tanner's. We descended the two steps into his dusky and odorous interior to buy, I remember, some rat poison. A little beyond the chemist's was the forge. You then walked along a very narrow path, under a fairly high wall, nodding here and there with weeds and tufts of grass, and so came to the iron garden-gates, and saw the high flat house behind its huge sycamore. A coach-house stood on the left of the house, and on the right a gate led into a kind of rambling orchard. The lawn lay away over to the left again, and at the bottom (for the whole garden sloped gently to a sluggish and rushy pond-like stream) was a meadow.

We arrived at noon, and entered the gates out of the hot dust beneath the glitter of the dark-curtained windows. Seaton led me at once through the little garden-gate to show me his tadpole pond, swarming with what (being myself not in the least interested in low life) seemed to me the most horrible creatures—of all shapes, consistencies, and sizes, but with which Seaton was obviously on the most intimate of terms. I can see his absorbed face now as, squatting on his heels he fished the slimy things out in his sallow palms. Wearying at last of these pets, we loitered about awhile in an aimless fashion. Seaton seemed to be listening, or at any rate waiting, for something to happen or for someone to come. But nothing did happen and no one came.

That was just like Seaton. Anyhow, the first view I got of his aunt was when, at the summons of a distant gong, we turned from the garden, very hungry and thirsty, to go into luncheon. We were approaching the house when Seaton suddenly came to a standstill. Indeed, I have always had the impression that he plucked at my sleeve. Something, at least, seemed to catch me back, as it were, as he cried, "Look out, there she is!"

She was standing at an upper window which opened wide on a hinge, and at first sight she looked an excessively tall and overwhelming figure. This, however, was mainly because the window reached all but to the floor of her bedroom. She was in reality rather an undersized woman, in spite of her long face and big head. She must have stood, I think, unusually still, with eyes fixed on us, though this impression may be due to Seaton's sudden warning and to my consciousness of the cautious and subdued air that had fallen on him at sight of her. I know that without the least reason in the world I felt a kind of guiltiness, as if I had been "caught." There was a silvery star pattern sprinkled on her black silk dress, and even from the ground I could see the immense coils of her hair and the rings on her left hand which was held fingering the small jet buttons of her bodice. She watched our united advance without stirring, until, imperceptibly, her eyes raised and lost themselves in the distance, so that it was out of an assumed reverie that she appeared suddenly to awaken to our presence beneath her when we drew close to the house.

"So this is your friend, Mr. Smithers, I suppose?" she said, bobbing to me.

"Withers, Aunt," said Seaton.

"It's much the same," she said, with eyes fixed on me. "Come in, Mr. Withers, and bring him along with you."

She continued to gaze at me—at least, I think she did so. I know that the fixity of her scrutiny and her ironical "Mr." made me feel peculiarly uncomfortable. None the less she was extremely kind and attentive to me, though, no doubt, her kindness and attention showed up more vividly against her complete neglect of Seaton. Only one remark that I have any recollection of she made to him: "When I look on my nephew, Mr. Smithers, I realize that dust we are, and dust shall become. You are hot, dirty, and incorrigible, Arthur."

She sat at the head of the table, Seaton at the foot, and I, before a wide waste of damask tablecloth, between them. It was an old and rather close dining-room, with windows thrown wide to the green garden and a wonderful cascade of fading roses. Miss Seaton's great chair faced this window, so that its rose-reflected light shone full on her yellowish face, and on just such chocolate eyes as my schoolfellow's, except that hers were more than half-covered by unusually long and heavy lids.

There she sat, steadily eating, with those sluggish eyes fixed for the most part on my face; above them stood the deep-lined fork between her eyebrows; and above that the wide expanse of a remarkable brow beneath its strange steep bank of hair. The lunch was copious, and consisted, I remember, of all such dishes as are generally considered too rich and too good for the schoolboy digestion—lobster mayonnaise, cold game sausages, an immense veal and ham pie farced with eggs, truffles, and numberless delicious flavours; besides kickshaws, creams, and sweetmeats. We even had a wine, a half-glass of old darkish sherry each.

Miss Seaton enjoyed and indulged an enormous appetite. Her example and a natural schoolboy voracity soon overcame my nervousness of her, even to the extent of allowing me to enjoy to the best of my bent so rare a spread. Seaton was singularly modest; the greater part of his meal consisted of almonds and raisins, which he nibbled surreptitiously and as if he found difficulty in swallowing them.

I don't mean that Miss Seaton "conversed" with me. She merely scattered trenchant remarks and now and then twinkled a baited question over my head. But her face was like a dense and involved accompaniment to her talk. She presently dropped the "Mr.", to my intense relief, and called me now Withers, or Wither, now Smithers, and even once towards the close of the meal distinctly Johnson, though how on earth my name suggested it, or whose face mine had reanimated in memory, I cannot conceive.

"And is Arthur a good boy at school, Mr. Wither?" was one of her many questions. "Does he please his masters? Is he first in his class? What does the reverend Dr. Gummidge think of him, eh?"

I knew she was jeering at him, but her face was adamant against the least flicker of sarcasm or facetiousness. I gazed fixedly at a blushing crescent of lobster.

"I think you're eighth, aren't you, Seaton?"

Seaton moved his small pupils towards his aunt. But she continued to gaze with a kind of concentrated detachment at me.

"Arthur will never make a brilliant scholar, I fear," she said, lifting a dexterously burdened fork to her wide mouth . . .

After luncheon she preceded me up to my bedroom. It was a jolly little bedroom, with a brass fender and rugs and a polished floor, on which it was possible, I afterwards found, to play "snow-shoes." Over the washstand was a little black-framed water-colour drawing, depicting a large eye with an extremely fishlike intensity in the spark of light on the dark pupil; and in "illuminated" lettering beneath was printed very minutely, "Thou God Seest ME," followed by a long looped monogram, "S.S.", in the corner. The other pictures were all of the sea: brigs on blue water; a schooner overtopping chalk cliffs; a rocky island of prodigious steepness, with two tiny sailors dragging a monstrous boat up a shelf of beach.

"This is the room, Withers, my poor dear brother William died in when a boy. Admire the view!"

I looked out of the window across the tree-tops. It was a day hot with sunshine over the green fields, and the cattle were standing swishing their tails in the shallow water. But the view at the moment was no doubt made more vividly impressive by the apprehension that she would presently inquire after my luggage, and I had brought not even a toothbrush. I need have had no fear. Hers was not that highly civilized type of mind that is stuffed with sharp, material details. Nor could her ample presence be described as in the least motherly.

"I would never consent to question a schoolfellow behind my nephew's back," she said, standing in the middle of the room, "but tell me, Smithers, why is Arthur so unpopular? You, I understand, are his only close friend." She stood in a dazzle of sun, and out of it her eyes regarded me with such leaden penetration beneath their thick lids that I doubt if my face concealed the least thought from her. "But there, there," she added very suavely, stooping her head a little, "don't trouble to answer me. I never extort an answer. Boys are queer fish. Brains might perhaps have suggested his washing his hands before luncheon; but—not my choice, Smithers. God forbid! And now, perhaps, you would like to go into the garden again. I cannot actually see from here, but I should not be surprised if Arthur is now skulking behind that hedge."

He was. I saw his head come out and take a rapid glance at the windows.

"Join him, Mr. Smithers; we shall meet again, I hope, at the teatable. The afternoon I spend in retirement."

Whether or not, Seaton and I had not been long engaged with the aid of two green switches in riding round and round a lumbering old grey horse we found in the meadow, before a rather bunched-up figure appeared, walking along the fieldpath on the other side of the water, with a magenta parasol studiously lowered in our direction throughout her slow progress, as if that were the magnetic needle and we the fixed Pole. Seaton at once lost all nerve and interest. At the next lurch of the old mare's heels he toppled over into the grass, and I slid off the sleek broad back to join him where he stood, rubbing his shoulder and sourly watching the rather pompous figure till it was out of sight.

"Was that your aunt, Seaton?" I enquired; but not till then.

He nodded.

"Why didn't she take any notice of us, then?"

"She never does."

"Why not?"

"Oh, she knows all right, without; that's the damn awful part of it." Seaton was one of the very few fellows at Gummidge's who had the ostentation to use bad language. He had suffered for it too. But it wasn't, I think, bravado. I believe he really felt certain things more intensely than most of the other fellows, and they were generally things that fortunate and average people do not feel at all—the peculiar quality, for instance, of the British schoolboy's imagination.

"I tell you, Withers," he went on moodily, slinking across the meadow with his hands covered up in his pockets, "she sees everything. And what she doesn't see, she knows without."

"But how?" I said, not because I was much interested, but because the afternoon was so hot and tiresome and purposeless, and it seemed more of a bore to remain silent. Seaton turned gloomily and spoke in a very low voice.

"Don't appear to be talking of her, if you wouldn't mind. It's—because she's in league with the Devil." He nodded his head and stooped to pick up a round flat pebble. "I tell you," he said, still stooping, "you fellows don't realize what it is. I know I'm a bit close and all that. But so would you be if you had that old hag listening to every thought you think."

I looked at him, then turned and surveyed one by one the windows of the house.

"Where's your *pater*?" I said awkwardly.

"Dead, ages and ages ago, and my mother too. She's not my aunt even by rights."

"What is she, then?"

"I mean she's not my mother's sister, because my grandmother married twice; and she's one of the first lot. I don't know what you call her, but anyhow she's not my real aunt."

"She gives you plenty of pocket-money."

Seaton looked steadfastly at me out of his flat eyes. "She can't give me what's mine. When I come of age half of the whole lot will be mine; and what's more"—he turned his back on the house—"I'll make her hand over every blessed shilling of it."

I put my hands in my pockets and stared at Seaton. "Is it much?"

He nodded.

"Who told you?" He got suddenly very angry; a darkish red came into his cheeks, his eyes glistened, but he made no answer, and we loitered listlessly about the garden until it was time for tea . . .

Seaton's aunt was wearing an extraordinary kind of lace jacket when we sidled sheepishly into the drawing-room together. She greeted me with a heavy and protracted smile, and bade me bring a chair close to the little table.

"I hope Arthur has made you feel at home," she said as she handed me my cup in her crooked hand. "He don't talk much to me; but then I'm an old woman. You must come again, Wither, and draw him out of his shell. You old snail!" She wagged her head at Seaton, who sat munching cake and watching her intently.

"And we must correspond, perhaps." She nearly shut her eyes at me. "You must write and tell me everything behind the creature's back." I confess I found her rather disquieting company. The evening drew on. Lamps were brought in by a man with a nondescript face and very quiet footsteps. Seaton was told to bring out the chessmen. And we played a game, she and I, with her big chin thrust over the board at every move as she gloated over the pieces and occasionally croaked "Check!"—after which she would sit back inscrutably staring at me. But the game was never finished. She simply hemmed me in with a gathering cloud of pieces that held me impotent, and yet one and all refused to administer to my poor flustered old king a merciful *coup de grâce*.

"There," she said, as the clock struck ten—"a drawn game, Withers. We are very evenly matched. A very creditable defence, Withers. You know your room. There's supper on a tray in the dining-room. Don't let the creature over-eat himself. The gong will sound three-quarters of an hour *before* a punctual breakfast." She held out her cheek to Seaton, and he kissed it with obvious perfunctoriness. With me she shook hands.

"An excellent game," she said cordially, "but my memory is poor, and"—she swept the pieces helter-skelter into the box—"the result will never be known." She raised her great head far back. "Eh?"

It was a kind of challenge, and I could only murmur: "Oh, I was absolutely in a hole, you know!" when she burst out laughing and waved us both out of the room.

Seaton and I stood and ate our supper, with one candlestick to light us, in a corner of the dining room. "Well, and how would you like it?" he said very softly, after cautiously poking his head round the doorway.

"Like what?"

"Being spied on—every blessed thing you do and think?"

"I shouldn't like it at all," I said, "if she does."

"And yet you let her smash you up at chess!"

"I didn't let her!" I said indignantly.

"Well, you funked it, then."

"And I didn't funk it either," I said, "she's so jolly clever with her knights."

Seaton stared at the candle. "Knights," he said slowly. "You wait, that's all." And we went upstairs to bed.

I had not been long in bed, I think, when I was cautiously awakened by a touch on my shoulder. And there was Seaton's face in the candlelight—and his eyes looking into mine.

"What's up?" I said, lurching on to my elbow.

"*Ssh!* Don't scurry," he whispered. "She'll hear. I'm sorry for waking you, but I didn't think you'd be asleep so soon."

"Why, what's the time, then?" Seaton wore, what was then rather unusual, a night-suit, and he hauled his big silver watch out of the pocket in his jacket.

"It's a quarter to twelve. I never get to sleep before twelve—not here."

"What do you do, then?"

"Oh, I read: and listen."

"Listen?"

Seaton stared into his candle-flame as if he were listening even then. "You can't guess what it is. All you read in ghost stories, that's all rot. You can't see much, Withers, but you know all the same."

"Know what?"

"Why, that they're there."

"Who's there?" I asked fretfully, glancing at the door.

"Why, in the house. It swarms with 'em. Just you stand still and listen outside my bedroom door in the middle of the night. I have, dozens of times; they're all over the place."

"Look here, Seaton," I said, "you asked me to come here, and I didn't mind chucking up a leave just to oblige you and because I'd promised; but don't get talking a lot of rot, that's all, or you'll know the difference when we get back."

"Don't fret," he said coldly, turning away. "I shan't be at school long. And what's more, you're here now, and there isn't anybody else to talk to. I'll chance the other."

"Look here, Seaton," I said, "you may think you're going to scare me with a lot of stuff about voices and all that. But I'll just thank you to clear out; and you may please yourself about pottering about all night."

He made no answer; he was standing by the dressing-table looking across his candle into the looking-glass; he turned and stared slowly round the walls.

"Even this room's nothing more than a coffin. I suppose she told you—'It's all exactly the same as when my brother William died'—trust her for that! And good luck to him, say I. Look at that." He raised his candle close to the little water-colour I have mentioned. "There's hundreds of eyes like that in this house; and even if God does see you, He takes precious good care you don't see Him. And it's just the same with them. I tell you what, Withers, I'm getting sick of all this. I shan't stand it much longer."

The house was silent within and without, and even in the yellowish radiance of the candle a faint silver showed through the open window on my blind. I slipped off the bedclothes, wide awake, and sat irresolute on the bedside.

"I know you're only guying me," I said angrily, "but why is the house full of—what you say? Why do you hear—what you *do* hear? Tell me that, you silly fool!"

Seaton sat down on a chair and rested his candlestick on his knee. He blinked at me calmly. "She brings them," he said, with lifted eyebrows.

"Who? Your aunt?"

He nodded.

"How?"

"I told you," he answered pettishly. "She's in league. You don't know. She as good as killed my mother; I know that. But it's not only her by a long chalk. She just sucks you dry. I know. And that's what she'll do for me; because I'm like her—like my mother, I mean. She simply hates to see me alive. I wouldn't be like that old she-wolf for a million pounds. And so"—he broke off, with a comprehensive wave of his candlestick—"they're always here. Ah, my boy, wait till she's dead! She'll hear something then, I can tell you. It's all very well now, but wait till then! I wouldn't be in her shoes when she has to clear out—for something. Don't you go and believe I care for ghosts, or whatever you like to call them. We're all in the same box. We're all under her thumb."

He was looking almost nonchalantly at the ceiling at the moment, when I saw his face change, saw his eyes suddenly drop like shot birds and fix themselves on the cranny of the door he had left just ajar. Even from where I sat I could see his cheek change colour; it went greenish. He crouched without stirring, like an animal. And I, scarcely daring to breathe, sat with creeping skin, sourly watching him. His hands relaxed, and he gave a kind of sigh.

"Was *that* one?" I whispered, with a timid show of jauntiness. He looked round, opened his mouth, and nodded. "What?" I said. He jerked his thumb with meaningful eyes, and I knew that he meant that his aunt had been there listening at our door cranny.

"Look here, Seaton," I said once more, wriggling to my feet. "You may think I'm a jolly noodle; just as you please. But your aunt has been civil to me and all that, and I don't believe a word you say about her, that's all, and never did. Every fellow's a bit off his pluck at night, and you may think it a fine sport to try your rubbish on me. I heard your aunt come upstairs before I fell asleep. And I'll bet you a level tanner she's in bed now. What's more, you can keep your blessed ghosts to yourself. It's a guilty conscience, I should think."

Seaton looked at me intently, without answering for a moment. "I'm not a liar, Withers; but I'm not going to quarrel either. You're the only chap I care a button for; or, at any rate, you're the only chap that's ever come here; and it's something to tell a fellow what you feel. I don't care a fig for fifty thousand ghosts; although I swear on my solemn oath that I know they're here. But she"—he turned deliberately—"you laid a tanner she's in bed, Withers; well, I know different. She's never in bed much of the night, and I'll prove it, too, just to show you I'm not such a nolly as you think I am. Come on!"

"Come on where?"

"Why, to see."

I hesitated. He opened a large cupboard and took out a small dark dressing-gown and a kind of shawl-jacket. He threw the jacket on the bed and put on the gown. His dusky face was colourless, and I could see by the way he fumbled at the sleeves he was shivering. But it was no good showing the white feather now. So I threw the tasselled shawl over my shoulders and, leaving our candle brightly burning on the chair, we went out together and stood in the corridor.

"Now then, listen!" Seaton whispered.

We stood leaning over the staircase. It was like leaning over a well, so still and chill the air was all around us. But presently, as I suppose happens in most old houses, began to echo and answer in my ears a medley of infinite small stirrings and whisperings. Now out of the distance an old timber would relax its fibres, or a scurry die away behind the perishing wainscot. But amid and behind such sounds as these I seemed to begin to be conscious, as it were, of the lightest of footfalls, sounds as faint as the vanishing remembrance of voices in a dream. Seaton was all in obscurity except his face; out of that his eyes gleamed darkly, watching me.

"You'd hear, too, in time, my fine soldier," he muttered. "Come on!"

He descended the stairs, slipping his lean fingers lightly along the balusters. He turned to the right at the loop, and I followed him barefooted along a thickly carpeted corridor. At the end stood a door ajar. And from here we very stealthily and in complete blackness ascended five narrow stairs. Seaton, with immense caution, slowly pushed open a door, and we stood together, looking into a great pool of duskiness, out of which, lit by the feeble clearness of a night-light, rose a vast bed. A heap of clothes lay on the floor; beside them two slippers dozed, with noses each to each, a foot or two apart. Somewhere a little clock ticked huskily. There was a close smell; lavender and eau de Cologne, mingled with the fragrance of ancient sachets, soap, and drugs. Yet it was a scent even more peculiarly compounded than that.

And the bed! I stared warily in; it was mounded gigantically, and it was empty.

Seaton turned a vague pale face, all shadows: "What did I say?" he muttered. "Who's—who's the fool now, I say? How are we going to get back without meeting her, I say? Answer me that! Oh, I wish to God you hadn't come here, Withers."

He stood audibly shivering in his skimpy gown, and could hardly speak for his teeth chattering. And very distinctly, in the hush that followed his whisper, I heard approaching a faint unhurried voluminous rustle. Seaton clutched my arm, dragged me to the right across the room to a large cupboard, and drew the door close to on us. And, presently, as with bursting lungs I peeped out into the long, low, curtained bedroom, waddled in that wonderful great head and body. I can see her now, all patched and lined with shadow, her tied-up hair (she must have had enormous quantities of it for so old a woman), her heavy lids above those flat, slow, vigilant eyes. She just passed across my ken in the vague dusk; but the bed was out of sight.

We waited on and on, listening to the clock's muffled ticking. Not the ghost of a sound rose up from the great bed. Either she lay archly listening or slept a sleep serener than an infant's. And when, it seemed, we had been hours in hiding and were cramped, chilled, and half suffocated, we crept out on all fours, with terror knocking at our ribs, and so down the five narrow stairs and back to the little candle-lit blue-and-gold bedroom.

Once there, Seaton gave in. He sat livid on a chair with closed eyes.

"Here," I said, shaking his arm, "I'm going to bed; I've had enough of this foolery; I'm going to bed." His lips quivered, but he made no answer. I poured out some water into my basin and, with that cold pictured azure eye fixed on us, bespattered Seaton's sallow face and forehead and dabbled his hair. He presently sighed and opened fish-like eyes.

"Come on!" I said. "Don't get shamming, there's a good chap. Get on my back, if you like, and I'll carry you into your bedroom."

He waved me away and stood up. So, with my candle in one hand, I took him under the arm and walked him along according to his direction down the corridor. His was a much dingier room than mine, and littered with boxes, paper, cages, and clothes. I huddled him into bed and turned to go. And suddenly, I can hardly explain it now, a kind of cold and deadly terror swept over me. I almost ran out of the room, with eyes fixed rigidly in front of me, blew out my candle, and buried my head under the bedclothes.

When I awoke, roused not by a gong, but by a long-continued tapping at my door, sunlight was raying in on cornice and bedpost, and birds were singing in the garden. I got up, ashamed of the night's folly, dressed quickly, and went downstairs. The breakfast room was sweet with flowers and fruit and honey. Seaton's aunt was standing in the garden beside the open French window, feeding a great flutter of birds. I watched her for a moment, unseen.

Her face was set in a deep reverie beneath the shadow of a big loose sun-hat. It was deeply lined, crooked, and, in a way I can't describe, fixedly vacant and strange. I coughed politely, and she turned with a prodigious smiling grimace to ask how I had slept. And in that mysterious fashion by which we learn each other's secret thoughts without a syllable said, I knew that she had followed every word and movement of the night before, and was triumphing over my affected innocence and ridiculing my friendly and too easy advances.

We returned to school, Seaton and I, lavishly laden, and by rail all the way. I made no reference to the obscure talk we had had, and resolutely refused to meet his eyes or to take up the hints he let fall. I was relieved—and yet I was sorry—to be going back, and strode on as fast as I could from the station, with Seaton almost trotting at my heels. But he insisted on buying more fruit and sweets—my share of which I accepted with a very bad grace. It was uncomfortably like a bribe, and, after all, I had no quarrel with his rum old aunt, and hadn't really believed half the stuff he had told me.

I saw as little of him as I could after that. He never referred to our visit or resumed his confidences, though in class I would sometimes catch his eye fixed on mine, full of a mute understanding, which I easily affected not to understand. He left Gummidge's, as I have said, rather abruptly, though I never heard of anything to his discredit. And I did not see him or have any news of him again till by chance we met one summer afternoon in the Strand.

He was dressed rather oddly in a coat too large for him and a bright silky tie. But we instantly recognized one another under the awning of a cheap jeweller's shop. He immediately attached himself to me and dragged me off, not too cheerfully, to lunch with him at an Italian restaurant near by. He chattered about our old school, which he remembered only with dislike and disgust; told me cold-bloodedly of the disastrous fate of one or two of the older fellows who had been among his chief tormentors; insisted on an expensive wine and the whole gamut of the foreign menu; and finally informed me, with a good deal of niggling, that he had come up to town to buy an engagement-ring.

And of course: "How is your aunt?" I enquired at last.

He seemed to have been awaiting the question. It fell like a stone into a deep pool, so many expressions flitted across his long, sad, sallow, un-English face.

"She's aged a good deal," he said softly, and broke off.

"She's been very decent," he continued presently after, and paused again. "In a way." He eyed me fleetingly. "I dare say you heard that—she—that is, that we—had lost a good deal of money."

"No," I said.

"Oh, yes!" said Seaton, and paused again.

And somehow, poor fellow, I knew in the clink and clatter of glass and voices that he had lied to me; that he did not possess, and never had possessed, a penny beyond what his aunt had squandered on his too ample allowance of pocket-money.

"And the ghosts?" I enquired quizzically.

He grew instantly solemn, and, though it may have been my fancy, slightly yellowed. But "You are making game of me, Withers," was all he said.

He asked for my address, and I rather reluctantly gave him my card.

"Look here, Withers," he said, as we stood together in the sunlight on the kerb, saying goodbye, "here I am, and—and it's all very well. I'm not perhaps as fanciful as I was. But you are practically the only friend I have on earth—except Alice . . . And there—to make a clean breast of it, I'm not sure that my aunt cares much about my getting married. She doesn't say so, of course. You know her well enough for that." He looked sidelong at the rattling gaudy traffic.

"What I was going to say is this: Would you mind coming down? You needn't stay the night unless you please, though, of course, you know you would be awfully welcome. But I should like you to meet my—to meet Alice; and then, perhaps, you might tell me your honest opinion of—of the other too."

I vaguely demurred. He pressed me. And we parted with a half promise that I would come. He waved his ball-topped cane at me and ran off in his long jacket after a bus.

A letter arrived soon after, in his small weak handwriting, giving me full particulars regarding route and trains. And without the least curiosity, even perhaps with some little annoyance that chance should have thrown us together again, I accepted his invitation and arrived one hazy midday at his out-of-the-way station to find him sitting on a low seat under a clump of "double" hollyhocks, awaiting me.

He looked preoccupied and singularly listless; but seemed, none the less, to be pleased to see me.

We walked up the village street, past the little dingy apothecary's and the empty forge, and, as on my first visit, skirted the house together, and, instead of entering by the front door, made our way down the green path into the garden at the back. A pale haze of cloud muffled the sun; the garden lay in a grey shimmer—its old trees, its snap-dragoned faintly glittering walls. But now there was an air of slovenliness where before all had been neat and methodical. In a patch of shallowly dug soil stood a worn-down spade leaning against a tree. There was an old decayed wheelbarrow. The roses had run to leaf and briar; the fruit-trees were unpruned. The goddess of neglect had made it her secret resort.

"You ain't much of a gardener, Seaton," I said at last, with a sigh of relief.

"I think, do you know, I like it best like this," said Seaton. "We haven't any man now, of course. Can't afford it." He stood staring at his little dark oblong of freshly turned earth. "And it always seems to me," he went on ruminatingly, "that, after all, we are all nothing better than interlopers on the earth, disfiguring and staining wherever we go. It may sound shocking blasphemy to say so; but then it's different here, you see. We are further away."

"To tell you the truth, Seaton, I *don't* quite see," I said; "but it isn't a new philosophy, is it? Anyhow, it's a precious beastly one."

"It's only what I think," he replied, with all his odd old stubborn meekness. "And one thinks as one *is*."

We wandered on together, talking little, and still with that expression of uneasy vigilance on Seaton's face. He pulled out his watch as we stood gazing idly over the green meadows and the dark motionless bulrushes.

"I think, perhaps, it's nearly time for lunch," he said. "Would you like to come in?"

We turned and walked slowly towards the house, across whose windows I confess my own eyes, too, went restlessly meandering in search of its rather disconcerting inmate. There was a pathetic look of bedraggledness, of want of means and care, rust and overgrowth and faded paint. Seaton's aunt, a little to my relief, did not share our meal. So he carved the cold meat, and dispatched a heaped-up plate by an elderly servant for his aunt's private consumption. We talked little and in half-suppressed tones, and sipped some Madeira which Seaton after listening for a moment or two fetched out of the great mahogany sideboard.

I played him a dull and effortless game of chess, yawning between the moves he himself made almost at haphazard, and with attention elsewhere engaged. Towards five o'clock came the sound of a distant ring, and Seaton jumped up, overturning the board, and so ended a game that else might have fatuously continued to this day. He effusively excused himself, and after some little while returned with a slim, dark, pale-faced girl of about nineteen, in a white gown and hat, to whom I was presented with some little nervousness as his "dear old friend and schoolfellow."

We talked on in the golden afternoon light, still, as it seemed to me, and even in spite of our efforts to be lively and gay, in a half-suppressed, lack-lustre fashion. We all seemed, if it were not my fancy, to be expectant, to be almost anxiously awaiting an arrival, the appearance of someone whose image filled our collective consciousness. Seaton talked least of all, and in a restless interjectory way, as he continually fidgeted from chair to chair. At last he proposed a stroll in the garden before the sun should have quite gone down.

Alice walked between us. Her hair and eyes were conspicuously dark against the whiteness of her gown. She carried herself not ungracefully, and yet with peculiarly little movement of her arms and body, and answered us both without turning her head. There was a curious provocative reserve in that impassive melancholy face. It seemed to be haunted by some tragic influence of which she herself was unaware.

And yet somehow I knew—I believe we all knew—that this walk, this discussion of their future plans, was a futility. I had nothing to base such scepticism on, except only a vague sense of oppression, a foreboding consciousness of some inert invincible power in the background, to whom optimistic plans and love-making and youth are as chaff and thistledown. We came back, silent, in the last light. Seaton's aunt was there—under an old brass lamp. Her hair was as barbarously massed and curled as ever. Her eyelids, I think, hung even a little heavier in age over their slow-moving inscrutable pupils. We filed in softly out of the evening, and I made my bow.

"In this short interval, Mr. Withers," she remarked amiably, "you have put off youth, put on the man. Dear me, how sad it is to see the young days vanishing! Sit down. My nephew tells me you met by chance—or act of Providence, shall we call it?—and in my beloved Strand! You, I understand, are to be best man—yes, best man! Or am I divulging secrets?" She surveyed Arthur and Alice with overwhelming graciousness. They sat apart on two low chairs and smiled in return.

"And Arthur—how do you think Arthur is looking?"

"I think he looks very much in need of a change," I said.

"A change! Indeed?" She all but shut her eyes at me and with an exaggerated sentimentality shook her head. "My dear Mr. Withers! Are we not *all* in need of a change in this fleeting, fleeting world?" She mused over the remark like a connoisseur. "And you," she continued, turning abruptly to Alice, "I hope you pointed out to Mr. Withers all my pretty bits?"

"We only walked round the garden," the girl replied; then, glancing at Seaton, added almost inaudibly, "it's a very beautiful evening."

"*Is* it?" said the old lady, starting up violently. "Then on this very beautiful evening we will go in to supper. Mr. Withers, your arm; Arthur, bring your bride."

We were a queer quartet, I thought to myself, as I solemnly led the way into the faded, chilly dining-room, with this indefinable old creature leaning wooingly on my arm—the large flat bracelet on the yellow-laced wrist. She fumed a little, breathing heavily, but as if with an effort of the mind rather than of the body; for she had grown much stouter and yet little more proportionate. And to talk into that great white face, so close to mine, was a queer experience in the dim light of the corridor, and even in the twinkling crystal of the candles. She was naïve; she was crafty and challenging; she was even arch; and all these in the brief, rather puffy passage from one room to the other, with these two tongue-tied children bringing up the rear. The meal was tremendous. I have never seen such a monstrous salad. But the dishes were greasy and over-spiced, and were indifferently cooked. One thing only was quite unchanged—my hostess's appetite was as gargantuan as ever. The heavy silver candelabra that lighted us stood before her high-backed chair. Seaton sat a little removed, his plate almost in darkness.

And throughout this prodigious meal his aunt talked, mainly to me, mainly *at* him, but with an occasional satirical sally at Alice and muttered explosions of reprimand to the servant. She had aged, and yet, if it be not nonsense to say so, seemed no older. I suppose to the Pyramids a decade is but as the rustling down of a handful of dust. And she reminded me of some such unshakeable prehistoricism. She certainly was an amazing talker—rapid, egregious, with a delivery that was perfectly overwhelming. As for Seaton—her flashes of silence were for him. On her enormous volubility would suddenly fall a hush; acid sarcasm would be left implied; and she would sit softly moving her great head, with eyes fixed full in a dreamy smile; but with her whole attention, one could see, slowly, joyously, absorbing his mute discomfiture.

She confided in us her views on a theme vaguely occupying at the moment, I suppose, all our minds. "We have barbarous institutions, and so must put up, I suppose, with a never-ending procession of fools—of fools *ad infinitum*. Marriage, Mr. Withers, was instituted in the privacy of a garden;

sub rosa, as it were. Civilization flaunts it in the glare of day. The dull marry the poor; the rich the effete; and so our New Jerusalem is peopled with naturals, plain and coloured, at either end. I detest folly; I detest still more (if I must be frank, dear Arthur) mere cleverness. Mankind has simply become a tailless host of uninstinctive animals. We should never have taken to Evolution, Mr. Withers. 'Natural Selection!'—little gods and fishes!—the deaf for the dumb. We should have used our brains—intellectual pride, the ecclesiastics call it. And by brains I mean—what do I mean, Alice?—I mean, my dear child," and she laid two gross fingers on Alice's narrow sleeve, "I mean courage. Consider it, Arthur. I read that the scientific world is once more beginning to be afraid of spiritual agencies. Spiritual agencies that tap, and actually float, bless their hearts! I think just one more of those mulberries—thank you.

"They talk about 'blind Love'," she ran on derisively as she helped herself, her eyes roving over the dish, "but why blind? I think, Mr. Withers, from weeping over its rickets. After all, it is we plain women that triumph, is it not so—beyond the mockery of time. Alice, now! Fleeting, fleeting is youth, my child. What's that you were confiding to your plate, Arthur? Satirical boy. He laughs at his old aunt: nay, but thou didst laugh. He detests all sentiment. He whispers the most acid asides. Come, my love, we will leave these cynics; we will go and commiserate with each other on our sex. The choice of two evils, Mr. Smithers!" I opened the door, and she swept out as if borne on a torrent of unintelligible indignation; and Arthur and I were left in the clear four-flamed light alone.

For a while we sat in silence. He shook his head at my cigarette-case, and I lit a cigarette. Presently he fidgeted in his chair and poked his head forward into the light. He paused to rise and shut again the shut door.

"How long will you be?" he asked me.

I laughed.

"Oh, it's not that!" he said, in some confusion. "Of course, I like to be with her. But it's not that. The truth is, Withers, I don't care about leaving her too long with my aunt."

I hesitated. He looked at me questioningly.

"Look here, Seaton," I said, "you know well enough that I don't want to interfere in your affairs, or to offer advice where it is not wanted. But don't you think perhaps you may not treat your aunt quite in the right way? As one gets old, you know, a little give and take. I have an old godmother, or something of the kind. She's a bit queer, too . . . A little allowance; it does no harm. But hang it all, I'm no preacher."

He sat down with his hands in his pockets and still with his eyes fixed almost incredulously on mine. "How?" he said.

"Well, my dear fellow, if I'm any judge—mind, I don't say that I am—but I can't help thinking she thinks you don't care for her; and perhaps takes your silence for—for bad temper. She has been very decent to you, hasn't she?"

" 'Decent'? My God!" said Seaton.

I smoked on in silence; but he continued to look at me with that peculiar concentration I remembered of old.

"I don't think, perhaps, Withers," he began presently, "I don't think you quite understand. Perhaps you are not quite our kind. You always did, just like the other fellows, guy me at school. You laughed at me that night you came to stay here—about the voices and all that. But I don't mind being laughed at—because I know."

"Know what?" It was the same old system of dull question and evasive answer.

"I mean I know that what we see and hear is only the smallest fraction of what is. I know she lives quite out of this. She *talks* to you; but it's all make-believe. It's all a 'parlour game.' She's not really with you; only pitting her outside wits against yours and enjoying the fooling. She's living on inside on what you're rotten without. That's what it is—a cannibal feast. She's a spider. It doesn't much matter what you call it. It means the same kind of thing. I tell you, Withers, she hates me; and you can scarcely dream what that hatred means. I used to think I had an inkling of the reason. It's oceans deeper than that. It just lies behind: herself against myself. Why, after all, how much do we really understand of anything? We don't even know our own histories, and not a tenth, not a tenth of the reasons. What has life been to me?—nothing but a trap. And when one sets oneself free for a while, it only begins again. I thought you might understand; but you are on a different level: that's all."

"What on earth are you talking about?" I said contemptuously, in spite of myself.

"I mean what I say," he said gutterally. "All this outside's only make-believe—but there! what's the good of talking? So far as this is concerned I'm as good as done. You wait."

Seaton blew out three of the candles and, leaving the vacant room in semi-darkness, we groped our way along the corridor to the drawing-room. There a full moon stood shining in at the long garden windows. Alice sat stooping at the door, with her hands clasped in her lap, looking out, alone.

"Where is she?" Seaton asked in a low tone.

She looked up; and their eyes met in a glance of instantaneous understanding, and the door immediately afterwards opened behind us.

"*Such* a moon!" said a voice, that once heard, remained unforgettably on the ear. "A night for lovers, Mr. Withers, if ever there was one. Get a shawl, my dear Arthur, and take Alice for a little promenade. I dare say we old cronies will manage to keep awake. Hasten, hasten, Romeo! My poor, poor Alice, how laggard a lover!"

Seaton returned with a shawl. They drifted out into the moonlight. My companion gazed after them till they were out of hearing, turned to me gravely, and suddenly twisted her white face into such a convulsion of contemptuous amusement that I could only stare blankly in reply.

"Dear innocent children!" she said, with inimitable unctuousness. "Well, well, Mr. Withers, we poor seasoned old creatures must move with the times. Do you sing?"

I scouted the idea.

"Then you must listen to my playing. Chess"—she clasped her forehead with both cramped hands—"chess is now completely beyond my poor wits."

She sat down at the piano and ran her fingers in a flourish over the keys. "What shall it be? How shall we capture them, those passionate hearts? That first fine careless rapture? Poetry itself." She gazed softly into the garden a moment, and presently, with a shake of her body, began to play the opening bars of Beethoven's "Moonlight" Sonata. The piano was old and woolly. She played without music. The lamplight was rather dim. The moonbeams from the window lay across the keys. Her head was in shadow. And whether it was simply due to her personality or to some really occult skill in her playing, I cannot say; I only know that she gravely and deliberately set herself to satirize the beautiful music. It brooded on the air, disillusioned, charged with mockery and bitterness. I stood at the window; far down the path I could see the white figure glimmering in that pool of colourless light. A few faint stars shone, and still that amazing woman behind me dragged out of the unwilling keys her wonderful grotesquerie of youth and love and beauty. It came to an end. I knew the player was watching me. "Please, please, go on!" I murmured, without turning. "*Please* go on playing, Miss Seaton."

No answer was returned to this honeyed sarcasm, but I realized in some vague fashion that I was being acutely scrutinized, when suddenly there followed a procession of quiet, plaintive chords which broke at last softly into the hymn, "A Few More Years Shall Roll."

I confess it held me spellbound. There is a wistful, strained plangent pathos in the tune; but beneath those masterly old hands it cried softly and bitterly the solitude and desperate estrangement of the world. Arthur and his lady-love vanished from my thoughts. No one could put into so hackneyed an old hymn tune such an appeal who had never known the meaning of the words. Their meaning, anyhow, isn't commonplace.

I turned a fraction of an inch to glance at the musician. She was leaning forward a little over the keys, so that at the approach of my silent scrutiny she had but to turn her face into the thin flood of moonlight for every feature to become distinctly visible. And so, with the tune abruptly terminated, we steadfastly regarded one another; and she broke into a prolonged chuckle of laughter.

"Not quite so seasoned as I supposed, Mr. Withers. I see you are a real lover of music. To me it is too painful. It evokes too much thought . . ."

I could scarcely see her little glittering eyes under their penthouse lids.

"And now," she broke off crisply, "tell me, as a man of the world, what do you think of my new niece?"

I was not a man of the world, nor was I much flattered in my stiff and dullish way of looking at things by being called one; and I could answer her without the least hesitation.

"I don't think, Miss Seaton, I'm much of a judge of character. She's very charming."

"A brunette?"

"I think I prefer dark women."

"And why? Consider, Mr. Withers; dark hair, dark eyes, dark cloud, dark night, dark vision, dark death, dark grave, dark DARK!"

Perhaps the climax would have rather thrilled Seaton, but I was too thick-skinned. "I don't know much about all that," I answered rather pompously. "Broad daylight's difficult enough for most of us."

"Ah," she said, with a sly inward burst of satirical laughter.

"And I suppose," I went on, perhaps a little nettled, "it isn't the actual darkness one admires, it's the contrast of the skin, and the colour of the eyes, and—and their shining. Just as," I went blundering on, too late to turn back, "just as you only see the stars in the dark. It would be a long day without any evening. As for death and the grave, I don't suppose we shall much notice that." Arthur and his sweetheart were slowly returning along the dewy path. "I believe in making the best of things."

"How very interesting!" came the smooth answer. "I see you are a philosopher, Mr. Withers. H'm! 'As for death and the grave, I don't suppose we shall much notice that.' Very interesting . . . And I'm sure," she added in a particularly suave voice, "I profoundly hope so." She rose slowly from her stool. "You will take pity on me again, I hope. You and I would get on famously—kindred spirits—elective affinities. And, of course, now that my nephew's going to leave me, now that his affections are centred on another, I shall be a very lonely old woman . . . Shall I not, Arthur?"

Seaton blinked stupidly. "I didn't hear what you said, Aunt."

"I was telling our old friend, Arthur, that when you are gone I shall be a very lonely old woman."

"Oh, I don't think so," he said in a strange voice.

"He means, Mr. Withers, he means, my dear child," she said, sweeping her eyes over Alice, "he means that I shall have memory for company—heavenly memory—the ghosts of other days. Sentimental boy! And did you enjoy our music, Alice? Did I really stir that youthful heart? . . . O, O, O," continued the horrible old creature, "you billers and cooers, I have been listening to such flatteries, such confessions! Beware, beware, Arthur, there's many a slip." She rolled her little eyes at me, she shrugged her shoulders at Alice, and gazed an instant stonily into her nephew's face.

I held out my hand. "Good night, good night!" she cried. "He that fights and runs away. Ah, good night, Mr. Withers; come again soon!" She thrust out her cheek at Alice, and we all three filed slowly out of the room.

Black shadow darkened the porch and half the spreading sycamore. We walked without speaking up the dusty village street. Here and there a crimson window glowed. At the fork of the high-road I said goodbye. But I had taken hardly more than a dozen paces when a sudden impulse seized me.

"Seaton!" I called.

He turned in the cool stealth of the moonlight.

"You have my address; if by any chance, you know, you should care to spend a week or two in town between this and the—the Day, we should be delighted to see you."

"Thank you, Withers, thank you," he said in a low voice.

"I dare say"—I waved my stick gallantly at Alice—"I dare say you will be doing some shopping; we could all meet," I added, laughing.

"Thank you, thank you, Withers—immensely," he repeated.

And so we parted.

* * *

But they were out of the jog-trot of my prosaic life. And being of a stolid and incurious nature, I left Seaton and his marriage, and even his aunt, to themselves in my memory, and scarcely gave a thought to them until one day I was walking up the Strand again, and passed the flashing gloaming of the second-rate jeweller's shop where I had accidentally encountered my old schoolfellow in the summer. It was one of those stagnant autumnal days after a night of rain. I cannot say why, but a vivid recollection returned to my mind of our meeting and of how suppressed Seaton had seemed, and of how vainly he had endeavoured to appear assured and eager. He must be married by now, and had doubtless returned from his honeymoon. And I had clean forgotten my manners, had sent not a word of congratulation, nor—as I might very well have done, and as I knew he would have been pleased at my doing—even the ghost of a wedding present. It was just as of old.

On the other hand, I pleaded with myself, I had had no invitation. I paused at the corner of Trafalgar Square, and at the bidding of one of those caprices that seize occasionally on even an unimaginative mind, I found myself pelting after a green bus, and actually bound on a visit I had not in the least intended or foreseen.

The colours of autumn were over the village when I arrived. A beautiful late afternoon sunlight bathed thatch and meadow. But it was close and hot. A child, two dogs, a very old woman with a heavy basket I encountered. One or two incurious tradesmen looked idly up as I passed by. It was all so rural and remote, my whimsical impulse had so much flagged, that for a while I hesitated to venture under the shadow of the sycamore-tree to enquire after the happy pair. Indeed I first passed by the faint-blue gates and continued my walk under the high, green and tufted wall. Hollyhocks had attained their topmost bud and seeded in the little cottage gardens beyond; the Michaelmas daisies were in flower; a sweet warm aromatic smell of fading leaves was in the air. Beyond the cottages lay a field where cattle were grazing, and beyond that I came to a little churchyard. Then the road wound on, pathless and houseless, among gorse and bracken. I turned impatiently and walked quickly back to the house and rang the bell.

The rather colourless elderly woman who answered my enquiry informed me that Miss Seaton was at home, as if only taciturnity forbade her adding, "But she doesn't want to see *you*."

"Might I, do you think, have Mr. Arthur's address?" I said.

She looked at me with quiet astonishment, as if waiting for an explanation. Not the faintest of smiles came into her thin face.

"I will tell Miss Seaton," she said after a pause. "Please walk in."

She showed me into the dingy undusted drawing-room, filled with evening sunshine and with the green-dyed light that penetrated the leaves overhanging the long French windows. I sat down and waited on and on, occasionally aware of a creaking footfall overhead. At last the door opened a little, and the great face I had once known peered round at me. For it was enormously changed; mainly, I think, because the aged eyes had rather suddenly failed, and so a kind of stillness and darkness lay over its calm and wrinkled pallor.

"Who is it?" she asked.

I explained myself and told her the occasion of my visit.

She came in, shut the door carefully after her, and, though the fumbling was scarcely perceptible, groped her way to a chair. She had on an old dressing-gown, like a cassock, of a patterned cinnamon colour.

"What is it you want?" she said, seating herself and lifting her blank face to mine.

"Might I just have Arthur's address?" I said deferentially. "I am so sorry to have disturbed you."

"H'm. You have come to see my nephew?"

"Not necessarily to see him, only to hear how he is, and, of course, Mrs. Seaton, too. I am afraid my silence must have appeared . . ."

"He hasn't noticed your silence," croaked the old voice out of the great mask; "besides, there isn't any Mrs. Seaton."

"Ah, then," I answered, after a momentary pause, "I have not seemed so black as I painted myself! And how is Miss Outram?"

"She's gone into Yorkshire," answered Seaton's aunt.

"And Arthur too?"

She did not reply, but simply sat blinking at me with lifted chin, as if listening, but certainly not for what I might have to say. I began to feel rather at a loss.

"You were no close friend of my nephew's, Mr. Smithers?" she said presently.

"No," I answered, welcoming the cue, "and yet, do you know, Miss Seaton, he is one of the very few of my old school-fellows I have come across in the last few years, and I suppose as one gets older one begins to value old associations . . ." My voice seemed to trail off into a vacuum. "I thought Miss Outram," I hastily began again, "a particularly charming girl. I hope they are both quite well."

Still the old face solemnly blinked at me in silence.

"You must find it very lonely, Miss Seaton, with Arthur away?"

"I was never lonely in my life," she said sourly. "I don't look to flesh and blood for my company. When you've got to be my age, Mr. Smithers (which God forbid), you'll find life a very different affair from what you seem to think it is now. You won't seek company then, I'll be bound. It's thrust on you." Her face edged round into the clear green light, and her eyes groped, as it were, over my vacant, disconcerted face. "I dare say, now," she said, composing her mouth, "I dare say my nephew told you a good many tarradiddles in his time. Oh, yes, a good many, eh? He was always a liar. What, now, did he say of me? Tell me, now." She leant forward as far as she could, trembling, with an ingratiating smile.

"I think he is rather superstitious," I said coldly, "but, honestly, I have a very poor memory, Miss Seaton."

"Why?" she said. "*I* haven't."

"The engagement hasn't been broken off, I hope."

"Well, between you and me," she said, shrinking up and with an immensely confidential grimace, "it has."

"I'm sure I'm very sorry to hear it. And where is Arthur?"

"Eh?"

"Where is Arthur?"

We faced each other mutely among the dead old bygone furniture. Past all my analysis was that large, flat, grey, cryptic countenance. And then, suddenly, our eyes for the first time really met. In some indescribable way out of that thick-lidded obscurity a far small something stooped and looked out at me for a mere instant of time that seemed of almost intolerable protraction. Involuntarily I blinked and shook my head. She muttered something with great rapidity, but quite inarticulately; rose and hobbled to the door. I thought I heard, mingled in broken mutterings, something about tea.

"Please, please, don't trouble," I began, but could say no more, for the door was already shut between us. I stood and looked out on the long-neglected garden. I could just see the bright weedy greenness of Seaton's tadpole pond. I wandered about the room. Dusk began to gather, the last birds in that dense shadowiness of trees had ceased to sing. And not a sound was to be heard in the house. I waited on and on, vainly speculating. I even attempted to ring the bell; but the wire was broken, and only jangled loosely at my efforts.

I hesitated, unwilling to call or to venture out, and yet more unwilling to linger on, waiting for a tea that promised to be an exceedingly comfortless supper. And as darkness drew down, a feeling of the utmost unease and disquietude came over me. All my talks with Seaton returned on me with a suddenly enriched meaning. I recalled again his face as we had stood hanging over the staircase, listening in the small hours to the inexplicable stirrings of the night. There were no candles in the room; every minute the autumnal darkness deepened. I cautiously opened the door and listened, and with some little dismay withdrew, for I was uncertain of my way out. I even tried the garden, but was confronted under a veritable thicket of foliage by a padlocked gate. It would be a little too ignominious to be caught scaling a friend's garden fence!

Cautiously returning into the still and musty drawing-room, I took out my watch, and gave the incredible old woman ten minutes in which to reappear. And when that tedious ten minutes had ticked by, I could scarcely distinguish its hands. I determined to wait no longer, drew open the door and, trusting to my sense of direction, groped my way through the corridor that I vaguely remembered led to the front of the house.

I mounted three or four stairs and, lifting a heavy curtain, found myself facing the starry fanlight of the porch. From here I glanced into the gloom of the dining-room. My fingers were on the latch of the outer door when I heard a faint stirring in the darkness above the hall. I looked up and became conscious of, rather than saw, the huddled old figure looking down on me.

There was an immense hushed pause. Then, "Arthur, Arthur," whispered an inexpressibly peevish rasping voice, "is that you? Is that you, Arthur?"

I can scarcely say why, but the question horribly startled me. No conceivable answer occurred to me. With head craned back, hand clenched on my umbrella, I continued to stare up into the gloom, in this fatuous confrontation.

"Oh, oh," the voice croaked. "It is *you*, is it? *That* disgusting man! . . . Go away out. Go away out."

At this dismissal, I wrenched open the door and, rudely slamming it behind me, ran out into the garden, under the gigantic old sycamore, and so out at the open gate.

I found myself half up the village street before I stopped running. The local butcher was sitting in his shop reading a piece of newspaper by the light of a small oil-lamp. I crossed the road and enquired the way to the station. And after he had with minute and needless care directed me, I asked casually if Mr. Arthur Seaton still lived with his aunt at the big house just beyond the village. He poked his head in at the little parlour door.

"Here's a gentleman enquiring after young Mr. Seaton, Millie," he said. "He's dead, ain't he?"

"Why, yes, bless you," replied a cheerful voice from within. "Dead and buried these three months or more—young Mr. Seaton. And just before he was to be married, don't you remember, Bob?"

I saw a fair young woman's face peer over the muslin of the little door at me.

"Thank you," I replied, "then I go straight on?"

"That's it, sir; past the pond, bear up the hill a bit to the left, and then there's the station lights before your eyes."

We looked intelligently into each other's faces in the beam of the smoky lamp. But not one of the many questions in my mind could I put into words.

And again I paused irresolutely a few paces further on. It was not, I fancy, merely a foolish apprehension of what the raw-boned butcher might "think" that prevented my going back to see if I could find Seaton's grave in the benighted churchyard. There was precious little use in pottering about in the muddy dark merely to discover where he was buried. And yet I felt a little uneasy. My rather horrible thought was that, so far as I was concerned—one of his extremely few friends—he had never been much better than "buried" in my mind.

Ivan Turgenev

Clara Militch

Ivan Turgenev was one of the few masters of supernatural horror fiction outside the English language in the nineteenth century. He was a Russian writer of enormous prestige and influence, and his supernatural works span his entire career, the best of them coming from his mature years. *Clara Militch* is a short novel and perhaps the best of all his works in the horror mode. Turgenev maintained that love is a supernatural phenomenon, an intriguing notion that underpins this story of requited love and horror. Turgenev's works were widely read in translation at the end of the nineteenth century. One might also note that in a contemporary scholarly edition of the text, the last word of the novella is "horror."

I

In the spring of 1878 there was living in Moscow, in a small wooden house in Shabolovka, a young man of five-and-twenty, called Yakov Aratov. With him lived his father's sister, an elderly maiden lady, over fifty, Platonida Ivanovna. She took charge of his house, and looked after his household expenditure, a task for which Aratov was utterly unfit. Other relations he had none. A few years previously, his father, a provincial gentleman of small property, had moved to Moscow together with him and Platonida Ivanovna, whom he always, however, called Platosha; her nephew, too, used the same name. On leaving the country-place where they had always lived up till then, the elder Aratov settled in the old capital, with the object of putting his son to the university, for which he had himself prepared him; he bought for a trifle a little house in one of the outlying streets, and established himself in it, with all his books and scientific odds and ends. And of books and odds and ends he had many—for he was a man of some considerable learning . . . "an out-and-out eccentric," as his neighbours said of him. He positively passed among them for a sorcerer; he had even been given the title of an "insectivist." He studied chemistry, mineralogy, entomology, botany, and medicine; he doctored patients gratis with herbs and metallic powders of his own invention, after the method of Paracelsus. These same powders were the means of his bringing to the grave his pretty, young, too delicate wife, whom he passionately loved, and by whom he had an only son. With the same powders he fairly ruined his son's health too, in the hope and intention of strengthening it, as he detected anæmia and a tendency to consumption in his constitution inherited from his mother. The name of "sorcerer" had been given him partly because he regarded himself as a descendant—not in the direct line, of course—of the great Bruce, in honour of whom he had called his son Yakov, the Russian form of James.

He was what is called a most good-natured man, but of melancholy temperament, pottering, and timid, with a bent for everything mysterious and occult. . . . A half-whispered ah! was his habitual exclamation; he even died with this exclamation on his lips, two years after his removal to Moscow.

His son, Yakov, was in appearance unlike his father, who had been plain, clumsy, and awkward; he took more after his mother. He had the same delicate pretty features, the same soft ash-coloured hair, the same little aquiline nose, the same pouting childish lips, and great greenish-grey languishing eyes, with soft eyelashes. But in character he was like his father; and the face, so unlike the father's face, wore the father's expression; and he had the triangular-shaped hands and hollow chest of the old Aratov, who ought, however, hardly to be called old, since he never reached his fiftieth year. Before his death, Yakov had already entered the university in the faculty of physics and mathematics; he did not, however, complete his course; not through laziness, but because, according to his notions, you could learn no more in the university than you could studying alone at home; and he did not go in for a diploma because he had no idea of entering the government service. He was shy with his fellow-students, made friends with scarcely any one, especially held aloof from women, and lived in great solitude, buried in books. He held aloof from women, though he had a heart of the tenderest, and was fascinated by beauty. . . . He had even obtained a sumptuous English keepsake, and (oh shame!) gloated adoringly over its "elegantly engraved" representations of the various ravishing Gulnaras and Medoras. . . . But his innate modesty always kept him in check. In the house he used to work in what had been his father's study, it was also his bed-room, and his bed was the very one in which his father had breathed his last.

The mainstay of his whole existence, his unfailing friend and companion, was his aunt Platosha, with whom he exchanged barely a dozen words in the day, but without whom he could not stir hand or foot. She was a long-faced, long-toothed creature, with pale eyes, and a pale face, with an invariable expression, half of dejection, half of anxious dismay. For ever garbed in a grey dress and a grey shawl, she wandered about the house like a spirit, with noiseless steps, sighed, murmured prayers—especially one favourite one, consisting of three words only, "Lord, succour us!"—and looked after the house with much good sense, taking care of every halfpenny, and buying everything herself. Her nephew she adored; she was in a perpetual fidget over his health—afraid of everything—not for herself but for him; and directly she fancied the slightest thing wrong, she would steal in softly, and set a cup of herb tea on his writing-table, or stroke him on the spine with her hands, soft as wadding. Yakov was not annoyed by these attentions—though the herb tea he left untouched—he merely nodded his head approvingly.

However, his health was really nothing to boast of. He was very impressionable, nervous, fanciful, suffered from palpitations of the heart, and sometimes from asthma; like his father, he believed that there are in nature, and in the soul of man, mysteries which may sometimes be divined, but to which one can never penetrate; he believed in the existence of certain powers and influences, sometimes beneficent, but more often malignant, . . . and he believed too in science, in its dignity and importance. Of late he had taken a great fancy to photography. The smell of the chemicals used in this pursuit was a source of great uneasiness to his old aunt—not on her own account again, but on Yasha's, on account of his chest; but for all the softness of his temper, there was not a little obstinacy in his composition, and he persisted in his favourite pursuit. Platosha gave in, and only sighed more than ever, and murmured, "Lord, succour us!" whenever she saw his fingers stained with iodine.

Yakov, as we have already related, had held aloof from his fellow-students; with one of them he had, however, become fairly intimate, and saw him frequently, even after the fellow-student had left the university and entered the service, in a position involving little responsibility. He had, in his own words, got on to the building of the Church of our Saviour, though, of course, he knew nothing whatever of architecture. Strange to say, this one solitary friend of Aratov's, by name Kupfer, a German, so far Russianised that he did not know one word of German, and even fell foul of "the Germans," this friend had apparently nothing in common with him. He was a black-haired, red-cheeked young man, very jovial, talkative, and devoted to the feminine society Aratov so assiduously avoided. It is true Kupfer both lunched and dined with him pretty often, and even, being a man of small means, used to borrow trifling sums of him; but this was not what induced the free and easy German to frequent the humble little house in Shabolovka so diligently. The spiritual purity, the idealism of Yakov pleased him, possibly as a contrast to what he was seeing and meeting every day; or possibly this very attachment to the youthful idealist betrayed him of German blood after all. Yakov liked Kupfer's simple-hearted frankness; and besides that, his accounts of the theatres, concerts, and balls, where he was always in attendance—of the unknown world altogether, into which Yakov could not make up his mind to enter—secretly interested and even excited the young hermit, without, however, arousing any desire to learn all this by his own experience. And Platosha made Kupfer welcome; it is true she thought him at times excessively unceremonious, but instinctively perceiving and realising that he was sincerely attached to her precious Yasha, she not only put up with the noisy guest, but felt kindly towards him.

II

At the time with which our story is concerned, there was in Moscow a certain widow, a Georgian princess, a person of somewhat dubious, almost suspicious character. She was close upon forty; in her youth she had probably bloomed with that peculiar Oriental beauty, which fades so quickly; now she powdered, rouged, and dyed her hair yellow. Various reports, not altogether favourable, nor altogether definite, were in circulation about her; her husband no one had known, and she had never stayed long in any one town. She had no children, and no property, yet she kept open house, in debt or otherwise; she had a salon, as it is called, and received a rather mixed society, for the most part young men. Everything in her house from her own dress, furniture, and table, down to her carriage and her servants, bore the stamp of something shoddy, artificial, temporary, . . . but the princess herself, as well as her guests, apparently desired nothing better. The princess was reputed a devotee of music and literature, a patroness of artists and men of talent, and she really was interested in all these subjects, even to the point of enthusiasm, and an enthusiasm not altogether affected. There was an unmistakable fibre of artistic feeling in her. Moreover she was very approachable, genial, free from presumption or pretentiousness, and, though many people did not suspect it, she was fundamentally good-natured, soft-hearted, and kindly disposed. . . . Qualities rare—and the more precious for their rarity—precisely in persons of her sort! "A fool of a woman!" a wit said of her: "but she'll get into heaven, not a doubt of it! Because she forgives everything, and everything will be forgiven her." It was said of her too that when she disappeared from a town, she always left as many creditors behind as persons she had befriended. A soft heart readily turned in any direction.

Kupfer, as might have been anticipated, found his way into her house, and was soon on an intimate—evil tongues said a too intimate—footing with her. He himself always spoke of her not only affectionately but with respect; he called her a heart of gold—say what you like! and firmly believed both in her love for art and her comprehension of art! One day after dinner at the Aratovs', in discussing the princess and her evenings, he began to persuade Yakov to break for once from his anchorite seclusion, and to allow him, Kupfer, to present him to his friend. Yakov at first would not even hear of it. "But what do you imagine?" Kupfer cried at last: "what sort of presentation are we talking about? Simply, I take you, just as you are sitting now, in your everyday coat, and go with you to her for an evening. No sort of etiquette is necessary there, my dear boy! You're learned, you know, and fond of literature and music"—(there actually was in Aratov's study a piano on which he sometimes struck minor chords)—"and in her house there's enough and to spare of all those goods! . . . and you'll meet there sympathetic people, no nonsense about them! And after all, you really can't at your age, with your looks (Aratov dropped his eyes and waved his hand deprecating-

756

ly), yes, yes, with your looks, you really can't keep aloof from society, from the world, like this! Why, I'm not going to take you to see generals! Indeed, I know no generals myself! . . . Don't be obstinate, dear boy! Morality is an excellent thing, most laudable. . . . But why fall a prey to asceticism? You're not going in for becoming a monk!"

Aratov was, however, still refractory; but Kupfer found an unexpected ally in Platonida Ivanovna. Though she had no clear idea what was meant by the word asceticism, she too was of the opinion that it would be no harm for dear Yasha to take a little recreation, to see people, and to show himself.

"Especially," she added, "as I've perfect confidence in Fyodor Fedoritch! He'll take you to no bad place! . . ." "I'll bring him back in all his maiden innocence," shouted Kupfer, at which Platonida Ivanovna, in spite of her confidence, cast uneasy glances upon him. Aratov blushed up to his ears, but ceased to make objections.

It ended by Kupfer taking him next day to spend an evening at the princess's. But Aratov did not remain there long. To begin with, he found there some twenty visitors, men and women, sympathetic people possibly, but still strangers, and this oppressed him, even though he had to do very little talking; and that, he feared above all things. Secondly, he did not like their hostess, though she received him very graciously and simply. Everything about her was distasteful to him: her painted face, and her frizzed curls, and her thickly-sugary voice, her shrill giggle, her way of rolling her eyes and looking up, her excessively low-necked dress, and those fat, glossy fingers with their multitude of rings! . . . Hiding himself away in a corner, he took from time to time a rapid survey of the faces of all the guests, without even distinguishing them, and then stared obstinately at his own feet. When at last a stray musician with a worn face, long hair, and an eyeglass stuck into his contorted eyebrow sat down to the grand piano and flinging his hands with a sweep on the keys and his foot on the pedal, began to attack a fantasia of Liszt on a Wagner motive, Aratov could not stand it, and stole off, bearing away in his heart a vague, painful impression; across which, however, flitted something incomprehensible to him, but grave and even disquieting.

III

Kupfer came next day to dinner; he did not begin, however, expatiating on the preceding evening, he did not even reproach Aratov for his hasty retreat, and only regretted that he had not stayed to supper, when there had been champagne! (of the Novgorod brand, we may remark in parenthesis). Kupfer probably realised that it had been a mistake on his part to disturb his friend, and that Aratov really was a man "not suited" to that circle and way of life. On his side, too, Aratov said nothing of the princess, nor of the previous evening. Platonida Ivanovna did not know whether to rejoice at the failure of this first experiment or to regret it. She decided at last that Yasha's health might suffer from such outings, and was comforted. Kupfer went away directly after dinner, and did not show himself again for a whole week. And it was not that he resented the failure of his suggestion, the good fellow was incapable of that, but he had obviously found some interest which was absorbing all his time, all his thoughts; for later on, too, he rarely appeared at the Aratovs', had an absorbed look, spoke little and quickly vanished. . . . Aratov went on living as before; but a sort of—if one may so express it—little hook was pricking at his soul. He was continually haunted by some reminiscence, he could not quite tell what it was himself, and this reminiscence was connected with the evening he had spent at the princess's. For all that, he had not the slightest inclination to return there again, and the world, a part of which he had looked upon at her house, repelled him more than ever. So passed six weeks.

And behold one morning Kupfer stood before him once more, this time with a somewhat embarrassed countenance. "I know," he began with a constrained smile, "that your visit that time was not much to your taste; but I hope for all that you'll agree to my proposal . . . that you won't refuse me my request!"

"What is it?" inquired Aratov.

"Well, do you see," pursued Kupfer, getting more and more heated: "there is a society here of amateurs, artistic people, who from time to time get up readings, concerts, even theatrical performances for some charitable object."

"And the princess has a hand in it?" interposed Aratov.

"The princess has a hand in all good deeds, but that's not the point. We have arranged a literary and musical matinée . . . and at this matinée you may hear a girl . . . an extraordinary girl! We cannot make out quite yet whether she is to be a Rachel or a Viardot . . . for she sings exquisitely, and recites and plays. . . . A talent of the very first rank, my dear boy! I'm not exaggerating. Well then, won't you take a ticket? Five roubles for a seat in the front row."

"And where has this marvellous girl sprung from?" asked Aratov.

Kupfer grinned. "That I really can't say. . . . Of late she's found a home with the princess. The princess you know is a protector of every one of that sort. . . . But you saw her, most likely, that evening."

Aratov gave a faint inward start . . . but he said nothing.

"She has even played somewhere in the provinces," Kupfer continued, "and altogether she's created for the theatre. There! you'll see for yourself!"

"What's her name?" asked Aratov.

"Clara . . ."

"Clara?" Aratov interrupted a second time. "Impossible!"

"Why impossible? Clara . . . Clara Militch; it's not her real name . . . but that's what she's called. She's going to sing a song of Glinka's . . . and of Tchaykovsky's; and then she'll recite the letter from *Yevgeny Oniegin*. Well; will you take a ticket?"

"And when will it be?"

"To-morrow . . . to-morrow, at half-past one, in a private drawing-room, in Ostozhonka. . . . I will come for you. A five-rouble ticket? . . . Here it is . . . no, that's a three-rouble one. Here . . . and here's the programme. . . . I'm one of the stewards."

Aratov sank into thought. Platonida Ivanovna came in at that instant, and glancing at his face, was in a flutter of agitation at once. "Yasha," she cried, "what's the matter with you? Why are you so upset? Fyodor Fedoritch, what is it you've been telling him?"

Aratov did not let his friend answer his aunt's question, but hurriedly snatching the ticket held out to him, told Platonida Ivanovna to give Kupfer five roubles at once.

She blinked in amazement. . . . However, she handed Kupfer the money in silence. Her darling Yasha had ejaculated his commands in a very imperative manner.

"I tell you, a wonder of wonders!" cried Kupfer, hurrying to the door. "Wait till tomorrow."

"Has she black eyes?" Aratov called after him.

"Black as coal!" Kupfer shouted cheerily, as he vanished.

Aratov went away to his room, while Platonida Ivanovna stood rooted to the spot, repeating in a whisper, "Lord, succour us! Succour us, Lord!"

IV

The big drawing-room in the private house in Ostozhonka was already half full of visitors when Aratov and Kupfer arrived. Dramatic performances had sometimes been given in this drawing-room, but on this occasion there was no scenery nor curtain visible. The organisers of the matinée had confined themselves to fixing up a platform at one end, putting upon it a piano, a couple of reading-desks, a few chairs, a table with a bottle of water and a glass on it, and hanging red cloth over the door that led to the room allotted to the performers. In the first row was already sitting the princess in a bright green dress. Aratov placed himself at some distance from her, after exchanging the barest of greetings with her. The public was, as they say, of mixed materials; for the most part young men from educational institutions. Kupfer, as one of the stewards, with a white ribbon on the cuff of his coat, fussed and bustled about busily; the princess was obviously excited, looked about her, shot smiles in all directions, talked with those next to her . . . none but men were sitting near her. The first to appear on the platform was a flute-player of consumptive appearance, who most conscientiously dribbled away—what am I saying?—piped, I mean—a piece also of consumptive tendency; two persons shouted bravo! Then a stout gentleman in spectacles, of an exceedingly solid, even surly aspect, read in a bass voice a sketch of Shtchedrin; the sketch was applauded, not the reader; then the pianist, whom Aratov had seen before, came forward and strummed the same fantasia of Liszt; the pianist gained an encore. He bowed with one hand on the back of the chair, and after each bow he shook back his hair, precisely like Liszt! At last after a rather long interval the red cloth over the door on to the platform stirred and opened wide, and Clara Militch appeared. The room resounded with applause. With hesitating steps, she moved forward on the platform, stopped and stood motionless, clasping her large handsome ungloved hands in front of her, without a curtsy, a bend of the head, or a smile.

She was a girl of nineteen, tall, rather broad-shouldered, but well-built. A dark face, of a half-Jewish half-gipsy type, small black eyes under thick brows almost meeting in the middle, a straight, slightly turned-up nose, delicate lips with a beautiful but decided curve, an immense mass of black hair, heavy even in appearance, a low brow still as marble, tiny ears . . . the whole face dreamy, almost sullen. A nature passionate, willful—hardly good-tempered, hardly very clever, but gifted—was expressed in every feature.

For some time she did not raise her eyes; but suddenly she started, and passed over the rows of spectators a glance intent, but not attentive, absorbed, it seemed, in herself. . . . "What tragic eyes she has!" observed a man sitting behind Aratov, a grey-headed dandy with the face of a Revel harlot, well known in Moscow as a prying gossip and writer for the papers. The dandy was an idiot, and meant to say something idiotic . . . but he spoke the truth. Aratov, who from the very moment of Clara's entrance had never taken his eyes off her, only at that instant recollected that he really had seen her at the princess's; and not only that he had seen her, but that he had even noticed that she had several times, with a peculiar insistency, gazed at him with her dark intent eyes. And now too—or was it his fancy?—on seeing him in the front row she seemed delighted, seemed to flush, and again gazed intently at him. Then, without turning round, she stepped away a couple of paces in the direction of the piano, at which her accompanist, a long-haired foreigner, was sitting. She had to render Glinka's ballad: "As soon as I knew you . . ." She began at once to sing, without changing the attitude of her hands or glancing at the music. Her voice was soft and resonant, a contralto; she uttered the words distinctly and with emphasis, and sang monotonously, with little light and shade, but with intense expression. "The girl sings with conviction," said the same dandy sitting behind Aratov, and again he spoke the truth. Shouts of "Bis!" "Bravo!" resounded over the room; but she flung a rapid glance on Aratov, who neither shouted nor clapped—he did not particularly care for her singing—gave a slight bow, and walked out without taking the hooked arm proffered her by the long-haired pianist. She was called back . . . not very soon, she reappeared, with the same hesitating steps approached the piano, and whispering a couple of words to the accompanist, who picked out and put before him another piece of music, began Tchaykovsky's song: "No, only he who knows the thirst to see." . . . This song she sang differently from the first—in a low voice, as though she were tired . . . and only the line next the last, "He knows what I have suffered," broke from her in a ringing, passionate cry. The last line, "And how I suffer" . . . she almost whispered, with a mournful prolongation of the last word. This song produced less impression on the audience than the Glinka ballad; there was much applause, however. . . . Kupfer was particularly conspicuous; folding his hands in a peculiar way, in the shape of a barrel, at each clap he produced an extraordinarily resounding report. The princess handed him a large, straggling nosegay for him to take to the singer; but she, seeming not to observe Kupfer's bowing figure, and outstretched hand with the nosegay, turned and went away, again without waiting for the pianist, who skipped forward to escort her more hurriedly than before, and when he found himself so unjustifiably deserted, tossed his hair as certainly Liszt himself had never tossed his!

During the whole time of the singing, Aratov had been watching Clara's face. It seemed to him that her eyes, through the drooping eyelashes, were again turned upon him; but he was especially struck by the immobility of the face, the forehead, the eyebrows; and only at her outburst of passion he caught through the hardly-parted lips the warm gleam of a close row of white teeth. Kupfer came up to him.

"Well, my dear boy, what do you think of her?" he asked, beaming all over with satisfaction.

"It's a fine voice," replied Aratov; "but she doesn't know how to sing yet; she's no real musical knowledge." (Why he said this, and what conception he had himself of "musical knowledge," the Lord only knows!)

Kupfer was surprised. "No musical knowledge," he repeated slowly. . . . "Well, as to that . . . she can acquire that. But what soul! Wait a bit, though; you shall hear her in Tatiana's letter."

He hurried away from Aratov, while the latter said to himself, "Soul! with that immovable face!" He thought that she moved and held herself like one hypnotised, like a somnambulist. And at the same time she was unmistakably . . . yes! unmistakably looking at him.

Meanwhile the matinée went on. The fat man in spectacles appeared again; in spite of his serious exterior, he fancied himself a comic actor, and recited a scene from Gogol, this time without eliciting a single token of approbation. There was another glimpse of the flute-player; another thunder-clap from the pianist; a boy of twelve, frizzed and pomaded, but with tearstains on his cheeks, thrummed some variations on a fiddle. What seemed strange was that in the intervals of the reading and music, from the performers' room, sounds were heard from time to time of a French horn; and yet this instrument never was brought into requisition. In the sequel it appeared that the amateur, who had been invited to perform on it, had lost courage at the moment of facing the public. At last Clara Militch made her appearance again.

She held a volume of Pushkin in her hand; she did not, however, glance at it once during her recitation. . . . She was obviously nervous, the little book shook slightly in her fingers. Aratov observed also the expression of weariness which now overspread all her stern features. The first line, "I write to you . . . what more?" she uttered exceedingly simply, almost naïvely, and with a naïve, genuine, helpless gesture held both hands out before her. Then she began to hurry a little; but from the beginning of the lines: "Another! no! To no one in the whole world I have given my heart!" she mastered her powers, gained fire; and when she came to the words, "My whole life has but been a pledge of a meeting true with thee," her hitherto thick voice rang out boldly and enthusiastically, while her eyes just as boldly and directly fastened upon Aratov. She went on with the same fervour, and only towards the end her voice dropped again; and in it, and in her face, the same weariness was reflected again. The last four lines she completely "murdered," as it is called; the volume of Pushkin suddenly slid out of her hand, and she hastily withdrew.

The audience fell to applauding desperately, encoring. . . . One Little-Russian divinity student bellowed in so deep a bass, "Mill-itch! Mill-itch!" that his neighbour civilly and sympathetically advised him "to take care of his voice, it would be the making of a protodeacon." But Aratov at once rose and made for the door. Kupfer overtook him. . . . "I say, where are you off to?" he called; "would you like me to present you to Clara?" "No, thanks," Aratov returned hurriedly, and he went homewards almost at a run.

V

He was agitated by strange sensations, incomprehensible to himself. In reality, Clara's recitation, too, had not been quite to his taste . . . though he could not quite tell why. It disturbed him, this recitation; it struck him as crude and inharmonious. . . . It was as though it broke something within him, forced itself with a certain violence upon him. And those fixed, insistent, almost importunate looks—what were they for? what did they mean?

Aratov's modesty did not for one instant admit of the idea that he might have made an impression on this strange girl, that he might have inspired in her a sentiment akin to love, to passion! . . . And indeed, he himself had formed a totally different conception of the still unknown woman, the girl to whom he was to give himself wholly, who would love him, be his bride, his wife. . . . He seldom dwelt on this dream—in spirit as in body he was virginal; but the pure image that arose at such times in his fancy was inspired by a very different figure, the figure of his dead ͺ ιother, whom he scarcely remembered, but whose portrait he treasured as ͼ sacred relic. The portrait was a water-colour, painted rather unskilfully by a lady who had been a neighbour of hers; but the likeness, as every one declared, was a striking one. Just such a tender profile, just such kind, clear eyes and silken hair, just such a smile and pure expression, was the woman, the girl, to have, for whom as yet he scarcely dared to hope. . . .

But this swarthy, dark-skinned creature, with coarse hair, dark eyebrows, and a tiny moustache on her upper lip, she was certainly a wicked, giddy . . . "gipsy" (Aratov could not imagine a harsher appellation)—what was she to him?

And yet Aratov could not succeed in getting out of his head this dark-skinned gipsy, whose singing and reading and very appearance were displeasing to him. He was puzzled, he was angry with himself. Not long before he had read Sir Walter Scott's novel, St. Ronan's Well (there was a complete edition of Sir Walter Scott's works in the library of his father, who had regarded the English novelist with esteem as a serious, almost a scientific, writer). The heroine of that novel is called Clara Mowbray. A poet who flourished somewhere about 1840, Krasov, wrote a poem on her, ending with the words:

> "Unhappy Clara! poor frantic Clara!
> Unhappy Clara Mowbray!"

Aratov knew this poem also. . . . And now these words were incessantly haunting his memory. . . . "Unhappy Clara! Poor, frantic Clara!" . . . (This was why he had been so surprised when Kupfer told him the name of Clara Militch.)

Platosha herself noticed, not a change exactly in Yasha's temper—no change in reality took place in it—but something unsatisfactory in his looks and in his words. She cautiously questioned him about the literary matinée at which he had been present; muttered, sighed, looked at him from in front, from the side, from behind; and suddenly clapping her hands on her thighs, she exclaimed: "To be sure, Yasha; I see what it is!"

"Why? what?" Aratov queried.

"You've met for certain at that matinée one of those long-tailed creatures" —this was how Platonida Ivanovna always spoke of all fashionably-dressed ladies of the period—"with a pretty dolly face; and she goes prinking *this* way . . . and pluming *that* way"—Platonida presented these fancied manœuvers in mimicry—"and making saucers like this with her eyes"—and she drew big, round circles in the air with her forefinger—"You're not used to that sort of thing. So you fancied . . . but that means nothing, Yasha . . . no-o-thing at all! Drink a cup of posset at night . . . it'll pass off! . . . Lord, succour us!"

Platosha ceased speaking, and left the room. . . . She had hardly ever uttered such a long and animated speech in her life. . . . While Aratov thought, "Auntie's right, I dare say. . . . I'm not used to it; that's all . . . "—it actually was the first time his attention had ever happened to be drawn to a person of the female sex . . . at least he had never noticed it before—"I mustn't give way to it."

And he set to work on his books, and at night drank some lime-flower tea; and positively slept well that night, and had no dreams. The next morning he took up his photography again as though nothing had happened. . . .

But towards evening his spiritual repose was again disturbed.

VI

And this is what happened. A messenger brought him a note, written in a large irregular woman's hand, and containing the following lines:

"If you guess who it is writes to you, and if it is not a bore to you, come to-morrow after dinner to the Tversky boulevard—about five o'clock—and wait. You shall not be kept long. But it is very important. Do come."

There was no signature. Aratov at once guessed who was his correspondent, and this was just what disturbed him. "What folly," he said, almost aloud; "this is too much. Of course I shan't go." He sent, however, for the messenger, and from him learned nothing but that the note had been handed him by a maidservant in the street. Dismissing him, Aratov read the letter through and flung it on the ground. . . . But, after a little while, he picked it up and read it again: a second time he cried, "Folly!"—he did not, however, throw the note on the floor again, but put it in a drawer. Aratov took up his ordinary occupations, first one and then another; but nothing he did was successful or satisfactory. He suddenly realised that he was eagerly expecting Kupfer! Did he want to question him, or perhaps even to confide in him? . . . But Kupfer did not make his appearance. Then Aratov took down Pushkin, read Tatiana's letter, and convinced himself again that the "gipsy girl" had not in the least understood the real force of the letter. And that donkey Kupfer shouts: Rachel! Viardot! Then he went to his piano, as it seemed, unconsciously opened it, and tried to pick out by ear the melody of Tchaykovsky's song; but he slammed it to again directly in vexation, and went up to his aunt to her special room, which was for ever baking hot, smelled of mint, sage, and other medicinal herbs, and was littered up with such a multitude of rugs, side-tables, stools, cushions, and padded furniture of all sorts, that any one unused to it would have found it difficult to turn round and oppressive to breathe in it. Platonida Ivanovna was sitting at the window, her knitting in her hands (she was knitting her darling Yasha a comforter, the thirty-eighth she had made him in the course of his life!), and was much astonished to see him. Aratov rarely went up to her, and if he wanted anything, used always to call, in his delicate voice, from his study: "Aunt Platosha!" However, she made him sit down, and sat all alert, in expectation of his first words, watching him through her spectacles with one eye, over them with the other. She did not inquire after his health nor offer him tea, as she saw he had not come for that. Aratov was a little disconcerted . . . then he began to talk . . . talked of his mother, of how she had lived with his father and how his father had got to know her. All this he knew very well . . . but it was just what he wanted to talk about. Unluckily for him, Platosha did not know how to keep up a conversation at all; she gave him very brief replies, as though she suspected that was not what Yasha had come for.

"Eh!" she repeated, hurriedly, almost irritably plying her knitting-needles. "We all know: your mother was a darling . . . a darling that she was. . . . And your father loved her as a husband should, truly and faithfully even in her grave; and he never loved any other woman": she added, raising her voice and taking off her spectacles.

"And was she of a retiring disposition?" Aratov inquired, after a short silence.

"Retiring! to be sure she was. As a woman should be. Bold ones have sprung up nowadays."

"And were there no bold ones in your time?"

"There were in our time too . . . to be sure there were! But who were they? A pack of strumpets, shameless hussies. Draggle-tails—for ever gadding about after no good. . . . What do they care? It's little they take to heart. If some poor fool comes in their way, they pounce on him. But sensible folk looked down on them. Did you ever see, pray, the like of such in our house?"

Aratov made no reply, and went back to his study. Platonida Ivanovna looked after him, shook her head, put on her spectacles again, and again took up her comforter . . . but more than once sank into thought, and let her knitting-needles fall on her knees.

Aratov up till very night kept telling himself, no! no! but with the same irritation, the same exasperation, he fell again into musing on the note, on the "gipsy girl," on the appointed meeting, to which he would certainly not go! And at night she gave him no rest. He was continually haunted by her eyes—at one time half-closed, at another wide open—and their persistent gaze fixed straight upon him, and those motionless features with their dominating expression. . . .

The next morning he again, for some reason, kept expecting Kupfer; he was on the point of writing a note to him . . . but did nothing, however, . . . and spent most of the time walking up and down his room. He never for one instant admitted to himself even the idea of going to this idiotic rendezvous . . . and at half-past three, after a hastily swallowed dinner, suddenly throwing on his cloak and thrusting his cap on his head, he dashed out into the street, unseen by his aunt, and turned towards the Tversky boulevard.

VII

Aratov found few people walking in it. The weather was damp and rather cold. He tried not to reflect on what he was doing, to force himself to turn his attention to every object that presented itself, and, as it were, persuaded himself that he had simply come out for a walk like the other people passing to and fro. . . . The letter of the day before was in his breast-pocket, and he was conscious all the while of its presence there. He walked twice up and down the boulevard, scrutinised sharply every feminine figure that came near him—and his heart throbbed. . . . He felt tired and sat down on a bench. And suddenly the thought struck him: "What if that letter was not written by her, but to some one else by some other woman?" In reality this should have been a matter of indifference to him . . . and yet he had to admit to himself that he did not want this to be so. "That would be too silly," he thought, "even sillier than *this!*" A nervous unrest began to gain possession of him; he began to shiver—not outwardly, but inwardly. He several times took his watch out of his waistcoat pocket, looked at the face, put it back, and each time forgot how many minutes it was to five. He fancied that every passer-by looked at him in a peculiar way, with a sort of sarcastic astonishment and curiosity. A wretched little dog ran up, sniffed at his legs, and began wagging its tail. He threatened it angrily. He was particularly annoyed by a factory lad in a greasy smock, who seated himself on a seat on the other side of the boulevard, and by turns whistling, scratching himself, and swinging his feet in enormous tattered boots, persistently stared at him. "And his master," thought Aratov, "is waiting for him, no doubt, while he, lazy scamp, is kicking up his heels here. . . ."

But at that very instant he felt that someone had come up and was standing close behind him . . . there was a breath of something warm from behind. . . .

He looked round. . . . She!

He knew her at once, though a thick, dark blue veil hid her features. He instantaneously leapt up from the seat, but stopped short, and could not utter a word. She too was silent. He felt great embarrassment; but her embarrassment was no less. Aratov, even through the veil, could not help noticing how deadly pale she had turned. Yet she was the first to speak.

"Thanks," she began in an unsteady voice, "thanks for coming. I did not expect . . ." She turned a little away and walked along the boulevard. Aratov walked after her.

"You have, perhaps, thought ill of me," she went on, without turning her head; "indeed, my conduct is very strange. . . . But I had heard so much about you . . . but no! I . . . that was not the reason. . . . If only you knew . . . There was so much I wanted to tell you, my God! . . . But how to do it . . . how to do it!"

Aratov was walking by her side, a little behind her; he could not see her face; he saw only her hat and part of her veil . . . and her long black shabby cape. All his irritation, both with her and with himself, suddenly came back to him; all the absurdity, the awkwardness of this interview, these explanations between perfect strangers in a public promenade, suddenly struck him.

"I have come on your invitation," he began in his turn. "I have come, my dear madam" (her shoulders gave a faint twitch, she turned off into a side passage, he followed her), "simply to clear up, to discover to what strange misunderstanding it is due that you are pleased to address me, a stranger to you . . . who . . . only *guessed*, to use your expression in your letter, that it was your writing to him . . . guessed it because during that literary matinée, you saw fit to pay him such . . . such obvious attention."

All this little speech was delivered by Aratov in that ringing but unsteady voice in which very young people answer at examinations on a subject in which they are well prepared. . . . He was angry; he was furious. . . . It was just this fury which loosened his ordinarily not very ready tongue.

She still went on along the walk with rather slower steps. . . . Aratov, as before, walked after her, and as before saw only the old cape and the hat, also not a very new one. His vanity suffered at the idea that she must now be thinking: "I had only to make a sign—and he rushed at once!"

Aratov was silent . . . he expected her to answer him; but she did not utter a word.

"I am ready to listen to you," he began again, "and shall be very glad if I can be of use to you in any way . . . though I am, I confess, surprised . . . considering the retired life I lead. . . ."

At these last words of his, Clara suddenly turned to him, and he beheld such a terrified, such a deeply-wounded face, with such large bright tears in the eyes, such a pained expression about the parted lips, and this face was so lovely, that he involuntarily faltered, and himself felt something akin to terror and pity and softening.

"Ah, why . . . why are you like that?" she said, with an irresistibly genuine and truthful force, and how movingly her voice rang out! "Could my turning to you be offensive to you? . . . is it possible you have understood nothing? . . . Ah, yes! you have understood nothing, you did not understand what I said to you, God knows what you have been imagining about me, you have not even dreamed what it cost me—to write to you! . . . You thought of nothing but yourself, your own dignity, your peace of mind! . . . But is it likely I" . . . (she squeezed her hands raised to her lips so hard that the fingers gave a distinct crack). . . . "As though I made any sort of demands of you, as though explanations were necessary first. . . . 'My dear madam, . . . I am, I confess, surprised, . . . if I can be of any use' . . . Ah! I am mad!—I was mistaken in you—in your face! . . . when I saw you the first time . . . ! Here . . . you stand. . . . If only one word. What, not one word?"

She ceased. . . . Her face suddenly flushed, and as suddenly took a wrathful and insolent expression. "Mercy! how idiotic this is!" she cried suddenly, with a shrill laugh. "How idiotic our meeting is! What a fool I am! . . . and you too. . . . Ugh!"

She gave a contemptuous wave of her hand, as though motioning him out of her road, and passing him, ran quickly out of the boulevard, and vanished.

The gesture of her hand, the insulting laugh, and the last exclamation, at once carried Aratov back to his first frame of mind, and stifled the feeling that had sprung up in his heart when she turned to him with tears in her eyes. He was angry again, and almost shouted after the retreating girl: "You may make a good actress, but why did you think fit to play off this farce on me?"

He returned home with long strides, and though he still felt anger and indignation all the way, yet across these evil, malignant feelings, unconsciously, the memory forced itself of the exquisite face he had seen for a single moment only. . . . He even put himself the question, "Why did I not answer her when she asked of me only a word? I had not time," he thought. "She did not let me utter the word . . . and what word could I have uttered?"

But he shook his head at once, and murmured reproachfully, "Actress!"

And again, at the same time, the vanity of the inexperienced nervous youth, at first wounded, was now, as it were, flattered at having any way inspired such a passion. . . .

"Though by now," he pursued his reflections, "it's all over, of course. . . . I must have seemed absurd to her." . . .

This idea was disagreeable to him, and again he was angry . . . both with her . . . and with himself. On reaching home, he shut himself up in his study. He did not want to see Platosha. The good old lady came twice to his locked door, put her ear to the keyhole, and only sighed and murmured her prayer.

"It has begun!" she thought. . . . "And he only five-and-twenty! Ah, it's early, it's early!"

VIII

All the following day Aratov was in very low spirits. "What is it, Yasha?" Platonida Ivanovna said to him: "you seem somehow all loose ends to-day!" . . . In her own peculiar idiom the old lady's expression described fairly accurately Aratov's mental condition. He could not work and he did not know himself what he wanted. At one time he was eagerly on the watch for Kupfer, again he suspected that it was from Kupfer that Clara had got his address . . . and from where else could she "have heard so much about him"? Then he wondered: was it possible his acquaintance with her was to end like this? Then he fancied she would write to him again; then he asked himself whether he ought not to write her a letter, explaining everything, since he did not at all like leaving an unfavorable impression of himself. . . . But exactly what to explain? Then he stirred up in himself almost a feeling of repulsion for her, for her insistence, her impertinence; and then again he saw that unutterably touching face and heard an irresistible voice; then he recalled her singing, her recitation—and could not be sure whether he had been right in his wholesale condemnation of it. In fact, he was all loose ends! At last he was heartily sick of it, and resolved to keep a firm hand over himself, as it is called, and to obliterate the whole incident, as it was unmistakably hindering his studies and destroying his peace of mind. It turned out not so easy to carry out this resolution . . . more than a week passed by before he got back into his old accustomed groove. Luckily Kupfer did not turn up at all; he was in fact out of Moscow. Not long before the incident, Aratov had begun to work at painting in connection with his photographic plans; he set to work upon it now with redoubled zest.

So, imperceptibly, with a few (to use the doctors' expression) "symptoms of relapse," manifested, for instance, in his once almost deciding to call upon the princess, two months passed . . . then three months . . . and Aratov was the old Aratov again. Only somewhere down below, under the surface of his life, something like a dark and burdensome secret dogged him wherever he went. So a great fish just caught on the hook, but not yet drawn up, will swim at the bottom of a deep stream under the very boat where the angler sits with a stout rod in his hand.

And one day, skimming through a not quite new number of the *Moscow Gazette,* Aratov lighted upon the following paragraph:

"With the greatest regret," wrote some local contributor from Kazan, "we must add to our dramatic record the news of the sudden death of our gifted actress Clara Militch, who had succeeded during the brief period of her engagement in becoming a favorite of our discriminating public. Our regret is the more poignant from the fact that Miss Militch by her own act cut short her young life, so full of promise, by means of poison. And this dreadful deed was the more awful through the talented actress taking the fatal drug in the theater itself. She had scarcely been taken home when to the universal grief, she expired. There is a rumor in the town that an unfortunate love affair drove her to this terrible act."

Aratov slowly laid the paper on the table. In outward appearance he remained perfectly calm . . . but at once something seemed to strike him a blow in the chest and the head—and slowly the shock passed on through all his limbs. He got up, stood still on the spot, and sat down again, again read through the paragraph. Then he got up again, lay down on the bed, and clasping his hands behind, stared a long while at the wall, as though dazed. By degrees the wall seemed to fade away . . . vanished . . . and he saw facing him the boulevard under the grey sky, and *her* in her black cape . . . then her on the platform . . . saw himself even close by her. That something which had given him such a violent blow in the chest at the first instant, began mounting now . . . mounting into his throat. . . . He tried to clear his throat; tried to call some one—but his voice failed him—and, to his own astonishment, tears rushed in torrents from his eyes . . . what called forth these tears? Pity? Remorse? Or was it simply his nerves could not stand the sudden shock?

Why, she was nothing to him? was she?

"But, perhaps, it's not true after all," the thought came as a sudden relief to him. "I must find out! But from whom? From the princess? No, from Kupfer . . . from Kupfer? But they say he's not in Moscow—no matter, I must try him first!"

With these reflections in his head, Aratov dressed himself in haste, called a cab and drove to Kupfer's.

IX

Though he had not expected to find him, he found him. Kupfer had, as a fact, been away from Moscow for some time, but he had now been back a week, and was indeed on the point of setting off to see Aratov. He met him with his usual heartiness, and was beginning to make some sort of explanation . . . but Aratov at once cut him short with the impatient question, "Have you heard it? Is it true?"

"Is what true?" replied Kupfer, puzzled.

"About Clara Militch?"

Kupfer's face expressed commiseration. "Yes, yes, my dear boy, it's true; she poisoned herself! Such a sad thing!"

Aratov was silent for a while. "But did you read it in the paper too?" he asked—"or perhaps you have been in Kazan yourself?"

"I have been in Kazan, yes; the princess and I accompanied her there. She came out on the stage there, and had a great success. But I didn't stay up to the time of the catastrophe . . . I was in Yaroslav at the time."

"In Yaroslav?"

"Yes—I escorted the princess there. . . . She is living now at Yaroslav."

"But you have trustworthy information?"

"Trustworthy . . . I have it at first-hand!—I made the acquaintance of her family in Kazan. But, my dear boy . . . this news seems to be upsetting you?

Why, I recollect you didn't care for Clara at one time? You were wrong, though! She was a marvelous girl—only what a temper! I was terribly brokenhearted about her!"

Aratov did not utter a word, he dropped into a chair, and after a brief pause, asked Kupfer to tell him . . . he stammered.

"What?" inquired Kupfer.

"Oh . . . everything," Aratov answered brokenly, "all about her family . . . and the rest of it. Everything you know!"

"Why, does it interest you? By all means!" And Kupfer, whose face showed no traces of his having been so terribly broken-hearted about Clara, began his story.

From his account Aratov learnt that Clara Militch's real name was Katerina Milovidov; that her father, now dead, had held the post of drawing-master in a school in Kazan, had painted bad portraits and holy pictures of the regulation type; that he had besides had the character of being a drunkard and a domestic tyrant; that he had left behind him, first a widow, of a shopkeeper's family, a quite stupid body, a character straight out of an Ostrovsky comedy; and secondly, a daughter much older than Clara and not like her—a very clever girl, and enthusiastic, only sickly, a remarkable girl—and very advanced in her ideas, my dear boy! That they were living, the widow and daughter, fairly comfortably, in a decent little house, obtained by the sale of the bad portraits and holy pictures; that Clara . . . or Katia, if you like, from her childhood up impressed every one with her talent, but was of an insubordinate, capricious temper, and used to be for ever quarrelling with her father; that having an inborn passion for the theatre, at sixteen she had run away from her parents' house with an actress . . .

"With an actor?" put in Aratov.

"No, not with an actor, with an actress, to whom she became attached. . . . It's true this actress had a protector, a wealthy gentleman, no longer young, who did not marry her simply because he happened to be married—and indeed I fancy the actress was a married woman." Furthermore Kupfer informed Aratov that Clara had even before her coming to Moscow acted and sung in provincial theatres, that, having lost her friend the actress—the gentleman, too, it seemed, had died, or else he had made it up with his wife—Kupfer could not quite remember this—she had made the acquaintance of the princess, "that heart of gold, whom you, my dear Yakov Andreitch," the speaker added with feeling, "were incapable of appreciating properly"; that at last Clara had been offered an engagement in Kazan, and that she had accepted it, though before then she used to declare that she would never leave Moscow! But then how the people of Kazan liked her—it was really astonishing! Whatever the performance was, nothing but nosegays and presents! nosegays and presents! A wholesale miller, the greatest swell in the province, had even presented her with a gold inkstand! Kupfer related all this with great animation, without giving expression, however, to any special sentimentality, and interspersing his narrative with the questions, "What is it to you?" and "Why do you ask?" when Aratov, who listened to him with devouring attention, kept asking for more and more details. All was told at last, and Kupfer was silent, rewarding himself for his exertions with a cigar.

"And why did she take poison?" asked Aratov. "In the paper it was stated . . ."

Kupfer waved his hand. "Well . . . that I can't say . . . I don't know. But the paper tells a lie. Clara's conduct was exemplary . . . no love affairs of any kind. . . . And indeed how should there be with her pride! She was proud—as Satan himself—and unapproachable! A headstrong creature! Hard as rock! You'll hardly believe it—though I knew her so well—I never saw a tear in her eyes!"

"But I have," Aratov thought to himself.

"But there's one thing," continued Kupfer, "of late I noticed a great change in her: she grew so dull, so silent, for hours together there was no getting a word out of her. I asked her even, 'Has any one offended you, Katerina Semyonovna?' For I knew her temper; she could never swallow an affront! But she was silent, and there was no doing anything with her! Even her triumphs on the stage didn't cheer her up; bouquets fairly showered on her . . . but she didn't even smile! She gave one look at the gold inkstand—and put it aside! She used to complain that no one had written the real part for her, as she conceived it. And her singing she'd given up altogether. It was my fault, my dear boy! . . . I told her that you thought she'd no musical knowledge. But for all that . . . why she poisoned herself—is incomprehensible! And the way she did it! . . ."

"In what part had she the greatest success?" . . . Aratov wanted to know in what part she had appeared for the last time, but for some reason he asked a different question.

"In Ostrovosky's *Gruna,* as far as I remember. But I tell you again she'd no love affairs! You may be sure of that from one thing. She lived in her mother's house. . . . You know the sort of shopkeepers' houses: in every corner a holy picture and a little lamp before it, a deadly stuffiness, a sour smell, nothing but chairs along the walls in the drawing-room, a geranium in the window, and if a visitor drops in, the mistress sighs and groans, as if they were invaded by an enemy. What chance is there for gallantry or lovemaking? Sometimes they wouldn't even admit me. Their servant, a muscular female, in a red sarafan, with an enormous bust, would stand right across the passage, and growl, 'Where are you coming?' No, I positively can't understand why she poisoned herself. Sick of life, I suppose," Kupfer concluded his cogitations philosophically.

Aratov sat with downcast head. "Can you give me the address of that house in Kazan?" he said at last.

"Yes; but what do you want it for? Do you want to write a letter there?"

"Perhaps."

"Well, you know best. But the old lady won't answer, for she can't read and write. The sister, though, perhaps . . . Oh, the sister's a clever creature! But I must say again, I wonder at you, my dear boy! Such indifference before . . . and now such interest! All this, my boy, comes from too much solitude!"

Aratov made no reply, and went away, having provided himself with the Kazan address.

When he was on his way to Kupfer's, excitement, bewilderment, expectation had been reflected on his face. . . . Now he walked with an even gait, with downcast eyes, and hat pulled over his brows; almost every one who met him sent a glance of curiosity after him . . . but he did not observe any one who passed . . . it was not as on the Tversky boulevard!

"Unhappy Clara! poor frantic Clara!" was echoing in his soul.

X

The following day Aratov spent, however, fairly quietly. He was even able to give his mind to his ordinary occupations. But there was one thing: both during his work and during his leisure he was continually thinking of Clara, of what Kupfer had told him the evening before. It is true that his meditations, too, were of a fairly tranquil character. He fancied that this strange girl interested him from the psychological point of view, as something of the nature of a riddle, the solution of which was worth racking his brains over. "Ran away with an actress living as a kept mistress," he pondered, "put herself under the protection of that princess, with whom she seems to have lived—and no *love affairs?* It's incredible! . . . Kupfer talked of pride! But in the first place we know" (Aratov ought to have said: we have read in books), . . . "we know that pride can exist side by side with levity of conduct; and secondly, how came she, if she were so proud, to make an appointment with a man who might treat her with contempt . . . and did treat her with it . . . and in a public place, moreover . . . in a boulevard!" At this point Aratov recalled all the scene in the boulevard, and he asked himself, Had he really shown contempt for Clara? "No," he decided, . . . "it was another feeling . . . a feeling of doubt . . . lack of confidence, in fact!" "Unhappy Clara!" was again ringing in his head. "Yes, unhappy," he decided again. . . . "That's the most fitting word. And, if so, I was unjust. She said truly that I did not understand her. A pity! Such a remarkable creature, perhaps, came so close . . . and I did not take advantage of it, I repulsed her. . . . Well, no matter! Life's all before me. There will be, very likely, other meetings, perhaps more interesting!

"But on what grounds did she fix on *me* of all the world?" He glanced into a looking-glass by which he was passing. "What is there special about me? I'm not a beauty, am I? My face . . . is like any face. . . . She was not a beauty either, though.

"Not a beauty . . . and such an expressive face! Immobile . . . and yet expressive! I never met such a face. . . . And talent, too, she has . . . that is, she had, unmistakable. Untrained, undeveloped, even coarse, perhaps . . . but unmistakable talent. And in that case I was unjust to her." Aratov was carried back in thought to the literary musical matinée . . . and he observed to himself how exceedingly clearly he recollected every word she had sung or recited, every intonation of her voice. . . . "That would not have been so had she been without talent. And now it is all in the grave, to which she has hastened of herself. . . . But I've nothing to do with that . . . I'm not to blame! It would be positively ridiculous to suppose that I'm to blame."

It again occurred to Aratov that even if she had had "anything of the sort" in her mind, his behavior during their interview must have effectually disillusioned her. . . . "That was why she laughed so cruelly, too, at parting. Besides, what proof is there that she took poison because of unrequited love? That's only the newspaper correspondents, who ascribe every death of that sort to unrequited love! People of a character like Clara's readily feel life repulsive . . . burdensome. Yes, burdensome. Kupfer was right; she was simply sick of life.

"In spite of her successes, her triumphs?" Aratov mused. He got a positive pleasure from the psychological analysis to which he was devoting himself. Remote till now from all contact with women, he did not even suspect all the significance for himself of this intense realization of a woman's soul.

"It follows," he pursued his meditations, "that art did not satisfy her, did not fill the void in her life. Real artists exist only for art, for the theatre. . . . Everything else is pale beside what they regard as their vocation. . . . She was a dilettante."

At this point Aratov fell to pondering again. "No, the word dilettante did not accord with that face, the expression of that face, those eyes. . . ."

And Clara's image floated again before him, with eyes, swimming in tears, fixed upon him, with clenched hands pressed to her lips. . . .

"Ah, no, no," he muttered, "what's the use?"

So passed the whole day. At dinner Aratov talked a great deal with Platosha, questioned her about the old days, which she remembered, but described very badly, as she had so few words at her command, and except her dear Yasha, had scarcely ever noticed anything in her life. She could only rejoice that he was nice and good-humored to-day; towards evening Aratov was so far calm that he played several games of cards with his aunt.

So passed the day . . . but the night!

XI

It began well; he soon fell asleep, and when his aunt went into him on tip-toe to make the sign of the cross three times over him in his sleep—she did so every night—he lay breathing as quietly as a child. But before dawn he had a dream.

He dreamed he was on a bare steppe, strewn with big stones, under a lowering sky. Among the stones curved a little path; he walked along it.

Suddenly there rose up in front of him something of the nature of a thin cloud. He looked steadily at it; the cloud turned into a woman in a white gown with a bright sash round her waist. She was hurrying away from him. He saw neither her face nor her hair . . . they were covered by a long veil. But he had an intense desire to overtake her, and to look into her face. Only, however much he hastened, she went more quickly than he.

On the path lay a broad flat stone, like a tombstone. It blocked up the way. The woman stopped. Aratov ran up to her; but yet he could not see her eyes . . . they were shut. Her face was white, white as snow; her hands hung lifeless. She was like a statue.

Slowly, without bending a single limb, she fell backwards, and sank down upon the tombstone. . . . And then Aratov lay down beside her, stretched out straight like a figure on a monument, his hands folded like a dead man's.

But now the woman suddenly rose, and went away. Aratov tried to get up too . . . but he could neither stir nor unclasp his hands, and could only gaze after her in despair.

Then the woman suddenly turned round, and he saw bright living eyes, in a living but unknown face. She laughed, she waved her hand to him . . . and still he could not move.

She laughed once more, and quickly retreated, merrily nodding her head, on which there was a crimson wreath of tiny roses.

Aratov tried to cry out, tried to throw off this awful nightmare. . . .

Suddenly all was darkness around . . . and the woman came back to him. But this was not the unknown statue . . . it was Clara. She stood before him, crossed her arms, and sternly and intently looked at him. Her lips were tightly pressed together, but Aratov fancied he heard the words, "If you want to know what I am, come over here!"

"Where?" he asked.

"Here!" he heard the wailing answer. "Here!"

Aratov woke up.

He sat up in bed, lighted the candle that stood on the little table by his bedside—but did not get up—and sat a long while, chill all over, slowly looking about him. It seemed to him as if something had happened to him since he went to bed; that something had taken possession of him . . . something was in control of him. "But is it possible?" he murmured unconsciously. "Does such a power really exist?"

He could not stay in his bed. He quickly dressed, and till morning he was pacing up and down his room. And, strange to say, of Clara he never thought for a moment, and did not think of her, because he had decided to go next day to Kazan!

He thought only of the journey, of how to manage it, and what to take with him, and how he would investigate and find out everything there, and would set his mind at rest. "If I don't go," he reasoned with himself, "why, I shall go out of my mind!" He was afraid of that, afraid of his nerves. He was convinced that when once he had seen everything there with his own eyes, every obsession would vanish like that nightmare. "And it will be a week lost over the journey," he thought; "what is a week? else I shall never shake it off."

The rising sun shone into his room; but the light of day did not drive away the shadows of the night that lay upon him, and did not change his resolution.

Platosha almost had a fit when he informed her of his intention. She positively sat down on the ground . . . her legs gave way beneath her. "To Kazan? why to Kazan?" she murmured, her dim eyes round with astonishment. She would not have been more surprised if she had been told that her Yasha was going to marry the baker woman next door, or was starting for

America. "Will you be long in Kazan?" "I shall be back in a week," answered Aratov, standing with his back half-turned to his aunt, who was still sitting on the floor.

Platonida Ivanova tried to protest more, but Aratov answered her in an utterly unexpected and unheard-of way: "I'm not a child," he shouted, and he turned pale all over, his lips trembled, and his eyes glittered wrathfully. "I'm twenty-six, I know what I'm about, I'm free to do what I like! I suffer no one . . . give me the money for the journey, pack my box with my clothes and linen . . . and don't torture me! I'll be back in a week, Platosha," he added, in a somewhat softer tone.

Platosha got up, sighing and groaning, and, without further protest, crawled to her room. Yasha had alarmed her. "I've no head on my shoulders," she told the cook, who was helping her to pack Yasha's things; "no head at all, but a hive full of bees all a-buz and a-hum! He's going off to Kazan, my good soul, to Ka-a-zan!" The cook, who had observed their dvornik the previous evening talking for a long time with a police officer, would have liked to inform her mistress of this circumstance, but did not dare, and only reflected, "To Kazan! if only it's nowhere farther still!" Platonida Ivanovna was so upset that she did not even utter her usual prayer. "In such a calamity the Lord God Himself cannot aid us!"

The same day Aratov set off for Kazan.

XII

He had no sooner reached that town and taken a room in a hotel than he rushed off to find out the house of the widow Milovidov. During the whole journey he had been in a sort of benumbed condition, which had not, however, prevented him from taking all the necessary steps, changing at Nizhni-Novgorod from the railway to the steamer, getting his meals at the stations, etc., etc. He was convinced as before that *there* everything would be solved; and therefore he drove away every sort of memory and reflection, confining himself to one thing, the mental rehearsal of the *speech,* in which he would lay before the family of Clara Militch the real cause of his visit. And now at last he reached the goal of his efforts, and sent up his name. He was admitted . . . with perplexity and alarm—still he was admitted.

The house of the widow Milovidov turned out to be exactly as Kupfer had described it; and the widow herself really was like one of the tradesmen's wives in Ostrovsky, though the widow of an official; her husband had held his post under government. Not without some difficulty, Aratov, after a preliminary apology for his boldness, for the strangeness of his visit, delivered the speech he had prepared, explaining that he was anxious to collect all the information possible about the gifted artist so early lost, that he was not led to this by idle curiosity, but by profound sympathy for her talent, of which he was the devoted admirer (he said that, devoted admirer!), that, in fact, it would be a sin to leave the public in ignorance of what it had lost—and why its hopes were not realized. Madame

Milovidov did not interrupt Aratov; she did not understand very well what this unknown visitor was saying to her, and merely opened her eyes rather wide and rolled them upon him, thinking, however, that he had a quiet respectable air, was well dressed . . . and not a pickpocket . . . hadn't come to beg.

"You are speaking of Katia?" she inquired, directly Aratov was silent.

"Yes . . . of your daughter."

"And you have come from Moscow for this?"

"Yes, from Moscow."

"Only on this account?"

"Yes."

Madame Milovidov gave herself a sudden shake. "Why, are you an author? Do you write for the newspapers?"

"No, I'm not an author—and hitherto I have not written for the newspapers."

The widow bowed her head. She was puzzled.

"Then, I suppose . . . it's from your own interest in the matter?" she asked suddenly. Aratov could not find an answer for a minute.

"Through sympathy, from respect for talent," he said at last.

The word "respect" pleased Madame Milovidov. "Eh!" she pronounced with a sigh . . . "I'm her mother, any way—and terribly I'm grieved for her. . . . Such a calamity all of a sudden! . . . But I must say it: a crazy girl she always was—and what a way to meet with her end! Such a disgrace. . . . Only fancy what it was for a mother? we must be thankful indeed that they gave her a Christian burial. . . ." Madame Milovidov crossed herself. "From a child up she minded no one—she left her parents' house . . . and at last—sad to say!—turned actress! Every one knows I never shut my doors upon her; I loved her, to be sure! I was her mother, any way! she'd no need to live with strangers . . . or to go begging! . . ." Here the widow shed tears . . ."But if you, my good sir," she began, again wiping her eyes with the ends of her kerchief, "really have any idea of the kind, and you are not intending anything dishonorable to us, but on the contrary, wish to show us respect, you'd better talk a bit with my other daughter. She'll tell you everything better than I can. . . . Annotchka!" called Madame Milovidov, "Annotchka, come here! Here is a worthy gentleman from Moscow wants to have a talk about Katia!"

There was a sound of something moving in the next room; but no one appeared. "Annotchka!" the widow called again, "Anna Semyonovna! come here, I tell you!"

The door softly opened, and in the doorway appeared a girl no longer very young, looking ill—and plain—but with very soft and mournful eyes. Aratov got up from his seat to meet her, and introduced himself, mentioning his friend Kupfer. "Ah! Fyodor Fedoritch?" the girl articulated softly, and softly she sank into a chair.

"Now, then, you must talk to the gentleman," said Madam Milovidov, getting up heavily: "he's taken trouble enough, he's come all the way from Moscow on purpose—he wants to collect information about Katia. And will you, my good sir," she added, addressing Aratov—"excuse me . . . I'm going to look after my housekeeping. You can get a very good account of everything from Annotchka; she will tell you about the theatre . . . and all the rest of it. She is a clever girl, well educated: speaks French, and reads books as well as her sister did. One may say indeed she gave her her education . . . she was older—and so she looked after it."

Madame Milovidov withdrew. On being left alone with Anna Semyonovna, Aratov repeated his speech to her; but realizing at the first glance that he had to do with a really cultivated girl, not a typical tradesman's daughter, he went a little more into particulars and made use of different expressions; but towards the end he grew agitated, flushed and felt that his heart was throbbing. Anna listened to him in silence, her hands folded on her lap; a mournful smile never left her face . . . bitter grief, still fresh in its poignancy, was expressed in that smile.

"You knew my sister?" she asked Aratov.

"No, I did not actually know her," he answered. "I met her and heard her once . . . but one need only hear and see your sister once to . . ."

"Do you wish to write her biography?" Anna questioned him again.

Aratov had not expected this inquiry; however, he replied promptly, "Why not? But above all, I wanted to acquaint the public . . ."

Anna stopped him by a motion of her hand.

"What is the object of that? The public caused her plenty of suffering as it is; and indeed Katia had only just begun life. But if you yourself—(Anna looked at him and smiled again a smile as mournful but more friendly . . . as though she were saying to herself, Yes, you make me feel I can trust you) . . . if you yourself feel such interest in her, let me ask you to come and see us this afternoon . . . after dinner. I can't just now . . . so suddenly . . . I will collect my strength . . . I will make an effort . . . Ah, I loved her too much!"

Anna turned away; she was on the point of bursting into sobs.

Aratov rose hurriedly from his seat, thanked her for her offer, said he should be sure . . . oh, very sure!—to come—and went off, carrying away with him an impression of a soft voice, gentle and sorrowful eyes, and burning in the tortures of expectation.

XIII

Aratov went back the same day to the Milovidovs and spent three whole hours in conversation with Anna Semyonovna. Madame Milovidov was in the habit of lying down directly after dinner—at two o'clock—and resting till evening tea at seven. Aratov's talk with Clara's sister was not exactly a conversation; she did almost all the talking, at first with hesitation, with embarrassment, then with a warmth that refused to be stifled. It was obvious that she had adored her sister. The confidence Aratov had inspired in her grew and strengthened; she was no longer stiff; twice she even dropped a few silent tears before him. He seemed to her to be worthy to hear an unreserved account of all she knew and felt . . . in her own secluded life nothing of this sort had ever happened before! . . . As for him . . . he drank in every word she uttered.

This was what he learned . . . much of it of course, half-said . . . much he filled in for himself.

In her early years, Clara had undoubtedly been a disagreeable child; and even as a girl, she had not been much gentler; self-willed, hot-tempered, sensitive, she had never got on with her father, whom she despised for his drunkenness and incapacity. He felt this and never forgave her for it. A gift for music showed itself early in her; her father gave it no encouragement, acknowledging no art but painting, in which he himself was so conspicuously unsuccessful though it was the means of support of himself and his family. Her mother Clara loved, . . . but in a careless way, as though she were her nurse; her sister she adored, though she fought with her and had even bitten her. . . . It is true she fell on her knees afterwards and kissed the place she had bitten. She was all fire, all passion, and all contradiction; revengeful and kind; magnanimous and vindictive; she believed in fate—and did not believe in God (these words Anna whispered with horror); she loved everything beautiful, but never troubled herself about her own looks, and dressed anyhow; she could not bear to have young men courting her, and yet in books she only read the pages which treated of love; she did not care to be liked, did not like caresses, but never forgot a caress, just as she never forgot a slight; she was afraid of death and killed herself! She used to say sometimes, "Such a one as I want I shall never meet . . . and no other will I have!" "Well, but if you meet him?" Anna would ask. "If I meet him . . . I will capture him." "And if he won't let himself be captured?" "Well, then . . . I will make an end of myself. It will prove I am no good." Clara's father—he used sometimes when drunk to ask his wife, "Who got you your blackbrowed she-devil there? Not I!"—Clara's father, anxious to get her off his hands as soon as possible, betrothed her to a rich young shopkeeper, a great blockhead, one of the so-called "refined" sort. A fortnight before the wedding-day—she was only sixteen at the time—she went up to her betrothed, her arms folded and her fingers drumming on her elbows—her favorite position—and suddenly gave him a slap on his rosy cheek with her large powerful hand! He jumped and merely gaped; it must be said he was head over ears in love with her . . . He asked: "What's that for?" She laughed scornfully and walked off. "I was there in the room," Anna related, "I saw it all, I ran after her and said to her, 'Katia, why did you do that, really?' And she answered me: 'If he'd been a real man he would have punished me, but he's no more pluck than a drowned hen! And then he asks, "What's that for?" If he loves me, and doesn't bear malice, he had better put up with it and not ask, "What's that for?" I will never be anything to him—never, never!' And indeed she did not marry him. It was soon after that she made the acquaintance of that actress, and left her home. Mother cried, but father only said, 'A stubborn beast is best away from the flock!' And he did not bother about her, or try to find her out. My father did not understand Katia. On the day before her flight," added Anna, "she almost smothered me in her embraces, and kept repeating: 'I can't, I can't help it! . . . My heart's torn, but I can't help it! your cage is too small . . . it cramps my wings! And there's no escaping one's fate. . . .'

"After that," observed Anna, "we saw each other very seldom. . . . When my father died, she came for a couple of days, would take nothing of her inheritance, and vanished again. She was unhappy with us . . . I could see that. Afterwards she came to Kazan as an actress."

Aratov began questioning Anna about the theater, about the parts in which Clara had appeared, about her triumphs. . . . Anna answered in detail, but with the same mournful, though keen fervor. She even showed Aratov a photograph, in which Clara had been taken in the costume of one of her parts. In the photograph she was looking away, as though turning from the spectators; her thick hair tied with a ribbon fell in a coil on her bare arm. Aratov looked a long time at the photograph, thought it like, asked whether Clara had taken part in public recitations, and learnt that she had not; that she had needed the excitement of the theatre, the scenery . . . but another question was burning on his lips.

"Anna Semyonovna!" he cried at last, not loudly, but with a peculiar force, "tell me, I implore you, tell me why did she . . . what led her to this fearful step?" . . .

Anna looked down. "I don't know," she said, after a pause of some instants. "By God, I don't know!" she went on strenuously, supposing from Aratov's gesture that he did not believe her. . . . "since she came back here certainly she was melancholy, depressed. Something must have happened to her in Moscow—what, I could never guess. But on the other hand, on that fatal day she seemed as it were . . . if not more cheerful, at least more serene than usual. Even I had no presentiment," added Anna with a bitter smile, as though reproaching herself for it.

"You see," she began again, "it seemed as though at Katia's birth it had been decreed that she was to be unhappy. From her early years she was convinced of it. She would lean her head on her hand, sink into thought, and say, 'I shall not live long!' She used to have presentiments. Imagine! she used to see beforehand, sometimes in a dream and sometimes awake, what was going to happen to her! 'If I can't live as I want to live, then I won't live,' . . . was a saying of hers too. . . . 'Our life's in our own hands, you know.' And she proved that!"

Anna hid her face in her hands and stopped speaking. "Anna Semyonovna," Aratov began after a short pause, "you have perhaps heard to what the newspapers ascribed . . . 'To an unhappy love affair?' " Anna broke in, at once pulling away her hands from her face. "That's a slander, a fabrication! . . . My pure, unapproachable Katia . . . Katia! . . . an unhappy, unrequited love? And shouldn't I have known of it? . . . Every one was in love with her . . . while she . . . And whom could she have fallen in love with here? Who among all the people here, who was worthy of her? Who was up to the standard of honesty, truth, purity . . . yes, above all, of purity which she, with all her faults, always held up as an ideal before her? . . . She repulsed! . . . she! . . ."

Anna's voice broke. . . . Her fingers were trembling. All at once she flushed crimson . . . crimson with indignation, and for that instant, and that instant only, she was like her sister.

Aratov was beginning an apology.

"Listen," Anna broke in again. "I have an intense desire that you should not believe that slander, and should refute it, if possible! You want to write an article or something about her: that's your opportunity for defending her memory! That's why I talk so openly to you. Let me tell you; Katia left a diary . . ."

Aratov trembled. "A diary?" he muttered.

"Yes, a diary . . . that is, only a few pages. Katia was not fond of writing . . . for months at a time she would write nothing, and her letters were so short. But she was always, always truthful, she never told a lie. . . . She, with her pride, tell a lie! I . . . I will show you this diary! You shall see for yourself whether there is the least hint in it of any unhappy love affair!"

Anna quickly took out of a table-drawer a thin exercise-book, ten pages, no more, and held it out to Aratov. He seized it eagerly, recognized the irregular sprawling handwriting, the handwriting of that anonymous letter, opened it at random, and at once lighted upon the following lines.

"Moscow, Tuesday . . . June.—Sang and recited at a literary matinée. To-day is a vital day for me. *It must decide my fate.* (These words were twice underlined.) I saw again . . ." Here followed a few lines carefully erased. And then, "No! no! no! . . . Must go back to the old way, if only . . ."

Aratov dropped the hand that held the diary, and his head slowly sank upon his breast.

"Read it!" cried Anna. "Why don't you read it? Read it through from the beginning. . . . It would take only five minutes to read it all, though the diary extends over two years. In Kazan she used to write down nothing at all. . . ."

Aratov got up slowly from his chair and flung himself on his knees before Anna.

She was simply petrified with wonder and dismay.

"Give me . . . give me that diary," Aratov began with failing voice, and he stretched out both hands to Anna. "Give it me . . . and the photograph . . . you are sure to have some other one, and the diary I will return. . . . But I want it, oh, I want it! . . ."

In his imploring words, in his contorted features there was something so despairing that it looked positively like rage, like agony . . . And he was in agony, truly. He could not himself have foreseen that such pain could be felt by him, and in a frenzy he implored forgiveness, deliverance . . .

"Give it me," he repeated.

"But . . . you . . . you were in love with my sister?" Anna said at last.

Aratov was still on his knees.

"I only saw her twice . . . believe me! . . . and if I had not been impelled by causes, which I can neither explain nor fully understand myself, . . . if there had not been some power over me, stronger than myself . . . I should not be entreating you . . . I should not have come here. I want . . . I must . . . you yourself said I ought to defend her memory!"

"And you were not in love with my sister?" Anna asked a second time.

Aratov did not at once reply, and he turned aside a little, as though in pain.

"Well, then! I was! I was—I'm in love now," he cried in the same tone of despair.

Steps were heard in the next room.

"Get up . . . get up . . ." said Anna hurriedly. "Mamma is coming."

Aratov rose.

"And take the diary and the photograph, in God's name! Poor, poor Katia! . . . But you will give me back the diary," she added emphatically. "And if you write anything, be sure to send it me. . . . Do you hear?"

The entrance of Madame Milovidov saved Aratov from the necessity of a reply. He had time, however, to murmur, "You are an angel! Thanks! I will send anything I write. . . ."

Madame Milovidov, half awake, did not suspect anything. So Aratov left Kazan with the photograph in the breast-pocket of his coat. The diary he gave back to Anna; but, unobserved by her, he cut out the page on which were the words underlined.

On the way back to Moscow he relapsed again into a state of petrifaction. Though he was secretly delighted that he had attained the object of his journey, still all thoughts of Clara he deferred till he should be back at home. He thought much more about her sister Anna. "There," he thought, "is an exquisite, charming creature. What delicate comprehension of everything, what a loving heart, what a complete absence of egoism! And how girls like that spring up among us, in the provinces, and in such surroundings too! She is not strong, and not good-looking, and not young; but what a splendid helpmate she would be for a sensible, cultivated man! That's the girl I ought to have fallen in love with!" Such were Aratov's reflections . . . but on his arrival in Moscow things put on quite a different complexion.

XIV

Platonida Ivanovna was unspeakably rejoiced at her nephew's return. There was no terrible chance she had not imagined during his absence. "Siberia at least!" she muttered, sitting rigidly still in her little room; "at least for a year!" The cook too had terrified her by the most well-authenticated stories of the disappearance of this and that young man of the neighborhood. The perfect innocence and absence of revolutionary ideas in Yasha did not in the least reassure the old lady. "For indeed . . . if you come to that, he studies photography . . . and that's quite enough for them to arrest him!" And behold, here was her darling Yasha back again, safe and sound. She observed, indeed, that he seemed thinner, and looked hollow in the face; natural enough, with no one to look after him! but she did not venture to question him about his journey. She asked at dinner. "And is Kazan a fine town?" "Yes," answered Aratov. "I suppose they're all Tartars living there?" "Not only Tartars." "And did you get a Kazan dressing-gown while you were there?" "No, I didn't." With that the conversation ended.

But as soon as Aratov found himself alone in his own room, he quickly felt as though something were enfolding him about, as though he were once more *in the power,* yes, in the power of another life, another being. Though he had indeed said to Anna in that sudden delirious outburst that he was in love with Clara, that saying struck even him now as senseless and frantic. No, he was not in love; and how could he be in love with a dead woman, whom he had not even liked in her lifetime, whom he had almost forgotten? No, but he was in *her* power . . . he no longer belonged to himself. He was *captured.* So completely captured, that he did not even attempt to free himself by laughing at his own absurdity, nor by trying to arouse if not a conviction, at least a hope in himself that it would all pass, that it was nothing but nerves, nor by seeking for proofs, nor by anything! "If I meet him, I will capture him," he recalled those words of Clara's Anna had repeated to him. Well, he was captured. But was not she dead? Yes, her body was dead . . . but her soul? . . . is not that immortal? . . . does it need corporeal organs to show its power? Magnetism has proved to us the influence of one living human soul over another living human soul. . . . Why should not this influence last after death, if the soul remains living? But to what end? What can come of it? But can we, as a rule, apprehend what is the object of all that takes place about us? These ideas so absorbed Aratov that he suddenly asked Platosha at tea-time whether she believed in the immortality of the soul. She did not for the first minute understand what his question was, then she crossed herself and answered. "She should think so indeed! The soul not immortal!" "And, if so, can it have any influence after death?" Aratov asked again. The old lady replied that it could . . . pray for us, that is to say; at least, when it had passed through all its ordeals, awaiting the last dread judgment. But for the first forty days the soul simply hovered about the place where its death had occurred.

"The first forty days?"

"Yes; and then the ordeals follow."

Aratov was astounded at his aunt's knowledge, and went off to his room. And again he felt the same thing, the same power over him. This power showed itself in Clara's image being constantly before him to the minutest details, such details as he seemed hardly to have observed in her lifetime; he saw . . . saw her fingers, her nails, the little hairs on her cheeks near her temples, the little mole under her left eye; he saw the slight movement of her lips, her nostrils, her eyebrows . . . and her walk, and how she held her head a little on the right side . . . he saw everything. He did not by any means take a delight in it all, only he could not help thinking of it and seeing it. The first night after his return he did not, however, dream of her . . . he was very tired, and slept like a log. But directly he waked up, she came back into his room again, and seemed to establish herself in it, as though she were the mistress, as though by her voluntary death she had purchased the right to it, without asking him or needing his permission. He took up her photograph, he began reproducing it, enlarging it. Then he took it into his head to fit it to the stereoscope. He had a great deal of trouble to do it . . . at last he succeeded. He fairly shuddered when through the glass he looked upon her figure, with the semblance of corporeal solidity given it by the stereoscope. But the figure was grey, as though covered with dust . . . and moreover the eyes—the eyes looked always to one side, as though turning away. A long,

long while he stared at them, as though expecting them to turn to him . . . he even half-closed his eyelids on purpose . . . but the eyes remained immovable, and the whole figure had the look of some sort of doll. He moved away, flung himself in an armchair, took out the leaf from her diary, with the words underlined, and thought, "Well, lovers, they say, kiss the words traced by the hand of the beloved—but I feel no inclination to do that—and the handwriting I think ugly. But that line contains my sentence." Then he recalled the promise he had made Anna about the article. He sat down to the table, and set to work upon it, but everything he wrote struck him as so false, so rhetorical . . . especially so false . . . as though he did not believe in what he was writing nor in his own feelings. . . . And Clara herself seemed so utterly unknown and uncomprehended! She seemed to withhold herself from him. "No!" he thought, throwing down the pen . . . "either authorship's altogether not my line, or I must wait a little!" He fell to recalling his visit to the Milovidovs, and all Anna had told him, that sweet, delightful Anna. . . . A word she had uttered—"pure"—suddenly struck him. It was as though something scorched him, and shed light. "Yes," he said aloud, "she was pure, and I am pure. . . . That's what gave her this power."

Thoughts of the immortality of the soul, of the life beyond the grave, crowded upon him again. Was it not said in the Bible: "Death, where is thy sting?" And in Schiller: "And the dead shall live!" *(Auch die Todten sollen leben!)*

And too, he thought, in Mitskevitch: "I will love thee to the end of time . . . and beyond it!" And an English writer had said: "Love is stronger than death." The text from Scripture produced particular effect on Aratov. . . . He tried to find the place where the words occurred. . . . He had no Bible; he went to ask Platosha for one. She wondered, she brought out, however, a very old book in a warped leather binding, with copper clasps, covered with candle wax, and handed it over to Aratov. He bore it off to his own room, but for a long time he could not find the text . . . he stumbled, however, on another: "Greater love hath no man than this, that a man lay down his life for his friends" (S. John xv. 13).

He thought: "That's not right. It ought to be: Greater *power* hath no man."

"But if she did not lay down her life for me at all? If she made an end of herself simply because life had become a burden to her? What if, after all, she did not come to that meeting for anything to do with love at all?"

But at that instant he pictured to himself Clara before their parting on the boulevard. . . . He remembered the look of pain on her face, and the tears and the words, "Ah, you understood nothing!"

No! he could have no doubt why and for whom she had laid down her life. . . .

So passed that whole day till night-time.

XV

Aratov went to bed early, without feeling specially sleepy, but he hoped to find repose in bed. The strained condition of his nerves brought about an exhaustion far more unbearable than the bodily fatigue of the journey and the railway. However, exhausted as he was, he could not get to sleep. He tried to read . . . but the lines danced before his eyes. He put out the candle, and darkness reigned in his room. But still he lay sleepless, with his eyes shut. . . . And it began to seem to him some one was whispering in his ear. . . . "The beating of the heart, the pulse of the blood," he thought. . . . But the whisper passed into connected speech. Some one was talking in Russian hurriedly, plaintively, and indistinctly. Not one separate word could he catch. . . . But it was the voice of Clara.

Aratov opened his eyes, raised himself, leaned on his elbow. . . . The voice grew fainter, but kept up its plaintive, hurried talk, indistinct as before. . . .

It was unmistakably Clara's voice.

Unseen fingers ran light arpeggios up and down the keys of the piano . . . then the voice began again. More prolonged sounds were audible . . . as it were moans . . . always the same over and over again. Then apart from the rest the words began to stand out . . . "Roses . . . roses . . . roses. . . ."

"Roses," repeated Aratov in a whisper. "Ah, yes! it's the roses I saw on the woman's head in the dream." . . . "Roses," he heard again.

"Is that you?" Aratov asked in the same whisper. The voice suddenly ceased.

Aratov waited . . . and waited, and dropped his head on the pillow. "Hallucinations of hearing," he thought. "But if . . . if she really were here, close at hand? . . . If I were to see her, should I be frightened? or glad? But what should I be frightened of? or glad of? Why, of this, to be sure; it would be a proof that there is another world, that the soul is immortal. Though, indeed, even if I did see something, it too might be a hallucination of the sight. . . ."

He lighted the candle, however, and in a rapid glance, not without a certain dread, scanned the whole room . . . and saw nothing in it unusual. He got up, went to the stereoscope . . . again the same grey doll, with its eyes averted. The feeling of dread gave way to one of annoyance. He was, as it were, cheated in his expectations . . . the very expectation indeed struck him as absurd.

"Well, this is positively idiotic!" he muttered, as he got back into bed, and blew out the candle. Profound darkness reigned once more.

Aratov resolved to go to sleep this time. . . . But a fresh sensation started up in him. He fancied some one was standing in the middle of the room, not far from him, and scarcely perceptibly breathing. He turned round hastily and opened his eyes. . . . But what could be seen in impenetrable darkness?

He began to feel for a match on his little bedside table . . . and suddenly it seemed to him that a sort of soft, noiseless hurricane was passing over the whole room, over him, through him, and the word "I!" sounded distinctly in his ears. . . .

"I! . . . I . . . !"

Some instants passed before he succeeded in getting the candle alight.

Again there was no one in the room; and he now heard nothing, except the uneven throbbing of his own heart. He drank a glass of water, and stayed still, his head resting on his hand. He was waiting.

He thought: "I will wait. Either it's all nonsense . . . or she is here. She is not going to play cat and mouse with me like this!" He waited, waited long . . . so long that the hand on which he was resting his head went numb . . . but not one of his previous sensations was repeated. Twice his eyes closed. . . . He opened them promptly . . . at least he believed that he opened them. Gradually they turned towards the door and rested on it. The candle burned dim, and it was once more dark in the room . . . but the door made a long streak of white in the half darkness. And now this patch began to move, to grow less, to disappear . . . and in its place, in the doorway, appeared a woman's figure. Aratov looked intently at it . . . Clara! And this time she was looking straight at him, coming towards him. . . . On her head was a wreath of red roses. . . . He was all in agitation, he sat up. . . .

Before him stood his aunt in a nightcap adorned with a broad red ribbon, and in a white dressing-jacket.

"Platosha!" he said with an effort. "Is that you?"

"Yes, it's I," answered Platonida Ivanovna . . . "I, Yasha darling, yes."

"What have you come for?"

"You waked me up. At first you kept moaning as it were . . . and then you cried out all of a sudden, 'Save me! help me!'"

"I cried out?"

"Yes, and such a hoarse cry, 'Save me!' I thought, Mercy on us! He's never ill, is he? And I came in. Are you quite well?"

"Perfectly well."

"Well, you must have had a bad dream then. Would you like me to burn a little incense?"

Aratov once more stared intently at his aunt, and laughed aloud. . . . The figure of the good old lady in her nightcap and dressing-jacket, with her long face and scared expression, was certainly very comic. All the mystery surrounding him, oppressing him—everything weird was sent flying instantaneously.

"No, Platosha dear, there's no need," he said. "Please forgive me for unwittingly troubling you. Sleep well, and I will sleep too."

Platonida Ivanovna remained a minute standing where she was, pointed to the candle, grumbled, "Why not put it out . . . an accident happens in a minute?" and as she went out, could not refrain, though only at a distance, from making the sign of the cross over him.

Aratov fell asleep quickly, and slept till morning. He even got up in a happy frame of mind . . . though he felt sorry for something. . . . He felt light and free. "What romantic fancies, if you come to think of it!" he said to himself with a smile. He never once glanced either at the stereoscope, or at the page torn out of the diary. Immediately after breakfast, however, he set off to go to Kupfer's.

What drew him there . . . he was dimly aware.

XVI

Aratov found his sanguine friend at home. He chatted a little with him, reproached him for having quite forgotten his aunt and himself, listened to fresh praises of that heart of gold, the princess, who had just sent Kupfer from Yaroslav a smoking-cap embroidered with fishscales . . . and all at once, sitting just opposite Kupfer and looking him straight in the face, announced that he had been a journey to Kazan.

"You have been to Kazan; what for?"

"Oh, I wanted to collect some facts about that . . . Clara Militch."

"The one that poisoned herself?"

"Yes."

Kupfer shook his head. "Well, you are a chap! And so quiet about it! Toiled a thousand miles out there and back . . . for what? Eh? If there'd been some woman in the case now! Then I can understand anything! anything! any madness!" Kupfer ruffled up his hair. "But simply to collect materials, as it's called among you learned people. . . . I'd rather be excused! There are statistical writers to do that job! Well, and did you make friends with the old lady and the sister? Isn't she a delightful girl?"

"Delightful," answered Aratov, "she gave me a great deal of interesting information."

"Did she tell you exactly how Clara took poison?"

"You mean . . . how?"

"Yes, in what manner?"

"No . . . she was still in such grief . . . I did not venture to question her too much. Was there anything remarkable about it?"

"To be sure there was. Only fancy; she had to appear on the stage that very day, and she acted her part. She took a glass of poison to the theatre with her, drank it before the first act, and went through all that act afterwards. With the poison inside her! Isn't that something like strength of will? Character, eh? And, they say, she never acted her part with such feeling, such passion! The public suspected nothing, they clapped, and called for her. . . . And directly the curtain fell, she dropped down there, on the stage. Convulsions . . . and convulsions, and within an hour she was dead! But didn't I tell you all about it? And it was in the papers too!"

Aratov's hands had grown suddenly cold, and he felt an inward shiver.

"No, you didn't tell me that," he said at last. "And you don't know what play it was?"

Kupfer thought a minute. "I did hear what the play was . . . there is a betrayed girl in it. . . . Some drama, it must have been. Clara was created for dramatic parts. . . . Her very appearance . . . But where are you off to?" Kupfer interrupted himself, seeing that Aratov was reaching after his hat.

"I don't feel quite well," replied Aratov. "Good-bye . . . I'll come in another time."

Kupfer stopped him and looked into his face. "What a nervous fellow you are, my boy! Just look at yourself. . . . You're as white as chalk."

"I'm not well," repeated Aratov, and, disengaging himself from Kupfer's detaining hands, he started homewards. Only at that instant it became clear to him that he had come to Kupfer with the sole object of talking of Clara . . .

"UNHAPPY CLARA, POOR FRANTIC CLARA. . . ."

On reaching home, however, he quickly regained his composure to a certain degree.

The circumstances accompanying Clara's death had at first given him a violent shock . . . but later on this performance "with the poison inside her," as Kupfer had expressed it, struck him as a kind of monstrous pose, a piece of bravado, and he was already trying not to think about it, fearing to arouse a feeling in himself, not unlike repugnance. And at dinner, as he sat facing Platosha, he suddenly recalled her midnight appearance, recalled that abbreviated dressing-jacket, the cap with the high ribbon—and why a ribbon on a nightcap?—all the ludicrous apparition which, like the scene-shifter's whistle in a transformation scene, had dissolved all his visions into dust! He even forced Platosha to repeat her description of how she had heard his scream, had been alarmed, had jumped up, could not for a minute find either his door or her own, and so on. In the evening he played a game of cards with her, and went off to his room rather depressed, but again fairly composed.

Aratov did not think about the approaching night, and was not afraid of it: he was sure he would pass an excellent night. The thought of Clara had sprung up within him from time to time; but he remembered at once how "affectedly" she had killed herself, and turned away from it. This piece of "bad taste" blocked out all other memories of her. Glancing cursorily into the stereoscope, he even fancied that she was averting her eyes because she was ashamed. Opposite the stereoscope on the wall hung a portrait of his mother. Aratov took it from its nail, scrutinised it a long while, kissed it and carefully put it away in a drawer. Why did he do that? Whether it was that it was not fitting for this portrait to be so close to that woman . . . or for some other reason Aratov did not inquire of himself. But his mother's portrait stirred up memories of his father . . . of his father, whom he had seen dying in this very room, in this bed. "What do you think of all this, Father?" he mentally addressed himself to him. "You understand all this; you too believed in Schiller's world of spirits. Give me advice!"

"Father would have advised me to give up all this idiocy," Aratov said aloud, and he took up a book. He could not, however, read for long, and feeling a sort of heaviness all over, he went to bed earlier than usual, in the full conviction that he would fall asleep at once.

And so it happened . . . but his hopes of a quiet night were not realised.

XVII

It had not struck midnight when he had an extraordinary and terrifying dream.

He dreamed that he was in a rich manorhouse of which he was the owner. He had lately bought both the house and the estate attached to it. And he kept thinking, "It's nice, very nice now, but evil is coming!" Beside him moved to and fro a little tiny man, his steward; he kept laughing, bowing, and trying to show Aratov how admirably everything was arranged in his house and his estate. "This way, pray, this way, pray," he kept repeating, chuckling at every word; "kindly look how prosperous everything is with you! Look at the horses . . . what splendid horses!" And Aratov saw a row of immense horses. They were standing in their stalls with their backs to him; their manes and tails were magnificent . . . but as soon as Aratov went near, the horses' heads turned towards him, and they showed their teeth viciously. "It's very nice," Aratov thought! "but evil is coming!" "This way, pray, this way," the steward repeated again, "pray come into the garden: look what fine apples you have!" The apples certainly were fine, red, and round; but as soon as Aratov looked at them, they withered and fell . . . "Evil is coming," he thought. "And here is the lake," lisped the steward, "isn't it blue and smooth? And here's a little boat of gold . . . will you get into it? . . . it floats of itself." "I won't get into it," thought Aratov, "evil is coming!" and for all that he got into the boat. At the bottom lay huddled up a little creature like a monkey; it was holding in its paws a glass full of a dark liquid. "Pray don't be uneasy," the steward shouted from the bank . . . "It's of no consequence! It's death! Good luck to you!" The boat darted swiftly along . . . but all of a sudden a hurricane came swooping down on it, not like the hurricane of the night before, soft and noiseless—no; a black, awful, howling hurricane! Everything was confusion. And in the midst of the whirling darkness Aratov saw Clara in a stage-dress; she was lifting a glass to her lips, listening to shouts of "Bravo! bravo!" in the distance, and some coarse voice shouted in Aratov's ear: "Ah! did you think it would all end in a farce? No; it's a tragedy! a tragedy!"

Trembling all over, Aratov awoke. In the room it was not dark. . . . A faint light streamed in from somewhere, and showed every thing in the gloom and stillness. Aratov did not ask himself whence this light came. . . . He felt one thing only: Clara was there, in that room . . . he felt her presence . . . he was again and for ever in her power!

The cry broke from his lips, "Clara, are you here?"

"Yes!" sounded distinctly in the midst of the lighted, still room.

Aratov inaudibly repeated his question. . . .

"Yes!" he heard again.

"Then I want to see you!" he cried, and he jumped out of bed.

For some instants he stood in the same place, pressing his bare feet on the chill floor. His eyes strayed about. "Where? where?" his lips were murmuring. . . .

Nothing to be seen, not a sound to be heard. . . . He looked round him, and noticed that the faint light that filled the room came from a night-light, shaded by a sheet of paper and set in a corner, probably by Platosha while he was asleep. He even discerned the smell of incense . . . also, most likely, the work of her hands.

He hurriedly dressed himself: to remain in bed, to sleep, was not to be thought of. Then he took his stand in the middle of the room, and folded his arms. The sense of Clara's presence was stronger in him than it had ever been.

And now he began to speak, not loudly, but with solemn deliberation, as though he were uttering an incantation.

"Clara," he began, "if you are truly here, if you see me, if you hear me—show yourself! . . . If the power which I feel over me is truly your power, show yourself! If you understand how bitterly I repent that I did not understand you, that I repelled you—show yourself! If what I have heard was truly your voice; if the feeling overmastering me is love; if you are now convinced that I love you, I, who till now have neither loved nor known any woman; if you know that since your death I have come to love you passionately, inconsolably; if you do not want me to go mad—show yourself, Clara!"

Aratov had hardly uttered this last word when all at once he felt that some one was swiftly approaching him from behind—as that day on the boulevard —and laying a hand on his shoulder. He turned round, and saw no one. But the sense of *her* presence had grown so distinct, so unmistakable, that once more he looked hurriedly about him. . . .

What was that? On an easy-chair, two paces from him, sat a woman, all in black. Her head was turned away, as in the stereoscope. . . . It was she! It was Clara! But what a stern, sad face!

Aratov slowly sank on his knees. Yes; he was right, then. He felt neither fear nor delight, not even astonishment. . . . His heart even began to beat more quietly. He had one sense, one feeling, "Ah! at last! at last!"

"Clara," he began, in a faint but steady voice, "why do you not look at me? I know that it is you . . . but I may fancy my imagination has created an image like *that one* . . ."—he pointed towards the stereoscope—"prove to me that it is you. . . . Turn to me, look at me, Clara!"

Clara's hand slowly rose . . . and fell again.

"Clara! Clara! turn to me!"

And Clara's head slowly turned, her closed lids opened, and her dark eyes fastened upon Aratov.

He fell back a little, and uttered a single, long-drawn-out, trembling "Ah!"

Clara gazed fixedly at him . . . but her eyes, her features, retained their former mournfully stern, almost displeased expression. With just that expression on her face she had come on to the platform on the day of the literary matinée, before she caught sight of Aratov. And, just as then, she suddenly flushed, her face brightened, her eyes kindled, and a joyful, triumphant smile parted her lips. . . .

"I have come!" cried Aratov. "You have conquered. . . . Take me! I am yours, and you are mine!"

He flew to her; he tried to kiss those smiling, triumphant lips, and he kissed them. He felt their burning touch: he even felt the moist chill of her teeth: and a cry of triumph rang through the half-dark room.

Platonida Ivanovna, running in, found him in a swoon. He was on his knees; his head was lying on the arm-chair; his outstretched arms hung powerless; his pale face was radiant with the intoxication of boundless bliss.

Platonida Ivanovna fairly dropped to the ground beside him; she put her arms round him, faltered, "Yasha! Yasha, darling! Yasha, dearest!" tried to lift him in her bony arms . . . he did not stir. Then Platonida Ivanovna fell to screaming in a voice unlike her own. The servant ran in. Together they somehow roused him, began throwing water over him—even took it from the holy lamp before the holy picture. . . .

He came to himself. But in response to his aunt's questions he only smiled, and with such an ecstatic face that she was more alarmed than ever, and kept crossing first herself and then him. . . . Aratov, at last, put aside her hand, and, still with the same ecstatic expression of face, said: "Why, Platosha, what is the matter with you?"

"What is the matter with you, Yasha darling?"

"With me? I am happy . . . happy, Platosha . . . that's what's the matter with me. And now I want to lie down, to sleep. . . ." He tried to get up, but felt such a sense of weakness in his legs, and in his whole body, that he could not, without the help of his aunt and the servant, undress and get into bed. But he fell asleep very quickly, still with the same look of blissful triumph on his face. Only his face was very pale.

XVIII

When Platonida Ivanovna came in to him next morning, he was still in the same position . . . but the weakness had not passed off and he actually preferred to remain in bed. Platonida Ivanovna did not like the pallor of his face at all. "Lord, have mercy on us! what is it?" she thought; "not a drop of blood in his face, refuses broth, lies there and smiles, and keeps declaring he's perfectly well!" He refused breakfast too. "What is the matter with you, Yasha?" she questioned him; "do you mean to lie in bed all day?" "And what if I did?" Aratov answered gently. This very gentleness again Platonida Ivanovna did not like at all. Aratov had the air of a man who has discovered a great, very delightful secret, and is jealously guarding it and keeping it to himself. He was looking forward to the night, not impatiently, but with curiosity. "What next?" he was asking himself; "what will happen?" Astonishment, incredulity, he had ceased to feel; he did not doubt that he was in communication with Clara, that they loved one another . . . that, too, he had no doubt about. Only . . . what could come of such love? He recalled that kiss . . . and a delicious shiver ran swiftly and sweetly through all his limbs. "Such a kiss," was his thought, "even Romeo and Juliet knew not! But next time I will be stronger. . . . I will master her. . . . She shall come with a wreath of tiny roses in her dark curls. . . .

"But what next? We cannot live together, can we? Then must I die so as to be with her? Is it not for that she has come; and is it not *so* she means to take me captive?

"Well; what then? If I must die, let me die. Death has no terrors for me now. It cannot, then, annihilate me? On the contrary, only *thus* and *there* can I be happy . . . as I have not been happy in life, as she has not. . . . We are both pure! Oh, that kiss!"

Platonida Ivanovna was incessantly coming into Aratov's room. She did not worry him with questions; she merely looked at him, muttered, sighed, and went out again. But he refused his dinner too: this was really too dreadful. The old lady set off to an acquaintance of hers, a district doctor, in whom she placed some confidence, simply because he did not drink and had a German wife. Aratov was surprised when she brought him in to see him; but Platonida Ivanovna so earnestly implored her darling Yashenka to allow Paramon Paramonitch (that was the doctor's name) to examine him—if only for her sake—that Aratov consented. Paramon Paramonitch felt his pulse, looked at his tongue, asked a question, and announced at last that it was absolutely necessary for him to "auscultate" him. Aratov was in such an amiable frame of mind that he agreed to this too. The doctor delicately uncovered his chest, delicately tapped, listened, hummed and hawed, prescribed some drops and a mixture, and, above all, advised him to keep quiet and avoid any excitement. "I dare say!" thought Aratov; "that idea's a little too late, my good friend!" "What is wrong with Yasha?" queried Platonida Ivanovna, as she slipped a three-rouble note into Paramon Paramonitch's hand in the doorway. The district doctor, who like all modern physicians—especially those who wear a government uniform—was fond of showing off with scientific terms, announced that her nephew's diagnosis showed all the symptoms of neurotic cardialgia, and there were febrile symptoms also. "Speak plainer, my dear sir; do," cut in Platonida Ivanovna; "don't terrify me with your Latin; you're not in your surgery!" "His heart's not right," the doctor explained; "and, well—there's a little fever too" . . . and he repeated his advice as to perfect quiet and absence of excitement. "But there's no danger, is there?" Platonida Ivanovna inquired severely. ("You dare rush off into Latin again," she implied.) "No need to anticipate any at present!"

The doctor went away . . . and Platonida Ivanovna grieved. . . . She sent to the surgery, though, for the medicine, which Aratov would not take, in spite of her entreaties. He refused any herb-tea too. "And why are you so uneasy, dear?" he said to her; "I assure you, I'm at this moment the sanest and happiest man in the whole world!" Platonida Ivanovna could only shake her head. Towards evening he grew rather feverish; and still he insisted that she should not stay in his room, but should go to sleep in her own. Platonida Ivanovna obeyed; but she did not undress, and did not lie down. She sat in an arm-chair, and was all the while listening and murmuring her prayers.

She was just beginning to doze, when suddenly she was awakened by a terrible piercing shriek. She jumped up, rushed into Aratov's room, and as on the night before, found him lying on the floor.

But he did not come to himself as on the previous night, in spite of all they could do. He fell the same night into a high fever, complicated by failure of the heart.

A few days later he passed away.

A strange circumstance attended his second fainting-fit. When they lifted him up and laid him on his bed, in his clenched right hand they found a small tress of a woman's dark hair. Where did this lock of hair come from? Anna Semyonovna had such a lock of hair left by Clara; but what could induce her to give Aratov a relic so precious to her? Could she have put it somewhere in the diary, and not have noticed it when she lent the book?

In the delirium that preceded his death, Aratov spoke of himself as Romeo . . . after the poison, spoke of marriage, completed and perfect; of his knowing now what rapture meant. Most terrible of all for Platosha was the minute when Aratov, coming a little to himself, and seeing her beside his bed, said to her, "Aunt, what are you crying for?—because I must die? But don't you know that love is stronger than death? . . . Death! death! where is thy sting? You should not weep, but rejoice, even as I rejoice. . . ."

And once more on the face of the dying man shone out the rapturous smile, which gave the poor old woman such cruel pain.

Robert W. Chambers

The Repairer of Reputations

Robert W. Chambers' first book, *The King in Yellow* (1895), is a monument in the development of horror literature in the U.S. In the stories therein, Chambers achieved a unique blend of Poe, Ambrose Bierce and the decadence of Wilde and Beardsley to produce a landmark collection. "The Yellow Sign" is generally accorded the primary status in the book as a masterpiece of horror, but the lead story, "The Repairer of Reputations," is in some ways an even more extraordinary achievement, a horrific tale that is also a sophisticated, avant garde work of science fiction set in New York twenty-five years in the future after the great war with Germany, a world of revolutions and suicide parlors, unconventional in many ways. Chambers became rich and famous as a novelist of romance and of historical adventure, and rarely returned to horror, never again reaching the heights of perfervid intensity of the stories in *The King in Yellow*. It is now obvious that great horror stories exist in all the sub-genres of fiction, and that SF, with its concern with alternate realities, is a particularly amenable genre for the horror writer. Many of the stories that contribute to the evolution of SF are also in fact horror, none more powerful than "The Repairer of Reputations."

I

"Ne raillon pas les fous; leur folie dure plus longtemps que la nôtre . . . Voilà toute la différence."

Toward the end of the year 1920 the Government of the United States had practically completed the programme, adopted during the last months of President Winthrop's administration. The country was apparently tranquil. Everybody knows how the Tariff and Labor questions were settled. The war with Germany, incident on that country's seizure of the Samoan Islands, had left no visible scars upon the republic, and the temporary occupation of Norfolk by the invading army had been forgotten in the joy over repeated naval victories and the subsequent ridiculous plight of General Von Gartenlaube's forces in the State of New Jersey. The Cuban and Hawaiian investments had paid one hundred per cent, and the territory of Samoa was well worth its cost as a coaling station. The country was in a superb state of defence. Every coast city had been well supplied with land fortifications; the army under the parental eye of the General Staff, organized according to the Prussian system, had been increased to 300,000 men with a territorial reserve of a million; and six magnificent squadrons of cruisers and battle-ships patrolled the six stations of the navigable seas, leaving a steam reserve amply fitted to control home waters. The gentlemen from the West had at last been constrained to acknowledge that a college for the training of diplomats was as necessary as law schools are for the training of barristers. Consequently we were no longer represented abroad by incompetent patriots. The nation was prosperous. Chicago, for a moment paralyzed after a second great fire, had risen from its ruins, white and imperial, and more beautiful than the white city which had been built for its plaything in 1893. Everywhere good architecture was replacing bad, and even in New York, a sudden craving for decency had swept away a great portion of the existing horrors. Streets had been widened, properly paved and lighted, trees had been planted, squares laid out, elevated structures demolished and underground roads built to replace them. The new government buildings and barracks were fine bits of architecture, and the long system of stone quays which completely surrounded the island had been turned into parks which proved a godsend to the population. The subsidizing of the state theatre and state opera brought its own reward. The United States National Academy of Design was much like European institutions of the same kind. Nobody envied the Secretary of Fine Arts, either his cabinet position or his portfolio. The Secretary of Forrestry and Game Preservation had a much easier time, thanks to the new system of National Mounted Police. We had profited well by the latest treaties with France and England; the exclusion of foreign-born Jews as a measure of national self-preservation, the settlement of the new independent negro state of Suanee, the checking of immigration, the new laws concerning naturalization, and the gradual centralization of power in the executive all contributed to national calm and prosperity. When the Government solved the Indian problem and squadrons of Indian cavalry scouts in native costume were substituted for the pitiable organizations tacked on to the tail of skeletonized regiments by a former Secretary of War, the nation drew a long sigh of relief. When, after the colossal Congress of Religions, bigotry and intolerance were laid in their graves and kindness and charity began to draw warring sects together, many thought the millennium had arrived, at least in the new world, which after all is a world by itself.

But self-preservation is the first law, and the United States had to look on in helpless sorrow as Germany, Italy, Spain and Belgium writhed in the throes of Anarchy, while Russia, watching from the Caucasus, stooped and bound them one by one.

In the city of New York the summer of 1899 was signalized by the dismantling of the Elevated Railroads. The summer of 1900 will live in the memories of New York people for many a cycle; the Dodge Statue was removed in that year. In the following winter began that agitation for the repeal of the laws prohibiting suicide, which bore its final fruit in the month of April, 1920, when the first Government Lethal Chamber was opened on Washington Square.

I had walked down that day from Dr. Archer's house on Madison Avenue, where I had been as a mere formality. Ever since that fall from my horse, four years before, I had been troubled at times with pains in the back of my head and neck, but now for months they had been absent, and the doctor sent me away that day saying there was nothing more to be cured in me. It was hardly worth his fee to be told that; I knew it myself. Still I did not grudge him the money. What I minded was the mistake which he made at first. When they picked me up from the pavement where I lay unconscious, and somebody had mercifully sent a bullet through my horse's head, I was carried to Doctor Archer, and he, pronouncing my brain affected, placed me in his private asylum where I was obliged to endure treatment for insanity. At last he decided that I was well, and I, knowing that my mind had always been as sound as his, if not sounder, "paid my tuition" as he jokingly called it, and left. I told him, smiling, that I would get even with him for his mistake, and he laughed heartily, and asked me to call once in a while. I did so, hoping for a chance to even up accounts, but he gave me none, and I told him I would wait.

The fall from my horse had fortunately left no evil results; on the contrary, it had changed my whole character for the better. From a lazy young man about town, I had become active, energetic, temperate, and above all—oh, above all else—ambitious. There was only one thing which troubled me. I laughed at my own uneasiness, and yet it troubled me.

During my convalescence I had bought and read for the first time *The King in Yellow*. I remember after finishing the first act that it occurred to me that I had better stop. I started up and flung the book into the fireplace; the volume struck the barred grate and fell open on the hearth in the fire-light. If I had not caught a glimpse of the opening words in the second act I should never have finished it, but as I stooped to pick it up, my eyes became riveted to the open page, and with a cry of terror, or perhaps it was of joy so poignant that I suffered in every nerve, I snatched the thing out of the coals and crept shaking to my bedroom, where I read it and reread it, and wept and laughed and trembled with a horror which at times assails me yet. This is the thing that troubles me, for I cannot forget Carcosa where black stars hang in the heavens; where the shadows of men's thoughts lengthen in the afternoon, when the twin suns sink into the Lake of Hali; and my mind will bear forever the memory of the Pallid Mask. I pray God will curse the writer, as the writer has cursed the world with this beautiful, stupendous creation, terrible in its simplicity, irresistible in its truth—a world which now trembles before the King in Yellow. When the French Government seized the translated copies which had just arrived in Paris, London, of course, became eager to read it. It is well known how the book spread like an infectious disease, from city to city, from continent to continent, barred out here, confiscated there, denounced by press and pulpit, censured even by the most advanced of literary anarchists. No definite principles had been violated in those wicked pages, no doctrine promulgated, no convictions outraged. It could not be judged by any known standard, yet, although it was acknowledged that the supreme note of art had been struck in *The King in Yellow*, all felt that human nature could not bear the strain, nor thrive on words in which the essence of purest poison lurked. The very banality and innocence of the first act only allowed the blow to fail afterward with more awful effect.

It was, I remember, the 13th day of April, 1920, that the first Government Lethal Chamber was established on the south side of Washington Square, between Wooster Street and South Fifth Avenue. The block which had formerly consisted of a lot of shabby old buildings, used as cafés and restaurants for foreigners, had been acquired by the Government in the winter of 1898. The French and Italian cafés and restaurants were torn down; the whole block was enclosed by a gilded iron railing, and converted into a lovely garden with lawns, flowers and fountains. In the centre of the garden stood a small, white building, severely classical in architecture, and surrounded by thickets of flowers. Six Ionic columns supported the roof, and the single door was of bronze. A splendid marble group of "The Fates" stood before the door, the work of a young American sculptor, Boris Yvain, who had died in Paris when only twenty-three years old.

The inauguration ceremonies were in progress as I crossed University Place and entered the square. I threaded my way through the silent throng of spectators, but was stopped at Fourth Street by a cordon of police. A regiment of United States lancers were drawn up in a hollow square around the Lethal Chamber. On a raised tribune facing Washington Park stood the Governor of New York, and behind him were grouped the Mayor of New York and Brooklyn, the Inspector-General of Police, the Commandant of the state troops, Colonel Livingston, military aide to the President of the United States, General Blount, commanding at Governor's Island, Major-General Hamilton, commanding the garrison of New York and Brooklyn, Admiral Buffby of the fleet in the North River, Surgeon General Lanceford, the staff of the National Free Hospital, Senators Wyse and Franklin of New York, and the Commissioner of Public Works. The tribune was surrounded by a squadron of hussars of the National Guard.

The Governor was finishing his reply to the short speech of the Surgeon-General. I heard him say: "The laws prohibiting suicide and providing punishment for any attempt at self-destruction have been repealed. The Government has seen fit to acknowledge the right of man to end an existence which may have become intolerable to him, through physical suffering or mental despair. It is believed that the community will be benefited by the removal of such people from their midst. Since the passage of this law, the number of suicides in the United States has not increased. Now that the Government has determined to establish a Lethal Chamber in every city, town and village in the country, it remains to be seen whether or not that class of human creatures from whose desponding ranks new victims of self-destruction fall daily will accept the relief thus provided." He paused, and turned to the white Lethal Chamber. The silence in the street was absolute. "There a painless death awaits him who can no longer bear the sorrows of this life. If death is welcome let him seek it there." Then quickly turning to the military aide of the President's household, he said, "I declare the Lethal Chamber open," and again facing the vast crowd, he cried in a clear voice: "Citizens of New York and of the United States of America, through me the Government declares the Lethal Chamber to be open."

The solemn hush was broken by a sharp cry of command, the squadron of hussars filed after the Governor's carriage, the lancers wheeled and formed along Fifth Avenue to wait for the commandant of the garrison, and the mounted police followed them. I left the crowd to gape and stare at the white marble Death Chamber, and, crossing South Fifth Avenue, walked along the western side of that thoroughfare to Bleecker Street. Then I turned to the right and stopped before a dingy shop which bore the sign,

HAWBERK, ARMORER.

I glanced into the doorway and saw Hawberk busy in his little shop at the end of the hall. He looked up at the same moment, and catching sight of me cried in his deep, hearty voice, "Come in, Mr. Castaigne!" Constance, his daughter, rose to meet me as I crossed the threshold, and held out her pretty hand, but I saw the blush of disappointment on her cheeks, and knew that it was another Castaigne she had expected, my cousin Louis. I smiled at her confusion and complimented her on the banner which she was embroidering from a colored plate. Old Hawberk sat riveting the worn greaves of some ancient suit of armor, and the ting! ting! ting! of his little hammer sounded pleasantly in the quaint shop. Presently he dropped his hammer, and fussed about for a moment with a tiny wrench. The soft clash of the mail sent a thrill of pleasure through me. I loved to hear the music of steel brushing against steel, the mellow shock of the mallet on thigh pieces, and the jingle of chain armor. That was the only reason I went to see Hawberk. He had never interested me personally, nor did Constance, except for the fact of her being in love with Louis. This did occupy my attention, and sometimes even kept me awake at night. But I knew in my heart that all would come right, and that I should arrange their future as I expected to arrange that of my kind doctor, John Archer. However, I should never have troubled myself about visiting them just then had it not been, as I say, that the music of the tinkling hammer had for me this strong fascination. I would sit for hours, listening and listening, and when a stray sunbeam struck the inlaid steel, the sensation it gave me was almost too keen to endure. My eyes would become fixed, dilating with a pleasure that stretched every nerve almost to breaking, until some movement of the old armorer cut off the ray of sunlight, then, still thrilling secretly, I leaned back and listened again to the sound of the polishing rag, swish! swish! rubbing rust from the rivets.

Constance worked with the embroidery over her knees, now and then pausing to examine more closely the pattern in the colored plate from the Metropolitan Museum.

"Who is this for?" I asked.

Hawberk explained that in addition to the treasures of armor in the Metropolitan Museum of which he had been appointed armorer, he also had charge of several collections belonging to rich amateurs. This was the missing greave of a famous suit which a client of his had traced to a little shop in Paris on the Quai d'Orsay. He, Hawberk, had negotiated for and secured the greave, and now the suit was complete. He laid down his hammer and read me the history of the suit, traced since 1450 from owner to owner until it was acquired by Thomas Stainbridge. When his superb collection was sold, this client of Hawberk's bought the suit, and since then the search for the missing greave had been pushed until it was, almost by accident, located in Paris.

"Did you continue the search so persistently without any certainty of the greave being still in existence?" I demanded.

"Of course," he replied coolly.

Then for the first time I took a personal interest in Hawberk.

"It was worth something to you," I ventured.

"No," he replied, laughing, "my pleasure in finding it was my reward."

"Have you no ambition to be rich?" I asked, smiling.

"My one ambition is to be the best armorer in the world," he answered gravely.

Constance asked me if I had seen the ceremonies at the Lethal Chamber. She herself had noticed cavalry passing up Broadway that morning, and had wished to see the inauguration, but her father wanted the banner finished, and she had stayed at his request.

"Did you see your cousin, Mr. Castaigne, there?" she asked, with the slighest tremor of her soft eyelashes.

"No," I replied carelessly. "Louis' regiment is manoeuvring out in Westchester County." I rose and picked up my hat and cane.

"Are you going upstairs to see the lunatic again?" laughed old Hawberk. If Hawberk knew how I loathe that word "lunatic," he would never use it in my presence. It rouses certain feelings within me which I do not care to explain. However, I answered him quietly: "I think I shall drop in and see Mr. Wilde for a moment or two."

"Poor fellow," said Constance, with a shake of her head, "it must be hard to live alone year after year, poor, crippled and almost demented. It is very good of you, Mr. Castaigne, to visit him as often as you do."

"I think he is vicious," observed Hawberk, beginning again with his hammer. I listened to the golden tinkle on the greave plates; when he had finished I replied:

"No, he is not vicious, nor is he in the least demented. His mind is a wonder chamber, from which he can extract treasures that you and I would give years of our lives to acquire."

Hawberk laughed.

I continued a little impatiently: "He knows history as no one else could know it. Nothing, however trivial, escapes his search, and his memory is so absolute, so precise in details, that were it known in New York that such a man existed, the people could not honor him enough."

"Nonsense," muttered Hawberk, searching on the floor for a fallen rivet.

"Is it nonsense," I asked, managing to suppress what I felt, "is it nonsense when he says that the tassets and cuissards of the enamelled suit of armor commonly known as the 'Prince's Emblazoned' can be found among a mass of rusty theatrical properties, broken stoves and ragpickers' refuse in a garret in Pell Street?"

Hawberk's hammer fell to the ground, but he picked it up and asked, with a great deal of calm, how I knew that the tassets and left cuissard were missing from the "Prince's Emblazoned."

"I did not know until Mr. Wilde mentioned it to me the other day. He said they were in the garret of 998 Pell Street."

"Nonsense," he cried, but I noticed his hand trembling under his leathern apron.

"Is this nonsense too?" I asked pleasantly. "Is it nonsense when Mr. Wilde continually speaks of you as the Marquis of Avonshire and of Miss Constance—"

I did not finish, for Constance had started to her feet with terror written on every feature. Hawberk looked at me and slowly smoothed his leathern apron. "That is impossible," he observed. "Mr. Wilde may know a great many things—"

"About armor, for instance, and the 'Prince's Emblazoned,'" I interposed, smiling.

"Yes," he continued, slowly, "about armor also—may be—but he is wrong in regard to the Marquis of Avonshire, who, as you know, killed his wife's traducer years ago, and went to Australia where he did not long survive his wife."

"Mr. Wilde is wrong," murmured Constance. Her lips were blanched but her voice was sweet and calm.

"Let us agree, if you please, that in this one circumstance Mr. Wilde is wrong," I said.

II

I climbed the three dilapidated flights of stairs, which I had so often climbed before, and knocked at a small door at the end of the corridor. Mr. Wilde opened the door and I walked in.

When he had double-locked the door and pushed a heavy chest against it, he came and sat down beside me, peering up into my face with his little light-colored eyes. Half a dozen new scratches covered his nose and cheeks, and the silver wires which supported his artificial ears had become displaced. I thought I had never seen him so hideously fascinating. He had no ears. The artificial ones, which now stood out at an angle from the fine wire, were his one weakness. They were made of wax and painted a shell pink, but the rest of his face was yellow. He might better have revelled in the luxury of some artificial fingers for his left hand, which was absolutely fingerless, but it seemed to cause him no inconvenience, and he was satisfied with his wax ears. He was very small, scarcely higher than a child of ten, but his arms were magnificently developed, and his thighs as thick as any athlete's. Still, the most remarkable thing about Mr. Wilde was that a man of his marvellous intelligence and knowledge should have such a head. It was flat and pointed, like the heads of many of those unfortunates whom people imprison in asylums for the weak-minded. Many called him insane but I knew him to be as sane as I was.

I do not deny that he was eccentric; the mania he had for keeping that cat and teasing her until she flew at his face like a demon, was certainly eccentric. I never could understand why he kept the creature, nor what pleasure he found in shutting himself up in his room with the surly, vicious beast. I remember once glancing up from the manuscript I was studying by the light of some tallow dips and seeing Mr. Wilde squatting motionless on his high chair, his eyes fairly blazing with excitement, while the cat, which had risen from her place before the stove, came creeping across the floor right at him. Before I could move she flattened her belly to the ground, crouched, trembled, and sprang into his face. Howling and foaming, they rolled over and over on the floor, scratching and clawing, until the cat screamed and fled under the cabinet, and Mr. Wilde turned over on his back, his limbs contracting and curling up like the legs of a dying spider. He *was* eccentric.

Mr. Wilde had climbed into his high chair, and, after studying my face, picked up a dog's-eared ledger and opened it.

"Henry B. Matthews," he read, "bookkeeper with Whysot Whysot and Company, dealers in church ornaments. Called April 3d. Reputation damaged on the race-track. Known as a welcher. Reputation to be repaired by August 1st. Retainer Five Dollars." He turned the page and ran his fingerless knuckles down the closely-written columns.

"P. Greene Dusenberry, Minister of the Gospel, Fairbeach, New Jersey. Reputation damaged in the Bowery. To be repaired as soon as possible. Retainer $100."

He coughed and added, "Called, April 6th."

"Then you are not in need of money, Mr. Wilde," I inquired.

"Listen," he coughed again.

"Mrs. C. Hamilton Chester, of Chester Park, New York City, called April 7th. Reputation damaged at Dieppe, France. To be repaired by October 1st. Retainer $500.

"Note.—C. Hamilton Chester, Captain U. S. S. 'Avalanche' ordered home from South Sea Squadron October 1st."

"Well," I said, "the profession of a Repairer of Reputations is lucrative."

His colorless eyes sought mine. "I only wanted to demonstrate that I was correct. You said it was impossible to succeed as a Repairer of Reputations; that even if I did succeed in certain cases, it would cost me more than I would gain by it. To-day I have five hundred men in my employ, who are poorly paid, but who pursue the work with an enthusiasm which possibly may be born of fear. These men enter every shade and grade of society; some even are pillars of the most exclusive social temples; others are the prop and pride of the financial world; still others hold undisputed sway among the 'Fancy and the Talent.' I choose them at my leisure from those who reply to my advertisements. It is easy enough, they are all cowards. I could treble the number in twenty days if I wished. So you see, those who have in their keeping the reputations of their fellow-citizens, *I* have in my pay."

"They may turn on you," I suggested.

He rubbed his thumb over his cropped ears, and adjusted the wax substitutes. "I think not," he murmured thoughtfully, "I seldom have to apply the whip, and then only once. Besides, they like their wages."

"How do you apply the whip?" I demanded.

His face for a moment was awful to look upon. His eyes dwindled to a pair of green sparks.

"I invite them to come and have a little chat with me," he said in a soft voice.

A knock at the door interrupted him, and his face resumed its amiable expression.

"Who is it?" he inquired.

"Mr. Steylette," was the answer.

"Come to-morrow," replied Mr. Wilde.

"Impossible," began the other, but was silenced by a sort of bark from Mr. Wilde.

"Come to-morrow," he repeated.

We heard somebody move away from the door and turn the corner by the stairway.

"Who is that?" I asked.

"Arnold Steylette, Owner and Editor in Chief of the great New York daily."

He drummed on the ledger with his fingerless hand, adding: "I pay him very badly, but he thinks it a good bargain."

"Arnold Steylette!" I repeated, amazed.

"Yes," said Mr. Wilde with a self-satisfied cough.

The cat, which had entered the room as he spoke, hesitated, looked up at him and snarled. He climbed down from the chair and squatting on the floor, took the creature into his arms and caressed her. The cat ceased snarling and presently began a loud purring which seemed to increase in timbre as he stroked her.

"Where are the notes?" I asked. He pointed to the table, and for the hundredth time I picked up the bundle of manuscript entitled

"THE IMPERIAL DYNASTY OF AMERICA."

One by one I studied the well-worn pages, worn only by my own handling, and although I knew all by heart, from the beginning, "When from Carcosa, the Hyades, Hastur, and Aldebaran," to "Castaigne, Louis de Calvados, born December 19th, 1877," I read it with an eager rapt attention, pausing to repeat parts of it aloud, and dwelling especially on "Hildred de Calvados, only son of Hildred Castaigne and Edythe Landes Castaigne, first in succession," etc., etc.

When I finished, Mr. Wilde nodded and coughed.

"Speaking of your legitimate ambition," he said, "how do Constance and Louis get along?"

"She loves him," I replied simply.

The cat on his knee suddenly turned and struck at his eyes, and he flung her off and climbed on to the chair opposite me.

"And Doctor Archer! But that's a matter you can settle any time you wish," he added.

"Yes," I replied, "Doctor Archer can wait, but it is time I saw my cousin Louis."

"It is time," he repeated. Then he took another ledger from the table and ran over the leaves rapidly.

"We are now in communication with ten thousand men," he muttered. "We can count on one hundred thousand within the first twenty-eight hours, and in forty-eight hours the state will rise *en masse*. The country follows the state, and the portion that will not, I mean California and the Northwest, might better never have been inhabited. I shall not send them the Yellow Sign."

The blood rushed to my head, but I only answered, "A new broom sweeps clean."

"The ambition of Cæsar and of Napoleon pales before that which could not rest until it had seized the minds of men and controlled even their unborn thoughts," said Mr. Wilde.

"You are speaking of the King in Yellow," I groaned with a shudder.

"He is a king whom Emperors have served."

"I am content to serve him," I replied.

Mr. Wilde sat rubbing his ears with his crippled hand. "Perhaps Constance does not love him," he suggested.

I started to reply, but a sudden burst of military music from the street below drowned my voice. The twentieth dragoon regiment, formerly in garrison at Mount St. Vincent, was returning from the manœuvres in Westchester County, to its new barracks on East Washington Square. It was my cousin's regiment. They were a fine lot of fellows, in their pale-blue, tight-fitting jackets, jaunty busbys and white riding breeches with the double yellow stripe, into which their limbs seemed molded. Every other squadron was armed with lances, from the metal points of which fluttered yellow and white pennons. The band passed, playing the regimental march, then came the colonel and staff, the horses crowding and trampling, while their heads bobbed in unison, and the pennons fluttered from their lance points. The troopers, who rode with the beautiful English seat, looked brown as berries from their bloodless campaign among the farms of Westchester, and the music of their sabres against the stirrups, and the jingle of spurs and carbines, was delightful to me. I saw Louis riding with his squadron. He was as handsome an officer as I have ever seen. Mr. Wilde, who had mounted a chair by the window, saw him too, but said nothing. Louis turned and looked straight at Hawberk's shop as he passed, and I could see the flush on his brown cheeks. I think Constance must have been at the window. When the last troopers had clattered by, and the last pennons vanished into South 5th Avenue, Mr. Wilde clambered out of his chair and dragged the chest away from the door.

"Yes," he said, "it is time that you saw your cousin Louis."

He unlocked the door and I picked up my hat and stick and stepped into the corridor. The stairs were dark. Groping about, I set my foot on something soft, which snarled and spit, and I aimed a murderous blow at the cat, but my cane shivered to splinters against the balustrade, and the beast scurried back into Mr. Wilde's room.

Passing Hawberk's door again I saw him still at work on the armor, but I did not stop, and stepping out into Bleecker Street, I followed it to Wooster, skirted the grounds of the Lethal Chamber, and crossing Washington Park, went straight to my rooms in the Benedick. Here I lunched comfortably, read the *Herald* and the *Meteor*, and finally went to the steel safe in my bedroom and set the time combination. The three and three-quarter minutes which it is necessary to wait, while the time lock is opening, are to me golden moments. From the instant I set the combination to the moment when I grasp the knobs and swing back the solid steel doors, I live in an ecstasy of expectation. Those moments must be like moments passed in Paradise. I know what I am to find at the end of the time limit. I know what the massive safe holds secure for me, for me alone, and the exquisite pleasure of waiting is hardly enhanced when the safe opens and I lift, from its velvet crown, a diadem of purest gold, blazing with diamonds. I do this every day, and yet the joy of waiting and at last touching again the diadem only seems to increase as the days pass. It is a diadem fit for a King among kings, an Emperor among emperors. The King in Yellow might scorn it, but it shall be worn by his royal servant.

I held it in my arms until the alarm on the safe rang harshly, and then tenderly, proudly, I replaced it and shut the steel doors. I walked slowly back into my study, which faces Washington Square, and leaned on the window sill. The afternoon sun poured into my windows, and a gentle breeze stirred the branches of the elms and maples in the park, now covered with buds and tender foliage. A flock of pigeons circled about the tower of the Memorial Church; sometimes alighting on the purple tiled roof, sometimes wheeling downward to the lotos fountain in front of the marble arch. The gardeners were busy with the flower beds around the fountain, and the freshly-turned earth smelled sweet and spicy. A lawn mower, drawn by a fat white horse, clinked across the green sward, and watering carts poured showers of spray over the asphalt drives. Around the statue of Peter Stuyvesant, which in 1897 had replaced the monstrosity supposed to represent Garibaldi, children played in the spring sunshine, and nurse girls wheeled elaborate baby-carriages with a reckless disregard for the pasty-faced occupants, which could probably be explained by the presence of half a dozen trim dragoon troopers languidly lolling on the benches. Through the trees, the Washington Memorial Arch glistened like silver in the sunshine, and beyond, on the eastern extremity of the square, the gray stone barracks of the dragoons and the white granite artillery stables were alive with color and motion.

I looked at the Lethal Chamber on the corner of the square opposite. A few curious people still lingered about the gilded iron railing, but inside the grounds the paths were deserted. I watched the fountains ripple and sparkle; the sparrows had already found this new bathing nook, and the basins were crowded with the dusty-feathered little things. Two or three white peacocks picked their way across the lawns, and a drab-colored pigeon sat so motionless on the arm of one of the Fates that it seemed to be a part of the sculptured stone.

As I was turning carelessly away, a slight commotion in the group of curious loiterers around the gates attracted my attention. A young man had entered, and was advancing with nervous strides along the gravel path which leads to the bronze doors of the Lethal Chamber. He paused a moment before the Fates, and as he raised his head to those three mysterious faces, the pigeon rose from its sculptured perch, circled about for a moment and wheeled to the east. The young man pressed his hands to his face, and then with an undefinable gesture sprang up the marble steps, the bronze doors closed behind him, and half an hour later the loiterers slouched away, and the frightened pigeon returned to its perch in the arms of Fate.

I put on my hat and went out into the park for a little walk before dinner. As I crossed the central driveway a group of officers passed, and one of them called out, "Hello, Hildred," and came back to shake hands with me. It was my cousin Louis, who stood smiling and tapping his spurred heels with his riding-whip.

"Just back from Westchester," he said; "been doing the bucolic; milk and curds, you know, dairy-maids in sunbonnets, who say 'haeow' and 'I don't think' when you tell them they are pretty. I'm nearly dead for a square meal at Delmonico's. What's the news?"

"There is none," I replied pleasantly. "I saw your regiment coming in this morning."

"Did you? I didn't see you. Where were you?"

"In Mr. Wilde's window."

"Oh, hell!" he began impatiently, "that man is stark mad! I don't understand why you————"

He saw how annoyed I felt by this outburst, and begged my pardon.

"Really, old chap," he said, "I don't mean to run down a man you like, but for the life of me, I can't see what the deuce you find in common with Mr. Wilde. He's not well-bred, to put it generously; he's hideously deformed; his head is the head of a criminally insane person. You know yourself he's been in an asylum————"

"So have I," I interrupted calmly.

Louis looked startled and confused for a moment, but recovered and slapped me heartily on the shoulder.

"You were completely cured," he began, but I stopped him again.

"I suppose you mean that I was simply acknowledged never to have been insane."

"Of course that—that's what I meant," he laughed.

I disliked his laugh because I knew it was forced, but I nodded gaily and asked him where he was going. Louis looked after his brother officers who had now almost reached Broadway.

"We had intended to sample a Brunswick cocktail, but to tell you the truth I was anxious for an excuse to go and see Hawberk instead. Come along, I'll make you my excuse."

We found old Hawberk, neatly attired in a fresh spring suit, standing at the door of his shop and sniffing the air.

"I had just decided to take Constance for a little stroll before dinner," he replied to the impetuous volley of questions from Louis. "We thought of walking on the park terrace along the North River."

At that moment Constance appeared and grew pale and rosy by turns as

Louis bent over her small gloved fingers. I tried to excuse myself, alleging an engagement up-town, but Louis and Constance would not listen, and I saw I was expected to remain and engage old Hawberk's attention. After all, it would be just as well if I kept my eye on Louis, I thought, and when they hailed a Spring Street horsecar, I got in after them and took my seat beside the armorer.

The beautiful line of parks and granite terraces overlooking the wharves along the North River, which were built in 1910 and finished in the autumn of 1917, had become one of the most popular promenades in the metropolis. They extended from the battery to 190th Street, overlooking the noble river and affording a fine view of the Jersey shore and the Highlands opposite. Cafés and restaurants were scattered here and there among the trees, and twice a week military bands from the garrison played in the kiosques on the parapets.

We sat down in the sunshine on the bench at the foot of the equestrian statue of General Sheridan. Constance tipped her sunshade to shield her eyes, and she and Louis began a murmuring conversation which was impossible to catch. Old Hawberk, leaning on his ivory-headed cane, lighted an excellent cigar, the mate to which I politely refused, and smiled at vacancy. The sun hung low above the Staten Island woods, and the bay was dyed with golden hues reflected from the sunwarmed sails of the shipping in the harbor.

Brigs, schooners, yachts, clumsy ferry-boats, their decks swarming with people, railroad transports carrying lines of brown, blue and white freight cars, stately sound steamers, *declassé* tramp steamers, coasters, dredgers, scows, and everywhere pervading the entire bay impudent little tugs puffing and whistling officiously;—these were the crafts which churned the sunlit waters as far as the eye could reach. In calm contrast to the hurry of sailing vessel and steamer, a silent fleet of white warships lay motionless in midstream.

Constance's merry laugh aroused me from my reverie.

"What *are* you staring at?" she inquired.

"Nothing—the fleet," I smiled.

Then Louis told us what the vessels were, pointing out each by its relative position to the old Red Fort on Governor's Island.

"That little cigar-shaped thing is a torpedo boat," he explained; "there are four more lying close together. They are the 'Tarpon,' the 'Falcon,' the 'Sea Fox' and the 'Octopus.' The gun-boats just above are the 'Princeton,' the 'Champlain,' the 'Still Water' and the 'Erie.' Next to them lie the cruisers 'Farragut' and 'Los Angeles,' and above them the battle-ships 'California' and 'Dakota,' and the 'Washington' which is the flag-ship. Those two squatty-looking chunks of metal which are anchored there off Castle William are the double-turreted monitors 'Terrible' and 'Magnificent'; behind them lies the ram, 'Osceola.'"

Constance looked at him with deep approval in her beautiful eyes. "What loads of things you know for a soldier," she said, and we all joined in the laugh which followed.

Presently Louis rose with a nod to us and offered his arm to Constance, and they strolled away along the river wall. Hawberk watched them for a moment and then turned to me.

"Mr. Wilde was right," he said. "I have found the missing tassets and left cuissard of the 'Prince's Emblazoned' in a vile old junk garret in Pell Street."

"998?" I inquired, with a smile.

"Yes."

"Mr. Wilde is a very intelligent man," I observed.

"I want to give him the credit of this most important discovery," continued Hawberk. "And I intend it shall be known that he is entitled to the fame of it."

"He won't thank you for that," I answered sharply; "please say nothing about it."

"Do you know what it is worth?" said Hawberk.

"No, fifty dollars, perhaps."

"It is valued at five hundred, but the owner of the 'Prince's Emblazoned' will give two thousand dollars to the person who completes his suit; that reward also belongs to Mr. Wilde."

"He doesn't want it! He refuses it!" I answered angrily. "What do you know about Mr. Wilde? He doesn't need the money. He is rich—or will be—richer than any living man except myself. What will we care for money then—what will we care, he and I, when—when————"

"When what?" demanded Hawberk, astonished.

"You will see," I replied, on my guard again.

He looked at me narrowly, much as Doctor Archer used to, and I knew he thought I was mentally unsound. Perhaps it was fortunate for him that he did not use the word lunatic just then.

"No," I replied to his unspoken thought, "I am not mentally weak; my mind is as healthy as Mr. Wilde's. I do not care to explain just yet what I have on hand, but it is an investment which will pay more than mere gold, silver and precious stones. It will secure the happiness and prosperity of a continent—yes, a hemisphere!"

"Oh," said Hawberk.

"And eventually," I continued more quietly, "it will secure the happiness of the whole world."

"And incidentally your own happiness and prosperity as well as Mr. Wilde's?"

"Exactly," I smiled. But I could have throttled him for taking that tone.

He looked at me in silence for a while and then said very gently, "Why don't you give up your books and studies, Mr. Castaigne, and take a tramp among the mountains somewhere or other? You used to be fond of fishing. Take a cast or two at the trout in the Rangelys."

"I don't care for fishing any more," I answered, without a shade of annoyance in my voice.

"You used to be fond of everything," he continued; "athletics, yachting, shooting, riding————"

"I have never cared to ride since my fall," I said quietly.

"Ah, yes, your fall," he repeated, looking away from me.

I thought this nonsense had gone far enough, so I turned the conversation back to Mr. Wilde; but he was scanning my face again in a manner highly offensive to me.

"Mr. Wilde," he repeated, "do you know what he did this afternoon? He came downstairs and nailed a sign over the hall door next to mine; it read:

Mr. Wilde,
Repairer of Reputations.
3d Bell.

Do you know what a Repairer of Reputations can be?"

"I do," I replied, suppressing the rage within.

"Oh," he said again.

Louis and Constance came strolling by and stopped to ask if we would join them. Hawberk looked at his watch. At the same moment a puff of smoke shot from the casemates of Castle William, and the boom of the sunset gun rolled across the water and was re-echoed from the Highlands opposite. The flag came running down from the flag-pole, the bugles sounded on the white decks of the warships, and the first electric light sparkled out from the Jersey shore.

As I turned into the city with Hawberk I heard Constance murmur something to Louis which I did not understand; but Louis whispered, "My darling," in reply; and again, walking ahead with Hawberk through the square I heard a murmur of "sweetheart," and "my own Constance," and I knew the time had nearly arrived when I should speak of important matters with my cousin Louis.

III

One morning early in May I stood before the steel safe in my bedroom, trying on the golden jewelled crown. The diamonds flashed fire as I turned to the mirror, and the heavy beaten gold burned like a halo about my head. I remembered Camilla's agonized scream and the awful words echoing through the dim streets of Carcosa. They were the last lines in the first act, and I dared not think of what followed—dared not, even in the spring sunshine, there in my own room, surrounded with familiar objects, reassured by the bustle from the street and the voices of the servants in the hallway outside. For those poisoned words had dropped slowly into my heart, as death-sweat drops upon a bed-sheet and is absorbed. Trembling, I put the diadem from my head and wiped my forehead, but I thought of Hastur and of my own rightful ambition, and I remembered Mr. Wilde as I had last left him, his face all torn and bloody from the claws of that devil's creature, and what he said—ah, what he said! The alarm bell in the safe began to whirr harshly, and I knew my time was up; but I would not heed it, and replacing the flashing circlet upon my head, I turned defiantly to the mirror. I stood for a long time absorbed in the changing expression of my own eyes. The mirror reflected a face which was like my own, but whiter, and so thin that I hardly recognized it. And all the time I kept repeating between my clenched teeth, "The day has come! the day has come!" while the alarm in the safe whirred and clamored, and the diamonds sparkled and flamed above my brow. I heard a door open but did not heed it. It was only when I saw two faces in the mirror;—it was only when another face rose over my shoulder, and two other eyes met mine. I wheeled like a flash and seized a long knife from my dressing-table, and my cousin sprang back very pale, crying: "Hildred! for God's sake!" Then as my hand fell, he said: "It is I, Louis, don't you know me?" I stood silent. I could not have spoken for my life. He walked up to me and took the knife from my hand.

"What is all this?" he inquired, in a gentle voice. "Are you ill?"

"No," I replied. But I doubt if he heard me.

"Come, come, old fellow," he cried, "take off that brass crown and toddle into the study. Are you going to a masquerade? What's all this theatrical tinsel anyway?"

I was glad he thought the crown was made of brass and paste, yet I didn't like him any the better for thinking so. I let him take it from my hand, knowing it was best to humor him. He tossed the splendid diadem in the air, and catching it, turned to me smiling.

"It's dear at fifty cents," he said. "What's it for?"

I did not answer, but took the circlet from his hands, and placing it in the safe, shut the massive steel door. The alarm ceased its infernal din at once. He watched me curiously, but did not seem to notice the sudden ceasing of the alarm. He did, however, speak of the safe as a biscuit box. Fearing lest he might examine the combination, I led the way into my study. Louis threw himself on the sofa and flicked at flies with his eternal riding-whip. He wore his fatigue uniform with the braided jacket and jaunty cap, and I noticed that his riding-boots were all splashed with red mud.

"Where have you been?" I inquired.

"Jumping mud creeks in Jersey," he said. "I haven't had time to change yet; I was rather in a hurry to see you. Haven't you got a glass of something? I'm dead tired; been in the saddle twenty-four hours."

I gave him some brandy from my medicinal store, which he drank with a grimace.

"Damned bad stuff," he observed. "I'll give you an address where they sell brandy that is brandy."

"It's good enough for my needs," I said indifferently. "I use it to rub my chest with." He stared and flicked at another fly.

"See here, old fellow," he began, "I've got something to suggest to you. It's four years now that you've shut yourself up here like an owl, never going anywhere, never taking any healthy exercise, never doing a damn thing but poring over those books up there on the mantelpiece."

He glanced along the row of shelves. "Napoleon, Napoleon, Napoleon!" he read. "For heaven sake, have you nothing but Napoleons there?"

"I wish they were bound in gold," I said. "But wait, yes, there is another book, *The King in Yellow*." I looked him steadily in the eye.

"Have you never read it?" I asked.

"I? No, thank God! I don't want to be driven crazy."

I saw he regretted his speech as soon as he had uttered it. There is only one word which I loathe more than I do lunatic and that word is crazy. But I controlled myself and asked him why he thought *The King in Yellow* dangerous.

"Oh, I don't know," he said, hastily. "I only remember the excitement it created and the denunciations from pulpit and press. I believe the author shot himself after bringing forth this monstrosity, didn't he?"

"I understand he is still alive," I answered.

"That's probably true," he muttered; "bullets couldn't kill a fiend like that."

"It is a book of great truths," I said.

"Yes," he replied, "of 'truths' which send men frantic and blast their lives. I don't care if the thing is, as they say, the very supreme essence of art. It's a crime to have written it and I for one shall never open its pages."

"Is that what you have come to tell me?" I asked.

"No," he said, "I came to tell you that I am going to be married."

I believe for a moment my heart ceased to beat, but I kept my eyes on his face.

"Yes," he continued, smiling happily, "married to the sweetest girl on earth."

"Constance Hawberk," I said mechanically.

"How did you know?" he cried, astonished. "I didn't know it myself until that evening last April, when we strolled down to the embankment before dinner."

"When is it to be?" I asked.

"It was to have been next September, but an hour ago a despatch came ordering our regiment to the Presidio, San Francisco. We leave at noon to-morrow. To-morrow," he repeated. "Just think, Hildred, to-morrow I shall be the happiest fellow that ever drew breath in this jolly world, for Constance will go with me."

I offered him my hand in congratulation, and he seized and shook it like the good-natured fool he was—or pretended to be.

"I am going to get my squadron as a wedding present," he rattled on. "Captain and Mrs. Louis Castaigne, eh, Hildred?"

Then he told me where it was to be and who were to be there, and made me promise to come and be best man. I set my teeth and listened to his boyish chatter without showing what I felt, but—

I was getting to the limit of my endurance, and when he jumped up, and, switching his spurs till they jingled, said he must go, I did not detain him.

"There's one thing I want to ask of you," I said quietly.

"Out with it, it's promised," he laughed.

"I want you to meet me for a quarter of an hour's talk to-night."

"Of course, if you wish," he said, somewhat puzzled. "Where?"

"Anywhere, in the park there."

"What time, Hildred?"

"Midnight."

"What in the name of—" he began, but checked himself and laughingly assented. I watched him go down the stairs and hurry away, his sabre banging at every stride. He turned into Bleecker Street, and I knew he was going to see Constance. I gave him ten minutes to disappear and then followed in his footsteps, taking with me the jewelled crown and the silken robe embroidered with the Yellow Sign. When I turned into Bleecker Street, and entered the doorway which bore the sign,

MR. WILDE,
REPAIRER OF REPUTATIONS.
3d Bell..

I saw old Hawberk moving about in his shop, and imagined I heard Constance's voice in the parlor; but I avoided them both and hurried up the trembling stairways to Mr. Wilde's apartment. I knocked, and entered without ceremony. Mr. Wilde lay groaning on the floor, his face covered with blood, his clothes torn to shreds. Drops of blood were scattered about over the carpet, which had also been ripped and frayed in the evidently recent struggle.

"It's that cursed cat," he said, ceasing his groans, and turning his colorless eyes to me; "she attacked me while I was asleep. I believe she will kill me yet."

This was too much, so I went into the kitchen and seizing a hatchet from the pantry, started to find the infernal beast and settle her then and there. My search was fruitless, and after a while I gave it up and came back to find Mr. Wilde squatting on his high chair by the table. He had washed his face and changed his clothes. The great furrows which the cat's claws had ploughed up in his face he had filled with collodion, and a rag hid the wound in his throat. I told him I should kill the cat when I came across her, but he only shook his head and turned to the open ledger before him. He read name after name of the people who had come to him in regard to their reputation, and the sums he had amassed were startling.

"I put on the screws now and then," he explained.

"One day or other some of these people will assassinate you," I insisted.

"Do you think so?" he said, rubbing his mutilated ears.

It was useless to argue with him, so I took down the manuscript entitled *Imperial Dynasty of America,* for the last time I should ever take it down in Mr. Wilde's study. I read it through, thrilling and trembling with pleasure. When I had finished, Mr. Wilde took the manuscript and, turning to the dark passage which leads from his study to his bedchamber, called out in a loud voice, "Vance." Then for the first time, I noticed a man crouching there in the shadow. How I had overlooked him during my search for the cat, I cannot imagine.

"Vance, come in," cried Mr. Wilde.

The figure rose and crept toward us, and I shall never forget the face that he raised to mine, as the light from the window illuminated it.

"Vance, this is Mr. Castaigne," said Mr. Wilde. Before he had finished speaking, the man threw himself on the ground before the table, crying and gasping, "Oh, God! Oh, my God! Help me! Forgive me—Oh, Mr. Castaigne, keep that man away. You cannot, you cannot mean it! You are different—save me! I am broken down—I was in a madhouse and now—when all was coming right—when I had forgotten the King—the King in Yellow and—but I shall go mad again—I shall go mad—"

His voice died into a choking rattle, for Mr. Wilde had leapt on him and his right hand encircled the man's throat. When Vance fell in a heap on the floor, Mr. Wilde clambered nimbly into his chair again, and rubbing his mangled ears with the stump of his hand, turned to me and asked me for the ledger. I reached it down from the shelf and he opened it. After a moment's searching among the beautifully written pages, he coughed complacently, and pointed to the name Vance.

"Vance," he read aloud, "Osgood Oswald Vance." At the sound of his voice, the man on the floor raised his head and turned a convulsed face to Mr. Wilde. His eyes were injected with blood, his lips tumefied. "Called April 28th," continued Mr. Wilde. "Occupation, cashier in the Seaforth National Bank; has served a term of forgery at Sing Sing, from whence he was transferred to the Asylum for the Criminal Insane. Pardoned by the Governor of New York, and discharged from the Asylum, January 19, 1918. Reputation damaged at Sheepshead Bay. Rumors that he lives beyond his income. Reputation to be repaired at once. Retainer $1,500.

"Note.—Has embezzled sums amounting to $30,000 since March 20th, 1919, excellent family, and secured present position through uncle's influence. Father President of Seaforth Bank."

I looked at the man on the floor.

"Get up, Vance," said Mr. Wilde in a gentle voice. Vance rose as if hypnotized. "He will do as we suggest now," observed Mr. Wilde, and opening the manuscript, he read the entire history of the Imperial Dynasty of America. Then in a kind and soothing murmur he ran over the important points with Vance, who stood like one stunned. His eyes were so blank and vacant that I imagined he had become half-witted, and remarked it to Mr. Wilde who replied that it was of no consequence anyway. Very patiently we pointed out to Vance what his share in the affair would be, and he seemed to understand after a while. Mr. Wilde explained the manuscript, using several volumes on Heraldry, to substantiate the result of his researches. He mentioned the establishment of the Dynasty in Carcosa, the lakes which connected Hastur, Aldebaron and the mystery of the Hyades. He spoke of Cassilda and Camilla, and sounded the cloudy depths of Demhe, and the Lake of Hali. "The scalloped tatters of the King in Yellow must hide Yhtill forever," he muttered, but I do not believe Vance heard him. Then by degrees he led Vance along the ramifications of the Imperial family, to Uoht and Thale, from Naotalba and Phantom of Truth, to Aldones, and then tossing aside his manuscript and notes, he began the wonderful story of the Last King. Fascinated and thrilled, I watched him. He threw up his head, his long arms were stretched out in a magnificent gesture of pride and power, and his eyes blazed deep in their sockets like two emeralds. Vance listened stupefied. As for me, when at last Mr. Wilde had finished, and pointing to me, cried, "The cousin of the King!" my head swam with excitement.

Controlling myself with a superhuman effort, I explained to Vance why I alone was worthy of the crown and why my cousin must be exiled or die. I made him understand that my cousin must never marry, even after renouncing all his claims, and how that least of all he should marry the daughter of the Marquis of Avonshire and bring England into the question. I showed him a list of thousands of names which Mr. Wilde had drawn up; every man whose name was there had received the Yellow Sign which no living human being dared disregard. The city, the state, the whole land, were ready to rise and tremble before the Pallid Mask.

The time had come, the people should know the son of Hastur, and the whole world bow to the Black Stars which hang in the sky over Carcosa.

Vance leaned on the table, his head buried in his hands. Mr. Wilde drew a rough sketch on the margin of yesterday's *Herald* with a bit of lead pencil. It was a plan of Hawberk's rooms. Then he wrote out the order and affixed the seal, and shaking like a palsied man, I signed my first writ of execution with my name Hildred-Rex.

Mr. Wilde clambered to the floor and unlocking the cabinet, took a long square box from the first shelf. This he brought to the table and opened. A new knife lay in the tissue paper inside and I picked it up and handed it to Vance, along with the order and the plan of Hawberk's apartment. Then Mr. Wilde told Vance he could go; and he went, shambling like an outcast of the slums.

I sat for a while watching the daylight fade behind the square tower of the Judson Memorial Church, and finally, gathering up the manuscript and notes, took my hat and started for the door.

Mr. Wilde watched me in silence. When I had stepped into the hall I looked back. Mr. Wilde's small eyes were still fixed on me. Behind him, the shadows gathered in the fading light. Then I closed the door behind me and went out into the darkening streets.

I had eaten nothing since breakfast, but I was not hungry. A wretched half-starved creature, who stood looking across the street at the Lethal Chamber, noticed me and came up to tell me a tale of misery. I gave him money, I don't know why, and he went away without thanking me. An hour later another outcast approached and whined his story. I had a blank bit of paper in my pocket, on which was traced the Yellow Sign and I handed it to him. He looked at it stupidly for a moment, and then with an uncertain glance at me, folded it with what seemed to me exaggerated care and placed it in his bosom.

The electric lights were sparkling among the trees, and the new moon shone in the sky above the Lethal Chamber. It was tiresome waiting in the square; I wandered from the Marble Arch to the artillery stables, and back again to the lotos fountain. The flowers and grass exhaled a fragrance which troubled me. The jet of the fountain played in the moonlight, and the musical splash of falling drops reminded me of the tinkle of chained mail in Hawberk's shop. But it was not so fascinating, and the dull sparkle of the moonlight on the water brought no such sensations of exquisite pleasure, as when the sunshine played over the polished steel of a corselet on Hawberk's knee. I watched the bats darting and turning above the water plants in the fountain basin, but their rapid, jerky flight set my nerves on edge, and I went away again to walk aimlessly to and fro among the trees.

The artillery stables were dark, but in the cavalry barracks the officers' windows were brilliantly lighted, and the sallyport was constantly filled with troopers in fatigue, carrying straw and harness and baskets filled with tin dishes.

Twice the mounted sentry at the gates was changed while I wandered up and down the asphalt walk. I looked at my watch. It was nearly time. The lights in the barracks went out one by one, the barred gate was closed, and every minute or two an officer passed in through the side wicket, leaving a rattle of accoutrements and a jingle of spurs on the night air. The square had become very silent. The last homeless loiterer had been driven away by the gray-coated park policeman, the car tracks along Wooster Street were deserted, and the only sound which broke the stillness was the stamping of the sentry's horse and the ring of his sabre against the saddle pommel. In the barracks, the officers' quarters were still lighted, and military servants passed and repassed before the bay windows. Twelve o'clock sounded from the new spire of St. Francis Xavier, and at the last stroke of the sad-toned bell a figure passed through the wicket beside the portcullis, returned the salute of the sentry, and crossing the street, entered the square and advanced toward the Benedick apartment house.

"Louis," I called.

The man pivoted on his spurred heels and came straight toward me.

"Is that you, Hildred?"

"Yes, you are on time."

I took his offered hand, and we strolled toward the Lethal Chamber.

He rattled on about his wedding and the graces of Constance, and their future prospects, calling my attention to his captain's shoulderstraps, and the triple gold arabesque on his sleeve and fatigue cap. I believe I listened as much to the music of his spurs and sabre as I did to his boyish babble, and at last we stood under the elms on the Fourth Street corner of the square opposite the Lethal Chamber. Then he laughed and asked me what I wanted with him. I motioned him to a seat on a bench under the electric light, and sat down beside him. He looked at me curiously, with that same searching glance which I hate and fear so in doctors. I felt the insult of his look, but he did not know it, and I carefully concealed my feelings.

"Well, old chap," he enquired, "what can I do for you?"

I drew from my pocket the manuscript and notes of the *Imperial Dynasty of America,* and looking him in the eye, said:

"I will tell you. On your word as a soldier, promise me to read this manuscript from beginning to end, without asking me a question. Promise me to read these notes in the same way, and promise me to listen to what I have to tell later."

"I promise, if you wish it," he said pleasantly. "Give me the paper, Hildred."

He began to read, raising his eyebrows with a puzzled whimsical air, which made me tremble with suppressed anger. As he advanced, his eyebrows contracted, and his lips seemed to form the word, "rubbish."

Then he looked slightly bored, but apparently for my sake read, with an attempt at interest, which presently ceased to be an effort. He started when in the closely-written pages he came to his own name, and when he came to mine he lowered the paper, and looked sharply at me for a moment. But he kept his word, and resumed his reading, and I let the half-formed question die on his lips unanswered. When he came to the end and read the signature of Mr. Wilde, he folded the paper carefully and returned it to me. I handed him the notes, and he settled back, pushing his fatigue cap up to his forehead, with a boyish gesture, which I remembered so well in school. I watched his face as he read, and when he finished I took the notes with the manuscript, and placed them in my pocket. Then I unfolded a scroll marked with the Yellow Sign. He saw the sign, but he did not seem to recognize it, and I called his attention to it somewhat sharply.

"Well," he said, "I see it. What is it?"

"It is the Yellow Sign," I said, angrily.

"Oh, that's it, is it?" said Louis, in that flattering voice, which Doctor Archer used to employ with me, and would probably have employed again, had I not settled his affair for him.

I kept my rage down and answered as steadily as possible, "Listen, you have engaged your word?"

"I am listening, old chap," he replied soothingly.

I began to speak very calmly.

"Dr. Archer, having by some means become possessed of the secret of the Imperial Succession, attempted to deprive me of my right, alleging that because of a fall from my horse four years ago, I had become mentally deficient. He presumed to place me under restraint in his own house in hopes of either driving me insane or poisoning me. I have not forgotten it. I visited him last night and the interview was final."

Louis turned quite pale, but did not move. I resumed triumphantly, "There are yet three people to be interviewed in the interests of Mr. Wilde and myself. They are my cousin Louis, Mr. Hawberk, and his daughter Constance."

Louis sprang to his feet and I arose also, and flung the paper marked with the Yellow Sign to the ground.

"Oh, I don't need that to tell you what I have to say," I cried with a laugh of triumph. "You must renounce the crown to me, do you hear, to *me*."

Louis looked at me with a startled air, but recovering himself said kindly, "Of course I renounce the—what is it I must renounce?"

"The crown," I said angrily.

"Of course," he answered, "I renounce it. Come, old chap, I'll walk back to your rooms with you."

"Don't try any of your doctor's tricks on me," I cried, trembling with fury. "Don't act as if you think I am insane."

"What nonsense," he replied. "Come, it's getting late, Hildred."

"No," I shouted, "you must listen. You cannot marry, I forbid it. Do you hear? I forbid it. You shall renounce the crown, and in reward I grant you exile, but if you refuse you shall die."

He tried to calm me but I was roused at last, and drawing my long knife barred his way.

Then I told him how they would find Dr. Archer in the cellar with his throat open, and I laughed in his face when I thought of Vance and his knife, and the order signed by me.

"Ah, you are the King," I cried, "but I shall be King. Who are you to keep me from Empire over all the habitable earth? I was born the cousin of a king, but I shall be King!"

Louis stood white and rigid before me. Suddenly a man came running up Fourth Street, entered the gate of the Lethal Temple, traversed the path to the bronze doors at full speed, and plunged into the death chamber with the cry of one demented, and I laughed until I wept tears, for I had recognized Vance, and knew that Hawberk and his daughter were no longer in my way.

"Go," I cried to Louis, "you have ceased to be a menace. You will never marry Constance now, and if you marry any one else in your exile, I will visit you as I did my doctor last night. Mr. Wilde takes charge of you to-morrow." Then I turned and darted into South Fifth Avenue, and with a cry of terror Louis dropped his belt and sabre and followed me like the wind. I heard him close behind me at the corner of Bleecker Street, and I dashed into the doorway under Hawberk's sign. He cried, "Halt, or I fire!" but when he saw that I flew up the stairs leaving Hawberk's shop below, he left me, and I heard him hammering and shouting at their door as though it were possible to arouse the dead.

Mr. Wilde's door was open, and I entered crying, "It is done, it is done! Let the nations rise and look upon their King!" but I could not find Mr. Wilde, so I went to the cabinet and took the splendid diadem from its case. Then I drew on the white silk robe, embroidered with the Yellow Sign, and placed the crown upon my head. At last I was King, King by my right in Hastur, King because I knew the mystery of the Hyades, and my mind had sounded the depths of the Lake of Hali. I was King! The first gray pencillings of dawn would raise a tempest which would shake two hemispheres. Then as I stood, my every nerve pitched to the highest tension, faint with the joy and splendor of my thought, without, in the dark passage, a man groaned.

I seized the tallow dip and sprang to the door. The cat passed me like a demon, and the tallow dip went out, but my long knife flew swifter than she, and I heard her screech, and I knew that my knife had found her. For a moment I listened to her tumbling and thumping about in the darkness, and then when her frenzy ceased, I lighted a lamp and raised it over my head. Mr. Wilde lay on the floor with his throat torn open. At first I thought he was dead, but as I looked, a green sparkle came into his sunken eyes, his mutilated hand trembled, and then a spasm stretched his mouth from ear to ear. For a moment my terror and despair gave place to hope, but as I bent over him his eyeballs rolled clean around in his head, and he died. Then while I stood, transfixed with rage and despair, seeing my crown, my empire, every hope and every ambition, my very life, lying prostrate there with the dead master, *they* came, seized me from behind, and bound me until my veins stood out like cords, and my voice failed with the paroxysms of my frenzied screams. But I still raged, bleeding and infuriated among them, and more than one policeman felt my sharp teeth. Then when I could no longer move they came nearer; I saw old Hawberk, and behind him my cousin Louis' ghastly face, and farther away, in the corner, a woman, Constance, weeping softly.

"Ah! I see it now!" I shrieked. "You have seized the throne and the empire. Woe! woe to you who are crowned with the crown of the King in Yellow!"

[EDITOR'S NOTE—Mr. Castaigne died yesterday in the Asylum for Criminal Insane.]

Oliver Onions

The Beckoning Fair One

Oliver Onions is one of the most powerful and elegant of all ghost story writers and his masterpiece is the novella, "The Beckoning Fair One." As a study of gradual mental deterioration, it is admired by Lovecraft, Blackwood and Aickman, and has been called the greatest single ghost story. It also represents complex levels of interpretation, all tightly woven and consistent. It is, for instance, an allegory of the fate of a man who rejects reality for art. It may well be a realistic portrayal of descent into psychosis. It is certainly a story that calls the nature of reality into doubt. Onions' first book of ghost stories, *Widdershins* (1911), is one of the rarest and best ghost books of the century; the stories are widely reprinted and influential, including the one herein. It is interesting to note the similarities between "The Beckoning Fair One" and "How Love Came to Professor Guildea" and "Clara Militch," its apparent precursors. It is in some ways superior even to "The Turn of the Screw."

1

The three or four "To Let" boards had stood within the low paling as long as the inhabitants of the little triangular "square" could remember, and if they had ever been vertical it was a very long time ago. They now overhung the palings each at its own angle, and resembled nothing so much as a row of wooden choppers, ever in the act of falling upon some passer-by, yet never cutting off a tenant for the old house from the stream of his fellows. Not that there was ever any great "stream" through the square; the stream passed a furlong and more away, beyond the intricacy of tenements and alleys and byways that had sprung up since the old house had been built, hemming it in completely; and probably the house itself was only suffered to stand pending the falling-in of a lease or two, when doubtless a clearance would be made of the whole neighborhood.

It was of bloomy old red brick, and built into its walls were the crowns and clasped hands and other insignia of insurance companies long since defunct. The children of the secluded square had swung upon the low gate at the end of the entrance-alley until little more than the solid top bar of it remained, and the alley itself ran past boarded basement windows on which tramps had chalked their cryptic marks. The path was washed and worn uneven by the spilling of water from the eaves of the encroaching next house, and cats and dogs had made the approach their own. The chances of a tenant did not seem such as to warrant the keeping of the "To Let" boards in a state of legibility and repair, and as a matter of fact they were not so kept.

For six months Oleron had passed the old place twice a day or oftener, on his way from his lodgings to the room, ten minutes' walk away, he had taken to work in; and for six months no hatchet-like notice-board had fallen across his path. This might have been due to the fact that he usually took the other side of the square. But he chanced one morning to take the side that ran past the broken gate and the rain-worn entrance alley, and to pause before one of the inclined boards. The board bore, besides the agent's name, the announcement, written apparently about the time of Oleron's own early youth, that the key was to be had at Number Six.

Now Oleron was already paying for his separate bedroom and workroom, more than an author who, without private means, habitually disregards his public, can afford; and he was paying in addition a small rent for the storage of the greater part of his grandmother's furniture. Moreover, it invariably happened that the book he wished to read in bed was at his working-quarters half a mile and more away, while the note or letter he had sudden need of during the day was as likely as not to be in the pocket of another coat hanging behind his bedroom door. And there were other inconveniences in having a divided domicile. Therefore Oleron, brought suddenly up by the hatchet-like notice-board, looked first down through some scanty privet bushes at the boarded basement windows, then up at the blank and grimy windows of the first floor, and so up to the second floor and the flat stone coping of the leads. He stood for a minute thumbing his lean and shaven jaw; then, with another glance at the board, he walked slowly across the square to Number Six.

He knocked, and waited for two or three minutes, but, although the door stood open, received no answer. He was knocking again when a long-nosed man in shirt-sleeves appeared.

"I was arsking a blessing on our food," he said in severe explanation.

Oleron asked if he might have the key of the old house; and the long-nosed man withdrew again.

Oleron waited for another five minutes on the step; then the man, appearing again and masticating some of the food of which he had spoken, announced that the key was lost.

"But you won't want it," he said. "The entrance door isn't closed, and a push'll open any of the others. I'm a agent for it, if you're thinking of taking it—"

Oleron recrossed the square, descended the two steps at the broken gate, passed along the alley, and turned in at the old wide doorway. To the right, immediately within the door, steps descended to the roomy cellars, and the staircase before him had a carved rail, and was broad and handsome and filthy. Oleron ascended it, avoiding contact with the rail and wall, and stopped at the first landing. A door facing him had been boarded up, but he pushed at that on his right hand, and an insecure bolt or staple yielded. He entered the empty first floor.

He spent a quarter of an hour in the place, and then came out again. Without mounting higher, he descended and recrossed the square to the house of the man who had lost the key.

"Can you tell me how much the rent is?" he asked.

The man mentioned a figure, the comparative lowness of which seemed accounted for by the character of the neighbourhood and the abominable state of unrepair of the place.

"Would it be possible to rent a single floor?"

The long-nosed man did not know; they might. . . .

"Who are they?"

The man gave Oleron the name of a firm of lawyers in Lincoln's Inn.

"You might mention my name—Barrett," he added.

Pressure of work prevented Oleron from going down to Lincoln's Inn that afternoon, but he went on the morrow, and was instantly offered the whole house as a purchase for fifty pounds down, the remainder of the purchase money to remain on mortgage. It took him half an hour to disabuse the lawyer's mind of the idea that he wished anything more of the place than to rent a single floor of it. This made certain hums and haws of a difference, and the lawyer was by no means certain that it lay within his power to do as Oleron suggested; but it was finally extracted from him that, provided the notice-boards were allowed to remain up, and that, provided it was agreed that in the event of the whole house letting, the arrangement should terminate automatically without further notice, something might be done. That the old place should suddenly let over his head seemed to Oleron the slightest of risks to take, and he promised a decision within a week. On the morrow he visited the house again, went through it from top to bottom, and then went home to his lodgings to take a bath.

He was immensely taken with that portion of the house he had already determined should be his own. Scraped clean and repainted, and with that old furniture of Oleron's grandmother's, it ought to be entirely charming. He went to the storage warehouse to refresh his memory of his half-forgotten belongings, and to take the measurements; and thence he went to a decorator's. He was very busy with his regular work, and could have wished that the notice-board had caught his attention either a few months earlier or else later in the year; but the quickest way would be to suspend work entirely until after his removal. . . .

A fortnight later his first floor was painted throughout in a tender, elder-flower white, the paint was dry, and Oleron was in the middle of his installation. He was animated, delighted; and he rubbed his hands as he polished and made disposals of his grandmother's effects—the tall lattice-paned china cupboard with its Derby and Mason and Spode, the large folding Sheraton table, the long, low bookshelves (he had had two of them "copied"), the chairs, the Sheffield candlesticks, the riveted rose-bowls. These things he set against his newly painted elder-white walls—walls of wood paneled in the happiest proportions, and molded and coffered to the low-seated window-recesses in a mood of gaiety and rest that the builders of rooms no longer know. The ceilings were lofty, and faintly painted with an old pattern of stars; even the tapering moldings of his iron fireplace were as delicately designated as jewelry; and Oleron walked about rubbing his hands, frequently stopping for the mere pleasure of the glimpses from white room to white room. . . .

"Charming, charming!" he said to himself. "I wonder what Elsie Bengough will think of this!"

He bought a bolt and a Yale lock for his door, and shut off his quarters from the rest of the house. If he now wanted to read in bed, his book could be had for stepping into the next room. All the time, he thought how exceedingly lucky he was to get the place. He put up a hat-rack in the little square hall, and hung up his hats and caps and coats; and passers through the small triangular square late at night, looking up over the little serried row of wooden "To Let" hatchets, could see the light within Oleron's red blinds, or else the sudden darkening of one blind and the illumination of another, as Oleron, candlestick in hand, passed from room to room, making final settlings of his furniture, or preparing to resume the work that his removal had interrupted.

2

As far as the chief business of his life—his writing—was concerned, Paul Oleron treated the world a good deal better than he was treated by it; but he seldom took the trouble to strike a balance, or to compute how far, at forty-four years of age, he was behind his points on the handicap. To have done so wouldn't have altered matters, and it might have depressed Oleron. He had chosen his path, and was committed to it beyond possibility of withdrawal. Perhaps he had chosen it in the days when he had been easily swayed by something a little disinterested, a little generous, a little noble; and had he ever thought of questioning himself, he would still have held to it that a life without nobility and generosity and disinterestedness was no life for him. Only quite recently, and rarely, had he even vaguely suspected that there was more in it than this; but it was no good anticipating the day when, he supposed, he would reach that maximum point of his powers beyond which he must inevitably decline, and be left face to face with the question whether it would not have profited him better to have ruled his life by less exigent ideals.

In the meantime, his removal into the old house with the insurance marks built into its brick merely interrupted *Romilly Bishop* at the fifteenth chapter.

As this tall man with the lean, ascetic face moved about his new abode, arranging, changing, altering, hardly yet into his working stride again, he gave the impression of almost spinster-like precision and nicety. For twenty years past, in a score of lodgings, garrets, flats, and rooms furnished and unfurnished, he had been accustomed to do many things for himself, and he had discovered that it saves time and temper to be methodical. He had arranged with the wife of the long-nosed Barrett, a stout Welsh woman with a falsetto voice, the Merionethshire accent of which long residence in London had not perceptibly modified, to come across the square each morning to prepare his breakfast and also to "turn the place out" on Saturday mornings; and for the rest, he even welcomed a little housework as a relaxation from the strain of writing.

His kitchen, together with the adjoining strip of an apartment into which a modern bath had been fitted, overlooked the alley at the side of the house; and at one end of it was a large closet with a door, and a square sliding hatch in the upper part of the door. This had been a powder-closet, and through the hatch the elaborately dressed head had been thrust to receive the click and puff of the powder-pistol. Oleron puzzled a little over this closet; then, as its use occurred to him, he smiled faintly, a little moved, he knew not by what. . . . He would have to put it to a very different purpose from its original one; it would probably have to serve as a larder. . . . It was in this closet that he made a discovery. The back of it was shelved, and, rummaging on an upper shelf that ran deeply into the wall, Oleron found a couple of mushroom-shaped old wooden wig-stands. He did not know how they had come to be there. Doubtless the painters had turned them up somewhere or other, and had put them there. But his five rooms, as a whole, were short of cupboard and closet-room; and it was only by the exercise of some ingenuity that he was able to find places for the bestowal of his household linen, his boxes, and his seldom-used but not-to-be-destroyed accumulation of papers.

It was early spring that Oleron entered on his tenancy, and he was anxious to have *Romilly* ready for publication in the coming autumn. Nevertheless, he did not intend to force its production. Should it demand longer in the doing, so much the worse; he realized its importance, its crucial importance, in his artistic development, and it must have its own length and time. In the workroom he had recently left he had been making excellent progress; *Romilly* had begun, as the saying is, to speak and act of herself; and he did not doubt she would continue to do so the moment the distraction of his removal was over. This distraction was almost over; he told himself it was time he pulled himself together again; and on a March morning he went out and returned again with two great bunches of yellow daffodils, placed one bunch on his mantelpiece between the Sheffield sticks and the other on the table before him, and took out the half-completed manuscript of *Romilly Bishop.*

But before beginning work he went to a small rosewood cabinet and took from a drawer his check-book and pass-book. He totted them up, and his monk-like face grew thoughtful. His installation had cost him more than he had intended it should, and his balance was rather less than fifty pounds, with no immediate prospect of more.

"Hm! I'd forgotten rugs and chintz curtains and so forth mounted up so," said Oleron. "But it would have been a pity to spoil the place for the want of ten pounds or so. . . . Well, *Romilly* simply *must* be out for the autumn, that's all. So here goes————"

He drew his papers toward him.

But he worked badly; or, rather, he did not work at all. The square outside had its own noises, frequent and new, and Oleron could only hope that he would speedily become accustomed to these. First came hawkers, with their carts and cries; at midday the children, returning from school, trooped into the square and swung on Oleron's gate; and when the children had departed again for afternoon school, an itinerant musician with a mandoline posted himself beneath Oleron's window and began to strum. This was a not unpleasant distraction, and Oleron, pushing up his window, threw the man a penny. Then he returned to his table again. . . .

But it was no good. He came to himself, at long intervals, to find that he had been looking about his room and wondering how it had formerly been furnished—whether a settee in buttercup or petunia satin had stood under the farther window, whether from the center molding of the light lofty ceiling had depended a glimmering crystal chandelier, or where the tambour-frame or the piquet-table had stood. . . .No, it was no good; he had far better be frankly doing nothing than getting fruitlessly tired; and he decided that he would take a walk, but, chancing to sit down for a moment, dozed in his chair instead.

"This won't do," he yawned when he awoke at half-past four in the afternoon; "I must do better than this to-morrow————"

And he felt so deliciously lazy that for some minutes he even contemplated the breach of an appointment he had for the evening.

The next morning he sat down to work without even permitting himself to answer one of his three letters—two of them tradesmen's accounts, the third a note from Miss Bengough, forwarded from his old address. It was a jolly day of white and blue, with a gay noisy wind and a subtle turn in the color of growing things; and over and over again, once or twice a minute, his room became suddenly light and then subsided again, as the shining white cloud rolled northeastward over the square. The soft fitful illumination was reflected in the polished surface of the table and even in the footworn old floor; and the morning noises had begun again.

Oleron made a pattern of dots on the paper before him, and then broke off to move the jar of daffodils exactly opposite the center of a creamy panel. Then he wrote a sentence that ran continuously for a couple of lines, after which it broke off into notes and jottings. For a time he succeeded in persuading himself that in making these memoranda he was really working; then he rose and began to pace his room. As he did so, he was struck by an idea. It was that the place might possibly be a little better for more positive color. It was, perhaps, a thought *too* pale—mild and sweet as a kind old face, but a little devitalized, even wan. . . . Yes, decidedly it would bear a robuster note—more and richer flowers, and possibly some warm and gay stuff for cushions for the window-seats. . . .

"Of course, I really can't afford it," he muttered, as he went for a two-foot and began to measure the width of the window recesses. . . .

In stooping to measure a recess, his attitude suddenly changed to one of interest and attention. Presently he rose again, rubbing his hands with gentle glee.

"Oho, oho!" he said. "These look to me very much like windowboxes, nailed up. We must look into this! Yes, those are boxes, or I'm . . . oho, this is an adventure!"

On that wall of his sitting-room there were two windows (the third was in another corner), and, beyond the open bedroom door, on the same wall, was another. The seats of all had been painted, repainted, and painted again; and Oleron's investigating finger had barely detected the old nailheads beneath the paint. Under the ledge over which he stooped an old keyhole also had been puttied up. Oleron took out his penknife.

He worked carefully for five minutes, and then went into the kitchen for a hammer and chisel. Driving the chisel cautiously under the seat, he started the whole lid slightly. Again using the penknife, he cut along the hinged edge and outward along the ends; and then he fetched a wedge and a wooden mallet.

"Now for our little mystery————" he said.

The sound of the mallet on the wedge seemed, in that sweet and pale apartment, somehow a little brutal—nay, even shocking. The paneling rang and rattled and vibrated to the blows like a sounding-board. The whole house seemed to echo; from the roomy cellarage to the garrets above, a flock of echoes seemed to awake; and the sound got a little on Oleron's nerve. All at once he paused, fetched a duster, and muffled the mallet. . . . When the edge was sufficiently raised he put his fingers under it and lifted. The paint flaked and starred a little; the rusty old nails squeaked and grunted; and the lid came up, laying open the box beneath. Oleron looked into it. Save for a couple of inches of scurf and mold and old cobwebs it was empty.

"No treasure there," said Oleron, a little amused that he should have fancied there might have been. "*Romilly* will still have to be out by the autumn. Let's have a look at the others."

He turned to the second window.

The raising of the two remaining seats occupied him until well into the afternoon. That of the bedroom, like the first, was empty; but from the second seat of his sitting-room he drew out something yielding and folded and furred over an inch thick with dust. He carried the object into the kitchen, and having swept it over a bucket, took a duster to it.

It was some sort of a large bag, of an ancient frieze-like material, and when unfolded it occupied the greater part of the small kitchen floor. In shape it was an irregular, a very irregular, triangle, and it had a couple of wide flaps, with the remains of straps and buckles. The patch that had been uppermost in the folding was of a faded yellowish brown; but the rest of it was of shades of crimson that varied according to the exposure of the parts of it.

"Now whatever can that have been?" Oleron mused as he stood surveying it. . . . "I give it up. Whatever it is, it's settled my work for today, I'm afraid————"

He folded the object up carelessly and thrust it into a corner of the kitchen; then, taking pans and brushes and an old knife, he returned to the sitting-room and began to scrape and to wash and to line with paper his newly discovered receptacles. When he had finished, he put his spare boots and books and papers into them; and he closed the lids again, amused with his little adventure, but also a little anxious for the hour to come when he should settle fairly down to his work again.

3

It piqued Oleron a little that his friend, Miss Bengough, should dismiss with a glance the place he himself had found so singularly winning. Indeed she scarcely lifted her eyes to it. But then she had always been more or less like that—a little indifferent to the graces of life, careless of appearances, and perhaps a shade more herself when she ate biscuits from a paper bag than when she dined with greater observance of the convenances. She was an unattached journalist of thirty-four, large, showy, fair as butter, pink as a dog-rose, reminding one of a florist's picked specimen bloom, and given to sudden and ample movements and moist and explosive utterances. She "pulled a better living out of the pool" (as she expressed it) than Oleron did; and by cunningly disguised puffs of drapers and haberdashers she "pulled" also the greater part of her very varied wardrobe. She left small whirlwinds of air behind her when she moved, in which her veils and scarves fluttered and spun.

Oleron heard the flurry of her skirts on his staircase and her single loud knock at his door when he had been a month in his new abode. Her garments brought in the outer air, and she flung a bundle of ladies' journals down on a chair.

"Don't knock off for me," she said across a mouthful of large-headed hatpins as she removed her hat and veil. "I didn't know whether you were straight yet, so I've brought some sandwiches for lunch. You've got coffee, I suppose?—No, don't get up—I'll find the kitchen————"

"Oh, that's all right, I'll clear these things away. To tell the truth, I'm rather glad to be interrupted," said Oleron.

He gathered his work together and put it away. She was already in the kitchen; he heard the running of water into the kettle. He joined her, and ten minutes later followed her back to the sitting-room with the coffee and sandwiches on a tray. They sat down, with the tray on a small table between them.

"Well, what do you think of the new place?" Oleron asked as she poured out coffee.

"Hm! . . . Anybody'd think you were going to get married, Paul."

He laughed.

"Oh, no. But it's an improvement on some of them, isn't it?"

"Is it? I suppose it is; I don't know. I liked the last place, in spite of the black ceiling and no watertap. How's *Romilly?*"

Oleron thumbed his chin.

"Hm! I'm rather ashamed to tell you. The fact is, I've not got on very well with it. But it will be all right on the night, as you used to say."

"Stuck?"

"Rather stuck."

"Got any of it you care to read to me? . . ."

Oleron had long been in the habit of reading portions of his work to Miss

Bengough occasionally. Her comments were always quick and practical, sometimes directly useful, sometimes indirectly suggestive. She, in return for his confidence, always kept all mention of her own work sedulously from him. His, she said, was "real work"; hers merely filled space, not always even grammatically.

"I'm afraid there isn't," Oleron replied, still meditatively dry-shaving his chin. Then he added, with a little burst of candor, "The fact is, Elsie, I've not written—not actually written—very much more of it—*any* more of it, in fact. But, of course, that doesn't mean I haven't progressed. I've progressed, in one sense, rather alarmingly. I'm now thinking of reconstructing the whole thing."

Miss Bengough gave a gasp. "Reconstructing!"

"Making Romilly herself a different type of woman. Somehow, I've begun to feel that I'm not getting the most out of her. As she stands, I've certainly lost interest in her to some extent."

"But—but————" Miss Bengough protested, "you had her so real, *so living*, Paul!"

Oleron smiled faintly. He had been quite prepared for Miss Bengough's disapproval. He wasn't surprised that she liked Romilly as she at present existed; she would. Whether she realized it or not, there was much of herself in his fictitious creation. Naturally Romilly would seem "real," "living," to her. . . .

"But are you really serious, Paul?" Miss Bengough asked presently, with a round-eyed stare.

"Quite serious."

"You're really going to scrap those fifteen chapters?"

"I didn't exactly say that."

"That fine, rich love-scene?"

"I should only do it reluctantly, and for the sake of something I thought better."

"And that beautiful, *beautiful* description of Romilly on the shore?"

"It wouldn't necessarily be wasted," he said a little uneasily.

But Miss Bengough made a large and windy gesture, and then let him have it.

"Really, you are *too* trying!" she broke out. "I do wish sometimes you'd remember you're human, and live in a world! You know I'd be the *last* to wish you to lower your standard one inch, but it wouldn't be lowering it to bring it within human comprehension. Oh, you're sometimes altogether too godlike! . . . Why, it would be a wicked, criminal waste of your powers to destroy those fifteen chapters! Look at it reasonably, now. You've been working for nearly twenty years; you've now got what you've been working for almost within your grasp; your affairs are at a most critical stage (oh, don't tell me; I know you're about at the end of your money); and here you are, deliberately proposing to withdraw a thing that will probably make your name, and to substitute for it something that ten to one nobody on earth will ever want to read—and small blame to them! Really, you try my patience!"

Oleron had shaken his head slowly as she had talked. It was an old story between them. The noisy, able practical journalist was an admirable friend—up to a certain point; beyond that . . . well, each of us knows that point beyond which we stand alone. Elsie Bengough sometimes said that had she had one-tenth part of Oleron's genius there were few things she could not have done—thus making that genius a quantitatively divisible thing, a sort of ingredient, to be added to or to be subtracted from in the admixture of his work. That it was a qualitative thing, essential, indivisible, informing, passed her comprehension. Their spirits parted company at that point. Oleron knew it. She did not appear to know it.

"Yes, yes, yes," he said a little wearily, by-and-by, "practically you're quite right, entirely right, and I haven't a word to say. If I could only turn *Romilly* over to you you'd make an enormous success of her. But that can't be, and I, for my part, am seriously doubting whether she's worth my while. You know what that means."

"What does it mean?" she demanded bluntly.

"Well," he said, smiling wanly, "what *does* it mean when you're convinced a thing isn't worth doing? You simply don't do it."

Miss Bengough's eyes swept the ceiling for assistance against this impossible man.

"What utter rubbish!" she broke out at last. "Why, when I saw you last you were simply oozing *Romilly*; you were turning her off at the rate of four chapters a week; if you hadn't moved you'd have had her three parts done by now. What on earth possessed you to move right in the middle of your most important work?"

Oleron tried to put her off with a recital of inconveniences, but she wouldn't have it. Perhaps in her heart she partly suspected the reason. He was simply mortally weary of the narrow circumstances of his life. He had had twenty years of it—twenty years of garrets and roof-chambers and dingy flats and shabby lodgings, and he was tired of dinginess and shabbiness. The reward was as far off as ever—or if it was not, he no longer cared as once he would have cared to put out his hand and take it. It is all very well to tell a man who is at the point of exhaustion that only another effort is required of him; if he cannot make it he is as far off as ever. . . .

"Anyway," Oleron summed up, "I'm happier here than I've been for a long time. That's some sort of a justification."

"And doing no work," said Miss Bengough pointedly.

At that a trifling petulance that had been gathering in Oleron came to a head.

"And why should I do nothing but work?" he demanded. "How much happier am I for it? I don't say I don't love my work—when it's done; but I hate doing it. Sometimes it's an intolerable burden that I simply long to be rid of. Once in many weeks it has a moment, one moment, of glow and thrill for me; I remember the days when it was all glow and thrill; and now I'm forty-four, and it's becoming drudgery. Nobody wants it; I'm ceasing to want it myself; and if any ordinary sensible man were to ask me whether I didn't think I was a fool to go on, I think I should agree that I was."

Miss Bengough's comely pink face was serious.

"But you knew all that, many, many years ago, Paul—and still you chose it," she said in a low voice.

"Well, and how should I have known?" he demanded. "I didn't know. I was told so. My heart, if you like, told me so, and I thought I knew. Youth always thinks it knows; then one day it discovers that it is nearly fifty————"

"Forty-four, Paul————"

"—forty-four, then—and it finds that the glamour isn't in front, but behind. Yes, I knew and chose, if *that's* knowing and choosing . . . but it's a costly choice we're called on to make when we're young!"

Miss Bengough's eyes were on the floor. Without moving them she said: "You're not regretting it, Paul?"

"Am I not?" he took her up. "Upon my word, I've lately thought I am! What *do* I get in return for it all?"

"You know what you get," she replied.

He might have known from her tone what else he could have had for the holding up of a finger—herself. She knew, but could not tell him, that he could have done no better thing for himself. Had he, any time these ten years, asked her to marry him, she would have replied quietly, "Very well; when?" He had never thought of it. . . .

"Yours is the real work," she continued quietly. "Without you we jackals couldn't exist. You and a few like you hold everything upon your shoulders."

For a minute there was a silence. Then it occurred to Oleron that this was common vulgar grumbling. It was not his habit. Suddenly he rose and began to stack cups and plates on the tray.

"Sorry you catch me like this, Elsie," he said, with a little laugh. . . . "No, I'll take them out; then we'll go for a walk, if you like. . . ."

He carried out the tray, and then began to show Miss Bengough round his flat. She made few comments. In the kitchen she asked what an old faded square of reddish frieze was, that Mrs. Barrett used as a cushion for her wooden chair.

"That? I should be glad if you could tell *me* what it is," Oleron replied as he unfolded the bag and related the story of its finding in the window-seat.

"I think I know what it is," said Miss Bengough. "It's been used to wrap up a harp before putting it into its case."

"By Jove, that's probably just what it was," said Oleron. "I could make neither head nor tail of it. . . ."

They finished the tour of the flat, and returned to the sitting-room.

"And who lives in the rest of the house?" Miss Bengough asked.

"I dare say a tramp sleeps in the cellar occasionally. Nobody else."

"Hm! . . . Well, I'll tell you what I think about it, if you like."

"I should like."

"You'll never work here."

"Oh?" said Oleron quickly. "Why not?"

"You'll never finish *Romilly* here. Why, I don't know, but you won't. I know it. You'll have to leave before you get on with that book."

He mused for a moment, and then said:

"Isn't that a little—prejudiced, Elsie?"

"Perfectly ridiculous. As an argument it hasn't a leg to stand on. But there it is," she replied, her mouth once more full of the large-headed hat pins.

Oleron was reaching down his hat and coat. He laughed.

"I can only hope you're entirely wrong," he said, "for I shall be in a serious mess if *Romilly* isn't out in the autumn."

4

As Oleron sat by his fire that evening, pondering Miss Bengough's prognostication that difficulties awaited him in his work, he came to the conclusion that it would have been far better had she kept her beliefs to herself. No man does a thing better for having his confidence damped at the outset, and to speak of difficulties is in a sense to make them. Speech itself becomes a deterrent act, to which other discouragements accrete until the very event of which warning is given is as likely as not to come to pass. He heartily confounded her. An influence hostile to the completion of *Romilly* had been born.

And in some illogical, dogmatic way women seem to have, she had attached this antagonistic influence to his new abode. Was ever anything so absurd! "You'll never finish *Romilly* here." . . . Why not? Was this her idea of the luxury that saps the spring of action and brings a man down to indolence and dropping out of the race? The place was well enough—it was entirely charming, for that matter—but it was not so demoralizing as all that! No; Elsie had missed the mark that time. . . .

He moved his chair to look round the room that smiled, positively smiled, in the firelight. He too smiled, as if pity was to be entertained for a maligned apartment. Even that slight lack of robust color he had remarked was not noticeable in the soft glow. The drawn chintz curtains—they had a flowered and trellised pattern, with baskets and oaten pipes—fell in long quiet folds to the window-seats; the rows of bindings in old bookcases took the light richly; the last trace of sallowness had gone with the daylight; and, if the truth must be told, it had been Elsie herself who had seemed a little out of the picture.

That reflection struck him a little, and presently he returned to it. Yes, the room had, quite accidentally, done Miss Bengough a disservice that afternoon. It had, in some subtle but unmistakable way, placed her, marked a contrast of qualities. Assuming for the sake of argument the slightly ridiculous proposition that the room in which Oleron sat *was* characterized by a certain sparsity and lack of vigor; so much the worse for Miss Bengough; she certainly erred on the side of redundancy and general muchness. And if one must contrast abstract qualities, Oleron inclined to the austere in taste. . . .

Yes, here Oleron had made a distinct discovery; he wondered he had not made it before. He pictured Miss Bengough again as she had appeared that afternoon—large, showy, moistly pink, with that quality of the prize bloom exuding, as it were, from her; and instantly she suffered in his thought. He even recognized now that he had noticed something odd at the time, and that unconsciously his attitude, even while she had been there, had been one of criticism. The mechanism of her was a little obvious; her melting humidity was the result of analyzable processes; and behind her there had seemed to lurk some dim shape emblematic of mortality. He had never, during the ten years of their intimacy, dreamed for a moment of asking her to marry him; nonetheless, he now felt for the first time a thankfulness that he had not done so. . . .

Then, suddenly and swiftly, his face flamed that he should be thinking thus of his friend. What! Elsie Bengough, with whom he had spent weeks and weeks of afternoons—she, the good chum, on whose help he would have counted had all the rest of the world failed him—she, whose loyalty to him would not, he knew, swerve as long as there was breath in her—Elsie to be even in thought dissected thus! He was an ingrate and a cad. . . .

Had she been there in that moment he would have abased himself before her.

For ten minutes and more he sat, still gazing into the fire, with that humiliating red fading slowly from his cheeks. All was still within and without, save for a tiny musical tinkling that came from his kitchen—the dripping of water from an imperfectly turned-off tap into the vessel beneath it. Mechanically he began to beat with his fingers to the faintly heard falling of the drops; the tiny regular movement seemed to hasten that shameful withdrawal from his face. He grew cool once more; and when he resumed his meditation he was all unconscious that he took it up again at the same point. . . .

It was not only her florid superfluity of build that he had approached in the attitude of criticism; he was conscious also of the wide differences between her mind and his own. He felt no thankfulness that up to a certain point their natures had ever run companionably side by side; he was now full of questions beyond that point. Their intellects diverged; there was no denying it; and, looking back, he was inclined to doubt whether there had been any real coincidence. True, he had read his writings to her and she had appeared to speak comprehendingly and to the point; but what can a man do who, having assumed that another sees as he does, is suddenly brought up sharp by something that falsifies and discredits all that has gone before? He doubted all now. . . . It did for a moment occur to him that the man who demands of a friend more than can be given to him is in danger of losing that friend, but he put the thought aside.

Again he ceased to think, and again moved his finger to the distant dripping of the tap. . . .

And now (he resumed by-and-by), if these things were true of Elsie Bengough, they were also true of the creation of which she was the prototype—Romilly Bishop. And since he could say of Romilly what for very shame he could not say of Elsie, he gave his thoughts rein. He did so in that smiling, fire-lighted room, to the accompaniment of the faintly heard tap.

There was no longer any doubt about it; he hated the central character of his novel. Even as he had described her physically she overpowered the senses; she was coarse-fibered, overcolored, rank. It became true the moment he formulated his thought; Gulliver had described the Brobdingnagian maids-of-honor thus: and mentally and spiritually she corresponded—was unsensitive, limited, common. The model (he closed his eyes for a moment) —the model stuck out through fifteen vulgar and blatant chapters to such a pitch that, without seeing the reason, he had been unable to begin the sixteenth. He marveled that it had only just dawned upon him.

And *this* was to have been his Beatrice, his vision! As Elsie she was to have gone into the furnace of his art, and she was to have come out the Woman all men desire! Her thoughts were to have been culled from his own finest, her form from his dearest dreams, and her setting wherever he could find one fit for her worth. He had brooded long before making the attempt; then one day he had felt her stir within him as a mother feels a quickening, and he had begun to write; and so he had added chapter to chapter. . . .

And those fifteen sodden chapters were what he had produced!

Again he sat softly moving his finger. . . .

Then he bestirred himself.

She must go, all fifteen chapters of her. That was settled. For what was to take her place his mind was a blank; but one thing at a time; a man is not excused from taking the wrong course because the right one is not immediately revealed to him. Better would come if it was to come; in the meantime—

He rose, fetched the fifteen chapters, and read them over before he should drop them into the fire.

But instead of putting them into the fire he let them fall from his hand. He became conscious of the dripping of the tap again. It had a tinkling gamut of four or five notes, on which it rang irregular changes, and it was foolishly sweet and dulcimer-like. In his mind Oleron could see the gathering of each drop, its little tremble on the lip of the tap, and the tiny percussion of its fall "Plink—plunk," minimized almost to inaudibility. Following the lowest note there seemed to be a brief phrase, irregularly repeated; and presently Oleron found himself waiting for the recurrence of this phrase. It was quite pretty. . . .

But it did not conduce to wakefulness, and Oleron dozed over his fire.

When he awoke again the fire had burned low and the flames of the candles were licking the rims of the Sheffield sticks. Sluggishly he rose, yawned, went his nightly round of door-locks, and window-fastenings, and passed into his bedroom. Soon, he slept soundly.

But a curious little sequel followed on the morrow. Mrs. Barrett usually tapped, not at his door, but at the wooden wall beyond which lay Oleron's bed; and then Oleron rose, put on his dressing-gown, and admitted her. He was not conscious that as he did so that morning he hummed an air; but Mrs. Barrett lingered with her hand on the doorknob and her face a little averted and smiling.

"De-ar me!" her soft falsetto rose. "But that will be a very o-ald tune, Mr. Oleron. I will not have heard it this for-ty years!"

"What tune?" Oleron asked.

"The tune, indeed, that you was humming, sir."

Oleron had his thumb in the flap of a letter. It remained there.

"*I* was humming? . . . Sing it, Mrs. Barrett."

Mrs. Barrett prut-prutted.

"I have no voice for singing, Mr. Oleron; it was Ann Pugh was the singer of our family; but the tune will be very o-ald, and it is called 'The Beckoning Fair One.' "

"Try to sing it," said Oleron, his thumb still in the envelope; and Mrs. Barrett, with much dimpling and confusion, hummed the air.

"They do say it was sung to a harp, Mr. Oleron, and it will be very o-ald," she concluded.

"And *I* was singing that?"

"Indeed you was. I would not be likely to tell you lies."

With a "Very well—let me have breakfast," Oleron opened his letter; but the trifling circumstance struck him as more odd than he would have admitted to himself. The phrase he had hummed had been that which he had associated with the falling from the tap on the evening before.

5

Even more curious than that the commonplace dripping of an ordinary water-tap should have tallied so closely with an actually existing air was another result it had, namely, that it awakened, or seemed to awaken, in Oleron an abnormal sensitiveness to other noises of the old house. It has been remarked that silence obtains its fullest and most impressive quality when it is broken by some minute sound; and, truth to tell, the place was never still. Perhaps the mildness of the spring air operated on its torpid old timbers; perhaps Oleron's fires caused it to stretch its old anatomy; and certainly a whole world of insect life bored and burrowed in its baulks and joists. At any rate Oleron had only to sit quiet in his chair and to wait for a minute or two in order to become aware of such a change in the auditory scale as comes upon a man who, conceiving the midsummer woods to be motionless and still, all at once finds his ear sharpened to the crepitation of a myriad insects.

And he smiled to think of man's arbitrary distinction between that which has life and that which has not. Here, quite apart from such recognizable sounds as the scampering of mice, the falling of plaster behind his paneling, and the popping of purses or coffins from his fire, was a whole house talking to him had he but known its language. Beams settled with a tired sigh into their old mortises; creatures ticked in the walls; joists cracked, boards complained; with no palpable stirring of the air window-sashes changed their positions with a soft knock in their frames. And whether the place had life in this sense or not, it had at all events a winsome personality. It needed but an hour of musing for Oleron to conceive the idea that, as his own body stood in friendly relation to his soul, so, by an extension and an attenuation, his habitation might fantastically be supposed to stand in some relation to himself. He even amused himself with the far-fetched fancy that he might so identify himself with the place that some future tenant, taking possession, might regard it as in a sense haunted. It would be rather a joke if he, a perfectly harmless author, with nothing on his mind worse than a novel he had discovered he must begin again, should turn out to be laying the foundation of a future ghost! . . .

In proportion, however, as he felt this growing attachment to the fabric of his abode, Elsie Bengough, from being merely unattracted, began to show a dislike of the place that was more and more marked. And she did not scruple to speak of her aversion.

"It doesn't belong to today at all, for you especially it's bad," she said with decision. "You're only too ready to let go your hold on actual things and to slip into apathy; *you* ought to be in a place with concrete floors and a patent gas-meter and a tradesman's lift. And it would do you all the good in the world if you had a job that made you scramble and rub elbows with your fellow-men. Now, if I could get you a job, for, say, two or three days a week, one that would allow you heaps of time for your proper work—would you take it?"

Somehow, Oleron resented a little being diagnosed like this. He thanked Miss Bengough, but without a smile.

"Thank you, but I don't think so. After all each of us has his own life to live," he could not refrain from adding.

"His own life to live! . . . How long is it since you were out, Paul?"

"About two hours."

"I don't mean to buy stamps or to post a letter. How long is it since you had anything like a stretch?"

"Oh, some little time perhaps. I don't know."

"Since I was here last?"

"I haven't been out much."

"And has *Romilly* progressed much better for your being cooped up?"

"I think she has. I'm laying the foundations of her. I shall begin the actual writing presently."

It seemed as if Miss Bengough had forgotten their tussle about the first *Romilly.* She frowned, turned half away, and then quickly turned again.

"Ah! . . . So you've still got that ridiculous idea in your head?"

"If you mean," said Oleron slowly, "that I've discarded the old *Romilly,* and am at work on a new one, you're right. I have still got that idea in my head."

Something uncordial in his tone struck her; but she was a fighter. His own absurd sensitiveness hardened her. She gave a "Pshaw!" of impatience.

"Where is the old one?" she demanded abruptly.

"Why?" asked Oleron.

"I want to see it. I want to show some of it to you. I want, if you're not wool-gathering entirely, to bring you back to your senses."

This time it was he who turned his back. But when he turned round again he spoke more gently.

"It's no good, Elsie. I'm responsible for the way I go, and you must allow me to go it—even if it should seem wrong to you. Believe me, I am giving thought to it. . . . The manuscript? I was on the point of burning it, but I didn't. It's in that window-seat, if you must see it."

Miss Bengough crossed quickly to the window-seat, and lifted the lid. Suddenly she gave a little exclamation, and put the back of her hand to her mouth. She spoke over her shoulder:

"You ought to knock those nails in, Paul," she said.

He strode to her side.

"What? What is it? What's the matter?" he asked. "I did knock them in—or, rather, pulled them out."

"You left enough to scratch with," she replied, showing her hand. From the upper wrist to the knuckle of the little finger a welling red wound showed.

"Good—Gracious!" Oleron ejaculated. . . . "Here, come to the bathroom and bathe it quickly—"

He hurried her to the bathroom, turned on warm water, and bathed and cleansed the bad gash. Then, still holding the hand, he turned cold water on it, uttering broken phrases of astonishment and concern.

"Good Lord, how did that happen! As far as I knew I'd . . . is this water too cold? Does that hurt? I can't imagine how on earth . . . there; that'll do—"

"No—one moment longer—I can bear it," she murmured, her eyes closed. . . .

Presently he led her back to the sitting-room and bound the hand in one of his handkerchiefs; but his face did not lose its expression of perplexity. He had spent half a day in opening and making serviceable the three window-boxes, and he could not conceive how he had come to leave an inch and a half of rusty nail standing in the wood. He himself had opened the lids of each of them a dozen times and had not noticed any nail; but there it was. . . .

"It shall come out now, at all events," he muttered, as he went for a pair of pincers. And he made no mistake about it that time.

Elsie Bengough had sunk into a chair, and her face was rather white; but in her hand was the manuscript of *Romilly*. She had not finished with *Romilly* yet. Presently she returned to the charge.

"Oh, Paul, it will be the greatest mistake you ever, *ever* made if you do not publish this!" she said.

He hung his head, genuinely distressed. He couldn't get that incident of the nail out of his head, and *Romilly* occupied a second place in his thoughts for the moment. But still she insisted; and when presently he spoke it was almost as if he asked her pardon for something.

"What can I say, Elsie? I can only hope that when you see the new version, you'll see how right I am. And if in spite of all you *don't* like her, well . . ." he made a hopeless gesture. "Don't you see that I *must* be guided by my own lights?"

She was silent.

"Come, Elsie," he said gently. "We've got along well so far; don't let us split on this."

The last words had hardly passed his lips before he regretted them. She had been nursing her injured hand, with her eyes once more closed; but her lips and lids quivered simultaneously. Her voice shook as she spoke.

"I can't help saying it, Paul, but you are so greatly changed."

"Hush, Elsie," he murmured soothingly; "you've had a shock; rest for a while. How could I change?"

"I don't know, but you are. You've not been yourself ever since you came here. I wish you'd never seen the place. It's stopped your work, it's making you into a person I hardly know, and it's made me horribly anxious about you. . . . Oh, how my hand is beginning to throb!"

"Poor child!" he murmured. "Will you let me take you to a doctor and have it properly dressed?"

"No—I shall be all right presently—I'll keep it raised—"

She put her elbow on the back of her chair, and the bandaged hand rested lightly on his shoulder.

At that touch an entirely new anxiety stirred suddenly within him. Hundreds of times previously, on their jaunts and excursions, she had slipped her hand within his arm as she might have slipped it into the arm of a brother, and he had accepted the little affectionate gesture as a brother might have accepted it. But now, for the first time, there rushed into his mind a hundred startling questions. Her eyes were still closed, and her head had fallen pathetically back; and there was a lost and ineffable smile on her parted lips. The truth broke in upon him. Good God! . . . And he had never divined it!

And stranger than all was that, now that he did see that she was lost in love of him, there came to him, not sorrow and humility and abasement, but something else that he struggled in vain against—something entirely strange and new, that, had he analyzed it, he would have found to be petulance and irritation and resentment and ungentleness. The sudden selfish prompting mastered him before he was aware. He all but gave it words. What was she doing there at all? Why was she not getting on with her own work? Why was she here interfering with his? Who had given her this guardianship over him that lately she had put forward so assertively?—"Changed?" It was she, not himself, who had changed. . . .

But by the time she had opened her eyes again he had overcome his resentment sufficiently to speak gently, albeit with reserve.

"I wish you would let me take you to a doctor."

She rose.

"No, thank you, Paul," she said. "I'll go now. If I need a dressing I'll get one; take the other hand, please. Good-by—"

He did not attempt to detain her. He walked with her to the foot of the stairs. Halfway along the narrow alley she turned.

"It would be a long way to come if you happened not to be in," she said: "I'll send you a postcard the next time."

At the gate she turned again.

"Leave here, Paul," she said, with a mournful look. "Everything's wrong with this house."

Then she was gone.

Oleron returned to his room. He crossed straight to the windowbox. He opened the lid and stood long looking at it. Then he closed it again and turned away.

"That's rather frightening," he muttered. "It's simply not possible that I should not have removed that nail. . . ."

6

Oleron knew very well what Elsie had meant when she had said that her next visit would be preceded by a postcard. She, too, had realized that at last, at last he knew—knew, and didn't want her. It gave him a miserable, pitiful pang, therefore, when she came again within a week, knocking at the door unannounced. She spoke from the landing; she did not intend to stay, she said; and he had to press her before she would so much as enter.

Her excuse for calling was that she had heard of an inquiry for short stories that he might be wise to follow up. He thanked her. Then, her business over, she seemed anxious to get away again. Oleron did not seek to detain her; even he saw through the pretext of the stories; and he accompanied her down the stairs.

But Elsie Bengough had no luck whatever in that house. A second accident befell her. Halfway down the staircase there was the sharp sound of splintering wood, and she checked a loud cry. Oleron knew the woodwork to be old, but he himself had ascended and descended frequently enough without mishap. . . .

Elsie had put her foot through one of the stairs.

He sprang to her side in alarm.

"Oh, I say! My poor girl!"

She laughed hysterically.

"It's my weight—I know I'm getting fat—"

"Keep still—let me clear these splinters away," he muttered between his teeth.

She continued to laugh and sob that it was her weight—she was getting fat—

He thrust downward at the broken boards. The extrication was no easy matter, and her torn boot showed him how badly the foot and ankle within it must be abraded.

"Good God—good God!" he muttered over and over again.

"I shall be too heavy for anything soon," she sobbed and laughed.

But she refused to reascend and to examine her hurt.

"No, let me go quickly—let me go quickly," she repeated.

"But it's a frightful gash!"

"No—not so bad—let me get away quickly—I'm—I'm not wanted."

At her words, that she was not wanted, his head dropped as if she had given him a buffet.

"Elsie!" he choked, brokenly and shocked.

But she too made a quick gesture, as if she put something violently aside.

"Oh, Paul, not *that*—not *you*—of course I do mean that too in a sense—oh, you know what I mean! . . . But if the other can't be, spare me this now! I—I wouldn't have come, but—but oh, I did, I *did* try to keep away!"

It was intolerable, heartbreaking; but what could he do—what could he say? He did not love her. . . .

"Let me go—I'm not wanted—let me take away what's left of me—"

"Dear Elsie—you are very dear to me—"

But again she made the gesture, as of putting something violently aside.

"No, not that—not anything less—don't offer me anything less—leave me a little pride—"

"Let me get my hat and coat—let me take you to a doctor," he muttered.

But she refused. She refused even the support of his arm. She gave another unsteady laugh.

"I'm sorry I broke your stairs, Paul. . . . You will go and see about the short stories, won't you?"

He groaned.

"Then if you won't see a doctor, will you go across the square and let Mrs. Barrett look at you? Look, there's Barrett passing now—"

The long-nosed Barrett was looking curiously down the alley, but as Oleron was about to call him he made off without a word. Elsie seemed anxious for nothing so much as to be clear of the place, and finally promised to go straight to a doctor, but insisted on going alone.

"Good-by," she said.

And Oleron watched her until she was past the hatchet-like "To Let" boards, as if he feared that even they might fall upon her and maim her.

That night Oleron did not dine. He had far too much on his mind. He walked from room to room of his flat, as if he could have walked away from Elsie Bengough's haunting cry that still rang in his ears. "I'm not wanted—don't offer me anything less—let me take away what's left of me—"

Oh, if he could only have persuaded himself that he loved her!

He walked until twilight fell, then, without lighting candles, he stirred up the fire and flung himself into a chair.

Poor, poor Elsie! . . .

But even while his heart ached for her, it was out of the question. If only he had known! If only he had used common observation! But those walks, those sisterly takings of the arm—what a fool he had been! . . . Well, it was too late now. It was she, not he, who must now act—act by keeping away. He would help her all he could. He himself would not sit in her presence. If she came, he would hurry her out again as fast as he could. . . . Poor, poor Elsie!

His room grew dark; the fire burned dead; and he continued to sit, wincing from time to time as a fresh tortured phrase rang again in his ears.

Then suddenly, he knew not why, he found himself anxious for her in a new sense—uneasy about her personal safety. A horrible fancy that even then she might be looking over an embankment down into dark water, that she might even now be glancing up at the hook on the door, took him. Women had been known to do those things. . . . Then there would be an inquest, and he himself would be called upon to identify her, and would be asked how she had come by an ill-healed wound on the hand and a bad abrasion of the ankle. Barrett would say that he had seen her leaving his house. . . .

Then he recognized that his thoughts were morbid. By an effort of will he put them aside, and sat for a while listening to the faint creakings and tickings and rappings within his paneling. . . .

If only he could have married her! . . . But he couldn't. Her face had risen before him again as he had seen it on the stairs, drawn with pain and ugly and swollen with tears. Ugly—yes, positively blubbered; if tears were women's weapons, as they were said to be, such tears were weapons turning against themselves . . . suicide again. . . .

Then all at once he found himself attentively considering her two accidents.

Extraordinary they had been, both of them. He *could not* have left that old nail standing in the wood; why, he had fetched tools specially from the kitchen; and he was convinced that that step that had broken beneath her weight had been as sound as the others. It was inexplicable. If these things could happen, anything could happen. There was not a beam nor a jamb in the place that might not fall without warning, not a plank that might not crash inward, not a nail that might not become a dagger. The whole place was full of life even now; as he sat there in the dark he heard its crowds of noises as if the house had been one great microphone. . . .

Only half conscious that he did so, he had been sitting for some time identifying these noises, attributing to each crack or creak or knock its material cause; but there was one noise which, again not fully conscious of the omission, he had not sought to account for. It had last come some minutes ago; it came again now—a sort of soft sweeping rustle that seemed to hold an almost inaudible minute crackling. For half a minute or so it had Oleron's attention; then his heavy thoughts were of Elsie Bengough again.

He was nearer to loving her in that moment than he had ever been. He thought how to some men their loved ones were but the dearer for those poor mortal blemishes that tell us we are but sojourners on earth, with a common fate not far distant that makes it hardly worth while to do anything but love for the time remaining. Strangling sobs, blearing tears, bodies buffeted by sickness, hearts and minds callous and hard with the rubs of the world— how little love there would be were these things a barrier to love! In that sense he did love Elsie Bengough. What her happiness had never moved in him her sorrow almost woke. . . .

Suddenly his meditation went. His ear had once more become conscious of that soft and repeated noise—the long sweep with the almost inaudible crackle in it. Again and again it came, with a curious insistence, and urgency. It quickened a little as he became increasingly attentive . . . it seemed to Oleron that it grew louder. . . .

All at once he started bolt upright in his chair, tense and listening. The silky rustle came again; he was trying to attach it to something. . . .

The next moment he had leapt to his feet, unnerved and terrified. His chair hung poised for a moment, and then went over, setting the fire-irons clattering as it fell. There was only one noise in the world like that which had caused him to spring thus to his feet. . . .

The next time it came Oleron felt behind him at the empty air with his hand, and backed slowly until he found himself against the wall.

"God in Heaven!" The ejaculation broke from Oleron's lips. The sound had ceased.

The next moment he had given a high cry.

"What is it? What's there? *Who's* there?"

A sound of scuttling caused his knees to bend under him for a moment; but that, he knew, was a mouse. That was not something that his stomach turned sick and his mind reeled to entertain. That other sound, the like of which was not in the world, had now entirely ceased; and again he called. . . .

He called and continued to call; and then another terror, a terror of the sound of his own voice, seized him. He did not dare to call again. His shaking hand went to his pocket for a match, but found none. He thought there might be matches on the mantelpiece—

He worked his way to the mantelpiece round a little recess, without for a moment leaving the wall. Then his hand encountered the mantelpiece, and groped along it. A box of matches fell to the hearth. He could just see them in the firelight, but his hand could not pick them up until he had cornered them inside the fender.

Then he rose and struck a light.

The room was as usual. He struck a second match. A candle stood on the table. He lighted it, and the flame sank for a moment and then burned up clear. Again he looked round.

There was nothing.

There was nothing; but there had been something, and might still be something. Formerly, Oleron had smiled at the fantastic thought that, by a merging and interplay of identities between himself and his beautiful room, he might be preparing a ghost for the future; it had not occurred to him *that there might have been a similar merging and coalescence in the past.* Yet with this staggering impossibility he was now face to face. Something did persist in the house; it had a tenant other than himself; and that tenant, whatsoever or whosoever, had appalled Oleron's soul by producing the sound of a woman brushing her hair.

7

Without quite knowing how he came to be there Oleron found himself striding over the loose board he had temporarily placed on the step broken by Miss Bengough. He was hatless and descending the stairs. Not until later did there return to him a hazy memory that he had left the candle burning on the table, had opened the door no wider than was necessary to allow the passage of his body, and had sidled out, closing the door softly behind him. At the foot of the stairs another shock awaited him. Something dashed with a flurry up from the disused cellars and disappeared out of the door. It was only a cat, but Oleron gave a childish sob.

He passed out of the gate, and stood for a moment under the "To Let" boards, plucking foolishly at his lip and looking up at the glimmer of light behind one of his red blinds. Then, still looking over his shoulder, he moved stumblingly up the square. There was a small public-house round the corner; Oleron had never entered it; but he entered it now, and put down a shilling that missed the counter by inches.

"B—b—bran—brandy," he said, and then stooped to look for the shilling.

He had the little sawdusted bar to himself; what company there was— carters and laborers and the small tradesmen of the neighborhood—was gathered in the farther compartment, beyond the space where the white-haired landlady moved among her taps and bottles. Oleron sat down on a hardwood settee with a perforated seat, drank half his brandy, and then, thinking he might as well drink it as spill it, finished it.

Then he fell to wondering which of the men whose voices he heard across the public-house would undertake the removal of his effects on the morrow.

In the meantime he ordered more brandy.

For he did not intend to go back to that room where he had left the candle burning. Oh no! He couldn't have faced even the entry and the staircase with the broken step—certainly not that pith-white, fascinating room. He would go back for the present to his old arrangement, of workroom and separate sleeping-quarters; he would go to his old landlady at once—presently— when he had finished his brandy—and see if she could put him up for the night. His glass was empty now. . . .

He rose, had it refilled, and sat down again.

And if anybody asked his reason for removing again? Oh, he had reason enough—reason enough! Nails that put themselves back into wood again and gashed people's hands, steps that broke when you trod on them, and women who came into a man's place and brushed their hair in the dark, were reasons enough! He was querulous and injured about it all. He had taken the place for himself, not for invisible women to brush their hair in; that lawyer fellow in Lincoln's Inn should be told so, too, before many hours were out; it was outrageous, letting people in for agreements like that!

A cut-glass partition divided the compartment where Oleron sat from the space where the white-haired landlady moved; but it stopped seven or eight inches above the level of the counter. There was no partition at the further bar. Presently Oleron, raising his eyes, saw that faces were watching him through the aperture. The faces disappeared when he looked at them.

He moved to a corner where he could not be seen from the other bar; but this brought him into line with the white-haired landlady.

She knew him by sight—had doubtless seen him passing and repassing; and presently she made a remark on the weather. Oleron did not know what he replied, but it sufficed to call forth the further remark that the winter had been a bad one for influenza, but that the spring weather seemed to be coming at last. . . . Even this slight contact with the commonplace steadied Oleron a little; an idle, nascent wonder whether the landlady brushed her hair every night, and, if so, whether it gave out those little electric cracklings, was shut down with a snap; and Oleron was better. . . .

With his next glass of brandy he was all for going back to his flat. Not go back? Indeed, he would go back! They should very soon see whether he was to be turned out of his place like that! He began to wonder why he was doing the rather unusual thing he was doing at that moment, unusual for him—sitting hatless, drinking brandy, in a public-house. Suppose he were to tell the white-haired landlady all about it—to tell her that a caller had scratched her hand on a nail, had later had the bad luck to put her foot through a rotten stair, and that he himself, in an old house full of squeaks and creaks and whispers, had heard a minute noise and had bolted from it in fright—what would she think of him? That he was mad, of course. . . . Pshaw! The real truth of the matter was that he hadn't been doing enough work to occupy him. He had been dreaming his days away, filling his head with a lot of moonshine about a new *Romilly* (as if the old one was not good enough), and now he was surprised that the devil should enter an empty head!

Yes, he would go back. He would take a walk in the air first—he hadn't walked enough lately—and then he would take himself in hand, settle the hash of that sixteenth chapter of *Romilly* (fancy, he had actually been fool enough to think of destroying fifteen chapters!) and thenceforward he would remember that he had obligations to his fellow men and work to do in the world. There was the matter in a nutshell.

He finished his brandy and went out.

He had walked for some time before any other bearing of the matter than that on himself occurred to him. At first, the fresh air had increased the heady effect of the brandy he had drunk; but afterwards his mind grew clearer than it had been since morning. And the clearer it grew, the less final did his boastful self-assurances become, and the firmer his conviction that, when all explanations had been made, there remained something that could not be explained. His hysteria of an hour before had passed; he grew steadily calmer; but the disquieting conviction remained. A deep fear took possession of him. It was a fear for Elsie.

For something in his place was inimical to her safety. Of themselves, her two accidents might not have persuaded him of this; but she herself had said it. *"I'm not wanted here. . . ."* And she had declared that there was something wrong with the place. She had seen it before he had. Well and good. One thing stood out clearly: namely, that if this was so, she must be kept away for quite another reason than that which had so confounded and humiliated Oleron. Luckily she had expressed her intention of staying away; she must be held to that intention. He must see to it.

And he must see to it all the more that he now saw his first example, never to set foot in the place again, was absurd. People did not do that kind of thing. With Elsie made secure, he could not with any respect to himself suffer himself to be turned out by a shadow, nor even by a danger merely because it was a danger. He had to live somewhere, and he would live there. He must return.

He mastered the faint chill of fear that came with the decision, and turned in his walk abruptly. Should fear grow on him again he would, perhaps, take one more glass of brandy. . . .

But by the time he reached the short street that led to the square he was too late for more brandy. The little public-house was still lighted, but closed, and one or two men were standing talking on the curb. Oleron noticed that a sudden silence fell on them as he passed, and he noticed further that the long-nosed Barrett, whom he passed a little lower down, did not return his good-night. He turned in at the broken gate, hesitated merely an instant in the alley, and then mounted his stairs again.

Only an inch of candle remained in the Sheffield stick, and Oleron did not light another one. Deliberately he forced himself to take it up and to make the tour of his five rooms before retiring. It was as he returned from the kitchen across his little hall that he noticed that a letter lay on the floor. He carried it into his sitting-room, and glanced at the envelope before opening it.

It was unstamped, and had been put into the door by hand. Its handwriting was clumsy, and it ran from beginning to end without comma or period. Oleron read the first line, turned to the signature, and then finished the letter.

It was from the man Barrett, and it informed Oleron that he, Barrett, would be obliged if Mr. Oleron would make other arrangements for the preparing of his breakfasts and the cleaning-out of his place. The sting lay in the tail, that is to say, the postscript. This consisted of a text of Scripture. It embodied an allusion that could only be to Elsie Bengough. . . .

A seldom-seen frown had cut deeply into Oleron's brow. So! That was it! Very well; they would see about that on the morrow. . . . For the rest, this seemed merely another reason why Elsie should keep away. . . .

Then his suppressed rage broke out. . . .

The foul-minded lot! The devil himself could not have given a leer at anything that had ever passed between Paul Oleron and Elsie Bengough, yet this nosing rascal must be prying and talking! . . .

Oleron crumpled the paper up, held it in the candle flame, and then ground the ashes under his heel.

One useful purpose, however, the letter had served: it had created in Oleron a wrathful blaze that effectually banished pale shadows. Nevertheless, one other puzzling circumstance was to close the day. As he undressed, he chanced to glance at his bed. The coverlets bore an impress as if somebody had lain on them. Oleron could not remember that he himself had lain down during the day—offhanded, he would have said that certainly he had not; but after all, he could not be positive. His indignation for Elsie, acting possibly with the residue of the brandy in him, excluded all other considerations; and he put out his candle, lay down, and passed immediately into a deep and dreamless sleep, which, in the absence of Mrs. Barrett's morning call, lasted almost once round the clock.

8

To the man who pays heed to that voice within him which warns him that twilight and danger are settling over his soul, terror is apt to appear an absolute thing, against which his heart must be safeguarded in a twink unless there is to take place an alteration in the whole range and scale of his nature. Mercifully, he has never far to look for safeguards. Of the immediate and small and common and momentary things of life, of usages and observances and modes and conventions, he builds up fortifications against the powers of darkness. He is even content that, not terror only, but joy also, should for working purposes be placed in the category of the absolute things; and the last treason he will commit will be that breaking down of terms and limits that strikes, not at one man, but at the welfare of the souls of all.

In his own person, Oleron began to commit this treason. He began to commit it by admitting the inexplicable and horrible to an increasing familiarity. He did it insensibly, unconsciously, by a neglect of the things that he now regarded it as an impertinence in Elsie Bengough to have prescribed. Two months before, the words "a haunted house," applied to his lovely bemusing dwelling, would have chilled his marrow; now his scale of sensation becoming depressed, he could ask "Haunted by what?" and remain unconscious that horror, when it can be proved to be relative, by so much loses its proper quality. He was setting aside the landmarks. Mists and confusion had begun to enwrap him.

And he was conscious of nothing so much as of a voracious inquisitiveness. He wanted *to know*. He was resolved to know. Nothing but the knowledge would satisfy him; and craftily he cast about for means whereby he might attain it.

He might have spared his craft. The matter was the easiest imaginable. As in time past he had known, in his writing, moments when his thoughts had seemed to rise of themselves and to embody themselves in words not to be altered afterwards, so now the questions he put himself seemed to be answered even in the moment of their asking. There was exhilaration in the swift, easy processes. He had known no such joy in his own power since the days when his writing had been a daily freshness and a delight to him. It was almost as if the course he must pursue was being dictated to him.

And the first thing he must do, of course, was to define the problem. He defined it in terms of mathematics. Granted that he had not the place to himself; granted that the old house had inexpressibly caught and engaged his spirit; granted that, by virtue of the common denominator of the place, this unknown co-tenant stood in some relation to himself: what next? Clearly, the nature of the other numerator must be ascertained.

And how? Ordinarily this would not have seemed simple, but to Oleron it was now pellucidly clear. The key, *of course*, lay in his half-written novel—or rather, in both *Romillys*, the old and the proposed new one.

A little while before, Oleron would have thought himself mad to have embraced such an opinion; now he accepted the dizzying hypothesis without a quiver.

He began to examine the first and second *Romillys*.

From the moment of his doing so the thing advanced by leaps and bounds. Swiftly he reviewed the history of the *Romilly* of the fifteen chapters. He remembered clearly now that he had found her insufficient on the very first morning on which he had sat down to work in his new place. Other instances of his aversion leaped up to confirm his obscure investigation. There had come the night when he had hardly forborne to throw the whole thing into the fire; and the next morning he had begun the planning of the new *Romilly*. It had been on that morning that Mrs. Barrett, overhearing him humming a brief phrase that the dripping of a tap the night before had suggested, had informed him that he was singing some air he had never in his life heard before, called "The Beckoning Fair One." . . .

The Beckoning Fair One! . . .

With scarcely a pause in thought he continued:

The first *Romilly* having been definitely thrown over, the second had instantly fastened herself upon him, clamoring for birth in his brain. He even fancied now, looking back, that there had been something like passion, hate almost, in the supplanting, and that more than once a stray thought given to his discarded creation had—(it was astonishing how credible Oleron found the almost unthinkable idea)—had offended the supplanter.

Yet that a malignancy almost homicidal should be extended to his fiction's poor mortal prototype. . . .

In spite of his inuring to a scale in which the horrible was now a thing to be fingered and turned this way and that, a "Good God!" broke from Oleron.

This intrusion of the first *Romilly*'s prototype into his thought again was a factor that for the moment brought his inquiry into the nature of his problem to a termination; the mere thought of Elsie was fatal to anything abstract. For another thing, he could not yet think of that letter of Barrett's, nor of a little scene that had followed it, without a mounting of color and a quick contraction of the brow. For wisely or not, he had had that argument out at once. Striding across the square on the following morning, he had bearded Barrett on his own doorstep. Coming back again a few minutes later, he had been strongly of opinion that he had only made matters worse. The man had been vagueness itself. He had not been able to be either challenged or brow-beaten into anything more definite than a muttered farrago in which the words "Certain things . . . Mrs. Barrett . . . respectable house . . . if the cap fits . . . proceedings that shall be nameless," had been constantly repeated.

"Not that I make any charge—" he had concluded.

"Charge!" Oleron had cried.

"I 'ave my idears of things, as I don't doubt you 'ave yours—"

"Ideas—mine!" Oleron had cried wrathfully, immediately dropping his voice as heads had appeared at windows of the square. "Look you here, my man; you've an unwholesome mind, which probably you can't help, but a tongue which you can help, and shall! If there is a breath of this repeated . . ."

"I'll not be talked to on my own doorstep like this by anybody . . ." Barrett had blustered. . . .

"You shall, and I'm doing it . . ."

"Don't you forget there's a Gawd above all, Who 'as said . . ."

"You're a low scandalmonger! . . ."

And so forth, continuing badly what was already badly begun. Oleron had returned wrathfully to his own house and thenceforward, looking out of his windows, had seen Barrett's face at odd times, lifting blinds or peering round curtains, as if he sought to put himself in possession of Heaven knew what evidence, in case it should be required of him.

The unfortunate occurrence made certain minor differences in Oleron's domestic arrangements. Barrett's tongue, he gathered, had already been busy; he was looked at askance by the dwellers of the square; and he judged it better, until he should be able to obtain other help, to make his purchases of provisions a little farther afield rather than at the small shops of the immediate neighborhood. For the rest, housekeeping was no new thing to him, and he would resume his old bachelor habits. . . .

Besides, he was deep in certain rather abstruse investigations, in which it was better that he should not be disturbed. He was looking out of his window one midday rather tired, not very well, and glad that it was not very likely he would have to stir out of doors, when he saw Elsie Bengough crossing the square towards his house. The weather had broken; it was a raw and gusty day; and she had to force her way against the wind that set her ample skirts bellying about her opulent figure and her veil spinning and streaming behind her.

Oleron acted swiftly and instinctively. Seizing his hat, he sprang to the door and descended the stairs at a run. A sort of panic had seized him. She must be prevented from setting foot in the place. As he ran along the alley he was conscious that his eyes went up to the eaves as if something drew them. He did not know that a slate might not accidentally fall. . . .

He met her at the gate, and spoke with curious volubleness.

"This is really too bad, Elsie! Just as I'm urgently called away! I'm afraid it can't be helped though, and that you'll have to think me an inhospitable beast." He poured it out just as it came into his head.

She asked if he was going to town.

"Yes, yes—to town," he replied. "I've got to call on—on Chambers. You know Chambers, don't you? No, I remember you don't; a big man you once saw me with. . . . I ought to have gone yesterday, and—" this he felt to be a brilliant effort—"and he's going out of town this afternoon. To Brighton. I had a letter from him this morning."

He took her arm and led her up the square. She had to remind him that his way to town lay in the other direction.

"Of course—how stupid of me!" he said, with a little loud laugh. "I'm so used to going the other way with you—of course; it's the other way to the bus. Will you come along with me? I am so awfully sorry it's happened like this. . . ."

They took the street to the bus terminus.

This time Elsie bore no signs of having gone through interior struggles. If she detected anything unusual in his manner she made no comment, and he, seeing her calm, began to talk less recklessly through silences. By the time they reached the bus terminus, nobody, seeing the pallid-faced man without an overcoat and the large ample-skirted girl at his side, would have supposed that one of them was ready to sink on his knees for thankfulness that he had, as he believed, saved the other from a wildly unthinkable danger.

They mounted to the top of the bus, Oleron protesting that he should not miss his overcoat, and that he found the day, if anything, rather oppressively hot. They sat down on a front seat.

Now that this meeting was forced upon him, he had something else to say that would make demands upon his tact. It had been on his mind for some time, and was, indeed, peculiarly difficult to put. He revolved it for some minutes, and then, remembering the success of his story of a sudden call to town, cut the knot of his difficulty with another lie.

"I'm thinking of going away for a little while, Elsie," he said.

She merely said: "Oh?"

"Somewhere for a change. I need a change. I think I shall go tomorrow, or the day after. Yes, tomorrow, I think."

"Yes," she replied.

"I don't quite know how long I shall be," he continued. "I shall have to let you know when I am back."

"Yes, let me know," she replied in an even tone.

The tone was, for her, suspiciously even. He was a little uneasy.

"You don't ask me where I'm going," he said, with a little cumbrous effort to rally her.

She was looking straight before her, past the bus-driver.

"I know," she said.

He was startled. "How, you know?"

"You're not going anywhere," she replied.

He found not a word to say. It was a minute or so before she continued, in the same controlled voice she had employed from the start.

"You're not going anywhere. You weren't going out this morning. You only came out because I appeared; don't behave as if we were strangers, Paul."

A flush of pink had mounted to his cheeks. He noticed that the wind had given her the pink of early rhubarb. Still he found nothing to say.

"Of course, you ought to go away," she continued. "I don't know whether you look at yourself often in the glass, but you're rather noticeable. Several people have turned to look at you this morning. So, of course, you ought to go away. But you won't, and I know why."

He shivered, coughed a little, and then broke silence.

"Then if you know, there's no use in continuing this discussion," he said curtly.

"Not for me, perhaps, but there is for you," she replied. "Shall I tell you what I know?"

"No," he said in a voice slightly raised.

"No?" she asked, her round eyes earnestly on him.

"No."

Again he was getting out of patience with her; again he was conscious of the strain. Her devotion and fidelity and love plagued him; she was only humiliating both herself and him. It would have been bad enough had he ever, by word or deed, given her cause for thus fastening herself on him . . . but there; that was the worst of that kind of life for a woman. Women such as she, business women, in and out of offices all the time, always, whether they realized it or not, made comradeship a cover for something else. They accepted the unconventional status, came and went freely, as men did, were honestly taken by men at their own valuation—and then it turned out to be the other thing after all, and they went and fell in love. No wonder there was gossip in shops and squares and public houses! In a sense the gossipers were in the right of it. Independent, yet not efficient; with some of womanhood's graces forgone, and yet with all the woman's hunger and need; half sophisticated yet not wise; Oleron was tired of it all. . . .

And it was time he told her so.

"I suppose," he said tremblingly, looking down between his knees, "I suppose the real trouble is in the life women who earn their own living are obliged to lead."

He could not tell in what sense she took the lame generality; she merely replied: "I suppose so."

"It can't be helped," he continued, "but you do sacrifice a good deal."

She agreed: a good deal; and then she added after a moment: "What, for instance?"

"You may or may not be gradually attaining a new status, but you're in a false position today."

It was very likely, she said; she hadn't thought of it much in that light—

"And," he continued desperately, "you're bound to suffer. Your most innocent acts are misunderstood; motives you never dreamed of are attributed to you; and in the end it comes to"—he hesitated a moment and then took the plunge—"to the sidelong look and the leer."

She took his meaning with perfect ease. She merely shivered a little as she pronounced the name.

"Barrett?"

His silence told her the rest.

Anything further that was to be said must come from her. It came as the bus stopped at a stage and fresh passengers mounted the stairs.

"You'd better get down here and go back, Paul," she said. "I understand perfectly—perfectly. It isn't Barrett. You'd be able to deal with Barrett. It's merely convenient for you to say it's Barrett. I know what it is . . . but you said I wasn't to tell you that. Very well. But before you go let me tell you why I came up this morning."

In a dull tone he asked her why. Again she looked straight before her as she replied:

"I came to force your hand. Things couldn't go on as they have been going, you know; and now that's all over."

"All over," he repeated stupidly.

"All over. I want you now to consider yourself, as far as I'm concerned, perfectly free. I make only one reservation."

He hardly had the spirit to ask her what that was.

"If *I* merely need *you*," she said, "please don't give that a thought; that's nothing; I shan't come near for that. But," she dropped her voice, "if *you're* in need of *me*, Paul—I shall know if you are, *and you will be*—then I shall come at no matter what cost. You understand that?"

He could only groan.

"So that's understood," she concluded. "And I think that's all. Now go back. I should advise you to walk back, for you're shivering—good-by—"

She gave him a cold hand, and he descended. He turned on the edge of the curb as the bus started again. For the first time in all the years he had known her, she parted from him with no smile and no wave of her long arm.

9

He stood on the curb plunged in misery, looking after her as long as she remained in sight; but almost instantly with her disappearance he felt the heaviness lift a little from his spirit. She had given him his liberty; true, there was a sense in which he had never parted with it, but now was no time for splitting hairs; he was free to act, and all was clear ahead. Swiftly the sense of lightness grew on him: it became a positive rejoicing in his liberty; and before he was halfway home he had decided what must be done next.

The vicar of the parish in which his dwelling was situated lived within ten minutes of the square. To his house Oleron turned his steps. It was necessary that he should have all the information he could get about this old house with the insurance marks and the sloping "To Let" boards, and the vicar was the person most likely to be able to furnish it. This last preliminary out of the way, and—aha! Oleron chuckled—things might be expected to happen!

But he gained less information than he had hoped for. The house, the vicar said, was old—but there needed no vicar to tell Oleron that; it was reputed (Oleron pricked up his ears) to be haunted—but there were few old houses about which some such rumor did not circulate among the ignorant; and the deplorable lack of Faith of the modern world, the vicar thought, did not tend to dissipate these superstitions. For the rest, his manner was the soothing manner of one who prefers not to make statements without knowing how they will be taken by his hearer. Oleron smiled as he perceived this.

"You may leave my nerves out of the question," he said. "How long has the place been empty?"

"A dozen years, I should say," the vicar replied.

"And the last tenant—did you know him—or her?" Oleron was conscious of a tingling of his nerves as he offered the vicar the alternative of sex.

"Him," said the vicar. "A man. If I remember rightly, his name was Madley; an artist. He was a great recluse; seldom went out of the place, and"—the vicar hesitated and then broke into a little gush of candor—"and since you appear to have come for this information, and since it is better that the truth should be told than that garbled versions should get about, I don't mind saying that this man Madley died there, under somewhat unusual circumstances. It was ascertained at the post-mortem that there was not a particle of food in his stomach, although he was found to be not without money. And his frame was simply worn out. Suicide was spoken of, but you'll agree with me that deliberate starvation is, to say the least, an uncommon form of suicide. An open verdict was returned."

"Ah!" said Oleron. . . . "Does there happen to be any comprehensive history of this parish?"

"No; partial ones only. I myself am not guiltless of having made a number of notes on its purely ecclesiastical history, its registers and so forth, which I shall be happy to show you if you would care to see them; but it is a large parish, I have only one curate, and my leisure, as you will readily understand . . ."

The extent of the parish and the scantiness of the vicar's leisure occupied the remainder of the interview, and Oleron thanked the vicar, took his leave, and walked slowly home.

He walked slowly for a reason, twice turning away from the house within a stone's-throw of the gate and taking another turn of twenty minutes or so. He had a very ticklish piece of work now before him; it required the greatest mental concentration; it was nothing less than to bring his mind, if he might, into such a state of unpreoccupation and receptivity that he should see the place as he had seen it on that morning when, his removal accomplished, he had sat down to begin the sixteenth chapter of the first *Romilly*.

For, could he recapture that first impression, he now hoped for far more from it. Formerly, he had carried no end of mental lumber. Before the influence of the place had been able to find him out at all, it had had the inertia of those dreary chapters to overcome. No results had shown. The process had been one of slow saturation, charging, filling up to a brim. But now he was light, unburdened, rid at last both of that *Romilly* and of her prototype. Now for the new unknown, coy, jealous, bewitching Beckoning Fair! . . .

At half-past two of the afternoon he put his key into the Yale lock, entered, and closed the door behind him. . . .

His fantastic attempt was instantly and astonishingly successful. He could have shouted with triumph as he entered the room; it was as if he had *escaped* into it. Once more, as in the days when his writing had had a daily freshness and wonder and promise for him, he was conscious of that new ease and mastery and exhilaration and release. The air of the place seemed to hold more oxygen; as if his own specific gravity had changed, his very tread seemed less ponderable. The flowers in the bowls, the fair proportions of the meadowsweet-colored panels and moldings, the polished floor, and the lofty and faintly starred ceiling, fairly laughed their welcome. Oleron actually laughed back, and spoke aloud.

"Oh, you're pretty, pretty!" he flattered it.

Then he lay down on his couch.

He spent that afternoon as a convalescent who expected a dear visitor might have spent it—in a delicious vacancy, smiling now and then as if in his sleep, and ever lifting drowsy and contented eyes to his alluring surroundings. He lay thus until darkness came, and, with darkness, the nocturnal noises of the old house. . . .

But if he waited for any specific happening, he waited in vain.

He waited similarly in vain on the morrow, maintaining, though with less ease, that sensitized late-like condition of his mind. Nothing occurred to give it an impression. Whatever it was which he so patiently wooed, it seemed to be both shy and exciting.

Then on the third day he thought he understood. A look of gentle drollery and cunning came into his eyes, and he chuckled.

"Oho, oho! . . . Well, if the wind sits in *that* quarter we must see what else there is to be done. What is there, now? . . . No, I won't send for Elsie; we don't need a wheel to break the butterfly on; we won't go to those lengths, my butterfly. . . ."

He was standing musing, thumbing his lean jaw, looking aslant; suddenly he crossed to his hall, took down his hat, and went out.

"My lady is coquettish, is she? Well, we'll see what a little neglect will do," he chuckled as he went down the stairs.

He sought a railway station, got into a train, and spent the rest of the day in the country. Oh, yes: Oleron thought *he* was the man to deal with Fair Ones who beckoned, and invited, and then took refuge in shyness and hanging back!

He did not return until after eleven that night.

"*Now*, my Fair Beckoner!" he murmured as he walked along the alley and felt in his pocket for his keys. . . .

Inside his flat, he was perfectly composed, perfectly deliberate, exceedingly careful not to give himself away. As if to intimate that he intended to retire immediately, he lighted only a single candle; and as he set out with it on his nightly round he affected to yawn. He went first into his kitchen. There was a full moon, and a lozenge of moonlight, almost peacock-blue by contrast with his candle-flame, lay on the floor. The window was uncurtained, and he could see the reflection of the candle, and, faintly, that of his own face, as he moved about. The door of the powder-closet stood a little ajar, and he closed it before sitting down to remove his boots on the chair with the cushion made of the folded harp-bag. From the kitchen he passed to the bathroom. There, another slant of blue moonlight cut the window-sill and lay across the pipes on the wall. He visited his seldom-used study, and stood for a moment gazing at the silvered roofs across the square. Then, walking straight through his sitting-room, his stockinged feet making no noise, he entered his bedroom and put the candle on the chest of drawers. His face all this time wore no expression save that of tiredness. He had never been wilier nor more alert.

His small bedroom fireplace was opposite the chest of drawers on which the mirror stood, and his bed and the window occupied the remaining sides of the room. Oleron drew down his blind, took off his coat, and then stooped to get his slippers from under the bed.

He could have given no reason for the conviction, but that the manifestation that for two days had been withheld was close at hand he never for an instant doubted. Nor, though he could not form the faintest guess of the shape it might take, did he experience fear. Startling or surprising it might be; he was prepared for that; but that was all; his scale of sensation had become depressed. His hand moved this way and that under the bed in search of his slippers. . . .

But for all his caution and method and preparedness, his heart all at once gave a leap and a pause that was almost horrid. His hand had found the slippers, but he was still on his knees; save for this circumstance he would have fallen. The bed was a low one; the groping for the slippers accounted for the turn of his head to one side; and he was careful to keep the attitude until he had partly recovered his self-possession. When presently he rose there was a drop of blood on his lower lip where he had caught at it with his teeth, and his watch had jerked out of the pocket of his waistcoat and was dangling at the end of its short leather guard. . . .

Then, before the watch had ceased its little oscillation, he was himself again.

In the middle of his mantelpiece there stood a picture, a portrait of his grandmother; he placed himself before this picture, so that he could see in the glass of it the steady flame of the candle that burned behind him on the chest of drawers. He could see also in the picture-glass the little glancings of light from the bevels and facets of the objects about the mirror and candle. But he could see more. These twinklings and reflections and re-reflections did not change their position; but there was one gleam that had motion. It was fainter than the rest, and it moved up and down through the air. It was the reflection of the candle on Oleron's black vulcanite comb, and each of its downward movements was accompanied by a silky and crackling rustle.

Oleron, watching what went on in the glass of his grandmother's portrait, continued to play his part. He felt for his dangling watch and began slowly to wind it up. Then, for a moment ceasing to watch, he began to empty his trousers pockets and to place methodically in a little row on the mantelpiece the pennies and half-pennies he took from them. The sweeping, minutely electric noise filled the whole bedroom, and had Oleron altered his point of observation, he could have brought the dim gleam of the moving comb so into position that it would almost have outlined his grandmother's head.

Any other head of which it might have been following the outline was invisible.

Oleron finished the emptying of his pockets; then, under cover of another simulated yawn, not so much summoning his resolution as overmastered by an exorbitant curiosity, he swung suddenly round. That which was being combed was still not to be seen, but the comb did not stop. It had altered its angle a little, and had moved a little to the left. It was passing, in fairly regular sweeps, from a point rather more than five feet from the ground, in a direction roughly vertical, to another point a few inches below the level of the chest of drawers.

Oleron continued to act to admiration. He walked to his little washstand in the corner, poured out water, and began to wash his hands. He removed his waistcoat, and continued his preparations for bed. The combing did not cease, and he stood for a moment in thought. Again his eyes twinkled. The next was very cunning—

"Hm! . . . *I think I'll read for a quarter of an hour,*" he said aloud. . . .

He passed out of the room.

He was away a couple of minutes; when he returned again the room was suddenly quiet. He glanced at the chest of drawers; the comb lay still, between the collar he had removed and a pair of gloves. Without hesitation Oleron put out his hand and picked it up. It was an ordinary eighteen-penny comb, taken from a card in a chemist's shop, of a substance of a definite specific gravity, and no more capable of rebellion against the Laws by which it existed than are the worlds that keep their orbits through the void. Oleron put it down again; then he glanced at the bundle of papers he held in his hand. What he had gone to fetch had been the fifteen chapters of the original *Romilly*.

"Hm!" he muttered as he threw the manuscript into a chair. . . . "As I thought. . . . She's just blindly, ragingly, murderously jealous."

On the night after that, and on the following night, and for many nights and days, so many that he began to be uncertain about the count of them, Oleron, courting, cajoling, neglecting, threatening, beseeching, eaten out with unappeased curiosity and regardless that his life was becoming one consuming passion and desire, continued his search for the unknown co-numerator of his abode.

10

As time went on, it came to pass that few except the postman mounted Oleron's stairs; and since men who do not write letters receive few, even the postman's tread became so infrequent that it was not heard more than once or twice a week. There came a letter from Oleron's publishers, asking when they might expect to receive the manuscript of his new book; he delayed for some days to answer it, and finally forgot it. A second letter came, which also he failed to answer. He received no third.

The weather grew bright and warm. The privet bushes among the chopper-like notice-boards flowered, and in the streets where Oleron did his shopping the baskets of flower-women lined the curbs. Oleron purchased flowers daily; his room clamored for flowers, fresh and continually renewed; and Oleron did not stint its demands. Nevertheless, the necessity for going out to buy them began to irk him more and more, and it was with a greater and ever greater sense of relief that he returned home again. He began to be conscious that again his scale of sensation had suffered a subtle change—a change that was not restoration to its former capacity, but an extension and enlarging that once more included terror. It admitted it in an entirely new form. *Lux orco, tenebræ Jovi.* The name of this terror was agoraphobia. Oleron had begun to dread air and space and the horror that might pounce upon the unguarded back.

Presently he so contrived it that his food and flowers were delivered daily at his door. He rubbed his hands when he had hit upon this expedient. That was better! Now he could please himself whether he went out or not. . . .

Quickly he was confirmed in his choice. It became his pleasure to remain immured.

But he was not happy—or if he was, his happiness took an extraordinary turn. He fretted discontentedly, could sometimes have wept for mere weakness and misery; and yet he was dimly conscious that he would not have exchanged his sadness for all the noisy mirth of the world outside. And speaking of noise: noise, much noise, now caused him the acutest discomfort. It was hardly more to be endured than that new-born fear that kept him, on the increasingly rare occasions when he did go out, sidling close to walls and feeling friendly railings with his hand. He moved from room to room softly and in slippers, and sometimes stood for many seconds closing a door so gently that not a sound broke the stillness that was in itself a delight. Sunday now became an intolerable day to him, for, since the coming of the fine weather, there had begun to assemble in the square under his windows each Sunday morning certain members of the sect to which the long-nosed Barrett adhered. These came with a great drum and large brass-bellied instruments; men and women uplifted anguished voices, struggling with their God; and Barrett himself, with upraised face and closed eyes and working brows, prayed that the sound of his voice might penetrate the ears of all unbelievers—as it certainly did Oleron's. One day, in the middle of one of these rhapsodies, Oleron sprang to his blind and pulled it down, and heard, as he did so, his own name made the object of a fresh torrent of outpouring.

And sometimes, but not as expecting a reply, Oleron stood still and called softly. Once or twice he called "Romilly!" and then waited; but more often his whispering did not take the shape of a name.

There was one spot in particular of his abode that he began to haunt with increasing persistency. This was just within the opening of his bedroom door. He had discovered one day that by opening every door in his place (always excepting the outer one, which he only opened unwillingly) and by placing himself on this particular spot, he could actually see to a greater or less extent into each of his five rooms without changing his position. He could see the whole of his sitting-room, all of his bedroom except the part hidden by the open door, and glimpses of his kitchen, bathroom, and of his rarely used study. He was often in this place, breathless and with his finger on his lip. One day, as he stood there, he suddenly found himself wondering whether this Madley, of whom the vicar had spoken, had ever discovered the strategic importance of the bedroom entry.

Light, moreover, now caused him greater disquietude than did darkness. Direct sunlight, of which as the sun passed daily round the house, each of his rooms had now its share, was like a flame in his brain; and even diffused light was a dull and numbing ache. He began, at successive hours of the day, one after another, to lower his crimson blinds. He made short and daring excursions in order to do this; but he was ever careful to leave his retreat open, in case he should have sudden need of it. Presently this lowering of the blinds had become a daily methodical exercise, and his rooms, when he had been his round, had the blood-red half-light of a photographer's darkroom.

One day, as he drew down the blind of his little study and backed in good order out of the room again, he broke into a soft laugh. "*That* bilks Mr. Barrett!" he said; and the baffling of Barrett continued to afford him mirth for an hour.

But on another day, soon after, he had a fright that left him trembling also for an hour. He had seized the cord to darken the window over the seat in which he had found the harp-bag, and was standing with his back well protected in the embrasure, when he thought he saw the tail of a black-and-white check skirt disappear round the corner of the house. He could not be sure—had he run to the window of the other wall, which was blinded, the skirt must have been already past—but he was *almost* sure that it was Elsie. He listened in an agony of suspense for her tread on the stairs. . . .

But no tread came, and after three or four minutes he drew a long breath of relief.

"By Jove, but that would have compromised me horribly!" he muttered. . . .

And he continued to mutter from time to time: "Horribly compromising . . . *no* woman would stand that . . . not *any* kind of woman . . . oh, compromising in the extreme!"

Yet he was not happy. He could not have assigned the cause of the fits of quiet weeping which took him sometimes; they came and went, like the fitful illumination of the clouds that travelled over the square; and perhaps, after all, if he was not happy, he was not unhappy. Before he could be unhappy something must have been withdrawn, and nothing had been granted. He was waiting for that granting, in that flower-laden, frightfully enticing apartment of his, with the pith-white walls tinged and subdued by the crimson blinds to a blood-like gloom.

He paid no heed to it that his stock of money was running perilously low, nor that he had ceased to work. Ceased to work? He had not ceased to work. They knew very little about it who supposed that Oleron had ceased to work! He was in truth only now beginning to work. He was preparing such a work . . . such a work . . . such a Mistress was a-making in the gestation of his Art. . . . Let him but get this period of probation and poignant waiting over and men should see. . . . How *should* men know her, this Fair One of Oleron's, until Oleron himself knew her? Lovely radiant creations are not thrown off like How-d'ye-do's. The men to whom it is committed to father them must weep wretched tears, as Oleron did, must swell with vain presumptuous hopes, as Oleron did, must pursue, as Oleron pursued, the capricious, fair, mocking, slippery, eager Spirit that, ever eluding, ever sees to it that the chase does not slacken. Let Oleron but hunt this Huntress a little longer . . . he would have her sparkling and panting in his arms yet. . . . Oh, no: they were very far from the truth who supposed that Oleron had ceased to work!

And if all else was falling away from Oleron, gladly he was letting it go. So do we all when our Fair Ones beckon. Quite at the beginning we wink, and promise ourselves that we will put Her Ladyship through her paces, neglect her for a day, turn her own jealous wiles against her, flout and ignore her when she comes wheedling; perhaps there lurks within us all the time a heartless sprite who is never fooled; but in the end all falls away. She beckons, beckons, and all goes. . . .

And so Oleron kept his strategic post within the frame of his bedroom door, and watched, and waited, and smiled, with his finger on his lips. . . . It was his duteous service, his worship, his troth-plighting, all that he had ever known of Love. And when he found himself, as he now and then did, hating the dead man Madley, and wishing that he had never lived, he felt that that, too, was an acceptable service. . . .

But, as he thus prepared himself, as it were, for a Marriage, and moped and chafed more and more that the Bride made no sign, he made a discovery that he ought to have made weeks before.

It was through a thought of the dead Madley that he made it. Since that night when he had thought in his greenness that a little studied neglect would bring the lovely Beckoner to her knees, and had made use of her own jealousy to banish her, he had not set eyes on those fifteen discarded chapters of *Romilly*. He had thrown them back into the window seat, forgotten their very existence. But his own jealousy of Madley put him in mind of hers, of her jilted rival of flesh and blood, and he remembered them. . . . Fool that he had been! Had he, then, expected his Desire to manifest herself while there still existed the evidence of his divided allegiance? What, and she with a passion so fierce and centered that it had not hesitated at the destruction, twice attempted, of her rival? Fool that he had been! . . .

But if *that* was all the pledge and sacrifice she required she should have it—ah, yes, and quickly!

He took the manuscript from the window seat, and brought it to the fire.

He kept his fire always burning now; the warmth brought out the last vestige of odor of the flowers with which his room was banked. He did not know what time it was; long since he had allowed his clock to run down—it had seemed a foolish measurer of time in regard to the stupendous things that were happening to Oleron; but he knew it was late. He took the *Romilly* manuscript and knelt before the fire.

But he had not finished removing the fastening that held the sheets together before he suddenly gave a start, turned his head over his shoulder, and listened intently. The sound he had heard had not been loud—it had been, indeed, no more than a tap, twice or thrice repeated—but it had filled Oleron with alarm. His face grew dark as it came again.

He heard a voice outside on his landing.

"Paul! . . . Paul! . . ."

It was Elsie's voice.

"Paul! . . . I know you're in . . . I want to see you. . . ."

He cursed her under his breath, but kept perfectly still. He did not intend to admit her.

"Paul! . . . You're in trouble . . . I believe you're in danger . . . at least come to the door! . . ."

Oleron smothered a low laugh. It somehow amused him that she, in such danger herself, should talk to him of *his* danger! . . . Well, if she was, serve her right; she knew, or said she knew, all about it. . . .

"Paul! . . . Paul! . . ."

"*Paul! . . . Paul! . . .*" He mimicked her under his breath.

"Oh, Paul, it's *horrible! . . .*"

Horrible was it? thought Oleron. Then let her get away. . . .

"I only want to help you, Paul. . . . I didn't promise not to come if you needed me. . . ."

He was impervious to the pitiful sob that interrupted the low cry. The devil take the woman! Should he shout to her to go away and not come back? No: let her call and knock and sob. She had a gift for sobbing; she mustn't think her sobs would move him. They irritated him, so that he set his teeth and shook his fist at her, but that was all. Let her sob.

"*Paul!* . . . *Paul!* . . ."

With his teeth hard set, he dropped the first page of *Romilly* into the fire. Then he began to drop the rest in, sheet by sheet.

For many minutes the calling behind his door continued; then suddenly it ceased. He heard the sound of feet slowly descending the stairs. He listened for the noise of a fall or a cry or the crash of a piece of the handrail of the upper landing; but none of these things came. She was spared. Apparently her rival suffered her to crawl abject and beaten away. Oleron heard the passing of her steps under the window; then she was gone.

He dropped the last page into the fire, and then, with a low laugh, rose. He looked fondly round his room.

"Lucky to get away like that," he remarked. "She wouldn't have got away if I'd given her as much as a word or a look! What devils these women are! . . . But no; I oughtn't to say that; one of 'em showed forbearance. . . ."

Who showed forbearance? And what was forborne? Ah, Oleron knew! . . . Contempt, no doubt, had been at the bottom of it, but that didn't matter: the pestering creature had been allowed to go unharmed. Yes, she was lucky; Oleron hoped she knew it. . . .

And now, now, now for his reward!

Oleron crossed the room. All his doors were open; his eyes shone as he placed himself within that of his bedroom.

Fool that he had been, not to think of destroying the manuscript sooner! . . .

How, in a houseful of shadows, should he know his own Shadow? How, in a houseful of noises, distinguish the summons he felt to be at hand? Ah, trust him! He would know! The place was full of a jugglery of dim lights. The blind at his elbow that allowed the light of a street lamp to struggle vaguely through—the glimpse of greeny blue moonlight seen through the distant kitchen door—the sulky glow of the fire under the black ashes of the burnt manuscript—the glimmering of the tulips and the moon-daisies and narcissi in the bowls and jugs and jars—these did not so trick and bewilder his eyes that he would not know his Own! It was he, not she, who had been delaying the shadowy Bridal; he hung his head for a moment in mute acknowledgment; then he bent his eyes on the deceiving, puzzling gloom again. He would have called her name had he known it—but now he would not ask her to share even a name with the other. . . .

His own face, within the frame of the door, glimmered white as the narcissi in the darkness. . . .

A shadow, light as fleece, seemed to take shape in the kitchen (the time had been when Oleron would have said that a cloud had passed over the unseen moon). The low illumination on the blind at his elbow grew dimmer (the time had been when Oleron would have concluded that the lamplighter going his round had turned low the flame of the lamp). The fire settled, letting down the black and charred papers; a flower fell from a bowl, and lay indistinct upon the floor; all was still; and then a stray draught moved through the old house, passing before Oleron's face. . . .

Suddenly, inclining his head, he withdrew a little from the doorjamb. The wandering draught caused the door to move a little on its hinges. Oleron trembled violently, stood for a moment longer, and then, putting his hand out to the knob, softly drew the door to, sat down on the nearest chair, and waited, as a man might await the calling of his name that should summon him to some weighty, high and privy Audience. . . .

11

One knows not whether there can be human compassion for anæmia of the soul. When the pitch of Life is dropped, and the spirit is so put over and reversed that that only is horrible which before was sweet and worldly and of the day, the human relation disappears. The sane soul turns appalled away, lest not merely itself, but sanity should suffer. We are not gods. We cannot drive our devils. We must see selfishly to it that devils do not enter into ourselves.

And this we must do even though Love so transfuse us that we may well deem our nature to be half divine. We shall but speak of honor and duty in vain. The letter dropped within the dark door will lie unregarded, or, if regarded for a brief instant between two unspeakable lapses, left and forgotten again. The telegram will be undelivered, nor will the whistling messenger (wiselier guided than he knows to whistle) be conscious as he walks away of the drawn blind that is pushed aside an inch by a finger and then fearfully replaced again. No: let the miserable wrestle with his own shadows; let him, if indeed he be so mad, clip and strain and enfold and crouch the succubus; but let him do so in a house into which not an air of Heaven penetrates, nor a bright finger of the sun pierces the filthy twilight. The lost must remain lost. Humanity has other business to attend to.

For the handwriting of the two letters that Oleron, stealing noiselessly one June day into his kitchen to rid his sitting-room of an armful of fetid and decaying flowers, had seen on the floor within his door, had had no more meaning for him than if it had belonged to some dim and far-away dream. And at the beating of the telegraph-boy upon the door, within a few feet of the bed where he lay, he had gnashed his teeth and stopped his ears. He had pictured the lad standing there, just beyond his partition, among packets of provisions and bundles of dead and dying flowers. For his outer landing was littered with these. Oleron had feared to open his door to take them in. After a week, the errand lads had reported that there must be some mistake about the order, and had left no more. Inside, in the red twilight, the old flowers turned brown and fell and decayed where they lay.

Gradually his power was draining away. The Abomination fastened on Oleron's power. The steady sapping sometimes left him for many hours of prostration gazing vacantly up at his red-tinged ceiling; idly suffering such fancies as came of themselves to have their way with him. Even the strongest of his memories had no more than a precarious hold upon his attention. Sometimes a flitting half-memory, of a novel to be written, a novel it was important that he should write, tantalized him for a space before vanishing again; and sometimes whole novels, perfect, splendid, established to endure, rose magically before him. And sometimes the memories were absurdly remote and trivial, of garrets he had inhabited and lodgings that had sheltered him, and so forth. Oleron had known a good deal about such things in his time, but all that was now past. He had at last found a place which he did not intend to leave until they fetched him out—a place that some might have thought a little on the green-sick side, that others might have considered to be a little too redolent of long-dead and morbid things for a living man to be mewed up in, but ah, so irresistible, with such an authority of its own, with such an associate of its own, and a place of such delights when once a man had ceased to struggle against its inexorable will! A novel? Somebody ought to write a novel about a place like that! There must be lots to write about in a place like that if one could but get to the bottom of it! It had probably already been painted, by a man called Madley who had lived there . . . but Oleron had not known this Madley—had a strong feeling that he wouldn't have liked him—would rather he had lived somewhere else—really couldn't stand the fellow—hated him, Madley, in fact. (Aha! That was a joke!) He seriously doubted whether the man had led the life he ought; Oleron was in two minds sometimes whether he wouldn't tell that long-nosed guardian of the public morals across the way about him; but probably he knew, and had made his praying hullabaloos for him also. That was his line. Why, Oleron himself had had a dust-up with him about something or other . . . some girl or other . . . Elsie Bengough her name was, he remembered. . . .

Oleron had moments of deep uneasiness about this Elsie Bengough. Or rather, he was not so much uneasy about her as restless about the things she did. Chief of these was the way in which she persisted in thrusting herself into his thoughts; and, whenever he was quick enough, he sent her packing the moment she made her appearance there. The truth was that she was not merely a bore; she had always been that; it had now come to the pitch where her very presence in his fancy was inimical to the full enjoyment of certain experiences. . . . She had no tact; really ought to have known that people are not at home to the thoughts of everybody all the time; ought in mere politeness to have allowed him certain seasons quite to himself; and was monstrously ignorant of things if she did not know, as she appeared not to know, that there were certain special hours when a man's veins ran with fire and daring and power, in which . . . well, in which he had a reasonable right to treat folk as he had treated that prying Barrett—to shut them out completely. . . . But no, up she popped: the thought of her, and ruined all. Bright towering fabrics, by the side of which even those perfect, magical novels of which he dreamed were dun and gray, vanished utterly at her intrusion. It was as if a fog should suddenly quench some fair-beaming star, as if at the threshold of some golden portal prepared for Oleron a pit should suddenly gape, as if a bat-like shadow should turn the growing dawn to murk and darkness again. . . . Therefore, Oleron strove to stifle even the nascent thought of her.

Nevertheless, there came an occasion on which this woman Bengough absolutely refused to be suppressed. Oleron could not have told exactly when this happened; he only knew by the glimmer of the street lamp on his blind that it was some time during the night, and that for some time she had not presented herself.

He had no warning, none, of her coming; she just came—was there. Strive as he would, he could not shake off the thought of her nor the image of her face. She haunted him.

But for her to come at *that* moment of all moments! . . . Really, it was past belief! How *she* could endure it, Oleron could not conceive! Actually, to look on, as it were, at the triumph of a Rival. . . . Good God! It was monstrous! tact—reticence—he had never credited her with an overwhelming amount of either: but he had never attributed mere—oh, there was no word for it! Monstrous—monstrous! Did she intend thenceforward. . . . Good God! To look on! . . .

Oleron felt the blood rush up to the roots of his hair with anger against her. "Damnation take her!" he choked. . . .

But the next moment his heat and resentment had changed to a cold sweat of cowering fear. Panic-stricken, he strove to comprehend what he had done. For though he knew not what, he knew he had done something, something fatal, irreparable, blasting. Anger he had felt, but not *this* blaze of ire that suddenly flooded the twilight of his consciousness with a white infernal light. *That* appalling flash was not his—not his *that* open rift of bright and searing Hell—not his, not his! His had been the hand of a child, preparing a puny blow; but what was *this other* horrific hand that was drawn back to strike in the same place? Had *he* set that in motion? Had *he* provided the spark that had touched off the whole accumulated power of that formidable and relentless place? He did not know. He only knew that that poor igniting particle in himself was blown out, that—Oh, impossible!—a clinging kiss (how else to express it?) had changed on his very lips to a gnashing and a removal, and that for very pity of the awful odds he must cry out to her against whom he had lately raged to guard herself. . . . guard herself. . . .

"*Look out!*" he shrieked aloud. . . .

The revulsion was instant. As if a cold slow billow had broken over him, he came to find that he was lying in his bed, that the mist and horror that had for so long enwrapped him had departed, that he was Paul Oleron, and that he was sick, naked, helpless, and unutterably abandoned and alone. His faculties, though weak, answered at last to his calls upon them; and he knew that it must have been a hideous nightmare that had left him sweating and shaking thus.

Yes, he was himself, Paul Oleron, a tired novelist, already past the summit of his best work, and slipping downhill again empty-handed from it all. He had struck short in his life's aim. He had tried too much, had overestimated his strength, and was a failure, a failure. . . .

It all came to him in the single word, enwrapped and complete; it needed no sequential thought; he was a failure. He had missed. . . .

And he had missed not one happiness, but two. He had missed the ease of this world, which men love, and he had missed also that other shining prize for which men forgo ease, the snatching and holding and triumphant bearing up aloft of which is the only justification of the mad adventurer who hazards the enterprise. And there was no second attempt. Fate has no morrow. Oleron's morrow must be to sit down to profitless, ill-done, unrequired work again, and so on the morrow after that, the morrow after that, and as many morrows as there might be. . . .

He lay there, weakly yet sanely considering it. . . .

And since the whole attempt had failed, it was hardly worth while to consider whether a little might not be saved from the general wreck. No good would ever come out of that half-finished novel. He had intended that it should appear in the autumn; was under contract that it should appear; no matter; it was better to pay forfeit to his publishers than to waste what days were left. He was spent; age was not far off; and paths of wisdom and sadness were the properest for the remainder of the journey. . . .

If only he had chosen the wife, the child, the faithful friend at the fireside, and let them follow an *ignis fatuus* that list! . . .

In the meantime it began to puzzle him exceedingly why he should be so weak, that his room should smell so overpoweringly of decaying vegetable matter, and that his hand, chancing to stray to his face in the darkness, should encounter a beard.

"Most extraordinary!" he began to mutter to himself.

"Have I been ill? Am I ill now? And if so, why have they left me alone? . . . Extraordinary! . . ."

He thought he heard a sound from the kitchen or bathroom. He rose a little on his pillow, and listened. . . . Ah! He was not alone, then! It certainly would have been extraordinary if they had left him ill and alone——Alone? Oh, no. He would be looked after. He wouldn't be left, ill, to shift for himself. If everybody else had forsaken him, he could trust Elsie Bengough, the dearest chum he had, for that . . . bless her faithful heart!

But suddenly a short, stifled, spluttering cry rang sharply out:

"*Paul!*"

It came from the kitchen.

And in the same moment it flashed upon Oleron, he knew not how, that two, three, five, he knew not how many minutes before, another sound, unmarked at the time, but suddenly transfixing his attention now, had striven to reach his intelligence. This sound had been the slight touch of metal on metal—just such a sound as Oleron made when he put his key into the lock.

"Hallo! . . . Who's that?" he called sharply from his bed.

He had no answer.

He called again. "Hallo! . . . Who's there? . . . Who is it?"

This time he was sure he heard noises, soft and heavy, in the kitchen.

"This is a queer thing altogether," he muttered. "By Jove, I'm as weak as a kitten, too. . . . Hallo, there! Somebody called, didn't they? . . . Elsie! Is that you? . . ."

Then he began to knock with his hand on the wall at the side of his bed. "Elsie! . . . Elsie! . . . You called, didn't you? . . . Please come here, whoever it is! . . ."

There was a sound as of a closing door, and then silence. Oleron began to get rather alarmed.

"It may be a nurse," he muttered: "Elsie'd have to get me a nurse, of course. She'd sit with me as long as she could spare the time, brave lass, and she'd get a nurse for the rest. . . . But it was awfully like her voice. . . . Elsie, or whoever it is! . . . I can't make this out at all. I must go and see what's the matter. . . ."

He put one leg out of bed. Feeling its feebleness, he reached with his hand for the additional support of the wall. . . .

But before putting out the other leg he stopped and considered, picking at his new-found beard. He was suddenly wondering whether he *dared* go into the kitchen. It was such a frightfully long way; no man knew what horror might not leap and huddle on his shoulders if he went so far; when a man has an overmastering impulse to get back into bed he ought to take heed of the warning and obey it. Besides, why should he go? What was there to go for? If it was that Bengough creature again, let her look after herself; Oleron was not going to have things cramp themselves on his defenseless back for the sake of such a spoil-sport as *she*! . . . If she was in, let her let herself out again, and the sooner the better for her! Oleron simply couldn't be bothered. He had his work to do. On the morrow, he must set about the writing of a novel with a heroine so winsome, capricious, adorable, jealous, wicked, beautiful, inflaming, and altogether evil, that men should stand amazed. She was coming over him now; he knew by the alteration of the very air of the room when she was near him; and that soft thrill of bliss that had begun to stir in him never came unless she was beckoning, beckoning. . . .

He let go the wall and fell back into bed again as—oh, unthinkable!—the other half of that kiss that a gnash had interrupted was placed (how else convey it?) on his lips, robbing him of very breath. . . .

12

In the bright June sunlight a crowd filled the square, and looked up at the windows of the old house with the antique insurance marks on its walls of red brick and the agents' notice-boards hanging like wooden choppers over the paling. Two constables stood at the broken gate of the narrow entrance alley, keeping folk back. The women kept to the outskirts of the throng, moving now and then as if to see the drawn red blinds of the old house from a new angle, and talking in whispers. The children were in the houses, behind closed doors.

A long-nosed man had a little group about him, and he was telling some story over and over again; and another man, little and fat and wide-eyed, sought to capture the long-nosed man's audience with some relation in which a key figured.

". . . and it was revealed to me that there'd been something that very afternoon," the long-nosed man was saying. "I was standing there, where Constable Saunders is—or rather, I was passing about my business, when they came out. There was no deceiving me, oh, no deceiving *me*! I saw her face. . . ."

"What was it like, Mr. Barrett?" a man asked.

"It was like hers whom our Lord said to, 'Woman, doth any man accuse thee?'—white as paper, and no mistake! Don't tell *me*! . . . And so I walks straight across to Mrs. Barrett, and 'Jane,' I says, 'this must stop, and stop at once; we are commanded to avoid evil,' I says, 'and it must come to an end now; let him get help elsewhere.' And she says to me, 'John,' she says, 'it's four-and-sixpence a week'—them was her words. 'Jane,' I says, 'if it was forty-six thousand pounds it should stop' . . . and from that day to this she hasn't set foot inside that gate."

There was a short silence: then,

"Did Mrs. Barrett ever . . . *see* anything, like?" somebody vaguely inquired.

Barrett turned austerely on the speaker.

"What Mrs. Barrett saw and Mrs. Barrett didn't see shall not pass these lips; even as it is written, keep thy tongue from speaking evil," he said.

Another man spoke.

"He was pretty near canned up in the *Wagon and Horses* that night, weren't he, Jim?"

"Yes, 'e 'adn't 'alf copped it. . . ."

"Not standing treat much, neither; he was in the bar, all on his own. . . ."

"So 'e was; we talked about it. . . ."

The fat, scared-eyed man made another attempt.

"She got the key off of me—she 'ad the number of it—she came into my shop of a Tuesday evening. . . ."

Nobody heeded him.

"Shut your heads," a heavy laborer commented gruffly, "she hasn't been found yet. 'Ere's the inspectors; we shall know more in a bit."

Two inspectors had come up and were talking to the constables who guarded the gate. The little fat man ran eagerly forward, saying that she had bought the key of him. "I remember the number, because of its being three ones and three threes—111333!" he exclaimed excitedly.

An inspector put him aside.

"Nobody's been in?" he asked of one of the constables.

"No, sir."

"Then you, Brackley, come with us; you, Smith, keep the gate. There's a squad on its way."

The two inspectors and the constable passed down the alley and entered the house. They mounted the wide carved staircase.

"This don't look as if he'd been out much lately," one of the inspectors muttered as he kicked aside a litter of dead leaves and paper that lay outside Oleron's door. "I don't think we need knock—break a pane, Brackley."

The door had two glazed panels; there was a sound of shattered glass; and Brackley put his hand through the hole his elbow had made and drew back the latch.

"Faugh!" . . . choked one of the inspectors as they entered. "Let some light and air in, quick. It stinks like a hearse——"

The assembly out in the square saw the red blinds go up and the windows of the old house flung open.

"That's better," said one of the inspectors, putting his head out of a window and drawing a deep breath. . . . "That seems to be the bedroom in there; will you go in, Simms, while I go over the rest? . . ."

They had drawn up the bedroom blind also, and the waxy-white, emaciated man on the bed had made a blinker of his hand against the torturing flood of brightness. Nor could he believe that his hearing was not playing tricks with him, for there were two policemen in his room, bending over him and asking where "she" was. He shook his head.

"This woman Bengough . . . goes by the name of Miss Elsie Bengough . . . d'ye hear? Where is she? . . . No good, Brackley; get him up; be careful with him; I'll just shove *my* head out of the window, I think. . . ."

The other inspector had been through Oleron's study and had found nothing, and was now in the kitchen, kicking aside an ankle-deep mass of vegetable refuse that cumbered the floor. The kitchen window had no blind, and was overshadowed by the blank end of the house across the alley. The kitchen appeared to be empty.

But the inspector, kicking aside the dead flowers, noticed that a shuffling track that was not of his making had been swept to a cupboard in the corner. In the upper part of the door of the cupboard was a square panel that looked as if it slid on runners. The door itself was closed.

The inspector advanced, put out his hand to the little knob, and slid the hatch along its groove.

Then he took an involuntary step back again.

Framed in the aperture, and falling forward a little before it jammed again in its frame, was something that resembled a large lumpy pudding, done up in a pudding-bag of faded browny red frieze.

"Ah!" said the inspector.

To close the hatch again he would have had to thrust that pudding back with his hand; and somehow he did not quite like the idea of touching it. Instead, he turned the handle of the cupboard itself. There was weight behind it, so much weight that, after opening the door three or four inches and peering inside, he had to put his shoulder to it in order to close it again. In closing it he left sticking out, a few inches from the floor, a triangle of black and white check skirt.

He went into the small hall.

"All right!" he called.

They had got Oleron into his clothes. He still used his hands as blinkers, and his brain was very confused. A number of things were happening that he couldn't understand. He couldn't understand the extraordinary mess of dead flowers there seemed to be everywhere; he couldn't understand why there should be police officers in his room; he couldn't understand why one of these should be sent for a four-wheeler and a stretcher; and he couldn't understand what heavy article they seemed to be moving about in the kitchen—his kitchen. . . .

"What's the matter?" he muttered sleepily. . . .

Then he heard a murmur in the square, and the stopping of a four-wheeler outside. A police officer was at his elbow again, and Oleron wondered why, when he whispered something to him, he should run off a string of words—something about "used in evidence against you." They had lifted him to his feet, and were assisting him towards the door. . . .

No, Oleron couldn't understand it at all.

They got him down the stairs and along the alley. Oleron was aware of confused angry shoutings; he gathered that a number of people wanted to lynch somebody or other. Then his attention became fixed on a little fat frightened-eyed man who appeared to be making a statement that an officer was taking down in a notebook.

"I'd seen her with him . . . they was often together . . . she came into my shop and said it was for him . . . I thought it was all right . . . 111333 the number was," the man was saying.

The people seemed to be very angry; many police were keeping them back; but one of the inspectors had a voice that Oleron thought quite kind and friendly. He was telling somebody to get somebody else into the cab before something or other was brought out; and Oleron noticed that a four-wheeler was drawn up at the gate. It appeared that it was himself who was to be put into it; and as they lifted him up he saw that the inspector tried to stand between him and something that stood behind the cab, but was not quick enough to prevent Oleron seeing that this something was a hooded stretcher. The angry voices sounded like a sea, something hard, like a stone, hit the back of the cab; and the inspector followed Oleron in and stood with his back to the window nearer the side where the people were. The door they had put Oleron in at remained open, apparently till the other inspector should come; and through the opening Oleron had a glimpse of the hatchet-like "To Let" boards among the privet-trees. One of them said that the key was at Number Six. . . .

Suddenly the raging of voices was hushed. Along the entrance-alley shuffling steps were heard, and the other inspector appeared at the cab door.

"Right away," he said to the driver.

He entered, fastened the door after him, and blocked up the second window with his back. Between the two inspectors Oleron slept peacefully. The cab moved down the square, the other vehicle went up the hill. The mortuary lay that way.

Fitz-James O'Brien

What Was It?

Fitz-James O'Brien was regarded as the heir apparent to Poe in America before his early death in the Civil War. He left behind only the excellent stories collected in his single, posthumous compilation (*The Life, Poems and Stories of . . .*). Three of his nine stories are significant contributions to the evolution of science fiction ("The Diamond Lens," "The Wondersmith," and "What Was It?"), but "What Was It?" is indeed a horror story of the physical sciences, and moreover a tale that catalogs other writers of the fantastic, from the Shakespeare of "The Tempest," and E.T.A. Hoffmann, to Mrs. Crowe, Charles Brockden Brown and Bulwer-Lytton. O'Brien manages to tame his invisible horror through science, rejecting the supernatural, which makes the story in a way an antihorror piece, but the juxtaposition of science and horror persists, from Poe through Lovecraft and beyond. "What Was It?" is a story substantially ahead of its time, with much of the feel of the 1890s fiction to come.

It is, I confess, with considerable diffidence that I approach the strange narrative which I am about to relate. The events which I purpose detailing are of so extraordinary a character that I am quite prepared to meet with an unusual amount of incredulity and scorn. I accept all such beforehand. I have, I trust, the literary courage to face unbelief. I have, after mature consideration, resolved to narrate, in as simple and straightforward a manner as I can compass, some facts that passed under my observation, in the month of July last, and which, in the annals of the mysteries of physical science, are wholly unparalleled.

I live at No.—Twenty-sixth Street, in New York. The house is in some respects a curious one. It has enjoyed for the last two years the reputation of being haunted. It is a large and stately residence, surrounded by what was once a garden, but which is now only a green enclosure used for bleaching clothes. The dry basin of what has been a fountain, and a few fruit-trees ragged and unpruned, indicate that this spot in past days was a pleasant, shady retreat, filled with fruits and flowers and the sweet murmur of waters.

The house is very spacious. A hall of noble size leads to a large spiral staircase winding through its centre, while the various apartments are of imposing dimensions. It was built some fifteen or twenty years since by Mr. A.——, the well-known New York merchant, who five years ago threw the commercial world into convulsions by a stupendous bank fraud. Mr. A——, as every one knows, escaped to Europe, and died not long after, of a broken heart. Almost immediately after the news of his decease reached this country and was verified, the report spread in Twenty-sixth Street that No.—was haunted. Legal measures had dispossessed the widow of its former owner, and it was inhabited merely by a care-taker and his wife, placed there by the house-agent in whose hands it had passed for purposes of renting or sale. These people declared that they were troubled with unnatural noises. Doors were opened without any visible agency. The remnants of furniture scattered through the various rooms were, during the night, piled one upon the other by unknown hands. Invisible feet passed up and down the stairs in broad daylight, accompanied by the rustle of unseen silk dresses, and the gliding of viewless hands along the massive balusters. The care-taker and his wife declared they would live there no longer. The house-agent laughed, dismissed them, and put others in their place. The noises and supernatural manifestations continued. The neighborhood caught up the story, and the house remained untenanted for three years. Several persons negotiated for it; but, somehow, always before the bargain was closed they heard the unpleasant rumors and declined to treat any further.

It was in this state of things that my landlady, who at that time kept a boarding-house in Bleecker Street, and who wished to move farther up town, conceived the bold idea of renting No.—Twenty-sixth Street. Happening to have in her house rather a plucky and philosophical set of boarders, she laid her scheme before us, stating candidly everything she had heard respecting the ghostly qualities of the establishment to which she wished to remove us. With the exception of two timid persons,—a sea-captain and a returned Californian, who immediately gave notice that they would leave,—all of Mrs. Moffat's guests declared that they would accompany her in her chivalric incursion into the abode of spirits.

Our removal was effected in the month of May, and we were charmed with our new residence. The portion of Twenty-sixth Street where our house is situated, between Seventh and Eighth Avenues, is one of the pleasantest localities in New York. The gardens back of the houses, running down nearly to the Hudson, form, in the summer time, a perfect avenue of verdure. The air is pure and invigorating, sweeping, as it does, straight across the river from the Weehawken heights, and even the ragged garden which surrounded the house, although displaying on washing days rather too much clothes-line, still gave us a piece of greensward to look at, and a cool retreat in the summer evenings, where we smoked our cigars in the dusk, and watched the fireflies flashing their dark-lanterns in the long grass.

Of course we had no sooner established ourselves at No.—than we began to expect the ghosts. We absolutely awaited their advent with eagerness. Our dinner conversation was supernatural. One of the boarders, who had purchased Mrs. Crowe's "Night Side of Nature" for his own private delectation, was regarded as a public enemy by the entire household for not having bought twenty copies. The man led a life of supreme wretchedness while he was reading this volume. A system of espionage was established, of which he was the victim. If he incautiously laid the book down for an instant and left the room, it was immediately seized and read aloud in secret places to a select few. I found myself a person of immense importance, it having leaked out that I was tolerably well versed in the history of supernaturalism, and had once written a story the foundation of which was a ghost. If a table or a wainscot panel happened to warp when we were assembled in the large drawing-room, there was an instant silence, and every one was prepared for an immediate clanking of chains and a spectral form.

After a month of psychological excitement, it was with the utmost dissatisfaction that we were forced to acknowledge that nothing in the remotest degree approaching the supernatural had manifested itself. Once the black butler asseverated that his candle had been blown out by some invisible agency while he was undressing himself for the night; but as I had more than once discovered this colored gentleman in a condition when one candle must have appeared to him like two, I thought it possible that, by going a step further in his potations, he might have reversed this phenomenon, and seen no candle at all where he ought to have beheld one.

Things were in this state when an incident took place so awful and inexplicable in its character that my reason fairly reels at the bare memory of the occurrence. It was the tenth of July. After dinner was over I repaired, with my friend Dr. Hammond, to the garden to smoke my evening pipe. Independent of certain mental sympathies which existed between the Doctor and myself, we were linked together by a vice. We both smoked opium. We knew each other's secret, and respected it. We enjoyed together that wonderful expansion of thought, that marvellous intensifying of the perceptive faculties, that boundless feeling of existence when we seem to have points of contact with the whole universe,—in short, that unimaginable spiritual bliss, which I would not surrender for a throne, and which I hope you, reader, will never—never taste.

Those hours of opium happiness which the Doctor and I spent together in secret were regulated with a scientific accuracy. We did not blindly smoke the drug of paradise, and leave our dreams to chance. While smoking, we carefully steered our conversation through the brightest and calmest channels of thought. We talked of the East, and endeavored to recall the magical panorama of its glowing scenery. We criticised the most sensuous poets,— those who painted life ruddy with health, brimming with passion, happy in the possession of youth and strength. If we talked of Shakespeare's "Tempest," we lingered over Ariel, and avoided Caliban. Like the Guebers, we turned our faces to the east, and saw only the sunny side of the world.

This skilful coloring of our train of thought produced in our subsequent visions a corresponding tone. The splendor of Arabian fairy-land dyed our dreams. We paced that narrow strip of grass with the tread and port of kings. The song of the *rana arborea*, while he clung to the bark of the ragged plum-tree, sounded like the strains of divine musicians. Houses, walls, and streets melted like rain-clouds, and vistas of unimaginable glory stretched away before us. It was a rapturous companionship. We enjoyed the vast delight more perfectly because, even in our most ecstatic moments, we were conscious of each other's presence. Our pleasures, while individual, were still twin, vibrating and moving in musical accord.

On the evening in question, the tenth of July, the Doctor and myself drifted into an unusually meta-physical mood. We lit our large meerschaums, filled with fine Turkish tobacco, in the core of which burned a little black nut of opium, that, like the nut in the fairy tale, held within its narrow limits wonders beyond the reach of kings; we paced to and fro, conversing. A strange perversity dominated the currents of our thought. They would *not* flow through the sun-lit channels into which we strove to divert them. For some unaccountable reason, they constantly diverged into dark and lonesome beds, where a continual gloom brooded. It was in vain ⌐at, after our old fashion, we flung ourselves on the shores of the East, and talked of its gay bazaars, of the splendors of the time of Haroun, of harems and golden palaces. Black afreets continually arose from the depths of our talk, and expanded, like the one the fisherman released from the copper vessel, until they blotted everything bright from our vision. Insensibly, we yielded to the occult force that swayed us, and indulged in gloomy speculation. We had talked some time upon the proneness of the human mind to mysticism, and the almost universal love of the terrible, when Hammond suddenly said to me, "What do you consider to be the greatest element of terror?"

The question puzzled me. That many things were terrible, I knew. Stumbling over a corpse in the dark; beholding, as I once did, a woman floating down a deep and rapid river, with wildly lifted arms, and awful, upturned face, uttering, as she drifted, shrieks that rent one's heart, while we, the spectators, stood frozen at a window which overhung the river at a height of sixty feet, unable to make the slightest effort to save her, but dumbly watching her last supreme agony and her disappearance. A shattered wreck, with no life visible, encountered floating listlessly on the ocean, is a terrible object, for it suggests a huge terror, the proportions of which are veiled. But now struck me, for the first time, that there must be one great and rul-embodiment of fear,—a King of Terrors, to which all others must succumb. What might it be? To what train of circumstances would it owe its existence?

"I confess, Hammond," I replied to my friend, "I never considered the subject before. That there must be one Something more terrible than any other thing, I feel. I cannot attempt, however, even the most vague definition."

"I am somewhat like you, Harry," he answered. "I feel my capacity to experience a terror greater than anything yet conceived by the human mind;—something combining in fearful and unnatural amalgamation hitherto supposed incompatible elements. The calling of the voices in Brockden Brown's novel of 'Wieland' is awful; so is the picture of the Dweller of the Threshold, in Bulwer's 'Zanoni'; but," he added, shaking his head gloomily, "there is something more terrible still than these."

"Look here, Hammond," I rejoined, "let us drop this kind of talk, for heaven's sake! We shall suffer for it, depend on it."

"I don't know what's the matter with me tonight," he replied, "but my brain is running upon all sorts of weird and awful thoughts. I feel as if I could write a story like Hoffman, to-night, if I were only master of a literary style."

"Well, if we are going to be Hoffmanesque in our talk, I'm off to bed. Opium and nightmares should never be brought together. How sultry it is! Good-night, Hammond."

"Good-night, Harry. Pleasant dreams to you."

"To you, gloomy wretch, afreets, ghouls, and enchanters."

We parted, and each sought his respective chamber. I undressed quickly and got into bed, taking with me, according to my usual custom, a book, over which I generally read myself to sleep. I opened the volume as soon as I had laid my head upon the pillow, and instantly flung it to the other side of the room. It was Goudon's "History of Monsters,"—a curious French work, which I had lately imported from Paris, but which, in the state of mind I had then reached, was anything but an agreeable companion. I resolved to go to sleep at once; so, turning down my gas until nothing but a little blue point of light glimmered on the top of the tube, I composed myself to rest.

The room was in total darkness. The atom of gas that still remained alight did not illuminate a distance of three inches round the burner. I desperately drew my arms across my eyes, as if to shut out the darkness, and tried to think of nothing. It was in vain. The confounded themes touched on by Hammond in the garden kept obtruding themselves on my brain. I battled against them. I erected ramparts of would-be blankness of intellect to keep them out. They still crowded upon me. While I was lying still as a corpse, hoping that by a perfect physical inaction I should hasten mental repose, an awful incident occurred. A Something dropped, as it seemed, from the ceiling, plum upon my chest, and the next instant I felt two bony hands encircling my throat, endeavoring to choke me.

I am no coward, and am possessed of considerable physical strength. The suddenness of the attack, instead of stunning me, strung every nerve to its highest tension. My body acted from instinct, before my brain had time to realize the terrors of my position. In an instant I wound two muscular arms around the creature, and squeezed it, with all the strength of despair, against my chest. In a few seconds the bony hands that had fastened on my throat loosened their hold, and I was free to breathe once more. Then commenced a struggle of awful intensity. Immersed in the most profound darkness, totally ignorant of the nature of the Thing by which I was so suddenly attacked, finding my grasp slipping every moment, by reason, it seemed to me, of the entire nakedness of my assailant, bitten with sharp teeth in the shoulder, neck, and chest, having every moment to protect my throat against a pair of sinewy, agile hands, which my utmost efforts could not confine,— these were a combination of circumstances to combat which required all the strength, skill and courage that I possessed.

At last, after a silent, deadly, exhausting struggle, I got my assailant under by a series of incredible efforts of strength. Once pinned, with my knee on what I made out to be its chest, I knew that I was victor. I rested for a moment to breathe. I heard the creature beneath me panting in the darkness, and felt the violent throbbing of a heart. It was apparently as exhausted as I was; that was one comfort. At this moment I remembered that I usually placed under my pillow, before going to bed, a large yellow silk pocket-handkerchief. I felt for it instantly; it was there. In a few seconds more I had, after a fashion, pinioned the creature's arms.

I now felt tolerably secure. There was nothing more to be done but to turn on the gas, and, having first seen what my midnight assailant was like, arouse the household. I will confess to being actuated by a certain pride in not giving the alarm before; I wished to make the capture alone and unaided.

Never losing my hold for an instant, I slipped from the bed to the floor, dragging my captive with me. I had but a few steps to make to reach the gas-burner; these I made with the greatest caution, holding the creature in a grip like a vise. At last I got within arm's-length of the tiny speck of blue light which told me where the gas-burner lay. Quick as lightning I released my grasp with one hand and let on the full flood of light. Then I turned to look at my captive.

I cannot even attempt to give any definition of my sensations the instant after I turned on the gas. I suppose I must have shrieked with terror, for in less than a minute afterward my room was crowded with the inmates of the house. I shudder now as I think of that awful moment. *I saw nothing!* Yes; I had one arm firmly clasped round a breathing, panting, corporeal shape, my other hand gripped with all its strength a throat as warm, and apparently fleshy, as my own; and yet, with this living substance in my grasp, with its body pressed against my own, and all in the bright glare of a large jet of gas, I absolutely beheld nothing! Not even an outline,—a vapor!

I do not, even at this hour, realize the situation in which I found myself. Imagination in vain tries to compass the awful paradox.

It breathed. I felt its warm breath upon my cheek. It struggled fiercely. It had hands. They clutched me. Its skin was smooth, like my own. There it lay, pressed close up against me, solid as stone,—and yet utterly invisible!

I wonder that I did not faint or go mad on the instant. Some wonderful instinct must have sustained me; for, absolutely, in place of loosening my hold on the terrible Enigma, I seemed to gain an additional strength in my moment of horror, and tightened my grasp with such wonderful force that I felt the creature shivering with agony.

Just then Hammond entered the room at the head of the household. As soon as he beheld my face—which, I suppose, must have been an awful sight to look at—he hastened forward, crying, "Great heaven, Harry! what has happened?"

"Hammond! Hammond!" I cried, "come here. O, this is awful! I have been attacked in bed by something or other, which I have hold of; but I can't see it,—I can't see it!"

Hammond, doubtless struck by the unfeigned horror expressed in my countenance, made one or two steps forward with an anxious yet puzzled expression. A very audible titter burst from the remainder of my visitors. This suppressed laughter made me furious. To laugh at a human being in my position! It was the worst species of cruelty. *Now*, I can understand why the appearance of a man struggling violently, as it would seem, with an airy nothing, and calling for assistance against a vision, should have appeared ludicrous. *Then*, so great was my rage against the mocking crowd that had I the power, I would have stricken them dead where they stood.

"Hammond! Hammond!" I cried again, despairingly, "for God's sake come to me. I can hold the—the thing but a short while longer. It is over-powering me. Help me! Help me!"

"Harry," whispered Hammond, approaching me, "you have been smoking too much opium."

"I swear to you, Hammond, that this is no vision," I answered, in the same low tone. "Don't you see how it shakes my whole frame with its struggles? If you don't believe me, convince yourself. Feel it,—touch it."

Hammond advanced and laid his hand in the spot I indicated. A wild cry of horror burst from him. He had felt it!

In a moment he had discovered somewhere in my room a long piece of cord, and was the next instant winding it and knotting it about the body of the unseen being that I clasped in my arms.

"Harry," he said, in a hoarse, agitated voice, for, though he preserved his presence of mind, he was deeply moved, "Harry, it's all safe now. You may let go, old fellow, if you're tired. The Thing can't move."

I was utterly exhausted, and I gladly loosed my hold.

Hammond stood holding the ends of the cord that bound the Invisible, twisted round his hand, while before him, self-supporting as it were, he beheld a rope laced and interlaced, and stretching tightly around a vacant space. I never saw a man look so thoroughly stricken with awe. Nevertheless his face expressed all the courage and determination which I knew him to possess. His lips, although white, were set firmly, and one could perceive at a glance that, although stricken with fear, he was not daunted.

The confusion that ensued among the guests of the house who were witnesses of this extraordinary scene between Hammond and myself,—who beheld the pantomime of binding this struggling Something,—who beheld me almost sinking from physical exhaustion when my task of jailer was over,—the confusion and terror that took possession of the bystanders, when they saw all this, was beyond description. The weaker ones fled from the apartment. The few who remained clustered near the door and could not be induced to approach Hammond and his Charge. Still, incredulity broke out through their terror. They had not the courage to satisfy themselves, and yet they doubted. It was in vain that I begged of some of the men to come near and convince themselves by touch of the existence in that room of a living being which was invisible. They were incredulous, but did not dare to undeceive themselves. How could a solid, living, breathing body be invisible, they asked. My reply was this. I gave a sign to Hammond, and both of us—conquering our fearful repugnance to touch the invisible creature—lifted it from the ground, manacled as it was, and took it to my bed. Its weight was about that of a boy of fourteen.

"Now, my friends," I said, as Hammond and myself held the creature suspended over the bed, "I can give you self-evident proof that here is a solid, ponderable body, which, nevertheless, you cannot see. Be good enough to watch the surface of the bed attentively."

I was astonished at my own courage in treating this strange event so calmly; but I had recovered from my first terror, and felt a sort of scientific pride in the affair, which dominated every other feeling.

The eyes of the bystanders were immediately fixed on my bed. At a given signal Hammond and I let the creature fall. There was the dull sound of a heavy body alighting on a soft mass. The timbers of the bed creaked. A deep impression marked itself distinctly on the pillow, and on the bed itself. The crowd who witnessed this gave a low cry, and rushed from the room. Hammond and I were left alone with our Mystery.

We remained silent for some time, listening to the low, irregular breathing of the creature on the bed, and watching the rustle of the bed-clothes as it impotently struggled to free itself from confinement. Then Hammond spoke.

"Harry, this is awful."

"Ay, awful."

"But not unaccountable."

"Not unaccountable! What do you mean? Such a thing has never occurred since the birth of the world. I know not what to think, Hammond. God grant that I am not mad, and that this is not an insane fantasy!"

"Let us reason a little, Harry. Here is a solid body which we touch, but which we cannot see. The fact is so unusual that it strikes us with terror. Is there no parallel, though, for such a phenomenon? Take a piece of pure glass. It is tangible and transparent. A certain chemical coarseness is all that prevents its being so entirely transparent as to be totally invisible. It is not *theoretically impossible*, mind you, to make a glass which shall not reflect a single ray of light,—a glass so pure and homogeneous in its atoms that the rays from the sun will pass through it as they do through the air, refracted but not reflected. We do not see the air, and yet we feel it."

"That's all very well, Hammond, but these are inanimate substances. Glass does not breathe, air does not breathe. This *thing* has a heart that palpitates,—a will that moves it,—lungs that play, and inspire and respire."

"You forget the phenomena of which we have so often heard of late," answered the Doctor, gravely. "At the meetings called 'spirit circles,' invisible hands have been thrust into the hands of those persons round the table,—warm, fleshy hands that seemed to pulsate with mortal life."

"What? Do you think, then, that this thing is—"

"I don't know what it is," was the solemn reply; "but please the gods I will, with your assistance, thoroughly investigate it."

We watched together, smoking many pipes, all night long, by the bedside of the unearthly being that tossed and panted until it was apparently wearied out. Then we learned by the low, regular breathing that it slept.

The next morning the house was all astir. The boarders congregated on the landing outside my room, and Hammond and myself were lions. We had to answer a thousand questions as to the state of our extraordinary prisoner, for as yet not one person in the house except ourselves could be induced to set foot in the apartment.

The creature was awake. This was evidenced by the convulsive manner in which the bed-clothes were moved in its efforts to escape. There was something truly terrible in beholding, as it were, those second-hand indications of the terrible writhings and agonized struggles for liberty which themselves were invisible.

Hammond and myself had racked our brains during the long night to discover some means by which we might realize the shape and general appearance of the Enigma. As well as we could make out by passing our hands over the creature's form, its outlines and lineaments were human. There was a mouth; a round, smooth head without hair; a nose, which, however, was little elevated above the cheeks; and its hands and feet felt like those of a boy. At first we thought of placing the being on a smooth surface and tracing its outline with chalk, as shoemakers trace the outline of the foot. This plan was given up as being of no value. Such an outline would give not the slightest idea of its conformation.

A happy thought struck me. We could take a cast of it in plaster of Paris. This would give us the solid figure, and satisfy all our wishes. But how to do it? The movements of the creature would disturb the setting of the plastic covering, and distort the mould. Another thought. Why not give it chloroform? It had respiratory organs,—that was evident by its breathing. Once reduced to a state of insensibility, we could do with it what we would. Doctor X——was sent for; and after the worthy physician had recovered from the first shock of amazement, he proceeded to administer the chloroform. In three minutes afterward we were enabled to remove the fetters from the creature's body, and a modeller was busily engaged in covering the invisible form with the moist clay. In five minutes more we had a mould, and before evening a rough facsimile of the Mystery. It was shaped like a man,— distorted, uncouth, and horrible, but still a man. It was small, not over four feet and some inches in height, and its limbs revealed a muscular development that was unparalleled. Its face surpassed in hideousness anything I had ever seen. Gustave Doré, or Callot, or Tony Johannot, never conceived anything so horrible. There is a face in one of the latter's illustrations to *Un Voyage où il vous plaira* which somewhat approaches the countenance of this creature, but does not equal it. It was the physiognomy of what I should fancy a ghoul might be. It looked as if it was capable of feeding on human flesh.

Having satisfied our curiosity, and bound every one in the house to secrecy, it became a question what was to be done with our Enigma? It was impossible that we should keep such a horror in our house; it was equally impossible that such an awful being should be let loose upon the world. I confess that I would have gladly voted for the creature's destruction. But who would shoulder the responsibility? Who would undertake the execution of this horrible semblance of a human being? Day after day this question was deliberated gravely. The boarders all left the house. Mrs. Moffat was in despair, and threatened Hammond and myself with all sorts of legal penalties if we did not remove the Horror. Our answer was, "We will go if you like, but we decline taking this creature with us. Remove it yourself if you please. It appeared in your house. On you the responsibility rests." To this there was, of course, no answer. Mrs. Moffat could not obtain for love or money a person who would even approach the Mystery.

The most singular part of the affair was that we were entirely ignorant of what the creature habitually fed on. Everything in the way of nutriment that we could think of was placed before it, but was never touched. It was awful to stand by, day after day, and see the clothes toss, and hear the hard breathing, and know that it was starving.

Ten, twelve days, a fortnight passed, and it still lived. The pulsations of the heart, however, were daily growing fainter, and had now nearly ceased. It was evident that the creature was dying for want of sustenance. While this terrible life-struggle was going on, I felt miserable. I could not sleep. Horrible as the creature was, it was pitiful to think of the pangs it was suffering.

At last it died. Hammond and I found it cold and stiff one morning in the bed. The heart had ceased to beat, the lungs to inspire. We hastened to bury it in the garden. It was a strange funeral, the dropping of that viewless corpse into the damp hole. The cast of its form I gave to Doctor X——, who keeps it in his museum in Tenth Street.

As I am on the eve of a long journey from which I may not return, I have drawn up this narrative of an event the most singular that has ever come to my knowledge.

Shirley Jackson

The Beautiful Stranger

Shirley Jackson's "The Beautiful Stranger" is an enigmatic, fantastic tale, a middle-class paranoid fantasy of utopia denied, perhaps a parody of the women's gothic romance, a tale of dread and doubt. Stephen King, in *Danse Macabre*, credits Jackson with influencing the invention of "the new American gothic," which is characterized as "a symbolic mirror," and summarizes a perceptive article by the scholar, John G. Park, about the growing obsession with the self-evident in the new gothic form, especially in Jackson's work. For our purposes in this anthology, though, it is Jackson's balancing of the psychological versus the supernatural in horror that is most salient. It is the tension created by the mysterious atmosphere, by the doubt as to the accuracy of the character's perception that leaves the reader in anxiety and wonder in *The Haunting of Hill House* and "The Beautiful Stranger," that is at the heart of the horroripilation. Jackson's best work is as complex and many-leveled as "The Turn of the Screw."

What might be called the first intimation of strangeness occurred at the railroad station. She had come with her children, Smalljohn and her baby girl, to meet her husband when he returned from a business trip to Boston. Because she had been oddly afraid of being late, and perhaps even seeming uneager to encounter her husband after a week's separation, she dressed the children and put them into the car at home a long half hour before the train was due. As a result, of course, they had to wait interminably at the station, and what was to have been a charmingly staged reunion, family embracing husband and father, became at last an ill-timed and awkward performance. Smalljohn's hair was mussed, and he was sticky. The baby was cross, pulling at her pink bonnet and her dainty lace-edged dress, whining. The final arrival of the train caught them in mid-movements, as it were; Margaret was tying the ribbons on the baby's bonnet, Smalljohn was half over the back of the car seat. They scrambled out of the car, cringing from the sound of the train, hopelessly out of sorts.

John Senior waved from the high steps of the train. Unlike his wife and children, he looked utterly prepared for his return, as though he had taken some pains to secure a meeting at least painless, and had, in fact, stood just so, waving cordially from the steps of the train, for perhaps as long as half an hour, ensuring that he should not be caught half-ready, his hand not lifted so far as to over-emphasize the extent of his delight in seeing them again.

His wife had an odd sense of lost time. Standing now on the platform with the baby in her arms and Smalljohn beside her, she could not for a minute remember clearly whether he was coming home, or whether they were yet standing here to say good-bye to him. They had been quarreling when he left, and she had spent the week of his absence determining to forget that in his presence she had been frightened and hurt. This will be a good time to get things straight, she had been telling herself; while John is gone I can try to get hold of myself again. Now, unsure at last whether this was an arrival or a departure, she felt afraid again, straining to meet an unendurable tension. This will not do, she thought, believing that she was being honest with herself, and as he came down the train steps and walked toward them she smiled, holding the baby tightly against her so that the touch of its small warmth might bring some genuine tenderness into her smile.

This will not do, she thought, and smiled more cordially and told him "hello" as he came to her. Wondering, she kissed him and then when he held his arm around her and the baby for a minute the baby pulled back and struggled, screaming. Everyone moved in anger, and the baby kicked and screamed, "No, no, no."

"What a way to say hello to Daddy," Margaret said, and she shook the baby, half-amused, and yet grateful for the baby's sympathetic support. John turned to Smalljohn and lifted him, Smalljohn kicking and laughing helplessly. "Daddy, Daddy," Smalljohn shouted, and the baby screamed, "No, no."

Helplessly, because no one could talk with the baby screaming so, they turned and went to the car. When the baby was back in her pink basket in the car, and Smalljohn was settled with another lollipop beside her, there was an appalling quiet which would have to be filled as quickly as possible with meaningful words. John had taken the driver's seat in the car while Margaret was quieting the baby, and when Margaret got in beside him she felt a little chill of animosity at the sight of his hands on the wheel; I can't bear to relinquish even this much, she thought; for a week no one has driven the car except me. Because she could see so clearly that this was unreasonable—John owned half the car, after all—she said to him with bright interest, "And how was your trip? The weather?"

"Wonderful," he said, and again she was angered at the warmth in his tone; if she was unreasonable about the car, he was surely unreasonable to have enjoyed himself quite so much. "Everything went very well. I'm pretty sure I got the contract, everyone was very pleasant about it, and I go back in two weeks to settle everything."

The stinger is in the tail, she thought. He wouldn't tell it all so hastily if he didn't want me to miss half of it; I am supposed to be pleased that he got the contract and that everyone was so pleasant, and the part about going back is supposed to slip past me painlessly.

"Maybe I can go with you, then," she said. "Your mother will take the children."

"Fine," he said, but it was much too late; he hesitated noticeably before he spoke.

"I want to go too," said Smalljohn. "Can I go with Daddy?"

They came into their house, Margaret carrying the baby, and John carrying his suitcase and arguing delightedly with Smalljohn over which of them was carrying the heavier weight of it. The house was ready for them; Margaret had made sure that it was cleaned and emptied of the qualities which attached so surely to her position of wife alone with small children; the toys which Smalljohn had thrown around with unusual freedom were picked up, the baby's clothes (no one, after all, came to call when John was gone) were taken from the kitchen radiator where they had been drying. Aside from the fact that the house gave no impression of waiting for any particular people, but only for anyone well-bred and clean enough to fit within its small trim walls, it could have passed for a home, Margaret thought, even for a home where a happy family lived in domestic peace. She set the baby down in the playpen and turned with the baby's bonnet and jacket in her hand and saw her husband, head bent gravely as he listened to Smalljohn. Who? she wondered suddenly; is he taller? That is not my husband.

She laughed, and they turned to her, Smalljohn curious, and her husband with a quick bright recognition; she thought, why, it is *not* my husband, and he knows that I have seen it. There was no astonishment in her; she would have thought perhaps thirty seconds before that such a thing was impossible, but since it was now clearly possible, surprise would have been meaningless. Some other emotion was necessary, but she found at first only peripheral manifestations of one. Her heart was beating violently, her hands were shaking, and her fingers were cold. Her legs felt weak and she took hold of the back of a chair to steady herself. She found that she was still laughing, and then her emotion caught up with her and she knew what it was: it was relief.

"I'm glad you came," she said. She went over and put her head against his shoulder. "It was hard to say hello in the station," she said.

Smalljohn looked on for a minute and then wandered off to his toybox. Margaret was thinking, this is not the man who enjoyed seeing me cry; I need not be afraid. She caught her breath and was quiet; there was nothing that needed saying.

For the rest of the day she was happy. There was a constant delight in the relief from her weight of fear and unhappiness, it was pure joy to know that there was no longer any residue of suspicion and hatred; when she called him "John" she did so demurely, knowing that he participated in her secret amusement; when he answered her civilly there was, she thought, an edge of laughter behind his words. They seemed to have agreed soberly that mention of the subject would be in bad taste, might even, in fact, endanger their pleasure.

They were hilarious at dinner. John would not have made her a cocktail, but when she came downstairs from putting the children to bed the stranger met her at the foot of the stairs, smiling up at her, and took her arm to lead her into the living room where the cocktail shaker and glasses stood on the low table before the fire.

"How nice," she said, happy that she had taken a moment to brush her hair and put on fresh lipstick, happy that the coffee table which she had chosen with John and the fireplace which had seen many fires built by John and the low sofa where John had slept sometimes, had all seen fit to welcome the stranger with grace. She sat on the sofa and smiled at him when he handed her a glass; there was an odd illicit excitement in all of it; she was "entertaining" a man. The scene was a little marred by the fact that he had given her a martini with neither olive nor onion; it was the way she preferred her martini, and yet he should not have, strictly, known this, but she reassured herself with the thought that naturally he would have taken some pains to inform himself before coming.

He lifted his glass to her with a smile; he is here only because I am here, she thought.

"It's nice to be here," he said. He had, then, made one attempt to sound like John, in the car coming home. After he knew that she had recognized him for a stranger, he had never made any attempt to say words like "coming home" or "getting back," and of course she could not, not without pointing her lie. She put her hand in his and lay back against the sofa, looking into the fire.

"Being lonely is worse than anything in the world," she said.

"You're not lonely now?"

"Are you going away?"

"Not unless you come too." They laughed at his parody of John.

They sat next to each other at dinner; she and John had always sat at formal opposite ends of the table, asking one another politely to pass the salt and the butter.

"I'm going to put in a little set of shelves over there," he said, nodding toward the corner of the dining room. "It looks empty here, and it needs things. Symbols."

"Like?" She liked to look at him; his hair, she thought, was a little darker than John's, and his hands were stronger; this man would build whatever he decided he wanted built.

"We need things together. Things we like, both of us. Small delicate pretty things. Ivory."

With John she would have felt it necessary to remark at once that they could not afford such delicate pretty things, and put a cold finish to the idea, but with the stranger she said, "We'd have to look for them; not everything would be right."

"I saw a little creature once," he said. "Like a tiny little man, only colored all purple and blue and gold."

She remembered this conversation; it contained the truth like a jewel set in the evening. Much later, she was to tell herself that it was true; John could not have said these things.

She was happy, she was radiant, she had no conscience. He went obediently to his office the next morning, saying good-bye at the door with a rueful smile that seemed to mock the present necessity for doing the things that John always did, and as she watched him go down the walk she reflected that this was surely not going to be permanent; she could not endure having him gone for so long every day, although she had felt little about parting from John; moreover, if he kept doing John's things he might grow imperceptibly more like John. We will simply have to go away, she thought. She was pleased, seeing him get into the car; she would gladly share with him—indeed, give him outright—all that had been John's, so long as he stayed her stranger.

She laughed while she did her housework and dressed the baby. She took satisfaction in unpacking his suitcase, which he had abandoned and forgotten in a corner of the bedroom, as though prepared to take it up and leave again if she had not been as he thought her, had not wanted him to stay. She put away his clothes, so disarmingly like John's, and wondered for a minute at the closet; would there be a kind of delicacy in him about John's things? Then she told herself no, not so long as he began with John's wife, and laughed again.

The baby was cross all day, but when Smalljohn came home from nursery school his first question was—looking up eagerly—"Where is Daddy?"

"Daddy has gone to the office," and again she laughed, at the moment's quick sly picture of the insult to John.

Half a dozen times during the day she went upstairs, to look at his suitcase and touch the leather softly. She glanced constantly as she passed through the dining room into the corner where the small shelves would be someday, and told herself that they would find a tiny little man, all purple and blue and gold, to stand on the shelves and guard them from intrusion.

When the children awakened from their naps she took them for a walk and then, away from the house and returned violently to her former lonely pattern (walk with the children, talk meaninglessly of Daddy, long for someone to talk to in the evening ahead, restrain herself from hurrying home: he might have telephoned), she began to feel frightened again; suppose she had been wrong? It could not be possible that she was mistaken; it would be unutterably cruel for John to come tonight.

Then, she heard the car stop and when she opened the door and looked up she thought, no, it is not my husband, with a return of gladness. She was aware from his smile that he had perceived her doubts, and yet he was so clearly a stranger that, seeing him, she had no need of speaking.

She asked him, instead, almost meaningless questions during that evening, and his answers were important only because she was storing them away to reassure herself while he was away. She asked him what was the name of their Shakespeare professor in college, and who was that girl he liked so before he met Margaret. When he smiled and said that he had no idea, that he would not recognize the name if she told him, she was in delight. He had not bothered to master all of the past, then; he had learned enough (the names of the children, the location of the house, how she liked her cocktails) to get to her, and after that, it was not important, because either she would want him to stay, or she would, calling upon John, send him away again.

"What is your favorite food?" she asked him. "Are you fond of fishing? Did you ever have a dog?"

"Someone told me today," he said once, "that he had heard I was back from Boston, and I distinctly thought he said that he heard I was dead in Boston."

He was lonely, too, she thought with sadness, and that is why he came, bringing a destiny with him: now I will see him come every evening through the door and think, this is not my husband, and wait for him, remembering that I am waiting for a stranger.

"At any rate," she said, "*you* were not dead in Boston, and nothing else matters."

She saw him leave in the morning with a warm pride, and she did her housework and dressed the baby; when Smalljohn came home from nursery school he did not ask, but looked with quick searching eyes and then sighed. While the children were taking their naps she thought that she might take them to the park this afternoon, and then the thought of another such afternoon, another long afternoon with no one but the children, another afternoon of widowhood, was more than she could submit to; I have done this too much, she thought, I must see something today beyond the faces of my children. No one should be so much alone.

Moving quickly, she dressed and set the house to rights. She called a high-school girl and asked if she would take the children to the park; without guilt, she neglected the thousand small orders regarding the proper jacket for the baby, whether Smalljohn might have popcorn, when to bring them home. She fled, thinking, I must be with people.

She took a taxi into town, because it seemed to her the only possible thing to do was to seek out a gift for him, her first gift to him, and she thought she would find him, perhaps, a little creature all blue and purple and gold.

She wandered through the strange shops in the town, choosing small lovely things to stand on the new shelves, looking long and critically at ivories, at small statues, at brightly colored meaningless expensive toys, suitable for giving to a stranger.

It was almost dark when she started home, carrying her packages. She looked from the window of the taxi into the dark streets, and thought with pleasure that the stranger would be home before her, and look from the window to see her hurrying to him; he would think, this is a stranger, I am waiting for a stranger, as he saw her coming. "Here," she said, tapping on the glass, "right here, driver." She got out of the taxi and paid the driver, and smiled as he drove away. I must look well, she thought, the driver smiled back at me.

She turned and started for the house, and then hesitated; surely she had come too far? This is not possible, she thought, this cannot be; surely our house was white?

The evening was very dark, and she could see only the houses going in rows, with more rows beyond them and more rows beyond that, and somewhere a house which was hers, with the beautiful stranger inside, and she lost out here.

Ambrose Bierce

The Damned Thing

Ambrose Bierce is, after Poe, the greatest American horror writer of the nineteenth century. He is one of the conduits through which Poe influenced Robert W. Chambers. He is relatively underrated nevertheless, since a large portion of his horror fiction is not supernatural at all but psychological fiction and is of a brutally and grotesquely ironic cast, darkly humorous stories of the absurd and surreal. "The Damned Thing" is one of his most impressive works, another in the hybrid line of O'Brien and Chambers that leads all the way to A. E. Van Vogt's "Black Destroyer" and John W. Campbell's "Who Goes There" and defines the sub-genre of "invisible, nonsupernatural horrific menace," one of the primary forms of the monster story that is also, characteristically, concerned with reality and perception. As the ghost and, indeed, the supernatural entirely have become less central to horror fiction, their place is in part taken by the newly imagined realities of SF (the first single author collection in the SF genre in the 1930s was *The Horror on the Asteroid* by Edmund Hamilton). Lovecraft's "At the Mountains of Madness," a sequel to Poe's "Narrative of Arthur Gordon Pym," was published in *Astounding,* an SF magazine in the 1930s, and Hugo Gernsback, the man who invented the idea of SF as a genre, mentioned H. G. Wells, Jules Verne and Edgar Allan Poe as the models for writers to follow, in the April 1926 editorial of his first issue of *Amazing Stories*. But it was O'Brien and Bierce (and, indeed, Wells) who are the virtual models, who took the seed from Poe and grew the first fertile forms. The evolution sketched in here spreads into substantial branches of horror fiction in the latter half of the twentieth century, an underemphasized but significant part of the SF genre worth a book in itself.

I: One Does Not Always Eat What is on the Table

By the light of a tallow candle which had been placed on one end of a rough table a man was reading something written in a book. It was an old account book, greatly worn; and the writing was not, apparently, very legible, for the man sometimes held the page close to the flame of the candle to get a stronger light on it. The shadow of the book would then throw into obscurity a half of the room, darkening a number of faces and figures; for besides the reader, eight other men were present. Seven of them sat against the rough log walls, silent, motionless, and the room being small, not very far from the table. By extending an arm anyone of them could have touched the

880

eighth man, who lay on the table, face upward, partly covered by a sheet, his arms at his sides. He was dead.

The man with the book was not reading aloud, and no one spoke; all seemed to be waiting for something to occur; the dead man only was without expectation. From the blank darkness outside came in, through the aperture that served for a window, all the ever unfamiliar noises of night in the wilderness—the long nameless note of a distant coyote; the stilly pulsing trill of tireless insects in trees; strange cries of night birds, so different from those of the birds of day; the drone of great blundering beetles, and all that mysterious chorus of small sounds that seem always to have been but half heard when they have suddenly ceased, as if conscious of an indiscretion. But nothing of all this was noted in that company; its members were not overmuch addicted to idle interest in matters of no practical importance; that was obvious in every line of their rugged faces—obvious even in the dim light of the single candle. They were evidently men of the vicinity—farmers and woodsmen.

The person reading was a trifle different; one would have said of him that he was of the world, worldly, albeit there was that in his attire which attested a certain fellowship with the organisms of his environment. His coat would hardly have passed muster in San Francisco; his foot-gear was not of urban origin, and the hat that lay by him on the floor (he was the only one uncovered) was such that if one had considered it as an article of mere personal adornment he would have missed its meaning. In countenance the man was rather prepossessing, with just a hint of sternness; though that he may have assumed or cultivated, as appropriate to one in authority. For he was a coroner. It was by virtue of his office that he had possession of the book in which he was reading; it had been found among the dead man's effects—in his cabin, where the inquest was now taking place.

When the coroner had finished reading he put the book into his breast pocket. At that moment the door was pushed open and a young man entered. He, clearly, was not of mountain birth and breeding: he was clad as those who dwell in cities. His clothing was dusty, however, as from travel. He had, in fact, been riding hard to attend the inquest.

The coroner nodded; no one else greeted him.

"We have waited for you," said the coroner. "It is necessary to have done with this business to-night."

The young man smiled. "I am sorry to have kept you," he said. "I went away, not to evade your summons, but to post to my newspaper an account of what I suppose I am called back to relate."

The coroner smiled.

"The account that you posted to your newspaper," he said, "differs, probably, from that which you will give here under oath."

"That," replied the other, rather hotly and with a visible flush, "is as you please. I used manifold paper and have a copy of what I sent. It was not written as news, for it is incredible, but as fiction. It may go as a part of my testimony under oath."

"But you say it is incredible."

"That is nothing to you, sir, if I also swear that it is true."

The coroner was silent for a time, his eyes upon the floor. The men about the sides of the cabin talked in whispers, but seldom withdrew their gaze from the face of the corpse. Presently the coroner lifted his eyes and said: "We will resume the inquest."

The men removed their hats. The witness was sworn.

"What is your name?" the coroner asked.

"William Harker."

"Age?"

"Twenty-seven."

"You knew the deceased, Hugh Morgan?"

"Yes."

"You were with him when he died?"

"Near him."

"How did that happen—your presence, I mean?"

"I was visiting him at this place to shoot and fish. A part of my purpose, however, was to study him and his odd, solitary way of life. He seemed a good model for a character in fiction. I sometimes write stories."

"I sometimes read them."

"Thank you."

"Stories in general—not yours."

Some of the jurors laughed. Against a sombre background humour shows high lights. Soldiers in the intervals of battle laugh easily, and a jest in the death chamber conquers by surprise.

"Relate the circumstances of this man's death," said the coroner. "You may use any notes or memoranda that you please."

The witness understood. Pulling a manuscript from his breast pocket he held it near the candle and turning the leaves until he found the passage that he wanted began to read.

2: What may Happen in a Field of Wild Oats

". . . The sun had hardly risen when we left the house. We were looking for quail, each with a shotgun, but we had only one dog. Morgan said that our best ground was beyond a certain ridge that he pointed out, and we crossed it by a trail through the *chaparral*. On the other side was comparatively level ground, thickly covered with wild oats. As we emerged from the *chaparral* Morgan was but a few yards in advance. Suddenly we heard, at a little distance to our right and partly in front, a noise as of some animal thrashing about in the bushes, which we could see were violently agitated.

" 'We've started a deer,' I said. 'I wish we had brought a rifle.'

"Morgan, who had stopped and was intently watching the agitated *chaparral*, said nothing, but had cocked both barrels of his gun and was holding it in readiness to aim. I thought him a trifle excited, which surprised me, for he had a reputation for exceptional coolness, even in moments of sudden and imminent peril.

" 'Oh, come,' I said. 'You are not going to fill up a deer with quail-shot, are you?'

"Still he did not reply; but catching a sight of his face as he turned it slightly toward me, I was struck by the intensity of his look. Then I understood that we had serious business in hand, and my first conjecture was that we had 'jumped' a grizzly. I advanced to Morgan's side, cocking my piece as I moved.

"The bushes were now quiet and the sounds had ceased, but Morgan was as attentive to the place as before.

" 'What is it? What the devil is it?' I asked.

" 'That Damned Thing!' he replied, without turning his head. His voice was husky and unnatural. He trembled visibly.

"I was about to speak further, when I observed the wild oats near the place of the disturbance moving in the most inexplicable way. I can hardly describe it. It seemed as if stirred by a streak of wind, which not only bent it, but pressed it down—crushed it so that it did not rise; and this movement was slowly prolonging itself directly toward us.

"Nothing that I had ever seen had affected me so strangely as this unfamiliar and unaccountable phenomenon, yet I am unable to recall any sense of fear. I remember—and tell it here because, singularly enough, I recollected it then—that once in looking carelessly out of an open window I momentarily mistook a small tree close at hand for one of a group of larger trees at a little distance away. It looked the same size as the others, but being more distinctly and sharply defined in mass and detail seemed out of harmony with them. It was a mere falsification of the law of aerial perspective, but it startled, almost terrified me. We so rely upon the orderly operation of familiar natural laws that any seeming suspension of them is noted as a menace to our safety, a warning of unthinkable calamity. So now the apparently causeless movement of the herbage and the slow, undeviating approach of the line of disturbance were distinctly disquieting. My companion appeared actually frightened, and I could hardly credit my senses when I saw him suddenly throw his gun to his shoulder and fire both barrels at the agitated grain! Before the smoke of the discharge had cleared away I heard a loud savage cry—a scream like that of a wild animal—and flinging his gun upon the ground, Morgan sprang away and ran swiftly from the spot. At the same instant I was thrown violently to the ground by the impact of something unseen in the smoke— some soft, heavy substance that seemed thrown against me with great force.

"Before I could get upon my feet and recover my gun, which seemed to have been struck from my hands, I heard Morgan crying out as if in mortal agony, and mingling with his cries were such hoarse, savage sounds as one hears from fighting dogs. Inexpressibly terrified, I struggled to my feet and looked in the direction of Morgan's retreat; and may Heaven in mercy spare me from another sight like that! At a distance of less than thirty yards was my friend, down upon one knee, his head thrown back at a frightful angle, hatless, his long hair in disorder and his whole body in violent movement from side to side, backward and forward. His right arm was lifted and seemed to lack the hand—at least, I could see none. The other arm was invisible. At times, as my memory now reports this extraordinary scene, I could discern but a part of his body; it was as if he had been partly blotted out—I cannot otherwise express it—then a shifting of his position would bring it all into view again.

"All this must have occurred within a few seconds, yet in that time Morgan assumed all the postures of a determined wrestler vanquished by superior weight and strength. I saw nothing but him, and him not always distinctly. During the entire incident his shouts and curses were heard, as if through an enveloping uproar of such sounds of rage and fury as I had never heard from the throat of man or brute!

"For a moment only I stood irresolute, then throwing down my gun, I ran forward to my friend's assistance. I had a vague belief that he was suffering from a fit, or some form of convulsion. Before I could reach his side he was down and quiet. All sounds had ceased, but with a feeling of such terror as even these awful events had not inspired I now saw again the mysterious movement of the wild oats, prolonging itself from the trampled area about the prostrate man toward the edge of a wood. It was only when it had reached the wood that I was able to withdraw my eyes and look at my companion. He was dead."

3: A Man though Naked may be in Rags

The coroner rose from his seat and stood beside the dead man. Lifting an edge of the sheet, he pulled it away, exposing the entire body, altogether naked and showing in the candle-light a clay-like yellow. It had, however, broad maculations of bluish black, obviously caused by extravasated blood from contusions. The chest and sides looked as if they had been beaten with a bludgeon. There were dreadful lacerations; the skin was torn in strips and shreds.

The coroner moved round to the end of the table and undid a silk handkerchief which had been passed under the chin and knotted on the top of the head. When the handkerchief was drawn away it exposed what had been the throat. Some of the jurors who had risen to get a better view repented their curiosity and turned away their faces. Witness Harker went to the open window and leaned out across the sill, faint and sick. Dropping the handkerchief upon the dead man's neck, the coroner stepped to an angle of the room and from a pile of clothing produced one garment after another, each of which he held up a moment for inspection. All were torn, and stiff with blood. The jurors did not make a closer inspection. They seemed rather uninterested. They had, in truth, seen all this before; the only thing that was new to them being Harker's testimony.

"Gentlemen," the coroner said, "we have no more evidence, I think. Your duty has been already explained to you; if there is nothing you wish to ask you may go outside and consider your verdict."

The foreman rose—a tall, bearded man of sixty, coarsely clad.

"I should like to ask one question, Mr. Coroner," he said. "What asylum did this yer last witness escape from?"

"Mr. Harker," said the coroner gravely and tranquilly, "from what asylum did you last escape?"

Harker flushed crimson again, but said nothing, and the seven jurors rose and solemnly filed out of the cabin.

"If you have done insulting me, sir," said Harker, as soon as he and the officer were left alone with the dead man, "I suppose I am at liberty to go?"

"Yes."

Harker started to leave, but paused, with his hand on the door latch. The habit of his profession was strong in him—stronger than his sense of personal dignity. He turned about and said:

"The book that you have there—I recognize it as Morgan's diary. You seemed greatly interested in it; you read in it while I was testifying. May I see it? The public would like—"

"The book will cut no figure in this matter," replied the official, slipping it into his coat pocket; "all the entries in it were made before the writer's death."

As Harker passed out of the house the jury reentered and stood about the table, on which the now covered corpse showed under the sheet with sharp definition. The foreman seated himself near the candle, produced from his breast pocket a pencil and scrap of paper and wrote rather laboriously the following verdict, which with various degrees of effort all signed:

"We, the jury, do find that the remains come to their death at the hands of a mountain lion, but some of us thinks, all the same, they had fits."

4: An Explanation from the Tomb

In the diary of the late Hugh Morgan are certain interesting entries having, possibly, a scientific value as suggestions. At the inquest upon his body the book was not put in evidence; possibly the coroner thought it not worth while to confuse the jury. The date of the first of the entries mentioned cannot be ascertained; the upper part of the leaf is torn away; the part of the entry remaining follows:

". . . would run in a half-circle, keeping his head turned always toward the centre, and again he would stand still, barking furiously. At last he ran away into the brush as fast as he could go. I thought at first that he had gone mad, but on returning to the house found no other alteration in his manner than what was obviously due to fear of punishment.

"Can a dog see with his nose? Do odours impress some cerebral centre with images of the thing that emitted them? . . .

"*Sept. 2.*—Looking at the stars last night as they rose above the crest of the ridge east of the house, I observed them successively disappear—from left to right. Each was eclipsed but an instant, and only a few at the same time, but along the entire length of the ridge all that were within a degree or two of the crest were blotted out. It was as if something had passed along between me and them; but I could not see it, and the stars were not thick enough to define its outline. Ugh! don't like this." . . .

Several weeks' entries are missing, three leaves being torn from the book.

"*Sept. 27.*—It has been about here again—I find evidences of its presence every day. I watched again all last night in the same cover, gun in hand, double-charged with buckshot. In the morning the fresh footprints were there, as before. Yet I would have sworn that I did not sleep—indeed, I hardly sleep at all. It is terrible, insupportable! If these amazing experiences are real I shall go mad; if they are fanciful I am mad already.

"*Oct.* 3.—I shall not go—it shall not drive me away. No, this is *my* house, *my* land. God hates a coward. . . .

"*Oct.* 5.—I can stand it no longer; I have invited Harker to pass a few weeks with me—he has a level head. I can judge from his manner if he thinks me mad.

"*Oct.* 7.—I have the solution of the mystery; it came to me last night—suddenly, as by revelation. How simple—how terribly simple!

"There are sounds that we cannot hear. At either end of the scale are notes that stir no chord of that imperfect instrument, the human ear. They are too high or too grave. I have observed a flock of blackbirds occupying an entire tree-top—the tops of several trees—and all in full song. Suddenly—in a moment—at absolutely the same instant—all spring into the air and fly away. How? They could not all see one another—whole tree-tops intervened. At no point could a leader have been visible to all. There must have been a signal of warning or command, high and shrill above the din, but by me unheard. I have observed, too, the same simultaneous flight when all were silent, among not only blackbirds, but other birds—quail, for example, widely separated by bushes—even on opposite sides of a hill.

"It is known to seamen that a school of whales basking or sporting on the surface of the ocean, miles apart, with the convexity of the earth between, will sometimes dive at the same instant—all gone out of sight in a moment. The signal has been sounded—too grave for the ear of the sailor at the masthead and his comrades on the deck—who nevertheless feel its vibrations in the ship as the stones of a cathedral are stirred by the bass of the organ.

"As with sounds, so with colours. At each end of the solar spectrum the chemist can detect the presence of what are known as 'actinic' rays. They represent colours—integral colours in the composition of light—which we are unable to discern. The human eye is an imperfect instrument; its range is but a few octaves of the real 'chromatic scale.' I am not mad; there are colours that we cannot see.

"And, God help me! the Damned Thing is of such a colour!"

Edith Wharton

Afterward

Edith Wharton, one of the great American writers in the tradition of realism, a close friend of Henry James, is also one of the finest of all American writers of supernatural fiction. James and Walter de la Mare are her models. Had John W. Campbell chosen, he could have used her as one of the models for the kind of tales he wanted to find for *Unknown*, ghost stories with a finely depicted everyday contemporary setting, except that her stories are basically for and of the upper and upper middle classes and Campbell produced for the "pulp" audience. Her influence on succeeding writers is difficult to trace, but her stories (collected in *Ghosts*) are masterful and endure. "Afterward" is indeed in the manner of de la Mare. Wharton gives us a character portrayal of meticulous clarity and substantial psychological depth, but the events are unsettling and ambiguous enough to impel the story over the border into our third category. It is essentially a story about perception and the nature of reality.

I

O h, there *is* one, of course, but you'll never know it."
The assertion, laughingly flung out six months earlier in a bright June garden, came back to Mary Boyne with a new perception of its significance as she stood, in the December dusk, waiting for the lamps to be brought into the library.

The words had been spoken by their friend Alida Stair, as they sat at tea on her lawn at Pangbourne, in reference to the very house of which the library in question was the central, the pivotal, "feature." Mary Boyne and her husband, in quest of a country place in one of the southern or southwestern counties, had, on their arrival in England, carried their problem straight to Alida Stair, who had successfully solved it in her own case; but it was not until they had rejected, almost capriciously, several practical and judicious suggestions that she threw out: "Well, there's Lyng, in Dorsetshire. It belongs to Hugo's cousins, and you can get it for a song."

The reason she gave for its being obtainable on these terms—its remoteness from a station, its lack of electric light, hot-water pipes, and other vulgar necessities—were exactly those pleading in its favour with two romantic Americans perversely in search of the economic drawbacks which were associated, in their tradition, with unusual architectural felicities.

"I should never believe I was living in an old house unless I was thoroughly uncomfortable," Ned Boyne, the more extravagant of the two, had jocosely insisted; "the least hint of 'convenience' would make me think it had been bought out of an exhibition, with the pieces numbered, and set up again." And they had proceeded to enumerate, with humorous precision, their various doubts and demands, refusing to believe that the house their cousin recommended was *really* Tudor till they learned it had no heating system, or that the village church was literally in the grounds till she assured them of the deplorable uncertainty of the water-supply.

"It's too uncomfortable to be true!" Edward Boyne had continued to exult as the avowal of each disadvantage was successively wrung from her; but he had cut short his rhapsody to ask, with a relapse to distrust: "And the ghost? You've been concealing from us the fact that there is no ghost!"

Mary, at the moment, had laughed with him, yet almost with her laugh, being possessed of several sets of independent perceptions, had been struck by a note of flatness in Alida's answering hilarity.

"Oh, Dorsetshire's full of ghosts, you know."

"Yes, yes; but that won't do. I don't want to have to drive ten miles to see somebody else's ghost. I want one of my own on the premises. *Is* there a ghost at Lyng?"

His rejoinder had made Alida laugh again, and it was then that she had flung back tantalizingly: "Oh, there *is* one, of course, but you'll never know it."

"Never know it?" Boyne pulled her up. "But what in the world constitutes a ghost except the fact of its being known for one?"

"I can't say. But that's the story."

"That there's a ghost, but that nobody knows it's a ghost?"

"Well—not till afterward, at any rate."

"Till afterward?"

"Not till long, long afterward."

"But if it's once been identified as an unearthly visitant, why hasn't its *signalement* been handed down in the family? How has it managed to preserve its incognito?"

Alida could only shake her head. "Don't ask me. But it has."

"And then suddenly—" Mary spoke up as if from cavernous depths of divination—"suddenly, long afterward, one says to one's self: *'That was it?'* "

She was startled at the sepulchral sound with which her question fell on the banter of the other two, and she saw the shadow of the same surprise flit across Alida's pupils. "I suppose so. One just has to wait."

"Oh, hang waiting!" Ned broke in. "Life's too short for a ghost who can only be enjoyed in retrospect. Can't we do better than that, Mary?"

But it turned out that in the event they were not destined to, for within three months of their conversation with Mrs. Stair they were settled at Lyng, and the life they had yearned for, to the point of planning it in advance in all its daily details, had actually begun for them.

It was to sit, in the thick December dusk, by just such a wide-hooded fireplace, under just such black oak rafters, with the sense that beyond the mullioned panes the downs were darkened to a deeper solitude: it was for the ultimate indulgence of such sensations that Mary Boyne, abruptly exiled from New York by her husband's business, had endured for nearly fourteen years the soul-deadening ugliness of a Middle Western town, and that Boyne had ground on doggedly at his engineering till, with a suddenness that still made her blink, the prodigious windfall of the Blue Star Mine had put them at a stroke in possession of life and the leisure to taste it. They had never for a moment meant their new state to be one of idleness; but they meant to give themselves only to harmonious activities. She had her vision of painting and gardening (against a background of gray walls), he dreamed of the production of his long-planned book on the "Economic Basis of Culture"; and with such absorbing work ahead no existence could be too sequestered: they could not get far enough from the world, or plunge deep enough into the past.

Dorsetshire had attracted them from the first by an air of remoteness out of all proportion to its geographical position. But to the Boynes it was one of the ever-recurring wonders of the whole incredibly compressed island—a nest of counties, as they put it—that for the production of its effects so little of a given quality went so far: that so few miles made a distance, and so short a distance a difference.

"It's that," Ned had once enthusiastically explained, "that gives such depth to their effects, such relief to their contrasts. They've been able to lay the butter so thick on every delicious mouthful."

The butter had certainly been laid on thick at Lyng: the old house hidden under a shoulder of the downs had almost all the finer marks of commerce with a protracted past. The mere fact that it was neither large nor exceptional made it, to the Boynes, abound the more completely in its special charm—the charm of having been for centuries a deep dim reservoir of life. The life had probably not been of the most vivid order: for long periods, no doubt, it had fallen as noiselessly into the past as the quiet drizzle of autumn fell, hour after hour, into the fish-pond between the yews; but these back-waters of existence sometimes breed, in their sluggish depths, strange acuities of emotion, and Mary Boyne had felt from the first the mysterious stir of intenser memories.

The feeling had never been stronger than on this particular afternoon when, waiting in the library for the lamps to come, she rose from her seat and stood among the shadows of the hearth. Her husband had gone off, after luncheon, for one of his long tramps on the downs. She had noticed of late that he preferred to go alone; and, in the tried security of their personal relations, had been driven to conclude that his book was bothering him, and that he needed the afternoons to turn over in solitude the problems left from the morning's work. Certainly the book was not going as smoothly as she had thought it would, and there were lines of perplexity between his eyes such as had never been there in his engineering days. He had often, then, looked fagged to the verge of illness, but the native demon of "worry" had never branded his brow. Yet the few pages he had so far read to her—the introduction, and a summary of the opening chapter—showed a firm hold on his subject, and an increasing confidence in his powers.

The fact threw her into deeper perplexity, since, now that he had done with "business" and its disturbing contingencies, the one other possible source of anxiety was eliminated. Unless it were his health, then? But physically he had gained since they had come to Dorsetshire, grown robuster, ruddier and fresher-eyed. It was only within the last week that she had felt in him the undefinable change which made her restless in his absence, and as tongue-tied in his presence as though it were *she* who had a secret to keep from him!

The thought that there *was* a secret somewhere between them struck her with a sudden rap of wonder, and she looked about her down the long room.

"Can it be the house?" she mused.

The room itself might have been full of secrets. They seemed to be piling themselves up, as evening fell, like the layers and layers of velvet shadow dropping from the low ceiling, the rows of books, the smoke-blurred sculpture of the hearth.

"Why, of course—the house is haunted!" she reflected.

The ghost—Alida's imperceptible ghost—after figuring largely in the banter of their first month or two at Lyng, had been gradually left aside as too ineffectual for imaginative use. Mary had, indeed, as became the tenant of a haunted house, made the customary inquiries among her rural neighbours, but, beyond a vague "They dü say so, ma'am," the villagers had nothing to impart. The elusive spectre had apparently never had sufficient identity for a legend to crystallize about it, and after a time the Boynes had set the matter down to their profit-and-loss account, agreeing that Lyng was one of the few houses good enough in itself to dispense with supernatural enhancements.

"And I suppose, poor ineffectual demon, that's why it beats its beautiful wings in vain in the void," Mary had laughingly concluded.

"Or, rather," Ned answered in the same strain, "why, amid so much that's ghostly, it can never affirm its separate existence as *the* ghost." And thereupon their invisible housemate had finally dropped out of their references, which were numerous enough to make them soon unaware of the loss.

Now, as she stood on the hearth, the subject of their earlier curiosity revived in her with a new sense of its meaning—a sense gradually acquired through daily contact with the scene of the lurking mystery. It was the house itself, of course, that possessed the ghost-seeing faculty, that communed visually but secretly with its own past; if one could only get into close enough communion with the house, one might surprise its secret, and acquire the ghost-sight on one's own account. Perhaps, in his long hours in this very room, where she never trespassed till the afternoon, her husband *had* acquired it already, and was silently carrying about the weight of whatever it had revealed to him. Mary was too well versed in the code of the spectral world not to know that one could not talk about the ghosts one saw: to do so was almost as great a breach of taste as to name a lady in a club. But this explanation did not really satisfy her. "What, after all, except for the fun of the shudder," she reflected, "would he really care for any of their old ghosts?" And thence she was thrown back once more on the fundamental dilemma: the fact that one's greater or less susceptibility to spectral influences had no particular bearing on the case, since, when one *did* see a ghost at Lyng, one did not know it.

"Not till long afterward," Alida Stair had said. Well, supposing Ned *had* seen one when they first came, and had known only within the last week what had happened to him? More and more under the spell of the hour, she threw back her thoughts to the early days of their tenancy, but at first only to recall a lively confusion of unpacking, settling, arranging of books, and calling to each other from remote corners of the house as, treasure after treasure, it revealed itself to them. It was in this particular connection that she presently recalled a certain soft afternoon of the previous October, when, passing from the first rapturous flurry of exploration to a detailed inspection of the old house, she had pressed (like a novel heroine) a panel that opened on a flight of corkscrew stairs leading to a flat ledge of the roof—the roof which, from below, seemed to slope away on all sides too abruptly for any but practised feet to scale.

The view from this hidden coign was enchanting, and she had flown down to snatch Ned from his papers and give him the freedom of her discovery. She remembered still how, standing at her side, he had passed his arm about her while their gaze flew to the long tossed horizon-line of the downs, and then dropped contentedly back to trace the arabesque of yew hedges about the fish-pond, and the shadow of the cedar on the lawn.

"And now the other way," he had said, turning her about within his arm; and closely pressed to him, she had absorbed, like some long satisfying draught, the picture of the gray-walled court, the squat lions on the gates, and the lime-avenue reaching up to the highroad under the downs.

It was just then, while they gazed and held each other, that she had felt his arm relax, and heard a sharp "Hullo!" that made her turn to glance at him.

Distinctly, yes, she now recalled that she had seen, as she glanced, a shadow of anxiety, of perplexity, rather, fall across his face; and, following his eyes, had beheld the figure of a man—a man in loose grayish clothes, as it appeared to her—who was sauntering down the lime-avenue to the court with the doubtful gait of a stranger who seeks his way. Her short-sighted eyes had given her but a blurred impression of slightness and grayishness, with something foreign, or at least unlocal, in the cut of the figure or its dress; but her husband had apparently seen more—seen enough to make him push past her with a hasty "Wait!" and dash down the stairs without pausing to give her a hand.

A slight tendency to dizziness obliged her, after a provisional clutch at the chimney against which they had been leaning, to follow him first more cautiously; and when she had reached the landing she paused again, for a less definite reason, leaning over the banister to strain her eyes through the silence of the brown sun-flecked depths. She lingered there till, somewhere in those depths, she heard the closing of a door; then, mechanically impelled, she went down the shallow flights of steps till she reached the lower hall.

The front door stood open on the sunlight of the court, and hall and court were empty. The library door was open, too, and after listening in vain for any sound of voices within, she crossed the threshold, and found her husband alone, vaguely fingering the papers on his desk.

He looked up, as if surprised at her entrance, but the shadow of anxiety had passed from his face, leaving it even, as she fancied, a little brighter and clearer than usual.

"What was it? Who was it?" she asked.

"Who?" he repeated, with the surprise still all on his side.

"The man we saw coming toward the house."

He seemed to reflect. "The man? Why, I thought I saw Peters; I dashed after him to say a word about the stable drains, but he had disappeared before I could get down."

"Disappeared? But he seemed to be walking so slowly when we saw him."

Boyne shrugged his shoulders. "So I thought; but he must have got up steam in the interval. What do you say to our trying a scramble up Meldon Steep before sunset?"

That was all. At the time the occurrence had been less than nothing, had, indeed, been immediately obliterated by the magic of their first vision from Meldon Steep, a height which they had dreamed of climbing ever since they had first seen its bare spine rising above the roof of Lyng. Doubtless it was the mere fact of the other incident's having occurred on the very day of their ascent to Meldon that had kept it stored away in the fold of memory from which it now emerged; for in itself it had no mark of the portentous. At the moment there could have been nothing more natural than that Ned should dash himself from the roof in the pursuit of dilatory tradesmen. It was the period when they were always on the watch for one or the other of the specialists employed about the place; always lying in wait for them, and rushing out at them with questions, reproaches or reminders. And certainly in the distance the gray figure had looked like Peters.

Yet now, as she reviewed the scene, she felt her husband's explanation of it to have been invalidated by the look of anxiety on his face. Why had the familiar appearance of Peters made him anxious? Why, above all, if it was of such prime necessity to confer with him on the subject of the stable drains, had the failure to find him produced such a look of relief? Mary could not say that any one of these questions had occurred to her at the time, yet, from the promptness with which they now marshalled themselves at her summons, she had a sense that they must all along have been there, waiting their hour.

II

Weary with her thoughts, she moved to the window. The library was now quite dark, and she was surprised to see how much faint light the outer world still held.

As she peered out into it across the court, a figure shaped itself far down the perspective of bare limes: it looked a mere blot of deeper gray in the grayness, and for an instant, as it moved toward her, her heart thumped to the thought, "It's the ghost!"

She had time, in that long instant, to feel suddenly that the man of whom, two months earlier, she had had a distant vision from the roof, was now, at his predestined hour, about to reveal himself as *not* having been Peters; and her spirit sank under the impending fear of the disclosure. But almost with the next tick of the clock the figure, gaining substance and character, showed itself even to her weak sight as her husband's; and she turned to meet him, as he entered, with the confession of her folly.

"It's really too absurd," she laughed out, "but I never *can* remember!"

"Remember what?" Boyne questioned as they drew together.

"That when one sees the Lyng ghost one never knows it."

Her hand was on his sleeve, and he kept it there, but with no response in his gesture or in the lines of his preoccupied face.

"Did you think you'd seen it?" he asked, after an appreciable interval.

"Why, I actually took *you* for it, my dear, in my mad determination to spot it!"

"Me—just now?" His arm dropped away, and he turned from her with a faint echo of her laugh. "Really, dearest, you'd better give it up, if that's the best you can do."

"Oh, yes, I give it up. Have *you*?" she asked, turning round on him abruptly.

The parlour-maid had entered with letters and a lamp, and the light struck up into Boyne's face as he bent above the tray she presented.

"Have *you*?" Mary perversely insisted, when the servant had disappeared on her errand of illumination.

"Have I what?" he rejoined absently, the light bringing out the sharp stamp of worry between his brows as he turned over the letters.

"Given up trying to see the ghost." Her heart beat a little at the experiment she was making.

Her husband, laying his letters aside, moved away into the shadow of the hearth.

"I never tried," he said, tearing open the wrapper of a newspaper.

"Well, of course," Mary persisted, "the exasperating thing is that there's no use trying, since one can't be sure till so long afterward."

He was unfolding the paper as if he had hardly heard her; but after a pause, during which the sheets rustled spasmodically between his hands, he looked up to ask, "Have you any idea *how long*?"

Mary had sunk into a low chair beside the fireplace. From her seat she glanced over, startled, at her husband's profile, which was projected against the circle of lamplight.

"No; none. Have *you*?" she retorted, repeating her former phrase with an added stress of intention.

Boyne crumpled the paper into a bunch, and then, inconsequently, turned back with it toward the lamp.

"Lord, no! I only meant," he explained, with a faint tinge of impatience, "is there any legend, any tradition, as to that?"

"Not that I know of," she answered; but the impulse to add "What makes you ask?" was checked by the reappearance of the parlour-maid, with tea and a second lamp.

With the dispersal of shadows, and the repetition of the daily domestic office, Mary Boyne felt herself less oppressed by that sense of something mutely imminent which had darkened her afternoon. For a few moments she gave herself to the details of her task, and when she looked up from it she was struck to the point of bewilderment by the change in her husband's face. He had seated himself near the farther lamp, and was absorbed in the perusal of his letters; but was it something he had found in them, or merely the shifting of her own point of view, that had restored his features to their normal aspect? The longer she looked the more definitely the change affirmed itself. The lines of tension had vanished, and such traces of fatigue as lingered were of the kind easily attributable to steady mental effort. He glanced up, as if drawn by her gaze, and met her eyes with a smile.

"I'm dying for my tea, you know; and here's a letter for you," he said.

She took the letter he held out in exchange for the cup she proffered him, and, returning to her seat, broke the seal with the languid gesture of the reader whose interests are all enclosed in the circle of one cherished presence.

Her next conscious motion was that of starting to her feet, the letter falling to them as she rose, while she held out to her husband a newspaper clipping.

"Ned! What's this? What does it mean?"

He had risen at the same instant, almost as if hearing her cry before she uttered it; and for a perceptible space of time he and she studied each other, like adversaries watching for an advantage, across the space between her chair and his desk.

"What's what? You fairly made me jump!" Boyne said at length, moving toward her with a sudden half-exasperated laugh. The shadow of apprehension was on his face again, not now a look of fixed foreboding, but a shifting vigilance of lips and eyes that gave her the sense of his feeling himself invisibly surrounded.

Her hand shook so that she could hardly give him the clipping.

"This article—from the *Waukesha Sentinel*—that a man named Elwell has brought suit against you—that there was something wrong about the Blue Star Mine. I can't understand more than half."

They continued to face each other as she spoke, and to her astonishment she saw that her words had the almost immediate effect of dissipating the strained watchfulness of his look.

"Oh, *that*!" He glanced down the printed slip, and then folded it with the gesture of one who handles something harmless and familiar. "What's the matter with you this afternoon, Mary? I thought you'd got bad news."

She stood before him with her undefinable terror subsiding slowly under the reassurance of his tone.

"You knew about this, then—it's all right?"

"Certainly I knew about it; and it's all right."

"But what *is* it? I don't understand. What does this man accuse you of?"

"Pretty nearly every crime in the calendar." Boyne had tossed the clipping down, and thrown himself into an armchair near the fire. "Do you want to hear the story? It's not particularly interesting—just a squabble over interests in the Blue Star."

"But who is this Elwell? I don't know the name."

"Oh, he's a fellow I put into it—gave him a hand up. I told you all about him at the time."

"I daresay. I must have forgotten." Vainly she strained back among her memories. "But if you helped him, why does he make this return?"

"Probably some shyster lawyer got hold of him and talked him over. It's all rather technical and complicated. I thought that kind of thing bored you."

His wife felt a sting of compunction. Theoretically, she deprecated the American wife's detachment from her husband's professional interests, but in practice she had always found it difficult to fix her attention on Boyne's report of the transactions in which his varied interests involved him. Besides, she had felt during their years of exile, that, in a community where the amenities of living could be obtained only at the cost of efforts as arduous as her husband's professional labours, such brief leisure as he and she could command should be used as an escape from immediate preoccupations, a flight to the life they always dreamed of living. Once or twice, now that this new life had actually drawn its magic circle about them, she had asked herself if she had done right; but hitherto such conjectures had been no more than the retrospective excursions of an active fancy. Now, for the first time, it startled her a little to find how little she knew of the material foundation on which her happiness was built.

She glanced at her husband, and was again reassured by the composure of his face; yet she felt the need of more definite grounds for her reassurance.

"But doesn't this suit worry you? Why have you never spoken to me about it?"

He answered both questions at once. "I didn't speak of it at first because it *did* worry me—annoyed me, rather. But it's all ancient history now. Your correspondent must have got hold of a back number of the *Sentinel*."

She felt a quick thrill of relief. "You mean it's over? He's lost his case?"

There was a just perceptible delay in Boyne's reply. "The suit's been withdrawn—that's all."

But she persisted, as if to exonerate herself from the inward charge of being too easily put off. "Withdrawn it because he saw he had no chance?"

"Oh, he had no chance," Boyne answered.

She was still struggling with a dimly felt perplexity at the back of her thoughts.

"How long ago was it withdrawn?"

He paused, as if with a slight return of his former uncertainty. "I've just had the news now; but I've been expecting it."

"Just now—in one of your letters?"

"Yes; in one of my letters."

She made no answer, and was aware only, after a short interval of waiting, that he had risen, and, strolling across the room, had placed himself on the sofa at her side. She felt him, as he did so, pass an arm about her, she felt his hand seek hers and clasp it, and turning slowly, drawn by the warmth of his cheek, she met his smiling eyes.

"It's all right—it's all right?" she questioned, through the flood of her dissolving doubts; and "I give you my word it was never righter!" he laughed back at her, holding her close.

III

One of the strangest things she was afterward to recall out of all the next day's strangeness was the sudden and complete recovery of her sense of security.

It was in the air when she woke in her low-ceiled, dusky room; it went with her downstairs to the breakfast-table, flashed out at her from the fire, and reduplicated itself from the flanks of the urn and the sturdy flutings of the Georgian teapot. It was as if, in some roundabout way, all her diffused fears of the previous day, with their moment of sharp concentration about the newspaper article—as if this dim questioning of the future, and startled return upon the past, had between them liquidated the arrears of some haunting moral obligation. If she had indeed been careless of her husband's affairs, it was, her new state seemed to prove, because her faith in him instinctively justified such carelessness; and his right to her faith had now affirmed itself in the very face of menace and suspicion. She had never seen him more untroubled, more naturally and unconsciously himself, than after the cross-examination to which she had subjected him: it was almost as if he had been aware of her doubts and had wanted the air cleared as much as she did.

It was as clear, thank Heaven! as the bright outer light that surprised her almost with a touch of summer when she issued from the house for her daily round of the gardens. She had left Boyne at his desk, indulging herself, as she passed the library door, by a last peep at his quiet face, where he bent, pipe in mouth, above his papers; and now she had her own morning's task to perform. The task involved, on such charmed winter days, almost as much happy loitering about the different quarters of her demesne as if spring were already at work there. There were such endless possibilities still before her, such opportunities to bring out the latent graces of the old place, without a single irreverent touch of alteration, that the winter was all too short to plan what spring and autumn executed. And her recovered sense of safety gave, on this particular morning, a peculiar zest to her progress through the sweet still place. She went first to the kitchen-garden, where the espaliered pear trees drew complicated patterns on the walls, and pigeons were fluttering and preening about the silvery-slated roof of their cot. There was something wrong about the piping of the hot-house, and she was expecting an authority from Dorchester, who was to drive out between trains and make a diagnosis of the boiler. But when she dipped into the damp heat of the greenhouses, among the spiced scents and waxy pinks and reds of old-fashioned exotics— even the flora of Lyng was in the note!—she learned that the great man had not arrived, and, the day being too rare to waste in an artificial atmosphere, she came out again and paced along the springy turf of the bowling-green to the gardens behind the house. At their farther end rose a grass terrace, looking across the fish-pond and yew hedges to the long house-front with its twisted chimney-stacks and blue roof angles all drenched in the pale gold moisture of the air.

Seen thus, across the level tracery of the gardens, it sent her, from open windows and hospitably smoking chimneys, the look of some warm human presence, of a mind slowly ripened on a sunny wall of experience. She had never before had such a sense of her intimacy with it, such a conviction that its secrets were all beneficent, kept, as they said to children, "for one's good," such a trust in its power to gather up her life and Ned's into the harmonious pattern of the long long story it sat there weaving in the sun.

She heard steps behind her, and turned, expecting to see the gardener accompanied by the engineer from Dorchester. But only one figure was in sight, that of a youngish slightly built man, who, for reasons she could not on the spot have given, did not remotely resemble her notion of an authority on hot-house boilers. The new-comer, on seeing her, lifted his hat, and paused with the air of a gentleman—perhaps a traveller—who wishes to make it known that his intrusion is involuntary. Lyng occasionally attracted the more cultivated traveller, and Mary half expected to see the stranger dissemble a camera, or justify his presence by producing it. But he made no gesture of any sort, and after a moment she asked, in a tone responding to the courteous hesitation of his attitude: "Is there any one you wish to see?"

"I came to see Mr. Boyne," he answered. His intonation, rather than his accent, was faintly American, and Mary, at the note, looked at him more closely. The brim of his soft felt hat cast a shade on his face, which, thus obscured, wore to her short-sighted gaze a look of seriousness, as of a person arriving "on business," and civilly but firmly aware of his rights.

Past experience had made her equally sensible to such claims; but she was jealous of her husband's morning hours, and doubtful of his having given any one the right to intrude on them.

"Have you an appointment with my husband?" she asked.

The visitor hesitated, as if unprepared for the question.

"I think he expects me," he replied.

It was Mary's turn to hesitate. "You see, this is his time for work: he never sees any one in the morning."

He looked at her a moment without answering; then, as if accepting her decision, he began to move away. As he turned, Mary saw him pause and glance up at the peaceful house-front. Something in his air suggested weariness and disappointment, the dejection of the traveller who has come from far off and whose hours are limited by the time-table. It occurred to her that if this were the case her refusal might have made his errand vain, and a sense of compunction caused her to hasten after him.

"May I ask if you have come a long way?"

He gave her the same grave look. "Yes—I have come a long way."

"Then, if you'll go to the house, no doubt my husband will see you now. You'll find him in the library."

She did not know why she had added the last phrase, except from a vague impulse to atone for her previous inhospitality. The visitor seemed about to express his thanks, but her attention was distracted by the approach of the gardener with a companion who bore all the marks of being the expert from Dorchester.

"This way," she said, waving the stranger to the house; and an instant later she had forgotten him in the absorption of her meeting with the boiler-maker.

The encounter led to such far-reaching results that the engineer ended by finding it expedient to ignore his train, and Mary was beguiled into spending the remainder of the morning in absorbed confabulation among the flower-pots. When the colloquy ended, she was surprised to find that it was nearly luncheon time, and she half expected, as she hurried back to the house, to see her husband coming out to meet her. But she found no one in the court but an under-gardener raking the gravel, and the hall, when she entered it, was so silent that she guessed Boyne to be still at work.

Not wishing to disturb him, she turned into the drawing-room, and there, at her writing table, lost herself in renewed calculations of the outlay to which the morning's conference had pledged her. The fact that she could permit herself such follies had not yet lost its novelty; and somehow, in contrast to the vague fears of the previous days, it now seemed an element of her recovered security, of the sense that, as Ned had said, things in general had never been "righter."

She was still luxuriating in a lavish play of figures when the parlour-maid, from the threshold, roused her with an enquiry as to the expediency of serving luncheon. It was one of their jokes that Trimmle announced luncheon as if she were divulging a state secret, and Mary, intent upon her papers, merely murmured an absent-minded assent.

She felt Trimmle wavering doubtfully on the threshold, as if in rebuke of such unconsidered assent; then her retreating steps sounded down the passage, and Mary, pushing away her papers, crossed the hall and went to the library door. It was still closed, and she wavered in her turn, disliking to disturb her husband, yet anxious that he should not exceed his usual measure of work. As she stood there, balancing her impulses, Trimmle returned with the announcement of luncheon, and Mary, thus impelled, opened the library door.

Boyne was not at his desk, and she peered about her, expecting to discover him before the book-shelves, somewhere down the length of the room; but her call brought no response, and gradually it became clear to her that he was not there.

She turned back to the parlour-maid.

"Mr. Boyne must be upstairs. Please tell him that luncheon is ready."

Trimmle appeared to hesitate between the obvious duty of obedience and an equally obvious conviction of the foolishness of the injunction laid on her. The struggle resulted in her saying: "If you please, madam, Mr. Boyne's not upstairs."

"Not in his room? Are you sure?"

"I'm sure, madam."

Mary consulted the clock. "Where is he, then?"

"He's gone out," Trimmle announced, with the superior air of one who has respectfully waited for the question that a well-ordered mind would have put first.

Mary's conjecture had been right, then. Boyne must have gone to the gardens to meet her, and since she had missed him, it was clear that he had taken the shorter way by the south door, instead of going round to the court. She crossed the hall to the French window opening directly on the yew garden, but the parlourmaid, after another moment of inner conflict, decided to bring out: "Please, madam, Mr. Boyne didn't go that way."

Mary turned back. "Where *did* he go? And when?"

"He went out of the front door, up the drive, madam." It was a matter of principle with Trimmle never to answer more than one question at a time.

"Up the drive? At this hour?" Mary went to the door herself, and glanced across the court through the tunnel of bare limes. But its perspective was as empty as when she had scanned it on entering.

"Did Mr. Boyne leave no message?"

Trimmle seemed to surrender herself to a last struggle with the forces of chaos.

"No, madam. He just went out with the gentleman."

"The gentleman? What gentleman?" Mary wheeled about, as if to front this new factor.

"The gentleman who called, madam," said Trimmle resignedly.

"When did a gentleman call? Do explain yourself, Trimmle!"

Only the fact that Mary was very hungry, and that she wanted to consult her husband about the greenhouses, would have caused her to lay so unusual an injunction on her attendant; and even now she was detached enough to note in Trimmle's eye the dawning defiance of the respectful subordinate who has been pressed too hard.

"I couldn't exactly say the hour, madam, because I didn't let the gentleman in," she replied, with an air of discreetly ignoring the irregularity of her mistress's course.

"You didn't let him in?"

"No, madam. When the bell rang I was dressing, and Agnes—"

"Go and ask Agnes, then," said Mary.

Trimmle still wore her look of patient magnanimity. "Agnes would not know, madam, for she had unfortunately burnt her hand in trimming the wick of the new lamp from town"—Trimmle, as Mary was aware, had always been opposed to the new lamp—"and so Mrs. Dockett sent the kitchen-maid instead."

Mary looked again at the clock. "It's after two! Go and ask the kitchen-maid if Mr. Boyne left any word."

She went in to luncheon without waiting, and Trimmle presently brought her there the kitchenmaid's statement that the gentleman had called about eleven o'clock, and that Mr. Boyne had gone out with him without leaving any message. The kitchen-maid did not even know the caller's name, for he had written it on a slip of paper, which he had folded and handed to her, with the injunction to deliver it at once to Mr. Boyne.

Mary finished her luncheon, still wondering, and when it was over, and Trimmle had brought the coffee to the drawing-room, her wonder had deepened to a first faint tinge of disquietude. It was unlike Boyne to absent himself without explanation at so unwonted an hour, and the difficulty of identifying the visitor whose summons he had apparently obeyed made his disappearance the more unaccountable. Mary Boyne's experience as the wife of a busy engineer, subject to sudden calls and compelled to keep irregular hours, had trained her to the philosophic acceptance of surprises; but since Boyne's withdrawal from business he had adopted a Benedictine regularity of life. As if to make up for the dispersed and agitated years, with their "stand-up" lunches, and dinners rattled down to the joltings of the dining-cars, he cultivated the last refinements of punctuality and monotony, discouraging his wife's fancy for the unexpected, and declaring that to a delicate taste there were infinite gradations of pleasure in the recurrences of habit.

Still, since no life can completely defend itself from the unforeseen, it was evident that all Boyne's precautions would sooner or later prove unavailable, and Mary concluded that he had cut short a tiresome visit by walking with his caller to the station, or at least accompanying him for part of the way.

This conclusion relieved her from further preoccupation, and she went out herself to take up her conference with the gardener. Thence she walked to the village post office, a mile or so away; and when she turned toward home the early twilight was setting in.

She had taken a foot-path across the downs, and as Boyne, meanwhile, had probably returned from the station by the highroad, there was little likelihood of their meeting. She felt sure, however, of his having reached the house before her; so sure that, when she entered it herself, without even pausing to enquire of Trimmle, she made directly for the library. But the library was still empty, and with an unwonted exactness of visual memory she observed that the papers on her husband's desk lay precisely as they had lain when she had gone in to call him to luncheon.

Then of a sudden she was seized by a vague dread of the unknown. She had closed the door behind her on entering, and as she stood alone in the long silent room, her dread seemed to take shape and sound, to be there breathing and lurking among the shadows. Her short-sighted eyes strained through them, half-discerning an actual presence, something aloof, that watched and knew; and in the recoil from that intangible presence she threw herself on the bell-rope and gave it a sharp pull.

The sharp summons brought Trimmle in precipitately with a lamp, and Mary breathed again at this sobering reappearance of the usual.

"You may bring tea if Mr. Boyne is in," she said, to justify her ring.

"Very well, madam. But Mr. Boyne is not in," said Trimmle, putting down the lamp.

"Not in? You mean he's come back and gone out again?"

"No, madam. He's never been back."

The dread stirred again, and Mary knew that now it had her fast.

"Not since he went out with—the gentleman?"

"Not since he went out with the gentleman."

"But who *was* the gentleman?" Mary insisted, with the shrill note of some one trying to be heard through a confusion of noises.

"That I couldn't say, madam." Trimmle, standing there by the lamp, seemed suddenly to grow less round and rosy, as though eclipsed by the same creeping shade of apprehension.

"But the kitchen-maid knows—wasn't it the kitchen-maid who let him in?"

"She doesn't know either, madam, for he wrote his name on a folded paper."

Mary, through her agitation, was aware that they were both designating the unknown visitor by a vague pronoun, instead of the conventional formula which, till then, had kept their allusions within the bounds of conformity. And at the same moment her mind caught at the suggestion of the folded paper.

"But he must have a name! Where's the paper?"

She moved to the desk, and began to turn over the documents that littered it. The first that caught her eye was an unfinished letter in her husband's hand, with his pen lying across it, as though dropped there at a sudden summons.

"My dear Parvis"—who was Parvis?—"I have just received your letter announcing Elwell's death, and while I suppose there is now no further risk of trouble, it might be safer—"

She tossed the sheet aside, and continued her search; but no folded paper was discoverable among the letters and pages of manuscript which had been swept together in a heap, as if by a hurried or a startled gesture.

"But the kitchen-maid *saw* him. Send her here," she commanded, wondering at her dullness in not thinking sooner of so simple a solution.

Trimmle vanished in a flash, as if thankful to be out of the room, and when she reappeared, conducting the agitated underling, Mary had regained her self-possession, and had her questions ready.

The gentleman was a stranger, yes—that she understood. But what had he said? And, above all, what had he looked like? The first question was easily enough answered, for the disconcerting reason that he had said so little— had merely asked for Mr. Boyne, and, scribbling something on a bit of paper, had requested that it should at once be carried in to him.

"Then you don't know what he wrote? You're not sure it *was* his name?"

The kitchen-maid was not sure, but supposed it was, since he had written it in answer to her enquiry as to whom she should announce.

"And when you carried the paper in to Mr. Boyne, what did he say?"

The kitchen-maid did not think that Mr. Boyne had said anything, but she could not be sure, for just as she had handed him the paper and he was opening it, she had become aware that the visitor had followed her into the library, and she had slipped out, leaving the two gentlemen together.

"But then, if you left them in the library, how do you know that they went out of the house?"

This question plunged the witness into a momentary inarticulateness, from which she was rescued by Trimmle, who, by means of ingenious circumlocutions, elicited the statement that before she could cross the hall to the back passage she had heard the two gentlemen behind her, and had seen them go out of the front door together.

"Then, if you saw the strange gentleman twice, you must be able to tell me what he looked like."

But with this final challenge to her powers of expression it became clear that the limit of the kitchen-maid's endurance had been reached. The obligation of going to the front door to "show in" a visitor was in itself so subversive of the fundamental order of things that it had thrown her faculties into hopeless disarray, and she could only stammer out, after various panting efforts: "His hat, mum, was different-like, as you might say—"

"Different? How different?" Mary flashed out, her own mind, in the same instant, leaping back to an image left on it that morning, and then lost under layers of subsequent impressions.

"His hat had a wide brim, you mean? and his face was pale—a youngish face?" Mary pressed her, with a white-lipped intensity of interrogation. But if the kitchen-maid found any adequate answer to this challenge, it was swept away for her listener down the rushing current of her own convictions. The stranger—the stranger in the garden! Why had Mary not thought of him before? She needed no one now to tell her that it was he who had called for her husband and gone away with him. But who was he, and why had Boyne obeyed him?

IV

It leaped out at her suddenly, like a grin out of the dark, that they had often called England so little—"such a confoundedly hard place to get lost in."

A confoundedly hard place to get lost in! That had been her husband's phrase. And now, with the whole machinery of official investigation sweeping its flashlights from shore to shore, and across the dividing straits; now, with Boyne's name blazing from the walls of every town and village, his portrait (how that wrung her!) hawked up and down the country like the image of a hunted criminal; now the little compact populous island, so policed, surveyed and administered, revealed itself as a Sphinx-like guardian of abysmal mysteries, staring back into his wife's anguished eyes as if with the wicked joy of knowing something they would never know!

In the fortnight since Boyne's disappearance there had been no word of him, no trace of his movements. Even the usual misleading reports that raise expectancy in tortured bosoms had been few and fleeting. No one but the kitchen-maid had seen Boyne leave the house, and no one else had seen "the gentleman" who accompanied him. All enquiries in the neighbourhood failed to elicit the memory of a stranger's presence that day in the neighbourhood of Lyng. And no one had met Edward Boyne, either alone or in company, in any of the neighbouring villages, or on the road across the downs, or at either of the local railway-stations. The sunny English noon had swallowed him as completely as if he had gone out into Cimmerian night.

Mary, while every official means of investigation was working at its highest pressure, had ransacked her husband's papers for any trace of antecedent complications, of entanglements or obligations unknown to her, that might throw a ray into the darkness. But if any such had existed in the background of Boyne's life, they had vanished like the slip of paper on which the visitor had written his name. There remained no possible thread of guidance except—if it were indeed an exception—the letter which Boyne had apparently been in the act of writing when he received his mysterious summons. That letter, read and reread by his wife, and submitted by her to the police, yielded little enough to feed conjecture.

"I have just heard of Elwell's death, and while I suppose there is now no further risk of trouble, it might be safer—" That was all. The "risk of trouble" was easily explained by the newspaper clipping which had apprised Mary of the suit brought against her husband by one of his associates in the Blue Star enterprise. The only new information conveyed by the letter was the fact of its showing Boyne, when he wrote it, to be still apprehensive of the results of the suit, though he had told his wife that it had been withdrawn, and though the letter itself proved that the plaintiff was dead. It took several days of cabling to fix the identity of the "Parvis" to whom the fragment was addressed, but even after these enquiries had shown him to be a Waukesha lawyer, no new facts concerning the Elwell suit were elicited. He appeared to have had no direct concern in it, but to have been conversant with the facts merely as an acquaintance, and possible intermediary; and he declared himself unable to guess with what object Boyne intended to seek his assistance.

This negative information, sole fruit of the first fortnight's search, was not increased by a jot during the slow weeks that followed. Mary knew that the investigations were still being carried on, but she had a vague sense of their gradually slackening, as the actual march of time seemed to slacken. It was as though the days, flying horror-struck from the shrouded image of the one inscrutable day, gained assurance as the distance lengthened, till at last they fell back into their normal gait. And so with the human imaginations at work on the dark event. No doubt it occupied them still, but week by week and hour by hour it grew less absorbing, took up less space, was slowly but inevitably crowded out of the foreground of consciousness by the new problems perpetually bubbling up from the cloudy caldron of human experience.

Even Mary Boyne's consciousness gradually felt the same lowering of velocity. It still swayed with the incessant oscillations of conjecture; but they were slower, more rhythmical in their beat. There were even moments of weariness when, like the victim of some poison which leaves the brain clear, but holds the body motionless, she saw herself domesticated with the Horror, accepting its perpetual presence as one of the fixed conditions of life.

These moments lengthened into hours and days, till she passed into a phase of stolid acquiescence. She watched the routine of daily life with the incurious eye of a savage on whom the meaningless processes of civilization make but the faintest impression. She had come to regard herself as part of the routine, a spoke of the wheel, revolving with its motion; she felt almost like the furniture of the room in which she sat, an insensate object to be dusted and pushed about with the chairs and tables. And this deepening apathy held her fast at Lyng, in spite of the entreaties of friends and the usual medical recommendation of "change." Her friends supposed that her refusal to move was inspired by the belief that her husband would one day return to the spot from which he had vanished, and a beautiful legend grew up about this imaginary state of waiting. But in reality she had no such belief: the depths of anguish enclosing her were no longer lighted by flashes of hope. She was sure that Boyne would never come back, that he had gone out of her sight as completely as if Death itself had waited that day on the threshold. She had even renounced, one by one, the various theories as to his disappearance which had been advanced by the press, the police, and her own agonised imagination. In sheer lassitude her mind turned from these alternatives of horror, and sank back into the blank fact that he was gone.

No, she would never know what had become of him—no one would ever know. But the house *knew*; the library in which she spent her long lonely evenings knew. For it was here that the last scene had been enacted, here that the stranger had come, and spoken the word which had caused Boyne to rise and follow him. The floor she trod had felt his tread; the books on the shelves had seen his face; and there were moments when the intense consciousness of the old dusky walls seemed about to break out into some audible revelation of their secret. But the revelation never came, and she knew it would never come. Lyng was not one of the garrulous old houses that betray the secrets entrusted to them. Its very legend proved that it had always been the mute accomplice, the incorruptible custodian, of the mysteries it had surprised. And Mary Boyne, sitting face to face with its silence, felt the futility of seeking to break it by any human means.

V

"I don't say it *wasn't* straight, and yet I don't say it *was* straight. It was business."

Mary, at the words, lifted her head with a start, and looked intently at the speaker.

When, half an hour before, a card with "Mr. Parvis" on it had been brought up to her, she had been immediately aware that the name had been a part of her consciousness ever since she had read it at the head of Boyne's unfinished letter. In the library she had found awaiting her a small sallow man with a bald head and gold eyeglasses, and it sent a tremor through her to know that this was the person to whom her husband's last known thought had been directed.

Parvis, civilly, but without vain preamble—in the manner of a man who has his watch in his hand—had set forth the object of his visit. He had "run over" to England on business, and finding himself in the neighbourhood of Dorchester, had not wished to leave it without paying his respects to Mrs. Boyne; and without asking her, if the occasion offered, what she meant to do about Bob Elwell's family.

The words touched the spring of some obscure dread in Mary's bosom.

Did her visitor, after all, know what Boyne had meant by his unfinished phrase? She asked for an elucidation of his question, and noticed at once that he seemed surprised at her continued ignorance of the subject. Was it possible that she really knew as little as she said?

"I know nothing—you must tell me," she faltered out; and her visitor thereupon proceeded to unfold his story. It threw, even to her confused perceptions, and imperfectly initiated vision, a lurid glare on the whole hazy episode of the Blue Star Mine. Her husband had made his money in that brilliant speculation at the cost of "getting ahead" of someone less alert to seize the chance; and the victim of his ingenuity was young Robert Elwell, who had "put him on" to the Blue Star scheme.

Parvis, at Mary's first cry, had thrown her a sobering glance through his impartial glasses.

"Bob Elwell wasn't smart enough, that's all; if he had been, he might have turned round and served Boyne the same way. It's the kind of thing that happens every day in business. I guess it's what the scientists call the survival of the fittest—see?" said Mr. Parvis, evidently pleased with the aptness of his analogy.

Mary felt a physical shrinking from the next question she tried to frame: it was as though the words on her lips had a taste that nauseated her.

"But then—you accuse my husband of doing something dishonourable?"

Mr. Parvis surveyed the question dispassionately. "Oh, no, I don't. I don't even say it wasn't straight." He glanced up and down the long lines of books, as if one of them might have supplied him with the definition he sought. "I don't say it *wasn't* straight, and yet I don't say it *was* straight. It was business." After all, no definition in his category could be more comprehensive than that.

Mary sat staring at him with a look of terror. He seemed to her like the indifferent emissary of some evil power.

"But Mr. Elwell's lawyers apparently did not take your view, since I suppose the suit was withdrawn by their advice."

"Oh, yes; they knew he hadn't a leg to stand on, technically. It was when they advised him to withdraw the suit that he got desperate. You see, he'd borrowed most of the money he lost in the Blue Star, and he was up a tree. That's why he shot himself when they told him he had no show."

The horror was sweeping over Mary in great deafening waves.

"He shot himself? He killed himself because of *that*?"

"Well, he didn't kill himself, exactly. He dragged on two months before he died." Parvis emitted the statement as unemotionally as a gramophone grinding out its "record."

"You mean that he tried to kill himself, and failed? And tried again?"

"Oh, he didn't have to *try* again," said Parvis grimly.

They sat opposite each other in silence, he swinging his eyeglasses thoughtfully about his finger, she, motionless, her arms stretched along her knees in an attitude of rigid tension.

"But if you knew all this," she began at length, hardly able to force her voice above a whisper, "how is it that when I wrote you at the time of my husband's disappearance you said you didn't understand his letter?"

Parvis received this without perceptible embarrassment: "Why, I didn't understand it—strictly speaking. And it wasn't the time to talk about it, if I had. The Elwell business was settled when the suit was withdrawn. Nothing I could have told you would have helped you to find your husband."

Mary continued to scrutinize him. "Then why are you telling me now?"

Still Parvis did not hesitate. "Well, to begin with, I supposed you knew more than you appear to—I mean about the circumstances of Elwell's death. And then people are talking of it now; the whole matter's been raked up again. And I thought if you didn't know you ought to."

She remained silent, and he continued: "You see, it's only come out lately what a bad state Elwell's affairs were in. His wife's a proud woman, and she fought on as long as she could, going out to work, and taking sewing at home when she got too sick—something with the heart, I believe. But she had his mother to look after, and the children, and she broke down under it, and finally had to ask for help. That called attention to the case, and the papers took it up, and a subscription was started. Everybody out there liked Bob Elwell, and most of the prominent names in the place are down on the list, and people began to wonder why—"

Parvis broke off to fumble in an inner pocket. "Here," he continued, "here's an account of the whole thing from the *Sentinel*—a little sensational, of course. But I guess you'd better look it over."

He held out a newspaper to Mary, who unfolded it slowly, remembering, as she did so, the evening when, in that same room, the perusal of a clipping from the *Sentinel* had first shaken the depths of her security.

As she opened the paper, her eyes, shrinking from the glaring head-lines, "Widow of Boyne's Victim Forced to Appeal for Aid," ran down the column of text to two portraits inserted in it. The first was her husband's, taken from a photograph made the year they had come to England. It was the picture of him that she liked best, the one that stood on the writing table upstairs in her bedroom. As the eyes in the photograph met hers, she felt it would be impossible to read what was said of him, and closed her lids with the sharpness of the pain.

"I thought if you felt disposed to put your name down—" she heard Parvis continue.

She opened her eyes with an effort, and they fell on the other portrait. It was that of a youngish man, slightly built, with features somewhat blurred by the shadow of a projecting hat-brim. Where had she seen that outline before? She stared at it confusedly, her heart hammering in her ears. Then she gave a cry.

"This is the man—the man who came for my husband!"

She heard Parvis start to his feet, and was dimly aware that she had slipped backward into the corner of the sofa, and that he was bending above her in alarm. She straightened herself, and reached out for the paper which she had dropped.

"It's the man! I should know him anywhere!" she persisted in a voice that sounded to her own ears like a scream.

Parvis's answer seemed to come to her from far off, down endless fog-muffled windings.

"Mrs. Boyne, you're not very well. Shall I call somebody? Shall I get a glass of water?"

"No, no, no!" She threw herself toward him, her hand frantically clutching the newspaper. "I tell you, it's the man! I *know* him! He spoke to me in the garden!"

Parvis took the journal from her, directing his glasses to the portrait. "It can't be, Mrs. Boyne. It's Robert Elwell."

"Robert Elwell?" Her white stare seemed to travel into space. "Then it was Robert Elwell who came for him."

"Came for Boyne? The day he went away from here?" Parvis's voice dropped as hers rose. He bent over, laying a fraternal hand on her, as if to coax her gently back into her seat. "Why, Elwell was dead! Don't you remember?"

Mary sat with her eyes fixed on the picture, unconscious of what he was saying.

"Don't you remember Boyne's unfinished letter to me—the one you found on his desk that day? It was written just after he'd heard of Elwell's death." She noticed an odd shake in Parvis's unemotional voice. "Surely you remember!" he urged her.

Yes, she remembered: that was the profoundest horror of it. Elwell had died the day before her husband's disappearance; and this was Elwell's portrait; and it was the portrait of the man who had spoken to her in the garden. She lifted her head and looked slowly about the library. The library could have borne witness that it was also the portrait of the man who had come in that day to call Boyne from his unfinished letter. Through the misty surgings of her brain she heard the faint boom of half-forgotten words— words spoken by Alida Stair on the lawn at Pangbourne before Boyne and his wife had ever seen the house at Lyng, or had imagined that they might one day live there.

"This was the man who spoke to me," she repeated.

She looked again at Parvis. He was trying to conceal his disturbance under what he probably imagined to be an expression of indulgent commiseration; but the edges of his lips were blue. "He thinks me mad; but I'm not mad," she reflected; and suddenly there flashed upon her a way of justifying her strange affirmation.

She sat quiet, controlling the quiver of her lips, and waiting till she could trust her voice; then she said, looking straight at Parvis: "Will you answer me one question, please? When was it that Robert Elwell tried to kill himself?"

"When—when?" Parvis stammered.

"Yes; the date. Please try to remember."

She saw that he was growing still more afraid of her. "I have a reason," she insisted.

"Yes, yes. Only I can't remember. About two months before, I should say."

"I want the date," she repeated.

Parvis picked up the newspaper. "We might see here," he said, still humouring her. He ran his eyes down the page. "Here it is. Last October— the—"

She caught the words from him. "The 20th, wasn't it?" With a sharp look at her, he verified. "Yes, the 20th. Then you *did* know?"

"I know now." Her gaze continued to travel past him. "Sunday, the 20th—that was the day he came first."

Parvis's voice was almost inaudible. "Came *here* first?"

"Yes."

"You saw him twice, then?"

"Yes, twice." She just breathed it at him. "He came first on the 20th of October. I remember the date because it was the day we went up Meldon Steep for the first time." She felt a faint gasp of inward laughter at the thought that but for that she might have forgotten.

Parvis continued to scrutinize her, as if trying to intercept her gaze.

"We saw him from the roof," she went on. "He came down the lime-avenue toward the house. He was dressed just as he is in that picture. My husband saw him first. He was frightened, and ran down ahead of me; but there was no one there. He had vanished."

"Elwell had vanished?" Parvis faltered.

"Yes." Their two whispers seemed to grope for each other. "I couldn't think what had happened. I see now. He *tried* to come then; but he wasn't dead enough—he couldn't reach us. He had to wait for two months to die; and then he came back again—and Ned went with him."

She nodded at Parvis with the look of triumph of a child who has worked out a difficult puzzle. But suddenly she lifted her hands with a desperate gesture, pressing them to her temples.

"Oh, my God! I sent him to Ned—I told him where to go! I sent him to this room!" she screamed.

She felt the walls of books rush toward her, like inward falling ruins; and she heard Parvis, a long way off, through the ruins, crying to her, and struggling to get at her. But she was numb to his touch, she did not know what he was saying. Through the tumult she heard but one clear note, the voice of Alida Stair, speaking on the lawn at Pangbourne.

"You won't know till afterward," it said. "You won't know till long, long afterward."

Algernon Blackwood

The Willows

Algernon Blackwood was one of the most prolific writers in all horror literature, and has been considered by some enthusiasts and experts as the greatest. H. P. Lovecraft (who did not impress Blackwood) called him "the one absolute and unquestioned master of weird atmosphere." His contributions to horror are many, but principally that he wrote many of his best works set outdoors, while horror had before him usually been set indoors. His nature or outdoor horror atmosphere is nowhere stronger than in "The Willows," which has been called the finest supernatural horror story in English. It stands in the center of the nature-of-reality stream in horror, midway between Bierce's "The Damned Thing" and Stephen King's "The Mist," closer to science fiction than the classic ghost story. In it, Blackwood captures part of the absolute essence of all horror literature: "And altogether the fear that hovered about me was such an unknown and immense kind of fear, so unlike anything I had ever felt before, that it woke a sense of awe and wonder in me that did much to counteract its worst effects." Horror, at its best, moves beyond fear to awe and wonder.

I

After leaving Vienna, and long before you come to Buda-Pesth, the Danube enters a region of singular loneliness and desolation, where its waters spread away on all sides regardless of a main channel, and the country becomes a swamp for miles upon miles, covered by a vast sea of low willow-bushes. On the big maps this deserted area is painted in a fluffy blue, growing fainter in color as it leaves the banks, and across it may be seen in large straggling letters the word *Sümpfe*, meaning marshes.

In high flood this great acreage of sand, shingle-beds, and willow-grown islands is almost topped by the water, but in normal seasons the bushes bend and rustle in the free winds, showing their silver leaves to the sunshine in an ever-moving plain of bewildering beauty. These willows never attain to the dignity of trees; they have no rigid trunks; they remain humble bushes, with rounded tops and soft outline, swaying on slender stems that answer to the least pressure of the wind; supple as grasses, and so continually shifting that they somehow give the impression that the entire plain is moving and *alive*. For the wind sends waves rising and falling over the whole surface, waves of leaves instead of waves of water, green swells like the sea, too, until the

909

branches turn and lift, and then silvery white as their under-side turns to the sun.

Happy to slip beyond the control of stern banks, the Danube here wanders about at will among the intricate network of channels intersecting the islands everywhere with broad avenues down which the waters pour with a shouting sound; making whirlpools, eddies, and foaming rapids; tearing at the sandy banks; carrying away masses of shore and willow-clumps; and forming new islands innumerable which shift daily in size and shape and possess at best an impermanent life, since the flood-time obliterates their very existence.

Properly speaking, this fascinating part of the river's life begins soon after leaving Pressburg, and we, in our Canadian canoe, with gipsy tent and frying-pan on board, reached it on the crest of a rising flood about mid-July. That very same morning, when the sky was reddening before sunrise, we had slipped swiftly through still-sleeping Vienna, leaving it a couple of hours later a mere patch of smoke against the blue hills of the Wienerwald on the horizon; we had breakfasted below Fischeramend under a grove of birch trees roaring in the wind; and had then swept on the tearing current past Orth, Hainburg, Petronell (the old Roman Carnuntum of Marcus Aurelius), and so under the frowning heights of Theben on a spur of the Carpathians, where the March steals in quietly from the left and the frontier is crossed between Austria and Hungary.

Racing along at twelve kilometers an hour soon took us well into Hungary, and the muddy waters—sure sign of flood—sent us aground on many a shingle-bed, and twisted us like a cork in many a sudden belching whirlpool before the towers of Pressburg (Hungarian, Poszony) showed against the sky; and then the canoe, leaping like a spirited horse, flew at top speed under the gray walls, negotiated safely the sunken chain of the Fliegende Brücke ferry, turned the corner sharply to the left, and plunged on yellow foam into the wilderness of islands, sand-banks, and swamp-land beyond—the land of the willows.

The change came suddenly, as when a series of bioscope pictures snaps down on the streets of a town and shifts without warning into the scenery of lake and forest. We entered the land of desolation on wings, and in less than half an hour there was neither boat nor fishing-hut nor red roof, nor any single sign of human habitation and civilization within sight. The sense of remoteness from the world of human kind, the utter isolation, the fascination of this singular world of willows, winds, and waters, instantly laid its spell upon us both, so that we allowed laughingly to one another that we ought by rights to have held some special kind of passport to admit us, and that we had, somewhat audaciously, come without asking leave into a separate little kingdom of wonder and magic—a kingdom that was reserved for the use of others who had a right to it, with everywhere unwritten warnings to trespassers for those who had the imagination to discover them.

Though still early in the afternoon, the ceaseless buffetings of a most tempestuous wind made us feel weary, and we at once began casting about for a suitable camping-ground for the night. But the bewildering character of the islands made landing difficult; the swirling flood carried us in-shore and then swept us out again; the willow branches tore our hands as we seized them to stop the canoe, and we pulled many a yard of sandy bank into the water before at length we shot with a great sideways blow from the wind into a backwater and managed to beach the bows in a cloud of spray. Then we lay panting and laughing after our exertions on hot yellow sand, sheltered from the wind, and in the full blaze of a scorching sun, a cloudless blue sky above, and an immense army of dancing, shouting willow bushes, closing in from all sides, shining with spray and clapping their thousand little hands as though to applaud the success of our efforts.

"What a river!" I said to my companion, thinking of all the way we had traveled from the source in the Black Forest, and how we had often been obliged to wade and push in the upper shallows at the beginning of June.

"Won't stand much nonsense now, will it?" he said, pulling the canoe a little farther into safety up the sand, and then composing himself for a nap.

I lay by his side, happy and peaceful in the bath of the elements—water, wind, sand, and the great fire of the sun—thinking of the long journey that lay behind us, and of the great stretch before us to the Black Sea, and how lucky I was to have such a delightful and charming traveling companion as my friend, the Swede.

We had made many similar journeys together, but the Danube, more than any other river I knew, impressed us from the very beginning with its *aliveness*. From its tiny bubbling entry into the world among the pinewood gardens of Donaueschingen, until this moment when it began to play the great river-game of losing itself among the deserted swamps, unobserved, unrestrained, it had seemed to us like following the growth of some living creature. Sleepy at first, but later developing violent desires as it became conscious of its deep soul, it rolled, like some huge fluid being, through all the countries we had passed, holding our little craft on its mighty shoulders, playing roughly with us sometimes, yet always friendly and well-meaning, till at length we had come inevitably to regard it as a Great Personage.

How, indeed, could it be otherwise, since it told us so much of its secret life? At night we heard it singing to the moon as we lay in our tent, uttering that odd sibilant note peculiar to itself and said to be caused by the rapid tearing of the pebbles along its bed, so great is its hurrying speed. We knew, too, the voice of its gurgling whirlpools, suddenly bubbling up on a surface previously quite calm; the roar of its shallows and swift rapids; its constant steady thundering below all mere surface sounds; and that ceaseless tearing of its icy waters at the banks. How it stood up and shouted when the rains fell flat upon its face! And how its laughter roared out when the wind blew upstream and tried to stop its growing speed! We knew all its sounds and voices, its tumblings and foamings, its unnecessary splashing against the bridges; that self-conscious chatter when there were hills to look on; the affected dignity of its speech when it passed through the little towns, far too important to laugh; and all these faint, sweet whisperings when the sun caught it fairly in some slow curve and poured down upon it till the steam rose.

It was full of tricks, too, in its early life before the great world knew it. There were places in the upper reaches among the Swabian forests, when yet the first whispers of its destiny had not reached it, where it elected to disappear through holes in the ground, to appear again on the other side of the porous limestone hills and start a new river with another name; leaving, too, so little water in its own bed that we had to climb out and wade and push the canoe through miles of shallows!

And a chief pleasure, in those early days of its irresponsible youth, was to lie low, like Brer Fox, just before the little turbulent tributaries came to join it from the Alps, and to refuse to acknowledge them when in, but to run for miles side by side, the dividing line well marked, the very levels different, the Danube utterly declining to recognize the newcomer. Below Passau, however, it gave up this particular trick, for there the Inn comes in with a thundering power impossible to ignore, and so pushes and incommodes the parent river that there is hardly room for them in the long twisting gorge that follows, and the Danube is shoved this way and that against the cliffs, and forced to hurry itself with great waves and much dashing to and fro in order to get through in time. And during the fight our canoe slipped down from its shoulder to its breast, and had the time of its life among the struggling waves. But the Inn taught the old river a lesson, and after Passau it no longer pretended to ignore new arrivals.

This was many days back, of course, and since then we had come to know other aspects of the great creature, and across the Bavarian wheat plain of Straubing she wandered so slowly under the blazing June sun that we could well imagine only the surface inches were water, while below there moved, concealed as by a silken mantle, a whole army of Undines, passing silently and unseen down to the sea, and very leisurely too, lest they be discovered.

Much, too, we forgave her because of her friendliness to the birds and animals that haunted the shores. Cormorants lined the banks in lonely places in rows like short black palings; gray crows crowded the shingle-beds; storks stood fishing in the vistas of shallower water that opened up between the islands, and hawks, swans, and marsh birds of all sorts filled the air with glinting wings and singing, petulant cries. It was impossible to feel annoyed with the river's vagaries after seeing a deer leap with a splash into the water at sunrise and swim past the bows of the canoe; and often we saw fawns peering at us from the underbrush, or looked straight into the brown eyes of a stag as we charged full tilt round a corner and entered another reach of the river. Foxes, too, everywhere haunted the banks, tripping daintily among the driftwood and disappearing so suddenly that it was impossible to see how they managed it.

But now, after leaving Pressburg, everything changed a little, and the Danube became more serious. It ceased trifling. It was halfway to the Black Sea, within scenting distance almost of other, stranger countries where no tricks would be permitted or understood. It became suddenly grown-up, and claimed our respect and even our awe. It broke out into three arms, for one thing, that only met again a hundred kilometers farther down, and for a canoe there were no indications which one was intended to be followed.

"If you take a side channel," said the Hungarian officer we met in the Pressburg shop while buying provisions, "you may find yourselves, when the flood subsides, forty miles from anywhere, high and dry, and you may easily starve. There are no people, no farms, no fishermen. I warn you not to continue. The river, too, is still rising, and this wind will increase."

The rising river did not alarm us in the least, but the matter of being left high and dry by a sudden subsidence of the waters might be serious, and we had consequently laid in an extra stock of provisions. For the rest, the officer's prophecy held true, and the wind, blowing down a perfectly clear sky, increased steadily till it reached the dignity of a westerly gale.

It was earlier than usual when we camped, for the sun was a good hour or two from the horizon, and leaving my friend still asleep on the hot sand, I wandered about in desultory examination of our hotel. The island, I found, was less than an acre in extent, a mere sandy bank standing some two or three feet above the level of the river. The far end, pointing into the sunset, was covered with flying spray which the tremendous wind drove off the crests of the broken waves. It was triangular in shape, with the apex upstream.

I stood there for several minutes, watching the impetuous crimson flood bearing down with a shouting roar, dashing in waves against the bank as though to sweep it bodily away, and then swirling by in two foaming streams on either side. The ground seemed to shake with the shock and rush, while the furious movement of the willow bushes as the wind poured over them increased the curious illusion that the island itself actually moved. Above, for a mile or two, I could see the great river descending upon me: it was like looking up the slope of a sliding hill, white with foam, and leaping up everywhere to show itself to the sun.

The rest of the island was too thickly grown with willows to make walking pleasant, but I made the tour, nevertheless. From the lower end the light, of course, changed, and the river looked dark and angry. Only the backs of the flying waves were visible, streaked with foam, and pushed forcibly by the great puffs of wind that fell upon them from behind. For a short mile it was visible, pouring in and out among the islands, and then disappearing with a huge sweep into the willows, which closed about it like a herd of monstrous antediluvian creatures crowding down to drink. They made me think of gigantic sponge-like growths that sucked the river up into themselves. They caused it to vanish from sight. They herded there together in such overpowering numbers.

Altogether it was an impressive scene, with its utter loneliness, its bizarre suggestion; and as I gazed, long and curiously, a singular emotion began to stir somewhere in the depths of me. Midway in my delight of the wild beauty, there crept, unbidden and unexplained, a curious feeling of disquietude, almost of alarm.

A rising river, perhaps, always suggests something of the ominous: many of the little islands I saw before me would probably have been swept away by the morning; this resistless, thundering flood of water touched the sense of awe. Yet I was aware that my uneasiness lay deeper far than the emotions of awe and wonder. It was not that I felt. Nor had it directly to do with the power of the driving wind—this shouting hurricane that might almost carry up a few acres of willows into the air and scatter them like so much chaff over the landscape. The wind was simply enjoying itself, for nothing rose out of the flat landscape to stop it, and I was conscious of sharing its great game with a kind of pleasurable excitement. Yet this novel emotion had nothing to do with the wind. Indeed, so vague was the sense of distress I experienced, that it was impossible to trace it to its source and deal with it accordingly, though I was aware somehow that it had to do with my realization of our utter insignificance before this unrestrained power of the elements about me. The huge-grown river had something to do with it too—a vague, unpleasant idea that we had somehow trifled with these great elemental forces in whose power we lay helpless every hour of the day and night. For here, indeed, they were gigantically at play together, and the sight appealed to the imagination.

But my emotion, so far as I could understand it, seemed to attach itself more particularly to the willow bushes, to these acres and acres of willows, crowding, so thickly growing there, swarming everywhere the eye could reach, pressing upon the river as though to suffocate it, standing in dense array mile after mile beneath the sky, watching, waiting, listening. And, apart quite from the elements, the willows connected themselves subtly with my malaise, attacking the mind insidiously somehow by reason of their vast numbers, and contriving in some way or other to represent to the imagination a new and mighty power, a power, moreover, not altogether friendly to us.

Great revelations of nature, of course, never fail to impress in one way or another, and I was no stranger to moods of the kind. Mountains overawe and oceans terrify, while the mystery of great forests exercises a spell peculiarly its own. But all these, at one point or another, somewhere link on intimately with human life and human experience. They stir comprehensible, even if alarming, emotions. They tend on the whole to exalt.

With this multitude of willows, however, it was something far different, I felt. Some essence emanated from them that besieged the heart. A sense of awe awakened, true, but of awe touched somewhere by a vague terror. Their serried ranks growing everywhere darker about me as the shadows deepened, moving furiously yet softly in the wind, woke in me the curious and unwelcome suggestion that we had trespassed here upon the borders of an alien world, a world where we were intruders, a world where we were not wanted or invited to remain—where we ran grave risks perhaps!

The feeling, however, though it refused to yield its meaning entirely to analysis, did not at the time trouble me by passing into menace. Yet it never left me quite, even during the very practical business of putting up the tent in a hurricane of wind and building a fire for the stew-pot. It remained, just enough to bother and perplex, and to rob a most delightful camping-ground of a good portion of its charm. To my companion, however, I said nothing, for he was a man I considered devoid of imagination. In the first place, I could never have explained to him what I meant, and in the second, he would have laughed stupidly at me if I had.

There was a slight depression in the center of the island, and here we pitched the tent. The surrounding willows broke the wind a bit.

"A poor camp," observed the imperturbable Swede when at last the tent stood upright; "no stones and precious little firewood. I'm for moving on early to-morrow—eh? This sand won't hold anything."

But the experience of a collapsing tent at midnight had taught us many devices, and we made the cosy gipsy house as safe as possible, and then set about collecting a store of wood to last till bedtime. Willow bushes drop no branches, and driftwood was our only source of supply. We hunted the shores pretty thoroughly. Everywhere the banks were crumbling as the rising flood tore at them and carried away great portions with a splash and a gurgle.

"The island's much smaller than when we landed," said the accurate Swede. "It won't last long at this rate. We'd better drag the canoe close to the tent, and be ready to start at a moment's notice. *I* shall sleep in my clothes."

He was a little distance off, climbing along the bank, and I heard his rather jolly laugh as he spoke.

"By Jove!" I heard him call, a moment later, and turned to see what had caused his exclamation; but for the moment he was hidden by the willows, and I could not find him.

"What in the world's this?" I heard him cry again, and this time his voice had become serious.

I ran up quickly and joined him on the bank. He was looking over the river, pointing at something in the water.

"Good Heavens, it's a man's body!" he cried excitedly. "Look!"

A black thing, turning over and over in the foaming waves, swept rapidly past. It kept disappearing and coming up to the surface again. It was about twenty feet from the shore, and just as it was opposite to where we stood it lurched round and looked straight at us. We saw its eyes reflecting the sunset, and gleaming an odd yellow as the body turned over. Then it gave a swift, gulping plunge, and dived out of sight in a flash.

"An otter, by gad!" we exclaimed in the same breath, laughing.

It *was* an otter, alive, and out on the hunt; yet it had looked exactly like the body of a drowned man turning helplessly in the current. Far below, it came to the surface once again, and we saw its black skin, wet and shining in the sunlight.

Then, too, just as we turned back, our arms full of driftwood, another thing happened to recall us to the river bank. This time it really was a man, and what was more, a man in a boat. Now a small boat on the Danube was an unusual sight at any time, but here in this deserted region, and at flood time, it was so unexpected as to constitute a real event. We stood and stared.

Whether it was due to the slanting sunlight, or the refraction from the wonderfully illumined water, I cannot say, but, whatever the cause, I found it difficult to focus my sight properly upon the flying apparition. It seemed, however, to be a man standing upright in a sort of flat-bottomed boat, steering with a long oar, and being carried down the opposite shore at a tremendous pace. He apparently was looking across in our direction, but the distance was too great and the light too uncertain for us to make out very plainly what he was about. It seemed to me that he was gesticulating and making signs at us. His voice came across the water to us shouting something furiously but the wind drowned it so that no single word was audible. There was something curious about the whole appearance—man, boat, signs, voice—that made an impression on me out of all proportion to its cause.

"He's crossing himself!" I cried. "Look, he's making the sign of the cross!"

"I believe you're right," the Swede said, shading his eyes with his hand and watching the man out of sight. He seemed to be gone in a moment, melting away down there into the sea of willows where the sun caught them in the bend of the river and turned them into a great crimson wall of beauty. Mist, too, had begun to rise, so that the air was hazy.

"But what in the world is he doing at nightfall on this flooded river?" I said, half to myself. "Where is he going at such a time, and what did he mean by his signs and shouting? D'you think he wished to warn us about something?"

"He saw our smoke, and thought we were spirits probably," laughed my companion. "These Hungarians believe in all sorts of rubbish: you remember the shopwoman at Pressburg warning us that no one ever landed here because it belonged to some sort of beings outside man's world! I suppose they believe in fairies and elementals, possibly demons too. That peasant in the boat saw people on the islands for the first time in his life," he added, after a slight pause, "and it scared him, that's all." The Swede's tone of voice was not convincing, and his manner lacked something that was usually there. I noted the change instantly while he talked, though without being able to label it precisely.

"If they had enough imagination," I laughed loudly—I remember trying to make as much *noise* as I could—"they might well people a place like this with the old gods of antiquity. The Romans must have haunted all this region more or less with their shrines and sacred groves and elemental deities."

The subject dropped and we returned to our stew-pot, for my friend was not given to imaginative conversation as a rule. Moreover, just then I remember feeling distinctly glad that he was not imaginative; his stolid, practical nature suddenly seemed to me welcome and comforting. It was an admirable temperament, I felt: he could steer down rapids like a red Indian, shoot dangerous bridges and whirlpools better than any white man I ever saw in a canoe. He was a grand fellow for an adventurous trip, a tower of strength when untoward things happened. I looked at his strong face and light curly hair as he staggered along under his pile of driftwood (twice the size of mine!), and I experienced a feeling of relief. Yes, I was distinctly glad just then that the Swede was—what he was, and that he never made remarks that suggested more than they said.

"The river's still rising, though," he added, as if following out some thoughts of his own, and dropping his load with a gasp. "This island will be under water in two days if it goes on."

"I wish the *wind* would go down," I said. "I don't care a fig for the river."

The flood, indeed, had no terrors for us; we could get off at ten minutes' notice, and the more water the better we liked it. It meant an increasing current and the obliteration of the treacherous shingle-beds that so often threatened to tear the bottom out of our canoe.

Contrary to our expectations, the wind did not go down with the sun. It seemed to increase with the darkness, howling overhead and shaking the willows round us like straws. Curious sounds accompanied it sometimes, like the explosion of heavy guns, and it fell upon the water and the island in great flat blows of immense power. It made me think of the sounds a planet must make, could we only hear it, driving along through space.

But the sky kept wholly clear of clouds, and soon after supper the full moon rose up in the east and covered the river and the plain of shouting willows with a light like the day.

We lay on the sandy patch beside the fire, smoking, listening to the noises of the night round us, and talking happily of the journey we had already made, and of our plans ahead. The map lay spread in the door of the tent, but the high wind made it hard to study, and presently we lowered the curtain and extinguished the lantern. The firelight was enough to smoke and see each other's face by, and the sparks flew about overhead like fireworks. A few yards beyond, the river gurgled and hissed, and from time to time a heavy splash announced the falling away of further portions of the bank.

Our talk, I noticed, had to do with the far-away scenes and incidents of our first camps in the Black Forest, or of other subjects altogether remote from the present setting, for neither of us spoke of the actual moment more than was necessary—almost as though we had agreed tacitly to avoid discussion of the camp and its incidents. Neither the otter nor the boatman, for instance, received the honor of a single mention, though ordinarily these would have furnished discussion for the greater part of the evening. They were, of course, distinct events in such a place.

The scarcity of wood made it a business to keep the fire going, for the wind, that drove the smoke in our faces wherever we sat, helped at the same time to make a forced draught. We took it in turn to make foraging expeditions into the darkness, and the quantity the Swede brought back always made me feel that he took an absurdly long time finding it; for the fact was I did not care much about being left alone, and yet it always seemed to be my turn to grub about among the bushes or scramble along the slippery banks in the moonlight. The long day's battle with wind and water—such wind and such water!—had tired us both, and an early bed was the obvious program. Yet neither of us made the move for the tent. We lay there, tending the fire, talking in desultory fashion, peering about us into the dense willow bushes, and listening to the thunder of wind and river. The loneliness of the place had entered our very bones, and silence seemed natural, for after a bit the sound of our voices became a trifle unreal and forced; whispering would have been the fitting mode of communication, I felt, and the human voice, always rather absurd amid the roar of the elements, now carried with it something almost illegitimate. It was like talking out loud in church, or in some place where it was not lawful, perhaps not quite *safe*, to be overheard.

The eeriness of this lonely island, set among a million willows, swept by a hurricane, and surrounded by hurrying deep waters, touched us both, I fancy. Untrodden by man, almost unknown to man, it lay there beneath the moon, remote from human influence, on the frontier of another world, an alien world, a world tenanted by willows only and the souls of willows. And we, in our rashness, had dared to invade it, even to make use of it!

Something more than the power of its mystery stirred in me as I lay on the sand, feet to fire, and peered up through the leaves at the stars. For the last time I rose to get firewood.

"When this has burnt up," I said firmly, "I shall turn in," and my companion watched me lazily as I moved off into the surrounding shadows.

For an unimaginative man I thought he seemed unusually receptive that night, unusually open to suggestion of things other than sensory. He too was touched by the beauty and loneliness of the place. I was not altogether pleased, I remember, to recognize this slight change in him, and instead of immediately collecting sticks, I made my way to the far point of the island where the moonlight on plain and river could be seen to better advantage. The desire to be alone had come suddenly upon me; my former dread returned in force; there was a vague feeling in me I wished to face and probe to the bottom.

When I reached the point of sand jutting out among the waves, the spell of the place descended upon me with a positive shock. No mere "scenery" could have produced such an effect. There was something more here, something to alarm.

I gazed across the waste of wild waters; I watched the whispering willows; I heard the ceaseless beating of the tireless wind; and, one and all, each in its own way, stirred in me this sensation of a strange distress. But the *willows* especially: for ever they went on chattering and talking among themselves, laughing a little, shrilly crying out, sometimes sighing—but what it was they made so much to-do about belonged to the secret life of the great plain they inhabited. And it was utterly alien to the world I knew, or to that of the wild yet kindly elements. They made me think of a host of beings from another plane of life, another evolution altogether, perhaps, all discussing a mystery known only to themselves. I watched them moving busily together, oddly shaking their big bushy heads, twirling their myriad leaves even when there was no wind. They moved of their own will as though alive, and they touched, by some incalculable method, my own keen sense of the *horrible*.

There they stood in the moonlight, like a vast army surrounding our camp, shaking their innumerable silver spears defiantly, formed all ready for an attack.

The psychology of places, for some imaginations at least, is very vivid; for the wanderer, especially, camps have their "note" either of welcome or rejection. At first it may not always be apparent, because the busy preparations of tent and cooking prevent, but with the first pause—after supper usually—it comes and announces itself. And the note of this willow-camp now became unmistakably plain to me: we were interlopers, trespassers; we were not welcomed. The sense of unfamiliarity grew upon me as I stood there watching. We touched the frontier of a region where our presence was resented. For a night's lodging we might perhaps be tolerated; but for a prolonged and inquisitive stay—No! by all the gods of the trees and the wilderness, no! We were the first human influences upon this island, and we were not wanted. *The willows were against us.*

Strange thoughts like these, bizarre fancies, borne I know not whence, found lodgment in my mind as I stood listening. What, I thought, if, after all, these crouching willows proved to be alive; if suddenly they should rise up, like a swarm of living creatures, marshaled by the gods whose territory we had invaded, sweep towards us off the vast swamps, booming overhead in the night—and then *settle down*! As I looked it was so easy to imagine they actually moved, crept nearer, retreated a little, huddled together in masses, hostile, waiting for the great wind that should finally start them a-running. I could have sworn their aspect changed a little, and their ranks deepened and pressed more closely together.

The melancholy shrill cry of a night bird sounded overhead, and suddenly I nearly lost my balance as the piece of bank I stood upon fell with a great splash into the river, undermined by the flood. I stepped back just in time, and went on hunting for firewood again, half laughing at the odd fancies that crowded so thickly into my mind and cast their spell upon me. I recalled the Swede's remark about moving on next day, and I was just thinking that I fully agreed with him, when I turned with a start and saw the subject of my thoughts standing immediately in front of me. He was quite close. The roar of the elements had covered his approach.

"You've been gone so long," he shouted above the wind, "I thought something must have happened to you."

But there was that in his tone, and a certain look in his face as well, that conveyed to me more than his actual words, and in a flash I understood the real reason for his coming. It was because the spell of the place had entered his soul too, and he did not like being alone.

"River still rising," he cried, pointing to the flood in the moonlight, "and the wind's simply awful."

He always said the same things, but it was the cry for companionship that gave the real importance to his words.

"Lucky," I cried back, "our tent's in the hollow. I think it'll hold all right." I added something about the difficulty of finding wood, in order to explain my absence, but the wind caught my words and flung them across the river, so that he did not hear, but just looked at me through the branches, nodding his head.

"Lucky if we get away without disaster!" he shouted, or words to that effect; and I remember feeling half angry with him for putting the thought into words, for it was exactly what I felt myself. There was disaster impending somewhere, and the sense of presentiment lay unpleasantly upon me.

We went back to the fire and made a final blaze, poking it up with our feet. We took a last look round. But for the wind the heat would have been unpleasant. I put this thought into words, and I remember my friend's reply struck me oddly: that he would rather have the heat, the ordinary July weather, than this "diabolical wind."

Everything was snug for the night; the canoe lying turned over beside the tent, with both yellow paddles beneath her; the provision sack hanging from a willow stem, and the washed-up dishes removed to a safe distance from the fire, all ready for the morning meal.

We smothered the embers of the fire with sand, and then turned in. The flap of the tent door was up, and I saw the branches and the stars and the white moonlight. The shaking willows and the heavy buffetings of the wind against our taut little house were the last things I remembered as sleep came down and covered all with its soft and delicious forgetfulness.

II

Suddenly I found myself lying awake, peering from my sandy mattress through the door of the tent. I looked at my watch pinned against the canvas, and saw by the bright moonlight that it was past twelve o'clock—the threshold of a new day—and I had therefore slept a couple of hours. The Swede was asleep still beside me; the wind howled as before something plucked at my heart and made me feel afraid. There was a sense of disturbance in my immediate neighborhood.

I sat up quickly and looked out. The trees were swaying violently to and fro as the gusts smote them, but our little bit of green canvas lay snugly safe in the hollow, for the wind passed over it without meeting enough resistance to make it vicious. The feeling of disquietude did not pass, however, and I crawled quietly out of the tent to see if our belongings were safe. I moved carefully so as not to waken my companion. A curious excitement was on me.

I was halfway out, kneeling on all fours, when my eye first took in that the tops of the bushes opposite, with their moving tracery of leaves, made shapes against the sky. I sat back on my haunches and stared. It was incredible, surely, but there, opposite and slightly above me, were shapes of some indeterminate sort among the willows, and as the branches swayed in the wind they seemed to group themselves about these shapes, forming a series of monstrous outlines that shifted rapidly beneath the moon. Close, about fifty feet in front of me, I saw these things.

My first instinct was to waken my companion, that he too might see them, but something made me hesitate—the sudden realization, probably, that I should not welcome corroboration; and meanwhile I crouched there staring in amazement with smarting eyes. I was wide awake. I remember saying to myself that I was *not* dreaming.

They first became properly visible, these huge figures, just within the tops of the bushes—immense, bronze-colored, moving, and wholly independent of the swaying of the branches. I saw them plainly and noted, now I came to examine them more calmly, that they were very much larger than human, and indeed that something in their appearance proclaimed them to be *not human* at all. Certainly they were not merely the moving tracery of the branches against the moonlight. They shifted independently. They rose upwards in a continuous stream from earth to sky, vanishing utterly as soon as they reached the dark of the sky. They were interlaced one with another, making a great column, and I saw their limbs and huge bodies melting in and out of each other, forming this serpentine line that bent and swayed and twisted spirally with the contortions of the wind-tossed trees. They were nude, fluid shapes, passing up the bushes, *within* the leaves almost—rising up in a living column into the heavens. Their faces I never could see. Unceasingly they poured upwards, swaying in great bending curves, with a hue of dull bronze upon their skins.

I stared, trying to force every atom of vision from my eyes. For a long time I thought they *must* every moment disappear and resolve themselves into the movements of the branches and prove to be an optical illusion. I searched everywhere for a proof of reality, when all the while I understood quite well that the standard of reality had changed. For the longer I looked the more certain I became that these figures were real and living, though perhaps not according to the standards that the camera and the biologist would insist upon.

Far from feeling fear, I was possessed with a sense of awe and wonder such as I have never known. I seemed to be gazing at the personified elemental forces of this haunted and primeval region. Our intrusion had stirred the powers of the place into activity. It was we who were the cause of the disturbance, and my brain filled to bursting with stories and legends of the spirits and deities of places that have been acknowledged and worshiped by men in all ages of the world's history. But, before I could arrive at any possible explanation, something impelled me to go farther out, and I crept forward on to the sand and stood upright. I felt the ground still warm under my bare feet; the wind tore at my hair and face; and the sound of the river burst upon my ears with a sudden roar. These things, I knew, were real, and proved that my senses were acting normally. Yet the figures still rose from the earth to heaven, silent, majestically, in a great spiral of grace and strength that overwhelmed me at length with a genuine deep emotion of worship. I felt that I must fall down and worship—absolutely worship.

Perhaps in another minute I might have done so, when a gust of wind swept against me with such force that it blew me sideways, and I nearly stumbled and fell. It seemed to shake the dream violently out of me. At least it gave me another point of view somehow. The figures still remained, still ascended into heaven from the heat of the night, but my reason at last began to assert itself. It must be a subjective experience, I argued—none the less real for that, but still subjective. The moonlight and the branches combined to work out these pictures upon the mirror of my imagination, and for some reason I projected them outwards and made them appear objective. I knew this must be the case, of course. I was the subject of a vivid and interesting hallucination. I took courage, and began to move forward across the open patches of sand. By Jove, though, was it all hallucination? Was it merely subjective? Did not my reason argue in the old futile way from the little standard of the known?

I only know that great column of figures ascended darkly into the sky for what seemed a very long period of time, and with a very complete measure of reality as most men are accustomed to gauge reality. Then suddenly they were gone!

And, once they were gone and the immediate wonder of their great presence had passed, fear came down upon me with a cold rush. The esoteric meaning of this lonely and haunted region suddenly flamed up within me and I began to tremble dreadfully. I took a quick look round—a look of horror that came near to panic—calculating vainly ways of escape; and then, realizing how helpless I was to achieve anything really effective, I crept back silently into the tent and lay down again upon my sandy mattress, first lowering the door-curtain to shut out the sight of the willows in the moonlight, and then burying my head as deeply as possible beneath the blankets to deaden the sound of the terrifying wind.

III

As though further to convince me that I had not been dreaming, I remember that it was a long time before I fell again into a troubled and restless sleep; and even then only the upper crust of me slept, and underneath there was something that never quite lost consciousness, but lay alert and on the watch.

But this second time I jumped up with a genuine start of terror. It was neither the wind nor the river that woke me, but the slow approach of something that caused the sleeping portion of me to grow smaller and smaller till at last it vanished altogether, and I found myself sitting bolt upright—listening.

Outside there was a sound of multitudinous little patterings. They had been coming, I was aware, for a long time, and in my sleep they had first become audible. I sat there nervously wide awake as though I had not slept at all. It seemed to me that my breathing came with difficulty, and that there was a great weight upon the surface of my body. In spite of the hot night, I felt clammy with cold and shivered. Something surely was pressing steadily against the sides of the tent and weighing down upon it from above. Was it the body of the wind? Was this the pattering rain, the dripping of the leaves? The spray blown from the river by the wind and gathering in big drops? I thought quickly of a dozen things.

Then suddenly the explanation leaped into my mind: a bough from the poplar, the only large tree on the island, had fallen with the wind. Still half caught by the other branches, it would fall with the next gust and crush us, and meanwhile its leaves brushed and tapped upon the tight canvas surface of the tent. I raised the loose flap and rushed out, calling to the Swede to follow.

But when I got out and stood upright I saw that the tent was free. There was no hanging bough; there was no rain or spray; nothing approached.

A cold, gray light filtered down through the bushes and lay on the faintly gleaming sand. Stars still crowded the sky directly overhead, and the wind howled magnificently, but the fire no longer gave out any glow, and I saw the east reddening in streaks through the trees. Several hours must have passed since I stood there before, watching the ascending figures, and the memory of it now came back to me horribly, like an evil dream. Oh, how tired it made me feel, that ceaseless raging wind! Yet, though the deep lassitude of a sleepless night was on me, my nerves were tingling with the activity of an equally tireless apprehension, and all idea of repose was out of the question. The river, I saw, had risen further. Its thunder filled the air, and a fine spray made itself felt through my thin sleeping shirt.

Yet nowhere did I discover the slightest evidences of anything to cause alarm. This deep, prolonged disturbance in my heart remained wholly unaccounted for.

My companion had not stirred when I called him, and there was no need to waken him now. I looked about me carefully, noting everything: the turned-over canoe; the yellow paddles—two of them, I'm certain; the provision sack and the extra lantern hanging together from the tree; and, crowding everywhere about me, enveloping all, the willows, those endless, shaking willows. A bird uttered its morning cry, and a string of ducks passed with whirring flight overhead in the twilight. The sand whirled, dry and stinging, about my bare feet in the wind.

I walked round the tent and then went out a little way into the bush, so that I could see across the river to the farther landscape, and the same profound yet indefinable emotion of distress seized upon me again as I saw the interminable sea of bushes stretching to the horizon, looking ghostly and unreal in the wan light of dawn. I walked softly here and there, still puzzling over that odd sound of infinite pattering, and of that pressure upon the tent that had wakened me. It *must* have been the wind, I reflected—the wind beating upon the loose, hot sand, driving the dry particles smartly against the taut canvas—the wind dropping heavily upon our fragile roof.

Yet all the time my nervousness and malaise increased appreciably.

I crossed over to the farther shore and noted how the coast line had altered in the night, and what masses of sand the river had torn away. I dipped my hands and feet into the cool current, and bathed my forehead. Already there was a glow of sunrise in the sky and the exquisite freshness of coming day. On my way back I passed purposely beneath the very bushes where I had seen the column of figures rising into the air, and midway among the clumps I suddenly found myself overtaken by a sense of vast terror. From the shadows a large figure went swiftly by. Some one passed me, as sure as ever man did. . . .

It was a great staggering blow from the wind that helped me forward again, and once out in the more open space, the sense of terror diminished strangely. The winds were about and walking, I remember saying to myself; for the winds often move like great presences under the trees. And altogether the fear that hovered about me was such an unknown and immense kind of fear, so unlike anything I had ever felt before, that it woke a sense of awe and wonder in me that did much to counteract its worst effects; and when I reached a high point in the middle of the island from which I could see the wide stretch of river, crimson in the sunrise, the whole magical beauty of it all was so overpowering that a sort of wild yearning woke in me and almost brought a cry up into the throat.

But this cry found no expression, for as my eyes wandered from the plain beyond to the island round me and noted our little tent half hidden among the willows, a dreadful discovery leaped out at me, compared to which my terror of the walking winds seemed as nothing at all.

For a change, I thought, had somehow come about in the arrangement of the landscape. It was not that my point of vantage gave me a different view, but that an alteration had apparently been effected in the relation of the tent to the willows, and of the willows to the tent. Surely the bushes now crowded much closer—unnecessarily, unpleasantly close. *They had moved nearer.*

Creeping with silent feet over the shifting sands, drawing imperceptibly nearer by soft, unhurried movements, the willows had come closer during the night. But had the wind moved them, or had they moved of themselves? I recalled the sound of infinite small patterings and the pressure upon the tent and upon my own heart that caused me to wake in terror. I swayed for a moment in the wind like a tree, finding it hard to keep my upright position on the sandy hillock. There was a suggestion here of personal agency, of deliberate intention, of aggressive hostility, and it terrified me into a sort of rigidity.

Then the reaction followed quickly. The idea was so bizarre, so absurd, that I felt inclined to laugh. But the laughter came no more readily than the cry, for the knowledge that my mind was so receptive to such dangerous imaginings brought the additional terror that it was through our minds and not through our physical bodies that the attack would come, and was coming.

The wind buffeted me about, and, very quickly it seemed, the sun came up over the horizon, for it was after four o'clock, and I must have stood on that little pinnacle of sand longer than I knew, afraid to come down at close quarters with the willows. I returned quietly, creepily, to the tent, first taking another exhaustive look round and—yes, I confess it—making a few measurements. I paced out on the warm sand the distances between the willows and the tent, making a note of the shortest distance particularly.

I crawled stealthily into my blankets. My companion, to all appearances, still slept soundly, and I was glad that this was so. Provided my experiences were not corroborated, I could find strength somehow to deny them, perhaps. With the daylight I could persuade myself that it was all a subjective hallucination, a fantasy of the night, a projection of the excited imagination.

Nothing further came to disturb me, and I fell asleep almost at once, utterly exhausted, yet still in dread of hearing again that weird sound of multitudinous pattering, or of feeling the pressure upon my heart that had made it difficult to breathe.

IV

The sun was high in the heavens when my companion woke me from a heavy sleep and announced that the porridge was cooked and there was just time to bathe. The grateful smell of frizzling bacon entered the tent door.

"River still rising," he said, "and several islands out in midstream have disappeared altogether. Our own island's much smaller."

"Any wood left?" I asked sleepily.

"The wood and the island will finish to-morrow in a dead heat," he laughed, "but there's enough to last us till then."

I plunged in the river from the point of the island, which had indeed altered a lot in size and shape during the night, and was swept down in a moment to the landing place opposite the tent. The water was icy, and the banks flew by like the country from an express train. Bathing under such conditions was an exhilarating operation, and the terror of the night seemed cleansed out of me by a process of evaporation in the brain. The sun was blazing hot; not a cloud showed itself anywhere; the wind, however, had not abated one little jot.

Quite suddenly then the implied meaning of the Swede's words flashed across me, showing that he no longer wished to leave post-haste, and had changed his mind. "Enough to last till to-morrow"—he assumed we should stay on the island another night. It struck me as odd. The night before he was so positive the other way. How had the change come about?

Great crumblings of the banks occurred at breakfast, with heavy splashings and clouds of spray which the wind brought into our frying-pan, and my fellow-traveler talked incessantly about the difficulty the Vienna-Pesth steamers must have to find the channel in flood. But the state of his mind interested and impressed me far more than the state of the river or the difficulties of the steamers. He had changed somehow since the evening before. His manner was different—a trifle excited, a trifle shy, with a sort of suspicion about his voice and gestures. I hardly know how to describe it now in cold blood, but at the time I remember being quite certain of one thing, viz., that he had become frightened!

He ate very little breakfast, and for once omitted to smoke his pipe. He had the map spread open beside him, and kept studying its markings.

"We'd better get off sharp in an hour," I said presently, feeling for an opening that must bring him indirectly to a partial confession at any rate. And his answer puzzled me uncomfortably: "Rather! If they'll let us."

"Who'll let us? The elements?" I asked quickly, with affected indifference.

"The powers of this awful place, whoever they are," he replied, keeping his eyes on the map. "The gods are here, if they are anywhere at all in the world."

"The elements are always the true immortals," I replied, laughing as naturally as I could manage, yet knowing quite well that my face reflected my true feelings when he looked up gravely at me and spoke across the smoke:

"We shall be fortunate if we get away without further disaster."

This was exactly what I had dreaded, and I screwed myself up to the point of the direct question. It was like agreeing to allow the dentist to extract the tooth; it *had* to come anyhow in the long run, and the rest was all pretense.

"Further disaster! Why, what's happened?"

"For one thing—the steering paddle's gone," he said quietly.

"The steering paddle gone!" I repeated, greatly excited, for this was our rudder, and the Danube in flood without a rudder was suicide. "But what——"

"And there's a tear in the bottom of the canoe," he added, with a genuine little tremor in his voice.

I continued staring at him, able only to repeat the words in his face somewhat foolishly. There, in the heat of the sun, and on this burning sand, I was aware of a freezing atmosphere descending round us. I got up to follow him, for he merely nodded his head gravely and led the way towards the tent a few yards on the other side of the fireplace. The canoe still lay there as I had last seen her in the night, ribs uppermost, the paddles, or rather, *the* paddle, on the sand beside her.

"There's only one," he said, stooping to pick it up. "And here's the rent in the base-board."

It was on the tip of my tongue to tell him that I had clearly noticed *two* paddles a few hours before, but a second impulse made me think better of it, and I said nothing. I approached to see.

There was a long, finely made tear in the bottom of the canoe where a little slither of wood had been neatly taken clean out; it looked as if the tooth of a sharp rock or snag had eaten down her length, and investigation showed that the hole went through. Had we launched out in her without observing it we must inevitably have foundered. At first the water would have made the wood swell so as to close the hole, but once out in midstream the water must have poured in, and the canoe, never more than two inches above the surface, would have filled and sunk very rapidly.

"There, you see, an attempt to prepare a victim for the sacrifice," I heard him saying, more to himself than to me, "two victims rather," he added as he bent over and ran his fingers along the slit.

I began to whistle—a thing I always do unconsciously when utterly nonplussed—and purposely paid no attention to his words. I was determined to consider them foolish.

"It wasn't there last night," he said presently, straightening up from his examination and looking anywhere but at me.

"We must have scratched her in landing, of course," I stopped whistling to say, "The stones are very sharp——"

I stopped abruptly, for at that moment he turned round and met my eye squarely. I knew just as well as he did how impossible my explanation was. There were no stones, to begin with.

"And then there's this to explain too," he added quietly, handing me the paddle and pointing to the blade.

A new and curious emotion spread freezingly over me as I took and examined it. The blade was scraped down all over, beautifully scraped, as though someone had sand-papered it with care, making it so thin that the first vigorous stroke must have snapped it off at the elbow.

"One of us walked in his sleep and did this thing," I said feebly, "or—or it has been filed by the constant stream of sand particles blown against it by the wind, perhaps."

"Ah," said the Swede, turning away, laughing a little, "you can explain everything!"

"The same wind that caught the steering paddle and flung it so near the bank that it fell in with the next lump that crumbled," I called out after him, absolutely determined to find an explanation for everything he showed me.

"I see," he shouted back, turning his head to look at me before disappearing among the willow bushes.

Once alone with these perplexing evidences of personal agency, I think my first thought took the form of "One of us must have done this thing, and it certainly was not I." But my second thought decided how impossible it was to suppose, under all the circumstances, that either of us had done it. That my companion, the trusted friend of a dozen similar expeditions, could have knowingly had a hand in it, was a suggestion not to be entertained for a moment. Equally absurd seemed the explanation that this imperturbable and densely practical nature had suddenly become insane and was busied with insane purposes.

Yet the fact remained that what disturbed me most, and kept my fear actively alive even in this blaze of sunshine and wild beauty, was the clear certainty that some curious alteration had come about in his *mind*—that he was nervous, timid, suspicious, aware of goings on he did not speak about, watching a series of secret and hitherto unmentionable events—waiting, in a word, for a climax that he expected, and, I thought, expected very soon. This grew up in my mind intuitively—I hardly knew how.

I made a hurried examination of the tent and its surroundings, but the measurements of the night remained the same. There were deep hollows formed in the sand, I now noticed for the first time, basin-shaped and of various depths and sizes, varying from that of a teacup to a large bowl. The wind, no doubt, was responsible for these miniature craters, just as it was for lifting the paddle and tossing it towards the water. The rent in the canoe was the only thing that seemed quite inexplicable; and, after all, it *was* conceivable that a sharp point had caught it when we landed. The examination I made of the shore did not assist this theory, but all the same I clung to it with that diminishing portion of my intelligence which I called my "reason." An explanation of some kind was an absolute necessity, just as some working explanation of the universe is necessary—however absurd—to the happiness of every individual who seeks to do his duty in the world and face the problems of life. The simile seemed to me at the time an exact parallel.

I at once set the pitch melting, and presently the Swede joined me at the work, though under the best conditions in the world the canoe could not be safe for traveling till the following day. I drew his attention casually to the hollows in the sand.

"Yes," he said, "I know. They're all over the island. But *you* can explain them, no doubt!"

"Wind, of course," I answered without hesitation. "Have you never watched those little whirlwinds in the street that twist and twirl everything into a circle? This sand's loose enough to yield, that's all."

He made no reply, and we worked on in silence for a bit. I watched him surreptitiously all the time, and I had an idea he was watching me. He seemed, too, to be always listening attentively to something I could not hear, or perhaps for something that he expected to hear, for he kept turning about and staring into the bushes, and up into the sky, and out across the water where it was visible through the openings among the willows. Sometimes he even put his hand to his ear and held it there for several minutes. He said nothing to me, however, about it, and I asked no questions. And meanwhile, as he mended that torn canoe with the skill and address of a red Indian, I was glad to notice his absorption in the work, for there was a vague dread in my heart that he would speak of the changed aspect of the willows. And, if he had noticed *that*, my imagination could no longer be held a sufficient explanation of it.

At length, after a long pause, he began to talk.

"Queer thing," he added in a hurried sort of voice, as though he wanted to say something and get it over. "Queer thing, I mean, about that otter last night."

I had expected something so totally different that he caught me with surprise, and I looked up sharply.

"Shows how lonely this place is. Otters are awfully shy things—"

"I don't mean that, of course," he interrupted. "I mean—do you think—did you think it really *was* an otter?"

"What else, in the name of heaven, what else?"

"You know, I saw it before you did, and at first it seemed—so *much* bigger than an otter."

"The sunset as you looked upstream magnified it, or something," I replied.

He looked at me absently a moment, as though his mind were busy with other thoughts.

"It had such extraordinary yellow eyes," he went on half to himself.

"That was the sun too," I laughed, a trifle boisterously. "I suppose you'll wonder next if that fellow in the boat——"

I suddenly decided not to finish the sentence. He was in the act again of listening, turning his head to the wind, and something in the expression of his face made me halt. The subject dropped, and we went on with our caulking. Apparently he had not noticed my unfinished sentence. Five minutes later, however, he looked at me across the canoe, the smoking pitch in his hand, his face exceedingly grave.

"I *did* rather wonder, if you want to know," he said slowly, "what that thing in the boat was. I remember thinking at the time it was not a man. The whole business seemed to rise quite suddenly out of the water."

I laughed again boisterously in his face, but this time there was impatience, and a strain of anger too, in my feeling.

"Look here now," I cried, "this place is quite queer enough without going out of our way to imagine things! That boat was an ordinary boat, and the man in it was an ordinary man, and they were both going downstream as fast as they could lick. And that otter *was* an otter, so don't let's play the fool about it!"

He looked steadily at me with the same grave expression. He was not in the least annoyed. I took courage from his silence.

"And for heaven's sake," I went on, "don't keep pretending you hear things, because it only gives me the jumps, and there's nothing to hear but the river and this cursed old thundering wind."

"You *fool*!" he answered in a low, shocked voice, "you utter fool. That's just the way all victims talk. As if you didn't understand just as well as I do!" he sneered with scorn in his voice, and a sort of resignation. "The best thing you can do is to keep quiet and try to hold your mind as firm as possible. This feeble attempt at self-deception only makes the truth harder when you're forced to meet it."

My little effort was over, and I found nothing more to say, for I knew quite well his words were true, and that *I* was the fool, not *he*. Up to a certain stage in the adventure he kept ahead of me easily, and I think I felt annoyed to be out of it, to be thus proved less psychic, less sensitive than himself to these extraordinary happenings, and half ignorant all the time of what was going on under my very nose. *He knew* from the very beginning, apparently. But at the moment I wholly missed the point of his words about the necessity of there being a victim, and that we ourselves were destined to satisfy the want. I dropped all pretense thenceforward, but thenceforward likewise my fear increased steadily to the climax.

"But you're quite right about one thing," he added, before the subject passed, "and that is that we're wiser not to talk about it, or even to think about it, because what one *thinks* finds expression in words, and what one *says*, happens."

That afternoon, while the canoe dried and hardened, we spent trying to fish, testing the leak, collecting wood, and watching the enormous flood of rising water. Masses of driftwood swept near our shores sometimes, and we fished for them with long willow branches. The island grew perceptibly smaller as the banks were torn away with great gulps and splashes. The weather kept brilliantly fine till about four o'clock, and then for the first time for three days the wind showed signs of abating. Clouds began to gather in the southwest, spreading thence slowly over the sky.

This lessening of the wind came as a great relief, for the incessant roaring, banging, and thundering had irritated our nerves. Yet the silence that came about five o'clock with its sudden cessation was in a manner quite as oppressive. The booming of the river had everything its own way then: it filled the air with deep murmurs, more musical than the wind noises, but infinitely more monotonous. The wind held many notes, rising, falling, always beating out some sort of great elemental tune; whereas the river's song lay between three notes at most—dull pedal notes, that held a lugubrious quality foreign to the wind, and somehow seemed to me, in my then nervous state, to sound wonderfully well the music of doom.

It was extraordinary, too, how the withdrawal suddenly of bright sunlight took everything out of the landscape that made for cheerfulness; and since this particular landscape had already managed to convey the suggestion of something sinister, the change of course was all the more unwelcome and noticeable. For me, I know, the darkening outlook became distinctly more alarming, and I found myself more than once calculating how soon after sunset the full moon would get up in the east, and whether the gathering clouds would greatly interfere with her lighting of the little island.

With this general hush of the wind—though it still indulged in occasional brief gusts—the river seemed to me to grow blacker, the willows to stand more densely together. The latter, too, kept up a sort of independent movement of their own, rustling among themselves when no wind stirred, and shaking oddly from the roots upwards. When common objects in this way become charged with the suggestion of horror, they stimulate the imagination far more than things of unusual appearance; and these bushes, crowding huddled about us, assumed for me in the darkness a bizarre *grotesquerie* of appearance that lent to them somehow the aspect of purposeful and living creatures. Their very ordinariness, I felt, masked what was malignant and hostile to us. The forces of the region drew nearer with the coming of night. They were focusing upon our island, and more particularly upon ourselves. For thus, somehow, in the terms of the imagination, did my really indescribable sensations in this extraordinary place present themselves.

I had slept a good deal in the early afternoon, and had thus recovered somewhat from the exhaustion of a disturbed night, but this only served apparently to render me more susceptible than before to the obsessing spell of the haunting. I fought against it, laughing at my feelings as absurd and childish, with very obvious physiological explanations, yet, in spite of every effort, they gained in strength upon me so that I dreaded the night as a child lost in a forest must dread the approach of darkness.

The canoe we had carefully covered with a waterproof sheet during the day, and the one remaining paddle had been securely tied by the Swede to the base of a tree, lest the wind should rob us of that too. From five o'clock onwards I busied myself with the stew-pot and preparations for dinner, it being my turn to cook that night. We had potatoes, onions, bits of bacon fat to add flavour, and a general thick residue from former stews at the bottom of the pot; with black bread broken up into it, the result was most excellent, and it was followed by a stew of plums with sugar and a brew of strong tea with dried milk. A good pile of wood lay close at hand, and the absence of wind made my duties easy. My companion sat lazily watching me, dividing his attentions between cleaning his pipe and giving useless advice—an admitted privilege of the off-duty man. He had been very quiet all the afternoon, engaged in re-caulking the canoe, strengthening the tent ropes, and fishing for driftwood while I slept. No more talk about undesirable things had passed between us, and I think his only remarks had to do with the gradual destruction of the island, which he declared was now fully a third smaller than when we first landed.

The pot had just begun to bubble when I heard his voice calling to me from the bank, where he had wandered away without my noticing. I ran up.

"Come and listen," he said, "and see what you make of it." He held his hand cupwise to his ear, as so often before.

"*Now* do you hear anything?" he asked, watching me curiously.

We stood there, listening attentively together. At first I heard only the deep note of the water and the hissings rising from its turbulent surface. The willows, for once, were motionless and silent. Then a sound began to reach my ears faintly, a peculiar sound—something like the humming of a distant gong. It seemed to come across to us in the darkness from the waste of swamps and willows opposite. It was repeated at regular intervals, but it was certainly neither the sound of a bell nor the hooting of a distant steamer. I can liken it to nothing so much as to the sound of an immense gong, suspended far up in the sky, repeating incessantly its muffled metallic note, soft and musical, as it was repeatedly struck. My heart quickened as I listened.

"I've heard it all day," said my companion. "While you slept this afternoon it came all round the island. I hunted it down, but could never get near enough to see—to localize it correctly. Sometimes it was overhead, and sometimes it seemed under the water. Once or twice, too, I could have sworn it was not outside at all, but *within myself*—you know—the way a sound in the fourth dimension is supposed to come."

I was too much puzzled to pay much attention to his words. I listened carefully, striving to associate it with any known familiar sound I could think of, but without success. It changed in direction, too, coming nearer, and then sinking utterly away into remote distance. I cannot say that it was ominous in quality, because to me it seemed distinctly musical, yet I must admit it set going a distressing feeling that made me wish I had never heard it.

"The wind blowing in those sand-funnels," I said, determined to find an explanation, "or the bushes rubbing together after the storm perhaps."

"It comes off the whole swamp," my friend answered. "It comes from everywhere at once." He ignored my explanations. "It comes from the willow bushes somehow——"

"But now the wind has dropped," I objected. "The willows can hardly make a noise by themselves, can they?"

His answer frightened me, first because I had dreaded it, and secondly, because I knew intuitively it was true.

"It is *because* the wind has dropped we now hear it. It was drowned before. It is the cry, I believe of the——"

I dashed back to my fire, warned by a sound of bubbling that the stew was in danger, but determined at the same time to escape from further conversation. I was resolute, if possible, to avoid the exchanging of views. I dreaded, too, that he would begin again about the gods, or the elemental forces, or something else disquieting, and I wanted to keep myself well in hand for what might happen later. There was another night to be faced before we escaped from this distressing place, and there was no knowing yet what it might bring forth.

"Come and cut up bread for the pot," I called to him, vigorously stirring the appetizing mixture. That stew-pot held sanity for us both, and the thought made me laugh.

He came over slowly and took the provision sack from the tree, fumbling in its mysterious depths, and then emptying the entire contents upon the ground-sheet at his feet.

"Hurry up!" I cried; "it's boiling."

The Swede burst out into a roar of laughter that startled me. It was forced laughter, not artificial exactly, but mirthless.

"There's nothing here!" he shouted, holding his sides.

"Bread, I mean."

"It's gone. There is no bread. They've taken it!"

I dropped the long spoon and ran up. Everything the sack contained lay upon the ground-sheet, but there was no loaf.

The whole dead weight of my growing fear fell upon me and shook me. Then I burst out laughing too. It was the only thing to do: and the sound of my own laughter also made me understand his. The strain of psychical pressure caused it—this explosion of unnatural laughter in both of us; it was an effort of repressed forces to seek relief; it was a temporary safety valve. And with both of us it ceased quite suddenly.

"How criminally stupid of me!" I cried, still determined to be consistent and find an explanation. "I clean forgot to buy a loaf at Pressburg. That chattering woman put everything out of my head, and I must have left it lying on the counter or——"

"The oatmeal, too, is much less than it was this morning," the Swede interrupted.

Why in the world need he draw attention to it? I thought angrily.

"There's enough for to-morrow," I said, stirring vigorously, "and we can get lots more at Komorn or Gran. In twenty-four hours we shall be miles from here."

"I hope so—to God," he muttered, putting the things back into the sack, "unless we're claimed first as victims for the sacrifice," he added with a foolish laugh. He dragged the sack into the tent, for safety's sake, I suppose, and I heard him mumbling on to himself, but so indistinctly that it seemed quite natural for me to ignore his words.

Our meal was beyond question a gloomy one, and we ate it almost in silence, avoiding one another's eyes, and keeping the fire bright. Then we washed up and prepared for the night, and, once smoking, our minds unoccupied with any definite duties, the apprehension I had felt all day long became more and more acute. It was not then active fear, I think, but the very vagueness of its origin distressed me far more than if I had been able to ticket and face it squarely. The curious sound I have likened to the note of a gong became now almost incessant, and filled the stillness of the night with a faint, continuous ringing rather than a series of distinct notes. At one time it was behind and at another time in front of us. Sometimes I fancied it came from the bushes on our left, and then again from the clumps on our right. More often it hovered directly overhead like the whirring of wings. It was really everywhere at once, behind, in front, at our sides and over our heads, completely surrounding us. The sound really defies description. But nothing within my knowledge is like that ceaseless muffled humming rising off the deserted world of swamps and willows.

We sat smoking in comparative silence, the strain growing every minute greater. The worst feature of the situation seemed to me that we did not know what to expect, and could therefore make no sort of preparation by way of defense. We could anticipate nothing. My explanations made in the sunshine, moreover, now came to haunt me with their foolish and wholly unsatisfactory nature, and it was more and more clear to me that some kind of plain talk with my companion was inevitable, whether I liked it or not. After all, we had to spend the night together, and to sleep in the same tent side by side. I saw that I could not get along much longer without the support of his mind, and for that, of course, plain talk was imperative. As long as possible, however, I postponed this little climax, and tried to ignore or laugh at the occasional sentences he flung into the emptiness.

Some of these sentences, moreover, were confoundedly disquieting to me, coming as they did to corroborate much that I felt myself: corroboration, too—which made it so much more convincing—from a totally different point of view. He composed such curious sentences, and hurled them at me in such an inconsequential sort of way, as though his main line of thought was secret to himself, and these fragments were the bits he found it impossible to digest. He got rid of them by uttering them. Speech relieved him. It was like being sick.

"There are things about us, I'm sure, that make for disorder, disintegration, destruction, *our* destruction," he said once, while the fire blazed between us. "We've strayed out of a safe line somewhere."

And another time, when the gong sounds had come nearer, ringing much louder than before, and directly over our heads, he said, as though talking to himself:

"I don't think a phonograph would show any record of that. The sound doesn't come to me by the ears at all. The vibrations reach me in another manner altogether, and seem to be within me, which is precisely how a fourth dimension sound might be supposed to make itself heard."

I purposely made no reply to this, but I sat up a little closer to the fire and peered about me into the darkness. The clouds were massed all over the sky and no trace of moonlight came through. Very still, too, everything was, so that the river and the frogs had things all their own way.

"It has that about it," he went on, "which is utterly out of common experience. It is *unknown*. Only one thing describes it really: it is a non-human sound; I mean a sound outside humanity."

Having rid himself of this indigestible morsel, he lay quiet for a time; but he had so admirably expressed my own feeling that it was a relief to have the thought out, and to have confined it by the limitation of words from dangerous wandering to and fro in the mind.

The solitude of that Danube camping-place, can I ever forget it? The feeling of being utterly alone on an empty planet! My thoughts ran incessantly upon cities and the haunts of men. I would have given my soul, as the saying is, for the "feel" of those Bavarian villages we had passed through by the score; for the normal, human commonplaces: peasants drinking beer, tables beneath the trees, hot sunshine, and a ruined castle on the rocks behind the red-roofed church. Even the tourists would have been welcome.

Yet what I felt of dread was no ordinary ghostly fear. It was infinitely greater, stranger, and seemed to arise from some dim ancestral sense of terror more profoundly disturbing than anything I had known or dreamed of. We had "strayed," as the Swede put it, into some region or some set of conditions where the risks were great, yet unintelligible to us; where the frontiers of some unknown world lay close about us. It was a spot held by the dwellers in some outer space, a sort of peephole whence they could spy upon the earth, themselves unseen, a point where the veil between had worn a little thin. As the final result of too long a sojourn here, we should be carried over the border and deprived of what we called "our lives," yet by mental, not physical, processes. In that sense, as he said, we should be the victims of our adventure—a sacrifice.

It took us in different fashion, each according to the measure of his sensitiveness and powers of resistance. I translated it vaguely into a personification of the mightily disturbed elements, investing them with the horror of a deliberate and malefic purpose, resentful of our audacious intrusion into their breeding-place; whereas my friend threw it into the unoriginal form at first of a trespass on some ancient shrine, some place where the old gods still held sway, where the emotional forces of former worshipers still clung, and the ancestral portion of him yielded to the old pagan spell.

At any rate, here was a place unpolluted by men, kept clean by the winds from coarsening human influences, a place where spiritual agencies were within reach and aggressive. Never, before or since, have I been so attacked by indescribable suggestions of a "beyond region," of another scheme of life, another evolution not parallel to the human. And in the end our minds would succumb under the weight of the awful spell, and we should be drawn across the frontier into *their* world.

Small things testified to this amazing influence of the place, and now in the silence round the fire they allowed themselves to be noted by the mind. The very atmosphere had proved itself a magnifying medium to distort every indication: the otter rolling in the current, the hurrying boatman making signs, the shifting willows, one and all had been robbed of its natural character, and revealed in something of its other aspect—as it existed across the border in that other region. And this changed aspect I felt was new not merely to me, but to the race. The whole experience whose verge we touched was unknown to humanity at all. It was a new order of experience, and in the true sense of the word *unearthly*.

"It's the deliberate, calculating purpose that reduces one's courage to zero," the Swede said suddenly, as if he had been actually following my thoughts. "Otherwise imagination might count for much. But the paddle, the canoe, the lessening food——"

"Haven't I explained all that once?" I interrupted viciously.

"You have," he answered dryly; "you have indeed."

He made other remarks too, as usual, about what he called the "plain determination to provide a victim"; but, having now arranged my thoughts better, I recognized that his was simply the cry of his frightened soul against the knowledge that he was being attacked in a vital part, and that he would be somehow taken or destroyed. The situation called for a courage and calmness of reasoning that neither of us could compass, and I have never before been so clearly conscious of two persons in me—the one that explained everything, and the other that laughed at such foolish explanations, yet was horribly afraid.

Meanwhile, in the pitchy night the fire died down and the woodpile grew small. Neither of us moved to replenish the stock, and the darkness consequently came up very close to our faces. A few feet beyond the circle of firelight it was inky black. Occasionally a stray puff of wind set the willows shivering about us, but apart from this not very welcome sound a deep and depressing silence reigned, broken only by the gurgling of the river and the humming in the air overhead.

We both missed, I think, the shouting company of the winds.

At length, at a moment when a stray puff prolonged itself as though the wind were about to rise again, I reached the point for me of saturation, the point where it was absolutely necessary to find relief in plain speech, or else to betray myself by some hysterical extravagance that must have been far worse in its effect upon both of us. I kicked the fire into a blaze, and turned to my companion abruptly. He looked up with a start.

"I can't disguise it any longer," I said; "I don't like this place, and the darkness, and the noises, and the awful feelings I get. There's something here that beats me utterly. I'm in a blue funk, and that's the plain truth. If the other shore was—different, I swear I'd be inclined to swim for it!"

The Swede's face turned very white beneath the deep tan of sun and wind. He stared straight at me and answered quietly, but his voice betrayed his huge excitement by its unnatural calmness. For the moment, at any rate, he was the strong man of the two. He was more phlegmatic, for one thing.

"It's not a physical condition we can escape from by running away," he replied, in the tone of a doctor diagnosing some grave disease; "we must sit tight and wait. There are forces close here that could kill a herd of elephants in a second as easily as you or I could squash a fly. Our only chance is to keep perfectly still. Our insignificance perhaps may save us."

I put a dozen questions into my expression of face, but found no words. It was precisely like listening to an accurate description of a disease whose symptoms had puzzled me.

"I mean that so far, although aware of our disturbing presence, they have not *found* us—not 'located' us, as the Americans say," he went on. "They're blundering about like men hunting for a leak of gas. The paddle and canoe and provisions prove that. I think they *feel* us, but cannot actually see us. We must keep our minds quiet—it's our minds they feel. We must control our thoughts, or it's all up with us."

"Death you mean?" I stammered, icy with the horror of his suggestion.

"Worse—by far," he said. "Death, according to one's belief, means either annihilation or release from the limitations of the senses, but it involves no change of character. *You* don't suddenly alter just because the body's gone. But this means a radical alteration, a complete change, a horrible loss of oneself by substitution—far worse than death, and not even annihilation. We happen to have camped in a spot where their region touches ours, where the veil between has worn thin"—horrors! he was using my very own phrase, my actual words—"so that they are aware of our being in their neighborhood."

"But *who* are aware?" I asked.

I forgot the shaking of the willows in the windless calm, the humming overhead, everything except that I was waiting for an answer that I dreaded more than I can possibly explain.

He lowered his voice at once to reply, leaning forward a little over the fire, an indefinable change in his face that made me avoid his eyes and look down upon the ground.

"All my life," he said, "I have been strangely, vividly, conscious of another region—not far removed from our own world in one sense, yet wholly different in kind—where great things go on unceasingly, where immense and terrible personalities hurry by, intent on vast purposes compared to which earthly affairs, the rise and fall of nations, the destinies of empires, the fate of armies and continents, are all as dust in the balance; vast purposes, I mean, that deal directly with the soul, and not indirectly with mere expressions of the soul——"

"I suggest just now—" I began, seeking to stop him, feeling as though I was face to face with a madman. But he instantly overbore me with his torrent that *had* to come.

"You think," he said, "it is the spirits of the elements, and I thought perhaps it was the old gods. But I tell you now it is—*neither*. These would be comprehensible entities, for they have relations with men, depending upon them for worship or sacrifice, whereas these beings who are now about us have absolutely nothing to do with mankind, and it is mere chance that their space happens just at this spot to touch our own."

The mere conception, which his words somehow made so convincing, as I listened to them there in the dark stillness of that lonely island, set me shaking a little all over. I found it impossible to control my movements.

"And what do you propose?" I began again.

"A sacrifice, a victim, might save us by distracting them until we could get away," he went on, "just as the wolves stop to devour the dogs and give the sleigh another start. But—I see no chance of any other victim now."

I stared blankly at him. The gleam in his eyes was dreadful. Presently he continued.

"It's the willows, of course. The willows *mask* the others, but the others are feeling about for us. If we let our minds betray our fear, we're lost, lost utterly." He looked at me with an expression so calm, so determined, so sincere, that I no longer had any doubts as to his sanity. He was as sane as any man ever was. "If we can hold out through the night," he added, "we may get off in the daylight unnoticed, or rather, *undiscovered*."

"But you really think a sacrifice would——"

That gong-like humming came down very close over our heads as I spoke, but it was my friend's scared face that really stopped my mouth.

"Hush!" he whispered, holding up his hand. "Do not mention them more than you can help. Do not refer to them *by name*. To name is to reveal: it is the inevitable clue, and our only hope lies in ignoring them, in order that they may ignore us."

"Even in thought?" He was extraordinarily agitated.

"Especially in thought. Our thoughts make spirals in their world. We must keep them *out of our minds* at all costs if possible."

I raked the fire together to prevent the darkness having everything its own way. I never longed for the sun as I longed for it then in the awful blackness of that summer night.

"Were you awake all last night?" he went on suddenly.

"I slept badly a little after dawn," I replied evasively, trying to follow his instructions, which I knew instinctively were true, "but the wind, of course——"

"I know. But the wind won't account for all the noises."

"Then you heard it too?"

"The multiplying countless little footsteps I heard," he said, adding, after a moment's hesitation, "and that other sound——"

"You mean above the tent, and the pressing down upon us of something tremendous, gigantic?"

He nodded significantly.

"It was like the beginning of a sort of inner suffocation?" I said.

"Partly, yes. It seemed to me that the weight of the atmosphere had been altered—had increased enormously, so that we should be crushed."

"And *that*," I went on, determined to have it all out, pointing upwards where the gong-like note hummed ceaselessly, rising and falling like wind. "What do you make of that?"

"It's *their* sound," he whispered gravely. "It's the sound of their world, the humming in their region. The division here is so thin that it leaks through somehow. But, if you listen carefully, you'll find it's not above so much as around us. It's in the willows. It's the willows themselves humming, because here the willows have been made symbols of the forces that are against us."

I could not follow exactly what he meant by this, yet the thought and idea in my mind were beyond question the thought and idea in his. I realized what he realized, only with less power of analysis than his. It was on the tip of my tongue to tell him at last about my hallucination of the ascending figures and the moving bushes, when he suddenly thrust his face again close into mine across the firelight and began to speak in a very earnest whisper. He amazed me by his calmness and pluck, his apparent control of the situation. This man I had for years deemed unimaginative, stolid!

"Now listen," he said. "The only thing for us to do is to go on as though nothing had happened, follow our usual habits, go to bed, and so forth; pretend we feel nothing and notice nothing. It is a question wholly of the mind, and the less we think about them the better our chance of escape. Above all, don't *think*, for what you think happens!"

"All right," I managed to reply, simply breathless with his words and the strangeness of it all; "all right, I'll try, but tell me one thing more first. Tell me what you make of those hollows in the ground all about us, those sand-funnels?"

"No!" he cried, forgetting to whisper in his excitement. "I dare not, simply dare not, put the thought into words. If you have not guessed, I am glad. Don't try to. *They* have put it into my mind; try your hardest to prevent their putting it into yours."

He sank his voice again to a whisper before he finished, and I did not press him to explain. There was already just about as much horror in me as I could hold. The conversation came to an end, and we smoked our pipes busily in silence.

Then something happened, something unimportant apparently, as the way it is when the nerves are in a very great state of tension, and this small thing for a brief space gave me an entirely different point of view. I chanced to look down at my sand-shoe—the sort we used for the canoe—and something to do with the hole at the toe suddenly recalled to me the London shop where I had bought them, the difficulty the man had in fitting me, and other details of the uninteresting but practical operation. At once, in its train, followed a wholesome view of the modern skeptical world I was accustomed to move in at home. I thought of roast beef and ale, motor-cars, policemen, brass bands, and a dozen other things that proclaimed the soul of ordinariness or utility. The effect was immediate and astonishing even to myself. Psychologically, I suppose, it was simply a sudden and violent reaction after the strain of living in an atmosphere of things that to the normal consciousness must seem impossible and incredible. But, whatever the cause, it momentarily lifted the spell from my heart, and left me for the short space of a minute feeling free and utterly unafraid. I looked up at my friend opposite.

"You damned old pagan!" I cried, laughing aloud in his face. "You imaginative idiot! You superstitious idolator! You——"

I stopped in the middle, seized anew by the old horror. I tried to smother the sound of my voice as something sacrilegious. The Swede, of course, heard it too—that strange cry overhead in the darkness—and that sudden drop in the air as though something had come nearer.

He had turned ashen white under the tan. He stood bolt upright in front of the fire, stiff as a rod, staring at me.

"After that," he said in a sort of helpless, frantic way, "we must go! We can't stay now; we must strike camp this very instant and go on—down the river."

He was talking, I saw, quite wildly, his words dictated by abject terror—the terror he had resisted so long, but which had caught him at last.

"In the dark?" I exclaimed, shaking with fear after my hysterical outburst, but still realizing our position better than he did. "Sheer madness. The river's in flood, and we've only got a single paddle. Besides, we only go deeper into their country! There's nothing ahead for fifty miles but willows, willows, willows!"

He sat down again in a state of semi-collapse. The positions, by one of those kaleidoscopic changes nature loves, were suddenly reversed, and the control of our forces passed over into my hands. His mind at last had reached the point where it was beginning to weaken.

"What on earth possessed you to do such a thing?" he whispered, with awe of genuine terror in his voice and face.

I crossed round to his side of the fire. I took both his hands in mine, kneeling down beside him and looking straight into his frightened eyes.

"We'll make one more blaze," I said firmly, "and then turn in for the night. At sunrise we'll be off full speed for Komorn. Now, pull yourself together a bit, and remember your own advice about *not thinking fear*!"

He said no more, and I saw that he would agree and obey. In some measure, too, it was a sort of relief to get up and make an excursion into the darkness for more wood. We kept close together, almost touching, groping among the bushes and along the bank. The humming overhead never ceased, but seemed to me to grow louder as we increased our distance from the fire. It was shivery work!

We were grubbing away in the middle of a thickish clump of willows where some driftwood from a former flood had caught high among the branches, when my body was seized in a grip that made me half drop upon the sand. It was the Swede. He had fallen against me, and was clutching me for support. I heard his breath coming and going in short gasps.

"Look! By my soul!" he whispered, and for the first time in my experience I knew what it was to hear tears of terror in a human voice. He was pointing to the fire, some fifty feet away. I followed the direction of his finger, and I swear my heart missed a beat.

There, in front of the dim glow, *something was moving.*

I saw it through a veil that hung before my eyes like the gauze drop-curtain used at the back of a theater—hazily a little. It was neither a human figure nor an animal. To me it gave the strange impression of being as large as several animals grouped together, like horses, two or three, moving slowly. The Swede, too, got a similar result, though expressing it differently, for he thought it was shaped and sized like a clump of willow bushes, rounded at the top, and moving all over upon its surface—"coiling upon itself like smoke," he said afterwards.

"I watched it settle downwards through the bushes," he sobbed at me. "Look, by God! It's coming this way! Oh, oh!"—he gave a kind of whistling cry. "*They've found us.*"

I gave one terrified glance, which just enabled me to see that the shadowy form was swinging towards us through the bushes, and then I collapsed backwards with a crash into the branches. These failed, of course, to support my weight, so that with the Swede on the top of me we fell in a struggling heap upon the sand. I really hardly knew what was happening. I was conscious only of a sort of enveloping sensation of icy fear that plucked the nerves out of their fleshly covering, twisted them this way and that, and replaced them quivering. My eyes were tightly shut; something in my throat choked me; a feeling that my consciousness was expanding, extending out into space, swiftly gave way to another feeling that I was losing it altogether, and about to die.

An acute spasm of pain passed through me, and I was aware that the Swede had hold of me in such a way that he hurt me abominably. It was the way he caught at me in falling.

But it was this pain, he declared afterwards, that saved me: it caused me to *forget them* and think of something else at the very instant when they were about to find me. It concealed my mind from them at the moment of discovery, yet just in time to evade their terrible seizing of me. He himself, he says, actually swooned at the same moment, and that was what saved him.

I only know that at a later time, how long or short is impossible to say, I found myself scrambling up out of the slippery network of willow branches, and saw my companion standing in front of me holding out a hand to assist me. I stared at him in a dazed way, rubbing the arm he had twisted for me. Nothing came to me to say, somehow.

"I lost consciousness for a moment or two," I heard him say. "That's what saved me. It made me stop thinking about them."

"You nearly broke my arm in two," I said, uttering my only connected thought at the moment. A numbness came over me.

"That's what saved *you!*" he replied. "Between us, we've managed to set them off on a false tack somewhere. The humming has ceased. It's gone—for the moment at any rate!"

A wave of hysterical laughter seized me again, and this time spread to my friend too—great healing gusts of shaking laughter that brought a tremendous sense of relief in their train. We made our way back to the fire and put the wood on so that it blazed at once. Then we saw that the tent had fallen over and lay in a tangled heap upon the ground.

We picked it up, and during the process tripped more than once and caught our feet in sand.

"It's those sand-funnels," exclaimed the Swede, when the tent was up again and the firelight lit up the ground for several yards about us. "And look at the size of them!"

All round the tent and about the fireplace where we had seen the moving shadows there were deep funnel-shaped hollows in the sand, exactly similar to the ones we had already found over the island, only far bigger and deeper, beautifully formed, and wide enough in some instances to admit the whole of my foot and leg.

Neither of us said a word. We both knew that sleep was the safest thing we could do, and to bed we went accordingly without further delay, having first thrown sand on the fire and taken the provision sack and the paddle inside the tent with us. The canoe, too, we propped in such a way at the end of the tent that our feet touched it, and the least motion would disturb and wake us.

In case of emergency, too, we again went to bed in our clothes, ready for a sudden start.

V

It was my firm intention to lie awake all night and watch, but the exhaustion of nerves and body decreed otherwise, and sleep after a while came over me with a welcome blanket of oblivion. The fact that my companion also slept quickened its approach. At first he fidgeted and constantly sat up, asking me if I "heard this" or "heard that." He tossed about on his cork mattress, and said the tent was moving and the river had risen over the point of the island; but each time I went out to look I returned with the report that all was well, and finally he grew calmer and lay still. Then at length his breathing became regular and I heard unmistakable sounds of snoring—the first and only time in my life when snoring has been a welcome and calming influence.

This, I remember, was the last thought in my mind before dozing off.

A difficulty in breathing woke me, and I found the blanket over my face. But something else besides the blanket was pressing upon me, and my first thought was that my companion had rolled off his mattress on to my own in his sleep. I called to him and sat up, and at the same moment it came to me that the tent was *surrounded*. That sound of multitudinous soft pattering was again audible outside, filling the night with horror.

I called again to him, louder than before. He did not answer, but I missed the sound of his snoring, and also noticed that the flap of the tent door was down. This was the unpardonable sin. I crawled out in the darkness to hook it back securely, and it was then for the first time I realized positively that the Swede was not there. He had gone.

I dashed out in a mad run, seized by a dreadful agitation, and the moment I was out I plunged into a sort of torrent of humming that surrounded me completely and came out of every quarter of the heavens at once. It was that same familiar humming—gone mad! A swarm of great invisible bees might have been about me in the air. The sound seemed to thicken the very atmosphere, and I felt that my lungs worked with difficulty.

But my friend was in danger, and I could not hesitate.

The dawn was just about to break, and a faint whitish light spread upwards over the clouds from a thin strip of clear horizon. No wind stirred. I could just make out the bushes and river beyond, and the pale sandy patches. In my excitement I ran frantically to and fro about the island, calling him by name, shouting at the top of my voice the first words that came into my head. But the willows smothered my voice, and the humming muffled it, so that the sound only traveled a few feet round me. I plunged among the bushes, tripping headlong, tumbling over roots, and scraping my face as I tore this way and that among the preventing branches.

Then, quite unexpectedly, I came out upon the island's point and saw a dark figure outlined between the water and the sky. It was the Swede. And already he had one foot in the river! A moment more and he would have taken the plunge.

I threw myself upon him, flinging my arms about his waist and dragging him shorewards with all my strength. Of course he struggled furiously, making a noise all the time just like that cursed humming, and using the most outlandish phrases in his anger about "going *inside* to Them," and "taking the way of the water and the wind," and God only knows what more besides, that I tried in vain to recall afterwards, but which turned me sick with horror and amazement as I listened. But in the end I managed to get him into the comparative safety of the tent, and flung him breathless and cursing upon the mattress, where I held him until the fit had passed.

I think the suddenness with which it all went and he grew calm, coinciding as it did with the equally abrupt cessation of the humming and pattering outside—I think this was almost the strangest part of the whole business perhaps. For he just opened his eyes and turned his tired face up to me so that the dawn threw a pale light upon it through the doorway, and said, for all the world just like a frightened child:

"My life, old man—it's my life I owe you. But it's all over now anyhow. They've found a victim in our place!"

Then he dropped back upon his blankets and went to sleep literally under my eyes. He simply collapsed, and began to snore again as healthily as though nothing had happened and he had never tried to offer his own life as a sacrifice by drowning. And when the sunlight woke him three hours later—hours of ceaseless vigil for me—it became so clear to me that he remembered absolutely nothing of what he had attempted to do that I deemed it wise to hold my peace and ask no dangerous questions.

He woke naturally and easily, as I have said, when the sun was already high in a windless hot sky, and he at once got up and set about the preparation of the fire for breakfast. I followed him anxiously at bathing, but he did not attempt to plunge in, merely dipping his head and making some remark about the extra coldness of the water.

"River's falling at last," he said, "and I'm glad of it."

"The humming has stopped too," I said.

He looked up at me quietly with his normal expression. Evidently he remembered everything except his own attempt at suicide.

"Everything has stopped," he said, "because——"

He hesitated. But I knew some reference to that remark he had made just before he fainted was in his mind, and I was determined to know it.

"Because 'They've found another victim'?" I said, forcing a little laugh.

"Exactly," he answered, "exactly! I feel as positive of it as though—as though—I feel quite safe again, I mean," he finished.

He began to look curiously about him. The sunlight lay in hot patches on the sand. There was no wind. The willows were motionless. He slowly rose to his feet.

"Come," he said; "I think if we look, we shall find it."

He started off on a run, and I followed him. He kept to the banks, poking with a stick among the sandy bays and caves and little back-waters, myself always close on his heels.

"Ah!" he exclaimed presently, "ah!"

The tone of his voice somehow brought back to me a vivid sense of the horror of the last twenty-four hours, and I hurried up to join him. He was pointing with his stick at a large black object that lay half in the water and half on the sand. It appeared to be caught by some twisted willow roots so that the river could not sweep it away. A few hours before the spot must have been under water.

"See," he said quietly, "the victim that made our escape possible!"

And when I peered across his shoulder I saw that his stick rested on the body of a man. He turned it over. It was the corpse of a peasant, and the face was hidden in the sand. Clearly the man had been drowned but a few hours before, and his body must have been swept down upon our island somewhere about the hour of the dawn—*at the very time the fit had passed.*

"We must give it a decent burial, you know."

"I suppose so," I replied. I shuddered a little in spite of myself, for there was something about the appearance of that poor drowned man that turned me cold.

The Swede glanced up sharply at me, and began clambering down the bank. I followed him more leisurely. The current, I noticed, had torn away much of the clothing from the body, so that the neck and part of the chest lay bare.

Halfway down the bank my companion suddenly stopped and held up his hand in warning; but either my foot slipped, or I had gained too much momentum to bring myself quickly to a halt, for I bumped into him and sent him forward with a sort of leap to save himself. We tumbled together on to the hard sand so that our feet splashed into the water. And, before anything could be done, we had collided a little heavily against the corpse.

The Swede uttered a sharp cry. And I sprang back as if I had been shot.

At the moment we touched the body there arose from its surface the loud sound of humming—the sound of several hummings—which passed with a vast commotion as of winged things in the air about us and disappeared upwards into the sky, growing fainter and fainter till they finally ceased in the distance. It was exactly as though we had disturbed some living yet invisible creatures at work.

My companion clutched me, and I think I clutched him, but before either of us had time properly to recover from the unexpected shock, we saw that a movement of the current was turning the corpse round so that it became released from the grip of the willow roots. A moment later it had turned completely over, the dead face uppermost, staring at the sky. It lay on the edge of the main stream. In another moment it would be swept away.

The Swede started to save it, shouting again something I did not catch about a "proper burial" and then abruptly dropped upon his knees on the sand and covered his eyes with his hands. I was beside him in an instant.

I saw what he had seen.

For just as the body swung round to the current the face and the exposed chest turned full towards us, and showed plainly how the skin and flesh were indented with small hollows, beautifully formed, and exactly similar in shape and kind to the sand-funnels that we had found all over the island.

"Their mark!" I heard my companion mutter under his breath. "Their awful mark!"

And when I turned my eyes again from his ghastly face to the river, the current had done its work, and the body had been swept away into midstream and was already beyond our reach and almost out of sight, turning over and over on the waves like an otter.

Thomas M. Disch

The Asian Shore

Thomas M. Disch's "The Asian Shore" is an extraordinary work of contemporary fiction about the nature of reality, about a singular transformation that is unsettling, disturbing, perhaps horrifying. It goes one step beyond Henry James' "The Jolly Corner," portraying a unique doppelganger situation that is altogether beyond conventional psychological investigation of character It is not a "category" story, neither supernatural nor science fiction, though it emerged originally out of SF, where it was first published. It is printed here comfortably among its kin in our third stream of horror, where it represents the ambiguous boundary of horror with existential dread. Disch is not often mentioned as a horror writer, but he has in fact a significant body of fiction in such collections as *Fun With Your New Head* (1971), *Getting Into Death* (1976), *102 H-Bombs* (1966), and the novel, *The Businessman* (1984), a body of work that seems of growing importance to the contemporary horror field.

1

There were voices on the cobbled street, and the sounds of motors. Footsteps, slamming doors, whistles, footsteps. He lived on the ground floor, so there was no way to avoid these evidences of the city's too abundant life. They accumulated in the room like so much dust, like the heaps of unanswered correspondence on the mottled tablecloth.

Every night he would drag a chair into the unfurnished back room—the guest room, as he liked to think of it—and look out over the tiled roofs and across the black waters of the Bosphorus at the lights of Usküdar. But the sounds penetrated this room too. He would sit there, in the darkness, drinking wine, waiting for her knock on the back door.

Or he might try to read: histories, books of travel, the long dull biography of Atatürk. A kind of sedation. Sometimes he would even begin a letter to his wife:

> *Dear Janice,*
> *No doubt you've been wondering what's become of me these last few months. . . .*

But the trouble was that once that part had been written, the frail

944

courtesies, the perfunctory reportage, he could not bring himself to say what *had* become of him.

Voices. . . .

It was just as well that he couldn't speak the language. For a while he had studied it, taxiing three times a week to Robert College in Bebek, but the grammar, based on assumptions wholly alien to any other language he knew, with its wavering boundaries between verbs and nouns, nouns and adjectives, withstood every assault of his incorrigibly Aristotelian mind. He sat at the back of the classroom, behind the rows of American teen-agers, as sullen as convicts, as comically out of context as the machineries melting in a Dali landscape—sat there and parroted innocuous dialogues after the teacher, taking both roles in turn, first the trustful, inquisitive John, forever wandering alone and lost in the streets of Istanbul and Ankara, then the helpful, knowing Ahmet Bey. Neither of these interlocutors would admit what had become increasingly evident with each faltering word that John spoke—that he would wander these same streets for years, inarticulate, cheated, and despised.

But these lessons, while they lasted, had one great advantage. They provided an illusion of activity, an obelisk upon which the eye might focus amid the desert of each new day, something to move toward and then something to leave behind.

After the first month it had rained a great deal, and this provided him with a good excuse for staying in. He had mopped up the major attractions of the city in one week, and he persisted at sightseeing long afterward, even in doubtful weather, until at last he had checked off every mosque and ruin, every museum and cistern cited in boldface in the pages of his Hachette. He visited the cemetery of Eyüp, and he devoted an entire Sunday to the land walls, carefully searching for, though he could not read Greek, the inscriptions of the various Byzantine emperors. But more and more often on these excursions he would see the woman or the child or the woman and the child together, until he came almost to dread the sight of any woman or any child in the city. It was not an unreasonable dread.

And always, at nine o'clock, or ten at the very latest, she would come knocking at the door of the apartment. Or, if the outer door of the building had not been left ajar by the people upstairs, at the window of the front room. She knocked patiently, in little clusters of three or four raps spaced several seconds apart, never very loud. Sometimes, but only if she were in the hall, she would accompany her knocking with a few words in Turkish, usually *Yavuz! Yavuz!* He had asked the clerk at the mail desk of the consulate what this meant, for he couldn't find it in his dictionary. It was a common Turkish name, a man's name.

His name was John. John Benedict Harris. He was an American.

She seldom stayed out there for more than half an hour any one night, knocking and calling to him, or to this imaginary Yavuz, and he would remain all that while in the chair in the unfurnished room, drinking Kavak and watching the ferries move back and forth on the dark water between Kabatas and Usküdar, the European and the Asian shore.

* * *

He had seen her first outside the fortress of Rumeli Hisar. It was the day, shortly after he'd arrived in the city, that he had come out to register at Robert College. After paying his fees and inspecting the library, he had come down the hill by the wrong path, and there it had stood, mammoth and majestically improbable, a gift. He did not know its name, and his Hachette was at the hotel. There was just the raw fact of the fortress, a mass of gray stone, its towers and crenelations, the gray Bosphorus below. He angled for a photograph, but even that far away it was too big—one could not frame the whole of it in a single shot.

He left the road, taking a path through dry brush that promised to circle the fortress. As he approached, the walls reared higher and higher. Before such walls there could be no question of an assault.

He saw her when she was about fifty feet away. She came toward him on the footpath, carrying a large bundle wrapped in newspaper and bound with twine. Her clothes were the usual motley of washed-out cotton prints that all the poorer women of the city went about in, but she did not, like most other women of her kind, attempt to pull her shawl across her face when she noticed him.

But perhaps it was only that her bundle would have made this conventional gesture of modesty awkward, for after that first glance she did at least lower her eyes to the path. No, it was hard to discover any clear portent in this first encounter.

As they passed each other he stepped off the path, and she did mumble some word in Turkish. Thank you, he supposed. He watched her until she reached the road, wondering whether she would look back, and she didn't.

He followed the walls of the fortress down the steep crumbling hillside to the shore road without finding an entrance. It amused him to think that there might not be one. Between the water and the barbicans there was only a narrow strip of highway.

An absolute daunting structure.

The entrance, which did exist, was just to the side of the central tower. He paid five lire admission and another two and a half lire to bring in his camera.

Of the three principal towers, visitors were allowed to climb only the one at the center of the eastern wall that ran along the Bosphorus. He was out of condition and mounted the enclosed spiral staircase slowly. The stone steps had evidently been pirated from other buildings. Every so often he recognized a fragment of a classic entablature of a wholly inappropriate intaglio design—a Greek cross or some crude Byzantine eagle. Each footfall became a symbolic conquest: one could not ascend these stairs without becoming implicated in the fall of Constantinople.

This staircase opened out into a kind of wooden catwalk clinging to the inner wall of the tower at a height of about sixty feet. The silolike space was resonant with the coo and flutter of invisible pigeons, and somewhere the wind was playing with a metal door, creaking it open, banging it shut. Here, if he so wished, he might discover portents.

He crept along the wooden platform, both hands grasping the iron rail stapled to the stone wall, feeling just an agreeable amount of terror, sweating nicely. It occurred to him how much this would have pleased Janice, whose enthusiasm for heights had equaled his. He wondered when, if ever, he would see her again, and what she would be like. By now undoubtedly she had begun divorce proceedings. Perhaps she was already no longer his wife.

The platform led to another stone staircase, shorter than the first, which ascended to the creaking metal door. He pushed it open and stepped out amid a flurry of pigeons into the full dazzle of the noon, the wide splendor of the elevation, sunlight above and the bright bow of water beneath—and, beyond the water, the surreal green of the Asian hills, hundred-breasted Cybele. It seemed, all of this, to demand some kind of affirmation, a yell. But he didn't feel up to yelling, or large gestures. He could only admire, at this distance, the illusion of tactility, hills as flesh, an illusion that could be heightened if he laid his hands, still sweaty from his passage along the catwalk, on the rough warm stone of the balustrade.

Looking down the side of the tower at the empty road he saw her again, standing at the very edge of the water. She was looking up at him. When he noticed her she lifted both hands above her head, as though signaling, and shouted something that, even if he could have heard it properly, he would surely not have understood. He supposed that she was asking to have her picture taken, so he turned the setting ring to the fastest speed to compensate for the glare from the water. She stood directly below the tower, and there seemed no way to frame an interesting composition. He released the shutter. Woman, water, asphalt road: it would be a snapshot, not a photograph, and he didn't believe in taking snapshots.

The woman continued to call up to him, arms raised in that same hieratic gesture. It made no sense. He waved to her and smiled uncertainly. It was something of a nuisance, really. He would have preferred to have this scene to himself. One climbed towers, after all, in order to be alone.

Altin, the man who had found his apartment for him, worked as a commission agent for carpet and jewelry shops in the Grand Bazaar. He would strike up conversations with English and American tourists and advise them what to buy, and where, and how much to pay. They spent one day looking and settled on an apartment building near Taksim, the commemorative traffic circle that served the European quarter of the city as a kind of Broadway. The several banks of Istanbul demonstrated their modern character here with neon signs, and in the center of the traffic circle, life-size, Atatürk led a small but representative group of his countrymen toward their bright, Western destiny.

The apartment was thought (by Altin) to partake of this same advanced spirit: it had central heating, a sit-down toilet, a bathtub, and a defunct but prestigious refrigerator. The rent was six hundred lire a month, which came to sixty-six dollars at the official rate but only fifty dollars at the rate Altin gave. He was anxious to move out of the hotel, so he agreed to a six-month lease.

He hated it from the day he moved in. Except for the shreds of a lousy sofa in the guest room, which he obliged the landlord to remove, he left everything as he found it. Even the blurry pinups from a Turkish girlie magazine remained where they were to cover the cracks in the new plaster. He was determined to make no accommodations: he might have to live in this city; it was not required that he *enjoy* it.

Every day he picked up his mail at the consulate. He sampled a variety of restaurants. He saw the sights and made notes for his book.

On Thursdays he visited a *hamam* to sweat out the accumulated poisons of the week and to be kneaded and stomped by a masseur.

He supervised the growth of his young mustache.

He rotted, like a jar of preserves left open and forgotten on the top shelf of a cupboard.

He learned that there was a special Turkish word for the rolls of dirt that are scraped off the skin after a steambath, and another that imitated the sound of boiling water: *fuker, fuker, fuker.* Boiling water signified, to the Turkish mind, the first stages of sexual arousal. It was roughly equivalent to the stateside notion of "electricity."

Occasionally, as he began to construct his own internal map of the unpromising alleyways and ruinous staircase streets of his neighborhood, he fancied that he saw her, that same woman. It was hard to be certain. She would always be some distance away, or he might catch just a glimpse out of the corner of his eye. If it were the same woman, nothing at this stage suggested that she was pursuing him. It was, at most, a coincidence.

In any case, he could not be certain. Her face had not been unusual, and he did not have the photograph to consult, for he had spoiled the entire roll of film removing it from the camera.

Sometimes after one of these failed encounters he would feel a slight uneasiness. It amounted to no more than that.

He met the boy in Üsküdar. It was during the first severe cold spell, in mid-November. His first trip across the Bosphorus, and when he stepped off the ferry onto the very soil (or, anyhow, the very asphalt) of this new continent, the largest of all, he could feel the great mass of it beckoning him toward its vast eastward vortex, tugging at him, sucking at his soul.

It had been his first intention, back in New York, to stop two months at most in Istanbul, learn the language; then into Asia. How often he had mesmerized himself with the litany of its marvels: the grand mosques of Kayseri and Sivas, of Beysehir and Afyon Karahisar; the isolate grandeur of Ararat and then, still moving east, the shores of the Caspian; Meshed, Kabul, the Himalayas. It was all these that reached out to him now, singing, stretching forth their siren arms, inviting him to their whirlpool.

And he? He refused. Though he could feel the charm of the invitation, he refused. Though he might have wished very much to unite with them, he still refused. For he had tied himself to the mast, where he was proof against their call. He had his apartment in that city which stood just outside their reach, and he would stay there until it was time to return. In the spring he was going back to the States.

But he did allow the sirens this much—that he would abandon the rational mosque-to-mosque itinerary laid down by his Hachette and entrust the rest of the day to serendipity. While the sun still shone that afternoon they might lead him where they would.

Asphalt gave way to cobbles, and cobbles to packed dirt. The squalor here was on a much less majestic scale than in Stambul, where even the most decrepit hovels had been squeezed by the pressure of population to heights of three and four stories. In Usküdar the same wretched buildings sprawled across the hills like beggars whose crutches had been kicked out from under them, supine; through their rags of unpainted wood one could see the scabbed flesh of mud-and-wattle. As he threaded his way from one dirt street to the next and found each of them sustaining this one unvarying tone, without color, without counterpoint, he began to conceive a new Asia, not of mountains and vast plains, but this same slum rolling on perpetually across grassless hills, a continuum of drabness, of sheer dumb extent.

Because he was short and because he would not dress the part of an American, he could go through these streets without calling attention to himself. The mustache too, probably, helped. Only his conscious, observing eyes (the camera had spoiled a second roll of film and was being repaired) would have betrayed him as a tourist today. Indeed, Altin had assured him (intending, no doubt, a compliment) that as soon as he learned to speak the language he would pass for a Turk.

It grew steadily colder throughout the afternoon. The wind moved a thick veil of mist over the sun and left it there. As the mists thinned and thickened, as the flat disk of sun, sinking westward, would fade and brighten, the vagaries of light whispered conflicting rumors about these houses and their dwellers. But he did not wish to stop and listen. He already knew more concerning these things than he wanted to. He set off at a quicker pace in the supposed direction of the landing stage.

The boy stood crying beside a public fountain, a water faucet projecting from a crude block of concrete, at the intersection of two narrow streets. Five years old, perhaps six. He was carrying a large plastic bucket of water in each hand, one bright red, the other turquoise. The water had splashed over his thin trousers and bare feet.

At first he supposed the boy cried only because of the cold. The damp ground must be near to freezing. To walk on it in bare wet feet. . . .

Then he saw the slippers. They were what he would have called shower slippers, small die-stamped ovals of blue plastic with single thongs that had to be grasped between the first and second toes.

The boy would stoop over and force the thongs between his stiff, cold-reddened toes, but after only a step or two the slippers would again fall off his numb feet. With each frustrated progress more water would slop over the sides of the buckets. He could not keep the slippers on his feet, and he would not walk off without them.

With this understanding came a kind of horror, a horror of his own helplessness. He could not go up to the boy and ask him where he lived, lift him and carry him—he was so small—to his home. Nor could he scold the child's parents for having sent him out on this errand without proper shoes or winter clothes. He could not even take up the buckets and have the child lead him to his home. For each of these possibilities demanded that he be able to *speak* to the boy, and this he could not do.

What *could* he do? Offer money? As well offer him, at such a moment, a pamphlet from the U.S. Information Agency!

There was, in fact, nothing, *nothing* he could do.

The boy had become aware of him. Now that he had a sympathetic audience he let himself cry in earnest. Lowering the two buckets to the ground and pointing at these and at the slippers, he spoke pleadingly to this grown-up stranger, to this rescuer, words in Turkish.

He took a step backward, a second step, and the boy shouted at him, what message of pain or uncomprehending indignation he would never know. He turned away and ran back along the street that had brought him to this crossway. It was another hour before he found the landing stage. It had begun to snow.

As he took his seat inside the ferry he found himself glancing at the other passengers, as though expecting to find her there among them.

The next day he came down with a cold. The fever rose through the night. He woke several times, and it was always their two faces that he carried with him from the dreams, like souvenirs whose origin and purpose have been forgotten; the woman at Rumeli Hisar, the child in Usküdar: some part of his mind had already begun to draw the equation between them.

2

It was the thesis of his first book that the quiddity of architecture, its chief claim to an esthetic interest, was its arbitrariness. Once the lintels were lying on the posts, once some kind of roof had been spread across the hollow space, then anything else that might be done was gratuitous. Even the lintel and the post, the roof, the space below, these were gratuitous as well. Stated thus it was a mild enough notion; the difficulty was in training the eye to see the whole world of usual forms—patterns of brick, painted plaster, carved and carpentered wood—not as "buildings" and "streets" but as an infinite series of free and arbitrary choices. There was no place in such a scheme for orders, styles, sophistication, taste. Every artifact of the city was anomalous, unique, but living there in the midst of it all you could not allow yourself too fine a sense of this fact. If you did . . .

It had been his task, these last three or four years, to re-educate his eye and mind to just this condition, of innocence. His was the very reverse of the Romantics' aims, for he did not expect to find himself, when this ideal state of "raw" perception was reached (it never would be, of course, for innocence, like justice, is an absolute; it may be approached but never attained), any closer to nature. Nature, as such, did not concern him. What he sought, on the contrary, was a sense of the great artifice of things, of structures, of the immense interminable wall that has been built just to exclude nature.

The attention that his first book had received showed that he had been at least partially successful, but he knew (and who better?) how far short his aim had fallen, how many clauses of the perceptual social contract he had never even thought to question.

So, since it was now a matter of ridding himself of the sense of the familiar, he had had to find some better laboratory for this purpose than New York, somewhere that he could be, more naturally, an alien. This much seemed obvious to him.

It had not seemed so obvious to his wife.

He did not insist. He was willing to be reasonable. He would talk about it. He talked about it whenever they were together—at dinner, at her friends' parties (his friends didn't seem to give parties), in bed—and it came down to this, that Janice objected not so much to the projected trip as to his entire program, the thesis itself.

No doubt her reasons were sound. The sense of the arbitrary did not stop at architecture; it embraced—or it would, if he let it—all phenomena. If there were no fixed laws that governed the furbelows and arabesques out of which a city is composed, there were equally no laws (or only arbitrary laws, which is the same as none at all) to define the relationships woven into the lattice of that city, relationships between man and man, man and woman, John and Janice.

And indeed this had already occurred to him, though he had not spoken of it to her before. He had often had to stop, in the midst of some quotidian ritual like dining out, and take his bearings. As the thesis developed, as he continued to sift away layer after layer of preconception, he found himself more and more astonished at the size of the demesne that recognized the sovereignty of convention. At times he even thought he could trace in his wife's slightest gesture or in her aptest phrase or in a kiss some hint of the Palladian rule book from which it had been derived. Perhaps with practice one would be able to document the entire history of her styles—here an echo of the Gothic Revival, there an imitation of Mies.

When his application for a Guggenheim was rejected, he decided he would make the trip by himself, using the bit of money that was still left from the book. Though he saw no necessity for it, he had agreed to Janice's request for a divorce. They parted on the best of terms. She had even seen him to the boat.

The wet snow would fall for a day, two days, forming knee-deep drifts in the open spaces of the city, in paved courtyards, on vacant lots. Cold winds polished the slush of streets and sidewalks to dull-gleaming lumpy ice. The steeper hills became impassable. The snow and the ice would linger a few days and then a sudden thaw would send it all pouring down the cobbled hillside in a single afternoon, brief alpine cataracts of refuse and brown water. A patch of tolerable weather might follow this flood, and then another blizzard. Altin assured him that this was an unusually fierce winter, unprecedented.

A spiral diminishing.

A tightness.

And each day the light fell more obliquely across the white hills and was more quickly spent.

One night, returning from a movie, he slipped on the iced cobbles just outside the door of his building, tearing both knees of his trousers beyond any possibility of repair. It was the only winter suit he had brought. Altin gave him the name of a tailor who could make another suit quickly and for less money than he would have had to pay for a readymade. Altin did all the bargaining with the tailor and even selected the fabric, a heavy wool-rayon blend of a sickly and slightly iridescent blue, the muted, imprecise color of the more unhappy breeds of pigeons. He understood nothing of the fine points of tailoring, and so he could not decide what it was about this suit—whether the shape of the lapels, the length of the back vent, the width of the pantlegs—that made it seem so different from other suits he had worn, so much . . . smaller. And yet it fitted his figure with the exactness one expects of a tailored suit. If he looked smaller now, and thicker, perhaps that was how he *ought* to look and his previous suits had been telling lies about him all these years. The color too performed some nuance of metamorphosis: his skin, balanced against this blue-gray sheen, seemed less "tan" than sallow. When he wore it he became, to all appearances, a Turk.

Not that he wanted to look like a Turk. Turks were, by and large, a homely lot. He only wished to avoid the other Americans who abounded here even at this nadir of the off-season. As their numbers decreased, their gregariousness grew more implacable. The smallest sign—a copy of *Newsweek* or the *Herald-Tribune*, a word of English, an airmail letter with its telltale canceled stamp—could bring them down at once in the full fury of their goodfellowship. It was convenient to have some kind of camouflage, just as it was necessary to learn their haunts in order to avoid them: Divan Yolu and Cumhuriyet Cadessi, the American Library and the consulate, as well as some eight or ten of the principal well-touristed restaurants.

Once the winter had firmly established itself he also put a stop to his sightseeing. Two months of Ottoman mosques and Byzantine rubble had brought his sense of the arbitrary to so fine a pitch that he no longer required the stimulus of the monumental. His own rooms—a rickety table, the flowered drapes, the blurry lurid pinups, the intersecting planes of walls and ceilings—could present as great a plentitude of "problems" as the grand mosques of Suleiman or Sultan Ahmet with all their mihrabs and minbers, their stalactite niches and faienced walls.

Too great a plenitude, actually. Day and night the rooms nagged at him. They diverted his attention from anything else he might try to do. He knew them with the enforced intimacy with which a prisoner knows his cell— every defect of construction, every failed grace, the precise incidence of the light at each hour of the day. Had he taken the trouble to rearrange the furniture, to put up his own prints and maps, to clean the windows and scrub the floors, to fashion some kind of bookcase (all his books remained in their two shipping cases), he might have been able to blot out these alien presences by the sheer strength of self-assertion, as one can mask bad odors with incense or the smell of flowers. But this would have been admitting defeat. It would have shown how unequal he was to his own thesis.

As a compromise he began to spend his afternoons in a café a short distance down the street on which he lived. There he would sit, at the table nearest the front window, contemplating the spirals of steam that rose from the small corolla of his tea glass. At the back of the long room, beneath the tarnished brass tea urn, there were always two old men playing backgammon. The other patrons sat by themselves and gave no indication that their thoughts were in any way different from his. Even when no one was smoking, the air was pungent with the charcoal fires of nargilehs. Conversation of any kind was rare. The nargilehs bubbled, tiny dice rattled in a leather cup, a newspaper rustled, a glass chinked against its saucer.

His red notebook always lay ready at hand on the table, and on the notebook his ballpoint pen. Once he had placed them there, he never touched them again till it was time to leave.

Though less and less in the habit of analyzing sensation and motive, he was aware that the special virtue of this café was as a bastion, the securest he possessed, against the now omnipresent influence of the arbitrary. If he sat here peacefully, observing the requirements of the ritual, a decorum as simple as the rules of backgammon, gradually the elements in the space about him would cohere. Things settled, unproblematically, into their own contours. Taking the flower-shaped glass as its center, this glass that was now only and exactly a glass of tea, his perceptions slowly spread out through the room, like the concentric ripples passing across the surface of an ornamental pond, embracing all its objects at last in a firm, noumenal grasp. Just so. The room was just what a room should be. It contained him.

He did not take notice of the first rapping on the café window, though he was aware, by some small cold contraction of his thoughts, of an infringement of the rules. The second time he looked up.

They were together. The woman and the child.

He had seen them each on several occasions since his trip to Usküdar three weeks before. The boy once on the torn-up sidewalk outside the consulate, and another time sitting on the railing of the Karaköy bridge. Once, riding in a *dolmus* to Taksim, he had passed within a scant few feet of the woman and they had exchanged a glance of unambiguous recognition. But he had never seen them together before.

But could he be certain, now, that it *was* those two? He saw a woman and a child, and the woman was rapping with one bony knuckle on the window for someone's attention. For his? If he could have seen her face. . . .

He looked at the other occupants of the café. The backgammon players. A fat, unshaven man reading a newspaper. A dark-skinned man with spectacles and a flaring mustache. The two old men, on opposite sides of the room, puffing on nargilehs. None of them paid any attention to the woman's rapping.

He stared resolutely at his glass of tea, no longer a paradigm of its own necessity. It had become a foreign object, an artifact picked up out of the rubble of a buried city, a shard.

The woman continued to rap at the window. At last the owner of the café went outside and spoke a few sharp words to her. She left without making a reply.

He sat with his cold tea another fifteen minutes. Then he went out into the street. There was no sign of them. He returned the hundred yards to his apartment as calmly as he could. Once inside he fastened the chain lock. He never went back to the café.

When the woman came that night, knocking at his door, it was not a surprise.

And every night, at nine or, at the very latest, ten o'clock.

Yavuz! Yavuz! Calling to him.

He stared at the black water, the lights of the other shore. He wondered, often, when he would give in, when he would open the door.

But it was surely a mistake. Some accidental *resemblance*. He was not Yavuz.

John Benedict Harris. An American.

If there had ever been one, if there had ever been a Yavuz.

The man who had tacked the pinups on the walls?

Two women, they might have been twins, in heavy eye make-up, garter belts, mounted on the same white horse. Lewdly smiling.

A bouffant hairdo, puffy lips. Drooping breasts with large brown nipples. A couch.

A beachball. Her skin dark. Bikini. Laughing. Sand. The water unnaturally blue.

Snapshots.

Had these ever been *his* fantasies? If not, why could he not bring himself to take them off the walls? He had prints by Piranesi. A blowup of Sagrada Familia in Barcelona. The Tchernikov sketch. He could have covered the walls.

He found himself trying to imagine this Yavuz . . . what he must be like.

3

Three days after Christmas he received a card from his wife, postmarked Nevada. Janice, he knew, did not believe in Christmas cards. It showed an immense stretch of white desert—a salt-flat, he supposed—with purple mountains in the distance, and above the purple mountains, a heavily retouched sunset. Pink. There were no figures in this landscape, or any sign of vegetation. Inside she had written:

"Merry Christmas! Janice."

The same day he received a manila envelope with a copy of *Art News*. A noncommittal note from his friend Raymond was paperclipped to the cover: "Thought you might like to see this. R."

In the back pages of the magazine there was a long and unsympathetic review of his book by F.R. Robertson. Robertson was known as an authority on Hegel's esthetics. He maintained that *Homo Arbitrans* was nothing but a compendium of truisms and—without seeming to recognize any contradiction in this—a hopelessly muddled reworking of Hegel.

Years ago he had dropped out of a course taught by Robertson after attending the first two lectures. He wondered if Robertson could have remembered this.

The review contained several errors of fact, one misquotation, and failed to mention his central argument, which was not, admittedly, dialectical. He decided he should write a reply and laid the magazine beside his typewriter to remind himself. The same evening he spilled the better part of a bottle of wine on it, so he tore out the review and threw the magazine into the garbage with his wife's card.

The necessity for a movie had compelled him into the streets and kept him in the streets, wandering from marquee to marquee, long after the drizzle of the afternoon had thickened to rain. In New York when this mood came over him he would take in a double bill of science-fiction films or Westerns on 42nd Street, but here, though cinemas abounded in the absence of televison, only the glossiest Hollywood kitsch was presented with the original soundtrack. B-movies were invariably dubbed in Turkish.

So obsessive was this need that he almost passed the man in the skeleton suit without noticing him. He trudged back and forth on the sidewalk, a sodden refugee from Halloween, followed by a small Hamelin of excited children. The rain had curled the corners of his poster (it served him now as an umbrella) and caused the inks to run. He could make out:

KIL G

STA   LDA

After Atatürk, the skeleton-suited Kiling was the principal figure of the new Turkish folklore. Every newsstand was heaped with magazines and comics celebrating his adventures, and here he was himself, or his avatar at least, advertising his latest movie. Yes, and there, down the side street, was the theater where it was playing: *Kiling Istanbulda.* Or: *Kiling in Istanbul.* Beneath the colossal letters a skull-masked Kiling threatened to kiss a lovely and obviously reluctant blonde, while on the larger poster across the street he gunned down two well-dressed men. One could not decide, on the evidence of such tableaux as these, whether Kiling was fundamentally good, like Batman, or bad, like Fantomas. So. . . .

He bought a ticket. He would find out. It was the name that intrigued him. It was, distinctly, an English name.

He took a seat four rows from the front just as the feature began, immersing himself gratefully into the familiar urban imagery. Reduced to black and white and framed by darkness, the customary vistas of Istanbul possessed a heightened reality. New American cars drove through the narrow streets at perilous speeds. An old doctor was strangled by an unseen assailant. Then for a long while nothing of interest happened. A tepid romance developed between the blond singer and the young architect, while a number of gangsters, or diplomats, tried to obtain possession of the doctor's black valise. After a confusing sequence in which four of these men were killed in an explosion, the valise fell into the hands of Kiling. But it proved to be empty.

The police chased Kiling over tiled rooftops. But this was a proof only of his agility, not of his guilt: the police can often make mistakes in these matters. Kiling entered, through a window, the bedroom of the blond singer, waking her. Contrary to the advertising posters outside, he made no attempt to kiss her. He addressed her in a hollow bass voice. The editing seemed to suggest that Kiling was actually the young architect whom the singer loved, but as his mask was never removed, this too remained in doubt.

He felt a hand on his shoulder.

He was certain it was she and he would not turn around. Had she followed him to the theater? If he rose to leave, would she make a scene? He tried to ignore the pressure of the hand, staring at the screen where the young architect had just received a mysterious telegram. His hands gripped tightly into his thighs. His hands: the hands of John Benedict Harris.

"Mr. Harris, hello!"

A man's voice. He turned around. It was Altin.

"Altin."

Altin smiled. His face flickered. "Yes. Do you think it is anyone?"

"Anyone else?"

"Yes."

"No."

"You are seeing this movie?"

"Yes."

"It is not in English. It is in Turkish."

"I know."

Several people in nearby rows were hissing for them to be quiet. The blond singer had gone down into one of the city's large cisterns. Binbirdirek. He himself had been there. The editing created an illusion that it was larger than it actually was.

"We will come up there," Altin whispered.

He nodded.

Altin sat on his right, and Altin's friend took the seat remaining empty on his left. Altin introduced his friend in a whisper. His name was Yavuz. He did not speak English.

Reluctantly he shook hands with Yavuz.

It was difficult, thereafter, to give his full attention to the film. He kept glancing sideways at Yavuz. He was about his own height and age, but then this seemed to be true of half the men in Istanbul. An unexceptional face, eyes that glistened moistly in the half-light reflected from the screen.

Kiling was climbing up the girders of the building being constructed on a high hillside. In the distance the Bosphorous snaked past misted hills.

There was something so unappealing in almost every Turkish face. He had never been able to pin it down: some weakness of bone structure, the narrow cheekbones; the strong vertical lines that ran down from the hollows of the eyes to the corner of the mouth; the mouth itself, narrow, flat, inflexible. Or some subtler disharmony among all these elements.

Yavuz. A common name, the mail clerk had said.

In the last minutes of the movie there was a fight between two figures dressed in skeleton suits, a true and a false Kiling. One of them was thrown to his death from the steel beams of the unfinished building. The villain, surely—but had it been the true or the false Kiling who died? And come to think of it, which of them had frightened the singer in her bedroom, strangled the old doctor, stolen the valise?

"Did you like it?" Altin asked as they crowded toward the exit.

"Yes, I did."

"And did you understand what the people said?"

"Some of it. Enough."

Altin spoke for a while to Yavuz, who then turned to address his new friend from America in rapid Turkish.

He shook his head apologetically. Altin and Yavuz laughed.

"He says to you that you have the same suit."

"Yes, I noticed that as soon as the lights came on."

"Where do you go now, Mr. Harris?"

"What time is it?"

They were outside the theater. The rain had moderated to a drizzle. Altin looked at his watch. "Seven o'clock. And a half."

"I must go home now."

"We will come with you and buy a bottle of wine. Yes?"

He looked uncertainly at Yavuz. Yavuz smiled.

And when she came tonight, knocking at his door and calling for Yavuz?

"Not tonight, Altin."

"No?"

"I am a little sick."

"Yes?"

"Sick. I have a fever. My head aches." He put his hand, mimetically, to his forehead, and as he did he *could* feel both the fever and the headache. "Some other time perhaps. I'm sorry."

Altin shrugged skeptically.

He shook hands with Altin and then with Yavuz. Clearly, they both felt they had been snubbed.

Returning to his apartment, he took an indirect route that avoided the dark side streets. The tone of the movie lingered, like the taste of a liqueur, to enliven the rhythm of cars and crowds, deepen the chiaroscuro of headlights and shop windows. Once, leaving the Eighth Street Cinema after *Jules et Jim*, he had discovered all the street signs of the Village translated into French; now the same law of magic allowed him to think that he could understand the fragmented conversation of passers-by. The meaning of an isolated phrase registered with the self-evident uninterpreted immediacy of "fact," the nature of the words mingling with the nature of things. Just so. Each knot in the net of language slipped, without any need of explication, into place. Every nuance of glance and inflection fitted, like a tailored suit, the contours of that moment, this street, the light, his conscious mind.

Inebriated by this fictive empathy, he turned into his own darker street at last and almost walked past the woman—who fitted, like every other element of the scene, so well the corner where she'd taken up her watch—without noticing her.

"You!" he said and stopped.

They stood four feet apart, regarding each other carefully. Perhaps she had been as little prepared for this confrontation as he.

Her thick hair was combed back in stiff waves from a low forehead, falling in massive parentheses to either side of her thin face. Pitted skin, flesh wrinkled in concentration around small pale lips. And tears—yes, tears—just forming in the corners of her staring eyes. With one hand she held a small parcel wrapped in newspaper and string, with the other she clutched the bulky confusion of her skirts. She wore several layers of clothing, rather than a coat, against the cold.

A slight erection stirred and tangled in the flap of his cotton underpants. He blushed. Once, reading a paperback edition of Krafft-Ebing, the same embarrassing thing had happened. That time it had been a description of necrophilia.

God, he thought, *if she notices!*

She whispered to him, lowering her gaze. To him, to Yavuz.

To come home with her . . . Why did he? . . . Yavuz, Yavuz, Yavuz . . . she needed . . . and his son. . . .

"I don't *understand* you," he insisted. "Your words make no sense to me. I am an American. My name is John Benedict Harris, not Yavuz. You're making a mistake—can't you see that?"

She nodded her head. "Yavuz."

"Not Yavuz! *Yok! Yok, yok!"*

And a word that meant "love" but not exactly that. Her hand tightened in the folds of her several skirts, raising them to show the thin, black-stockinged ankles.

"No!"

She moaned.

. . . wife . . . his home . . . Yalova . . . his life.

"Damn you, go away!"

Her hand let go her skirts and darted quickly to his shoulder, digging into the cheap cloth. Her other hand shoved the wrapped parcel at him. He pushed her back but she clung fiercely, shrieking his name: *Yavuz!* He struck her face.

She fell on the wet cobbles. He backed away. The greasy parcel was in his left hand. She pushed herself up to her feet. Tears flowed along the vertical channels from eyes to mouth. A Turkish face. Blood dripped slowly out of one nostril. She began to walk away in the direction of Taksim.

"And don't return, do you understand? Stay away from me!" His voice cracked.

When she was out of sight he looked at the parcel in his hands. He knew he ought not to open it, that the wisest course was to throw it into the nearest garbage can. But even as he warned himself, his fingers had snapped the string.

A large lukewarm doughy mass of *borek.* And an orange. The saliva sprouted in his mouth at the acrid smell of the cheese.

No!

He had not had dinner that night. He was hungry. He ate it. Even the orange.

During the month of January he made only two entries in his notebook. The first, undated, was a long extract copied from A. H. Lybyer's book on the Janissaries, the great slave-corps of the sultans, *The Government of the Ottoman Empire in the Time of Suleiman the Magnificent.* The passage read:

> Perhaps no more daring experiment has been tried on a large scale upon the face of the earth than that embodied in the Ottoman Ruling Institution. Its nearest ideal analogue is found in the Republic of Plato, its nearest actual parallel in the Mamluk system of Egypt; but it was not restrained within the aristocratic Hellenic limitations of the first, and it subdued and outlived the second. In the United States of America men have risen from the rude work of the backwoods to the presidential chair, but they have done so by their own effort and not through the gradations of a system carefully organized to push them forward. The Roman Catholic Church can still train a peasant to become a pope, but it has never begun by choosing its candidates almost exclusively from families which profess a hostile religion. The Ottoman system deliberately took slaves and made them ministers of state. It took boys from the sheep-run and the plough-tail and made them courtiers and the husbands of princesses; it took young men whose ancestors had borne the Christian name for centuries and made them rulers in the greatest of Muhammadan states, and soldiers and generals in invincible armies whose chief joy it was to beat down the Cross and elevate the Crescent. It never asked its novices "Who was your father?" or "What do you know?" or even "Can you speak our tongue?" but it studied their faces and their frames and said: "You shall be a soldier and, if you show yourself worthy, a general," or "You shall be a scholar and a gentleman and, if the ability lies in you, a governor and a prime minister." Grandly disregarding the fabric of fundamental customs which is called "human nature," and those religious and social prejudices which are thought to be almost as deep as life itself, the Ottoman system took children forever from parents, discouraged family cares among its members through their most active years, allowed them no certain hold on property, gave them no definite promise that their sons and daughters would profit by their success and sacrifice, raised and lowered them with no regard for ancestry or previous distinction, taught them a strange law, ethics, and religion, and ever kept them conscious of a sword raised above their heads

which might put an end at any moment to a brilliant career along a matchless path of human glory.

The second and briefer entry was dated the twenty-third of January and read as follows:

Heavy rains yesterday. I stayed in drinking. She came around at her usual hour. This morning when I put on my brown shoes to go out shopping they were wet through. Two hours to dry them out over the heater. Yesterday I wore only my sheepskin slippers—I did not leave the building once.

4

A human face is a construction, an artifact. The mouth is a little door, and the eyes are windows that look at the street, and all the rest of it, the flesh, the bone beneath, is a wall to which any manner of ornament may be affixed, gewgaws of whatever style or period one takes a fancy to—swags hung below the cheeks and chin, lines chiseled or smoothed away, a recession emphasized, a bit of vegetation here and there. Each addition or subtraction, however minor in itself, will affect the entire composition. Thus, the hair that he had trimmed a bit closer to the temples restores hegemony to the vertical elements of a face that is now noticeably *narrower.* Or is this exclusively a matter of proportion and emphasis? For he has lost weight too (one cannot stop eating regularly without some shrinkage), and the loss has been appreciable. A new darkness has given definition to the always incipient pouches below his eyes, a darkness echoed by the new hollowness of his cheeks.

But the chief agent of metamorphosis is the mustache, which has grown full enough now to obscure the modeling of his upper lip. The ends, which had first shown a tendency to droop, have developed, by his nervous habit of twisting them about his fingers, the flaring upward curve of a scimitar (or *pala,* after which in Turkey this style of mustache is named: *pala biyik).* It is this, the baroque mustache, not a face, that he sees when he looks in a mirror.

Then there is the whole question of "expression," its quickness, constancy, the play of intelligence, the characteristic "tone" and the hundreds upon hundreds of possible gradations within the range of that tone, the eyes' habits of irony and candor, the betraying tension or slackness of a lip. Yet it is scarcely necessary to go into this at all, for his face, when he sees it, or when anyone sees it, could not be said to *have* an expression. What was there, after all, for him to express?

The blurring of edges, whole days lost, long hours awake in bed, books scattered about the room like little animal corpses to be nibbled at when he grew hungry, the endless cups of tea, the tasteless cigarettes. Wine, at least, did what it was supposed to do—it took away the sting. Not that he felt the sting these days with any poignance. But perhaps without the wine he would have.

He piled the nonreturnable bottles in the bathtub, exercising in this act (if in no other) the old discrimination, the "compulsive tact" he had made so much of in his book.

The drapes were always drawn. The lights were left burning at all hours, even when he slept, even when he was out, three sixty-watt bulbs in a metal chandelier hanging just out of plumb.

Voices from the street impinged. Vendors in the morning, and the metallic screak of children. At night the radio in the apartment below, drunken arguments. Scatterings of words, like illuminated signs glimpsed driving on a thruway, at high speeds, at night.

Two bottles of wine were not enough if he started early in the afternoon, but three could make him sick.

And though the hours crawled, like wounded insects, so slowly across the floor, the days rushed by in a torrent. The sunlight slipped across the Bosphorus so quickly that there was scarcely time to rise and see it.

One morning when he woke there was a balloon on a stick propped in the dusty flower vase atop his dresser. A crude Mickey Mouse was stenciled on the bright red rubber. He left it there, bobbing in the vase, and watched it shrivel day by day, the face turning small and black and wrinkled.

The next time it was ticket stubs, two of them, from the Kabatas-Usküdar ferry.

Till that moment he had told himself it was a matter only of holding out until the spring. He had prepared himself for a siege, believing that an assault was not possible. Now he realized that he would actually have to go out there and fight.

Though it was mid-February, the weather accommodated his belated resolution with a series of bright blue days, a wholly unseasonable warmth that even tricked early blossoms from a few unsuspecting trees. He went through Topkapi once again, giving a respectful, indiscriminate and puzzled attention to the celadon ware, to golden snuffboxes, to pearly-embroidered pillows, to the portrait miniatures of the sultans, to the fossil footprint of the Prophet, to Iznik tiles, to the lot. There it was, all spread out before him, heaps and masses of it: beauty. Like a salesclerk tying price tags to items of merchandise, he would attach this favorite word of his, provisionally, to these sundry bibelots, then step back a pace or two to see how well or poorly it "matched." Was *this* beautiful? Was *that*?

Amazingly, none of it was beautiful. The priceless baubles all just sat there on their shelves, behind the thick glass, as unrespondent as the drab furniture back in his own room.

He tried the mosques: Sultan Ahmet, Beyazit, Sehazade, Yeni Camii, Laleli Camii. The old magic, the Vitruvian trinity of "commodity, firmness, and delight," had never failed him so enormously before. Even the shock of scale, the gape-mouthed peasant reverence before thick pillars and high domes, even this deserted him. Go where he would through the city, he could not get out of his room.

Then the land walls, where months before he had felt himself rubbing up against the very garment of the past. He stood at the same spot where he had stood then, at the point where Mehmet the Conqueror had breached the walls. Quincunxes of granite cannonballs decorated the grass; they reminded him of the red balloon.

As a last resort he returned to Eyüp. The false spring had reached a tenuous apogee, and the February light flared with deceiving brilliance from the thousand facets of white stone blanketing the steep hillside. Small flocks of three or four sheep browsed between the graves. The turbaned shafts of marble jutted in every direction but the vertical (which it was given to the cypresses to define) or lay, higgledy-piggledy, one atop another. No walls, no ceilings, scarcely a path through the litter: this was an architecture supremely abstract. It seemed to him to have been piled up here, over the centuries, just to vindicate the thesis of his book.

And it worked. It worked splendidly. His mind and his eye came alive. Ideas and images coalesced. The sharp slanting light of the late afternoon caressed the jumbled marble with a cold careful hand, like a beautician adding the last touches to an elaborate coiffure. Beauty? Here it was. Here it was abundantly!

He returned the next day with his camera, redeemed from the repair shop where it had languished for two months. To be on the safe side he had asked the repairman to load it for him. He composed each picture with mathematical punctilio, fussing over the depth of field, crouching or climbing atop sepulchers for a better angle, checking each shot against the reading on the light meter, deliberately avoiding picturesque solutions and easy effects. Even taking these pains he found that he'd gone through the twenty exposures in under two hours.

He went up to the small café on the top of the hill. Here, his Hachette had noted respectfully, the great Pierre Loti had been wont to come of a summer evening, to drink a glass of tea and look down the sculptured hills and through the pillars of cypress at the Fresh Waters of Europe and the Golden Horn. The café perpetuated the memory of this vanished glory with pictures and mementos. Loti, in a red fez and savage mustachios, glowered at the contemporary patrons from every wall. During the First World War, Loti had remained in Istanbul, taking the part of his friend, the Turkish sultan, against his native France.

He ordered a glass of tea from a waitress who had been got up as a harem girl. Apart from the waitress he had the café to himself. He sat on Pierre Loti's favorite stool. It was delicious. He felt right at home.

He opened his notebook and began to write.

Like an invalid taking his first walk out of doors after a long convalescence, his renascent energies caused him not only the predictable and welcome euphoria of resurrection but also a pronounced intellectual giddiness, as though by the simple act of rising to his feet he had thrust himself up to some really dangerous height. This dizziness became most acute when, in trying to draft a reply to Robertson's review, he was obliged to return to passages in his own book. Often as not what he found there struck him as incomprehensible. There were entire chapters that might as well have been written in ideograms or futhorc, for all the sense they made to him now. But occasionally, cued by some remark so irrelevant to any issue at hand as to be squeezed into an embarrassed parenthesis, he would spring off toward the most unforeseen—and undesirable—conclusions. Or rather, each of these tangents led, asymptotically, to a single conclusion: to wit, that his book, or any book he might conceive, was worthless, and worthless not because his thesis was wrong but precisely because it might be right.

There was a realm of judgment and a realm of fact. His book, if only because it was a book, existed within the bounds of the first. There was the trivial fact of its corporeality, but, in this case as in most others, he discounted that. It was a work of criticism, a systematization of judgment, and to the extent that his system was complete, its critical apparatus must be able to measure its own scales of mensuration and judge the justice of its own decrees. But could it? Was not his "system" as arbitrary a construction as any silly pyramid? What was it, after all? A string of words, of more or less agreeable noises, politely assumed to correspond to certain objects and classes of objects, actions and groups of actions, in the realm of fact. And by what subtle magic was this correspondence to be verified? Why, by just the assertion that it was so!

This, admittedly, lacked clarity. It had come to him thick and fast, and it was colored not a little by cheap red wine. To fix its outlines a bit more firmly in his own mind he tried to "get it down" in his letter to *Art News:*

> Sirs:
> I write to you concerning F.R. Robertson's review of my book, though the few words I have to say bear but slightly upon Mr. Robertson's oracles, as slightly perhaps as these bore upon *Homo Arbitrans.*
> Only this—that, as Gódel has demonstrated in mathematics, Wittgenstein in philosophy, and Duchamp, Cage, and Ashbery in their respective fields, the final statement of any system is a self-denunciation, a demonstration of how its particular little tricks are done—not by magic (as magicians have always known) but by the readiness of the magician's audience to be deceived, which readiness is the very glue of the social contract.
> Every system, including my own and Mr. Robertson's, is a system of more or less interesting lies, and if one begins to call these lies into question, then one ought really to begin with the first. That is to say, with the very questionable proposition on the title page: *Homo Arbitrans* by John Benedict Harris.
> Now I ask you, Mr. Robertson, what could be more improbable than that? More tentative? More arbitrary?

He sent the letter off, unsigned.

5

He had been promised his photos by Monday, so Monday morning, before the frost had thawed on the plate-glass window, he was at the shop. The same immodest anxious interest to see his pictures of Eyüp possessed him as once he had felt to see an essay or a review in print. It was as though these items, the pictures, the printed words, had the power to rescind, for a little while, his banishment to the realm of judgment, as though they said to him: "Yes, look, here we are, right in your hand. We're real, and so you must be too."

The old man behind the counter, a German, looked up mournfully to gargle a mournful *ach*. "Ach, Mr. Harris! Your pictures are not aready yet. Come back soon at twelve o'clock."

He walked through the melting streets that were, this side of the Golden Horn, jokebooks of eclecticism. No mail at the consulate, which was only to be expected. Half-past ten.

A pudding at a pudding shop. Two lire. A cigarette. A few more jokes: a bedraggled caryatid, an Egyptian tomb, a Greek temple that had been changed by some Circean wand into a butcher shop. Eleven.

He looked, in the bookshop, at the same shopworn selection of books that he had looked at so often before. Eleven-thirty. Surely, they would be ready by now.

"You are here, Mr. Harris. Very good."

Smiling in anticipation, he opened the envelope, removed the slim, warped stack of prints.

No.

"I'm afraid these aren't mine." He handed them back. He didn't want to feel them in his hand.

"What?"

"Those are the wrong pictures. You've made a mistake."

The old man put on a pair of dirty spectacles and shuffled through the prints. He squinted at the name on the envelope. "You are Mr. Harris."

"Yes, that is the name on the envelope. The envelope's all right, the pictures aren't."

"It is not a mistake."

"These are *somebody else's* snapshots. Some family picnic. You can see that."

"I myself took out the roll of film from your camera. Do you remember, Mr. Harris?"

He laughed uneasily. He hated scenes. He considered just walking out of the shop, forgetting all about the pictures. "Yes, I do remember. But I'm afraid you must have gotten that roll of film confused with another. I *didn't* take these pictures. I took pictures at the cemetery in Eyüp. Does that ring a bell?"

Perhaps, he thought, "ring a bell" was not an expression a German would understand.

As a waiter whose honesty has been called into question will go over the bill again with exaggerated attention, the old man frowned and examined each of the pictures in turn. With a triumphant clearing of his throat he laid one of the snapshots face up on the counter. "Who is that, Mr. Harris?"

It was the boy.

"Who! I . . . I don't know his name."

The old German laughed theatrically, lifting his eyes to a witnessing heaven. "It is you, Mr. Harris! It is you!"

He bent over the counter. His fingers still refused to touch the print. The boy was held up in the arms of a man whose head was bent forward as though he were examining the close-cropped scalp for lice. Details were fuzzy, the lens having been mistakenly set at infinity.

Was it his face? The mustache resembled his mustache, the crescents under the eyes, the hair falling forward. . . .

But the angle of the head, the lack of focus—there was room for doubt.

"Twenty-four lire please, Mr. Harris."

"Yes. Of course." He took a fifty-lire note from his billfold. The old man dug into a lady's plastic coin purse for change.

"Thank you, Mr. Harris."

"Yes. I'm . . . sorry."

The old man replaced the prints in the envelope, handed them across the counter.

He put the envelope in the pocket of his suit. "It was my mistake."

"Good-bye."

"Yes, good-bye."

He stood on the street, in the sunlight, exposed. Any moment either of them might come up to him, lay a hand on his shoulder, tug at his pantleg. He could not examine the prints here. He returned to the sweetshop and spread them out in four rows on a marble-topped table.

Twenty photographs. A day's outing, as commonplace as it had been impossible.

Of these twenty, three were so overexposed as to be meaningless, and should not have been printed at all. Three others showed what appeared to be islands or different sections of a very irregular coastline. They were unimaginatively composed, with great expanses of bleached-out sky and glaring water. Squeezed between these, the land registered merely as long dark blotches flecked with tiny gray rectangles of buildings. There was also a view up a steep street of wooden houses and naked wintry gardens.

The remaining thirteen pictures showed various people, and groups of people, looking at the camera. A heavyset woman in black, with black teeth, squinting into the sun—standing next to a pine tree in one picture, sitting uncomfortably on a natural stone formation in the second. An old man, dark-skinned, bald, with a flaring mustache and several days' stubble of beard. Then these two together—a very blurred print. Three little girls standing in front of a middle-aged woman, who regarded them with a pleased, proprietorial air. The same three girls grouped around the old man, who seemed to take no notice of them whatever. And a group of five men: the spread-legged shadow of the man taking this picture was roughly stenciled across the pebbled foreground.

And the woman. Alone. The wrinkled sallow flesh abraded to a smooth white mask by the harsh midday light.

Then the boy snuggling beside her on a blanket. Nearby small waves lapped at a narrow shingle.

Then these two still together with the old woman and the three little girls. The contiguity of the two women's faces suggested a family resemblance.

The figure that could be identified as himself appeared in only three of the pictures: once holding the boy in his arms; once with his arm around the woman's shoulders, while the boy stood before them scowling; once in a group of thirteen people, all of whom had appeared in one or another of the previous shots. Only the last of these three was in focus. He was one of the least noticeable figures in this group, but the mustached face smiling so rigidly into the camera was undeniably his own.

He had never seen these people, except, of course, for the woman and the boy. Though he had, hundreds of times, seen people just like them in the streets of Istanbul. Nor did he recognize the plots of grass, the stands of pine, the boulders, the shingle beach, though once again they were of such a generic type that he might well have passed such places a dozen times without taking any notice of them. Was the world of fact really as characterless as *this*? That it *was* the world of fact he never for a moment doubted.

And what had *he* to place in the balance against these evidences? A name? A face?

He scanned the walls of the sweetshop for a mirror. There was none. He lifted the spoon, dripping, from his glass of tea to regard the reflection of his face, blurred and inverted, in the concave surface. As he brought the spoon closer, the image grew less distinct, then rotated through one hundred eighty degrees to present, upright, the mirror image of his staring, dilated eye.

He stood on the open upper deck as the ferry churned, hooting, from the deck. Like a man stepping out of doors on a blustery day, the ferry rounded the peninsular tip of the old city, leaving the quiet of the Horn for the rough wind-whitened waters of the Sea of Marmara. A cold south wind stiffened the scarlet star and crescent on the stern mast.

From this vantage the city showed its noblest silhouette: first the great gray horizontal mass of the Topkapi walls, then the delicate swell of the dome of St. Irena, which had been built (like a friend carefully chosen to demonstrate, by contrast, one's own virtues) just to point up the swaggering impossibility of the neighboring Holy Wisdom, that graceless and abstract issue of the union commemorated on every capital within by the twined monograms of the demon-emperor Justinian and his whore and consort Theodora; then, bringing both the topographic and historic sequence to an end, the proud finality of the Blue Mosque.

The ferry began to roll in the rougher water of the open sea. Clouds moved across the sun at quicker intervals to mass in the north above the dwindling city. It was four-thirty. By five o'clock he would reach Heybeli, the island identified by both Atlin and the mail clerk at the consulate as the setting of the photographs.

The airline ticket to New York was in his pocket. His bags, all but the one he would take on the plane, had been packed and shipped off in a single afternoon and morning of head-long drunken fear. Now he was safe. The certain knowledge that tomorrow he would be thousands of miles away had shored up the crumbling walls of confidence like the promise of a prophet who cannot err, Tiresias in balmy weather. Admittedly this was the shameful safety of a rout so complete that the enemy had almost captured his baggage train—but it was safety for all that, as definite as tomorrow. Indeed, this "tomorrow" was more definite, more present to his mind and senses, than the actual limbo of its preparation, just as, when a boy, he had endured the dreadful tedium of Christmas Eve by projecting himself into the morning that would have to follow and which, when it did finally arrive, was never so real, by half, as his anticipations.

Because he was this safe, he dared today confront the enemy (if the enemy would confront *him*) head on. It risked nothing, and there was no telling what it might yield. Though if it were the *frisson* that he was after, then he should have stayed and seen the thing through to its end. No, this last excursion was more a gesture than an act, bravado rather than bravery. The very self-consciousness with which he had set out seemed to ensure that nothing really disastrous could happen. Had it not always been their strategy before to catch him unaware?

Finally, of course, he could not explain to himself why he had gone to the ferry, bought his ticket, embarked, except that each successive act seemed to heighten the delectable sense of his own inexorable advance, a sensation at once of almost insupportable tension and of dreamlike lassitude. He could no more have turned back along this path, once he had entered on it, than at the coda of a symphony he could have refused to listen. Beauty? Oh yes, intolerably! He had *never* known anything so beautiful as this.

The ferry pulled into the quay of Kinali Ada, the first of the islands. People got on and off. Now the ferry turned directly into the wind, toward Burgaz. Behind them the European coast vanished into the haze.

The ferry had left the Burgaz dock and was rounding the tiny islet of Kasik. He watched with fascination as the dark hills of Kasik, Burgaz, and Kinali slipped slowly into perfect alignment with their positions in the photograph. He could almost hear the click of the shutter.

And the other relationships between these simple sliding planes of sea and land—was there not something nearly as *familiar* in each infinitesimal shift of perspective? When he looked at these islands with his eyes half-closed, attention unfocused, he could almost . . .

But whenever he tried to take this up, however gently, between the needle-tipped compasses of analysis, it crumbled into dust.

It began to snow just as the ferry approached Heybeli. He stood at the end of the pier. The ferry was moving eastward, into the white air, toward BÜYÜK ADA.

He looked up a steep street of wooden houses and naked wintry gardens. Clusters of snowflakes fell on the wet cobbles and melted. At irregular intervals street lamps glowed yellow in the dusk, but the houses remained dark. Heybeli was a summer resort. Few people lived here in the winter months. He walked halfway up the hill, then turned to the right. Certain details of woodwork, the proportion of a window, a sagging roof caught his attention momentarily, like the flicker of wings in the foliage of a tree twenty, fifty, a hundred yards ahead.

The houses were fewer, spaced farther apart. In the gardens snow covered the leaves of cabbages. The road wound up the hill toward a stone building. It was just possible to make out the flag waving against the gray sky. He turned onto a footpath that skirted the base of the hill. It led into the pines. The thick carpet of fallen needles was more slippery than ice. He rested his cheek against the bark of a tree and heard, again, the camera's click, systole and diastole of his heart.

He heard the water, before he saw it, lapping on the beach. He stopped. He focused. He recognized the rock. He walked toward it. So encompassing was his sense of this scene, so inclusive, that he could feel the footsteps he left behind in the snow, feel the snow slowly covering them again. He stopped.

It was here he had stood with the boy in his arms. The woman had held the camera to her eye with reverent awkwardness. He had bent his head forward to avoid looking directly into the glare of the setting sun. The boy's scalp was covered with the scabs of insect bites.

He was ready to admit that all this had happened, the whole impossible event. He did admit it. He lifted his head proudly and smiled, as though to say: *All right—and then? No matter what you do, I'm safe! Because, really, I'm not here at all. I'm already in New York.*

He laid his hands in a gesture of defiance on the outcropping of rock before him. His fingers brushed the resilient thong of the slipper. Covered with snow, the small oval of blue plastic had completely escaped his attention.

He spun around to face the forest, then round again to stare at the slipper lying there. He reached for it, thinking to throw it into the water, then drew his hand back.

He turned back to the forest. A man was standing just outside the line of the trees, on the path. It was too dark to discern any more of his features than that he had a mustache.

On his left the snowy beach ended in a wall of sandstone. To his right the path swung back into the forest, and behind him the sea dragged the shingle back and forth.

"Yes?"

The man bent his head attentively, but said nothing.

"Well, yes? Say it."

The man walked back into the forest.

The ferry was just pulling in as he stumbled up to the quay. He ran onto it without stopping at the booth to buy a ticket. Inside under the electric light he could see the tear in his trousers and a cut on the palm of his right hand. He had fallen many times, on the pine needles, over rocks in furrowed fields, on cobbles.

He took a seat by the coal stove. When his breath returned to him, he found that he was shivering violently. A boy came round with a tray of tea. He bought a glass for one lire. He asked the boy, in Turkish, what time it was. It was ten o'clock.

The ferry pulled up to the dock. The sign over the ticket booth said BüyüK ADA. The ferry pulled away from the dock.

The ticket taker came for his ticket. He held out a ten-lire note and said, "Istanbul."

The ticket taker nodded his head, which meant no.

"*Yok.*"

"No? How much then? *Kac para?*"

"*Yok Istanbul—Yalova.*" He took the money offered him and gave him back in exchange eight lire and a ticket to Yalova on the Asian coast.

He had got onto a ferry going in the wrong direction. He was not returning to Istanbul, but to Yalova.

He explained, first in slow precise English, then in a desperate fragmentary Turkish, that he could not go to Yalova, that it was impossible. He produced his airline ticket, pointed at the eight o'clock departure time, but he could not remember the Turkish word for "tomorrow." Even in his desperation he could see the futility of all this: between BüyüK ADA and Yalova there were no more stops, and there would be no ferries returning to Istanbul that night. When he got to Yalova he would have to get off the boat.

A woman and a boy stood at the end of the wooden dock, at the base of a cone of snowy light. The lights were turned off on the middle deck of the ferry. The man who had been standing so long at the railing stepped, stiffly, down to the dock. He walked directly toward the woman and the boy. Scraps of paper eddied about his feet then, caught up in a strong gust, sailed out at a great height over the dark water.

The man nodded sullenly at the woman, who mumbled a few rapid words of Turkish. Then they set off, as they had so many times before, toward their home, the man leading the way, his wife and son following a few paces behind, taking the road along the shore.

Robert Aickman

The Hospice

Robert Aickman's stories always maintain a certain level of doubt as to the nature of what is literally going on. He builds an atmosphere of growing dread and fear out of this doubt and never for a moment reveals whatever firm grounding might explain the events rationally. Horrifying things are glimpsed out of the corner of the eye but when the head turns to look at them, they are gone. This is a story of a man who has lost his way and wandered over the border into the absurd and the surreal. Both the reader and the viewpoint-character experience simultaneous disorientation and in the end more questions are raised than answered. "The Hospice" is classic Aickman, a paradigm of our third variety of horror, wherein the moral structures are deconstructed (as in Jackson's "The Summer People") and the psychological conceits unreliable—all details and every effect contribute to profound and unsettling instability suggestive of undefinable horror, which is most certainly there.

It was somewhere at the back of beyond. Maybury would have found it difficult to be more precise.

He was one who, when motoring outside his own territory, preferred to follow a route "given" by one of the automobile organizations, and, on this very occasion, as on other previous ones, he had found reasons to deplore all deviation. This time it had been the works manager's fault. The man had not only poured ridicule on the official route, but had stood at the yard gate in order to make quite certain that Maybury set off by the short cut which, according to him, all the fellows in the firm used, and which departed in the exactly opposite direction.

The most that could be said was that Maybury was presumably at the outer edge of the immense West Midlands conurbation. The outer edge it by now surely must be, as he seemed to have been driving for hours since he left the works, going round and round in large or small circles, asking the way and being unable to understand the answers (when answers were vouchsafed), all the time seemingly more off-course than ever.

Maybury looked at his watch. He *had* been driving for hours. By rights he should have been more than halfway home—considerably more. Even the dashboard light seemed feebler than usual; but by it Maybury saw that soon he would be out of petrol. His mind had not been on that particular matter of petrol.

Dark though it was, Maybury was aware of many trees, mountainous and

970

opaque. It was not, however, that there were no houses. Houses there must be, because on both sides of the road, there were gates; broad single gates, commonly painted white: and, even where there were no gates, there were dim entrances. Presumably it was a costly nineteenth-century housing estate. Almost identical roads seemed to curve away in all directions. The straight-forward had been genteelly avoided. As often in such places, the racer-through, the taker of a short cut, was quite systematically penalized. Probably this attitude accounted also for the failure to bring the street lighting fully up-to-date.

Maybury came to a specific bifurcation. It was impossible to make any reasoned choice, and he doubted whether it mattered much in any case.

Maybury stopped the car by the side of the road, then stopped the engine in order to save the waning petrol while he thought. In the end, he opened the door and stepped out into the road. He looked upwards. The moon and stars were almost hidden by the thick trees. It was quiet. The houses were set too far back from the road for the noise of the television sets to be heard, or the blue glare thereof seen. Pedestrians are nowadays rare in such a district at any hour, but now there was no traffic either, nor sound of traffic more remote. Maybury was disturbed by the silence.

He advanced a short distance on foot, as one does at such times. In any case, he had no map, but only a route, from which he had departed quite hopelessly. None the less, even that second and locally preferred route, the one used by all the fellows, had seemed perfectly clear at the time, and as the manager had described it. He supposed that otherwise he might not have been persuaded to embark upon it; not even overpersuaded. As things were, his wonted expedient of merely driving straight ahead until one found some definite sign or other indication would be dubious, because the petrol might run out first.

Parallel with each side of each road was a narrow made-up footway, with a central gravelly strip. Beyond the strip to Maybury's left was a wilderness of vegetation, traversed by a ditch, beyond which was the hedge-line of the different properties. By the light of the occasional street-lamp, Maybury could see that sometimes there was an owner who had his hedge trimmed, and sometimes an owner who did not. It would be futile to walk any further along the road, though the air was pleasantly warm and aromatic. There were Angela and their son, Tony, awaiting him; and he must resume the fight to rejoin them.

Something shot out at him from the boskage on his left.

He had disturbed a cat, returned to its feral habitude. The first he knew of it was its claws, or conceivably its teeth, sunk into his left leg. There had been no question of ingratiation or cuddling up. Maybury kicked out furiously. The strange sequel was total silence. He must have kicked the cat a long way, because on the instant there was no hint of it. Nor had he seen the color of the cat, though there was a pool of light at that point on the footway. He fancied he had seen two flaming eyes, but he was not sure even of that. There had been no mew, no scream.

Maybury faltered. His leg really hurt. It hurt so much that he could not bring himself to touch the limb, even to look at it in the lamplight.

He faltered back to the car, and, though his leg made difficulties even in starting it, set off indecisively down the road along which he had just walked. It might well have become a case of its being wise for him to seek a hospital. The deep scratch or bite of a cat might well hold venom, and it was not pleasant to think where the particular cat had been treading, or what it might have been devouring. Maybury again looked at his watch. It was fourteen minutes past eight. Only nine minutes had passed since he had looked at it last.

The road was beginning to straighten out, and the number of entrances to diminish, though the trees remained dense. Possibly, as so often happens, the money had run out before the full development had reached this region of the property. There were still occasional houses, with entries at long and irregular intervals. Lamp posts were becoming fewer also, but Maybury saw that one of them bore a hanging sign of some kind. It was most unlikely to indicate a destination, let alone a destination of use to Maybury, but he eased and stopped none the less, so urgently did he need a clue of some kind. The sign was shaped like a club in a pack of cards, and read:

THE HOSPICE

S_O GOOD FARE _ON
M_E ACCOMMODA^{TI}

The modest words relating to accommodation were curved round the downward pointing extremity of the club.

Maybury decided almost instantly. He was hungry. He was injured. He was lost. He was almost without petrol.

He would enquire for dinner and, if he could telephone home, might even stay the night, though he had neither pyjamas nor electric razor. The gate, made of iron, and more suited, Maybury would have thought, to a farmyard bullpen, was, none the less, wide open. Maybury drove through.

The drive had likewise been surfaced with rather unattractive concrete, and it appeared to have been done some time ago, since there were now many potholes, as if heavy vehicles passed frequently. Maybury's headlights bounced and lurched disconcertingly as he proceeded, but suddenly the drive, which had run quite straight, again as on a modern farm, swerved, and there, on Maybury's left, was The Hospice. He realized that the drive he had come down, if indeed it had been a drive, was not the original main entrance. There was an older, more traditional drive, winding away between rhododendron bushes. All this was visible in bright light from a fixture high above the cornice of the building: almost a floodlight, Maybury thought. He supposed that a new entry had been made for the vehicles of the various suppliers when the place had become—whatever exactly it had become, a private hotel? a guest house? a club? No doubt the management aspired to cater for the occupants of the big houses, now that there were no longer servants in the world.

Maybury locked the car and pushed at the door of the house. It was a solid Victorian door, and it did not respond to Maybury's pressure. Maybury was discouraged by the need to ring, but he rang. He noticed that there was a second bell, lower down, marked NIGHT. Surely it could not yet be Night? The great thing was to get in, to feed (the works had offered only packeted sandwiches and flavourless coffee by way of luncheon), to ingratiate himself: before raising questions of petrol, whereabouts, possible accommodation for the night, a telephone call to Angela, disinfectant for his leg. He did not much care for standing alone in a strange place under the bright floodlight, uncertain what was going to happen.

But quite soon the door was opened by a lad with curly fair hair and an untroubled face. He looked like a young athlete, as Maybury at once thought. He was wearing a white jacket and smiling helpfully.

"Dinner? Yes, certainly, sir. I fear we've just started, but I'm sure we can fit you in."

To Maybury, the words brought back the seaside boarding houses where he had been taken for holidays when a boy. Punctuality in those days had been almost as important as sobriety.

"If you can give me just a couple of minutes to wash . . ."

"Certainly, sir. This way, please."

Inside, it was not at all like those boarding houses of Maybury's youth. Maybury happened to know exactly what it *was* like. The effect was that produced by the efforts of an expensive and, therefore, rather old-fashioned furniture emporium if one placed one's whole abode and most of one's cheque-book in its hands. There were hangings on all the walls, and every chair and sofa was upholstered. Colours and fabrics were harmonious but rich. The several standard lamps had immense shades. The polished tables derived from Italian originals. One could perhaps feel that a few upholstered occupants should have been designed and purveyed to harmonize also. As it was, the room was empty, except for the two of them.

The lad held open the door marked "Gentlemen" in script, but then followed Maybury in, which Maybury had not particularly expected. But the lad did not proceed to fuss tiresomely, with soap and towel, as happens sometimes in very expensive hotels, and happened formerly in clubs. All he did was stand about. Maybury reflected that doubtless he was concerned to prevent all possible delay, dinner having started.

The dining-room struck Maybury, immediately he entered, as rather too hot. The central heating must be working with full efficiency. The room was lined with hangings similar to those Maybury had seen in the hall, but apparently even heavier. Possibly noise reduction was among the objects. The ceiling of the room had been brought down in the modern manner, as if to serve the stunted; and any window or windows had disappeared behind swathes.

It is true that knives and forks make a clatter, but there appeared to be no other immediate necessity for costly noise abatement, as the diners were all extremely quiet; which at first seemed the more unexpected in that most of them were seated, fairly closely packed, at a single long table running down the central axis of the room. Maybury soon reflected, however, that if he had been wedged together with a party of total strangers, he might have found little to say to them either.

This was not put to the test. On each side of the room were four smaller tables, set endways against the walls, every table set for a single person, even though big enough to accommodate four, two on either side; and at one of these, Maybury was settled by the handsome lad in the white jacket.

Immediately, soup arrived.

The instantaneity of the service (apart from the fact that Maybury was late) could be accounted for by the large number of the staff. There were quite certainly four men, all, like the lad, in white jackets; and two women, both in dark blue dresses. The six of them were noticeably deft and well set-up, though all were past their first youth. Maybury could not see more because he had been placed with his back to the end wall which contained the service door (as well as, on the other side, the door by which the guests entered from the lounge). At every table, the single place had been positioned in that way, so that the occupant saw neither the service door opening and shutting, nor, in front of him, the face of another diner.

As a matter of fact, Maybury was the only single diner on that side of the room (he had been given the second table down, but did not think that anyone had entered to sit behind him at the first table); and, on the other side of the room, there was only a single diner also, he thought, a lady, seated at the second table likewise, and thus precisely parallel with him.

There was an enormous quantity of soup, in what Maybury realized was an unusually deep and wide plate. The amplitude of the plate had at first been masked by the circumstance that round much of its wide rim was inscribed, in large black letters, THE HOSPICE; rather in the style of a baby's plate, Maybury thought, if both lettering and plate had not been so immense. The soup itself was unusually weighty too: it undoubtedly contained eggs as well as pulses, and steps had been taken to add "thickening" also.

Maybury was hungry, as has been said, but he was faintly disconcerted to realize that one of the middle-aged women was standing quietly behind him as he consumed the not inconsiderable number of final spoonfuls. The spoons seemed very large also, at least for modern usages. The woman removed his empty plate with a reassuring smile.

The second course was there. As she set it before him, the woman spoke confidentially in his ear of the third course: "It's turkey tonight." Her tone was exactly that in which promise is conveyed to a little boy of his favourite dish. It was as if she were Maybury's nanny; even though Maybury had never had a nanny, not exactly. Meanwhile, the second course was a proliferating elaboration of pasta; plainly home-made pasta, probably fabricated that morning. Cheese, in fairly large granules, was strewn across the heap from a large porcelain bowl without Maybury being noticeably consulted.

"Can I have something to drink? A lager will do."

"We have nothing like that, sir." It was as if Maybury knew this perfectly well, but she was prepared to play with him. There might, he thought, have been some warning that the place was unlicensed.

"A pity," said Maybury.

The woman's inflections were beginning to bore him; and he was wondering how much the rich food, all palpably fresh, and home-grown, and of almost unattainable quality, was about to cost him. He doubted very much whether it would be sensible to think of staying the night at The Hospice.

"When you have finished your second course, you may have the opportunity of a word with Mr. Falkner." Maybury recollected that, after all, he had started behind all the others. He must doubtless expect to be a little hustled while he caught up with them. In any case, he was not sure whether or not the implication was that Mr. Falkner might, under certain circumstances, unlock a private liquor store.

Obviously it would help the catching-up process if Maybury ate no more than two-thirds of the pasta fantasy. But the woman in the dark blue dress did not seem to see it like that.

"Can't you eat any more?" she enquired baldly, and no longer addressing Maybury as sir.

"Not if I'm to attempt another course," replied Maybury, quite equably.

"It's turkey tonight," said the woman. "You know how turkey just slips down you?" She still had not removed his plate.

"It's very good," said Maybury firmly. "But I've had enough."

It was as if the woman were not used to such conduct, but, as this was no longer a nursery, she took the plate away.

There was even a slight pause, during which Maybury tried to look round the room without giving an appearance of doing so. The main point seemed to be that everyone was dressed rather formally: all the men in "dark suits," all the women in "long dresses." There was a wide variety of age, but, curiously again, there were more men than women. Conversation still seemed far from general. Maybury could not help wondering whether the solidity of the diet did not contribute here. Then it occurred to him that it was as if most of these people had been with one another for a long time, during which things to talk about might have run out, and possibly with little opportunity for renewal through fresh experience. He had met that in hotels. Naturally, Maybury could not, without seeming rude, examine the one-third of the assembly which was seated behind him.

His slab of turkey appeared. He had caught up, even though by cheating. It was an enormous pile, steaming slightly, and also seeping slightly with a colourless, oily fluid. With it appeared five separate varieties of vegetable in separate dishes, brought on a tray; and a sauceboat, apparently for him alone, of specially compounded fluid, dark red and turgid. A sizeable mound of stuffing completed the repast. The middle-aged woman set it all before him swiftly but, this time, silently, with unmistakable reserve.

The truth was that Maybury had little appetite left. He gazed around, less furtively, to see how the rest were managing. He had to admit that, as far as he could see, they were one and all eating as if their lives depended on it: old as well as young, female as well as male; it was as if all had spent a long, unfed day in the hunting field. "Eating as if their lives depended on it," he said again to himself; then, struck by the absurdity of the phrase when applied to eating, he picked up his knife and fork with resolution.

"Is everything to your liking, Mr. Maybury?"

Again he had been gently taken by surprise. Mr. Falkner was at his shoulder: a sleek man in the most beautiful dinner jacket, an instantly ameliorative maître d'hôtel.

"Perfect, thank you," said Maybury. "But how did you know my name?"

"We like to remember the names of all our guests," said Falkner, smiling.

"Yes, but how did you find out *my* name in the first place?"

"We like to think we are proficient at that too, Mr. Maybury."

"I am much impressed," said Maybury. Really he felt irritated (irritated, at least), but his firm had trained him never to display irritation outside the family circle.

"Not at all," said Falkner genially. "Whatever our vocation in life, we may as well do what we can to excel." He settled the matter by dropping the subject. "Is there anything I can get for you? Anything you would like?"

"No, thank you very much. I have plenty."

"Thank *you*, Mr. Maybury. If you wish to speak to me at any time, I am normally available in my office. Now I will leave you to the enjoyment of your meal. I may tell you, in confidence, that there is steamed fruit pudding to follow."

He went quietly forward on his round of the room, speaking to perhaps one person in three at the long, central table; mainly, it seemed, to the older people, as was no doubt to be expected. Falkner wore very elegant black suède shoes, which reminded Maybury of the injury to his own leg, about which he had done nothing, though it might well be septic, even endangering the limb itself, perhaps the whole system.

He was considerably enraged by Falkner's performance about his name, especially as he could find no answer to the puzzle. He felt that he had been placed, almost deliberately, at an undignified disadvantage. Falkner's patronizing conduct in this trifling matter was of a piece with the nannying attitude of the waitress. Moreover, was the unexplained discovery of his name such a trifle, after all? Maybury felt that it had made him vulnerable in other matters also, however undefined. It was the last straw in the matter of his eating any more turkey. He no longer had any appetite whatever.

He began to pass everything systematically through his mind, as he had been trained to do; and almost immediately surmised the answer. In his car was a blue-bound file which on its front bore his name: "Mr. Lucas Maybury"; and this file he supposed that he must have left, name-upwards, on the driving seat, as he commonly did. All the same, the name was merely typed on a sticky label, and would not have been easy to make out through the car window. But he then remembered the floodlight. Even so, quite an effort had been necessary on someone's part, and he wondered who had made that effort. Again he guessed the answer: it was Falkner himself who had been snooping. What would Falkner have done if Maybury had parked the car outside the floodlighted area, as would have been perfectly possible? Used a torch? Perhaps even skeleton keys?

That was absurd.

And how much did the whole thing matter? People in business often had these little vanities, and often had he encountered them. People would do almost anything to feed them. Probably he had one or two himself. The great thing when meeting any situation was to extract the essentials and to concentrate upon them.

To some of the people Falkner was speaking for quite a period of time, while, as Maybury noticed, those seated next to them, previously saying little in most cases, now said nothing at all, but confined themselves entirely to eating. Some of the people at the long table were not merely elderly, he had observed, but positively senile: drooling, watery-eyed, and almost hairless; but even they seemed to be eating away with the best. Maybury had the horrid idea about them that eating was all they did do. "They lived for eating": another nursery expression, Maybury reflected; and at last he had come upon those of whom it might be true. Some of these people might well relate to rich foods as alcoholics relate to excisable spirits. He found it more nauseating than any sottishness; of which he had seen a certain amount.

Falkner was proceeding so slowly, showing so much professional consideration, that he had not yet reached the lady who sat by herself parallel with Maybury, on the other side of the room. At her Maybury now stared more frankly. Black hair reached her shoulders, and she wore what appeared to be a silk evening dress, a real "model," Maybury thought (though he did not really know), in many colours; but her expression was of such sadness, suffering, and exhaustion that Maybury was sincerely shocked, especially as once she must, he was sure, have been beautiful, indeed, in a way, still was. Surely so unhappy, even tragic, a figure as that could not be ploughing through a big slab of turkey with five vegetables? Without caution or courtesy, Maybury half rose to his feet in order to look.

"Eat up, sir. Why you've hardly started!" His tormentor had quietly returned to him. What was more, the tragic lady *did* appear to be eating.

"I've had enough. I'm sorry, it's very good, but I've had enough."

"You said that before, sir, and, look, here you are, still eating away." He knew that he had, indeed, used those exact words. Crises are met by clichés.

"I've eaten quite enough."

"That's not necessarily for each of us to say, is it?"

"I want no more to eat of any kind. Please take all this away and just bring me a black coffee. When the time comes, if you like. I don't mind waiting." Though Maybury did mind waiting, it was necessary to remain in control.

The woman did the last thing Maybury could have expected her to do. She picked up his laden plate (he had at least helped himself to everything) and, with force, dashed it on the floor. Even then the plate itself did not break, but gravy and five vegetables and rich stuffing spread across the thick, patterned, wall-to-wall carpet. Complete, in place of comparative, silence followed in the whole room; though there was still, as Maybury even then observed, the muted clashing of cutlery. Indeed, his own knife and fork were still in his hands.

Falkner returned round the bottom end of the long table.

"Mulligan," he asked, "how many more times?" His tone was as quiet as ever. Maybury had not realized that the alarming woman was Irish.

"Mr. Maybury," Falkner continued. "I entirely understand your difficulty. There is naturally no obligation to partake of anything you do not wish. I am only sorry for what has happened. It must seem very poor service on our part. Perhaps you would prefer to go into our lounge? Would you care simply for some coffee?"

"Yes," said Maybury, concentrating upon the essential. "I should, please. Indeed, I had already ordered a black coffee. Could I possibly have a pot of it?"

He had to step with care over the mess on the floor, looking downwards. As he did so, he saw something most curious. A central rail ran the length of the long table a few inches above the floor. To this rail, one of the male guests was attached by a fetter round his left ankle.

Maybury, now considerably shaken, had rather expected to be alone in the lounge until the coffee arrived. But he had no sooner dropped down upon one of the massive sofas (it could easily have seated five in a row, at least two of them stout) than the handsome boy appeared from somewhere and proceeded merely to stand about, as at an earlier phase of the evening. There were no illustrated papers to be seen, nor even brochures about Beautiful Britain, and Maybury found the lad's presence irksome. All the same, he did not quite dare to say, "There's nothing I want." He could think of nothing to say or to do; nor did the boy speak, or seem to have anything particular to do either. It was obvious that his presence could hardly be required there when everyone was in the dining room. Presumably they would soon be passing on to fruit pudding. Maybury was aware that he had yet to pay his bill. There was a baffled but considerable pause.

Much to his surprise, it was Mulligan who in the end brought him the coffee. It was a single cup, not a pot; and even the cup was of such a size that Maybury, for once that evening, could have done with a bigger. At once he divined that coffee was outside the régime of the place, and that he was being specially compensated, though he might well have to pay extra for it. He had vaguely supposed that Mulligan would have been helping to mop up in the dining-room. Mulligan, in fact, seemed quite undisturbed.

"Sugar, sir?" she said.

"One lump, please," said Maybury, eyeing the size of the cup.

He did not fail to notice that, before going, she exchanged a glance with the handsome lad. He was young enough to be her son, and the glance might mean anything or nothing.

While Maybury was trying to make the most of his meagre coffee and to ignore the presence of the lad, who must surely be bored, the door from the dining-room opened, and the tragic lady from the other side of the room appeared.

"Close the door, will you?" she said to the boy. The boy closed the door, and then stood about again, watching them.

"Do you mind if I join you?" the lady asked Maybury.

"I should be delighted."

She was really rather lovely in her melancholy way, her dress was as splendid as Maybury had supposed, and there was in her demeanour an element that could only be called stately. Maybury was unaccustomed to that.

She sat, not at the other end of the sofa, but at the centre of it. It struck

Maybury that the rich way she was dressed might almost have been devised to harmonize with the rich way the room was decorated. She wore complicated, oriental-looking earrings, with pink translucent stones, like rosé diamonds (perhaps they *were* diamonds); and silver shoes. Her perfume was heavy and distinctive.

"My name is Cécile Céliména," she said. "How do you do? I am supposed to be related to the composer, Chaminade."

"How do you do?" said Maybury. "My name is Lucas Maybury, and my only important relation is Solway Short. In fact, he's my cousin."

They shook hands. Her hand was very soft and white, and she wore a number of rings, which Maybury thought looked real and valuable (though he could not really tell). In order to shake hands with him, she turned the whole upper part of her body towards him.

"Who is that gentleman you mention?" she asked.

"Solway Short? The racing motorist. You must have seen him on the television."

"I do not watch the television."

"Quite right. It's almost entirely a waste of time."

"If you do not wish to waste time, why are you at The Hospice?"

The lad, still observing them, shifted, noticeably, from one leg to the other.

"I am here for dinner. I am just passing through."

"Oh! You are going then?"

Maybury hesitated. She was attractive and, for the moment, he did not wish to go. "I suppose so. When I've paid my bill and found out where I can get some petrol. My tank's almost empty. As a matter of fact, I'm lost. I've lost my way."

"Most of us here are lost."

"Why here? What makes you come here?"

"We come for the food and the peace and the warmth and the rest."

"A tremendous *amount* of food, I thought."

"That's necessary. It's the restorative, you might say."

"I'm not sure that I quite fit in," said Maybury. And then he added: "I shouldn't have thought that you did either."

"Oh, but I do! Whatever makes you think not?" She seemed quite anxious about it, so that Maybury supposed he had taken the wrong line.

He made the best of it. "It's just that you seem a little different from what I have seen of the others."

"In what way, different?" she asked, really anxious, and looking at him with concentration.

"To start with, more beautiful. You are very beautiful," he said, even though the lad was there, certainly taking in every word.

"That is kind of you to say." Unexpectedly she stretched across the short distance between them and took his hand. "What did you say your name was?"

"Lucas Maybury."

"Do people call you Luke?"

"No, I dislike it. I'm not a Luke sort of person."

"But your wife can't call you Lucas?"

"I'm afraid she does." It was a fishing question he could have done without.

"Lucas? Oh no, it's such a cold name." She was still holding his hand.

"I'm very sorry about it. Would you like me to order you some coffee?"

"No, no. Coffee is not right; it is stimulating, wakeful, overexciting, unquiet." She was gazing at him again with sad eyes.

"This is a curious place," said Maybury, giving her hand a squeeze. It was surely becoming remarkable that none of the other guests had yet appeared.

"I could not live without The Hospice," she replied.

"Do you come here often?" It was a ludicrously conventional form of words.

"Of course. Life would be impossible otherwise. All those people in the world without enough food, living without love, without even proper clothes to keep the cold out."

During dinner it had become as hot in the lounge, Maybury thought, as it had been in the dining-room.

Her tragic face sought his understanding. None the less, the line she had taken up was not a favourite of his. He preferred problems to which solutions were at least possible. He had been warned against the other kind.

"Yes," he said. "I know what you mean, of course."

"There are millions and millions of people all over the world with no clothes at all," she cried, withdrawing her hand.

"Not quite," Maybury said, smiling. "Not quite that. Or not yet."

He knew the risks perfectly well, and thought as little about them as possible. One had to survive, and also to look after one's dependents.

"In any case," he continued, trying to lighten the tone, "that hardly applies to you. I have seldom seen a more gorgeous dress."

"Yes," she replied with simple gravity. "It comes from Rome. Would you like to touch it?"

Naturally, Maybury would have liked, but, equally naturally, was held back by the presence of the watchful lad.

"Touch it," she commanded in a low voice. "God, what are you waiting for? Touch it." She seized his left hand again and forced it against her warm, silky breast. The lad seemed to take no more and no less notice than of anything else.

"Forget. Let go. What is life for, for God's sake?" There was a passionate earnestness about her which might rob any such man as Maybury of all assessment, but he was still essentially outside the situation. As a matter of fact, he had never in his life lost *all* control, and he was pretty sure by now that, for better or for worse, he was incapable of it.

She twisted round until her legs were extended the length of the sofa, and her head was on his lap, or more precisely on his thighs. She had moved so deftly as not even to have disordered her skirt. Her perfume wafted upwards.

"Stop glancing at Vincent," she gurgled up at him. "I'll tell you something about Vincent. Though you may think he looks like a Greek God, the simple fact is that he hasn't got what it takes, he's impotent."

Maybury was embarrassed, of course. All the same, what he reflected was

that often there were horses for courses, and often no more to be said about a
certain kind of situation than that one thing.

It did not matter much what he reflected, because when she had spoken,
Vincent had brusquely left the room through what Maybury supposed to be
the service door.

"Thank the Lord," he could not help remarking naïvely.

"He's gone for reinforcements," she said. "We'll soon see."

Where were the other guests? Where, by now, could they be? All the same,
Maybury's spirits were authentically rising, and he began caressing her more
intimately.

Then, suddenly, it seemed that everyone was in the room at once, and this
time all talking and fussing.

She sat herself up, none too precipitately, and with her lips close to his ear,
said, "Come to me later. Number 23."

It was quite impossible for Maybury to point out that he was not staying
the night in The Hospice.

Falkner had appeared.

"To bed, all," he cried genially, subduing the crepitation on the instant.

Maybury, unentangled once more, looked at his watch. It seemed to be
precisely ten o'clock. That, no doubt, was the point. Still, it seemed very
close upon a heavy meal.

No one moved much, but no one spoke either.

"To bed, all of you," said Falkner again, this time in a tone which might
almost be described as roguish. Maybury's lady rose to her feet.

All of them filtered away, Maybury's lady among them. She had spoken no
further word, made no further gesture.

Maybury was alone with Falkner.

"Let me remove your cup," said Falkner courteously.

"Before I ask for my bill," said Maybury, "I wonder if you could tell me
where I might possibly find some petrol at this hour?"

"Are you out of petrol?" enquired Falkner.

"Almost."

"There's nothing open at night within twenty miles. Not nowadays.
Something to do with our new friends, the Arabs, I believe. All I can suggest
is that I syphon some petrol from the tank of our own vehicle. It is a quite
large vehicle and it has a large tank."

"I couldn't possibly put you to that trouble." In any case, he, Maybury,
did not know exactly how to do it. He had heard of it, but it had never arisen
before in his own life.

The lad, Vincent, reappeared, still looking pink, Maybury thought, though
it was difficult to be sure with such a glowing skin. Vincent began to lock up;
a quite serious process, it seemed, rather as in great-grandparental days,
when prowling desperadoes were to be feared.

"No trouble at all, Mr. Maybury," said Falkner. "Vincent here can do it
easily, or another member of my staff."

"Well," said Maybury, "if it would be all right . . ."

"Vincent," directed Falkner, "don't bolt and padlock the front door yet.
Mr. Maybury intends to leave us."

"Very good," said Vincent, gruffly.

"Now if we could go to your car, Mr. Maybury, you could then drive it round to the back. I will show you the way. I must apologise for putting you to this extra trouble, but the other vehicle takes some time to start, especially at night."

Vincent had opened the front door for them.

"After you, Mr. Maybury," said Falkner.

Where it had been excessively hot within, it duly proved to be excessively cold without. The floodlight had been turned off. The moon had "gone in," as Maybury believed the saying was; and all the stars had apparently gone in with it.

Still, the distance to the car was not great. Maybury soon found it in the thick darkness, with Falkner coming quietly step by step behind him.

"Perhaps I had better go back and get a torch?" remarked Falkner.

So there duly was a torch. It brought to Maybury's mind the matter of the office file with his name on it, and, as he unlocked the car door, there the file was, exactly as he had supposed, and, assuredly, name uppermost. Maybury threw it across to the back seat.

Falkner's electric torch was a heavy service object which drenched a wide area in cold, white light.

"May I sit beside you, Mr. Maybury?" He closed the offside door behind him.

Maybury had already turned on the headlights, torch or no torch, and was pushing at the starter, which seemed obdurate.

It was not, he thought, that there was anything wrong with it, but rather that there was something wrong with him. The sensation was exactly like a nightmare. He had of course done it hundreds of times, probably thousands of times; but now, when after all it really mattered, he simply could not manage it, had, quite incredibly, somehow lost the simple knack of it. He often endured bad dreams of just this kind. He found time with part of his mind to wonder whether this was not a bad dream. But it was to be presumed not, since now he did not wake, as we soon do when once we realize that we are dreaming.

"I wish I could be of some help," remarked Falkner, who had shut off his torch, "but I am not accustomed to the make of car. I might easily do more harm than good." He spoke with his usual bland geniality.

Maybury was irritated again. The make of car was one of the commonest there is: trust the firm for that. All the same, he knew it was entirely his own fault that he could not make the car start, and not in the least Falkner's. He felt as if he were going mad. "I don't quite know what to suggest," he said; and added: "If, as you say, there's no garage."

"Perhaps Cromie could be of assistance," said Falkner. "Cromie has been with us quite a long time and is a wizard with any mechanical problem."

No one could say that Falkner was pressing Maybury to stay the night, or even hinting towards it, as one might expect. Maybury wondered whether the funny place was not, in fact, full up. It seemed the most likely answer. Not that Maybury wished to stay the night: far from it.

"I'm not sure," he said, "that I have the right to disturb anyone else."

"Cromie is on night duty," replied Falkner. "He is always on night duty. That is what we employ him for. I will fetch him."

He turned on the torch once more, stepped out of the car, and disappeared into the house, shutting the front door behind him, lest the cold air enter.

In the end, the front door reopened, and Falkner re-emerged. He still wore no coat over his dinner suit, and seemed to ignore the cold. Falkner was followed by a burly but shapeless and shambling figure, whom Maybury first saw indistinctly standing behind Falkner in the light from inside the house.

"Cromie will soon put things to rights," said Falkner, opening the door of the car. "Won't you, Cromie?" It was much as one speaks to a friendly retriever.

But there was little, Maybury felt, that was friendly about Cromie. Maybury had to admit to himself that on the instant he found Cromie alarming, even though, what with one thing and another, there was little to be seen of him.

"Now what exactly seems wrong, Mr. Maybury?" asked Falkner. "Just tell Cromie what it is."

Falkner himself had not attempted to re-enter the car, but Cromie forced himself in and was sprawling in the front seat, next to Maybury, where Angela normally sat. He really did seem a very big, bulging person, but Maybury decisively preferred not to look at him, though the glow cast backwards from the headlights provided a certain illumination.

Maybury could not acknowledge that for some degrading reason he was unable to operate the starter, and so had to claim there was something wrong with it. He was unable not to see Cromie's huge, badly misshapen, yellow hands, both of them, as he tugged with both of them at the knob, forcing it in and out with such violence that Maybury cried out: "Less force. You'll wreck it."

"Careful, Cromie," said Falkner from outside the car. "Most of Cromie's work is on a big scale," he explained to Maybury.

But violence proved effective, as so often. Within seconds, the car engine was humming away.

"Thank you very much," said Maybury.

Cromie made no detectable response, nor did he move.

"Come on out, Cromie," said Falkner. "Come on out of it."

Cromie duly extricated himself and shambled off into the darkness.

"Now," said Maybury, brisking up as the engine purred. "Where do we go for the petrol?"

There was the slightest of pauses. Then Falkner spoke from the dimness outside. "Mr. Maybury, I have remembered something. It is not petrol that we have in our tank. It is, of course, diesel oil. I must apologise for such a stupid mistake."

Maybury was not merely irritated, not merely scared: he was infuriated. With rage and confusion he found it impossible to speak at all. No one in the modern world could confuse diesel oil and petrol in that way. But what could he possibly do?

Falkner, standing outside the open door of the car, spoke again. "I am extremely sorry, Mr. Maybury. Would you permit me to make some amends by inviting you to spend the night with us free of charge, except perhaps for the dinner?"

Within the last few minutes Maybury had suspected that this moment was bound to come in one form or another.

"Thank you," he said less than graciously. "I suppose I had better accept."

"We shall try to make you comfortable," said Falkner.

Maybury turned off the headlights, climbed out of the car once more, shut and, for what it was worth, locked the door, and followed Falkner back into the house. This time Falkner completed the locking and bolting of the front door that he had instructed Vincent to omit.

"I have no luggage of any kind," remarked Maybury, still very much on the defensive.

"That may solve itself," said Falkner, straightening up from the bottom bolt and smoothing his dinner jacket. "There's something I ought to explain. But will you first excuse me a moment?" He went out through the door at the back of the lounge.

Hotels really have become far too hot, thought Maybury. It positively addled the brain.

Falkner returned. "There is something I ought to explain," he said again. "We have no single rooms, partly because many of our visitors prefer not to be alone at night. The best we can do for you in your emergency, Mr. Maybury, is to offer you the share of a room with another guest. It is a large room and there are two beds. It is a sheer stroke of good luck that at present there is only one guest in the room, Mr. Bannard. Mr. Bannard will be glad of your company, I am certain, and you will be quite safe with him. He is a very pleasant person, I can assure you. I have just sent a message up asking him if he can possibly come down, so that I can introduce you. He is always very helpful, and I think he will be here in a moment. Mr. Bannard has been with us for some time, so that I am sure he will be able to fit you up with pyjamas and so forth."

It was just about the last thing that Maybury wanted from any point of view, but he had learned that it was of a kind that is peculiarly difficult to protest against, without somehow putting oneself in the wrong with other people. Besides, he supposed that he was now committed to a night in the place, and therefore to all the implications, whatever they might be, or very nearly so.

"I should like to telephone my wife, if I may," Maybury said. Angela had been steadily on his mind for some time.

"I fear that's impossible, Mr. Maybury," replied Falkner. "I'm so sorry."

"How can it be impossible?"

"In order to reduce tension and sustain the atmosphere that our guests prefer, we have no external telephone. Only an internal link between my quarters and the proprietors."

"But how can you run an hotel in the modern world without a telephone?"

"Most of our guests are regulars. Many of them come again and again, and the last thing they come for is to hear a telephone ringing the whole time with all the strain it involves."

"They must be half round the bend," snapped Maybury, before he could stop himself.

"Mr. Maybury," replied Falkner, "I have to remind you of two things. The first is that I have invited you to be our guest in the fuller sense of the word. The second is that, although you attach so much importance to efficiency, you none the less appear to have set out on a long journey at night with very little petrol in your tank. Possibly you should think yourself fortunate that you are not spending the night stranded on some motorway."

"I'm sorry," said Maybury, "but I simply must telephone my wife. Soon she'll be out of her mind with worry."

"I shouldn't think so, Mr. Maybury," said Falkner smiling. "Concerned, we must hope; but not quite out of her mind."

Maybury could have hit him, but at that moment a stranger entered.

"Ah, Mr. Bannard," said Falkner, and introduced them. They actually shook hands. "You won't mind, Mr. Bannard, if Mr. Maybury shares your room?"

Bannard was a slender, bony little man, of about Maybury's age. He was bald, with a rim of curly red hair. He had slightly glaucous grey-green eyes of the kind that often go with red hair. In the present environment, he was quite perky, but Maybury wondered how he would make out in the world beyond. Perhaps, however, this was because Bannard was too shrimp-like to look his best in pyjamas.

"I should be delighted to share my room with anyone," replied Bannard. "I'm lonely by myself."

"Splendid," said Falkner coolly. "Perhaps you'd lead Mr. Maybury upstairs and lend him some pyjamas? You must remember that he is a stranger to us and doesn't yet know all our ways."

"Delighted, delighted," exclaimed Bannard.

"Well, then," said Falkner. "Is there anything you would like, Mr. Maybury, before you go upstairs?"

"Only a telephone," rejoined Maybury, still recalcitrant. He simply did not believe Falkner. No one in the modern world could live without a telephone, let alone run a business without one. He had begun uneasily to wonder if Falkner had spoken the whole truth about the petrol and the diesel fuel either.

"Anything you would like that we are in a position to provide, Mr. Maybury?" persisted Falkner, with offensive specificity.

"There's no telephone *here*," put in Bannard, whose voice was noticeably high, even squeaky.

"In that case, nothing," said Maybury. "But I don't know what my wife will do with herself."

"None of us knows that," said Bannard superfluously, and cackled for a second.

"Good-night, Mr. Maybury. Thank you, Mr. Bannard."

Maybury was almost surprised to discover, as he followed Bannard upstairs, that it seemed a perfectly normal hotel, though overheated and decorated over-heavily. On the first landing was a full-size reproduction of a chieftain in scarlet tartan by Raeburn. Maybury knew the picture, because it had been chosen for the firm's calendar one year, though ever since they had used girls. Bannard lived on the second floor, where the picture on the landing was smaller, and depicted ladies and gentlemen in riding dress taking refreshments together.

"Not too much noise," said Bannard. "We have some very light sleepers amongst us."

The corridors were down to half-illumination for the night watches, and distinctly sinister. Maybury crept foolishly along and almost stole into Bannard's room.

"No," said Bannard in a giggling whisper. "Not Number 13, not yet. Number 12 A."

As a matter of fact Maybury had not noticed the number on the door that Bannard was now cautiously closing, and he did not feel called upon to rejoin.

"Do be quiet taking your things off, old man," said Bannard softly. "When once you've woken people who've been properly asleep, you can never quite tell. It's a bad thing to do."

It was a large square room, and the two beds were in exactly opposite corners, somewhat to Maybury's relief. The light had been on when they entered. Maybury surmised that even the unnecessary clicking of switches was to be eschewed.

"That's your bed," whispered Bannard, pointing jocularly.

So far Maybury had removed only his shoes. He could have done without Bannard staring at him and without Bannard's affable grin.

"Or perhaps you'd rather we did something before settling down?" whispered Bannard.

"No, thank you," replied Maybury. "It's been a long day." He was trying to keep his voice reasonably low, but he absolutely refused to whisper.

"To be sure it has," said Bannard, rising to much the volume that Maybury had employed. "Night-night then. The best thing is to get to sleep quickly." His tone was similar to that which seemed habitual with Falkner.

Bannard climbed agilely into his own bed, and lay on his back peering at Maybury over the sheets.

"Hang your suit in the cupboard," said Bannard, who had already done likewise. "There's room."

"Thank you," said Maybury. "Where do I find the pyjamas?"

"Top drawer," said Bannard. "Help yourself. They're all alike."

And, indeed, the drawer proved to be virtually filled with apparently identical suits of pyjamas.

"It's between seasons," said Bannard. "Neither proper summer, nor proper winter."

"Many thanks for the loan," said Maybury, though the pyjamas were considerably too small for him.

"The bathroom's in there," said Bannard.

When Maybury returned, he opened the door of the cupboard. It was a big cupboard and it was almost filled by a long line of (presumably) Bannard's suits.

"There's room," said Bannard once more. "Find yourself an empty hanger. Make yourself at home."

While balancing his trousers on the hanger and suspending it from the rail, Maybury again became aware of the injury to his leg. He had hustled so rapidly into Bannard's pyjamas that, for better or for worse, he had not even looked at the scar.

"What's the matter?" asked Bannard on the instant. "Hurt yourself, have you?"

"It was a damned cat scratched me," replied Maybury, without thinking very much.

But this time he decided to look. With some difficulty and some pain, he rolled up the tight pyjama leg. It was a quite nasty gash and there was much dried blood. He realized that he had not even thought about washing the wound. In so far as he had been worrying about anything habitual, he had been worrying about Angela.

"Don't show it to me," squeaked out Bannard, forgetting not to make a noise. All the same, he was sitting up in bed and staring as if his eyes would pop. "It's bad for me to see things like that. I'm upset by them."

"Don't worry," said Maybury. "I'm sure it's not as serious as it looks." In fact, he was far from sure; and he was aware also that it had not been quite what Bannard was concerned about.

"I don't want to know anything about it," said Bannard.

Maybury made no reply but simply rolled down the pyjama leg. About his injury too there was plainly nothing to be done. Even a request for Vaseline might lead to hysterics. Maybury tried to concentrate upon the reflection that if nothing worse had followed from the gash by now, then nothing worse might ever follow.

Bannard, however, was still sitting up in bed. He was looking pale. "I come here to forget things like that," he said. "We all do." His voice was shaking.

"Shall I turn the light out?" enquired Maybury. "As I'm the one who's still up?"

"I don't usually do that," said Bannard, reclining once more, none the less. "It can make things unnecessarily difficult. But there's you to be considered too."

"It's your room," said Maybury, hesitating.

"All right," said Bannard. "If you wish. Turn it out. Tonight anyway." Maybury did his injured leg no good when stumbling back to his bed. All the same, he managed to arrive there.

"I'm only here for one night," he said more to the darkness than to Bannard. "You'll be on your own again tomorrow."

Bannard made no reply, and, indeed, it seemed to Maybury as if he were no longer there, that Bannard was not an organism that could function in the dark. Maybury refrained from raising any question of drawing back a curtain (the curtains were as long and heavy as elsewhere), or of letting in a little night air. Things, he felt, were better left more or less as they were.

It was completely dark. It was completely silent. It was far too hot.

Maybury wondered what the time was. He had lost all touch. Unfortunately, his watch lacked a luminous dial.

He doubted whether he would ever sleep, but the night had to be endured somehow. For Angela it must be even harder—far harder. At the best, he had never seen himself as a first-class husband, able to provide a superfluity, eager to be protective. Things would become quite impossible, if he were to lose a leg. But, with modern medicine, that might be avoidable, even at the worst: he should be able to continue struggling on for some time yet.

As stealthily as possible he insinuated himself from between the burning blankets and sheets on to the surface of the bed. He lay there like a dying fish, trying not to make another movement of any kind.

He became almost cataleptic with inner exertion. It was not a promising recipe for slumber. In the end, he thought he could detect Bannard's breathing, far, far away. So Bannard was still there. Fantasy and reality are different things. No one could tell whether Bannard slept or waked, but it had in any case become a quite important aim not to resume general conversation with Bannard. Half a lifetime passed.

There could be no doubt, now, that Bannard was both still in the room and also awake. Perceptibly, he was on the move. Maybury's body contracted with speculation as to whether Bannard in the total blackness was making towards his corner. Maybury felt that he was only half his normal size.

Bannard edged and groped interminably. Of course Maybury had been unfair to him in extinguishing the light, and the present anxiety was doubtless no more than the price to be paid.

Bannard himself seemed certainly to be entering into the spirit of the situation: possibly he had not turned the light on because he could not reach the switch; but there seemed more to it than that. Bannard could be thought of as committed to a positive effort in the direction of silence, in order that Maybury, the guest for a night, should not be disturbed. Maybury could hardly hear him moving at all, though perhaps it was a gamble whether this was consideration or menace. Maybury would hardly have been surprised if the next event had been hands on his throat.

But, in fact, the next event was Bannard reaching the door and opening it, with vast delicacy and slowness. It was a considerable anticlimax, and not palpably outside the order of nature, but Maybury did not feel fully reassured as he rigidly watched the column of dim light from the passage slowly widen and then slowly narrow until it vanished with the faint click of the handle. Plainly there was little to worry about, after all, but Maybury had probably reached that level of anxiety where almost any new event merely causes new stress. Soon, moreover, there would be the stress of Bannard's return. Maybury half realized that he was in a grotesque condition to be so upset, when Bannard was, in fact, showing him all possible consideration. Once more he reflected that poor Angela's plight was far worse.

Thinking about Angela's plight, and how sweet, at the bottom of everything, she really was, Maybury felt more wakeful than ever, as he awaited Bannard's return, surely imminent, surely. Sleep was impossible until Bannard had returned.

But still Bannard did not return. Maybury began to wonder whether something had gone wrong with his own time faculty, such as it was; something, that is, of medical significance. That whole evening and night, from soon after his commitment to the recommended route, he had been in doubt about his place in the universe, about what people called the state of his nerves. Here was evidence that he had good reason for anxiety.

Then, from somewhere within the house, came a shattering, earpiercing scream, and then another, and another. It was impossible to tell whether the din came from near or far; still less whether it was female or male. Maybury had not known that the human organism could make so loud a noise, even in the bitterest distress. It was shattering to listen to; especially in the enclosed, hot, total darkness. And this was nothing momentary: the screaming went on and on, a paroxysm, until Maybury had to clutch at himself not to scream in response.

He fell off the bed and floundered about for the heavy curtains. Some light on the scene there must be; if possible, some new air in the room. He found the curtains within a moment, and dragged back first one, and then the other.

There was no more light than before.

Shutters, perhaps? Maybury's arm stretched out gingerly. He could feel neither wood nor metal.

The light switch. It must be found.

While Maybury fell about in the darkness, the screaming stopped on a ghoulish gurgle: perhaps as if the sufferer had vomited immensely and then passed out; or perhaps as if the sufferer had in mercy passed away altogether. Maybury continued to search.

It was harder than ever to say how long it took, but in the end he found the switch, and the immediate mystery was explained. Behind the drawn-back curtains was, as the children say, just wall. The room apparently had no window. The curtains were mere decoration.

All was silent once more: once more extremely silent. Bannard's bed was turned back as neatly as if in the full light of day.

Maybury cast off Bannard's pyjamas and, as quickly as his state permitted, resumed his own clothes. Not that he had any very definite course of action. Simply it seemed better to be fully dressed. He looked vaguely inside his pocket-book to confirm that his money was still there.

He went to the door and made cautiously to open it and seek some hint into the best thing for him to do, the best way to make off.

The door was unopenable. There was no movement in it at all. It had been locked at the least; perhaps more. If Bannard had done it, he had been astonishingly quiet about it: conceivably experienced.

Maybury tried to apply himself to thinking calmly.

The upshot was that once more, and even more hurriedly, he removed his clothes, disposed of them suitably, and resumed Bannard's pyjamas.

It would be sensible once more to turn out the light; to withdraw to bed, between the sheets, if possible; to stand by, as before. But Maybury found that turning out the light, the resultant total blackness, were more than he could face, however expedient.

Ineptly, he sat on the side of his bed, still trying to think things out, to plan sensibly. Would Bannard, after all this time, ever, in fact, return? At least during the course of that night?

He became aware that the electric light bulb had begun to crackle and fizzle. Then, with no further sound, it simply failed. It was not, Maybury thought, some final authoritative lights-out all over the house. It was merely that the single bulb had given out, however unfortunately from his own point of view: an isolated industrial incident.

He lay there, half in and half out, for a long time. He concentrated on the thought that nothing had actually happened that was dangerous. Ever since his schooldays (and, indeed, during them) he had become increasingly aware that there were many things strange to him, most of which had proved in the end to be apparently quite harmless.

Then Bannard was creeping back into the dark room. Maybury's ears had picked up no faint sound of a step in the passage, and, more remarkable, there had been no noise, either, of a turned key, let alone, perhaps, of a drawn bolt. Maybury's view of the bulb failure was confirmed by a repetition of the widening and narrowing column of light, dim, but probably no dimmer than before. Up to a point, lights were still on elsewhere. Bannard, considerate as before, did not try to turn on the light in the room. He shut the door with extraordinary skill, and Maybury could just, though only just, hear him slithering into his bed.

Still, there was one unmistakable development: at Bannard's return, the dark room had filled with perfume; the perfume favoured, long ago, as it seemed, by the lady who had been so charming to Maybury in the lounge. Smell is, in any case, notoriously the most recollective of the senses.

Almost at once, this time, Bannard not merely fell obtrusively asleep, but was soon snoring quite loudly.

Maybury had every reason to be at least irritated by everything that was happening, but instead he soon fell asleep himself. So long as Bannard was asleep, he was at least in abeyance as an active factor in the situation; and many perfumes have their own drowsiness, as Iago remarked. Angela passed temporarily from the forefront of Maybury's mind.

Then he was awake again. The light was on once more, and Maybury supposed that he had been awakened deliberately, because Bannard was standing there by his bed. Where and how had he found a new light bulb? Perhaps he kept a supply in a drawer. This seemed so likely that Maybury thought no more of the matter.

It was very odd, however, in another way also.

When Maybury had been at school, he had sometimes found difficulty in distinguishing certain boys from certain other boys. It had been a very large school, and boys do often look alike. None the less, it was a situation that Maybury thought best to keep to himself, at the time and since. He had occasionally made responses or approaches based upon misidentifications: but had been fortunate in never being made to suffer for it bodily, even though he had suffered much in his self-regard.

And now it was the same. Was the man standing there really Bannard? One obvious thing was that Bannard had an aureole or fringe of red hair, whereas this man's fringe was quite grey. There was also a different expression and general look, but Maybury was more likely to have been mistaken about that. The pyjamas seemed to be the same, but that meant little.

"I was just wondering if you'd care to talk for a bit," said Bannard. One had to assume that Bannard it was; at least to start off with. "I didn't mean to wake you up. I was just making sure."

"That's all right, I suppose," said Maybury.

"I'm over my first beauty sleep," said Bannard. "It can be lonely during the night." Under all the circumstances it was a distinctly absurd remark, but undoubtedly it was in Bannard's idiom.

"What was all that screaming?" enquired Maybury.

"I didn't hear anything," said Bannard. "I suppose I slept through it. But I can imagine. We soon learn to take no notice. There are sleepwalkers for that matter, from time to time."

"I suppose that's why the bedroom doors are so hard to open?"

"Not a bit," said Bannard, but he then added, "Well, partly, perhaps. Yes, partly. I think so. But it's just a knack really. We're not actually locked in, you know." He giggled. "But what makes you ask? You don't need to leave the room in order to go to the loo. I showed you, old man."

So it really must be Bannard, even though his eyes seemed to be a different shape, and even a different colour, as the hard light caught them when he laughed.

"I expect I was sleepwalking myself," said Maybury warily.

"There's no need to get the wind up," said Bannard, "like a kid at a new school. All that goes on here is based on the simplest of natural principles: eating good food regularly, sleeping long hours, not taxing the overworked brain. The food is particularly important. You just wait for breakfast, old man, and see what you get. The most tremendous spread, I promise you."

"How do you manage to eat it all?" asked Maybury. "Dinner alone was too much for me."

"We simply let Nature have its way. Or rather, perhaps, *her* way. We give Nature her head."

"But it's not *natural* to eat so much."

"That's all you know," said Bannard. "What you are, old man, is effete." He giggled as Bannard had giggled, but he looked somehow unlike Maybury's recollection of Bannard. Maybury was almost certain there was some decisive difference.

The room still smelt of the woman's perfume; or perhaps it was largely Bannard who smelt of it, Bannard who now stood so close to Maybury. It was embarrassing that Bannard, if he really had to rise from his bed and wake Maybury up, did not sit down; though preferably not on Maybury's blanket.

"I'm not saying there's no suffering here," continued Bannard. "But where in the world are you exempt from suffering? At least no one rots away in some attic—or wretched bed-sitter, more likely. Here there are no single rooms. We all help one another. What can you and I do for one another, old man?"

He took a step nearer and bent slightly over Maybury's face. His pyjamas really reeked of perfume.

It was essential to be rid of him; but essential to do it uncontentiously. The prospect should accept the representative's point of view as far as possible unawares.

"Perhaps we could talk for just five or ten minutes more," said Maybury, "and then I should like to go to sleep again, if you will excuse me. I ought to explain that I slept very little last night owing to my wife's illness."

"Is your wife pretty?" asked Bannard. "Really pretty? With this and that?" He made a couple of gestures, quite conventional though not aforetime seen in drawing rooms.

"Of course she is," said Maybury. "What do you think?"

"Does she really turn you on? Make you lose control of yourself?"

"Naturally," said Maybury. He tried to smile, to show he had a sense of humour which could help him to cope with tasteless questions.

Bannard now not merely sat on Maybury's bed, but pushed his frame against Maybury's legs, which there was not much room to withdraw, owing to the tightness of the blanket, as Bannard sat on it.

"Tell us about it," said Bannard. "Tell us exactly what it's like to be a married man. Has it changed your whole life? Transformed everything?"

"Not exactly. In any case, I married years ago."

"So now there is someone else. *I* understand."

"No, actually there is not."

"Love's old sweet song still sings to you?"

"If you like to put it like that, yes. I love my wife. Besides, she's ill. And we have a son. There's him to consider too."

"How old is your son?"

"Nearly sixteen."

"What colour are his hair and eyes?"

"Really, I'm not sure. No particular colour. He's not a baby, you know."

"Are his hands still soft?"

"I shouldn't think so."

"Do you love your son, then?"

"In his own way, yes, of course."

"I should love him were he mine, and my wife too." It seemed to Maybury that Bannard said it with real sentiment. What was more, he looked at least twice as sad as when Maybury had first seen him: twice as old, and twice as sad. It was all ludicrous, and Maybury at last felt really tired, despite the lump of Bannard looming over him, and looking different.

"Time's up for me," said Maybury. "I'm sorry. Do you mind if we go to sleep again?"

Bannard rose at once to his feet, turned his back on Maybury's corner, and went to his bed without a word, thus causing further embarrassment.

It was again left to Maybury to turn out the light, and to shove his way back to bed through the blackness.

Bannard had left more than a waft of the perfume behind him; which perhaps helped Maybury to sleep once more almost immediately, despite all things.

Could the absurd conversation with Bannard have been a dream? Certainly what happened next was a dream: for there was Angela in her nightdress with her hands on her poor head, crying out "Wake up! Wake up! Wake up!" Maybury could not but comply, and in Angela's place, there was the boy, Vincent, with early morning tea for him. Perforce the light was on once more: but that was not a matter to be gone into.

"Good morning, Mr. Maybury."

"Good morning, Vincent."

Bannard already had his tea.

Each of them had a pot, a cup, jugs of milk and hot water, and a plate of bread and butter, all set on a tray. There were eight large triangular slices each.

"No sugar," cried out Bannard genially. "Sugar kills appetite."

Perfect rubbish, Maybury reflected; and squinted across at Bannard, recollecting his last rubbishy conversation. By the light of morning, even if it were but the same electric light, Bannard looked much more himself, fluffy red aureole and all. He looked quite rested. He munched away at his bread and butter. Maybury thought it best to go through the motions of following suit. From over there Bannard could hardly see the details.

"Race you to the bathroom, old man," Bannard cried out.

"Please go first," responded Maybury soberly. As he had no means of conveying the bread and butter off the premises, he hoped, with the aid of the towel, to conceal it in his skimpy pyjamas jacket, and push it down the water closet. Even Bannard would probably not attempt to throw his arms round him and so uncover the offence.

Down in the lounge, there they all were, with Falkner presiding indefinably but genially. Wan though authentic sunlight trickled in from the outer world, but Maybury observed that the front door was still bolted and chained. It was the first thing he looked for. Universal expectation was detectable: of breakfast, Maybury assumed. Bannard, at all times shrimpish, was simply lost in the throng. Cécile he could not see, but he made a point of not looking very hard. In any case, several of the people looked new, or at least different. Possibly it was a further example of the phenomenon Maybury had encountered with Bannard.

Falkner crossed to him at once: the recalcitrant but still privileged outsider. "I can promise you a good breakfast, Mr. Maybury," he said confidentially. "Lentils. Fresh fish. Rump steak. Apple pie made by ourselves, with lots and lots of cream."

"I mustn't stay for it," said Maybury. "I simply mustn't. I have my living to earn. I must go at once."

He was quite prepared to walk a couple of miles; indeed, all set for it. The automobile organisation, which had given him the route from which he should never have diverged, could recover his car. They had done it for him before, several times.

A faint shadow passed over Falkner's face, but he merely said in a low voice, "If you really insist, Mr. Maybury—"

"I'm afraid I have to," said Maybury.

"Then I'll have a word with you in a moment."

None of the others seemed to concern themselves. Soon they all filed off, talking quietly among themselves, or, in many cases, saying nothing.

"Mr. Maybury," said Falkner, "you can respect a confidence?"

"Yes," said Maybury steadily.

"There was an incident here last night. A death. We do not talk about such things. Our guests do not expect it."

"I am sorry," said Maybury.

"Such things still upset me," said Falkner. "None the less I must not think about that. My immediate task is to dispose of the body. While the guests are preoccupied. To spare them all knowledge, all pain."

"How is that to be done?" enquired Maybury.

"In the usual manner, Mr. Maybury. The hearse is drawing up outside the door even as we speak. Where you are concerned, the point is this. If you wish for what in other circumstances I could call a lift, I could arrange for you to join the vehicle. It is travelling quite a distance. We find that best." Falkner was progressively unfastening the front door. "It seems the best solution, don't you think, Mr. Maybury? At least it is the best I can offer. Though you will not be able to thank Mr. Bannard, of course."

A coffin was already coming down the stairs, borne on the shoulders of four men in black, with Vincent, in his white jacket, coming first, in order to leave no doubt of the way and to prevent any loss of time.

"I agree," said Maybury. "I accept. Perhaps you would let me know my bill for dinner?"

"I shall waive that too, Mr. Maybury," replied Falkner, "in the present circumstances. We have a duty to hasten. We have others to think of. I shall simply say how glad we have all been to have you with us." He held out his hand. "Good-bye, Mr. Maybury."

Maybury was compelled to travel with the coffin itself, because there simply was not room for him on the front seat, where a director of the firm, a corpulent man, had to be accommodated with the driver. The nearness of death compelled a respectful silence among the company in the rear compartment, especially when a living stranger was in the midst; and Maybury alighted unobtrusively when a bus stop was reached. One of the undertaker's men said that he should not have to wait long.

Philip K. Dick

A Little Something for Us Tempunauts

Philip K. Dick was often regarded as the greatest science fiction writer in English during the 1960s and 1970s. Many of his most famous novels and stories are in the horror mode—yet he is rarely discussed as a horror writer of great powers and achievement—worthy of a place beside Robert Aickman and at the same time a legitimate heir of Robert W. Chambers and Ambrose Bierce. Science fiction has a long tradition of stories that question the nature of reality but none is more disturbing than "A Little Something for Us Tempunauts," written at the height of Dick's career. Bodies of work from such writers as Dick and Wolfe and Disch in the SF field in recent decades demand the broadening of the older definitions of horror literature, and require discarding criteria based on content in favor of the effect itself.

Wearily, Addison Doug plodded up the long path of synthetic redwood rounds, step by step, his head down a little, moving as if he were in actual physical pain. The girl watched him, wanting to help him, hurt within her to see how worn and unhappy he was, but at the same time she rejoiced that he was there at all. On and on, toward her, without glancing up, going by feel . . . like he's done this many times, she thought suddenly. Knows the way too well. Why?

"Addi," she called, and ran toward him. "They said on the TV you were dead. All of you were killed!"

He paused, wiping back his dark hair which was no longer long; just before launch they had cropped it. But he had evidently forgotten. "You believe everything you see on TV?" he said, and came on again, haltingly, but smiling now. And reaching up for her.

God, it felt good to hold him, and to have him clutch at her again, with more strength than she had expected. "I was going to find somebody else," she gasped. "To replace you."

"I'll knock your head off if you do," he said. "Anyhow, that isn't possible; nobody could replace me."

"But what about the implosion?" she said. "On re-entry; they said—"

"I forget," Addison said, in the tone he used when he meant, I'm not going to discuss it. The tone had always angered her before, but not now. This time she sensed how awful the memory was. "I'm going to stay at your place a couple days," he said, as together they moved up the path toward the open front door of the tilted A-frame house. "If that's okay. And Benz and Crayne will be joining me, later on; maybe even as soon as tonight. We've got a lot to talk over and figure out."

"Then all three of you survived." She gazed up into his careworn face. "Everything they said on TV . . ." She understood, then. Or believed she did. "It was a cover story. For—political purposes, to fool the Russians. Right? I mean, the Soviet Union'll think the launch was a failure because on re-entry—"

"No," he said. "A chrononaut will be joining us, most likely. To help figure out what happened. General Toad said one of them is already on his way here; they got clearance already. Because of the gravity of the situation."

"Jesus," the girl said, stricken. "Then who's the cover story for?"

"Let's have something to drink," Addison said. "And then I'll outline it all for you."

"Only thing I've got at the moment is California brandy."

Addison Doug said, "I'd drink anything right now, the way I feel." He dropped to the couch, leaned back, and sighed a ragged, distressed sigh, as the girl hurriedly began fixing both of them a drink.

The FM-radio in the car yammered, ". . . grieves at the stricken turn of events precipitating out of an unheralded . . ."

"Official nonsense babble," Crayne said, shutting off the radio. He and Benz were having trouble finding the house, having only been there once before. It struck Crayne that this was a somewhat informal way of convening a conference of this importance, meeting at Addison's chick's pad out here in the boondocks of Ojai. On the other hand, they wouldn't be pestered by the curious. And they probably didn't have much time. But that was hard to say; about that no one knew for sure.

The hills on both sides of the road had once been forests, Crayne observed. Now housing tracts and their melted, irregular, plastic roads marred every rise in sight. "I'll bet this was nice once," he said to Benz, who was driving.

"The Los Padres National Forest is near here," Benz said. "I got lost in there when I was eight. For hours I was sure a rattler would get me. Every stick was a snake."

"The rattler's got you now," Crayne said.

"All of us," Benz said.

"You know," Crayne said, "it's a hell of an experience to be dead."

"Speak for yourself."

"But technically—"

"If you listen to the radio and TV." Benz turned toward him, his big gnome face bleak with admonishing sternness. "We're no more dead than anyone else on the planet. The difference for us is that our death date is in the past, whereas everyone else's is set somewhere at an uncertain time in the future. Actually, some people have it pretty damn well set, like people in cancer wards; they're as certain as we are. More so. For example, how long can we stay here before we go back? We have a margin, a latitude that a terminal cancer victim doesn't have."

Crayne said caustically, "The next thing you'll be telling us to cheer us up is that we're in no pain."

"Addi is. I watched him lurch off earlier today. He's got it psychosomatically—made it into a physical complaint. Like God's kneeling on his neck; you know, carrying a much-too-great burden that's unfair, only he won't complain out loud . . . just points now and then at the nail hole in his hand." He grinned.

"Addi has got more to live for than we do."

"Every man has more to live for than any other man. I don't have a cute chick to sleep with, but I'd like to see the semi's rolling along the Riverside Freeway at sunset a few more times. It's not what you have to live for; it's that you want to live to see it, to be there—that's what is so damn sad."

They rode on in silence.

In the quiet living room of the girl's house the three tempunauts sat around smoking, taking it easy; Addison Doug thought to himself that the girl looked unusually foxy and desirable in her stretched-tight white sweater and micro-skirt and he wished, wistfully, that she looked a little less interesting. He could not really afford to get embroiled in such stuff at this point. He was too tired.

"Does she know," Benz said, indicating the girl, "what this is all about? I mean, can we talk openly? It won't wipe her out?"

"I haven't explained it to her yet," Addison said.

"You goddam well better," Crayne said.

"What is it?" the girl said, stricken, sitting upright with one hand directly between her breasts. As if clutching at a religious artifact that isn't there, Addison thought.

"We got snuffed on re-entry," Benz said. He was, really, the cruelest of the three. Or at least the most blunt. "You see, Miss . . ."

"Hawkins," the girl whispered.

"Glad to meet you, Miss Hawkins." Benz surveyed her in his cold, lazy fashion. "You have a first name?"

"Merry Lou."

"Okay, Merry Lou," Benz said. To the other two men he observed, "Sounds like the name a waitress has stitched on her blouse. Merry Lou's my name and I'll be serving you dinner and breakfast and lunch and dinner and breakfast for the next few days or however long it is before you all give up and go back to your own time; that'll be fifty-three dollars and eight cents, please, not including tip. And I hope y'all never come back, y'hear?" His voice had begun to shake; his cigarette, too. "Sorry, Miss Hawkins," he said then. "We're all screwed up by the implosion at re-entry time. As soon as we got here in ETA we learned about it. We've known longer than anyone else; we knew as soon as we hit Emergence Time."

"But there's nothing we could do," Crayne said.

"There's nothing anyone can do," Addison said to her, and put his arm around her. It felt like a déjà vu thing but then it hit him. We're in a closed time loop, he thought, we keep going through this again and again, trying to solve the re-entry problem, each time imagining it's the first time, the only time . . . and never succeeding. Which attempt is this? Maybe the millionth;

we have sat here a million times, raking the same facts over and over again and getting nowhere. He felt bone-weary, thinking that. And he felt a sort of vast philosophical hate toward all other men, who did not have this enigma to deal with. We all go to one place, he thought, as the Bible says. But . . . for the three of us, we have been there already. Are lying there now. So it's wrong to ask us to stand around on the surface of Earth afterward and argue and worry about it and try to figure out what malfunctioned. That should be, rightly, for our heirs to do. We've had enough already.

He did not say this aloud, though—for their sake.

"Maybe you bumped into something," the girl said.

Glancing at the others, Benz said sardonically, "Maybe we 'bumped into something.'"

"The TV commentators keep saying that," Merry Lou said, "about the hazard in re-entry of being out of phase spatially and colliding right down to the molecular level with tangent objects, any one of which—" She gestured. "You know. 'No two objects can occupy the same space at the same time.' So everything blew up, for that reason." She glanced around questioningly.

"That is the major risk factor," Crayne acknowledged. "At least theoretically, as Doctor Fein at Planning calculated when they got into the hazard question. But we had a variety of safety locking devices provided that functioned automatically. Re-entry couldn't occur unless these assists had stabilized us spatially so we would not overlap. Of course, all those devices, in sequence, might have failed. One after the other. I was watching my feedback 'metric scopes on launch, and they agreed, every one of them, that we were phased properly at that time. And I heard no warning tones. Saw none, neither." He grimaced. "At least it didn't happen then."

Suddenly Benz said, "Do you realize that our next-of-kin are now rich? All our Federal and commercial life insurance payoff. Our 'next of kin'—God forbid, that's us, I guess. We can apply for tens of thousands of dollars, cash on the line. Walk into our brokers' offices and say, 'I'm dead; lay the heavy bread on me.'"

Addison Doug was thinking, the public memorial services. That they have planned, after the autopsies. That long line of black-draped Cads going down Pennsylvania Avenue, with all the government dignitaries and double-domed scientist types—*and we'll be there*. Not once but twice. Once in the oak hand-rubbed brass-fitted flag-draped caskets, but also . . . maybe riding in open limos, waving at the crowds of mourners.

"The ceremonies," he said aloud.

The others stared at him, angrily, not comprehending. And then, one by one, they understood; he saw it on their faces.

"No," Benz grated. "That's—impossible."

Crayne shook his head emphatically. "They'll order us to be there, and we will be. Obeying orders."

"Will we have to *smile*?" Addison said. "To fucking *smile*?"

"No," General Toad said slowly, his great wattled head shivering about on his broomstick neck, the color of his skin dirty and mottled, as if the mass of decorations on his stiff-board collar had started part of him decaying away. "You are not to smile, but on the contrary are to adopt a properly grief-stricken manner. In keeping with the national mood of sorrow at this time."

"That'll be hard to do," Crayne said.

The Russian chrononaut showed no response; his thin beaked face, narrow within his translating earphones, remained strained with concern.

"The nation," General Toad said, "will become aware of your presence among us once more for this brief interval; cameras of all major TV networks will pan up on you without warning, and at the same time, the various commentators have been instructed to tell their audiences something like the following." He got out a piece of typed material, put on his glasses, cleared his throat and said, " 'We seem to be focusing on three figures riding together. Can't quite make them out. Can you?' " General Toad lowered the paper. "At this point they'll interrogate their colleagues extempore. Finally they'll exclaim, 'Why Roger,' or Walter or Ned, as the case may be, according to the individual network—"

"Or Bill," Crayne said. "In case it's the Bufonidae network, down there in the swamp."

General Toad ignored him. "They will severally exclaim, "Why Roger, I believe we're seeing the three tempunauts themselves! Does this indeed mean that somehow the difficulty—?" And then the colleague commentator says in his somewhat more somber voice, 'What we're seeing at this time I think, David, or Henry or Pete or Ralph, whichever it is, 'consists of mankind's first verified glimpse of what the technical people refer to as Emergence Time Activity or ETA. Contrary to what might seem to be the case at first sight, these are *not*—repeat not—our three valiant tempunauts as such, as we would ordinarily experience them, but more likely picked up by our cameras as the three of them are temporarily suspended in their voyage to the future, which we initially had reason to hope would take place in a time continuum roughly a hundred years from now . . . but it would seem that they somehow undershot and are here now, at this moment, which of course is, as we know, our present.' "

Addison Doug closed his eyes and thought, Crayne will ask him if he can be panned up on by the TV cameras holding a balloon and eating cotton candy. I think we're all going nuts from this, all of us. And then he wondered, How many times have we gone through this idiotic exchange?

I can't prove it, he thought wearily. But I know it's true. We've sat here, done this miniscule scrabbling, listened to and said all this crap, many times. He shuddered. Each rinky dink word . . .

"What's the matter?" Benz said acutely.

The Soviet chrononaut spoke up for the first time. "What is the maximum interval of ETA possible to your three-man team? And how large a percent has been exhausted by now?"

After a pause Crayne said, "They briefed us on that before we came in here today. We've consumed approximately one-half of our maximum total ETA interval."

"However," General Toad rumbled, "we have scheduled the Day of National Mourning to fall within the expected period remaining to them of ETA time. This required us to speed up the autopsy and other forensic findings, but in view of public sentiment, it was felt . . ."

The autopsy, Addison Doug thought, and again he shuddered; this time he could not keep his thoughts within himself and he said, "Why don't we adjourn this nonsense meeting and drop down to Pathology and view a few tissue sections enlarged and in color, and maybe we'll brainstorm a couple of vital concepts that'll aid medical science in its quest for explanations? Explanations—that's what we need. Explanations for problems that don't exist yet; we can develop the problems later." He paused. "Who agrees?"

"I'm not looking at my spleen up there on the screen," Benz said. "I'll ride in the parade but I won't participate in my own autopsy."

"You could distribute microscopic purple-stained slices of your own gut to the mourners along the way," Crayne said. "They could provide each of us with a doggy bag; right, General? We can strew tissue sections like confetti. I still think we should smile."

"I have researched all the memoranda about smiling," General Toad said, riffling the pages stacked before him, "and the consensus at policy is that smiling is not in accord with national sentiment. So that issue must be ruled closed. As far as your participating in the autopsical procedures which are now in progress—"

"We're missing out as we sit here," Crayne said to Addison Doug. "I always miss out."

Ignoring him, Addison addressed the Soviet chrononaut. "Officer N. Gauki," he said in his microphone, dangling on his chest, "what in your mind is the greatest terror facing a time traveler? That there will be an implosion due to coincidence on re-entry, such as has occurred in our launch? Or did other traumatic obsessions bother you and your comrade during your own brief but highly successful time flight?"

N. Gauki after a pause answered, "R. Plenya and I exchanged views at several informal times. I believe I can speak for us both when I respond to your question by emphasizing our perpetual fear that we had inadvertently entered a closed time loop and would never break out."

"You'd repeat it forever?" Addison Doug asked.

"Yes, Mr. A. Doug," the chrononaut said, nodding somberly.

A fear that he had never experienced before overcame Addison Doug. He turned helplessly to Benz and muttered, "Shit." They gazed at each other.

"I really don't believe this is what happened." Benz said to him in a low voice, putting his hand on Doug's shoulder; he gripped hard, the grip of friendship. "We just imploded on re-entry, that's all. Take it easy."

"Could we adjourn soon?" Addison Doug said in a hoarse, strangling voice, half-rising from his chair. He felt the room and the people in it rushing in at him, suffocating him. Claustrophobia, he realized. Like when I was in grade school, when they flashed a surprise test on our teaching machines, and I saw I couldn't pass it. "Please," he said simply, standing. They were all looking at him, with different expressions. The Russian's face was especially sympathetic, and deeply lined with care. Addison wished—"I want to go home," he said to them all, and felt stupid.

*   *   *

He was drunk. It was late at night, at a bar on Hollywood Boulevard; fortunately Merry Lou was with him, and he was having a good time. Everyone was telling him so, anyhow. He clung to Merry Lou and said, "The great unity in life, the supreme unity and meaning, is man and woman. Their absolute unity; right?"

"I know," Merry Lou said. "We studied that in class." Tonight, at his request, Merry Lou was a small blonde girl, wearing purple bellbottoms and high heels and an open midriff blouse. Earlier she had had a lapis lazuli in her navel, but during dinner at Ting Ho's it had popped out and been lost. The owner of the restaurant had promised to keep on searching for it, but Merry Lou had been gloomy ever since. It was, she said, symbolic. But of what she did not say. Or anyhow he could not remember; maybe that was it. She had told him what it meant, and he had forgotten.

An elegant young black at a nearby table, with an Afro and striped vest and overstuffed red tie, had been staring at Addison for some time. He obviously wanted to come over to their table but was afraid to; meanwhile, he kept on staring.

"Did you ever get the sensation," Addison said to Merry Lou, "that you knew exactly what was about to happen? What someone was going to say? Word for word? Down to the slightest detail? As if you had already lived through it once before?"

"Everybody gets into that space," Merry Lou said. She sipped a Bloody Mary.

The black rose and walked toward them. He stood by Addison. "I'm sorry to bother you, sir."

Addison said to Merry Lou, "He's going to say, 'Don't I know you from somewhere? Didn't I see you on TV?'"

"That was precisely what I intended to say," the black said.

Addison said, "You undoubtedly saw my picture on page forty-six of the current issue of *Time*, the section on new medical discoveries. I'm the G.P. from a small town in Iowa catapulated to fame by my invention of a widespread, easily available cure for eternal life. Several of the big pharmaceutical houses are already bidding on my vaccine."

"That might have been where I saw your picture," the black said, but he did not appear convinced. Nor did he appear drunk; he eyed Addison Doug intensely. "May I seat myself with you and the lady?"

"Sure," Addison Doug said. He now saw, in the man's hand, the ID of the U.S. security agency that had ridden herd on the project from the start.

"Mr. Doug," the security agent said as he seated himself beside Addison, "you really shouldn't be here shooting off your mouth like this. If I recognized you, some other dude might and freak out. It's all classified until the Day of Mourning. Technically, you're in violation of a Federal Statute by being here; did you realize that? I should haul you in. But this is a difficult situation; we don't want to do something uncool and make a scene. Where are your two colleagues?"

"At my place," Merry Lou said. She had obviously not seen the ID. "Listen," she said sharply to the agent, "why don't you get lost? My husband here has been through a grueling ordeal, and this is his only chance to unwind."

Addison looked at the man. "I knew what you were going to say before you came over here." Word for word, he thought. I am right, and Benz is wrong and this will keep happening, this replay.

"Maybe," the security agent said, "I can induce you to go back to Miss Hawkins' place voluntarily. Some info arrived—" he tapped the tiny earphone in his right ear—"just a few minutes ago, to all of us, to deliver to you, marked urgent, if we located you. At the launch site ruins . . . they've been combing through the rubble, you know?"

"I know," Addison said.

"They think they have their first clue. Something was brought back by one of you. From ETA, over and above what you took, in violation of all your pre-launch training."

"Let me ask you this," Addison Doug said. "Suppose somebody does see me? Suppose somebody does recognize me? So what?"

"The public believes that even though re-entry failed, the flight into time, the first American time-travel launch, was successful. Three U.S. tempunauts were thrust a hundred years into the future—roughly twice as far as the Soviet launch of last year. That you only went a *week* will be less of a shock if it's believed that you three chose deliberately to remanifest at this continuum because you wished to attend, in fact felt compelled to attend—"

"We wanted to be in the parade," Addison interrupted. "Twice."

"You were drawn to the dramatic and somber spectacle of your own funeral procession, and will be glimpsed there by the alert camera crews of all major networks. Mr. Doug, really, an awful lot of high-level planning and expense have gone into this to help correct a dreadful situation; trust us, believe me. It'll be easier on the public, and that's vital, if there's ever to be another U.S. time shot. And that is, after all, what we all want."

Addison Doug stared at him. "We want what?"

Uneasily, the security agent said, "To take further trips into time. As you have done. Unfortunately, you yourself cannot ever do so again, because of the tragic implosion and death of the three of you. But other tempunauts—"

"We want what? Is that what we want?" Addison's voice rose; people at nearby tables were watching now. Nervously.

"Certainly," the agent said. "And keep your voice down."

"I don't want that," Addison said. "I want to stop. To stop forever. To just lie in the ground, in the dust, with everyone else. To see no more summers—the *same* summer."

"Seen one, you've seen them all," Merry Lou said hysterically. "I think he's right, Addi; we should get out of here. You've had too many drinks, and it's late, and this news about the—"

Addison broke in, "What was brought back? How much extra mass?"

The security agency said, "Preliminary analysis shows that machinery weighing about one hundred pounds was lugged back into the time-field of the module and picked up along with you. This much mass—" The agent gestured. "That blew up the pad right on the spot. It couldn't begin to compensate for that much more than had occupied its open area at launch time."

"Wow!" Merry Lou said, eyes wide. "Maybe somebody sold one of you a quadraphonic phono for a dollar ninety-eight including fifteen-inch air-suspension speakers and a lifetime supply of Neil Diamond records." She tried to laugh, but failed; her eyes dimmed over. "Addi," she whispered, "I'm sorry. But it's sort of—weird. I mean, it's absurd; you all were briefed, weren't you, about your return weight? You weren't even to add so much as a piece of paper to what you took. I even saw Doctor Fein demonstrating the reasons on TV. And one of you hoisted a hundred pounds of machinery into the field? You must have been trying to self-destruct, to do that!" Tears slid from her eyes; one tear rolled out onto her nose and hung there. He reached reflexively to wipe it away, as if helping a little girl rather than a grown one.

"I'll fly you to the analysis site," the security agent said, standing up. He and Addison helped Merry Lou to her feet; she trembled as she stood a moment, finishing her Bloody Mary. Addison felt acute sorrow for her, but then, almost at once, it passed. He wondered why. One can weary even of that, he conjectured. Of caring for someone. If it goes on too long—on and on. Forever. And, at last, even after that, into something no one before, not God Himself, maybe, had ever had to suffer and in the end, for all His great heart, succumb to.

As they walked through the crowded bar toward the street, Addison Doug said to the security agent, "Which one of us—"

"They know which one," the agent said as he held the door to the street open for Merry Lou. The agent stood, now, behind Addison, signaling for a gray Federal car to land at the red parking area. Two other security agents, in uniform, hurried toward them.

"Was it me?" Addison Doug asked.

"You better believe it," the security agent said.

The funeral procession moved with aching solemnity down Pennsylvania Avenue, three flag-draped caskets and dozens of black limousines passing between rows of heavily coated, shivering mourners. A low haze hung over the day, gray outlines of buildings faded into the rain-drenched murk of the Washington March day.

Scrutinizing the lead Cadillac through prismatic binoculars, TV's top news and public events commentator Henry Cassidy droned on at his vast unseen audience. ". . . sad recollections of that earlier train among the wheatfields carrying the coffin of Abraham Lincoln back to burial and the nation's capital. And what a sad day this is, and what appropriate weather, with its dour overcast and sprinkles!" In his monitor he saw the zoomar lens pan up on the fourth Cadillac, as it followed those with the caskets of the dead tempunauts.

His engineer tapped him on the arm.

"We appear to be focusing on three unfamiliar figures so far not identified, riding together," Henry Cassidy said into his neck mike, nodding agreement. "So far I'm unable to quite make them out. Are your location and vision any better from where you're placed, Everett?" he inquired of his colleague and pressed the button that notified Everett Branton to replace him on the air.

"Why, Henry," Branton said in a voice of growing excitement, "I believe we're actually eyewitness to the three American tempunauts as they remanifest themselves on their historic journey into the future!"

"Does this signify," Cassidy said, "that somehow they have managed to solve and overcome the—"

"Afraid not, Henry," Branton said in his slow, regretful voice. "What we're eyewitnessing to our complete surprise consists of the Western world's first verified glimpse of what the technical people refer to as Emergence Time Activity."

"Ah yes, ETA," Cassidy said brightly, reading it off the official script the Federal authorities had handed him before air time.

"Right, Henry. Contrary to what *might* seem to be the case at first sight, these are not—repeat *not*—our three brave tempunauts as such, as we would ordinarily experience them—"

"I grasp it now, Everett," Cassidy broke in excitedly, since his authorized script read CASS BREAKS IN EXCITEDLY. "Our three tempunauts have momentarily suspended in their historic voyage to the future, which we believe will span across to a time-continuum roughly a century from now. . . . It would seem that the overwhelming grief and drama of this unanticipated day of mourning has caused them to . . ."

"Sorry to interrupt, Henry," Everett Branton said, "but I think, since the procession has momentarily halted on its slow march forward, that we might be able to . . ."

"No!" Cassidy said, as a note was handed him in a swift scribble, reading: *Do not interview 'nauts. Urgent. Dis. previous inst.* "I don't think we're going to be able to . . ." he continued, ". . . to speak briefly with tempunauts Benz, Crayne, and Doug, as you had hoped, Everett. As we had all briefly hoped to." He wildly waved the boom-mike back; it had already begun to swing out expectantly toward the stopped Cadillac. Cassidy shook his head violently at the mike technician and his engineer.

Perceiving the boom-mike swinging at them, Addison Doug stood up in the back of the open Cadillac. Cassidy groaned. He wants to speak, he realized. Didn't they reinstruct *him*? Why am I the only one they get across to? Other boom-mikes representing other networks plus radio station interviewers on foot now were rushing out to thrust up their microphones into the faces of the three tempunauts, especially Addison Doug's. Doug was already beginning to speak, in response to a question shouted up to him by a reporter. With his boom-mike off, Cassidy couldn't hear the question, nor Doug's answer. With reluctance, he signaled for his own boom-mike to trigger on.

". . . before," Doug was saying loudly.

"In what manner, 'All this has happened before'?" the radio reporter, standing close to the car, was saying.

"I mean," U.S. tempunaut Addison Doug declared, his face red and strained, "that I have stood here in this spot and said again and again, and all of you have viewed this parade and our deaths at re-entry endless times, a closed cycle of trapped time which must be broken."

"Are you seeking," another reporter jabbered up at Addison Doug, "for a solution to the re-entry implosion disaster which can be applied in retrospect so that when you do return to the past you will be able to correct the malfunction and avoid the tragedy which cost—or for you three, will cost—your lives?"

Tempunaut Benz said, "We are doing that, yes."

"Trying to ascertain the cause of the violent implosion and eliminate the cause before we return," tempunaut Crayne added, nodding. "We have learned already that for reasons unknown, a mass of nearly one hundred pounds of miscellaneous Volkswagen motor parts, including cylinders, the head . . ."

This is awful, Cassidy thought. "This is amazing!" he said aloud, into his neck mike. "The already tragically deceased U.S. tempunauts, with a determination that could emerge only from the rigorous training and discipline to which they were subjected—and we wondered why at the time but can clearly see why now—have already analyzed the mechanical slipup responsible, evidently, for their own deaths, and have begun the laborious process of sifting through and eliminating causes of that slipup so that they can return to their original launch site and re-enter without mishap."

"One wonders," Branton mumbled onto the air and into his feedback earphone, "what the consequences of this alteration of the near past will be. If in re-entry they do *not* implode and are *not* killed, then they will not—well, it's too complex for me, Henry, these time paradoxes that Doctor Fein at the Time Extrusion Labs in Pasadena has so frequently and eloquently brought to our attention."

Into all the microphones available, of all sorts, tempunaut Addison Doug was saying, more quietly now, "We must now eliminate the cause of re-entry implosion. The only way out of this trap is for us to die. Death is the only solution for this. For the three of us." He was interrupted as the procession of Cadillacs began to move forward.

Shutting off his mike momentarily, Henry Cassidy said to his engineer, "Is he nuts?"

"Only time will tell," his engineer said in a hard-to-hear voice.

"An extraordinary moment in the history of the United States' involvement in time travel," Cassidy said then, into his now live mike. "Only time will tell—if you will pardon the inadvertent pun—whether tempunaut Doug's cryptic remarks, uttered impromptu at this moment of supreme suffering for him, as in a sense to a lesser degree it is for all of us, are the words of a man deranged by grief or an accurate insight into the macabre dilemma that in theoretical terms we knew all along might eventually confront—confront and strike down with its lethal blow—a time-travel launch, either ours or the Russians'."

He segued then, to a commercial.

"You know," Branton's voice muttered in his ear, not on the air but just to the control room and to him, "if he's right they ought to let the poor bastards die."

"They ought to release them," Cassidy agreed. "My God, the way Doug looked and talked, you'd imagine he'd gone through this for a thousand years and then some! I wouldn't be in his shoes for anything."

"I'll bet you fifty bucks," Branton said, "they have gone through this before. Many times."

"Then we have, too," Cassidy said.

Rain fell now, making all the lined-up mourners shiny. Their faces, their eyes, even their clothes—everything glistened in wet reflections of broken, fractured light, bent and sparkling, as, from gathering gray formless layers above them, the day darkened.

"Are we on the air?" Branton asked.

Who knows? Cassidy thought. He wished the day would end.

The Soviet chrononaut N. Gauki lifted both hands impassionedly and spoke to the Americans across the table from him in a voice of extreme urgency. "It is the opinion of myself and my colleague R. Plenya, who for his pioneering achievements in time travel has been certified a Hero of the Soviet People, and rightly so, that based on our own experience and on theoretical material developed both in your own academic circles and in the Soviet Academy of Sciences of the USSR, we believe that tempunaut A. Doug's fears may be justified. And his deliberate destruction of himself and his team mates at re-entry, by hauling a huge mass of auto back with him from ETA, in violation of his orders, should be regarded as the act of a desperate man with no other means of escape. Of course, the decision is up to you. We have only advisory position in this matter."

Addison Doug played with his cigarette lighter on the table and did not look up. His ears hummed, and he wondered what that meant. It had an electronic quality. Maybe we're within the module again, he thought. But he did not perceive it; he felt the reality of the people around him, the table, the blue plastic lighter between his fingers. No smoking in the module during re-entry, he thought. He put the light carefully away in his pocket.

"We've developed no concrete evidence whatsoever," General Toad said, "that a closed-time loop has been set up. There's only the subjective feelings of fatigue on the part of Mr. Doug. Just his belief that he's done all this repeatedly. As he says, it is very probably psychological in nature." He rooted pig-like among the papers before him. "I have a report, not disclosed to the media, from four psychiatrists at Yale on his psychological makeup. Although unusually stable, there is a tendency toward cyclothymia on his part, culminating in acute depression. This naturally was taken into account long before the launch, but it was calculated that the joyful qualities of the two others in the team would offset this functionally. Anyhow, that depressive tendency in him is exceptionally high, now." He held the paper out, but no one at the table accepted it. "Isn't it true, Doctor Fein," he said, "that an acutely depressed person experiences time in a peculiar way, that is, circular time, time repeating itself, getting nowhere, around and around? The person gets so psychotic that he refuses to let go of the past. Re-runs it in his head constantly."

"But you see," Dr. Fein said, "this subjective sensation of being trapped is perhaps all we would have." This was the research physicist whose basic work had laid the theoretical foundation for the project. "If a closed loop did unfortunately lock into being."

"The general," Addison Doug said, "is using words he doesn't understand."

"I researched the ones I was unfamiliar with," General Toad said. "The technical psychiatric terms . . . I know what they mean."

To Addison Doug, Benz said, "Where'd you get all those VW parts, Addi?"

"I don't have them yet," Addison Doug said.

"Probably picked up the first junk he could lay his hands on," Crayne said. "Whatever was available, just before we started back."

"Will start back," Addison Doug corrected.

"Here are my instructions to the three of you," General Toad said. "You are not in any way to attempt to cause damage or implosion or malfunction during re-entry, either by lugging back extra mass or by any other method that enters your mind. You are to return as scheduled and in replica of the prior simulations. This especially applies to you, Mr. Doug." The phone by his right arm buzzed. He frowned, picked up the receiver. An interval passed, and then he scowled deeply and set the receiver back down, loudly.

"You've been overruled," Dr. Fein said.

"Yes, I have," General Toad said. "And I must say at this time that I am personally glad because my decision was an unpleasant one."

"Then we can arrange for implosion at re-entry," Benz said after a pause.

"The three of you are to make the decision," General Toad said. "Since it involves your lives. It's been entirely left up to you. Whichever way you want it. If you're convinced you're in a closed time loop, and you believe a massive implosion at re-entry will abolish it—" He ceased talking, as tempunaut Doug rose to his feet. "Are you going to make another speech, Doug?" he said.

"I just want to thank everyone involved," Addison Doug said. "For letting us decide." He gazed haggard-faced and wearily around at all the individuals seated at the table. "I really appreciate it."

"You know," Benz said slowly, "blowing us up at re-entry could add nothing to the chances of abolishing a closed loop. In fact that could do it, Doug."

"Not if it kills us all," Crayne said.

"You agree with Addi?" Benz said.

"Dead is dead," Crayne said. "I've been pondering it. What other way is more likely to get us out of this? Than if we're dead? What possible other way?"

"You may be in no loop," Dr. Fein pointed out.

"But we may be," Crayne said.

Doug, still on his feet, said to Crayne and Benz, "Could we include Merry Lou in our decision-making?"

"Why?" Benz said.

"I can't think too clearly any more," Doug said. "Merry Lou can help me; I depend on her."

"Sure," Crayne said. Benz, too, nodded.

General Toad examined his wristwatch stoically and said, "Gentlemen, this concludes our discussion."

Soviet chrononaut Gauki removed his headphones and neck mike and hurried toward the three U.S. tempunauts, his hand extended; he was apparently saying something in Russian, but none of them could understand it. They moved away somberly, clustering close.

"In my opinion you're nuts, Addi," Benz said. "But it would appear that I'm the minority now."

"If he *is* right," Crayne said, "if—one chance in a billion—if we are going back again and again forever, that would justify it."

"Could we go see Merry Lou?" Addison Doug said. "Drive over to her place now?"

"She's waiting outside," Crayne said.

Striding up to stand beside the three tempunauts, General Toad said, "You know, what made the determination go the way it did was the public reaction to how you, Doug, looked and behaved during the funeral procession. The NSC advisors came to the conclusion that the public would, like you, rather be certain it's over for all of you. That it's more of a relief to them to know you're free of your mission than to save the project and obtain a perfect re-entry. I guess you really made a lasting impression on them, Doug. That whining you did." He walked away then, leaving the three of them standing there alone.

"Forget him," Crayne said to Addison Doug. "Forget everyone like him. We've got to do what we have to."

"Merry Lou will explain it to me," Doug said. She would know what to do, what would be right.

"I'll go get her," Crayne said, "and after that the four of us can drive somewhere, maybe to her place, and decide what to do. Okay?"

"Thank you." Addison Doug said, nodding; he glanced around for her hopefully, wondering where she was. In the next room, perhaps, somewhere close. "I appreciate that," he said.

Benz and Crayne eyed each other. He saw that, but did not know what it meant. He knew only that he needed someone, Merry Lou most of all, to help him understand what the situation was. And what to finalize on to get them out of it.

Merry Lou drove them north from Los Angeles in the superfast lane of the freeway toward Ventura, and after that inland to Ojai. The four of them said very little. Merry Lou drove well, as always; leaning against her, Addison Doug felt himself relax into a temporary sort of peace.

"There's nothing like having a chick drive you," Crayne said, after many miles had passed in silence.

"It's an aristocratic sensation," Benz murmured. "To have a woman do the driving. Like you're nobility being chauffeured."

Merry Lou said, "Until she runs into something. Some big slow object."

Addison Doug said, "When you saw me trudging up to your place . . . up the redwood round path the other day. What did you think? Tell me honestly."

"You looked," the girl said, "as if you'd done it many times. You looked worn and tired and—ready to die. At the end." She hesitated. "I'm sorry, but that's how you looked, Addi. I thought to myself, he knows the way too well."

"Like I'd done it too many times."

"Yes," she said.

"Then you vote for implosion," Addison Doug said.

"Well—"

"Be honest with me," he said.

Merry Lou said, "Look in the back seat. The box on the floor."

With a flashlight from the glove compartment the three men examined the box. Addison Doug, with fear, saw its contents. VW motor parts, rusty and worn. Still oily.

"I got them from behind a foreign car garage near my place," Merry Lou said. "On the way to Pasadena. The first junk I saw that seemed as if it'd be heavy enough. I had heard them say on TV at launch time that anything over fifty pounds up to—"

"It'll do it," Addison Doug said. "It did do it."

"So there's no point in going to your place," Crayne said. "It's decided. We might as well head south toward the module. And initiate the procedure for getting out of ETA. And back to re-entry." His voice was heavy but evenly pitched. "Thanks for your vote, Miss Hawkins."

She said, "You are all so tired."

"I'm not." Benz said. "I'm mad. Mad as hell."

"At me?" Addison Doug said.

"I don't know," Benz said. "It just—Hell." He lapsed into brooding silence then. Hunched over, baffled and inert. Withdrawn as far as possible from the others in the car.

At the next freeway junction she turned the car south. A sense of freedom seemed now to fill her, and Addison Doug felt some of the weight, the fatigue, ebbing already.

On the wrist of each of the three men the emergency alert receiver buzzed its warning tone; they all started.

"What's that mean?" Merry Lou said, slowing the car.

"We're to contact General Toad by phone as soon as possible," Crayne said. He pointed. "There's a Standard Station over there; take the next exit, Miss Hawkins. We can phone in from there."

A few minutes later Merry Lou brought her car to a halt beside the outdoor phone booth. "I hope it's not bad news," she said.

"I'll talk first," Doug said, getting out. Bad news, he thought with labored amusement. Like what? He crunched stiffly across to the phone booth, entered, shut the door behind him, dropped in a dime and dialed the toll-free number.

"Well, do I have news!" General Toad said when the operator had put him on the line. "It's a good thing we got hold of you. Just a minute—I'm going to let Doctor Fein tell you this himself. You're more apt to believe him than me." Several clicks, and then Doctor Fein's reedy, precise, scholarly voice, but intensified by urgency.

"What's the bad news?" Addison Doug said.

"Not bad, necessarily," Dr. Fein said. "I've had computations run since our discussion, and it would appear—by that I mean it is statistically probable but still unverified for a certainty—that you are right, Addison. You are in a closed time loop."

Addison Doug exhaled raggedly. You nowhere autocratic mother, he thought. You probably knew all along.

"However," Dr. Fein said excitedly, stammering a little, "I also calculate —we jointly do, largely through Cal Tech—that the greatest likelihood of maintaining the loop is to implode on re-entry. Do you understand, Addison? If you lug all those rusty VW parts back and implode, then your statistical chances of closing the loop forever is greater than if you simply re-enter and all goes well."

Addison Doug said nothing.

"In fact, Addi—and this is the severe part that I have to stress—implosion at re-entry, especially a massive, calculated one of the sort we seem to see shaping up—do you grasp all this, Addi? Am I getting through to you? For Chrissake, Addi? Virtually *guarantees* the locking in of an absolutely unyielding loop such as you've got in mind. Such as we've all been worried about from the start." A pause. "Addi? Are you there?"

Addison Doug said, "I want to die."

"That's your exhaustion from the loop. God knows how many repetitions there've been already of the three of you—"

"No," he said and started to hang up.

"Let me speak with Benz and Crayne," Dr. Fein said rapidly. "Please, before you go ahead with re-entry. Especially Benz; I'd like to speak with him in particular. Please, Addison. For their sake; your almost total exhaustion has—"

He hung up. Left the phone booth, step by step.

As he climbed back into the car, he heard their two alert receivers still buzzing. "General Toad said the automatic call for us would keep your two receivers doing that for a while," he said. And shut the car door after him. "Let's take off."

"Doesn't he want to talk to us?" Benz said.

Addison Doug said, "General Toad wanted to inform us that they have a little something for us. We've been voted a special Congressional Citation for valor or some damn thing like that. A special medal they never voted anyone before. To be awarded posthumously."

"Well, hell—that's about the only way it can be awarded," Crayne said.

Merry Lou, as she started up the engine, began to cry.

"It'll be a relief," Crayne said presently, as they returned bumpily to the freeway, "when it's over."

It won't be long now, Addison Doug's mind declared.

On their wrists the emergency alert receivers continued to put out their combined buzzing.

"They will nibble you to death," Addison Doug said. "The endless wearing down by various bureaucratic voices."

The others in the car turned to gaze at him inquiringly, with uneasiness mixed with perplexity.

"Yeah," Crayne said. "These automatic alerts are really a nuisance." He sounded tired. As tired as I am, Addison Doug thought. And, realizing this, he felt better. It showed how right he was. It showed how right he was.

Great drops of water struck the windshield; it had now begun to rain. That pleased him too. It reminded him of that most exalted of all experiences within the shortness of his life: the funeral procession moving slowly down Pennsylvania Avenue, the flag-draped caskets. Closing his eyes, he leaned back and felt good at last. And heard, all around him once again, the sorrow-bent people. And, in his head, dreamed of the special Congressional Medal. For weariness, he thought. A medal for being tired.

He saw, in his head, himself in other parades too, and in the deaths of many. But really it was one death and one parade. Slow cars moving along the street in Dallas, and with Dr. King as well. . . . He saw himself return again and again, in his closed cycle of life, to the national mourning that he could not and they could not forget. He would be there; they would always be there; it would always be, and every one of them would return together again and again forever. To the place, the moment, they wanted to be. The event which meant the most to all of them.

This was his gift to them, the people, his country. He had bestowed upon the world a wonderful burden. The dreadful and weary miracle of eternal life.